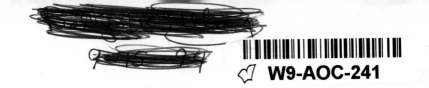

THREE BESTSELLING NOVELS

LARRY McMURTRY

THREE BESTSELLING NOVELS

LARRY McMURTRY

LONESOME DOVE

LEAVING CHEYENNE

THE LAST PICTURE SHOW

WINGS BOOKS

New York • *Avenel, New Jersey*

This edition contains the complete and unabridged texts of the original editions. They have been completely reset for this volume.

This 1994 edition is published by Wings Books,
distributed by Random House Value Publishing, Inc.,
40 Engelhard Avenue, Avenel, New Jersey 07001,
by arrangement with Simon & Schuster Inc.

                    Random House
New York • Toronto • London • Sydney • Auckland

Printed and bound in the United States of America

Library of Congress Cataloging-in-Publication Data

McMurtry, Larry.
    [Novels.   Selections]
    Three complete novels : Lonesome dove, The last picture show ;
Leaving Cheyenne / Larry McMurtry.
        p.   cm.
    ISBN 0-517-10069-X
    1. Man-woman relationships—Texas—Fiction.   2. Cattle drives—
West (U.S.)—Fiction.   3. Cowboys—West (U.S.)—Fiction.
4. Teenage boys—Texas—Fiction.   5. Ranch life—Texas—Fiction.
I. Title.   II. Title: 3 complete novels.
PS3563.A319A6   1994
813'.54—dc20   94-4907
                                                        CIP

8   7   6   5   4   3   2   1

Contents

LONESOME DOVE
1

LEAVING CHEYENNE
615

THE LAST PICTURE SHOW
791

LONESOME DOVE

For Maureen Orth,
and
In memory of
the nine McMurtry boys
(1878–1983)
"Once in the saddle they
Used to go dashing . . ."

All American lies at the end of the wilderness road, and our past is not a dead past, but still lives in us. Our forefathers had civilization inside themselves, the wild outside. We live in the civilization they created, but within us the wilderness still lingers. What they dreamed, we live, and what they lived, we dream.

T. K. Whipple, *Study Out the Land*

PART I

1

WHEN AUGUSTUS CAME OUT on the porch the blue pigs were eating a rattlesnake—not a very big one. It had probably just been crawling around looking for shade when it ran into the pigs. They were having a fine tug-of-war with it, and its rattling days were over. The sow had it by the neck, and the shoat had the tail.

"You pigs git," Augustus said, kicking the shoat. "Head on down to the creek if you want to eat that snake." It was the porch he begrudged them, not the snake. Pigs on the porch just made things hotter, and things were already hot enough. He stepped down into the dusty yard and walked around to the springhouse to get his jug. The sun was still high, sulled in the sky like a mule, but Augustus had a keen eye for sun, and to his eye the long light from the west had taken on an encouraging slant.

Evening took a long time getting to Lonesome Dove, but when it came it was a comfort. For most of the hours of the day—and most of the months of the year—the sun had the town trapped deep in dust, far out in the chaparral flats, a heaven for snakes and horned toads, roadrunners and stinging lizards, but a hell for pigs and Tennesseans. There was not even a respectable shade tree within twenty or thirty miles; in fact, the actual location of the nearest decent shade was a matter of vigorous debate in the offices—if you wanted to call a roofless barn and a couple of patched-up corrals offices—of the Hat Creek Cattle Company, half of which Augustus owned.

His stubborn partner, Captain W. F. Call, maintained that there was excellent shade as close as Pickles Gap, only twelve miles away, but Augustus wouldn't allow it. Pickles Gap was if anything a more worthless community than Lonesome Dove. It had only sprung up because a fool from north Georgia named Wesley Pickles had gotten himself and his family lost in the mesquites for about ten days. When he finally found a clearing, he wouldn't leave it, and Pickles Gap came into being, mainly attracting travelers like its founder, which is to say people too weakwilled to be able to negotiate a few hundred miles of mesquite thicket without losing their nerve.

The springhouse was a little lumpy adobe building, so cool on the inside that Augustus would have been tempted to live in it had it not been for its popularity with black widows, yellow jackets and centipedes. When he opened the door he didn't immediately see any centipedes but he did immediately hear the nervous buzz of a rattlesnake that was evidently smarter than the one the pigs were eating. Augustus could just make out the snake, coiled in a corner, but decided not to shoot it; on a quiet spring evening in Lonesome Dove, a shot could cause complications. Everybody in town would hear it and conclude either that the Comanches were down from the plains or the Mexicans up from the river. If any of the customers of the Dry Bean, the town's one saloon, happened to be drunk

9

or unhappy—which was very likely—they would probably run out into the street and shoot a Mexican or two, just to be on the safe side.

At the very least, Call would come stomping up from the lots, only to be annoyed to discover it had just been a snake. Call had no respect whatsoever for snakes, or for anyone who stood aside for snakes. He treated rattlers like gnats, disposing of them with one stroke of whatever tool he had in hand. "A man that slows down for snakes might as well walk," he often said, a statement that made about as much sense to an educated man as most of the things Call said.

Augustus held to a more leisurely philosophy. He believed in giving creatures a little time to think, so he stood in the sun a few minutes until the rattler calmed down and crawled out a hole. Then he reached in and lifted his jug out of the mud. It had been a dry year, even by the standards of Lonesome Dove, and the spring was just springing enough to make a nice mud puddle. The pigs spent half their time rooting around the springhouse, hoping to get into the mud, but so far none of the holes in the adobe was big enough to admit a pig.

The damp burlap the jug was wrapped in naturally appealed to the centipedes, so Augustus made sure none had sneaked under the wrapping before he uncorked the jug and took a modest swig. The one white barber in Lonesome Dove, a fellow Tennessean named Dillard Brawley, had to do his barbering on one leg because he had not been cautious enough about centipedes. Two of the vicious red-legged variety had crawled into his pants one night and Dillard had got up in a hurry and had neglected to shake out the pants. The leg hadn't totally rotted off, but it had rotted sufficiently that the family got nervous about blood poisoning and persuaded he and Call to saw it off.

For a year or two Lonesome Dove had had a real doctor, but the young man had lacked good sense. A *vaquero* with a loose manner that everybody was getting ready to hang at the first excuse anyway passed out from drink one night and let a blister bug crawl in his ear. The bug couldn't find its way out, but it could move around enough to upset the *vaquero*, who persuaded the young doctor to try and flush it. The young man was doing his best with some warm salt water, but the *vaquero* lost his temper and shot him. It was a fatal mistake on the *vaquero*'s part: someone blasted his horse out from under him as he was racing away, and the incensed citizenry, most of whom were nearby at the Dry Bean, passing the time, hung him immediately.

Unfortunately no medical man had taken an interest in the town since, and Augustus and Call, both of whom had coped with their share of wounds, got called on to do such surgery as was deemed essential. Dillard Brawley's leg had presented no problem, except that Dillard screeched so loudly that he injured his vocal cords. He got around good on one leg, but the vocal cords had never fully recovered, which ultimately hurt his business. Dillard had always talked too much, but after the trouble with the centipedes, what he did was whisper too much. Customers couldn't relax under their hot towels for trying to make out Dillard's whispers. He hadn't really been worth listening to, even when he had two legs, and in time many of his customers drifted off to the Mexican barber. Call even used the Mexican, and Call didn't trust Mexicans *or* barbers.

Augustus took the jug back to the porch and placed his rope-bottomed chair so as to utilize the smidgin of shade he had to work with. As the sun sank, the shade would gradually extend itself across the porch, the wagon yard, Hat Creek, Lonesome Dove and, eventually, the Rio Grande. By the time the shade had reached the river, Augustus would have mellowed with the evening and be ready for some intelligent conversation, which usually involved talking to himself. Call would work until slap dark if he could find anything to do, and if he couldn't find anything he would make up something—and Pea Eye was too much of a corporal to quit before the Captain quit, even if Call would have let him.

The two pigs had quietly disregarded Augustus's orders to go to the creek, and were under one of the wagons, eating the snake. That made good sense, for the creek was just as dry as the wagon yard, and farther off. Fifty weeks out of the year Hat Creek was nothing but a sandy ditch, and the fact that the two pigs didn't regard it as a fit wallow was a credit to their intelligence. Augustus often praised the pigs' intelligence in a running argument he had been having with Call for the last few years. Augustus maintained that pigs were smarter than all horses and most people, a claim that galled Call severely.

"No slop-eating pig is as smart as a horse," Call said, before going on to say worse things.

As was his custom, Augustus drank a fair amount of whiskey as he sat and watched the sun ease out of the day. If he wasn't tilting the rope-bottomed chair, he was tilting the jug. The days in Lonesome Dove were a blur of heat and as dry as chalk, but mash whiskey took some of the dry away and made Augustus feel nicely misty inside—foggy and cool as a morning in the Tennessee hills. He seldom got downright drunk, but he did enjoy feeling misty along about sundown, keeping his mood good with tasteful swigs as the sky to the west began to color up. The whiskey didn't damage his intellectual powers any, but it did make him more tolerant of the raw sorts he had to live with: Call and Pea Eye and Deets, young Newt, and old Bolivar, the cook.

When the sky had pinked up nicely over the western flats, Augustus went around to the back of the house and kicked the kitchen door a time or two. "Better warm up the sowbelly and mash a few beans," he said. Old Bolivar didn't answer, so Augustus kicked the door once or twice more, to emphasize his point, and went back to the porch. The blue shoat was waiting for him at the corner of the house, quiet as a cat. It was probably hoping he would drop something—a belt or a pocketknife or a hat—so he could eat it.

"Git from here, shoat," Augustus said. "If you're that hungry go hunt up another snake." It occurred to him that a leather belt couldn't be much tougher or less palatable than the fried goat Bolivar served up three or four times a week. The old man had been a competent Mexican bandit before he ran out of steam and crossed the river. Since then he had led a quiet life, but it *was* a fact that goat kept turning up on the table. The Hat Creek Cattle Company didn't trade in them, and it was unlikely that Bolivar was buying them out of his own pocket—stealing goats was probably his way of keeping up his old skills. His old skills did not include cooking. The goat meat tasted like it had been fried in tar, but Augustus was the only member of the establishment sensitive enough to raise a complaint. "Bol, where'd you get the tar you fried this goat in?" he asked regularly, his quiet attempt at wit falling as usual on deaf ears. Bolivar ignored all queries, direct or indirect.

Augustus was getting about ready to start talking to the sow and the shoat when he saw Call and Pea Eye walking up from the lots. Pea Eye was tall and lank, had never been full in his life, and looked so awkward that he appeared to be about to fall down even when he was standing still. He looked totally helpless, but that was another case of looks deceiving. In fact, he was one of the ablest men Augustus had ever known. He had never been an outstanding Indian fighter, but if you gave him something he could work at deliberately, like carpentering or blacksmithing, or well-digging or harness repair, Pea was excellent. If he had been a man to do sloppy work, Call would have run him off long before.

Augustus walked down and met the men at the wagons. "It's a little early for you two to be quittin', ain't it, girls?" he said. "Or is this Christmas or what?"

Both men had sweated their shirts through so many times during the day that they were practically black. Augustus offered Call the jug, and Call put a foot on a wagon tongue and took a swig just to rinse the dry out of his mouth. He spat a mouthful of perfectly good whiskey in the dust and handed the jug to Pea Eye.

"Girls yourself," he said. "It ain't Christmas." Then he went on to the house, so abruptly that Augustus was a little taken aback. Call had never been one for fine manners, but if the day's work had gone to his satisfaction he would usually stand and pass the time a minute.

The funny thing about Woodrow Call was how hard he was to keep in scale. He wasn't a big man—in fact, was barely middle-sized—but when you walked up and looked him in the eye it didn't seem that way. Augustus was four inches taller than his partner, and Pea Eye three inches taller yet, but there was no way you could have convinced Pea Eye that Captain Call was the short man. Call had him buffaloed, and in that respect Pea had plenty of company. If a man meant to hold his own with Call it was necessary to keep in mind that Call wasn't as big as he seemed. Augustus was the one man in south Texas who could usually keep him in scale, and he built on his advantage whenever he could. He started many a day by pitching Call a hot biscuit and remarking point-blank, "You know, Call, you ain't really no giant."

A simple heart like Pea could never understand such behavior. It gave Augustus a laugh sometimes to consider that Call could hoodwink a man nearly twice his size, getting Pea to confuse the inner with the outer man. But of course Call himself had such a single-track mind that he scarcely realized he was doing it. He just did it. What made it a fascinating trick was that Call had never noticed that he had a trick. The man never wasted five minutes appreciating himself; it would have meant losing five minutes off whatever job he had decided he wanted to get done that day.

"It's a good thing I ain't scairt to be lazy," Augustus told him once.

"You may think so. I don't," Call said.

"Hell, Call, if I worked as hard as you, there'd be no thinking done at all around this outfit. You stay in a lather fifteen hours a day. A man that's always in a lather can't think nothin' out."

"I'd like to see you think the roof back on that barn," Call said.

A strange little wind had whipped over from Mexico and blown the roof off clean as a whistle, three years before. Fortunately it only rained in Lonesome Dove once or twice a year, so the loss of the roof didn't result in much suffering for the stock, when there was stock. It mostly meant suffering for Call, who had never been able to locate enough decent lumber to build a new roof. Unfortunately a rare downpour had occurred only about a week after the wind dropped the old roof in the middle of Hat Creek. It had been a real turd-floater, and also a lumber-floater, washing much of the roof straight into the Rio Grande.

"If you think so much, why didn't you think of that rain?" Call asked. Ever since, he had been throwing the turd-floater up to Augustus. Give Call a grievance, however silly, and he would save it like money.

Pea Eye wasn't spitting out any mash whiskey. He had a skinny neck—his Adam's apple bulged so when he drank that it reminded Augustus of a snake with a frog stuck in its gullet.

"Call looks mad enough to kick the stump," Augustus said, when Pea finally stopped to breathe.

"She bit a hunk out of him, that's why," Pea said. "I don't know why the Captain wants to keep her."

"Fillies are his only form of folly," Augustus said. "What's he doing letting a horse bite him? I thought you boys were digging the new well?"

"Hit rock," Pea said. "Ain't room for but one man to swing a pick down in that hole, so Newt swung it while I shod horses. The Captain took a ride. I guess he thought he had her sweated down. He turned his back on her and she bit a hunk out."

The mare in question was known around town as the Hell Bitch. Call had bought her in Mexico, from some *caballeros* who claimed to have killed an Indian to get her—a Comanche, they said. Augustus doubted that part of the story: it was unlikely one Comanche had been riding around by himself in that part of Mexico, and if there had been two Comanches the *caballeros* wouldn't have lived to do any horse trading. The mare was a dapple gray, with a white muzzle and a white streak down her forehead, too tall to be pure Indian pony and too short-barreled to be pure thoroughbred. Her disposition did suggest some time spent with Indians, but which Indians and how long was anybody's guess. Every man who saw her wanted to buy her, she was that stylish, but Call wouldn't even listen to an offer, though Pea Eye and Newt were both anxious to see her sold. They had to work around her every day and suffered accordingly. She had once kicked Newt all the way into the blacksmith's shop and nearly into the forge. Pea Eye was at least as scared of her as he was of Comanches, which was saying a lot.

"What's keeping Newt?" Augustus asked.

"He may have went to sleep down in that well," Pea Eye said.

Then Augustus saw the boy walking up from the lots, so tired he was barely moving. Pea Eye was half drunk by the time Newt finally made the wagons.

"'I god, Newt, I'm glad you got here before fall," Augustus said. "We'd have missed you during the summer."

"I been throwin' rocks at the mare," Newt said, with a grin. "Did you see what a hunk she bit out of the Captain?"

Newt lifted one foot and carefully scraped the mud from the well off the sole of his boot, while Pea Eye continued to wash the dust out of his throat.

Augustus had always admired the way Newt could stand on one leg while cleaning the other boot. "Look at that, Pea," he said. "I bet you can't do that."

Pea Eye was so used to seeing Newt stand on one leg to clean his boot that he couldn't figure out what it was Gus thought he couldn't do. A few big swigs of liquor sometimes slowed his thinking down to a crawl. This usually happened at sundown, after a hard day of well-digging or horseshoeing; at such times Pea was doubly glad he worked with the Captain, rather than Gus. The less talk the Captain had to listen to, the better humor he was in, whereas Gus was just the opposite. He'd rattle off five or six different questions and opinions, running them all together like so many unbranded cattle—it made it hard to pick out one and think about it carefully and slowly, the only ways Pea Eye liked to think. At such times his only recourse was to pretend the questions had hit him in his deaf ear, the left one, which hadn't really worked well since the day of their big fight with the Keechis—what they called the Stone House fight. It had been pure confusion, since the Indians had been smart enough to fire the prairie grass, smoking things up so badly that no one could see six feet ahead. They kept bumping into Indians in the smoke and having to shoot point-blank; a Ranger right next to Pea had spotted one and fired too close to Pea's ear.

That was the day the Indians got away with their horses, which made Captain Call about as mad as Pea had ever seen him. It meant they had to walk down the Brazos for nearly two hundred miles, worrying constantly about what would happen if the Comanches discovered they were afoot. Pea Eye hadn't noticed he was half deaf until they had walked most of the way out.

Fortunately, while he was worrying the question of what it was he couldn't do, old Bolivar began to whack the dinner bell, which put an end to discussion. The old dinner bell had lost its clapper, but Bolivar had found a crowbar that somebody had managed to break, and he laid into the bell so hard that you couldn't have heard the clapper if there had been one.

The sun had finally set, and it was so still along the river that they could hear the horses swishing their tails, down in the lots—or they could until Bolivar laid into the bell. Although he probably knew they were standing around the wagons, in easy hearing distance, Bolivar continued to pound the bell for a good five minutes. Bolivar pounded the bell for reasons of his own; even Call couldn't control him in that regard. The sound drowned out the quiet of sunset, which annoyed Augustus so much that at times he was tempted to go up and shoot the old man, just to teach him a lesson.

"I figure he's calling bandits," Augustus said, when the ringing finally stopped. They started for the house, and the pigs fell in with them, the shoat eating a lizard he had caught somewhere. The pigs liked Newt even better than Augustus— when he didn't have anything better to do he would feed them scraps of rawhide and scratch their ears.

"If them bandits were to come, maybe the Captain would let me start wearing a gun," Newt said wistfully. It seemed he would never get old enough to wear a gun, though he was seventeen.

"If you was to wear a gun somebody would just mistake you for a gunfighter and shoot you," Augustus said, noting the boy's wistful look. "It ain't worth it. If Bol ever calls up any bandits I'll lend you my Henry."

"That old man can barely cook," Pea Eye remarked. "Where would he get any bandits?"

"Why, you remember that greasy bunch he had," Augustus said. "We used to buy horses from 'em. That's the only reason Call hired him to cook. In the business we're in, it don't hurt to know a few horsethieves, as long as they're Mexicans. I figure Bol's just biding his time. As soon as he gains our trust his bunch will sneak up some night and murder us all."

He didn't believe anything of the kind—he just liked to stimulate the boy once in a while, and Pea too, though Pea was an exceptionally hard man to stimulate, being insensitive to most fears. Pea had just sense enough to fear Comanches— that didn't require an abundance of sense. Mexican bandits did not impress him.

Newt had more imagination. He turned and looked across the river, where a big darkness was about to settle. Every now and then, about sundown, the Captain and Augustus and Pea and Deets would strap on guns and ride off into that darkness, into Mexico, to return about sunup with thirty or forty horses or perhaps a hundred skinny cattle. It was the way the stock business seemed to work along the border, the Mexican ranchers raiding north while the Texans raided south. Some of the skinny cattle spent their lives being chased back and forth across the Rio Grande. Newt's fondest hope was to get old enough to be taken along on the raids. Many a night he lay in his hot little bunk, listening to old Bolivar snore and mumble below him, peering out the window toward Mexico, imagining the wild doings that must be going on. Once in a while he even heard gunfire, though seldom more than a shot or two, from up or down the river—it got his imagination to working all the harder.

"You can go when you're grown," the Captain said, and that was all he said. There was no arguing with it, either—not if you were just hired help. Arguing with the Captain was a privilege reserved for Mr. Gus.

They no sooner got in the house than Mr. Gus began to exercise the privilege. The Captain had his shirt off, letting Bolivar treat his mare bite. She had got him just above the belt. Enough blood had run down into his pants that one pants leg was caked with it. Bol was about to pack the bite with his usual dope, a mixture of axle grease and turpentine, but Mr. Gus made him wait until he could get a look at the wound himself.

"I god, Woodrow," Augustus said. "As long as you've worked around horses it looks like you'd know better than to turn your back on a Kiowa mare."

Call was thinking of something and didn't answer for a minute. What he was thinking was that the moon was in the quarter—what they called the rustler's moon. Let it get full over the pale flats and some Mexicans could see well enough to draw a fair bead. Men he'd ridden with for years were dead and buried, or at least dead, because they'd crossed the river under a full moon. No moon at all was nearly as bad: then it was too hard to find the stock, and too hard to move it. The quarter moon was the right moon for a swing below the border. The brush country to the north was already thick with cattlemen, making up their spring herds and getting trail crews together; it wouldn't be a week before they began to drift into Lonesome Dove. It was time to go gather cattle.

"Who said she was Kiowa?" he said, looking at Augustus.

"I've reasoned it out," Augustus said. "You could have done the same if you ever stopped working long enough to think."

"I can work and think too," Call said. "You're the only man I know whose brain don't work unless it's in the shade."

Augustus ignored the remark. "I figure it was a Kiowa on his way to steal a woman that lost that mare," he said. "Your Comanche don't hunger much after señoritas. White women are easier to steal, and don't eat as much besides. The Kiowa are different. They fancy señoritas."

"Can we eat or do we have to wait till the argument's over?" Pea Eye asked.

"We starve if we wait for that," Bolivar said, plunking a potful of sowbelly and beans down on the rough table. Augustus, to the surprise of no one, was the first to fill his plate.

"I don't know where you keep finding these Mexican strawberries," he said, referring to the beans. Bolivar managed to find them three hundred and sixty-five days a year, mixing them with so many red chilies that a spoonful of beans was more or less as hot as a spoonful of red ants. Newt had come to think that only two things were certain if you worked for the Hat Creek Cattle Company. One was that Captain Call would think of more things to do than he and Pea Eye and Deets could get done, and the other was that beans would be available at all meals. The only man in the outfit who didn't fart frequently was old Bolivar himself—he never touched beans and lived mainly on sourdough biscuits and chickory coffee, or rather cups of brown sugar with little puddles of coffee floating on top. Sugar cost money, too, and it irked the Captain to spend it, but Bolivar could not be made to break a habit. Augustus claimed the old man's droppings were so sugary that the blue shoat had taken to stalking him every time he went to shit, which might have been true. Newt had all he could do to keep clear of the shoat, and his own droppings were mostly bean.

By the time Call got his shirt on and came to the table, Augustus was reaching for a second helping. Pea and Newt were casting nervous glances at the pot, hoping for seconds themselves but too polite to grab before everyone had been served. Augustus's appetite was a kind of natural calamity. Call had watched it with amazement for thirty years and yet it still surprised him to see how much Augustus ate. He didn't work unless he had to, and yet he could sit down night after night and out-eat three men who had put in a day's labor.

In their rangering days, when things were a little slow the boys would sit around and swap stories about Augustus's eating. Not only did he eat a lot, he ate it fast. The cook that wanted to hold him at the grub for more than ten minutes had better have a side of beef handy.

Call pulled out a chair and sat down. As Augustus was ladling himself a big scoop of beans, Call stuck his plate under the ladle. Newt thought it such a slick move that he laughed out loud.

"Many thanks," Call said. "If you ever get tired of loafing I guess you could get a job waiting tables."

"Why, I had a job waiting tables once," Augustus said, pretending he had meant to serve Call the beans. "On a riverboat. I wasn't no older than Newt when I had that job. The cook even wore a white hat."

"What for?" Pea Eye asked.

"Because it's what real cooks are supposed to wear," Augustus said, looking at Bolivar, who was stirring a little coffee into his brown sugar. "Not so much a hat as a kind of big white cap—it looked like it could have been made out of a bedsheet."

"I'd be damned if I'd wear one," Call said.

"Nobody would be loony enough to hire you to cook, Woodrow," Augustus said. "The cap is supposed to keep the cook's old greasy hairs from falling into the food. I wouldn't be surprised if some of Bol's hairs have found their way into this sow bosom."

Newt looked at Bolivar, sitting over by the stove in his dirty serape. Bolivar's hair looked like it had had a can of secondhand lard poured over it. Once every few months Bol would change clothes and go visit his wife, but his efforts at improving his appearance never went much higher than his mustache, which he occasionally tried to wax with grease of some kind.

"How come you to quit the riverboat?" Pea Eye asked.

"I was too young and pretty," Augustus said. "The whores wouldn't let me alone."

Call was sorry it had come up. He didn't like talk about whores—not anytime, but particularly not in front of the boy. Augustus had little shame, if any. It had long been a sore spot between them.

"I wish they'd drownt you then," Call said, annoyed. Conversation at the table seldom led to any good.

Newt kept his eyes on his plate, as he usually did when the Captain grew annoyed.

"Drown me?" Augustus said. "Why, if anybody had tried it, those girls would have clawed them to shreds." He knew Call was mad, but wasn't much inclined to humor him. It was his dinner table as much as Call's, and if Call didn't like the conversation he could go to bed.

Call knew there was no point in arguing. That was what Augustus wanted: argument. He didn't really care what the question was, and it made no great difference to him which side he was on. He just plain loved to argue, whereas Call hated to. Long experience had taught him that there was no winning arguments with Augustus, even in cases where there was a simple right and wrong at issue. Even in the old days, when they were in the thick of it, with Indians and hardcases to worry about, Augustus would seize any chance for a dispute. Practically the closest call they ever had, when the two of them and six Rangers got surprised by the Comanches up the Prairie Dog Fork of the Red and were all digging holes in the bank that could have turned out to be their graves if they hadn't been lucky and got a cloudy night and sneaked away, Augustus had kept up a running argument with a Ranger they called Ugly Bobby. The argument was entirely about coon dogs, and Augustus had kept it up all night, though most of the Rangers were so scared they couldn't pass water.

Of course the boy lapped up Augustus's stories about riverboats and whores. The boy hadn't been anywhere, so it was all romance to him.

"Listening to you brag about women don't improve the taste of my food," he said, finally.

"Call, if you want better food you have to start by shooting Bolivar," Augustus said, reminded of his own grievance against the cook.

"Bol, I want you to quit whackin' that bell with that crowbar," he said. "You can do it at noon if you want to but let off doin' it at night. A man with any sense can tell when it's sundown. You've spoilt many a pretty evening for me, whackin' that bell."

Bolivar stirred his sugary coffee and held his peace. He whacked the dinner bell because he liked the sound, not because he wanted anybody to come and eat. The men could eat when they liked—he would whack the bell when *he* liked. He enjoyed being a cook—it was a good deal more relaxing than being a bandit—but that didn't mean that he intended to take orders. His sense of independence was undiminished.

"Gen-eral Lee freed the slaves," he remarked in a surly tone.

Newt laughed. Bol never had been able to get the war straight, but he had been genuinely sorry when it ended. In fact, if it had kept going he would probably have stayed a bandit—it was a safe and profitable profession with most of the Texans gone. But the ones who came back from the war were mostly bandits themselves, and they had better guns. The profession immediately became overcrowded. Bolivar knew it was time to quit, but once in a while he got the urge for a little shooting.

"It wasn't General Lee, it was Abe Lincoln who freed the slaves," Augustus pointed out.

Bolivar shrugged. "No difference," he said.

"A big difference," Call said. "One was a Yankee and one wasn't."

Pea Eye got interested for a minute. The beans and sowbelly had revived him. He had been very interested in the notion of emancipation and had studied over it a lot while he went about his work. It was obviously just pure luck that he himself hadn't been born a slave, but if he had been unlucky Lincoln would have freed him. It gave him a certain admiration for the man.

"He just freed Americans," he pointed out to Bolivar.

Augustus snorted. "You're in over your head, Pea," he said. "Who Abe Lincoln freed was a bunch of Africans, no more American than Call here."

Call pushed back his chair. He was not about to sit around arguing slavery after a long day, or after a short one either.

"I'm as American as the next," he said, taking his hat and picking up a rifle.

"You was born in Scotland," Augustus reminded him. "I know they brought you over when you was still draggin' on the tit, but that don't make you no less a Scot."

Call didn't reply. Newt looked up and saw him standing at the door, his hat on and his Henry in the crook of his arm. A couple of big moths flew past his head, drawn to the light of the kerosene lamp on the table. With nothing more said, the Captain went out the door.

2

CALL WALKED THE RIVER for an hour, though he knew there was no real need. It was just an old habit he had, left over from wilder times: checking, looking for a sign of one kind or another, honing his instincts, as much as anything. In his years as a Ranger captain it had been his habit to get off by himself for a time, every night, out of camp and away from whatever talking and bickering were going on. He had discovered early on that his instincts needed privacy in which to operate. Sitting around a fire being sociable, yawning and yarning, might be fine in safe country, but it could cost you an edge in country that wasn't so safe. He liked to get off by himself, a mile or so from camp, and listen to the country, not the men.

Of course, real scouting skills were superfluous in a place as tame as Lonesome Dove, but Call still liked to get out at night, sniff the breeze and let the country talk. The country talked quiet; one human voice could drown it out, particularly if it was a voice as loud as Augustus McCrae's. Augustus was notorious all over Texas for the strength of his voice. On a still night he could be heard at least a mile, even if he was more or less whispering. Call did his best to get out of range of Augustus's voice so that he could relax and pay attention to other sounds. If nothing else, he might get a clue as to what weather was coming—not that there was much mystery about the weather around Lonesome Dove. If a man looked straight up at the stars he was apt to get dizzy, the night was so clear. Clouds were scarcer than cash money, and cash money was scarce enough.

There was really little in the way of a threat to be looked for, either. A coyote might sneak in and snatch a chicken, but that was about the worst that was likely to happen. The mere fact that he and Augustus were there had long since discouraged the local horsethieves.

Call angled west of the town, toward a crossing on the river that had once been favored by the Comanches in the days when they had the leisure to raid into Mexico. It was near a salt lick. He had formed the habit of walking up to the crossing almost every night, to sit for a while on a little bluff, just watching. If the moon was high enough to cast a shadow, he sheltered beside a clump of chaparral. If the Comanches ever came again, it stood to reason they would make for their old crossing, but Call knew well enough that the Comanches weren't going to come again. They were all but whipped, hardly enough warriors left free to terrorize the upper Brazos, much less the Rio Grande.

The business with the Comanches had been long and ugly—it had occupied Call most of his adult life—but it was really over. In fact, it had been so long since he had seen a really dangerous Indian that if one had suddenly ridden up to the crossing he would probably have been too surprised to shoot—exactly the kind of careless attitude he was concerned to guard against in himself. Whipped they might be, but as long as there was one free Comanche with a horse and a gun it would be foolish to take them lightly.

He tried hard to keep sharp, but in fact the only action he had scared up in six months of watching the river was one bandit, who might just have been a *vaquero* with a thirsty horse. All Call had had to do in that instance was click the hammer of his Henry—in the still night the click had been as effective as a shot. The man wheeled back into Mexico, and since then nothing had disturbed the crossing except a few mangy goats on their way to the salt lick.

Even though he still came to the river every night, it was obvious to Call that Lonesome Dove had long since ceased to need guarding. The talk about Bolivar calling up bandits was just another of Augustus's overworked jokes. He came to the river because he liked to be alone for an hour, and not always be crowded. It seemed to him he was pressed from dawn till dark, but for no good reason. As a Ranger captain he was naturally pressed to make decisions—and decisions that might mean life or death to the men under him. That had been a natural pressure—one that went with the job. Men looked to him, and kept looking, wanting to know he was still there, able to bring them through whatever scrape they might be in. Augustus was just as capable, beneath all his rant, and would have got them through the same scrapes if it had been necessary, but Augustus wouldn't bother rising to an occasion until it became absolutely necessary. He left the worrying to Call—so the men looked to Call for orders, and got drunk with Augustus. It never ceased to gripe him that Augustus could not be made to act like a Ranger except in emergencies. His refusal was so consistent that at times both Call and the men would almost hope for an emergency so that Gus would let up talking and arguing and treat the situation with a little respect.

But somehow, despite the dangers, Call had never felt pressed in quite the way he had lately, bound in by the small but constant needs of others. The physical work didn't matter: Call was not one to sit on a porch all day, playing cards or gossiping. He intended to work; he had just grown tired of always providing the example. He was still the Captain, but no one had seemed to notice that there was no troop and no war. He had been in charge so long that everyone assumed all thoughts, questions, needs and wants had to be referred to him, however simple these might be. The men couldn't stop expecting him to captain, and he couldn't stop thinking he had to. It was ingrained in him, he had done it so long, but he was aware that it wasn't appropriate anymore. They weren't even peace officers: they just ran a livery stable, trading horses and cattle when they could find a buyer. The work they did was mostly work he could do in his sleep, and yet, though his day-to-day responsibilities had constantly shrunk over the last ten years, life did not seem easier. It just seemed smaller and a good deal more dull.

Call was not a man to daydream—that was Gus's department—but then it wasn't really daydreaming he did, alone on the little bluff at night. It was just thinking back to the years when a man who presumed to stake out a Comanche trail would do well to keep his rifle cocked. Yet the fact that he had taken to thinking back annoyed him, too: he didn't want to start working over his memories, like an old man. Sometimes he would force himself to get up and walk two or three more miles up the river and back, just to get the memories out of his head. Not until he felt alert again—felt that he could still captain if the need arose—would he return to Lonesome Dove.

===

After supper, when Call left for the river, Augustus, Pea Eye, Newt, Bolivar and the pigs repaired to the porch. The pigs nosed around in the yard, occasionally catching a lizard or a grasshopper, a rat snake or an unwary locust. Bolivar brought out a whetstone and spent twenty minutes or so sharpening the fine bone-handled knife that he wore at his belt. The handle was made from the horn of a mule deer and the thin blade flashed in the moonlight as Bolivar carefully drew it back and forth across the whetstone, spitting on the stone now and then to dampen its surface.

Although Newt liked Bolivar and considered him a friend, the fact that Bol felt it necessary to sharpen the knife every night made him a little nervous. Mr. Gus's constant joking about bandits—although Newt knew it was joking—had its effect. It was a mystery to him why Bol sharpened the knife every single night, since he never cut anything with it. When he asked him about it Bol smiled and tested the blade gently with his thumb.

"It's like a wife," he said. "Every night you better stroke it."

That made no sense to Newt, but got a laugh from Augustus.

"If that's the case your wife is likely pretty rusty by now, Bol," he said. "She don't get sharpened more than twice a year."

"She is old," Bolivar said.

"The older the violin, the sweeter the music," Augustus said. "Us old folks appreciate whetting just as much as the young, or maybe more. You ought to bring her up here to live, Bol. Think of the money you'd save on whetstones."

"That knife would cut through a man's naik like it was butter," Pea Eye said. He had an appreciation of such things, being the owner of a fine Bowie knife himself. It had a fourteen-inch blade and he had bought it from a soldier who had personally commissioned it from Bowie. He didn't sharpen it every night like Bol did his, but he took it out of its big sheath once in a while to make sure it hadn't lost its edge. It was his Sunday knife and he didn't use it for ordinary work like butchering or cutting leather. Bolivar never used his for ordinary work either, though once in a while, if he was in a good mood, he would throw it and stick it in the side of a wagon, or maybe shave off a few fine curls of rawhide with it. Newt would then feed the rawhide to the pigs.

Augustus himself took a dim view of the utility of knives, particularly of fancy knives. He carried a plain old clasp in his pocket and used it mainly for cutting his toenails. In the old days, when they all lived mostly off game, he had carried a good skinning knife as a matter of necessity, but he had no regard at all for the knife as a fighting weapon. So far as he was concerned, the invention of the Colt revolver had rendered all other short-range weapons obsolete. It was a minor irritant that he had to spend virtually every night of his life listening to Bol grind his blade away.

"If I have to listen to something, I'd rather listen to you whet your wife," he said.

"I don't bring her," Bol said. "I know you. You would try to corrupt her."

Augustus laughed. "No, I ain't much given to corrupting old women," he said. "Ain't you got any daughters?"

"Only nine," Bolivar said. Abruptly, not even getting up, he threw the knife at the nearest wagon, where it stuck, quivering for a moment. The wagon was only about twenty feet away, so it was no great throw, but he wanted to make a point about his feeling for his daughters. Six were married already, but the three left at home were the light of his life.

"I hope they take after their mother," Augustus said. "If they take after you you're in for a passel of old maids." His Colt was hanging off the back of the chair and he reached around and got it, took it out of its holster, and idly twirled the chamber a time or two, listening to the pretty little clicks.

Bolivar was sorry he had thrown the knife, since it meant he would have to get up and walk across the yard to retrieve it. At the moment his hip joints hurt, as well as several other joints, all the result of letting a horse fall on him five years before.

"I am better looking than a buzzard like you," he said, pulling himself up.

Newt knew Bolivar and Mr. Gus were just insulting one another to pass the time, but it still made him nervous when they did it, particularly late in the day, when they had both been hitting their respective jugs for several hours. It was a peaceful night, so still that he could occasionally hear the sound of the piano down at the Dry Bean saloon. The piano was the pride of the saloon, and, for that matter, of the town. The church folks even borrowed it on Sundays. Luckily the church house was right next to the saloon and the piano had wheels. Some of the deacons had built a ramp out at the back of the saloon, and a board track across to the church, so that all they had to do was push the piano right across to the church. Even so, the arrangement was a threat to the sobriety of the deacons, some of whom considered it their duty to spend their evenings in the saloon, safeguarding the piano.

Once they safeguarded it so well on Saturday night that they ran it off its rail on Sunday morning and broke two legs off it. Since there weren't enough sober men in church that morning to carry it inside, Mrs. Pink Higgins, who played it, had to sit out in the street and bang away at the hymns, while the rest of the congregation, ten ladies and a preacher, stayed inside and sang. The arrangement was made more awkward still by the fact that Lorena Wood came out on the backstairs of the saloon, practically undressed, and listened to the hymns.

Newt was deeply in love with Lorena Wood, though so far he had not even had an opportunity to speak to her. He was painfully aware that if the chance for personal speech ever did arise he would have no idea what to say. On the rare occasions when he had an errand that took him by the saloon he lived in terror, afraid some accident might occur which would actually force him to speak to her. He *wanted* to speak to Lorena, of course—it represented the very summit of his life's hopes—but he didn't want to have to do it until he had decided on the best thing to say, which so far he had not, though Lorena had been in town for several months, and he had been in love with her from the moment he first glimpsed her face.

On an average day, Lorena occupied Newt's thoughts about eight hours, no matter what tasks occupied his hands. Though normally an open young man, quick to talk about his problems—to Pea Eye and Deets, at least—he had never so much as uttered Lorena's name aloud. He knew that if he did utter it a terrible amount of ribbing would ensue, and while he didn't mind being ribbed about most things, his feeling for Lorena was too serious to admit frivolity. The men who made up the Hat Creek outfit were not great respecters of feeling, particularly tender feeling.

There was also the danger that someone might slight her honor. It wouldn't be the Captain, who was not prone to jesting about women, or even to mentioning them. But the thought of the complications that might arise from an insult to Lorena had left Newt closely acquainted with the mental perils of love long before he had had an opportunity to sample any of its pleasures except the infinite pleasure of contemplation.

Of course, Newt knew that Lorena was a whore. It was an awkward fact, but it didn't lessen his feelings for her one whit. She had been abandoned in Lonesome Dove by a gambler who decided she was bad for his luck; she lived over the Dry Bean and was known to receive visitors of various descriptions, but Newt was not a young man to choke on such details. He was not absolutely sure what whores did, but he assumed that Lorena had come by her profession as accidentally as he had come by his. It was pure accident that he happened to be a horse wrangler for the Hat Creek outfit, and no doubt an equally pure one that had made Lorena a whore. What Newt loved about her was her nature, which he could see in her face. It was easily the most beautiful face that had ever been seen in Lonesome Dove, and he had no doubt that hers was the most beautiful nature, too. He intended to say something along those lines to her when he finally spoke to her. Much of his time on the porch after supper was spent in trying to figure out what words would best express such a sentiment.

That was why it irritated him slightly when Bol and Mr. Gus started passing insults back and forth, as if they were biscuits. They did it almost every night, and pretty soon they'd be throwing knives and clicking pistols, making it very hard for him to concentrate on what he would say to Lorena when they first met. Neither Mr. Gus nor Bolivar had lived their lives as peaceful men, and it seemed to him they might both be itching for one last fight. Newt had no doubt that if such a fight occurred Mr. Gus would win. Pea Eye claimed that he was a better pistol shot than Captain Call, though it was hard for Newt to imagine anyone being better at anything than Captain Call. He didn't want the fight to happen, because it would mean the end of Bol, and despite a slight nervousness about Bol's bandit friends, he did like Bol. The old man had given him a serape once, to use as a blanket, and had let him have the bottom bunk when he was sick with jaundice. If Mr. Gus shot him it would mean Newt had one less friend. Since he had no family, this was not a thought to be taken lightly.

"What do you reckon the Captain does out there in the dark?" he asked.

Augustus smiled at the boy, who was hunched over on the lower step, as nervous as a red pup. He asked the same question almost every night when he thought there might be a fight. He wanted Call around to stop it, if it ever started.

"He's just playin' Indian fighter," he said.

Newt doubted that. The Captain was not one to play. If he felt he had to go off and sit in the dark every night, he must think it important.

Mention of Indians woke Pea Eye from an alcoholic doze. He hated Indians, partly because for thirty years fear of them had kept him from getting a good night's sleep. In his years with the Rangers he never closed his eyes without expecting to open them and find some huge Indian getting ready to poke him with something sharp. Most of the Indians he had actually seen had all been scrawny little men, but it didn't mean the huge one who haunted his sleep wasn't out there waiting.

"Why, they could come," he said. "The Captain's right to watch. If I wasn't so lazy I'd go help him."

"He don't want you to help him," Augustus said testily. Pea's blind loyalty to Call was sometimes a trial. He himself knew perfectly well why Call headed for the river every night, and it had very little to do with the Indian threat. He had made the point many times, but he made it again.

"He heads for the river because he's tired of hearing us yap," he said. "He ain't a sociable man and never was. You could never keep him in camp, once he had his grub. He'd rather sit off in the dark and prime his gun. I doubt he'd find an Indian if one was out there."

"He used to find them," Pea said. "He found that big gang of them up by Fort Phantom Hill."

"'I god, Pea," Augustus said. "Of course he found a few here and there. They used to be thicker than grass burrs, if you remember. I'll guarantee he won't scratch up none tonight. Call's got to be the one to out-suffer everybody, that's the pint. I won't say he's a man to hunt glory like some I've knowed. Glory don't interest Call. He's just got to do his duty nine times over or he don't sleep good."

There was a pause. Pea Eye had always been uncomfortable with Gus's criticisms of the Captain, without having any idea how to answer them. If he came back at all he usually just adopted one of the Captain's own remarks.

"Well, somebody's got to take the hard seat," he said.

"Fine with me," Augustus said. "Call can suffer for you and me and Newt and Deets and anybody else that don't want to do it for themselves. It's been right handy having him around to assume them burdens all these years, but if you think he's doing it for us and not because it's what he happens to like doing, then you're a damn fool. He's out there sitting behind a chaparral bush congratulating himself on not having to listen to Bol brag on his wife. He knows as well as I do there isn't a hostile within six hundred miles of here."

Bolivar stood over by the wagon and relieved himself for what seemed to Newt like ten or fifteen minutes. Often when Bol started to relieve himself Mr. Gus would yank out his old silver pocket watch and squint at it until the pissing stopped. Sometimes he even got a stub of a pencil and a little notebook out of the old black vest he always wore and wrote down how long it took Bolivar to pass his water.

"It's a clue to how fast he's failing," Augustus pointed out. "An old man finally dribbles, same as a fresh calf. I best just keep a record, so we'll know when to start looking for a new cook."

For once, though, the pigs took more interest in Bol's performance than Mr. Gus, who just drank a little more whiskey. Bol yanked his knife out of the side of the wagon and disappeared into the house. The pigs came to Newt to get their ears scratched. Pea Eye slumped against the porch railing—he had begun to snore.

"Pea, wake up and go to bed," Augustus said, kicking at his leg until he waked him. "Newt and I might forget and leave you out here, and if we done that these critters would eat you, belt buckle and all."

Pea Eye got up without really opening his eyes and stumbled into the house.

"They wouldn't really eat him," Newt said. The blue shoat was on the lower step, friendly as a dog.

"No, but it takes a good threat to get Pea moving," Augustus said.

Newt saw the Captain coming back, his rifle in the crook of his arm. As always, Newt felt relieved. It eased something inside him to know the Captain was back. It made it easier to sleep. Lodged in his mind somewhere was the worry that maybe some night the Captain *wouldn't* come back. It wasn't a worry that he would meet with some accident and be killed, either: it was a worry that he might just leave. It seemed to Newt that the Captain was probably tired of them all, and with some justice. He and Pea and Deets did their best to pull their weight, but Mr. Gus never pulled any weight at all, and Bol sat around and drank tequila most of the day. Maybe the Captain would just saddle up the Hell Bitch some night and go.

Once in a great while Newt dreamed that the Captain not only left, but took him with him, to the high plains that he had heard about but never seen. There was never anyone else in the dreams: just him and the Captain, horseback in a beautiful grassy country. Those were sweet dreams, but just dreams. If the Captain did leave he would probably just take Pea along, since Pea had been his corporal for so many years.

"I don't see any scalps," Augustus said, when Call came up.

Call ignored him, leaned his rifle against the porch rail and lit a smoke.

"This would have been a good night to cross some stock," he said.

"Cross 'em and do what with 'em?" Augustus asked. "I ain't seen no cattle buyers yet."

"We could actually take the cattle to them," Call said. "It's been done. It ain't against the law for you to work."

"It's against my law," Augustus said. "Them buyers ain't nailed down. They'll show up directly. Then we'll cross the stock."

"Captain, can I go next time?" Newt asked. "I believe I'm getting old enough."

Call hesitated. Pretty soon he was going to have to say yes, but he wasn't ready to just then. It wasn't really fair to the boy—he would have to learn sometime—but still Call couldn't quite say it. He had led boys as young, in his day, and seen them killed, which was why he kept putting Newt off.

"You'll get old quick if you keep sitting up all night," he said. "Work to do tomorrow. You best go to bed."

The boy went at once, looking a little disappointed.

"Night, son," Augustus said, looking at Call when he said it. Call said nothing.

"You should have let him sit," Augustus said, a little later. "After all, the boy's only chance for an education is listening to me talk."

Call let that one float off. Augustus had spent a year in a college, back in Virginia somewhere, and claimed to have learned his Greek letters, plus a certain amount of Latin. He never let anyone forget it.

They could hear the piano from down at the Dry Bean. An old-timer named Lippy Jones did all the playing. He had the same problem Sam Houston had had, which was a hole in his belly that wouldn't quite heal shut. Someone had shot Lippy with a big bore gun; instead of dying he ended up living with a leak. With a handicap like that, it was lucky he could play the piano.

Augustus got up and stretched. He took his Colt and holster off the back of the chair. So far as he was concerned the night was young. He had to step over the shoat to get off the porch.

"You oughtn't to be so stubborn about that boy, Woodrow," he said. "He's spent about enough of his life shoveling horseshit."

"I'm a sight older than him and I still shovel my share of it," Call said.

"Well, that's your choice," Augustus said. "It's my view that there are more fragrant ways to make a fortune. Card playing, for one. I believe I'll straggle down to that gin palace and see if I can scare up a game."

Call was about finished with his smoke. "I don't mind your card playin', if that's all it is," he said.

Augustus grinned. Call never changed. "What else would it be?" he asked.

"You never used to gamble this regular," Call said. "You better watch that girl."

"Watch her for what?"

"To see she don't get you to marry her," Call said. "You're just enough of an old fool to do it. I won't have that girl around."

Augustus had a good laugh. Call was given to some funny notions, but that was one of the funniest, to think that a man of his years and experience would marry a whore.

"See you for breakfast," he said.

Call sat on the steps a little while longer, listening to the blue pigs snore.

3

LORENA HAD NEVER LIVED in a place where it was cool—it was her one aim. It seemed to her she had learned to sweat at the same time she had learned to breathe, and she was still doing both. Of all the places she had heard men talk about, San Francisco sounded the coolest and nicest, so it was San Francisco she set her sights on.

Sometimes it seemed like slow going. She was nearly twenty-four and hadn't got a mile past Lonesome Dove, which wasn't fast progress considering that she had only been twelve when her parents got nervous about Yankees and left Mobile.

That much slow progress would have discouraged most women, but Lorena didn't allow her mind to dwell on it. She had her flat days, of course, but that was mostly because Lonesome Dove itself was so flat. She got tired of looking out the window all day and seeing nothing but brown land and gray chaparral. In the middle of the day the sun was so hot the land looked white. She could see the river from her window, and Mexico. Lippy told her she could make a fortune if she cared to establish herself in Mexico, but Lorena didn't care to. From what she could see of the country it didn't look any more interesting than Texas, and the men stunk just as bad as Texans, if not worse.

Gus McCrae claimed to have been to San Francisco, and would talk to her for hours about how blue the water was in the bay, and how the ships came in from everywhere. In the end he overtalked it, like he did everything. Once or twice Lorena felt she had a clear picture of it, listening to Gus, but by the time he finally quit talking she would have lost it and just be lying there, wishing it would cool off.

In that respect, Gus was unusual, for most men didn't talk. He would blab right up until he shoved his old carrot in, and then would be blabbing again, before it was even dry. Generous as he was by local standards—he gave her five dollars in gold every single time—Lorena still felt a little underpaid. It should have been five dollars for wetting his carrot and another five dollars for listening to all the blab. Some of it was interesting, but Lorena couldn't keep her mind on so much talk. It didn't seem to hurt Gus's feelings any. He talked just as cheerful whether she was listening or not, and he never tried to talk her into giving him two pokes for the price of one, as most of the younger men did.

It was peculiar that he was her most regular customer, because he was also her oldest. She made a point of not letting anything men did surprise her much, but secretly it did surprise her a little that a man as old as Gus would still be so partial to it. In that respect he put a lot of younger men to shame, including Mosby Marlin, who had held her up for two years over in east Texas. Compared to Gus, Mosby couldn't even be said to have a carrot, though he did have a kind of little stringy radish that he was far too proud of.

She had only been seventeen when she met Mosby, and both her parents were dead. Her pa fell out in Vicksburg, and her ma only made it to Baton Rouge, so it was Baton Rouge where she was stranded when Mosby found her. She hadn't done any sporting up to that time, though she had developed early and had even had some trouble with her own pa, though he was feverish to the point of delirium when the trouble happened. He died soon after. She knew Mosby was a drunkard from the first, but he told her he was a Southern gentleman and he had an expensive buggy and a fine pair of horses, so she believed him.

Mosby claimed that he wanted to marry her, and Lorena believed that too, and let him drag her off to a big old drafty house near a place called Gladewater. The house was huge, but it didn't even have glass in the windows or rugs or anything; they had to set smoke pots in the rooms to keep the mosquitoes from eating them alive, which the mosquitoes did anyway. Mosby had a mother and two mean sisters and no money, and no intention of marrying Lorena anyway, though he kept claiming he would for a while.

In fact, the womenfolk treated Lorena worse than they treated the nigras, and they didn't treat the nigras good. They didn't treat Mosby good, either, or one another good—about the only creatures that ever saw any kindness around that house were Mosby's hounds. Mosby assured her he'd set the hounds on her if she ever tried to run away.

It was in the nights, when Lorena had to lay there with the smoke from the smoke pots so thick she couldn't breathe, and the clouds of mosquitoes nearly as thick as the smoke, and Mosby constantly bothering her with his radish, that Lorena's spirits sunk so low she ceased to want to talk. She became a silent woman. Soon after, the sporting started, because Mosby lost so much money one night that he offered two of his friends a poke in exchange for his debt. Lorena was so surprised that she didn't have time to arm herself, and the men had their way, but the next morning when the two were gone she went at Mosby with his own quirt and cut his face so badly they put her in the cellar for two days and didn't even bring her food.

Two or three months later it happened again with some more friends, and this time Lorena didn't fight. She was so tired of Mosby and his radish and the smoke pots that she was willing to consider anything different. The mother and the mean sisters wanted to drive her out of the house, and Lorena would have been glad to go, but Mosby threw such a fit that one of the sisters ran off herself to live with an aunt.

Then one night Mosby just plain sold a poke to a traveling man of some kind: he seemed to be planning to do it regular, only the second man he sold her to happened to take a fancy to Lorena. His name was John Tinkersley, the tallest and prettiest man Lorena had seen up to that point, and the cleanest. When he asked her if she was really married to Mosby she said no. Tinkersley suggested then and there that she accompany him to San Antonio. Lorena was glad to agree. Mosby was so shocked by her decision that he offered to go get the preacher and marry her on the spot, but by that time Lorena had figured out that being married to Mosby would be even worse than what she had already been through. Mosby tried for a while to work himself up to a fight, but he was no match for Tinkersley and he knew it. The best he could salvage was to sell Tinkersley a horse for Lorena, plus the sidesaddle that belonged to the sister who had run off.

San Antonio was a big improvement over Gladewater, if only because there were no smoke pots and few mosquitoes. They kept two rooms in a hotel—not the finest in town but fine enough—and Tinkersley bought Lorena some pretty clothes. Of course he financed that by selling the horse and the sidesaddle, which disappointed Lorena a little. She had discovered that she liked riding. She would have been happy to ride on to San Francisco, but Tinkersley had no interest in that. Clean and tall and pretty as he was, he turned out, in the end, to be no better bargain than Mosby. If he had a soft spot, it was for himself, not for her. He even spent money getting his fingernails cut, which was something Lorena had never dreamed a man would do. For all that, he was a hard man. Fighting with Mosby had been like fighting with a little boy, whereas the first time she talked back to Tinkersley he hit her so hard her head cracked a washpot on the bureau behind her. Her ears rang for three days. He threatened to do worse than that, too, and Lorena didn't suppose they were idle threats. She held her tongue around Tinkersley from then on. He made it clear that marriage wasn't what he had had in mind when he took her away from Mosby, which was all right in itself, since she had already got out of the habit of thinking about marriage.

That didn't mean she was in the habit of thinking about herself as a sporting woman, but it was precisely that habit that Tinkersley expected her to acquire.

"Well, you're already trained, ain't you?" he said. Lorena didn't consider what had happened in Gladewater any training for anything, but then it was clear there wasn't anything respectable she was trained for, even if she could get away from Tinkersley without being killed. For a few days she had thought Tinkersley might love her, but he soon made it clear that she meant about as much to him as a good saddle. She knew that for the time being the sporting life was about her only choice. At least the hotel room was nice and there were no mean sisters. Most of the sports who came to see her were men Tinkersley gambled with in the bar down below. Once in a while a nice one would even give her a little money directly, instead of leaving it with Tinkersley, but Tinkersley was smart about such things and he found her hiding place and cleaned her out the day they took the stage to Matamoros. He might not have done it if he hadn't had a string of losses, but the fact that he was handsome didn't mean that he was a good gambler, as several of the sports pointed out to Lorena. He was just a middling gambler, and he had such a run of bad luck in San Antonio that he decided there might be less competition down on the border.

It was on that trip that they had the real fight. Lorena felt swollen with anger about the money—swollen enough, finally, not to be scared of him. What she wanted was to kill him for being so determined to leave her absolutely nothing. If she had known more about guns she *would* have killed him. She thought with a gun you just pulled the trigger, but it turned out his had to be cocked first. Tinkersley was lying on the bed drunk, but not so drunk he didn't notice when she stuck his own gun in his stomach. When she realized it wasn't going to go off she had just time to hit him in the face with it, a lick that actually won the fight for her, although before he gave up and went to look for a doctor to stitch his jaw up Tinkersley did bite her on the upper lip as they were rolling around, Lorena still hoping the gun would shoot.

The bite had left a faint little scar just above her upper lip; to Lorena's amusement it was that trifling scar that seemed to make men crazy for a time with her. Of course it wasn't just the scar—she had developed well and had also gotten prettier as she got older. But the scar played its part. Tinkersley got drunk in Lonesome Dove the day he left her, and he told everyone in the Dry Bean that she was a murderous woman. So she had a reputation in the town before she even unpacked her clothes. Tinkersley had left her with no money at all, but fortunately she could cook when she had to; the Dry Bean was the only place in Lonesome Dove that served food, and Lorena had been able to talk Xavier Wanz, who owned it, into letting her do the cooking until the cowboys got over being scared of her and began to approach her.

Augustus was the man who got it started. While he was pulling off his boots the first time he smiled at her.

"Where'd you get that scar?" he asked.

"Somebody bit me," Lorena said.

Once Gus became a regular, she had no trouble making a living in the town, although in the summer, when the cowboys were mostly off on the trail, pickings sometimes grew slim. While she was well past the point of trusting men, she soon perceived that Gus was in a class by himself, at least in Lonesome Dove. He wasn't mean, and he didn't treat her like most men treated a sporting woman. She knew he would probably even help her if she ever really needed help. It seemed to her he had got rid of something other men hadn't got rid of—some meanness or some need. He was the one man besides Lippy she would sometimes talk to— a little. With most of the sports she had nothing at all to say.

In fact, her silence soon came to be widely commented on. It was part of her, like the scar, and, like the scar, it drew men to her even though it made them deeply uneasy. It was not a trick, either, although she knew it unnerved the sports and made matters go quicker. Silent happened to be how she felt when men were with her.

In respect to her silence, too, Gus McCrae was different. At first he seemed not to notice it—certainly he didn't let it bother him. Then it began to amuse him, which was not a reaction Lorena had had from anyone else. Most men chattered like squirrels when they were with her, no doubt hoping she would say something back. Of course Gus was a great blabber, but his blabbing wasn't really like the chattering the other sports did. He was just full of opinion, which he freely poured out, as much for his own amusement as for anything. Lorena had never particularly looked at life as if it was something funny, but Gus did. Even her lack of talk struck him as funny.

One day he walked in and sat down in a chair, the usual look of amusement on his face. Lorena assumed he was going to take his boots off and she went over to the bed, but when she looked around he was sitting there, one foot on the other knee, twirling the rowel of his spur. He always wore spurs, although it was not often she saw him on horseback. Once in a while, in the early morning, the bawling of cattle or the nickering of horses would awaken her and she would look out the window and see him and his partner and a gang of riders trailing their stock through the low brush to the east of town. Gus was noticeable, since he rode a big black horse that looked like it could have pulled three stagecoaches by itself. But he kept his spurs on even when he wasn't riding so he would have them handy when he wanted something to jingle.

"Them's the only musical instruments I ever learned to play," he told her once.

Since he just sat there twirling his spur and smiling at her, Lorena didn't know whether to get undressed or what. It was July, blistering hot. She had tried sprinkling the bedsheets, but the heat dried them sometimes before she could even lay down.

"I god, it's hot," Gus said. "We could all be living in Canada just as cheap. I doubt I've even got the energy to set my post."

Why come then? Lorena thought.

Another unusual thing about Gus was that he could practically tell what she was thinking. In this case he looked abashed and dug a ten-dollar gold piece out of his pocket, which he pitched over to her. Lorena felt wary. It was five dollars too much, even if he did decide to set his post. She knew old men got crazy sometimes and wanted strange things—Lippy was a constant problem, and he had a hole in his stomach and could barely keep up his piano playing. But it turned out she had no need to worry about Gus.

"I figured out something, Lorie," he said. "I figured out why you and me get along so well. You know more than you say and I say more than I know. That means we're a perfect match, as long as we don't hang around one another more than an hour at a stretch."

It made no sense to Lorena, but she relaxed. There was no likelihood he would try anything crazy on her.

"This is ten dollars," she said, thinking maybe he just hadn't noticed what kind of money he was handing over.

"You know, prices are funny," he said. "I've known a good many sporting girls and I've always wondered why they didn't price more flexible. If I was in your place and I had to traipse upstairs with some of these old smelly sorts, I'd want a sight of money, whereas if it was some good-looking young sprout who kept himself barbered up, why a nickel might be enough."

Lorena remembered Tinkersley, who had had the use of her for two years, taken all she brought in, and then left her without a cent.

"A nickel wouldn't be enough," she said. "I can do without the barbering."

But Augustus was in a mood for discussion. "Say you put two dollars as your low figure," he said. "That's for the well-barbered sprout. What would the high figure be, for some big rank waddy who couldn't even spell? The pint I'm making is that all men ain't the same, so they shouldn't be the same price, or am I wrong? Maybe from where you sit all men *are* the same."

Once she thought about it, Lorena saw his point. All men weren't quite the same. A few were nice enough that she might notice them, and a goodly few were mean enough that she couldn't help noticing them, but the majority were neither one nor the other. They were just men, and they left money, not memories. So far it was only the mean ones who had left memories.

"Why'd you give me this ten?" she asked, willing to be a little curious, since it seemed it was going to be just talk anyway.

"Hoping to get you to talk a minute," Augustus said, smiling. He had the most white hair she had ever seen on a man. He mentioned once that it had turned white when he was thirty, making his life more dangerous, since the Indians would have considered the white scalp a prize.

"I was married twice, you remember," he said. "Should have been married a third time but the woman made a mistake and didn't marry me."

"What's that got to do with this money?" Lorena asked.

"The pint is, I ain't a natural bachelor," Augustus said. "There's days when a little bit of talk with a female is worth any price. I figure the reason you don't have much to say is you probably never met a man who liked to hear a woman talk. Listening to women ain't the fashion in this part of the country. But I expect you got a life story like everybody else. If you'd like to tell it, I'm the one that'd like to hear it."

Lorena thought that over. Gus didn't seem uncomfortable. He just set there, twirling his rowel.

"In these parts what your business is all about is woman's company anyway," he said. "Now in a cold clime it might be different. A cold clime will perk a boy up and make him want to wiggle his bean. But down here in this heat it's mostly company they're after."

There was something to that. Men looked at her sometimes like they wished she would be their sweetheart—the young ones particularly, but some of the old ones too. One or two had even wanted her to let them keep her, though where they meant to do the keeping she didn't know. She was already living in the only spare bedroom in Lonesome Dove. Little marriages were what they wanted—just something that would last until they started up the trail. Some girls did it that way—hitched up with one cowboy for a month or six weeks and got presents and played at being respectable. She had known girls who did it that way in San Antonio. The thing that struck her was that the girls seemed to believe it as much as the cowboys did. They would act just as silly as respectable girls, getting jealous of one another and pouting all day if their boys didn't act to suit them. Lorena had no interest in conducting things that way. The men who came to see her would have to realize that she was not interested in playacting.

After a bit, she decided she wasn't interested in telling Augustus her life story, either. She buttoned her dress back up and handed him the ten dollars.

"It ain't worth ten dollars," she said. "Even if I could remember it all."

Augustus stuck the money back in his pocket. "I ought to know better than to try and buy conversation," he said, still grinning. "Let's go down and play some cards."

4

WHEN AUGUSTUS LEFT CALL sitting on the steps he took a slow stroll through the wagon yard and down the street, stopping for a moment on the sandy bottom of Hat Creek to strap on his pistol. The night was quiet as sleep, no night when he expected to have to shoot anybody, but it was only wise to have the pistol handy in case he had to whack a drunk. It was an old Colt dragoon with a seven-inch barrel and, as he was fond of saying, weighed about as much as the leg he strapped it to. One whack would usually satisfy most drunks, and two whacks would drop an ox if Augustus cared to put his weight into it.

The border nights had qualities that he had come to admire, different as they were from the qualities of nights in Tennessee. In Tennessee, as he remembered, nights tended to get mushy, with a cottony mist drifting into the hollows. Border nights were so dry you could smell the dirt, and clear as dew. In fact, the nights were so clear it was tricky; even with hardly any moon the stars were bright enough that every bush and fence post cast a shadow. Pea Eye, who had a jumpy disposition, was always shying from shadows, and he had even blazed away at innocent chaparral bushes on occasion, mistaking them for bandits.

Augustus was not particularly nervous, but even so he had hardly started down the street before he got a scare: a little ball of shadow ran right at his feet. He jumped sideways, fearing snakebite, although his brain knew snakes didn't roll like balls. Then he saw an armadillo hustle past his feet. Once he saw what it was, he tried to give it a kick to teach it not to walk in the street scaring people, but the armadillo hurried right along as if it had as much right to the street as a banker.

The town was not roaring with people, nor was it bright with lights, though a light was on at the Pumphreys', whose daughter was about to have a baby. The Pumphreys ran a store; the baby their daughter was expecting would arrive in the world to find itself fatherless, since the boy who had married the Pumphrey girl had drowned in the Republican River in the fall of the year, with the girl only just pregnant.

There was only one horse hitched outside the Dry Bean when Augustus strolled up—a rangy sorrel that he recognized as belonging to a cowboy named Dishwater Boggett, so named because he had once rushed into camp so thirsty from a dry drive that he wouldn't wait his turn at the water barrel and had filled up on some dishwater the cook had been about to throw out. Seeing the sorrel gave Augustus a prime feeling because Dish Boggett loved card playing, though he lacked even minimal skills. Of course he also probably lacked ante money, but that didn't necessarily rule out a game. Dish was a good hand and could always get hired—Augustus didn't mind playing for futures with such a man.

When he stepped in the door, everybody was looking peeved, probably because Lippy was banging away at "My Bonnie Lies Over the Ocean," a song that he loved to excess and played as if he hoped it could be heard in the capital of Mexico. Xavier Wanz, the little Frenchman who owned the place, was nervously wiping his tables with a wet rag. Xavier seemed to think keeping the tables well wiped was the crucial factor in his business, though Augustus was often forced to point out to him that such a view was nonsense. Most of the patrons of the Dry Bean were so lacking in fastidiousness that they wouldn't have noticed a dead skunk on the tables, much less a few crumbs and spilled drinks.

Xavier himself had a near-monopoly on fastidiousness in Lonesome Dove. He wore a white shirt the year round, clipped his little mustache once a week and even wore a bow tie, or, at least, a black shoestring that did its best to serve as a bow tie. Some cowpoke had swiped Xavier's last real bow tie, probably meaning to try and impress some girl somewhere up the trail. Since the shoestring was limp, and not stiff like a bow tie should be, it merely added to the melancholy of Xavier's appearance, which would have been melancholy enough without it. He had been born in New Orleans and had ended up in Lonesome Dove because someone had convinced him Texas was the land of opportunity. Though he soon discovered otherwise, he was too proud or too fatalistic to attempt to correct his mistake. He approached day-to-day life in the Dry Bean with a resigned temper, which on occasion stopped being resigned and became explosive. When it exploded, the placid air was apt to be rent by Creole curses.

"Good evening, my good friend," Augustus said. He said it with as much gravity as he could muster, since Xavier appreciated a certain formality.

In return, Xavier nodded stiffly. It was hard to extend the amenities when Lippy was at the height of a performance.

Dish Boggett was sitting at one of the tables with Lorena, hoping to persuade her to give him a poke on credit. Though Dish was barely twenty-two, he wore a walrus mustache that made him look years older than he was, and much more solemn. In color the mustache was stuck between yellow and brown—kind of prairie-dog-colored, Augustus thought. He frequently suggested to Dish that if he wanted to eat prairie dog he ought to remember to pick his teeth, a reference to the mustache whose subtlety was lost on Dish.

Lorena had her usual look—the look of a woman who was somewhere else. She had a fine head of blond hair, whose softness alone set her apart in a country where most women's hair had a consistency not much softer than saddle strings. Her cheeks hollowed a little—it gave her a distracting beauty. Augustus's experience had taught him that hollow-cheeked beauty was a dangerous kind. His two wives had both been fat-cheeked and trustworthy but had possessed little resistance to the climate. One had expired of pleurisy in only the second year of their marriage, while the other had been carried off by scarlet fever after the seventh. But the woman Lorena put him most in mind of was Clara Allen, whom he had loved hardest and deepest, and still loved. Clara's eyes were direct and sparkled with interest, whereas Lorena's were always side-looking. Still, there was something about the girl that reminded him of Clara, who had chosen a stolid horse trader when she decided to marry.

"I god, Dish," he said, going over to the table, "I never expected to see you loafing down here in the south this time of the year."

"Loan me two dollars, Gus," Dish said.

"Not me," Augustus said. "Why would I loan money to a loafer? You ought to be trailing cattle by this time of year."

"I'll be leaving next week to do just that," Dish said. "Loan me two dollars and I'll pay you in the fall."

"Unless you drown or get stomped or shoot somebody and get hung," Augustus said. "No sir. Too many perils ahead. Anyway, I've known you to be sly, Dish. You've probably got two dollars and just don't want to spend it."

Lippy finished his concert and came and joined them. He wore a brown bowler hat he had picked up on the road to San Antonio some years before. Either it had blown out of a stagecoach or the Indians had snatched some careless drummer and not bothered to take his hat. At least those were the two theories Lippy had worked out in order to explain his good fortune in finding the hat. In Augustus's view the hat would have looked better blowing around the country for two years than it did at present. Lippy only wore it when he played the piano; when he was just gambling or sitting around attending to the leak from his stomach he frequently used the hat for an ashtray and then sometimes forgot to empty the ashes before putting the hat back on his head. He only had a few strips of stringy gray hair hanging off his skull, and the ashes didn't make them look much worse, but ashes represented only a fraction of the abuse the bowler had suffered. It was also Lippy's pillow, and had had so many things spilled on it or in it that Augustus could hardly look at it without gagging.

"That hat looks about like a buffalo cud," Augustus said. "A hat ain't meant to be a chamber pot, you know. If I was you I'd throw it away."

Lippy was so named because his lower lip was about the size of the flap on a saddlebag. He could tuck enough snuff under it to last a normal person at least a month; in general the lip lived a life of its own, there toward the bottom of his face. Even when he was just sitting quietly, studying his cards, the lip waved and wiggled as if it had a breeze blowing across it, which in fact it did. Lippy had something wrong with his nose and breathed with his mouth wide open.

Accustomed as she was to hard doings, it had still taken Lorena a while to get used to the way Lippy slurped when he was eating, and she had once had a dream in which a cowboy walked by Lippy and buttoned the lip to his nose as if it were the flap of a pocket. But her disgust was nothing compared to Xavier's, who suddenly stopped wiping tables and came over and grabbed Lippy's hat off his head. Xavier was in a bad mood, and his features quivered like those of a trapped rabbit.

"Disgrace! I won't have this hat. Who can eat?" Xavier said, though nobody was trying to eat. He took the hat around the bar and flung it out the back door. Once as a boy he had carried slops in a restaurant in New Orleans that actually used tablecloths, a standard of excellence which haunted him still. Every time he looked at the bare tables in the Dry Bean he felt a failure. Instead of having tablecloths, the tables were so rough you could get a splinter just running your hand over them. Also, they weren't attractively round, since the cowboys could not be prevented from whittling on their edges—over the years sizable chunks had been whittled off, giving most of the tables an unbalanced look.

He himself had a linen tablecloth which he brought out once a year, on the anniversary of the death of his wife. His wife had been a bully and he didn't miss her, but it was the only occasion sufficient to provide an excuse for the use of a tablecloth in Lonesome Dove. His wife, whose name had been Therese, had bullied horses, too, which is why his team had run off and flung themselves and the buggy into a gully, the buggy landing right on top of Therese. At the annual dinner in her honor Xavier proved that he was still a restaurateur of discipline by getting drunk without spilling a drop on the fine tablecloth. Augustus was the only one invited to the dinners, but he only came every three or four years, out of politeness; not only were the occasions mournful and silly—everyone in Lonesome Dove had been glad to see the last of Therese—they were mildly dangerous. Augustus was neither as disciplined a drinker as Xavier nor as particular about tablecloths, either, and he knew that if he spilled liquor on the precious linen the situation would end badly. He would not likely have to shoot Xavier, but it might be necessary to whack him on the head, and Augustus hated to hit such a small head with such a large pistol.

To Xavier's mind, Lippy's hat was the final exacerbation. No man of dignity would allow such a hat in his establishment, much less on the head of an employee, so from time to time he seized it and flung it out the door. Perhaps a goat would eat it; they were said to eat worse. But the goats ignored the hat, and Lippy always went out and retrieved it when he remembered that he needed an ashtray.

"Disgrace!" Xavier said again, in a somewhat happier tone.

Lippy was unperturbed. "What's wrong with that hat?" he asked. "It was made in Philadelphia. Says so inside it."

It did say so, but Augustus, not Lippy, was the one who had originally made the point. Lippy could not have read a word as big as Philadelphia, and he had only the vaguest notion of where the city was. All he knew was that it must be a safe and civilized place if they had time to make hats instead of fighting Comanches.

"Xavier, I'll make you a deal," Augustus said. "Loan Dish here two dollars so we can get a little game going, and I'll rake that hat into a towsack and carry it home to my pigs. It's the only way you'll ever get rid of it."

"If you wear it again I will burn it," Xavier said, still inflamed. "I will burn the whole place. Then where will you go?"

"If you was to burn that pianer you best have a swift mule waiting," Lippy said, his lip undulating as he spoke. "The church folks won't like it."

Dish found the conversation a burden to listen to. He had delivered a small horse herd in Matamoros and had ridden nearly a hundred miles upriver with Lorie in mind. It was funny he would do it, since the thought of her scared him, but he had just kept riding and here he was. He mainly did his sporting with Mexican whores, but now and then he found he wanted a change from small brown women. Lorena was so much of a change that at the thought of her his throat clogged up and he lost his ability to talk. He had already been with her four times and had a vivid memory of how white she was: moon-pale and touched with shadows, like the night outside. Only not like the night, exactly—he could ride through the night peacefully, and a ride with Lorena was not peaceful. She used some cheap powder, a souvenir of her city living, and the smell of it seemed to follow Dish for weeks. He didn't like just paying her, though—it seemed to him it would be better if he brought her a fine present from Abilene or Dodge. He could get away with that with the señoritas—they liked the idea of presents to look forward to, and Dish was careful never to renege. He always came back from Dodge with ribbons and combs.

But somehow he could not get up the nerve even to make the suggestion to Lorena. It was hard enough to make a plain business offer. Often she seemed not to hear questions when they were put to her. It was hard to make a girl realize you had special feelings for her when she wouldn't look at you, didn't hear you, and made your throat clog up. It was even harder to live with the thought that the girl in question didn't want you to have the special feelings, particularly if you were about to go up the trail and not see her for many months.

Confusing as these feelings were, they were made even worse for Dish by the realization that he couldn't afford even the transaction that the girl would accept. He was down to his last two bits, having lost a full month's wages in a game in

Matamoros. He had no money, and no eloquence with which to persuade Lorena to trust him, but he did have a dogged persistence and was prepared to sit in the Dry Bean all night in hope that his evident need would finally move her.

Under the circumstances it was a sore trial to Dish that Augustus had come in. It seemed to him that Lorie had been getting a little friendlier, and if nothing had happened to distract her he might soon have prevailed. At least it had been just him and her at the table, which had been nice in itself. But now it was him and her and Augustus and Lippy, making it difficult, if not impossible, for him to plead his case—though all he had really been doing by way of pleading was to look at her frequently with big hopeful eyes.

Lippy began to feel unhappy about the fact that Xavier had thrown his hat out the door. Augustus's mention of the pigs put the whole matter in a more ominous light. After all, the pigs might come along and eat the hat, which was one of the solidest comforts in his meager existence. He would have liked to go and retrieve the hat before the pigs came along, but he knew that it wasn't really wise to provoke Xavier unduly when he was in a bad mood anyway. He couldn't see out the back door because the bar was in the way—for all he knew the hat might already be gone.

"I wisht I could get back to St. Louis," he said. "I hear it's a right busy town." He had been reared there, and when his heart was heavy he returned to it in his thoughts.

"Why, hell, go," Augustus said. "Life's a short affair. Why spend it here?"

"Well, you are," Dish said, in a surly tone, hoping Gus would take the hint and set out immediately.

"Dish, you sound like you've got a sour stomach," Augustus said. "What you need is a good satisfying game of cards."

"Nothing of the kind," Dish said, casting a bold and solicitous glance at Lorena.

Looking at her, though, was like looking at the hills. The hills stayed as they were. You could go to them, if you had the means, but they extended no greeting.

Xavier stood at the door, staring into the dark. The rag he used to wipe the tables was dripping onto his pants leg, but he didn't notice.

"It's too bad nobody in town ain't dead," Augustus remarked. "This group has the makings of a first-rate funeral party. What about you, Wanz? Let's play cards."

Xavier acquiesced. It was better than nothing. Besides, he was a devilish good cardplayer, one of the few around who was a consistent match for Augustus. Lorena was competent—Tinkersley had taught her a little. When the Dry Bean was full of cowboys she was not allowed to sit in, but on nights when the clientele consisted of Augustus, she often played.

When she played, she changed, particularly if she won a little—Augustus frequently did his best to help her win a little, just to see the process take place. The child in her was briefly reborn—she didn't chatter, but she did occasionally laugh out loud, and her cloudy eyes cleared and became animated. Once in a while, when she won a really good pot, she would give Augustus a little punch with her fist. It pleased him when that happened—it was good to see the girl enjoying herself. It put him in mind of family games, the kind he had once played with his lively sisters in Tennessee. The memory of those games usually put him to drinking more than he liked to—and all because Lorie ceased being a sulky whore for a little while and reminded him of happy girls he had once known.

They played until the rustler's moon had crossed to the other side of town. Lorena brightened so much that Dish Boggett fell worse in love with her than ever; she filled him with such an ache that he didn't mind that Xavier won half of his next month's wages. The ache was very much with him when he finally decided there was no hope and stepped out into the moonlight to unhitch his horse.

Augustus had come with him, while Lippy sneaked out the back door to retrieve his hat. The light in Lorena's room came on while they were standing there, and Dish looked up at it, catching just her shadow as she passed in front of the lamp.

"Well, Dish, so you're leaving us," Augustus said. "Which outfit's lucky enough to have you this trip?"

The quick glimpse of Lorena put Dish in such perplexity of spirit that he could hardly focus on the question.

"Reckon I'm going with the UU's," he said, his eyes still on the window.

The cause of Dish's melancholy was not lost on Augustus.

"Why that's Shanghai Pierce's bunch," he said.

"Yup," Dish said, starting to lift his foot to his stirrup.

"Now hold on a minute, Dish," Augustus said. He fished in his pocket and came out with two dollars, which he handed to the surprised cowboy.

"If you're riding north with old Shang we may never meet again this side of the bourn," Augustus said, deliberately adopting the elegiac tone. "At the very least you'll get your hearing ruint. That voice of his could deafen a rock."

Dish had to smile. Gus seemed unaware that one of the more persistent topics of dispute on the Texas range was whether his voice was louder than Shanghai Pierce's. It was commonly agreed that the two men had no close rivals when it came to being deafening.

"Why'd you give me this money?" Dish asked. He had never been able to figure Gus out.

"You asked me for it, didn't you?" Augustus said. "If I'd given it to you before the game started I might as well have handed it to Wanz, and he don't need no two dollars of mine."

There was a pause while Dish tried to puzzle out the real motive, if there was one.

"I'd not want it thought I'd refuse a simple loan to a friend," Augustus said. "Specially not one who's going off with Shanghai Pierce."

"Oh, Mr. Pierce don't go with us," Dish said. "He goes over to New Orleans and takes the train."

Augustus said nothing, and Dish soon concluded that he was to get the loan, even if the aggravation of Mr. Pierce's company wasn't involved.

"Well, much obliged then," Dish said. "I'll see you in the fall if not sooner."

"There's no need for you to ride off tonight," Augustus said. "You can throw your blanket down on our porch, if you like."

"I might do that," Dish said. Feeling rather awkward, he rehitched his horse and went to the door of the Dry Bean, wanting to get upstairs before Lorie turned off her light.

"I believe I left something," he said lamely, at the door of the saloon.

"Well, I won't wait, Dish," Augustus said. "But we'll expect you for breakfast if you care to stay."

As he strolled away he heard the boy's footsteps hitting the stairs at the back of the saloon. Dish was a good boy, not much less green than Newt, though a more experienced hand. Best to help such boys have their moment of fun, before life's torments snatched them.

From a distance, standing in the pale street, he saw two shadows against the yellow box of light from Lorie's room. She wasn't that set against Dish, it seemed to him, and she had been pepped up from the card playing. Maybe even Lorie would be surprised and find a liking for the boy. Occasionally he had known sporting women to marry and do well at it—if Lorie were so inclined Dish Boggett would not be a bad man to settle on.

The light had gone off at the Pumphreys' and the armadillo was no longer there to roll its shadow at him. The pigs were stretched out on the porch, lying practically snout to snout. Augustus was about to kick them off to make room for the guest he more or less expected, but they looked so peaceful he relented and went around to the back door. If Dish Boggett, with his prairie dog of a mustache, considered himself too refined to throw his bedroll beside two fine pigs, then he could rout them out himself.

5

WHATEVER SUBJECT Augustus had on his mind when he went to bed was generally still sitting there when he woke up. He was such a short sleeper that the subject had no time to slip out of mind. Five hours was as much as he ever slept at a stretch, and four hours was more nearly his average.

"A man that sleeps all night wastes too much of life," he often said. "As I see it the days was made for looking and the nights for sport."

Since sport was what he had been brooding about when he got home, it was still in his thoughts when he arose, which he did about 4 A.M., to see to the breakfast—in his view too important a meal to entrust to a Mexican bandit. The heart of his breakfast was a plenitude of sourdough biscuits, which he cooked in a Dutch oven out in the backyard. His pot dough had been perking along happily for over ten years, and the first thing he did upon rising was check it out. The rest of the breakfast was secondary, just a matter of whacking off a few slabs of bacon and frying a panful of pullet eggs. Bolivar could generally be trusted to deal with the coffee.

Augustus cooked his biscuits outside for three reasons. One was because the house was sure to heat up well enough anyway during the day, so there was no point in building any more of a fire than was necessary for bacon and eggs. Two was because biscuits cooked in a Dutch oven tasted better than stove-cooked biscuits, and three was because he liked to be outside to catch the first light. A man that depended on an indoor cookstove would miss the sunrise, and if he missed sunrise in Lonesome Dove, he would have to wait out a long stretch of heat and dust before he got to see anything so pretty.

Augustus molded his biscuits and went out and got a fire going in the Dutch oven while it was still good dark—just enough of a fire to freshen up his bed of mesquite coals. When he judged the oven was ready he brought the biscuits and his Bible out in the backyard. He set the biscuits in the oven, and sat down on a big black kettle that they used on the rare occasions when they rendered lard. The kettle was big enough to hold a small mule, if anybody had wanted to boil one, but for the last few years it had remained upside down, making an ideal seat.

The eastern sky was red as coals in a forge, lighting up the flats along the river. Dew had wet the million needles of the chaparral, and when the rim of the sun edged over the horizon the chaparral seemed to be spotted with diamonds. A bush in the backyard was filled with little rainbows as the sun touched the dew.

It was tribute enough to sunup that it could make even chaparral bushes look beautiful, Augustus thought, and he watched the process happily, knowing it would only last a few minutes. The sun spread reddish-gold light through the shining bushes, among which a few goats wandered, bleating. Even when the sun rose above the low bluffs to the south, a layer of light lingered for a bit at the level of the chaparral, as if independent of its source. Then the sun lifted clear, like an immense coin. The dew quickly died, and the light that filled the bushes like red dust dispersed, leaving clear, slightly bluish air.

It was good reading light by then, so Augustus applied himself for a few minutes to the Prophets. He was not overly religious, but he did consider himself a fair prophet and liked to study the styles of his predecessors. They were mostly too long-winded, in his view, and he made no effort to read them verse for verse— he just had a look here and there, while the biscuits were browning.

While he was enjoying a verse or two of Amos the pigs walked around the corner of the house, and Call, at almost the same moment, stepped out the back door, pulling on his shirt. The pigs walked over and stood directly in front of Augustus. The dew had wet their blue coats.

"They know I've got a soft heart," he said to Call. "They're hoping I'll feed them this Bible.

"I hope you pigs didn't wake up Dish," he added, for he had checked and seen that Dish was there, sleeping comfortably with his head on his saddle and his hat over his eyes, only his big mustache showing.

To Call's regret he had never been able to come awake easily. His joints felt like they were filled with glue, and it was an irritation to see Augustus sitting on the black kettle looking as fresh as if he'd slept all night, when in fact he had probably played poker till one or two o'clock. Getting up early and feeling awake was the one skill he had never truly perfected—he got up, of course, but it never felt natural.

Augustus lay down the Bible and walked over to look at Call's wound.

"I oughta slop some more axle grease on it," he said. "It's a nasty bite."

"You tend to your biscuits," Call said. "What's Dish Boggett doing here?"

"I didn't ask the man his business," Augustus said. "If you die of gangrene you'll be sorry you didn't let me dress that wound."

"It ain't a wound, it's just a bite," Call said. "I was bit worse by bedbugs down in Saltillo that time. I suppose you set up reading the Good Book all night."

"Not me," Augustus said. "I only read it in the morning and the evening, when I can be reminded of the glory of the Lord. The rest of the day I'm just reminded of what a miserable stink hole we stuck ourselves in. It's hard to have fun in a place like this, but I do my best."

He went over and put his hand on top of the Dutch oven. It felt to him like the biscuits were probably ready, so he took them out. They had puffed up nicely and were a healthy brown. He took them quickly into the house and Call followed. Newt was at the table, sitting straight upright, a knife in one hand and a fork in the other, but sound asleep.

"We come to this place to make money," Call said. "Nothing about fun was in the deal."

"Call, you don't even like money," Augustus said. "You've spit in the eye of every rich man you've ever met. You like money even less than you like fun, if that's possible."

Call sighed, and sat down at the table. Bolivar was up and stumbling around the stove, shaking so that he spilled coffee grounds on the floor.

"Wake up, Newt," Augustus said. "If you don't you'll fall over and stick yourself in the eye with your own fork."

Call gave the boy a little shake and his eyes popped open.

"I was having a dream," Newt said, sounding very young.

"Your tough luck, then, son," Augustus said. "Morning around here is more like a nightmare. Now look what's happened!"

In an effort to get the coffee going, Bolivar had spilled a small pile of coffee grounds into the grease where the eggs and bacon were frying. It seemed a small enough matter to him, but it enraged Augustus, who liked to achieve an orderly breakfast at least once a week.

"I guess it won't hurt the coffee none to taste like eggs," he said testily. "Most of the time your eggs taste like coffee."

"I don't care," Bolivar said. "I feel sick."

Pea Eye came stumbling through about that time, trying to get his pizzle out of his pants before his bladder started to flood. It was a frequent problem. The pants he wore had about fifteen small buttons, and he got up each morning and buttoned every one of them before he realized he was about to piss. Then he would come rushing through the kitchen trying to undo the buttons. The race was always close, but usually Pea would make it to the back steps before the flood commenced. Then he would stand there and splatter the yard for five minutes or so. When he could hear sizzling grease in one ear and the sound of Pea Eye pissing in the other, Augustus knew that the peace of the morning was over once again.

"If a woman ever stumbled onto this outfit at this hour of the day she'd screech and poke out her eyes," Augustus said.

At that point someone did stumble onto it, but only Dish Boggett, who had always been responsive to the smell of frying bacon.

It was a surprise to Newt, who immediately snapped awake and tried to get his cowlick to lay down. Dish Boggett was one of his heroes, a real cowboy who had been up the trail all the way to Dodge City more than once. It was Newt's great ambition: to go up the trail with a herd of cattle. The sight of Dish gave him hope, for Dish wasn't somebody totally out of reach, like the Captain. Newt didn't imagine that he could ever be what the Captain was, but Dish seemed not that much different from himself. He was known to be a top hand, and Newt welcomed every chance to be around him; he liked to study the way Dish did things.

"Morning, Dish," he said.

"Why, howdy there," Dish said, and went to stand beside Pea Eye and attend to the same business.

It perked Newt up that Dish didn't treat him like a kid. Someday, if he was lucky, maybe he and Dish would be cowboys together. Newt could imagine nothing better.

Augustus had fried the eggs hard as marbles to compensate for the coffee grains, and when they looked done to him he poured the grease into the big three-gallon syrup can they used for a grease bucket.

"It's poor table manners to piss in hearing of those at the table," he said, directing his remarks to the gentlemen on the porch. "You two are grown men. What would your mothers think?"

Dish looked a little sheepish, whereas Pea was merely confused by the question. His mother had passed away in Georgia when he was only six. She had not had time to give him much training before she died, and he had no idea what she might think of such an action. However, he was sure she would not have wanted him to go in his pants.

"I had to hurry," he said.

"Howdy, Captain," Dish said.

Call nodded. In the morning he had the advantage of Gus, since Gus had to cook. With Gus cooking, he got his choice of the eggs and bacon, and a little food always brought him to life and made him consider all the things that ought to be done during the day. The Hat Creek outfit was just a small operation, with just enough land under lease to graze small lots of cattle and horses until buyers could be found. It amazed Call that such a small operation could keep three grown men and a boy occupied from sunup until dark, day after day, but such was the case. The barn and corrals had been in such poor shape when he and Gus bought the place that it took constant work just to keep them from total collapse. There was nothing important to do in Lonesome Dove, but that didn't mean there was enough time to keep up with the little things that needed doing. They had been six weeks sinking a new well and were still far from deep enough.

When Call raked the eggs and bacon onto his plate, such a crowd of possible tasks rushed into his mind that he was a minute responding to Dish's greetings.

"Oh, hello, Dish," he said, finally. "Have some bacon."

"Dish is planning to shave his mustache right after breakfast," Augustus said. "He's getting tired of livin' without women."

In fact, with the aid of Gus's two dollars, Dish had been able to prevail on Lorena. He had awakened on the porch with a clear head, but when Augustus mentioned women he remembered it all and suddenly felt weak with love. He had been keenly hungry when he sat down at the table, his mouth watering for the eggs and fryback, but the thought of Lorena's white body, or the portion of it he had got to see when she lifted her nightgown, made him almost dizzy for a moment. He continued to eat, but the food had lost its taste.

The blue shoat came to the door and looked in at the people, to Augustus's amusement. "Look at that," he said. "A pig watching a bunch of human pigs." Though he had been outpositioned at the frying pan, he was in prime shape to secure his share of the biscuits, half a dozen of which he had already sopped in honey and consumed.

"Throw that pig them eggshells," he said to Bolivar. "He's starving."

"I don't care," Bolivar said, sucking coffee-colored sugar out of a big spoon. "I feel sick."

"You're repeating yourself, Bol," Augustus said. "If you're planning on dying today I hope you dig your grave first."

Bolivar looked at him sorrowfully. So much talk in the morning gave him a headache to go with his shakes. "If I dig a grave it will be yours," he said simply.

"Going up the trail, Dish?" Newt asked, hoping to turn the conversation to more cheerful matters.

"I hope to," Dish said.

"It would take a hacksaw to cut these eggs," Call said. "I've seen bricks that was softer."

"Well, Bol spilled coffee in them," Augustus said, "I expect it was hard coffee."

Call finished the rocklike eggs and gave Dish the onceover. He was a lank fellow, loose-built, and a good rider. Five or six more like him and they could make up a herd themselves and drive it north. The idea had been in his mind for a year or more. He had even mentioned it to Augustus, but Augustus merely laughed at him.

"We're too old, Call," he said. "We've forgot everything we need to know."

"You may have," Call said. "I ain't."

Seeing Dish put Call in mind of his idea again. He was not eager to spend the rest of his life on well-digging or barn repair. If they made up a fair herd and did well with it, they would make enough to buy some good land north of the brush country.

"Are you signed to go with someone then?" he asked Dish.

"Oh, no, I ain't signed on," Dish said. "But I've gone before, and I imagine Mr. Pierce will hire me again—or if not him someone else."

"We might give you work right here," Call said.

That got Augustus's attention. "Give him work doing what?" he asked. "Dish here's a top hand. He don't cotton to work that requires walking, do you, Dish?"

"I don't, for a fact," Dish said, looking at the Captain but seeing Lorena. "I've done a mess of it though. What did you have in mind?"

"Well, we're going down to Mexico tonight," Call said. "Going to see what we can raise. We might make up a herd ourselves, if you wanted to wait a day or two while we look it over."

"That mare bite's drove you crazy," Augustus said. "Make up a herd and do what with it?"

"Drive it," Call said.

"Well, we might drive it over to Pickles Gap, I guess," Augustus said. "That ain't enough work to keep a hand like Dish occupied for the summer."

Call got up and carried his dishes to the washtub. Bolivar wearily got off his stool and picked up the water bucket.

"I wish Deets would come back," he said.

Deets was a black man; he had been with Call and Augustus nearly as long as Pea Eye. Three days before, he had been sent to San Antonio with a deposit of money, a tactic Call always used, since few bandits would suspect a black man of having any money on him.

Bolivar missed him because one of Deet's jobs was to carry water.

"He'll be back this morning," Call said. "You can set your clock by Deets."

"You might set yours," Augustus said. "I wouldn't set mine. Old Deets is human. If he ever run into the right dark-complexioned lady you might have to wind your clock two or three times before he showed up. He's like me. He knows that some things are more important than work."

Bolivar looked at the water bucket with irritation. "I'd like to shoot this damn bucket full of holes," he said.

"I don't think you could hit that bucket if you was sitting on it," Augustus said. "I've seen you shoot. You ain't the worst shot I ever knew—that would be Jack Jennell—but you run him a close race. Jack went broke as a buffalo hunter quicker than any man I ever knew. He couldn't have hit a buffalo if one had swallowed him."

Bolivar went out the door with the bucket, looking as if it might be a while before he came back.

Dish meanwhile was doing some hard thinking. He had meant to leave right after breakfast and ride back to the Matagorda, where he had a sure job. The Hat

Creek outfit was hardly known as a trail-driving bunch, but on the other hand Captain Call was not a man to indulge in idle talk. If he was contemplating a drive he would probably make one. Meanwhile there was Lorena, who might come to see him in an entirely different light if he could spend time with her for a few days running. Of course, getting to spend time with her was expensive, and he had not a cent, but if word got around that he was working for the Hat Creek outfit he could probably attract a little credit.

One thing Dish prided himself on was his skill at driving a buggy; it occurred to him that since Lorena seemed to spend most of her time cooped up in the Dry Bean, she might appreciate a buggy ride along the river in a smart buggy, if such a creature could be found in Lonesome Dove. He got up and carried his plate to the wash bucket.

"Captain, if you mean it I'd be pleased to stay the day or two," Dish said.

The Captain had stepped out on the back porch and was looking north, along the stage road that threaded its way through the brush country toward San Antonio. The road ran straight for a considerable distance before it hit the first gully, and Captain Call had his eyes fixed on it. He seemed not to hear Dish's reply, although he was only a few feet away. Dish stepped out on the porch to see what it was that distracted the man. Far up the road he could see two horsemen coming, but they were so far yet that it was impossible to tell anything about them. At moments, heat waves from the road caused a quavering that made them seem like one horseman. Dish squinted but there was nothing special about the riders that his eye could detect. Yet the Captain had not so much as turned his head since they appeared.

"Gus, come out here," the Captain said.

Augustus was busy cleaning his plate of honey, a process that involved several more biscuits.

"I'm eating," he said, though that was obvious.

"Come see who's coming," the Captain said, rather mildly, Dish thought.

"If it's Deets my watch is already set," Augustus said. "Anyway, I don't suppose he's changed clothes, and if I have to see his old black knees sticking out of them old quilts he wears for pants it's apt to spoil my digestion."

"Deets is coming all right," Call said. "The fact is, he ain't by himself."

"Well, the man's always aimed to marry," Augustus said. "I imagine he just finally met up with that dark-complexioned lady I was referring to."

"He ain't met no lady," Call said with a touch of exasperation. "Who he's met is an old friend of ours. If you don't come here and look I'll have to drag you."

Augustus was about through with the biscuits anyway. He had to use a forefinger to capture the absolute last drop of honey, which was just as sweet licked off a finger as it was when eaten on good sourdough biscuits.

"Newt, did you know honey is the world's purest food?" he said, getting up.

Newt had heard enough lectures on the subject to have already forgotten more than most people ever know about the properties of honey. He hurried his plate to the tub, more curious than Mr. Gus about who Deets could have found.

"Yes, sir, I like it myself," he said, to cut short the talk of honey.

Augustus was a step behind the boy, idly licking his forefinger. He glanced up the road to see what Call could be so aroused about. Two riders were coming, the one on the left clearly Deets, on the big white gelding they called Wishbone. The other rider rode a pacing bay; it took but a moment for recognition to strike. The rider seemed to slump a little in the saddle, in the direction of his horse's off side, a tendency peculiar to only one man he knew. Augustus was so startled that he made the mistake of running his sticky fingers through his own hair.

"'I god, Woodrow," he said. "That there's Jake Spoon.""

6

THE NAME STRUCK NEWT like a blow, so much did Jake Spoon mean to him. As a very little boy, when his mother had still been alive, Jake Spoon was the man who came most often to see her. It had begun to be clear to him, as he turned over his memories, that his mother had been a whore, like Lorena, but this realization tarnished nothing, least of all his memories of Jake Spoon. No man had been kinder, either to him or his mother—her name had been Maggie. Jake had given him hard candy and pennies and had set him on a pacing horse and given him his first ride; he had even had old Jesus, the bootmaker, make him his first pair of boots; and once when Jake won a lady's saddle in a card game he gave the saddle to Newt and had the stirrups cut down to his size.

Those were the days before order came to Lonesome Dove, when Captain Call and Augustus were still Rangers, with responsibilities that took them up and down the border. Jake Spoon was a Ranger too, and in Newt's eyes the most dashing of them all. He always carried a pearl-handled pistol and rode a pacing horse—easier on the seat, Jake claimed. The dangers of his profession seemed to sit lightly on him.

But then the fighting gradually died down along the border and the Captain and Mr. Gus and Jake and Pea Eye and Deets all quit rangering and formed the Hat Creek outfit. But the settled life seemed not to suit Jake, and one day he was just gone. No one was surprised, though Newt's mother was so upset by it that for a time he got a whipping every time he asked when Jake was coming back. The whippings didn't seem to have much to do with him, just with his mother's disappointment that Jake had left.

Newt stopped asking about Jake, but he didn't stop remembering him. It was barely a year later that his mother died of fever; the Captain and Augustus took him in, although at first they argued about him. At first Newt missed his mother so much that he didn't care about the arguments. His mother and Jake were both gone and arguments were not going to bring them back.

But when the worst pain passed and he began to earn his keep around the Hat Creek outfit by doing the numerous chores that the Captain set him, he often drifted back in his mind to the days when Jake Spoon had come to see his mother. It seemed to him that Jake might even be his father, though everyone told him his name was Newt Dobbs, not Newt Spoon. Why it was Dobbs, and why everyone was so sure, was a puzzle to him, since no one in Lonesome Dove seemed to know anything about a Mr. Dobbs. It had not occurred to him to ask his mother while she was alive—last names weren't used much around Lonesome Dove, and he didn't realize that the last name was supposed to come from the father. Even Mr. Gus, who would talk about anything, seemed to have no information about Mr. Dobbs. "He went west when he shouldn't have," was his only comment on the man.

Newt had never asked Captain Call to amplify that information—the Captain preferred to volunteer what he wanted you to know. In his heart, though, Newt didn't believe in Mr. Dobbs. He had a little pile of stuff his mother had left, just a few beads and combs and a little scrapbook and some cutout pictures from magazines that Mr. Gus had been kind enough to save for him, and there was nothing about a Mr. Dobbs in the scrapbook and no picture of him amid the pictures, though there was a scratchy picture of his grandfather, Maggie's father, who had lived in Alabama.

If, as he suspected, there had been no Mr. Dobbs, or if he had just been a gentleman who stopped at the rooming house a day or two—they had lived in the rooming house when Maggie was alive—then it might be that Jake Spoon was really his father. Perhaps no one had informed him of it because they thought it more polite to let Jake do so himself when he came back.

Newt had always assumed Jake *would* come back, too. Scraps of news about him had blown back down the cow trails—word that he was a peace officer in Ogallala, or that he was prospecting for gold in the Black Hills. Newt had no idea where the Black Hills were, or how you went about finding gold in them, but one of the reasons he was eager to head north with a cow herd was the hope of running into Jake somewhere along the way. Of course he wanted to wear a gun and become a top hand and have the adventure of the drive—maybe they would even see buffalo, though he knew there weren't many left. But underneath all his other hopes was the oldest yearning he had, one that could lie covered over for months and years and still be fresh as a toothache: the need to see Jake Spoon.

Now the very man was riding toward them, right there beside Deets, on a pacing horse as pretty as the one he had ridden away ten years before. Newt forgot Dish Boggett, whose every move he had been planning to study. Before the two riders even got very close Newt could see Deet's big white teeth shining in his black face, for he had gone away on a routine job and was coming back proud of more than having done it. He didn't race his horse up to the porch or do anything silly, but it was plain even at a distance that Deets was a happy man.

Then the horses were kicking up little puffs of dust in the wagon yard and the two were almost there. Jake wore a brown vest and a brown hat, and he still had his pearl-handled pistol. Deets was still grinning. They rode right up to the back porch before they drew rein. It was obvious that Jake had come a long way, for the pacing bay had no flesh on him.

Jake's eyes were the color of coffee, and he wore a little mustache. He looked them all over for a moment, and then broke out a slow grin.

"Howdy, boys," he said. "What's for breakfast?"

"Why, biscuits and fatback, Jake," Augustus said. "The usual fare. Only we won't be serving it up for about twenty-four hours. I hope you've got a buffalo liver or a haunch of venison on you to tide you over."

"Gus, don't tell me you've et," Jake said, swinging off the bay. "We rode all night, and Deets couldn't think of nothing to talk about except the taste of them biscuits you make."

"While you was talking, Gus was eating them," Call said. He and Jake shook hands, looking one another over.

Jake looked at Deets a minute. "I knowed we should have telegraphed from Pickles Gap," he said, then turned with a grin and shook Gus's hand.

"You always was a hog, Gus," Jake said.

"And you were usually late for meals," Augustus reminded him.

Then Pea Eye insisted on shaking hands, though Jake had never been very partial to him. "By gosh, Jake, you stayed gone a while," Pea Eye said.

While they were shaking Jake noticed the boy, standing there by some lank cowhand with a heavy mustache. "My lord," he said. "Are you little Newt? Why you're plumb growed. Who let that happen?"

Newt felt so full of feeling that he could hardly speak. "It's me, Jake," he said. "I'm still here."

"What do you think, Captain?" Deets asked, handing Call the receipt from the bank. "Didn't I find the prodigal?"

"You found him," Call said. "I bet he wasn't in church, either."

Deets had a laugh at that. "No, sir," he said. "Not in church."

Jake was introduced to Dish Boggett, but once he shook hands he turned and had another look at Newt as if the fact that he was nearly grown surprised him more than anything else in Lonesome Dove.

"I swear, Jake," Augustus said, looking at the bay horse, "you've rode that horse right down to the bone."

"Give him a good feed, Deets," Call said. "I judge it's been a while since he's had one."

Deets led the horses off toward the roofless barn. It was true that he made his pants out of old quilts, for reasons that no one could get him to explain. Colorful as they were, quilts weren't the best material for riding through mesquite and chaparral. Thorns had snagged the pants in several places, and cotton ticking was sticking out. For headgear Deets wore an old cavalry cap he had found somewhere—it was in nearly as bad shape as Lippy's bowler.

"Didn't he have that cap when I left?" Jake asked. He took his own hat off and slapped the dust off his pants leg with it. He had curly black hair, but Newt saw to his surprise that there was a sizable bald spot on the top of his head.

"He found that cap in the fifties, to the best of my recollection," Augustus said. "You know Deets is like me—he's not one to quit on a garment just because it's got a little age. We can't all be fine dressers like you, Jake."

Jake turned his coffee eyes on Augustus and broke out another slow grin. "What'd it take to get you to whip up another batch of them biscuits?" he said. "I've come all the way from Arkansas without tasting a good bite of bread."

"From the looks of that pony it's been fast traveling," Call said, which was as close to prying as he intended to get. He had run with Jake Spoon off and on for twenty years, and liked him well; but the man had always worried him a little, underneath. There was no more likable man in the west, and no better rider, either; but riding wasn't everything, and neither was likableness. Something in Jake didn't quite stick. Something wasn't quite consistent. He could be the coolest man in the company in one fight, and in the next be practically worthless.

Augustus knew it too. He was a great sponsor of Jake's and had stayed fond of him although for years they were rivals for Clara Allen, who eventually showed them both the door. But Augustus felt, with Call, that Jake wasn't long on backbone. When he left the Rangers Augustus said more than once that he would probably end up hung. So far that hadn't happened, but riding up at breakfast time on a gant horse was an indication of trouble. Jake prided himself on pretty horses, and would never ride a horse as hard as the bay had been ridden if trouble wasn't somewhere behind him.

Jake saw Bolivar coming from the old cistern with a bucketful of water. Bolivar was a new face, and one that had no interest in his homecoming. A little cool water sloshed over the edges of the bucket, looking very good to a man with a mouth as dusty as Jake's.

"Boys, I'd like a drink and maybe even a wash, if you can spare one," he said. "My luck's been running kinda muddy lately, but I'd like to get water enough in me that I can at least spit before I tell you about it."

"Why, sure," Augustus said. "Go fill the dipper. You want us to stay out here and hold off the posses?"

"There ain't no posses," Jake said, going in the house.

Dish Boggett felt somewhat at a loss. He had been all ready to hire on, and then this new man rode up and everyone had sort of forgotten him. Captain Call, a man known for being all business, seemed a little distracted. He and Gus just stood there as if they expected a posse despite what Jake Spoon had said.

Newt noticed it too. Mr. Gus ought to go in and cook Jake some biscuits, but he just stood there, thinking about something, evidently. Deets was on his way back from the lots.

Dish finally spoke up. "Captain, like I said, I'd be glad to wait if you have some plans to make up a herd," he said.

The Captain looked at him strangely, as if he might have forgotten his name, much less what he was doing there. But it wasn't the case.

"Why, yes, Dish," he said. "We might be needing some hands, if you don't mind doing some well-digging while you wait. Pea, you best get these boys started."

Dish was almost ready to back out then and there. He had drawn top wages for the last two years without being asked to do anything that couldn't be done from a horse. It was insensitive of the Captain to think that he could just order him off, with a boy and an old idiot like Pea Eye, to wrestle a spade and crowbar all day. It scratched his pride, and he had a notion to go get his horse and let them keep their well-digging. But the Captain was looking at him hard, and when Dish looked up to say he had changed his mind, their eyes met and Dish didn't say it. There had been no real promises made, much less talk of wages, but somehow Dish had taken one step too far. The Captain was looking at him eye to eye, as if to see if he was going to stand by his own words or if he meant to wiggle like a fish and change his mind. Dish had only offered to stay because of Lorie, but suddenly it had all gotten beyond her. Pea and Newt were already walking toward the barn. It was clear from the Captain's attitude that unless he wanted to lose all reputation, he had trapped himself into at least one day's well-digging.

It seemed to him he ought to at least say something to salvage a little pride, but before he could think of anything Gus came over and clapped him on the shoulder.

"You should have rode on last night, Dish," he said with an irritating grin. "You may never see the last of this outfit now."

"Well, you was the one that invited me," Dish said, highly annoyed. Since there was no help for it short of disgrace, he started for the lots.

"If you come to Chiny you can stop digging," Augustus called after him. "That's the place where the men wear pigtails."

"I wouldn't ride him if I were you," Call said. "We may need him."

"I didn't send him off to dig no well," Augustus said. "Don't you know that's an insult to his dignity? I'm surprised he went. I thought Dish had more grit."

"He said he'd stay," Call said. "I ain't feeding him three times a day to sit around and play cards with you."

"No need to now," Augustus said. "I got Jake for that. I bet you don't get Jake down in your well."

At that moment Jake stepped out on the back porch, his sleeves rolled up and his face red from the scrubbing he had given it with the old piece of sacking they used for a towel.

"That old *pistolero's* been cleaning his gun on this towel," Jake said. "It's filthy dirty."

"If it's just his six-shooter he's cleaning on it you oughtn't to complain," Augustus said. "There's worse things he could wipe on it."

"Hell, don't you men ever wash?" Jake asked. "That old Mex didn't even want to give me a pan of water."

It was the kind of remark Call had no patience with, but that was Jake, more interested in fancy arrangements than in the more important matters.

"Once you left, our standards slipped," Augustus said. "The majority of this outfit ain't interested in refinements."

"That's plain," Jake said. "There's a damn pig on the back porch. What about them biscuits?"

"Much as I've missed you, I ain't overworking my sourdough just because you and Deets couldn't manage to get here in time," Augustus said. "What I will do is fry some meat."

He fried it, and Jake and Deets ate it, while Bolivar sat in the corner and sulked at the thought of two more breakfasts to wash up after. It amused Augustus to watch Jake eat—he was so fastidious about it—but the sight put Call into a black fidget. Jake could spend twenty minutes picking at some eggs and a bit of bacon. It was obvious to Augustus that Call was trying to be polite and let Jake get some food in his belly before he told his story, but Call was not a patient man and had already controlled his urge to get to work longer than was usual. He stood in the door, watching the whitening sky and looking restless enough to bite himself.

"So where have you been, Jake?" Augustus asked, to speed things up.

Jake looked thoughtful, as he almost always did. His coffee-colored eyes always seemed to be traveling leisurely over scenes from his own past, and they gave the impression that he was a man of sorrows—an impression very appealing to the ladies. It disgusted Augustus a little that ladies were so taken in by Jake's big eyes. In fact, Jake Spoon had had a perfectly easy life, doing mostly just what he pleased and keeping his boots clean; what his big eyes concealed was a slow-working brain. Basically Jake just dreamed his way through life and somehow got by with it.

"Oh, I've been seeing the country," he said. "I was up to Montana two years ago. I guess that's what made me decide to come back, although I've been meaning to get back down this way and see you boys for some years."

Call came back in the room and straddled a chair, figuring he might as well hear it.

"What's Montana got to do with us?" he asked.

"Why, Call, you ought to see it," Jake said. "A prettier country never was."

"How far'd you go?" Augustus asked.

"Way up, past the Yellowstone," Jake said. "I was near to the Milk River. You can smell Canady from there."

"I bet you can smell Indians too," Call said. "How'd you get past the Cheyenne?"

"They shipped most of them out," Jake said. "Some of the Blackfeet are still troublesome. But I was with the Army, doing a little scouting."

That hardly made sense. Jake Spoon might scout his way across a card table, but Montana was something else.

"When'd you take to scouting?" Call asked dryly.

"Oh, I was just with a feller taking some beef to the Blackfeet," Jake said. "The Army came along to help."

"A lot of damn help the Army would be, driving beef," Gus said.

"They helped us keep our hair," Jake said, laying his knife and fork across his plate as neatly as if he were eating at a fancy table.

"My main job was to skeer the buffalo out of the way," he said.

"Buffalo," Augustus said. "I thought they was about gone."

"Pshaw," Jake said. "I must have seen fifty thousand up above the Yellowstone. The damn buffalo hunters ain't got the guts to take on them Indians. Oh, they'll finish them, once the Cheyenne and the Sioux finally cave in, and they may have even since I left. The damn Indians have the grass of Montana all to themselves. And has it got grass. Call, you ought to see it."

"I'd go today if I could fly," Call said.

"Be safer to walk," Augustus said. "By the time we walked up there maybe they would have licked the Indians."

"That's just it, boys," Jake said. "The minute they're licked there's going to be fortunes made in Montana. Why, it's cattle land like you've never seen, Call. High grass and plenty of water."

"Chilly, though, ain't it?" Augustus asked.

"Oh, it's got weather," Jake said. "Hell, a man can wear a coat."

"Better yet, a man can stay inside," Augustus said.

"I've yet to see a fortune made inside," Call said. "Except by a banker, and we ain't bankers. What did you have in mind, Jake?"

"Getting to it first," Jake said. "Round up some of these free cattle and take 'em on up. Beat all the other sons of bitches, and we'd soon be rich."

Augustus and Call exchanged looks. It was odd talk to be hearing from Jake Spoon, who had never been known for his ambition—much less for a fondness for cows. Pretty whores, pacing horses, and lots of clean shirts had been his main requirements in life.

"Why, Jake, what reformed you?" Gus asked. "You was never a man to hanker after fortune."

"Living with the cows from here to Montana would mean a change in your habits, if I remember them right," Call said.

Jake grinned his slow grin. "You boys," he said. "You got me down for lazier than I am. I ain't no lover of cow shit and trail dust, I admit, but I've seen something that you haven't seen: Montana. Just because I like to play cards don't mean I can't smell an opportunity when one's right under my nose. Why, you boys ain't even got a barn with a roof on it. I doubt it would bust you to move."

"Jake, if you ain't something," Augustus said. "Here we ain't seen hide nor hair of you for ten years and now you come riding in and want us to pack up and go north to get scalped."

"Well, Gus, me and Call are going bald anyway," Jake said. "You're the only one whose hair they'd want."

"All the more reason not to carry it to a hostile land," Augustus said. "Why don't you just calm down and play cards with me for a few days? Then when I've won all your money we'll talk about going places."

Jake whittled down a match and began to meticulously pick his teeth.

"By the time you clean me, Montana will be all settled up," he said. "I don't clean quick."

"What about that horse?" Call asked. "You didn't gant him like that just so you could get here and help us beat the rush to Montana. What's this about your luck running thick?"

Jake looked a little more sorrowful as he picked his teeth. "Kilt a dentist," he said. "A pure accident, but I kilt him."

"Where'd this happen?" Call asked.

"Fort Smith, Arkansas," Jake said. "Not three weeks ago."

"Well, I've always considered dentistry a dangerous profession," Augustus said. "Making a living by yanking people's teeth out is asking for trouble."

"He wasn't even pulling my tooth," Jake said. "I didn't even know there was a dentist in the town. I got in a little argument in a saloon and a damn mule skinner threw down on me. Somebody's old buffalo rifle was leaning against the wall right by me and that's what I went for. Hell, I was sitting on my own pistol—I never wouldn't have got to it in time. I wasn't even playin' cards with the mule skinner."

"What riled him then?" Gus asked.

"Whiskey," Jake said. "He was bull drunk. Before I even noticed, he took a dislike to my dress and pulled his Colt."

"Well, I don't know what took you to Arkansas in the first place, Jake," Augustus said. "A fancy dresser like yourself is bound to excite comment in them parts."

Call had found, over the years, that it only did to believe half of what Jake said. Jake was not a bald liar, but once he thought over a scrape, his imagination sort of worked on it and shaded it in his own favor.

"If the man pointed a gun at you and you shot him, then that was self-defense," Call said. "I still don't see where the dentist comes in."

"It was bad luck all around," Jake said. "I never even shot the mule skinner. I did shoot, but I missed, which was enough to scare him off. But of course I shot that dern buffalo gun. It was just a little plank saloon we were sitting in. A plank won't stop a fifty-caliber bullet."

"Neither will a dentist," Augustus observed. "Not unless you shoot down on him from the top, and even then I expect the bullet would come out his foot."

Call shook his head—Augustus could think of the damndest things.

"So where was the dentist?" he asked.

"Walking along on the other side of the street," Jake said. "They got big wide streets in that town, too."

"But not wide enough, I guess," Call said.

"Nope," Jake said. "We went to the door to watch the mule skinner run off and saw the dentist laying over there dead, fifty yards away. He had managed to get in the exact wrong spot."

"Pea done the same thing once," Augustus said. "Remember, Woodrow? Up in the Wichita country? Pea shot at a wolf and missed and the bullet went over a hill and kilt one of our horses."

"I won't forget that," Call said. "It was little Billy it killed. I hated to lose that horse."

"Of course we couldn't convince Pea he'd done it," Augustus said. "He don't understand trajectory."

"Well, I understand it," Jake said. "Everybody in town liked that dentist."

"Aw, Jake, that won't stick," Augustus said. "Nobody really likes dentists."

"This one was the mayor," Jake said.

"Well, it was accidental death," Call said.

"Yeah, but I'm just a gambler," Jake said. "They all like to think they're respectable back in Arkansas. Besides, the dentist's brother was the sheriff, and somebody told him I was a gunfighter. He invited me to leave town a week before it happened."

Call sighed. All the gunfighter business went back to one lucky shot Jake had made when he was a mere boy starting out in the Rangers. It was funny how one shot could make a man's reputation like that. It was a hip shot Jake made because he was scared, and it killed a Mexican bandit who was riding toward them on a dead run. It was Call's opinion, and Augustus's too, that Jake hadn't even been shooting at the bandit—he was probably shooting in hopes of bringing down the horse, which might have fallen on the bandit and crippled him a little. But Jake shot blind from the hip, with the sun in his eyes to boot, and hit the bandit right in the Adam's apple, a thing not likely to occur more than once in a lifetime, if that often.

But it was Jake's luck that most of the men who saw him make the shot were raw boys too, with not enough judgment to appreciate how lucky a thing it was. Those that survived and grew up told the story all across the West, so there was hardly a man from the Mexican border to Canada who hadn't heard what a dead pistol shot Jake Spoon was, though any man who had fought with him through the years would know he was no shot at all with a pistol and only a fair shot with a rifle.

Call and Augustus had always worried about Jake because of his unearned reputation, but he was a lucky fellow and there were not many men around dumb enough to enjoy pistol fights, so Jake managed to get by. It was ironic that the shot which finally got him in trouble was as big an accident as the shot that had made his fame.

"How'd you get loose from the sheriff?" Call asked.

"He was gone when it happened," Jake said. "He was up in Missouri, testifying on some stage robbers. I don't know if he's even back to Fort Smith yet."

"They wouldn't have hung you for an accident, even in Arkansas," Call said.

"I am a gambler, but that's one I didn't figure to gamble on," Jake said. "I just went out the back door and left, hoping July would get too busy to come after me."

"July's the sheriff?" Gus asked.

"Yes, July Johnson," Jake said. "He's young, but he's determined. I just hope he gets busy."

"I don't know why a lawman would want a dentist for a brother," Augustus said rather absently.

"If he warned you out of the town you should have left," Call said. "There's plenty of other towns besides Fort Smith."

"Jake probably had him a whore," Augustus said. "He usually does."

"You're one to talk, Gus," Jake said.

They all fell silent for a time while Jake thoughtfully picked his teeth with the sharpened match. Bolivar was sound asleep, sitting on his stool.

"I should have rode on, Call," Jake said apologetically. "But Fort Smith's a pretty town. It's on the river, and I like to have a river running by me. They eat catfish down there. I got where it kinda suited my tooth."

"I'd like to see the fish that could keep me in a place I wasn't wanted," Call said. Jake had always been handy with excuses.

"That's what we'll tell the sheriff when he shows up to take you back," Augustus said. "Maybe he'll take you fishing while you're waiting to be hung."

Jake let it pass. Gus would have his joke, and he and Call *would* disapprove of him when he got in some unlucky scrape. It had always been that way. But the three of them were *compañeros* still, no matter how many dentists he killed. Call and Gus had been the law themselves and didn't always bow and scrape to it. They would not likely let some young sheriff take him off to hang because of an accident. He was willing to take a bit of ribbing. When trouble came, if it did, the boys would stick and July Johnson would have to ride back home empty-handed.

He stood up and walked to the door to look over the hot, dusty little town.

"I hardly thought to find you boys still here," he said. "I thought you'd have some big ranch somewhere by now. This town was a two-bit town when we came here and it looks to me like it's lost about fifteen cents since then. Who's left that we all know?"

"Xavier and Lippy," Augustus said. "Therese got kilt, thank God. A few of the boys are left but I forget who. Tom Bynum's left."

"He would be," Jake said. "The Lord looks after fools like Tom."

"What do you hear of Clara?" Augustus asked. "I suppose since you traveled the world you've been to see her. Dropped in for supper, innocent-like, I guess."

Call stood up to go. He had heard enough to know why Jake had come back, and didn't intend to waste the day listening to him jaw about his travels, particularly not if it meant having to hear any talk about Clara Allen. He had heard enough about Clara in the old days, when Gus and Jake had both been courting her. He had been quite happy to think it all ended when she married, but it hadn't ended, and listening to Gus pine over her was almost as bad as having him and Jake fighting about her. Now, with Jake back, it would all start again, though Clara Allen had been married and gone for over fifteen years.

Deets stood up when Call did, ready for work. He hadn't said a word while eating, but it was clear he took much pride in being the one who had seen Jake first.

"Well, it ain't a holiday," Call said. "Work to do. Me and Deets will go see if we can help them boys."

"That Newt surprised me," Jake said. "I had it in mind he was still a spud. Is Maggie still here?"

"Maggie's been dead nine years," Augustus said. "You wasn't hardly over the hill when it happened."

"I swear," Jake said. "You mean you've had little Newt for nine years?"

There was a long silence, in which only Augustus felt comfortable. Deets felt so uncomfortable that he stepped in front of the Captain and went out the door.

"Why, yes, Jake," Gus said. "We've had him since Maggie died."

"I swear," Jake said again.

"It was only the Christian thing," Augustus said. "Taking him in, I mean. After all, one of you boys is more than likely his pa."

Call put on his hat, picked up his rifle and left them to their talk.

7

JAKE SPOON STOOD in the door of the low house, watching Call and Deets head for the barn. He had been looking forward to being home from the moment he looked out the door of the saloon and saw the dead man laying in the mud across the wide main street of Fort Smith, but now that he was home it came back to him how nervous things could be if Call wasn't in his best mood.

"Deets's pants are a sight, ain't they," he said mildly. "Seems to me he used to dress better."

Augustus chuckled. "He used to dress worse," he said. "Why, he had that sheepskin coat for fifteen years. You couldn't get in five feet of him without the lice jumping on you. It was because of that coat that we made him sleep in the barn. I ain't finicky except when it comes to lice."

"What happened to it?" Jake asked.

"I burned it," Augustus said. "Done it one summer when Deets was off on a trip with Call. I told him a buffalo hunter stole it. Deets was ready to track him and get his coat back, but I talked him out of it."

"Well, it was his coat," Jake said. "I don't blame him."

"Hell, Deets didn't need it," Augustus said. "It ain't cold down here. Deets was just attached to it because he had it so long. You remember when we found it, don't you? You was along?"

"I may have been along but I don't remember," Jake said, lighting a smoke.

"We found that coat in an abandoned cabin up on the Brazos," Augustus said. "I guess the settlers that run out decided it was too heavy to carry. It weighed as much as a good-sized sheep, which is why Call gave it to Deets. He was the only one of us stout enough to carry it all day. Don't you remember that, Jake? It was the time we had that scrape up by Fort Phantom Hill."

"I remember a scrape, but the rest is kinda cloudy," Jake said. "I guess all you boys have got to do is sit around and talk about old times. I'm young yet, Gus. I got a living to make."

In fact, what he did remember was being scared every time they crossed the Brazos, since it would just be ten or twelve of them and no reason not to think they would run into a hundred Comanches or Kiowas. He would have been glad to quit rangering if he could have thought of a way to do it that wouldn't look bad, but there was no way. In the end he came through twelve Indian fights and many scrapes with bandits only to get in real trouble in Fort Smith, Arkansas, as safe a town as you could find.

Now that he had come back, it was just to be reminded of Maggie, who had always threatened to die if he ever left her. Of course, he had thought it just girlish talk, the kind of thing all women said when they were trying to hold a fellow. Jake had heard such talk all the way up the trail, in San Antonio and Fort Worth,

Abilene and Dodge, in Ogallala and Miles City—the talk of whores pretending to be in love for one. But Maggie had actually died, when he had only supposed she would just move on to another town. It was a sad memory to come home to, though from what he knew of the situation, Call had done her even worse than he had.

"Jake, I notice you've not answered me about Clara," Augustus said. "If you've been to see her I'd like to hear about it, even though I begrudge you every minute."

"Oh, you ain't got much begrudging to do," Jake said. "I just seen her for a minute, outside a store in Ogallala. That dern Bob was with her, so all I could do was tip my hat and say good morning."

"I swear, Jake, I thought you'd have more gumption than that," Augustus said. "They live up in Nebraska, do they?"

"Yes, on the North Platte," Jake said. "Why, he's the biggest horse trader in the territory. The Army gets most of its horses from him, what Army's in those parts, and the Army wears out a lot of horses. I reckon he's close to rich."

"Any young uns?" Augustus asked.

"Two girls, I believe," Jake said. "I heard her boys died. Bob wasn't too friendly—I wasn't asked to supper."

"Even old dumb Bob's got enough sense to keep the likes of you away from Clara," Augustus said. "How did she look?"

"Clara?" Jake said. "Not as pretty as she once was."

"I guess it's a hard life up in Nebraska," Gus said.

After that, neither of them had any more to say for a few minutes. Jake thought it ill-spoken of Gus to bring Clara up, a woman he no longer had any sympathy for since she had shown him the door and married a big dumb horse trader from Kentucky. Even losing her to Gus wouldn't have been so bitter a blow, since Gus had been her beau before he met her.

Augustus felt his own pangs—irked, mainly, that Jake had had a glimpse of Clara, whereas he himself had to make do with an occasional scrap of gossip. At sixteen she had been so pretty it took your breath, and smart too—a girl with some sand, as she had quickly shown when both her parents had been killed in the big Indian raid of '56, the worst ever to rake that part of the country. Clara had been in school in San Antonio when it happened, but she came right back to Austin and ran the store her parents had started—the Indians had tried to set fire to it but for some reason it didn't catch.

Augustus felt he might have won her that year, but as luck would have it he was married then, to his second wife, and by the time she died Clara had developed such an independent mind that winning her was no longer an easy thing.

In fact, it proved an impossible thing. She wouldn't have him, or Jake either, and yet she married Bob Allen, a man so dumb he could hardly walk through a door without bumping his head. They soon went north; since then, Augustus had kept his ears open for news that she was widowed—he didn't wish Clara any unpleasantness, but horse trading in Indian country was risky business. If Bob should meet an untimely end—as better men had—then he wanted to be the first to offer his assistance to the widow.

"That Bob Allen's lucky," he remarked. "I've known horse traders who didn't last a year."

"Why, hell, you're a horse trader yourself," Jake said. "You boys have let yourselves get stuck. You should have gone north long ago. There's plenty of opportunity left up north."

"That may be, Jake, but all you've done with it is kill a dentist," Augustus said. "At least we ain't committed no ridiculous crimes."

Jake smiled. "Have you got anything to drink around here?" he asked. "Or do you just sit around all day with your throat parched."

"He gets drunk," Bolivar said, waking up suddenly.

Augustus stood up. "Let's go for a stroll," he said. "This man don't like folks idling in his kitchen after a certain hour."

They walked out into the hot morning. The sky was already white. Bolivar followed them out, picking up a rawhide lariat that he kept on a pile of firewood back by the porch. They watched him walk off into the chaparral, the rope in his hand.

"That old *pistolero* ain't very polite," Jake said. "Where's he going with that rope?"

"I didn't ask him," Gus said. He went around to the springhouse, which was empty of rattlesnakes for once. It amused him to think how annoyed Call would be when he came up at noon and found them both drunk. He handed Jake the jug, since he was the guest. Jake uncorked it and took a modest swig.

"Now if we had some shade to drink this in, we'd be in good shape," Jake said. "I don't suppose there's a sporting woman in this town, is there?"

"You are a scamp," Augustus said, taking the jug. "Are you so rich that's all you can think about?"

"I can think about it, rich or poor," Jake said.

They squatted in the shade of the springhouse for a bit, their backs against the adobe, which was still cool on the side the sun hadn't struck. Augustus saw no need to mention Lorena, since he knew Jake would soon discover her for himself and probably have her in love with him within the week. The thought of Dish Boggett's bad timing made him smile, for it was certain Jake's return would doom whatever chance Dish might have had. Dish had committed himself to a day of well-digging for nothing, for when it came to getting women in love with him Jake Spoon had no equal. His big eyes convinced them he'd be lost without them, and none of them seemed to want him just to go on and be lost.

While they were squatting by the springhouse, the pigs came nosing around the house looking for something to eat. But there wasn't so much as a grasshopper in the yard. They stopped and looked at Augustus a minute.

"Get on down to the saloon," he said. "Maybe you'll find Lippy's hat."

"Folks that keep pigs ain't no better than farmers," Jake said. "I'm surprised at you and Call. If you gave up being lawmen I thought you'd at least stay cattlemen."

"I thought you'd own a railroad by now, for that matter," Augustus said. "Or a whorehouse, at least. I guess life's been a disappointment to us both."

"I may not have no fortune, but I've never said a word to a pig, either," Jake said. Now that he was home and back with friends, he was beginning to feel sleepy. After a few more swigs and a little more argument, he stretched out as close to the springhouse as he could get, so as to have shade for as long as possible. He raised up an elbow to have one more go at the jug.

"How come Call lets you sit around and guzzle this mash all day?" he asked.

"Call ain't never been my boss," Augustus said. "It's no say-so of his when I drink."

Jake looked off across the scrubby pastures. There were tufts of grass here and there, but mostly the ground looked hard as flint. Heat waves were rising off it like fumes off kerosene. Something moved in his line of vision, and for a moment he thought he saw some strange brown animal under a chaparral bush. Looking more closely he saw that it was the old Mexican's bare backside.

"Hell, why'd he take a rope if all he meant to do was shit?" he asked. "Where'd you get the greasy old bastard?"

"We're running a charitable home for retired criminals," Augustus said. "If you'd just retire you'd qualify."

"Dern, I forgot how ugly this country is," Jake said. "I guess if there was a market for snake meat, this would be the place to get rich."

With that he put his hat over his face, and within no more than two minutes began a gentle snoring. Augustus returned the jug to the springhouse. It occurred to him that while Jake was napping he might pay a visit to Lorie; once she fell under Jake's spell he would probably require her to suspend professional activities for a while.

Augustus viewed this prospect philosophically; it was his experience that a man's dealings with women were invariably prone to interruptions, often of a more lasting nature than Jake Spoon was apt to prompt.

He left Jake sleeping and strolled down the middle of Hat Creek. As he passed the corrals, he saw Dish straining at the windlass to bring a big bucket of dirt out of the new well. Call was in the lot, working with the Hell Bitch. He had her snubbed to a post and was fanning her with a saddle blanket. Dish was as wet with sweat as if he'd just crawled out of a horse trough. He'd sweated through the hatband of his hat, and had even sweated through his belt.

"Dish, you're plumb wet," Augustus said. "If there was a well there, I'd figure you fell in it."

"If folks could drink sweat you wouldn't need no well," Dish said. It seemed to Augustus that his tone was a shade unfriendly.

"Look at it this way, Dish," Augustus said. "You're storing up manna in heaven, working like this."

"Heaven be damned," Dish said.

Augustus smiled. "Why, the Bible just asks for the sweat of your brow," he said. "You're even sweating from the belt buckle, Dish. That ought to put you in good with the Seraphim."

The reference was lost on Dish, who bitterly regretted his foolishness in allowing himself to be drawn into such undignified work. Augustus stood there grinning at him as if the sight of a man sweating was the most amusing thing in the world.

"I ought to kick you down this hole," Dish said. "If you hadn't loaned me that money I'd be halfway to the Matagorda by now."

Augustus walked over to the fence to watch Call work the mare. He was about to throw the saddle on her. He had her snubbed close, but she still had her eye turned so she could watch him in case he got careless.

"You ought to blindfold her," Augustus said. "I thought you knowed that much."

"I don't want her blindfolded," Call said.

"If she was blindfolded she might bite the post next time instead of you," Augustus said.

Call got her to accept the blanket and picked up his saddle. Snubbed as she was, she couldn't bite him, but her hind legs weren't snubbed. He kept close to her shoulder as he prepared to ease on the saddle. The mare let go with her near hind foot. It didn't get him but it got the saddle and nearly knocked it out of his hand. He kept close to her shoulder and got the saddle in position again.

"Remember that horse that bit off all that old boy's toes—all the ones on the left foot, I mean?" Augustus said. "That old boy's name was Harwell. He went to the war and got killed at Vicksburg. He never was much of a hand after he lost his toes. Of course, the horse that bit 'em off had a head the size of a punkin. I don't suppose a little mare like that could take off five toes in one bite."

Call eased the saddle on her, and the minute the stirrups slapped against her belly the mare went as high as she could get, and the saddle flew off and landed twenty feet away. Augustus got a big laugh out of it. Call went to the barn and returned with a short rawhide rope.

"If you want help just ask me," Augustus said.

"I don't," Call said. "Not from you."

"Call, you ain't never learned," Augustus said. "There's plenty of gentle horses in this world. Why would a man with your responsibilities want to waste time with a filly that's got to be hobbled and blindfolded before you can even keep a saddle on her?"

Call ignored him. In a moment the mare tentatively lifted the near hind foot with the thought of kicking whatever might be in range. When she did he caught the foot with the rawhide rope and took a hitch around the snubbing post. It left the mare standing on three legs, so she could not kick again without throwing herself. She watched him out of the corner of her eye, trembling a little with indignation, but she accepted the saddle.

"Why don't you trade her to Jake?" Augustus said. "If they don't hang him, maybe he could teach her to pace."

Call left the mare saddled, snubbed, and on three legs, and came to the fence to have a smoke and let the mare have a moment to consider the situation.

"Where's Jake?" he asked.

"Catching a nap," Augustus said. "I reckon the anxiety wore him out."

"He ain't changed a bit," Call said. "Not a dern bit."

Augustus laughed. "You're one to talk," he said. "When's the last time you changed? It must have been before we met, and that was thirty years ago."

"Look at her watch us," Call said. The mare *was* watching them—even had her ears pointed at them.

"I wouldn't take it as no compliment," Augustus said. "She ain't watching you because she loves you."

"Say what you will," Call said, "I never seen a more intelligent filly."

Augustus laughed again. "Oh, that's what you look for, is it? Intelligence," he said. "You and me's got opposite ideas about things. It's intelligent creatures you got to watch out for. I don't care if they're horses or women or Indians or what. I learned long ago there's much to be said for dumbness. A dumb horse may step in a hole once in a while, but at least you can turn your back on one without losing a patch of hide."

"I'd rather my horses didn't step in no holes," Call said. "You reckon somebody's really on Jake's trail?"

"Hard to judge," Augustus said. "Jake was always nervous. He's seen more Indians that turned out to be sage bushes than any man I know."

"A dead dentist ain't a sage bush," Call said.

"No—in that case it's the sheriff that's the unknown factor," Gus said. "Maybe he didn't like his brother. Maybe some outlaw will shoot him before he can come after Jake. Maybe he'll get lost and end up in Washington, D.C. Or maybe he'll show up tomorrow and whip us all. I wouldn't lay money."

They fell silent for a moment, the only sound the grinding of the windlass as Dish drew up another bucket of dirt.

"Why not go north?" Call said, taking Augustus by surprise.

"Why, I don't know," Augustus said. "I've never given the matter no thought, and so far as I know you haven't either. I do think we're a shade old to do much Indian fighting."

"There won't be much," Call said. "You heard Jake. It's the same up there as it is down here. The Indians will soon be whipped. And Jake does know good country when he sees it. It sounds like a cattleman's paradise."

"No, it sounds like a goddamn wilderness," Augustus said. "Why, there ain't even a house to go to. I've slept on the ground enough for one life. Now I'm in the mood for a little civilization. I don't have to have oprys and streetcars, but I do enjoy a decent bed and a roof to keep out the weather."

"He said there were fortunes to be made," Call said. "It stands to reason he's right. Somebody's gonna settle it up and get that land. Suppose we got there first. We could buy you forty beds."

The surprising thing to Augustus was not just what Call was suggesting but how he sounded. For years Call had looked at life as if it were essentially over. Call had never been a man who could think of much reason for acting happy, but then he had always been one who knew his purpose. His purpose was to get done what needed to be done, and what needed to be done was simple, if not easy. The settlers of Texas needed protection, from Indians on the north and bandits on the south. As a Ranger, Call had had a job that fit him, and he had gone about the work with a vigor that would have passed for happiness in another man.

But the job wore out. In the south it became mainly a matter of protecting the cattle herds of rich men like Captain King or Shanghai Pierce, both of whom had more cattle than any one man needed. In the north, the Army had finally taken the fight against the Comanches away from the Rangers, and had nearly finished it. He and Call, who had no military rank or standing, weren't welcomed by the Army; with forts all across the northwestern frontier the free-roving Rangers found that they were always interfering with the Army, or else being interfered with. When the Civil War came, the Governor himself called them in and asked them not to go—with so many men gone they needed at least one reliable troop of Rangers to keep the peace on the border.

It was that assignment that brought them to Lonesome Dove. After the war, the cattle market came into existence and all the big landowners in south Texas began to make up herds and trail them north, to the Kansas railheads. Once cattle became the game and the brush country filled up with cowboys and cattle traders, he and Call finally stopped rangering. It was no trouble for them to cross the river and bring back a few hundred head at a time to sell to the traders who were too lazy to go into Mexico themselves. They prospered in a small way; there was enough money in their account in San Antonio that they could have considered themselves rich, had that notion interested them. But it didn't; Augustus knew that nothing about the life they were living interested Call, particularly. They had enough money that they could have bought land, but they hadn't, although plenty of land could still be had wonderfully cheap.

It was that they had roved too long, Augustus concluded, when his mind turned to such matters. They were people of the horse, not of the town; in that they were more like the Comanches than Call would ever have admitted. They had been in Lonesome Dove nearly ten years, and yet what little property they had acquired was so worthless that neither of them would have felt bad about just saddling up and riding off from it.

Indeed, it seemed to Augustus that that was what both of them had always expected would happen. They were not of the settled fraternity, he and Call. From time to time they talked of going west of the Pecos, perhaps rangering out there; but so far only the rare settler had cared to challenge the Apache, so there was no need for Rangers.

Augustus had not expected that Call would be satisfied just to rustle Mexican cattle forever, but neither had he expected him to suddenly decide to strike out for Montana. Yet it was obvious the idea had taken hold of the man.

"I tell you what, Call," Augustus said. "You and Deets and Pea go on up there to Montany and build a nice snug cabin with a good fireplace and at least one bed, so it'll be waiting when I get there. Then clear out the last of the Cheyenne and the Blackfeet and any Sioux that look rambunctious. When you've done that, me and Jake and Newt will gather up a herd and meet you on Powder River."

Call looked almost amused. "I'd like to see the herd you and Jake could get there with," he said. "A herd of whores, maybe."

"I'm sure it would be a blessing if we could herd a few up that way," Augustus said. "I don't suppose there's a decent woman in the whole territory yet."

Then the thought struck him that there could be no getting to Montana without crossing the Platte, and Clara lived on the Platte. Bob Allen or no, she would ask *him* to supper, if only to show off her girls. Jake's news might be out of date. Maybe she had even run her husband off since Jake had passed through. Anyway, husbands had been got around a few times in the history of the world, if only to the extent of having to set a place for an old rival at the supper table. Such thoughts put the whole prospect in a more attractive light.

"How far do you reckon it is to Montany, Call?" he asked.

Call looked north across the dusty flats, as if estimating in his mind's eye the great rise of the plains, stretching even farther than hearsay, away and beyond the talk of men. Jake that morning had mentioned the Milk River, a stream he had never heard of. He knew the country he knew, and had never been lost in it, but the country he knew stopped at the Arkansas River. He had known men speak of the Yellowstone as if it were the boundary of the world; even Kit Carson, whom he had met twice, had not talked of what lay north of it.

But then his memory went back to a camp they had made on the Brazos, many years before, with an Army captain; there was a Delaware scout with him who had been farther than any man they knew—all the way to the headwaters of the Missouri.

"Remember Black Beaver, Gus?" he asked. "He'd know how far it was."

"I remember him," Augustus said. "It was always a puzzle to me how such a short-legged Indian could cover so much ground."

"He claimed to have been all the way from the Columbia to the Rio Grande," Call said. "That's knowing the country, I'd say."

"Well, he was an Indian," Augustus said. "He didn't have to go along establishing law and order and making it safe for bankers and Sunday-school teachers, like we done. I guess that's why you're ready to head off to Montany. You want to help establish a few more banks."

"That's aggravating," Call said. "I ain't a banker."

"No, but you've done many a banker a good turn," Augustus said. "That's what we done, you know. Kilt the dern Indians so they wouldn't bother the bankers."

"They bothered more than bankers," Call said.

"Yes, lawyers and doctors and newspapermen and drummers of every description," Augustus said.

"Not to mention women and children," Call said. "Not to mention plain settlers."

"Why, women and children and settlers are just cannon fodder for lawyers and bankers," Augustus said. "They're part of the scheme. After the Indians wipe out enough of them you get your public outcry, and we go chouse the Indians out of the way. If they keep coming back then the Army takes over and chouses them worse. Finally the Army will manage to whip 'em down to where they can be squeezed onto some reservation, so the lawyers and bankers can come in and get civilization started. Every bank in Texas ought to pay us a commission for the work we done. If we hadn't done it, all the bankers would still be back in Georgia, living on poke salad and turnip greens."

"I don't know why you stuck with it, if that's the way you think," Call said. "You should have gone home and taught school."

"Hell, no," Augustus said. "I wanted a look at it before the bankers and lawyers get it."

"Well, they ain't got to Montana," Call said.

"If we go they won't be far behind," Augustus said. "The first ones that get there will hire you to go hang all the horsethieves and bring in whichever Indians have got the most fight left, and you'll do it and the place will be civilized. Then you won't know what to do with yourself, no more than you have these last ten years."

"I ain't a boy," Call said. "I'll be dead before all that happens. Anyhow, I ain't going there to law. I'm going there to run cattle. Jake said it was a cattleman's paradise."

"You ain't a cattleman, Call," Augustus said. "No more than I am. If we was to get a ranch I don't know who would run it."

It seemed to Call the mare had probably stood on three legs long enough, and he had surely jawed with Gus long enough. Sometimes Gus sang a strange tune. He had killed as many Indians as any Ranger, and had seen enough of their butchery that you'd think he knew why he was doing it; and yet when he talked he seemed to be on their side.

"As to the ranch," he said, "the boy could run it. He's nearly grown."

Augustus puzzled over that for a moment, as if it had never occurred to him. "Well, maybe so, Call," he said. "I guess he could run it if he was a mind to, and if you would let him."

"I don't know why he wouldn't be a mind to," Call said, and walked over to the mare.

8

BY THE MIDDLE of the afternoon it was so hot nobody could think. At least Newt couldn't, and the other hands didn't seem to be thinking very fast either. All they could find to argue about was whether it was hotter down in the well digging or up in the sun working the windlass. Down in the well they all worked so close together and sweated so much that it practically made a fog, while up in the sun fog was no problem. Being down in the well made Newt nervous, particularly if Pea was with him, because when Pea got to working the crowbar he didn't always look where he was jabbing and once had almost jabbed it through Newt's foot. From then on Newt worked spraddle-legged, so as to keep his feet out of the way.

They were going at it hard when the Captain came riding back, having lathered the mare good by loping her along the river for about twenty miles. He rode her right up to the well.

"Hello, boys," he said. "Ain't the water flowing yet?"

"It's flowin'," Dish said. "A gallon or two of it flowed outa me."

"Be thankful you're healthy," Call said. "A man that couldn't sweat would die in this heat."

"I don't suppose you'd trade for that mare," Dish asked. "I like her looks."

"You ain't the first that's liked them," Call said. "I'll keep her, I believe. But you boys can stop work now and catch a little rest. We have to go to Mexico tonight."

They all went over and sat in the alleyway of the barn—it had a little shade in it. The minute they sat down Deets began to patch his pants. He kept a big needle and some heavy thread in a cigar box in the saddle shed—given any chance he would get out his needle and start patching. He was woolly-headed and his wool was just getting gray.

"If I was you I'd give up on them pants," Dish said. "If you've got to wear quilts you best find a new one and start over."

"No, sir," Deets said genially. "These pants got to last."

Newt was a little excited. The Captain hadn't separated him off from the rest of the men when he told them to rest. It might mean he was going to get to go to Mexico at last. On the other hand, he had been down in the well, so the Captain might just have forgotten him.

"I do fancy that mare," Dish said, watching the Captain unsaddle her.

"I don't see why," Pea said. "She near kilt the Captain just yesterday. Bit a hunk out of him the size of my foot."

They all looked at Pea's foot, which was about the size and shape of a scoop shovel.

"I'd say that passes belief," Dish said. "Her whole head ain't the size of your foot."

"If that chunk had come out of you, you'd have thought it was big enough, I guess," Pea said mildly.

After Dish had caught his breath he pulled his case knife out of his pocket and asked if anyone wanted a game of root-the-peg. Newt had a pocketknife too and was quick to take him up. The game involved flipping the knives in various ways and making them stick in the dirt. Dish won and Newt had to dig a peg out of the ground with his teeth. Dish drove the peg in so far that Newt had dirt up his nose before he finally got it out.

The sight amused Pea no end. "By gosh, Newt, if we break the crowbar you can finish digging the well with your nose," he said.

While they were sitting around, idly experimenting with a few new knife throws, they heard the clop of horses and looked up to see two riders approaching from the east at an easy trot.

"Now who would that be?" Pea asked. "It's an odd time of day to visit."

"Well, if it ain't old Juan Cortinas it's probably just a couple of bank robbers," Dish said, referring to a Mexican cattle thief who was hailed, south of the river, as a great hero due to the success of his raids against the Texans.

"No, it ain't Cortinas," Pea Eye said, squinting at the riders. "He always rides a gray."

Dish could hardly believe anyone would be so dumb as to believe Juan Cortinas would just ride into Lonesome Dove with only one man.

The men stopped on the far side of the lots to read the sign Augustus had put up when the Hat Creek outfit had gone in business. All Call wanted on the sign was the simple words Hat Creek Livery Stable, but Augustus could not be persuaded to stop at a simple statement like that. It struck him that it would be best to put their rates on the sign. Call had been for tacking up one board with the name on it to let people know a livery stable was available, but Augustus thought that hopelessly unsophisticated; he bestirred himself and found an old plank door that had blown off somebody's root cellar, perhaps by the same wind that had taken their roof. He nailed the door onto one corner of the corrals, facing the road, so that the first thing most travelers saw when entering the town was the sign. In the end he and Call argued so much about what was to go on the sign that Call got disgusted and washed his hands of the whole project.

That suited Augustus fine, since he considered that he was the only person in Lonesome Dove with enough literary talent to write a sign. When the weather was fair he would go sit in the shade the sign cast and think of ways to improve it; in the two or three years since they had put it up he had thought of so many additions to the original simple declaration that practically the whole door was covered.

At first he had started out spare and just put the name of the firm, "Hat Creek Cattle Company and Livery Emporium," but that caused controversy in itself. Call claimed nobody knew what an emporium was, including himself, and he still didn't despite Augustus's many long-winded attempts to explain it to him. All Call knew was that they didn't run one, and he didn't want one, whatever it was, and there was no way something like that could fit with a cattle company.

However, Augustus had his way, and "Emporium" went on the sign. He mainly put it in because he wanted visitors to know there was at least one person in Lonesome Dove who knew how to spell important words.

Next he had put his name and Call's, his first because he was two years older and felt seniority should be honored. Call didn't care—his pride ran in other directions. Anyway he soon came to dislike the sign so much that he would just as soon not have had his name on it at all.

Pea Eye badly wanted his name on the sign, so one year Augustus lettered it in for him as a Christmas present. Pea, of course, couldn't read, but he could look, and once he got his name located on the sign he was quick to point it out to anyone who happened to be interested. He had already pointed it out to Dish, who wasn't interested particularly. Unfortunately it had been three decades since anyone had called Pea anything but Pea, and even Call, who had been the man to accept him into the Rangers, couldn't remember his real first name, though he knew his last name was Parker.

Having no wish to embarrass the man, Augustus had written him in as "P. E. Parker, Wrangler." He had wanted to list him as a blacksmith, since in truth Pea was a superior blacksmith and only an average wrangler, but Pea Eye thought he could sit a horse as well as anyone and didn't wish to be associated publicly with a lower trade.

Newt recognized that he was rightly too young to have his name on the sign and never suggested the possibility to anyone, though it would have pleased him mightily if someone had suggested it for him. No one did, but then Deets had to wait nearly two years before his name appeared on the sign, and Newt resigned himself to waiting too.

Of course, it had not occurred to Augustus to put Deets's name on, Deets being a black man. But when Pea's name was added there was a lot of discussion about it, and around that time Deets developed a tremendous case of the sulks—unlike him and perplexing to Call. Deets had ridden with him for years, through all weathers and all dangers, over country so barren they had more than once had to kill a horse to have meat, and in all those years Deets had given cheerful service. Then, all because of the sign, he went into a sulk and stayed in it until Augustus finally spotted him looking wistfully at it one day and figured it out. When Augustus told Call about his conclusion, Call was further outraged. "That damn sign's ruint this outfit," he said, and went into a sulk himself. He had known Augustus was vain but would never have suspected Deets or Pea of such a failing.

Of course Augustus was happy to add Deets's name to the sign, although, as in the case of Pea, there was some trouble with the particulars. Simply writing "Deets" on the sign didn't work. Deets couldn't read either, but he could see that his name was far too short in comparison with the others. At least it was short in comparison with the other names on the sign, and Deets wanted to know why.

"Well, Deets, you just got one name," Augustus said. "Most people got two. Maybe you've got two and just forgot one of them."

Deets sat around thinking for a day or two, but he could not remember ever having another name, and Call's recollection bore him out. At that point even Augustus began to think the sign was more trouble than it was worth, since it was turning out to be so hard to please everyone. The only solution was to think up another name to go with Deets, but while they were debating various possibilities, Deets's memory suddenly cleared.

"Josh," he said, one night after supper, to the surprise of everyone. "Why, I'm Josh. Can you write that, Mr. Gus?"

"Josh is short for Joshua," Augustus said. "I can write either one of them. Joshua's the longest."

"Write the longest," Deets said. "I'm too busy for a short name."

That made no particular sense, nor were they ever able to get Deets to specify how he happened to remember that Josh was his other name. Augustus wrote him on the sign as "Deets, Joshua," since he had already written the "Deets." Fortunately Deets's vanity did not extend to needing a title, although Augustus was tempted to write him in as a prophet—it would have gone with the "Joshua," but Call had a fit when he mentioned it.

"You'll have us the laughingstock of this whole county," Call said. "Suppose somebody come up to Deets and asked him to prophesy?"

Deets himself thought that was an amusing prospect. "Why, I could do it, Captain," he said. "I'd prophesy hot and I'd prophesy dry and I'd charge 'em a dime."

Once the names were settled the rest of the sign was a simple matter. There were two categories, things for rent and things for sale. Horses and rigs were available for rental, or at least horses and one rig, a spring buggy with no springs that they had bought from Xavier Wanz after his wife, Therese, had got smashed by it. For sale Augustus listed cattle and horses. As an afterthought he added, "Goats and Donkeys Neither Bought nor Sold," since he had no patience with goats and Call even less with donkeys. Then, as another afterthought, he had added, "We Don't Rent Pigs," which occasioned yet another argument with Call.

"Why, they'll think we're crazy here when they see that," he said. "Nobody in their right mind would want to rent a pig. What would you do with a pig once you rented it?"

"Why, there's plenty of useful tasks pigs can do," Augustus said. "They could clean the snakes out of a cellar, if a man had a cellar. Or they can soak up mud puddles. Stick a few pigs in a mud puddle and pretty soon the puddle's gone."

It was a burning day, and Call was sweated down. "If I could find anything as cool as a mud puddle I'd soak it up myself," he said.

"Anyhow, Call, a sign's a kind of a tease," Augustus said. "It ought to make a man stop and consider just what it is he wants out of life in the next few days."

"If he thinks he wants to rent a pig he's not a man I'd want for a customer," Call said.

The caution about pigs ended the sign to Augustus's satisfaction, at least for a while, but after a year or two had passed, he decided it would add dignity to it all if the sign ended with a Latin motto. He had an old Latin schoolbook that had belonged to his father; it was thoroughly battered from having been in his saddlebags for years. It had a few pages of mottoes in the back, and Augustus spent many happy hours poring over them, trying to decide which might look best at the bottom of the sign. Unfortunately the mottoes had not been translated, perhaps because by the time the students got to the back of the book they were supposed to be able to read Latin. Augustus had had only a fleeting contact with the language and had no real opportunity to improve his knowledge; once he had been caught in an ice storm on the plains and had torn out a number of pages of the grammar in order to get a fire started. He had kept himself from freezing, but at the cost of most of the grammar and vocabulary; what was left didn't help him much with the mottoes at the end of the book. However, it was his view that Latin was mostly for looks anyway, and he devoted himself to the mottoes in order to find one with the best look. The one he settled on was *Uva uvam vivendo varia fit*, which seemed to him a beautiful motto, whatever it meant. One day when nobody was around he went out and lettered it onto the bottom of the sign, just below "We Don't Rent Pigs." Then he felt that his handiwork was complete. The whole sign read:

HAT CREEK CATTLE COMPANY
AND LIVERY EMPORIUM

CAPT. AUGUSTUS MC CRAE

CAPTAIN W. F. CALL

} PROPS.

P. E. PARKER   WRANGLER

DEETS, JOSHUA

FOR RENT: HORSES AND RIGS

FOR SALE: CATTLE AND HORSES

GOATS AND DONKEYS NEITHER BOUGHT NOR SOLD

WE DON'T RENT PIGS.

UVA UVAM VIVENDO VARIA FIT.

Augustus didn't say a word about the motto, and it was a good two months before anybody even noticed it, which showed how unobservant the citizens of Lonesome Dove really were. It galled Augustus severely that no one appreciated the fact that he had thought to write a Latin motto on a sign that all visitors could see as they rode in, though in fact those riding in took as little note of it as those already in, perhaps because getting to Lonesome Dove was such a hot, exhausting business. The few people who accomplished it were in no mood to stop and study erudite signs.

More galling still was the fact that no member of his own firm had noticed the motto, not even Newt, from whom Augustus expected a certain alertness. Of course two members of the firm were totally illiterate—three, if he chose to count Bolivar—and wouldn't have known Latin from Chinese. Still, the way they casually treated the sign as just part of the landscape caused Augustus to brood a good deal about the contempt that familiarity breeds.

Call did finally notice the motto one day, but only because his horse happened to throw a shoe across the road from the sign. When he got down to pick up the shoe he glanced over and noticed some curious writing below the part about pigs. He had a notion that the words were Latin but that didn't explain what they were doing on the sign. Augustus was on the porch at the time, consulting his jug and keeping out of the way.

"What the hell did you do now?" Call asked. "Wasn't the part about the pigs bad enough for you? What's the last part say?"

"It says a little Latin," Augustus said, undisturbed by his partner's surly tone.

"Why Latin?" Call asked. "I thought it was Greek you knew."

"I did know my letters once," he said. He was fairly drunk, and feeling melancholy about all the sinking he had done in the world. Throughout the rough years the Greek alphabet had leaked out of his mind a letter at a time—in fact, the candle of knowledge he had set out with had burned down to a sorry stub.

"So what's it say, that Latin?" Call asked.

"It's a motto," Augustus said. "It just says itself." He was determined to conceal for as long as possible the fact that he didn't know what the motto meant, which anyway was nobody's business. He had written it on the sign—let others read it.

Call was quick to see the point. "You don't know yourself," he said. "It could say anything. For all you know it invites people to rob us."

Augustus got a laugh out of that. "The first bandit that comes along who can read Latin is welcome to rob us, as far as I'm concerned," he said. "I'd risk a few nags for the opportunity of shooting at an educated man for a change."

After that, the argument about the motto, or the appropriateness of the sign as a whole, surfaced intermittently when there was nothing else to argue about around the place. Of the people who actually had to live closest to the sign, Deets liked it best, since in the afternoon the door it was written on afforded a modest spot of shade in which he could sit and let his sweat dry.

No one else got much use out of it, and it was unusual to see two horsemen on a hot afternoon stop and read the sign instead of loping on into Lonesome Dove to wet their dusty gullets.

"I guess they're professors," Dish said. "They sure like to read."

Finally the men trotted on around to the barn. One was a stocky red-faced man of about the age of the Captain; the other was a tiny feist of a fellow with a pocked face and a big pistol strapped to his leg. The red-faced man was obviously the boss. His black horse was no doubt the envy of many a man. The little man rode a *grulla* that was practically swaybacked.

"Men, I'm Wilbarger," the older man said. "That's a damned amusing sign."

"Well, Mr. Gus wrote it," Newt said, trying to be friendly. It would certainly please Mr. Gus that somebody with a liking for signs had finally come along.

"However, if I had a mind to rent pigs I'd be mighty upset," Wilbarger said. "A man that likes to rent pigs won't be stopped."

"He'd be stopped if he was to show up here," Newt said, after a bit. Nobody else spoke up and he felt that Wilbarger's remark demanded an answer.

"Well, is this a cow outfit or have you boys run off from a circus?" Wilbarger asked.

"Oh, we cow a little," Pea said. "How much cowing are you likely to need?"

"I need forty horses, which it says on that sign you sell," Wilbarger said. "A dern bunch of Mexicans run off dern near all of our remuda two nights back. I've got a herd of cattle gathered up the other side of the Nueces, and I don't plan to walk 'em to Kansas on foot. A feller told me you men could supply horses. Is that true?"

"Yep," Pea Eye said. "What's more, we can even chase Mexicans."

"I've got no time to discuss Mexicans," Wilbarger said. "If you gentlemen could just trot out about forty well-broke horses we'll pay you and be on our way."

Newt felt a little embarrassed. He was well aware that forty horses was out of the question, but he had hated to come right out and say so. Also, as the youngest member of the outfit, it was not his responsibility to be the spokesman.

"You best talk to the Captain about it," he suggested. "The Captain handles all the deals."

"Oh," Wilbarger said, wiping the sweat off his brow with his forearm. "If I'd noticed a captain I'd have picked him to talk to in the first place, instead of you circus hands. Does he happen to live around here?"

Pea pointed at the house, fifty yards away, in the chaparral.

"I expect he's home," he said.

"You men oughta publish a newspaper," Wilbarger said. "You're plumb full of information."

His pockmarked companion found the remark wonderfully funny. To every-one's surprise, he let out a cackle of a laugh, like the sound a hen might make if the hen were mad about something.

"Which way's the whorehouse?" he asked, when he finished his cackle.

"Chick, you're a sight," Wilbarger said, and turned his horse and trotted off toward the house.

"Which way's the whorehouse?" Chick asked again.

He was looking at Dish, but Dish had no intention of revealing Lorena's where-abouts to an ugly little cowboy on a swaybacked horse.

"It's over in Sabinas," Dish said matter-of-factly.

"Which?" Chick asked, caught a little off guard.

"Sabinas," Dish repeated. "Just wade the river and ride southeast for about a day. You'll likely strike it."

Newt thought it extremely clever of Dish to come out with such a remark, but Chick clearly didn't appreciate the cleverness. He was frowning, which tensed his small face up and made his deep pockmarks look like holes that went clear through his cheeks.

"I didn't ask for no map of Mexico," he said. "I've been told there's a yellow-haired girl right in this town."

Dish slowly got to his feet. "Well, just my sister," he said.

Of course it was a rank lie, but it got the job done. Chick was not convinced by the information, but Wilbarger had ridden off and left him, and he was conscious of being outnumbered and disliked. To imply that a cowboy's sister was a sporting woman might lead to prolonged fisticuffs, if not worse—and Dish Boggett looked to be a healthy specimen.

"In that case some fool has tolt me wrong," Chick said, turning his horse toward the house.

Pea Eye, who liked to take life one simple step at a time, had not appreciated the subtleties of the situation.

"Where'd you get a sister, Dish?" he asked. Pea's mode of living was modeled on the Captain's. He barely went in the Dry Bean twice a year, preferring to wet his whistle on the front porch, where he would be assured of a short walk to bed if it got too wet. When he saw a woman it made him uncomfortable; the danger of deviating from proper behavior was too great. Generally when he spotted a female in his vicinity he took the modest way and kept his eyes on the ground. Nonetheless, he had chanced to look up one morning as they were trailing a herd of Mexican cattle through Lonesome Dove. He had seen a yellow-haired girl looking out an open window at them. Her shoulders were bare, which startled him so that he dropped a rein. He had not forgotten the girl, and he occasionally stole a glance at the window if he happened to be riding by. It was a surprise to think she might have been Dish's sister.

"Pea, when was you born?" Dish asked, grinning at Newt.

The question threw Pea into confusion. He had been thinking about the girl he had seen in the window; to be asked when he was born meant stopping one line of thought and trying to shift to another, more difficult line.

"Why you'd best ask the Captain that, Dish," he said mildly. "I can't never remember."

"Well, since we got the afternoon off I believe I'll take a stroll," Dish said. He ambled off toward town.

The prospect of getting to go with the men that night kept crowding into Newt's mind.

"Where do you go when you go down south?" he asked Pea, who was still ruminating on the subject of his own birth.

"Oh, we just lope around till we strike some stock," Pea said. "The Captain knows where to look."

"I hope I get to go," Newt said.

Deets clapped him on the shoulder with a big black hand.

"You in a hurry to get shot at, my lord," he said. Then he walked over and stood looking down into the unfinished well.

Deets was a man of few words but many looks. Newt had often had the feeling that Deets was the only one in the outfit who really understood his wishes and needs. Bolivar was kind from time to time, and Mr. Gus was usually kind, though his kindness was of a rather absentminded nature. He had many concerns to talk and argue about, and it was mostly when he got tired of thinking about everything else that he had the time to think about Newt.

The Captain was seldom really harsh with him unless he made a pure mess of some job, but the Captain never passed him a kind word, either. The Captain did not go around handing out kind words—but if he was in the mood to do so Newt knew he would be the last to get one. No compliment ever came to him from the Captain, no matter how well he worked. It was a little discouraging: the harder he tried to please the Captain, the less the Captain seemed to be pleased. When Newt managed to do some job right, the Captain seemed to feel that he had been put under an obligation, which puzzled Newt and made him wonder what was the point of working well if it was only going to irritate the Captain. And yet all the Captain seemed to care about was working well.

Deets noticed his discouragement and did what he could to help pick his spirits up. Sometimes he helped out with jobs that were too much for Newt, and whenever a chance for complimenting a piece of work came, Deets paid the compliment himself. It was a help, though it couldn't always make up for the feeling Newt had that the Captain held something against him. Newt had no idea what it could be, but it seemed there was something. Deets was the only one beside himself who seemed to be aware of it, but Newt could never work up the nerve to question Deets about it directly—he knew Deets wouldn't want to talk about such things. Deets didn't talk much anyway. He tended to express himself more with his eyes and his hands.

While Newt was thinking of night and Mexico, Dish Boggett strolled happily toward the Dry Bean saloon, thinking of Lorena. All day, laboring at the windlass or in the well, he had thought of her. The night had not gone as well as he had hoped it would—Lorena had not given him anything that could be construed as encouragement—but it occurred to Dish that maybe she just needed more time to get used to the notion that he loved her. If he could stay around a week or two she might get used to it, and even come to like it.

Behind the general store, an old Mexican saddlemaker was cutting a steerhide into strips from which to make a rope. It occurred to Dish that he might be more presentable if he walked down to the river and washed off some of the sweat that had dried on him during the day, but walking to the river meant losing time and he decided to let that notion slide. What he did do was stop just back of the Dry Bean to tuck his shirttail in more neatly and dust off his pants.

It was while he was attending to his shirttail that he suddenly got a shock. He had stopped about twenty feet behind the building, which was just two stories of frame lumber. It was a still, hot afternoon, no breeze blowing. A strong fart could have been heard far up the street, but it was no fart that caught Dish's ear. When he first heard the steady crackling, creaking sound he thought nothing of it, but a second or two later something dawned on him that almost made him feel sick. In spite of himself he stepped closer to the building, to confirm his fear.

From the corner just over his head, where Lorena had her room, came a crackling and a creaking sound such as two people can make in a bad bed with a cornshuck mattress over a weak spring. Lorena had such a bed; only last night it had made the same noise beneath them, loud enough that Dish wondered briefly, before pleasure overtook him, if anybody besides themselves was hearing it.

Now he was hearing it, standing with his shirttail half tucked in, while someone else was making it with Lorena. Memories of her body mingled with the sound, causing such a painful feeling in Dish's breast that for a second he couldn't move. He felt almost paralyzed, doomed to stand in the heat beneath the very room he had been hoping to enter himself. *She* was part of the sound—he knew just what chords she contributed to the awful music. Anger began to fill him, and for a moment its object was Xavier Wanz, who could at least have seen that Lorena had a cotton-tick mattress instead of those scratchy cornshucks, which weren't even comfortable to sleep on.

In a second, though, Dish's anger passed Xavier by, and surged in the direction of the man in the room above him, who was also above Lorena, using her body to produce the crackling and the creaking. He had no doubt it was the pockmarked weasel on the swaybacked gray, who had probably pretended to ride up to the house and then cut back down the dry bed of the creek straight to the saloon. It would be a move he would soon regret.

Dish belted his pants and strode grimly around the saloon to the north side. It was necessary to go all the way around the building to get out of hearing of the bed sounds. He fully meant to kill the little weasel when he came out of the saloon. Dish was no gunfighter, but some things could not be borne. He took out his pistol and checked his loads, surprised at how fast life could suck you along; that morning he had awoke with no plans except to be a cowboy, and now he was about to become a man-killer, which would put his whole future in doubt. The man might have powerful friends, who would hunt him down. Still, feeling what he felt, he could see no other course to follow.

He holstered his pistol and stepped around the corner, expecting to stand by the swaybacked gray until the cowboy came out, so the challenge could be given.

But stepping around the corner brought another shock. There was no swaybacked gray tied to the hitch rail in front of the saloon. In fact, there were no horses at all in front of the saloon. Over at the Pumphreys' store a couple of big strapping boys were loading rolls of barbed wire into a wagon. Otherwise the street was empty.

It put Dish in a deep quandary. He had been more than ready to commit murder, but now he had no victim to commit it on. For a moment he tried to convince himself he hadn't heard what he had heard. Perhaps Lorena was just bouncing on the cornshucks for the sake of bouncing. But that theory wouldn't hold. Even a lighthearted girl wouldn't want to bounce on a cornshuck mattress on a hot afternoon, and anyway Lorena wasn't a lighthearted girl. Some man had prompted the bouncing: the question was, Who?

Dish looked inside, only to discover that the Dry Bean was as empty as a church house on Saturday night. There was no sign of Xavier or Lippy, and, worse, the creaking hadn't stopped. He could still hear it from the front door. It was too much for Dish. He hurried off the porch and up the street, but it soon hit him that he had no place to go, not unless he wanted to collect his horse and strike out for the Matagorda, leaving Captain Call to think what he would.

Dish wasn't quite ready to do that—at least not until he found out who his rival was. Instead, he walked up one side of the street and down the other, feeling silly for doing it. He went all the way to the river, but there was nothing to see there except a strip of brown water and a big coyote. The coyote stood in the shallow, eating a frog.

Dish sat by the river an hour, and when he got back to the Dry Bean everything was back to normal. Xavier Wanz was standing at the door with a wet rag in his hand, and Lippy was sitting on the bar shaving a big corn off his thumb with a straight razor. They didn't count for much, in Dish's view.

What counted was that Lorena, looking prettily flushed, was sitting at a table with Jake Spoon, the coffee-eyed stranger with the pearl-handled pistol. Jake had his hat pushed back on his head and was addressing her, with his eyes at least, as if he had known her for years. There was a single glass of whiskey sitting on the table. From the doorway Dish saw Lorena take a sip out of the glass and then casually hand it to Jake, who took more than a sip.

The sight embarrassed Dish profoundly—it went to the pit of his stomach, like the sound of the creaking bed when he first heard it. He had never seen his ma and pa drink from the same glass, and they had been married people. And yet, the day before, he had been practically unable to get Lorie to look at him at all, and him a top hand, not just some drifter.

In a flash, as he stood half-through the swinging doors, Dish's whole conception of woman changed; it was as if lightning had struck, burning his old notions to a crisp in one instant. Nothing was going to be as he had imagined it—maybe nothing ever would again. He started to go back out the door, so he could at least go off and adjust to his new life alone, but he had lingered a moment too long. Both Jake and Lorena looked up from one another and saw him in the door. Lorena didn't change expression, but Jake at once gave him a friendly look and lifted his hand.

"Hooray," he said. "Come on in, son. I hope you're the start of a crowd. If there's anything I can't stand it's a dern gloomy saloon."

Lippy, content beneath his bowler, turned and shook his lip in Dish's direction for a moment. Then he blew the shavings of his corn off the bar.

"Dish ain't much of a crowd," he said.

Dish stepped in, wishing once again that he had never heard of the town of Lonesome Dove.

Jake Spoon waved at Xavier. "Davie, bring your poison," he said. He refused to call Xavier anything but Davie. "Anybody's that's had to dig a dern well in this heat deserves a free drink and I'm buying it," Jake added.

He motioned at a chair, and Dish took it, feeling red in the face one second and pale the next. He longed to know what Lorena was feeling about it all, and when Jake turned his head a minute, he cast her a glance. Her eyes were unusually bright, but they didn't see him. They returned continually to Jake, who was paying her no particular mind. She tapped her fingers on the table three or four times, a little absently, as if keeping time with her own thoughts, and she drank two more sips from Jake's glass. There were tiny beads of sweat above her upper lip, one right at the edge of the faint scar, but she didn't look bothered by the heat or anything else.

Dish could hardly pull his eyes away, she was so pretty, and when he did he caught Jake Spoon looking at him. But Jake's look was entirely friendly—he seemed plain glad for company.

"If I was to try well-digging, I doubt I'd survive an hour," he said. "You boys ought to stand up to Call and make him dig his own well."

At that point Xavier brought out a bottle and a glass. Jake took the bottle himself and poured liberally. "This is better likker than they got in Arkansas," he said.

"Arkansas," Xavier said contemptuously, as if the word spoke for itself.

At that point Dish felt himself lose belief in what was happening. There was no place he would rather not be than at a table with Lorie and another man, yet that appeared to be where he was. Lorie didn't seem to mind him being there, but on the other hand it was clear she would not have minded if he were a thousand miles away. Xavier stood by his elbow, with the rag dripping onto his pants leg, and Jake Spoon drank whiskey and looked friendly. With Jake's hat pushed back, Dish could see a little strip of white skin right at his forehead, skin the sun never struck.

For a time Dish lost all sense of what life was about. He even lost the sense that he was a cowboy, the strongest sense he had to work with. He was just a fellow with a glass in his hand, whose life had suddenly turned to mud. The day before he had been a top hand, but what did that mean anymore?

Though the day was hot and bright, Dish felt cold and cloudy, so puzzled by the strange business called life that he couldn't think where to look, much less what to say. He took a drink and then another and then several, and, though life remained cloudy, the inside of the cloud began to be warm. By the middle of the second bottle he had stopped worrying about Lorie and Jake Spoon and was sitting by the piano, singing "My Bonnie Lies Over the Ocean," while Lippy played.

9

AUGUSTUS WAS on the front porch, biding his time, when Wilbarger rode up. Biding his time seemed to him the friendly thing to do, inasmuch as Jake Spoon had ridden a long way and had likely been scared to seek out womankind during his trip. Jake was one of those men who seemed to stay in rut the year round, a great source of annoyance to Call, who was never visibly in rut. Augustus was subject to it, but, as he often said, he wasn't going to let it drive him like a mule—a low joke that still went over the heads of most of the people who heard it. He enjoyed a root, as he called it, but if conditions weren't favorable, could make do with whiskey for lengthy spells. It was clear that with Jake just back, conditions wouldn't be too favorable that afternoon, so he repaired to his jug with the neighborly intention of giving Jake an hour or two to whittle down his need before he followed along and tried to interest him in a card game.

Wilbarger of course was a surprise. He trotted his big black horse right up to the porch, which surprised the blue pigs as much as it did Augustus. They woke up and grunted at the horse.

Wilbarger looked enviously at Augustus's jug. "By God, I bet that ain't persimmon juice you're drinking," he said. "I wish I could afford an easy life."

"If you was to dismount and stop scaring my pigs you'd be welcome to a drink," Augustus said. "We can introduce ourselves later."

The shoat got up and walked right under the black horse, which was well broke enough that it didn't move. Wilbarger was more shocked than the horse. In fact, Augustus was shocked himself. The shoat had never done such a thing before, though he had always been an unpredictable shoat.

"I guess that's one of the pigs you don't rent," Wilbarger said. "If I'd been riding my mare she'd have kicked it so far you'd have had to hunt to find your bacon."

"Well, that pig had been asleep," Augustus said. "I guess it didn't expect a horse to be standing there when it woke up."

"Which are you, Call or McCrae?" Wilbarger asked, tired of discussing pigs.

"I'm McCrae," Augustus said. "Call wouldn't put up with this much jabbering."

"Can't blame him," Wilbarger said. "I'm Wilbarger."

At that moment Call stepped out of the house. In fact his bite had pained him all day and he had been in the process of making himself a poultice of cactus pulp. It took a while to make, which is why he had come in early.

As he came out on the porch a small man on a gray came riding around the house.

"Why, hell, you had us surrounded and we didn't even know it," Augustus said. "This is Captain Call, standing here with his shirttail out."

"I'm Wilbarger," Wilbarger said. "This is my man Chick."

"You're free to get down," Call said.

"Oh, well," Wilbarger said, "why get down when I would soon just have to climb back up? It's unnecessary labor. I hear you men trade horses."

"We do," Call said. "Cattle too."

"Don't bother me about cattle," Wilbarger said. "I got three thousand ready to start up the trail. What I need is a remuda."

"It's a pity cattle can't be trained to carry riders," Augustus said. The thought had just occurred to him, so, following his habit, he put it at once into speech.

Both Call and Wilbarger looked at him as if he were daft.

"You may think it a pity," Wilbarger said. "I can call it a blessing. I suppose you wrote that sign."

"That's right," Augustus said. "Want me to write you one?"

"No, I ain't ready for the sanatorium yet," Wilbarger said. "I never expected to meet Latin in this part of Texas but I guess education has spread."

"How'd you round up that much stock without horses?" Call asked, hoping to get the conversation back around to business.

"Oh, well, I just trained a bunch of jackrabbits to chase 'em out of the brush," Wilbarger said, a bit testy.

"In fact some dern Mexicans stole our horses," he added. "I had heard you men hung all the Mexican horsethieves when you was Rangers, but I guess you missed a few."

"Why, hell, we hung ever one of 'em," Augustus said, glad to see that their visitor was of an argumentative temper. "It must be the new generation that stole your nags. We ain't responsible for them."

"This is idle talk," Wilbarger said. "I happen to be responsible for three thousand cattle and eleven men. If I could buy forty horses, good horses, I'd feel happier. Can you oblige me?"

"We expect to have a hundred head available at sunup tomorrow," Call said. Gus's talkativeness had one advantage—it often gained him a minute or two in which to formulate plans.

"I had no intention of spending the night here," Wilbarger said. "Anyway, I don't need a hundred head, or fifty either. How many could I get this afternoon?"

Augustus dug out his old brass pocket watch and squinted at it.

"Oh, we couldn't sell horses now," he said. "We're closed for the day."

Wilbarger abruptly dismounted and automatically loosened his horse's girth a notch or two to give him an easier breath.

"I never expected to hear talk like this," he said. "I never heard of a livery stable closing in bright daylight."

"Oh, the *stable* don't close," Augustus said. "We can stable anything you want us to. It's just the horse-trading part of the operation that's closed."

Wilbarger walked up to the porch. "If that jug's for rent I'll rent a swig," he said. "I guess that jug's about the only thing that's still open in this town."

"It's open and it's free," Augustus said, handing it to him.

While Wilbarger was drinking, Augustus looked at Call. The remark about the hundred horses had struck him as bold talk, even if they were planning a swing through Mexico. Their main object on recent swings had been cattle. Now and again they ran into a few horses and threw them in with the cattle, but seldom more than ten or twelve in one night. Where the other ninety were to come from Augustus didn't know.

"Ain't there a whore in this town?" Chick asked. He was still horseback. The remark took everybody by surprise. Wilbarger seemed quite displeased with it.

"Chick, I thought you had a few manners," he said. "Talking that kind of talk down at the lots is one thing. Talking it up here when I'm trying to discuss business with these gentlemen is something else."

"Well, them boys at the lots wouldn't tell me," Chick said, with a touch of a whine.

"That's because they're God-fearing boys," Augustus said. "You wouldn't catch them boys with no Jezebel."

"Is that her name?" Chick asked. "It ain't the name I heard."

"He's never learned to curb his passions," Wilbarger said. "I hope you'll excuse him."

"A loose tongue is never welcome," Augustus said mildly.

"Horses," Wilbarger said, returning to the more important subject. "This business about being closed is an irritation. I'd hoped to be back to my herd by sunup. It's held in a bad place. The mosquitoes will eat most of my crew if I don't hurry. If I could just get enough ponies to get me started I might be able to pick up some extras as I go north."

"That's a risk," Call said.

"I know it's a risk—what ain't?" Wilbarger said. "How many could you sell me this afternoon?"

Call was tired of beating around the bush.

"Three," he said.

"Three this afternoon and a hundred tomorrow," Wilbarger said. "You must know a man with lots of horses to sell. I wish I knew him."

"He mostly sells to us," Augustus said. "We're lavish with money."

Wilbarger handed back the jug. "You're lavish with time, too," he said. "My time. We couldn't go visit this man right now, could we?"

Call shook his head. "Sunup," he said.

Wilbarger nodded, as if that was what he had expected. "All right," he said. "If you've left me a choice, I don't notice it."

He walked back to the black horse, tightened the girth and pulled himself back into the saddle.

"You men won't disappoint me, will you?" he asked. "I'm mean as a tom turkey when I'm disappointed."

"We've always been taken at our word," Call said. "You can count on forty horses at sunup, thirty-five dollars a horse."

"We'll be here," Wilbarger said. "You won't have to hunt us up."

"Wait a minute," Call said. "What's your horse brand, or do you have one?"

"I have one," Wilbarger said. "I brand HIC on the left hip."

"Are your horses shod?" Call asked.

"All shod," Wilbarger said. "Bring 'em if you see 'em."

"What's HIC stand for?" Augustus asked.

"Well, it's Latin," Wilbarger said. "Easier than what you wrote on that sign."

"Oh," Augustus said. "Where'd you study Latin?"

"Yale college," Wilbarger said. Then he and Chick trotted off.

"I figure he's a liar," Augustus said. "A man that went to Yale college wouldn't need to trail cattle for a living."

"How do you know?" Call said. "Maybe the family went broke. Or maybe he just wanted an outdoor life."

Augustus looked skeptical. It was a shock to think there was someone in town more educated than himself.

"Caught you off, didn't he?" Call said. "You didn't even know what that short little word means."

"Why, it's short for hiccough," Augustus said blithely. "It's a curious thing to brand on a horse, if you ask me."

"You figure Jake's drunk?" Call asked.

"Why, no," Augustus said. "I figure he's happier than he was this morning, though. Why?"

"Because I want him sober tonight," Call said. "I want you both sober."

"I could be sober as the day I was born and not find no hundred horses," Augustus said. "Those figures don't make sense. Wilbarger just needs forty, and we can't find that many anyway. What will we do with the other sixty if we was to find them?"

"We'll need a remuda ourselves, if we go to Montana," Call said.

Augustus sat the jug down and sighed. "I could kick Jake," he said.

"Why?"

"For putting that idea in your head," Augustus said. "Jake's an easy fellow. Ideas like that float right through his head and out the other side. But no dern idea has ever made it through your head. Your brain would bog a mule. Here I've been living in a warm climate most of my life and you want me to move to a cold climate."

"Why not, if it's better country?" Call asked.

Augustus was silent for a time. "I don't want to argue Montana right now," he said. "I thought we was still arguing tonight. Where are we aiming to steal a hundred horses?"

"The Hacienda Flores," Call said.

"I knowed it," Augustus said. "We ain't going on a cowhunt, we're launching an assault."

The Hacienda Flores was the largest ranch in Coahuila. It was there when the Rio Grande was just a river, not a boundary; the *vaqueros* would cross that river as casually as they crossed any stream. Millions of acres that had once been part of the Hacienda were now part of Texas, but *vaqueros* still crossed the river and brought back cattle and horses. They were, in their view, merely bringing back their own. The ranch headquarters was only thirty miles away and it was there that they kept the main part of a horse herd several hundred strong, with many of the horses wearing Texas brands.

"If I didn't know better I'd say you were trying to scare up a war," Augustus said. "Old Pedro Flores ain't gonna make us a gift of a hundred horses, even if he did steal all of them himself."

"Everything's got its risks," Call said.

"Yeah, and you're as fond of risk as Jake is of women," Augustus said. "Suppose we get away with the horses. What then?"

"Sell Wilbarger forty and keep the rest," Call said. "Pick up some cattle and head north."

"Head north who with?" Augustus asked. "We don't exactly add up to a cattle crew."

"We can hire cowboys," Call said. "There's plenty of young cowhands around here."

Augustus sighed again and stood up. It looked like the easy life was over for a while. Call had idled too long, and now he was ready to make up for it by working six times as hard as a human should work.

On the other hand it would be satisfying to run off some of Pedro's horses. Pedro was an old rival, and rivalry still had its interest.

"Jake would have done better to let them hang him," he said. "You know how he suffers when he has to work."

"Where are you going?" Call asked, when Augustus started to walk off.

"Why, down to tell Jake the news," Augustus said. "He might want to oil his gun."

"I guess we'll take the boy," Call said. He had been thinking about it. If they were going to get a hundred horses they would need every hand.

"Why, good," Augustus said. "I'll tell Newt. He'll probably be so pleased he'll fall off the fence."

═══

But Newt wasn't sitting on the fence when he heard the news. He was standing in the sandy bottom of Hat Creek, listening to Dish Boggett vomit. Dish was upstream a little ways, acting very sick. He had come walking up from the saloon with Jake Spoon and Mr. Gus, not walking too straight but on his feet. Then he had stumbled over to the edge of the creek and started vomiting. Now he was down on his hands and knees, still vomiting. The sounds coming out of him reminded Newt of the sucking sound a cow makes pulling her foot out of a muddy bog.

Newt had been sick at his stomach a few times, but never that sick, and he was worried. Dish sounded like he was going to die. Newt would not have thought anybody could get so sick in such a short space of time. Mr. Jake and Mr. Gus didn't seem worried, though. They stood on the banks of the creek, chatting amiably, while Dish hung his head and made the sound like the bogged cow.

With Dish in such trouble, Newt could hardly enjoy the good news Mr. Gus had told him—though it was news he had waited for for years. Instead of floating with happiness, he was too worried about Dish to feel much of anything else.

"Want me to go get Bolivar?" he asked. Bolivar was the house doctor.

Mr. Gus shook his head. "Bolivar can't get a man over being drunk," he said. "Call should have kept you boys working. If Dish had stayed down in that well he never would have been tempted."

"A fish couldn't drink no faster than that boy drank," Jake said. "If fishes drink."

"They don't drink what he drunk," Augustus said. He knew perfectly well that Dish had been love-smitten, and that it had been his undoing.

"I hope the Captain don't see him," Newt said. The Captain was intolerant of drinking unless it was done at night and in moderation.

No sooner had he said it than they saw the Captain come out of the house and walk toward them. Dish was still on his hands and knees. About that time Bolivar began to beat the dinner bell with the crowbar, though it was much earlier than their usual supper hour. He had evidently not cleared his action with the Captain, who looked around in annoyance. The clanging of iron on iron didn't do much to improve Dish's condition—he began to make the boggy sound again.

Jake looked at Augustus. "Call's apt to fire him," he said. "Ain't there any excuses we can make for him?"

"Dish Boggett is a top hand," Augustus said. "He can make his own excuses."

Call walked up and looked at the stricken cowboy, whose stomach was still heaving. "What happened to him?" he asked, frowning.

"I didn't see it," Augustus said. "I think he may have swallowed a hunk of barbed wire."

Dish meanwhile heard a new voice above him and turned his head enough to see that the Captain had joined the group of spectators. It was an eventuality he had been dreading, even in his sickness. He had no memory of what had happened in the Dry Bean, except that he had sung a lot of songs, but even in the depths of his drunkenness he had realized he would have to answer for it all to Captain Call. At some point he had lost sight of Lorena, forgot he was in love with her and even forgot she was sitting across the room with Jake, but he never quite forgot that he was supposed to ride that night with Captain Call. In his mind's eye he had seen them riding, even as he drank and sang, and now the Captain had come, and it was time to begin the ride. Dish didn't know if he had the strength to stand up, much less mount a horse, much less stay aboard one and round up livestock, but he knew his reputation was at stake and that if he didn't give it a try he would be disgraced forever. His stomach had not quite quit heaving, but he managed to take a deep breath and get to his feet. He made a pretense of walking up the bank as if nothing was wrong, but his legs had no life in them and he was forced to drop to his knees and crawl up, which only added embarrassment to his misery, the bank being scarcely three feet high and little more than a slope.

Call stepped close enough to the young cowboy to smell whiskey and realized he was only sick drunk. It was the last thing he had expected, and his immediate impulse was to fire the boy on the spot and send him back to Shanghai Pierce, who was said to be tolerant of the bottle. But before he opened his mouth to do it he happened to note that Gus and Jake were grinning at one another as if it were all a capital joke. To them no doubt it was—jokes had always interested them more than serious business. But since they were so full of this particular joke, it occurred to Call that they had probably tricked Dish somehow and got him drunk on purpose, in which case it was not entirely the boy's fault. They were wily foxes, and worse about joking when the two of them were together. It was just like them to pull such a stunt at the time when it was least appropriate—just the kind of thing they had done all through their years as Rangers.

Dish meanwhile had gained the top of the bank and made it to his feet. When he stood up, his head cleared for a moment and he felt a wild optimism—maybe he was over being drunk. A second later his hopes were shattered. He started to walk off toward the lots to saddle his horse, stubbed his toe on a mesquite root that poked up through the dirt and fell flat on his face.

Newt's hopes had risen too, when Dish stood up, and he was horribly embarrassed when his friend sprawled in the dirt. It was a mystery to him how Dish could get so drunk in such a short space of time, and why he would do it, with such an important night ahead. Bolivar was still banging the bell with the crowbar, making it that much more difficult to think.

Jake Spoon was unaccustomed to Bolivar's habits and grimaced unhappily as the banging continued.

"Who asked that old man to make such a racket?" he asked. "Why don't somebody shoot him?"

"If we shoot him we'll have Gus for a cook," Call said. "In that case we'll have to eat talk, or else starve to death listening."

"You could do worse than to listen to me," Augustus said.

Dish Boggett had risen again. His eyes had a wide, glassy look, and he held himself carefully, as if afraid that another fall would break him like glass.

"What happened to you?" Call asked.

"Why, Captain," Dish said, "I wish I could say."

"Why can't you say?"

"Because I can't remember," Dish said.

"Aw, he's all right," Augustus said. "He just wanted to see how fast he could drink two bottles of whiskey."

"Who put him up to that?" Call asked.

"Not me," Augustus said.

"Not me, neither," Jake said, grinning. "All I done was offer to hunt a funnel. I believe he could have got it down a little faster if he'd had a funnel."

"I can ride, Captain," Dish said. "Once I get on a horse it'll all wear off."

"I hope you're right," Call said. "I'll not keep a man in my crew who can't do his job."

Bolivar was still clanging the bell, which caused Jake to look more out of temper.

"Hell, if this is the Fourth of July I'll set off my own firecrackers," he said, taking out his pistol. Before anybody could say a word, he shot three times in the general direction of the house. The clanging continued as if the shots hadn't happened, but Newt, at least, was shocked. It seemed a reckless way to act, even if Bol was making too much noise.

"If you're that trigger-happy, no wonder you're on the run," Augustus said. "If you want to stop the noise, go hit him in the head with a brick."

"Why walk when you can shoot?" Jake asked with another grin.

Call said nothing. He had noticed that Jake actually raised his barrel enough to eliminate any danger to their cook. It was typical—Jake always liked to act meaner than he was.

"If you men want grub, you better go get it," he said. "Sundown would be the time to leave."

After supper Jake and Augustus went outside to smoke and spit. Dish sat on the Dutch oven, sipping black coffee and squeezing his temples with one hand—each temple felt like someone had given it a sharp rap with a small ax. Deets and Newt started for the lots to catch the horses, Newt very conscious of the fact that he was the only one in the group without a sidearm. Deets had an old Walker Colt the size of a ham, which he only wore when he went on trips, since even he wouldn't have been stout enough to carry it all day without wearing down.

The Captain had gone to the lots ahead of them, since it took a little time to get the Hell Bitch saddled. He had her snubbed to the post when Deets and Newt arrived. When Newt walked in the barn to get a rope, the Captain turned and handed him a holstered pistol and a gun belt.

"Better to have it and not need it than to need it and not have it," he added, a little solemnly.

Newt took the gun and slipped it out of its holster. It smelled faintly of oil— the Captain must have oiled it that day. It was not the first time he had held a pistol, of course. Mr. Gus had given him thorough training in pistol shooting and had even complimented him on his skill. But holding one and actually having one of your own were two different things. He turned the cylinder of the Colt and listened to the small, clear clicks it made. The grip was wood, the barrel cool and blue; the holster had kept a faint smell of saddle soap. He slipped the gun back in its holster, put the gun belt around his waist and felt the gun's solid weight against his hip. When he walked out into the lots to catch his horse, he felt grown and complete for the first time in his life. The sun was just easing down toward the Western horizon, the bullbats were dipping toward the stone stock tank that Deets and the Captain had built long ago. Deets had already caught Mr. Gus's horse, a big solid sorrel they called Mud Pie, and was catching his own mount. Newt shook out a loop, and on the first throw caught his own favorite, a dun gelding he called Mouse. He felt he could even rope better with the gun on his hip.

"Oh, my, they done put a gun on you, ain't they," Deets said with a big grin. "I guess next thing you'll be boss of us all."

No thought that ambitious had ever crossed Newt's mind. The summit of his hopes had been to be one of the crew—to be allowed to go along and do whatever there was to do. But Deets had said it as a joke, and Newt was in the perfect mood to take a joke.

"That's right," he said. "I 'spect they'll make me boss any day. And the first thing I'll do is raise your wages."

Deets slapped his leg and laughed, the thought was so funny. When the rest of the outfit finally wandered down from the house they found the two of them grinning back and forth at one another.

"Look at 'em," Augustus said. "You'd think they just discovered teeth."

As the day died and the afterglow stretched upward in the soft, empty sky, the Hat Creek outfit, seven strong, crossed the river and rode southeast, toward the Hacienda Flores.

10

THE FIRST DIFFERENCE Newt noticed about being grown up was that time didn't pass as slow. The minute they crossed the river the Captain struck southeast in a long trot, and in no time the land darkened and they were riding by moonlight, still in a long trot. Since he had never been allowed in Mexico, except once in a while in one of the small villages down the river when they were buying stock legitimately, he didn't really know what to expect, but he hadn't expected it to be quite so dark and empty. Pea Eye and Mr. Gus were always talking about how thick the bandits were, and yet the seven of them rode for two hours into country that seemed to contain nothing except itself. They saw no lights, heard no sounds—they just rode, across shallow gullies, through thinning chaparral, farther and farther from the river. Once in a while the Captain stepped up the pace and they traveled in a short lope, but mostly he stuck with the trot. Since Mouse had an easy trot and a hard lope, Newt was happy with the gait.

He was in the middle of the company. It was Pea Eye's traditional job to watch the rear. Newt rode beside Dish Boggett, who had not said one word since leaving and whose state Newt couldn't judge, though at least he hadn't fallen off his horse. The thin moon lit the sky but not the ground. The only landmarks were shadows, low shadows, mostly made by chaparral and mesquite. Of course, it was not Newt's place to worry about the route, but it occurred to him that he had better try to keep some sense of where he was in case he got separated from the outfit and had to find his own way back. But the farther they rode, the more lost he felt; about all he knew for sure was that the river was on his left. He tried to watch the Captain and Mr. Gus and to recognize the landmarks they were guiding the outfit by. But he could detect nothing. They did not seem to be paying much attention to the terrain. It was only when they loped over a ridge and surprised a sizable herd of longhorns that the Captain drew rein. The cattle, spooked by the seven riders, were already running away.

By this time the stars were bright, and the Milky Way like a long speckled cloud. Without a word the Captain got off. Stepping to the end of his rein, he began to relieve himself. One by one the other men dismounted and did the same, turning slightly so as not to be pointed at one another. Newt thought he had better do what the others were doing, but to his embarrassment could not make water. All he could do was button up again and hope nobody had noticed.

In the silence that followed the pissing they could still hear the sound of running cattle, the only sound to be heard other than the breath of the horses or the occasional jingling spur. The Captain seemed to feel the horses deserved a short rest; he stayed on the ground, looking in the direction of the fleeing cattle.

"Them cattle could be had for the taking," he said. "Anybody get a count?"

"No, I never," Augustus said, as if he would be the only one who could possibly have made a count.

"Oh, was them cattle?" Jake said. "I thought they was dern antelope. They went over the ridge so fast I never got a look."

"It's lucky they run west," Call said.

"Lucky for who?" Augustus asked.

"For us," Call said. "We can come back and pick them up tomorrow night. I bet it was four hundred or more."

"Them of us that wants to can, I guess," Augustus said. "I ain't worked two nights running since I can remember."

"You *never* worked two nights running," Jake said as he swung back up on his horse. "Not unless you was working at a lady, anyhow."

"How far have we come, Deets?" Call asked. Deets had one amazing skill—he could judge distances traveled better than any man Call had ever known. And he could do it in the daytime, at night, in all weathers, and in brush.

"It's five miles yet to the out camp," Deets said. "It's a little ways north, too."

"Let's bear around it," Call said.

Augustus considered that an absurd precaution. "'I god," he said. "The dern camp's five miles away. We can likely slip past it without going clear around by Mexico City."

"It don't hurt to give it room," Call said. "We might scare some more cattle. I've known men who could hear the sound of running cattle a long way off."

"I couldn't hear Jehovah's trumpet from no five miles off," Augustus said. "Anyway, we ain't the only thing in this country that can spook cattle. A lobo wolf can spook them, or a lion."

"I didn't ask for a speech," Call said. "It's foolish to take chances."

"Some might think it foolish to try and steal horses from the best-armed ranch in northern Mexico," Augustus said. "Pedro must work about a hundred *vaqueros.*"

"Yes, but they're spread around, and most of them can't shoot," Call said.

"Most of us can't, either," Augustus said. "Dish and Newt ain't never spilt blood, and one of 'em's drunk anyway."

"Gus, you'd talk to a possum," Jake said.

"I wisht we had one along," Augustus said. "I've seen possums that could out-think this crowd."

After that, the talk died and they all slipped back into the rhythm of the ride. Newt tried hard to stay alert, but their pace was so steady that after a while he stopped thinking and just rode, Deets in front of him, Dish beside him, Pea behind. If he had been sleepy he could almost have gone to sleep at a high trot, it was all so regular.

Dish Boggett had ridden off the worst of his drunk, though there were moments when he still felt queasy. Dish had spent most of his life on a horse and could ride in any condition short of paralysis; he had no trouble keeping his place in the group. In time his head quit throbbing and he felt well enough to take an interest in the proceedings at hand. He was not troubled by any sense of being lost, or any apprehension about Mexican bandits. He was confident of his mount and prepared to outrun any trouble that couldn't be otherwise handled. His main trouble was that he was riding just behind Jake Spoon and thus was reminded of what had happened in the saloon every time he looked up. He knew he had become a poor second in Lorena's affections to the man just in front of him, and the knowledge rankled. The one consoling thought was that there might be gunplay before the night was over—Dish had never been in a gun battle but he reasoned that if bullets flew thick and fast Jake might stop one of them, which could change the whole situation. It wasn't exactly that Dish hoped he'd be killed outright—maybe just wounded enough that they'd have to leave him someplace downriver where there might be a doctor.

More than once they spotted bunches of longhorn cattle, all of whom ran like deer at the approach of the horsemen.

"Why, hell, if we was to start to Montana with cattle like these, we'd be there in a week," Augustus said. "A horse couldn't keep up with them, nor a steam locomotive neither."

"The big camp, Captain," Deets said, "it's over the ridge."

"We don't want the camp, we want the horse herd," Augustus said in his full voice.

"Talk up, Gus," Jake said. "If you talk a little louder they'll probably bring the horse herd to us, only they'll be riding it."

"Well, they're just a bunch of bean eaters," Augustus said. "As long as they don't fart in my direction I ain't worried."

Call turned south. The closer they were to action, the more jocularity bothered him. It seemed to him that men who had been in bad fights and seen death and injury ought to develop a little respect for the dangers of their trade. The last thing he wanted to do at such times was talk—a man who was talking couldn't listen to the country, and might miss hearing something that would make the crucial difference.

Gus's disregard of common sense in such matters was legendary. Jake appeared to have the same disregard, but Call knew his was mostly bluff. Gus started the joking, and Jake felt like he had to keep up his end of it, because he wanted to be thought a cool customer.

In fact, though, Gus McCrae *was* a cool customer, perhaps the coolest Call had ever known—and he had known many men who didn't scare easy. His disregard of danger was so complete that Call initially thought he must want to die. He had known men who did want to die—who for some reason had ended up with a dislike of life—and most of them had got the death they wanted. In Texas, in his time, getting killed was easy.

But Gus loved to live and had no intention of letting anyone do him out of any of his pleasures. Call finally decided his coolness was just a by-product of his general vanity and overconfidence. Call himself spent plenty of time on self-appraisal. He knew what he could certainly do, and what he might do if he was lucky, and what he couldn't do barring a miracle. The problem with Gus was that he regarded himself as the miracle, in such situations. He treated danger with light contempt or open scorn, and scorn was about all he seemed to have for Pedro Flores, although Pedro had held onto his stony empire through forty violent years.

Of course, when trouble came Gus was reliable, but the only man in the outfit who was really much help as a planner was Deets. Nobody expected Deets to talk, which left him free to pay attention, and he paid careful attention, often noticing things that Call had overlooked, or confirming judgments that Call felt uncertain about. Even Gus was quick to admit that Deets had the best hearing in the outfit, although Deets himself claimed to rely just as much on his sense of smell—a claim Augustus poked fun at.

"What does trouble smell like then?" he asked. "I never noticed it had an odor. You right sure you ain't just smelling yourself?"

But Deets would never explain himself or allow Gus to draw him very deeply into argument. "How do the coyote know?" he sometimes replied.

When they had ridden south two or three more miles, Call drew rein. "There's another out camp off this way," he said. "His wranglers stay in it. I doubt there's more than one or two of them, but we don't want one to get loose to warn the big house. We best sneak in and catch them. Me and Deets can do it."

"Them *vaqueros* are probably drunk by now," Augustus said. "Drunk and asleep both."

"We'll split," Call said. "You and Jake and Pea and Dish go get the horses. We'll catch the wranglers."

Only after he said it did he remember the boy. He had forgotten he was along. Of course it would have been safer for the boy to go after the horse herd, but the order had been given and he never liked to change his plan once one was struck.

Augustus dismounted and tightened his cinch a notch. "I hope we don't strike too many gullies," he said. "I dislike jumping gullies in the dark."

Newt's heart gave a little jump when he realized the Captain meant to keep him with him. It must mean the Captain thought he was worth something, after all, though he had no idea how to catch a wrangler, Mexican or otherwise.

Once the group split up, Call slowed his pace. He was inwardly annoyed with himself for not sending the boy with Gus. He and Deets had worked together so long that very little talk was needed between them. Deets just did what needed to be done, silently. But the boy wouldn't know what needed to be done and might blunder into the way.

"You reckon they keep a dog?" Call asked—a dog was likely to bark at anything, and a smart *vaquero* would heed it and take immediate precautions.

Deets shook his head. "A dog would already be barking," he said. "Maybe the dog got snakebit."

Newt gripped his reins tightly and mashed his hat down on his head every few minutes—he didn't want to lose his hat. Two worries see-sawed in his mind: that he might get killed or that he might make a stupid blunder and displease the Captain. Neither was pleasant to contemplate.

Call stopped and dismounted when it seemed to him they were about a quarter of a mile from the camp. The boy did the same, but Deets, for some reason, still sat his horse. Call looked at him and was about to speak, but Deets lifted his big hand. He apparently heard something they didn't hear.

"What is it?" Call whispered.

Deets got down, still listening. "Don't know," he said. "Sounded like singin'."

"Why would the *vaqueros* be singing this time of night?" Call asked.

"Nope, white folks singin'," Deets said.

That was even more puzzling. "Maybe you hear Gus," Call said. "Surely he wouldn't be crazy enough to sing now."

"I'm going a little closer," Deets said, handing Newt his reins.

Newt felt awkward, once Deets left. He was afraid to speak, so he simply stood, holding the two horses.

It embarrassed Call that his own hearing had never been as good as it should be. He listened but could hear nothing at all. Then he noticed the boy, who looked tense as a wire.

"Do you hear it?" he asked.

At any other time the question would have struck Newt as simple. Either he heard something or he didn't. But under the press of action and responsibilities, the old certainties dissolved. He did think he heard something, but he couldn't say what. The sound was so distant and indistinct that he couldn't even be sure it was a sound. The harder he strained to hear, the more uncertain he felt about what he heard. He would never have suspected that a simple thing like sound could produce such confusion.

"I might hear it," Newt said, feeling keenly that the remark was inadequate. "It's a real thin sound," he added. "Haven't they got birds down here? It could be a bird."

Call drew his rifle from his saddle scabbard. Newt started to get his, but Call stopped him.

"You won't need it, and you might just drop it," he said. "I dropped one of mine once, and had to go off and leave it."

Deets was suddenly back with them, stepping quietly to the Captain's side.

"They're singing, all right," he said.

"Who?"

"Some white folks," Deets said. "Two of 'em. Got 'em a mule and a donkey."

"That don't make no sense at all," Call said. "What would two white men be doing in one of Pedro Flores' camps?"

"We can go look," Deets said.

They followed Deets in single file over a low ridge, where they stopped. A flickering light was visible some hundred yards away. When they stopped, Deets's judgment was immediately borne out. The singing could be plainly heard. The song even sounded familiar.

"Why, it's 'Mary McCrae,' " Newt said. "Lippy plays it."

Call hardly knew what to think. They slipped a little closer, to the corner of what had once been a large rail corral. It was obvious that the camp was no longer much used, because the corral was in poor repair, rails scattered everywhere. The hut that once belonged to the wranglers was roofless—smoke from the singers' fire drifted upward, whiter than the moonlight.

"This camp's been burnt out," Call whispered.

He could hear the singing plainly, which only increased his puzzlement. The voices weren't Mexican, nor were they Texan. They sounded Irish—but why were Irishmen having a singing party in one of Pedro Flores' old cow camps? It was an odd situation to have stumbled onto. He had never heard of an Irish *vaquero*. The whole business was perplexing, but he couldn't just stand around and wonder about it. The horse herd would soon be on the move.

"I guess we better catch 'em," he said. "We'll just walk in from three sides. If you see one of them make a break for it try to shoot his horse."

"No horses," Deets reminded him. "Just a mule and a donkey."

"Shoot it anyway," Call said.

"What if I hit the man?" Newt said.

"That's his worry," Call said. "Not letting him ride away is your worry."

They secured their horses to a little stunted tree and turned toward the hut. The singing had stopped but the voices could still be heard, raised in argument.

At that point the Captain and Deets walked off, leaving Newt alone with his nervousness and a vast weight of responsibility. It occurred to him that he was closest to their own horses. If the men were well-trained bandits, they might like nothing better than to steal three such horses. The singing might be a trick, a way of throwing the Captain off guard. Perhaps there were more than two men. The others could be hidden in the darkness.

No sooner had it occurred to him that there might be more bandits than he began to wish it hadn't occurred to him. The thought was downright scary. There were lots of low bushes, mostly chaparral, between him and the hut, and there could be a bandit with a Bowie knife behind any one of them. Pea had often explained to him how effective a good bowie knife was in the hands of someone who knew where to stick it—descriptions of stickings came back to his mind as he eased forward. Before he had gone ten steps he had become almost certain that his end was at hand. It was clear to him that he would be an easy victim for a bandit with the least experience. He had never shot anyone, and he couldn't see well at night. His own helplessness was so obvious to him that he quickly came to feel numb—not too numb to dread what might happen, but too dull-feeling to be able to think of a plan of resistance.

He even felt a flash of irritation with the Captain for being so careless as to leave him on the side of the house where their horses were. Captain Call's trust, which he had never really expected to earn, had immediately become excessive, leaving him with responsibilities he didn't feel capable of meeting.

But time was moving forward, and he himself was walking slowly toward the house, his pistol in one hand. The hut had seemed close when the Captain and Deets were standing with him, but once they left it had somehow gotten farther away, leaving him many dangerous shadows to negotiate. The one reassuring aspect was that the men in the shadows were talking loudly and probably wouldn't hear him coming unless he lost control completely and shot off his gun.

When he got within thirty yards of the house he stopped and squatted behind a bush. The hut had never been more than a lean-to with a few piles of adobe bricks stacked up around it; its walls were so broken and full of holes that it was easy to look in. Newt saw that both the men arguing were short and rather stout. Also, they were unarmed, or appeared to be. Both had on dirty shirts, and the older of the two men was almost bald. The other one looked young, perhaps no older than himself. They had a bottle, but it evidently didn't have much left in it, because the older one wouldn't pass it to the young one.

It was not hard to make out the drift of their conversation either. The subject of the debate was their next meal.

"I say we eat the mule," the younger man said.

"Nothing of the sort," the other said.

"Then give me a drink," the younger said.

"Go away," the older man said. "You don't deserve my liquor and you won't eat my mule. I'm beholden to this mule, and so are you. Didn't it bring you all this way with no complaint?"

"To the desert to die, you mean?" the young one said. "I'm to thank a mule for that?"

Newt could just make out a thin mule and a small donkey, tethered at the entrance of the hut, beyond the fire.

"If it comes to it we'll eat the donkey," the bald man said. "What can you do with a donkey anyway?"

"Train it to sit on its ass and eat sugar cubes," the young one said. Then he giggled at his own wit.

Newt edged a little closer, his fear rapidly diminishing. Men who could engage in such conversation didn't seem very dangerous. Just as he was relaxing a hand suddenly gripped his shoulder and for a second he nearly fainted with fright, thinking the bowie knife would hit him next. Then he realized it was Deets. Motioning for him to follow, Deets walked right up to the hut. He did not appear to be worried in the least. When they were a few feet from the broken adobe wall, Newt saw Captain Call step into the circle of firelight from the other side.

"You men just hold steady," he said, in a calm, almost friendly, voice.

It evidently didn't sound as friendly to the men around the fire.

"Murderers!" the young one yelled. He sprang to his feet and darted past the Captain so fast the Captain didn't even have time to trip him or hit him with his rifle barrel. For a fat man he moved fast, springing on the back of the mule before the other two could even move. Newt expected the Captain to shoot him or at least step over and knock him off the mule, but to his surprise the Captain just stood and watched, his rifle in the crook of his arm. The boy—for he was no older—pounded the mule desperately with his heels and the mule responded with a short leap and then went crashing down, throwing the boy over its head and almost back to the spot he had left. Looking more closely, Newt saw why the Captain had not bothered to stop the escape: the mule was hobbled.

The sight of a man so addled as to try and get away on a hobbled mule was too much for Deets. He slapped his leg with his big hand and laughed a deep laugh, resting his rifle for a moment on the low adobe wall.

"You see, it's a poor mule," the boy said indignantly, springing up. "Its legs won't work."

Deets laughed even louder, but the baldheaded man sighed and looked at the Captain in a rather jolly way.

"He's my brother but he ain't smart," he said quietly. "The Lord gave him a fine baritone voice and I guess he thought that was enough to do for a poor Irish boy."

"I'm smarter than yourself at least," the boy said, kicking dirt at his brother. He seemed quite prepared to take the quarrel farther, but his brother merely smiled.

"You must unhobble the mule if you want his legs to work," he said. "It's details like that you're always forgetting, Sean."

The mule had managed to get to its feet and was standing quietly by the Captain.

"Well, I didn't hobble him," Sean said. "I was riding the donkey."

The baldheaded man hospitably held the bottle out to the Captain.

"It's only a swallow," he said, "but if you're thirsty, you're welcome."

"Much obliged, but I'll pass," the Captain said. "Do you men know where you are?"

"We ain't in Ireland," the boy said. "I know that much."

"You wouldn't have a bag of potatoes about you, sir, would you?" the older said. "We do miss our spuds."

Call motioned for Deets and Newt to join the group. When they did the bald man stood up.

"Since you've not bothered to murder us, I'll introduce myself," he said. "I'm Allen O'Brien and this is young Sean."

"Are those your only animals?" Call asked. "Just a donkey and a mule?"

"We had three mules to start with," Allen said. "I'm afraid our thirst got the better of us. We traded two mules for a donkey and some liquor."

"And some beans," Sean said. "Only the beans were no good. I broke my tooth trying to eat one."

It was Call's turn to sigh. He had expected *vaqueros,* and instead had turned up two helpless Irishmen, neither of whom even had an adequate mount. Both the mule and the donkey looked starved.

"How'd you men get here?" he asked.

"That would be a long story," Allen said. "Are we far from Galveston? That was our destination."

"You overshot it by a wide mark," Call said. "This hut you're resting in belongs to a man named Pedro Flores. He ain't a gentle man, and if he finds you tomorrow I expect he'll hang you."

"Oh, he will," Deets agreed. "He'll be mad tomorrow."

"Fine, we'll go with you," Allen said. He courteously offered the bottle to both Deets and Newt, and when they refused drained it with one gulp and flung it into the darkness.

"Now we're packed," he said.

"Get the horses," Call said to Newt, looking at the Irishmen. They were none of his business and he could just ride off and leave them, but the theft he was about to commit would put their lives in considerable danger: Pedro Flores would vent his anger on whatever whites lay to hand.

"I've no time for a long explanation," he said. "We've got some horses to the south of here. I'll send a man back with two of them as soon as I can. Be ready— we won't wait for you."

"You mean leave tonight?" the boy said. "What about sleep?"

"Just be ready," Call said. "We'll want to move fast when we move, and you'll never make it on that mule and that jackass."

Newt felt sorry for the two. They seemed friendly. The younger one was holding the sack of dried beans. Newt didn't feel he could leave without a word about the beans.

"You have to soak them beans," he said. "Soak them a while and it softens them up."

The Captain was already loping away, and Newt didn't dare linger any longer.

"There's no water to soak them in," Sean said. He was very hungry, and inclined to despair at such times.

Deets was the last to leave. Allen O'Brien walked over, as he was mounting.

"I hope you'll not forget us," he said. "I do fear we're lost."

"The Captain said we'll get you, we'll get you," Deets said.

"Maybe they'll bring a wagon," Sean said. "A wagon would suit me best."

"A cradle would suit you best," his brother said.

They listened as the sound of loping horses grew faint and was lost in the desert night.

11

AUGUSTUS SOON FOUND the horse herd in a valley south of the old line camp. Call had predicted its location precisely, but had overestimated its size. A couple of horses whinnied at the sight of riders but didn't seem particularly disturbed.

"Probably all Texas horses anyway," Augustus said. "Probably had enough of Mexico."

"I've had enough of it and I just got here," Jake said, lighting his smoke. "I never liked it down here with these chili-bellies."

"Why, Jake, you should stay and make your home here," Augustus said. "That sheriff can't follow you here. Besides, think of the women."

"I got a woman," Jake said. "That one back in Lonesome Dove will do me for a while."

"She'll do you, all right," Augustus said. "That girl's got more spunk than you have."

"What would you know about it, Gus?" Jake asked. "I don't suppose you've spent time with her, a man your age."

"The older the violin, the sweeter the music," Augustus said. "You never knowed much about women."

Jake didn't answer. He had forgotten how much Gus liked argument.

"I guess you think all women want you to marry them and build 'em a house and raise five or six brats," Augustus said. "But it's my view that very few women are fools, and only a fool would pick you for a chore like that, Jake. You'll do fine for a barn dance or a cakewalk, or maybe a picnic, but house building and brat raising ain't exactly your line."

Jake kept quiet. He knew that silence was the best defense once Augustus got wound up. It might take him a while to talk himself out, if left alone, but any response would just encourage him.

"This ain't no hundred horses," he said, after a bit. "Maybe we got the wrong herd."

"Nope, it's right," Augustus said. "Pedro just learned not to keep all his remuda in one place. It's almost forty horses here. It won't satisfy Woodrow, but then practically nothing does."

He had no sooner spoken than he heard three horses coming from the north.

"If that ain't them, we're under attack," Jake said.

"It's them," Augustus said. "A scout like you, who's traveled in Montana, ought to recognize his own men."

"Gus, you'd exasperate a preacher," Jake said. "I don't know what your dern horses sound like."

It was an old trick of theirs, trying to make him feel incompetent—as if a man was incompetent because he couldn't see in the dark, or identify a local horse by the sound of its trot.

"'I god, you're techy, Jake," Augustus said, just as Call rode up.

"Is this all there is or did you trot in and run the rest off?" he asked.

"Do them horses look nervous?" Augustus asked.

"Dern," Call said. "Last time we was through here there was two or three hundred horses."

"Maybe Pedro's going broke," Augustus said. "Mexicans can go broke, same as Texans. What'd you do with the *vaqueros?*"

"We didn't find none. We just found two Irishmen."

"Irishmen?" Augustus asked.

"They just lost," Deets said.

"Hell, I can believe they're lost," Jake said.

"On their way to Galveston," Newt said, thinking it might help clarify the situation.

Augustus laughed. "I guess it ain't hard to miss Galveston if you start from Ireland," he said. "However, it takes skill to miss the dern United States entirely and hit Pedro Flores' ranch. I'd like to meet men who can do that."

"You'll get your chance," Call said. "They don't have mounts, unless you count a mule and a donkey. I guess we better help them out of their fix."

"I'm surprised they ain't naked, too," Augustus said. "I'd had thought some bandit would have stolen their clothes by now."

"Have you counted these horses, or have you been sitting here jawing?" Call said brusquely. The night was turning out to be more complicated and less profitable than he had hoped.

"I assigned that chore to Dish Boggett," Augustus said. "It's around forty."

"Not enough," Call said. "You take two and go back and get the Irishmen."

He took his rope off his saddle and handed it to the boy.

"Go catch two horses," he said. "You better make hackamores."

Newt was so surprised by the assignment he almost dropped the rope. He had never roped a horse in the dark before—but he would have to try. He trotted off toward the horse herd, sure they would probably stampede at the sight of him. But he had a piece of luck. Six or eight horses trotted over to sniff at his mount and he easily caught one of them. As he was making a second loop and trying to lead the first horse over to Pea, Dish Boggett trotted over without being asked and casually roped another horse.

"What are we gonna do, brand 'em?" he asked.

Newt was irritated, for he would have liked to complete the assignment himself, but since it was Dish he said nothing.

"Lend 'em to some men we found," he said. "Irishmen."

"Oh," Dish said. "I hate to lend my rope to an Irishman. I might be out a good rope."

Newt solved that by putting his own rope on the second horse. He led them back to where the Captain was waiting. As he did, Mr. Gus began to laugh, causing Newt to worry that he had done something improperly after all—he couldn't imagine what.

Then he saw that they were looking at the horse brands—H I C on the left hips.

"It just goes to show that even sinners can accomplish Christian acts," Augustus said. "Here we set out to rob a man and now we're in a position to return valuable property to a man who's already been robbed. That's curious justice, ain't it?"

"It's a wasted night, is what it is," Call said.

"If it was me I'd make the man pay a reward for them horses," Jake said. "He'd never have seen them agin if it hadn't been for us."

Call was silent. Of course they could not charge a man for his own horses.

"That's all right, Call," Augustus said. "We'll make it up off the Irishmen. Maybe they got rich uncles—bank directors or railroad magnates or something. They'll be so happy to see those boys alive again that they'll likely make us partners."

Call ignored him, trying to think of some way to salvage the trip. Though he had always been a careful planner, life on the frontier had long ago convinced him of the fragility of plans. The truth was, most plans did fail, to one degree or another, for one reason or another. He had survived as a Ranger because he was quick to respond to what he had actually found, not because his planning was infallible.

In the present case he had found two destitute travelers and a herd of recently stolen horses. But it was still four hours till sunup and he was reluctant to abandon his original ambition, which was to return with a hundred Mexican horses. It was still possible, if he acted decisively.

"All right," he said, quickly sorting over in his head who should be assigned to do what. "These are mainly Wilbarger's horses. The reason they're so gentle is because they've been run to a frazzle, and they're used to Texans besides."

"I'd catch one and ride him home, if I could find one that paces," Jake said. "I'm about give out from bouncing on this old trotter you boys gave me."

"Jake's used to feather pillows and Arkansas whores," Augustus said. "It's a pity he has to associate with hard old cobs like us."

"You two can jabber tomorrow," Call said. "Pedro's horses have got to be somewhere. I'd like to make a run at them before I quit. That means we have to split three ways."

"Leave me split the shortest way home," Jake said, never too proud to complain. "I've bounced my ass over enough of Mexico."

"All right," Call said. "You and Deets and Dish take these horses home."

He would have liked to have Deets with him, but Deets was the only one he knew for certain could take the Wilbarger horses on a line for Lonesome Dove. Dish Boggett, though said to be a good hand, was an untested quality, whereas Jake was probably lost himself.

"Gus, that leaves you the Irishmen," he said. "If they can ride, you ought to catch up with these horses somewhere this side of the river. Just don't stop to play no poker with them."

Augustus considered the situation for a minute.

"So that's your strategy, is it?" he said. "You and Newt and Pea get to have all the fun and the rest of us are stuck with the chores."

"Why, I was trying to make it easy for you, Gus," Call said. "Seeing as you're the oldest and most decrepit."

"See you for breakfast, then," Augustus said, taking the lead ropes from Newt. "I just hope the Irishmen don't expect a buggy."

With that he galloped off. The rest of them trotted down to where Pea and Dish were sitting, waiting.

"Pea, you come with me," Call said. "And you—" looking at the boy. Though it would expose Newt to more danger, he decided he wanted the boy with him. At least he wouldn't pick up bad habits, as he undoubtedly would have if he'd been sent along with Gus.

"All you three have to do is get these horses to town by sunup," he added. "If we ain't back, give Wilbarger his."

"What are you planning to do, stay here and get married?" Jake asked.

"My plans ain't set," he said. "Don't you worry about us. Just keep them horses moving."

He looked at Deets when he said that. He could not formally make Deets the leader over two white men, but he wanted him to know that he had the responsibility of seeing that the horses got there. Deets said nothing, but when he trotted off to start the horses he took the point as if it was his natural place. Dish Boggett loped around to the other point, leaving Jake to bring up the rear.

Jake seemed largely uninterested in the proceedings, which was his way.

"Call, you're some friend," he said. "I ain't been home a whole day and you already got me stealing horses."

But he loped off after the herd and was soon out of sight. Pea Eye yawned as he watched him go.

"I swear," he said. "Jake's just like he used to be."

<hr>

An hour later they found the main horse herd in a narrow valley several miles to the north. Call estimated it to be over a hundred horses strong. The situation had its difficulty, the main one being that the horses were barely a mile from the Flores headquarters, and on the wrong side of it at that. It would be necessary to bring them back past the hacienda, or else take them north to the river, a considerably longer route. If Pedro Flores and his men chose to pursue, they would have a fine chance of catching them out in the open, in broad daylight, several miles from help. It would be himself and Pea and the boy against a small army of *vaqueros*.

On the other hand, he didn't relish leaving the horses, now that he had found them. He was tempted just to move them right past the hacienda and hope everyone there had gone to bed drunk.

"Well, we're here," he said. "Let's take 'em."

"It's a bunch," Pea said. "We won't have to come back for a while."

"We won't never come back," Call said. "We'll sell some and take the rest with us to Montana."

Life was finally starting, Newt thought. Here he was below the border, about to run off a huge horse herd, and in a few days or weeks he would be going up the trail to a place he had barely even heard of. Most of the cowpokes who went north from Lonesome Dove just went to Kansas and thought that was far—but Montana must be twice as far. He couldn't imagine what such a place would look like. Jake had said it had buffalo and mountains, two things he had never seen, and snow, the hardest thing of all to imagine. He had seen ridges and hills, and so had a notion about mountains, and he had seen pictures of buffalo in the papers that the stage drivers sometimes left Mr. Gus.

Snow, however, was an entirely mysterious thing. Once or twice in his lifetime there had been freezes in Lonesome Dove—he had seen thin ice on the water bucket that sat on the porch. But ice wasn't snow, which was supposed to stack up on the ground so high that people had to wade through it. He had seen pictures of people sledding over it, but still couldn't imagine what it would actually feel like to be in snow.

"I guess we'll just go for home," Call said. "If we wake 'em up we wake 'em up."

He looked at the boy. "You take the left point," he said. "Pea will be on the right, and I'll be behind. If trouble comes, it'll come from behind, and I'll notice it first. If they get after us hot and heavy we can always drop off thirty or forty horses and hope that satisfies them."

They circled the herd and quietly started it moving to the northwest, waving a rope now and then to get the horses in motion but saying as little as possible. Newt could not help feeling a little odd about it all, since he had somehow had it in his mind that they were coming to Mexico to buy horses, not steal them. It was puzzling that such a muddy little river like the Rio Grande should make such a difference in terms of what was lawful and what not. On the Texas side, horse stealing was a hanging crime, and many of those hung for it were Mexican cowboys who came across the river to do pretty much what they themselves were doing. The Captain was known for his sternness where horsethieves were concerned, and yet, here they were, running off a whole herd. Evidently if you crossed the river to do it, it stopped being a crime and became a game.

Newt didn't really feel that what they were doing was wrong—if it had been wrong, the Captain wouldn't have done it. But the thought hit him that under Mexican law what they were doing might be a hanging offense. It put a different slant on the game. In imagining what it would be like to go to Mexico, he had always supposed the main danger would come in the form of bullets, but he was no longer so sure. On the ride down he hadn't been worried, because he had a whole company around him.

But once they started back, instead of having a whole company around him, he seemed to have no one. Pea was far across the valley, and the Captain was half a mile to the rear. If a bunch of hostile *vaqueros* sprang up, he might not even be able to find the other two men. Even if he wasn't captured immediately, he could easily get lost. Lonesome Dove might be hard to locate, particularly if he was being chased.

If caught, he knew he could expect no mercy. The only thing in his favor was that there didn't seem to be any trees around to hang him from. Mr. Gus had once told a story about a horsethief who had to be hung from the rafter of a barn because there were no trees, but so far as Newt could tell there were no barns in Mexico either. The only thing he knew clearly was that he was scared. He rode for several miles, feeling very apprehensive. The thought of hanging—a new thought—wouldn't leave his mind. It became so powerful at one point that he squeezed his throat with one hand, to get a little notion of how it felt not to breathe. It didn't feel so bad when it was just his hand, but he knew a rope would feel a lot worse.

But the miles passed and no *vaqueros* appeared. The horses strung out under the moonlight in a long line, trotting easily. They were well past the hacienda, and the night seemed so peaceful that Newt began to relax a little. After all, the Captain and Pea and the others had done such things many times. It was just a night's work, and one that would soon be over.

Newt wasn't tired, and as he became less scared he began to imagine how gratifying it would be to ride into Lonesome Dove with such a large herd of horses. Everyone who saw them ride in would realize that he was now a man—even Lorena might see it if she happened to look out her window at the right time. He and the Captain and Pea were doing an exceptional thing. Deets would be proud of him, and even Bolivar would take notice.

All went peaceful and steady, and the thin moon hung brightly in the west. It seemed to Newt that it must be one of the longest nights of the year. He kept looking to the east, hoping to see a little redness on the horizon, but the horizon was still black.

He was thinking about the morning, and how nice it would be to cross the river and bring the horses through the town, when the peaceful night suddenly went off like a bomb. They were on the long chaparral plain not far south of the river and were easing the horses around a particularly dense thicket of chaparral, prickly pear and low mesquite when it happened. Newt had dropped off the point a little distance, to allow the horses room to skirt the thicket, when he heard shots from behind him. Before he had time to look around, or even touch his own gun, the horse herd exploded into a dead run and began to spread out. He saw what looked like half the herd charging right at him from the rear; some of the horses nearest him veered and went crashing into the chaparral. Then he heard Pea's gun sound from the other side of the thicket, and at that point lost all capacity for sorting out what was happening. When the race started, most of the herd was behind him, and the horses ahead of him were at least going in the same direction he was. But in a few seconds, once the whole mass of animals was moving at a dead run over the uncertain terrain, he suddenly noticed a stream of animals coming directly toward him from the right. The new bunch had simply cut around the chaparral thicket from the north and collided with the first herd. Before Newt even had time to consider what was happening, he was engulfed in a mass of animals, a few of which went down when the two herds ran together. Then, over the confused neighing of what seemed like hundreds of horses he began to hear yells and curses—Mexican curses. To his shock he saw a rider engulfed in the mass like himself, and the rider was not the Captain or Pea Eye. He realized then that two horse herds had run together, theirs headed for Texas, the other coming from Texas, both trying to skirt the same thicket, though from opposite directions.

The realization was unhelpful, though, because the horses behind him had caught up with him and all were struggling for running room. For a second he thought of trying to force his way to the outside, but then he saw two riders already there, struggling to turn the herd. They were not succeeding, but they were not his riders, either, and it struck him that being in the middle of the herd offered a certain safety, at least.

It quickly became clear that their herd was much the larger, and was forcing the new herd to curve into its flow. Soon all the horses were running northwest, Newt still in the middle of the bunch. Once a big wild-eyed gelding nearly knocked Mouse down; then Newt heard shots to his left and ducked, thinking the shots were meant for him. Just as he ducked Mouse leaped a sizable chaparral bush. With his eyes toward the gunfire Newt was unprepared for the leap, and lost a stirrup and one rein but held onto the saddle horn and kept his seat. From then on he concentrated on riding, though he still occasionally heard shots. He kept low over his horse, an unnecessary precaution, for the running herd threw up so much dust that he could not have seen ten feet in front of him even if it had been daylight. He was grateful for the dust—it was choking him, but it was also keeping him from getting shot, a more important consideration.

After a few miles the horses were no longer bunched so tightly. It occurred to Newt that he ought to angle out of the herd and not just let himself be carried along like a cow chip on a river, but he didn't know what such a move might mean. Would he be required to shoot at the *vaqueros* if they were still there? He was almost afraid to take his pistol out of its holster for fear Mouse would jump another bush and he'd drop it.

While he was running along, trying not to fall off and hoping he and the horses wouldn't suddenly go over a cutbank or pile into a deep gully of some kind, he heard a sound that was deeply reassuring: the sound of the Captain's rifle, the big Henry. Newt heard it shoot twice. It had to be the Captain because he was the only man on the border who carried a Henry. Everyone else had already switched to the lighter Winchesters.

The shots meant the Captain was all right. They came from ahead, which was odd, since the Captain had been behind, but then the *vaqueros* had been ahead, too. Somehow the Captain had managed to get to the front of the run and deal with them.

Newt looked back over his shoulder and saw red in the east. It was just a line of red, like somebody had drawn it with a crayon, over the thick black line of the land, but it meant that the night was ending. He didn't know where they were, but they still had a lot of horses. The horses were well spread by then, and he eased out of the herd. Despite the red in the east, the land seemed darker than it had all night; he could see nothing and just exerted himself to keep up, hoping they were going in the right direction. It felt a little odd to be alive and unharmed after such a deep scare, and Newt kept looking east, wishing the light would hurry so he could see around him and know whether it was safe to relax. For all he knew, Mexicans with Winchesters could be a hundred yards behind him.

He wished the Captain would shoot again; he had never been in a situation in which he felt so uncertain about everything. Squint as he could, Newt could see nothing but dark land and white dust. Of course the sun would soon solve the problem, but what would he see when he could see? The Captain and Pea could be ten miles away, and he himself could be riding into Mexico with Pedro Flores' *vaqueros*.

Then, coming over a little rise in the ground, he saw something that gave him heart: a thin silver ribbon to the northwest that could only be the river. The fading moon hung just above it. Across it, Texas was in sight, no less dark than Mexico, but there. The deep relief Newt felt at the sight of it washed away most of his fear. He even recognized the curve of the river—it was the old Comanche crossing, only a mile above Lonesome Dove. Whoever he was with had brought him home.

To his dismay, the sight of such a safe, familiar place made him want to cry. It seemed to him that the night had lasted many days—days during which he had been worried every moment that he would do something wrong and make a mistake that meant he would never come back to Lonesome Dove, or else come back disgraced. Now it was over and he was almost back, and relief seemed to run through him like warm water, some of which leaked out his eyes. It made him glad it was still dark—what would the men think, if they saw him? There was so much dust on his face that when he quickly wiped away the tears of relief his fingers rubbed off moist smears of dirt.

In a few minutes more, as the herd neared the river, the darkness loosened and began to gray. The red on the eastern horizon was no longer a line but spread upward like an opened fan. Soon Newt could see the horses moving through the first faint gray light—a lot of horses. Then, just as he thought he had brought the flood within himself under control, the darkness loosened its hold yet more and the first sunlight streamed across the plain, filtering through the cloud of dust to touch the coats of the tired horses, most of whom had slowed to a rapid trot. Ahead, waiting on the bank of the river, was Captain Call, the big Henry in the crook of his arm. The Hell Bitch was lathered with sweat, but her head was up and she slung it restlessly as she watched the herd approach—even pointing her keen ears at Mouse for a moment. Neither the Captain nor the gray mare looked in the least affected by the long night or the hard ride, yet Newt found himself so moved by the mere sight of them sitting there that he had to brush away yet another tear and smudge his dusty cheek even worse.

Down the river aways he could see Pea, sitting on the rangy bay they called Sardine. Of the hostile *vaqueros* they had met there was no sign. There were so many questions Newt wanted to ask about what they had done and where they had been that he hardly knew where to begin; yet, when he rode up to the Captain, keeping Mouse far enough away from the Hell Bitch that she wouldn't try to take a bite out of him, he didn't ask any questions. They would have poured out of him if it had been Mr. Gus or Deets or Pea, but since it was the Captain, the questions just stayed inside. All he said, at the end of the most exciting and important night of his life, was a simple good morning.

"It is a good one, ain't it?" Call said, as he watched the huge herd of horses—well over a hundred of them—pour over the low banks and spread out down the river to drink. Pea had ridden Sardine into the water stirrup deep to keep the herd from spreading too far south.

Call knew that it had been rare luck, running into the four Mexican horsethieves and getting most of the horses they had just brought over from Texas. The Mexicans had thought they had run into an army—who but an army would have so many horses?—and had not really stayed to make a fight, though he had had to scare off one *vaquero* who kept trying to turn the herd.

As for the boy, it was good that he had picked up a little experience and come through it all with nothing worse than a dirty face.

They sat together silently as the top half of the sun shot long ribbons of light across the brown river and the drinking horses, some of whom lay down in the shallows and rolled themselves in the cooling mud. When the herd began to move in twos and threes up the north bank, Call touched the mare and he and the boy moved out into the water. Call loosened his rein and let the mare drink. He was as pleased with her as he was with the catch. She was surefooted as a cat, and far from used up, though the boy's mount was so done in he would be worthless for a week. Pea's big bay was not much better. Call let the mare drink all she wanted before gathering his rein. Most of the horses had moved to the north bank, and the sun had finished lifting itself clear of the horizon.

"Let's ease on home," he said to the boy. "I hope Wilbarger's got his pockets full of money. We've got horses to sell."

12

IF WILBARGER WAS IMPRESSED at the sight of so many horses, he gave no sign of it. The small herd had already been penned, and he and Deets and the man called Chick were quietly separating out horses with the H I C brand on them. Dish Boggett worked the gate between the two corrals, letting Wilbarger's horses run through and waving his rope in the face of those he didn't claim. Jake Spoon was nowhere in sight, nor was there any sign of Augustus and the Irishmen.

The new herd was far too large to pen. Call had always meant to fence a holding pasture for just such an eventuality, but he had never gotten around to it. In the immediate case it didn't matter greatly; the horses were tired from their long run and could be left to graze and rest. After breakfast he would send the boy out to watch them.

Wilbarger paused from his work a moment to look at the stream of horses trotting past, then went back to his cutting, which was almost done. Since there was already enough help in the pen, there was nothing for Newt to do but stand by the fence and watch. Pea had already climbed up on what they called the "opry seat"—the top rail of the corral—to watch the proceedings. His bay and Newt's Mouse, just unsaddled, took a few steps and then lay down and rolled themselves in the dust.

Call was not quite ready to rest the mare. When Wilbarger finished his sorting and came over to the fence, it was her, not the Captain, that he had his eye on.

"Good morning," he said. "Let's trade. You keep them thirty-eight splendid horses I just sorted out and I'll take that mean creature you're astraddle of. Thirty-eight for one is generous terms, in my book."

"Keep your book," Call said, not surprised at the offer.

Pea Eye was so startled by what he was hearing that he almost fell off the fence. "You mean you'd give up all them horses for the chance of having a hunk bit out of you?" he asked. He knew men fancied the Captain's mare, but that anyone would fancy her to that extent was almost more than he could credit.

Dish Boggett walked over, slapping the dust off his chaps with a coiled rope.

"Is that your last word on the subject?" Wilbarger asked. "I'm offering thirty-eight for one. You won't get a chance like that every day of your life."

Dish snorted. He fancied the gray mare himself. "It'd be like tradin' a fifty-dollar gold piece for thirty-eight nickels," he said. He was in a foul temper anyway. The minute they had the horses penned, Jake Spoon had unsaddled and walked straight to the Dry Bean, as if that were where he lived.

Wilbarger ignored him too. "This outfit is full of opinion," he said. "If opinions was money you'd all be rich." He looked at Call.

"I won't trade this mare," Call said. "And that ain't an opinion."

"No, it's more like a damn hard fact," Wilbarger said. "I live on a horse and yet I ain't had but good ones my whole life."

"This is my third," Call said.

Wilbarger nodded. "Well, sir," he said, "I'm obliged to you for getting here on time. It's plain the man you deal with knows where there's a den of thieves."

"A big den," Call said.

"Well, let's go, Chick," Wilbarger said. "We won't get home unless we start."

"You might as well stay for breakfast," Call said. "A couple more of your horses are on their way."

"What are they doing, traveling on three legs?" Wilbarger asked.

"They're with Mr. McCrae," Call said. "He travels at his own pace."

"Talks at it, too," Wilbarger said. "I don't think we'll wait. Keep them two horses for your trouble."

"We brought in some nice stock," Call said. "You're welcome to look it over, if you're still short."

"Not interested," Wilbarger said. "You won't rent pigs and you won't trade that mare, so I might as well be on my way."

Then he turned to Dish Boggett. "Want a job, son?" he asked. "You look all right to me."

"I got a job," Dish said.

"Running off Mexican horses isn't a job," Wilbarger said. "It's merely a gamble. You've the look of a cowboy, and I'm about to start up the trail with three thousand head."

"So are we," Call said, amused that the man would try to hire a hand out from under him with him sitting there.

"Going where?" Wilbarger asked.

"Going to Montana," Call said.

"I wouldn't," Wilbarger said. He rode over to the gate, leaned over to open it, and rode out, leaving the gate for Chick to close. When Chick tried to lean down and shut the gate his hat fell off. Nobody walked over to pick it up for him, either—he was forced to dismount, which embarrassed him greatly. Wilbarger waited, but he looked impatient.

"Well, we may see you up the trail, then," he said to Call. "I wouldn't aim for Montana, though. Too far, too cold, full of bears and I don't know about the Indians. They may be beat but I wouldn't count on it. You might end up making some a present of a fine herd of beef."

"We'll try not to," Call said.

Wilbarger rode off, Chick following at the rear of the small horse herd. As Chick rode past, Dish Boggett was greatly tempted to rope him off his horse and box his ears as a means of relieving his feelings about Lorie and Jake Spoon—but the Captain was sitting there, so he merely gave Chick a hard stare and let him go.

"By gosh, I could eat," Pea Eye said. "I sure hope Gus ain't lost."

"If he's lost I don't know what we'll do for biscuits," he added, since nobody commented on his remark.

"You could always get married," Dish observed dryly. "There's plenty of women who can make biscuits."

It was not the first time Pea had had that particular truth pointed out to him. "I know there is," he said. "But that don't mean there's one of 'em that would have me."

Deets gave a rich chuckle. "Why, the widow Cole would have you," he said. "She'd be pleased to have you." Then, well aware that the widow Cole was something of a sore spot with Pea, he walked off toward the house.

Mention of Mary Cole made Pea Eye very uncomfortable. From time to time, throughout his life, it had been pointed out to him that he might marry—Gus McCrae was very fond of pointing it out, in fact.

But once in a while, even if nobody mentioned one, the thought of women entered his head all on its own, and once it came it usually tended to stay for several hours, filling his noggin like a cloud of gnats. Of course, a cloud of gnats was nothing in comparison to a cloud of Gulf coast mosquitoes, so the thought of women was not *that* bothersome, but it was a thought Pea would rather not have in his head.

He had never known what to think about women, and still didn't, but so far as actions went he was content to take his cue from the Captain, whose cue was plain. The Captain left them strictly alone, and had all the years Pea had been with him, excepting only one puzzling instance that had occurred years before, which Pea only remembered once every year or two, usually when he was dreaming. He had gone down to the saloon to get an ax someone had borrowed and not returned, and while he was getting the ax he heard a young woman crying out words and grievances to someone who was with her in her room.

The woman doing the crying was the whore named Maggie, Newt's mother, whom Jake Spoon took such a fancy to later. It was only after Pea had found the ax and was halfway home with it that it occurred to him that Maggie had been talking to the Captain, and had even called him by his first name, which Pea had never used in all his years of service.

The knowledge that the Captain was in the room with a whore struck Pea hard, sort of like the bullet that had hit him just behind the shoulder blades in the big Indian scrape up by Fort Phantom Hill. When the bullet hit he felt a solid whack and then sort of went numb in the brain—and it was the same with the notion that struck him as he was carrying the ax home from the saloon: Maggie was talking to the Captain in the privacy of her room, whereas so far as he knew no one had ever heard of the Captain doing more than occasionally tipping his hat to a lady if he met one in the street.

Overhearing that snatch of conversation was an accident Pea was slow to forget. For a month or two after it happened he went around feeling nervous, expecting life to change in some bold way. And yet nothing changed at all. They all soon went up the river to try and catch some bandits raiding out of Chihuahua, and the Captain, so far as he could tell, was the same old Captain. By the time they came back, Maggie had had her child, and soon after, Jake Spoon moved in with her for a while. Then he left and Maggie died and Gus went down one day and got Newt from the Mexican family that had taken him upon Maggie's death.

The years had gone on passing, most of them slow years, particularly after they quit rangering and went into the horse-and-cattle business. The only real result of overhearing the conversation was that Pea was cautious from then on about who he let borrow the ax. He liked life slow and didn't want any more mysteries or sharp surprises.

Though he was content to stick with the Captain and Gus and do his daily work, he found that the problem of women was one that didn't entirely go away. The question of marriage, about which Deets felt so free to chuckle, was a persistent one. Gus, who had been married twice and who whored whenever he could find a whore, was the main reason it was so persistent. Marriage was one of Gus's favorite subjects. When he got to talking about it the Captain usually took his rifle and went for a walk, but by that time Pea would usually be comfortable on the porch and a little sleepy with liquor, so he was the one to get the full benefit of Gus's opinions, one of which was that Pea was just going to waste by not marrying the widow Cole.

The fact that Pea had only spoken to Mary Cole five or six times in his life, most of them times when she was still married to Josh Cole, didn't mean a thing to a bystander like Gus, or even a bystander like Deets; both of them seemed to take it for granted that Mary regarded him as a fit successor to Josh. The thing that seemed to clinch it, in their view, was that, while Mary was an unusually tall woman, she was not as tall as Pea. She had been a good foot taller than Josh Cole, a mild fellow who had been in Pickles Gap buying a milk cow when a bad storm hit. A bolt of lightning fried both Josh and his horse—the milk cow had only been singed, but it still affected her milk. Mary Cole never remarried, but, in Gus's view, that was only because Pea Eye had not had the enterprise to walk down the street and ask her.

"Why, Josh was just a half-pint," Gus said frequently. "That woman needs a full pint. It'd be a blessing for her to have a man around who could reach the top shelf."

Pea had never considered that height might be a factor in relations such as marriage. After brooding about it for several months it occurred to him that Gus was tall too, and educated as well.

"Hell, you're tall," he said one night. "You ought to marry her yourself. The both of you can read."

He knew Mary could read because he had been in church once or twice when the preacher had asked her to read the Psalms. She had a kind of low, scratchy voice, unusual in a woman; once or twice, listening to it made Pea feel funny, as if someone was tickling the little hairs at the back of his neck.

Gus vehemently denied that he would be a suitable mate for Mary Cole. "Why, no, Pea, it wouldn't do," he said. "I've done been wrung through the wringer of marriage twice. What a widow wants is someone fresh. It's what all women want, widows or not. If a man's got experience it's bound to be that he got it with another woman, and that don't never sit well. A forthright woman like Mary probably considers that she can give you all the experience you're ever likely to need."

To Pea it was all just a troublesome puzzle. He could not remember how the subject had come up in the first place, since he had never said a word about wanting to marry. Whatever else it meant, it meant leaving the Captain, and Pea didn't plan to do that. Of course, Mary didn't live very far away, but the Captain always liked to have his men handy in case something came up sudden. There was no knowing what the Captain would think if he were to try and marry. One day he pointed out to Gus that he was far from being the only available man in Lonesome Dove. Xavier Wanz was available, not to mention Lippy. A number of the traveling men who passed through were surely unmarried. But when he raised the point, Gus just ignored him.

Some nights, laying on the porch, he felt a fool for even thinking about such things, and yet think he did. He had lived with men his whole life, rangering and working; during his whole adult life he couldn't recollect spending ten minutes alone with a woman. He was better acquainted with Gus's pigs than he was with Mary Cole, and more comfortable with them too. The sensible thing would be to ignore Gus and Deets and think about things that had some bearing on his day's work, like how to keep his old boot from rubbing a corn on his left big toe. An Army mule had tromped the toe ten years before, and since then it had stuck out slightly in the wrong direction, just enough to make his boot rub a corn. The only solution to the problem was to cut holes in his boot, which worked fine in dry weather but had its disadvantages when it was wet and cold. Gus had offered to rebreak the toe and set it properly, but Pea didn't hate the corn that bad. It did seem to him that it was only common sense that a sore toe made more difference in his life than a woman he had barely spoken to; yet his mind didn't see it that way. There were nights when he lay on the porch too sleepy to shave his corn, or even to worry about the problem, when the widow Cole would pop to the surface of his consciousness like a turtle on the surface of a pond. At such times he would pretend to be asleep, for Gus was so sly he could practically read minds, and would surely tease him if he figured out that he was thinking about Mary and her scratchy voice.

Even more persistent than the thought of her reading the Psalms was another memory. One day he had been passing her house just as a little thunderstorm swept through the town, scaring the dogs and cats and rolling tumbleweeds down the middle of the street. Mary had hung a washing and was out in her backyard trying to get it in before the rain struck, but the thunderstorm proved too quick for her. Big drops of rain began to splatter in the dust, and the wind got higher, causing the sheets on Mary's clothesline to flap so hard they popped like guns. Pea had been raised to be helpful, and since it was obvious that Mary was going to have a hard time with the sheets, he started over to offer his assistance.

But the storm had a start on both of them, and before he even got there the rain began to pour down, turning the white dust brown. Most women would have seen at that point that the wash was a lost cause and run for the house, but Mary wasn't running. Her skirt was already so wet it was plastered to her legs, but she was still struggling with one of the flapping sheets. In the struggle, two or three small garments that she had already gathered up blew out of her hand and off across the yard, which had begun to look like a shallow lake. Pea hurried to retrieve the garments and then helped Mary get the wet sheet off the line—she was evidently just doing it out of pure stubbornness, since the sun was shining brightly to the west of the storm and would obviously be available to dry the sheet again in a few minutes.

It was Pea's one close exposure to an aspect of womankind that Gus was always talking about—their penchant for flying directly in the face of reason. Mary was as wet on the top as on the bottom, and the flapping sheet had knocked one of the combs out of her hair, causing it to come loose. The wash was as wet as it had been before she hung it up in the first place, and yet she wasn't quitting. She was taking clothes off the line that would just have to be hung back on in fifteen minutes, and Pea was helping her do it as if it all made some sense. While he was steadying the clothesline he happened to notice something that gave him almost as hard a jolt as the bolt of lightning that killed Josh Cole: the clothes he had rescued were undergarments—white bloomers of the sort that it was obvious Mary was wearing beneath the skirt that was so wet against her legs. Pea was so shocked that he almost dropped the underpants back in the mud. She was bound to think it bold that he would pick up her undergarments like that—yet she was determined to have the sheets off the line and all he could do was stand there numb with embarrassment. It was a blessing that rain soon began to pour off his hat brim in streams right in front of his face, making a little waterfall for him to hide behind until the ordeal ended. With the water running off his hat he only caught blurred glimpses of what was going on—he could not judge to what extent Mary had been shocked by his helpful but thoughtless act.

To his surprise, nothing terrible happened. When she finally had the sheet under control, Mary took the bloomers from him as casually as if they were handkerchiefs or table napkins or something. To his vast surprise, she seemed to be rather amused at the sight of him standing there with a stream of water pouring off his hat and falling just in front of his nose.

"Pea, it's a good thing you know how to keep your mouth shut," she said. "If you opened it right now you'd probably drown. Many thanks for your help."

She was the kind of forthright woman who called men by their first names, and she was known to salt her speech rather freely with criticism.

"We've the Lord to thank for this bath," she said. "I personally didn't need it, but I'm bound to say it might work an improvement where you're concerned. You ain't as bad-looking as I thought, now that you're nearly clean."

By the time she got to her back porch the rain was slackening and the sun was already striking little rainbows through the sparkle of drops that still fell. Pea had walked on home, the water dripping more slowly from his hat. He never mentioned the incident to anyone, knowing it would mean unmerciful teasing if it ever got out. But he remembered it. When he lay on the porch half drunk and it floated up in his mind, things got mixed into the memory that he hadn't even known he was noticing, such as the smell of Mary's wet flesh. He hadn't meant to smell her, and hadn't made any effort to, and yet the very night after it happened the first thing he remembered was that Mary had smelled different from any other wet thing he had ever smelled. He could not find a word for what was different about Mary's smell—maybe it was just that, being a woman, she smelled cleaner than most of the wet creatures he came in contact with. It had been more than a year since the rainstorm, and yet Mary's smell was still part of the memory of it. He also remembered how she seemed to bulge out of her corset at the top and the bottom both.

It was not every night that he remembered Mary, though. Much of the time he found himself wondering about the generalities of marriage. The principal aspect he worried over most was that marriage required men and women to live together. He had tried many times to envision how it would be to be alone at night under the same roof with a woman—or to have one there at breakfast and supper. What kind of talk would a woman expect? And what kind of behavior. It stumped him: he couldn't even make a guess. Once in a while it occurred to him that he could tell Mary he would like to marry her but didn't consider himself worthy to live under the same roof with her. If he put it right she might take a liberal attitude and allow him to continue to live down the street with the boys, that being what he was used to. He would plan, of course, to make himself available for chores when she required him—otherwise life could go on in its accustomed way.

He was even tempted to sound out Gus on the plan—Gus knew more about marriage than anyone else—but every time he planned to bring it up he either got sleepy first or decided at the last second he had better keep quiet. If the plan was ridiculous in the eyes of an expert, then Pea wouldn't know what to think, and besides, Gus would never let up teasing.

=

They were all scattered around the table, finishing one of Bol's greasy breakfasts, when they heard the sound of horses in the yard. The next minute Augustus trotted up and dismounted, with the two Irishmen just a few yards behind him. Instead of being bareback the Irishmen were riding big silver-studded Mexican saddles and driving eight or ten skinny horses before them. When they reached the porch they just sat on their horses, looking unhappy.

Dish Boggett had not really believed there were any Irishmen down in Mexico, and when he stepped out on the back porch and saw them he burst right out laughing.

Newt felt a little sorry for the two of them, but he had to admit they were a comical sight. The Mexican saddles were all clearly meant for men with longer legs. Their feet did not come anywhere near the stirrups. Even so, the Irishmen seemed disinclined to dismount.

Augustus jerked the saddle off his tired horse and turned him loose to graze.

"Get down, boys," he said to the Irishmen. "You're safe now, as long as you don't eat the cooking. This is what we call home."

Allen O'Brien had both hands around the big Mexican saddle horn. He had been holding it so tightly for the last two hours that he was not sure he could turn it loose. He looked down with apprehension.

"I'd not realized how much taller a horse is than a mule," he said. "It seems a long ways down."

Dish regarded the remark as the most comical he had ever heard. It had never occurred to him that there could be such a thing as a grown man who didn't know how to dismount from a horse. The sight of the two Irishmen stuck with their short legs dangling down the sides of the horses struck him as so funny that he doubled over with laughter.

"I guess we'll have to build 'em a ladder, by God," he said, when he could catch his breath.

Augustus too was mildly amused by the Irishmen's ignorance. "Why, boys, you just have to flop over and drop," he said.

Allen O'Brien accomplished the dismounting with no real trouble, but Sean was reluctant to drop once he flopped over. He hung from the saddle horn for several seconds, which puzzled the horse, so that it began to try and buck a little. It was too thin and too tired to do much, but Sean did get jerked around a little, a sight so funny that even Call laughed. Allen O'Brien, once safe on the ground, immediately joined in the laughter out of relief. Sean finally dropped and stood glaring at his brother.

"Well, I don't see Jake—that figures," Augustus said, taking himself a big dipper of water and squishing a few mouthfuls around and spitting them out, to clear the dust from his throat. He then offered the dipper to Allen O'Brien, who imitated the squishing and spitting, thinking it must be a custom of the new country he found himself in.

"You took your time, I see," Call said. "I was about to start back with a burial party."

"Shucks," Augustus said. "Bringing these boys in was such a light task that I went over to Sabinas and stopped off at the whorehouse."

"That explains the saddles," Call said.

"Yes, and the horses too," Augustus said. "All the bandits was dead drunk by the time we got there. These Irish boys can't maintain much of a pace riding bareback so we helped ourselves to a few saddles and the best of the nags."

"Them horses wouldn't make good soap," Dish said, looking at the horses Augustus had brought back.

"If I wasn't so hungry I'd argue the point," Augustus said. "Bile them horses for a week or two and they'd produce a fine soap."

Young Sean O'Brien could not conceal his disappointment with America.

"If this is America, where's the snow?" he asked, to everyone's surprise. His image of the new country had been strongly influenced by a scene of Boston Harbor in winter that he had seen in an old magazine. There had been lots of snow, and the hot backyard he found himself in was nothing like what he had expected. Instead of ships with tall masts there was just a low adobe house, with lots of old saddles and pieces of rotting harness piled under a little shed at one corner. Worse still, he could not see a spot of green anywhere. The bushes were gray and thorny, and there were no trees at all.

"No, son, you've overshot the snow," Augustus said. "What we have down here is sand."

Call felt his impatience rising. The night had been far more successful than he could have hoped. They could keep the best horses and sell the rest—the profits would easily enable them to hire a crew and outfit a wagon for the trip north. Then all they would have to do would be gather the cattle and brand them. If everyone would work like they should, it could all be accomplished in three weeks, and they could be on the trail by the first of April—none too soon, considering the distance they had to go. The problem would be getting everyone to work like they should. Jake was already off with his whore, and Augustus hadn't had breakfast.

"You men go eat," Call said to the Irishmen; having rescued them, he could do no less than feed them.

Allen O'Brien was looking dejectedly at the few buildings that made up Lonesome Dove. "Is this all there is to the town?" he asked.

"Yes, and it's worse than it looks," Augustus said.

To the embarrassment of everyone, Sean O'Brien began to cry. It had been an extremely tense night, and he hadn't expected to survive it. All during the ride he had expected to fall off his horse and become paralyzed. He associated paralysis with falls because a cousin of his had fallen off a cottage he was thatching and had been paralyzed ever since. The horse Sean had been given seemed to him at least as tall as a cottage, and he felt he had good reason to worry. He had spent a long boat ride growing more and more homesick for the green land he had left. When they were put ashore at Vera Cruz he had not been too disappointed; it was only Mexico they were in, and no one had ever told him Mexico was green.

But now they were in America, and all he could see was dust and low bushes with thorns, and almost no grass at all. He had expected coolness and dew and green grass on which to stretch out for a long nap. The bare hot yard was a cruel letdown, and besides, Sean was an easy weeper. Tears ran out of his eyes whenever he thought of anything sad.

His brother Allen was so embarrassed by the sight of Sean's tears that he walked straight into the house and sat down at the table. They had been asked to eat—if Sean preferred to stand in the yard crying, that was his problem.

Dish concluded that the young Irishman was probably crazy. Only someone crazy would break out crying in front of several grown men.

Augustus saved the day by going over and taking Sean by the arm. He spoke kindly to him and led him toward the house. "Let's go eat, son," he said. "It won't look quite so ugly on a full stomach."

"But where's the grass?" Sean asked, snuffling.

Dish Boggett let out a whoop. "I guess he was meaning to graze," he said.

"Why, no, Dish," Augustus said. "He was just reared in a place where the grass covers the ground—not in no desert, like you."

"I was reared on the Matagorda," Dish said. "We got grass knee high over there."

"Gus, we need to talk a minute," Call said.

But Augustus had already led the boy through the door, and Call had to follow him in.

A surprised Bolivar watched the Irishmen put away sowbelly and beans. He was so startled by their appearance that he picked up a shotgun that he kept by the cookstove and put it across his lap. It was his goat-gun, a rusty .10 gauge, and he liked to have it handy if anything unusual happened.

"I hope you don't decide to shoot that thing off in here," Augustus said. "It'd take a wall out if you did—not to mention us."

"I don't shoot yet," Bol said sullenly, keeping his options open.

Call waited until Augustus filled his plate, since there would be no getting his attention until he had food before him. The young Irish boy had stopped crying and was putting away beans faster even than Augustus—starvation was probably all that was wrong with him.

"I'm going to go see if I can hire some hands," Call said. "You better move them horses this afternoon."

"Move 'em where?" Augustus asked.

"Upriver, as far as you want," Call said.

"These Irishmen have fine voices," Augustus remarked. "It's a pity there ain't two more of 'em—we'd have a barbershop quartet."

"It would be a pity if you lost them horses while I'm off hiring the hands, too," Call pointed out.

"Oh, you mean you want me to sleep out on the ground for several nights just to keep Pedro from stealing these horses back?" Gus asked. "I'm out of practice sleeping on the ground."

"What was you planning to sleep on on the way to Montana?" Call asked in turn. "We can't take the house with us, and there ain't many hotels between here and there."

"I hadn't been planning on going to Montana," Augustus said. "That's your plan. I may come if I feel like it. Or you may change your mind. I know you never have changed your mind about anything yet, but there's a first time for everything."

"You'd argue with a stump," Call said. "Just watch them horses. We may never get that lucky again."

Call saw there was no point in losing any more time. If Augustus was not of a mind to be serious, nothing could move him.

"Jake did come back, didn't he?" Augustus asked.

"His horse is here," Call said. "I guess he probably come with it. Do you think he'll work, once we start?"

"No, and I won't, either," Augustus said. "You better hire these Irish boys while you got the chance."

"It's work we're looking for," Allen said. "What we don't know we'll gladly learn."

Call refrained from comment. Men who didn't know how to get on and off a horse would not be much use around a cow outfit.

"Where you goin' hiring?" Augustus asked.

"I might go to the Raineys'," Call said. "As many boys as they got they ought to be able to spare a few."

"I sparked Maude Rainey once upon a time," Augustus said, tilting back his chair. "If we hadn't had the Comanches to worry with, I expect I'd have married her. Her name was Grove before she married. She lays them boys like hens lay eggs, don't she?"

Call left, to keep from having to talk all day. Deets was catching a short nap on the back porch, but he sat up when Call came out. Dish Boggett and the boy were roping low bushes, Dish teaching the boy a thing or two about the craft of roping. That was good, since nobody around the Hat Creek outfit could rope well enough to teach him anything. Call himself could rope in an emergency, and so could Pea, but neither of them were ropers of the first class.

"Practice up, boys," he said. "As soon as we gather some cattle there's gonna be a pile of roping to do."

Then he caught his second-best horse, a sorrel gelding they called Sunup, and headed northeast toward the brush country.

13

LORENA HAD STOPPED expecting ever to be surprised, least of all by a man, and then Jake Spoon walked in the door and surprised her. The surprise started the minute before he even spoke to her. Partly it was that he seemed to know her the minute he saw her.

She had been sitting at a table expecting Dish Boggett to come back with another two dollars he had borrowed somewhere. It was an expectation that brought her no pleasure. It was clear Dish expected something altogether different from what the two dollars would buy him. That was why, in general, she preferred older men to young ones. The older ones were more likely to be content with what they paid for; the young ones almost always got in love with her, and expected it to make a difference. It got so she never said a word to the young men, thinking that the less she said the less they would expect. Of course they went right on expecting, but at least it saved her having to talk. She could tell Dish Boggett was going to pester her as long as he could afford to, and when she heard boot heels and the jingle of spurs on the porch she assumed it was him, coming back for a second round.

Instead, Jake had walked in. Lippy gave a whoop, and Xavier was excited enough that he came out from behind the bar and shook Jake's hand. Jake was polite and glad to see them, and took the trouble to ask their health and make a few jokes, but even before he had drunk the free drink Xavier offered him he had begun to make a difference in the way she felt. He had big muddy brown eyes and a neat mustache that turned down at the corners, but of course she had seen big eyes and mustaches before. What made the difference was that Jake was so at home and relaxed even after he saw her sitting there. Most men got nervous when they saw her, aware that their wives wouldn't like them being in the same room with her, or else made nervous by the thought of what they wanted from her, which they couldn't get without some awkward formalities of a sort that few of them could handle smoothly.

But Jake was the opposite of nervous. Before he even spoke to her he smiled at her several times in the most relaxed way—not in the bragging way Tinkersley had when he smiled. Tinkersley's smile had said plainly enough that he felt she ought to be grateful for the chance to do whatever he wanted her to do. Of course she was grateful to him for taking her away from Mosby and the smoke pots, but once she had been away for a while she came to hate Tinkersley's smile.

Lorena felt puzzled for a moment. She didn't ignore the men who walked through the door of the Dry Bean. It didn't do to ignore men. The majority of them were harmless, with nothing worse than a low capacity to irritate—they were worse than chiggers but not as bad as bedbugs, in her view. Still, there was no doubt that there were some mean ones who plain had it in for women, and it was best to try and spot those and take precautions. But as far as trusting the general run of men, there was no need, since she had no intention of ever expecting anything from one of them again. She didn't object to sitting in on a card game once in a while—she even enjoyed it, since making money at cards was considerably easier and more fun than doing it the other way—but a good game of cards once in a while was about as far as her expectations went.

Immediately Jake Spoon began to change the way her thinking worked. Before he even brought his bottle to the table to sit with her, she began to want him to. If he had taken the bottle and gone to sit by himself, she would have felt disappointed, but of course he didn't. He sat down, asked her if she'd like some refreshments and looked her right in the face for a while in a friendly, easygoing way.

"My goodness," he said, "I never expected to find nobody like you here. We didn't see much beauty when I lived in these parts. Now if this was San Francisco, I wouldn't be so surprised. I reckon that's where you really belong."

It seemed a miracle to Lorie that a man had walked in who could figure that out so quick. In the last year she had begun to doubt her own ability to get to San Francisco and even to doubt that it was as cool and nice as she had been imagining it to be, and yet she didn't want to give up the notion, because she had no other notion to put in its place. It might be silly to even think about it, but it was the best she had.

Then Jake came along and right away mentioned exactly the right place. Before the afternoon was over she had laid aside her caution and her silence and told Jake more about herself than she had ever told anyone. Lippy and Xavier listened from a distance in astonished silence. Jake said very little, though he patted her hand from time to time and poured her a drink when her glass was empty. Once in a while he would say, "My goodness," or "That damned dog, I ought to go find him and shoot him," but mostly he just looked friendly and confident, sitting there with his hat tipped back.

When she got through with her story, he explained that he had killed a dentist in Fort Smith, Arkansas, and was a wanted man, but that he had hopes of eluding the law, and if he did, he would certainly try to see that she got to San Francisco, where she belonged. The way he said it made a big impression on Lorie. A sad tone came into his voice from time to time, as if it pained him to have to remember that mortality could prevent him from doing her such a favor. He sounded like he expected to die, and probably soon. It wasn't a whine, either—just a low note off his tongue and a look in his eye; it didn't interrupt for a minute his ability to enjoy the immediate pleasures of life.

It gave Lorie the shivers when Jake talked like that, and made her feel that she wanted to play a part in keeping him alive. She was used to men thinking they needed her desperately just because they wanted to get their carrots in her, or wanted her to be their girl for a few days or weeks. But Jake wasn't asking for anything like that. He just let her see that he felt rather impermanent and might not be able to carry out all that he wished. Lorena wanted to help him. She was surprised, but the feeling was too strong to deny. She didn't understand it, but she felt it. She knew she had a force inside her, but her practice had been to save it entirely for herself. Men were always hoping she would bestow some of it on them, but she never had. Then, with little hesitation, she began to offer it to Jake. He was a case. He didn't ask for help, but he knew how to welcome it.

She was the one who suggested they go upstairs, mainly because she was tired of Lippy and Xavier listening to everything they said. On the way up she noticed that Jake was favoring one foot. It turned out one of his ankles had been broken years before, when a horse fell on him—the ankle was apt to swell if he had to ride hard for long stretches, as he had just done. She helped him ease his boot off and got him some hot water and Epsom salts. After he had soaked his foot for a while he looked amused, as if he had just thought of something pleasant.

"You know, if there was a tub around here, I'd just have a bath and trim my mustache," he said.

There was a washtub sitting on the back porch. Lorena carried it up when she needed a bath, and the six or eight buckets of water it took to fill it. Xavier used it more often than she did. He could tolerate dirt on his customers, but not on himself. Lippy gave no thought to baths so far as anyone knew.

Lorena offered to go get the washtub, since Jake had one boot off, but he wouldn't hear of it. He took the other boot off and limped down by himself and got the tub. Then he bribed Lippy to heat up some water. It took a while, since the water had to be heated on the cookstove.

"Why, Jake, you could buy a bath from the Mexican barber for ten cents," Lippy pointed out.

"That may be true, but I prefer the company in this establishment," Jake said.

Lorena thought maybe he would want her to leave the room while he bathed, since so far he had treated her modestly, but he had nothing like that in mind. He latched her door, so Lippy couldn't pop in and catch a glimpse of something it wasn't his business to see.

"Lippy will eye the girls," Jake said—no news to Lorena.

"I wisht it was a bigger tub," he said. "We could have us a wash together."

Lorena had never heard of such a thing. It surprised her how coolly Jake stripped off for his wash. Like all men who weren't pure gamblers, he was burned brown on his face and neck and hands, and was fish-white on the rest of his body. Most of her customers were brown down to their collar, and white below. The great majority of them were reluctant to show anything of their bodies, though it was bodies they had come to satisfy. Some wouldn't even unbuckle their belts. Lorena often made them wait while she undressed—if she didn't, whatever she was wearing got mussed up. Also, she liked undressing in front of men because it scared them. A few would get so scared they had to back out of the whole business—though they always scrupulously paid her and apologized and made excuses. They came in thinking they wanted to persuade her out of her clothes, but when she matter-of-factly took them off, it often turned the tables.

Gus was an exception, of course. He liked her naked and he liked her clothed. Seeing one body would remind him of other bodies, and he would sit on the bed and scratch himself and talk about various aspects of women that only he would have had anything to say about: the varieties of bosoms, for example.

Jake Spoon wasn't as talkative as Gus, but he was just as immodest. He sat happily in the tub until the water got cold. He even asked if she'd like to give him a haircut. She didn't mind trying, but quickly saw that she was making a mess of it and stopped with only a small portion of his curly black hair removed.

Once he toweled himself off he turned and led her to the bed. He stopped before he got there and looked as though he was going to offer her money. Lorena had wondered if he would, and when he stopped, she turned quickly so he could undo the long row of buttons down the back of her dress. She felt impatient—not for the act, but for Jake to go ahead and assume responsibility for her. She had never supposed that she would want such a thing from a man, but she was not bothered by the fact that she had changed her mind in the space of an hour, or that she was a little drunk when she changed it. She felt confident that Jake Spoon would get her out of Lonesome Dove, and she didn't intend to allow money to pass between them—or anything else that might cause him to leave without her.

Jake immediately stepped over and helped her undo the buttons. It was plain she wasn't the first woman he had undressed, because he even knew how to unhook the dress at the neck, something most of her customers would never have thought of.

"You've had this one awhile, I reckon," he said, looking rather critically at the dress once he got it off her.

That, too, surprised her, for no man had ever commented, favorably or unfavorably, upon her clothes—not even Tinkersley, who had given her the money to buy the very dress Jake was holding, just a cheap cotton dress which was fraying at the collar. Lorena felt a touch of shame that a man would notice the fraying. She had often meant to make a new dress or two—that being the only way to get one, in Lonesome Dove—but she was awkward with a needle and was still getting by on the dresses she had bought in San Antonio.

In the months there she had had several offers to go to San Antonio with men who would probably have bought her dresses, but she had always declined. San Antonio was in the wrong direction, she hadn't liked any of the men, and anyway didn't really need new dresses, since she was attracting more business than she wanted just wearing the old ones.

Jake's comment had been mildly made, but it threw Lorena slightly off. She realized he was a finicky man—she could not get away with being lazy about herself, any longer. A man who noticed a frayed collar with a near-naked woman standing right in front of him was a new kind of man to Lorena—one who would soon notice other things, some perhaps more serious than a collar. She felt disheartened; some glow had seeped from the moment. Probably he had already been to San Francisco and seen finer women than her. Perhaps when it came time to leave he wouldn't want to bother with someone so ill-dressed. Perhaps the surprise that had walked into her life would simply walk back out of it.

But her sinking confidence was only momentary. Jake put the dress aside, watched her draw her shift off over her head, and sat beside her when she lay down. He was perfectly at ease.

"Well, Lorie, you take the prize," he said. "I had not a hope of being this lucky when I headed back here. Why, you're as fine as flowers."

When he began to stroke her she noticed that his hands were like a woman's, his fingers small and his fingernails clean. Tinkersley had had clean fingernails, but Jake wasn't arrogant like Tinkersley, and he gave the impression of having nothing but time. Most men crawled on top of her at once, but Jake just sat on the bed, smiling at her. When he smiled, her confidence returned. With most men, there was a moment when they moved their eyes away. But Jake kept looking at her, right in the eye. He looked at her so long that she began to feel shy. She felt more naked than she had ever felt, and when he bent to kiss her, she flinched. She did not like kissing, but Jake merely grinned when she flinched, as if her shyness was funny. His breath was as clean as his hands. Many a sour breath had ruffled her hair and affronted her nostrils, but Jake's was neither rank nor sour. It had a clean cedary flavor to it.

When it was over, Jake took a nap, and instead of getting up and dressing, Lorie lay with him, thinking. She thought of San Francisco, and just thinking about it made her think that she could do anything. She didn't even feel like moving to wipe the sheets. Let them be. She would be going soon, and Xavier could burn them for all she cared.

When Jake woke he looked at her and grinned, and his hand, warm now, went right back to work.

"If I ain't careful I'm apt to sprout up again," he said.

Lorena wanted to ask him why his breath smelled like cedar but she didn't know if she ought, since he had just come to town. But then she asked him, a little shocked at hearing her own voice make the question.

"Why, I passed a cedar grove and cut myself some toothpicks," Jake said. "There's nothing that sweetens the breath like a cedar toothpick, unless it's mint, and mint don't grow in these parts."

Then he kissed her again, as if to make her a present of his sweet breath. Between kisses he talked to her about San Francisco, and what might be the best route to take. Even after he slid between her legs again and made the old bed-spring whine and the sorry mattress crackle, he kept talking a little.

When he finally got up and stretched and suggested they go downstairs, Lorena felt more cheerful than she had for years. Xavier and Lippy, who were used to her long sulks, hardly knew what to think. Neither did Dish Boggett, who happened to walk in. Dish sat down and drank a bottle of whiskey before anybody noticed. Then he got to singing, and everybody laughed at him. Lorena laughed as loud as Lippy, whose lip waved like a flag when he was amused.

Only later, when Jake left to ride south with Captain Call, did Lorena feel impatient. She wanted Jake to come back. The time with him had been so relaxed it almost seemed like a wakeful dream of some kind. She wanted to have the dream again.

That night, when a skinny cowboy named Jasper Fant came in from the river and approached her, Lorie just stared at him silently until he got embarrassed and backed off, never having actually said a word. Staring was all she had to do. Jasper consulted with Lippy and Xavier, and by the end of the week, all the cowboys along the river knew that the only sporting woman in Lonesome Dove had abruptly given up the sport.

14

WHEN JAKE FINALLY came ambling up to the house, having spent the better part of the day asleep in Lorena's bed, Augustus was already nuzzling his jug from time to time. He was sitting on the front porch, waving off flies and watching the two Irishmen, who were sleeping as if dead under the nearest wagon. They had gone to sleep in the wagon's meager shade; the shade had moved, but not the Irishmen. The boy had no hat. He slept with his arm across his face. Jake didn't even glance at them as he walked past, a fact Augustus noted. Jake had never been renowned for his interest in people unless the people were whores.

"Where's Call?" Jake asked when he got to the porch.

"You didn't expect to find Woodrow Call sitting in the shade, did you?" Augustus asked. "That man was born to work."

"Yes, and you was born to talk too much," Jake said. "I need to borrow ten dollars."

"Oh?" Augustus said. "Has Lorie upped her rates?"

Jake ignored the question, which was only meant to rile him, and reached for the jug.

"No, the girl's as generous as a preacher's widow," Jake said. "She wouldn't take money from a gentleman like me. I hope she charged you plenty, though, for I know you've been there before me."

"I've always tried to keep a step ahead of you, Jake," Augustus said. "But to answer your question, Call's gone to round up a dern bunch of cowboys so we can head out for Montana with a dern bunch of cows and suffer for the rest of our lives."

"Well, dern," Jake said. "I admit I was a fool to mention it."

He settled himself on the lower step and set the jug halfway between them so they could both reach it. He was mildly chagrined that Call had left before he could borrow the money—extracting money from Augustus had always been a long and wearisome business. Call was easier when it came to money—he didn't like to lend it, but he would rather lend it than talk about it, whereas Augustus would rather talk than do anything.

Also, it was bothersome that Call had seized on the idea of Montana so abruptly, though it had always been his view that if you could just hit Call with the right idea, he would apply his energies and make a fortune, which he might then share with the man who brought along the idea.

Now that he was back, though, he wouldn't mind spending a few warm idle months in Lonesome Dove. Lorie was more of a beauty than he had expected to find. Her room over the saloon wasn't much, but it was better accommodation than they could expect on the way to Montana.

As usual, though, life moved faster than he had intended it to. Call would come back with a lot of cowboys and he would practically have to marry Lorie in order to get out of going up the trail. Then, if he did set his foot down and stay in Lonesome Dove, who knew but what some lawman from Fort Smith would show up and drag him off to hang? Just as he had been in the mood to slow down, his own loose mouth had gotten him in trouble.

"Maybe he won't find no cattle to drive, or no hands, neither," he suggested, knowing it was wishful thinking.

"He'll find the cattle, and if he can't find the hands he'll drive 'em himself," Augustus said. "And make us help him."

Jake tipped his hat back and said nothing. The blue shoat wandered around the corner of the house and stood there looking at him, which for some reason Jake found peculiarly irritating. Gus and his pig were aggravating company.

"I ought to shoot that pig right betwixt the eyes," he said, feeling more irritable the longer he sat. There was not much good in anything that he could see. Either it was back to Montana and probably get scalped, or stay in Texas and probably get hung. And if he wasn't careful the girl would get restless and actually expect him to take her to San Francisco. The main problem with women was that they were always wanting something like San Francisco, and once they began to expect it they would get testy if it didn't happen. They didn't understand that he talked of pleasant things and faraway places just to create a happy prospect that they could look forward to for a while. It wasn't meant to really happen, and yet women never seemed to grasp that; he had been in ticklish spots several times as their disappointment turned to anger. It was something, how mad women could get.

"Was you ever threatened by a woman, Gus?" he asked, thinking about it.

"No, not what you'd call threatened," Augustus said. "I was hit with a stove lid once or twice."

"Why?" Jake asked.

"Why, no reason," Augustus said. "If you live with Mexicans you can expect to eat beans, sooner or later."

"Who said anything about Mexicans?" Jake said, a little exasperated. Gus was the derndest talker.

Augustus chuckled. "You was always slow to see the point, Jake," he said. "If you fool with women you'll get hit by a stove lid, sooner or later, whereas if you live with Mexicans you have to expect beans in your diet."

"I'd like to see a woman that can hit me with a stove lid," Jake said. "I will take an insult once in a while, but I'd be damned if I'd take that."

"Lorie's apt to hit you with worse if you try to wiggle out of taking her to San Francisco," Augustus said, delighted that an opportunity had arisen to catch Jake out so early in his visit.

Jake let that one float. Of course Gus would know all about the girl. Not that it took brains to know about women: they spread their secrets around like honey in a flytrap. Of course Lorie would want to go to San Francisco, by common agreement the prettiest town in the west.

Augustus stood up and lifted his big pistol off the back of his chair. "I guess we ought to wake up them Irishmen before they bake," he said. He walked over and kicked at their feet for a while until they began to stir. Finally Allen O'Brien sat up, looking groggy.

"Lord, it's warm, ain't it?" he said.

"Why, this is spring, son," Augustus remarked. "If you're looking for warm come back on the Fourth of July. We usually thaw out by then."

When he was sure both Irishmen were awake he went back to the house and came out with his rifle. "Well, let's go," he said to Jake.

"Go where?" Jake asked. "I just got set down."

"To hide them horses," Augustus said. "Pedro Flores is no quitter. He'll be coming."

Jake felt sour. He wished again that circumstances hadn't prompted him to come back. He had already spent one full night on horseback, and now the boys were expecting him to spend another, all on account of a bunch of livestock he had no interest in in the first place.

"I don't know as I'm coming," he said. "I just got here. If I'd known you boys did nothing but chouse horses around all night, I don't know that I would have come."

"Why, Jake, you lazy bean," Augustus said, and walked off. Jake had a stubborn streak in him, and once it was activated even Call could seldom do much with him. The Irish boy was standing up, trying to get the sleep out of his eyes.

"Come on, boys," Augustus said. "Time to ride the river."

"You want us to ride some more?" Sean asked. He had rolled over during his nap and had grass burrs in his shirt.

"You'll soon catch on to riding," Augustus said. "It's easier than you might think."

"Do you have any mules?" Sean asked. "I'm better at riding mules."

"Son, we're fresh out," Augustus said. "Can either of you boys shoot?"

"No, but we can dig potatoes," Allen said—he didn't want the man to think they were totally incompetent.

"You boys took the wrong ship," Augustus said. "I doubt there's ten spuds in this whole country."

He caught them the gentlest horses out of the small bunch that were still penned, and taught them how to adjust their stirrups so their feet wouldn't dangle—he hadn't had time for that refinement in Sabinas. Just then Jake came walking along, a Winchester in the crook of his arm. No doubt he had concluded it would be easier to stay up all night than to explain to Call why he hadn't.

Soon the Irishmen were mounted and were cautiously walking their mounts around the pen.

"It's new to them but they're a quick-witted race," Augustus said. "Give 'em a week and they'll be ridin' like Comanches."

"I don't know that I'll pause a week," Jake said. "You boys have got hard to tolerate. I might take that yellow-haired gal and mosey off to California."

"Jake, you're a dern grasshopper," Augustus said. "You ride in yesterday talking Montana, and today you're talking California."

Once the Irishmen had got fairly competent at mounting and dismounting, Augustus gave them each a Winchester and made them shoot at a cactus a time or two.

"You've got to learn sometime," he said. "If you can learn to ride and shoot before Captain Call gets back, he might hire you."

The O'Brien boys were so awed to find themselves with deadly weapons in their hands that they immediately forgot to be nervous about their horses. Sean had never held a gun before, and the flat crack of the bullet when he shot at the cactus was frightening. It occurred to him that if they were expected to shoot, they could also expect to be shot at—an unappealing thought.

"Do we ask their names before we shoot them?" he inquired.

"It ain't necessary," Augustus assured him. "Most of them are named Jesus anyway."

"Well, I ain't named Jesus," Jake said. "You boys try not to do your learning in my direction. I've been known to get riled when I'm shot at."

When the two Irishmen came trotting up to the horse herd behind Augustus and Jake, Dish Boggett could hardly believe his eyes. He had always heard that the Hat Creek outfit was peculiar, but arming men who didn't even know how to dismount from their horses was not so much peculiar as insane.

Augustus took the lead on a big white horse named Puddin' Foot, and Jake Spoon followed him. Jake looked sour as clabber, which suited Dish fine. Maybe Lorena hadn't fallen quite in love with him, after all.

Dish rode over and poked Newt, who was asleep on his horse. Dish himself had napped from time to time, the day being hot and the horse herd placid.

"You ought to see what's coming," he said. "Gus has put them dern midgets a-horseback."

Newt had a hard time getting his eyes open. As soon as the chase was over, sleep had begun trying to pull him down. If Pedro Flores had ridden up and offered to shoot him he didn't think he would much care, since it would at least mean more sleep. He knew cowboys were supposed to be able to stay in the saddle two or three days at a stretch without sleep, but he was guiltily aware that he had not yet learned the trick. When Dish poked him, his hat fell off, and when he got down to get it his legs felt as heavy as if somebody had put lead in his boots. He would have liked to say something to Sean O'Brien, who looked as tired as he was, but he couldn't think of a word to say.

Augustus, who had had no chance to examine Call's big catch, rode into the herd and eased through to the other side, where Deets and Pea were waiting. He took his time about it, giving the animals a critical inspection as he went past. Not more than forty of them struck him as prime mounts. A lot were undersized, some had saddle sores, and the whole bunch of them were skinny from overwork or underfeeding, or probably no feeding. Except for a prize stud or two, Pedro Flores had probably never wasted an oat on a horse in his life.

"These nags is barely worth a night's sleep," he said to Deets and Pea. "If we was aiming to start a soap factory they might do, but so far as I know, we ain't. I've a notion to keep the best fifty and run the rest off."

"My lord," Pea said, aghast at what Gus had suggested. "The Captain would shoot all of us if we run off any of these horses."

"I don't doubt he'd foam at the mouth," Augustus said. "What do you think, Deets?"

"They skinny," Deets said. "Might get fat, if we give 'em enough time."

"You might grow wings, if I give you enough time," Augustus said. They looked across the river. The sun was slipping fast—in an hour or two they could expect a loud visit.

"Here's the plan," he said. "Pedro won't bother coming to town, knowing our habits like he does. We'll pen the prime stock and hide the skinny little rabbits up in some thicket. Then if we don't like the looks of his army, we can skedaddle and let him drive his own soap factory back home."

Pea Eye felt deeply uneasy about the plan. When the Captain was around, things were done in a more straightforward fashion. Gus was always coming up with something sly. However, Pea's opinion hadn't been asked—he watched as

Gus and Deets began to cut the herd. Soon Dish Boggett figured out what was happening and rode over to help them. Dish was always a willing hand except when it came to digging wells.

Jake sat with the boy and the Irishmen and watched the proceedings without much interest. He had himself a smoke but didn't offer anybody else one.

Newt watched too, trying to decide if he ought to go help. Mr. Gus and Deets and Dish were doing the work so efficiently he decided he'd just be in the way, so he stayed put, hoping Jake would say something to him. There had been no chance to renew their friendship since Jake had come home.

As sunset approached, Newt felt more and more anxious. The Captain being gone always affected him that way. He knew Mr. Gus was supposed to be one of the coolest hands on the border, and he was confident Jake could handle practically anything that came up, but despite those two he couldn't stop himself from feeling anxious when the Captain was gone.

Young Sean O'Brien felt anxious too, only his anxiety was of a different nature. The prospect of shooting and being shot at had loomed larger and larger in his thinking until he could think of little else. Since Newt looked friendly, he decided to seek his counsel in the matter.

"What part of a man is it best to shoot at?" he asked, addressing himself to Newt.

Jake Spoon chuckled. "His horse," he said. "Just aim for his horse. There ain't many of them chili-bellies that will bother you once they're afoot."

With that he touched spurs to his horse and trotted around to the other side of the herd.

"Is that right?" Sean asked. "You're supposed to shoot the horse?"

"If Jake says so, it's right," Newt said loyally, though the advice had surprised him too.

"Have you shot many?" Sean asked.

Newt shook his head. "Nope," he said. "Last night was the first time I even got to go. I never even shot at a man, or a horse either."

"You shoot the horse," Sean said, when his brother Allen rode up. Allen said nothing. He was thinking of his little wife, Sary, whom he had left in Ireland. She had wept for weeks before he left, thinking it wrong that he should leave her. He had got his dander up and left anyway, and yet now he missed her so that tears as wet as hers sprang from his eyes almost every time he thought of her. Though normally a cheerful and even a merry man, the absence of Sary had affected him more than he had supposed anything could. In his mind's eye he saw her small redheaded figure moving through the chores of the day, now cooking spuds, now wringing milk from the tired teat of their old milk cow. He ignored all talk when he was thinking of Sary, refusing to let it distract him. How would she feel if she could know what he had got himself into, sitting on a horse with a heavy gun beneath his leg?

On the other side of the herd Augustus had finished separating out the prime stock and was about to divide up the crew. Deets and Dish were holding the cut at a little distance from the main herd.

"Well, girls," Augustus said, "you might as well take these nags in and put 'em to bed. Me and this fine bunch of hands will ease the others upriver."

Dish Boggett could hardly believe his good fortune. He had been braced for a scratch night of brush-busting, but it seemed old Gus had a mind to spare him.

"All right," he said. "Tell me what you want for supper, Gus, and I'll go eat it for you once we get these penned."

Augustus ignored the sally. "Deets, you watch close," he said. "This young spark will probably have to go and get drunk, or maybe married before the night is over."

Dish waved and started the horses; just as he did, Jake came loping over.

"Where are they going?" he asked.

"Back to town," Augustus said. "Be the safest place for the good stock, I figure."

"Why, damn," Jake said, plainly chagrined. "You could have sent me back. I'm the one that's worn to a frazzle."

"Somebody's got to help me protect these boys," Augustus said. "As I recall, you made a name for yourself by shooting Mexican bandits—I thought you'd welcome the chance to polish your reputation a little."

"I'd rather shoot *you*," Jake said, pretty grumpily. "You've caused me more hell than all the bandits in Mexico."

"Now Jake, be fair," Augustus said. "You was just hoping to go back and get your bean in that girl again. I feel young Dish should have his shot before you ruin her completely."

Jake snorted. The young cowboy was the least of his worries.

"If you like these Irishmen so much, you watch them," he said. "Send me little Newt, and we'll take one side. Are we supposed to be going anywhere in particular?"

"No," Augustus said. "Just try to keep them out of Mexico." He waved at Newt, who soon came loping over.

"Son, Jake Spoon has requested your help," he said. "If you and him watch the east me and Pea and them shortcakes will take the west."

The boy's face lit up as if he had just been given a new saddle. He had practically worshipped Jake Spoon once, and would clearly be willing to again, given the encouragement. Augustus felt a momentary pang—he liked Jake, but felt him to be too leaky a vessel to hold so much hope. But then, all vessels leaked to some degree.

"Will we just keep riding or will we stop and wait for the Mexicans?" Newt asked, anxious to know the right thing to do.

"Keep riding," Augustus said. "Let 'em catch us, if they're men enough. And if they do, try not to shoot up all your ammunition. We might need some tomorrow."

With that he turned and, in a few minutes, with the inexpert help of the Irishmen, got the hundred horses moving north in the fading light.

15

THE MINUTE they got the herd penned, Dish felt himself getting restless. He had a smoke, leaning on the gate of the big corral. He knew he had a clear duty to stay with the horses. Though the darky was obviously a superior hand, he could hardly be expected to hold the place against a swarm of bandits.

The problem was that Dish could not believe in the swarm of bandits. Under the red afterglow the town was still as a church. Now and then there was the bleat of a goat or the call of a bullbat, but that was all. It was so peaceful that Dish soon convinced himself there was no need for two men to waste the whole evening in a dusty corral. The bandits were theoretical, but Lorena was real, and only two hundred yards away.

Leaning on the gate, Dish had no trouble imagining favorable possibilities. Jake Spoon was only human—and he was oversure of himself, at that. He might have rushed his suit. Dish could understand it; he would have rushed one himself, had he known how. Perhaps Lorie had not welcomed such boldness—perhaps she had recognized that Jake was not a man to depend on.

By the time he had mulled the prospect for thirty minutes, Dish was in a fever. He had to have another shot or else carry some sharp regrets with him up the trail. Some might think it irresponsible—Captain Call, for one, certainly would—but he could not stand all night in chunking distance of Lorena and not go see her.

"Well, it all looks safe," he said to Deets, who had seated himself against a big water trough, his rifle across his lap.

"Quiet so far," Deets agreed.

"I reckon it'll be some while before anything happens, if anything does," he said. "I believe I'll just stroll over to that saloon and bathe my throat."

"Yes, sir, you go along," Deets said. "I can look after the stock."

"You just shoot, if you need help," Dish said. "I'll get back here in a minute if there's trouble."

He took his horse, so he wouldn't be caught afoot in the event of trouble, and went trotting off.

Deets was just as glad to see him leave, for the young man's restlessness made him an uncomfortable companion. It was not a restlessness other men could talk to—only a woman could cure it.

Deets had had such restlessness once, and had had no woman to cure it, but years and hard work had worn the edge off it, and he could relax and enjoy the quiet of the night, if he was let alone. He liked sitting with his back against the water trough, listening to the horses settling themselves. From time to time one would come to the trough and drink, sucking the water into its mouth in long draughts. Across the pen two horses were stamping and snorting nervously, but

Deets didn't get up to go look. Probably it was just a snake that had snaked too close to the pen. A snake wasn't going to fool with horses if it could help it.

The possibility of attack didn't worry him. Even if a few *vaqueros* did make a pass at the town, they would be nervous, sure of being outgunned. He could sleep—he had the knack of going in and out of sleep easily and quickly—but despite the long night and day he wasn't sleepy. Relaxing, at times, was as good as sleeping. A sleeping man would miss the best of the evening, and the moonrise as well. Deets had always been partial to the moon, watched it often, thought about it much. To him it was a more interesting and a more affecting thing than the sun, which shone on every day in much the same fashion.

But the moon changed. It moved around the sky; it waxed and waned. On the nights when it rose full and yellow over the plains around Lonesome Dove, it seemed so close that a man could almost ride over with a ladder and step right onto it. Deets had even imagined doing it, a few times—propping a ladder against the old full moon, and stepping on. If he did it, one thing was sure: Mr. Gus would have something to talk about for a long time. Deets had to grin at the mere thought of how excited Mr. Gus would get if he took off and rode the moon. For he thought of it like a ride, something he might just do for a night or two when things were slow. Then, when the moon came back close to Lonesome Dove, he would step off and walk back home. It would surprise them all.

Other times, though, the moon rode so high that Deets had to come to his senses and admit that no man could really ride on it. When he imagined himself up there, on the thin little hook that hung above him white as a tooth, he almost got dizzy from his own imagining and had to try harder to pay attention to what was happening on the ground.

Still, when there was nothing to see around him but a few horses sucking water, he could always rest himself by watching the moon and the sky. He loved clear nights and hated clouds—when it was cloudy he felt deprived of half the world. His fear of Indians, which was deep, was tied to his sense that the moon had powers that neither white men nor black men understood. He had heard Mr. Gus talk about the moon moving the waters, and though he had glimpsed the ocean many times, by the Matagorda, he had not been able to get a sense of how the moon moved it.

But he was convinced that Indians understood the moon. He had never talked with an Indian about it, but he knew they had more names for it than white people had, and that suggested a deeper understanding. The Indians were less busy and would naturally have more time to study such things. It had always seemed to Deets that it was lucky for the whites that the Indians had never gained full control over the moon. He had dreamed once, after the terrible battle of Fort Phantom Hill, that the Indians had managed to move the moon over by one of those little low hills that were all over west Texas. They had got it to pause by the edge of a mountain so they could leap their horses onto it. It still occurred to him at times that such a thing might have happened, and that there were Comanches or possibly Kiowa riding around on the moon. Often, when the moon was full and yellow, and close to the earth, he got the strong feeling that Indians were on it. It was a fearful feeling, one he had never discussed with any man. The Indians hated the whites and if they got control of the moon—which was said to control the waters—then terrible things might happen. The Indians could have the moon suck all the water out of the wells and rivers, or else turn it all to salt, like the ocean. That would be the end, and a hard end at that.

But when the moon was just a little white hook, Deets tended to lose his worries. After all, water was still sweet, except for an alkaline river or two, like the Pecos. Perhaps if the Indians got on the moon, they had all fallen off.

Sometimes Deets wished that he could have had some schooling, so as to maybe learn the answers to some of the things that puzzled and intrigued him. Night and day itself was something to ponder: there had to be a reason for the sun to fall, lie hidden and then rise again from the opposite side of the plain, and other reasons for the rain, the thunder and the slicing north wind. He knew the big motions of nature weren't accidents; it was just that his life had not given him enough information to grasp the way of things.

And yet Indians, who could not even talk a normal language, seemed to understand more about it even than Mr. Gus, who could talk a passel about the motions of nature or anything else you wanted to hear talked about. Mr. Gus had even tried to tell him the world was round, though Deets regarded that as just joking talk. But it was Mr. Gus who put his name on the sign so that everyone who could read would realize he was part of the outfit—it made up for a lot of joking.

Deets rested happily by the water trough, now and then glancing at the moon. The ground shadows hid him completely, and any *vaquero* foolish enough to try and slip in would get a sharp surprise.

===

Dish himself got something of a surprise when he walked into the Dry Bean, for Lorena was not alone, as he had been imagining her to be. She sat at a table with Xavier and Jasper Fant, the skinny little waddie from upriver. Dish had met Jasper once or twice and rather liked him, though at this time he would have liked him a lot better if he had stayed upriver, where he belonged. Jasper had a sickly look to him, but in fact was as healthy as the next man and had an appetite to rival Gus McCrae's.

"There's Dish," Lorena said, when he came in the door. "Now we can have a game."

Lippy, as usual, was kibbitzing, putting in his two cents' worth whether they were wanted or not.

"Not unless he's been to the bank, we can't," he said. "Xavier cleaned Dish out last night, and he ain't active enough to make his fortune back in one day."

"Don't mean he can't take a hand," Jasper said, giving Dish a friendly nod. "Xavier's cleaned me out too and I'm still playing."

"We all got weaknesses," Lippy observed. "Wanz's is playing poker for credit. That's why he can't afford to pay his pianer player an honest wage."

Xavier endured these witticisms silently. He was in a worse mood than usual, and he knew why. Jake Spoon had come to town and promptly deprived him of a whore, an asset vital to an establishment such as his in an out-of-the-way place like Lonesome Dove. Many a traveler, who might not ordinarily come that far, would, because of Lorie. There was no woman like her on the border. She was not friendly, but because of her, men came and stayed to drink away the night. He would not be likely to get another such whore: there were Mexican women as pretty, but few cowboys would ride the extra miles for a Mexican woman, those being plentiful in most parts of south Texas.

Besides, he himself bought Lorie once a week, if not more. Once in a period of restless enthusiasm he had bought her six times in five days—after which, being ashamed of his extravagance, if not his lust, he abstained for two weeks. It was a happy convenience having Lorie in the place, and a fine change from his wife, Therese, who had been stingy with her favors and a bully to boot. Once Therese had denied him anything resembling a favor for a period of four months, which, for a man of Xavier's temperament, was a painful thing. He had been required to hunt Mexican women himself during that period, and had come close to feeling the wrath of a couple of Mexican husbands.

By contrast, Lorie was restful, and he had come to love her. She did not exhibit the slightest fondness for him, but neither did she raise the slightest objection when he felt like buying her, a fact Lippy was deeply resentful of. She refused to be bought by Lippy at any price.

Now Jake Spoon had spoiled it all, and the only way Xavier could vent his annoyance was by winning money from Jasper Fant, most of which he would never collect.

"Where's Jake?" Lorie asked—a shock to Dish. His hopes, which had been soaring as he walked through the dark to the saloon, flopped down to boot level. For her to inquire about the man so shamelessly bespoke a depth of attachment that Dish could barely imagine. It was not likely she would ever inquire at all about him, even if he stepped out the door and vanished for a year.

"Why, Jake's with Gus and the boys," he said, sitting down to make the best face of it he could.

It was not much of a face, for Lorie had never seemed prettier to him. She had pushed up the sleeves of her dress, and when it came her turn to handle the cards her white arms all but mesmerized him. He could hardly think to bet for watching Lorie's arms and her firm lips. Her arms were plumpish, but more graceful than any Dish had ever seen. He could not think what he was doing, he wanted her so much; it caused him to play so badly that in an hour he had lost three months' wages.

Jasper Fant fared no better, whether from love of Lorie or lack of skill, Dish didn't know. Didn't know, and didn't care. All he was conscious of was that somehow he would have to outlast Jake, for there could be no woman for him except the one across the table. The very friendliness with which she treated him stung like a scorpion bite, for there was nothing special in it. She was almost as friendly to Lippy, a pure fool, and with a hole in his stomach to boot.

The card game soon became a torture for everyone but Lorie, who won hand after hand. It pleased her to think how surprised Jake would be when he came back and saw her winnings. He would know she wasn't helpless, at least. Xavier himself didn't lose much—he never lost much—but he wasn't playing with his usual alertness. Lorie knew that might be because of her, but she didn't care. She had always liked playing cards, and liked it even better now that it was all she had to do until Jake came back. She even liked Dish and Jasper, a little. It was a relief not to have to hold herself out of the fun because of what they wanted. She knew they felt hopeless, but then she had felt hopeless enough times, waiting for them to work up their nerve, or else borrow two dollars. Let them get a taste.

"Dish, we might as well stop," Jasper said. "We'll barely get out of debt this year as it is."

"I'll take a hand," Lippy said. "I might be rusty but I'm willing."

"Let him play," Xavier said suddenly. It was a house rule that Lippy was not allowed to gamble. His style was extravagant and his resources meager. Several times his life had been endangered when strangers discovered he had no means of paying them the sums he had just lost.

But Xavier had lost faith in house rules since it had also been a house rule that Lorena was a whore, and now she wasn't anymore. If a whore could retire so abruptly, Lippy might as well play cards.

"What's he gonna pay me with when I win?" Lorena asked.

"Sweet music," Lippy said cheerfully. "I'll play your favorite song."

It was not much enticement, Lorena thought, since he played her favorite songs every time she came in the room as it was, hoping his skill at the keyboard would finally move her to let him buy a poke.

She wasn't about to start that, but she did play him a few hands—the cowboys were too sunk even to drink. The boys said goodnight to her politely, hoping she would think kindly of them, but she didn't. Boys didn't interest her as much as cards.

Outside, Jasper paused in the street and had a smoke with Dish.

"Hired on yet?" Jasper asked. He had a mustache no thicker than a shoestring, and a horse that was not much thicker than the mustache.

"I think so," Dish said. "I'm working for these Hat Creek boys right now. They're thinking of getting up a drive."

"You mean they hire you to play cards?" Jasper asked. He fancied himself a joker.

"Oh, I was just resting," Dish said. "I'm helping their darky guard some stock."

"Guard it from what?"

"From the Mexicans we stole it from," Dish said. "The Captain went off to hire a crew."

"Hell," Jasper said. "If the Mexicans knew the Captain was gone they'd come and take back Texas."

"I reckon not," Dish said. He felt the remark was slightly insulting. The Captain was not the only man in Texas who could fight.

"He can hire me, if he wants to, when he gets back," Jasper said.

"He probably will," Dish said. Jasper had a reputation for being reliable, if not brilliant.

Though aware that Dish might be touchy on the subject, Jasper was curious about what had happened to change Lorie so. He looked wishfully at the light in her window.

"Is that girl got married, or what?" he asked. "Every time I jingled my money she looked at me like she was ready to carve my liver."

Dish resented the question. He was not so coarse as to enjoy discussing Lorie with just any man who happened to ask. On the other hand, it was hard to see Jasper Fant as a rival. He looked half starved, and probably was.

"It's a scoundrel named Jake Spoon," Dish said. "I reckon he's beguiled her."

"Oh, so that's it," Jasper said. "I believe I've heard the name. A *pistolero* of some kind, ain't he?"

"I wouldn't know what he is," Dish said, in a tone that was meant to let Jasper know he had no great interest in discussing the matter further. Jasper took the hint and the two of them rode over to the Hat Creek pens in silence, their minds on the white-armed woman in the saloon. She was no longer unfriendly, but it seemed to both of them that things had gone a little better before the change.

16

BY THE END of the first day's hiring, Call had collected four boys, none of them yet eighteen. Young Bill Spettle, the one they called Swift Bill, was no older than Newt, and his brother Pete only a year older than Bill. So desperate were their family circumstances that Call was almost hesitant to take them. The widow Spettle had a brood of eight children, Bill and Pete being the oldest. Ned Spettle, the father of them all, had died of drink two years before. It looked to Call as if the family was about to starve out. They had a little creek-bottom farm not far north of Pickles Gap, but the soil was poor and the family had little to eat but sowbelly and beans.

The widow Spettle, however, was eager for him to take the boys, and would hear no protest from Call. She was a thin woman with bitter eyes. Call had heard from someone that she had been raised rich, in the East, with servants to comb her hair and help her into her shoes when she got up. It might just have been a story—it was hard for him to imagine a grownup who would need to be helped into their own shoes—but if even part of it was true she had come a long way down. Ned Spettle had never got around to putting a floor in the shack of a house he built. His wife was rearing eight children on the bare dirt. He had heard it said that Ned had never got over the war, which might have explained it. Plenty hadn't. It accounted for the shortage of grown men of a certain age, that war. Call himself felt a kind of guilt at having missed it, though the work he and Gus had done on the border had been just as dangerous, and just as necessary.

"Take 'em," the widow Spettle said, looking at her boys as if she wondered why she'd borne them. "I reckon they'll work as hard as any."

Call knew the boys had helped take a small herd to Arkansas. He paid the widow a month's wage for each boy, knowing she would need it. There was evidently not a shoe in the family—even the mother was barefoot, a fact that must shame her, if the servant story were true.

He didn't take the Spettle boys with him, for he had brought no spare horses. But the boys started at once for Lonesome Dove on foot, each of them carrying a blanket. They had one pistol between them, a Navy Colt with half its hammer knocked off. Though Call assured them he would equip them well once they got to Lonesome Dove, they wouldn't leave the gun.

"We've never shot airy other gun," Swift Bill said, as if that meant they couldn't.

When he took his leave, Mrs. Spettle and the six remaining children scarcely noticed him. They stood in the hot yard, with a scrawny hen or two scratching around their bare feet, watching the boys and crying. The mother, who had scarcely touched her sons before they left, stood straight up and cried. Three of the children were girls, but the other three were boys in their early teens, old enough, at least, to be of use to their mother.

"We'll take good care of them," Call said, wasting words. The young girls hung onto the widow's frayed skirts and cried. Call rode on, though with a bad feeling in his throat. It was better that the boys go; there was not enough work for them there. And yet they were the pride of the family. He would take as good care of them as he could, and yet what did that mean, with a drive of twenty-five hundred miles to make?

He made the Rainey ranch by sundown, a far more cheerful place than the Spettle homestead. Joe Rainey had a twisted leg, the result of an accident with a buckboard, but he got around on the leg almost as fast as a healthy man. Call was not as fond of Maude, Joe's fat red-faced wife, as Augustus was, but then he had to admit he was not as fond of any woman as Augustus was.

Maude Rainey was built like a barrel, with a bosom as big as buckets and a voice that some claimed would make hair fall out. It was the general consensus around Lonesome Dove that if she and Augustus had married their combined voices would have deafened whatever children they might have produced. She talked at the table like some men talked when they were driving mules.

Still, she and Joe had managed to produce an even dozen children so far, eight of them boys and all of them strapping. Among them the Raineys probably ate as much food in one meal as the Spettles consumed in a week. As near as Call could determine they all devoted most of their waking hours to either growing or butchering or catching what they ate. Augustus's blue pigs had been purchased from the Raineys and were the first thing Maude thought to inquire about when Call rode up.

"Have you et that shoat yet?" Maude asked, before he could even dismount.

"No, we ain't," Call said. "I guess Gus is saving him for Christmas, or else he just likes to talk to him."

"Well, step down and have a wash at the bucket," Maude said. "I'm cooking one of that shoat's cousins right this minute."

It had to be admitted that Maude Rainey set a fine table. Call had no sooner got his sleeves rolled up and his hands clean than supper began. Joe Rainey just had time to mumble a prayer before Maude started pushing around the cornbread. Call was faced with more meats than he had seen on one table since he could remember: beefsteak and pork chops, chicken and venison, and a stew that appeared to contain squirrel and various less familiar meats. Maude got red in the face when she ate, as did everyone else at her table, from the steam rising off the platters.

"This is my varmint stew, Captain," Maude said.

"Oh," he asked politely, "what kind of varmints?"

"Whatever the dogs catch," Maude said. "Or the dogs themselves, if they don't manage to catch nothing. I won't support a lazy dog."

"She put a possum in," one of the little girls said. She seemed as full of mischief as her fat mother, who, fat or not, had made plenty of mischief among the men of the area before she settled on Joe.

"Now, Maggie, don't be giving away my recipes," Maude said. "Anyway, the Captain's likely et possum before."

"At least it ain't a goat," Call said, trying to make conversation. It was an unfamiliar labor, since at his own table he mostly worked at avoiding it. But he knew women liked to talk to their guests, and he tried to fit into the custom.

"We've heard a rumor that Jake is back and on the run," Joe Rainey said. He wore a full beard, which at the moment was shiny with pork drippings. Joe had a habit of staring straight ahead. Though Call assumed he had a neck joint like other men, he had never seen him use it. If you happened to be directly in front of him, Joe would look you in the eye; but if you were positioned a little to the side, his look went floating on by.

"Yes, Jake arrived," Call said. "He's been to Montana and says it's the prettiest country in the world."

"It's probably filt with women, then," Maude said. "I remember Jake. If he can't find a woman he gets so restless he'll scratch."

Call saw no need to comment on Jake's criminal status, if any. Fortunately the Raineys were too busy eating to be very curious. The children, who had been well brought up, didn't try for the better meats, but made do with a platter of chicken and some fryback and cornbread. One little tad, evidently the runt of the family, got nothing but cornbread and chicken gizzards, but he knew better than to complain. With eleven brothers and sisters all bigger than him, complaint would have been dangerous.

"Well, what's Gus up to?" Maude asked. "I been sitting here waiting for him to come over and try to take me away from Joe, but I don't guess he's coming. Has he still got his craving for buttermilk?"

"Yes, he drinks it by the gallon," Call said. "I fancy it myself, so we compete."

He felt Maude's statement not in the best of taste, but Joe Rainey continued to stare straight ahead and drip into his beard.

Call finally asked if he could hire a couple of the boys. Maude sighed, and looked down her double row of children. "I'd rather sell pigs than hire out boys," she said, "but I guess they've got to go see the world sometime."

"What's the pay?" Joe asked, always the practical man.

"Why, forty dollars and found, I reckon," Call said. "Of course we'll furnish the mounts."

That night he slept in a wagon in the Raineys' yard. He had been offered a place in the loft, but it was piled so high with children that he hardly trusted himself in it. Anyway, he preferred the out-of-doors, though the out-of-doors at the Raineys' was more noisy than he was used to. The pigs grunted all night, looking for lizards or something to eat. Then there was a barn owl that wouldn't stop calling, so he had a time getting to sleep.

The next morning he got a promise from Maude that her two oldest boys would get themselves to Lonesome Dove by the end of the week. The boys themselves—Jimmy and Ben Rainey—scarcely said a word. Call rode off feeling satisfied, believing he had enough of a crew to start gathering cattle. Word would get out, and a few more men would probably trickle in.

They had to get the cattle and get them branded. At least they had the luxury of surplus horses, or did if Gus and Jake hadn't contrived to fiddle around and lose them.

He worried about that possibility most of the way home. Not that Gus wasn't competent—so far as sheer ability went, Gus was as competent as any man he'd ever known. There had been plenty of times when he'd wondered if he himself could match Gus, if Gus really tried. It was a question that never got tested, because Gus seldom tried. As a team, the two of them were perfectly balanced; he did more than he needed to, while Gus did less.

Gus himself often joked about it. "If you got killed I might work harder," he said. "I might get in a righteous frame of mind if I had that stimulation. But you ain't kilt, so what's the point?"

Call wasted no time getting back, wishing all the way that he had the mare. She had spoiled him—made him too aware of the limitations of his other mounts. The fact that she was dangerous made him like her the more. She made him extra watchful, which was good.

When he got within fifteen miles of Lonesome Dove he cut west, thinking they would be holding the herd in that direction. He rode around the southern edge of the bad brush country and struck the trail of the horses. They had been going back south, over their own tracks, which was curious. Gus had taken them back to town. Probably he had a reason, but it was not one Call could guess, so he loped on home.

When he approached the town he saw the horses, grazing upriver a little ways, with Deets and Newt and the Irishmen holding them. They looked to be all there, so evidently nothing had happened.

One thing about Gus McCrae, he was easily found. By three in the afternoon, any afternoon, he would be sitting on the porch, drawing occasionally from his jug. When Call rode up, he was sitting there taking a nap. There was no sign of Jake.

"You're a fine guard," he said, dismounting.

Augustus had his hat over his eyes, but he removed it and looked at Call.

"How's Maude Rainey?" he asked.

"She's in good health," Call said. "She fed me twice."

"Good thing it was just twice," Augustus said. "If you'd stayed a week you'd have had to rent an ox to get home on."

"She's anxious to sell you some more pigs," Call said, taking the jug and rinsing his mouth with whiskey.

"If Joe was to get kilt I might court her again," Augustus speculated.

"I hope you will," Call said. "Them twelve young ones ought to have a good father. What are the horses doing back here so soon?"

"Why, grazing, most likely," Augustus said.

"Didn't Pedro make a try?"

"No, he didn't, and for a very good reason," Augustus said.

"What reason would that be?"

"Because he died," Augustus said.

"Well, I swear," Call said, stunned. "Is that the truth?"

"I ain't seen the corpse," Augustus said, "but I imagine it's true. Jasper Fant rode in looking for work and had the news, though the scamp didn't give it to me until I had wasted most of the night."

"I wonder what killed him," Call said. Pedro Flores had been a factor in their lives off and on for thirty years, though probably they had not actually seen him more than six or seven times. It was surprising, hearing he was gone, and though it should have been a relief, it wasn't, exactly. It was too much of a surprise.

"Jasper wasn't up on the details," Augustus said. "He just heard it from a *vaquero*. But I allow it's true, because it explains why you could lope in with a boy and an idiot and saunter off with his remuda."

"Well, I swear," Call said again. "I never expected that."

"Oh, well," Augustus said, "I never either, but then I don't know why not. Mexicans don't have no special dispensation. They die like the rest of us. I expect Bol will die one of these days, and then we won't have nobody to whack the dinner bell with the crowbar."

"Pedro was tough, though," Call said.

After all, the man had more or less held nearly a hundred-mile stretch of the border, and for nearly thirty years. Call had known many men who died, but somehow had not expected it of Pedro, though he himself had fired several bullets at him.

"I'd like to know what took him," Call said.

"He might have choked on a pepper," Augustus said. "Them that can't be killed by knives or bullets usually break their necks falling off the porch or something. Remember Johnny Norvel, dying of that bee sting? I guess Johnny had been shot twenty times, but a dern bee killed him."

It was true. The man had rangered with them, and yet the bee sting had given him a seizure of some kind, and no one could bring him out of it.

"Well, it will about finish the Flores operation," Augustus said. "He just had three boys, and we hung the only one of 'em with any get-up-and-go."

To Augustus's surprise, Call sat down on the porch and took a big swallow from the jug. He felt curious—not sick but suddenly empty—it was the way a kick in the stomach could make you feel. It was an odd thing, but true, that the death of an enemy could affect you almost as much as the death of a friend. He had experienced it before, when news reached them that Kicking Wolf was dead. Some young soldier on his second patrol had made a lucky shot and killed him, on the Clear Fork of the Brazos—and Kicking Wolf had kept two companies of Rangers busy for twenty years. Killed by a private. Call had been shoeing a horse when Pea brought him that piece of news, and he felt so empty for a spell that he had to put off finishing the job.

That had been ten years ago, and he and Gus soon quit rangering. So far as Call was concerned, the death of Kicking Wolf meant the end of the Comanches, and thus the end of their real job. There were other chiefs, true, and the final fights were yet to be fought, but he had never had the vengeful nature of some Rangers and had no interest in spending a decade mopping up renegades and stragglers.

Pedro Flores was a far cry from being the fighter Kicking Wolf had been. Pedro seldom rode without twenty or thirty *vaqueros* to back him up, whereas Kicking Wolf, a small man no bigger than the boy, would raid San Antonio with five or six braves and manage to carry off three women and scare all the whites out of seven or eight counties just by traveling through them. But Pedro was of the same time, and had occupied them just as long.

"I didn't know you liked that old bandit so much," Augustus said.

"I didn't like him," Call said. "I just didn't expect him to die."

"He probably never expected it neither," Augustus said. "He was a rough old cob."

After a few minutes the empty feeling passed, but Call didn't get to his feet. The sense that he needed to hurry, which had been with him most of his life, had disappeared for a space.

"We might as well go on to Montana," he said. "The fun's over around here."

Augustus snorted, amused by the way his friend's mind worked.

"Call, there never was no fun around here," he said. "And besides, you never had no fun in your life. You wasn't made for fun. That's my department."

"I used the wrong word, I guess," Call said.

"Yes, but why did you?" Augustus said. "That's the interesting part."

Call didn't feel like getting drawn into an argument, so he kept quiet.

"First you run out of Indians, now you've run out of bandits, that's the point," Augustus said. "You've got to have somebody to outwit, don't you?"

"I don't know why I'd need anybody when I've got you," Call said.

"I don't see why we just don't take over northern Mexico, now that Pedro's dead," Augustus said. "It's just down the dern street. I'm sure there's still a few folks down there who'd give you a fight."

"I don't need a fight," Call said. "It won't hurt us to make some money."

"It might," Augustus said. "I might drown in the Republican River, like the Pumphrey boy. Then you'd get all the money. You wouldn't even know how to have fun with it. You'd probably use it to buy gravestones for old bandits you happened to like."

"If you drown in the Republican River, I'll give your part to Jake," Call said. "I guess he'd know how to spend it."

With that he mounted and rode off, meaning to find Jasper Fant and hire him, if he really wanted to work.

17

BY THE TIME Jake Spoon had been in Lonesome Dove ten days, Lorena knew she had a job to do—namely the job of holding him to his word and making sure he took her to San Francisco as he had promised to do.

Of course Jake had not given her any direct notice that he intended to do differently. He moved in with her immediately and was just as pleasant about everything as he had been the first day. He had not taken a cent of money from her, and they seldom passed an hour together without him complimenting her in some way—usually on her voice, or her looks, or the fine texture of her hair, or some delicacy of manner. He had a way of appearing always mildly surprised by her graces, and if anything his sentiments only grew warmer as they got to know one another better. He repeated several times his dismay at her having been stuck for so long in a dismal hole like Lonesome Dove.

But after a week, Lorena became aware of a curious thing: Jake was more attached to her than she was to him. The fact struck her late one afternoon while she was watching him nap. He had insisted on a root, and gone right to sleep afterward; while the sweat was cooling on them she realized she wasn't excited about him in the way she had been the first day. The first day had been one of the big days of her life, because of the smooth way Jake had shown up and taken over, ending her long period of tension and discomfort.

She still felt peaceful with him; they had never quarreled and he had not demonstrated the slightest inclination to meanness. But it was clear to her already that he was one of those men somebody had to take care of. He had fooled her for a few days into thinking he would do the taking care of, but that wasn't so. He was a clever cardplayer and could make money, but that was just part of it. Jake had to have company. When he slept, or when he was amused, or was just lolling around telling stories, the childish part of him showed, and it was a big part. Before the week was over it seemed to her that he was all play.

The realization didn't disturb her calm, though. It meant he needed her more than he would admit; she recognized the need and didn't care whether he admitted it or not. If Jake had been as firm as he pretended to be, it would have left her with little security. He could have just walked off.

But he wouldn't. He liked talk, woman's talk, and the comforts of the bed. He even liked it that she lived above the saloon, since it meant a game was handy if he felt like playing.

Since the Hat Creek outfit had been gathering cattle and getting ready for their drive, games were handier than they had been for a while. Several cowboys drifted into Lonesome Dove, looking for work; some of them had enough snap left at night to wander in and cut the cards. A tall cowboy named Needle Nelson showed up from north of San Antonio, and a cheerful cowboy from Brownsville named Bert Borum.

At first Xavier was cheered by all the new customers, until it occurred to him that they would only be there for a week or two. Then the thought of how empty the saloon would soon be filled him with gloom, and he stood by the door most of the night, his washrag dripping down his leg.

Lippy was kept plenty busy, for the cowboys were always requesting songs. Lippy liked the company. He was proud of his talent at the keyboard and would pound out any song that was requested.

Jake took pains to teach Lorena a few things about card playing that she didn't know. She came to wonder how Jasper and Bert and Needle Nelson got by on so little sleep, for the Captain worked them hard all day and the games went on half the night. The only cowboy likely to pull a sour face if she sat in was Dish Boggett, who wouldn't get over being in love with her. It amused her that he sat there looking so solemn, with his big mustache. Jake did not even seem to notice that the man was in love with her. She was tempted to tease Jake a little, but he had told her plain out he was a jealous man: for all she knew, he might shoot Dish, which would be a pity. Dish was nice enough—it was just that he couldn't compare with Jake Spoon.

When the gathering and branding of cattle had been going on for about ten days, Lorena began to feel a crisis coming. She heard the boys speculate that the branding would be done in another week, which meant they were close to starting the drive. The boys were saying they were already late.

"Hell, we'll be crossing the Yellowstone on the dern ice, if we don't get started," Needle Nelson said. He was a funny-looking man, thin as a wire, and with an Adam's apple that looked as big as a turkey egg.

"Why, I doubt we'll make the Yellowstone," Jasper Fant said. "Most of us will get drownt before we get that far."

"Needle won't," Dish Boggett suggested. "There ain't a river up that way deep enough he couldn't walk through it and not get his hat wet."

"I can swim, anyway," Needle remarked.

"I'd like to see you swim with fifty or sixty cattle on top of you, or maybe your own horse," Jasper said.

"Ain't no fifty or sixty cattle going to *be* on top of me," Needle replied, unruffled. "Nor no dern horse neither."

Bert Borum thought Needle was hilarious—he thought pretty near everything was hilarious. He was one of those men who have a laugh you like to hear.

"I'm getting me a float before I cross airy river," he declared.

"What kind of float?" Dish inquired.

"Ain't decided," Bert said. "Might tie a few jugs to my horse. Jugs are good floats."

"Where would you get a dern jug on a cattle drive?" Jasper asked. "If the Captain was to catch you with a jug, he'd want to know who drank the whiskey out of it."

Jake was tolerant of the cowboys but careful to keep himself a bit apart from them. He never chimed in when they talked about the life they would have on the trail, and he never spoke to Lorena about the fact that the herd would be leaving in ten days. He didn't work much on the branding, either, though once in a while he spent a night helping them gather more stock. Mostly he let it appear that the drive had nothing to do with him.

Lorena didn't press him, but she kept an eye on him. If he wanted to stay, that was one thing, but if he planned on going he was going to have to figure a way to take her. He wasn't leaving without her, whatever he might think about the matter.

Then, before the issue came to a head, something happened that took Lorena completely unaware. It was a blistering day, the saloon totally empty except for Lippy. Xavier, who had a taste for fish, had gone off to the river to see if he could catch any. Lorena was sitting at a table, practicing one or two card tricks Jake had taught her, when who should walk in but Gus. His shirt was as wet from sweat as if he'd been underwater a week, and even his hatband was sweated through. He went around behind the bar, got himself a bottle and brought it over to the table, grinning a big grin despite the heat.

She noted that he brought her a glass, which struck her as bold, but then Gus would do anything, as Jake was always saying.

"What I can't figure out is why there ain't but two sinners in this saloon," Gus said.

Lorena made no comment, but Lippy piped up.

"I've tried to sin all my life—ain't you gonna count me?" he asked.

"No, you got a hole in your stomach," Augustus said. "You paid for yours, but so far me and Lorie have got off scot-free."

Gus poured a little whiskey in her glass, and filled his to just below the brim.

"I want a poke," he said, as casual as if he were asking her to loan him two bits.

Lorena was so taken aback that she didn't know what to say. She looked at Lippy, who was just sitting there listening, as if it were his right.

Gus, of course, was not the slightest bit embarrassed by what he was suggesting. He took his hat off and hung it on a chair, looking at her pleasantly.

Lorena felt sorely at a loss. She had never expected Gus to commit such a blunder, for it was well known that he and Jake were good friends. Gus must know that Jake was living with her; and yet he walked in and asked, as if it made no difference.

She sat silent, showing her puzzlement, which only seemed to amuse Gus.

"I wisht you wouldn't sit there thinking about it," he said. "Just sell me the poke and be done with it. I hate to sit and watch a woman think."

"Why?" she asked, finding her voice again. She felt the beginnings of indignation. "I guess I got the right to think, if I want to," she added.

Gus just grinned. "Oh, you got the right," he said. "It's just that it's fearsome for a man to have a woman start thinking right in front of him. It always leads to trouble."

He paused and drank a healthy swallow of whiskey.

"I'm with Jake now," Lorena said, merely stating the obvious.

"I know that, honey," Augustus said. "The minute I looked up the road and seen Jake coming, I knew you and him would settle in. Jake's a good hand to settle in with, I admit—a sight better than me. But the fact is he went out to the cow camp at the wrong time and Call put him to work. Call don't appreciate Jake's restful qualities like you and me do. He's been fretting for a week because Jake wasn't working, and now that he's got him you can bet he'll keep him a day or two."

Lorena looked at Lippy, wishing he wasn't there. But Lippy sat, astonished at what he was hearing. His lip hung down like a flap of some kind, as it always did when he forgot himself.

"Jake ain't got the stuff to stand up to Call," Augustus said. "He's gonna have to stay out there and brand dogies for a while. So there ain't no reason for you not to sell me a poke."

"I told you the reason," Lorena said. "Jake takes care of me now," she added.

"No he don't," Gus said. "You take care of him."

It was the very truth Lorena had discovered for herself, and it stumped her that Gus would not only know it but come right out with it as if it were an ordinary fact.

"Jake Spoon has never taken care of nobody," Gus said. "Not even himself. He's the world's child, and the main point about him is that he'll always find somebody to take care of him. It used to be me and Call, but right now it's you. That's fine and good, but it's no reason you should go out of business entirely. You can sell me a poke and still take care of Jake."

Lorena knew that was true, as far as it went. Jake was not hard to take care of, and probably not hard to fool. It wouldn't enter his head that she would sell a poke, now that she had him. He had plenty of pride and not a little vanity. It was one of the things she liked about him. Jake thought well of his looks; he was not a dressy man, like Tinkersley, but he nonetheless took pains with his appearance and knew that women fancied him. She had never seen him mad, but she knew he would not like anyone to make light of him.

"I believe he'd shoot the man that touches me," she said.

"I believe it too," Lippy said. "Jake's mighty partial to Lorie."

"Hell, you're partial to her yourself," Gus said. "We're all partial to her. But Jake ain't exactly a killer."

"He killed that man in Arkansas," Lorena said.

Augustus shrugged. "He fired off a buffalo gun and the bullet happened to hit a dentist," he said. "I don't call that no crime of passion."

Lorena didn't like it that Gus acted like Jake wasn't much. He had a reputation for being a cool man in a fight.

"He kilt that bandit," Lippy said. "Hit him right in the Adam's apple, I've heard."

"The truth of that is, the bandit rode into the bullet," Augustus said. "He was unlucky, like the dentist."

Lorena just sat. The situation was so unexpected that she could not think about it clearly. Of course she had no intention of going upstairs with Gus, but he couldn't just be scared off with a look like some cowboy. Gus was not afraid of looks—or of Jake either, it seemed.

"I'll give you fifty dollars," Gus said with a big grin.

Lippy nearly fell off his stool. He had never seen or imagined anything so rash. Fifty dollars for one poke? Then it occurred to him he would cheerfully give as much, if he had it, to get under Lorena's skirts. A man could always get more money, but there wasn't but one Lorie, not on the border, anyway.

"Hell, I would too," he said, just to register the offer.

"I didn't know you was so rich," Augustus said, a little amused.

"Well, I ain't now, but I might be," Lippy said. "Business is picking up."

"Pshaw," Augustus said. "Once we start the drive you'll be lucky to earn a nickel in a month."

Lorena decided her best out was to pretend to be frightened of Jake's vengeance, though now that she thought about it she knew Gus was probably right. She had met one or two men who were proven killers, and Jake didn't have their manner at all.

"I won't do it," she said. "He'll kill us if he finds out."

"How would he find out?" Gus asked.

"Lippy might tell him," she said.

Augustus looked at Lippy. It was true that the man was a dreadful gossip, and a gossip, moreover, who had scant materials to work with. It would not be easy for him to resist mentioning that he had heard a man offer fifty dollars for a poke.

"I'll give you ten dollars to keep your mouth shut," Augustus said. "And if you betray me I'll shoot another hole in your stomach."

"Gimme the ten," Lippy said, his astonishment growing. That made sixty dollars Gus would be spending. He had never heard of anyone spending such an amount on their pleasure, but then, so far as he knew, there was no one anywhere like Gus, a man who seemed to care nothing for money.

Gus handed over the money and Lippy pocketed it, knowing he had struck a bargain he had better keep, at least until Gus died. Gus was no one to fool with. He had seen several men try, usually over card games, and most all of them had got whacked over the head with Gus's big gun. Gus didn't shoot unless he had to, but he was not loath to whack a man. Lippy was dying to tell Xavier what he'd missed by going fishing, but he knew he had better postpone the pleasure for a few years. One hole in his stomach was enough.

Lorena felt her indignation growing. She was beginning to feel cornered, something she had not expected to have to feel again. Jake was supposed to have ended that, and yet he hadn't. Of course he probably never suspected his own friend would make such a move behind his back, and yet it still seemed negligent of him, for he knew Gus's ways.

"You can pay him if you want but I ain't going," she said. "Jake's my sweetheart."

"I ain't trying to cut him out," Augustus said. "I just want a poke."

Lorena felt her silence coming back. It was the only way to deal with such a situation. She sat for a few minutes, not talking, hoping he would go away. But it didn't work. He just sat and drank, perfectly friendly and in no hurry. Once she thought about it, the sum grew on her a little. It was something, to be offered fifty dollars. She would have thought it crazy in anyone except Gus, but Gus was clearly not crazy. In a way it was a big compliment that he would offer fifty dollars just for that.

"Go get a Mexican woman," she said. "Why waste your money?"

"Because you're my preference," Augustus said. "I'll tell you what, let's cut the cards. If you're high, I'll give you the money and forget the poke. If I'm high, I'll give you the money and you give me the poke."

Lorena thought she might as well. After all, it was just gambling, which was what Jake did. If she won it would all seem like a joke, something that Gus had cooked up to pass the time. Besides, she would have fifty dollars and could send to San Antonio for some new dresses, so Jake wouldn't be so critical of her wardrobe. She could tell him she beat Gus to the tune of fifty dollars, which would astonish him, since he played with Gus all the time and seldom won more than a few dollars.

Then, in a second, Gus beat her. She came up with a ten of spades, and him with the queen of hearts. It was her sense that he'd cheated, though she couldn't have said how. She had not realized before what a determined man he was. He had come in for a purpose and she had not been clever enough to head him off. He paid her the fifty dollars at once—it had not been a bluff. When he had had the poke and was dressing, she found that she felt pretty cheerful and was not in a mood to hurry him out. After all, Gus had paid her many visits and given her nothing to hold against him. The fifty dollars was flattering, and she rather liked it that she was his preference even though he was Jake's best friend. She had stopped feeling silent and was content to let him loll for a few minutes.

"Well, do you and Jake aim to marry?" he asked, looking at her cheerfully.

"He ain't mentioned it," she said. "He's taking me to San Francisco, though."

Augustus snorted. "I figured that was his game," he said.

"He promised," Lorena said. "I mean to hold him to it, Gus."

"You'll need my help then," Augustus said. "Jake is a slippery eel. The only way to keep him around is to chain him to a wagon."

"I can keep him around," Lorena said confidently.

"Oh, he fancies you," Augustus said. "But that don't mean he'll stay around. My guess is he'll use the drive as an excuse when the time comes."

"If he goes with it, then I'm going too," she said.

"Why, Lorie, you're welcome, as far as I'm concerned," Augustus said. "The problem is Call. He ain't very tolerant of women."

That was no news. Captain Call was one of the few men in the region who had never been to visit her. In fact, so far as she could remember, he had never been in the saloon.

"It's a free country, ain't it?" she said. "I guess I can go where I want."

Gus got off the bed and tucked his carrot back in his pants.

"It's not very free if you happen to work for Call," he said.

"You think Lippy will tell on us?" she asked. To her surprise, she felt no guilt at all about operating behind Jake's back. So far as she was concerned she was still his sweetheart. It had happened only because Gus had been too quick for her in a card game—it didn't affect the situation one way or another.

"He won't tell," Augustus said. "Lippy's got more sense than you might think. What he figures is that if he keeps quiet he might make another ten dollars some-time. Which is right. He might."

"Well, not unless we play a hand," Lorena said. "I don't trust your cut."

Augustus grinned. "A man who wouldn't cheat for a poke don't want one bad enough," he said as he took his hat.

18

AUGUSTUS RODE BACK to camp a little after sunset, thinking the work would have stopped by then. The cattle were being held in a long valley near the river, some five miles from town. Every night Call went across the river with five or six hands and came back with two or three hundred Mexican cattle—longhorns mostly, skinny as rails and wild as deer. Whatever they got they branded the next day, with the part of the crew that had rested doing the hard end of the work. Only Call worked both shifts. If he slept, it was an hour or two before breakfast or after supper. The rest of the time he worked, and so far as anyone could tell the pace agreed with him. He had taken to riding the Hell Bitch two days out of three, and the mare seemed no more affected by the work than he was.

Bolivar had not taken kindly to being moved to a straggly camp out in the brush, with no dinner bell to whack or crowbar to whack it with. He kept his ten-gauge near the chuck box and scowled at everybody. The Irishmen were so intimidated that they were always the last ones in line. As a consequence they got little to eat and were no longer as fat as they had been the day they arrived.

It seemed the Irishmen *were* part of the outfit, though. Their total inexperience was offset by an energy and a will to learn that impressed even Call. He let them stay in the first place, because he was so short-handed he couldn't afford to turn away any willing hand. By the time more competent men arrived the Irishmen had gotten over their fear of horses and worked with a will. Not being cowboys, they had no prejudice against working on the ground. Once shown the proper way to throw a roped animal, they cheerfully flung themselves on whatever the ropers drug up to the branding fire, even if it was a two-year-old bull with lots of horn and a mean disposition. They had no great finesse, but they were dogged, and would eventually get the creature down.

This willingness to work on the ground was indispensable, for most cowboys would rather eat poison than be forced to dismount. They all fancied themselves ropers, and swelled like toads if asked to do work they considered beneath their dignity.

Since there were few goats to steal near the camp, Bol's menus relied heavily on beef, with the usual admixture of beans. He had brought along a sack of chilies, and he dumped them liberally into his beans, feeling free to augment the dish with pieces of whatever varmints strayed into his path—rattlesnakes mostly, with an occasional armadillo.

For several days the crew ate the fiery beans without complaint, only the Irishmen showing pronounced ill effects. Young Sean had difficulty with the peppers. He could not eat the beans without weeping, but, with all the work, his appetite raged to such a point that he could not avoid the beans. He ate them and wept. Most of the crew liked the boy and had decided to treat his frequent weepings as simply a mild aberration, related in some way to his nationality.

Then one day Jasper Fant caught Bolivar skinning a rattlesnake. He assumed Bolivar was merely going to make himself a rattlesnake belt, but he happened to turn around as Bol sliced the snake right into the stewpot, a sight which agitated him greatly. He had heard that people ate snake but had never expected to do so himself. When he told the other hands what he had seen they were so aroused that they wanted to hang Bolivar on the spot, or at least rope him and drag him through the prickly pear to improve his manners. But when they approached Augustus with the information about the snake, he laughed at them.

"You boys must have been raised on satin pillows," he said. "If you'd rangered you'd have got a taste for snake long ago."

He then proceeded to give them a lecture on the culinary properties of rattlesnake—a lecture that Jasper, for one, received rather stiffly. It might be superior to chicken, rabbit and possum, as Gus claimed, but that didn't mean he wanted to eat it. His visits to the stewpot became a source of irritation to everyone; he would fish around in the pot for several minutes, seeking portions of meat that he could feel confident hadn't come from a snake. Such delicacy exacerbated the rest of the crew, who were usually so hungry by suppertime that they could ill abide waits.

Call and Jake rode in while Augustus was eating. The sight of Gus with his plate full put Jake in a low temper, since he himself had handled branding irons all day while Gus had amused himself in town and stayed fresh. They had branded over four hundred cattle since sunup, enough to make Jake wish he had never brought up the notion of taking cattle to Montana.

"Hello, girls," Augustus said. "You look like you've done a heavy laundry. Wait till I finish my beef and I'll help you off your horses."

"I don't want off mine," Jake said. "Hand me a plate and I'll eat on the way to town."

Call felt irritated. It was the first full day Jake had put in since the work started, and mostly he had lazed through it.

"Why? Must you go?" he asked, trying to keep it mild. "We're going to make our last drag tonight. We have to get started, you know."

Jake dismounted and walked over to the grub, pretending he hadn't heard. He didn't want an argument with Call if he could avoid one. In truth, he had not been thinking very far ahead since drifting back to Lonesome Dove. He had often thought of the fortune that could be made in cattle in Montana, but then a man could think of a fortune without actually having to go and make one. The only good thing to be said for trailing cattle that far north was that it beat hanging in Arkansas, or rotting in some jail.

Then there was Lorie. So far she hadn't had a single fit, but that didn't mean she wouldn't if she found out he was leaving. On the other hand, he couldn't very well take her—no one in his memory had ever tried to bring a woman into one of Call's camps.

It was all vexing, having decisions to make, and yet having no time to think them through. He got himself a hunk of beef and some of the old Mexican's peppery stew and went back to where Call and Gus were sitting. He felt distinctly irritated with Call—the man never seemed to need any of the things other humans needed, like sleep or women. Life for Call was work, and he seemed to think everyone else ought to see it the same way.

"Why, Jake, you look plumb grumpy," Augustus said, when Jake sat down and began to eat. "Honest work don't agree with you, I guess."

"No, I'm about as cooked as this beef," Jake said.

Newt and the two Irishmen were holding the herd. The Irishmen were particularly good night herders because they could sing; their melodies seemed to soothe the cattle. In fact, the whole camp enjoyed the Irish singing. Newt couldn't sing a lick, but he had rapidly developed into such a skilled cowhand that Call felt a little guilty for having held him back so long.

"I'm sure partial to the evening," Augustus said. "The evening and the morning. If we just didn't have to have the rest of the dern day I'd be a lot happier."

"If we have a good drag tonight we can start north on Monday," Call said. "How does that suit you, Jake?"

"Oh, fine," Jake said. "But you boys don't have to try and suit me with your drive. I've been thinking of spending some time in San Antonio."

"That's a big disappointment," Augustus said. "It's a long way to Montany. I was counting on you to keep up the conversation."

"Well, count agin," Jake said, deciding on the spot that he wouldn't go.

Call knew there was no point in reminding Jake that the whole drive had been his idea. The man was willful as a child in some respects. Show him what he ought to do and he would dig in his heels and refuse. It was particularly irritating in this instance, because nobody in the outfit had ever been farther north than Kansas. Jake knew the country and could be a big help.

"Jake, we wish you'd come," he said. "We were relying on you to help us choose the route."

"No, Jake don't like to help his *compañeros*," Augustus said. "He's got his own fancies to cultivate. The fact that he caused all this don't mean a thing to him."

"Did I cause it?" Jake asked, trying to keep the talk light.

"Of course you caused it," Augustus said. "Who was it said Montana is a cowman's paradise?"

"Well, it is," Jake said.

"Then you should have picked a cattleman to mention it to," Augustus said. "Not two old laws like us."

"Hell, you're cattlemen now," Jake said. "All it takes is cows."

"Are you aiming to marry Lorie?" Augustus asked, changing his tack.

"Marry her?" Jake asked, astonished. "Why would I marry her?"

"You could do worse," Augustus said. "An old scamp like you's apt to break down any time. It would be nice to have a young woman to rub your back and bring you soup."

"I ain't near as old as you," Jake reminded him. "Why don't you marry her?" It was talk he didn't care to hear.

Swift Bill Spettle had let a horse kick him that morning and had a knot on his forehead as big as a goose egg.

"You best let Bol rub some ointment on that bump," Call suggested. The Spettle boys were mighty green, but they were not afraid to work.

Call got up and went to get his supper. As soon as he left, Augustus stretched his legs and grinned at Jake.

"I played a hand with Lorie this afternoon," he said. "I believe you've made her restless, Jake."

"How's that?"

"She does seem to be looking forward to San Francisco," Augustus said.

Jake felt himself getting more and more peevish. Lorena should have known better than to play cards with Gus, or even to talk to him, though she could hardly be blamed for listening. It was well known that Gus would talk to a stump if he couldn't find a human.

"I doubt she'll want to spend no time in San Antonio," Augustus said. "That's where she was before she came here, and women don't like to go backwards. Most women will never back up an inch their whole lives."

"I can't see that it's any of your affair what we do," Jake said. "I guess she'd go to San Antonio if I say to. If she don't, she'll just get left."

"Bring her on the drive," Augustus said. "She might like Montany. Or if she gets tired of looking at the ass end of these cows, you could always stop in Denver."

It was something, the talent Gus had for saying the very thing that a man might have been half thinking. Jake had more than once considered Denver, regretted more than once that he hadn't stopped there instead of going to Fort Smith. Going along with a drive would be a good enough way to get back to Denver. Of course, that didn't settle the question of Lorie, exactly.

"You know as well as I do Call would never allow no woman in this camp," he said. It was surprising that Gus would even suggest such a thing.

"Call ain't God," Augustus said. "He don't have to get his way every day of the month. If she was my sweetheart, I'd bring her, and if he didn't like it he could bite himself."

"You couldn't afford her, Gus, no better card player than you are," Jake said, standing up. "I believe I'll go to town. I don't feel like bumping around Mexico tonight."

Without another word he got his horse and left. Call watched him go and walked back over to Gus. "Do you think he'll come on the drive?" he asked.

"Not unless you let him bring his girl," Augustus said.

"Why, is Jake that crazy?" Call asked. "Does he want to bring that girl?"

"It never occurred to him, but it has now," Augustus said. "I invited her."

Call was impatient to get off, but Gus's remark stopped him. Gus was never one to do the usual, but this was stretching things, even for him.

"You done what?"

"Told him he ought to bring Lorie along," Augustus said. "She'd improve the company."

"I won't have it," Call said at once. "Goddamn you. You know better than that."

"Ain't you late for work?" Augustus asked. "I can't enjoy the night for all this jabbering."

Call decided it was some joke. Even Gus wouldn't go that far. "I'm going," he said. "You watch this end."

Augustus lay back, his head against his saddle. It was a clear night, the stars just beginning to appear. Needle, Bert, Pea, Deets and Dish were waiting to go to Mexico. The rest of the boys were holding the herd. Bol was peeing on the campfire, causing it to sputter. Call turned his horse and rode toward the river.

19

NEWT'S MIND had begun to dwell on the north for long stretches. Particularly at night, when he had nothing to do but ride slowly around and around the herd, listening to the small noises the bedded cattle made, or the sad singing of the Irishmen, he thought of the north, trying to imagine what it must be like.

He had grown up with the sun shining, with mesquite and chaparral, armadillos and coyotes, Mexicans and the shallow Rio Grande. Only once had he been to a city: San Antonio. Deets had taken him on one of his banking trips, and Newt had been in a daze from all there was to see.

Once, too, he had gone with Deets and Pea to deliver a small bunch of horses to Matagorda Bay, and had seen the great gray ocean. Then, too, he had felt dazed, staring at the world of water.

But even the sight of the ocean had not stirred him so much as the thought of the north. All his life he had heard talk of the plains that had no end, and of Indians and buffalo and all the creatures that lived on them. Mr. Gus had even talked of great bears, so thick that bullets couldn't kill them, and deerlike creatures called elk, twice the size of ordinary deer.

Now, in only a few days, he would be going north, a prospect so exciting that for hours at a stretch he was taken away from himself, into imaginings. He continued to do his normal work, although his mind wasn't really on it. He could imagine himself and Mouse out in a sea of grass, chasing buffalo. He could scare himself to the point where his breath came short, just imagining the great thick bears.

Before the Irishmen had been there a week, he had made friends with Sean O'Brien. At first the conversation was one-sided, for Sean was full of worries and prone to talking a blue streak; once he found that Newt would listen and not make fun of him, the talk gushed out, most of it homesick talk. He missed his dead mother and said over and over again that he would not have left Ireland if she hadn't died. He would cry immediately at the thought of his mother, and when Newt revealed that his mother was also dead, the friendship became closer.

"Did you have a pa?" Newt asked one day, as they were resting by the river after a stretch of branding.

"Yes, I had one, the bastard," Sean said grimly. "He only came home when he was a mind to beat us."

"Why would he beat you?" Newt asked.

"He liked to," Sean said. "He was a bastard, Pa. Beat Ma and all of us whenever he could catch us. We laid for him once and was gonna brain him with a shovel, but he was a lucky one. The night was dark and we never seen him."

"What happened to him?" Newt asked.

"Ha, the drunkard," Sean said. "He fell down a well and drownded. Saved us killing him and going to jail, I guess."

Newt had always missed having a father, but the fact that Sean spoke so coldly of his put the matter in a different light. Perhaps he was not so unlucky, after all.

He was riding around the herd when Jake Spoon trotted past on his way to Lonesome Dove.

"Going to town, Jake?" Newt asked.

"Yes, I think I will," Jake said. He didn't stop to pass the time; in a second he was out of sight in the shadows. It made Newt's spirits fall a little, for Jake had seldom said two words to him since he came back. Newt had to admit that Jake was not much interested in him, or the rest of them either. He gave the impression of not exactly liking anything around the Hat Creek outfit.

Listening to the talk around the campfire at night, Newt learned that the cowboys were unanimously hostile to Jake for fixing it so that Lorena was no longer a whore. Dish, he knew, was particularly riled, though Dish never said much when the other boys were talking about it.

"Hell," Needle said, "there never was but one thing worth doing on this border, and now a man can't even do that."

"A man can do it plenty over in Mexico," Bert observed. "Cheaper too."

"That's what I like about you, Bert," Augustus said, as he whittled a mesquite twig into a toothpick. "You're a practical man."

"No, he just likes them brown whores," Needle said. Needle kept a solemn look on his face at all times, seldom varying his expression.

"Gus, I've heard it said you had a fancy for that woman yourself," Jasper Fant said. "I wouldn't have suspected it in a man as old as you."

"What would you know about anything, Jasper?" Augustus asked. "Age don't slow a man's whoring. It's lack of income that does that. No more prosperous than you look, I wouldn't think you'd know much about it."

"We oughtn't to talk this way around these young boys," Bert said. "I doubt a one of 'em's even had a poke, unless it was at a milk cow."

A general laugh went up.

"These young uns will have to wait until we get to Ogallala," Augustus said. "I've heard it's the Sodom of the plains."

"If it's worse than Fort Worth I can't wait to get there," Jasper said. "I've heard there's whores you can marry for a week, if you stay in town that long."

"It won't matter how long we stay," Augustus said. "I'll have skinned all you boys of several years' wages before we get that far. I'd skin you out of a month or two tonight, if somebody would break out the cards."

That was all it took to get a game started. Apart from telling stories and speculating about whores, it seemed to Newt the cowboys would rather play cards than anything. Every night, if there were as many as four who weren't working, they'd spread a saddle blanket near the campfire and play for hours, mostly using their future wages as money. Already the debts which existed were so complicated it gave Newt a headache to think about them. Jasper Fant had lost his saddle to Dish Boggett, only Dish was letting him keep it and use it.

"A man dumb enough to bet his saddle is dumb enough to eat gourds," Mr. Gus had said when he heard about that bet.

"I have et okra," Jasper replied, "but I have never yet et no gourd."

So far neither Newt nor the Rainey or Spettle boys had been allowed to play. The men felt it would be little short of criminal to bankrupt young men at the outset of their careers. But sometimes when nobody was using the deck, Newt borrowed it and he and the others played among themselves. Sean O'Brien joined in. They usually played for pebbles, since none of them had any money.

Talking to Sean had made Newt curious about Ireland. Sean said the grass was thick as a carpet there. The description didn't help much for Newt had never seen a carpet. The Hat Creek outfit possessed no rugs of any kind, or anything that was green. Newt had a hard time imagining how a whole country could be covered with green grass.

"What do you do in Ireland?" he asked.

"Mostly dig spuds," Sean said.

"But aren't there horses and cows?" Newt asked.

Sean thought for a moment, but could only remember about a dozen cows in the vicinity of his village, which was near the sea. He had slept beside their own old milk cow on many a cold night, but he figured if he tried to lie down beside one of the animals they called cows in America the cow would be fifty miles away before he got to sleep.

"There are cows," he said, "but you don't find them in bunches. There'd be no place to put them."

"What do you do with all the grass then?" Newt asked.

"Why, nothing," Sean said. "It just grows."

The next morning, while helping Deets and Pea build the branding fires, Newt mentioned that Sean said he brought his milk cow into the house and slept with her. Deets had a good laugh at the thought of a cow in a house. Pea stopped working for about ten minutes while he thought the matter over. Pea never liked to give his opinion too quickly.

"It wouldn't work around the Captain," he said finally, that being his opinion.

"How long do you think it will take us to get up north?" Newt asked Deets, the acknowledged expert on times and distances.

Though he had laughed about the cow in the house, Deets had not been his usual cheerful self for the last few days. He felt a change coming. They were leaving Lonesome Dove, where life had been quiet and steady, and Deets could not understand the reason for it. The Captain was not prone to rash moves—and yet it seemed rash to Deets to just pick up and go north. Usually when he thought about the Captain's decisions he agreed with him, but this time he couldn't. He was going, but he felt uneasy in his mind. He remembered one thing the Captain had drilled into them many times during the rangering years: that a good start made for a good campaign.

Now, it seemed to him, the Captain had forgotten his own rule. Jake Spoon came home one day, and the next day the Captain was ready to go, with a crew that was just a patched-together bunch, a lot of wild cattle, and horses most of which were only half broke. Besides that, it was nearly April, late to be starting out to go so far. He had been on the plains in summer and seen how quickly the water holes dried up.

Deets felt a foreboding, a sense that they were starting on a hard journey to a far place. And now here was the boy, too excited about the prospect to keep his mind on the work.

"Chop them sticks," Deets said. "Don't be worrying about the time. It'll be fall, I expect, before we get there."

Deets watched the boy, hoping he wouldn't chop his foot off cutting the wood. He knew how to handle an ax, but he was forgetful once he got his mind on something. He didn't stop working, he just worked absently, thinking about something else.

They were friends, though, he and Newt. The boy was young and had all his hopes, while Deets was older and had fewer. Newt sometimes asked so many questions that Deets had to laugh—he was like a cistern, from which questions flowed instead of water. Some Deets answered and some he didn't. He didn't tell Newt all he knew. He didn't tell him that even when life seemed easy, it kept on getting harder. Deets liked his work, liked being part of the outfit and having his name on the sign; yet he often felt sad. His main happiness consisted of sitting with his back against the water tank at night, watching the sky and the changing moon.

He had known several men who blew their heads off, and he had pondered it much. It seemed to him it was probably because they could not take enough happiness just from the sky and the moon to carry them over the low feelings that came to all men.

Those feelings hadn't come to the boy yet. He was a good boy, as gentle as the gray doves that came to peck for gravel on the flats behind the barn. He would try to do any task that was asked of him, and if he worried overmuch it was that he wasn't good enough at his work to please the Captain. But then the whole outfit worried about that—all, at least, except Mr. Gus. Deets himself had fallen short a few times over the years and had felt the Captain's displeasure afflict him like a bruise.

"I swan," Pea said, "Jake's slipped off again. He sure don't take to branding."

"Mr. Jake, he don't take to *work*," Deets said with a chuckle. "It don't have to be branding."

Newt went on chopping wood, a little bothered by the fact that Jake had such a bad reputation with the men. They all considered him to be a man who shirked his duties. Mr. Gus worked even less and nobody seemed to feel that way about him. It was puzzling and, to Newt's mind, unfair. Jake had just returned. Once he got rested, perhaps he would be more interested in the work.

While he was puzzling about it, he took a bad swing with the ax and a piece of mesquite he was trying to split flew right up and almost hit Deets in the head. It would have, except that Deets had evidently been expecting just such an accident. He quickly ducked. Newt was embarrassed—at the moment he had made his slip, his mind had drifted to Lorena. He was wondering what spending a day with her would actually be like. Would they just sit in the saloon playing cards, or what? Since he had not spoken to her, it was hard for him to know what the two of them could do for a whole day, but he liked to think about it.

Deets didn't say a word or even look at Newt accusingly, but Newt was still mortified. There were times when Deets seemed almost to be able to read his mind; what would he think if he knew he had been thinking about Lorena?

After that, he reminded himself that Lorena was Jake's woman, and tried to pay better attention to splitting the tough wood.

20

THE MINUTE Jake stepped in the door of the Dry Bean Lorena saw that he was in a sulk. He went right over to the bar and got a bottle and two glasses. She was sitting at a table, piddling with a deck of cards. It was early in the evening and no one was around except Lippy and Xavier, which was a little surprising. Usually three or four of the Hat Creek cowboys would be there by that time.

Lorena watched Jake closely for a few minutes to see if she was the cause of his sulk. After all, she had sold Gus the poke that very afternoon—it was not impossible that Jake had found out, some way. She was not one who expected to get away with much in life. If you did a thing hoping a certain person wouldn't find out, that person always did. When Gus tricked her and she gave him the poke, she was confident the matter would get back to Jake eventually. Lippy was only human, and things that happened to her got told and repeated. She didn't exactly want Jake to know, but she wasn't afraid of him, either. He might hit her, or he might shoot Gus: she found she couldn't easily predict him, which was one reason she didn't care if he found out. After that, she would know him a lot better, whatever he did.

But when he sat down at the table and set a glass in front of her she soon realized it was not her who had put the tight look in his face. She saw nothing unfriendly in his eyes. She took a sip or two of whiskey, and about that time Lippy came over and sat down at the table with them as if he'd been invited.

"Well, you've come in by yourself, I see," Lippy said, pushing his dirty bowler back off his wrinkled forehead.

"I did, and by God I intend to be by myself," Jake said irritably. He got up and without another word took his bottle and glass and headed for the stairs.

It put her out of sorts with Lippy, for it was still hot in her room and she would rather have stayed in the saloon, where there was at least a breath of breeze.

But with Jake so out of sorts there was nothing to do but go upstairs. She gave Lippy a cool look as she got up, which surprised him so it made his lip drop.

"Why air you looking at me that way?" he asked. "I never tolt on you."

Lorena didn't answer. A look was better than words, where Lippy was concerned.

Then, the very minute she got in the room, Jake decided he wanted a poke, and in a hurry. He had drunk a half glass of whiskey while he was climbing the stairs, and a big shot of whiskey nearly always made him want it. He was dusty as could be from a day with the cattle, and would usually have waited for a bath, or at least washed the grit off his face and hands in the washbasin, but this time he didn't wait. He even tried to kiss her with his hat on, which didn't work at all. His hat was as dusty as the rest of him. The dust got in her nose and made her sneeze. His haste was unusual—he was a picky man, apt to complain if the sheets weren't clean enough to suit him.

138

But this time he didn't seem to notice that dust was sifting out of his clothes onto the floor. When he opened his pants and pulled his shirttail out a little trickle of sand came with it. The night was stifling and Jake so sandy that by the time he got through there was so much dirt in the bed that they might as well have been wallowing around on the ground. There were little lines of mud on her belly where sweat had caked the dust. She didn't resent it, particularly—it was better than smoke pots and mosquitoes.

It was only when Jake sat up to reach for his whiskey bottle that he noticed the dust.

"Dern, I'm sandy," he said. "I should have bathed in the river."

He sighed, poured himself a whiskey and sat with his back against the wall, idly running a hand up and down her leg. Lorena waited, taking a sip or two of whiskey. Jake looked tired.

"Well, these boys," he said. "They are aggravating devils."

"Which boys?" she asked.

"Call and Gus," he said. "Just because I mentioned Montana to 'em they expect me to help 'em drive them dern cattle up there."

Lorena watched him. He looked out the window and wouldn't meet her eye.

"I'll be damned if I'll do it," he said. "I ain't no dern cowpuncher. Call just got it in his head to go, for some reason. Well, let him go."

But she knew that bucking Gus and the Captain was no easy thing for Jake. He looked at her finally, a sadness in his eyes, as if he was asking her to think of a way to help him.

Then he grinned, his little smart lazy grin. "Gus thinks we ought to marry," he said.

"I'd rather go to San Francisco," Lorena said.

Jake stroked her leg again. "Well, we will," he said. "But don't Gus come up with some notions! He thinks I ought to bring you along on the drive."

Then he looked at her again, as if trying to fathom what was in her thoughts. Lorena let him look. Tired as he was, with his shirt open, there seemed nothing in the man to fear. It was hard to know what he himself feared. He was proud as a turkey cock around other men, irritable and quick to pass an insult. Sitting on her bed, with his clothes unbuttoned, he seemed anything but tough.

"What was old Gus up to all afternoon?" he asked. "He never got back till sundown."

"The same thing you was just up to," Lorena said.

Jake lifted his eyebrows, not really surprised. "I knowed it, that scamp," he said. "Left me to work so he could come and pester you."

Lorena decided to tell it. That would be better than if he found it out from somebody else. Besides, though she considered herself his sweetheart, she didn't consider him her master. He had not really mastered anything except poking, though he had improved her card game a little.

"Gus offered me fifty dollars," she said.

Jake lifted his eyebrows again in his tired way, as if there was nothing he could possibly be told that would really surprise him. It angered her a little, his acting as if he knew everything in advance.

"He's a fool with money," Jake said.

"I turned him down," Lorena said. "I told him I was with you."

Jake's eyes came alive for a moment and he gave her a smart slap on the cheek, so quick she scarcely saw it coming. Though it stung her cheek, there was no real anger in it—it was nothing to some of the licks she had taken from Tinkersley. Jake hit her the once as if that was the rule in a game they were playing, and then the life went out of his eyes again and he looked at her with only a tired curiosity.

"I reckon he got his poke," he said. "If he didn't you can hit me a lick."

"We cut the cards for it and he cheated," Lorena said. "I can't prove it but I know it. He gave me the fifty dollars anyway."

"I ought to told you never to cut the cards with that old cud," Jake said. "Not unless you're ready for what he's ready for. He's the best card cheat I ever met. He don't cheat often, but when he does you ain't gonna catch him."

He wiped some of the mud off her belly. "Now that you're rich you can loan me twenty," he said.

"Why should I?" Lorena said. "You didn't earn it and you didn't stop it."

Besides, he had money from his own card playing. If she knew anything, it was not to give a man money. That was nothing more than an invitation to get sold with their help.

Jake looked amused. "Keep it then," he said. "But if it had been any other man than Gus I would have shot you."

"If you'd known," she said, getting up.

Jake stood looking out the window while she stripped the bed. He sipped his whiskey but didn't mention the trail again.

"Are you going with the herd?" she asked.

"Ain't decided," he said. "They'll be here till Monday."

"I plan to leave when you leave," she said. "With the herd or not."

Jake looked around. She was standing in her shift, a little red spot on one cheek where he had slapped her, a lick that made no impression on her at all. It seemed to him there was never much time with women. Before you could look at one twice, you were into an argument, and they were telling you what was going to happen.

"You'd look a sight in a cow camp," he said. "All them dern cowboys are in love with you anyway. I'd had to kill half of 'em before we got to the Red River, if you go along."

"They won't bother me," she said. "Gus is the only one with the guts to try it."

Jake chuckled. "Yes, he'd want to cut the cards twice a day," he said.

It seemed to him harder, as he got older, to find a simple way of life. On the one hand there were his friends, who expected something of him; on the other there was Lorie, who expected something else. He himself had no fixed ideas about what to do, though he thought it would be pleasant to live in a warm town where he could find a card game. Having a pretty woman to stay with made life happier, of course, but not if it meant having to take the woman to San Francisco.

Of course he could run: he wasn't chained to the bedpost or to the friends either. There was Mexico, right out the window. But what would that get him? Mexico was even more violent than Texas. Mexicans were always hanging Texans to make up for all the Mexicans Texans hung. If hanging was all he had to look forward to, he'd rather take his in Arkansas.

Lorie was watching him with a strange heat in her eyes. It wasn't because he had slapped her either. He felt she was reading his mind—somehow most women could read his mind. He had only really out-maneuvered one, a little redheaded whore in Cheyenne who was all heart and no brain. Lorena wasn't going to be fooled. Her look put him on the defensive. Most men would have beat her black and blue for what she had done that afternoon, and yet she hadn't even made an attempt to conceal it. She played by her own rules. It struck him that she might be the one to kill the sheriff from Arkansas, if it came to that. She wouldn't balk at it, if he could keep her wanting him.

"You don't need to stand there looking out of sorts," he said. "I won't run off without you."

"I ain't out of sorts," Lorena said. "You are. You don't want to stay and you don't want to go."

Jake looked at her mildly. "I've been up that way," he said. "It's rough. Why don't we go up to San Antonio and gamble for a spell?"

"Tinkersley took me there," Lorena said. "I don't want to go back."

"You're a hard one to please," Jake said, getting a little testy suddenly.

"I ain't," Lorena said. "You please me fine. I just want to go to San Francisco, like you promised."

"Well, if you don't like San Antone there's Austin, or Fort Worth," Jake said. "There's lots of nice towns that ain't as hard to get to as San Francisco."

"I don't care if it's hard," Lorena said. "Let's just go."

Jake sighed and offered her more of his whiskey. "Lay back down," he said. "I'll rub your back."

"I don't need my back rubbed," she said.

"Lorie, we can't leave tonight," he said. "I was just offering to be friendly."

She had not meant to press him so, but a decision had become important to her. She had spent too many nights in the little hot room they were in. Taking the gritty sheets off the bed made her realize it. She had changed them many times because the men she lay under were as gritty as Jake had been. It was something that had repeated itself once too often. Now she was done with it. She wanted to throw the sheets, and maybe the mattress and the bed, too, out the window. She was through with the room and everything that went with it, and Jake Spoon might as well know it.

"Honey, you look like you've caught a fever," Jake said, not realizing it was a fever of impatience to be done with Lonesome Dove and everything in it. "If you're set on it, I reckon we'll go, but I don't fancy living in no cow camp. Call wouldn't have it anyway. We can ride with them during the day and make our own camp."

Lorena was satisfied. Where they camped made no difference to her. Then Jake started talking about Denver, and how when they got there it would be easy to make their way across to San Francisco. She only half listened. Jake washed off as best he could in the little washbasin. She had only one spare sheet, so she put it on the bed while he was washing.

"Let's leave tomorrow," she said.

"But the herd don't leave till Monday," he reminded her.

"It ain't our herd," she said. "We don't have to wait for it."

There was something different about her, Jake had to admit. She had a beautiful face, a beautiful body, but also a distance in her such as he had never met in a woman. Certain mountains were that way, like the Bighorns. The air around them was so clear you could ride toward them for days without seeming to get any closer. And yet, if you kept riding, you would get to the mountains. He was not so sure he would ever get to Lorie. Even when she took him, there was a distance between them. And yet she would not let him leave.

When they blew out the lamp a shaft of moonlight came in the window and cut across their bodies. Lorie let him rub her back, since he enjoyed doing it. She was not sleepy. In her mind she had already left Lonesome Dove; she was simply waiting for the night to end so they could really leave. Jake got tired of the back rub and tried to roll her over for another poke but she wouldn't have it. She pushed his carrot away, a response he didn't like at all.

"What's the matter now?" he asked.

Lorie didn't answer. There was nothing to say. He made a second try and she pushed it away again. She knew he hated to be denied but didn't care. He would have to wait. Listening to his heavy, frustrated breathing, she thought for a while that he might be going to make a fight over it, but he didn't. His feelings were hurt, but pretty soon he yawned. He kept twisting and turning, hoping she would relent. From time to time he nudged her hip, as if by accident. But he had worked all day; he was tired. Soon he slept. Lorie lay awake, looking out the window, waiting for it to be time to leave.

21

JAKE AWOKE not long after dawn to find Lorena up before him. She sat at the foot of the bed, her face calm, watching the first red light stretch over the mesquite flats. He would have liked to sleep, to hide in sleep for several days, make no decisions, work no cattle, just drowse. But not even sleep was really under his control. The thought that he had to get up and leave town—with Lorie—was in the front of his mind, and it melted his drowsiness. For a minute or two he luxuriated in the fact that he was sleeping on a mattress. It might be a poor one stuffed with corn shucks, but it was better than he would get for the next several months. For months it would just be the ground, with whatever weather they happened to catch.

He looked at Lorie for a minute, thinking that perhaps if he scared her with Indian stories she would change her mind.

But when he raised up on one elbow to look at her in the fresh light, the urge to discourage her went away. It was a weakness, but he could not bear to disappoint women, even if it was ultimately for their own good. At least he couldn't disappoint them to their faces. Leaving them was his only out, and he knew he wasn't ready to leave Lorie. Her beauty blew the sleep right out of his brain, and all she was doing was looking out a window, her long golden hair spilling over her shoulders. She wore an old threadbare cotton shift that should have been thrown away long ago. She didn't own a decent dress, and had nothing to show her beauty to advantage, yet most of the men on the border would ride thirty miles just to sit in a saloon and look at her. She had the quality of not yet having really started her life—her face had a freshness unusual in a woman who had been sporting for a while. The thought struck him that the two of them might do well in San

Francisco, if they could just get there. There were men of wealth there, and Lorie's beauty would soon attract them.

"You don't look like you've changed your mind," he said. "I guess I've got to get up and go buy you a horse."

"Take my money," she said. "Don't get one that's too tall."

She gave him Gus's fifty dollars.

"Hell, I don't need all this," he said. "There ain't a horse in town worth fifty dollars, unless it's that mare of Call's, and she ain't for sale."

But he took the money, thinking it a fine joke on Gus that the money from his poke would buy Lorie a mount to ride to Montana, or however far they went. He had known perfectly well Gus would try something of the sort, for Gus would never let him have a woman to himself. Gus liked to be a rival more than anything else, Jake figured. And as for Lorie going through with it—well, it relieved him of a certain level of responsibility for her. If she was going to keep that much independence, so would he.

Lorena kept looking out the window. It was as if her mind had already left Lonesome Dove and moved up the trail. Jake sat up and put his arms around her. He loved the way she smelled in the mornings; he liked to sniff at her shoulders or her throat. He did it again. She didn't reject these little morning attentions, but she didn't encourage them either. She waited for him to leave and go buy the horse, running over in her mind the few things she could take with her.

There was not much. Her favorite thing was a mother-of-pearl comb Tinkersley had bought her when they first got to San Antonio. She had a thin gold ring that had been her mother's, and one or two other trifles. She had never liked to buy things; in Lonesome Dove it didn't matter, for there was nothing much to buy.

Jake sat and scratched himself for a while, smelling Lorie's flesh and hoping she would encourage him, but since she didn't, he finally got dressed and went off to see about horses and equipment.

Before Jake had been gone ten minutes Lorena got a surprise. There was a timid knock at her door. She opened it a peek and there was Xavier, standing on the stairs in tears. He just stood there looking as if it was the end of the world, tears running down his cheeks and dripping onto his shirt. She didn't know what to make of it, but since she wasn't dressed, she didn't want to let him in.

"Is it true, what Jake says?" he asked. "You are leaving today?"

Lorena nodded. "We're going to San Francisco," she said.

"I want to marry you," Xavier said. "Do not go. If you go I don't want to live. I will burn the place down. It's a filthy place anyway. I will burn it tomorrow."

Well, it's your place, she thought. Burn it if you want to. But she didn't say it. Xavier had not been unkind to her. He had given her a job when she didn't have a penny, and had paid promptly for whatever services he required. Now he was standing on the stairs, so wrought up he could hardly see.

"I'm going," she said.

Xavier shook his head in despair. "But Jake is not true," he said. "I know him. He will leave you somewhere. You will never get to San Francisco."

"I'll get there," Lorena said. "If Jake don't stay, I'll get there with someone else."

He shook his head. "You will die somewhere," he said. "He'll take you the wrong way. We could marry. I will sell this place. We can go to Galveston and take a boat for California. We can get a restaurant, there. I have Therese's money. We can get a clean restaurant, with tablecloths. You won't have to see men anymore."

Except I'd have to see you, she thought.

"Let me come in," he said. "I will give you anything . . . more than Gus."

She shook her head. "Jake would kill you," she said. "You go on now."

"I can't," he said, still crying. "I am dying for you. If he kills me I would be better. I will give you anything."

Again she shook her head, not quite sure what to think. She had seen Xavier have fits before, but usually fits of anger. This fit was different. His chest was heaving and his eyes poured tears.

"You should marry me," he said. "I will be good to you. I am not like these men. I have manners. You would see how kind I would be. I would never leave you. You could have an easy life."

Lorena just kept shaking her head. The most interesting thing he said was about the boat. She didn't know much, but she knew Galveston was closer than Denver. Why was Jake wanting to ride to Denver, if they could take a boat?

"You better leave," she said. "I don't want Jake to catch you up here. He might shoot you."

"No!" Xavier exclaimed. "I will shoot *him!* I have a shotgun. I will shoot him when he comes back if you don't let me in."

Lorena hardly knew what to think. It was crazy behavior. Xavier didn't seem to want to budge from the stairs. He did own a shotgun. It was not likely Jake would let someone as pitiful as Xavier shoot him, but then if he shot Xavier, that would be almost as bad. He already had his Arkansas trouble from shooting someone. They might not get to leave if there was a shooting, and Xavier looked desperate enough to do anything.

Then Xavier began to pull money out of his pocket. It was hard to say how much he held out to her, but it was a good deal more than fifty dollars. It might even be a hundred dollars. The sight of it made her feel tired. No matter what plans she made or how she tried to live, some man would always be looking at her and holding out money. Without giving it much thought, Mosby had started something that nothing seemed to stop. She thought Jake had stopped it, but he hadn't. His talk about killing men was just talk. If he had cared that much he would have shot Gus, friend or no friend. It was hard to believe he would even shoot Xavier—probably he would just give her another slap and forget about it.

"Please," Xavier said. "Please. I need you."

At least it might calm him down, she thought, opening the door. Also, he was usually quick as a rabbit when he came to her.

"I ain't messin' this bed," she said. "It's the last sheet."

Xavier didn't care. He put the money on her little chest of drawers and turned to her. Lorie shut the door and leaned against it, lifting her shift. With a grateful look Xavier dropped his pants. Soon his legs were trembling so she was afraid he would collapse before he was done. But he didn't. When he finished he put his head against her bosom for a moment, wetting her breasts with his tears even as she felt his drip on her thigh.

Then he stepped back and pulled up his pants.

"Goodbye," he said.

"Well, I ain't left yet," she said. "We're not going till afternoon."

Xavier looked at her once more, and left. His look startled her. It was like the look in her Pa's eyes, when he died in Baton Rouge. She watched him go down the stairs. He went slowly, as if feeling for each stair. He had scarcely been in her room two minutes, but her shift was wet with his tears. Men were all strange, but Xavier was stranger than many.

When he finally made it to the bottom she turned and hid the money. It was just one more secret she had from Jake.

22

LATE THAT AFTERNOON, as the boys were sitting around Bolivar's cook fire, getting their evening grub, Augustus looked up from his plate and saw Jake and Lorena ride into camp. They were riding two good horses and leading a pack horse. The most surprising thing was that Lorena was wearing pants. So far as he could remember, he had never seen a woman in pants, and he considered himself a man of experience. Call had his back turned and hadn't seen them, but some of the cowboys had. The sight of a woman in pants scared them so bad they didn't know where to put their eyes. Most of them began to concentrate heavily on the beans in their plates. Dish Boggett turned white as a sheet, got up without a word to anybody, got his night horse and started for the herd, which was strung out up the valley.

It was Dish's departure that got Call's attention. He looked around and saw the couple coming.

"We got you to thank for this," he said to Gus.

"I admit I was inspired," Augustus said. He knew his friend was in a silent fury, but he himself thought the visit might provide a little amusement. It had been in short supply lately. The only thing there had been to laugh at was Allen O'Brien getting pitched into a pile of prickly pears by a bronc. When he emerged he even had thorns in his beard.

But that was a normal hazard, the horses being unreliable and the prickly pear abundant.

A woman in pants was far more unusual. Jake rode right up to the cook fire, though Augustus could tell from his manner that he was nervous.

"Howdy, boys," he said. "Mind if we make a meal?"

"Course not, you're as welcome around here as money, Jake," Augustus said. "You and Lorie too."

Call watched the proceedings silently, unable to decide who he was more aggravated at, Gus or Jake. Surely the latter knew better than to bring a woman into a cow camp. It was difficult enough to keep men peaceful even if they didn't have a woman to argue about.

"Woodrow, you know Lorie, I reckon," Jake said, although he knew it wasn't true. Call's silence had always made him nervous.

"We've not met," Call said, touching his hat but not looking at the woman. He didn't want to get angry at Jake in front of all the hands, and all but Dish and the two Rainey boys were lounging around eating their evening meal. Or, at least, they *had* been lounging. Now they were sitting as stiffly as if they were in church. Some looked paralyzed. For a moment the only sound in the camp was the jingle of a bit as the woman's horse slung its head.

Augustus walked over to help Lorena dismount. The sight of the boys all sitting like statues made him want to laugh. The sudden appearance of a Comanche would not have affected them as much.

He recognized the brown mare Lorie rode as having belonged to Mary Pumphrey, the young widow.

"I would not have thought Mary would give up her mare," he said.

"Jake bought her," Lorena said, grateful that Gus had come over to offer her help. Jake had not so much as looked at her since they rode into camp. She had never seen Captain Call up close before, but she could tell Jake was mighty uneasy about him.

It depressed her a little that she was left to depend on Gus's courtesy from the very outset. He took her over to the cook fire and saw that she got a good helping of food, talking casually all the while, mainly about the qualities of the Pumphrey mare. Jake followed and got some grub but he was silent when he did it.

Still, it had felt good to ride out of Lonesome Dove. She had not seen Xavier again. The Dry Bean had been empty as they made their preparations. The pants had been Jake's idea. He had known a woman mule skinner in Montana who had worn pants.

While Jake had been fixing the pack horse Lippy had come out on the steps of the saloon and waved his lip at her one more time.

"I never tolt on you, Lorie," he said. He looked like he might cry too. You'll just have to cry, she thought. He took his bowler off and turned it around and around in his hand until it made her nervous.

"You'll have to pardon the grub," Augustus said. "Bol has learned to season but he forgot to learn to cook."

Bolivar was resting comfortably against a wagon wheel and ignored the sally. He was wavering in his mind whether to stay or go. He did not like travel—the thought of it made him unhappy. And yet, when he went home to Mexico he felt unhappy too, for his wife was disappointed in him and let him know it every day. He had never been sure what she wanted—after all, their children were beautiful—but whatever it was, he had not been able to give it to her. His daughters were his delight, but they would soon all marry and be gone, leaving him no protection from his wife. Probably he would shoot his wife if he went home. He had shot an irritating horse, right out from under himself. A man's patience sometimes simply snapped. He had shot the horse right between the ears and then found it difficult to get the saddle off, once the horse fell. Probably he would shoot his wife in the same way, if he went home. Many times he had been tempted to shoot one or another of the members of the Hat Creek outfit, but of course if he did that he would be immediately shot in return. Every day he thought he might go home, but he didn't. It was easier to stay and cut up a few snakes into the cook pot than to listen to his wife complain.

So he stayed, day by day, paying no attention to what anyone said. That in itself was a luxury he wouldn't have at home, for a disappointed woman was not easy to ignore.

Jake ate without tasting his food, wishing he had never come back to Lonesome Dove. It was going to be no pleasure riding north, if Call was so disapproving. He had meant to take Call aside and quietly explain it, but somehow he could not think of the best words to use. Call's silences had a way of making him lose track of his thoughts—some of which were perfectly good thoughts, in their way.

As they ate, the dusk deepened. Sean O'Brien, on the far side of the herd, began to sing his night song, an Irish melody whose words did not carry across the long plain where the cattle stood. But in the still night the sound carried; somehow it made Newt want to cry. He was sitting stiffly only a few feet from Lorena. He had been looking at her closely for the first time—hardly daring to, and yet feeling that he was safe because of the dusk. She was more beautiful than he had imagined, but she did not look happy—it gave him a painful feeling to see her unhappiness, and the song made it worse. His eyes filled up. It was no wonder Sean cried so much, Newt thought—his songs made you want to cry even when you couldn't hear the words.

"This is a lucky herd," Augustus said.

"And how is that?" Jake asked, a little testy. In some moods he could tolerate Gus's talk, but at other times the very sound of Gus's voice made him want to take out a gun and shoot the man. It was a loud voice—the sound of it made it hard to think, when it wasn't easy to think anyway. But the most aggravating aspect to it was that Gus always sounded cheerful, as if there was no trouble in the world that could catch him. At times when life seemed all trouble, the sight of Gus, untouched by all that went on around him, was difficult to bear.

"Why, it's the only herd on the trail that's got two Irish baritones to sing to it," Augustus said.

"He sings too sad," Needle Nelson said, for the sound of Sean's voice affected him as it had Newt. It brought to mind his mother, who had died when he was eight, and also a little sister he had been fond of, who had succumbed to a fever when only four.

"It's the Irish nature," Augustus said.

"No, it's just Sean," Allen O'Brien said. "He's just a crybaby."

Call came walking over. He felt he had to know what Jake meant to do.

"Well, Jake, have you made your plans?" he asked, being as formal as possible.

"Oh, we've decided to try our luck in Denver for the time being," Jake said. "I believe we'd both enjoy the cool weather."

"It's a hard trip," Call observed.

"Why tell that to Jake?" Augustus asked. "He's a traveled man and ain't put off by hardship. Feather beds ain't his style."

He had meant it as blatant irony, since of course feather beds were exactly Jake's style, but the discussion was so solemn that his flourish went unnoticed.

"We had hoped to sort of ease along with the bunch of you," Jake said, his eyes down. "We'll make our own camp, so as not to be in the way. Might could help out a little if things get tight. The water might be a little chancy, once we hit the plains."

"If I'd liked water better I guess I'd have stayed a riverboater, and you boys would have missed out on some choice conversation over the years," Augustus said.

"Hell, it's taken ten years off my life, listening to you talk," Jake said.

"Jake, you are surly tonight," Augustus said mildly. "I guess leaving the easy pickings around here has put you out of sorts."

Pea Eye was carefully whetting his bowie knife on the sole of one boot. Though they were still perfectly safe, as far as he knew, Pea had already begun to have bad dreams about the big Indian whose ferocity had haunted his sleep for years. The dreams had been so bad that he had already started sleeping with the unsheathed bowie knife in his hand, so he would be in the habit of it by the time they hit Indian country. This precaution caused certain problems for the young hands whose duty it was to wake him for his shift at night herding. It put them in danger of getting stabbed, a fact which troubled Jasper Fant particularly. Jasper was sensitive to danger. Usually he chose to wake Pea by kicking him in one foot, although even that wasn't really safe—Pea was tall and who knew when he might snap up and make a lunge. Jasper had concluded that the best way would be to pelt him with small rocks, although such caution would only earn him the scorn of the rest of the hands.

"I wouldn't have wanted to miss hearing you talk, Gus," Pea said, though he could not offhand remember a single thing Gus had said over the years. But he could remember, night after night, drowsing off to the sound of Gus's voice.

"I'm ready to start, if we got to start," Augustus said. "We got enough cattle now to stock five ranches."

Call knew that was true, but he found it difficult to resist running over to Mexico every few nights to add more cattle. They were easy to get, without Pedro Flores to contend with.

"It does seem a pity you're so independent, Jake," Augustus said. "If you come in with us you could be a cattle baron yet."

"Nope, I'd rather be pore than chew the dust," Jake said, standing up. Lorie stood up too. She felt her silence coming back. It was men watching her while trying to pretend they weren't watching her that brought it on. Few of them were bold enough just to look straight at her. They had to be sneaky about it. Being among them in the camp was worse than the saloon, where at least she had her room. In the camp there was nothing she could do but sit and listen to the talk pass her by.

"I guess we'll try to find a ridge to camp on," Jake said. "It would be nice to be upwind from these smelly beasts."

"Good God, Jake, if you're that finicky you ought to have been a barber," Augustus said. "Then you could smell hair oil and toilet water all day and never be offended." He walked over and helped Lorena mount. The brown mare was restless and kept slinging her head.

"I may take to barbering yet," Jake said, annoyed that Gus had seen fit to help Lorie again. She was going to have to learn to mount sometime, with over a thousand miles of riding ahead.

"I hope you'll come back for breakfast," Augustus said. "We eat about an hour before sunrise. Woodrow Call likes to put in a full day, as you may remember."

"For that matter we intend to have our breakfast sent out by the hotel," Jake said sarcastically, spurring his horse.

Call watched them go, annoyed. Augustus noticed, and chuckled.

"Even you can't stop inconvenient things from happening, Call," he said. "Jake can only be controlled up to a point, and Lorie's a woman. She can't be controlled at all."

Call didn't want to argue about it. He picked up his Henry and walked out of the circle of firelight, meaning to have a few minutes to himself. Passing behind the wagon, he bumped into Newt, who had evidently been holding his water while the woman was in camp and had just slipped off to relieve himself.

"Sorry, Captain," he said.

"You ought to go get Dish," Call said. "I don't know why he rode off. It ain't his shift. I guess we'll start tomorrow. We can't take all the cattle in Mexico."

He stood silently a moment. The mood to walk had left him.

Newt was surprised. The Captain never shared his decisions with him, and yet it seemed that the decision to leave had just been made, right there behind the wagon.

"Captain," he asked, "how far is it, up north?" It was something he couldn't stop wondering about, and since the Captain hadn't walked away, the question just popped out.

Then he immediately felt silly for asking it. "I guess it's a mighty far piece, up north," he said, as if to relieve the Captain of the need to answer.

It struck Call that they should have educated the boy a little better. He seemed to think north was a place, not just a direction. It was another of Gus's failings—he considered himself a great educator, and yet he rarely told anyone anything they needed to know.

"It's a ways farther than you've been," Call said, not sure the boy had ever been anywhere. Probably they had at least taken him to Pickles Gap at some point.

"Oh, I been north," Newt said, not wanting the Captain to think him completely untraveled. "I been north clear to San Antone—remember?"

Call remembered then—Deets had taken him once.

"Where we're going is a sight farther," he said.

23

"WELL, I'M GOING TO MISS WANZ," Augustus said, as he and Call were eating their bacon in the faint morning light. "Plus I already miss my Dutch ovens. You would want to move just as my sourdough got right at its prime."

"I'd like to think there's a better reason for living in a place than you being able to cook biscuits," Call said. "Though I admit they're good biscuits."

"You ought to admit it, you've et enough of them," Augustus said. "I still think we ought to just hire the town and take it with us. Then we'd have a good barkeep and someone to play the pianer."

With Call suddenly determined to leave that very day, Augustus found himself regretful, nostalgic already for things he hadn't particularly cared for but hated to think of losing.

"What about the well?" he asked. "Another month and we'd have it dug."

"We?" Call asked. "When did you hit a lick on that well?"

He looked around and saw to his astonishment that Augustus's two pigs were laying under the wagon, snuffling. In the half dark he had thought it was Bolivar snoring.

"Who asked them dern pigs?" he said.

"I guess they tracked us," Augustus said. "They're enterprising pigs."

"I guess you're planning to take them too?"

"It's still a free country," Augustus said. "They can come if they want the inconvenience. Wonder where Jake camped."

At that point the late shift came riding in—Newt, Pea, Dish Boggett and Jasper Fant, plus a fifth man, who hadn't been part of the shift.

"Why, it's Soupy Jones," Call said.

"Godamighty," Augustus said. "The man must of have lost his wits, what few he had."

Soupy had rangered with them a few months, before they quit. He was brave but lazy, a fine cardplayer, and by all odds the best horseman any of them had ever known. His love of being horseback was so strong that he could seldom be induced to dismount, except to sleep or eat.

"I thought Soupy married," Call said, as the boys unsaddled their night horses.

"That was the gossip," Augustus said. "Married a rich woman and became a sheriff, I heard. Well, maybe she run off with a preacher. If she didn't, I don't know why he's out this time of night."

Soupy, a short man, came walking over with Pea Eye.

"Look what rode up," Pea Eye said. "I near mistook him for a bandit since it was pitch-dark."

"'I god, Soupy, you should have waited till we lit the lanterns," Augustus said, standing up to shake hands. "A sharp bunch of gun hands like us, you're lucky not to be shot."

"Aw, Gus," Soupy said, not knowing what else to say. He had always been nonplused by Gus's witticisms.

"Morning, Captain," he said, as Call shook his hand.

"Have some grub," Call said. He had always been fond of the man, despite his unwillingness to dismount if there was something to do on the ground.

"Where'd you come from, Soupy?" Augustus asked. "Didn't we hear you was mayor of someplace. Or was it governor?"

"I was just in Bastrop, Gus," Soupy said. "Bastrop don't have no mayor, or governor either. It's barely a town."

"Well, we're barely an outfit," Augustus said, "though we got two fine pigs that just joined us last night. Are you looking for employment?"

"Yes, my wife died," Soupy said. "She was never strong," he added, in the silence that followed the remark.

"Well, you're hired, at least," Call said.

"I lost two wives myself," Augustus remarked.

"I heard Jake was around but I don't see him," Soupy said. He and Jake had been close buddies once, and it was partly curiosity about him that made Soupy want to rejoin the Hat Creek outfit.

"Well, he is," Call said, not anxious to have to explain the situation.

"Jake won't camp with us old cobs," Augustus said. "He's traveling with a valet, if you know what that is."

"No, but if it's traveling with Jake I bet it wears skirts," Soupy said—a remark which for some reason seemed to catch everybody wrong. Or everybody but Gus, who laughed long and hard. Feeling a little confused, but happy to have been hired, Soupy went off with Pea Eye to get breakfast.

"I'm going in and pry up that sign I wrote so we can take it with us," Augustus said. "I may pry up one of my Dutch ovens and bring it too."

"Bol ain't said that he's going," Call said. It was a mild anxiety. If Bol quit and they had to depend on Gus to do the cooking, the whole trip would be in jeopardy. Apart from biscuits, his cooking was of the sort that caused tempers to flare.

In fact, Bolivar was standing by the cook fire, staring into it with an expression of deep gloom. If he heard the remark he gave no sign.

"Oh, Bol's got the adventurer's spirit," Augustus said. "He'll go. If he don't, he'll just have to go home and whet his wife more often than he cares to."

With that he went and got the two mules that constituted their wagon team. The bigger mule, a gray, was named Greasy, and the smaller, a bay, they called Kick Boy, out of respect for his lightning rear hooves. They had not been worked very much, there seldom having been a need to take the wagon anywhere. It was theoretically for rent, but rarely got rented more than once a year. Greasy and Kick Boy were an odd-looking team, the former being nearly four hands higher than the latter. Augustus hitched them to the wagon, while Call went to inspect the remuda, meaning to weed out any horses that looked sickly.

"Don't weed out too many," Augustus said. "We might need to eat 'em."

Dish Boggett, who had had little sleep and had not enjoyed the little, found the remark irritating.

"Why would we need to eat the dern horses, with three thousand cattle right in front of us?" he asked. He had spent hours riding around the herd, with a tight wad of anger in his breast.

"I can't say, Dish," Augustus said. "We might want to change our fare, for all I know. Or the Sioux Indians might run off the cattle. Of course, they might run off the horses too."

"Happened to us in that Stone House fight," Pea remarked. "They set fire to the grass and I couldn't see a dern thing."

"Well, I ain't you," Dish informed him. "I bet I could see my own horse, fire or no fire."

"I'm going to town," Augustus said. "You boys will stand and jabber all day. Any of you want anything brought? It has to be something that will fit in this wagon."

"Bring me five hundred dollars, that'll fit," Jasper said.

There was general laughter, which Augustus ignored. "What I ought to bring is a few coffins," he said. "Most of you boys will probably be drownt before we hit the Powder River."

"Bring a few jugs, if you see any," Jasper said. The fear of drowning was strong in him, and Gus's remark spoiled his mood.

"Jasper, I'll bring a boat if I notice one," Augustus said. He caught Bolivar staring at him malevolently.

"Come on, if you're coming, Bol," he said. "No reason for you to go north and drown."

Bol was indeed feeling terrible. They only talked of going, not of coming back. It might be he would never see Mexico again, or his lovely daughters, if he left. And yet, when he looked across the river and thought of his village, he just felt tired. He was too tired to deal with a disappointed woman, and much too tired to be a bandit.

Instead of climbing in the wagon, he turned away and sat down near the pigs. They had found a cool spot where the water barrel had dripped, and were lying on their stomachs, watching the proceedings alertly.

"If I ain't back in a month, you girls feel free to start without me," Augustus said. Then he drove off, amused that Dish Boggett looked so out of sorts just from being in love with a woman who didn't want him. It was a peril too common to take seriously.

A half mile from the main camp he came upon the very woman who had given Dish the pain. She was attempting to cook some fryback, and was getting no help from Jake Spoon, who hadn't even provided her with a good fire. Jake was sitting on his bedding, his hair sticking up in back, trying to dig a thorn out of his hand with a pocketknife.

Augustus stopped the team and got down to chat a minute.

"Jake, you look like you slept standing on your head," he said. "Is that a bullet you're digging out? Has she shot you already?"

"Who invited you to breakfast?" Jake said.

"I've et," Augustus said. "I just stopped by to set the table, so you two could dine in style."

"Hello, Gus," Lorie said.

"Don't start no conversation, else he'll stay all day," Jake said. "I'd forgotten what a pest you are, Gus."

He had got the thorn in his thumb hobbling the horses the night before, and had been unable to get it out in the dark. Now his thumb was swollen to twice its size, for a green mesquite thorn was only slightly less poisonous than a rattlesnake. Besides, he had slept badly on the stony ground, and Lorie had refused him again, when all he wanted was a little pleasure to take his mind off his throbbing thumb. They were camped only two miles from town and could easily have ridden back and slept comfortably in the Dry Bean, but when he suggested it Lorie showed her stubborn streak and refused. He could go back if he cared to—she wasn't. So he had stayed and slept poorly, worrying most of the night about snakes. As much camping as he had done, it was a fear that never left him.

"It's a wonder you ain't froze to death years ago, if that's the best fire you can make," Augustus said. He began to gather sticks.

"You don't need to bother," Lorena said. "I've already burned the meat." It was good Gus had stopped, for Jake was in a temper already, just because she had turned away from him the night before. He had a quick pride; any refusal made him angry. As for sleeping on the ground, she didn't mind. It was at least fairly cool.

"I never expected to find you to be still in bed at this hour, Jake," Augustus said. "You'll have a time keeping up with us if you don't improve your habits. By the way, Soupy hired on this morning. He inquired about you."

"There goes the easy money," Jake said. "Soupy will win ever cent you boys can earn in the next ten years. He's been known to win from me, and that ain't easy."

"Well, I'm going to town," Augustus said. "Want me to pick you up a Bible or a few hymnbooks?"

"Nope, we're leaving," Jake said. "Soon as we pack."

"That won't be soon," Augustus said. "You've scattered stuff over three acres just making this one little camp."

That was true. They had unpacked in the dark and made a mess of it. Jake was looking for a whiskey bottle that wasn't where he thought he'd put it. It was plain camping wasn't a neat way of life. There was no place to wash, and they were carrying very little water, which was the main reason she had refused Jake. She liked a wash and felt he could wait until they camped near a river and could splash a little of the dust off before bedding down.

Augustus watched them eat the poor burned breakfast. It was eternally amusing, the flow of human behavior. Who could have predicted Jake would be the one to take Lorena out of Lonesome Dove? She had been meaning to leave since the day she arrived, and now Jake, who had slipped from the grasp of every woman who had known him, was firmly caught by a young whore from Alabama.

The quality of determination had always intrigued him. Lorie had it, and Jake didn't. Hers was nothing compared to W. F. Call's, but hers would probably be sufficient to get her to San Francisco, where no doubt she would end up a respectable woman.

After accepting a cup of coffee from Lorie, he took a look at Jake's thumb, which was swollen and turning white.

"You better be sure you got all that thorn out," Gus said. "If you didn't you'll probably lose the hand, and maybe the arm that goes with it."

"I won't lose no arm, and if I did I could still beat you dealing one-handed," Jake said. "I hope you invite us to breakfast one of these days, to repay the favor."

When Augustus reached Lonesome Dove, the one street was still and empty, with only one horse twitching its tail in front of the Pumphreys' store. The dust his wagon stirred hung straight as a column before settling back into the street. Augustus stopped in front of the deserted blacksmith shop. The blacksmith, an uncommunicative man named Roy Royce, had ridden out of town some months before and had not come back.

Augustus found a small crowbar among the tools the man had cavalierly abandoned, and rode up the street to the Hat Creek corrals, where he easily pried his sign off the fence. The Dutch ovens were more resistant. They showed signs of crumbling, so he left them. There would be no time for leisurely biscuit making on the trail anyway.

He walked through the house and had a look at the roofless barn, amused at how little trace remained of their ten years' residence. They had lived the whole time as if they might leave at any minute, and now that was exactly what they had done. The barn would stay roofless, the well only partially dug. The rattlesnakes could take the springhouse, for all he cared—he had already removed his whiskey jug. It would be a while before he had such a good shady porch to sit on, drinking the afternoon out. In Texas he had drunk to take his mind off the heat; in Montana, no doubt, it would be to take his mind off the cold. He didn't feel sad. The one thing he knew about Texas was that he was lucky to be leaving it alive—and, in fact, he had a long way to go before he could be sure of accomplishing that much.

He drove down to the saloon for a last word with Xavier. At first he thought the saloon was empty, but then he saw Xavier sitting at a little table near the shadowy end of the bar. He had not bothered to shave for two days, a sign of profound demoralization.

"Dern, Wanz, you look poorly," Augustus said. "I see the morning rush ain't started yet."

"It will never start," Xavier said in a desperate voice.

"Just because you lost your whore don't mean the sun won't rise again," Augustus assured him. "Take a trip to San Antonio and recruit another whore."

"I would have married her," Xavier said, feeling too hopeless even to conceal that he was hopeless.

"I ain't surprised," Augustus said gently. It was one thing to make light of a young man's sorrows in love, but another to do it when the sorrower was Xavier's age. There were men who didn't get over women. He himself, fortunately, was not one of them, though he had felt fairly black for a year after Clara married. It was curious, for Xavier had had stuff enough to survive a hellion like Therese, but was devastated by the departure of Lorena, who could hardly, with reason, have been expected to stay in one room over a saloon all her life.

"I would have taken her to San Francisco," Xavier said. "I would have given her money, bought her clothes."

"In my opinion the woman made a poor bargain," Augustus said. "I seen her not an hour ago, trying to cook over a dern smoky fire. But then we don't look at life like women do, Wanz. They don't always appreciate convenience."

Xavier shrugged. Gus often talked about women, but he had never listened and didn't intend to start. It wouldn't bring Lorena back, or make him feel less hopeless. It had seemed a miracle, the day she walked in the door, with nothing but her beauty. From the first he had planned to marry her someday. It didn't matter that she was a whore. She had intelligence, and he felt sure her intelligence would one day guide her to him. She would see, in time, how much kinder he was than other men; she would recognize that he treated her better, loved her more.

Yet it hadn't worked. She went with him willingly enough when he requested it, but no more willingly than she went with other men. Then Jake had come and taken her, just taken her, as easily as picking a hat off a rack. Often Xavier had passed the boring hours by dreaming of how happy Lorie would be when he made his proposal, offering to free her from whoring and every form of drudgery. But when he offered, she had merely shaken her head, and now his dreams were ruined.

He remembered that when he declared his love her eyes hadn't changed at all—it was as if he had suggested she sweep out the bar. She had only tolerated him to avoid a scene with Jake, and had seemed scarcely aware that he had given her nearly two hundred dollars, four times as much as Gus. It was enough to buy her passage to San Francisco. But she had merely taken it and shut the door. It was cruel, love.

"Well, it's too bad you ain't a cowboy," Augustus said. "You look like you could use a change of air. Where's Lippy?"

Xavier shrugged. The last thing that would interest him was the whereabouts of Lippy.

Augustus drank a glass but said no more. He knew he could not talk Xavier out of his depression.

"If Jake gets killed, tell her I will come," Xavier said—there was always that prospect. After all, he had only met Therese because her first husband had fallen off a roof and broken his neck. A man like Jake, a traveler and a gambler, might meet a violent end at any time.

"I doubt it'll happen," Augustus said, not wishing to encourage faint hopes.

When he went out he found Lippy sitting in the wagon with his bowler on his head.

"How'd you get in my wagon?" Augustus asked.

"Jumped off the roof and this is where I landed," Lippy said. He liked to joke.

"Jump back on the roof then," Augustus said. "I'm going to Montana."

"I'm hiring on," Lippy said. "The pianer playin's over around here. Wanz won't feed me and I can't cook. I'll starve to death."

"It might beat drowning in the Republican River," Augustus said. Lippy had a little bag packed and sitting between his feet. It was clear he was packed and ready.

"Let's go," he said.

"Well, we got two Irishmen, I guess we can always use a man with a hole in his stomach," Augustus said. Lippy had been a fair horseman once. Maybe Call would let him look after the remuda.

As they rode out of town the widow Cole was hanging out her washing. Hot as the sun was, it seemed to Augustus it would be dry before she got it on the line. She kept a few goats, one of which was nibbling on the rope handle of her laundry basket. She was an imposing woman, and he felt a pang of regret that he and she had not got on better, but the truth was they fell straight into argument even if they only happened to meet in the street. Probably her husband, Joe Cole, had bored her for twenty years, leaving her with a taste for argument. He himself enjoyed argument, but not with a woman who had been bored all her life. It could lead to a strenuous existence.

As they passed out of town, Lippy suddenly turned sentimental. Under the blazing sun the town looked white—the only things active in it were the widow and her goats. There were only about ten buildings, hardly enough to make a town, but Lippy got sentimental anyway. He remembered when there had been another saloon, one that kept five Mexican whores. He had gone there often and had great fun in the days before he got the wound in his belly. He had never forgotten the merry whores—they were always sitting on his lap. One of them, a girl named Maria, would sleep with him merely because she liked the way he played the piano. Those had been the years.

At the thought of them his eyes teared up, making his last look at Lonesome Dove a watery one. The dusty street wavered in his vision as if under a heavy rain.

Augustus happened to notice that Lippy was crying, tears running down both sides of his nose into the floppy pocket of his lip. Lippy normally cried when he got drunk, so the sight was nothing new, except that he didn't seem drunk. "If you're sick you can't go," he said sternly. "We don't want no sickly hands."

"I ain't sick, Gus," Lippy said, a little embarrassed by his tears. Soon he felt a little better. Lonesome Dove was hidden—he could barely see the top of the little church house across the chaparral flats.

"It's funny, leaving a place, ain't it?" he said. "You never do know when you'll get back."

24

ALTHOUGH HE KNEW they wouldn't leave until the heat of the day was over, Newt felt so excited that he didn't miss sleep and could hardly eat. The Captain had made it final: they were leaving that day. He had told all the hands that they ought to see to their equipment; once they got on the trail, opportunities for repair work might be scarce.

In fact, the advice only mattered to the better-equipped hands: Dish, Jasper, Soupy Jones and Needle Nelson. The Spettle brothers, for example, had no equipment at all, unless you called one pistol with a broken hammer equipment. Newt had scarcely more; his saddle was an old one and he had no slicker and only one blanket for a bedroll. The Irishmen had nothing except what they had been loaned.

Pea seemed to think the only important equipment was his bowie knife, which he spent the whole day sharpening. Deets merely got a needle and some pieces of rawhide and sewed a few rawhide patches on his old quilted pants.

When they saw Mr. Augustus ride up with Lippy, some of the hands thought it might be a joke, but the Captain at once put him in charge of the horses, an action that moved Dish Boggett to scorn.

"Half the remuda will run off once they see him flop that lip," he said.

Augustus was inspecting the feet of his main horse, a large buckskin he called old Malaria, not a graceful mount but a reliable one.

"It might surprise you, Dish," he said, "but Lippy was once a considerable hand. I wouldn't talk if I were you. You may end up with a hole in your own stomach and have to play whorehouse piano for a living."

"If I do I'll starve," Dish said. "I never had the opportunity of piano lessons."

Once it was clear he was not going to be constantly affronted by the sight of Jake and Lorena, Dish's mood improved a little. Since they were traveling along the same route, an opportunity might yet arise to demonstrate that he was a better man than Jake Spoon. She might need to be saved from a flood or a grizzly bear—grizzly bears were often the subject of discussion around the campfire at night. No one had ever seen one, but all agreed they were almost impossible to kill. Jasper Fant had taken to worrying about them constantly, if only as a change from worrying about drowning.

Jasper's obsession with drowning had begun to oppress them all. He had talked so much about it that Newt had come to feel it would be almost a miracle if someone didn't drown at every river.

"Well, if we see one of them bears, Pea can stick him with that knife he keeps sharpening," Bert Borum said. "It ought to be sharp enough to kill a dern elephant by now."

Pea took the criticism lightly. "It never hurts to be ready," he said, quoting an old saying of the Captain's.

Call himself spent the day on the mare, weeding out the weaker stock, both cattle and horses. He worked with Deets. About noon, they were resting under a big mesquite tree. Deets was watching a little Texas bull mount a cow not far away. The little bull hadn't come from Mexico. He had wandered in one morning, unbranded, and had immediately whipped three larger bulls that attempted to challenge him. He was not exactly rainbow-colored, but his hide was mottled to an unusual extent—part brown, part red, part white, and with a touch here and there of yellow and black. He looked a sight, but he was all bull. Much of the night he could be heard baying; the Irishmen had come to hate him, since his baying drowned out their singing.

In fact, none of the cowboys liked him—he would occasionally charge a horse, if his temper was up, and was even worse about men on foot. Once, Needle Nelson had dismounted meaning to idle away a minute or two relieving himself, and the little bull had charged him so abruptly that Needle had had to hop back on his horse while still pissing. All the hands had a fine laugh at his expense. Needle had been so angered that he wanted to rope and cut the bull, but Call intervened. Call thought the bull well made though certainly a peculiar mix of colors, and wanted to keep him.

"Let him be," he said. "We'll need some bulls in Montana."

Augustus had been highly amused. "Good God, Call," he said. "You mean you want to fill this paradise we're going to with animals that look like that?"

"He ain't bad-looking if you don't count his color," Call said.

"Be damned to his color and his disposition too," Needle said. He knew he would be a long time living down having to mount his horse with his dingus flopping.

"Well, I reckon it's time to go," Call said to Deets. "We'll never get there if we don't start."

Deets was not so sure they would get there anyway, but he kept his doubts to himself. The Captain usually managed to do what he meant to do.

"I want you to be the scout," the Captain said. "We got plenty of men to keep the stock moving. I want you to find us water and a good bed ground every night."

Deets nodded modestly, but inside he felt proud. Being made scout was more of an honor than having your name on a sign. It was proof that the Captain thought highly of his abilities.

When they got back to the wagon Augustus was oiling his guns. Lippy fanned himself with his bowler, and most of the other hands were just sitting around wishing it was cooler.

"Have you counted the stock yet?" Call asked Augustus. The man possessed a rare skill when it came to counting animals. He could ride through a herd and count it, something Call had never been able to do.

"No, I ain't got around to that task," Augustus said. "Maybe I will if you tell me what difference it makes."

"It would be useful to know how many we're starting out with," Call said. "If we get there with ninety percent we'll be lucky."

"Yes, lucky if we get there with ninety percent of ourselves," Augustus said. "It's your show, Call. Myself, I'm just along to see the country."

Dish Boggett had been dozing under the wagon. He sat up so abruptly that he bumped his head on the bottom of the wagon. He had had a terrible dream in which he had fallen off a cliff. The dream had started nice, with him riding along on the point of a herd of cattle. The cattle had become buffalo and the buffalo had started running. Soon they began to pour over a cutbank of some kind. Dish saw it in plenty of time to stop his horse, but his horse wouldn't stop, and before he knew it he went off the bank, too. The ground was so far below, he could barely see it. He fell and fell, and to make matters worse his horse turned over in the air, so that Dish was upside down and on the bottom. Just as he was about to be mashed, he woke up, lathered in sweat.

"See what I mean?" Augustus said. "Dish has already cracked his noggin and we ain't even left."

Call got a plate of food and went off by himself to eat. It was something he had always done—moved apart, so he could be alone and think things out a little. In the old days, when he first developed the habit, the men had not understood. Occasionally one would follow him, wanting to chat. But they soon learned better—nothing made Call sink deeper into silence than for someone to come around and start yapping when he wanted to be by himself.

Virtually all his life he had been in the position of leading groups of men, yet the truth was he had never liked groups. Men he admired for their abilities in action almost always brought themselves down in his estimation if he had to sit around and listen to them talk—or watch them drink or play cards or run off after women. Listening to men talk usually made him feel more alone than if he were a mile away by himself under a tree. He had never really been able to take part in the talk. The endless talk of cards and women made him feel more set apart—and even a little vain. If that was the best they could think of, then they were lucky they had him to lead them. It seemed immodest, but it was a thought that often came to him.

And the more he stayed apart, the more his presence made the men nervous.

"It's hard for normal men to relax around you, Call," Augustus told him once. "You ain't never been relaxed yourself, so you don't know what you're missing."

"Pshaw," Call said. "Pea goes to sleep around me half the time. I guess that's relaxed."

"No, that's worn out," Augustus said. "If you didn't work him sixteen hours a day he'd be as nervous as the rest."

When Call had eaten, he took his plate back to Bolivar, who seemed to have decided to go along. He had made no move to leave, at least. Call wanted him along, and yet somehow didn't feel quite right about it. It didn't seem proper that a man with a wife and daughters would go away without even informing them, on a journey from which he might never return. The old *pistolero* didn't owe the Hat Creek outfit that kind of effort, and Call reluctantly raised the subject with him.

"Bol, we're leaving today," he said. "You can have your wages, if you'd rather."

Bol just looked annoyed, shook his head and didn't say a word.

"I'm glad you're with us, Bol," Augustus said. "You'll make a fine Canadian."

"What is Canada?" Charlie Rainey asked. He had never been sure.

"The land of the northern lights," Augustus said. The heat had caused a dearth of conversation and made him welcome almost any question.

"What's them?" the boy wondered.

"Why, they light up the sky," Augustus said. "I don't know if you can see 'em from Montany."

"I wonder when we'll see Jake again?" Pea Eye said. "That Jake sure don't keep still."

"He was just here yesterday, we don't need to marry him," Dish said, unable to conceal his irritation at the mere mention of the man.

"Well, I've oiled my guns," Augustus said. "We might as well go and put the Cheyenne nation to flight, if the Army hasn't."

Call didn't answer.

"Ain't you even sorry to leave this place, now that we've made it so peaceful?" Augustus asked.

"No," Call said. "We ought to left right after we come."

It was true. He had no affection for the border, and a yearning for the plains, dangerous as they were.

"It's a funny life," Augustus said. "All these cattle and nine-tenths of the horses is stolen, and yet we was once respected lawmen. If we get to Montana we'll have to go into politics. You'll wind up governor if the dern place ever gets to be a state. And you'll spend all your time passing laws against cattle thieves."

"I wish there was a law I could pass against you," Call said.

"I don't know what Wanz is going to do without us," Augustus said.

25

IN THE LATE AFTERNOON they strung a rope corral around the remuda, so each hand could pick himself a set of mounts, each being allowed four picks. It was slow work, for Jasper Fant and Needle Nelson could not make up their minds. The Irishmen and the boys had to take what was left after the more experienced hands had chosen.

Augustus did not deign to make a choice at all. "I intend to ride old Malaria all the way," he said, "or if not I'll ride Greasy."

Once the horses were assigned, the positions had to be assigned as well.

"Dish, you take the right point," Call said. "Soupy can take the left and Bert and Needle will back you up."

Dish had assumed that, as a top hand, he would have a point, and no one disputed his right, but both Bert and Needle were unhappy that Soupy had the other point. They had been with the outfit longer, and felt aggrieved.

The Spettle boys were told to help Lippy with the horse herd, and Newt, the Raineys and the Irishmen were left with the drags. Call saw that each of them had bandanas, for the dust at the rear of the herd would be bad.

They spent an hour patching on the wagon, a vehicle Augustus regarded with scorn. "That dern wagon won't get us to the Brazos," he said.

"Well, it's the only wagon we got," Call said.

"You didn't assign me no duties, nor yourself either," Augustus pointed out.

"That simple," Call said. "I'll scare off bandits and you can talk to Indian chiefs."

"You boys let these cattle string out," he said to the men. "We ain't in no big hurry."

Augustus had ridden through the cattle and had come back with a count of slightly over twenty-six hundred.

"Make it twenty-six hundred cattle and two pigs," he said. "I guess we've seen the last of the dern Rio Grande. One of us ought to make a speech, Call. Think of how long we've rode this river."

Call was not willing to indulge him in any dramatics. He mounted the mare and went over to help the boys get the cattle started. It was not a hard task. Most of the cattle were still wild as antelope and instinctively moved away from the horsemen. In a few minutes they were on the trail, strung out for more than a mile. The point riders soon disappeared in the low brush.

Lippy and the Spettle boys were with the wagon. With the dust so bad, they intended to keep the horses a fair distance behind.

Bolivar sat on the wagon seat, his ten-gauge across his lap. In his experience trouble usually came quick, when it came, and he meant to keep the ten-gauge handy to discourage it.

Newt had heard much talk of dust, but had paid little attention to it until they actually started the cattle. Then he couldn't help noticing it, for there was nothing else to notice. The grass was sparse, and every hoof sent up its little spurt of dust. Before they had gone a mile he himself was white with it, and for moments actually felt lost, it was so thick. He had to tie the bandana around his nose to get a good breath. He understood why Dish and the other boys were so anxious to draw assignments near the front of the herd. If the dust was going to be that bad all the way, he might as well be riding to Montana with his eyes shut. He would see nothing but his own horse and the few cattle that happened to be within ten yards of him. A grizzly bear could walk in and eat him and his horse both, and they wouldn't be missed until breakfast the next day.

But he had no intention of complaining. They were on their way, and he was part of the outfit. After waiting for the moment so long, what was a little dust?

Once in a while, though, he dropped back a little. His bandana got sweaty, and the dust caked on it so that he felt he was inhaling mud. He had to take it off and beat it against his leg once in a while. He was riding Mouse, who looked like he could use a bandana of his own. The dust seemed to make the heat worse, or else the heat made the dust worse.

The second time he stopped to beat his bandana, he happened to notice Sean leaning off his horse as if he were trying to vomit. The horse and Sean were both white, as if they had been rolled in powder, though the horse Sean rode was a dark bay.

"Are you hurt?" he asked anxiously.

"No, I was trying to spit," Sean said. "I've got some mud in my mouth. I didn't know it would be like this."

"I didn't either," Newt said.

"Well, we better keep up," he added nervously—he didn't want to neglect his responsibilities. Then, to his dismay, he looked back and saw twenty or thirty cattle standing behind them. He had ridden right past them in the dust. He immediately loped back to get them, hoping the Captain hadn't noticed. When he turned back, two of the wild heifers spooked. Mouse, a good cow horse, twisted and jumped a medium-sized chaparral bush in an effort to gain a step on the cows. Newt had not expected the jump and lost both stirrups, but fortunately diverted the heifers so that they turned back into the main herd. He found his heart was beating fast, partly because he had almost been thrown and partly because he had nearly left thirty cattle behind. With such a start, it seemed to him he would be lucky to get to Montana without disgracing himself.

Call and Augustus rode along together, some distance from the herd. They were moving through fairly open country, flats of chaparral with only here and there a strand of mesquite. That would soon change: the first challenge would be the brush country, an almost impenetrable band of thick mesquite between them and San Antonio. Only a few of the hands were experienced in the brush, and a bad run of some kind might cost them hundreds of cattle.

"What do you think, Gus?" Call asked. "Think we can get through the brush, or had we better go around?"

Augustus looked amused. "Why, these cattle are like deer, only faster," he said. "They'll get through the brush fine. The problem will be the hands. Half of them will probably get their eyes poked out."

"I still don't know what you think," Call said.

"The problem is, I ain't used to being consulted," Augustus said. "I'm usually sitting on the porch drinking whiskey at this hour. As for the brush, my choice would be to go through. It's that or go down to the coast and get et by the mosquitoes."

"Where do you reckon Jake will end up?" Call asked.

"In a hole in the ground, like you and me," Augustus said.

"I don't know why I ever ask you a question," Call said.

"Well, last time I seen Jake he had a thorn in his hand," Augustus said. "He was wishing he'd stayed in Arkansas and taken his hanging."

They rode up on a little knobby hill and stopped for a moment to watch the cattle. The late sun shone through the dust cloud, making the white dust rosy. The riders to each side of the herd were spread wide, giving the cattle lots of room. Most of them were horned stock, thin and light, their hides a mixture of colors. The riders at the rear were all but hidden in the rosy dust.

"Them boys on the drags won't even be able to get down from their horses unless we take a spade and spade 'em off a little," Augustus said.

"It won't hurt 'em," Call said. "They're young."

In the clear late afternoon light they could see all the way back to Lonesome Dove and the river and Mexico. Augustus regretted not tying a jug to his saddle— he would have liked to sit on the little hill and drink for an hour. Although Lonesome Dove had not been much of a town, he felt sure that a little whiskey would have made him feel sentimental about it.

Call merely sat on the hill, studying the cattle. It was clear to Augustus that he was not troubled in any way by leaving the border or the town.

"It's odd I partnered with a man like you, Call," Augustus said. "If we was to meet now instead of when we did, I doubt we'd have two words to say to one another."

"I wish it could happen, then, if it would hold you to two words," Call said. Though everything seemed peaceful, he had an odd, confused feeling at the thought of what they had undertaken. He had quickly convinced himself it was necessary, this drive. Fighting the Indians had been necessary, if Texas was to be settled. Protecting the border was necessary, else the Mexicans would have taken south Texas back.

A cattle drive, for all its difficulty, wasn't so imperative. He didn't feel the old sense of adventure, though perhaps it would come once they got beyond the settled country.

Augustus, who could almost read his mind, almost read it as they were stopped on the little knob of a hill.

"I hope this is hard enough for you, Call," he said. "I hope it makes you happy. If it don't, I give up. Driving all these skinny cattle all that way is a funny way to maintain an interest in life, if you ask me."

"Well, I didn't," Call said.

"No, but then you seldom ask," Augustus said. "You should have died in the line of duty, Woodrow. You'd know how to do that fine. The problem is you don't know how to live."

"Whereas you do?" Call asked.

"Most certainly," Augustus said. "I've lived about a hundred to your one. I'll be a little riled if I end up being the one to die in the line of duty, because this ain't my duty and it ain't yours, either. This is just fortune hunting."

"Well, we wasn't finding one in Lonesome Dove," Call said. He saw Deets returning from the northwest, ready to lead them to the bed-ground. Call was glad to see him—he was tired of Gus and his talk. He spurred the mare on off the hill. It was only when he met Deets that he realized Augustus hadn't followed. He was still sitting on old Malaria, back on the little hill, watching the sunset and the cattle herd.

PART II

26

JULY JOHNSON HAD BEEN RAISED not to complain, so he didn't complain, but the truth of the matter was, it had been the hardest year of his life: a year in which so many things went wrong that it was hard to know which trouble to pay attention to at any given time.

His deputy, Roscoe Brown—forty-eight years of age to July's twenty-four—assured him cheerfully that the increase in trouble was something he had better get used to.

"Yep, now that you've turned twenty-four you can't expect no mercy," Roscoe said.

"I don't expect no mercy," July said. "I just wish things would go wrong one at a time. That way I believe I could handle it."

"Well, you shouldn't have got married then," Roscoe said.

It struck July as an odd comment. He and Roscoe were sitting in front of what passed for a jail in Fort Smith. It just had one cell, and the lock on that didn't work—when it was necessary to jail someone they had to wrap a chain around the bars.

"I don't see what that has to do with it," July said. "Anyway, how would you know? You ain't never been married."

"No, but I got eyes," Roscoe said. "I can see what goes on around me. You went and got married and the next thing you know you turned yellow. Makes me glad I stayed a bachelor. You're still yellow," he went on to point out.

"It ain't Elmira's fault I got jaundice," July said. "I caught it in Missouri at that dern trial."

It was true that he was still fairly yellow, and fairly weak, and Elmira was losing patience with both states.

"I wish you'd turn back white," she had said that morning, although he was noticeably less jaundiced than he had been two weeks before. Elmira was short, skinny, brunette, and had little patience. They had only been married four months, and one of the surprises, from July's point of view, was her impatience. She wanted the chores done immediately, whereas he had always proceeded at a methodical pace. The first time she bawled him out about his slowness was only two days after the wedding. Now it seemed she had lost whatever respect she had ever had for him. Once in a while it occurred to him that she had never had any anyway, but if that was so, why had she married him?

"Uh-oh, here comes Peach," Roscoe said. "Ben must have been a lunatic to marry that woman."

"According to you, all us Johnsons are lunatics," July said, a little irritated. It was not Roscoe's place to criticize his dead brother, though it was perfectly true that Peach was not his favorite sister-in-law. He had never known why Ben nicknamed her "Peach," for she was large and quarrelsome and did not resemble a peach in any way.

Peach was picking her way across the main street of Fort Smith, which was less of a quagmire than usual, since it had been dry lately. She was carrying a red rooster for some reason. She was the largest woman in town, nearly six feet tall, whereas Ben had been the runt of the Johnson family. Also, Peach talked a blue streak and Ben had seldom uttered three words a week, although he had been the mayor of the town. Now Peach still talked a blue streak and Ben was dead.

That fact, well known to everyone in Fort Smith for the last six weeks, was no doubt what Peach was coming to take up with him.

"Hello, July," Peach said. The rooster flapped a few times but she shook him and he quieted down.

July tipped his hat, as did Roscoe.

"Where'd you find the rooster?" Roscoe asked.

"It's my rooster, but he won't stay home," Peach said. "I found him down by the store. The skunks will get him if he ain't careful."

"Well, if he ain't careful he deserves it," Roscoe said.

Peach had always found Roscoe an irritating fellow, not as respectful as he might be. He was little better than a criminal himself, in her view, and she was opposed to his being deputy sheriff, although it was true that there was not much to choose from in Fort Smith.

"When are you aiming to start after that murderer?" she asked July.

"Why, pretty soon," he said, although he felt tired at the thought of starting after anybody.

"Well, he'll get over in Mexico or somewhere if you sit around here much longer," Peach said.

"I expect to find him down around San Antonio," July said. "I believe he has friends there."

Roscoe had to snort at that remark. "That's right," he said. "Two of the most famous Texas Rangers that ever lived, that's his friends. July will be lucky not to get hung himself. If you ask me, Jake Spoon ain't worth it."

"It's nothing to do with what *he's* worth," Peach said. "Ben was the one who was worth it. He was my husband and July's brother and the mayor of this town. Who else do you think seen to it your salary got paid?"

"The salary I get don't take much seeing to," Roscoe said. "A dern midget could see to it." At thirty dollars a month he considered himself grievously underpaid.

"Well, if you was earning it, the man wouldn't have got away in the first place," Peach continued. "You could have shot him down, which would have been no more than he deserved."

Roscoe was uneasily aware that he was held culpable in some quarters for Jake's escape. The truth was, the killing had confused him, for he had been a good deal fonder of Jake than of Ben. Also it was a shock and a surprise to find Ben lying in the street with a big hole in him. Everyone else had been surprised too—Peach herself had fainted. Half the people in the saloon seemed to think the mule skinner had shot Ben, and by the time Roscoe got their stories sorted out Jake was long gone. Of course it had been mostly an accident, but Peach didn't see it that way. She wanted nothing less than to see Jake hang, and probably would have if Jake had not had the good sense to leave.

July had heard it all twenty-five or thirty times, the versions differing a good deal, depending upon the teller. He felt derelict for not having made a stronger effort to run Jake out of town before he himself left for the trial in Missouri. Of course it would have been convenient if Roscoe had promptly arrested the man, but Roscoe never arrested anybody except old man Darton, the one drunk in the county Roscoe felt he could handle.

July had no doubt that he could find Jake Spoon and bring him back for trial. Gamblers eventually showed up in a town somewhere, and could always be found. If he hadn't had the attack of jaundice he could have gone right after him, but now six weeks had passed, which would mean a longer trip.

The problem was, Elmira didn't want him to go. She considered it an insult that he would even consider it. The fact that Peach didn't like her and had snubbed her repeatedly didn't help matters. Elmira pointed out that the shooting had been an accident, and made it plain that she thought he ought not to let Peach Johnson bully him into making a long trip.

While July was waiting for Peach to leave, the rooster, annoyed at being held so tightly, gave Peach's hand a couple of hard pecks. Without an instant's hesitation Peach grabbed him by the head, swung him a few times and wrung his neck. His body flew off a few feet and lay jerking. Peach pitched the head over in some weeds by the jailhouse porch. She had not got a drop of blood on her—the blood was pumping out of the headless rooster into the dust of the street.

"That'll teach him to peck me," Peach said. "At least I'll get to eat him, instead of a skunk having the pleasure."

She went over and picked the rooster up by the feet and held him out from her body until he quit jerking.

"Well, July," she said, "I hope you won't wait too long to start. Just because you're a little yellow don't mean you can't ride a horse."

"You Johnsons marry the dernest women," Roscoe said, when Peach was safely out of hearing.

"What's that?" July said, looking at Roscoe sternly. He would not have his deputy criticizing his wife.

Roscoe regretted his quick words. July was touchy on the subject of his new wife. It was probably because she was several years older and had been married before. In Fort Smith it was generally considered that she had made a fool of July, though since she was from Kansas no one knew much about her past.

"Why, I was talking about Ben and Sylvester," Roscoe said. "I guess I forgot you're a Johnson, since you're the sheriff."

The remark made no sense—Roscoe's remarks often made no sense, but July had too much on his mind to worry about it. It seemed he was faced every single day with decisions that were hard to make. Sometimes, sitting at his own table, it was hard to decide whether to talk to Elmira or not. It was not hard to tell when Elmira was displeased, though. Her mouth got tight and she could look right through him and give no indication that she even saw him. The problem was trying to figure out what she was displeased about. Several times he had tried asking if anything was wrong and had been given bitter, vehement lectures on his short-comings. The lectures were embarrassing because they were delivered in the presence of Elmira's son, now his stepson, a twelve-year-old named Joe Boot. Elmira had been married in Missouri to a fellow named Dee Boot, about whom she had never talked much—she just said he died of smallpox.

Elmira also often lectured Joe as freely as she lectured July. One result was that he and Joe had become allies and good friends; both of them spent much of their time just trying to avoid Elmira's wrath. Little Joe spent so much time around the jail that he became a kind of second deputy. Like Elmira, he was skinny, with big eyes that bulged a little in his thin face.

Roscoe was fond of the boy, too. Often he and Joe went down to the river to fish for catfish. Sometimes if they made a good catch July would bring Roscoe home for supper, but those occasions were seldom successful. Elmira thought little of Roscoe Brown, and though Roscoe was as nice to her as he could be, the fish suppers were silent, tense affairs.

"Well, July, I guess you're between a rock and a hard place," Roscoe said. "You either got to go off and fight them Texas Rangers or else stay here and fight Peach."

"I could send you after him," July said. "You're the one that let him get away."

Of course he was only teasing. Roscoe could hardly handle old man Darton, who was nearly eighty. He wouldn't stand much of a chance against Jake Spoon and his friends.

Roscoe almost tipped over in his chair, he was so astonished. The notion that he might be sent on a job like that was ridiculous—living with Elmira must have made July go crazy if he was thinking such thoughts.

"Peach ain't gonna let it rest," July said, as much to himself as to Roscoe.

"Yes, it's your duty to catch the man," Roscoe said, anxious to get himself as far off the hook as possible. "Benny was your brother, even if he was a dentist."

July didn't say it, but the fact that Benny had been his brother had little to do with his decision to go after Jake Spoon. Benny had been the oldest and he himself the youngest of the ten Johnson boys. All but the two of them went away after they grew up, and Benny seemed to feel that July should have gone away too. He was reluctant to give July the sheriff's job when it came open, although there had been no other candidate than Roscoe. July got the job, but Benny remained resentful and had balked at even providing a new lock for the jail's one cell. In fact, Benny had never done one kind thing for him that July could remember. Once when he pulled a bad tooth of July's he had charged the full fee.

July's feelings of responsibility had to do with the town, not the man who was killed. Since pinning on the sheriff's badge two years before, his sense of responsibility for the town had grown steadily. It seemed to him that as sheriff he had a lot more to do with the safety and well-being of the citizens than Benny had as mayor. The rivermen were the biggest problem—they were always drinking and fighting and cutting one another up. Several times he had had to pile five or six into the little cell.

Lately more and more cowboys passed through the town. Once the wild men of Shanghai Pierce had come through, nearly destroying two saloons. They were not bad men, just rowdy and wild to see a town. They tended to scare people's livestock and rope their pets, and were intolerant of any efforts to curb their play. They were not gunmen, but they could box—July had been forced to crack one or two of them on the jaw and keep them in jail overnight.

Little Joe worshiped the cowboys—it was plain to July that he would run off with one of the outfits, given the chance. When not doing chores he would spend hours practicing with an old rope he had found, roping stumps, or sometimes the milk-pen calf.

July was prepared to accept a certain rowdiness on the part of the cowboys as they passed through, but he felt no leniency at all for men like Jake Spoon. Gamblers offended him, and he had warned several out of town.

Roscoe loved to whittle better than any man July had ever known. If he was sitting down, which was usually the case, he was seldom without a whittling stick in his hands. He never whittled them into anything, just whittled them away, and the habit had come to irritate July.

"I guess if I leave you'll whittle up the whole dern town before I get back," he said.

Roscoe held his peace. He could tell July was in a touchy mood—and who could blame him, with a wife like Elmira and a sister-in-law like Peach. He enjoyed his whittling but of course he was not going to whittle down any houses. July often exaggerated when he was in a bad mood.

July stood up. He wasn't very tall, but he was sturdy. Roscoe had once seen him lift an anvil down at the blacksmith's shop, and he had just been a boy then.

"I'm going home," July said.

"Well, send little Joe over, if he ain't busy," Roscoe said. "We'll play some dominoes."

"It's milking time," July said. "He's got to milk. Anyway, Ellie don't like him playing dominoes with you. She thinks it'll make him lazy."

"Why, it ain't made me lazy, and I've played dominoes all my life," Roscoe said.

July knew the statement was absurd. Roscoe was only a deputy because he was lazy. But if there was one thing he didn't want to get into, it was an argument over whether Roscoe was lazy, so he gave him a wave and walked on off.

27

WHEN JULY GOT HOME it was nearly dusk. Home was just a cabin on the edge of town. As he passed the horse pen he saw that little Joe had roped the milk-pen calf again—it was easy to do, for the calf seldom moved.

"You've got that calf broke," July said. "You could probably saddle him and ride him if you wanted to."

"I milked," Joe said. He got the pail, and the two walked to the cabin together. It was a fairly good cabin, although it didn't yet have a wood floor—just well-packed dirt. July felt bad about bringing his bride to a cabin without a wood floor, but being sheriff didn't pay much and it was the best he could do.

It was a high cabin with a little sleeping loft in it. July had initially supposed that was where they would put the boy, but, in fact, Elmira had put *them* in the sleeping loft and assigned the boy a pallet on the floor.

When they got there she had already cooked the supper—just bacon and corn-bread—and was sitting up in the loft with her feet dangling. She liked to sit and let her feet dangle down into the cabin. Elmira liked being alone and spent most of her time in the loft, occasionally doing a little sewing.

"Don't you slosh that milk," she said, when Joe came in with the pail.

"Ain't much to slosh," Joe said.

It was true—the milk cow was playing out. Joe put his rope over by his pallet. It was his most prized possession. He had found it in the street one morning, after some cowboys had passed through. He didn't dare use it for several days, assuming the cowboy who had lost it would come back and look for it. But none did, so gradually he began to practice on the milk-pen calf. If he had had a horse, he would have thought seriously of leaving and trying to get on with a cow outfit, but they only had two horses and July needed both of those.

"The food's on," Elmira said, but she made no move to come down from the loft and eat it with them.

She seldom did eat with them. It bothered July a good deal, though he made no complaint. Since their little table was almost under the loft he could look up and see Elmira's bare legs as he ate. It didn't seem normal to him. His mother had died when he was six, yet he could remember that she always ate with the family; she would never have sat with her legs dangling practically over her husband's head. He had been at supper at many cabins in his life, but in none of them had the wife sat in the loft while the meal was eaten. It was a thing out of the ordinary, and July didn't like for things to be out of the ordinary in his life. It seemed to him it was better to do as other people did—if society at large did things a certain way it had to be for a good reason, and he looked upon common practices as rules that should be obeyed. After all, his job was to see that common practices were honored—that citizens weren't shot, or banks robbed.

He had arrested plenty of people who misbehaved, yet he could not bring himself to say a word to his wife about her own unusual behavior.

Joe didn't share July's discomfort with the fact that his mother seldom came to the table. When she did come it was usually to scold him, and he got scolded enough as it was—besides, he liked eating with July, or doing anything else with July. So far as he was concerned, marrying July was the best thing his mother had ever done. She scolded July as freely as she scolded him, which didn't seem right to Joe. But then July accepted it and never scolded back, so perhaps that was the way of the world: women scolded, and men kept quiet and stayed out of the way as much as possible.

"Want some buttermilk?" July asked, going to the crock.

"No, sir," Joe said. He hated buttermilk, but July loved it so that he always asked anyway.

"You ask him that every night," Elmira said from the edge of the loft. It irritated her that July came home and did exactly the same things day after day.

"Stop asking him," she said sharply. "Let him get his own buttermilk if he wants any. It's been four months now and he ain't drunk a drop—looks like you'd let it go."

She spoke with a heat that surprised July. Elmira could get angry about almost anything, it seemed. Why would it matter if he invited the boy to have a drink of buttermilk? All he had to do was say no, which he had.

"Well, it's good," he said quietly.

Joe almost wished he had taken a glass, since it would have kept July out of trouble. But it was too late.

After that one remark the meal went smoothly, mainly because no one said another word. Joe and July ate their cornbread and bacon, and Elmira hung her feet in the air.

"You take that medicine," she said to July, as soon as he had finished. "If you don't, I guess you'll be yellow the rest of your life."

"He ain't as yellow as he was," Joe said, feeling that it was incumbent on him to take up for July a little bit, since July would never take up for himself. He had no real fear of his mother—she whipped him plenty, but her anger never lasted long, and if she was really mad he could always outrun her.

"He's too yellow for me," Elmira said. "If I'd wanted a yellow husband I'd have married a Chinaman."

"What's a Chinaman?" Joe asked.

"Go get a bucket of water," Elmira said.

July sat at the table, feeling a little sad, while the boy drew a bucket of water. At least they had a well—the river was nearly a mile away, which would have been a long carry.

Joe brought the bucket in and went back outside. It was stuffy in the small cabin. There were a lot of fireflies out. For amusement he caught a few and let them flicker in his hand.

"Want a bath?" July asked his wife. "I'll fetch some more water if you do."

Elmira didn't answer because she didn't really hear him. It was peculiar, but July almost never said anything that she did hear anymore. It seemed to her that the last thing she heard were their marriage vows. After that, though she heard his voice, she didn't really hear his words. Certainly he was nothing like Dee Boot when it came to conversation. Dee could talk all week and never say the same thing twice, whereas it seemed to her July had never said anything different since they'd married.

That in itself didn't bother her, though. If there was one thing she didn't need to do, it was to talk to a man.

"I been thinking I might better go on and catch Jake Spoon," July said. He said everything in the same tone of voice, making it doubly difficult to pay attention to him, but Elmira caught his meaning.

"Do what?" she asked.

"Go get Jake Spoon," July said. "I'm over my jaundice enough to ride."

"Let him go," Elmira said. "Who wants him, anyway?"

July was not about to tell her Peach wanted him. "Well, he killed Benny," he said.

"I say let him go," Elmira said. "That was an accident."

She came downstairs and dipped her face in the cool water, then wiped it on an old piece of sacking they used for a towel.

"He shouldn't have run," July said. "He might have got off."

"No, Peach would have shot him," Elmira said. "She's the one don't care about the law."

That was a possibility. Peach had an uncontrollable temper.

"Well, I've got to catch him—it's my job," he said.

Elmira felt like laughing. July was flattering himself if he thought he could catch a man like Jake Spoon. But then, if she laughed she would be giving herself away. July had no idea that she knew Jake Spoon, but she had known Jake even before she knew Dee. He and Dee had been buddies up in Kansas. Jake even asked her to marry him once, in a joking way—for Jake was not the marrying kind and she hadn't been then, either. He had always kidded her, in the days when she was a sporting girl in Dodge, that she would end up respectable, though even he couldn't have guessed that she'd marry a sheriff. It amused him no end when he found out. She had seen him twice in the street after he came to Fort Smith, and she could tell by the way he grinned and tipped his hat to her that he thought it one of the world's finest jokes. If he had ever come to the cabin and seen that it had a dirt floor, he would have realized it was one of those jokes that aren't funny.

And yet she had not hesitated when July proposed, though she had only known him three days. It was the buffalo hunters who convinced her she had better change her way of life. One had taken a fancy to her, a man so big and rough that she feared to refuse him, though she should have—in all her days she had never been used so hard. And the buffalo hunters were numerous. Had it not been for Dee, they might have finished her. But Dee had always been partial to her and loaned her enough money to make a start in a town where she had no reputation: St. Jo, Missouri, which was where July came to testify. She met him in court, for she had no job at the time and was watching the trial to pass the hours.

She just had a dusty little room in a boardinghouse in St. Jo, and the boy a cubbyhole in the attic. Dee snuck in twice, in the dead of night, so as not to tarnish her reputation. He liked Joe, too, and had the notion that he ought to grow up to be something. It was the last time she saw Dee that they had worked out the smallpox story.

"I'm going north, Ellie—I'm tired of sweating," he said. "You go south and you'll be fine. If anybody asks say your husband died of smallpox—you can get to be a widow without ever having been married. I might get the smallpox anyway, unless I'm lucky."

"I'd go north with you, Dee," she said quietly, not putting much weight on it. Dee didn't care to have much weight put on things.

But Dee just grinned and pulled at his little blond mustache.

"Nope," he said. "You got to go respectable. I bet you make a schoolmarm yet."

Then he had given her a sweet kiss, told her to look after his boy, and left her with ten dollars and the memory of their reckless years together in Abilene and Dodge. She had known he wouldn't take her north—Dee traveled alone. It was only when he settled in a town to gamble that he liked a woman. But he had offered to go shoot the buffalo hunter who had used her so hard. She had pretended she didn't know the man's name. Dee wasn't a hard man, certainly not as hard as the buffalo hunter. He would have been the one to end up dead.

As for July, it had been no trick to marry him. He was like some of the young cowboys who had never touched a woman or even spoken to one. In two days he was hers. She soon knew that he made no impression on her. His habits never varied. He did the same things in the same way every day. Nine days out of ten he even forgot to wipe the buttermilk off his upper lip. But he wasn't hard like the buffalo hunters. With him she was safe from that kind of treatment, at least.

When she heard Jake was in town she thought she might just run away with him, though she knew he was even less dependable than Dee. But once he shot Benny she had to give up that little dream, the only little dream she had.

Since then, life had been very boring. She spent most of her days sitting in the loft, letting her feet dangle, remembering the old days with Dee and Jake.

July was sitting in the dark, buttermilk on his lip, looking at her as patiently as if he were a calf. The very look of him, so patient, made her want to torment him any way she could.

July knew that for some reason he irritated Elmira—she reacted crossly to almost everything he said or suggested. Sometimes he wondered if all men only made their wives look hostile and sullen. If it wasn't the case, then he wondered what made the difference.

He had always taken pains to be as nice as possible, sharing all the chores with little Joe and sparing her inconveniences whenever he could. Yet it seemed the more polite he tried to be, the more he stumbled or said the wrong thing or generally upset her. At night it had gotten so he could hardly put a hand on her, she looked at him so coldly. She could lie a foot from him and make him feel that he was miles away. It all made him feel terrible, for he had come to love her more than anything.

"Wipe your lip, July," she said. "I wish you'd ever learn, or else stop drinking that buttermilk."

Embarrassed, he wiped it. When Elmira was annoyed she made him so nervous that he couldn't really remember whether he had eaten, or what.

"You ain't sick, are you?" he asked. There were fevers going around, and if she had one it would explain why she felt so testy.

"I ain't sick," she said.

Since he had started the business about Jake, he thought he might as well finish it. She was mad anyway.

"If I start after Spoon now, I expect I could be back in a month," he said.

Ellie just looked at him. It was all right with her if he was gone for a year. The only reason she objected to his going was that she knew Peach was behind it; if somebody was going to tell the man what to do, it ought to be her, not Peach.

"Take Joe with you," she said.

Such a thought had never occurred to July, though it had crossed his mind that he might take Roscoe.

"Why, you'll need him," July said. "You've got the chores."

Elmira shrugged. "I can milk that old cow," she said. "The chores ain't hard. We ain't raising cotton, you know. I want you to take Joe. He needs to see the world."

It was true the boy might be useful on a long trip. There would be someone to help him watch the prisoner, once there was a prisoner. But it meant leaving Ellie alone, which he didn't like.

As if reading his mind, she sat down at the table and looked at him.

"I been alone before, July," she said. "It ain't gonna hurt me. Roscoe can help if I need something I can't carry."

That was true, of course—not that Roscoe would be particularly obliging about it. Roscoe claimed to have a bad back and would complain for days if forced to do anything resembling manual labor.

"There could be a fight," July said, remembering that Jake Spoon was said to have difficult friends. "I don't expect it, but you never know with a gambler."

"I don't reckon they'd shoot a boy," Elmira said. "You take Joe. He's got to grow up sometime."

Then, to escape the stuffy cabin, she went outside and sat on a stump for a while. The night was thick with fireflies. In a little while she heard July come out. He didn't say anything. He just sat.

Despite his politeness and constant kindness, Elmira felt a bitterness toward him. The thing he didn't know was that she was with child. He wouldn't know it, either, if she could help it. She had just married out of fright—she didn't want him or the child either. And yet she was scared to try and stop the child—in Abilene she had known a girl who bled to death from trying to stop a baby. She had died on the stairs outside Elmira's room on a bitter cold night; blood had run all the way down the stairs and frozen in the night into red ice. The girl, whose name was Jenny, had stuck to the stairs. They had had to heat water in order to get her loose.

The sight had been enough to discourage her from trying to stop a baby. Yet the thought that she had one made her bitter. She didn't want to go through it all again, and she didn't want to live with July Johnson. It was just that the buffalo hunter had been so rough; it had scared her into thinking she had to find a different life.

Life in Fort Smith was different, too—so dull that she found little reason to raise herself from her quilts, most days. The women of the town, though they had no reason to suspect her, suspected her anyway and let her alone. Often she was tempted just to walk into a saloon where there was a girl or two she might have talked to, but instead she had given way to apathy, spending whole days sitting on the edge of her sleeping loft, doing nothing.

Watching the fireflies sparkle in the woods behind the cabin, Elmira waited, listening. Sure enough, in a few minutes, she heard the little metallic clicks, as July slowly rotated the chambers in his pistol before going back to town to make his rounds. It set her teeth on edge that he would do it every night.

"Guess I'll go have a look," he said. "Won't be long."

It was what he said every night. It was true, too. Unless the rivermen were fighting, he was never long. Mainly he hoped that when he came to bed she'd want him. But she didn't want him. She had kept him at a distance since she was sure about the baby. It hurt his feelings, but she didn't care.

As she heard him walk off through the darkness, her spirits sank even lower. It seemed there was no winning in life. She wanted July and Joe to be gone, suddenly, so she would not have to deal with them every day. Their needs were modest enough, but she no longer wanted to face them. She had reached a point where doing anything for anyone was a strain. It was like heavy work, it was so hard.

It came to her more strongly every day how much she missed Dee Boot. He was the exact opposite of July Johnson. July could be predicted down to the least gesture, whereas Dee was always doing what a person least expected. Once, in Abilene, to get revenge on a madam he hadn't liked, he had pretended to bring her a nice pie from the bakery, and indeed he had got the baker to produce what looked like a perfect piecrust—but he had gone over to the livery stable and filled the piecrust with fresh horse turds. The madam, a big, mean woman named Sal, had actually cut into it before she sensed the joke.

Elmira smiled to herself, remembering some of the funny things Dee did. They had known one another for nearly fifteen years, since she had found herself stranded, as a girl, way up in Kansas. It hadn't been all Dee, of course; there had been plenty of others. Some had lasted only a few minutes, some a week or two or a month, but somehow she and Dee always found themselves back together. It irritated her that he had been content just to pull his mustache and head for the north without her. He seemed to think it would be easy for her to be respectable. Of course, it was her fault for picking July. She hadn't expected his politeness to irritate her so much.

After the night deepened, the moon came out and rose above the pines. Elmira sat on the stump and watched it, glad to be alone. The thought that July and Joe would be going off caused her spirits to lift—it occurred to her that once they left there would be nothing to stop her from leaving too. Boats went up the Arkansas nearly every week. It might be that Dee Boot was missing her as much as she missed him. He wouldn't mind that she was with child—such things he took lightly.

It made her smile to think of finding Dee. While July tracked one gambler, she would track another, in the opposite direction. When July got back, with or without Jake, and discovered that his wife was gone, it might surprise him so much he would even forget to drink his buttermilk.

28

THE NEXT MORNING, an hour before dawn, July and Joe left the cabin and caught their horses. Joe was almost stunned with excitement at getting to go with July. His friend Roscoe Brown had been stunned, too, when July went by the jail and told Roscoe they were going.

"You'll get that boy kilt before I even teach him all my domino tricks," Roscoe said. It puzzled him that July would do such a thing.

Joe was not tempted to question the miracle. The main thing that bothered him was that he lacked a saddle, but July took care of that by borrowing an old single-tree from Peach Johnson. She was so pleased July was finally going after her husband's killer that she would have given them the saddle—rats had eaten most of it, anyway.

Elmira got up and cooked them breakfast, but the food did nothing to ease the heaviness of heart which July felt. All night he had hoped she might turn to him, it being his last night at home for a while—but she hadn't. Once he had accidentally touched her, turning on the pallet they slept on, and she had stiffened. It was clear to July that she wasn't going to miss him, though he was certainly going to miss her. It was peculiar, but she showed no sign of being sorry to see Joe go, either. Yet Joe was her son and he was her husband—if she didn't love her husband and her son, who did she love? For all she knew would be gone for months, and yet she was just as brisk with them as if it was an ordinary day. She saw to it that Joe drew another bucket of water before he left, and then jumped on July for nearly forgetting his jaundice medicine.

Yet, for all her bad temper, it was no relief to leave. He felt apprehension so strongly that at one point it seemed to tighten his throat and nearly caused him to choke on a bite of corn bread. He felt he was being carried along through his life as a river might carry a chip. There seemed to be no way he could stop anything that was happening, although it all felt wrong.

The only relief he could find was in the knowledge that he was doing his job and earning the thirty dollars a month the town paid him. There were a few tight-fisted citizens who didn't think there was thirty dollars' worth of sheriffing to do in Fort Smith in a given month. Going after a man who had killed the mayor was the kind of work people seemed to think a sheriff ought to do, although it would probably be less dangerous than having to stop two rivermen from carving one another up with knives.

They left Elmira standing in the door of the cabin and rode through the dark town to the jail, but before they got there Red, Joe's horse, suddenly bowed up, began to buck, and threw him. Joe was not hurt, but he was dreadfully embarrassed to be thrown right at the outset of such an important trip.

"It's just Red," July said. "He's got to have his buck. He's gotten rid of me a time or two that way."

Roscoe slept on a couch in the jail and was up and stumbling around in his bare feet when they got there. July got a rifle and two boxes of bullets and then got down a shotgun too.

"That's my shotgun," Roscoe said. He was not in the best of tempers. He hated to have his sleeping quarters invaded before it was even light.

"We'll need to eat," July said. "Joe can shoot a rabbit now and then if we don't see no deer."

"You'll probably see a Comanche Indian and they'll cook both of you as if you was dern rabbits," Roscoe said.

"Oh, they're about whipped, I reckon," July said.

"'Bout?" Roscoe said. "Well, I 'bout knocked out a wasp's nest last year, but the two I missed near stung me to death. 'Bout ain't good enough where Comanches are concerned. You must be planning to make San Antonio in one day, since you're starting this early," he added, still grumpy from having been routed out of bed.

July let him grumble and took a saddle scabbard off one of the other rifles so there'd be something to put the shotgun in.

By the time light had begun to show over the river, they were ready to go. Roscoe was awake enough by then to feel apprehensive. Being deputy was an easy job while July was around, but the minute he left it became heavy with responsibility. Anything could happen, and he would be the one who would have to handle it.

"Well, I hope the dern Comanches don't decide they want Fort Smith," he said morosely. Several times he had dreams of a troop of wild Indians riding right down the street and filling him full of arrows while he sat in front of the jail, whittling.

"They won't," July said, anxious to get away before Roscoe thought up other bad things that might happen.

Roscoe noted that Joe was bareheaded, another sign of July's recklessness. It occurred to him that he had an old black felt hat. It was hanging on a peg, and he went back in and got it for the boy.

"Here, you take this," he said, surprised at his own generosity.

When Joe put it on, his head disappeared nearly down to his mouth, which was grinning.

"If he wears that he'll probably ride off a cliff," July said, although it was true the boy needed a hat.

"He can tie it on with some string," Roscoe said. "It'll keep that dern sun out of his eyes."

Now that they were ready, July felt strangely unwilling to leave. It was getting good light—far down the street they could see the river shining, and beyond it a faint glow of red on the horizon. In its awakening hour the town seemed peaceful, lovely, calm. A rooster began to crow.

Yet July had a sense that something was terribly wrong. More than once it occurred to him that Elmira might have some strange disease that caused her to act the way she was acting. She had less appetite than most people, for one thing—she just nibbled at her food. Now he had no one to trust her to except Roscoe Brown, who was only slightly less afraid of her than he would be of a Comanche.

"You look after Ellie," he said sternly. "If she needs her groceries carried, you carry them."

"Okay, July," Roscoe said.

July got on his horse, adjusted his bedroll and sat looking at the river. They weren't carrying much bedding, but then the warm weather was coming.

"Take her a fish now and then, if you catch one," he said.

To Roscoe Brown it seemed a strange instruction. Elmira had made it plain that she didn't like fish.

"Okay, July," he said again, though he didn't mean to waste his time offering fish to a woman who didn't like them.

July could think of no more instructions. Roscoe knew the town as well as he did.

"Joe, be careful," Roscoe said. For some reason it affected him to see the boy going. It was a poor saddle he had, too. But the boy still grinned out from under the old hat.

"We'll catch him," Joe said proudly.

"Well, I'll try not to let nobody shoot no more dentists," Roscoe said.

July regarded the remark as irrelevant, for Roscoe knew well enough that the town had been without a dentist since Benny's death. "Just watch old man Darton," he said. "We don't want him to fall off the ferry."

The old man lived in a shack on the north bank and merely came over for liquor. Once in a while he eluded Roscoe, and twice already he had fallen into the river. The ferrymen didn't like him anyway, and if it happened again they might well let him drown.

"I'll handle the old scamp," Roscoe said confidently. Old man Darton was one responsibility he felt he could handle any day.

"Well, I guess we'll see you when we see you, Roscoe," July said. Then he turned his horse away from the river and the glowing sky, and he and little Joe were soon out of town.

29

SIX DAYS LATER responsibility descended upon Roscoe Brown with a weight far beyond anything he had ever felt. As usual, it fell out of a clear blue sky—as fine a day as one could want, with the Arkansas River sparkling down at the end of the street. Roscoe, having no pressing duties, was sitting in front of the jail whittling, when he noticed Peach Johnson coming up the street with little Charlie Barnes at her side. Charlie was a banker, and the only man in town to wear a necktie every day. He was also the main deacon in the church, and, by common consent the man most likely to marry Peach if she ever remarried. Charlie was a widower, and richer by far than Benny had ever been. Nobody liked him, not even Peach, but she was too practical a woman to let that stop her if she took a notion to marry.

· When Roscoe saw them coming he snapped shut his whittling knife and put the stick he had been whittling in his shirt pocket. There was no law against whittling, but he didn't want to get a reputation as an idler, particularly not with a man who was as apt as not to end up the next mayor of Fort Smith.

"Morning, folks," he said, when the two walked up.

"Roscoe, I thought July gave you instructions to look after Elmira," Peach said.

"Well, he said take her a fish if I caught one, but I ain't caught any lately," Roscoe said. He felt a little guilty without even knowing what was wrong, for Elmira had not once crossed his mind since July left.

"If I know July—and I do know July—I bet he said more than that," Peach said.

"Well, he said to carry her some groceries if she asked, but she ain't asked," he said.

"When have you seen her?" Charlie Barnes asked. He was looking stern, though it was hard for a man so short and fat to really muster much sternness.

The question stumped Roscoe. Probably he had seen Elmira recently, but when he thought about it he couldn't think when. The woman was not much for traipsing around town. Right after the marriage she had been seen in the stores some, spending July's money, but he couldn't recollect having seen her in a store in recent days.

"You know Elmira," he said. "She don't come out much. Mainly she just stays in the cabin."

"Well, she ain't in it now," Peach said.

"We think she's gone," Charlie Barnes said.

"Why, where would she go?" Roscoe said.

Peach and Charlie didn't answer, and a silence fell.

"Maybe she just took a walk," Roscoe said, although he knew that sounded weak.

"That's what I thought yesterday," Peach said. "She wasn't there yesterday and she ain't there today. I doubt she'd take no overnight walk."

Roscoe had to admit it was unlikely. The nearest town, Catfish Grove, was fourteen miles away, and not much of a destination at that.

"Maybe she just don't want to answer the door," he said. "She takes a lot of naps."

"Nope, I went in and looked," Peach said. "There ain't a soul in that cabin, and there wasn't yesterday, neither."

"We think she's gone," Charlie Barnes said again. He was not a talkative man. ·

Roscoe got up from his comfortable seat. If Elmira was indeed gone, that constituted a serious problem. Peach and Charlie stood there as if they expected him to do something, or tell them right off where she had gone.

"I wonder if something got her?" he asked, thinking out loud. There were still plenty of bears in the woods, and some said there were panthers, though he himself had never seen one.

"If she wandered off, anything could have got her," Peach said. "Could have been an animal or it could have been a man."

"Why, Peach, I don't know why a man would want her," Roscoe said, only to realize that the remark probably sounded funny. After all, Peach was related to her.

"I don't either, but I ain't a man," Peach said, giving Charlie Barnes a hard look. Roscoe thought it unlikely that Charlie wanted Elmira. It might be that he didn't even want Peach.

He walked to the edge of the porch and looked up the street, hoping to see Elmira standing in it. In all his years as a deputy he had never heard of a woman just getting lost, and it seemed unfair that it should happen to July's wife. There was nobody in the street but a farmer with a mule team.

"Why, I'll go have a look," he said. "Maybe she just went visiting."

"Who would she visit?" Peach asked. "She ain't been out of that cabin more than twice since July married her. She don't know the names of five people in this town. I was just going to take her some dumplings, since July is gone off. If I hadn't done it I doubt she would have even been missed."

From her tone Roscoe got the clear implication that he had been remiss in his duty. In fact, he had meant to look in on Elmira at some point, but the time had passed so quickly he had forgotten to.

"Well, I'll go right up there," he said, trying to sound cheerful. "I expect she'll turn up."

"We think she's gone," Charlie Barnes said, for the third time.

Roscoe decided to go at once to keep from having to hear Charlie Barnes repeat himself all morning. He tipped his hat to Peach and started for the cabin, but to his dismay Peach and Charlie stayed right at his heels. It disturbed him to have company, but there was nothing he could do about it. It seemed to him curious that Peach would take Elmira dumplings, for the two women were known not to get along; it crossed his mind that Elmira had seen Peach coming and gone into hiding.

Sure enough, the cabin was empty. There was no sign that anybody had been in it for a day or two. A slab of corn bread sat on the cookstove, already pretty well nibbled by the mice.

"She mostly sat in the loft," Roscoe said, mainly to hear himself talk. Hearing himself was better than hearing Peach.

"There ain't nothing up there but a pallet," Peach said.

That proved to be the truth. It was not much of a pallet, either—just a couple of quilts. July, being the youngest of the Johnson family, had never had any money and had not accumulated much in the way of goods.

Roscoe racked his brain to try and think if there was anything missing, but he had never been in the loft before and could not think of a possession that might have been missing—just Elmira.

"Didn't she have shoes on, when they got hitched?" he asked.

Peach looked disgusted. "Of course she had shoes on," she said. "She wasn't that crazy."

"Well, I don't see no shoes in this cabin, men's or women's," Roscoe said. "If she's gone, I guess she wore 'em."

They went out and walked around the cabin. Roscoe was hoping to find a trail, but there were weeds all around the cabin, wet with dew, and all he did was get his pants legs wet. He was growing more and more uneasy—if Elmira was just in hiding from Peach he wished she'd give up and come out. If July came back and found his new wife missing, there was no telling how upset he'd be.

It seemed to him the most likely explanation was bears, though he knew it wasn't a foolproof explanation. If a bear had just walked in and got her, there would have been some blood on the floor. On the other hand, no bear had ever walked into Fort Smith and got a woman, though one had entered a cabin near Catfish Grove and carried off a baby.

"I guess a bear got her unless she's hiding," he said, unhappily. Being a deputy sheriff had suddenly gotten a lot harder.

"We think she's gone," Charlie Barnes said, with irritating persistence. If a bear had got her, of course she would be gone.

"He means we think she's left," Peach said.

That made no sense at all, since the woman had just married July.

"Left to go where?" he said. "Left to do what?"

"Roscoe, you ain't got the sense God gave a turkey," Peach said, abandoning her good manners. "If she left, she just left—left. My guess is she got tired of living with July."

That was such a radical thought that merely trying to think it gave Roscoe the beginnings of a headache.

"My God, Peach," he said, feeling stunned.

"There's no need to swear, Roscoe," Peach said. "We all seen it coming. July's a fool or he wouldn't have married her."

"It could have been a bear, though," Roscoe said. All of a sudden, it seemed the lesser of two evils. If Elmira was dead July might eventually get over it—if she had run off, there was no telling what he might do.

"Well, where's the tracks, then?" Peach asked. "If a bear came around, all the dogs in this town would have barked, and half the horses would have run away. If you ask me, Elmira's the one that run away."

"My God," Roscoe said again. He knew he was going to get blamed, no matter what.

"I bet she took that whiskey boat," Peach said. In fact, a boat had headed upriver only a day or two after July left.

It was the only logical explanation. No stage had passed through in the last week. A troop of soldiers had come through, going west, but soldiers wouldn't have taken Elmira. The boat had been filled with whiskey traders, headed up for Bents' Fort. Roscoe had seen a couple of the boatmen staggering on the street, and when the boat had left with no fights reported, he had felt relieved. Whiskey traders were rough men—certainly not the sort married women ought to be traveling with.

"You better go see what you can find out, Roscoe," Peach said. "If she's run off, July's gonna want to know about it."

That was certainly true. July doted on Elmira.

It took no more than a walk to the river to confirm what Peach had suspected. Old Sabin, the ferryman, had seen a woman get on the whiskey boat the morning it left.

"My God, why didn't you tell me?" Roscoe asked.

Old Sabin just shrugged. It was none of his business who got on boats other than his own.

"I figert it was a whore," he said.

Roscoe walked slowly back to the jail, feeling extremely confused. He wanted badly for it all to be a mistake. On the way up the street he looked in every store, hoping he would find Elmira in one of them spending money like a normal woman. But she wasn't there. At the saloon he asked Renfro, the barkeep, if he knew of a whore who had left town lately, but there were only two whores in town, and Renfro said they were both upstairs asleep.

It was just the worst luck. He had worried considerably about the various bad things that might happen while July was gone, but the loss of Elmira had not been among his worries. Men's wives didn't usually leave on a whiskey barge. He had heard of cases in which they didn't like wedded life and went back to their families, but Elmira hadn't even had a family, and there was no reason for her not to like wedded life, since July had not worked her hard at all.

Once it was plain that she was gone, Roscoe felt in the worst quandary of his life. July was gone too, off in the general direction of San Antonio. It might be a month before he got back, at which point someone would have to tell him the bad news. Roscoe didn't want to be the someone, but then he was the person whose job it was to sit around the jail, so he would probably have to do it.

Even worse, he would have to sit there for a month or two worrying about July's reaction when he finally got back. Or it could be three months or six months— July had been known to be slow. Roscoe knew he couldn't take six months of anxiety. Of course it just proved that July had been foolish to marry, but that didn't make the situation any easier to live with.

In less than half an hour it seemed that every single person in Fort Smith found out that July Johnson's wife had run off on a whiskey barge. It seemed the Johnson family provided almost all the excitement in the town, the last excitement having been Benny's death. Such a stream of people came up to question Roscoe about the disappearance that he was forced to give up all thought of whittling, just at a time when having a stick to whittle on might have settled his nerves.

People who had seldom laid eyes on Elmira suddenly showed up at the jail and began to question him about her habits, as if he was an authority on them— though all he had ever seen the woman do was cook a catfish or two.

One of the worst was old lady Harkness, who had once taught school somewhere or other in Mississippi and had treated grownups like schoolchildren ever since. She helped out a little in her son's general store, where evidently there wasn't work enough to keep her busy. She marched across the street as if she had been appointed by God to investigate the whole thing. Roscoe had already discussed it with the blacksmith and the postmaster and a couple of cotton farmers, and was hoping for a little time off in which to think it through. Old lady Harkness didn't let that stop her.

"Roscoe, if you was my deputy, I'd arrest you," she said. "What do you mean lettin' somebody run off with July's wife?"

"Nobody run off with her," Roscoe said. "She just run off with herself, I guess."

"What do you know about it?" old lady Harkness said. "I don't guess she'd just have got on a boatful of men if she wasn't partial to one of them. When are you going after her?"

"I ain't," Roscoe said, startled. It had never occurred to him to go after Elmira.

"Well, you will unless you're good for nothing, I guess," the old lady said. "This ain't much of a town if things like that can happen and the deputy just sit there."

"It never was much of a town," Roscoe reminded her, but the point, which was obvious, merely seemed to anger her.

"If you ain't up to getting the woman, then you better go get July," she said. "He might want his wife back before she gets up there somewhere and gets scalped."

She then marched off, much to Roscoe's relief. He went in and took a drink or two from a bottle of whiskey he kept under his couch and usually only used as a remedy for toothache. He was careful not to drink too much, since the last thing he needed was for the people in Fort Smith to get the notion he was a drunk. But then, the next thing he knew, despite his care, the whiskey bottle was empty, and he seemed to have drunk it, although it did not feel to him like he was drunk. In the still heat he got drowsy and went to sleep on the couch, only to awake in a sweat to find Peach and Charlie Barnes staring down at him.

It was very upsetting, for it seemed to him the day had started out with Peach and Charlie staring down at him. In his confusion it occurred to him that he might have dreamed the whole business about Elmira running off. Only there were Peach and Charlie again; the dream might be starting over. He wanted to wake up before it got to the part about the whiskey barge, but it turned out he was awake, after all.

"Is she still gone?" he asked, hoping by some miracle that Elmira had showed up while he was sleeping.

"Of course she's still gone," Peach said. "And you're drunk on the job. Get up from there and go get July."

"But July went to Texas," Roscoe said. "The only place I've ever been to is Little Rock, and it's in the other direction."

"Roscoe, if you can't find Texas you're a disgrace to your profession," Peach said.

Peach had a habit of misunderstanding people, even when the point was most obvious.

"I can find Texas," he said. "The point is, kin I find July?"

"He's riding with a boy, and he's going to San Antonio," Peach said. "I guess if you ask around, someone will have seen them."

"Yeah, but what if I miss 'em?" Roscoe asked.

"Then I guess you'll end up in California," she said.

Roscoe found that he had a headache, and listening to Peach made it worse.

"His wife's gone," Charlie Barnes said.

"Dern it, Charlie, shut up!" Peach said. "He knows that. I don't think he's forgot *that*."

Roscoe had not forgotten it. Overnight it had become the dominant fact of his life. Elmira was gone and he was expected to do something about it. Moreover, his choices were limited. Either he went upriver and tried to find Elmira or he had to go to Texas and look for July. He himself was far from sure that either action was wise.

Trying to recover his wits, with a headache and Peach and Charlie Barnes staring at him for the second time that day, was not easy. Mainly Roscoe felt aggrieved that July had put him in such a position. July had been doing well enough without a wife, it seemed to Roscoe; but if he *had* to marry, he could have been a little more careful and at least married someone who would have the courtesy to stay around Fort Smith—about the least that one ought to be able to ask of a wife. Instead, he had made the worst possible choice and left Roscoe to suffer the consequences.

"I ain't much of a traveler," Roscoe said, for actually his one trip, to Little Rock, had been one of the nightmares of his life, since he had ridden the whole way in a cold rain and had run a fever for a month as a result.

Nonetheless, the next morning he found himself saddling up the big white gelding he had ridden for the last ten years, a horse named Memphis, the town of his origin. Several of the townspeople were there at the jail, watching him pack his bedroll and tie on his rifle scabbard, and none of them seemed worried that he was about to ride off and leave them unprotected. Although Roscoe said little, he felt very pettish toward the citizens of Fort Smith, and toward Peach Johnson and Charlie Barnes in particular. If Peach had just minded her own business, nobody would even have discovered that Elmira was missing until July returned, and then July would have been able to take care of the problem, which rightly was his problem anyway.

"Well, I hope nobody don't rob the bank while I'm gone," he said to the little crowd watching him. He wanted to suggest worse possibilities, such as Indian raids, but, in fact, the Indians had not molested Fort Smith in years, though the main reason he rode white horses was that he had heard somewhere that Indians were afraid of them.

The remark about the bank being robbed was aimed at Charlie Barnes, who blinked a couple of times in response. It had never been robbed, but if it had been, Charlie might have died on the spot, not out of fright but because he hated to lose a nickel.

The little jail, which had been more or less Roscoe's home for the last few years, had never seemed more appealing to him. Indeed, he felt like crying every time he looked at it, but of course it would not do to cry in front of half the town. It was another beautiful morning, with the hint of summer—Roscoe had always loved the summer and hated the cold, and he wondered if he would get back in time to enjoy the sultry days of July and August, when it was so hot even the river hardly seemed to move. He was much given to premonitions—had had them all his life—and he had a premonition now. It seemed to him that he wouldn't get back. It seemed to him he might be looking his last on Fort Smith, but the townspeople gave him no chance to linger or be sorry.

"Elmira'll be to Canada before you get started," Peach pointed out.

Reluctantly, Roscoe climbed up on Memphis, a horse so tall it was only necessary to be on him to have a view. "Well, I hate to go off and leave you without no deputy," he said. "I doubt if July will like it. He put me in charge of this place."

Nobody said a word to that.

"If July gets back and I ain't with him, you tell him I went looking," Roscoe said. "We may just circle around for a while, me and July. First I'll look for him, then he can look for me. And if the town goes to hell in the meantime, don't blame it on Roscoe Brown."

"Roscoe, we got the fort over there half a mile away," Peach said. "I guess the soldiers can look after us as good as you can."

That was true, of course. There wouldn't even be a Fort Smith if there hadn't been a fort first. Still, the soldiers didn't concern themselves much with the town.

"What if Elmira comes back?" Roscoe asked. No one had raised that possibility. "Then I'd be gone and won't know it."

"Why would she come back?" Peach asked. "She just left."

Roscoe found it hard even to remember Elmira, though he had done practically nothing but think about her for the last twenty-four hours. All he really knew was that he hated to ride out of the one town he felt at home in. That everyone was eager for him to go made him feel distinctly bitter.

"Well, the soldiers ain't gonna help you if old man Darton goes on a tear," he said. "July told me to be sure and watch him."

But the little group of citizens seemed not to be worried by the thought of what old man Darton might do. They watched him silently.

Unable to think of any other warnings, or any reason for his staying that might convince anyone, Roscoe gave Memphis a good kick—he was a steady horse once he hit his stride, but he did start slow—and the big-footed gelding kicked a little dust on Charlie Barnes's shiny shoes, getting underway. Roscoe took one last look at the river and headed for Texas.

30

THE FIRST GOOD WASH Lorena got was in the Nueces River. They had had a bad day trying to fight their way through mesquite thickets, and when they came to the river she just decided to stop, particularly since she found a shady spot where there wasn't any mesquite or prickly pear.

Jake had no part in the decision because Jake was drunk. He had been steadily drinking whiskey all day as they rode, and was so unsteady in his seat that Lorena wasn't even sure they were still going in the right direction. But they were ahead of the cattle—from every clearing she could look back and see the dust the herd raised. It was a fair way back, but directly behind them, which made her feel reassured. It would not be pleasant to be lost, with Jake so drunk.

Of course, he only drank because his hand was paining him. Probably he hadn't gotten all the thorn out—his thumb had turned from white to purple. She was hoping they would strike a town that had a doctor, but there seemed to be nothing in that part of the country but prickly pear and mesquite.

It was bad luck, Jake having an accident so soon after they started, but it was just a thorn. Lorena supposed the worst it could do was fester. But when he got off his horse, his legs were so unsteady he could barely wobble over to the shade. She was left to tie the horses and make the camp, while Jake lay propped up against the tree and continued to pull on his bottle.

"Dern, it's hot," he said, when she stopped for a minute to look at his hand. "I wonder where the boys are camped tonight. We might go over and get up a game of cards."

"You'd lose," she said. "You're too drunk to shuffle."

There was a flash of anger in Jake's eyes. He didn't like being criticized. But he made no retort.

"I'm going to have a wash," Lorena said.

"Don't drown," he said. "Be a pity if you was to drown on your way to San Francisco."

It was clear he was angry—he hated to be denied, or to see her take the lead over him in anything. Lorena met his anger with silence. She knew he couldn't stay mad very long.

The river was green and the water cold underneath the surface. She waded in and stood chest-deep, letting the water wash away the layers of dust and sweat. As she was wading out, feeling clean and light, she got a scare: a big snapping turtle sat on the bank right where she had entered the river. It was big as a tub and so ugly Lorena didn't want to get near it. She waded upstream, and just as she got out heard a shot—Jake was shooting his pistol at the turtle. He walked down to the water, probably just because he liked to see her naked.

"You are a sight," he said, grinning. Then he shot at the turtle again and missed. He shot four times, all the bullets plopping into the mud. The turtle, unharmed, slid off into the water.

"I was never no shot with my left hand," Jake said.

Lorena sat down on a grassy place in the sun and let the water drip off her legs. As soon as she sat down Jake came over and began to rub her back. He had a feverish look in his eye.

"I don't know where I got such a fancy for you," he said. "You are a sight to see."

He stretched out beside her and pulled her back. It was odd to look up beyond his head and see the white sky above them instead of the cracked boards in the ceiling above her head in the Dry Bean. More than usual, it made her feel not there—far from Jake and what he was doing. Crowded up in a room, it was difficult for her to keep herself—on the grass, with the sky far above, it was easy.

But it was not easy for Jake to finish—he was sicker than she had suspected. His legs were trembling and his body strained at hers. She looked in his face and saw he was frightened—he groaned, trying to grip her shoulder with his sore hand. Then, despite himself, he slipped from her; he tried to push back in, but kept slipping away. Finally he gave up and collapsed on her, so tired that he seemed to pass out.

When he sat up, she eased out from under him. He looked around with no recognition. She dressed and helped him dress, then got him propped against a big shade tree. She made a little fire, thinking some coffee might help him. While she was getting the pot out of the pack she heard a splashing and looked up to see a black man ride his horse into the river from the other side. Soon the horse was swimming, but the black man didn't seem frightened. The horse waded out, dripping, and the black man dismounted and let it shake itself.

"How do, miss," the black man said. Jake had fallen into a drowse and didn't even know the man was there.

"Mister Jake taking a nap?" he asked.

"He's sick," Lorena said.

The man walked over and squatted by Jake a moment, then gently lifted his hand. Jake woke up.

"Why, it's old Deets," he said. "We're all right now, Lorie. Deets will see us through."

"I been looking for a good place to cross the herd," Deets said. "Captain made me the scout."

"Well, he's right," Jake said. "We'd all have been lost twenty years ago if it hadn't been for you."

"You full of fever," Deets said. "Let me get that sticker out of your hand."

"I thought I got it all the other day," Jake said. "I'd as soon have you cut my hand off as dig around in there."

"Oh, no," Deets said. "You got to keep your hand. Might need you to shoot a bandit if one gets after me."

He went back and rummaged in his saddlebag, bringing out a large needle.

"I got to keep a needle," he said to Lorena. "Got to sew my pants from time to time."

Then, after heating the needle and letting it cool, he carefully probed the swelling at the base of Jake's thumb. Jake yelped when he began, and then yelped again a little later, but he didn't resist.

"Goddamn the dern thorns," he said weakly.

Then, with a wide grin, Deets held up the needle. The tiny yellow tip of the thorn was on it. "Now you be cuttin' the cards agin," he said.

Jake looked relieved, though still flushed with fever.

"I'll play you right now, Deets," he said. "You're the only one in the whole dern outfit with any money."

The black man just grinned and returned the needle to the little packet in his saddlebag. Then he accepted the cup of coffee which Lorie offered.

"Miss, you oughta get him on across the river," he said, when he handed back the coffee cup.

"Why?" Lorena asked. "We done made camp. He'll want to rest."

"Rest on the other side," Deets said. "Gonna come a storm tonight. The river be up tomorrow."

It seemed hard to believe. There was not a cloud in the sky. But the man had spoken in a tone that indicated he knew what he was talking about.

The girl looked sad, Deets thought. He glanced at the sun, which was dropping.

"I can help," he said. "I'll get you settled." The black man had them packed in no time, tying their bedrolls high so as to keep them out of the river.

"Dern, we didn't use this camp much," Jake said, when he realized they were moving. But when Deets mentioned the storm, he simply mounted and rode into the river. He was soon across.

It was a good thing Deets had offered to help. Lorena's mare balked and wouldn't take the water. She would go in chest-deep and then whirl and climb back up the bank, showing the whites of her eyes and trying to run. Despite herself, Lorena felt her fear rising. Once, already, the mare had nearly fallen. She might really fall, trapping Lorena beneath the green water. She tried to control her fear—she would have to get across many rivers if she was to get to San Francisco—but the mare kept flouncing and trying to turn and Lorena couldn't help being afraid. She could see Jake on the other bank. He didn't look very concerned.

The third time the mare turned, the black man was suddenly beside her. "Let me have her," he said.

When he took the reins Lorena felt a deeper fright than she had ever known. She gripped the horse's mane so tightly the horsehairs cut into her hands. Then she shut her eyes—she couldn't bear to see the water coming over her. The mare took a leap, and there was a different feeling. They were swimming. She heard the black man's voice talking soothingly to the mare. The water lapped at her waist, but it came no higher; after a moment she opened her eyes. They were nearly across the river. The black man was looking back watchfully, lifting her reins a bit so as to keep the horse's head out of the water. Then there was the suck of the water against her legs as they started to climb out of the river. With a smile, the black man handed her back her wet reins. She was gripping the mane so tightly it took an act of will to turn her hands loose.

"Why, she's a fine swimmer," Deets said. "You be fine on this horse, Miss."

Lorena had clenched her teeth so tightly she couldn't even speak to thank the man, though she felt a flush of gratitude. Had it not been for him she felt sure she would have drowned. Jake by this time had untied his bedroll and thrown it down under a big mesquite. It had been nothing to him, her having to cross the river. Though the fright had begun to relax its grip, Lorena still didn't feel that she had control of her limbs so that she could simply step off the horse and walk as she had always walked. She felt angry at Jake for taking it all so lightly.

.

Deets smiled at Lorena tolerantly and turned his own horse back toward the river.

"Make your fire and do your cooking now," he said. "Then blow out the fire. It's gonna come a bad wind. If the fire gets loose you might have trouble."

He glanced south, at the sky.

"The wind's gonna come about sundown," he said. "First it will be sand and then lightning. Don't tie the horses to no big trees."

Despite herself, Lorena felt her spirits sinking. She had always feared lightning above all things, and here she was without even a house to hide in. She saw it was going to be harder than she had imagined. Here it was only the second day and she had already had a fright like death. Now lightning was coming. For a moment it all felt hopeless—better she had just sat in the Dry Bean for life, or married Xavier. She had gone over to Jake in a minute, and yet, the truth was Xavier would probably have taken care of her better. It was all foolish, her dream of San Francisco.

She looked again at the black man, meaning to try and thank him for helping her across the river, but he was looking at her kindly, and she didn't say anything.

"I got to go lead the Captain to the crossing," he said.

Lorena nodded. "Tell Gus hello," she said.

"I'll tell him," Deets said, and rode into the Nueces for the third time.

31

"WELL, HERE'S WHERE we all find out if we was meant to be cowboys," Augustus said—for he had no doubt that Deets would soon be proved right about the coming storm. "Too bad it couldn't wait a day or two until some of you boys had more practice," he added. "I expect half of you will get trampled before the night is over, leaving me no way to collect my just debts."

"We have to expect it," Call said. "It's the stormy time of the year."

Still, a sandstorm at night, with a herd that wasn't trailbroken and a green crew of men, was not going to be anything to look forward to.

"You reckon we could make it across the river before it hits?" he asked, but Deets shook his head. They were several miles from the Nueces and the sun was low.

"It's a steep crossing," Deets said. "You don't want to hit it in the dark."

Newt had just come off the drags for a drink of water, and the first thing he heard was talk of sandstorm. It didn't seem to him that it would make much difference; his world was mostly sand anyway. He had to rinse his mouth five or six times before he could even eat a plate of beans without swallowing grit with them.

Call felt uncertain. He had never had to plan for a storm in brushy country, with a fresh herd of cattle. There were so many factors to consider that he felt passive for a moment—an old feeling he knew well from his years of rangering.

Often, in a tight situation, his mind would seem to grow tired from so much hard thinking. He would sink for a time into a blankness, only to come out of it in the midst of an action he had not planned. He was never conscious of the trigger that set him back in motion, but something always pulled it, and he would find himself moving before he was conscious that it was time to move.

Already he could feel a change in the wind. The day had been still, but there was a hot breath against his cheek, coming from the south. He had waited out many such winds in Lonesome Dove, with the sand whirling up from Mexico so fast it felt like birdshot when it hit the skin. The Hell Bitch looked around restlessly, well aware of what was coming.

"It's gonna be a muddy sundown, boys," Augustus said.

In fact, the sun was barely visible, only its edges showing yellow and the disc itself dark as if in an eclipse. To the west and south the sand was rising in the clear sky like a brown curtain, though far above it the evening star was still bright.

Bolivar stopped the wagon and went back to dig around in the piles of bedrolls, looking for his serape.

"Go tell Dish and Soupy to hold up the cattle," Call said to Newt. The boy felt proud to have been given a commission and loped around the herd until he came to the point. The cattle were behaving quietly, just walking along, grazing when there was anything to graze on. Dish was slouched at ease in his saddle.

"I guess this means you've been promoted," he said, when Newt rode up. "Or else I been demoted."

"We're getting a storm," Newt said. "The Captain says to hold 'em up."

Dish looked at the sky and loosened his bandana. "I wish the dern storms would learn to get here in the daytime," he said with a grin. "I don't know why, but they generally strike just when I'm ready to catch a nap."

His attitude toward the storm was contemptuous, as befitted a top hand. Newt tried to imitate his manner but couldn't bring it off. He had never been out in a sandstorm at night, with thousands of cattle to control, and was not looking forward to the experience, which began almost immediately. Before he could get around the herd to Soupy, the sand was blowing. The sun disappeared as if someone had popped a lid over it, and a heavy half-light filled the plains for a few minutes.

"By God, it looks like a good one comin'," Soupy said, adjusting his bandana over his nose and pulling his hat down tight on his head. The loss of hats due to sudden gusts of wind had become a larger problem than Newt would have thought it could be. They were always blowing off, spooking the horses or cattle or both. He was grateful to Deets for having fixed a little rawhide string onto his so that he had been spared the embarrassment of losing it at crucial times.

Newt had meant to go back to the wagon, but the storm gave him no time. While Soupy was fixing his bandana, they looked around and saw streams of sand like small, low clouds blowing in the dim light through the mesquite just to the south. The little clouds of sand seemed like live things, slipping around the mesquite and by the chaparral as a running wolf might, sliding under the bellies of the cattle and then rising a little, to blow over their backs. But behind the little sand streams came a river, composed not of water but of sand. Newt only glanced once, to get his directions, and the sand filled his eyes so that he was immediately blind.

It was in his first moment of blindness that the cattle began to run, as if pushed into motion by the river of sand. Newt heard Soupy's horse break into a run, and

Mouse instantly was running too, but running where, Newt had no idea. He dug a finger into his eyes, hoping to get the sand out, but it was like grinding them with sandpaper. Tears flowed, but the sand turned them to mud on his lashes. Now and then he could get a blurred glimpse out of one eye, and at the first glimpse was horrified to discover that he was in among the cattle. A horn nudged his leg, but Mouse swerved and nothing more happened. Newt stopped worrying about seeing and concentrated on keeping his seat. He knew Mouse could leap any bush not higher than his head. He felt a horrible sense of failure, for surely he had not done his job. The Captain had not meant for him to stay near the head of the herd; he was there because he had not moved quick enough, and it was his fault if he was doomed, as he assumed he was. Once he thought he heard a whoop and was encouraged, but the sound was instantly sucked away by the wind—the wind keened like a cry, its tone rising over the lower tone of the pounding hooves. When Newt began to be able to see again, it did him little good, for it was then almost pitch-dark.

Over the roar of the wind and the running herd he suddenly heard the popping of tree limbs. A second later a mesquite limb hit him in the face and brush tore at him from all sides. He knew they had hit a thicket and assumed it was his end— Mouse faltered and almost went to his knees, but managed to right himself. All Newt could do was duck as low over the horn as possible and hold his arms in front of his face.

To his great relief the running cattle soon slowed. The brush was so thick it checked them as a herd, though the same thicket soon divided them into several groups. The bunch Newt was with soon slowed to a trot and then a walk. Mouse's sides were slick with sweat. Newt felt it was a miracle that he was still alive. Then he heard pistol shots ahead and to his right—a string of cracks, the sound instantly taken by the wind. The wind seemed to be increasing. When he tried to straighten up in the saddle it was like pushing with his back against a heavy door. He tried to turn Mouse, because he still hoped to get back to the rear, where he belonged, but Mouse wouldn't turn. It angered Newt—he was supposed to be making the decisions, not Mouse. The horse would circle, but he wouldn't go into the wind, and Newt finally gave up, aware that he probably couldn't find the wagon or the main herd anyway.

In the short lulls in the wind he could hear the clicking of long horns, as the cattle bumped into one another in the darkness. They were walking slowly, and Newt let Mouse walk along beside them. He had worried as much as he could, and he simply rode, his mind blank. It seemed like he had been riding long enough for the night to be over, but it wasn't, and the sand still stung his skin. He was surprised suddenly by a flicker of light to the west—so quick and so soon lost that he didn't at first recognize it as lightning. But it flickered again and soon was almost constant, though still far away. At first Newt welcomed it—it enabled him to see that he was still with the several hundred cattle, and also helped him avoid thickets.

But as the lightning came closer thunder came with it—the sound seemed to roll over them like giant boulders. Mouse flinched, and Newt began to flinch too. Then, instead of running across the horizon like snakes' tongues, the lightning began to drive into the earth, with streaks thick as poles, and with terrible cracks.

In one of the flashes Newt saw Dish Boggett, not thirty yards away. Dish saw him, too, and came toward him. In the next flash Newt saw Dish pulling on a yellow slicker.

"Where's Soupy?" Dish asked. Newt had no idea.

"He must have got turned wrong," Dish said. "We've got most of the cattle. You should have brought a slicker. We're going to get some rain."

As the flashes continued, Newt strained his eyes to keep Dish in sight, but soon lost him. To his amazement he saw that the cattle seemed to have caught the lightning—little blue balls of it rolled along their horns. While he was watching the strange sight, a horse bumped his. It was Deets.

"Ride off the cattle," he said. "Don't get close to them when they got the lightning on their horns. Get away from 'em."

Newt needed no urging, for the sight was scary and he remembered Dish describing how lightning had hit a cowboy he knew and turned him black. He wanted to ask Deets some questions, but between one flash and another Deets vanished.

The wind had become fitful, gusting and then dying, and instead of beating steadily at his back, the sand was fitful too, swirling around him one moment and gone the next. In the flashes of lightning he could see that the sky was clearing high to the east, but a wall of clouds loomed to the west, the lightning darting underneath them.

Almost before the last of the sand had stung his eyes, it seemed, the rain began, pelting down in big scattered drops that felt good after all the grit. But the drops got thicker and less scattered and soon the rain fell in sheets, blown this way and that at first by the fitful wind. Then the world simply turned to water. In a bright flash of lightning Newt saw a wet, frightened coyote run across a few feet in front of Mouse. After that he saw nothing. The water beat down more heavily even than the wind and the sand: it pounded him and ran in streams off his hat brim. Once again he gave up and simply sat and let Mouse do what he wanted. As far as he knew, he was completely lost, for he had moved away from the cattle in order to escape the lightning and had no sense that he was anywhere near the herd. The rain was so heavy that at moments he felt it might drown him right on his horse. It blew in his face and poured into his lip from his hat brim. He had always heard that cowboying involved considerable weather, but had never expected so many different kinds to happen in one night. An hour before, he had been so hot he thought he would never be cool again, but the drenching water had already made him cold.

Mouse was just as dejected and confused as he was. The ground was covered with water—there was nothing to do but splash along. To make matters worse they hit another thicket and had to back out, for the wet mesquite had become quite impenetrable. When they finally got around it the rain had increased in force. Mouse stopped and Newt let him—there was no use proceeding when they didn't know where they needed to proceed. The water pouring off his hat brim was an awkward thing—one stream in front, one stream behind. A stream of water poured right in front of his nose while another sluiced down his back.

Then Mouse began to move again and Newt heard the splashing of a horse ahead. He didn't know if it carried a friendly rider, but Mouse seemed to think so, for he was trotting through the hock-high water, trying to locate the other horse. In one of the weakening flashes of lightning Newt saw cattle trotting along, fifty yards to his right. Suddenly, with no warning, Mouse began to slide. His back feet almost went out from under him—they had struck a gully, and Newt felt water rising up his legs. Fortunately it wasn't a deep gully; Mouse regained his balance and struggled through it, as scared as Newt.

There was nothing to do but plod on. Newt remembered how happy he had been when dawn finally came after the night they had gone to Mexico. If he could just see such a dawn again he would know how to appreciate it. He was so wet it didn't seem as if he could ever be dry, or that he could do such a simple thing as sit in the bright sun again feeling hot, or stretch out on the grass and sleep. As it was, he couldn't even yawn without water blowing in his mouth.

Soon he got too tired to think and could only hope that it would finally be morning. But the night went on and on. The lightning died and the hard rain stopped, but a drizzle continued; they hit intermittent patches of thick brush and had to back and turn and go on as best they could. When he had crossed the gully, one boot had filled with water. Newt wanted to stop and empty it—but what if he dropped it and couldn't find it in the dark? Or got it off and couldn't get it back on? A fine sight he would make, if he ever saw camp again, riding in with one boot in his hand. Thinking about the ridicule that would involve, he decided just to let the boot squish.

All the same, he felt proud of Mouse, for many horses would have fallen, sliding into a gully.

"Good horse," he said. "If we just keep going maybe it'll get light."

Mouse swung his head to get his wet forelock out of his eyes, and kept on plodding through the mud.

32

J AKE HAD FORGOTTEN to hobble the horses—he remembered it when the first lightning struck and Lorena's young mare suddenly snapped her rein and ran off. It was dark and the sand was still blowing. He managed to get the hobbles on his own horse and the pack mule, but had to let the mare go.

"She won't go far," he said, when he got back to Lorie. She was huddled under a blanket, her back against a big mesquite tree and her legs half buried in the sand.

"No better than she likes to swim. I expect we'll find her on this side of the river," Jake said.

Lorena didn't answer. The lightning filled her with such tension that she didn't think she could endure it. If it went on much longer she felt it would twist her like a wire.

She held the blanket around her as tightly as she could, and her teeth were clenched as they had been when she crossed the river. She kept trying to think about something besides the lightning, but she couldn't. She kept thinking of how it would feel if it hit her—it was said to be like a burn, but how could a burn travel through your body in an instant?

Then the lightning began to strike in the trees nearby, with cracks so loud that it made her head ring. She didn't mind the wet. Jake had tried to rig a tarp, but it wasn't big enough.

A bolt hit just behind them, with a sound so loud that it took her breath. I want to go back, she thought. When she got her breath back she was crying, the tears mingling with the rain on her face.

"We got to get out from under this dern tree," Jake yelled.

Lorena didn't move. He was crazy. The tree was all that was keeping them from death. Out in the open the lightning would immediately strike them.

But Jake began to pull at her. "Come on," he said. "We'll get under the bank. It might strike the tree."

The lightning had become constant—she could see every whisker on Jake's face in the glare. He looked old. But he wouldn't leave her under the tree. In the flashes she could see the river. The river had almost got her and now he wanted her to go back to it. When he pulled, she fought. The tree was the only protection she had and she didn't want to leave it.

"Dern it, come on!" Jake said. "This ain't no place to sit out a lightning storm."

Every time he pulled, the tightness inside her broke out a little and she struck at him. The first blow hit him in the eye and he slipped and sat down in the mud. Then it was dark. When the lightning flashed again, she saw Jake trying to get up, a look of surprise on his face. But he grabbed her in the darkness and began to drag her away from the tree. She kicked at him and they both went down, but a bolt struck so loud and so near that she forgot to fight. She let him pull her toward the river, dragging the tarp. Another bolt hit so near it shook the ground, almost causing Jake to fall in the water. There was not much overhang to the bank, and the tarp was so muddy he could barely drag it, but he pulled it over them and sat close to her, shivering. In the flashes the light was so bright that she could see every wavelet on the river. She wondered where the turtle was, but before she could look it was pitch-dark again. In the next flash she saw the horses jumping and trying to shake off their hobbles. She shut her eyes but when the bolts hit she felt the light on her eyelids. There was nothing to do but wait to die. Jake was shivering against her. She felt her muscles coiling up, getting tighter and tighter.

"Well, I wish we'd brought our feather bed," Jake said, trying to make light of it.

She opened her eyes to blackness and a second later saw the lightning come to earth just across the river, cracking into the tree where they had made their first camp. The tree split at the top, then darkness fell, and when the next flash came the split part had fallen to the ground.

"We got ol' Deets to thank that we're still alive," Jake said. "That one would have got us if we'd stayed put."

You didn't thank him, Lorena thought. She put her head against her knees and waited.

33

BY DAWN the rain had stopped completely and the sky was cloudless. The first sunlight sparkled on the wet thickets and the hundreds of puddles scattered among them, on the wet hides of the cattle and the dripping horses.

At the head of the main bunch of cattle, Call surveyed the situation without too much apprehension. Unless there was a lightning victim somewhere, they had come through the storm well. The cattle had walked themselves out and were docile for the time being. Deets had been to look, and Soupy, Jasper and Needle had the rest of the herd a mile or two east. The wagon was stuck in a gully, but when the hands gathered they soon had enough ropes on it to pull it out. Bol refused to budge from the wagon seat while the pullout took place. Lippy had got out to help push and consequently was covered in mud practically up to his lip.

Newt had been extremely surprised, when dawn came, to discover that he was in his natural position in relation to the herd: behind it. He was too tired even to feel very relieved. All he wanted was to stretch out and sleep. Several times he dozed off, sitting straight up in the saddle. Mouse was just as tired, and kept to a slow walk.

Deets reported that all the hands were well and accounted for with one exception: Mr. Gus. He had been with the main herd for a while but now he was nowhere to be seen.

"He probably rode off to the café to get his breakfast," Dish Boggett said. "Or else went in to San Antone to get himself a shave."

"He might have went to see Mr. Jake," Deets said. "Want me to go look?"

"Yes, have a look," Call said. "I want to cross the river as soon as possible and it would be convenient to have Gus along."

"It ain't much of a river," Dish said. "I could near jump across it if I had a long-legged horse."

When asked how many cattle he thought might be lost Dish estimated no more than twenty-five head, if that many.

"Well, you nearly lost me," Jasper Fant said, when they were all standing around the wagon. Bol had some dry wood that he had kept under a tarp, but the preparation of victuals was going too slowly to suit most of the hands.

"I'm so tired I won't be worth nothing for a week," Jasper added.

"When was you ever worth anything?" Dish inquired. He himself was in rather good fettle. It always improved his mood to have his skill recognized, as it clearly was by all hands. He had managed to turn the main part of the herd out of the worst of the brush and keep it together. Even Captain Call had seemed impressed.

The only cowboy who had not performed up to caliber in the emergency was Sean O'Brien, who had been walking out to catch his night horse when the storm hit. He was such a poor roper that Newt usually roped his horses for him, if he happened to be around. This time, of course, he hadn't been. The Spettles, responsible for the remuda, were afraid Sean's awkward roping would cause the whole herd to bolt; Bill Spettle had roped a horse for him, but it wasn't one he could ride. Sean had promptly been bucked off, and when the remuda did bolt, Sean's horse ran with it. Sean had been forced to ride in the wagon all night, more worried for his life than his reputation. Bolivar had made it clear that he didn't like passengers.

While breakfast was cooking most of the cowboys pulled off their shirts and spread them on bushes to dry. A few took off their pants, too, but only the few who possessed long underwear. Dish Boggett was one of the few who had carefully wrapped his extra clothes in an oilcloth, so he soon had on dry pants and a shirt, which somewhat increased his sense of superiority to the rest of the crew.

"You boys look like a dern bunch of wet chickens," he said.

It was true that the crew presented an odd appearance, though Newt wouldn't have compared them to chickens. Most of them were burned a deep brown on the face, neck and hands, but the rest of their bodies, which the sun never touched, were stark white. Bert Borum was the funniest-looking without a shirt, for he had a round fat belly with curly black hair on it that ran right down into his pants.

Pea Eye walked around in a pair of all-enveloping long johns which he had worn continuously for the last several years. He had his knife and gun belt on over his underwear, in case of sudden attack.

"There ain't no point in gettin' too dry," he pointed out. "We got to cross the river after a while."

"I'd just as soon go around it," Needle said. "I've crossed it many times but I've been lucky."

"I'll be glad to cross it—maybe I'll get a wash," Lippy said. "I can't do much under all this mud."

"Why, that ain't a river, it's just a creek," Dish said. "The last time I crossed it I didn't even notice it."

"I guess you'll notice it if five or six of them heifers get on top of you," Jasper said.

"It's just the first of many," Bert said. "How many rivers is it between here and the Yellowstone?"

The question set everyone to counting and arguing, for as soon as they decided they had an accurate count, someone would think of another stream, and there would be a discussion as to whether it should count as a river.

The Rainey boys were sleeping under the wagon. Both had dropped like rocks once they dismounted, oblivious to wet clothes and too tired to be interested in food. The Raineys liked their sleep, whereas the Spettles could do without it. They seemed unaffected by the strenuous night—they sat apart, as silent as always.

"I wish they'd talk, so we'd know what they were thinking," Sean said. The silent Spettles made him nervous.

Call was annoyed with Gus, who had still not returned. Pea had reported seeing him just after dawn, riding east in evident health. Call noticed the Texas bull, standing about fifty yards away. He was watching the two pigs, who were rooting around a chaparral bush. Probably they were trying to root out a ground squirrel, or perhaps a rattlesnake. The bull took a few steps toward them, but the pigs ignored him.

Needle Nelson was scared of the bull. The minute he noticed him he went to get his rifle out of his saddle scabbard. "If he comes at me, I aim to shoot him," Needle said. "He'll never live to cross the Yellowstone unless he leaves me be."

Lippy, too, disliked the bull, and climbed up on the wagon when he saw how close the bull was.

"He won't charge the camp," Call said—though in fact he was not so sure the bull wouldn't.

"Why, he charged Needle," Jasper said. "Needle had to get going so fast he near forgot his dingus."

At that there was a general laugh, though Needle Nelson didn't join in. He kept his rifle propped against a wagon wheel while he was eating.

The bull continued to watch the pigs.

34

AS SOON AS THE SUN got high enough to be warm, Lorena spread their gear on trees and bushes to dry. It seemed astonishing to her that she was alive and unhurt after such a night. Her spirits rose rapidly and she was even reconciled to having to ride the pack mule. But Jake wouldn't hear of that. His own spirits were low.

"I hate to squish every move I make," he said. "It ain't supposed to get this wet in these parts."

Now that the scare was over, Lorena found that she didn't mind that things were damp. It beat being hot, in her book. The only awkward part was that the few foodstuffs they had brought had been soaked. The flour was ruined, the salt a lump. At least the bacon and coffee weren't ruined, and they had a little of each before Jake rode off to look for her horse.

Once he left, she went down to the river to wash the mud off her legs. Then, since the sun was already hot, she found a grassy place that wasn't too wet and lay down to have a nap. Looking up at the sky, her spirits rose even more. The sky was perfectly clear and blue, only whitened with sun over to the east. Being outside felt good—she had spent too much time in little hot rooms, looking at ceilings.

While she was resting, who should come riding up with her mare but Gus.

"I hope there's still some coffee in the pot," he said, when he dismounted. "I've usually had ten biscuits by this time of day, not to mention some honey and a few eggs. Got any eggs, Lorie?"

"No, but we got bacon," she said. "I'll fry you some."

Augustus looked around with amusement at the muddy camp.

"I don't see young Jake," he said. "Is he off preaching a sermon, or did he wash away?"

"He went to look for the horse, only I guess he went in the wrong direction," Lorie said.

Augustus took out his big clasp knife and cut the bacon for her. For a woman who had spent the night being drenched she looked wonderfully fresh, young and beautiful. Her hair was not yet dry; the wet ends were dark. Occasionally a little line of water ran down her bare arm. Bending over the fire, her face was relaxed in a way he had never seen it. The strain that always showed in Lonesome Dove—the strain of always holding herself apart—had disappeared, making her look girlish.

"Why, Lorie," he said, "I guess traveling agrees with you. You look pretty as the morning."

Lorena smiled. It was funny. Out in the open she felt more at ease with Gus than she had in the saloon.

"How long has Jake been gone?" he asked.

"Not long," she said. "He rode down the river, looking for tracks."

Augustus laughed. "Why, Jake couldn't track an elephant if he was more than ten steps behind it," he said. "I guess we ought to call him back before he gets lost."

He drew his pistol and fired a couple of shots into the air.

A few minutes later, as he was finishing the bacon, Jake came galloping into camp, rifle in hand. Lorena was going around from bush to bush, collecting the clothes, which the hot sun had already dried.

"Gus, I didn't know we was gonna have to have you for breakfast every day of the whole trip," Jake said.

"You was never grateful for nothing, Jake," Augustus said. "Here I returned a fifty-dollar horse that you couldn't have found in a week, and all you can do is gripe about my company."

"Well, there's such a thing as too much of your dern company," Jake said, looking to see if Lorie was out of hearing.

"Are you jealous, or what?" Augustus asked.

"Why wouldn't I be, when you've tried to poke every woman I ever looked at?" Jake said.

"Whoa, now," Augustus said. "I'm just eating my bite of bacon. But I will say you should have brought a tent if you mean to take a sprightly girl like Lorie out in the weather."

Jake didn't intend to spend any time bantering about women with Gus. It was good they had the horse back, of course. "I reckon we'll pack up and move on to San Antonio," he said, just as Lorena came back with an armful of dry clothes.

"I don't want to go to San Antone," she said. "I been there."

Jake was taken aback. "Why, it's a good gambling town," he said. "We ain't rich yet. It wouldn't hurt us to stop for a week, while the boys get the herd started good. Then we can catch up."

"I don't like to go back to places," Lorena said. "It's bad luck."

"Yes, and it would be worse luck to get up the trail and run out of money."

"That's all right, Jake," Augustus said, flinging the dregs of his coffee into a chaparral bush. "I'll be glad to keep tabs on Lorie while you run into town and lose your wad."

"What makes you think I'd lose it?" Jake said, his face darkening.

"You'd lose it if I was around," Augustus said, "and if I wasn't handy, you'd probably get in a scrape and shoot another dentist. Besides, if anybody with a badge on is trying to hunt you up, I'd think the first place they'd look is San Antonio."

"If anybody with a badge on comes looking for me he's apt to find more of me than he wants," Jake said. "Let's get packed, Lorie. We might make town tomorrow, if we push on."

"I don't want to go to San Antonio," Lorena said again. She knew Jake hated to be contradicted, but she didn't much care.

Before she could think, he whipped around and slapped her—not hard, but it was a slap.

"Dern it all, I guess you'll go where I say go," he said, his face red with anger.

Lorena felt embarrassed to have been hit in front of Gus, but he seemed uninterested in what she and Jake did. Of course he was just being polite—what else could he do?

She remembered all the money Xavier had pressed on her. It was lucky she had it.

She looked at Augustus again and saw that he was quietly watching, waiting to see how she would handle Jake, who was glaring at her, expecting her to cry, probably. But it had taken all the fury of the storm to make her cry; a little pop from him was just something to be ignored. She turned her back on him and walked off to start the packing.

In a minute Jake cooled down sufficiently to come over and squat by the fire. "I don't know what's wrong with Lorie," he said. "She's getting touchy."

Augustus chuckled. "You're the one that's touchy," he said. "She didn't slap you."

"Well, by God, why would she buck me?" Jake asked. "I'm the one that decides where we go and when we stop."

"You may be and you may not be," Augustus said. "Maybe it ain't that simple."

"It'll be that simple or she'll have soon seen the last of me," Jake said.

"I doubt she'll miss you, Jake," Augustus said. "You got your charms but then I got my charms too. I'll come and make camp with her if you decide you've had enough of her sass. I ain't violent like you, neither."

"I didn't hurt her," Jake said. He felt a little guilty about the slap—it had upset him to ride in and see her sitting there with Gus, and then she bucked him. Gus always managed to aggravate whatever situation he was in with a woman.

"I've got to go," Augustus said. "Captain Call will be mad as a hornet if I don't get back. Much obliged for the breakfast."

"That's two you owe us," Jake said. "I hope you'll ride into town and buy us a feed when you're up that way."

"Why, the two of you won't be in town," Augustus said. He trotted down to where Lorena was quietly packing the mule.

"Don't forget to hobble that mare," he said. "I guess she ain't as tired of Lonesome Dove as we are. She was on her way home when I came across her."

"I'll hobble her," Lorena said. She gave Gus a grin—Jake's little flare-up had not affected her good spirits.

"If you get any prettier you won't be safe around me," Augustus said. "I might be forced to cut the cards with you again."

"No, I told you we're gonna play a hand next time," Lorena said. "It'll give me a better chance."

"You look out for yourself," Augustus said. "If that scamp runs off and leaves you, why, come and get me. You can find us by the dust."

"He won't leave," Lorena said. "He'll be fine."

She watched Gus swim the muddy river. He waved from the other bank and soon disappeared into the brush. She went on packing. Soon Jake couldn't stand it and walked over.

"You oughtn't to provoke me like that," he said, looking a little hangdog. He tried putting his hands on her, but Lorena shrugged them off and went to the other side of the pack mule.

"I wasn't provoking you," she said. "I just said I wasn't going back to San Antone."

"Dern it, I'd like to gamble a little somewhere between here and Denver," Jake said.

"Go gamble," she said. "I never said you couldn't. I'll stay in camp."

"Oh, no doubt you've made arrangements with Gus," Jake said. "I guess he's planning to come over and teach you card tricks," he said bitterly, and turned on his heel.

Lorena didn't mind. It was too pretty a day. The fact that Gus had found her horse was a good sign. She felt like riding, even though the country was brushy. She felt like a lope, in fact. Jake could sulk if he wanted to. She was looking forward to the trip.

35

THE DAY SOON GREW HOT, and the cattle, tired from their all-night walk, were sluggish and difficult to move. Call had to put half the crew on the drags to keep going. Still, he was determined to get across the Nueces, for Deets had said he expected it to storm again that night.

There was no avoiding the brush entirely, but Deets had found a route that took them slightly downriver, around the worst of the thickets. As they got close to the river they began to encounter swarms of mosquitoes, which attacked horses and men alike, settling on them so thickly that they could be wiped off like stains. All the men covered their faces as best they could, and the few who had gloves put them on. The horses were soon flinching, stamping and swishing their tails, their withers covered with mosquitoes. The cattle were restive too, mosquitoes around their eyes and in their nostrils.

Newt was soon so covered with blood from mashed mosquitoes that he looked as if he had been wounded in battle. Sean, who rode near him, was no better. Any inconvenience made Sean think of home, and the mosquitoes were a big inconvenience.

"I'd like to be going to Ireland," he told Newt. "If I only knew where the boats were, I'd be going." His face was lumpy from mosquito bites.

"I guess we'll drown the skeeters when we hit the river," Newt said. It was the only thing that promised relief. He had been dreading the river, but that was before the mosquitoes hit.

To make matters worse, one particular red cow had begun to irritate him almost beyond endurance. She had developed a genius for wiggling into thickets and just stopping. Shouting made no impression on her at all—she would stand in the thicket looking at him, well aware that she was safe. Once Newt dismounted, planning to scare her on foot, but she lowered her head menacingly and he abandoned that idea.

Time and again she hid in a thicket, and time and again, after shouting himself hoarse, he would give up and force his horse into the thicket after her. The cow would bolt out, popping limbs with her horns, and run as if she meant to lead the herd. But when the next thicket appeared, she would wiggle right in. She was so much trouble that he was sorely tempted to leave her—it seemed to him the boys were driving the herd and he was just driving the one red cow.

Once the mosquitoes hit, the cow's dilatoriness became almost more than Newt could endure. The cow would stand in a thicket and look at him silently and stupidly, moving only when she had to and stopping again as soon as she could find a convenient thicket. Newt fought down a terrible urge just to pull his gun and shoot her—that would show the hussy! Nothing less was going to make any impression on her—he had never felt so provoked by a single animal before. But he couldn't shoot her and he couldn't leave her; the Captain wouldn't approve of either action. He had already shouted himself hoarse. All he could do was pop her out of thicket after thicket.

Call had taken the precaution of buying a lead steer from the Pumphreys—a big, docile longhorn they called Old Dog. The steer had never been to Montana, of course, but he had led several herds to Matagorda Bay. Call figured the old steer would at least last until they had the herd well trail-broken.

"Old Dog's like me," Augustus said, watching Dish Boggett edge the old steer to the front of the herd in preparation for the crossing.

"How's that?" Call asked. "Lazy, you mean?"

"Mature, I mean," Augustus said. "He don't get excited about little things."

"You don't get excited about nothing," Call said. "Not unless it's biscuits or whores. So what was Jake up to?" he asked. It rankled him that the man was being so little help. Jake had done many irritating things in his rangering days, but nothing as aggravating as bringing a whore along on a cattle drive.

"Jake was up to being Jake," Augustus said. "It's a full-time job. He requires a woman to help him with it."

Dish had gradually eased Old Dog to the front of the herd, working slowly and quietly. The old steer was twice as big as most of the scrawny yearlings that made up the herd. His horns were long and they bent irregularly, as if they were jointed.

Just before the men reached the river they came out into a clearing a mile or more wide. It was a relief, after the constant battle with the mesquite and chaparral. The grass was tall. Call loped through it with Deets, to look at the crossing. Dish trotted over to Augustus on the trim sorrel he called Mustache, a fine cow horse whose eyes were always watching to see that no rebellious cow tried to make a break for freedom. Dish uncoiled his rope and made a few practice throws at a low mesquite seedling. Then he even took a throw, for a joke, at a low-flying buzzard that had just risen off the carcass of an armadillo.

"I guess you're practicing up so you can rope a woman, if we make it to Ogallala," Augustus said.

"You don't have to rope women in that town, I hear," Dish said. "They rope you."

"It's a long way to Nebrasky," Augustus said. "You'll be ready to be roped by then, Dish."

"Where'd you go for half the morning?" Dish asked. He was hoping Gus would talk a little about Lorena, though part of him didn't want to hear it, since it would involve Jake Spoon.

"Oh, Miss Lorena and I like to take our coffee together in the morning," Augustus said.

"I hope the weather didn't treat her too bad," Dish said, feeling wistful suddenly. He could think of nothing pleasanter than taking coffee with Lorena in the morning.

"No, she's fine," Augustus said. "The fresh air agrees with her, I guess."

Dish said no more, and Augustus decided not to tease him. Occasionally the very youngness of the young moved him to charity—they had no sense of the swiftness of life, nor of its limits. The years would pass like weeks, and loves would pass too, or else grow sour. Young Dish, skilled cowhand that he was, might not live to see the whores of Ogallala, and the tender feelings he harbored for Lorena might be the sweetest he would ever have.

Looking at Dish, so tight with his need for Lorena, whom he would probably never have, Augustus remembered his own love for Clara Allen—it had pained him and pleased him at once. As a young woman Clara had such grace that just looking at her could choke a man; then, she was always laughing, though her life had not been the easiest. Despite her cheerful eyes, Clara was prone to sudden angers, and sadnesses so deep that nothing he could say or do would prompt her to answer him, or even to look at him. When she left to marry her horse trader, he felt that he had missed the great opportunity of his life; for all their fun together he had not quite been able to touch her, either in her happiness or her sadness. It wasn't because of his wife, either—it was because Clara had chosen the angle of their relation. She loved him in certain ways, wanted him for certain purposes, and all his straining, his tricks, his looks and his experience could not induce her to alter the angle.

The day she told him she was going to marry the horse trader from Kentucky, he had been too stunned to say much. She just told him plainly, with no fuss: Bob was the kind of man she needed, and that was that. He could remember the moment still: they had been standing in front of her little store, in Austin, and she had taken his hand and held it for a time.

"Well, Clara," he said, feeling very lame, "I think you are a fool but I wish you happiness. I guess I'll see you from time to time."

"You won't if I can help it, Gus," she said. "You leave me be for the next ten years or so. Then come and visit."

"Why ten years?" he asked, puzzled.

Clara grinned—her humor never rested for long. "Why, I'll be a wife," she said. "I won't be wanting to be tempted by the likes of you. But once I've got the hang of married life I'll want you to come."

It made no sense at all to Augustus. "Why?" he asked. "Planning to run off after ten years, or what?"

"No," Clara said. "But I'd want my children to know you. I'd want them to have your friendship."

It struck him that he was already years late—it had been some sixteen years since Clara held his hand in front of the store. He had not watched the time closely, but it wouldn't matter. It might only mean that there would be more children for him to be friends with.

"I may just balk in Ogallala," he said out loud.

Dish was surprised. "Well, balk any time you want to, Gus," he said.

Augustus was put out with himself for having spoken his thoughts. Still, the chance of settling near Clara and her family appealed to him more than the thought of following Call into another wilderness. Clara was an alert woman who, even as a girl, had read all the papers; he would have someone to talk to about the events of the times. Call had no interest in the events of the times, and a person like Pea Eye wouldn't even know what an event was. It would be nice to chat regularly with a woman who kept up—though of course it was possible that sixteen years on the frontier had taken the edge off Clara's curiosity.

"Can you read, Dish?" he asked.

"Well, I know my letters," Dish said. "I can read some words. Of course there's plenty I ain't had no practice with."

A few hundred yards away they could see Call and Deets riding along the riverbank, studying the situation.

"I wisht we was up to the Red River," Dish said. "I don't like this low country."

"I wish we was to the Yellowstone, myself," Augustus said. "Maybe Captain Call would be satisfied with that."

When they reached the river it seemed that it was going to be the smoothest crossing possible. Old Dog seemed to have an affinity for Deets and followed him right into the water without so much as stopping to sniff. Call and Dish, Augustus and Pea and Needle Nelson spread out on the downriver side, but the cattle showed no signs of wanting to do anything but follow Old Dog.

The water was a muddy brown and the current fast, but the cattle only had to swim a few yards. One or two small bunches attempted to turn back, but with most of the crew surrounding them they didn't make a serious challenge.

Despite the smoothness, Newt felt a good deal afraid and shut his eyes for a second when his horse went to swimming depth and the water came over the saddle. But he got no wetter, and he opened his eyes to see that he was almost across the river. He struck the far bank almost at the same time as a skinny brown longhorn; Mouse and the steer struggled up the bank side by side.

It was just as Newt turned to watch the last of the cattle cross that a scream cut the air, so terrible that it almost made him faint. Before he could even look toward the scream Pea Eye went racing past him, with the Captain just behind him. They both had coiled ropes in their hands as they raced their horses back into the water—Newt wondered what they meant to do with the ropes. Then his eyes found Sean, who was screaming again and again, in a way that made Newt want to cover his ears. He saw that Sean was barely clinging to his horse, and that a lot of brown things were wiggling around him and over him. At first, with the screaming going on, Newt couldn't figure out what the brown things were—they seemed like giant worms. His mind took a moment to work out what his eyes were seeing. The giant worms were snakes—water moccasins. Even as the realization struck him, Mr. Gus and Deets went into the river behind Pea Eye and the Captain. How they all got there so fast he couldn't say, for the screams had started just as Mouse and the steer reached the top of the bank, so close that Newt could see the droplets of water on the steer's horns.

Then the screams stopped abruptly as Sean slipped under the water—his voice was replaced almost at once by the frenzied neighing of the horse, which began to thrash in the water and soon turned back toward the far bank. As he gained a footing and rose out of the water he shook three snakes from his body, one slithering off his neck.

Pea Eye and the Captain were beating about themselves with their coiled ropes. Newt saw Sean come to the surface downstream, but he wasn't screaming any more. Pea leaned far off his horse and managed to catch Sean's arm, but then his horse got frightened of the snakes and Pea lost his hold. Deets was close by. When Sean came up again Pea got him by the collar and held on. Sean was silent, though Newt could see that his mouth was open. Deets got Pea's horse by the bridle and kept it still. Pea managed to get his hands under Sean's arms and drag him across the saddle. The snakes had scattered, but several could be seen on the surface of the river. Dish Boggett had his rifle drawn but was too shaken by the sight to shoot. Deets waved him back. Suddenly there was a loud crack—Mr. Gus had shot a snake with his big Colt. Twice more he shot and two more snakes disappeared. The Captain rode close to Pea and helped him support Sean's body.

In a minute Pea's horse was across the deep water and found its footing. Call and Deets held the horse still while Pea took the dying boy in his arms—then Deets led the horse ashore. Augustus rode out of the water behind Call. The cattle were still crossing, but no cowboys were crossing with them. Bert, the Rainey boys and Allen O'Brien were on the south bank, not eager to take the water. A mile back, across the long clearing, the wagon and the horses had just come in sight.

Pea handed the boy down to Dish and Deets. Call quickly took his slicker off his saddle and they laid the boy on it. His eyes were closed, his body jerking slightly. Augustus cut the boy's shirt off—there were eight sets of fang marks, including one on his neck.

"That don't count the legs," Augustus said. "There ain't no point in counting the legs."

"What done it?" Dish asked. He had seen the snakes plainly and had even wanted to shoot them, but he couldn't believe it or understand it.

"It was his bad luck to strike a nest of them, I guess," Augustus said. "I never seen a nest of snakes in this river before and I've crossed it a hundred times. I never seen that many snakes in any river."

"The storm got 'em stirred up," Deets said.

Call knelt by the boy, helpless to do one thing for him. It was the worst luck—to come all the way from Ireland and then ride into a swarm of water moccasins. He remembered, years before, in a hot droughty summer, stopping to water his horse in a drying lake far up the Brazos—he had ridden his horse in so he could drink and had happened to look down and see that the muddy shallows of the lake were alive with cottonmouths. The puddles were like nests, filled with wiggling snakes, as brown as chocolate. Fortunately he had not ridden into such a puddle. The sight unnerved him so that he shot a snake on reflex—a useless act, to shoot one where there were hundreds.

He had seen the occasional snake in rivers along the coast but never more than one or two together; there had been at least twenty, probably more, around the boy. On the south bank, the horse he had ridden was rolling over and over in the mud, ignored by the frightened cowboys. Maybe the horse was bitten too.

Pea, who had been the first to the rescue, swimming his mount right into the midst of the snakes, suddenly felt so weak he thought he would fall off his horse. He dismounted, clinging to the horn in case his legs gave out.

Augustus noticed how white he was and went to him.

"Are you snake-bit, Pea?" he asked, for in the confusion a man could get wounds he wasn't aware of. He had known more than one man to take bullets without noticing it; one Ranger had been so frightened when his wound was pointed out to him that he died of fright, not the bullet.

"I don't think I'm bit," Pea said. "I think I whupped them off."

"Get your pants down," Call said. "One could have struck you down low."

They could find no wound on Pea—meanwhile, the cattle had begun to drift, with no one watching them cross. Some were making the bank a hundred yards downstream. The cowboys on the south bank had still not crossed.

"Gus, you and Deets watch him," Call said, mounting. "We've got to keep the cattle from drifting."

He noticed Newt sitting beside Pea's horse, his face white as powder.

"Come help us," he said, as Pea and Dish loped off toward the cattle.

Newt turned his horse and followed the Captain, feeling that he was doing wrong. He should have said something to Sean, even if Sean couldn't hear him. He wanted to tell Sean to go on and find a boat somewhere and go back to Ireland quick, whatever the Captain might think. Now he knew Sean was going to die, and that it was forever too late for him to find the boat, but he wanted to say it anyway. He had had a chance to say it, but had missed it.

He trotted beside the Captain, feeling that he might vomit, and also feeling disloyal to Sean.

"He wanted to go back to Ireland!" he said suddenly, tears pouring out of his eyes. He was so grieved he didn't care.

"Well, I expect he did," the Captain said quietly.

Newt held his reins, still crying, and let Mouse do the work. He remembered Sean's screams, and how much the snakes had looked like giant wiggly worms. When at last the cattle were started back toward the main herd the Captain put his horse back into the river, which startled Newt. He didn't see how anybody could just ride back into a river that could suddenly be filled with snakes, but this time no snakes appeared. Newt saw that Mr. Gus and Deets had not moved, and wondered if Sean was dead yet. He kept feeling he ought to leave the cattle and go talk to Sean, even if it was too late for Sean to answer, but he was afraid to. He didn't know what to do, and he sat on his horse and cried until he started vomiting. He had to lean over and vomit beneath his horse's neck.

In his mind he began to wish for some way to undo what had happened—to make the days run backward, to the time when they were still in Lonesome Dove. He imagined Sean alive and well—and did what he had not done, told him to go off to Galveston and find a boat to take him home. But he kept looking back, and there was Deets and Mr. Gus, kneeling by Sean. He longed to see Sean sit up and be all right, but Sean didn't, and Newt could only sit hopelessly on his horse and hold the cattle.

Augustus and Deets could do little for Sean except sit with him while his life was ending.

"I guess it would have been better if Pea had just let him drown," Augustus said. "He was an unlucky young sprout."

"Mighty unlucky," Deets said. He felt an unsteadiness in his limbs. Though he had seen much violent death, he had not seen one more terrible than the one that had just occurred. He felt he would never again cross a river without remembering it.

Before his brother crossed the river, Sean O'Brien died. Augustus covered the boy with his slicker just as the horse herd came clambering up the bank. The herd passed so close that when some of the horses stopped to shake themselves the fine spray wet Deets's back. The Spettle boys came out of the river wide-eyed with fright, clinging to their wet mounts. On the far bank Call had the other men helping to ease the wagon down the steep crossing.

"Now if them snakes had come at Bol, he would have had a chance," Augustus said. "He has his ten-gauge."

"The storm stirred them up," Deets said again. He felt guilty, for he had chosen the crossing in preference to one up the river, and now a boy was dead.

"Well, Deets, life is short," Augustus said. "Shorter for some than for others. This is a bad way to start a trip."

Bolivar was unhappy. He didn't think the wagon would make it, even across such a small river, but he was not willing to leave it either. He sat grimly on the wagon seat, Lippy beside him, while the cowboys got ropes on the wagon.

"You mean Sean's dead?" Allen O'Brien asked the Captain, so stunned he could barely speak.

"Yes, he's dead," Call said—he had seen Gus cover the corpse.

"It's me that done it," Allen said, tears on his round face. "I never should have brought the boy. I knew he was too young."

Call said nothing more. The boy's age had had nothing to do with what had happened, of course; even an experienced man, riding into such a mess of snakes, wouldn't have survived. He himself might not have, and he had never worried about snakes. It only went to show what he already knew, which was that there were more dangers in life than even the sharpest training could anticipate. Allen O'Brien should waste no time on guilt, for a boy could die in Ireland as readily as elsewhere, however safe it might appear.

Jasper and Bert had seen the snakes, and Jasper was so terrified that he couldn't look at the water. Soupy Jones was almost as scared. The Rainey boys looked as if they might fall off their horses.

More than anything, Jasper wanted to quit. He had crossed the Nueces many times, and yet, as the moment approached when he would have to do it again, he felt he couldn't. Pea and Dish and the others who had already crossed seemed to him like the luckiest men in the world.

"Captain, do you reckon them snakes are gone?" he asked.

"Well, they're scattered," Call said.

As they got ready to go in Jasper drew his pistol, but Call shook his head. "No shooting," he said. He had no confidence that any of the men could shoot from a swimming horse and hit anything, as Gus had.

"Just quirt 'em if you see any," he added.

"I hope none don't crawl in this wagon," Lippy said, his lip quivering with apprehension.

The wagon floated better than expected—Bolivar barely got his feet wet. Jasper flinched once when he saw a stick he thought was a snake, but the moccasins had scattered and were not seen again.

Allen O'Brien dismounted and stood and cried over his brother. Jasper Fant cried, too, mostly from relief that he was still alive.

While they were having their cry, Deets and Pea got shovels from the wagon and dug a grave, back from the river a hundred yards, beside a live oak tree. Then they cut off part of one of the wagon sheets, wrapped the dead boy in it and carried him in the wagon to the grave. They laid him in it and Deets and Pea soon covered him, while most of the crew stood around, not knowing what to do or say.

"If you'd like to sing or something, do it," Call said. Allen stood a moment, started singing an Irish song in a quavering voice, then broke down crying and couldn't finish it.

"I don't have no pianer or I'd play one of the church hymns," Lippy said.

"Well, I'll say a word," Augustus said. "This was a good, brave boy, for we all saw that he conquered his fear of riding. He had a fine tenor voice, and we'll all miss that. But he wasn't used to this part of the world. There's accidents in life and he met with a bad one. We may all do the same if we ain't careful."

He turned and mounted old Malaria. "Dust to dust," he said. "Lets the rest of us go on to Montana."

He's right, Call thought. The best thing to do with a death was to move on from it. One by one the cowboys mounted and went off to the herd, many of them taking a quick last look at the muddy grave under the tree.

Augustus waited for Allen O'Brien, who was the last to mount. He was so weak from shock, it seemed he might not be able to, but he finally got on his horse and rode off, looking back until the grave was hidden by the tall gray grass. "It seems too quick," he said. "It seems very quick, just to ride off and leave the boy. He was the babe of our family," he added.

"If we was in town we'd have a fine funeral," Augustus said. "But as you can see, we ain't in town. There's nothing you can do but kick your horse."

"I wish I could have finished the song," Allen said.

36

THE WHISKEY BOAT STANK, and the men on it stank, but Elmira was not sorry she had taken passage. She had a tiny little cubbyhole among the whiskey casks, with a few planks and some buffalo skins thrown over it to keep the rain out, but she spent most of her time sitting at the rear of the boat, watching the endless flow of brown water. Some days were so hot that the air above the water shimmered and the shore became indistinct; other days a chill rain blew and she wrapped herself in one of the buffalo robes and kept fairly dry. The rain was welcome, for it discouraged the fleas. They made her sleep uneasy, but it was a small price to pay for escaping from Fort Smith. She had lived where there were fleas before, and worse things than fleas.

As the boat inched its way up the Arkansas, the brown river gradually narrowed, and as it narrowed the boatmen and whiskey traders grew more restless. They drank so much whiskey themselves that Elmira felt they would be lucky to have any left to sell. Though she often felt them watching her as she sat at the end of the boat, they let her alone. Only Fowler, the chief trader, ever spoke more than a word or two to her. Fowler was a burly man with a dirty yellow beard and one eyelid that wouldn't behave. It twitched and jerked up and down erratically, so that looking at him was disconcerting: one minute he would be looking at you out of both eyes, and then the eyelid would droop and he would only be looking with an eye and a half.

Fowler drank continuously—all day and all night, so far as Elmira could tell. When she woke, from the fleas or the rocking of the boat, she would always hear his hoarse voice, talking to anyone who would listen. He kept a heavy rifle in the crook of his arm, and his eyes were always scanning the banks.

Mainly Fowler talked of Indians, for whom he had a pure hatred. He had been a buffalo hunter and had had many run-ins with them. When the buffalo ran out he began to traffic in whiskey. So far neither he nor any of his men had offered Elmira the slightest offense. It surprised her. They were a rough-looking bunch, and she had taken a big gamble in getting on the boat. No one in Fort Smith had seen her leave, as far as she knew, and the boatmen could have killed her and thrown her to the turtles without anyone's being the wiser. The first few nights in her cubbyhole she had been wakeful and a little frightened, expecting one of the men to stumble in and fall on her. She waited, thinking it would happen—if it did, she would only have her old life back, which had been part of the point of leaving. She would stop being July Johnson's wife, at least. It might be rough for a while, but eventually she would find Dee and life would improve.

But the men avoided her, day or night—all except Fowler, who wandered the boat constantly. Once, standing beside her, he knelt suddenly and cocked his rifle, but what he thought was an Indian turned out to be a bush. "The heat's got my eye jumping," he said, spitting a brown stream of tobacco into the water.

Elmira also watched the distant banks, which were green with the grass of spring. As the river gradually narrowed, she saw many animals: deer, coyote, cattle—but no Indians. She remembered stories heard over the years about women being carried off by Indians; in Kansas she had had such a woman pointed out to her, one who had been rescued and brought back to live with whites again. To her the woman seemed no different from other women, though it was true that she seemed cowed; but then, many women were cowed by events more ordinary. It was hard to see how the Indians could be much worse than the buffalo hunters, two of whom were on board. The sight of them brought back painful memories. They were big men with buffalo-skin coats and long shaggy hair—they looked like the animals they hunted. At night, in her cubbyhole, she would sometimes hear them relieving themselves over the side of the boat; they would stand just beyond the whiskey casks and pour their water into the Arkansas.

For some reason the sound reminded her of July, perhaps because she had never heard him make it. July was reticent about such things and would walk far into the woods when he had to go, to spare her any embarrassment. She found his reticence and shyness strangely irritating—it sometimes made her want to tell him what she had really done before they married. But she held back that truth, and every other truth she knew; she ceased talking to July Johnson at all.

In the long days and nights, with no one to talk to but Fowler, and him only occasionally, Elmira found herself thinking more and more about Dee. Joe she didn't think about, had never thought about much. He had never seemed hers, exactly, though she had certainly borne him. But from the first she had looked at him with detachment and only mild interest, and the twelve years since his birth had been a waiting period—waiting for the time for when she could send him away and belong only to herself again. It occurred to her that the one good thing about marrying July Johnson was that he would do to leave Joe with.

With Dee, she could belong to herself, for if ever a man belonged to himself, it was Dee. You never knew where Dee would be from one day to the next; when he was there he was always eager to share the fun, but then, before you could look around he had vanished, off to another town or another girl.

Soon the skies above the river got wider and wider as the river wound out of the trees and cut through the plains. The nights were cool, the mornings warming quickly, so that when Elmira woke the river behind her would be covered with a frosting of mist, and the boat would be lost in the mist completely, until the sun could break through. Several times ducks and geese, taking off in the mist, almost flew into her as she stood at the rear of the boat wrapped in the buffalo robe. When the mist was heavy the splash of birds or the jumping of fish startled her; once she was frightened by the heavy beat of wings as one of the huge gray cranes flew low over the boat. As the mist thinned she would see the cranes standing solemnly in the shallows, ignoring the strings of ducks that swam nearby. Pockets of mist would linger on the water for an hour or more after the sun had risen and the sky turned a clear blue.

At night many sounds came from the banks, the most frequent being the thin howling of coyotes. From time to time during the day they would see a coyote or a gray wolf on the bank, and the hunters would sharpen their aim by shooting at the animals. They seldom killed one, for the river was still too wide; sometimes Elmira would see the bullets kick mud.

When there was no rain she liked the nights and would often slip to the rear of the boat and listen to the gurgle and suck of the water. There were stars by the millions; one night the full moon seemed to rise out of the smoky river. The moon was so large that at first it seemed to touch both banks. Its light turned the evening mist to a color like pearl. But then the moon rose higher and grew yellow as a melon.

It was the morning after the full moon that a fight broke out between one of the whiskey traders and a buffalo hunter. Elmira, waking, heard loud argument, which was nothing new—almost every night there was loud argument, once the men got drunk. Once or twice they fought with fists, bumping against the casks that formed the walls of her room, but those fights ran their course. She had seen many men fight and was not much disturbed.

But the morning fight was different—she was awakened by a high scream. It ended in a kind of moan and she heard a body fall to the deck of the boat. Then she heard heavy breathing, as the winner of the fight caught his breath. The man soon walked away and a heavy silence fell—so heavy that Elmira wondered if everyone had left the boat. She began to feel frightened. Maybe Indians had got on the boat and killed all the whiskey traders. She huddled in her quilts, wondering what to do, but then she heard Fowler's gruff voice. It had just been a fight of some kind.

When the sun came up she went to her place at the rear of the boat. It was very still. The men were up, sitting in a group at the far end. When she looked, she saw a man lying face down near the place where the fight had taken place. He wasn't moving. She recognized him as one of the whiskey traders by his red hair.

A few minutes later Fowler and a couple of the men came and stood looking at the body. Then, as Elmira watched, they took off his belt and boots, rolled him over and cleaned out his pockets. The front of his body was stiff with blood. When the men had everything valuable off his body they simply picked the man up and threw him overboard. He floated in the water face down, and as the boat went on, Elmira looked and saw the body bump the boat. That's the end of you, she thought. She didn't know the man's name. She wished he would sink so she wouldn't have to see him. It was still misty, though, and soon the body was lost in the mist.

A little later Fowler brought her a plate of breakfast.

"What was the fight about?" she asked.

"'Bout you," Fowler said, his eyelid drooping.

That was a surprise. The men seemed to have almost no interest in her. Also, if the fight was over her, it was unusual that the victim had not tried to claim her.

"About me how?" she asked.

Fowler looked at her with his eye and a half.

"Well, you're the only woman we got," he said. "There's some would take advantage of you. Only the one talking it the most is kilt now."

"I guess he is," she said. "Which one killed him?"

"Big Zwey," Fowler said.

Big Zwey was the worst-looking of the buffalo hunters. He had an oily beard and fingernails as black as tar. It was peculiar to think that a buffalo hunter had been her protector after what she had been through with them.

"Why'd he do it?" she asked. "What difference does it make to him what happens to me?"

"He fancies you," Fowler said. "Wants to marry you, he says."

"Marry me?" Elmira said. "He can't marry me."

Fowler chuckled. "He don't know that," he said. "Big Zwey ain't quite normal."

None of you are quite normal, Elmira thought, and I must not be either, or I wouldn't be here.

"You took a chance, gettin' on a boat with men like us," Fowler said.

Elmira didn't respond. Often, from then on, she felt Big Zwey's eyes on her, though he never spoke to her or even came near her. None of the other men did either—probably afraid they would be killed and dumped overboard if they approached her. Sometimes Zwey would sit watching her for hours, from far down the boat. It made her feel bitter. Already he thought she belonged to him, and the other men thought so too. It kept them away from her, but in their eyes she didn't belong to herself. She belonged to a buffalo hunter who had never even spoken to her.

Their fright made her contemptuous of them, and whenever she caught one of them looking at her she met the look with a cold stare. From then on she said nothing to anyone and spent her days in silence, watching the brown river as it flowed behind.

37

TRAVELING WAS EVEN WORSE than Roscoe had supposed it would be, and he had supposed it would be pure hell.

Before he had been gone from Fort Smith much more than three hours, he had the bad luck to run into a bunch of wild pigs. For some reason Memphis, his mount, had an unreasoning fear of pigs, and this particular bunch of pigs had a strong dislike of white horses, or perhaps of deputy sheriffs. Before Roscoe had much more than noticed the pigs he was in a runaway. Fortunately the pines were not too thick, or Roscoe felt he would not have survived. The pigs were led by a big brown boar that was swifter than most pigs; the boar was nearly on them before Memphis got his speed up. Roscoe yanked out his pistol and shot at the boar till the pistol was empty, but he missed every time, and when he tried to reload, racing through the trees with a lot of pigs after him, he just dropped his bullets. He had a rifle but was afraid to get it out for fear he'd drop that too.

Fortunately the pigs weren't very determined. They soon stopped, but Memphis couldn't be slowed until he had run himself out. After that he was worthless for the rest of the day. In the afternoon, stopping to drink at a little creek, he bogged to his knees. Roscoe had to get off and whip him on the butt five or six times with a lariat rope before he managed to lunge out of the mud, by which time Roscoe himself was covered with it. He also lost one boot, sucked so far down in the mud he could barely reach it. He hadn't brought an extra pair of boots, mainly because he didn't own one, and was forced to waste most of the afternoon trying to clean the mud off the ones he had.

He made his first camp barely ten miles from town. What mostly worried him wasn't that he was too close to the town but that he was too close to the pigs. For all he knew, the pigs were still tracking him; the thought that they might arrive just after he went to sleep kept him from getting to sleep until almost morning. Roscoe was a town man and had spent little time sleeping in the woods. He slept blissfully on the old settee in the jail, because there you didn't have to worry about snakes, wild pigs, Indians, bandits, bears or other threats—just the occasional rowdy prisoner, who could be ignored.

Once the night got late, the woods were as noisy as a saloon, only Roscoe didn't know what most of the noises meant. To him they meant threats. He sat with his back to a tree all night, his pistol in his hand and his rifle across his lap. Finally, about the time it grew light, he got too tired to care if bears or pigs ate him, and he stretched out for a little while.

The next day he felt so tired he could barely stay in the saddle, and Memphis was almost as tired. The excitement of the first day had left them both worn out. Neither had much interest in their surroundings, and Roscoe had no sense at all that he was getting any closer to catching up with July. Fortunately there was a well-marked Army trail between Fort Smith and Texas, and he and Memphis plodded along it all day, stopping frequently to rest.

Then, as the sun was falling, he had what seemed like a stroke of luck. He heard someone yelling, and he rode into a little clearing near the trail only to discover that the reason there was a clearing was that a farmer had cut down the trees. Now the man was trying to get the clearing even clearer by pulling up the stumps, using a team of mules for the purpose. The mules were tugging and pulling at a big stump, with the farmer yelling at them to pull harder.

Roscoe had little interest in the work, but he did have an interest in the presence of the farmer, which must mean that a cabin was somewhere near. Maybe he could sleep with a roof over his head for one more night. He rode over and stopped a respectful distance away, so as not to frighten the mule team. The stump was only partly out—quite a few of its thick roots were still running into the ground.

At that point the farmer, who was wearing a floppy hat, happened to notice Roscoe. Immediately the action stopped, as the farmer looked him over. Roscoe rode a little closer, meaning to introduce himself, when to his great surprise the farmer took off his hat and turned out not to be a he. Instead the farmer was a good-sized woman wearing man's clothes. She had brown hair and had sweated through her shirt.

"Well, are you gonna get off and help or are you just going to set there looking dumb?" she asked, wiping her forehead.

"I'm a deputy sheriff," Roscoe replied, thinking that would be all the explanation that was needed.

"Then take off your star, if it's that heavy," the woman said. "Help me cut these roots. I'd like to get this stump out before dark. Otherwise we'll have to work at night, and I hate to waste the coal oil."

Roscoe hardly knew what to think. He had never tried to pull up a stump in his life, and didn't want to start. On the other hand he didn't want to sleep in the woods another night if he could help it.

The woman was looking Memphis over while she caught her breath. "We might could hitch that horse to the team," she said. "My mules ain't particular."

"Why, this horse wouldn't know what to do if it was hitched," Roscoe said. "It's a riding horse."

"Oh, I see," the woman said. "You mean it's dumb or too lazy to work."

It seemed the world was full of outspoken women. The woman farmer reminded Roscoe a little of Peach.

Somewhat reluctantly he got down and tied Memphis to a bush at the edge of the field. The woman was waiting impatiently. She handed Roscoe an ax and he began to cut the thick, tough roots while the woman encouraged the team. The stump edged out of the ground a little farther, but it didn't come loose. Roscoe hadn't handled an ax much in the last few years and was awkward with it. Cutting roots was not like cutting firewood. The roots were so tough the ax tended to bounce unless the hit was perfect. Once he hit a root too close to the stump and the ax bounced out of his hand and nearly hit the woman on the foot.

"Dern, I never meant to let it get loose from me," Roscoe said.

The woman looked disgusted. "If I had a piece of rawhide I'd tie it to your hand," she said. "Then the two of you could flop around all you wanted to. What town hired you to be deputy sheriff anyway?"

"Why, Fort Smith," Roscoe said. "July Johnson's the sheriff."

"I wish he'd been the one that showed up," the woman said. "Maybe he'd know how to chop a root."

Then she began to pop the mules again and Roscoe continued to whack at the roots, squeezing the ax tightly so it wouldn't slip loose again. In no time he was sweating worse than the woman, sweat dripping into his eyes and off his nose. It had been years since he had sweated much, and he didn't enjoy the sensation.

While he was half blinded by the sweat, the mules gave a big pull and one of the roots that he'd been about to cut suddenly slipped out of the ground, uncurled and lashed at him like a snake. The root hit him just above the knees and knocked him backward, causing him to drop the ax again. He tried to regain his balance but lost it and fell flat on his back. The root was still twitching and curling as if it had a life of its own.

The woman didn't even look around. The mules had the stump moving, and she kept at them, popping them with the reins and yelling at them as if they were deaf, while Roscoe lay there and watched the big stump slowly come out of the hole where it had been for so many years. A couple of small roots still held, but the mules kept going and the stump was soon free.

Roscoe got slowly to his feet, only to realize that he could barely walk.

The woman seemed to derive a certain amusement from the way he hobbled around trying to gain control of his limbs.

"Who did they send you off to catch?" she asked. "Or did they just decide you wasn't worth your salary and run you out of town?"

Roscoe felt aggrieved. Even strangers didn't seem to think he was worth his salary, and yet in his view he did a fine job of keeping the jail.

"I'm after July Johnson," he said. "His wife run off."

"I wish she'd run this way," the woman said. "I'd put her to work helping me clear this field. It's slow work, doing it alone."

And yet the woman had made progress. At the south edge of the field, where Memphis was tied, forty or fifty stumps were lined up.

"Where's your menfolks?" Roscoe asked.

"Dead or gone," the woman said. "I can't find no husband that knows how to stay alive. My boys didn't care for the work, so they left about the time of the war and didn't come back. What's your name, Deputy?"

"Roscoe Brown," Roscoe said.

"I'm Louisa," the woman said. "Louisa Brooks. I was born in Alabama and I wish I'd stayed. Got two husbands buried there and there's another buried on this property here. Right back of the house, he's buried, that was Jim," she added. "He was fat and I couldn't get him in the wagon so I dug the hole and there he lies."

"Well, that's a shame," Roscoe said.

"No, we didn't get on," Louisa said. "He drank whiskey and talked the Bible too, and I like a man that does one thing or the other. I told him once he could fall dead for all I care, and it wasn't three weeks before the fool just did it."

Though Roscoe had been hopeful of staying the night, he was beginning to lose his inclination. Louisa Brooks was almost as scary as wild pigs, in his view. The mules drug the stump over to where the others were and Roscoe walked over and helped Louisa untie it.

"Roscoe, you're invited to supper," she said, before he could make up his mind to go. "I bet you can eat better than you chop."

"Oh, I ought to get on after July," Roscoe said, halfheartedly. "His wife run off."

"I meant to run off, before Jim went and died," Louisa said. "If I had, I wouldn't have had to bury him. Jim was fat. I had to hitch a mule to him to drag him out of the house. Spent all day pulling up stumps and then had to work half the night planting a husband. How old are you getting to be?"

"Why, forty-eight, I guess," Roscoe said, surprised to be asked.

Louisa took off her hat and fanned herself with it as they followed the mules down one edge of the field. Roscoe led his horse.

"The skinny ones last longer than the fat ones," Louisa said. "You'll probably last till you're about sixty."

"Or longer, I hope," Roscoe said.

"Can you cook?" Louisa asked. She was a fair-looking woman, though large.

"No," Roscoe admitted. "I generally eat at the saloon or else go home with July."

"I can't neither," Louisa said. "Never interested me. What I like is farming. I'd farm day and night if it didn't take so much coal oil."

That seemed curious. Roscoe had never heard of a woman farmer, though plenty of black women picked cotton during the season. They came to a good-sized clearing without a stump in it. There was a large cabin and a rail corral. Louisa unharnessed the mules and put them in the pen.

"I'd leave 'em out but they'd run off," she said. "They don't like farming as much as I do. I guess we'll have corn bread for supper. It's about all I eat."

"Why not bacon?" Roscoe asked. He was quite hungry and would have appreciated a good hunk of bacon or a chop of some kind. Several chickens were scratching around the cabin—any one of them would have made good eating but he didn't feel he ought to mention it, since he was the guest.

"I won't have no pigs around," Louisa said. "Too smart. I won't bother with animals I have to outwit. I'd rather just farm."

True to her word, Louisa served up a meal of corn bread, washed down with well water. The cabin was roomy and clean, but there was not much food in it. Roscoe was puzzled as to how Louisa could keep going with nothing but corn bread in her. It occurred to him that he had not seen a milk cow anywhere, so evidently she had even dispensed with such amenities as milk and butter.

She herself munched a plate of corn bread contentedly, now and then fanning herself. It was hot and still in the cabin.

"I doubt you'll catch that sheriff," she said, looking Roscoe over.

Roscoe doubted it too, but felt that he had to make a show of trying, at least. What was more likely was that if he rode around long enough July would eventually come and find him.

"Well, he went to Texas," he said. "Maybe I'll strike someone that's seen him."

"Yes, and maybe you'll ride right into a big mess of Comanche Indians," Louisa said. "You do that and you'll never enjoy another good plate of corn bread."

Roscoe let the remark pass. The less said about Indians the better, in his view. He munched corn bread for a while, preferring not to think about any of the various things that might happen to him in Texas.

"Was you ever married?" Louisa asked.

"No, ma'am," Roscoe said. "I was never even engaged."

"In other words you've went to waste," Louisa said.

"Well, I've been a deputy sheriff for a good spell," Roscoe said. "I keep the jail."

Louisa was watching him closely in a way that made him a little uncomfortable. The only light in the cabin came from a small coal-oil lamp on the table. A few small bugs buzzed around the lamp, their movements casting shadows on the table. The corn bread was so dry that Roscoe kept having to dip dipperfuls of water to wash it down.

"Roscoe, you're in the wrong trade," Louisa said. "If you could just learn to handle an ax you might make a good farmer."

Roscoe didn't know what to say to that. Nothing was less likely than that he would make a farmer.

"Why'd that sheriff's wife run off?" Louisa asked.

"She didn't say," Roscoe said. "Maybe she said to July but I doubt it, since he left before she did."

"Didn't like Arkansas, I guess," Louisa said. "He might just as well let her go, if that's the case. I like it myself, though it ain't no Alabama."

After that the conversation lagged. Roscoe kept wishing there was something to eat besides corn bread, but there wasn't. Louisa continued to watch him from the other side of the table.

"Roscoe, have you had any experience with women at all?" she asked, after a bit.

To Roscoe it seemed a bold question, and he took his time answering it. Once about twenty years earlier he had fancied a girl named Betsie and had been thinking about asking her to take a walk with him some night. But he was shy, and while he was getting around to asking, Betsie died of smallpox. He had always regretted that they never got to take their walk, but after that he hadn't tried to have much to do with women.

"Well, not much," he admitted, finally.

"I got the solution to both our problems," Louisa said. "You let that sheriff find his own wife and stay here and we'll get married."

She said it in the same confident, slightly loud voice that she always seemed to use—after a day of yelling at mules it was probably hard to speak in a quiet voice.

Despite the loudness, Roscoe assumed he had misunderstood her. A woman didn't just out and ask a man to marry. He pondered what she had said a minute, trying to figure out where he might have missed her meaning. It stumped him, though, so he chewed slowly on his last bite of cornbread.

"What was it you said?" he asked, finally.

"I said we oughta get married," Louisa said loudly. "What I like about you is you're quiet. Jim talked every second that he didn't have a whiskey bottle in his mouth. I got tired of listening. Also, you're skinny. If you don't last, you'll be easy to bury. I've buried enough husbands to take such things into account. What do you say?"

"I don't want to," Roscoe said. He was aware that it sounded impolite but was too startled to say otherwise.

"Well, you ain't had time to think about it," Louisa said. "Give it some thought while you're finishing the corn bread. Much as I hate burying husbands, I don't want to live alone. Jim wasn't much good but he was somebody in the bed, at least. I've had six boys in all but not a one of 'em stayed around. Had two girls but they both died. That's eight children. I always meant to have ten but I've got two to go and time's running out."

She munched her corn bread for a while. She seemed to be amused, though Roscoe couldn't figure out what might be amusing.

"How big was your family?" she asked.

"There was just four of us boys," Roscoe said. "Ma died young."

Louisa was watching him, which made him nervous. He remembered that he was supposed to be thinking about the prospect of marrying her while he finished the cornbread, but in fact his appetite was about gone anyway and he was having to choke it down. He began to feel more and more of a grievance against more and more people. The start of it all was Jake Spoon, who had no business coming to Fort Smith in the first place. It seemed to him that a chain of thoughtless actions, on the part of many people he knew, had resulted in his being stuck in a cabin in the wilderness with a difficult widow woman. Jake should have kept his pistol handier, and not resorted to a buffalo gun. Benny Johnson should have been paying attention to his dentistry and not walking around in the street in the middle of the day. July shouldn't have married Elmira if she was going to run off, and of course Elmira certainly had no business getting on the whiskey boat.

In all of it no one had given much consideration to him, least of all the townspeople of Fort Smith. Peach Johnson and Charlie Barnes, in particular, had done their best to see that he had to leave.

But if the townspeople of Fort Smith had not considered him, the same couldn't be said for Louisa Brooks, who was giving him a good deal more consideration than he was accustomed to.

"I was never a big meat eater," she said. "Living off corn bread keeps you feeling light on your feet."

Roscoe didn't feel light on his feet, though. Both his legs pained him from where the root had struck them. He choked down the last of the corn bread and took another swallow or two of the cool well water.

"You ain't a bad-looking feller," Louisa said. "Jim was prone to warts. Had 'em on his hands and on his neck both. So far as I can see you don't have a wart on you."

"No, don't believe so," Roscoe admitted.

"Well, that's all the supper," Louisa said. "What about my proposition?"

"I can't," Roscoe said, putting it as politely as he knew how. "If I don't keep on till I find July I might lose my job."

Louisa looked exasperated. "You're a fine guest," she said. "I tell you what, let's give it a tryout. You ain't had enough experience of women to know whether you like the married life or not. It might suit you to a T. If it did, you wouldn't have to do risky work like being a deputy."

It was true that being a deputy had become almost intolerably risky—Roscoe had to grant that. But judging from July's experience, marriage had its risks too.

"I don't favor mustaches much," Louisa said. "But then life's a matter of give and take."

They had eaten the corn bread right out of the pan, so there were no dishes to wash. Louisa got up and threw a few crumbs out the door to her chickens, who rushed at them greedily, two of them coming right into the cabin.

"Don't you eat them chickens?" Roscoe asked, thinking how much better the corn bread would have tasted if there had been a chicken to go with it.

"No, I just keep 'em to control the bugs," Louisa said. "I ate enough chicken in Alabama to last me a lifetime."

Roscoe felt plenty nervous. The question of sleeping arrangements could not be postponed much longer. He had looked forward briefly to sleeping in the cabin, where he would feel secure from snakes and wild pigs, but that hope was dashed. He hadn't spent a night alone with a woman in his whole life and didn't plan to start with Louisa, who stood in the doorway drinking a dipper of water. She squished a swallow or two around in her mouth and spat it out the door. Then she put the dipper back in the bucket and leaned over Roscoe, so close he nearly tipped over backward in his chair out of surprise.

"Roscoe, you've went to waste long enough," she said. "Let's give it a tryout."

"Well, I wouldn't know how to try," Roscoe said. "I've been a bachelor all my life."

Louisa straightened up. "Men are about as worthless a race of people as I've ever encountered," she said. "Look at the situation a minute. You're running off to catch a sheriff you probably can't find, who's in the most dangerous state in the union, and if you do find him he'll just go off and try to find a wife that don't want to live with him anyway. You'll probably get scalped before it's all over, or hung, or a Mexican will get you with a pigsticker. And it'll all be to try and mend something that won't mend anyway. Now I own a section of land here and I'm a healthy woman. I'm willing to take you, although you've got no experience either at farming or matrimony. You'd be useful to me, whereas you won't be a bit of use to that sheriff or that town you work for either. I'll teach you how to handle an ax and a mule team, and guarantee you all the corn bread you can eat. We might even have some peas to go with it later in the year. I can cook peas. Plus I've got one of the few feather mattresses in this part of the country, so it'd be easy sleeping. And now you're scared to try. If that ain't cowardice, I don't know what is."

Roscoe had never expected to hear such a speech, and he had no idea how to reply to it. Louisa's approach to marriage didn't seem to resemble any that he had observed, though it was true he had not spent much time studying the approaches to matrimony. Still, he had only ridden into Louisa's field an hour before sundown, and it was not yet much more than an hour after dark. Her proposal seemed hasty to him by any standards.

"Well, we ain't much acquainted," he said. "How do you know we'd get along?"

"I don't," Louisa said. "That's why I offered just to give it a tryout. If you don't like it you can leave, and if I can't put up with you I expect I could soon run you off. But you ain't even got the gumption to try. I'd say you're scared of women."

Roscoe had to admit that was true, except for a whore now and then. But he only admitted it to himself, not to Louisa. After some reflection he decided it was best to leave her charge unanswered.

"I guess I'll bed down out back," he said.

"Well, fine," Louisa said. "Just watch out for Ed."

That was a surprise. "Who's Ed?" he asked.

"Ed's a snake," Louisa said. "Big rattler. I named him after my uncle, because they're both lazy. I let Ed stay around because he holds down the rodents. He don't bother me and I don't bother him. But he hangs out around to the back, so watch out where you throw down your blanket."

Rosco did watch. He stepped so gingerly, getting his bedding arranged, that it took him nearly twenty minutes to settle down. Then he couldn't get the thought of the big snake off his mind. He had never heard of anyone naming a snake before, but then nothing she did accorded with any procedure he was familiar with. The fact that she had mentioned the snake meant that he had little chance of getting to sleep. He had heard that snakes had a habit of crawling in with people, and he definitely didn't want to be crawled in with. He wrapped his blanket around him tightly to prevent Ed from slipping in, but it was a hot sultry night and he was soon sweating so profusely that he couldn't sleep anyway. There were plenty of grass and weeds around, and every time anything moved in the grass he imagined it to be the big rattler. The snake might get along with Louisa, but that didn't mean he would accept strangers.

Hours passed and he still couldn't get to sleep, though he was plenty tired. It was clear that if the sleeping didn't improve he was going to be dead on his feet long before he got back to Fort Smith. His eyelids would fall, but then he'd hear something and jerk awake, a process that went on until he was too tired to care whether he died or not. He had been propped up against the wall of the cabin, but he slowly slid down and finally slept, flat on his back.

When he awoke he got a shock almost worse than if he had found the rattler curled on his chest: Louisa was standing astraddle of him. Roscoe was so tired that it was only his brain that had come awake, it seemed. He would ordinarily have reacted quickly to the sight of anyone standing astraddle of him, much less a woman, but in this case his limbs were so heavy with sleep that he couldn't move a one: opening his eyes was effort enough. It was nearly sunup, still sultry and humid. He saw that Louisa was barefoot and that her feet and ankles were wet from the dewy grass. He couldn't see her face or judge her disposition, but he felt a longing to be back on his couch in the jail, where crazy things didn't happen. Although he was just in his long johns, the blanket was up about his chest, so at least she hadn't caught him indecent.

For a second he took a sleepy comfort from that reflection, but a second later it ceased to be true. Louisa stuck one of her wet feet under the blanket and kicked it off. Roscoe was so anchored in sleep he still couldn't react. Then, to his extreme astonishment, Louisa squatted right atop his middle and reached into his long johns and took hold of his tool. Nothing like that had ever happened to him, and he was stunned, though his tool wasn't. While the rest of him had been heavy with sleep, it had become heavy with itself.

"Why you're a tom turkey, ain't you," Louisa said.

To Roscoe's astonishment, Louisa proceeded to squat right down on him. Instead of being covered with a blanket, he was covered with her skirts. At that point the sun broke through the mist, lighting the clearing and adding to his embarrassment, for anyone could have ridden up and seen that something mighty improper was happening.

As it was, though, only three or four of Louisa's chickens watched the act, but even the fact that the chickens were standing around added to Roscoe's embarrassment. Maybe the chickens weren't really watching, but they seemed to be. Meanwhile Louisa was wiggling around without much interest in what he thought about it all. Roscoe decided the best approach was to pretend a dream was happening, though he knew quite well it wasn't. But Louisa's vigor was such that even if Roscoe had got his thoughts in place they would soon have been jarred awry. A time or two he was practically lifted off the ground by her efforts; he was scooted off his tarp and back into the weeds and was forced to open his eyes again in hopes of being able to spot a bush he could grab, to hold himself in place. About the time Louisa moved him completely off the tarp, matters came to a head. Despite the chickens and the weeds and the danger of witnesses, he felt a sharp pleasure. Louisa apparently did too, soon afterward, for she wiggled even more vigorously and grunted loudly. Then she sat on him for several minutes, scratching at the chigger bites on his wet ankles. He soon sank right out of her, but Louisa was in no hurry to get up. She seemed in a quiet humor. Once in a while she clucked a time or two at the chickens. Roscoe felt his neck begin to itch from the weeds. A swarm of gnats hung right over his face, and Louisa considerately swatted them away.

"There's Ed," Louisa said. Sure enough, a big rattler was crawling over a log about ten yards away. Louisa continued to sit, unconcerned about the snake or anything else.

"Are you a one-timer or are you feisty, Roscoe?" she asked after a while.

Roscoe had a notion that he knew what she meant. "I'm mostly a no-timer," he said.

Louisa sighed. "You ain't hopeless, but you sure ain't feisty," she said after a while, wiping the sweat off her face with the sleeve of her dress. "Let's go see if the corn bread's done."

She got up and went back around the house. Roscoe quickly got dressed and drug his gear around the corner, dumping it in a heap beside the door.

When he went in, Louisa sat another pan of corn bread on the table and they had breakfast.

"Well, what's it going to be, marriage or Texas?" Louisa asked after a while.

Roscoe knew it had to be Texas, but it was not so simple a matter to think out as it had been before Louisa came out and sat down on him. For one thing, he had no desire to go to Texas; he felt his chances of finding July to be very slim, and July's of finding Elmira completely hopeless. In the meantime it had become clear to him that Louisa had her charms, and that the fact that they were being offered him on a trial basis was a considerable enticement. He was beginning to feel that Louisa was right: he had mostly been wasted, and might have more feistiness in him than anyone, himself included, had suspected. There was no likelihood of his getting to use much of this capacity in Texas, either.

"It's a hard choice," he said, though one thing that made it a little easier was the knowledge that life with Louisa involved more than featherbeds. It also involved pulling up stumps all day, an activity he had no interest in or aptitude for.

"Well, I don't take back nothing I said," Louisa declared. "You men are a worthless race. You're good for a bounce now and then, and that's about it. I doubt you'd make much of a farmer."

For some reason Roscoe felt melancholy. For all her loud talk, Louisa didn't seem to be as disagreeable to him as he had first thought her to be. It seemed to him she might be persuaded to tone down her farming, maybe even move into a town and settle for putting in a big garden, if it was presented to her right. But he couldn't, because there was the problem of July, who had given him a job and been good to him. The point was, he owed July. Even if he never found him, he had to make the effort, or know that he had failed a friend. Had it not been for that obligation he would have stayed a day or two and considered Louisa's offer.

"It ain't that I ain't obliged," he said. "I'm obliged. The dern thing about it is July. Even if Elmira ain't coming back, he's got to be told. It's my dern job, too. July's the only friend I got in that town except Joe. Joe's Elmira's boy."

Then a happy thought occurred to him. Maybe July had made a slow start. He might not be too far ahead. Perhaps his jaundice had come back on him, in which case he might have had to hole up for a few days. If he himself was lucky he might strike July in a week or two and break the news. Once that was done, his obligation would be satisfied and there would be nothing to keep him from coming back for another visit with Louisa—provided he could find the farm a second time.

"I could come by on my way back," he said. "July's been sick—he may have had to hole up. I might not have to look no more than a month."

Louisa shrugged. "Suit yourself but don't expect me to hold you no stall," she said. "Somebody feistier than you might ride in tomorrow for all I know."

Roscoe found nothing to say. Obviously he was taking a risk.

"What's the story on this July?" Louisa asked. "That wife of his sounds like a woman of ill fame. What kind of sheriff would marry a woman of ill fame?"

"Well, July's slow," Roscoe said. "He's the sort that don't talk much."

"Oh, that sort," Louisa said. "The opposite of my late husband, Jim."

She took a pair of men's brogans from beside the table and began to lace them on her bare feet.

"The thing about men that don't talk much is that they don't usually learn much, either," Louisa said. She got her sunbonnet off a nail on the wall and tucked her thick brown hair under it.

"You don't blabber, but I believe you've got it in you to learn," she said. "I'm going to do some farming."

"What do I owe you for the grub?" Roscoe asked.

"I'd hate to think I'd charge for corn bread," Louisa said. They went out and Roscoe began to roll up his bedroll. He was preoccupied and made such a sloppy job of it that Louisa burst out laughing. She had a happy laugh. One corner of his tarp hung down over his horse's flank.

"Roscoe, you're a disgrace in most respects," Louisa said. "I bet you lose that bedroll before you get to Texas."

"Well, should I stop back?" Roscoe asked, for she seemed in a fair humor.

"Why, I guess so," Louisa said. "I've put up with worse than you, and probably will again."

Roscoe rode off, though Memphis didn't take kindly to having the tarp flopping at his flank, so he had to get down and retie the roll. When he finally got it tied and remounted to ride on, he saw that Louisa had already hitched her mules to a stump and was giving them loud encouragement as they strained at the harness. It seemed to him he had never met such a curious woman. He gave her a wave that she didn't see, and rode on west with very mixed feelings. One moment he felt rather pleased and rode light in the saddle, but the next moment the light feeling would turn heavy. A time or two Roscoe could barely hold back the tears, he felt so sad of a sudden—and it would have been hard to say whether the sadness came because of having to leave Louisa or because of the uncertain journey that lay ahead.

38

JOE KNEW RIGHT OFF that something was bothering July, because he didn't want to talk. It was not that July had ever been a big talker, like Roscoe could be if he was in the mood, but he was seldom as silent as he was the first week of the trip. Usually he would talk about horses or fishing or cowboys or the weather or something, but on the trip west it just seemed he didn't want to talk at all.

At first it made a problem because Joe had never been on such an important journey, and there were many things he wanted to ask about. For one thing, he was curious to know how they were going to go about catching Jake Spoon. Also, he was curious about Indians, and about the famous Texas Rangers Roscoe said were protecting Jake. He wanted to know how far it was to Texas and if they would see an ocean on the trip.

Once he started asking these questions it became clear at once that it was a strain for July even to listen, much less answer. It cost him such an effort to respond that Joe soon gave up asking and just rode along in silence, waiting for the land to change and the Indians to appear.

In fact they rode so hard that Joe soon stopped missing the talk. Although still curious, he discovered that travel was harder than he had expected it to be. Besides hating to talk, July also seemed to hate to stop. When they came to a creek he would let the horses water, and now and then he got down to relieve himself; otherwise they rode from first light until it was too dark to see. On nights when there was a moon they rode well into the night.

It was a strange business, traveling, Joe decided. July went at it hard. Yet Joe didn't wish for a minute that he had stayed home. Going with July was the most exciting thing he had ever done by far.

Several times they came upon farms. July asked the farmers if they had seen Jake, and twice was told that yes, Jake had spent the night. But they themselves didn't spend the night, and rarely even took a meal. Once on a hot afternoon July did accept a glass of buttermilk from a farmer's wife. Joe got one too. There were several little girls on that farm, who giggled every time they looked at Joe, but he ignored them. The farmer's wife asked them twice to stay overnight, but they went on and made camp in a place thick with mosquitoes.

"Does Texas have mosquitoes too?" Joe asked.

July didn't answer. He knew the boy was starved for talk, and that he himself had been a sorry companion on the trip, but in fact he had no talk in him. He was so filled with worry that the only way he could contain it was just to keep silent and concentrate on the travel. He knew he was pushing both the boy and the horses harder than he ought to, but he couldn't keep from it. Only hard, constant travel allowed him to hold down the worry—which was all to do with Elmira.

Almost from the day they left, he felt something was wrong. He had had a feeling that something bad had happened, and no matter how hard he tried to concentrate on the job at hand, the worry wouldn't leave. It was all he could do to keep from turning the horses around and heading back for Fort Smith.

At first Joe was cheerful and eager, but he was not a particularly strong boy, and he was not used to riding sixteen hours a day. He didn't complain, but he did grow tired, sleeping so deeply when they stopped that July could barely get him awake when it was time to move on. Often he rode in a doze for miles at a stretch. Once or twice July was tempted to leave him at one of the farms they passed. Joe was a willing worker and could earn his keep until he could come back and get him. But the only reason for doing that would be to travel even harder, and the horses couldn't stand it. Besides, if he left the boy, it would be a blow to his pride, and Joe didn't have too much pride as it was.

For several days they bore southwest, through the pine woods. It had been a rainy spring and their big problem was mosquitoes. The trees dripped and the puddles lay everywhere. July hardly noticed the mosquitoes himself, but Joe and the horses suffered, particularly at night.

"Pretty soon I'll be all bump," Joe said, grinning, as they slogged through a clearing. He looked up to see a broad, muddy river curving down from the north.

"I guess that's the Red," July said. "That means we're about to Texas."

When they rode up to the banks of the river they were greeted by an amazing sight. Though running freely, the river was shallow and evidently boggy. Evidence for the bogginess was visible in the form of a tall man over toward the far bank. He was standing in knee-high water, between a gaunt horse and a little brown pack mule, both of which had sunk past their hocks in the river mud.

"I've heard this river was half quicksand," July said.

From Roscoe, Joe had heard terrible stories about quicksand—in the stories, men and horses and even wagons were slowly swallowed up. He had suspected the stories were exaggerated, and the man and his animals proved it. All might be bogged, but none were sinking. The man wore a tall beaver hat and a long frock coat. Both animals had numerous parcels tied to them, and the man was amusing himself by untying the parcels and pitching them into the river. One by one they began to float away. To their astonishment he even threw away his bedroll.

"The man must be a lunatic," July said. "He must think that horse will float if he gets off some weight. That horse ain't gonna float."

The man noticed them and gave a friendly wave, then proceeded to unburden the mule of most of its pack. Some floated and some merely lay in the shallow water.

July rode upstream until he found a place where both deer and cattle had crossed. The water was seldom more than a foot deep. They crossed a reddish bar of earth, and it seemed for a moment they might bog, but July edged south and soon found firm footing. In a few minutes they were on the south bank, whereas the man in the beaver hat had made no progress at all. He was so cool about his predicament that it was hard to tell if he even wished to make progress.

"Let me have your rope," July said to Joe. He tied their two ropes together and managed to fling the man a line. After that it was no great trouble to drag the horse and the pack mule out. The man waded out with them.

"Thank you, men," he said. "I believe if my mule hadn't got out soon, he would have learned to live on fish. They're self-reliant creatures."

"I'm July Johnson and this is Joe," July said. "You didn't need to throw away your baggage."

"I've suffered no loss," the man said. "I'm glad I found a river to unload that stuff in. Maybe the fish and the tadpoles will make better use of it than I have."

"Well, I've never seen a fish that used a bedroll," July said.

Joe had never met a man so careless that he would throw his possessions in a river. But the man seemed as cheerful as if he'd just won a tub of money.

"My name's Sedgwick," he said. "I'm traveling through this country looking for bugs."

"I bet you found plenty," July said.

"What do you do with bugs?" Joe asked, feeling that the man was the strangest he had ever met.

"I study them," the man said.

Joe hardly knew what to say. What was there to study about a bug? Either it bit you or it didn't.

"I've left about a thousand bugs in Little Rock," the man said. "That's why I threw away my equipment. I'm out of the mood to study bugs and am thinking of going to Texas to preach the Gospel. I've heard that Texans can use some good straight Gospel."

"Why study a bug?" Joe asked again, his curiosity getting the better of him.

"There's more than a million species of insect and only one species of human being," the man said. "When we finish up with this planet the insects will take over. You may not think it, seeing all this fair land, but the days of the human race are numbered. The insects are waiting their turn."

July decided the man was mildly touched, but probably no danger to himself or anyone. "I'd watch these crossings, if I were you. Cross where the deer cross and you'll be all right," he said.

The man turned his blue eyes on July for a moment. "Why, son, I'm fine," he said. "You're the one in trouble. I can see you carry a weight on your heart. You're hurrying along to do something you may not want to do. I see by your badge that you're a lawman. But the crimes the law can understand are not the worst crimes. I have often sinned worse than the murderer, and yet I try to live in virtue."

July was so taken aback he hardly knew what to say. This Mr. Sedgwick was one of the queerest men he had ever met.

"This boy looks a little peaked," Mr. Sedgwick said. "You can leave him with me, if you like. I'll bring him along slow, fatten him up and teach him about the insect kingdom as we travel. I doubt he's had much chance to get an education."

July was half tempted. The stranger seemed kindly. On the other hand he wore a sidearm under his coat, so perhaps he wasn't as kindly as he looked.

"It may be we'll meet down the road," July said, ignoring the offer.

"Perhaps," Mr. Sedgwick said. "I see you're in a hurry to get someplace. It's a great mistake to hurry."

"Why?" Joe asked, puzzled by almost everything the traveler said.

"Because the grave's our destination," Mr. Sedgwick said. "Those who hurry usually get to it quicker than those who take their time. Now, me, I travel, and when I'll get anywhere is anybody's guess. If you two hadn't come along I'd have likely stood there in the river for another hour or two. The moving waters are ever a beautiful sight."

Mr. Sedgwick turned and walked down the riverbank without another word. From time to time he squatted to peer closely at the ground.

"I reckon he's spotted a bug," Joe said.

July didn't answer. Crazy or not, the tall traveler had been smart enough to figure out that the sheriff of Fort Smith was traveling with a heavy heart.

39

THE DEATH OF the young Irishman cast a heavy gloom over the cow camp. Call could do nothing about it. For the next week it seemed no one talked of anything but the death.

At night while they were having their grub, or just waiting for their turn at night herding to start, the cowboys talked endlessly about deaths they had witnessed, deaths they had heard about. Most of them had lived through rough times and had seen men die, but no one of their acquaintance had ridden into a nest of snakes in a river, and they could not keep the subject off their tongues.

The worst, by far, was Jasper Fant, who was so unnerved by what he had seen that for a time Call felt he might be losing his mind. Jasper had never been reticent, but now it seemed he had to be talking every waking minute as a means of holding his own fears in balance.

Allen O'Brien had the opposite response. He rode all day in silence, as nervous and withdrawn as the Spettle brothers. He would sit by the fire crying while the others talked of memorable deaths.

The cattle, still fresh to the trail, were not easily controlled. The brush was bad, the weather no better. It rained for three days and the mosquitoes were terrible. The men were not used to the night work and were irritable as hens. Bert Borum and Soupy Jones had an argument over how to hobble a horse and almost came to blows. Lippy had been put in charge of firewood, and the wood he cut didn't suit Bolivar, who was affronted by Lippy's very presence. Deets had fallen into one of his rare glooms, probably because he felt partly to blame for the boy's death.

Dish Boggett was proving a treasure as a point man. He kept the point all day, true as a rule, and little happened with the cattle that he didn't see.

By contrast the Rainey boys were disappointing. Both had taken homesick, missing their jolly mother and her well-stocked table. They drug around listlessly, not actually shirking their work but taking a long time to do it.

Augustus roamed freely about the outfit. Sometimes he rode ahead of the herd, which put Dish Boggett in a bad mood—nobody was supposed to be ahead of him except the scout. Other days Augustus would idle along with his pigs, who frequently stopped to wallow in puddles or root rats out of their holes.

Everyone had been dreading the next river, which was the San Antonio. There was much controversy about how far north moccasins could live—were they in the Cimarron, the Arkansas, the Platte? No one knew for sure, but everyone knew there were plenty in the San Antonio river.

One morning after breakfast Deets came back to say he had found a shallow crossing only a mile or two from the camp.

"What's the snake population?" Augustus asked. It was another gray wet day and he was wearing his big yellow slicker.

"Seen a few turtles, that's all," Deets said. "If they're there, they're hid."

"I hope they ain't there," Augustus said. "If a mouse snake was to show itself now, half these waddies would climb a tree."

"I'm more worried about Indians," Pea Eye said.

It was true. The minute they left Lonesome Dove he had begun to have his big Indian dreams. The same big Indian he had dreamed about for years had come back to haunt his sleep. Sometimes just dozing on his horse he would dream about the Indian. He slept poorly, as a result, and felt he would be tired and good for nothing by the time they reached Montana.

"It's curious how things get in your head," he said. "I've got an Indian in mine."

"I expect your ma told you you'd be stolt, when you was young," Augustus said.

He and Call rode over to the crossing and looked carefully for snakes, but saw none.

===

"I wish you'd stop talking about that boy's death," Call said. "If you would maybe they'd get over it."

"Wrong theory," Augustus said. "Talk's the way to kill it. Anything gets boring if you talk about it enough, even death."

They sat on the bank of the river, waiting for the herd to come in sight. When it did, the Texas bull was walking along beside Old Dog. Some days the bull liked to lead, other days he did nothing but fight or worry the heifers.

"This ain't a well-thought-out journey," Augustus remarked. "Even if we get these cattle to Montana, who are we gonna sell 'em to?"

"The point ain't to sell 'em next week," Call said. "The point is to get the land. The people will be coming."

"Why are we taking that ugly bull?" Augustus asked. "If the land's all that pretty, it don't need a lot of ugly cattle on it."

To their relief the crossing went off well. The only commotion was caused by Jasper, who charged the river at a gallop and caused his horse to stumble and nearly fall.

"That might have worked if there'd been a bridge," Soupy Jones said, laughing.

Jasper was embarrassed. He knew he couldn't run a horse across a river, but at the last minute a fear of snakes had overcome him and blocked out his common sense.

Newt was too tired to be afraid of anything. He had not adjusted to night herding. While his horse was watering, Mr. Gus rode up beside him. The clouds had broken to the west.

"I wish the sun would come out and fry these skeeters," Augustus said.

The wagon was slowly approaching the crossing, Bolivar driving and Lippy riding in the back. Behind came the horse herd and the Spettle boys.

It was strange, Newt thought, that one river could be so peaceful and another suddenly boil up with snakes and kill Sean. Several times, mostly at night, he had imagined Sean was still alive. Being so sleepy made it harder to keep from mixing dreams with what was actually happening. He even had conversations with the other hands that seemed like they were conversations in dreams. He had never known the sadness of losing a friend, and had begun to consider what a long way they had to go.

"I hope don't nobody else get killed," he said.

"Well, it's hard to calculate the odds in this kind of a situation," Augustus said. "We may not have another bad injury the whole way. On the other hand, half of us may get wiped out. If we have much bad luck I doubt I'll make it myself."

"Why?" Newt asked, startled to hear him say such a thing.

"Because I ain't spry like I used to be," Augustus said. "Used to be I was quick to duck any kind of trouble. I could roll off a horse quicker than a man can blink. I'm still faster than some folks, but I ain't as fast as I was."

The wagon made the crossing easily, and the two blue pigs, who had been ambling along behind it, walked in and swam the San Antonio river.

"Look at them," Augustus said happily. "Ain't they swimmers?"

40

AS THE DAYS PASSED, Lorena found she liked the traveling more and more. The nights were no easier—almost every night the lightning flickered and thunderstorms rolled over them. Often, while she and Jake slept, big drops of rain would hit them in the face and force them to grab for the tarp. Soon the blankets seemed permanently damp, causing Jake to grumble and complain. But the tarp was hot and stiff, and he himself never thought to keep it handy. She would have to stumble around and arrange it in the dark, while Jake cussed the weather.

But no matter how uncomfortable the nights, the sky usually cleared in the morning. She liked to sit on the blankets and feel the sun getting warmer. She watched her arms getting slowly tanned and felt that a life of travel was what she was meant for. Her mare had gotten used to the travel too and no longer looked back toward Lonesome Dove.

Lorena might love the traveling, but it was clear that Jake didn't. More and more he was inclined to sulk. The fact that she had refused to go into San Antonio festered like the thorn he had had in his hand. Every day he brought it up, but she had said all she intended to say on the subject and just shook her head. Often she traveled all day in silence, thinking her thoughts and ignoring Jake's complaints.

"Dern you, why can't you talk?" he said one night as she was making the camp-fire. Deets, who stopped by their camp almost every day to see that they were all right, had shown her how to make a fire. He had also taught her how to pack the mule and do various other chores that Jake mostly neglected.

"I can talk," Lorena said.

"Well, you don't," Jake said. "I never seen a woman keep so quiet."

He spoke hotly—indeed, had been angry at her most of the trip. He was spoiling for a battle of some kind, but Lorena didn't want to battle. She had nothing against Jake, but she didn't feel she had to jump every time he whistled, which seemed to be what he expected. Jake was very fussy, complaining about the way she cooked the bacon or laid out the blankets. She ignored him. If he didn't like the way she did things, he was free to do them different—but he never did them different. He just fussed at her.

"We could be sleeping in a fine hotel tonight," he said. "San Antonio ain't but an hour's ride."

"Go sleep in one, if you want to," Lorena said. "I'll stay in camp."

"I guess you do wish I'd leave," Jake said. "Then you could whore with the first cowpoke that came along."

That was too silly to answer. She had not whored since the day she met him, unless you counted Gus. She sipped her coffee.

"That's your game, ain't it?" Jake said, his eyes hot.

"No," Lorena said.

"Well, you're a goddamn liar, then," Jake said. "Once a whore, always a whore. I won't stand for it. Next time I'll take a rope to you."

After he ate his bacon he saddled and rode off without another word—to go gamble, she supposed. Far from being scared, Lorena was relieved. Jake's angers were light compared to some she had known, but it was no pleasure having him around when he was so hot. Probably he thought to scare her, riding off so quick and leaving her in camp, but she felt no fear at all. The herd and all the boys were only a mile away. No one would be likely to bother her with the cow camp so close.

She sat on her blankets, enjoying the night. It was deep dusk, and birds—bull-bats—were whooshing around—she could see them briefly as shadows against the darkening sky. She and Jake had camped in a little clearing. While she was sipping her coffee, a possum walked within ten feet of her, stopped a moment to look at her stupidly, and walked on. After a while she heard faraway singing—the Irishman was singing to the cattle herd. Deets had told them about the terrible death of his brother.

Before she could get to sleep a horse came racing toward the camp. It was only Jake, running in in the hope of scaring her. He raced right into camp, which was irritating because it raised dust that settled in the blankets. He had ridden into town and bought whiskey, and then had rushed back, thinking to catch her with Gus or one of the cowhands. He was jealous every hour of the day.

He yanked his saddle off the horse and passed her the whiskey bottle, which was already half empty.

"I don't want none," she said.

"I guess there's nothing I could ask that you'd do," Jake said. "I wish that dern Gus would show up. At least we could have a card game."

Lorena lay back on her blanket and didn't answer. Anything she said would only make him worse.

Watching her lie there, calm and silent, Jake felt hopeless and took another long drink from the whiskey bottle. He considered himself a smart man, and yet he had got himself in a position that would have embarrassed a fool. He had no business traveling north with a woman like Lorie, who had her own mind and wouldn't obey the simplest order unless it happened to suit her. The more he drank, the sorrier he felt for himself. He wished he had just told Lorie no, and left her to sweat it out in Lonesome Dove. Then at least he could be in camp with the men, where there were card games to be had, not to mention protection. Despite himself, he could not stop worrying about July Johnson.

Then he remembered Elmira, whom he had sported with a few times in Kansas. What a trick on July to have married a whore and not know it.

He offered Lorena the bottle again, but she just lay there.

"Why won't you drink?" Jake asked. "Are you too good to get drunk?"

"I don't want to," she said. "You'll be drunk enough for both of us."

"By God, I guess I'll find out if there's anything you'll still do," Jake said, yanking open his pants and rolling onto her.

Lorena let him, thinking it might put him in a better humor. She watched the stars. But when Jake finished and reached for his bottle again, he seemed no happier. She reached for the bottle and took one swallow—her throat was dry. Jake wasn't angry anymore, but he looked sad.

"Lie down and sleep," Lorena said. "You don't rest enough."

Jake was thinking that Austin was only two days away. Maybe he could take Lorena to Austin and sneak off and leave her. Once he rejoined the boys, there would be little she could do about it. After all, she would be safer there than she would be on the trail. Beautiful as she was, she would do well in Austin.

Yet she was uncommonly beautiful. It had always been his trouble—he liked the beauties. It gave her a power he didn't appreciate, otherwise he would never have been talked into a trip that was little more than absurd. He was slowed to the pace of Call's cow herd and tied to a woman who attracted every man she saw. Even then, he didn't know if he could leave her. For all her difficult ways, he wanted her and couldn't tolerate the thought of her taking up with Gus or anyone else. He felt she would stick by him if things got bad. He didn't like being alone or having to take orders from Call.

"Have you ever been to a hanging?" he asked.

"No," Lorena said. The question surprised her.

Jake offered her the bottle and she took another swallow. "I expect they'll hang me someday," he said. "I was told by a fortune-teller that such would be my fate."

"Maybe the fortune-teller didn't know," Lorie said.

"I've seen many a hanging," Jake said. "We hung plenty of Mexicans when we were Rangers. Call never wasted no time when it came to hangings."

"He wouldn't, I guess," Lorena said.

Jake chuckled. "Did he ever come visit you all that time you were there?" he asked.

"No," Lorena said.

"Well, he had a whore once," Jake said. "He tried to sneak around, but me and Gus found out about it. We both used to spark her once in a while, so we both knew. I guess he thought he got away with it."

Lorena knew the type. Many men came to her hoping no one would know.

"Her name was Maggie," Jake said. "She was the one had little Newt. I was gone when she died. Gus said she wanted to marry Call and give up the life, but I don't know if it's true. Gus will say anything."

"So whose boy is he?" Lorena asked. She had seen the boy often, looking at her window. He was old enough to come to her, but he probably had no money, or else was just too shy.

"Newt? Why, who knows?" Jake said. "Maggie was a whore."

Then he sighed and lay down beside her, running his hand up and down her body. "Lorie, me and you was meant for feather beds," he said. "We wasn't meant for these dusty blankets. If we could find a nice hotel I'd show you some fun."

Lorena didn't answer. She would rather keep traveling. When Jake had his feel he went to sleep.

41

BEFORE THE HERD HAD PASSED San Antonio they nearly lost Lippy in a freak accident with the wagon. It was a hot day and the herd was moseying along at a slow rate. The mosquitoes were thinning a little, to everyone's satisfaction, and the cowboys were riding along half asleep in their saddles when the trouble started.

The herd had just crossed a little creek when Newt heard stock running and looked back to see the wagon racing for the creek like Comanches were after it. Bol was not on the seat, either—the mules ran unchecked. Lippy was on the seat, but he didn't have the reins and couldn't stop the team.

Jim Rainey was in the rear, and, thinking to be helpful, turned back to try and head the mules. In fact, the mules refused to be headed, and all Jim accomplished was to turn them out of the easy track where the herd had crossed, which caused them to strike the creek at a place where the bank dropped off about three feet. Newt saw there was going to be a terrible wreck, but short of shooting the mules, had no way to stop it. What he couldn't understand was why Lippy didn't jump. He sat on the seat, frozen and helpless, as the mules raced right off the cutbank.

As they were going off, Newt saw that the tail of Lippy's old brown coat had gotten pinched in the wagon seat—which explained his not having jumped. The wagon tipped straight down, bounced once, and turned completely over just as it hit the water. The mules, still hitched to it, fell backwards on top of the mess. All four wagon wheels were spinning in the air when Newt and the Raineys jumped off their horses. The trouble was, they had no idea what to do next.

Fortunately Augustus had seen the commotion and in a minute was in the water, on old Malaria. He threw a loop over one of the spinning wheels and spurred the big horse vigorously, pulling the wagon to a tilt on one edge.

"Fish him out, boys, otherwise we'll have to go all the way to Montana without no pianer player," he said—though privately he doubted his efforts would do any good. The wagon had landed smack on top of Lippy. If he wasn't drowned he probably had a broken neck.

When the wagon tilted, Newt saw Lippy's legs. He and the Raineys waded in and tried to get him loose, but the coat was still pinched in the seat. All they could do was get his head above water, though his head was so covered with mud that it was difficult at first to know if he was dead or alive. Fortunately Pea soon rode up and cut the coat loose with his bowie knife.

"He's a mudhead, ain't he," Pea said, carefully wiping his knife on his pants leg. "Now I guess he'll be mad at me for ten years because I ruined his coat."

Lippy was limp as a rag and hadn't moved a muscle. Newt felt sick to his stomach. Once more, on a perfectly nice day with everything going well, death had struck and taken another of his friends. Lippy had been part of his life since he could remember. When he was a child, Lippy had occasionally taken him into the saloon and let him bang on the piano. Now they would have to bury him as they had buried Sean.

Strangely, neither Pea nor Mr. Gus was much concerned. The mules had regained their feet and stood in the shallow water, swishing their tails and looking sleepy. Call rode up about that time. He had been at the head of the herd, with Dish Boggett.

"Ain't nobody gonna unhitch them mules?" he asked. A big sack of flour had been thrown out of the wagon and lay in the river getting ruined. Newt had not noticed it until the Captain pointed at it.

"Well, I ain't," Augustus said. "The boys can, their feet are already wet."

It seemed to Newt everyone was being mighty callous about Lippy, who lay on the riverbank. Then, to his surprise, Lippy, whose head was still covered with mud, rolled over and began to belch water. He belched and vomited for several minutes, making a horrible sound, but Newt's relief that he was not dead was so great that he welcomed the sound and waded out to help the Raineys unhitch the mules.

It soon became clear that the wagon bed had been damaged beyond repair in the accident. When it was righted, all the goods that had been in it floated in the shallow water.

"What a place for a shipwreck," Augustus said.

"I never seen a wagon break in two before," Pea said.

The wagon bed, old and rotten, had burst upon impact. Several cowboys rode up and began to fish their bedrolls out of the muddy water.

"What became of Bol?" Pea asked. "Wasn't he driving the wagon?"

Lippy was sitting up, wiping mud off his head. He ran one finger under his loose lip as if he expected to find a tadpole or a small fish, but all he found was mud. About that time the Spettle boys rode up, and crossed the horse herd.

"Seen the cook?" Augustus asked.

"Why, he's walking along carrying his gun," Bill Spettle said. "Them pigs are with him."

Bolivar soon came in sight a couple of hundred yards away, the blue pigs walking along beside him.

"I heared a shot," Lippy said. "About that time them mules took to running. I guess a bandit shot at us."

"No competent bandit would waste a bullet on you or Bol either," Augustus said. "There ain't no reward for either of you."

"It sounded like a shotgun," Bill Spettle volunteered.

"Bol might have been taking target practice," Augustus said. "He might have fired at a cowpie."

"It don't matter what it was," Call said. "The damage is done."

Augustus was enjoying the little break the accident produced. Walking along all day beside a cow herd was already proving monotonous—any steady work had always struck him as monotonous. It was mainly accidents of one kind and another that kept life interesting, in his view, the days otherwise being mainly repetitious things, livened up mostly by the occasional card game.

It was made even more interesting a few minutes later when Bolivar walked up and handed in his resignation. He didn't even look at the smashed wagon.

"I don't want to go this way," he said, addressing himself to the Captain. "I am going back."

"Why, Bol, you won't stand a chance," Augustus said. "A renowned criminal like you. Some young sheriff out to make a reputation will hang you before you get halfway to the border."

"I don't care," Bol said. "I am going back."

In fact, he expected to be fired anyway. He had been dozing on the wagon seat, dreaming about his daughters, and had accidentally fired off the ten-gauge. The recoil had knocked him off the wagon, but even so it had been hard to get free of the dream. It turned into a dream in which his wife was angry, even as he awoke and saw the mules dashing away. The pigs were rooting in a rat's nest, under a big cactus. Bol was so enraged by the mules' behavior that he would have shot one of them, only they were already well out of range.

He had not seen the wagon go off the creek bank, but he was not surprised that it was broken. The mules were fast. He would probably not have been able to hit one of them even with a rifle, distracted as he was by the dream.

The fall convinced him he had lived long enough with Americans. They were not his *compañeros*. Most of his *compañeros* were dead, but his country wasn't dead, and in his village there were a few men who liked to talk about the old days when they had spent all their time stealing Texas cattle. In those years his wife had not been so angry. As he walked toward the busted wagon and the little group of men, he decided to go back. He was tired of seeing his family only in dreams. Perhaps this time when he walked in, his wife would be glad to see him.

At any rate, the Americanos were going too far north. He had not really believed Augustus when he said they would ride north for several months. Most of what Augustus said was merely wind. He supposed they would ride for a few days and then sell the cattle, or else start a ranch. He himself had never been more than two days' hard ride from the border in his life. Now a week had passed and the Americanos showed no sign of stopping. Already he was far from the river. He missed his family. Enough was enough.

Call was not especially surprised. "All right, Bol, do you want a horse?" he asked. The old man had cooked for them for ten years. He deserved a mount.

"*Sí*," Bol said, remembering that it was a long walk back to the river, and then three days more to his village.

Call caught the old man a gentle gelding. "I've got no saddle to give you," he said, when he presented Bol with the horse.

Bol just shrugged. He had an extra serape and soon turned it into a saddle blanket. Apart from the gun, it was his only possession. In a moment he was ready to start home.

"Well, Bol, if you change your mind, you can find us in Montana," Augustus said. "It may be that your wife's too rusty for you now. You may want to come back and cook up a few more goats and snakes."

"*Gracias, Capitán,*" Bol said, when Call handed him the reins to the gelding. Then he rode off, without another word to anybody. It didn't surprise Augustus, since Bol had worked for them all those years without saying a word to anybody unless directly goaded into it—usually by Augustus.

But his departure surprised and saddened Newt. It spoiled his relief that Lippy was alive—after all, he had lost another friend, Bol instead of Lippy. Newt didn't say so, but he would rather have lost Lippy. He didn't want Lippy to die, of course, but he wouldn't have minded if he had decided to return to Lonesome Dove.

But Bol rode away from them, his old gun resting across the horse's withers. For a moment Newt felt so sad that he almost embarrassed himself by crying. He felt his eyes fill up. How could Bol just go? He had always been the cook, and yet in five minutes he was as lost to them as if he *had* died. Newt turned and made a show of spreading out the bedrolls, but it was mainly to conceal the fact that he felt sad. If people kept leaving, they'd be down to nobody before they even got north of Texas.

Riding away, Bolivar too felt very sad. Now that he was going, he was not sure why he had decided to go. Perhaps it was because he didn't want to face embarrassment. After all, he had fired the shot that caused the mules to run. Also, he didn't want to get so far north that he couldn't find his way back to the river. As he rode away he decided he had made another stupid choice. So far, in his opinion, almost every decision of his life had been stupid. He didn't miss his wife that much—they had lost the habit of one another and might not be able to reacquire it. He felt a little bitter as he rode away. The *Capitán* should not have let him go. After all, he was the only man among them who could cook. He didn't really like the Americanos, but he was used to them. It was too bad they had suddenly decided to get so many cattle and go north. Life in Lonesome Dove had been easy. Goats were plentiful and easy to catch, and his wife was the right distance away. When he grew bored, he could beat the dinner bell with the broken crowbar. For some reason it gave him great satisfaction to beat the dinner bell. It had little to do with dinner, or anything. It was just something he liked to do. When he stopped he could hear the echoes of his work fading into Mexico.

He decided that, since he was in no hurry, he would stop in Lonesome Dove and beat the bell a few more times. He could say it was the *Capitán*'s orders. The thought was comforting. It made up for the fact that most of his decisions had been stupid. He rode south without looking back.

42

"WELL, IF WE WASN'T DOOMED to begin with, we're doomed now," Augustus said, watching Bolivar ride away. He enjoyed every opportunity for pronouncing doom, and the loss of a cook was a good one.

"I expect we'll poison ourselves before we get much farther, with no regular cook," he said. "I just hope Jasper gets poisoned first."

"I never liked that old man's cooking anyway," Jasper said.

"You'll remember it fondly, once you're poisoned," Augustus said.

Call felt depressed by the morning's events. He did not particularly lament the loss of the wagon—an old wired-together wreck at best—but he did lament the loss of Bol. Once he formed a unit of men he didn't like to lose one of them, for any reason. Someone would have to assume extra work, which seldom sat well with whoever had to do it. Bolivar had been with them ten years and it was trying to lose him suddenly, although Call had not really expected him to come when he first announced the trip. Bolivar was a Mexican. If he didn't miss his family, he'd miss his country, as the Irishman did. Every night now, Allen O'Brien sang his homesick songs to the cattle. It soothed the cattle but not the men—the songs were too sorrowful.

Augustus noticed Call standing off to one side, looking blue. Once in a while Call would fall into blue spells—times when he seemed almost paralyzed by doubts he never voiced. The blue spells never came at a time of real crisis. Call thrived on crisis. They were brought on by little accidents, like the wagon breaking.

"Maybe Lippy can cook," Augustus suggested, to see if that would register with Call.

Lippy had found an old piece of sacking and was wiping the mud off his head. "No, I never learned to cook, I just learned to eat," Lippy said.

Call got on his horse, hoping to shake off the low feeling that had settled over him. After all, nobody was hurt, the herd was moving well, and Bol was no great loss. But the low feeling stayed. It was as if he had lead in his legs.

"You might try to load that gear on them mules," he said to Pea.

"Maybe we can make a two-wheel cart," Pea said. "There ain't much wrong with the front of the wagon. It's the back end that's busted up."

"Dern, Pea, you're a genius for figuring that out," Augustus said.

"I guess I'll go into San Antonio," Call said. "Maybe I can hire a cook and buy a new wagon."

"Fine, I'll join you," Augustus said.

"Why?" Call asked.

"To help judge the new chef," Augustus said. "You'd eat a fried stove lid if you was hungry. I'm interested in the finer points of cooking, myself. I'd like to give the man a tryout before we hire him."

"I don't see why. He won't have nothing much tenderer than a stove lid to cook around this outfit anyway," Jasper said. He had been very disappointed in the level of the grub.

"Just don't get nobody who cooks snakes," he warned. "If I have to eat any more snakes I'm apt to give notice."

"That's an idle threat, Jasper," Augustus said. "You wouldn't know where to go if you was to quit. For one thing, you'd be skeert to cross a river."

"You ought to let him be about that," Call said, when they had ridden out of earshot. Jasper's fear of water was nothing to joke about. Call had seen grown men get so scared of crossing rivers that it was practically necessary to knock them out at every crossing—and a shaky man was apt to panic and spook the herd. Under normal circumstances, Jasper Fant was a good hand, and there was nothing to be gained by riding him about his fear of water.

On the way to San Antonio they passed two settlements—nothing more than a church house and a few little stores, but settlements anyway, and not ten miles apart.

"Now look at that," Augustus said. "The dern people are making towns everywhere. It's our fault, you know."

"It ain't our fault and it ain't our business, either," Call said. "People can do what they want."

"Why, naturally, since we chased out the Indians and hung all the good bandits," Augustus said. "Does it ever occur to you that everything we done was probably a mistake? Just look at it from a nature standpoint. If you've got enough snakes around the place you won't be overrun with rats or varmints. The way I see it, the Indians and the bandits have the same job to do. Leave 'em be and you won't constantly be having to ride around these dern settlements."

"You don't have to ride around them," Call said. "What harm do they do?"

"If I'd have wanted civilization I'd have stayed in Tennessee and wrote poetry for a living," Augustus said. "Me and you done our work too well. We killed off most of the people that made this country interesting to begin with."

Call didn't answer. It was one of Gus's favorite themes, and if given a chance he would expound on it for hours. Of course it was nonsense. Nobody in their right mind would want the Indians back, or the bandits either. Whether Gus had ever been in his right mind was an open question.

"Call, you ought to have married and had six or eight kids," Augustus remarked. If he couldn't get anywhere with one subject he liked to move on to another. Call's spirits hadn't improved much. When he was low it was hard to get him to talk.

"I can't imagine why you think so," Call said. "I wonder what's become of Jake?"

"Why, Jake's moseying along—starved for a card game, probably," Augustus said.

"He ought to leave that girl and throw in with us," Call said.

"You ain't listening," Augustus said. "I was trying to explain why you ought to marry. If you had a passel of kids, then you'd always have a troop to boss when you felt like bossing. It would occupy your brain and you wouldn't get gloomy as often."

"I doubt that marriage could be worse than having to listen to you," Call said, "but that ain't much of a testimonial for it."

They reached San Antonio late in the day, passing near one of the old missions. A Mexican boy in a brown shirt was bringing in a small herd of goats.

"Maybe we ought to take a few goats to Montana," Augustus said. "Goats can be melodious, more so than your cattle. They could accompany the Irishman and we'd have more of a singsong."

"I'll settle for more of a wagon," Call said.

Fortunately they were able to buy one almost at once from a big livery stable north of the river. It was necessary to buy two more mules to pull the wagon back to the herd. Fortunately the mules were cheap, twenty dollars a head, and the big German who ran the livery stable threw in the harness.

Augustus volunteered to drive the wagon back to the herd on condition he could have a drink and a meal first. He hadn't been to San Antonio in years and he marveled at the new establishments that had sprung up.

"Why, this place'll catch New Orleans if it don't stop growing," he said. "If we'd put in a barbershop ten years ago we'd be rich now."

There was a big saloon on the main street that they'd frequented a lot in their rangering days. It was called the Buckhorn, because of the owner's penchant for using deer horns for coat and hat racks. His name was Willie Montgomery, and he had been a big crony of Augustus's at one time. Call suspected him of being a card sharp, but if so he was a careful card sharp.

"I guess Willie will be so glad to see us he'll offer us a free dinner, at least," Augustus said, as they trotted over to the saloon. "Maybe a free whore, too, if he's prospering."

But when they strode in, there was no sign of Willie or anyone they recognized. A young bartender with slick hair and a string tie gave them a look when they stepped to the bar, but seemed as if he could scarcely be troubled to serve them. He was wiping out glasses with a little white towel and setting each one carefully on a shelf. The saloon was mostly empty, just a few cardplayers at a table in the back.

Augustus was not one to stand patiently and be ignored by a bartender. "I'd like a shot of whiskey and so would my companion, if it ain't too much trouble," he said.

The bartender didn't look around until he had finished polishing the glass he had in his hand.

"I guess it ain't, old-timer," he said. "Rye, or what will it be?"

"Rye will do, provided it gets here quick," Augustus said, straining to be polite.

The young bartender didn't alter his pace, but he did provide two glasses and walked slowly back to get a bottle of whiskey.

"You dern cowboys ought to broom yourselves off before you walk in here," he said with an insolent look. "We can get all the sand we need without the customers bringing it to us. That'll be two dollars."

Augustus pitched a ten-dollar gold piece on the bar and as the young man took it, suddenly reached out, grabbed his head and smashed his face into the bar, before the young man could even react. Then he quickly drew his big Colt, and when the bartender raised his head, his broken nose gushing blood onto his white shirtfront, he found himself looking right into the barrel of a very big gun.

"Besides the liquor, I think we'll require a little respect," he said. "I'm Captain McCrae and this is Captain Call. If you care to turn around, you can see our pictures when we was younger. Among the things we don't put up with is dawdling service. I'm surprised Willie would hire a surly young idler like you."

The cardplayers were watching the proceedings with interest, but the young bartender was too surprised at having suddenly had his nose broken to say anything at all. He held his towel to his nose, which was still pouring blood. Augustus calmly walked around the bar and got the picture he had referred to, which was propped up by the mirror with three or four others of the same vintage. He laid the picture on the bar, took the glass the young bartender had just polished, slinging it lazily into the air back in the general direction of the cardplayers, and then the roar of the big Colt filled the saloon.

Call glanced around in time to see the glass shatter. Augustus had always been a wonderful pistol shot—it was pleasing to see he still was. All of the cardplayers scurried for cover except a fat man in a big hat. Looking more closely, Call remembered him—his name was Ned Tym, and he was a seasoned gambler, too seasoned to be disturbed by a little flying glass. When it stopped flying, Ned Tym coolly took his hat off and blew the glass from the brim.

"Well, the Texas Rangers is back in town," he said. "Hello, Gus. Next time I see a circus I'll ask them if they need a trick shot."

"Why, Ned, is that you?" Augustus said. "My old eyes are failing. If I'd recognized you I'd have shot your hat off and saved a glass. Where do you keep your extra aces these days?"

Before Ned Tym could answer, a man in a black coat came running down the stairs at the back of the saloon. He wasn't much older than the bartender.

"What's going on here, Ned?" the man asked, prudently stopping by the card table. Augustus still held the big pistol in his hand.

"Oh, nothing, John," Ned said. "Captain McCrae and Captain Call happened in and Captain McCrae gave us a little demonstration with his pistol, that's all."

"It ain't all," the bartender said, in a loud voice. "The old son of a bitch broke my nose."

With a movement so graceful it seemed almost gentle, Augustus reached across the bar and rapped the bartender above the ear with his gun barrel. A tap was enough. The bartender slid out of sight and was seen no more.

"Why'd you do that?" the man in the black coat asked. He was angry, but, even more, he seemed surprised. Call glanced at him and judged him no threat—he sipped his whiskey and left the theatrics to Augustus.

"I'm surprised you have to ask why I did that," Augustus said, holstering his gun. "You heard the name he called me. If that's city ways, they don't appeal to me. Besides, he was a dawdling bartender and deserved a lick. Do you own this place, or what's your gripe?"

"I own it," the man said. "I don't allow shooting in it, either."

"What became of Wee Willie Montgomery?" Augustus asked. "You didn't have to whack the bartender just to get a glass of whiskey when he owned it."

"Willie's woman run off," Ned Tym informed them. "He decided to chase her, so he sold the place to Johnny here."

"Well, I can't say that I think he made a good choice," Augustus said, turning back to the bar. "Probably chose bad in the woman department too. Maybe if he's lucky she'll get plumb away."

"No, they're living up in Fort Worth," Ned said. "Willie was determined not to lose her."

Call was looking at the picture Augustus had fetched from behind the bar. It was of himself and Gus and Jake Spoon, taken years before. Jake was grinning and had a pearl-handled pistol stuck in his belt, whereas he and Gus looked solemn. It had been taken in the year they chased Kicking Wolf and his band all the way to the Canadian, killing over twenty of them. Kicking Wolf had raided down the Brazos, messing up several families of settlers and scaring people in the little settlements. Driving them back to the Canadian had made the Rangers heroes for a time, though Call had known it was hollow praise. Kicking Wolf hadn't been taken or killed, and there was nothing to keep him on the Canadian for long. But for a few weeks, everywhere they went there was some photographer with his box, wanting to take their picture. One had cornered them in the Buckhorn and made them stand stiffly while he got his shot.

The young man in the black coat went over behind the bar and looked at the fallen bartender.

"Why did you have to break his nose," he asked.

"He'll thank me someday," Augustus said. "It will make him more appealing to the ladies. He looked too much like a long-tailed rat, as it was. With no better manners than he had, I expect he was in for a lonely life."

"Well, I won't have this!" the young man said loudly. "I don't know why you old cowboys think you can just walk in and do what you please. What's that picture doing on the bar?"

"Why, it's just a picture of us boys, back in the days when they wanted to make us senators," Augustus said. "Willie kept it on the mirror there so when we happened in we could see how handsome we used to look."

"I'm a notion to call the sheriff and have the two of you arrested," the young man said. "Shooting in my bar is a crime, and I don't care what you done twenty years ago. You can get out of here and be quick about it or you'll end up spending your night in jail." He got angrier as he spoke.

"Oh, now, John, I wouldn't threaten these gentlemen if I was you," Ned Tym said, appalled at what he was hearing. "This is Captain Call and Captain McCrae."

"Well, what's that to me?" the man said, whirling on Ned. "I never heard of them and I won't have these old cowboys coming in here and making this kind of mess."

"They ain't old cowboys," Ned said. "They're Texas Rangers. You've heard of them. You've just forgot."

"I don't know why I would have," the man said. "I just lived here two years, miserable ones at that. I don't necessarily keep up with every old-timer who ever shot at an Indian. It's mostly tall tales anyway, just old men bragging on themselves."

"John, you don't know what you're talking about," Ned said, growing more alarmed. "Captain Call and Captain McCrae would be the last ones to brag."

"Well, that's your opinion," John said. "They look like braggarts to me."

Call was beginning to feel annoyed, for the young man was giving them unmannerly looks and talking to them as if they were trash; but then it was partly Gus's fault. The fact that the bartender had been a little slow and insolent hadn't necessarily been a reason to break his nose. Gus was touchy about such things though. He enjoyed having been a famous Texas Ranger and was often put out if he didn't receive all the praise he thought he had coming.

Gus held the picture out so the young man could see it.

"You have to admit that's us," he said. "Why would you keep our picture propped up behind your bar and then expect us to stand there and be treated like spit when we walk in?"

"Oh, well, I never even noticed them dern pictures," John said. "I ought to have thrown all that old junk out, but I never got around to it. Just drink your drink and skedaddle or be ready to go to jail. Here comes the sheriff now."

Sure enough, in about a minute, Tobe Walker stepped into the bar. He was a heavyset man with a walrus mustache who looked older than his years. Call was amused to see him, for what the angry young man didn't know was that Tobe had been in their Ranger troop for four years, just before they quit. He had only been sixteen then, but he made a good Ranger. Tobe had looked up to both of them as if they were gods, and was an unlikely man to arrest them. His eyes widened when he saw them.

"Why, can it be?" he asked. "Captain Call?"

"Well, Tobe," Call said, shaking his hand.

Augustus, too, was highly amused by the turn of events.

"'I god, Tobe," he said, "I guess it's your duty to handcuff us and march us off to jail."

"Why would I do that?" Tobe asked. "There's times when I think I ought to jail myself, but I don't know why I'd want to jail you two."

"Because you're hired to keep the peace and these old soaks have been disturbing it," John said. The fact that Tobe obviously recognized them only made him more testy.

Tobe became immediately frosty. "What's that you say, John?" he asked.

"I guess you heard me, sheriff, unless you're deaf," John said. "These men came in here and broke my bartender's nose. Then one of them shot off a gun for no reason. Then they pistol-whipped the bartender. I offered them a chance to leave, but since they haven't, I'm a notion to file charges and let the law take its course."

He said his little say so pompously that it struck the three of them as funny. Augustus laughed out loud, Call and Tobe smiled, and even Ned Tym chimed in with a chuckle.

"Son, you've misjudged our reputation," Augustus said. "We was the law around here when you was still sucking a teat. So many people think we saved them from the Indians that if you was to bring charges against us, and any of the boys that rangered with us got wind of it, they'd probably hang *you.* Anyway, whacking a surly bartender ain't much of a crime."

"John, I'd advise you to stop your name-calling," Tobe said. "You're acting too hot. You'd best just apologize and bring me a whiskey."

"I'll be damned if I'll do either one," John said, and without another word stepped over the fallen bartender and went back upstairs.

"What's he got, a whore up there?" Augustus asked hopefully. He was beginning to feel restive and would have liked some female company.

"Yes, John keeps a *señorita,*" Tobe said. "I guess you'll have to excuse him. He's from Mobile and I've heard it said people in those parts are hotheaded."

"Well, it ain't a local prerogative," Augustus said. "We've got hotheads in our crew, and ain't none of them from Mobile, Alabama."

They got a whiskey bottle, sat down at a table and chatted for a while, talking of old times. Tobe inquired after Jake, and they carefully refrained from mentioning that he was on the run from the law. While they were talking, the bartender got up and staggered out the back way. His nose had stopped bleeding but his shirt was drenched in blood.

"Hell, he looks like he's been butchered," Tobe said cheerfully.

Ned Tym and his friends soon resumed their card game, but the other players' nerves were shaken and Ned soon drained them of money.

Tobe Walker looked wistful when they told him they were taking a herd to Montana. "If I hadn't married, I bet I'd go with you," he said. "I imagine there's some fair pastures up there. Being a lawman these days is mostly a matter of collaring drunks, and it does get tiresome."

When they left, he went off dutifully to make his rounds. Augustus hitched the new mules to the new wagon. The streets of San Antonio were silent and empty as they left. The moon was high and a couple of stray goats nosed around the walls of the old Alamo, hoping to find a blade of grass. When they had first come to Texas in the Forties people had talked of nothing but Travis and his gallant losing battle, but the battle had mostly been forgotten and the building neglected.

"Well, Call, I guess they forgot us, like they forgot the Alamo," Augustus said.

"Why wouldn't they?" Call asked. "We ain't been around."

"That ain't the reason—the reason is we didn't die," Augustus said. "Now Travis lost his fight, and he'll get in the history books when someone writes up this place. If a thousand Comanches had cornered us in some gully and wiped us out, like the Sioux just done Custer, they'd write songs about us for a hundred years."

It struck Call as a foolish remark. "I doubt there was ever a thousand Comanches in one bunch," he said. "If there had been they would have taken Washington, D.C."

But the more Augustus thought about the insults they had been offered in the bar—a bar where once they had been hailed as heroes—the more it bothered him.

"I ought to have given that young pup from Mobile a rap or two," he said.

"He was just scared," Call said. "I'm sure Tobe will lecture him next time he sees him."

"It ain't the pint, Woodrow," Augustus said. "You never do get the pint."

"Well, what is it, dern it?" Call asked.

"We'll be the Indians, if we last another twenty years," Augustus said. "The way this place is settling up it'll be nothing but churches and dry-goods stores before you know it. Next thing you know they'll have to round up us old rowdies and stick us on a reservation to keep us from scaring the ladies."

"I'd say that's unlikely," Call said.

"It's dern likely," Augustus said. "If I can find a squaw I like, I'm apt to marry her. The thing is, if I'm going to be treated like an Indian, I might as well act like one. I think we spent our best years fighting on the wrong side."

Call didn't want to argue with nonsense like that. They were nearly to the edge of town, passing a few adobe hovels where the poorer Mexicans lived. In one of them a baby cried. Call was relieved to be leaving. With Gus on the prod, anything could happen. In the country, if he got mad and shot something, it would probably be a snake, not a rude bartender.

"We didn't fight on the wrong side," Call said. "What's a miracle is that you stayed on the right side of the law for as long as you have. Jake's too cowardly to be much of an outlaw, but you ain't."

"I may be one yet," Augustus said. "It'd be better than ending up like Tobe Walker, roping drunks for a living. Why, the man nearly cried when we left, he wanted to come so bad. Tobe used to be quick, and look at him now, fat as a gopher."

"It's true he's put on weight, but then Tobe was always chunky built," Call said. On that one, though, he suspected Gus was right. Tobe had looked at them sadly when they mounted to ride away.

43

AS FAR AS ROSCOE WAS CONCERNED, travel started bad and got worse. For one thing, it seemed he would never find Texas, a fact that preyed on his mind. From all indications it was a large place, and if he missed it he would be laughed out of Fort Smith—assuming he ever got back.

When he started out, he supposed that the easiest way to find Texas would be just to ask the settlers he encountered, but the settlers proved a remarkably ignorant lot. Most of them seemed never to have been more than a few hundred feet from the place they happened to be settled. Many were unable to give directions to the next settlement, much less to a place as remote as Texas. Some were able to point in the general direction of Texas, but after riding a few miles, dodging thickets and looking for suitable crossings on the many creeks, Roscoe could not be sure he was still proceeding in that direction.

Fortunately the problem of direction was finally solved one afternoon when he ran into a little party of soldiers with a mule team. They claimed to be heading for someplace called Buffalo Springs, which was in Texas. There were only four soldiers, two horseback and two in the wagon, and they had relieved the tedium of travel by getting drunk. They were generous men, so generous that Roscoe was soon drunk too. His relief at finding men who knew where Texas was caused him to imbibe freely. He was soon sick to his stomach. The soldiers considerately let him ride in the wagon—not much easier on his stomach, for the wagon had no springs. Roscoe became so violently ill that he was forced to lie flat in the wagon bed with his head sticking out the back end, so that when the heaves hit him he could vomit, or at least spit, without anyone losing time.

An afternoon passed in that way, with Roscoe alternately vomiting and lying on his back in the wagon, trying to recover his equilibrium. When he lay on his back the hot sun beat right down in his face, giving him a hard headache. The only way to block the sun was to put his hat over his face, but when he did that the close atmosphere in the hat, which smelled like the hair lotion Pete Peters, the barber back in Fort Smith, had used liberally, made him sick to his stomach again.

Soon Roscoe had nothing left in him to throw up but his guts, and he was expecting to see them come up any time. When he finally sat up, feeling extremely weak, he found that they had come to the banks of a wide, shallow river. The soldiers had ignored his illness, but they couldn't ignore the river.

"This is the Red," one soldier said. "That's Texas right across yonder."

Roscoe crawled out of his wagon, thinking to ride Memphis across, but found he couldn't make the climb into the saddle. Of course, Memphis was a tallish horse, but normally the saddle was reachable. Suddenly it wavered in the heat. It wasn't that the saddle was rising, it was that Roscoe's legs were sinking. He found himself sitting on the ground, holding to one stirrup.

The soldiers laughed at his plight and pitched him on Memphis as if he were a sack of potatoes.

"It's a good thing you run into us, Deputy," one soldier said. "If you'd kept on going west into the Territory, the dern Indians would have got you and et your testicles off."

"Et my what?" Roscoe asked, appalled at the casual way the soldier dropped such a terrible remark.

"I've heard that's what occurs if you let 'em catch you alive," the soldier said.

"Well, what's the Indian situation in Texas then?" Roscoe asked. The soldiers seemed completely uninformed on the subject. They were from Missouri. All they knew about Indians was that they liked to do bad things to white captives. One mentioned that a soldier he knew had been shot with an arrow at such close range that the arrow went in one ear and the point came out the other side of the soldier's head.

The soldiers seemed to enjoy telling such stories, but Roscoe couldn't share their enthusiasm. He lay awake most of the night, thinking about testicles and arrows in the head.

The next afternoon the soldiers turned west, assuring him that he only had to hold a course southwest and he would eventually hit San Antonio. Though recovered from his drunk, he didn't feel very vigorous—lack of proper sleeping conditions was slowly breaking down his health, it seemed.

That evening, as dusk was falling, he was about to reconcile himself to another night spent propped against a tree. He didn't like sleeping sitting up, but it meant he could be up and running quicker, if the need arose. But before he could select a tree to lean against he spotted a cabin a little distance ahead.

When he approached, he saw an old man with a tobacco-stained beard sitting on a stump skinning a small animal—a possum, as it turned out. Roscoe felt encouraged. The old man was the first person he had seen in Texas, and perhaps would be a source of accurate information about the road.

"Howdy," he said loudly, for the old man had not looked up from his skinning and Roscoe considered it dangerous to take people by surprise.

The old man didn't look up, but a form appeared in the doorway of the cabin—a girl, Roscoe thought, though in the dusk he couldn't be sure.

"Mind if I stop for the night?" Roscoe asked, dismounting.

The old man squinted at him briefly. "If you want supper you'll have to kill your own varmint," he said. "And leave the gal alone, she's mine, bought and paid for."

That struck Roscoe as strange. The old man's manner was anything but friendly. "Well, it's a little too late to go possum-huntin'," Roscoe said, trying to make light talk. "I've got a biscuit I can eat."

"Leave the gal alone," the old man said again.

The old man, a hard-looking customer, didn't look up again until he had finished skinning the possum. All Roscoe could do was stand around uneasily. The silence was heavy. Roscoe almost wished he had ridden on and spent the night sitting up against a tree. The level of civilization in Texas definitely wasn't very high if the old man was an example of it.

"Come get the varmint," the old man said to the girl.

She slipped out and took the bloody carcass without a word. In the dusk it was hard to make out much about her except that she was thin. She was barefoot and had on a dress that looked like it was made from part of a cotton sack.

"I gave twenty-eight skunk hides for her," the old man said suddenly. "You got any whiskey?"

In fact, Roscoe did have a bottle that he had bought off the soldiers. He could already smell frying meat—the possum, no doubt—and his appetite came back. He had nothing in his stomach and could think of little he would rather eat than a nice piece of fried possum. Around Fort Smith the Negroes kept the possums thinned out; they were seldom available on the tables of white folks.

"I got a bottle in my bag," Roscoe said. "You're welcome to share it."

He assumed that such an offer would assure him a place at the table, but the assumption was wrong. The old man took the whiskey bottle when he offered it, and then sat right on the stump and drank nearly all of it. Then he got up without a word and disappeared into the dark cabin. He did not reappear. Roscoe sat on the stump—the only place there was to sit—and the darkness got deeper and deeper until he could barely see the cabin fifteen feet away. Evidently the old man and the girl had no light, for the cabin was pitch-dark.

When it became plain he was not going to be invited for supper, Roscoe ate the two biscuits he had saved. He felt badly treated, but there was little he could do about it. When he finished the biscuits he pitched his bedroll up against the side of the cabin. As soon as he stretched out, the moon came up and lit the little clearing so brightly it made it hard to sleep.

Then he heard the old man say, "Fix the pallet." The cabin was crudely built, with cracks between the logs big enough for a possum to crawl through, it seemed to Roscoe. He heard the old man stumbling around. "Goddamn you, come here," the old man said. Roscoe began to feel unhappy that he had stopped at the cabin. Then he heard a whack, as if the old man had hit the girl with a belt or a razor strap or something. There was a scuffle which he couldn't help but hear, and the strap landed a couple more times. Then the girl began to whimper.

"What's that?" Roscoe said, thinking that if he spoke up the old man might let be. But it didn't work. The scuffling continued and the girl kept whimpering. Then it seemed they fell against the cabin, not a foot from Roscoe's head. "If you don't lay still I'll whup you tomorrow till you'll wisht you had," the old man said. He sounded out of breath. Roscoe tried to think of what July would do in such a situation. July had always cautioned him about interfering in family disputes—the most dangerous form of law work, July claimed. July had once tried to stop a woman who was going after her husband with a pitchfork and had been wounded in the leg as a result.

In this case, Roscoe didn't know if it was even a family dispute that he was hearing. The old man had just said he bought the girl, though of course slavery had been over for years, and in any case the girl was white. The girl seemed to be putting up a good fight, despite her whimpering, for the old man was breathing hard and cursing her when he could get his breath. Roscoe wished more than ever that he had never spotted the cabin. The old man was a sorry customer, and the girl could only be having a miserable life with him.

The old man soon got done with the girl, but she whimpered for a long time— an unconscious whimpering, such as a dog makes when it is having a bad dream. It disturbed Roscoe's mind. She seemed too young a girl to have gotten herself into such a rough situation, though he knew that in the hungry years after the war many poor people with large families had given children to practically anyone who would take them, once they got of an age to do useful work.

Roscoe woke up soaked, though not from rain. He had rolled off his blanket in the night and been soaked by the heavy dew. As the sun rose water sparkled on the grass blades near his eyes. In the cabin he could hear the old man snoring loudly. There was no sound from the girl.

Since there was no likelihood he would be offered breakfast, Roscoe mounted and rode off, feeling pretty sorry for the girl. The old man was a rascal who had not even thanked him for the whiskey. If Texans were all going to be like him, it could only be a sorry trip.

A mile or two along in the day, Memphis began to grow restive, flicking his ears and looking around. Roscoe looked, but saw nothing. The country was pretty heavily wooded. Roscoe thought maybe a wolf was following them, or possibly some wild pigs, but he could spot nothing. They covered five or six miles at a leisurely pace.

Roscoe was half asleep in the saddle when a bad thing happened. Memphis brushed against a tree limb that had a wasp's nest on it. The nest broke loose from the limb and fell right in Roscoe's lap. It soon rolled off the saddle, but not before twenty or thirty wasps buzzed up. When Roscoe awoke, all he could see was wasps. He was stung twice on the neck, twice on the face, and once on the hand as he was battling them.

It was a rude awakening. He put Memphis into a lope and soon outran the wasps, but two had got down his shirt, and these stung him several more times before he could crush them to death against his body. He quickly got down from his horse and took off his shirt to make sure no more wasps were in it.

While he was standing there, smarting from yellow-jacket stings, he saw the girl—the same skinny girl who had been in the cabin, wearing the same cotton-sack dress. She tried to duck behind a bush but Roscoe happened to look up just at the right second and see her. Roscoe hastily put his shirt back on, though the wasp stings were stinging like fire and he would have liked to spit on them at least. But a man couldn't be rubbing spit on himself with a girl watching.

"Well, come on out, since you're here," Roscoe said, thinking it interesting that the girl had easily kept up with Memphis for six miles. For all he knew the old man had sent her to request more whiskey, or something.

The girl came slowly to him, shy as a rabbit. She was still barefoot and her legs were scratched from all the rough country. She stopped twenty feet away, as if not sure how close she was supposed to come. She was rather a pretty girl, Roscoe thought, although her brown hair was dirty and she had bruises on her thin arms from the old man's rough treatment.

"How come you to follow?" Roscoe asked. It was the first good look he had had at her—she seemed not more than fourteen or fifteen.

The girl just stood, too shy to talk.

"I didn't get your name," Roscoe said, trying to be polite.

"Ma called me her Janey," the girl said. "I run off from old Sam."

"Oh," Roscoe said, wishing that the wasps had picked another time to sting him, and also that the girl named Janey had picked another time to run off.

"I near kilt him this morning," the girl said. "He used me bad and I ain't really his anyway, it's just he give Bill some skunk pelts for me. I was gonna take the ax and kill him but then you come by and I run off to go with you."

The girl had a low husky voice, lower than a boy's, and once over her first moment of shyness wasn't loath to talk.

"I seen you get stung," she said. "There's a creek just along there. Mud poultices are the best for them yellow-jacket stings. You mix 'em with spit and it helps."

That of course was common knowledge, though it was thoughtful of the girl to mention it. The running-away business he thought he better deal with at once.

"I'm a deputy sheriff," Roscoe said. "I'm headed down to Texas to find a man. I must travel fast, and I've got but one horse."

He stopped, feeling sure the girl would take the hint. Instead, something like a smile crossed her face for an instant.

"You call this fast travelin'?" she asked. "I could have been two miles ahead of you just running on foot. I done already walked all the way here from San Antone, and I guess I can keep up with you unless you lope."

The remark almost swayed Roscoe in the girl's favor. If she had been to San Antonio, she might know how to get back. He himself had been plagued from the start by a sense of hopelessness about finding his way, and would have welcomed a guide.

But a runaway girl was not the sort of guide he had in mind. After all, the only reason he was looking for July was to report on a runaway woman. How would it look if he showed up with another? July would think it highly irregular, and if the folks back in Fort Smith got wind of it it could easily be made to look bad. After all, old Sam hadn't kept her around just because she could fry a possum in the dark.

The memory of the frying possum crossed his mind, reminding him that he was very hungry. What with the wasp stings on top of the hunger, it was difficult to express himself clearly, or even to think clearly, for that matter.

As if reading his hunger from his expression, the girl quickly moved to strengthen her case. "I can catch varmints," she said. "Bill taught me the trick. Mostly I can outrun 'em. I can fish if you've got a hook."

"Oh," Roscoe said, "I guess you caught that possum then."

The girl shrugged. "I can walk faster than possums can run," she said. "If we can get to the creek I'll fix them stings."

The stings were burning like fire. Roscoe decided there would be no impropriety in letting the girl go as far as the creek. He considered offering to let her ride double, but before he could mention it she ran on ahead. Not only could she walk faster than a possum could run, she could run faster than Memphis could walk. He had to put the horse into a trot to keep up with her. By the time they got to the creek, Roscoe felt lightheaded from the combination of hunger and wasp stings. His vision was swimming again, as it had when he was drunk. A wasp had got him close to one eye; soon the eye swelled shut. His head felt larger than it usually did. It was a very inconvenient life, and, as usual when traveling got bad, he felt resentful of July for having married a woman who would run off.

The girl beat him to the creek and began making mud poultices and spitting in them. She immediately dismantled a couple of crawdad houses to get the kind of mud she required. Fortunately the creek had a high bank, which cast a little shade. Roscoe sat in the shade and allowed the girl to pack the mud poultices over the stings on his face. She even managed to get one on the swelling near his eye.

"You get that shirt off," she said, startling Roscoe so that he obeyed. The mud felt cool.

"Old Sam et crawdads," she said, as she sat back to survey her handiwork. "He can't shoot worth a dern so he had to live off the varmints I could catch."

"Well, I wish you could catch a fat rabbit," Roscoe said. "I'm plumb starved."

The next moment the girl was gone. She disappeared over the bank. Roscoe felt silly, for of course he had not really meant for her to go catch a rabbit. She might be fast, but rabbits were surely faster.

His feeling of lightheadedness came back and he lay down in the cool shade, thinking a little nap wouldn't hurt. He shut his eyes for a moment, and when he opened them he saw a surprising sight—or two sights, really. One was a dead cottontail lying near him. The other was the girl, who was wading down the edge of the creek, a short stick in her hands. Suddenly a big bullfrog jumped off the bank. While the frog was in the air, the girl hit it with the stick and knocked it far up the bank. She scrambled up after it, and Roscoe stood up to watch, although he had only one eye to watch with. She had knocked the frog into some weeds, which slowed its hopping some. The frog cleared the weeds once, but it couldn't jump far, and the girl was soon on it with her stick. A moment later she came down the bank holding the squashed frog by the legs. Its pink tongue was hanging out.

"Got a rabbit and a frog," she said. "You want 'em fried up?"

"I never et no frog," Roscoe said. "Who eats frogs?"

"You just eat the legs," the girl said. "Gimme your knife."

Roscoe handed it over. The girl rapidly skinned the cottontail, which was indeed plump. Then she whacked the knife into the frog, threw the top half into the creek and peeled the skin off the legs with her teeth. Roscoe had a few simple utensils in his saddlebag, which she got without a word from him. Roscoe assumed the stings must be affecting him because he felt like he was in a dream. He wasn't asleep, but he felt no inclination to move. The top half of the frog, its dangling guts pale in the water, drifted over to shore. Two gray turtles surfaced and began to nibble at the guts. Roscoe mainly watched the turtles while the girl made a little fire and cooked the rabbit and the frog legs. To his surprise, the frog legs kept hopping out of the pan as if the frog was still alive.

However, when she got them cooked, he ate one and was very pleased with the taste. Then he and the girl divided the rabbit and ate it to the last bite, throwing the bones into the creek. The combination of rabbit and frog innards had caused quite a congregation of turtles to collect.

"Niggers eat turtles," the girl said, cracking a rabbit bone between her teeth.

"They eat most anything," Roscoe said. "I guess they can't be choosy."

After the meal, Roscoe felt less lightheaded. The girl sat a few feet away, staring into the waters of the creek. She seemed just a child. Her legs were muddy from wading in the creek, her arms still bruised from her troubles with old Sam. Some of the bruises were blue, others had faded to yellow. The cotton-sack dress was torn in several places.

The problem of what to do about her began to weigh on Roscoe's mind. It had been nice of her to feed him, but that didn't answer the question of what was to be done with her. Old Sam had not looked like a man who would take kindly to losing something he regarded as his property. He might be trailing them at that very moment, and since they weren't far from the cabin he might be about to catch up.

"I guess that old man will be coming after you," Roscoe said, feeling nervous.

"Nope," the girl said.

"Well, he said you was his," Roscoe said. "Why wouldn't he come after you?"

"He's got rheumatism in his knees," the girl said.

"Don't he have a horse?"

"No, it foundered," she said. "Besides, I took the big pan and whacked him across the knees to keep him still a few days."

"My goodness," Roscoe said. "You're a rough customer, I guess."

The girl shook her head. "I ain't rough," she said. "Old Sam was rough."

She took the utensils to the creek and washed them before putting them back in the packs.

Roscoe was painfully aware that he had to make a decision. It was near midday and he had only covered a few miles. The girl was a handy person to have along on a trip, he had to admit. On the other hand, she was a runaway, and it would all be hard to explain to July.

"Don't you have no folks?" he asked, hoping there was a relative somewhere ahead whom he could leave the girl with.

She shook her head. "They died," she said. "I had a brother but the Indians run off with him. Ma died and Pa went crazy and shot himself. I lived with a Dutchman till Bill got me."

"My lord," Roscoe said. "Who was this Bill?"

A look of unhappiness crossed the girl's face. "Bill was taking me to Fort Worth," she said. "Then he run across old Sam up there by Waco and they got drunk and Sam traded for me."

She never explained who Bill was, but Roscoe let it go. He decided to put off deciding what to do about her for at least a day. His wasp stings were paining him and he didn't feel he could make a competent decision when he could only see out of one eye. Maybe they would hit a settlement and he could find some nice family who needed help. They might take her off his hands.

The only problem was the one horse. It didn't seem right for him to ride and her to walk. Of course, she weighed next to nothing. It wouldn't hurt Memphis to carry them both.

"You best come for a day or two," he said. "Maybe we can find you someplace better than where you left. I'd hate for you to have to go back."

"I ain't going back," the girl said. "Old Sam would kill me."

When Roscoe offered her a stirrup up, she looked at him strangely.

"I don't mind the walk," she said.

"Well, we got to hurry," he said. "July's way ahead. Jump up here."

The girl did. Memphis looked annoyed, but he was too lazy to put up a fuss. The girl hooked her toes in the girth and held onto the saddle strings.

"It's high, ain't it?" she said. "I can see over the bushes."

"You tell me if I go wrong," Roscoe said, as they splashed across the creek. "I can't afford to miss that San Antone."

44

NORTH OF SAN ANTONIO the country finally began to open up, to the relief of everyone. Two weeks of mesquite had tried everyone's patience. Gradually the mesquite thinned and the country became less heavily wooded. The grass was better and the cattle easier to handle. They grazed their way north so slowly most days that Newt felt it would take forever just to get out of Texas, much less make it to Montana.

He still worked the drags; as the grass improved the work was a little less dusty. He mainly rode along with the Rainey boys, discussing things they might see up the trail. A major topic of speculation was whether the Indians had actually been whipped or not.

At night around the campfire there were always Indian stories being told, mostly by Mr. Gus. Once the crew had settled into the rhythm of night work, the Captain took to doing what he always done: he removed himself from the company a little distance. Almost every night he would catch the Hell Bitch and ride away. It puzzled some of the men.

"Reckon he don't like the way we smell?" Bert Borum asked.

"If that's what it is, I don't blame him," Jasper said. "Pea needs to wash his underwear more than twice a year."

"The Captain likes to go off," Pea said, ignoring the remark about his underwear.

Augustus was in a card game with the Irishman and Lippy. The stakes were theoretical, since he had already won six months of their wages.

"Woodrow likes to be out where he can sniff the wind," he said. "It makes him feel smart. Of course he would be the first one massacred if there was any smart Indians left."

"I hope there ain't none," Lippy remarked.

"They wouldn't want you," Augustus said. "They don't bother with crazies."

"I wisht we'd get a cook," Jasper said. "I'm dern tired of eating slop."

It was a common complaint. Since Bolivar's departure the food had been uneven, various men trying their hand at cooking. Call had ridden into several settlements, hoping to find someone they could hire as cook, but he had had no luck. Augustus usually cooked breakfast, catering to his own interest entirely and drawing many complaints because he favored scrambling eggs—a style several hands, Dish Boggett in particular, found revolting.

"I like my eggs with just a light fry," Dish said, morning after morning, only to watch helplessly as Augustus turned them into batter and poured them into a big skillet. "Don't do that, Gus," he said. "You'll get the white and the yellow all mixed up."

"They're going to get mixed up in your stomach anyway," Augustus pointed out.

Dish was not the only one who hated scrambled eggs. "I don't eat the white of eggs if I can help it," Jasper said. "I hear it causes blindness."

"Where'd you hear nonsense like that?" Augustus asked, but Jasper couldn't remember.

However, by breakfast time everyone was usually so hungry they ate whatever they could get, complaining with every bite.

"This coffee would float a stove lid," Call said one morning. He always rode in in time for breakfast.

"I generally eat mine with a spoon," Lippy said.

"This is a free country we live in," Augustus reminded them. "Anyone who don't like this coffee can spit it out and make their own."

No one cared to do anything that extreme. Since Call didn't believe in stopping for a meal at noon, breakfast was a necessity, whoever cooked it.

"We got to get a cook, even if it's a bad one," Augustus said. "It's too dangerous for a valuable man like me. I might get shot yet, over eggs."

"Well, Austin ain't far," Call said. "We can try there."

The day was fine and the herd moving nicely, with Dish holding the point as if he had held it all his life. Austin was only twenty miles to the east. Call was ready to go but Augustus insisted on changing his shirt.

"I might meet a lady," he said. "You can look for the cook."

They rode east and soon picked up the wagon trail into Austin, but they had not followed it far when Augustus suddenly swung his horse to the north.

"That ain't the way to Austin," Call said.

"I just remembered something," Augustus said.

He loped off without another word. Call turned the Hell Bitch and followed. He thought perhaps Gus was thirsty—they weren't far from a little creek that fed into the Guadalupe.

Sure enough, it was the little spring-fed creek that Augustus had been looking for. It ran through a small grove of live oaks, spread along the slope of a good-sized hill. Gus and old Malaria stopped on the hill, looking down at the creek and a little pool it formed below the trees. Gus was just sitting and looking, which was odd—but then Gus *was* odd. Call rode up, wondering what had drawn Gus's attention to the spot, and was shocked to see that Gus had tears in his eyes. They wet his cheeks and glistened on the ends of his mustache.

Call didn't know what to say because he had no idea what was wrong. Gus sometimes laughed until he cried, but he seldom just cried. Moreover, it was a fine day. It was puzzling, but he decided not to ask.

Gus sat for five minutes, not saying a word. Call got down and relieved himself to pass the time. He heard Gus sigh and looked up to see him wiping his eyes with a bandana.

"What has come over you?" Call asked finally.

Augustus took off his hat for a moment to let his head cool. "Woodrow, I doubt you'd understand," he said, looking at the grove and the pool.

"Well if I don't, I don't," Call said. "I sure don't so far."

"I call this Clara's orchard," Augustus said. "Me and her discovered it one day while on a buggy ride. We come out here on picnics many a time."

"Oh," Call said. "I might have known it would have something to do with her. I doubt there's another human being over whom you'd shed a tear."

Augustus wiped his eyes with his fingers. "Well, Clara was lovely," he said. "I expect it was the major mistake of my life, letting her slip by. Only you don't understand that, because you don't appreciate women."

"If she didn't want to marry you I don't guess there was much you could have done about it," Call said, feeling awkward. The subject of marriage was not one he was comfortable with.

"It weren't that simple," Augustus said, looking at the creek and the little grove of trees and remembering all the happiness he had had there. He turned old Malaria and they rode on toward Austin, though the memory of Clara was as fresh in his mind as if it were her, not Woodrow Call, who rode beside him. She had had her vanities, mainly clothes. He used to tease her by saying he had never seen her in the same dress twice, but Clara just laughed. When his second wife died and he was free to propose, he did one day, on a picnic to the place they called her orchard, and she refused instantly, without losing a trace of her merriment.

"Why not?" he asked.

"I'm used to my own ways," she said. "You might try to make me do something I wouldn't want to do."

"Don't I indulge your every whim?" he asked.

"Yes, but that's because you haven't got me," Clara said. "I bet you'd change fast if I ever let you get the upper hand."

But she had never let him get the upper hand, though it seemed to him she had surrendered it without a fight to a dumb horse trader from Kentucky.

Call was a little embarrassed for Augustus.

"When was you the happiest, Call?" Augustus asked.

"Happiest about what?" Call asked.

"Just about being a live human being, free on the earth," Augustus said.

"Well, it's hard to single out any one particular time," Call said.

"It ain't for me," Augustus said. "I was happiest right back there by that little creek. I fell short of the mark and lost the woman, but the times were sweet."

It seemed an odd choice to Call. After all, Gus had been married twice.

"What about your wives?" he asked.

"Well, it's peculiar," Augustus said. "I never was drawn to fat women, and yet I married two of them. People do odd things, all except you. I don't think you ever wanted to be happy anyway. It don't suit you, so you managed to avoid it."

"That's silly," Call said.

"It ain't, either," Augustus said. "I don't guess I've watched you punish yourself for thirty years to be totally wrong about you. I just don't know what you done to deserve the punishment."

"You've got a strange way of thinking," Call said.

They had hardly ridden three miles from the grove when they spotted a little camp at the foot of a limestone bluff. It was near a pool and a few trees.

"I bet that's Jake," Call said.

"No, it's just Lorie," Augustus said. "She's resting by a tree. I bet Jake's gone to town and left her."

Call looked again, but the camp was a half a mile away and all he could see was the horses and the pack mule. Throughout his years as a Ranger, Augustus had always been renowned for his remarkable eyesight. Time and again, on the high plains and in the Pecos country, it had been proven that he could see farther than other people. In the shimmering mirages the men were always mistaking sage bushes for Indians. Call himself could shade his eyes and squint and still not be certain, but Augustus would merely glance at the supposed Indian for a moment, laugh and go back to card playing or whiskey drinking or whatever he might be doing.

"Yep, that's a big tribe of sage bushes," he would say.

Pea, particularly, stood in awe of Augustus's vision, his own being notably weak. Sometimes on a hunt Augustus would try in vain to show Pea Eye an antelope or a deer.

"I might could see it if we could get closer," Pea would say.

"Pea, I don't know what keeps you from riding off a cliff," Augustus responded. "If we get closer the animal will just get farther."

"Let's hire Lorie to cook," Augustus said.

"Let's don't," Call said. "Bring her into that camp and there'd be fights ever day, even if she was a decent woman."

"I don't know why you're so down on whores, Woodrow," Augustus said. "You had yours, as I remember."

"Yes, that was my mistake," Call said, annoyed that Gus would bring it up.

"It ain't a mistake to behave like a human being once in a while," Augustus said. "Poor Maggie got her heart broke, but she gave you a fine son before she quit."

"You don't know that and I don't want to talk about it," Call said. "He could be yours, or Jake's, or some damn gambler's."

"Yes, but he ain't, he's yours," Augustus said. "Anybody with a good eye can see it. Besides, Maggie told me. She and I were good friends."

"I don't know about friends," Call said. "I'm sure you were a good customer."

"The two can overlap," Augustus pointed out, well aware that his friend was not happy to have such a subject broached. Call had been secretive about it when it was happening and had been even more secretive about it since.

When they rode into the little camp, Lorena was sitting under the tree, quietly watching them. She had evidently just bathed in the pool, for her long blond hair was wet. Once in a while she squeezed water off a strand with her fingers. She had a bruise below one eye.

"I god, Lorie, it looks like an easy life," Augustus said. "You got your own swimming hole. Where's Jake?"

"He went to town," Lorena said. "He's done been gone two days."

"Must be in a good game," Augustus said. "Jake will play for a week if he's ahead."

Call thought it was unconscionable to leave any woman alone that long in such rough country.

"When do you expect him back?" he asked.

"He said he wasn't coming back," Lorena said. "He left mad. He's been mad the whole way up here. He said I could have the horse and the mule and go where I pleased."

"I doubt he meant it," Augustus said. "What do you think?"

"He'll be back," Lorena said.

Call was not so sure. Jake had never been one to load himself with responsibilities unnecessarily.

To his annoyance, Gus got down and hitched his horse to a bush. Then he unsaddled.

"I thought you was going to Austin," Call said.

"Woodrow, you go," Augustus said. "I ain't in the mood for city life just now. I'll stay here and play cards with Lorie until that scamp shows up."

Call was very annoyed. One of Gus's worst traits was an inability to stick to a plan. Call might spend all night working out a strategy, and Augustus might go along with it for ten minutes and then lose patience and just do whatever came into his mind. Of course, going into town to hire a cook was no great project, but it was still irritating that Gus would just drop off. But Call knew it was pointless to argue.

"Well, I hope you get back to the herd tonight, in case I'm late," he said. "There should be somebody with some experience around."

"Oh, I don't know," Augustus said. "It's time that outfit got a little practice in doing without us. They probably think the sun won't come up unless you're there to allow it."

Rather than re-argue yet another old argument, Call turned the Hell Bitch. Even experienced men were apt to flounder badly in crises if they lacked leadership. He had seen highly competent men stand as if paralyzed in a crisis, though once someone took command and told them what to do they might perform splendidly. A loose group like the Hat Creek outfit wouldn't even know how to decide who was to decide, if both he and Gus were gone.

He put the Hell Bitch into a lope—it was a pleasure to watch the easy way the mare ate up the miles. With such a horse under him he could soon forget most of his vexations.

Then, for no reason, between one stride and the next, the Hell Bitch suddenly rolled out of her easy gait into a flying buck. Call was riding along relaxed and, before he could even jerk her head up, he lost a stirrup and knew he was thrown. Well, goddamn you, you finally got me, he thought, and a second later was on the ground. But he had taken a wrap around his hand with one rein and held on, hoping the rein wouldn't snap. The rein held, and Call got to his feet and caught the other rein.

"Well, your little plan failed," he said to the mare. He knew that with a little better luck she would have been loose and gone. She didn't fight at all when he remounted, and she showed no sign of wanting to buck anymore. Call kept her in a trot for a mile or two before letting her go back to the lope. He didn't expect her to try it again. She was too intelligent to waste her energies at a time when she knew he would be set for trouble. Somehow she had sensed that he had his mind on other things when she exploded. In a way it pleased him—he had never cared for totally docile horses. He liked an animal that was as alert as he was—or, in the mare's case, even more alert. She had been aware of his preoccupations, whereas he had had no inkling of her intentions.

Now she was content to ignore her own failure, but he had no doubt that if she judged the time to be right she would try again. He decided to find some braided horsehair reins when he got to Austin—the thin leather rein he was using could easily have snapped. Braided horsehair would give him an advantage if he got thrown again, and he had never been exceptional at riding bucking horses.

"You try what you like," he said. He had begun, more and more, to talk out loud to her when they were alone. "I'll tell you this: I aim to ride you across the Yellowstone, and if I don't it'll be because one of us gets killed first."

The gray mare loped on toward Austin, once again easily eating up the miles.

45

LORENA WAS AMUSED that Gus had stopped. He was not a man to miss a chance. If he thought to trick her again, he would have to work hard at it, but she was relieved to have him stay. The two days since Jake had left were wearisome. Although she knew he would come back in time, she was less and less certain that it mattered, for Jake had taken a grudge against her and she suspected he would be slow to give it up. It was puzzling to her, thinking back on it, why she had been so quick to trust him. Somehow he had convinced her he was the answer to all her problems. She had felt an overpowering feeling of need and trust when he had sat down and began talking to her so friendly. He had seemed as eager to hear her talk as she had been to hear his.

Only a month had passed, and in the last few days he had made it perfectly clear that he had no interest in ever hearing her talk again and would prefer that she didn't. It made her sad. If she was always going to be so mistaken about men, she would be lucky ever to get to San Francisco.

At times, waiting, she had almost decided just to take the horse and the mule and try to find her way back to Lonesome Dove. Xavier had said he would marry her and take her anywhere she wanted to go. She remembered the day he had come into the room—his wild eyes, his threat to kill Jake. When she had nothing to do but sit around and think about it, her capacity for mistakes discouraged her so that she considered drowning herself in the little pool. But it was a sunny, pretty morning, and when she went into the pool a little later, it was only to wash her hair in the cool water. For a moment she put her head under and opened her eyes, but it felt silly—to die in such an element was only ridiculous. She began to wonder if perhaps she was touched—if that was why she made mistakes. Her mother had been touched. She often babbled of people no one knew. She talked to dead relatives, dead babies, speaking to them as if they were still alive. Lorena wondered if it was mistakes that had made her mother do that. Perhaps, after so many mistakes, your mind finally broke loose and wandered back and forth between past and present.

"Lorie, you look downcast," Augustus said. "Not four or five days ago you felt keen and looked more beautiful than the sky. What's that scamp done to cause such a change?"

"I don't know, Gus," Lorena said. "Seems like I change every day."

"Oh, like most people do," he said, watching her. She had a sad look in her eyes.

"I didn't used to down in Lonesome Dove," she said. "I mainly just felt the same from one day to the next."

"Yes, hopeless," Augustus said. "You didn't expect nothing. Then Jake come along and started you expecting again."

"I didn't expect this," Lorena said.

"No, but he got you hoping, at least," Augustus said. "The trouble is, Jake ain't a man to support nobody's hopes but his own."

Lorena shrugged. It hadn't been Jake's fault. He hadn't asked her to turn herself over to him, although he had accepted readily enough when she did.

"I guess I'm in a fix," she said. "He ain't gonna take me to California."

"Nope," Augustus said. "It's too bad Call's ornery about women or we could make you a cook and all the cowhands could fall in love with you. Dish is near crazy with love for you as it is."

"That won't get him much," Lorena said. Dish had been her last customer before Jake. He had a white body, like all the rest, and was so excited he was hardly with her any time.

"Well, he's got you to think about," Augustus said. "That's more important than you might think. A young man needs a woman to think about."

"I guess he's free to think all he wants," Lorena said. "Why'd you stop off, Gus?"

"Hoping for a poke," Augustus said. "What's it gonna be this time, draw poker?"

"No, blackjack," Lorena said. "I'm luckier at it. What do I get if I win?"

Augustus grinned. "I'll be *your* whore," he said. "You can have a poke on demand."

"Why would I want one?" Lorena asked. The notion of a man being a whore amused her a little, it was so unusual.

"Think about it a minute," Augustus said. "Suppose it all worked the other way, and men were the whores. You just walk into a saloon and jingle your money and buy anyone you wanted. And he'd have to take his clothes off and do what you said to."

"I never seen one I wanted," Lorena said. "'Cept Jake, and that didn't last any time."

"I know it's hard to think about," Augustus said. "You been the one wanted all this time. Just suppose it was the opposite and you could buy what you wanted in the way of a man."

Lorena decided Gus was the craziest man she had ever known. He didn't look crazy, but his notions were wild.

"Suppose I was a whore," he said. "I've always figured I'd make a good one. If you win this hand I'll give you a free poke and all you'll have to figure out is how to enjoy it."

"I wouldn't enjoy it," Lorena said. She had never enjoyed it, and it would take more than Gus's talk to change her opinion.

"Did you never play games?" Augustus asked.

"I played spin the bottle," Lorena said, remembering that she had played it with her brother, who had been sickly and had stayed in Alabama with her grandmother.

"Well, it's a kind of game we're talking about," Augustus said. "Games are played for fun. You've thought about it as a business too long. If you win the card game you ought to pretend you're a fancy lady in San Francisco who don't have nothing to do but lay around on silk sheets and have a nigger bring you buttermilk once in a while. And what my job is is to make you feel good."

"I don't like buttermilk," Lorena said. To her surprise, Gus suddenly stroked her cheek. It took her aback and she put her head down on her knees. Gus put his hand under her wet hair and rubbed the back of her neck.

"Yes, that's your problem," he said. "You don't like buttermilk, or nothing else. You're like a starving person whose stomach is shrunk up from not having any food. You're shrunk up from not wanting nothing."

"I want to get to San Francisco," Lorena said. "It's cool, they say."

"You'd be better off if you could just enjoy a poke once in a while," Augustus said, taking one of her hands in his and smoothing her fingers. "Life in San Francisco is still just life. If you want one thing too much it's likely to be a disappointment. The healthy way is to learn to like the everyday things, like soft beds and buttermilk—and feisty gentlemen."

Lorena didn't answer. She shut her eyes and let Gus hold her hand. She was afraid he would try more, without paying her or even playing cards, but he didn't. It was a very still morning. Gus seemed content to hold her hand and sit quietly. She could hear the horses swishing their tails.

Then Gus let her hand go and stood up and took off his shirt and pants. Lorena wondered what made him behave so strangely—they were supposed to play cards first. Gus had on flannel underwear that had been pink once. It was so worn the color had almost faded to white. It was full of holes and his white chest hair stuck out of some of the holes. He also took off his boots and socks.

"You had your bath, but I ain't had one," he said, and went to the water hole and waded right in, underwear and all. The water was cold, but Gus went splashing off across the pool. He ducked his head under a few times and then swam back.

"Dern, that water was so cold it shriveled my pod," he said. He sat down on a big rock to let the heat dry him. Then, looking beyond her, he apparently saw something she couldn't see.

"Lorie, would you mind handing me my gun belt?" he asked.

"Why?" she asked.

"I see an Indian coming and I can't tell if he's friendly," Augustus said. "He's riding a pacing horse and that ain't a good sign."

His old pistol was so heavy she had to use both hands to pass the gun belt to him.

"Jake rides a pacing horse," she said.

"Yes, and he's a scamp," Augustus said.

Lorena looked west, but she could see no one. The rolling plain was empty.

"Where is he?" she asked.

"He'll be a while yet," Augustus said.

"How do you know he's an Indian, if he's that far?" she asked.

"Indians got their own way of riding, that's why," Augustus said. "This one might have killed a Mexican or at least stole one's horse."

"How do you know?" she asked.

"He's got silver on his saddle, like Mexicans go in for," Augustus said. "I seen the sun flashing on it."

Lorena looked again and saw a tiny speck. "I don't know how you can see that far, Gus," she said.

"Call don't neither," Augustus said. "Makes him mad. He's better trained than me but ain't got the eyesight."

Then he grinned at her, and put his hat on to shade his eyes. He was watching the west in a way that made her apprehensive.

"You want the rifle?" she asked.

"No, I've shot many a sassy bandit with this pistol," he said. "I'm glad to have my hat, though. It don't do to go into a scrape bareheaded."

The rider was close enough by then that she too could see the occasional flash of sun on the saddle. A few minutes later he rode into camp. He was a big man, riding a bay stallion. Gus had been right: he was an Indian. He had long, tangled black hair and wore no hat—just a bandana tied around his head. His leather leggings were greasy and his boots old, though he wore a pair of silver spurs with big rowels. He had a large knife strapped to one leg and carried a rifle lightly across the pommel of his saddle.

He looked at them without expression—in fact, not so much at them as at their horses. Lorena wished Augustus would say something, but he sat quietly, watching the man from under the brim of his old hat. The man had a very large head, squarish and heavy.

"I'd like to water," he said, finally. His voice was as heavy as his head.

"It's free water," Augustus said. "I hope you like it cold. We ain't got time to warm it for you."

"I like it wet," the man said and trotted past them to the pool. He dismounted and squatted quickly, raising the water to his mouth in a cupped hand.

"Now that's a graceful skill," Augustus said. "Most men just drop on their bellies to drink out of a pond, or else dip water in their hats, which means the water tastes like hair."

The bay stallion waded a few steps into the pool and drank deeply.

The man waited until the horse had finished drinking, then came walking back, his spurs jingling lightly as he walked. Again he glanced at their horses, before looking at them.

"This is Miss Wood," Augustus said, "and I'm Captain McCrae. I hope you've had breakfast because we're low on grub."

The man looked at Augustus calmly and a little insolently, it seemed to Lorena.

"I'm Blue Duck," he said. "I've heard of you, McCrae. But I didn't know you was so old."

"Oh, I wasn't till lately," Augustus said. It seemed to Lorena that he too had a touch of insolence in his manner. Though Gus was sitting in his underwear, apparently relaxed, Lorena didn't think there was anything relaxed about the situation. The Indian called Blue Duck was frightening. Now that he stood close to them his head seemed bigger than ever, and his hands too. He held the rifle in the crook of his arm, handling it like a toy.

"Where's Call if you're McCrae?" Blue Duck asked.

"Captain Call went to town," Augustus said. "He's shopping for a cook."

"I was told I best kill both of you if I killed one," the Indian said. "It's my bad luck he's gone."

"Well, he'll be back," Augustus said, the insolence more pronounced in his voice. "You can sit over there in the shade and wait if you'd enjoy a chance at us both."

Blue Duck looked him in the eye for a moment, and with a light movement swung back on his horse.

"I can't wait all day just for the chance to shoot two worn-out old Rangers," he said. "There are plenty that need killing besides you two."

"I guess Charlie Goodnight must have run you off," Augustus said. "Otherwise you wouldn't be off down here in respectable country riding some dead Mexican's saddle."

The man smiled a hard smile. "If you ever bring that goddamned old tongue of yours north of the Canadian I'll cut it out and feed it to my wolf pups," he said. "That and your nuts too."

Without another look he rode past them and on out of the camp.

Lorena looked at Gus, half expecting him to shoot the man, but Gus just pushed his hat brim up and watched him ride away. Lorena almost wished Gus *would* shoot him, for she felt the man was a killer, although she had no basis for the judgment. He had not looked at her and didn't seem to be interested in her, yet he felt dangerous. Sometimes the minute a man stepped into her room she would know he was dangerous and would hurt her if she gave him the opportunity. Even Tinkersley had been that way. Some days he was harmless, other days dangerous. She could tell, even with her back to him, if he was in a mood to slap her. If he was in such a mood, he would hit her no matter how small she walked. But she wasn't really afraid with Tinkersley—his angers had a short life. He hit hard, but he only hit once.

The man called Blue Duck was much more frightening. He might not hit at all—or he might do something worse.

"Pack up, Lorie," Augustus said. "You best stay near us for a night or two."

"Who is he?" she asked.

"One we ought to have hung ten years ago," Augustus said. "Couldn't catch him. He's a Comanchero. He's got a greasy bunch of murderers and child-stealers. He used to work the Red River country from New Mexico all the way across to Arkansas, hitting settlers. They'd butcher the grownups and take the horses and kids."

"Why couldn't you catch him?" she asked.

"He was better at doing without water than we were," Augustus said. "He knew them dry plains and we didn't. Then the Army blocked us. MacKenzie said he'd get him, only he didn't."

"Would he have tried to kill you if Captain Call had been here?"

"I wonder," Augustus said. "I guess he thinks he's that good."

"Do you think he is?" she asked.

"You never know," Augustus said. "I don't underestimate him, though he'd have to step quick to beat me and Call both."

"He didn't even look at me," Lorena said. "I don't think he'll come back."

"I imagine he took you in long before he got to camp," Augustus said. "I ain't the only one in the world with good eyesight."

"I want to wait for Jake," Lorena said. "I told him I'd wait."

"Don't be foolish," Augustus said. "You didn't know Blue Duck was around when you told him. The man might decide he wants to use you for fish bait."

Lorena felt it was a test of Jake. She was frightened of the man, and part of her wanted to go with Gus. But she had trusted herself to Jake and she still hoped that he would make good.

"I don't want to go to that cow camp," she said. "They all look at me."

Augustus was watching the ridge where Blue Duck had disappeared. "I should have just shot him," he said. "Or he should have shot me. He was the last person I was expecting to see. We had heard that he was dead. I been hearing for years that he was dead, but that was him."

Lorena didn't believe the man was interested in her. Even if men avoided looking at her she could feel their interest, if they had any. The man called Blue Duck had been more interested in the horses.

"I don't know that Jake can protect you, even if he comes back," Augustus said.

It made her a little sad for Jake that all his friends doubted his abilities. He was not respected. Probably Gus was right: she should quit Jake. Gus himself was a more able man, she had no doubt. He might take her to California. He had made it clear he had no great interest in the cattle drive. He talked a lot of foolishness, but he had never been mean. He was still sitting on the big rock, idly scratching himself through a hole in the wet underwear.

"Gus, we could go to California," she said. "I'd go with you and let Jake take his chances."

Augustus looked at her and smiled. "Why, I'm complimented, Lorie," he said. "Mighty complimented."

"Let's go then," she said, impatient suddenly.

"No, I'm bound for Ogallala, honey," he said.

"Where's that?"

"In Nebraska," he said.

"What's there?" Lorena asked, for she had never heard anyone mention such a place.

"A woman named Clara," Augustus said.

Lorena waited, but he said no more than that. She didn't want to ask. It was always something, she thought—something to keep her from getting to the one place she wanted to be. It made her bitter—she remembered some of the things Gus had blabbed to her since she had known him.

"I guess you ain't so practical, then," she said.

Augustus was amused. "Do I claim to be practical?" he asked.

"You claim it but you ain't," Lorena said. "You're going all the way to Nebraska for a woman. I'm a woman, and I'm right here. You could have the pokes, if that's all it is."

"By God, I got you talking anyway," Augustus said. "I never thought I'd be that lucky."

Lorena felt her little anger die, the old discouragement take its place. Once again she found herself alone in a hot place, dependent on men who had other things on their mind. It seemed life would never change. The discouragement went so deep in her that she began to cry. It softened Gus. He put an arm around her and wiped the tears off her cheeks with his finger.

"Well, I guess you do want to get to California," he said. "I'll strike a deal. If we both make it to Denver I'll buy you a train ticket."

"I'll never make no Denver," Lorena said. "I'll never make it out of this Texas."

"Why, we're half out already," Augustus said. "Texas don't last much north of Fort Worth. You're young, besides. That's the big difference in us. You're young and I ain't." He got up and put on his clothes.

"Dern, I wonder where that greasy bandit was going," he said. "I've heard of him killing in Galveston; maybe that's where he's going. I wish now I'd have shot him while he was drinking."

He tried again to get Lorena to come over to the cow camp, but Lorena just shook her head. She wasn't going anywhere, and what's more, she was through talking. It did no good, never had.

"This is a worrisome situation," Augustus said. "I probably ought to track that man or send Deets to do it. Deets is a better tracker than me. Jake ain't back and I ain't got your faith in him. I best send one of the hands to guard you until we know where that bandit's headed."

"Don't send Dish," Lorena said. "I don't want Dish coming around."

Augustus chuckled. "You gals are sure hard on the boys that love you," he said. "Dish Boggett's got a truer heart than Jake Spoon, although neither one of them has much sense."

"Send me the black man," she said. "I don't want none of them others."

"I might," Augustus said. "Or I might come back myself. How would that suit you?"

Lorena didn't answer. She felt the anger coming back. Because of some woman named Clara she wasn't getting to San Francisco, when otherwise Gus would have taken her. She sat silently on the rock.

"Lorie, you're a sight," he said. "I guess I bungled this opportunity. You'd think I'd get smoother, experienced as I am."

She kept silent. Gus was nearly out of sight before she looked up. She still felt the anger.

46

"NEWT, YOU LOOK like you just wiggled out of a flour sack," Pea Eye said. He had taken to making the remark almost every evening. It seemed to surprise him that Newt and the Rainey boys came riding in from the drags white with dust, and he always had the same thing to say about it. It was beginning to annoy Newt, but before he could get too annoyed, Mr. Gus surprised him out of his wits by telling him to lope over to Jake's camp and keep watch for Lorena until Jake got back.

"I wish I could clean up first," Newt said, acutely conscious of how dirty he was.

"He ain't sending you to marry her," Dish Boggett said, very annoyed that Gus had chosen Newt for the assignment. The thought that Jake Spoon had gone off and left Lorena unattended was irritation enough.

"I doubt Newt can even find her," he added to Gus, after the boy left.

"She's barely a mile from here," Augustus said. "He can find her."

"I would have been glad to take on the chore," Dish pointed out.

"I've no doubt you would," Augustus said. "Then Jake would have showed up and you two would have a gunfight. I doubt you could hit one another, but you might hit a horse or something. Anyway, we can't spare a top hand like you," he added, thinking the compliment might soothe Dish's feelings. It didn't. He immediately walked off in a sulk.

Captain Call rode in just as Newt was leaving.

"So where's the new cook?" Augustus asked.

"He'll be along tomorrow," Call said. "Why are you sending the boy off?"

Newt heard the question and felt unhappy for a moment. Almost everybody called him Newt, but the Captain still called him "the boy."

"Lorie can't be left by herself tonight," Augustus said. "I don't reckon you seen Jake."

"I never hit the right saloon," Call said. "I was after a cook. He's there, though. I heard his name mentioned several times."

"Hear anyone mention Blue Duck?" Augustus asked.

Call was unsaddling the mare. At the mention of the Comanchero he stopped. "No, why would I?" he asked.

"He stopped and introduced himself," Augustus said. "Over at Jake's camp."

Call could hardly credit the information. He looked at Gus closely to see if it was some kind of joke. Blue Duck stole white children and gave them to the Comanches for presents. He took scalps, abused women, cut up men. What he didn't steal he burned, always fleeing west onto the waterless reaches of the *llano estacado*, to unscouted country where neither Rangers nor soldiers were eager to follow. When he and Call quit the Rangers, Blue Duck had been a job left undone. Stories of his crimes trickled as far down as Lonesome Dove.

"You seen him?" Call asked. In all these years he himself had never actually seen Blue Duck.

"Yep," Augustus said.

"Maybe it wasn't him," Call said. "Maybe it was somebody claiming to be him. This ain't his country."

"It was him," Augustus said.

"Then why didn't you kill him?" Call asked. "Why didn't you bring the woman into camp? He'll butcher her and the boy too if he comes back."

"That's two questions," Augustus said. "He didn't introduce himself at first, and once he did, he was ready. It would have been touch and go who got kilt. I might have got him or at least wounded him, but I'd have probably got wounded in the process and I don't feel like traveling with no wound."

"Why'd you leave the woman?"

"She didn't want to come and I don't think he's after her," Augustus said. "I think he's after horses. I sent Deets to track him—he won't get Lorie with Deets on his trail, and if he's circling and means to make a play for our horses, Deets will figure it out."

"Maybe," Call said. "Maybe that killer will figure it out first and lay for Deets. I'd hate to lose Deets."

Pea Eye, who had been standing around waiting for the Irishman to cook the evening's meat, suddenly felt his appetite going. Blue Duck sounded just like the big Indian of his dreams, the one who was always in the process of knifing him when he woke up.

Call turned the Hell Bitch loose in the remuda and came back to the cook wagon. Augustus was eating a beefsteak and a big plate of beans.

"Is this cook you hired a Mexican?" Augustus asked.

Call nodded. "I don't like sending that boy off to sit up with a whore," he said.

"He's young and innocent," Augustus said. "That's why I picked him. He'll just moon over her a little. If I'd sent one of the full-grown rowdies, Jake might have come back and shot him. I doubt he'd shoot Newt."

"I doubt he'll even come back, myself," Call said. "That girl ought to have stayed in Lonesome Dove."

"If you was a young girl, with life before you, would you want to settle in Lonesome Dove?" Augustus asked. "Maggie done it, and look how long she lasted."

"She might have died anyplace," Call said. "I'll die someplace, and so will you—it might not be no better place than Lonesome Dove."

"It ain't dying I'm talking about, it's living," Augustus said. "I doubt it matters where you die, but it matters where you live."

Call got up and went to catch his night horse. Without thinking, he caught the Hell Bitch again, though he had just turned her loose. One of the Spettle boys looked at him curiously and said nothing. Call saddled the Hell Bitch anyway and rode around the herd to see that all was in place. The cattle were calm, most of them already bedded down. Needle Nelson, perennially sleepy, dozed in his saddle.

In the fading light, Call saw a horseman coming. It was Deets, which made him feel better. More and more it seemed Deets was the one man in the outfit he could have a comfortable word with from time to time. Gus turned every word into an argument. The other men were easy to talk to, but they didn't know anything. If one stopped to think about it, it was depressing how little most men learned in their lifetimes. Pea Eye was a prime example. Though loyal and able and brave, Pea had never displayed the slightest ability to learn from his experience, though his experience was considerable. Time and again he would walk up on the wrong side of a horse that was known to kick, and then look surprised when he got kicked.

Deets was different. Deets observed, he remembered; rarely would he volunteer advice, but when asked, his advice was always to the point. His sense of weather was almost as good as an Indian's, and he was a superlative tracker.

Call waited, anxious to know where Blue Duck had gone, or whether it had really been him. "What's the news?" he asked.

Deets looked solemn. "I lost him," he said. "He went southeast about ten miles. Then I lost him. He went into a creek and never came out."

"That's odd," Call said. "You think it was Blue Duck?"

"Don't know, Captain," Deets said.

"Do you think he's gone, then?" Call asked.

Deets shook his head. "Don't think so, Captain," he said. "We better watch the horses."

"Dern," Call said. "I thought we might have a peaceful night for once."

"Full moon coming," Deets said. "We can spot him if he bothers us tonight."

They sat together and watched the moon rise. Soon it shed a pale, cool light over the bed-grounds. The Texas bull began to low. He was across the herd, in the shadows, but in the still air his lowing carried far across the little valley, echoing off the limestone bluffs to the west.

"Well, go get some grub," Call said to Deets. "I'm going over to them bluffs. He might have a gang or he might not. You get between our camp and Jake's camp so you can help if he comes for the girl. Be watchful."

He loped over to the bluffs, nearly a mile away, picked his way to the top and spread his bedroll on the bluff's edge. In the clear night, with the huge moon, he could see far across the bedded herd, see the bright wick of the campfire, blocked occasionally when someone led a horse across in front of it.

Behind him the mare kicked restlessly at the earth for a moment as if annoyed, and then began to graze.

Call got his rifle out of the scabbard and cleaned it, though it was in perfect order. Sometimes the mere act of cleaning a gun, an act he had performed thousands of times, would empty his mind of jarring thoughts and memories—but this time it didn't work. Gus had jarred him with mention of Maggie, the bitterest memory of his life. She had died in Lonesome Dove some twelve years before, but the memory had lost none of its salt and sting, for what had happened with her had been unnecessary and was now uncorrectable. He had made mistakes in battle and led men to their deaths, but his mind didn't linger on those mistakes; at least the battles had been necessary, and the men soldiers. He could feel that he had done as well as any man could have, given the raw conditions of the frontier.

But Maggie had not been a fighting man—just a needful young whore, who had for some reason fixed on him as the man who could save her from her own mistakes. Gus had known her first, and Jake, and many other men, whereas he had only visited her out of curiosity to find out what it was that he had heard men talk and scheme about for so long. It turned out not to be much, in his view—a brief, awkward experience, where the pleasure was soon drowned in embarrassment and a feeling of sadness. He ought not to have gone back twice, let alone a third time, yet something drew him back—not so much the need of his own flesh as the helplessness and need of the woman. She had such frightened eyes. He never met her in the saloon but came up the back stairs, usually after dark; she would be standing just inside the door waiting, her face anxious. Some weakness in him brought him back every few nights, for two months or more. He had never said much to her, but she said a lot to him. She had a small, quick voice, almost like a child's. She would talk constantly, as if to cover his embarrassment at what they had met to do. Some nights he would sit for half an hour, for he came to like her talk, though he had long since forgotten what she had said. But when she talked, her face would relax for a while, her eyes lose their fright. She would clasp his hand while she talked—one night she buttoned his shirt. And when he was ready to leave—always a need to leave, to be away, would come over him—she would look at him with fright in her face again, as if she had one more thing to say but couldn't say it.

"What is it?" he asked one night, turning at the top of the stairs. It was as if her need had pulled the question out of him.

"Can't you just say my name?" she asked. "Can't you just say it once?"

The question so took him by surprise that it was the one thing of all those she had said that stayed with him through the years. Why was it important that he say her name?

"Why, yes," he said, puzzled. "Your name's Maggie."

"But you don't never say it," she said. "You don't never call me nothin'. I just wish you'd say it once when you come."

"I don't know what that would amount to," he said honestly.

Maggie sighed. "I'd just feel happy if you did," she said. "I'd just feel so happy."

Something in the way she said it had disturbed him terribly. She looked as if she would cry or run down the stairs after him. He had seen despair in men and women, but had not expected to see it in Maggie on that occasion. Yet despair was what he saw.

Two nights later he had started to go to her again, but stopped himself. He had taken his gun and walked out of Lonesome Dove to the Comanche crossing and sat the night. He never went to see Maggie again, though once in a while he might see her on the street. She had had the boy, lived four years, and died. According to Gus she had stayed drunk most of her last year. She had gotten thick with Jake for a spell, but then Jake left.

Over all those years, he could still remember how her eyes fixed on him hopefully when he entered, or when he was ready to leave. It was the most painful part of the memory—he had not asked her to care for him that much, yet she had. He had only asked to buy what other men had bought, but she had singled him out in a way he had never understood.

He felt a heavy guilt, though, for he *had* gone back time after time, and had let the need grow without even thinking about it or recognizing it. And then he left.

"Broke her heart," Gus said, many times.

"What are you talking about?" Call said. "She was a whore."

"Whores got hearts," Augustus said.

The bitter truth was that Gus was right. Maggie hadn't even seemed like a whore. There was nothing hard about her—in fact, it was obvious to everyone that she was far too soft for the life she was living. She had tender expressions—more tender than any he had ever seen. He could still remember her movements— those more than her words. She could never quite get her hair to stay fixed, and was always touching it nervously with one hand. "It won't behave," she said, as if her hair were a child.

"You take care of her, if you're so worried," he said to Gus, but Gus shrugged that off. "She ain't in love with me, she's in love with you," he pointed out.

It was the point in all his years with Gus when they came closest to splitting the company, for Gus would not let up. He wanted Call to go back and see Maggie.

"Go back and do what?" Call asked. He felt a little desperate about it. "I ain't a marrying man."

"She ain't proposed, has she?" Gus asked sarcastically.

"Well, go back and do what?" Call asked.

"Sit with her—just sit with her," Gus said. "She likes your company. I don't know why."

Instead, Call sat by the river, night after night. There was a period when he wanted to go back, when it would have been nice to sit with Maggie a few minutes and watch her fiddle with her hair. But he chose the river, and his solitude, think- ing that in time the feeling would pass, and best so: he would stop thinking about Maggie, she would stop thinking about him. After all, there were more talkative men than him—Gus and Jake, for two.

But it didn't pass—all that passed were years. Every time he heard of her being drunk, or having some trouble, he would feel uneasy and guilty, as if he were to blame. It didn't help that Gus piled on the criticism, so much so that twice Call was on the point of fighting him. "You like to have everyone needing you, but you're right picky as to who you satisfy," Gus had said in the bitterest of the fights.

"I don't much want nobody needing me," Call said.

"Then why do you keep running around with this bunch of half-outlaws you call Texas Rangers? There's men in this troop who won't piss unless you point to a spot. But when a little thing like Maggie, who ain't the strongest person in the world, gets a need for you, you head for the river and clean your gun."

"Well, I might need my gun," Call said. But he was aware that Gus always got the better of their arguments.

All his life he had been careful to control experience as best he could, and then something had happened that was forever beyond his control, just because he had wanted to find out about the business with women. For years he had stayed to himself and felt critical of men who were always running to whores. Then he had done it himself and made a mockery of his own rules. Something about the girl, her timidity or just the lonely way she looked, sitting by her window, had drawn him. And somehow, within the little bits of pleasure, a great pain had been con- cealed, one that had hurt him far more than the three bullets he had taken in bat- tle over the years.

When the boy was born it got worse. For the first two years he was in torment over what to do. Gus claimed Maggie had said the boy was Call's, but how could she know for sure? Maggie hadn't had it in her to refuse a man. It was the only reason she was a whore, Call had decided—she just couldn't turn away any kind of love. He felt it must all count as love, in her thinking—the cowboys and the gamblers. Maybe she just thought it was the best love she could get.

A few times he almost swayed, almost went back to marry her, though it would have meant disgrace. Maybe the boy was his—maybe it was the proper thing to do, although it would mean leaving the Rangers.

A time or two he even stood up to go to her, but his resolve always broke. He just could not go back. The night he heard she was dead he left the town without a word to anyone and rode up the river alone for a week. He knew at once that he had forever lost the chance to right himself, that he would never again be able to feel that he was the man he had wanted to be. The man he had wanted to be would never have gone to Maggie in the first place. He felt like a cheat—he was the most respected man on the border, and yet a whore had a claim on him. He had ignored the claim, and the woman died, but somehow the claim remained, like a weight he had to carry forever.

The boy, growing up in the village, first with a Mexican family and then with the Hat Creek outfit, was a living reminder of his failure. With the boy there he could never be free of the memory and the guilt. He would have given almost anything just to erase the memory, not to have it part of his past, or in his mind, but of course he couldn't do that. It was his forever, like the long scar on his back, the result of having let a horse throw him through a glass window.

Occasionally Gus would try to get him to claim the boy, but Call wouldn't. He knew that he probably should, not out of certainty so much as decency, but he couldn't. It meant an admission he couldn't make—an admission that he had failed someone. It had never happened in battle, such failure. Yet it had happened in a little room over a saloon, because of a small woman who couldn't keep her hair fixed. It was strange to him that such a failure could seem so terrible, and yet it did. It was such a torment when he thought of it that he eventually tried to avoid all situations in which women were mentioned—only that way could he keep the matter out of mind for a stretch of time.

But it always came back, for sooner or later men around the campfires or the wagon or the outfit would begin to talk of whores, and the thought of Maggie would sting his mind as sweat stings a cut. He had only seen her for a few months. The memory should have died, and yet it wouldn't. It had a life different from any other memory. He had seen terrible things in battle and had mostly forgotten them, and yet he couldn't forget the sad look in Maggie's eyes when she mentioned that she wished he'd say her name. It made no sense that such a statement could haunt him for years, but as he got older, instead of seeming less important it became more important. It seemed to undermine all that he was, or that people thought he was. It made all his trying, his work and discipline, seem fraudulent, and caused him to wonder if his life had made sense at all.

What he wanted most was what he could never have: for it not to have happened—any of it. Better by far never to have known the pleasure than to have the pain that followed. Maggie had been a weak woman, and yet her weakness had all but slaughtered his strength. Sometimes just the thought of her made him feel that he shouldn't pretend to lead men anymore.

Sitting on the low bluff, watching the moon climb the dark sky, he felt the old sadness again. He felt, almost, that he didn't belong with the very men he was leading, and that he ought to just leave: ride west, let the herd go, let Montana go, be done with the whole business of leading men. It was peculiar to seem so infallible in their eyes and yet feel so empty and sad when he thought of himself.

Call could faintly hear the Irishman still singing to the cattle. Once more the Texas bull lowed. He wondered if all men felt such disappointment when thinking of themselves. He didn't know. Maybe most men didn't think of themselves.

Probably Pea Eye gave no more thought to his life than he did to which side of a horse he approached. Probably, too, Pea Eye had no Maggie—which was only another irony of his leadership. Pea had been faithful to his tenets, whereas he had not.

And yet, Call remembered, that very day he had seen Gus McCrae cry over a woman who had been gone fifteen years and more: Gus, of all men he knew, the most nonchalant.

Finally he felt a little better, as he always did if he stayed alone long enough. The breeze flickered over the little bluff. Occasionally the Hell Bitch pawed the ground. At night he let her graze on the end of a long rope, but this time he carefully wrapped the end of the rope around his waist before lying back against his saddle to sleep. If Blue Duck was really in the vicinity a little extra caution might pay.

47

As NEWT RODE through the dusk, he felt so anxious that he began to get a headache. Often that would happen when he felt a lot was expected of him. By the time he had ridden a couple of miles he began to have strong apprehensions. What if he missed Lorena's camp? Mr. Gus had said it was due east, but Newt couldn't be sure he was traveling due east. If he missed the camp there was no doubt in his mind that he would be disgraced. It would make him a permanent laughingstock, and Dish Boggett would probably refuse to have anything more to do with him—it was widely known that Dish was partial to Lorena.

It was a great relief to him when Mouse nickered and Lorena's horse nickered back. At least that disgrace had been avoided. He loped on to the little camp, and at first couldn't see Lorena at all, just the horse and the mule. Then he finally saw her sitting with her back against a tree.

He had spent most of the ride rehearsing things he might say to her, but at the sight of her he completely forgot them all. He slowed Mouse to a walk in hope of thinking up something to say before he had to speak, but for some reason his mind wouldn't work. He also found that he couldn't breathe easily.

Lorena looked up when she saw him coming, but she didn't rise. She sat with her back against the tree and waited for him to explain himself. Newt could see her pale face, but it was too dark to tell anything about her expression.

"It's just me," Newt managed to say. "My name's Newt," he added, realizing that Lorena probably didn't know it.

Lorena didn't speak. Newt remembered having heard men comment on the fact that she didn't talk much. Well, they were right. The only sound from the camp was the sound of crickets. His pride at having been given such an important errand began to fade.

"Mr. Gus said to come," he pointed out.

Lorena was sorry Gus had sent him. The bandit hadn't returned and she didn't feel in danger. She had a feeling Jake would be coming—even angry, he wouldn't want to do without her three nights in a row. She didn't want the boy around. The alone feeling had come back, the feeling that had been with her most of her life. In a way she was glad it had. Being alone was easier and more restful than having to talk to a boy. Anyway, why send a boy? He wouldn't be able to stand up to a bandit.

"You go on back," she said. It tired her to think of having the boy around all night.

Newt's spirits fell. It was just what he had feared she would say. He had been ordered to come and look after her, and he couldn't just blithely disobey an order. But neither did he want to disobey Lorena. He sat where he was, on Mouse, in the grip of terrible indecision. He almost wished something would happen—a sudden attack of Mexicans or something. He might be killed, but at least he wouldn't have to make a choice between disobeying Mr. Gus and disobeying Lorena.

"Mr. Gus said I was to stay," he said nervously.

"Gus can lump it," Lorena said. "You go on back."

"I guess I'll just tell him you said you were all right," Newt said, feeling hopeless.

"How old are you?" Lorena asked suddenly, to his immense surprise.

"I'm seventeen," Newt said. "I knew Jake when I was real little."

"Well, you ride on back," she said. "I don't need looking after."

She said it with more friendliness in her voice, but it didn't make it easier to do. He could see her plainly in the white night. She sat with her knees drawn up.

"Well, goodbye, then," he said. Lorena didn't answer. He turned back toward the herd, feeling a worse failure than ever.

Then it occurred to Newt that he would just have to trick her. He could watch without her knowing it. That way he wouldn't have to go back to camp and admit that Lorena didn't want him in camp with her. If he did that, the cowboys would make jokes about it all the way to Montana, making out that he had tried to do things he hadn't tried to do. He wasn't even sure what you were supposed to try to do. He had a sort of cloudy sense, but that was all.

He trotted what he judged to be about a half a mile from Lorena's camp before stopping and dismounting. His new plan for watching Lorena involved leaving Mouse—if he tried to sneak back on Mouse, Lorena's mare might nicker. He would have to tie Mouse and sneak back on foot, a violation of a major rule of cowboying. You were never supposed to be separated from your horse. The rule probably had to do with Indian fighting, Newt supposed: you would obviously be done for if the Indians caught you on foot.

But it was such a beautiful, peaceful night, the moon new and high, that Newt decided to chance it. Lorena might already be asleep, it was so peaceful. On such a night it would be little risk to tie Mouse for a few hours. He looped his rein over a tree limb and went walking back toward Lorena's. He stopped at a little stand of live oak about a hundred yards from the camp, sat down with his back against a tree and drew his pistol. Just holding it made him feel ready for anything.

Resting with his back against the tree, Newt let himself drift back into the old familiar daydreams in which he got better and better as a cowboy until even the Captain had to recognize that he was a top hand. His prowess was not lost on Lorena, either. He didn't exactly dream that they got married, but she did ask him to get off his horse and talk for a while.

But while they were talking he began to feel that something was wrong. Lorena's face was there and then it wasn't. Somehow the daydream had become a night dream, and the night dream was ending. He woke up very frightened, though at first he didn't know why he was frightened. He just knew that something was wrong. He still sat under the tree, the gun in his hand, only there was a sound that was wrong, a sound like drumming. For a second it confused him—then he realized what it was: the cattle were running. Instantly he was running too, running for Mouse. He wasn't sure how close the cattle were or whether they were running in his direction, but he didn't stop to listen. He knew he had to get to Mouse and then ride back to Lorena, to help her in case the cattle swerved her way. He began to hear men yelling to the west, obviously the boys trying to turn the cattle. Then suddenly a bunch of running cattle appeared right in front of him, fifty or sixty of them. They ran right past him and on toward the bluffs.

Newt ran as hard as he could, not because he was afraid of being trampled but because he had to get Mouse and try to be some help. He kept running until he was covered with sweat and could barely get breath into his lungs. He was hoping none of the cowboys saw him afoot. He held onto the gun as he ran.

Finally he had to slow down. His legs refused to keep up the speed and he trotted the last two hundred yards to where he had tied Mouse. But the horse wasn't there! Newt looked around to be sure he had the right place. He had used a boulder as a landmark, and the boulder was where it should be—but not the horse. Newt knew the stampede might have scared him and caused him to break the rein, but there was no broken rein hanging from the tree where Mouse had been tied.

Before he could stop himself, Newt began to cry. He had lost the Mouse, an unforgivable thing, and all because he thought he had conceived a good plan for watching Lorena. He hated to think what the Captain would say when he had to confess. He ran one way and then the other for a while, thinking there might be two identical boulders—that the horse might still be there. But it wasn't true. The horse was just gone. He sat down under the tree where Mouse should have been, sure that he was ruined as a cowboy unless a miracle happened. He didn't think one would.

The cattle were still running. He could feel the earth shake and hear the drumming of their hooves, though they weren't close. Probably the boys had managed to get them circling.

Newt finally got his breath back and stopped crying, but he didn't get up because there was no reason to. He felt a terrible anger at Mouse for having run off and put him in such a position. If Mouse had suddenly walked up, Newt felt he would cheerfully have shot him.

But Mouse didn't walk up. Newt heard a few shots, quite a ways to the north—just the boys, firing to turn the herd. Then the drumming got fainter and finally stopped. Newt knew the run was over. He sat where he was, wondering why, of all people, he had to be so unlucky. Then he noticed that it was beginning to get light. He must have slept most of the night over by Lorena's camp.

He got up and trudged through the faint light back toward the wagon, and had not walked a quarter of a mile before he heard a loping horse and turned to see Pea clipping along a ridge, right toward him. Though caught afoot, Newt still felt a certain relief. Pea was his friend, and wouldn't judge him as harshly as the others would.

Even in the cool morning Pea's horse was white with sweat, so it had been a hard run.

"Dern, you're alive after all," Pea said. "I figured you was. The Captain's about to have a fit. He decided you got trampled, and he and Gus are having at it because Gus was the one sent you off."

"Why did he think I got trampled?" Newt asked.

"Because your horse was mixed in with the cattle when we finally got 'em turned," Pea said. "They all think you're a dead hero. Maybe I'll get to be a hero when I tell 'em I found you."

Newt climbed upon Pea's weary horse, almost too tired to care that his reputation had been saved.

"What'd he do, jump over a bush and throw you?" Pea asked. "I was always skittish about them small horses—they can get out from under you too quick."

"He'll play hell doing it again," Newt said, feeling very angry at Mouse. He ordinarily wouldn't have spoken so strongly in the presence of Pea, or any adult, but his feelings were ragged. Somehow Pea's explanation of what had happened made more sense than the truth—so much so that Newt began to half believe it himself. Being thrown was not particularly admirable, but it happened to all cowboys sooner or later, and it was a lot easier to admit to than what had actually occurred.

As they trotted over a ridge, Newt could see the herd about a mile away. It seemed curious that the Captain would get upset at the thought that he had been trampled—if he had let himself get thrown he deserved to be trampled—but he was too sleepy to care what anybody thought.

"Looky there," Pea said. "I reckon that's the new cook."

Newt had let his eyelids fall. It was not easy to get them up again, even to see the new cook. He was so sleepy things looked blurred when he did open his eyes. Then he saw a donkey with a pack on its back, walking slowly along.

"I didn't know a donkey could cook," he said irritably, annoyed that Pea would josh him when he was so tired.

"No, the cook's over there," Pea said. "He's got a fair lead on the donkey."

Sure enough, a short man was walking through the grass some fifty yards ahead of the donkey. He was traveling slow: it was just that his donkey was traveling slower. The man wore a sombrero with a hole in the top.

"I guess the Captain found us another old bandit," Pea said. "He ain't much taller than a rock."

It was true that the new cook was very short. He was also very stout-looking. He carried a rifle casually over one shoulder, holding it by the barrel. When he heard them riding up he stopped and whistled at the donkey, but the donkey paid no attention.

Newt saw that the new cook was old. His brown face was nothing but wrinkles. When they rode up he stopped and courteously took off his sombrero, and his short hair was white. But his eyes were friendly.

"Howdy," Pea said. "We're with the Hat Creek outfit. Are you the new cook?"

"I am Po Campo," the man said.

"If you was to spur up that donkey you'd get there a lot quicker," Pea said. "We're all practically starved."

Po Campo smiled at Newt.

"If I tried to ride that donkey it would stop and I'd never get there at all," Po said. "Besides, I don't ride animals."

"Why not?" Pea asked, amazed.

"It's not civilized," the old man said. "We're animals too. How would you like it if somebody rode you?"

Such a question was too much for Pea. He didn't consider himself an animal, and in his whole life had never given one minute's thought to the possibility of being ridden.

"You mean you just walk everywhere?" Newt asked. The notion of a man who didn't ride horses was almost too strange to be believed. It was particularly strange that such a man was coming to cook for a crew of cowboys, some of whom hated to dismount even to eat.

Po Campo smiled. "It's a good country to walk in," he said.

"We got to hurry," Pea said, a little alarmed to be having such a conversation.

"Get down and walk with me, young man," Po Campo said. "We might see some interesting things if we keep our eyes open. You can help me gather breakfast."

"You'll likely see the Captain, if you don't speed along a little faster," Pea said. "The Captain don't like to wait on breakfast."

Newt slid off the horse. It was a surprise to Pea and even a little bit of a surprise to himself, but he did it anyway. The wagon was only two or three hundred yards away. It wouldn't take long to walk it, but it would postpone for a few minutes having to explain why he had lost his horse.

"I'll just walk on in with him," he said to Pea.

"By God, if this keeps up I guess we'll all be afoot before long," Pea said. "I'll just lope on over and tell the Captain neither one of you is dead."

He started to leave and then looked down at Po Campo.

"Do you use a lot of pepper in your cooking?" he asked.

"As much as I can find," Po Campo said.

"Well, that's all right, we're used to it," Pea said.

To Newt's surprise, Po Campo put a friendly hand on his shoulder. He almost flinched, for it was rare for anyone to touch him in friendship. If he got touched it was usually in a wrestling match with one of the Raineys.

"I like to walk slow," Po Campo said. "If I walk too fast I might miss something."

"There ain't much to miss around here," Newt said. "Just grass."

"But grass is interesting," the old man said. "It's like my serape, only it's the earth it covers. It covers everything and one day it will cover me."

Though the old man spoke cheerfully, the words made Newt sad. He remembered Sean O'Brien. He wondered if the grass had covered Sean yet. He hoped it had—he had not been able to rid himself of the memory of the muddy grave they had put Sean in, back by the Nueces.

"How many men in this outfit?" Po Campo asked.

Newt tried to count in his head, but his brain was tired and he knew he was missing a few hands.

"There's a bunch of us," he said. "More than ten."

"Have you got molasses?" Po Campo asked.

"There's a barrel in the wagon but we ain't used it yet," Newt said. "Might be saving it for Christmas."

"Maybe I'll fry up some grasshoppers tonight," Po Campo said. "Grasshoppers make good eating if you fry them crisp and dip them in a little molasses."

Newt burst out laughing at the thought of anyone eating a grasshopper. Po Campo was evidently a joker.

"What's your donkey's name?" he asked, feeling a little fresher for having had his laugh.

"I call her Maria after my sister," Po Campo said. "My sister was slow too."

"Do you really cook grasshoppers?" Newt asked.

"When I can get them," Po Campo said. "The old ones taste better than the young ones. It isn't that way with animals, but it is with grasshoppers. The old ones are brittle, like old men. They are easy to get crisp."

"I doubt you'll get anybody to eat one," Newt said, beginning to believe Po Campo was serious. After all the trouble there had been over snakes in the stew, it was hard to imagine what would happen if Po Campo fried up some grasshoppers.

Newt liked the old man and didn't want him to get off on the wrong foot with the crew, which, after all, was a touchy crew.

"Maybe you oughta just cook some beef," he suggested. "That's what we're mostly used to."

Po Campo chuckled again. "Worms make good butter, you know," he said. "Slugs particularly."

Newt didn't know what to say to that. It occurred to him that the Captain might have been a little hasty when he hired the cook. Po Campo was even friendlier than Bol, but still, a man who thought you could dip grasshoppers in molasses and use worms for butter was not likely to become popular with a finicky eater like Jasper Fant, who liked his beef straight.

"Mr. Gus used to make the biscuits, but he had to leave his ovens behind," Newt said. He was hungry, and the memory of how good Mr. Gus's biscuits had tasted when they lived in Lonesome Dove came over him so strongly that for a second he felt faint.

Po Campo looked at Newt quickly and hitched up his pants. "I'll make you something better than biscuits," he said, but he didn't mention what it might be.

"I hope it ain't worms," Newt said.

48

"YOU THINK that Indian's around here somewhere?" Call asked.

"How would I know?" Augustus said. "He didn't inform me of his business. He just said he'd cut our balls off if we come north of the Canadian."

"I'd like to know why these cattle ran," Call said. "It was a still night and we had 'em bedded down."

"Cattle don't just run in the rain," Augustus said. "They can run on still nights too."

"I don't like it that Deets lost the man's track," Call said. "A man that Deets can't track is a slippery man."

"Hell," Augustus said. "Deets is just rusty. You're rusty too. The two of you have lost your skills. Running a livery stable don't prepare you for tracking Comancheros."

"I suppose you ain't rusty, though," Call said.

"My main skills are talking and cooking biscuits," Augustus said. "And getting drunk on the porch. I've probably slipped a little on the biscuits in the last few days, and I've lost the porch, but I can still talk with the best of them."

"Or the worst," Call said.

They were standing by the wagon, hoping the new cook would come in time to cook breakfast. Pea Eye loped up and unfolded himself in the direction of the ground.

"Your getting off a horse reminds me of an old crane landing in a mud puddle," Augustus said.

Pea ignored the remark—it was necessary to ignore most of those Gus made or else you got bogged down in useless conversation.

"Well, Newt's alive," he said. "He got throwed off, is all."

"Why didn't you bring him?" Call asked, relieved.

"We met the cook and he wanted company," Pea said. "The cook claims he don't ride on animals, so they're walking. There they come now."

Sure enough, they could see the boy and the old man a couple of hundred yards away. They were moving in the general direction of the camp, but not rapidly.

"If the cook's as slow as Newt, they won't be here till next week," Gus said.

"What are they doing?" Call asked. They were certainly doing something. Instead of simply coming to camp they were walking around in circles, as if looking for lost objects.

"The cook's got a donkey, only he don't ride it," Pea Eye remarked. "He says it ain't civilized to ride animals."

"Why, the man's a philosopher," Augustus said.

"That's right—I just hired him to talk to you," Call said. "It would free the rest of us so maybe we could work."

A few minutes later Newt and Po Campo walked up to the wagon, trailed at a good distance by the donkey. It turned out they had been gathering bird's eggs. They were carrying them in the old man's serape, which they had stretched between them, like a hammock.

"*Buenos días,*" Po Campo said to the group at large. "If that donkey ever gets here we'll have breakfast."

"Why can't we have it now?" Augustus asked. "You're here and I see you brought the eggs."

"Yes, but I need my skillet," Po Campo said. "I'm glad I spotted those plovers. It's not every day I find this many plover's eggs."

"It's not every day I eat them," Augustus said. "What'd you say your name was?"

"Po Campo," the old man said. "I like this boy here. He helped me gather these eggs, although he's bunged up from gettin' throwed."

"Well, I'm Augustus McCrae," Augustus said. "You'll have to do the best you can with this rough old crew."

Po Campo whistled at his donkey. "Plover's eggs are better than quail's eggs," he said. "More taste, although quail's eggs aren't bad if you boil them and let them cool."

He went around the camp shaking hands with each man in turn. By the time he had finished meeting the crew the donkey had arrived, and in a remarkably short time Po Campo had unpacked a huge skillet, made himself a little grill with a couple of branding irons laid across two chunks of firewood, and had scrambled up sixty or seventy plover's eggs. He sprinkled in a few spices from his pack and cooked the eggs until they could be cut in slices, like an egg pie. After sampling his own wares and grunting cryptically, he gave each man a slice. Some, like Jasper, were reluctant to sample such exotic fare, but once they had eaten a bite or two their reluctance disappeared.

"Dern, this is the best bird-egg pie I ever tasted," Jasper admitted. "It's better than hen's eggs."

"Don't you even know an omelet when you see one, Jasper?" Augustus said. He was miffed to see the new cook become a hero in five minutes, whereas he had cooked excellent biscuits for years and drawn little praise.

"It's just a plain omelet, made from plover's eggs," he added, for emphasis. "I could have scrambled one up if I'd known you boys had a taste for such things."

"Tonight I intend to fry some grasshoppers," Po Campo remarked. He was watching the two blue pigs—they in their turn were watching him. They had come out from under the wagon in order to eat the eggshells.

"If you're thinking of them pigs, don't bother," Augustus said. "If they want grasshoppers, let them catch their own. They're quick as rabbits."

"No, I am going to fry some for Newt," Po Campo said. "He claims he has never eaten a good fried grasshopper dipped in molasses. It makes a good dessert if you fry them crisp."

The crew burst out laughing at the thought of eating grasshoppers. Po Campo chuckled too. He had already dismantled his little grill and was scouring the frying pan with a handful of weeds.

Call felt relieved. It was easy to see Po Campo had a way with men. Everyone looked happy except Gus, who was in a sulk because he had been outcooked. Gus always liked to be the best at whatever there was to do.

"I liked that bird's-egg pie but I draw the line at eating insects," Jasper said.

"I wish I had some sweet potatoes," Augustus said. "I'd show you girls how to make a pie."

"I hear you cook good biscuits," Po Campo said, smiling at him.

"That's right," Augustus said. "There's an art to biscuit making, and I learned it."

"My wife was good at it too," Po Campo remarked. "I liked her biscuits. She never burned them on the bottom."

"Where's she live, Mexico?" Augustus asked, curious as to where the short old man had come from.

"No, she lives in hell, where I sent her," Po Campo said quietly, startling everyone within hearing. "Her behavior was terrible, but she made good biscuits."

There was a moment of silence, the men trying to decide if they were supposed to believe what they had just heard.

"Well, if that's where she is, I expect we'll all get to eat her biscuits, one of these days," Augustus said. Even he was a little startled. He had known men who had killed their wives, but none so cool about admitting it as Po Campo.

"That's why I hope I go to heaven," Po Campo said. "I don't want nothing more to do with that woman."

"This here ain't Montana," Call said. "Let's start the cattle."

=====

That night, true to his word, Po Campo fried some grasshoppers. Before he got around to it he fed the crew a normal meal of beefsteak and beans and even conjured up a stew whose ingredients were mysterious but which all agreed was excellent. Allen O'Brien thought it was better than excellent—it changed his whole outlook on life, and he pressed Po Campo to tell him what was in it.

"You saw me gathering it," Po Campo said. "You should have watched better."

True to his principles, he had refused to ride the donkey or climb up on the wagon seat beside Lippy. "I better walk," he said. "I might miss something."

"Might miss getting snakebit," Lippy said. Since the incident on the Nueces he had developed such a terror of snakes that he slept in the wagon and even stood on the wagon seat to urinate.

Po Campo had walked all day, a hundred yards or so west of the herd, trailing two sacks he had tucked in his belt. Now and then he would put something in one of them, but nobody saw what unless it was the pigs, who trailed the old man closely. All that could be said was that his stew was wonderfully flavorsome. Deets ate so many helpings that he grew embarrassed about his appetite.

It was Deets who first got up his nerve to sample the fried grasshoppers. Since the new cook had the crew in such a good mood, Call allowed him to use a little of the molasses they were saving for special occasions. Just having someone who could cook decently was a special occasion, though, like the men, he put no stock in eating grasshoppers.

But Po Campo had caught a big sackful, and when his grease was hot he sprinkled them into it five or six at a time. When he judged they were done he used the tip of a big knife to flick them out onto a piece of cheesecloth. Soon he had forty or fifty fried, and no one rushing to eat them.

"Eat them," he said. "They're better than potatoes."

"May be, but they don't look like potatoes," Allen O'Brien said. "They look like bugs."

"Dish, you're a top hand, you ought to take the first helping," Augustus said. "None of us would want to cut you out of your turn."

"You're welcome to my dang turn," Dish said. "I pass on eatin' bugs."

"What's holding you back, Gus?" Needle Nelson asked.

"Wisdom," Augustus said.

Finally Deets walked over and picked up one of the grasshoppers. He was inclined to trust a man who could cook such flavorsome stew. He grinned, but didn't eat it right away.

"Put a little molasses on it," Po Campo urged.

Deets dipped the grasshopper in the little dish of molasses.

"I don't guess it will kill him but I bet it makes him vomit," Lippy said, watching the proceedings from the safety of the wagon seat.

"I wish you'd fry up some of these mosquitoes," Augustus said. "I doubt they'd make good eating, but at least we'd be rid of them."

Then Deets ate the grasshopper. He crunched it, chewed, and then reached for another, grinning his big grin. "Tastes just like candy," he said.

After he had eaten three or four he offered one to Newt, who covered it liberally with molasses. To his surprise, it tasted fine, though mostly what tasted was the molasses. The grasshopper itself just tasted crunchy, like the tailbones of a catfish.

Newt ate another of his own accord and Deets ate four or five more. Then Deets persuaded Pea Eye to try one and Pea ate two or three. To everyone's surprise, Call strolled over and ate a couple; in fact, he had a sweet tooth and couldn't resist the molasses. Dish decided he had to eat one to keep up his reputation, and then the Rainey boys each ate a couple to imitate Newt. Pete Spettle walked over and ate two and then Soupy, Needle and Bert each tried one. The remaining grasshoppers went quick, and before Jasper could make up his mind to try one they were all gone.

"Dern you all for a bunch of greedy pigs," he said, wishing someone had thought to save him at least one.

"Now I've seen everything," Augustus said. "Cowboys eating bugs." His pride had not allowed him to sample them—it would only mean another triumph for Po Campo.

"Did I tell you worms make good butter?" Po Campo said.

"Anybody who tries to butter my biscuit with a worm had better have a long stride," Soupy Jones remarked. "This outfit is getting crazier all the time."

While the crew was standing around discussing the merits of grasshoppers they heard a galloping horse approaching camp.

"I hope it's the mail," Augustus said.

"It's Mr. Jake," Deets said, long before the horse came in sight.

Jake Spoon rode right up to the campfire and jumped off his horse, which was lathered with sweat. He looked around wildly, as if expecting to see someone.

"Ain't Lorie here?" he asked.

"No," Augustus said, feeling sick suddenly. The night's stampede had caused him to forget Lorena completely. He had even forgotten that Jake had been out of pocket. He had drowsed all day, relieved that Newt was safe and supposing that Lorie had been fine or Newt wouldn't have left her.

"Gus, you better not be hiding her," Jake said in a shaky voice. He had whiskey on his breath.

"We're not hiding her," Call said quietly. "She ain't been here."

Newt was about to go on night guard. He was just repairing a cinch that had begun to fray. At the sight of Jake he felt a deep apprehension. All day he had believed that he had gotten away with his stupidity in leaving his horse. Now a new and worse fear struck him. Something had happened to the woman he had been sent to guard.

"Well, by God, she's gone, and I'd like to know where she went," Jake said.

"Maybe she moved camp," Augustus said, not wanting to face what he knew. "Or maybe you missed it—you look like you've had a few."

"I've had a whole bottle," Jake said. "But I ain't drunk, and even if I was I could find my own dern camp. Anyway, the camping stuff is there. It's just Lorie and the two horses that are gone."

Call sighed. "What about tracks?" he asked.

Jake looked disgusted. "I didn't look for no tracks," he said. "I figured she come over here and married Gus. They're such sweethearts they have to have breakfast together every morning. Anyhow, where else would she go? She ain't got a map."

Jake looked tired and shaky; he also looked worried.

"Where in tarnation could she go?" he asked the crowd at large. "I guess I can find her tomorrow. She can't be far off."

Augustus's saddle lay a few feet away. He had been meaning to spread a tarp by it and use the saddle for a pillow. Instead he picked it up, went over and untied his rope. Without another word he headed for the remuda.

"Where's he going?" Jake asked. "I can't figure him out."

The sight of Jake, half drunk and useless, filled Call with disgust. Incompetents invariably made trouble for people other than themselves. Jake had refused to take part in the work, had brought his whore along and then let her get stolen.

"She was there last night," Newt said, very worried. "Mr. Gus sent me to watch. I watched till the cattle got to running."

Augustus came back, leading a big sorrel he called Jerry. The horse had an erratic disposition but was noted for his speed and wind.

"You ought to wait and look at the tracks," Call said. "You don't know what happened. She could have ridden into town. Jake might have missed her."

"No, Blue Duck stole her," Augustus said. "It's my fault for not shooting the son of a bitch while he was drinking. I didn't know who he was at the time, but I should have shot him on suspicion. And then I plumb forgot about it all day. I'm getting too foolish to live."

"Blue Duck was here?" Jake said, looking sick.

"Yep," Augustus said, saddling the sorrel. "I didn't worry much because Deets tracked him way south. But I guess he fooled us both."

"Why, there was talk of him over at Fort Worth," Jake said. "He runs a big gang of murderers. They lay by the trails and murder travelers for whatever they've got on 'em. Why didn't you just bring her to camp, if you knew he was around?"

"I should have, for sure," Augustus said. "But she didn't want to come. She had faith in you for some reason."

"Well, this is aggravating," Jake said. "She wouldn't come to town either. She would have been safe in town. But she wouldn't come."

"What's your plan, Gus?" he asked, when he saw that Augustus was almost ready to leave.

"My plan is to go get Lorie back," Augustus said.

"I hope you catch the man before he gets home," Call said. "Otherwise you'll be up against a gang."

Augustus shrugged. "It's just one gang," he said.

"I'm going with you," Dish Boggett said, surprising everyone.

"I didn't ask for volunteers and I don't want any," Augustus said.

"It's none of your say anyway, you pup!" Jake said hotly.

"I ain't no pup and you're a gambling lowlife who let her get stolen," Dish said coolly. He and Jake faced off, both tense as wires, but Augustus mounted and rode his horse in between them.

"Now, girls," he said, "let's not get to gunfighting. I'm going and you two are staying here."

"It's a free country," Dish said, looking up at Augustus angrily.

"Not for you, it ain't," Augustus said. "You've got to stay here and keep this cow herd pointed for the north star."

"That's right," Call said quickly. Losing Gus was all right—he seldom worked anyway. But Dish was their best hand. He had already turned two stampedes—something no one else in the outfit had the skill to manage.

Dish didn't like it, but, faced with the Captain's orders, there was not much he could do about it. The thought of Lorena in the hands of an outlaw made him feel sick, and his rage at Jake Spoon for exposing her to such danger was terrible. He turned and walked away.

"Are we leaving tonight?" Jake asked. "My horse is rode down."

"You ain't leaving at all, Jake," Augustus said. "At least not with me. I'm likely to have to travel hard, and I won't have time for conversation."

Jake flared up again. "By God, I'll go if I please," he said. "She's my woman."

Augustus ignored him. "I hate to leave just when you're breaking in a new cook," he said to Call. "I guess by the time I get back you'll all be nibbling on spiders and centipedes."

Deets came over, looking worried. "You best watch close," he said. "He gave me the slip—might give you the slip."

"Oh, you probably had your mind on grasshoppers or something, Deets," Augustus said.

"You got enough shells?" Call asked.

"I don't know, I ain't counted the gang yet," Augustus said. "If I run out I can always throw rocks at them."

With that and a nod he rode off. Call felt a little confused. Though the woman was no responsibility of his, he felt like he should be going too. Here he was, stuck with a bunch of cattle, while Gus was riding off to do the work they ought to have done long ago. It didn't feel right.

Meanwhile, Jake was working himself into a fury over Gus's behavior.

"I should have shot him!" he said. "By God, what does he mean, leaving me? I brought the woman, I guess I've got a right to go fetch her back."

"You should have stuck closer," Call remarked.

"I meant to," Jake said guiltily. "I only meant to stay in Austin one night. But then I got some good hands and thought I'd make it two. She could have come with me but she wouldn't. Loan me a horse, why don't you? I don't want Gus to get too much of a start."

"He said he didn't want you," Call said. "You know him. If he don't want you he won't take you."

"He wouldn't let us alone," Jake said, as if talking to himself. "He was always coming for breakfast."

Then his eyes fell on Newt, who was feeling guilty enough. "You was sent to watch her," Jake said. "I'd say you did a hell of a poor job."

Newt didn't reply. It was true—he had, and it made him feel worse that Jake was the one to say it. He mounted his night horse and rode quickly out of camp. He knew he was going to cry and didn't want any of the boys to see him. Soon he did cry, so much that the tears dripped off his face and wet the cantle of his saddle.

Back in camp, Jake was still stomping around in a fury. "That boy ain't worth his wages," he said. "I should have given him a lick or two."

Call didn't like his tone. "You sit down," he said. "He don't need a lick. He came back to help with the stampede, which is what he was supposed to do. Probably Blue Duck started the cattle running some way and then went and got the woman. It ain't the boy's fault."

Then Jake spotted Po Campo, who was sitting propped against a wagon wheel, his serape wrapped around him.

"Who's this, another bandit?" Jake asked.

"No, just a cook," Po Campo said.

"Well, you look like a bandit to me," Jake said. "Maybe that goddamned Indian sent you to poison us all."

"Jake, you sit down or get out," Call said. "I won't hear this wild talk."

"By God, I'll get out," Jake said. "Loan me a horse."

"No, sir," Call said. "We need all we've got. You can buy one in Austin."

Jake looked like he might collapse from nervousness and anger. All the boys who weren't on night guard watched him silently. The men's disrespect showed in their faces, but Jake was too disturbed to notice.

"By God, you and Gus are fine ones," Jake said. "I never thought to be treated this way." He climbed on his tired horse and rode out of camp mumbling to himself.

"Jake must have got his nerves stretched," Pea Eye said mildly.

"He won't get far on that horse," Deets said.

"He don't need to get far," Call said. "I imagine he'll just sleep off the whiskey and be back in the morning."

"You don't want me to go with Mr. Gus?" Deets asked. It was clear he was worried.

Call considered it. Deets was a fine tracker, not to mention a cool hand. He could be of some help to Gus. But the girl was none of his affair, and they needed Deets's scouting skills. Water might get scarcer and harder to find once they struck the plains.

"We don't want to lose Mr. Gus," Deets said.

"Why, I doubt anything would happen to Gus," Pea Eye said, surprised that anyone would think something might. Gus had always been there, the loudest person around. Pea Eye tried to imagine what might happen to him but came up with nothing—his brain made no picture of Gus in trouble.

Call agreed with him. Augustus had always proved to be a good deal more capable than most outlaws, even famous ones.

"No, you stay with us, Deets," Call said. "Gus likes the notion of whipping out a whole gang of outlaws all by himself."

Deets let be, but he didn't feel easy. The fact that he had lost the track worried him. It meant the Indian was better than him. He might be better than Mr. Gus, too. The Captain always said it was better to have two men, one to look in front and one to look behind. Mr. Gus would not have anyone to look behind.

Deets worried all the next day. Augustus did not come back, and no more was seen of Jake Spoon.

49

LORENA DIDN'T SEE the man come. She wasn't asleep, or even thinking about sleep. What she was thinking was that it was about time for Jake to show up. Much as he liked card playing, he liked his carrot better. He would be back before long.

Then, without her hearing a step or feeling any danger, Blue Duck was standing in front of her, the rifle still held in his big hand like a toy. She saw his legs and the rifle when she looked up, but a cloud had passed over the moon and she couldn't see his face—not at first.

A cold fear struck her. She knew she had been wrong not to go to the cow camp. She had even sent the boy away. She should have gone, but she had the silly notion that Jake would show up and scare the bandit off if he came back.

"Let's git," Blue Duck said.

He had already caught her horse, without her hearing. Lorena felt so scared she was afraid she couldn't walk. She didn't want to look at the man—she might start running and then he would kill her. He had the worst voice she had ever heard. It was low, like the lowing of that bull she kept hearing at night, but there was death in it too.

She looked down for a moment at the bedding; she had been combing her hair and her little box with her comb in it was there. But the man pushed her toward the horse.

"No, thanks, we'll travel light," he said.

She managed to mount, but her legs were shaking. She felt his hand on her ankle. He took a rawhide string and tied her ankle to her stirrup. Then he went around and tied the other ankle.

"I guess that'll hold you," he said, and caught the pack-horse.

Then they were moving, her horses snubbed to his by a short rope. To the west, where the cow camp was, she heard shouts, and the drumming sound of the cattle running. Blue Duck rode right toward the sound. In a minute they were in the running cattle; Lorena was so frightened she kept her eyes closed, but she could feel the heat of the animals' bodies. Then they were through the cattle. She looked, hoping to see Gus or one of the cowboys—anyone who might help her. But she saw no one.

When the sound of the stampede died, Lorena let go all hope. She had been stolen by a man Gus said was bad. The man put the horses into a lope, and it seemed to Lorena they were going to lope forever. Blue Duck didn't look back and didn't speak. At first she was only conscious of how scared she was, though she felt flickers of anger at Jake for letting it happen. She knew it was as much her fault as Jake's, but she soon stopped caring whose fault it was. She knew she was as good as dead, and would never get to see San Francisco, the one thing she had always looked forward to. Soon even that loss and the prospect of death ceased to mean much, she grew so tired. She had never ridden so hard. Before morning, all she could think of was stopping, although for all she knew, when they did stop something bad would happen. But in time it came to seem to be worth it just to stop.

Yet when they did stop, in the faint dawn, it was only for five minutes. They had crossed many creeks during the night. Her legs had been wet several times. In a little creek scarcely five feet wide he decided to let the horses water. He untied Lorena's ankles and nodded for her to get down. She did, and almost fell, her limbs were so weak and numb. It was dark in the little creek bed, but light on the ridge above it. As she stood by her horse, holding onto a stirrup until some feeling came back in her legs, Blue Duck opened his trousers and made water, while the horses drank.

"Get to it, if you plan to," he said, hardly looking at her.

Lorena couldn't. She was too scared. And it didn't occur to her to drink, an omission she would soon regret. Blue Duck drank and then motioned for her to mount again. He quickly retied her ankles. They were moving again as the dawn came. At first the light made her hopeful. Jake or somebody might be riding after them. They might pass a town or a farm—somebody might see that she was being stolen.

But the country they rode through was completely empty. It was a country of rocky hills and ridges and a hot, cloudless sky. A blankness came to her, replacing her foolish hope. Blue Duck never looked back. He seemed to be taking the horses through the roughest country he could find, but he never slackened his pace.

As the day grew hotter, she became thirsty, so thirsty that it was painful to remember that she had stood near a creek and hadn't drunk. She could remember the sound the creek made as it ran over the rocks. At moments it haunted her; most of the time she was too tired to remember anything. It seemed to her the horses would die if they just rode all day. They rode at a steady trot. In time she regretted, too, that she had not relieved herself—she had been too scared. Hours passed and they crossed creek after creek, but the man didn't stop again. He just kept riding. The need to relieve herself became an agony—it was mixed with thirst and fatigue, until she didn't know which was worse. Then she realized that her pants were wet and her thighs stinging—she had gone while she was dozing. Soon her thighs felt scalded from the urine and the constant rubbing of the saddle. The pain was minor compared to her thirst. During the afternoon, with the sun beating down so hot that her shirt was as wet from sweat as if she had swum a river in it, she thought she was going to break down, that she would have to beg the man for water. Her lips were cracked and the sweat off her face ran into the cracks and stung her, but she licked at it. At least it was wet and even a second of wetness on her tongue felt good. She had never been so thirsty in her life, and had not imagined it could be such a pain. The most terrible part was when they crossed water—for creeks were numerous. She would look down at the water as they crossed, and she wanted to beg. She leaned over at one of the deeper creeks, trying to get a little water in her hand, but she couldn't reach it, though it splashed beneath the horse's belly. She cried then, tears mingling with the sweat. Her head throbbed from the beating sunlight, and she began to lose hold on life for minutes at a time. She felt she might cross over. What a joke it would be on the man if, when he got her wherever he was taking her, she was dead. He wouldn't get much from her dead.

But she didn't die—she just got thirstier and thirstier. Her tongue began to bother her. It seemed to fill her mouth, and when she licked at the drops of sweat it felt as large as her hand.

Then, as she was dreaming of water, she opened her eyes to find that they were stopped by a sizable stream. Blue Duck was untying her ankles.

"I'd say you wet your pants," he said.

Lorena didn't care what he said. Her legs wouldn't work, but she wanted the water so bad she crawled to it, getting her pants muddy, and her arms. She couldn't drink fast enough—in gulping the water she got some up her nose. While she was drinking, Blue Duck waded in beside her and pulled her up by her hair.

"Don't drink so fast," he said. "You'll founder."

Then he pushed her head under and held it there. Lorena thought he meant to drown her and tried to grab his legs to pull herself out; but evidently he just wanted to give her a bath, because he soon let go and walked back to the horses. Lorena sat in the water, her clothes soaked, not caring. She drank until she couldn't drink any more. Blue Duck had unsaddled the horses, and they were standing in the river, drinking.

When she waded out of the river, Blue Duck was sitting under a tree, chewing on a piece of dried meat. He fished in his saddlebag and gave her a piece. Lorena didn't feel hungry—but then she remembered she had not felt thirsty that morning, either. She took the piece of jerky.

"We'll rest a spell till it's dark," he said.

She looked at the sun, which was not high. It wouldn't be much of a rest. She nibbled at the meat, which was so hard her teeth could barely dent it. She went and sat in the shade of a small tree growing by the creek.

Blue Duck hobbled the horses, then came and looked down at her. "I got a treatment for women that try to run away," he said casually. "I cut a little hole in their stomachs and pull out a gut and wrap it around a limb. Then I drag them thirty or forty feet and tie them down. That way they can watch the coyotes come and eat their guts."

He went back and lay down under a tree, adjusted his saddlebags for a pillow, and was soon asleep.

Lorena was too tired for his threat to scare her much. She wasn't going to run away and give him a reason to cut a hole in her stomach. She did think she was going to die, though. She felt death had her, in the form of the Comanchero. She wouldn't live to be cut or be gnawed by coyotes. She would die if he touched her, she felt. She was too tired to care much. The one thing that crossed her mind was that she should have gone with Xavier. He was a man of his word, and no worse in most respects than other men. And yet she had been determined to go riding off with Jake, who had not even looked after her three weeks. Jake was probably still in Austin, playing cards. She didn't particularly blame him—playing cards beat most things you could do.

She dozed for what seemed like a minute and woke to find Blue Duck shaking her. It was dusk, the sun just down.

"Let's git," he said. "We don't want to miss the cool of the evening."

Once again they rode all night. Lorena slept in the saddle and would have fallen off if she hadn't been tied in the stirrups. At dawn he let her down again, by another creek, and this time she did as he did—peed and drank. They rode all day again through empty country, never seeing a horseman, a town, even an animal. The only thing she noticed was that there were fewer trees. She grew so tired of riding that she would have been glad to die, if only because it meant being stopped. She wanted sleep more than she had ever wanted anything. The sun blazed all day. When she dozed, sweat stood on her eyelids and wet her face when she awoke.

Blue Duck took so little interest in her that she couldn't understand why he had stolen her. He scarcely looked back all day. He untied her when they stopped, tied her again when they mounted. Once, drinking at a creek that was barely a trickle, the hand she was bracing herself with slipped and she got mud on her nose. The sight seemed to amuse him slightly.

"Monkey John will like that yellow hair," he said. "He'll 'bout have to marry you when he sees that."

Later, as he was tying her back on her horse, he mentioned her hair again.

"It's too bad the tribes played out," he said. "A few years back all I would have had to do was scalp you. I could have got a bunch for a scalp like yours."

He reached up and idly fingered her hair. "I hope that goddamn old Ranger hurries along," he said. "I owe him a few."

"Gus?" she said. "Gus won't come. I ain't his."

"He's coming," Blue Duck said. "I don't know if it's for you or for me, but he's coming. I oughta just gut you and leave you here and let him bury whatever the buzzards and the varmints don't eat."

Lorena didn't look at him, for fear that if she looked he'd do it.

"Only I told the boys I'd bring them a woman," he said. "I doubt they thought I'd find the likes of you. They'll probably give me most of their money and all their hides when they see you."

That day her mare played out. She had been stumbling more and more, as she tired. In the heat of the afternoon she stopped and stood with her head down.

"I guess who ever picked this one was just planning to ride to church," Blue Duck said. He untied Lorena and put her on the pack-horse. They rode off and left the mare. The pack-horse lasted only a day, and when he stopped, Blue Duck made her get up behind him on the big sorrel. If it bothered the horse to carry two riders, he didn't show it. Lorena held to the saddle strings and tried not to touch Blue Duck, although he paid her no mind.

Riding at his back, she noticed something she had not seen before: a white necklace of some kind. It was a bone necklace, and after looking at it for a time she realized it was made of fingers—human fingers.

That evening, when they stopped to rest, Blue Duck saw her glance at the necklace. He grinned in the way that made her think of death.

"Easiest way to get the rings off," he said. "Just take the fingers. It's no harder than breaking off a little stick if you know how."

That night he tied her hand and foot and rode off. Lorena didn't speak, didn't question him. Maybe he was leaving her for the buzzards, but she felt she would rather die than say something that might anger him. She didn't try to get untied either, for fear he was watching, waiting for her to make some attempt to escape. She slept, and she awoke as he was cutting her bounds. Another horse was standing there.

"It ain't much of a horse, but it's only got to last about a day," he said.

There was no saddle—he had not bothered to take the saddle off the dying packhorse. He passed a cord under the horse's belly and tied her ankles.

She had thought the riding hard even when she had a saddle but quickly realized how easy that had been. She slipped from side to side and had to cling to the horse's mane to stay on. Blue Duck rode as before, seldom looking back. It was night and she was tired, but there was no dozing. Despite her grip on the mane, she almost slid off several times. With her feet tied, if she fell she could just roll under the horse's belly and be kicked to death. The horse was narrow-backed and not very smooth-gaited; she could find no way to sit that didn't jar her, and long before morning she thought if they didn't stop she would be cut in two.

But she wasn't, though her hands were raw from gripping the horsehair so tightly. Minute by minute, for hours, it seemed to her that she couldn't go on— that she might as well give up and slide under the animal's belly. There was no reason to stay alive anyway: Blue Duck had her.

When he untied her at a creek, she stumbled into it to drink, no longer caring if she got wet or muddy. Again he gave her only a piece of hard dried meat. She barely had the strength to get back on the horse; she had to claw her way up using the mane. Blue Duck didn't help her and he tied her ankles anyway, though it was obvious she was too weak to run away. She felt a flash of anger—why did he keep tying her when she could barely walk?

The country had begun to flatten out. The grass was higher than any she had seen. When she looked up and flung the sweat out of her eyes it seemed she could see a farther distance than she had ever seen before. Waves of heat shimmered over the grass—once she looked up and thought she saw a giant tree far ahead, but when she looked again it was gone.

Blue Duck rode on through the high grass, never slowing, seldom looking back. She felt hatred growing, pushing through her fear. If she fell, he probably wouldn't even stop. He only wanted her for his men. He didn't care how much she hurt or how tired she was. He hadn't cared to keep her saddle or even her saddle blanket, though the blanket would have kept the horse's hard back from bruising her so. She felt like she had felt when she had tried to shoot Tinkersley. If she ever got a chance she would kill the man, in revenge for all the painful hours she had spent watching his indifferent back.

Well before sundown they came to a broad riverbed with just a little thin ribbon of brown water visible across an expanse of reddish sand.

"Keep in my tracks," Blue Duck said. "If you don't you're apt to bog."

Just as he was about to put his horse into the sand, he held up. Across the river Lorena saw four riders watching them.

"It's Ermoke and three of his boys," Blue Duck said. "I guess they've been off scalping."

Lorena felt a chill, just looking at the riders. Jake had said most of the Indians still running loose were renegades. He made light of them. He had dealt with renegades before, he said, and could do it again. Except that he was still in Austin, playing cards, and there were the renegades.

She wanted to turn her horse and flee, hopeless as that was, but while she sat in a cold sweat of fear Blue Duck turned and caught her bridle, wrapping her reins around his saddle horn.

They went cautiously across the sand, Blue Duck occasionally back-tracking a few yards to find a route he liked better. Lorena kept her eyes down. She didn't want to look at the men waiting on the other side.

Twice, despite all Blue Duck's caution, it seemed they had gone wrong. His horse started to bog, and then hers. But both times, by heavy spurring, Blue Duck got the big sorrel to lunge free, pulling her horse free. Once, in one of the lunges, she was thrown far up on her horse's neck. But finally they found a solid crossing and trotted through the few yards of brown water.

As they rode out of the river the four men waiting whipped up their mounts and raced down to meet them. One of them carried a lance strung with patches of hair. Lorena had never seen a scalp before, but she felt sure the patches were scalps. Most seemed old and dusty, but one, a patch of shiny black hair, was still crusted with blood. All of the men were Indians, heavily armed.

The leader, who carried the lance with the collection of scalps, had a hard face, with a thin wisp of mustache at each corner of his mouth. It was as if the hairs curled out of his mouth. She glanced only once and then kept her eyes away, for they were all looking at her and their looks were bad. She knew she had come to a hard place and had no one to help her. She heard the leader speak to Blue Duck and then felt their horses crowd around her. Several hands reached out to feel and pull her hair. She could smell the men and feel them, but she didn't look up. She didn't want to see them. Their rank, sweaty smell was almost enough to make her sick. One of them, amused by her hair, pulled it till her scalp stung, and he laughed a strange, jerky laugh. They crowded so close around her on their hot horses that for a moment she felt she might faint. She had never been in such a hard place, not even when Mosby's sisters locked her in the basement.

Two of the men dismounted and one of them started to untie her ankles, but Blue Duck whistled.

"Let's go," he said. "I reckon she'll keep till sundown."

Ermoke, the leader, the man with the wisps of hair at the corners of his mouth, retied her ankles so tightly that the rawhide cut her. He took her bridle and led her from then on. The other three men rode behind her.

At the sight, Blue Duck laughed. "I guess they don't want to take no chances on you getting away," he said. "Fresh women is scarce in these parts."

Lorena began to wish there was some way just to die. If there was, she would have done it. But she was tied, and there was no way.

They rode until the sun was gone and the western sky red with afterglow. Then Blue Duck reined in and quickly dropped the saddle off his horse.

"Okay, Ermoke," he said. "Go on and have a taste. We'll stop until the moon rises."

Before he had finished speaking, the men had cut her ankles free and were dragging her off the horse. They didn't even wait to tie their horses. When Lorena would open her eyes for a second she saw the darkening sky through the legs of the waiting horses. The man with the jerky laugh had a bugle and also less lust than the rest. After covering her once, he sat in the grass playing bugle calls. Now and then, watching what was happening, he would laugh the jerky laugh. Lorena had expected death, but it wasn't death she got—just the four men. Ermoke, the leader, wouldn't leave her. The other men began to complain. When she opened her eyes, she looked for the moon. But the moon was late and she only saw the horses, still standing over her. Blue Duck had gone away, and when he returned Ermoke was with her again.

"Let's go," Blue Duck said. "That's enough of a taste."

When Ermoke ignored him, Blue Duck walked over and kicked him in the ribs so hard that Lorena was rolled over with the Indian.

"You better mind," Blue Duck said. Ermoke got up, holding his side.

While they retied her ankles, the laughing bugler blew a few more notes.

50

IT WAS JULY JOHNSON'S view that all gamblers were lazy, and most of them cocky; Jake Spoon was known to be both. Maybe instead of riding all the way to south Texas he would decide to test his luck in Fort Worth, it being a fair-sized cow town.

July thought it was a possibility worth investigating, for if he could run into Jake there it would save himself and little Joe hundreds of miles. It would also mean he could get back to Elmira quicker. Getting back to Elmira occupied his mind a lot more than catching Jake Spoon. He rode along all day thinking about her, which made him a poor companion for Joe, who didn't seem to miss her at all.

Actually, as much as anything, July wanted to stop in Fort Worth to post her a letter he had written. It seemed to him she might be getting lonesome and would enjoy some mail. Yet the letter he composed, though he had labored over it several nights, was such a poor composition that he had debated sending it. He hesitated, for if it struck her wrong she would make fun of it. But he felt a need to write and lamented the fact that he was such a poor hand at it. The letter was very short.

DEAR ELLIE—

We have come a good peace and have been lucky with the weather, it has been clear.

No sign of Jake Spoon yet but we did cross the Red River and are in Texas, Joe likes it. His horse has been behaving all right and neither of us has been sick.

I hope that you are well and have not been bothered too much by the skeeters.

YOUR LOVING HUSBAND,
JULY

He studied over the letter for days and wanted to put in that he missed her or perhaps refer to her as his darling, but he decided it was too risky—Elmira sometimes took offense at such remarks. Also he was bothered by spelling and didn't know if he had done a good job with it. Several of the words didn't look right to him, but he had no way of checking except to ask Joe, and Joe had only had a year or two of schooling so far. He was particularly worried about the word "skeeters," and scratched it in the dirt one night while they were camped, to ask Joe's opinion.

"It looks too long," Joe said, glad to be asked. "I'd take out a letter or two."

July studied the matter for several minutes and finally decided he might spare one of the "e" letters. But when he took it out the word looked too short, so when he recopied the letter, he put it back in.

"I bet she'll be glad to get the letter," Joe said, to cheer July up. July had been nothing but gloomy since they left Fort Smith.

Actually, he didn't think his mother would care one way or another whether she got a letter from July. His mother didn't think much of July—she had told him so in no uncertain terms several times.

Joe himself was happy enough to be gone from Fort Smith, though he missed Roscoe somewhat. Otherwise he took a lively interest in the sights along the way, though for a while the sights consisted mostly of trees. Gradually they began to get out into more open country. One day, to his delight, they surprised a small bunch of buffalo, only eight animals. The buffalo ran off, and he and July raced after them for a while to get a better look. After a couple of miles they came to a little river and they stopped to watch the buffalo cross. Even July forgot his gloom for a few minutes at the sight of the big, dusty animals.

"I'm glad there's some left," he said. "I know the hide hunters have about killed them off."

Late that day they rode into Fort Worth. The number of houses amazed Joe, and the wide, dusty streets were filled with wagons and buggies. July decided they ought to go to the post office first, though at the last minute he became so worried about his letter that he almost decided not to mail it. He wanted badly to mail it, and yet he didn't want to.

It seemed to Joe that they rode past about fifty saloons, looking for the post office. Fort Smith only had three saloons and one livery stable, whereas Fort Worth had a big wagon yard and stores galore. They even met a small herd of wild-looking longhorn cattle being driven right through the streets by four equally wild-looking cowboys. The cattle, for all their wild looks, behaved so well that they didn't get to see the cowboys actually rope one, a sight Joe longed to see.

At the post office July debated several more minutes and finally took his letter in, purchased a stamp and mailed it. The postal clerk was an old man wearing eyeglasses. He scrutinized the address on the letter and then looked at July.

"Arkansas, is that where you're from?" he asked.

"Why, yes," July said.

"Johnson your name?" the man asked.

"Why, yes," July said again. "I'm surprised you know."

"Oh, just guessing," the man said. "I think I got a letter for you here somewhere."

July remembered they had told Peach and Charlie they might stop in Fort Worth and try to get wind of Jake and, of course, Elmira. He had only mentioned it—it had never occurred to him that anyone might want to write him. At the thought that the letter might be from Elmira, his heart beat faster. If it was, he intended to ask for his own letter back so he could write her a proper answer.

The old clerk took his time looking for the letter—so much time that July grew nervous. He had not been expecting mail, but now that the prospect had arisen he could hardly wait to know who his letter was from and what it said.

But he was forced to wait, as the old man scratched around in piles of dusty papers and looked in fifteen or twenty pigeonholes. "Dern," the old man said. "I remember you having a letter. I hope some fool ain't thrown it away by mistake."

Three cowboys came in, all with letters they had written to their sisters or sweethearts, and all of them had to stand there waiting while the old man continued his search. July's heart began to sink. Probably the old man had a poor memory, and if there was a letter it was for somebody else.

One of the cowboys, a fiery fellow with a red mustache, finally could not contain his impatience. "Are you looking for your galoshes, or what?" he asked the old man.

The old man ignored him, or else couldn't hear him. He was humming as he looked.

"It ought to be a hanging crime for the post office to work so slow," the impatient fellow said. "I could have carried this letter by hand in less time than this."

Just as he said it, the old man found July's letter under a mail bag. "Some fool set a mailbag on it," he said, handing it to July.

"I guess men grow old and die standing here waiting to buy a dern stamp," the fiery fellow said.

"If you're planning to cuss I'll ask you to do it outside," the clerk said, unperturbed.

"I guess it's a free country," the cowboy said. "Anyway, I ain't cussing."

"I hope you can afford a stamp," the old man said. "We don't give credit around here."

July didn't wait to hear the end of the argument. He could tell by the handwriting on the envelope that the letter was from Peach, not Elmira. The realization knocked his spirits down several pegs. He knew he had no reason to expect a letter from Elmira in the first place, but he was longing to see her, and the thought that she might have written had been comforting.

Joe was sitting on the board sidewalk outside the post office, watching the steady stream of buggies, wagons and horseback riders go by.

July had looked perked up when he went in, but not when he came out. "It's from Peach," he said. He opened the letter and leaned against a hitch rail to try and make out Peach's handwriting, which was rather hen-scratchy:

Dear July—

Ellie took off just after you did. My opinion is she won't be back, and Charlie thinks the same.

Roscoe's a poor deputy, you ought to dock his wages over this. He didn't even notice she was gone but I called it to his attention.

Roscoe has started after you, to give you the news, but it is not likely he'll find you—he is a man of weak abilities. I think the town is a sight better off without him.

We think Ellie left on a whiskey boat, I guess she took leave of her senses. If that's the case it would be a waste of time to go looking for her, Charlie thinks the same. You had better just go on and catch Jake Spoon, he deserves to pay the price.

Your sister-in-law,
Mary Johnson

July had forgotten that Peach had a normal name like Mary before his brother gave her the nickname. Ben had found Peach in Little Rock and had even lived there two months in order to court her.

"What'd it say?" Little Joe asked.

July didn't want to think about what it said. It was pleasanter to try and keep his mind off the facts—the main fact being the one his mind was most reluctant to approach. Ellie had left. She didn't want to be married to him. Then why had she married him? He couldn't understand that, or why she had left.

He looked at Joe, angry with the boy for a moment though he knew it was wrong to be. If Joe had stayed in Fort Smith, Ellie couldn't have left so easily. Then he remembered that it was Ellie who had insisted that the boy come along. None of it was Joe's fault.

"It's bad news," July said.

"Did Ma leave?" Joe asked.

July nodded, surprised. If the boy could figure it out so easily, it must mean that he was the fool for having missed something so obvious that even a boy could see it.

"How could you guess?" he asked.

"She don't like to stay in one place too long," Joe said. "That's her way."

July sighed and looked at the letter again. He decided he didn't believe the part about the whiskey boat. Even if Ellie had taken leave of her senses she wouldn't travel on a whiskey boat. He had left her money. She could have taken a stage.

"What are we gonna do now?" Joe asked.

July shook his head. "I ain't got it thought through," he said. "Roscoe's coming."

Joe's face brightened. "Roscoe?" he said. "Why'd he want to come?"

"Don't imagine he wanted to," July said. "I imagine Peach made him."

"When'll he show up?" Joe asked.

"No telling," July said. "No telling when, and no telling where, either. He don't have no sense of direction. He could be going east, for all we know."

That possibility alone made his quandary more difficult. His wife had left for parts unknown, his deputy was wandering in other parts unknown, and the man he was supposed to catch was in yet other parts unknown.

In fact, July felt he had reached a point in his life where virtually nothing was known. He and Joe were on a street in Fort Worth, and that was basically the sum of his knowledge.

"I guess we better go find your mother," he said, though even as he said it he knew it meant letting Jake Spoon get away. It also meant letting Roscoe Brown stay lost, wherever he was lost.

"Ellie might be in trouble," he said, talking mainly to himself.

"Maybe Roscoe's found out where she is," Joe suggested.

"I doubt it," July said. "I doubt Roscoe even knows where *he* is."

"Ma probably just went to look for Dee," Joe said.

"Who?" July asked, startled.

"Dee," Joe said. "Dee Boot."

"But he's dead," July said, looking very disturbed. "Ellie told me he died of smallpox."

From the look on July's face, Joe knew he had made a mistake in mentioning Dee. Of course, it was his mother's fault. She had never told him that Dee had died—if he had. Joe didn't believe he was dead either. It was probably just something his mother had told July for reasons of her own.

"Ain't he your pa?" July asked.

"Yep," Joe said proudly.

"She said he died of smallpox," July said. "She said it happened in Dodge."

Joe didn't know how to correct his blunder. July looked as if the news had made him sick.

"I don't think she'd lie to me," July said out loud, but again talking to himself. He didn't mean it and couldn't think why he had said it. Probably she had lied to him right along, about wanting to be married and everything. Probably Dee Boot was alive, in which case Elmira must be married to two men. It seemed hard to believe, since she didn't seem to enjoy being married much.

"Let's go," July said. "I can't think in all this bustle."

"Ain't you gonna look for Jake in the saloons?" Joe asked. After all, that was what they had come to Fort Worth to do.

But July mounted and rode off so fast that Joe was afraid for a second he would lose him amid the wagons. He had to jump on his horse and lope, just to catch up.

They rode east, back in the direction they had come from. Joe didn't ask any questions, nor did July give him the chance. It was almost evening when they started, and they rode until two hours after dark before they camped.

"We better find Roscoe," July said that night, when they were camped. "He might know more than Peach thinks he does."

Suddenly he had a terrible longing to see Roscoe, a man who had irritated him daily for years. Roscoe might know something about Ellie—she might have explained herself to him, and Roscoe might have had his reasons for concealing the information from Peach. It was quite possible he knew exactly where Ellie was, and why she left.

By the time he lay down to sleep he was more than half convinced that Roscoe knew the truth and would put his mind at ease. Even so, as it was, his mind was far from at ease. He was tense with anger at Peach for being so open with her opinions, particularly the one about Ellie being gone for good.

Joe was sleeping with his mouth open, snoring softly. July wondered that he could sleep so soundly with his mother missing.

The stars were out and July lay awake all night, looking at them and wondering what to do. It occurred to him that Ellie was probably camped under the same stars, the same sky. He began to have strange thoughts. The stars looked so close together. As a boy he had enjoyed good balance and could cross creeks by stepping on stones and rocks. If only he could be in the sky and use the stars like stepping-stones. In no time he could find Ellie. If she went toward Kansas, then she was only a few stars to the north, and yet, on the earth, it would take him days to get to her.

The plains were still and silent, so silent that July felt that if he spoke Ellie ought to be able to hear him. If she was watching the stars, as he was, why wouldn't she know that he was thinking of her?

The longer he lay awake, the stranger he felt. He felt he was probably going crazy from all the strain. Of course the stars couldn't help. They were stars, not mirrors. They couldn't show Ellie what he was feeling. He dozed for a little while and had a dream that she had come back. They were sitting in the loft of their little cabin and she was smiling at him.

When he awoke and realized the dream wasn't true, he felt so disappointed that he cried. It had seemed so real, and Ellie had even touched him, smiling. He tried to go back to sleep so the dream would return, but he couldn't. The rest of the night he lay awake, remembering the sweetness of the dream.

51

IN THE MORNING, when July was making coffee, they began to hear the sounds of cattle. They were camped near a little creek and the flats were misty, so he couldn't see much, but over the mists he could hear cattle bawling and cowboys hollering at them. Probably a herd had been bedded nearby and the boys were trying to get them moving.

Joe was yawning and trying to get awake. The hardest part of traveling was trying to start early. Just when he was sleeping best, July would get up and start saddling his horse.

By the time the sun was beginning to thin out the mists, they had had their coffee and a bite of bacon and were horseback. The herd was in sight, spread out over the plain for three or four miles, thousands of cattle in it. Neither July nor Joe had ever seen a herd so large, and they paused for a moment to look at it. The morning plains were still dewy.

"How many is it?" Joe asked. He had never dreamed there could be so many cattle in one place.

"I don't know. Thousands," July said. "I've heard south Texas is nothing but cattle."

Though the herd was in progress, the camp crew wasn't. The cook was packing his pots and skillets into a wagon.

"I guess we ought to ask them if they've seen Roscoe," July said. "He could be south of us. Or they might have news of Jake."

They loped over to the wagon just as the wrangler turned loose the horse herd. The horses, fifty or sixty of them, were jumping and frisking, kicking up their heels and nickering at one another, glad to be moving. July and Joe waited until the wrangler had them headed north before trotting on toward the wagon. The cook wore an old black hat, and had a long, dirty beard.

"You're too late, boys," he said. "The hands just et me out of breakfast."

"Well, we've et," July said, noticing for the first time a man sitting on a tarp by the ashes of the campfire. The unusual thing about the man was that he was reading a book. His horse, a fine-looking black, was saddled and grazing a few yards away.

"Where would I find the boss?" July asked, addressing himself to the old cook.

"I'm the boss, that's why I've got time to read," the reading man said. "My name's Wilbarger." He wore iron-rimmed spectacles.

"I like to snatch a minute for Mr. Milton, and the morning's my only hope," Wilbarger added. "At night I'm apt to be in a stampede, and you can't read Mr. Milton during a stampede—not and take his sense. My days are mostly taken up with lunkheads and weather and sick horses, but I sometimes get a moment of peace after breakfast."

The man looked at them sternly through his glasses. Joe, who had hated what little schooling he'd had, was at a loss to know why a grown man would sit around and read on a pretty day.

"I'm sorry to interrupt you," July said.

"Are you a lawman?" Wilbarger asked in his impatient way.

"I am," July said.

"Then you're going to have to listen to some complaints about the law in this state," Wilbarger said. "I've never seen a place with less law. The farther south you go, the worse the horsethieves get. Along that border they're thicker than ticks."

"Well, I ain't from Texas, I'm from Arkansas," July said.

"It's a weak excuse," Wilbarger said, marking his place with a grass blade and standing up. "I didn't notice much law in Arkansas either. There's law of sorts in New Orleans, but out here it's every man for himself."

"Well, there's Texas Rangers but I guess they mostly fight the Indians," July said, wondering where the conversation would end.

"Yes, I met a couple," Wilbarger said. "They were excellent horsethieves themselves. They stole my remuda back from some sly Mexicans. Are you looking for a killer or what?"

"Yes, a man named Jake Spoon," July said. "He killed a dentist in Fort Smith."

Wilbarger tucked his book carefully into his bedroll and tossed the bedroll in the back of the wagon.

"You've overshot Mr. Spoon," he said. "He was recently seen in the town of Lonesome Dove, where he won twenty dollars from a hand of mine. However, he's headed this way. He partnered up with the gentlemen who got my horses back. If I were you I'd camp here and put this boy in school. They'll be along in two or three weeks."

"I thank you for the information," July said. "I don't suppose you've run across a man named Roscoe Brown along the trail."

"Nope, who'd he kill?" Wilbarger asked.

"Nobody," July said. "He's my deputy. It may be that he's lost."

"The name Roscoe don't inspire confidence," Wilbarger said. "People named Roscoe ought to stick to clerking. However, it's summertime. At least your man won't freeze to death. Any more people you're looking for?"

"No, just them two," July said, refraining from mentioning Elmira.

Wilbarger mounted. "I hope you hang Spoon promptly," he said. "I expect he's a card cheat, and card cheats undermine society faster than anything. If you find your deputy, see if you can't steer him into clerking."

With that he trotted over to the cook. "Are you coming with us, Bob?" he asked.

"No," the cook said. "I'm planning to marry and settle down here in north Texas."

"I hope you marry somebody who can cook," Wilbarger said. "If you do, let me know. When she gets ready to leave you, I'll hire her."

He looked around at Joe. "Need a job, son?" he asked. "We need a boy that don't ask questions and is handy with an ax. I don't know about your chopping skills, but you ain't asked a question yet."

Wilbarger seemed serious, and July was tempted to let Joe do it. Going north with a herd would be good experience for him. The main advantage, though, was that he himself could then travel alone, with just his thoughts. Without Joe to look after, he could better accomplish the main task ahead, which was to find Elmira.

Joe was startled. He had never expected to be offered a job with a cow outfit, and hearing the words was a thrill. But of course he couldn't take it—he had been assigned to July.

"Much obliged," he said. "I reckon I can't."

"Well, the job's open," Wilbarger said. "We may meet again. I've got to lope up to the Red River to see if I think the water's fresh enough for my stock."

"What'll you do if it ain't?" Joe asked. He had never known anyone who just said one unusual thing after another, as Wilbarger did. How could the water in a river not be fresh enough for cows?

"Well, I could piss in it to show it what I thought of it," Wilbarger said.

"Could you use any company?" July asked. "We're going up that way."

"Oh, I can always use good conversation, when I can get it," Wilbarger said. "I was brought up to expect good conversation, but then I run off to the wilderness and it's been spotty ever since. Why are you going north when the man you want is to the south?"

"I've got other business as well," July said. He didn't want to describe it though. He hadn't meant to ask Wilbarger if they could ride along. He wouldn't ordinarily have done it, but then his life was no longer ordinary. His wife was lost, and his deputy also. He felt more confused than he ever had in his life, whereas Wilbarger was a man who seemed far less confused than most. He seemed to know his mind immediately, whatever the question put to him.

Wilbarger started at once and loped several miles without speaking. Joe loped with him. The country was open, lightly spotted with elm and post oak. They came to a fair-sized stream and Wilbarger stopped to water his horse.

"Have you been to Colorado?" July asked.

"Yes, once," Wilbarger said. "Denver's no worse than most towns out here. I intend to avoid that country, though. The Indians in those parts ain't entirely reformed, and the outlaws are meaner than the Indians, with less excuse."

It was not comforting talk when one's wife was said to be on a whiskey boat going up the Arkansas.

"Planning a trip to Colorado?" Wilbarger asked.

"I don't know," July said. "Maybe."

"Well, if you go up on the plains and get scalped, there'll be that much less law in Arkansas," Wilbarger said. "But then there might not be that much crime in Arkansas now. I guess most of the crime's moved to Texas."

July wasn't listening. He was trying to convince himself that Peach was wrong—that Elmira had just gone wandering for a few days. When Wilbarger started to move on, July did not.

"Thanks for the company," he said. "I think we better go look for my deputy."

"There's a perfectly straight trail from Fort Smith into Texas," Wilbarger said. "Captain Marcy laid it out. If that deputy can't even stay in a road, I expect you ought to fire him."

Then he loped away without saying goodbye. Joe wished they were going with him. In only a few hours the man had paid him several compliments and had offered to hire him. He found himself feeling resentful both of July and Roscoe. July didn't seem to know what he wanted to do, and as for Roscoe, if he couldn't stay in a road, then he deserved to be lost. He wished he had spoken up and grabbed the job when Wilbarger offered it.

But the moment had been missed—Wilbarger was already out of sight, and they were still sitting there. July looked depressed, as he had ever since they had left Fort Smith. Finally, without a word, he turned east, back toward Arkansas. Joe wished he was old enough to point out to July that nothing he was doing made any sense. But he knew July probably wouldn't even hear him in the state he was in. Joe felt annoyed, but he kept quiet and followed along.

52

THE AMAZING THING about Janey, in Roscoe's view, was that she knew her way. Almost as amazing was that she liked to walk. The first day or two it felt a little wrong that he was riding and she was walking, but she was just a slip of a girl, and he was a grown man and a deputy besides. He pointed out to her that she was welcome to ride—she weighed practically nothing, and anyway they weren't traveling fast enough to tire a horse.

But Janey didn't want to ride. "I'll walk and all you have to do is keep up," she said. Of course it was no trouble for a man on horseback to keep up with a girl on foot, and Roscoe began to relax and even to enjoy the trip a little. It was pretty weather. All he had to do was trot along and think. What he mostly thought about was how surprised July would be when they showed up and told him the news.

Not only could Janey keep them on the trail but she was also extremely useful when it came to rounding up grub. Once they got settled in a camp at night she would disappear and come back five minutes later with a rabbit or a possum or a couple of squirrels. She could even catch birds. Once she came back with a fat brownish bird of a sort Roscoe had never seen.

"Now what bird is that?" he asked.

"Prairie chicken," Janey said. "There was two but one got away."

They ate the prairie chicken and it was as good as any regular chicken Roscoe had ever had. Janey cracked open the bones with her teeth and sucked out the marrow.

The only problem with her at all, from Roscoe's point of view, was that she was tormented by bad dreams and whimpered at night. Roscoe loaned her a blanket, thinking she might be cold, but that wasn't it. Even wrapped in a blanket she still whimpered, and because of that didn't sleep much. He would awake in the grayness just before dawn and see Janey sitting up, stirring the little campfire and scratching her ankles. She was barefoot, of course, and her ankles and shins were scratched by the rough grass she went through each day.

"Did you never have any shoes?" he asked once.

"Never did," Janey said, as if it didn't matter.

The only times she would consent to crawl up on the horse was when they had a sizable creek to cross. She didn't like wading in deep water.

"'Fraid of them snappers," she said. "If one of them was to bite me I'd die."

"They're mighty slow," Roscoe said. "It's easy to outrun 'em."

"I dream about them," Janey said, not reassured. "They just keep coming, and I can't run."

Except for snapping turtles and sleep, she seemed to fear nothing. Many times coiled rattlers would sing at them as they traveled, and Janey would never give the snakes a glance. Old Memphis was more nervous about snakes than she was, and Roscoe more nervous than either one of them. He had once heard of a man being bitten by a rattlesnake that had gotten up in a tree. According to the story, the snake had dropped right off a limb and onto the man and had bitten him in the neck. Roscoe imagined how unpleasant it could be to have a snake drop on one's neck—he took care to ride under as few limbs as possible and was glad to see the trees thinning out as they rode west.

It seemed they were on a fairly good trail, for every day they encountered three or four travelers, sometimes more. Once they caught up with a family plodding along in a wagon. It was such a large family that it looked like a small town on the move, particularly if you wanted to count the livestock. The old man of the family, who was driving the team, didn't seem talkative, but his wife was.

"We're from Missouri," she said. "We're going west and I guess we'll stop when we feel like it. We've got fourteen young 'uns and are hoping to establish a farm."

Eight or nine of the young ones were riding in the wagon. They stared at Roscoe and Janey, as silent as owls.

Several times they met soldiers going east toward Fort Smith. The soldiers were a taciturn lot and passed without much talk. Roscoe attempted to inquire about July, but the soldiers made it clear that they had better things to do than keep a lookout for Arkansas sheriffs.

Janey was shy of people. She had keen eyesight and would usually see other travelers before Roscoe did. Often when she saw one she disappeared, darting off the trail and hiding in weeds and tall grass until the stranger passed.

"What are you hiding for?" Roscoe asked. "Them soldiers ain't after you."

"Bill might be with them," Janey said.

"Bill who?"

"Bill," she repeated. "He gave me to old Sam. I ain't going with Bill again."

She continued to hide at the approach of strangers, and once in a while Roscoe had to admit that it was well she did. There were some rough customers traveling the trail. One day they met two dirty-looking men with greasy beards and six or seven guns between them. Roscoe had an anxious moment, for the men stopped him and asked to borrow tobacco. The fact that he was traveling without any didn't sit well with them, and they looked as if they might contest the issue.

"I reckon you're lying," one said. He was a small fellow but had mean little eyes and was generally more frightening than his companion, a man the size of an ox, who seemed to take no interest in the conversation.

"Why would a man travel without nothing to smoke?" the little one asked.

"It never agreed with me," Roscoe explained. "I had to give it up."

"If you was more dried up I guess we could smoke you," the little one said, with mean intent.

But the men rode on, and Roscoe soon forgot about them and began to feel drowsy. The day was muggy, and occasionally he would see lightning flicker in the west.

After a while it struck him that something was missing, and he figured out that it was Janey. Usually, once the travelers were out of sight, she reappeared. Memphis had come to trust her and would follow her like a pet goat.

Only this time she wasn't there to follow. Roscoe looked all around and there wasn't a soul in sight, though the plain stretched out and he could see for miles. He was alone, and by no means sure of his direction. It scared him. He had come to depend on the girl, even though she was a loud sleeper. He yelled a time or two, but got no response. The fact that he could see so far scared him a little. He had been raised in a land of trees and was not used to country that looked so long and empty. How he could have lost Janey in such an open place was a mystery to him. He sat still for a while, hoping she would pop up, but she didn't, and finally he rode on at a slow walk.

An hour passed, and then another, and Roscoe was forced to consider the possibility that he might have lost the girl. One of the snakes she took so little notice of could have bitten her. She could be dying somewhere back along the trail.

If she wasn't going to reappear it was his duty to go back and find her, and, as sunset was not far off, and it looked like thunderstorms were on the way, he had better hurry.

He turned and started back at a trot, but had not gone twenty paces before Janey popped up from behind a bush and jumped right up on Memphis.

"They're followin'," she said. "I been watching. I guess they want to kill you."

"Well, they won't find no tobacco, even if they do," Roscoe said.

Still, the little one had had a bad pair of eyes, and he could easily believe they meant to harm him. He wheeled the horse around and started to put him into a run, but Janey jerked on the reins.

"They're in front of us," she said. "They got around you while you was poking along."

Roscoe had never felt so at a loss. There was not so much as a tree in sight, and it was a long way back to Fort Smith. He didn't see how the men could expect to ambush him in the open plain.

"Dern," he said, feeling hopeless. "I can't figure which way to run."

Janey pointed north. "Up that way," she said. "There's a gully."

Roscoe couldn't see what good a gully would do but he took her advice, and they set off north at a dead run. Memphis was shocked to be spurred into a run, but once he got started he ran with a will.

Once again, Janey was right. They had only been running half a mile when they struck a big gully. Roscoe stopped and looked around. Not a soul was in sight, which made him feel silly. What were they to do next?

"Can you shoot?" Janey asked.

"Well, I have shot," Roscoe said. "There ain't been nobody much to shoot at in Fort Smith. Sometimes July and I shoot at pumpkins, or bottles and things. July's a good shot, but I'm just fair. I expect I could hit that big fellow but I don't know about the little one."

"Gimme the pistol, I'll shoot 'em for you," Janey said.

"What'd you ever shoot?" he asked, surprised.

"Give it to me," Janey said, and when he slowly handed it over, she hopped off the horse, climbed out of the gully and disappeared.

Five minutes later, before he could even untie his tarp, it began to rain. Lightning started hitting the ground, and it rained torrents. Roscoe got totally soaked. In ten minutes there was a little river running down the middle of the gully, though the gully had been bone dry when they rode up. The thunder crashed and it grew dark.

Roscoe felt that he had never hated travel so much, not even when the pigs chased him. He was alone and likely either to be drowned or shot before the night was over, or even well begun.

He remembered how snug and secure the jail was, back in Fort Smith, how nice it was to come in slightly drunk and have a comfortable couch to lie on. It was a life he fervently wished he had never left.

The rain increased until it seemed to Roscoe it was raining as hard as it could possibly rain. He didn't try to seek shelter, for there was none. It was uncomfortable to be so soaked, but since the water was probably all that was keeping him from being murdered by the little man with the mean eyes, it was silly to complain. Roscoe just sat, hoping that the little creek that filled the gully wouldn't rise enough to drown him.

The storm turned out to be just a heavy shower. In ten minutes the rain lightened, and soon it was barely sprinkling. The sun had set, but to the west there was a clear band of sky under the clouds, and the clouds were thinning. The band of sky became red with afterglow. Above it, as the clouds thinned, there was a band of white, and then a deep blue, with the evening star in it. Roscoe dismounted and stood there dripping, aware that he ought to be planning some form of defense but unable to think of any. It seemed to him the storm might have discouraged the two men—maybe one of them had even been struck by lightning.

Before he could draw much comfort from that line of speculation he heard his own gun go off. A second or two later it went off again, and then again. The sound came from just north of the gully. As he could not be any wetter, and could not stand the suspense of not knowing what was going on, he waded the little creek and climbed the bank, only to look and see the barrels of a shotgun not a yard from his face. The ox of a man held the shotgun; in his big hands it looked tiny, though the barrels in Roscoe's face seemed as big as cannons.

"Clamber on up here, traveler," the big man said.

July had told him never to argue with a loaded gun, and Roscoe had no intention of disobeying his instructions. He climbed up the muddy bank and saw that Janey was involved in a tussle with the little outlaw. He had her down and was astraddle of her and was trying to tie her, but Janey was wiggling desperately. She was covered with mud, and in the wet, slick grass was proving hard to subdue. The man cuffed her twice, but the blows had no effect that Roscoe could see.

The big man with the shotgun seemed to find the tussle amusing. He walked over for a closer look, though he continued to keep the shotgun pointed at Roscoe.

"Why don't you just shoot her?" he asked the little man. "She was willing to shoot you."

The little man didn't answer. He was breathing hard but he continued to try and tie Janey's wrists.

Roscoe had to admire Janey's spunk. The situation looked hopeless, but she kept struggling, twisting around and scratching at the man when she could. Finally the big man stepped in and planted a muddy boot on one of her arms, enabling his companion to tie her wrists. The little man cuffed her again for good measure, and sat back to get his breath. He looked around at Roscoe, his eyes as bad as ever.

"Where'd you get this feisty rabbit?" he asked. "She dern near shot me and she nicked Hutto."

"We're from Arkansas," Roscoe said. He felt foolish for having given Janey the pistol. After all, he was the deputy. On the other hand, if they had seen him shoot, the men might have shot back.

"Let's just shoot them and take the horse," Hutto, the big man said. "We could have done it this afternoon and saved all this time."

"Yeah, and the dern soldiers would have found them," the other said. "You can't just leave bodies lying right in the road no more. Somebody's apt to take an interest."

"Jim, you're too nervous," Hutto said. "Anyway, this ain't a road, and we ain't far from the Territory. Let's shoot 'em and take what they got."

"What *have* they got, by God?" Jim asked. "Go bring the horse."

Hutto brought Memphis and the two amused themselves for a few minutes by going through the bedroll and the saddlebags. One kept Roscoe covered with the shotgun while the other emptied the contents of the saddlebags carelessly on the wet grass. What they saw was very disappointing to them.

"All right, Jim, I told you they looked like a waste of time," Hutto said.

"Well, there's a horse, at least," Jim said. Then he gave Roscoe a mean look.

"Strip off them duds," he said.

"What?" Roscoe asked.

"Strip off them duds," the man repeated. He picked up Roscoe's pistol, which had fallen in the grass, and pointed it at him.

"Why must I?" Roscoe asked.

"Well, your underwear might fit me," Jim suggested. "You ain't got much else to offer."

Roscoe was forced to take off every bit of clothing. He felt miserable taking off his boots, for he knew that wet as they were he'd be lucky to get them back on. But then, if he was dead it wouldn't matter. When he got down to his long johns he became embarrassed, for after all Janey was sitting there watching. She was wet and muddy, and hadn't said a word.

The man seemed to think he might have money sewed in his long johns, and insisted he take them off. Hutto poked him with the barrels of the shotgun, something he couldn't ignore. He took them off and stood there naked, hoping Janey wouldn't look.

Of course the men found the thirty dollars he was carrying in his old wallet—it represented a month's wages, and was all he had to finish the trip with. But they had found that before they made him strip. They seemed reluctant to believe it was all the money he had, and casually proceeded to pick his clothes apart with their knives.

"The thirty dollars is all I got," he said several times.

"I guess you wouldn't be the first man to lie," Jim said, picking at the seams of his pants to see if he had any greenbacks sewed in them.

Roscoe was appalled, for the clothes that were being destroyed were the only ones he owned. Then he remembered that he was going to be killed anyway and felt a little better. It was very embarrassing to him to have to stand there naked.

The men weren't watching Janey—they were too intent on trying to find money in his saddlebags. While they were all ignoring her she had been quietly scooting backwards on the slick grass. Jim had his back to her and Hutto was winding Roscoe's old pocket watch. Roscoe happened to look and saw that Janey was quietly creeping away; they had tied her hands but had neglected her feet. Suddenly she began to run. It was deep dusk and in a second she had got into the tall grass north of the gully. She made no sound, but Hutto must have sensed something, for he whirled and let go a blast with the shotgun. Roscoe flinched. Hutto fired the other barrel, and Jim turned and shot three times with Roscoe's own pistol, which he had stuck in his belt.

Roscoe peered into the dusk, but there was no sign of Janey. The bandits looked too, with no better luck.

"Reckon we hit her?" Jim asked.

"Nope," Hutto said. "She got in that tall grass."

"Well, she could be hit," Jim said.

"I could be General Lee, only I ain't," Hutto remarked, looking disgusted. "Why didn't you tie her feet?"

"Why didn't *you?*" Jim retorted.

"I wasn't sitting on her," Hutto said.

"You watch this one and I'll go catch her," Jim said. "I bet once I do she won't get away for a while."

"Why, Jim, you can't catch her," Hutto said. "In this dark? Remember how she ambushed us? If she was a better shot we'd both be corpses, and if she's got a rifle hid out there somewhere we may be corpses yet."

"I ain't scared of her," Jim said. "Dern her, I should have cracked her with a gun barrel a time or two."

"You should have shot her," Hutto said. "I know you expected to amuse yourself, but look how it turned out. The girl got away and the deputy only had thirty dollars and some dirty underwear."

"She can't be far," Jim said. "Let's camp and look for her in the morning."

"Well, you can, but I'm going," Hutto said. "A girl that size ain't worth tracking."

Just as he said it, a good-sized rock came flying through the air and hit him right in the mouth. He was so surprised he slipped and sat down. The rock had smashed his lips; blood poured down his chin. A second later another hit Jim in the ribs. Jim drew a pistol and fired several times in the direction the rocks came from.

"Oh, stop wasting shells," Hutto said. He spat out a mouthful of blood.

Two more rocks came flying in, both aimed at Jim. One hit him right in the elbow, causing him to double over in pain. The other flew over his head.

Hutto seemed to think the whole thing was funny. He sat on the muddy ground, laughing and spitting great mouthfuls of blood. Jim crouched down, pistol drawn, watching for rocks.

"This beats all I ever heard of," Hutto said. "Here we are in a rock fight with a girl no bigger than a minute, and she's winning. If news of this gets out we'll have to retire."

He looked at Roscoe, who was standing stock-still. One of the rocks had just missed him—he didn't want to move and risk interfering with Janey's aim.

"By God, when I get her she'll wish she'd kept a-running," Jim said, cocking his gun. A second later a rock hit him on the shoulder and the gun went off. Furious, he fired into the darkness until the pistol was empty.

"Well, we'll sure have to kill this deputy now," Hutto remarked. He wiggled a loose tooth with a bloody finger. "If he was to tell about this, our reputation as desperados would be ruint forever."

"Then why don't you get up and help me rush her?" Jim said angrily.

"Oh, I think we should just sit and let her chunk us to death," Hutto said. "I think it serves us right for being idiots. You was scared of this deputy, when he ain't no more dangerous than a chicken. Maybe next time you'll be content to shoot when I want to shoot."

Jim opened his pistol. He was trying to reload and watch for rocks, too, squinting into the darkness. Another rock came in low and he managed to turn and take it on his thigh, but it caused him to drop three bullets.

Roscoe was beginning to feel more hopeful. He was remembering all the varmints Janey had brought into camp—probably she had used them to sharpen her aim. His hope was she'd start throwing for the head before the men got around to killing him.

Hutto was calmer than Jim. He reached over, got his shotgun and broke the breach.

"I'll tell you, Jim," he said, "you just keep sitting there drawing her fire. I'll load up with some buckshot. Maybe if she don't brain you before the moon rises, I can catch the angle and shoot her. Or at least chase her out of chunkin' range."

He reached into the pocket of his buckskin coat for some shells, and as he did, a miracle happened—for in Roscoe's mind a miracle it was. He stood there, naked and wet, sure to be murdered within a few minutes unless a slip of a girl, armed only with rocks, could defeat two grown men armed with guns. He himself was so sure of being killed that he felt rather detached from what was happening, and invested only faint hope in Janey's chances of saving him.

Nobody saw July come. Hutto was reaching in his pocket for shells and Jim was trying to fish those he had dropped out of the mud. Roscoe was watching Jim, whom he liked least. He was hoping to see a big rock hit Jim right between the eyes, perhaps cracking his skull. It wouldn't stop Hutto from killing him, but it would be some consolation if Jim got his skull cracked first.

Then, at the same moment, Jim, Hutto, and he himself all became aware that someone was there who hadn't been. It was July Johnson, standing behind Jim with his pistol drawn and cocked.

"You won't need them shells," July said quietly. "Just leave 'em lie."

"Well, you son of a bitch," Jim said, "what gives you the right to pull a gun on me?"

Jim looked up, and just as he did, the rock Roscoe had been hoping for sailed in and hit him right in the throat. He dropped his gun and fell over backwards. He lay there clutching his throat and trying desperately to draw breath.

Hutto had two shotgun shells in his hand but he didn't try to shove them in the shotgun. "I've had bad luck before, but nothing to top this," he said, ignoring July and looking at Roscoe. "Can't you at least make that gal stop throwing rocks?"

Roscoe was having trouble believing what he saw. He felt he had missed a step or two in the proceedings somehow.

"Are you gonna get your clothes on or are you just going to stand there?" July asked.

It sounded like July, and it looked like July, so Roscoe was forced to conclude that he was saved. He had been in the process of adjusting to impending death, and it seemed to him a part of him must already have left for the other place, because he felt sort of absent and dull. Ordinarily he would not have stood around on a muddy prairie naked, and yet in some ways it was easier than having to pick up the pieces of his life again, which meant, first off, having to literally pick up pieces of his clothes.

"They cut up my duds," he said to July. "I doubt I'll ever be able to get them boots back on, wet as they are."

"Joe, bring the handcuffs," July said.

Joe walked into camp with two sets of handcuffs. It shocked him to see Roscoe naked.

"I never seen so many young 'uns," Hutto said. "Can this one throw rocks too?"

"Who *is* throwing the rocks?" July asked. He had been about to step in before the rock-throwing started, but the rock-thrower's accuracy had been so startling that he had waited a few minutes to watch the outcome.

"That's Janey," Roscoe said, buttoning up what was left of his best shirt. "She practices chunking varmints. It's how we been getting our grub."

July quickly handcuffed Jim, who was still writhing around on the grass. The blow to the throat seemed to have damaged his windpipe—he gasped loudly for air, like a drowning man.

"You might shoot me, but you ain't putting no dern cuffs on me," Hutto said when July approached him.

"This is July Johnson, and I wouldn't fight him," Roscoe said. For some reason he felt rather friendly to Hutto, though it was Hutto who had been most inclined to kill him.

Hutto didn't fight but neither did he get handcuffed, for the simple reason that his wrists were too big. July was forced to tie him with a saddle string, a method he would rather have avoided. A man as large as Hutto would eventually stretch out any rope or piece of rawhide if he kept trying.

Roscoe managed to get his pants to hold together pretty well although they were full of holes. As predicted, he could not get his boots on. Joe helped, but the two of them made no headway.

"It's a good thing you shot," Joe said. "We was already camped, but July recognized your gun."

"Oh, was that it?" Roscoe said, reluctant to admit that it had been Janey who shot.

Once the men were handcuffed and tied, July got them onto their horses and tied their feet to the stirrups. Hutto and Jim he knew by reputation, for they had harried the east Texas trails for the last year or two, mostly robbing settlers but occasionally killing those who put up a fight. He had expected to find Roscoe eventually, but not the two bandits. Now something would have to be done with them before he could even ask Roscoe all the questions he wanted to ask about

Elmira. Also, there was the rock-thrower—Janey, Roscoe had called her. Why was a Janey traveling with Roscoe? Indeed, where was she? The rock-throwing had stopped but no one had appeared.

Now that the danger was past, Roscoe began to feel that there were many awkward matters awaiting explanation. He had forgotten about Elmira and her departure for several days, although her departure was the reason he was in Texas. Also, he would have to explain to July why he was traveling with a young girl. It seemed better to talk about the miracle of July's appearance, but July didn't want to say much about it.

"I never expected to see you right then," Roscoe said. "Then there you were, pointing that gun."

"This is the main trail to Texas from Fort Smith," July pointed out. "If I was looking for you that's where I'd likely be."

"Yeah, but I didn't know you was looking for me," Roscoe said. "You don't usually."

"Peach wrote and told me you was on the way," July said. It was all the explanation he planned to offer until he could get Roscoe alone.

"I guess we're caught, but what next?" Hutto asked. He did not like to be left out of conversations. Jim, who still had to suck hard to get his breath, showed no inclination to talk.

"You say there's a girl?" July asked.

"Yep, Janey."

"Call her in," July said.

Roscoe made an effort, but it went awkwardly. "Come on, July's here," he said loudly into the darkness. "It's safe, he's the sheriff I work for," he added, just as loudly.

There was no sound from the darkness, and no sign of Janey. Roscoe could tell July was impatient. It made him nervous. He remembered how Janey had disappeared for two hours that afternoon. If she thought July would wait two hours, she didn't know much about him.

"Come on in, we've got these men tied," he said, without much hope that Janey would obey.

She didn't. There was not a sound to be heard, except for some coyotes singing about a mile away.

"I suspect that girl has Indian blood," Hutto said. "She had us ambushed, fair and square, and if she was as good with a pistol as she is with a rock we'd be dead."

"What's the matter with her?" July asked. "Why won't she come?"

"I don't know," Roscoe said. "She don't take to company, I guess."

July thought it a very odd business. Roscoe had never been one to womanize. In fact, around Fort Smith his skill in avoiding various widow women had often been commented on. And yet he had somehow taken up with a girl who could throw rocks more accurately than most men could shoot.

"I don't intend to spend the night here," July said. "Has she got a horse?"

"No, but she's quick of foot," Roscoe said. "She's been keeping ahead of me without no trouble. Where are we going?"

"To Fort Worth," July said. "The sheriff there will probably be glad to get these men."

"Yes, he will, the son of a bitch," Hutto said.

Roscoe felt bad about going off and leaving Janey, but he couldn't think what to do about it. July tied the two outlaws' horses to a single lead rope and instructed

Roscoe and Joe to stay close behind them. It had clouded up and was almost pitch-dark, but that had no effect on July's pace, which was fast. Having to deliver the outlaws to justice was taking him out of his way, but there was nothing else for it.

When they had been riding about an hour, Roscoe got the scare of his life, for suddenly someone jumped on the horse behind him. For a terrifying second he thought Jim must have gotten loose and come to strangle him or stick a knife in him. Memphis was startled, too, and jumped sideways into Joe's horse.

Then he heard the person panting and knew it was Janey.

"I couldn't keep up no longer," she said. "I thought he'd slow down but he just keeps going."

Joe was so startled to see a girl materialize behind Roscoe that he didn't say a word. He found it hard to credit that the person who had thrown the rocks could be a girl. Yet he had seen the rocks hit the men. How could a girl throw so hard and straight?

July had appropriated Hutto's shotgun, loaded it and put it across his saddle—he assumed it would make the prisoners think twice before starting trouble. His one thought was to get back to Fort Worth, turn the men over and start at once to look for Elmira.

They rode all night, and when the plains got gray they were no more than five miles from Fort Worth. He glanced back at the prisoners and was startled to see the girl, riding behind Roscoe. She looked very young. Her bare legs were as thin as a bird's. Roscoe was slumped over the horn, asleep, and the girl held the reins. She was also watching the two prisoners, both of whom were plenty wide-awake. July got down and checked Hutto's knots, which indeed were slipping.

"I guess you're Janey," he said to the girl. She nodded. July handed her the shotgun to hold while he retied Hutto.

"My God, don't do that, she's apt to cut us in two," Jim said. His voice had a husky croak from the blow on his throat—it pained him to speak, but the sight of the girl with the shotgun clearly pained him more.

Joe had managed to get the sleep out of his eyes, and was rather aggrieved that July had given the gun to the girl. She was no older than he was and she was female. He felt he ought to have been given the shotgun.

"You don't give a man much of a chance, do you?" Hutto said, as July retied him. He was a messy sight from all the dried blood on his mouth and his beard, but he seemed cheerful.

"Nope," July said.

"If they don't hang us, you better watch out for Jim," Hutto said. "Jim hates to have anyone point a gun at him. He's got a vengeful nature, too."

Jim did seem vengeful. His eyes were shining with hatred, and he was looking at the girl. The look was so hot that many men would have flinched from it, but the girl didn't.

All the while Roscoe slumped over his horse's neck, snoring away. They were nearly on the outskirts of Fort Worth before he woke up, and it was not until July handed the prisoners over to the sheriff that he began to feel alive.

Janey had acted like she wanted to bolt when they came into town—the sight of so many wagons and people clearly upset her—but she held on. July found a livery stable, for it would be necessary to rest the horses for a while. It was run by a woman, who kindly offered to scrape up a little breakfast for the youngsters. It consisted of corn bread and bacon, which they ate sitting on big washtubs outside the woman's house.

Roscoe's clothes were practically in ribbons, so much so that the woman laughed when she saw him. She offered to mend his clothes for another fifty cents, but Roscoe had to decline, since he had nothing to wear while the work was being done.

"This is a big-looking town," Roscoe said. "I guess I can buy myself some clothes."

"Not for no fifty cents," the woman said. "That's nothing but a sack the girl's wearing. You ought to get her something decent to wear while you're buying."

"Well, I might," Roscoe said. It was true that Janey's dress was a mere rag.

Janey seemed to think Fort Worth was quite a sight. She was over her fright, and she looked around with interest.

"Is that girl your daughter?" the woman asked.

"No," Roscoe said. "I never saw her till last week."

"Well, she's somebody's daughter and she deserves better than a sack to wear," the woman said. "That boy's dressed all right, how come you skimped on the girl?"

"No opportunity," Roscoe said. "I just found her up in the country."

The woman had a red face, and it got redder when she was angry, as she now clearly was. "I don't know what to think of you men," she said, and went in her house and slammed the door.

"Where *did* you get her?" July asked.

"I didn't get her, exactly," Roscoe said. He felt on the defensive. It was clear that people would think the worst of him, whatever he did. No doubt in Fort Smith the word would be out that instead of sticking to orders he had run off with the first young girl he could find.

"She run off and followed me," he added. July looked noncommittal.

"A dern old man beat her and used her hard, and that's why she run off," Roscoe elaborated. "Can we go to a saloon? I'd sure fancy a beer."

July took him to a saloon and bought him a beer. Now that he had Roscoe alone he felt curiously reluctant to mention Elmira. Even hearing her name spoken would be painful.

"What about Ellie?" he said finally. "Peach said she left."

"Well, Peach is right," Roscoe said. "Or if she didn't leave, then she's hiding. Or else a bear got her."

"Did you see bear tracks?" July asked.

"No," Roscoe admitted.

"Then a bear didn't get her," July said.

"She probably left on the whiskey boat," Roscoe said, trying to hide behind his beer glass.

"I don't see why," July said softly, almost to himself. He didn't see why. He had never done anything to disturb her that he could remember. He had never hit her, or even spoken harshly to her. What would prompt a woman to run off when nothing was wrong? Of course, it wasn't true that *nothing* had been wrong. Something had been. He just didn't know what. He didn't know why she had married him if she didn't like him, and he had the sense that she didn't. It was true that Peach had hinted a few times that people got married for reasons other than liking, but Peach was known to be cynical.

Now, in the saloon, he remembered Peach's hints. Maybe Ellie had never liked him. Maybe she had married him for reasons she hadn't wanted to mention. Thinking about it all made him feel very sad.

"Did you talk to her at all after I left?" he asked Roscoe.

"No," Roscoe admitted.

July didn't speak for five minutes. Roscoe turned over in his mind various excuses for not seeing Elmira, but in truth, it had never once occurred to him to go and see her. He slowly drank his beer.

"What about Jake?" he asked.

"He's to the south," July said. "He's coming with a trail herd. I want to find Ellie. Once that's done we'll look for Jake."

He fished some money out of his pocket and paid for the beers. "Maybe you ought to take the young ones and go back to Arkansas," he said. "I'm going after Ellie."

"I'll come with you," Roscoe said. Now that he had found July, he had no intention of losing him again. He had had plenty of trouble coming, and yet worse might occur if he tried to go back on his own.

"I expect if we paid that woman she'd board the girl," July said. "You go buy some duds. You'll be a laughingstock if you try to travel in those you got on."

The woman at the livery stable agreed to board Janey for three dollars a month. July paid for two months. When told she was to stay in Fort Worth, Janey didn't say a word. The woman spoke to her cheerfully about getting some better clothes, but Janey sat on the washtub, silent.

The woman offered to take Joe, too, and board him free if he would help out around the livery stable. July was tempted, but Joe looked so unhappy that he relented and decided to let him stay with them. Then Roscoe showed up, in clothes that looked so stiff it was a wonder he could even walk in them.

"I guess you might break them clothes in by Christmas," the livery-stable woman said, laughing. "You look like you're wearing stovepipes."

"I can't help it if they're black," Roscoe said. "It was all they had that fit."

He felt sorry about leaving Janey. What if old Sam got well and tracked them to Fort Worth and found her? He offered her two dollars in case she had expenses, but Janey just shook her head. When they rode off, she was still sitting on the big washtub.

Joe was glad she wasn't coming. She made him feel that he didn't do things very well.

He didn't have long to enjoy being glad, though. That night they camped on the plains, twenty miles north of Fort Worth. July felt it was all right to sleep without a guard, as there were trail herds on both sides of them. They could hear the night herders singing to the cattle.

In the morning, when Joe opened his eyes, Janey was squatting by the cold campfire. She still wore her sack. Even July had not heard her come. When July woke up she handed him back the six dollars he had given the woman. July just took it, looking surprised. Joe felt annoyed. It was wrong of the girl to come without July's permission. If the Indians carried her off, he for one would not be too sorry—although, when he thought about it, he realized he himself might be an easier catch. The girl had followed them at night, across the plains. It was something he couldn't have done.

All that day the girl ran along on her own, never getting far behind. She was not like any of the girls Joe had known in Fort Smith, none of whom could have kept up for five minutes. Joe didn't know what to make of her, and neither did July, or even Roscoe, who had found her. But soon they were far out on the plains, and it was clear to everyone that Janey was along for the trip.

53

LONG BEFORE THE WHISKEY BOAT STOPPED, Elmira knew she was going to have trouble with Big Zwey. The man had never approached her, or even spoken to her, but every time she went out of her shed to sit and watch the water, she felt his eyes on her. And when they loaded the whiskey in wagons and started across the plains for Bents' Fort, his eyes followed her in whatever wagon she chose to ride for the day.

It seemed to her it might be the fact that she was so small that made Big Zwey so interested. It was a problem she had had before. Huge men seemed to like her because she was so tiny. Big Zwey was even larger than the buffalo hunter who had caused her to run to July.

Sometimes in the evening, when he brought her her food, Fowler would sit and talk with her a bit. He had a scar which ran over his nose and down across his lips into his beard. He had a rough look, but his eyes were dreamy.

"This whiskey-hauling business has about petered out," he said one evening. "Indians kept the trade going. Now they've about got them all penned up, down in these parts. I may go up north."

"Are there many towns up north?" she asked, remembering that Dee had mentioned going north. Dee liked his comforts—hotels and barbershops and such. Once she had offered to cut his hair and had made a mess of it. Dee had been good-natured about it, but he did remark that it paid to stick to professionals. He was vain about his looks.

"There's Ogallala," Fowler said. "That's on the Platte. There's towns in Montana, but that's a long way."

Big Zwey had a deep voice. She could sometimes hear him talking to the men, even over the creak of the wagon wheels. He wore a long buffalo coat and seldom took it off, even when the days were hot.

One morning there was great excitement. Just as the morning mists began to thin, the man on guard claimed to have seen six Indians on a ridge. He was a young men, very nervous. If there were Indians, they did not reappear. During the day the men surprised three buffalo and killed one of them. That night Fowler brought Elmira samples of the liver and the tongue—the best parts, he said.

The men had talked about the Fort so much that Elmira had supposed it was a real town, but it was just a few scattered buildings, none in good repair. There was only one woman there, the wife of a blacksmith, and she had gone crazy due to the death of all five of her children. She sat in a chair all day, saying nothing to anyone.

Fowler did his best for Elmira. He got the traders to let her have a little room—just a tiny, dirty closet, really. It was next to a warehouse where piles of buffalo skins were stored. The smell of the skins was worse than anything that had happened on the river. Her room was full of fleas that had escaped from the skins. She spent much of her time scratching.

Though the Fort was nothing much to see, it was a busy place, with riders coming and going all the time. Watching them, Elmira wished she was a man so she could just buy a horse and ride away. The men let her alone, but they did look at her whenever she left her room. There were several wild-looking Mexicans who scared her worse than the buffalo hunters.

After a week of scratching, she began to realize she had done a foolish thing, taking the whiskey boat. In Fort Smith, all she had felt was an overwhelming desire to go. The day she left she felt that her life depended on getting out of Fort Smith that day—she had a fear that July would suddenly show up again.

She didn't regret leaving, but neither did she calculate on landing in a place as bad as Bent's Fort. In the cow towns, stages came and went, at least—if you didn't like Dodge you could always go to Abilene. But no stage came to Bent's Fort—just a wagon track that soon disappeared into the emptiness of the plains.

Though she had not been bothered, the men at the Fort looked very rough. "They don't think you're worth robbing," Fowler said, but she wasn't sure he was right. Some of the Mexicans looked like they might do worse than rob her if the mood struck them. Once, sitting under the little shed outside her room, she saw a fight between two Mexicans. She heard a yell and saw each man pull a knife. They went at one another like butchers. Their clothes were soon bloody, but evidently the cuts were not serious, for after a while they stopped fighting and went back to gambling together.

Fowler said there might be a party of hunters going north, and that perhaps they would take her, but a week passed and the party didn't materialize. Then one day Fowler brought her a little plate of food, under her shed. He looked at her sheepishly, as if he had something to say but didn't want to say it.

"Big Zwey wants to marry you," he said finally, in an apologetic tone.

"Well, I'm already married," she said.

"What if he just wants to marry you temporary?" Fowler asked.

"It's always temporary," Elmira said. "Why don't he ask himself?"

"Zwey ain't much of a talker," Fowler said.

"I've heard him talk," she said. "He talks to the men."

Fowler laughed and said no more. Elmira felt angry. She was in a spot if some man was wanting to marry her. Someone had thrown a fresh buffalo skin into the warehouse and she could hear the flies buzzing on it from where she sat.

"He'll take you to Ogallala, if you'll do it," Fowler said. "You might think about it. He ain't as bad as some."

"How would you know?" she asked. "You ain't been married to him."

Fowler shrugged. "He might be your best bet," he said. "I'm going back downriver next week. A couple of hide haulers are taking a load to Kansas, and they might take you, but it'd be a hard trip. You'd have to smell them stinkin' hides all the way. Anyway, the hide haulers are rough," he said. "I think Zwey would treat you all right."

"I don't want to go to Kansas," she said. "I been to Kansas."

What ruined that was that she was pregnant, and showing. Some of the saloons weren't particular, but it was always harder to get work if you were pregnant. Besides, she didn't want to work, she wanted Dee, who wouldn't mind that she was pregnant.

Big Zwey began to spend hours just watching her. He didn't pretend to gamble or do anything else, he just watched her. She sat under her shed in one patch of shade, and he sat in another about thirty yards away, just watching. He didn't pretend to gamble or do anything else.

Once when he was watching, some riders spotted a little herd of buffalo. The other hunters were wild to go after them, but Zwey wouldn't go. They yelled at him and argued with him, but he just sat. Finally they went off without him. One hunter tried to borrow his gun, but Zwey wouldn't give it up. He sat there with his big rifle across his lap, looking at Elmira.

It became amusing to her, her power over the man. He had never spoken to her, not one word, and yet he would sit for hours, thirty yards away. It was something, what must go through men's minds where women were concerned, to cause them to behave so strangely.

One morning she came out of her closet earlier than usual—she had a touch of morning sickness and wanted some fresh air. When she opened the door, she almost bumped into Big Zwey, who had just been standing outside her door. Her sudden appearance embarrassed him so that he gave her one appalled look and turned and went off, practically at a trot, putting a safe distance between them. He was a very heavy man, and the sight of him trying to run made her laugh out loud, something she hadn't done in a while. He didn't turn to look back at her again until he was safely back in his spot, and then he turned fearfully, as if he expected to be shot for having stood by her door.

"Tell him I'll go," she said to Fowler that evening. "I guess he ain't so bad."

"You tell him," Fowler said.

The next morning she walked over to where Big Zwey sat. When he saw her coming, it seemed for a second like he might bolt, but she was too close. Instead, he sat as if paralyzed, fear in his eyes.

"I'll go if you think you can get me to Ogallala," she said. "I'll pay you what it's worth to you."

Zwey didn't say anything.

"How'll we travel?" she asked. "I ain't much good at riding horses."

Big Zwey didn't respond for about a minute. Elmira was about to lose patience when he brushed his mouth with the back of his hand, as if to clean it.

"Could get that there hide wagon," he said, pointing to a rundown piece of equipment a few yards away. To Elmira the wagon didn't look like it could travel ten yards, much less all the way to Nebraska.

"Could get the blacksmith to fix it," Big Zwey said. Now that he had spoken to her and not been struck by lightning, he felt a little easier.

"Did you mean just us two to go?" Elmira asked.

The question gave him so much pause that she almost wished she hadn't asked it. He fell silent again, his eyes troubled.

"Might take Luke," he said.

Luke was a weaselly little buffalo hunter with only a thumb and one finger on his left hand. He carried dice and gambled when he could get anyone to gamble with him. Once on the boat she had asked Fowler about him, and Fowler said a butcher had cut his fingers off with a cleaver, for some reason.

"When can we go?" she asked. It turned out to be a decision Big Zwey wasn't immediately up to making. He pondered the matter for some time but reached no conclusion.

"I want to get out of here," she said. "I'm tired of smelling buffalo hides."

"Get that blacksmith to fix that wagon," Zwey responded. He stood up, picking up the tongue of the wagon and began to drag it toward the blacksmith's shop, a hundred yards away. The next morning, the wagon, more or less patched, was sitting outside her closet. When she walked over to inspect it she saw that Luke was in it, sleeping off a drunk. He slept with his mouth open, showing black teeth, and not many of them at that.

Luke had ignored her on the trip upriver, but when he woke up he hopped out of the wagon and came right over, a grin on his weaselly face.

"Big Zwey and I have partnered up," he said. "Can you drive a wagon?"

"I guess I could if we go slow," she said.

Luke had spiky red hair that stuck out in all directions. A skinning knife a foot long was slung in a scabbard under one shoulder. He grinned constantly, exposing his black teeth and, unlike Zwey, was not a bit afraid to look her in the eye. He had an insolent manner and spat tobacco juice constantly while he talked.

"Zwey went to buy some mules," he said. "We got two horses but they won't do for the wagon. Anyway, we might get some hides while you're driving the wagon."

"I don't like the smell of hides," she said pointedly, but not pointedly enough for Luke to get the message.

"You get where you don't smell 'em after a while," he said. "I don't hardly even notice it, I've smelled 'em so much."

Luke had a little quirt and was always nervously popping himself on the leg with it. "You skeert of Indians?" he asked.

"I don't know," Elmira said. "I guess I don't like 'em much."

"I've already killed five of them," Luke said.

Big Zwey finally arrived leading two scrawny mules and carrying a harness he had traded for. The harness was in bad repair but there was plenty of rawhide around, and they soon had it tied together fairly well. Luke was quite dexterous with his thumb and little finger. He did better than Zwey, whose hands were too big for harness making.

She soon got the hang of driving the mules. There was not much to it, for the mules were content to follow the two men on horseback. It was only when the men loped off to hunt that the mules were likely to balk. On the second day out, with the men gone, she crossed a creek whose banks were so steep and rough that she felt sure the wagon would turn over. She was ready to jump and take her chances, but by a miracle it stayed upright.

That day the men killed twenty buffalo. Elmira had to wait in the sun all day while they skinned them out. Finally she got down and sat under the wagon, which provided a little shade. The men piled the bloody, smelly hides into the wagon, which didn't suit the mules. They hated the smell of hides as much as she did.

Big Zwey had lapsed back into silence, leaving all the talking to Luke, who chattered away whether anybody listened to him or not.

Often Elmira had a nervous stomach. The jostling of the wagon took getting used to. The plains looked smooth in the distance, but they were surprisingly rough to pass over. Big Zwey had given her a blanket to put over the rough seat—it kept her from getting splinters but didn't cushion the bumps.

Alone with the two men, in the middle of the great, empty prairie, she felt apprehensive. In the cow towns there had been lots of girls around—if a man got mean, she could yell. On the boat it hadn't seemed as dangerous, because the men were always fighting and gambling among themselves. But at night on the prairie there were only the three of them, and nothing much to keep anyone busy.

Big Zwey sat and looked at her through the campfire, and Luke looked, too, while he talked. She didn't know if Big Zwey considered that in some way he had married her already. She worried that he might suddenly come over and want the marriage to begin, though so far he had been too shy even to speak to her much. For all she knew he might expect her to be married to Luke, too, and she didn't want that. The thought made her so nervous that she couldn't eat the buffalo meat they offered her—anyway, it was tougher than any meat she had ever tried to chew. She chewed on one bite until her jaws got tired and then spat it out.

But when she went to the wagon and made the one blanket into a kind of bed, neither man followed. She lay awake for a long time, apprehensive, but the men sat by the fire, occasionally looking her way but making no move to disturb her. Luke got his dice out and soon they were playing. Elmira was able to sleep, but awoke to the roll of thunder a few hours later. The men were asleep by the dying fire. Across the prairie she began to see lightning darting down the sky, and within a few minutes big drops of water hit her. In a minute she was wet. She jumped down and crawled under the wagon. It wasn't much protection but it was some. Soon lightning was crashing all around and the thunder came in big, flat cracks, as if a building had fallen down. It frightened her so that she hugged her knees and trembled. When the lightning struck, the whole prairie would be bathed for a second in white light.

The rainstorm soon passed, but she lay awake for the rest of the night, listening to water drip off the wagon. It grew very dark. She didn't know what might have happened to the men.

But in the morning they were right where they had gone to sleep, wet as muskrats but ready to drink a pot of coffee. Neither even commented on the storm. Elmira decided they were used to hard traveling and that she had better get used to it too.

Soon she began to talk to the mules as they plodded along. She didn't say much, and the mules didn't answer, but it made the long hot days pass a little faster.

54

AUGUSTUS SPENT HALF THE FIRST DAY finding the tracks, for Blue Duck had been cool enough to lead Lorena through the stampeding cattle, so that their tracks would be blotted out by the thousands of cattle tracks. It was a fine trick, and one not many men would dare to try.

Years had passed since Augustus had done any serious tracking. He rode around all morning, trying to remember the last man he had tracked, just to give himself perspective. It seemed to him that the last man had been an incompetent horsethief named Webster Witter, who had rustled horses in the Blanco country at one time. He and Call had gone after him one day by themselves and caught him and hung him before sundown. But the tracking had been elemental, due to the fact that the man had been driving forty stolen horses.

The thing he remembered best about Webster Witter was that he had been a tall man and they caught him out in the scrub and had to hang him to a short tree. It was that or take him back, and Call was against taking him back. Call believed summary justice was often the only justice, and in those days he was right, since they had to depend on circuit judges who often as not didn't show up.

"If we take him back he'll bribe the jailer, or dig out or something, and we'll have to catch him at it again," Call said. It never occurred to Call just to shoot someone he could hang, and in this instance Augustus didn't suggest it, for they had rushed out without much ammunition and were traveling in rough country.

Fortunately, Webster's neck broke when they whipped the horse out from under him, otherwise he could have stood there and laughed at them, for the limb of the mesquite sagged badly and both his feet drug the ground.

That had been at least twelve years ago, and Augustus soon concluded that his tracking skills had rusted to the point of being unusable. The only horse tracks he found for the first three hours belonged to Hat Creek horses. He almost decided to go back and get Deets, though he knew Call would be reluctant to surrender him.

Finally, by circling wide to the northwest, Augustus crossed the three horses' tracks. Blue Duck had tried the one trick—crossing the stampede—but that was all. After that the tracks bore straight for the northwest, so unerringly that Augustus soon found he didn't need to pay much attention to them. If he lost them he could usually pick them up within half a mile.

He rode as hard as he dared, but he had only one horse and couldn't afford to ruin him. At each watering he let him have a few minutes of rest. He rode all night, and the next day the tracks were still bearing northwest. He felt unhappy with himself for he wasn't catching up. Lorena was getting a taste of hard travel the like of which she had never imagined. Probably she would have worse to deal with than hard travel unless she was very lucky, and Augustus knew it was his fault. He should have packed her into camp the minute he discovered who Blue Duck was; in retrospect he couldn't imagine why he hadn't. It was the kind of lapse he had been subject to all his life: things that were clearly dangerous didn't worry him enough.

He tried to swallow his regrets and concentrate on finding her: after all, it had happened, and why he had let it no longer particularly mattered. Blue Duck was a name from their past. Having him show up in their midst fifteen years later had thrown his reasoning off.

The second day he stopped tracking altogether, since it was plain Blue Duck was heading for the Staked Plains. That took in a lot of territory, of course, but Augustus thought he knew where Blue Duck would go: to an area north and west of the Palo Duro Canyon—it was there he had always retreated to when pursued.

Once Call and he had sat on the western edge of the great canyon, looking across the brown waterless distances to the west. They had finally decided to end their pursuit there while they had a fair chance of getting back alive. It wasn't Indians they feared so much as lack of water. It had been midsummer and the plains looked seared, what grass there was, brown and brittle. Call was frustrated; he hated to turn back before he caught his man.

"There's got to be water out there," Call said. "They cross it, and they can't drink dirt."

"Yes, but they know where it is and we don't," Augustus pointed out. "They can kill their horses getting to it—they got more horses. But if we kill ours it's a dern long walk back to San Antonio."

That afternoon he crossed the Clear Fork of the Brazos and passed a half-built cabin, abandoned and empty. It was a vivid enough reminder of the power of the Comanches—their massacres caused plenty of settlers to retreat while they still had legs to retreat on. Call and he had watched through the Fifties as the line of the frontier advanced only to collapse soon after. The men and women who came up the Trinity and the Brazos were no strangers to hardship—but hardship was one thing, terror another. The land was spacious and theirs for the taking, but land couldn't cancel out fear—a fact that Call never understood. It annoyed him that the whites gave up and retreated.

"I wish they'd stick," he said many times. "If they would, there'd soon be enough of them to beat back the Indians."

"You ain't never laid in bed all night with a scared woman," Augustus said. "You can't start a farm if you've got to live in a fort. Them that starts the farms have got to settle off by themselves, which means they're easy to cut off and carve up."

"Well, they could leave the women for a while," Call said. "Send for them when it's safe."

"Yes, but a man that goes to the trouble to take a wife don't generally want to go off and leave her," Augustus pointed out. "It means doing the chores all by yourself. Besides, without a wife handy you won't be getting no kids, and kids are a wonderful source of free labor. They're cheaper than slaves by a damn sight."

They had argued the point for years, but fruitlessly, for Call had no sympathy for human weakness. Augustus put it down to a lack of imagination. Call could never imagine what it was like to be scared. They had been in tight spots, but usually that meant action, and in battles things happened too fast for fear to paralyze the mind of a man like Call. He couldn't imagine what it was like to go to bed every night scared that you and your family would feel the knives of the Comanches before sunrise.

That night Augustus stopped to rest his horse, making a cold camp on a little bluff and eating some jerky he had brought along. He was in the scrubby post-oak country near the Brazos and from his bluff could see far across the moonlit valleys.

It struck him that he had forgotten emptiness such as existed in the country that stretched around him. After all, for years he had lived within the sound of the piano from the Dry Bean, the sound of the church bell in the little Lonesome Dove church, the sound of Bol whacking the dinner bell. He even slept within the sound of Pea Eye's snoring, which was as regular as the ticking of a clock.

But here there was no sound, not any. The coyotes were silent, the crickets, the locusts, the owls. There was only the sound of his own horse grazing. From him to the stars, in all directions, there was only silence and emptiness. Not the talk of men over their cards, nothing. Though he had ridden hard he felt strangely rested, just from the silence.

The next day he found the carcass of Lorie's mare. By the end of the day he was out of the scrub. When he crossed the Wichita he angled west. He had not seen Blue Duck's tracks in two days but he didn't care. He had always had confidence in his instincts and felt he knew where the man would stop. Possibly he was bound for Adobe Walls, one of the Bents' old forts. This one, on the Canadian, had never been much of a success. The Bents had abandoned it, and it became a well-known gathering place for buffalo hunters, as well as for anyone crossing the plains.

It was spring—what few buffalo were left would be moving north, and what buffalo hunters were left would be gathered at the old fort, getting ready for a last hide harvest. Buffalo hunters were not known to be too particular about their company; though Blue Duck and his men had picked off plenty of them over the years, the new crop would probably overlook that fact if he turned up with a prize like Lorena.

Also, there were still renegade bands of Kiowas and Comanches loose on the plains. The bands were supposedly scattered—at least that was the talk in south Texas—and the trade in captives virtually dead.

But Augustus wasn't in south Texas anymore, and as he rode through the empty country he had plenty of time to consider that maybe the talk hadn't been all that accurate—talk often wasn't. The bands were doomed, but they might last another year or two, whereas he was advancing into their country in the here and now. He wasn't afraid for himself, but he was afraid for Lorena. Blue Duck might be dealing with some renegade chief with a taste for white women. Lorena would put a nice cap on a career largely devoted to stealing children.

If Blue Duck intended to trade her to an Indian, he would probably take her farther west, through the region known as the Quitaque, and then north to a crossing on the Canadian where the Comanches had traded captives for decades. Nearby was the famous Valley of Tears, spoken of with anguish by such captives as had been recovered. There the Comancheros divided captives, mothers being separated from their children and sold to different bands, the theory being that if they were isolated they would be less likely to organize escapes.

As he moved into the Quitaque, a parched country where shallow red canyons stretched west toward the Palo Duro, Augustus would see little spiraling dust devils rising from the exposed earth far ahead of him. During the heat of the day mirages in the form of flat lakes appeared, so vivid that a time or two he almost convinced himself there was water ahead, although he knew there wasn't.

He decided to head first for the big crossing on the Canadian. If there was no sign of Blue Duck there he could always follow the river over to the Walls. He crossed the Prairie Dog Fork of the Red River—plenty of prairie dogs were in evidence, too—and rode west to the edge of the Palo Duro. Several times he saw small herds of buffalo, and twice rode through valleys of bleached bones, places where hunters had slaughtered several hundred animals at a time. By good luck he found a spring and spent the night by it, resting his horse for the final push.

Late the next day he came into the breaks of the Canadian, a country of shallow, eroded gullys. He could see where the river curved east, across the plains. He rode east for several miles, hoping to cross Blue Duck's tracks. He didn't, which convinced him he had guessed wrong in coming so far west. The man had probably gone directly to the Walls and pitched Lorena into the laps of a bunch of buffalo hunters.

Before he had time to lament his error, though, Augustus saw a sight which took his mind off it completely. He saw a speck moving across the plains north, toward the river. At first he thought it might be Blue Duck, but if so he was traveling without Lorena—there was only one speck. His horse saw the speck too. Augustus drew his rifle in the case the speck turned out to be hostile. He loped toward it only to discover an old man with a dirty white beard, pushing a wheelbarrow across the plains. The wheelbarrow contained buffalo bones. And as if that wasn't unusual enough, Augustus found that he even knew the man.

His name was Aus Frank, and he had started as a mountain man, trapping beaver. He had once kept a store in Waco but for some reason got mad and robbed the bank next to his store—the bank had thought they were getting along with him fine until the day he walked in and robbed them. Augustus and Call were in Waco at the time, and though Call was reluctant to bother with bank robbers—he felt bankers were so stupid they deserved robbing—they were persuaded to go after him. They caught him right away, but not without a gun battle. The battle took place in a thicket on the Brazos, where Aus Frank had stopped to cook some venison. It went on for two hours and resulted in no injuries; then Aus Frank ran out of ammunition and had been easy enough to arrest. He cursed them all the way back to Waco and broke out of jail the day they left town. Augustus had not heard of him since—yet there he was wheeling a barrow full of buffalo bones across the high plains.

He didn't seem to be armed, so Augustus rode right up to him, keeping his rifle across his saddle. The old robber could well have a pistol hidden in the bones, though unless his aim had improved, he was not much of a threat even if he did.

"Hello, Aus," Augustus said, as he rode up. "Have you gone in the bone business, or what?"

The old man squinted at him for a moment, but made no reply. He kept on wheeling his barrow full of bones over the rough ground. Tobacco drippings had stained his beard until most of it was a deep brown.

"I guess you don't remember me," Augustus said, falling in beside him. "I'm Captain McCrae. We shot at one another all afternoon once, up on the Brazos. You was in one thicket and me and Captain Call was in the next one. We pruned the post oaks with all that shooting, and then we stuck you in jail and you crawled right out again."

"I don't like you much," Aus Frank said, still trundling. "Put me in the goddamn jail."

"Well, why'd you rob that bank?" Augustus said. "It ain't Christian to rob your neighbors. It ain't Christian to hold a grudge, neither. Wasn't you born into the Christian religion?"

"No," Aus Frank said. "What do you want?"

"A white girl," Augustus said. "Pretty one. An outlaw carried her off. You may know him. His name is Blue Duck."

Aus Frank stopped the wheelbarrow. He needed to spit and leaned over and spat a large mouthful of tobacco juice directly into the hole of a red-ant bed. The ants, annoyed, scurried about in all directions.

Augustus laughed. Aus Frank had always been an original. In Waco, as he remembered, he had caused controversy because he never seemed to sleep. The lantern in his store would be on at all hours of the night, and the man would often be seen roaming the streets at three in the morning. Nobody knew what he was looking for, or if he found it.

"Now that's a new trick," Augustus said. "Spitting on ants. I guess that's all you've got to do besides haul bones."

Aus Frank resumed his walk, and Augustus followed along, amused at the strange turns life took. Soon they came down into the valley of the Canadian. Augustus was amazed to see an enormous pyramid of buffalo bones perhaps fifty yards from the water. The bones were piled so high, it seemed to him Aus Frank must have a ladder to use in his piling, though he saw no sign of one. Down the river a quarter of a mile there was another pyramid, just as large.

"Well, Aus, I see you've been busy," Augustus said. "You'll be so rich one of these days some bank will come along and rob you. Who do you sell these bones to?"

Aus Frank ignored the question. While Augustus watched, he pushed his wheelbarrow up to the bottom of the pyramid of bones and began to throw the bones as high as possible up the pyramid. Once or twice he got a leg bone or thigh bone all the way to the top, but most of the bones hit midway and stuck. In five minutes the big wheelbarrow was empty. Without a word Aus Frank took the wheelbarrow and started back across the prairie.

Augustus decided to rest while the old man worked. Such camp as there was was rudimentary. Aus had dug a little cave in one of the red bluffs south of the river, and his gear was piled in front of it. There was a buffalo gun and a few pots and pans, and that was it. The main crossing was a mile downriver, and Augustus rode down to inspect it before unsaddling. There were horse tracks galore, but not those he was looking for. He saw five pyramids of bones between the crossing and Aus Frank's camp, each containing several tons of bones.

Back at the camp, Augustus rested in the shade of the little bluff. Aus Frank continued to haul in bones until sundown. After pitching his last load up on the pyramid, he wheeled the barrow to his camp, turned it over and sat on it. He looked at Augustus for two or three minutes without saying anything.

"Well, are you going to invite me for supper or not?" Augustus asked.

"Never should have arrested me," Aus Frank said. "I don't like that goddamn bank."

"You didn't stay in jail but four hours," Augustus reminded him. "Now that I've seen how hard you work, I'd say you probably needed the rest. You could have studied English or something. I see you've learned it finally."

"I don't like the goddamn bank," Aus repeated.

"Let's talk about something else," Augustus suggested. "You're just lucky you didn't get shot on account of that bank. Me and Call were both fine shots in those days. The thicket was the only thing that saved you."

"They cheated me because I couldn't talk good," Aus Frank said.

"You got a one-track mind, Aus," Augustus said. "You and half of mankind. How long you been up here on the Canadian river?"

"I come five years," Aus said. "I want a store."

"That's fine, but you've outrun the people," Augustus said. "They won't be along for another ten years or so. I guess by then you'll have a helluva stock of buffalo bones. I just hope there's a demand for them."

"Had a wagon," Aus Frank said. "Got stole. Apaches got it."

"That so?" Augustus said. "I didn't know the Apaches lived around here."

"Over by the Pecos," Aus said. "I quit the mountains. Don't like snow."

"I'll pass on snow myself, when I have the option," Augustus said. "This is a lonely place you've settled in, though. Don't the Indians bother you?"

"They leave me be," Aus said. "That one you're hunting, he's a mean one. He kilt Bob. Built a fire under him and let him sizzle.

"He don't bother me, though," he added. "Kilt Bob and let me be."

"Bob who?"

"Old Bob, that I was in the mountains with," Aus said.

"Well, his burning days are over, if I find him," Augustus said.

"He's quick, Blue Duck," Aus said. "Has some Kiowas with him. They ate my dog."

"How many Kiowas?" Augustus asked.

"It was a big dog," Aus said. "Killed two wolves. I had a few sheep once but the Mexicans run them off."

"It's a chancy life out here on the plains," Augustus said. "I bet you get a nice breeze in the winter, too."

"Them Kiowas ate that dog," Aus repeated. "Good dog."

"Why ain't Blue Duck killed you?" Augustus asked.

"Laughs at me," Aus said. "Laughs at my bones. He says he'll kill me when he gets ready."

"How many Kiowas does he run around with?" Augustus asked again. The old man was evidently not used to having anyone to talk to. His remarks came out a little jerky.

"Six," Aus Frank said.

"Who's over at the Walls?" Augustus asked.

The old man didn't answer. Darkness had fallen, and Augustus could barely see him sitting on his wheelbarrow.

"No beaver in this river," Aus Frank said after several minutes.

"No, a beaver would be foolish to be in this river," Augustus said. "There ain't a tree within twenty miles, and beavers like to gnaw trees. You should have stayed up north if you like beavers."

"I'd rather gather these bones," the old man said. "You don't have to get your feet wet."

"Did you get to Montana when you was a beaverman?"

Augustus waited several minutes for a reply, but the old man never answered. When the moon came up, Augustus saw that he had fallen asleep sitting on his wheelbarrow, his head fallen over in his arms.

Augustus was tired and hungry. He lay where he was, thinking about food, but making no effort to get up and fix any, if there was any to be fixed. While he was thinking he ought to get up and eat, he fell asleep.

Deep in the night a sound disturbed him, and he came awake and drew his pistol. It was well on toward morning—he could tell that by the moon—but the sound was new to him.

Cautiously he turned over, only to see at once that the source of the sound was Aus Frank. He had risen in the night and collected another load of buffalo bones. Now he was heaving them up on the pyramid. The sound that had awakened Augustus was the sound of bones, clicking and rattling as they slid down the sides of the pyramid.

Augustus holstered his pistol and walked over to watch the old man.

"You're an unusual fellow, Aus," he said. "I guess you just work night and day. You should have partnered up with Woodrow Call. He's as crazy about work as you are. The two of you might own the world by now if you'd hooked up."

Aus Frank didn't respond. He had emptied the wheelbarrow, and he pushed it up the slope, away from the river.

Augustus caught his horse and rode east. On his way he saw Aus Frank again, working under the moonlight. He had plenty to work with, for the plain around was littered with buffalo bones. It looked as if a whole herd had been wiped out, for a road of bones stretched far across the plain.

He remembered when he had first come to the high plains, years before. For two days he and Call and the Rangers had ridden parallel to the great southern buffalo herd—hundreds of thousands of animals, slowly grazing north. It had been difficult to sleep at night because the horses were nervous around so many animals, and the sounds of the herd were constant. They had ridden for nearly a hundred miles and seldom been out of sight of buffalo.

Of course they had heard that the buffalo were being wiped out, but with the memory of the southern herd so vivid, they had hardly credited the news. Discussing it in Lonesome Dove they had decided that the reports must be exaggerated—thinned out, maybe, but not wiped out. Thus the sight of the road of bones stretching over the prairie was a shock. Maybe roads of bones were all that was left. The thought gave the very emptiness of the plains a different feel. With those millions of animals gone, and the Indians mostly gone in their wake, the great plains were truly empty, unpeopled and ungrazed.

Soon the whites would come, of course, but what he was seeing was a moment between, not the plains as they had been, or as they would be, but a moment of true emptiness, with thousands of miles of grass resting unused, occupied only by remnants—of the buffalo, the Indians, the hunters. Augustus thought they were crazed remnants, mostly, like the old mountain man who worked night and day gathering bones to no purpose.

"No wonder you never worked out in Waco, Aus," he said, speaking as much to himself as to the old man. Aus Frank was not in a talkative mood, or a listening mood either. He had filled his wheelbarrow and was heading back to camp.

"I'm going to the Walls to kill that big renegade for you," Augustus said. "Need anything?"

Aus Frank stopped, as if thinking it over.

"I wisht they hadn't killed that dog," he said. "I liked that dog. It was them Kiowas that killed it, not the Mexicans. Six Kiowas."

"Well, I got six bullets," Augustus said. "Maybe I'll send the rascals where your dog went."

"Them Kiowas shot Bob's horse," Aus added. "That's how come they caught him. Built a fire under him and cooked him. That's their way."

Then he lifted his wheelbarrow full of bones and walked off toward the Canadian River.

The light was just coming, the plains black in the distance, the sky gray where it met the land. Though dawn was his favorite hour, it was also an hour at which Augustus most keenly felt himself to be a fool. What was it but folly to be riding along the Canadian River alone, easy pickings for an outlaw gang, and hungry to boot? A chain of follies had put him there: Call's abrupt decision to become a cattleman and his own decision, equally abrupt, to try and rescue a girl foolish enough to be taken in by Jake Spoon. None of it was sensible, yet he had to admit there was something about such follies that he liked. The sensible way, which he had pursued once or twice in his life, had always proved boring, usually within a few days. In his case it had led to nothing much, just excessive drunkenness and reckless card playing. There was more enterprise in certain follies, it seemed to him.

As the sun lit the grass, he rode east along the road of buffalo bones.

55

MONKEY JOHN HATED IT that she wouldn't talk. "By God, I'll cut your tongue out if you ain't gonna use it," he said once, and he knocked her down and sat on her, his big knife an inch from her face, until Dog Face threatened to shoot him if he didn't let her be. Lorena expected him to do it. He was the worst man she had ever known, worse even than Ermoke and the Kiowas, though they were bad enough. She shut her eyes, expecting to feel the knife, but Dog Face cocked his pistol and Monkey John didn't cut her. He continued to sit on her chest though, arguing with Dog Face about her silence.

"What do you care if she talks?" Dog Face said. "I wouldn't talk to you either, you goddamn old runt."

"She can talk, goddamn her," Monkey John said. "Duck said she talked to him."

"It's her business if she don't want to talk," Dog Face insisted. He was a thin scarecrow of a man, but he had crazy eyes, and Monkey John never pushed him too far.

"By God, we bought her," Monkey John said. "Give all them hides for her. She oughta do what we say."

"You get your damn money's worth," Dog Face said. "Most of them hides was mine anyway.

"You old runt," he added.

Monkey John was old and short. His hair was a dirty white and he was under five feet, but that didn't keep him from being mean. Twice he had grabbed sticks out of the fire and beat her with them. There was nothing she could do but curl up as tight as she could. Her back and legs were soon burned and bruised and she knew Monkey John would do worse than that if he ever got her alone long enough, but Dog Face owned half of her and he stuck close to be sure his investment didn't get too damaged.

Though she had seen Dog Face and Monkey John give Blue Duck the skins in trade for her, it seemed they weren't full owners, for whenever the Kiowas showed up, every two or three days, they drug her off to their camp for their share, and the two white men didn't try to stop them. There was no love lost between the white men and the Kiowas, but both sides were too afraid of Blue Duck to get into it with one another.

Blue Duck was the only man of the bunch who seemed to take no interest in her. He had stolen her to sell, and he had sold her. It was clear that he didn't care what they did to her. When he was in camp he spent his time cleaning his gun or smoking and seldom even looked her way. Monkey John was bad, but Blue Duck still scared her more. His cold, empty eyes frightened her more than Monkey John's anger or Dog Face's craziness. Blue Duck had scared the talk completely out of her. She had never been much for talk, but her silence in the camp was different from her old silence. In Lonesome Dove she had often hidden her words, but she could find them if she needed them; she had brought them out quick enough when Jake came along.

Now speech had left her; fear took its place. The two white men talked constantly of killing. Blue Duck didn't talk about it, but she knew he could do it whenever it pleased him. She didn't expect to live to the end of any day—only the fact that the men weren't tired of her yet kept her alive. When they did tire they would kill her. She thought about how it would happen but couldn't picture it in her mind. She only hoped it wasn't Blue Duck that finally did it. She was so dirty and stank so that it seemed strange the men would even want to use her, but of course they were even dirtier and stank worse. They camped not far from a creek, but none of the men ever washed. Monkey John told her several times what he would do to her if she tried to run away—terrible things, on the order of what Blue Duck had threatened, on the morning after he kidnapped her, only worse if possible. He said he would sew her up with rawhide threads so tight she couldn't make water and then would watch her till she burst.

Lorena tried to shut her mind when he talked like that. She knew the trick of not talking, and was learning not to hear. At night she wondered sometimes if she could just learn to die. She wanted to, and imagined how angry they would be if they woke up one morning and she was dead so they could get no more from her.

But she couldn't learn that trick. She thought of being dead, but she didn't die, and she didn't try to escape either. She didn't know where she was, for the plains stretched around, empty and bare, as far as she could see. They had horses and they would catch her and do something to her, or else give her to the Kiowas. Monkey John threatened that too, describing what the Kiowas would do if they got the chance. At night that was mostly what the men talked about—what the Indians did to people they caught. She believed it. Often with the Kiowas she felt a deep fright come over her. They did what they wanted with her but it wasn't enough—she could see them looking at her after they finished, and the looks made her more scared even than the things Monkey John threatened. The Kiowas just looked, but there was something in their looks that made her wish she could be dead and not have to think about it.

Blue Duck came and went. Some days he would be there at the camp, sharpening his knife. Other days he would ride off. Sometimes the Kiowas went with him, other days they sat around their camp doing nothing. Monkey John swore at them, but the Kiowas didn't listen. They laughed at the old man and gave him looks of the sort they gave Lorena. It wasn't only women they could do things to.

One day the Kiowas found a crippled cow, left by some herd. The cow had a split hoof and could barely hobble along on three legs. The Kiowas poked it with their lances and got it in sight of camp. Then one hit it in the head with an ax and the cow fell dead. The Kiowas split open the cow's stomach and began to pull out her guts. They sliced off strips of the white guts and squeezed out what was in them, eating it greedily. That's what he said he'd do to me, Lorena thought. Pull out my guts like that cow.

"Look at them dern gut eaters," Dog Face said. "I'd be derned if I'd eat guts raw."

"You might if you was hungry," Monkey John said.

"They ain't hungry, they got the whole cow," Dog Face pointed out.

If there was hope for her, Lorena knew it lay with Dog Face. He was rough and crazy, but he wasn't hard like the old man. He might cuff her if she disappointed him, but he didn't beat her with hot sticks or kick her stomach like the old man did. At times she caught Dog Face looking at her in a friendly way. He was getting so he didn't like Monkey John to hurt her or even touch her. He was cautious about what he said, for the old man would flare up in an instant, but when Monkey John bothered her, Dog Face got restless and would often take his gun and leave the camp. Monkey John didn't care—he played with her roughly whether anyone was in camp or not.

One night Blue Duck rode in from one of his mysterious trips with some whiskey, which he dispensed freely both to the two white men and to the Kiowas. Blue Duck drank with them, but not much, whereas in an hour Monkey John, Dog Face and the Kiowas were very drunk. It was a hot night but they built a big campfire and sat around it, passing the bottle from hand to hand.

Lorena began to feel frightened. Blue Duck had not so much as looked at her, but she felt something was about to happen. He had several bottles of whiskey, and as soon as the men finished one he handed them another. Monkey John was particularly sloppy when he drank. The whiskey ran out of the corners of his mouth and into his dirty beard. Once he stood up and made water without even turning his back.

"You could go off aways," Dog Face said. "I don't want to sit in your piss."

The old man continued to make water, most of it hitting the campfire and making a spitting sound, but some splattering on the ground near where Dog Face sat.

"I could but I ain't about to," the old man said. "Scoot back if you're afraid of a little piss."

Blue Duck spread a blanket near the fire and began to roll dice on it. The Kiowas immediately got excited. Ermoke grabbed the dice and rolled them several times. Each of the Kiowas had a try, but Monkey John scoffed at their efforts.

"Them gut eaters can't throw dice," he said.

"You better be quiet," Blue Duck said. "Ermoke wouldn't mind frying your liver."

"He tries it and I'll blow a hole in him you could catch rain water through," Monkey John said.

"Let's gamble," Blue Duck said. "I ain't had a game in a while."

"Gamble for what?" Dog Face asked. "All I got is my gun and I'd be in pretty shape without that. Or my horses."

"Put up your horses then," Blue Duck said. "You might win."

Dog Face shook his head.

"I don't know much," Dog Face said. "But I know better than to bet my dern horses. There ain't nowhere to walk to from this Canadian that a man can get to on foot."

Yet an hour later he lost his horses to Blue Duck. Monkey John lost his on the first roll. Before long Blue Duck had won all the horses, though many of the Indians were so drunk they hardly seemed to know what was happening.

Blue Duck had a heavy, square face—he kept shaking the dice in his big hand. Sometimes he would play with a strand of his shaggy hair, as a girl would. Sometimes Lorena thought maybe she could grab a gun and shoot him—the men left their rifles laying around. But the gun hadn't worked when she tried to shoot Tinkersley, and if she tried to shoot Blue Duck and didn't kill him she would be in for it. She might be in for it anyway, though it seemed to her the men were scared of him too. Even Monkey John was cautious when Blue Duck was around. They might be glad to see him dead. She didn't try it. It was because she was so frightened of him that she wanted to, yet the same fright kept her from it.

"Well, now I've won the livestock," Blue Duck said. "Or most of it."

"Most of it, hell, you've won it all," Monkey John said. "We're stuck on this god-damn river."

"I ain't won the girl," Blue Duck said.

"A woman ain't livestock," Dog Face said.

"This one is," Blue Duck said. "I've bought and sold better animals than her many times."

"Well, she's ours," Monkey John said.

"She's just half yours," Blue Duck reminded him. "Ermoke and his boys own a half interest."

"We was aiming to buy them out," Dog Face said.

Blue Duck laughed his heavy laugh. "By the time you raise the money, there won't be much left to buy," he said. "You'd do better to buy a goat."

"Don't want no goddamn goat," Dog Face said. He was nervous about the turn the conversation was taking.

"Let's gamble some more," Blue Duck said, shaking the dice at Ermoke. "Bet me your half interest in the woman. If you win I'll let you have your horses back."

Ermoke shook his head, looking at Lorena briefly across the campfire.

"No," he said. "We want the woman."

"Come on, let's gamble," Blue Duck said, a threatening tone in his voice. All the Kiowas looked at him. The two white men kept quiet.

The Kiowas began to argue among themselves. Lorena didn't understand their gabble, but it was clear some wanted to gamble and some didn't. Some wanted their horses back. Ermoke finally changed his mind, though he kept looking across the fire at her. It was as if he wanted her to know he had his plans for her, however the game turned out.

All the Kiowas finally agreed to gamble except one, the youngest. He didn't want it. He was skinny and very young-looking, no more than sixteen, but he was more interested in her than the rest. Sometimes, in the Kiowa camp, he had two turns, or even three. The older men laughed at his appetite and tried to distract him when he covered her, but he ignored them.

Now he balked. He didn't look up, just kept his eyes down and shook his head. The Kiowas yelled at him but he didn't respond. He just kept shaking his head. He didn't want to risk his interest in her.

"That damn chigger's holding up the game," Blue Duck said to Ermoke. He stood up and walked a few steps into the darkness. In a minute, they heard him making water. The Kiowas were still drinking whiskey. Now Ermoke was in the mood to gamble, and he reached over and shook the young man, trying to get him to agree, but the young man looked sullenly at the ground.

Suddenly there was a shot, startling them all, and the young man flopped backwards. Blue Duck stepped back into the firelight, a rifle in his hands. The Indians were speechless. Blue Duck sat down, the rifle across his lap, and rattled the dice again. The young Indian's feet were still in the light, but the feet didn't move.

"By God, life's cheap up here on the goddamn Canadian," Monkey John said.

"Cheap, and it might get cheaper," Blue Duck said.

Then the gambling started again. The dead boy was ignored. In a few minutes Blue Duck had won her back—not only what the Indians owned but what the white men owned too. Dog Face didn't want to play, but he also didn't want to die. He played and lost, and so did Monkey John.

"I think you're a goddamn cheat," Monkey John said, drunk enough to be reckless. "I think you cheated me out of our horses, and now you've cheated us out of this woman."

"I don't want the woman," Blue Duck said. "You men can have her back as a gift, and your horses too, provided you do me one favor."

"I bet it's a hell of a big favor," Dog Face said. "What do you want us to do, attack a fort?"

Blue Duck chuckled. "There's an old man following me," he said. "He went west, but he'll be coming along one of these days. I want you to kill him.

"Hear that, Ermoke?" he added. "You can have your horses back, and the woman too. Just kill that old man. I hear he's coming down the river."

"I'd like to know who you hear it from?" Monkey John asked.

"He's been following me ever since I stole the woman," Blue Duck said. "He ain't no tracker, though. He went off across the Quitaque. But now he's figured it out and he'll be coming."

"By God, he must want her bad, to come all this way," Monkey John said.

"Kill him tomorrow," Blue Duck said, looking at Ermoke. "Take some of the horses and go find some help."

Ermoke was drunk and angry. "We do it," he said. "Then we take the woman."

"The hell you will," Dog Face said. "We're in on this and she's half ours, and you ain't taking her nowhere."

"You shut up, or I'll kill you like I killed that chigger," Blue Duck said.

"You get some help," he said again, looking at Ermoke. "I doubt you five can kill that old man."

"Hell, what is he?" Monkey John said. "Five against one's nice odds."

"These five can't shoot," Blue Duck said. "They can whoop and holler, but they can't shoot. That old man can."

"That makes a difference," Dog Face agreed. "I can shoot. If he gets past Ermoke, I'll finish him."

"Somebody better settle him," Blue Duck said. "Otherwise you'll all be dead."

The Kiowas stood up and drug the dead boy away. Lorena heard them arguing in the darkness. Blue Duck sat where he was, his rifle across his lap; he seemed half asleep.

Monkey John got up and came over to her. "Who is this old man?" he asked. "You got a husband?"

Lorena stayed in her silence. It infuriated Monkey John. He grabbed her by the hair and cuffed her, knocking her over. Then he grabbed a stick of wood and was about to beat her with it when Dog Face intervened.

"Put it down," he said. "You've beat her enough."

"Let her answer me then," Monkey John said. "She can talk. Duck says so."

Dog Face picked up his rifle. Monkey John still had the stick.

"You'd pull a gun on me over a whore?" Monkey John said.

"I ain't gonna shoot you but I'll break your head if you don't let her be," Dog Face said.

Monkey John was too drunk to listen. He charged Dog Face and swung the stick at him but Dog Face wasn't as drunk. He hit Monkey John with the barrel of his rifle. The old man went loop-legged and dropped his stick. Then he dropped, too, falling on the stick.

"I'd have let him beat her," Blue Duck said.

"I ain't you," Dog Face said.

In the night Lorena tried to sort it out in her mind. She had been hungry so much, tired so much, scared so much, that her mind didn't work well anymore. Sometimes she would try to remember something and couldn't—it was as if her mind and memory had gone and hidden somewhere until things were better. Dog Face had given her an old blanket; otherwise she would have had to sleep on the ground in what was left of her clothes. She wrapped the blanket around her and tried to think back over the talk. It meant Gus was coming—it was Gus Blue Duck wanted the Kiowas to kill. She had almost forgotten he was following her, life had gotten so hard. The Kiowas had been sent to kill him, so Gus might never arrive. It was hard to believe that Gus would get her out—the times when she had known him had been so different from the hard times. She didn't think she would ever get out. Blue Duck was too bad. Dog Face was her only chance, and Dog Face was scared of Blue Duck. Sooner or later Blue Duck would give her to Ermoke or someone just as hard. If that was going to happen it was better that her mind had gone to hide.

In the gray dawn she saw the Kiowas leave. Blue Duck talked to them in Indian talk and gave them some bullets to kill Gus with. He woke Dog Face and shook Monkey John more or less awake. "If he gets past Ermoke, you two kill him," he said. Then he left.

Monkey John looked awful. He had a bloody lump on his head, and a hangover. He had slept with his face in the dirt all night and an ant had stung him several times, leaving one eye swollen nearly shut. He got to his feet but he could hardly stand.

"How's he think I can shoot?" he asked Dog Face. "I can't see but from one eye, and it's the wrong eye."

"Put some mud on it, it's just ant bites," Dog Face said. He was cleaning his gun.

56

AUGUSTUS WAS A LITTLE put out with himself for doing such a poor job of tracking. He had gambled on Blue Duck heading west, when in fact he had crossed the Red and gone straight north. It was the kind of gamble Call would never take. Call would have tracked all the way, or let Deets track.

The country near the Canadian was rough and broken, and he dropped south to where the plains flattened out. He wanted to spare his horse as much as possible.

He rode east all morning, a bad feeling in his heart. He had meant to catch Blue Duck within a day, but he hadn't. The renegade had out-traveled him. It would have been rough on Lorie, such traveling. He should have borrowed Call's mare, but the thought hadn't occurred to him until too late. By this time Lorie could be dead, or ruined. He had helped recover several captives from the Comanches in his rangering days, and often the recovery came too late if the captives were women. Usually their minds were gone and they were only interested in dying, which they mostly did once they got back to people who would let them die.

He was thinking about Lorie when the Indians broke for him. Where they had hidden he didn't know, for he was in the center of a level plain. He first heard a little cutting sound as bullets zipped into the grass, ten yards from his horse. Later, the sound of bullets cutting grass was more distinct in his memory than the sounds of shots. Before he really heard the shots he had his horse in a dead run, heading south. It seemed to him there were ten or twelve Indians, but he was more concerned with outrunning them than with getting a count. But within minutes he knew he wasn't going to be able to outrun them. He had pushed his horse too hard and soon was steadily losing ground.

There was plenty of ground to lose, too. He had hoped for a creek or a bank or a gully—something he could get down into and make his stand—but he was on the flat prairie as far as the eye could see. He contemplated turning and trying to charge through them; if he killed three or four they might get discouraged. But if there was even one man among them with any sense they'd just shoot the horse, and there he'd be.

He glimpsed something white on the prairie slightly to the east and headed for it—it turned out just to be more buffalo bones, another place where a sizable herd of animals had been slaughtered. As Augustus raced through the bones he saw a wallow, a place where many buffalo had laid down and rolled in the dirt. It was only a slight depression on the plain, not more than a foot deep, but he decided it was the best he was going to get. The Indians were barely a minute behind him. He jumped down, pulled his rifle and cartridge rolls clear of the horse and dropped them in the buffalo wallow. Then he drew his knife, wrapped the bridle reins tightly around one hand, and jabbed the knife into the horse's neck, slashing the jugular vein. Blood poured out and the horse leaped and plunged desperately but Augustus held on, though sprayed with blood. When the horse fell, he managed to turn him so that the horse lay across one end of the wallow, his blood pumping out into the dust. Once the horse tried to rise, but Augustus jerked him back and he didn't try again.

It was a desperate trick, but the only one he could think of that increased his chances—most horses shied from the smell of fresh blood. He needed the horse for a breastworks anyway and could have shot him, but he had saved a bullet, and the blood smell might work for him.

As soon as he was sure the horse was beyond rising, he picked up his rifle. The Indians were shooting, though still far out of effective range. Again he heard the zing of bullets cutting the prairie grass. Augustus rested the rifle barrel across the dying horse's withers and waited. The Indians were yelling as they raced down on him—one or two carried lances, but those were mainly for show, or to puncture him with if they caught him alive.

Sure enough, when they were fifty or sixty yards away, their horses caught the first whiffs of fresh blood, still pumping from the torn throat of the dying horse. They slowed and began to rear and shy, and as they did, Augustus started shooting. The Indians were dismayed; they flailed at the horses with their rifles, but the horses were spooked. Two stopped dead and Augustus immediately shot their riders. He could have asked for no better target than an Indian stopped fifty yards away on a horse that wouldn't move. The two men dropped and lay still. Augustus replaced the two cartridges and wiped the sweat out of his eyes.

The blood had bought him a chance—without it he would have been overrun and killed, no matter how fast or well he had shot. Now the Indians were trying to force their horses into a charge, but it wasn't working—the horses kept swerving and shying. Some tried to circle to the south, and when they turned, Augustus shot two more. Then one Indian did a gallant thing—he threw a blanket over his horse's head and got the confused horse to charge blind. The man seemed to be the leader; at least he carried the longest lance. He charged at the wallow, rifle in one hand, lance in the other, though when he tried to lever the rifle with one hand he dropped it. Augustus almost laughed, but the Indian kept up the charge with only a lance, a brave thing. Augustus shot him when he was no more than thirty feet away; he let him get that close in hopes of grabbing his horse. The Indian fell dead, but the horse shied away and Augustus didn't feel he could afford to chase him.

The remaining Indians were discouraged. Five Indians were dead, and the battle not five minutes old. Augustus replaced his cartridges and killed a sixth as the Indians were retreating. He might have got one or two more, but decided against risking long shots when his situation was so chancy. There might be more Indians available nearby, though he considered it unlikely. Probably they had charged with all they had—in which case he had killed half of them.

With no shooting to do for a little while, Augustus took stock of the situation and decided the worst part of it was that he had no one to talk to. He had been within a minute or two of death, which could not be said to be boring, exactly—but even desperate battle was lacking in something if there was no one to discuss it with. What had made battle interesting over the years was not his opponents but his colleagues. It was fascinating, at least to him, to see how the men he had fought with most often reacted to the stimulus of attack.

Pea Eye, for example, was mostly concerned with not running out of bullets. He was extremely conservative in his choice of targets, so conservative that he often spent a whole engagement sighting at people but never pulling the trigger.

"Could have wasted a shell," he said, if someone pointed this out to him. It was true that when he did shoot he rarely missed, but that was because he rarely shot at anything over thirty yards away.

Call was interesting to observe in a battle too. It took a fight to bring out the fighter in him, and a fighter was mostly what he was. Call was a great attacker. Once the enemy was sighted, he liked to go after them, and would often do so in defiance of the odds. He might plan elaborately before a battle, but once it was joined his one desire was to close with the enemy and destroy him. Call had destruction in him and would go on killing when there was no need. Once his blood heated, it was slow to cool. Call himself had never been beaten for good—only death could accomplish that—and he reasoned that if an enemy was alive he wasn't beaten either—not for good.

Augustus knew that reasoning wasn't accurate—men could get enough of fighting and turn from it. Some would do almost anything to avoid the fear it produced.

Deets understood that. He would never fire on a fleeing man, whereas Call would pursue a man fifty miles and kill him if the man had attacked him. Deets fought carefully and shrewdly—he would have known the trick about fresh blood. But Deets's great ability was in preventing ambushes. He would seem to feel them coming, often a day or two early, when he could have had no particular clues. "How'd you know?" they would ask him and Deets would have no answer. "Just knew," he said.

The six remaining Indians had retreated well beyond rifle range, but they weren't gone. He could see them holding council, but they were three hundred yards away and the heat waves created a wavery mirage between him and them.

Unless there were more Indians, Augustus didn't consider that he was in a particularly serious situation. It was hot and the blowflies were already buzzing over the horse blood, but those were trivial discomforts. He had filled his canteen that morning, and the Canadian was no more than ten miles to the north. More than likely the Indians would decide they had missed their big chance and go away. They might try to get him at night, but he didn't plan to be there. Come dark he would head for the river.

All afternoon the six Indians stayed where they were. Occasionally they would fire a shot his way, hoping to get lucky. Finally one rode off to the east, returning about an hour later with a white man who set up a tripod and began to shoot at him with a fifty-caliber buffalo gun.

That was an inconvenient development. Augustus had to hastily dig himself a shallow hole on the other side of the horse, where the blood and the blowflies were worse. They were not worse, though, than the impact of a fifty-caliber bullet, several of which hit the horse in the next hour. Augustus kept digging. Fortunately the man was not a particularly good shot—many of the bullets sang overhead, though one or two hit his saddle and ricocheted.

Once when the buffalo hunter was reloading, Gus took a quick shot at him, raising his barrel to compensate for the range. The shot missed the white man but wounded one of the Indian horses. The horse's scream unnerved the shooter, who moved his tripod back another fifty yards. Augustus kept low and waited for darkness, which was only another hour away.

The shooter kept him pinned until full dark—but as soon as it was too dark to shoot, Augustus yanked his saddle loose from the dead mount and walked west, stopping to take what bullets he could salvage from the men he had killed. None had many, but one had a fairly good rifle, and Augustus took it as insurance. He hated carrying the saddle, but it was a shield of sorts; if he got caught in open country it might be the only cover he would have.

While he was going from corpse to corpse collecting ammunition, he was startled to hear the sudden rattle of shots from the east. That was puzzling. Either the Indians had fallen to fighting among themselves or someone else had come on the scene. Then the shots ceased and he heard the sound of running horses—the Indians leaving, most probably.

This new development put him in a quandary. He was prepared for a good hard walk to the river, carrying a heavy saddle, but if there were strangers around they might be friendly, and he might not have to carry the saddle. Possibly the scout for a cattle herd had stumbled into the little group of hostiles, though the main trail routes lay to the east.

At any rate, he didn't feel he should ignore the possibility, so he turned back toward the shooting. There was still a little light in the sky, though it was dark on the ground. From time to time Augustus stopped to listen and at first heard nothing: the plains were still.

The third time he stopped, he thought he heard voices. They were faint, but they were white, an encouraging sign. He went cautiously toward them, trying to make as little noise as possible. It was hard to carry a saddle without it creaking some, but he was afraid to put it down for fear he could not find his way back to it in the dark. Then he heard a horse snort and another horse jingle his bit. He was getting close. He stopped to wait for the moon to rise. When it did, he moved a little closer, hoping to see something. Instead he heard what sounded like a subdued argument.

"We don't know how many there is," one voice said. "There could be five hundred Indians around here, for all we know."

"I can go find them," another voice said. It was a girlish voice, which surprised him.

"You hush," the first voice said. "Just because you can catch varmints don't mean you can sneak up on Indians."

"I could find 'em," the girlish voice insisted.

"They'll find you and make soup of you if you ain't lucky," was the reply.

"I don't think there's no five hundred," a third voice said. "I don't think there's five hundred Indians left in this part of the country."

"Well, if there was even a hundred, we'd have all we could do," the first voice pointed out.

"I'd like to know who they were shooting at when we rode up," the other man said. "I don't believe it was buffalo, though I know it was a buffalo gun."

Augustus decided he wouldn't get a better opportunity than that, so he cleared his throat and spoke in the loudest tones he could muster without actually shouting.

"They were shooting at me," he said. "I'm Captain McCrae, and I'm coming in."

He took a few steps to the side when he said it, for he had known men to shoot from reflex when they were frightened. Nothing was more dangerous than walking into the camp of a bunch of men who had their nerves on edge.

"Don't get nervous and shoot, I'm friendly," he said, just as he saw the outline of their horses against the sky.

"I hate this walking around in the dark," he added loudly—not that it was much of an observation. It was designed to keep the strangers from getting jumpy.

Then he saw four people standing by the horses. It was too dark to tell much about any of them, but he dumped the saddle on the ground and went over to shake hands.

"Howdy," he said, and the men shook hands, though none of them had yet said anything. The surprise of his appearance had evidently left them speechless.

"Well, here we are," Augustus said. "I'm Augustus McCrae and I'm after an outlaw named Blue Duck. Have you seen any sign of the man?"

"No, we just got here," one of the men said.

"I know about him, though," July said. "My name is July Johnson. I'm sheriff from Fort Smith, Arkansas, and this is my deputy, Roscoe Brown."

"July Johnson?" Augustus asked.

"Yes," July said.

"By God, that's a good one," Augustus said. "We were expecting you down in Lonesome Dove, and here you are practically in Kansas. If you're still after Jake Spoon, you've missed him by about three hundred miles."

"I have more urgent business," July said rather solemnly.

To Augustus he seemed young, although it was hard to tell in the dark. Mainly it was his voice that seemed young.

"I see you brought family," Augustus said. "Most lawmen don't travel with their children. Or did you pick up these two sprats along the way?"

Nobody answered. They simply stood, as if the question was too complicated for an answer.

"Did the Indians kill your horse?" July asked.

"No, I killed him," Augustus said. "Used him for a fort. There ain't much to hide behind on these plains. I heard shooting. Did you kill any more of them bucks?"

"Don't think so," July said. "I might have hit the buffalo hunter. We never expected to find Indians."

"I killed six this afternoon," Augustus said. "I think there was twelve to begin with, not counting the buffalo hunter. I expect they work for Blue Duck. He stole a woman and I'm after him. I think he sent them bucks to slow me down."

"I hope there ain't too much of a bunch," Roscoe said. "I never kilt one before."

In fact he had never killed anyone before, or even given the possibility much thought. Sudden death was not unknown in Fort Smith, but it was not common, either. It had been a big shock when the Indians turned their guns on them and began to shoot at them. Not until he saw July draw his rifle and start firing did it dawn on him that they were under attack. He had hastily drawn his pistol and shot several times—it had not affected the Indians but it angered July.

"You're just wasting bullets, they're way out of pistol range," he said. But then the Indians ran, so it didn't matter so much.

"What's your plan, Mr. Johnson?" Augustus asked politely. "If your business is urgent you might not want to slow down long enough to help me catch this Blue Duck."

That was true. July didn't want to slow down at all until he found Elmira. If he had been alone, he would have traveled twenty hours a day and rested four. But he was hardly alone. Roscoe was nervous as a cat and spent all day talking about his worries. Joe didn't complain, but the hard traveling had worn him out and he rode along in a doze most of the time and slept like a dead thing when they stopped.

The only one who didn't suffer from the pace was Janey, who mainly walked. July had to admit that she was unusually helpful. When they stopped, she did whatever chores there were to do without being asked. And she was always up and ready to leave when he was, whereas Joe and Roscoe were so sluggish in the morning that it took them half an hour just to get their horses saddled.

Now, out of the blue, a Texas Ranger had showed up—one of the very ones who had partnered with Jake Spoon. He was afoot and a long way from help, and they couldn't just ride off and leave him. Besides, there were hostile Indians around, which made the whole situation more worrisome.

"I haven't planned, very much," July said honestly. "Seems like every time I make a plan something happens to change it."

"Well, life's a twisting stream," Augustus said. "Speaking of which, the Canadian river ain't but a short way to the north. Them bucks are probably camped somewhere on it."

"What would you advise?" July asked. "You know the country."

"It's a steep-banked river," Augustus said. "If we have to fight Indians we'd be in a lot better position there than out on this plain."

"You say the man stole a woman?" July asked.

"Yes," Augustus said. "A girl who was traveling with us."

"We best go on to the river, I guess," July said. "You can ride with me and Roscoe can tote your saddle."

"If this boy ain't armed, maybe he'd like a rifle," Augustus said. "One of them bucks I shot had a pretty good Winchester, and this boy looks old enough to shoot."

He handed the rifle to Joe, who was so stunned by the gift that he could barely say thank you. "Is it loaded already?" he asked, rubbing the smooth stock with one hand.

"You dern right it's loaded," Augustus said. "Just make sure you shoot one of them, and not one of us."

He climbed up behind July and they all rode north. Joe felt intensely proud, now that he was armed. He kept one hand on the stock of the rifle, expecting that any minute the Indians might attack.

But the ride to the river was uneventful. It seemed they had not been riding long before they saw the silver band of the river in the moonlight. July stopped so abruptly that Joe almost bumped into his horse. He and Mr. McCrae were look- ing at something downriver. At first Joe couldn't see anything to look at, but then he noticed a tiny flame of light, far downriver.

"That'd be them," Augustus said. "I guess they ain't worried about us, or they wouldn't be so bold with their campfire. They don't know it, but the wrath of the Lord is about to descend upon them. I dislike bold criminals of whatever race, and I believe I'll go see that they pay their debts."

"I'd best go with you," July said. "You don't know how many there are."

"Let's go make camp," Augustus said. "Then we'll think it out."

They rode upriver a mile, stopping where the mouth of a canyon sloped down to the riverbed.

"This is as good as we'll get," Augustus said. "What I'd like is the loan of a horse for the night. I'll have him back by breakfast, and maybe a few others to boot."

"You want to go at them alone?" July asked.

"It's my job," Augustus said. "I doubt there's many of them. I just hope Blue Duck is there."

Roscoe could not believe what he was hearing. He felt very scared as it was, and yet this stranger was preparing to ride off by himself.

"Why, there could be ten of them," he said. "Do you think you could kill ten men?"

"They're easier to scare at night," Augustus said. "I expect I'll just run most of them off. But I do intend to kill Mr. Duck if I see him. He's stole his last woman."

"I think I ought to go," July said. "I could be of some help. Roscoe can stay here with the young ones."

"No, I'd rather you stay with your party, Mr. Johnson," Augustus said. "I'd feel better about it in my mind. You've got an inexperienced deputy and two young people to think about. Besides, you said you had urgent business. These things are chancy. You might stop a bullet and never get your business finished."

"I think I ought to go," July said. It was in his mind that Ellie could even be in the camp. Somebody could have stolen *her* as easily as the Texas woman. The whiskey traders wouldn't have put up much fight. Of course, it wasn't likely she was there, but then what was likely anymore? He felt he ought to have a look, at least.

In any case, the man could use help, and it should be no great risk to leave Roscoe and the young ones in camp for a few hours. They all needed the rest.

Augustus realized he could probably use help, since he didn't know how many men he was facing. However, he didn't have a high opinion of the average man's ability as a fighter. The majority of men couldn't fight at all and even most outlaws were the merest amateurs when it came to battle. Few could shoot well, and even fewer had any mind for strategy.

The problem was that Blue Duck was evidently one of the few who could think. He had planned the theft of Lorena perfectly. Also, he had survived twenty years or more in a rough country, at a rough game, and could be expected to be formidable, if he was around.

But probably he wasn't there. Probably he had sold the woman and left, sending a few Kiowas down the trail to take care of whoever came along. It would likely just be a matter of shooting down two or three renegade buffalo hunters who had been too lazy to find honest work once the herds petered out.

Augustus was undecided as to whether he would be better off by himself or with a country sheriff from Arkansas. All he knew about the sheriff was that Jake Spoon had run from him, which wasn't much to go on. The young man had had no experience with plains fighting and perhaps not much with any fighting. There was no telling if he could even take care of himself in a scrape. If he couldn't, he would be better left—but then, who would know until the fighting started?

"What happens to us if you two both get kilt?" Roscoe asked. It was a question that loomed large in his mind.

"Head back southeast as fast as you can," Augustus said. "Once you make it down below the Red River you'll probably be all right. If you go east a ways you ought to run into some herds."

"Why, we'll be back," July said. "I ought to go help Captain McCrae, but we'll be back."

Augustus didn't feel right about it, but he made no further effort to stop July Johnson. They let the horses rest for an hour, then put Augustus's saddle on Roscoe's big gelding, and left. When they rode up on the ridge above the river they saw again the little spark of light to the east, and made for it.

"If it ain't prying, what is this urgent business you're on?" Augustus asked.

July was hesitant about answering. Roscoe and Joe had both looked at him strangely as he left, and the look bothered him. It was as if both of them were his children—both looked to him for care. Only Janey seemed comfortable being left on the Canadian.

"Well, sir, it's my wife," July said. "She's gone from home. It might be that she got stolen too."

Augustus felt that was interesting. They were both chasing women across the plains. He said no more. A man whose wife had left was apt to be sore about it and touchy. He changed the subject at once.

"It was your brother Jake shot?" he asked.

"Yes," July said. "I guess it was accidental, but I've got to take him back. Only I'd like to find Elmira first."

They rode in silence for seven or eight miles over broken country. Augustus was thinking what a curious man Jake Spoon was, that he would let a woman be stolen and just go on playing cards, or whatever he was doing.

Every time they topped a ridge and saw the tiny flame of the campfire, July tried to calm himself, tried to remind himself that it would be almost a miracle if Elmira were there. Yet he couldn't help hoping. Sometimes he felt so bad about things that he didn't know if he could keep going much longer without knowing where she was.

Finally, with the camp not more than a mile away, Augustus drew rein. He dismounted to listen. In the still night, on the open plain, voices could carry a ways, and he might be able to get a sense of how many they were up against.

July dismounted, too, and waited for Augustus to tell him what the plan was. They were only a hundred yards from the river, and while they were listening they heard something splash through the water downstream from where they stood.

"It could be a buffalo," July whispered. "We seen a few."

"More likely a horse," Augustus said. "Buffalo wouldn't cross that close to camp."

He looked at the young man, worried by the nervousness in his voice. "Have you done much of this kind of thing, Mr. Johnson?" he asked.

"No," July admitted. "I ain't done none. About the worst we get in Arkansas are robbers."

"Let's walk our horses a little closer," Augustus said. "Don't let 'em whinny. If we can get within a hundred yards of their camp we're in good shape. Then I favor charging right into them. They'll hear us before they see us, which will scare them, and we'll be on them before they have time to think. Use your handgun and save your rifle—this'll be close-range work. If there's any left, we'll turn and make a second run at them."

"We mustn't trample the women," July said.

"We won't," Augustus said. "Have you ever killed?"

"No," July said. "I've never had to."

I wish you'd stayed with your party, Augustus thought, but he didn't say it.

57

DOG FACE WAS DYING, and he knew it. A bullet had hit a rib and turned downward into his gut. The bullet hadn't come out, and nobody was trying to get it out, either. He lay on a saddle blanket in his death sweat, and all Blue Duck wanted to know was how many men there had been in the party that shot him.

"Three horses," one of the Kiowas said, but Dog Face couldn't remember if it had been two or three.

"It was gettin' dark," he said. One whole side of his body was wet with blood. He wanted to see the girl, but Blue Duck squatted by his side, blocking his view.

"You never hit McCrae?" he asked.

"He forted up behind his horse," Dog Face said. "I might have put one in him. I don't know."

"We'll kill him tomorrow," Monkey John said. "He ain't got no horse and maybe he's crippled."

"I doubt it," Blue Duck said. "I expect tomorrow he'll walk in and finish the rest of you, unless he does it tonight."

"I hurt bad," Dog Face said. "Go on and shoot me."

Blue Duck laughed. "You won't catch me wasting a bullet on you," he said. "Monkey can cut your damn throat if he wants to."

But Monkey wouldn't come near him. Monkey John was worried, and so were the Kiowas. They all kept cocking and uncocking their pistols. They asked for whiskey, but Blue Duck wouldn't give them any.

Dog Face looked at the girl. She sat with her arms wrapped around her knees. Blue Duck went and saddled his horse. When he came back to the fire he kicked the girl. He kicked her several times, until she fell over and lay curled up.

"What'd she do?" Dog Face asked.

Blue Duck walked over and kicked him in the side, causing him to scream with pain and roll off the blanket.

"Mind your own goddamn business," Blue Duck said.

"You gonna leave?" Monkey John asked nervously.

"That's right," Blue Duck said. "I aim to look for a better crew. The whole bunch of you couldn't kill one man. You never even attacked that second bunch. It was probably just a cowboy or two."

Dog Face tried to roll back on his blanket, but his strength was gone. The Kiowas had already taken his gun and divided his ammunition among themselves, so he couldn't even shoot himself. He had a razor in his pack and might have managed to cut his own throat, but his pack was on the other side of the fire and he knew he would never be able to crawl to it.

Blue Duck kicked Lorena twice more. "You ain't worth selling," Blue Duck said. "The Kiowas can have you."

"What about me?" Monkey John asked. "What about my half interest?"

"I won back your half interest," Blue Duck said. "I won the Kiowas' half too."

"Then how come you're giving her to the goddamn Kiowas?" Monkey John said. "Give her to me."

"No, I want them to carve her up," Blue Duck said. "It might put some spirit in them, so they can go out tomorrow and run that old Ranger to ground."

"Hell, I'm as mean as they are," Monkey John said. "I can finish him, if he comes around here."

Blue Duck mounted. "You ain't half as mean as they are," he said. "And if McCrae comes around here you better step quick or you'll be plugged. He got Ermoke, and Ermoke was three times the fighter you are."

He opened his pack, took out a bottle of whiskey and pitched it to the Indians. Then he said something to them in their language and rode away toward the river.

Lorena lay where she had fallen, listening to Dog Face moan. With each breath he let out a throaty moan. His wound had bloody bubbles on it. Lorena got up on her hands and knees and vomited from fear. The Kiowas were all looking at her as they drank. She wanted to run but felt too weak. Anyway, they would soon catch her if she ran. She crawled away from the vomit and sank back, too tired and scared to move. Monkey John sat back from the fire, clutching his rifle. He didn't even look at her—he wouldn't help her. She was just in for it.

"Help her, Monkey," Dog Face said weakly.

"Hell, I can't help her," Monkey John said. "You heard him. He gave her to them."

One of the Kiowas understood the talk and was angered. He pulled his knife and stood over Dog Face threateningly. Dog Face continued to moan. Then the Kiowa sat on his chest and Dog Face screamed, a weak scream. The rest of the Indians jumped for him. He was too weak even to lift a hand. One Kiowa cut his belt and two more pulled his pants off. Before Lorena could even turn her head, they castrated him. Another slashed a knife across his forehead and began to rip off his hair. Dog Face screamed again, but it was soon muffled as the Kiowas held his head and stuffed his own bloody organs into his mouth, shoving them down his throat with the handle of a knife. His hair was soon ripped off and the Kiowa took the scalp and tied it to his lance. Dog Face struggled for breath, a pool of blood beneath his legs. Yet he wasn't dead. Lorena had her face in her arms, but she could still hear him moan and gurgle for breath. She wished he would die—it shouldn't take so long just to die.

She expected any minute they would fall on her, but they didn't. What they had done to Dog Face put them in a good mood, and they passed around the whiskey bottle.

Monkey John was probably as scared as she was. He sat silently by the fire, his rifle in his hands, pulling at his dirty beard. Once in a while the Kiowas would jabber at him in their own language, but he didn't answer.

Lying with her face almost on the ground, she was the first to hear the horses—only she didn't really know what it was, or take any hope from it. It was something running—maybe Blue Duck was coming back to reclaim her.

The Kiowas, singing and drinking, two with bloody knives still in their hands, didn't hear the running, but Monkey John suddenly heard it. He jumped to his feet and raised his rifle, but before he could fire she heard a gun go off in the darkness and Monkey John dropped the rifle and slumped to a sitting position, his mouth open as if he were about to say something.

Lorena saw that, and just as she saw it the two horses raced right over Monkey John without touching him and were into the Kiowas. One Kiowa screamed, a sound more hopeless and frightening even than the scream of Dog Face. Before she thought about it being Gus, she saw him yank his horse almost down right in the middle of the Kiowas. He shot the one that screamed and then the two that held the knives, shooting from his horse right into their chests. Another Kiowa grabbed the lance with Dog Face's scalp on it, but Gus shot him before he could lift it. He shot another just as the man was picking up his rifle. The last Kiowa fled into the darkness, and Gus turned his horse after him. "Finish any that ain't finished," he said to the other man. But that man had barely dismounted before there was a shot in the darkness. He stood by his horse listening. There was another shot, and then the sound of a horse loping back. Lorena thought it was over but Monkey John shot with his pistol at the man standing by the fire. He missed completely and the man slowly raised his own pistol, but before he could fire Gus rode back into the firelight and shot with his rifle, knocking Monkey John back into the pack.

Then Gus turned her over and was holding her in his arms, his rifle still in one hand.

"Where's Blue Duck, Lorie?" he asked. "Was he here tonight?"

Lorena had a hard struggle to get her mind back to Blue Duck. She had stopped talking, and though she wanted to talk, the words wouldn't come. She stared at Gus and began to cry but she couldn't get out an answer to the question.

"Was he here tonight?" Gus asked again. "Just answer that and I won't bother you no more until you feel better."

Lorena nodded. Blue Duck had been there. It was all she could do.

Gus stood up. "Go back to your party," Gus said to the other man. "Go now."

"I didn't shoot a one," the other man said. "You shot the whole bunch."

"It ain't important," Augustus said. "I can't leave this girl and she ain't in shape to travel fast. Go back to your party. If Lorie can ride we'll come when we can."

"Did you kill the one that ran off?" July asked.

"Yes," Augustus said. "A man can't outrun a horse. You get along. There's a dangerous man loose along this river and I doubt that deputy of yours can handle him."

What if I can't, either? July thought, looking down at Dog Face. He had managed to pull his genitals out of his mouth, and still lay breathing. Looking at the pool of blood he lay in, July felt his stomach start to come up. He turned away to keep from vomiting.

"I'll tidy up these dead," Augustus said. "I know this is a shock to you, Mr. Johnson. It's different from a barroom scrape in Arkansas. But you got to choke it down and get back to your people."

"Are you going to kill him?" July asked, referring to Dog Face.

"Yes, if he don't travel soon," Augustus said.

Before July was over the second ridge, he heard the gun again.

58

"RECKON WE'LL HEAR IT when they fight?" Joe asked.

"We won't hear it much," Roscoe said. "That campfire was way off. Anyway, maybe it's just cowboys and there won't be no fight."

"But we saw Indians," Joe said. "I bet it's them."

"It might be them," Roscoe admitted. "But maybe they just kept running."

"I hope they didn't run this direction," Joe said. He hated to admit how scared he was, but he was a good deal more scared than he could remember being before in his life. Usually when they camped he was so glad to be stopped he just unrolled his blanket and went to sleep, but though he unrolled his blanket as usual, he didn't go to sleep. It was the first time he had been separated from July on the whole trip, and he was surprised at how much scarier it felt. They had been forbidden to build a fire, so all they could do was sit in the dark. Of course it wasn't cold, but a fire would have made things more cheerful.

"I guess July will kill 'em," he said several times.

"That Texas Ranger done killed six," Roscoe said. "Maybe he'll kill 'em and July can save his ammunition."

Joe held his new rifle. Several times he cocked the hammer and then eased it back down. If the Indians came, he hoped they'd wait for daylight, so he'd have a better chance for a shot.

Janey sat off by herself. She had seen the Indians first and had run back to tell July. Roscoe hadn't believed her at first, but July had. He had got off several shots once the Indians started firing.

Roscoe felt bothered by the fact that there were no more trees. All his life he had lived amid trees and had given little thought to what a comfort they were.

Trees had been so common that it was a shock to ride out on the plains and discover that there was a part of earth where there weren't any. Occasionally they might see a few along the rivers, but not many, and those were more bushes than trees. You couldn't lean against them, which was a thing he liked to do. He had got so he could even sleep pretty well leaning against a tree.

But now July had left him on a river where there wasn't even a bush. He would have to sleep flat out on the ground or else sit up all night. The sky was pale with moonlight, but it didn't provide enough light to see well by. Soon Roscoe began to get very nervous. Everywhere he looked he began to see things that could have been Indians. He decided to cock his pistol, in case some of the things were Indians.

When he cocked his pistol, Joe cocked his rifle. "Did you see one?" he asked.

"It might have been one," Roscoe said.

"Where?" Janey asked.

When Roscoe pointed, she immediately went running off toward it. Roscoe could hardly believe his eyes—but she had always been a wild girl.

"It was just a bush," Janey said, when she came back.

"You better be glad of that," he said. "If it had been an Indian you'd have got scalped."

"Reckon they've had the fight yet?" Joe asked. "I'll be glad when they get back."

"It might be morning before they get back," Roscoe said. "We better just rest. The minute July gets back he'll wanta go on looking for your mother."

"I guess she's found Dee," Joe said. "She likes Dee."

"Then how come she married July, dern it?" Roscoe asked. "It was the start of all this, you know. We'd be back in Arkansas playing dominoes if she hadn't married July."

Every time Roscoe tried to think back along the line of events that had led to his being in a place where there was no trees to lean against, he strayed off the line and soon got all tangled up in his thinking. It was probably better not to try and think back down the line of life.

"I can't get to sleep for nothin'," Joe said.

Roscoe was glad he hadn't had to go with the other men. He remembered how weak he had felt that afternoon when he realized it was bullets that were hitting in the grass around him. It had sounded like bees sounded in the leaves, but of course it was bullets.

While he was thinking about it he nodded for a few minutes—it seemed like a few minutes—asleep with his gun cocked. He had a little dream about the wild pigs, not too frightening. The pigs were not as wild as they had been in real life. They were just rooting around a cabin and not trying to harm him, yet he woke in a terrible fright and saw something incomprehensible. Janey was standing a few feet in front of him, with a big rock raised over her head. She was holding it with both hands—why would she do such a thing at that time of night? She wasn't making a sound; she just stood in front of him holding the rock. It was not until she flung it that he realized someone else was there. But someone was: someone big. In his surprise, Roscoe forgot he had a pistol. He quickly stood up. He didn't see where the rock went, but Janey suddenly dropped to her knees. She looked around at him. "Shoot at him," she said. Roscoe remembered the pistol, which was cocked, but before he could raise it, the big shadow that Janey had thrown the rock at slid close to him and shoved him—not a hard shove, but it made him drop the pistol. He knew he was awake and not dreaming, but he didn't have any more strength than he would have had in a dream in terms of moving quick. He saw the big shadow standing by him but he had felt no fear, and the shadow didn't shove him again. Roscoe felt warm and sleepy and sat back down. It was like he was in a warm bath. He hadn't had too many warm baths in his life, but he felt like he was in one and was ready for a long snooze. Janey was crawling, though—crawling right over his legs. "Now what are you doing?" he said, before he saw that her eyes were fixed on the pistol he had dropped. She wanted the pistol, and for some reason crawled right over his legs to get to it. But before she got to it the shadow came back. "Why, you're a fighter, ain't you?" the shadow man said. "If I wasn't in such a hurry I'd show you a trick or two." Then he raised his arms and struck down at her; Roscoe couldn't see if it was with an ax or what, but the sound was like an ax striking wood, and Janey stopped moving and lay across his legs. "Joe?" Roscoe said; he had just remembered that he had made Joe stop cocking and uncocking his rifle so he could get to sleep.

"Was that his name?" the shadow man said. Roscoe knew it must be a man, for he had a heavy voice. But he couldn't see the man's face. He just seemed to be a big shadow, and anyway Roscoe couldn't get his mind fixed on it, or on where Joe was or when July would be back, or on anything much, he felt so warm and tired. The big shadow stood astraddle of him and reached down for his belt but Roscoe had let go all concern, he felt so tired. He felt everything would have to stop for a while; it was as if the darkness itself was pushing his eyelids down. Then the warm sleep took him.

July found them an hour later, already stiff in death. He had raced as fast as he could over the rough country, not wanting to take the time to follow the river itself but too unsure of his position to go very far from it. From time to time he stopped, listening for shots, but the dark plains were quiet and peaceful, though it was on them that he had just seen the most violent and terrible things he had ever witnessed in his life. The only sound he heard was the wind singing over the empty miles of grass; in the spring night the wind sang gently.

July had never felt so inadequate. He was not even sure he could find his way back to where they had left the others. He was a sheriff, paid to fight when necessary, but nothing in his experience had prepared him for the slaughter he had just witnessed. Captain McCrae had killed six men, whereas he had not even fired his gun when the old bandit was aiming at him. It had all seemed so rapid, all those deaths in a minute or two. Captain McCrae had not seemed disturbed, whereas he felt such confusion he could scarcely think. He had met rough men in Arkansas and backed several of them down and arrested them, but this was different: the dying buffalo hunter had had nothing but a patch of blood between his legs. Death and worse happened on the plains.

When he saw the canyon where he had left his party he stopped to listen but heard nothing. It made him fearful, for Joe's horse would always whinny at his. But this time there was no whinny and he saw no horses. He dismounted and walked slowly down the canyon. Maybe they had forgotten to hobble the horses and they had grazed away. Roscoe was forgetful in such matters.

"Roscoe?" he said, when he came in sight of the camp.

He could see the three forms on the ground as if asleep, but he knew they weren't asleep because Janey lay across Roscoe's legs.

The only sound in the camp was the sound of flies buzzing on blood.

July didn't want to see it. He knew he had to, but he didn't want to.

He felt a terrible need to turn things back, all the way back to the time when he and Roscoe and Joe and Elmira had all been in Arkansas. He knew it could never be. Something had happened which he would never be free of. He had even lost the chance to stay and die with his people, though Captain McCrae had offered him that chance. "I'd feel better in my mind if you'd stay with your party," he had said.

He had not stayed, but when he had gone, he hadn't fought, either. He had done nothing but ride twice over the same stretch of prairie, while death had come to both camps. He had no doubt that if he had stayed with Roscoe and the children, it would have come to him too. The man who had killed them must be a fighter on the order of Captain McCrae.

For a time, July did not go into the camp. He couldn't. He stood and listened to the flies buzz over them. He didn't want to see what had been done to them. Now, when he did find Elmira, it would only be to tell her that her son was dead. And if he lived to return to Fort Smith it would be without Roscoe Brown, a loyal man who had never asked for much.

The strange girl who could catch rabbits would catch no more rabbits.

After a time, July took his knife and began to dig graves. He climbed out of the canyon and dug them on the plain. Digging with a knife was slow work, but it was the only digging tool he had. The loose dirt he threw out with his hands. He was still digging at sunup, yet the graves were pitifully shallow affairs. He would have to do better than that, or the coyotes would get the corpses. Once in a while he looked down at the bodies. Joe lay apart from the other two, sprawled on his blanket as if asleep.

July began to gather rocks to pile on the graves. There were plenty along the canyon, though some had to be pried out of the dirt. While he was carrying one, he saw two riders far across the plain, black dots in the bright sunlight. His horse whinnied, eager for company.

When Augustus rode up with Lorena, the Arkansas sheriff was still digging. Augustus rode over to the canyon edge and looked down.

"More dead to tidy up," he said, dismounting. He had given Lorena Roscoe's horse, which had an easy gait, and was riding on the best of the Indian ponies, a skinny paint.

"It's my fault," July said. "If I'd done what you said, maybe they'd be alive."

"And maybe you'd be dead and I'd have had to tidy you up," Augustus said. "Don't be reviling yourself. None of us is such fine judges of what to do."

"You told me to stay," July said.

"I know I did, son," Augustus said. "I'm sure you wish you had. But yesterday's gone on down the river and you can't get it back. Go on with your digging and I'll tidy up."

He turned to Lorena and helped her down. "You stay here, darling," he said.

But when he started down the canyon, Lorena followed him. She didn't want Gus to be far away.

"No, I don't want you to go down there and see this mess," Augustus said. "Sit right here, where you can watch me. I won't be out of sight."

He turned to July. "Sit with her," he said. "She don't have much to say right now. Just sit with her, Mr. Johnson."

July stopped his work. The woman didn't look at him. Her sad eyes were fixed on Captain McCrae as he made his way down the canyon. Her legs were black and blue and there was a yellowing bruise on one cheek. She didn't turn her head or look at him at all.

"My name is July Johnson," he said, to be polite, but the woman didn't appear to hear.

Augustus went quickly to the camp and tied each body in a blanket. Blue Duck had been so confident of his victims that he hadn't even bothered to shoot. The deputy and the girl had been knifed, ripped open from navel to breastbone. Evidently it hadn't been enough for the girl, because her head had been smashed in too. So had the boy's, probably with the butt of the rifle Gus had given him. The deputy had been castrated as well. Using saddle strings, Gus tied the blankets as tightly around them as he could. It was strange that three such people had been on the Canadian, but then, that was the frontier—people were always wandering where they had no business being. He himself had done it and got away with it—had been a Ranger in Texas rather than a lawyer in Tennessee. The three torn specimens he was tying into their shrouds had not been so lucky.

He carried the bodies up to the prairie, laid them in their shallow graves and helped July pile rocks on the graves, a pitiful expedient that wouldn't deter the varmints for long. In the other camp he had merely laid the buffalo hunters and the dead Kiowas in a line and left them.

"I guess he took Joe's horse," July said.

"Yes, and his life," Augustus said. "I'm sure he had more interest in the horse."

"If you're going after him I'd like to try and help," July said.

"I got nothing to go after him on," Augustus said. "He's better mounted than us, and this ain't no place to go chasing a man who's got you out-horsed. He's headed for the Purgatory this time, I bet."

"The what?" July asked.

"It's a river up in Colorado," Augustus said. "He's probably got another gang there. We best let him go this time."

"I hate to," July said. He had begun to imagine confronting the man and shooting him down.

"Son, this is a sad thing," Augustus said. "Loss of life always is. But the life is lost for good. Don't you go attempting vengeance. You've got more urgent business. If I ever run into Blue Duck I'll kill him. But if I don't, somebody else will. He's big and mean, but sooner or later he'll meet somebody bigger and meaner. Or a snake will bite him or a horse will fall on him, or he'll get hung, or one of his renegades will shoot him in the back. Or he'll just get old and die."

He went over and tightened the girth on his saddle.

"Don't be trying to give back pain for pain," he said. "You can't get even measures in business like this. You best go find your wife."

July looked across the river at the unending prairie. If I find her she'll hate me worse now, he thought.

Augustus watched him mount, thinking how young he looked. He couldn't be much over twenty. But he was old enough to have found a wife and lost her—not that it took long to lose one, necessarily.

"Where is this Adobe Walls place?" July asked.

"It ain't far down the river," Augustus said, "but I'd pass by it if I were you. Your wife ain't there. If she went up the Arkansas I'd imagine she's up in Kansas, in one of the towns."

"I would hate to miss her," July said.

If she's at Adobe Walls, you'd do better to miss her, Augustus thought, but he didn't say it. He shook hands with the young sheriff and watched him mount and ride across the river. Soon he dipped out of sight, in the rough breaks to the north. When he reappeared on the vast plain, he was only a tiny speck.

Augustus went to Lorena. He had spent most of the night simply holding her in his arms, hoping that body heat would finally help her stop trembling and shaking. She had not said a word so far, but she would look him in the face, which was a good sign. He had seen women captives too broken even to raise their eyes.

"Come on, Lorie," he said. "Let's take a little ride."

She stood up obediently, like a child.

"We'll just ride over east a ways and see if we can find us some shade," Augustus said. "Then we'll loll around for a couple of weeks and let Call and the boys catch up with us. They'll be coming with the cattle pretty soon. By then I expect you'll be feeling better."

Lorena didn't answer, but she mounted without help and rode beside him all day.

59

CALL EXPECTED GUS to be back in a day or two. Maybe he'd have the girl and maybe he wouldn't, but it was not likely he'd be gone long. Gus was a hard traveler and usually overtook whoever he was after promptly, arrested them or dispatched them, and got back.

For a day or two he didn't give Gus's absence much thought. He was irritated with Jake Spoon for having been so troublesome and undependable, but then, he partly had himself to blame for that. He should have set Jake straight before they left Lonesome Dove—informed him in no uncertain terms that the girl wasn't coming.

When the third day passed and Gus wasn't back, Call began to be uneasy. Augustus had survived so much that Call didn't give his safety much thought. Even men accustomed all their lives to sudden death didn't expect it to happen to Gus McCrae. The rest of them might fall by the wayside, their mortality taking gentle or cruel forms, but Gus would just go on talking.

Yet five days passed, and then a week, and he didn't return. The herd crossed the Brazos without incident, and then the Trinity, and there was still no Gus.

They camped west of Fort Worth and Call allowed the men to go into town. It would be the last town they would see until they hit Ogallala, and it might be that some of them wouldn't live to hit Ogallala. He let them go carouse, keeping just the boys, to help him hold the herd. Dish Boggett volunteered to stay, too—he still had his thoughts on Lorena and was not about to leave camp while there was a chance that Gus would bring her back.

"Dern, he's behaving like a deacon," Soupy said. "I expect to hear him preach a sermon any day."

Needle Nelson took a more charitable view. "He's just in love," he said. "He don't want to go trashing around with us."

"By God, he'll wish he had before we hit Nebraska," Jasper Fant said. "You don't see me waiting. I'd like to drink a couple of more bottles of good whiskey before I have to cross any more of them cold rivers. They got real cold rivers up north, I hear. Some of them even got ice in them, I guess."

"If I was to see a chunk of ice in a river, I'd rope it and we could use it to water our drinks," Bert Borum said.

Bert was inordinately proud of his skill with a rope, the men thought. He was indeed quick and accurate, but the men were tired of hearing him brag on himself and were constantly on the lookout for things he could rope that might cause him to miss. Once Bert had silenced them for a whole day by roping a coyote on the first throw, but they were not the sort of men to keep silent long.

"Go rope that dern bull, if you're so good at roping," Needle Nelson said, referring to the Texas bull. The bull seemed to resent it when the cowboys sat in groups—he would position himself fifty yards away and paw the earth and bellow. Needle was in favor of shooting him but Call wouldn't allow it.

"I can rope the son of a bitch fast enough," Bert said. "Getting the rope off would be the problem."

"Getting you buried would be the problem if you was to rope that bull," Dish said. The fact that he chose to restrain himself and not get drunk in Fort Worth increased his sense of superiority somewhat, and many of the crew had had about all of Dish's sense of superiority as they could take, particularly since he was restraining himself for love of a young woman who clearly didn't give a hoot about him.

"If you're so in love, why didn't you go bring her back and leave Gus here?" Jasper asked. "Gus is a damn sight more entertaining than you are, Dish."

At that Dish turned and jumped him but Call soon broke it up. "If you want to fight, collect your wages first," he said.

The Rainey boys were feeling grownup and wanted Newt to talk the Captain into letting them go to town. "I wanta try a whore," Ben Rainey said.

Newt declined to make the request.

"Just ask him," Ben said.

"I'll ask him when we get to Nebraska," Newt said.

"Yeah, and if I drown in the Red River I won't ever get to try no whore," Ben said.

Call began to be very worried about Gus. It was unusual for him to be gone so long with only one man to chase. Of course, Blue Duck might have had a gang waiting, and Gus might have ridden into an ambush. He had not done any serious fighting in years. Even Pea Eye had begun to worry about him.

"Here we are all the way to Fort Worth and Gus still ain't back," Pea Eye said.

Po Campo didn't go to Fort Worth either. He sat with his back to one of the wheels of the wagon, whittling one of the little female figures he liked to carve. As he walked along during the day he kept his eye out for promising chunks of wood and, if he saw one, would pitch it in the wagon. Then at night he whittled. He would start with a fairly big chunk, and after a week or so would have it whittled into a little wooden woman about two inches high.

"I hope he comes back," Po Campo said. "I enjoy his acquaintance, although he doesn't like my cooking."

"Well, we wasn't used to eating bugs and such when you first came," Pea Eye said. "I expect he'll work up a taste for it when he comes back. It never used to take him so long to catch a bandit."

"He won't catch Blue Duck," Po Campo said.

"Why, do you know the man?" Call asked, surprised.

"I know him," Po Campo said. "There is no worse man. Only the devil is worse and the devil won't bother us on this trip."

That was surprising talk. Call looked at the old man closely, but Po Campo was just sitting by the wagon wheel, wood shavings all over his short legs. He noticed Call's look and smiled.

"I lived on the *llano* once," he said. "I wanted to raise sheep but I was foolish. The wolves killed them and the Comanches killed them and the weather killed them. Then Blue Duck killed my three sons. After that I left the *llano*."

"Why don't you think Gus will catch him?" Call asked.

Po Campo considered the question. Deets was sitting near him. He loved to watch the old man whittle. It seemed miraculous to Deets that Po could take a plain chunk of wood and make it into a little woman figure. He watched to see if he could figure out how it happened, but so far he had not been able to. Po Campo kept turning the wood in his hand, the shavings dropping in his lap, and then finally it would be done.

"I didn't like the horse Captain Gus took," Po Campo said. "He won't catch Blue Duck on that horse. Blue Duck always has the best horse in the country—that's why he always gets away."

"He don't have the best horse in this country," Call said. "I do."

"Yes, that's true, she is a fine mare," Po said. "You might catch up with him but Captain Gus won't. Blue Duck will sell the woman. Captain Gus might get her back if the Indians don't finish him. I wouldn't make a bet."

"I'd make one, if I had money," Deets said. "Mister Gus be fine."

"I didn't think there was much left in the way of Indians," Call said.

"There are young renegades," Po said. "Blue Duck always finds them. Some are left. The *llano* is a big place."

That was certainly true. Call remembered the few times they had ventured on it. After a day or two the men would grow anxious because of the emptiness. "There's too much of this nothing," Pea said. He would say it two or three times a day, like a refrain, as the mirages shimmered in the endless distances. Even a man with a good sense of direction could get lost with so few surface features to guide him. Water was always chancy.

"I miss Gus," Pea Eye said. "I get to expecting to hear him talk and he ain't here. My ears sort of get empty."

Call had to admit that he missed him too, and that he was worried. He had had at least one disagreement a day with Gus for as many years as he could remember. Gus never answered any question directly, but it was possible to test an opinion against him, if you went about it right. More and more Call felt his absence, though fortunately they were having uneventful times—the cattle were fairly well trail-broken and weren't giving any trouble. The crew for the most part had been well behaved, no more irritable or contrary than any other group of men. The weather had been ideal, water plentiful, and the spring grass excellent for grazing.

A thought that nagged Call was that he had let Gus go off alone to do a job that was too big for him—a job they ought to have done together. Often, during the day, as he rode ahead of the herd, he would look to the northwest, hoping to see Gus returning. More and more the thought came to him that Gus was probably dead. Men simply vanished into the *llano* to die somewhere and lie without graves, their bones eventually scattered by varmints. Of course, Gus was a famous man, in his way. If Blue Duck had killed him he might brag, and word would eventually get back. But what if some young renegade who didn't know he was famous killed him? Then he would simply be gone.

The thought that Gus was dead began to weigh on Call. It came to him several times a day, at moments, and made him feel empty and strange. They had not had much of a talk before Gus left. Nothing much had been said. He began to wish that somehow things could have been rounded off a little better. Of course he knew death was no respecter. People just dropped when they dropped, whether they had rounded things off or not. Still, it haunted him that Gus had just ridden off and might not ride back. He would look over the cattle herd strung out across the prairie and feel it was all worthless, and a little absurd. Some days he almost felt like turning the cattle loose and paying off the crew. He could take Pea and Deets and maybe the boy, and they would look for Gus until they found him.

The crew came back from Fort Worth hung over and subdued. Jasper Fant's head was splitting to such an extent that he couldn't bear to ride—he got off his horse and walked the last two miles, stopping from time to time to vomit. He tried to get the other boys to wait on him—in his state he could have been easily robbed and beaten, as he pointed out—but his companions were indifferent to his fate. Their own headaches were severe enough.

"You can walk to China for all I care," Needle said, expressing the sentiments of the group. They rode on and left Jasper to creep along as best he could.

Po Campo had anticipated their condition and had a surprise waiting for them—a sugary cobbler made with dewberries he had picked.

"Sugar is the thing for getting over liquor," he said. "Eat a lot and then lie down for a few minutes."

"Did Jasper quit?" Call asked.

"No, he's enjoying the dry heaves somewhere between here and town," Soupy Jones allowed. "Last I heard of him he sounded like he was about to vomit up his socks."

"What's the news of Jake?" Call inquired.

The question produced a remarkable collection of black looks.

"He's a haughty son of a bitch," Bert Borum said. "He acted like he never knowed a one of us."

"He tolt me I smelled like cowshit," Needle said. "He was sitting there gambling and had some whore hanging over him."

"I wouldn't say he misses that one that got took," Soupy said.

Jasper Fant finally straggled in. Everyone was standing around grinning, though he couldn't see why.

"Something must have happened funnier than what I been doing," he said.

"A lot of things are funnier than vomiting," Pea Eye said.

"Jasper missed the cobbler, that's the laugh," Allen O'Brien said, not feeling too frisky himself. "I used to be better at hangovers, back in Ireland. Of course, then I had one every day," he reflected. "I had more practice."

When Jasper realized he had missed a dewberry cobbler, one of his favorite dishes, he threatened to quit the outfit, since they were so ungrateful. But he was too weak to carry out his threat. Po Campo forced him to eat a big spoonful of molasses as a headache cure, while the rest of the crew got the herd on the move.

"I guess the next excitement will be the old Red River," Dish Boggett said, as he took the point.

60

JUST AS THE WORLD had been drying out nicely and the drive becoming enjoyable, in Newt's view, it suddenly got very wet again. Two days before they hit the Red River low black clouds boiled out of the northwest like smoke off grease. It was springlike and fair in the morning, but before it was even afternoon the world turned to water.

It rained so hard for two hours that it was difficult even to see the cattle. Newt moped along on Mouse, feeling chilled and depressed. By this time, they were on a rolling plain bare of trees. There was nothing to get under except the sky. They made a wet camp and Po Campo poured hot coffee down them by the gallon, but it still promised to be a miserable night. Po and Deets, the acknowledged experts on weather, discussed the situation and admitted they didn't know when it might stop raining.

"It probably won't rain a week," Po Campo said, which cheered nobody up.

"Dern, it better not rain no week," Jasper said. "Them rivers will be like oceans."

That night they all herded, not because the cattle were particularly restless but because it was drier on a horse than on the sopping ground. Newt began to think it had been a mistake to leave Lonesome Dove if it was going to be so wet. He remembered how dry and clear the days had been there. He and Mouse stumbled through the night somehow, though before morning he was so tired he had lost all interest in living.

The next day was no better. The skies were like iron, and Mr. Gus wasn't back. He had been gone a long time, it seemed, and so had Lorena. Dish Boggett grew increasingly worried and took to confiding in Newt now and then. Newt respected his feelings, whereas the other hands were distinctly callous when it came to Dish's feelings.

"Because of Jake we lost 'em both, I guess," Dish said. "Jake is a goddamn bastard."

It was painful to Newt to have to think of Jake that way. He still remembered how Jake had played with him when he was a little child, and that Jake had made his mother get a lively, merry look in her eyes. All the years Jake had been gone, Newt had remembered him fondly and supposed that if he ever did come back he would be a hero. But it had to be admitted that Jake's behavior since his return had not been heroic at all. It bordered on the cowardly, particularly his casual return to card playing once Lorena had been stolen.

"If she's alive and Gus gets her back, I still aim to marry her," Dish said, as rain poured off his hat in streams.

"Dern, we should be herding fish," he said, a little later, holding the point nonetheless, though he hardly felt like it. If Lorena was indeed dead, he meant to stay clear of other women and grieve for her for a lifetime.

It was still raining when they came to the low banks of the Red River. The river was up somewhat, but it was still not a very wide channel or a very deep one. What worried Call was the approach to it—over a hundred yards of wet, rusty-colored sand. The Red was famous for its quicksands.

Deets sat with him, looking at the river thoughtfully. It had long represented the northern boundary of their activity. The land beyond the rusty sands was new to them.

"Do you think we ought to wait and let it go down?" Call asked.

"It ain't going down," Deets pointed out. "Still raining."

Dish came over to watch as Deets probed for a crossing, several times checking his horse and moving to the side to seek firmer footing.

"I guess this will spoil Jasper's digestion," he said, for Jasper's sensitivity on the subject of rivers was becoming more pronounced. "We bogged sixty head of Mr. Pierce's cattle in this very river, although that was over toward Arkansas. I must have had a hundred pounds of mud on my clothes before we got them out."

Deets put his horse into the surging water and was soon across the channel, but had to pick his way across another long expanse of sand before he was safely on the north bank. Evidently he didn't like the crossing, because he waved the others back with his hat and loped away downriver. He was soon out of sight in the rain, but came back in an hour with news of a far better crossing downstream. By then the whole crew was nervous, for the Red was legendary for drowning cowboys, and the fact that they had nothing to do but sit and drip increased general anxiety.

But their fears were unfounded. The rain slowed and the sun broke through as they were easing the cattle across the mud flats toward the brownish water. Deets had found a gravel bar that made the entrance to the river almost as good as a road. Old Dog led the herd right in and was soon across and grazing on the long wet grass of the Oklahoma Territory. Five or six of the weaker cows bogged as they were coming out, but they were soon extracted. Dish and Soupy took off their clothes and waded into the mud and got ropes on the cows, and Bert Borum pulled them out.

The sight of the sun put the men in high spirits. Hadn't they crossed the Red River and lived to tell about it? That night the Irishman sang for hours, and a few of the cowboys joined in—they had gradually learned a few of the Irish songs.

Sometimes Po Campo sang in Spanish. He had a low, throaty voice that always seemed like it was about to die for lack of breath. The songs bothered some of the men, they were so sad.

"Po, you're a jolly fellow, how come you only sing about death?" Soupy asked. Po had a little rattle, made from a gourd, and he shook it when he sang. The rattle, plus his low throaty voice, made a curious effect.

The sound could make the hairs stand upon Pea Eye's neck. "That's right, Po. You do sing sad, for a happy man," Pea Eye observed once, as the old man shook his gourd.

"I don't sing about myself," Campo said. "I sing about life. I am happy, but life is sad. The songs don't belong to me."

"Well, you sing them, who do they belong to?" Pea asked.

"They belong to those who hear them," Po said. He had given Deets one of the little women figures he whittled—Deets was very proud of it, and kept it in the pocket of his old chaps.

"Don't give none of them to me," Pea Eye said. "They're too sad. I'll get them nervous dreams."

"If you hear them, they belong to you," Po said. It was hard to see his eyes. They were deep-set anyway, and he seldom took his big-brimmed hat off.

"I wish we had a fiddle," Needle said. "If we had a fiddle, we could dance."

"Dance with who?" Bert asked. "I don't see no ladies."

"Dance with ourselves," Needle said.

But they didn't have a fiddle—just Po Campo shaking his rattle and the Irishman singing of girls.

Even on a nice clear night the sad singing and the knowledge that there were no ladies was enough to make the men feel low. They ended up talking of their sisters, those that had them, most nights.

Call heard little of the talk or the singing, for he continued to make his camp apart. He thought it best. If the herd ran, he would be in a better position to head it.

Gus's absence depressed him. It could only mean that something had gone wrong, and they might never find out what.

One night, cleaning his rifle, he was startled by the sound of his own voice. He had never been one to talk to himself, but as he cleaned the gun, he had been having, in his head, the conversation with Gus that there had not been time to have before Gus left. "I wish you'd killed the man when you had a chance," he said. "I wish you'd never encouraged Jake to bring that girl."

The words had just popped out. He was doubly glad he was alone, for if the men had heard him they would have thought him daft.

But no one heard him except the Hell Bitch, who grazed at the end of a long rope. Every night he slipped one end of the rope beneath his belt and then looped it around his wrist, so there would be no chance of her taking fright and suddenly jerking loose from him. Call had become so sensitive to her movements that if she even raised her head to sniff the air he would wake up. Usually it was no more than a deer, or a passing wolf. But the mare noticed, and Call rested better, knowing she would watch.

61

AUGUSTUS FIGURED THAT two or three days' ride east would put them in the path of the herds, but on the second day the rains struck, making travel unpleasant. He cut Lorena a crude poncho out of a tarp he had picked up at the buffalo hunter's camp, but even so it was bad traveling. The rains were chill and it looked like they might last, so he decided to risk Adobe Walls—the old fort offered the only promise of shelter.

They got there to find the place entirely deserted and most of the buildings in ruins.

"Not enough buffalo," Augustus said. "It wasn't two years ago that they had that big fight here, and now look at it. It looks like it's been empty fifty years." The only signs of life were the rattlesnakes, of which there were plenty, and mice, which explained the snakes. A few owls competed with the snakes for the mice.

They found a room whose roof was more-or-less intact, and whose fireplace even worked once Augustus poked loose an owl's nest. He broke up the remains of an old wagon to make a fire.

"This weather'll slow Call up," Augustus said. "I expect they all think we're dead by now."

Lorena still had not spoken. She found her silence hard to give up—it seemed her best weapon against the things that could happen. Talk didn't help when things were worst—no one was listening. If the Kiowas had got to do what they would have liked to do, she could have screamed her voice out and no one would have heard.

Gus was perfectly patient with her silence. He didn't seem to mind it. He just went on talking as if they were having a conversation, talking of this and that. He didn't talk about what had happened to her but treated her as he always had in Lonesome Dove.

Though she didn't talk, she couldn't stand to have Gus out of her sight. At night she rolled in his blanket with him—it was only then that she felt warm. But if he stood up to do some errand she watched him, and if the errand took him outside she got up and went out too.

The second day the rains still poured. Gus poked around the fort to see if he could find anything useful and came across a large box of buttons.

"There was a woman here during that fight, I recollect," he said. "I guess she took off so fast she left her button box."

There were all sizes of buttons—it gave Augustus an idea. He had a pack of cards in his saddlebags, which he quickly produced. "Let's play a few hands," he said. "The buttons can be our money." He spread a blanket near the fireplace and sorted the buttons into piles according to size. There were some large horn buttons that must have been meant for coats.

"Them'll be our fifty-dollar gold pieces," he said. "These here will be tens and these little ones can be fives. This is a high-stakes game we're playing."

"Don't you cheat, Gus," Lorena said suddenly. "If you cheat I won't give you no pokes."

Augustus was so pleased to hear her talk that tears came into his eyes. "We're just playing for buttons, honey," he said.

For the first hand or two Lorena made mistakes—she had forgotten what the cards meant. But it quickly came back to her and she played avidly, even laughing once when she won a hand. But the playing soon tired her—it seemed anything tired her if she did it long. And she still trembled at the least thing.

When Gus saw that she was tiring he made a pallet for her by the fireplace and sat by her while she napped. Her bruises were healing. She was much thinner than she had been when Blue Duck took her away—her cheeks had hollowed. Outside, the rain pelted the long prairies. The roof had a leak in one corner and a little stream of water dripped down one wall.

They stayed in the Walls for two days, comfortably out of the wet. That first evening, by good luck, Augustus happened to see a deer grazing just outside the wagon yard. That night they had venison and Lorena ate with real appetite for the first time.

"Eat like that, and you'll soon be the most beautiful woman in Texas again," Augustus said.

Lorena said nothing. That night she woke up crying and shaking. Augustus held her and crooned to her as if she were a child. But she didn't go back to sleep. She lay on the pallet, her eyes wide open. An hour or two before dawn the rain stopped, and soon a bright sun shone above the wet prairie.

"I wish we could stay here," Lorena said, when she saw Gus making preparations to leave.

"We might not last long if we did," Augustus said. "Every mangy renegade that's left loose knows about this place. If a bunch of them showed up at once we'd be in trouble."

Lorena understood that, but she didn't want to go. Lying on the pallet and playing cards for buttons was fine, so long as it was just Gus who was there. She didn't want to see other men, for any reason at all. She didn't want them to see her. There was a strong feeling within her that she should stay hidden. She wanted Gus to hide her.

"I don't want them," she said, looking at Gus.

"You won't have to have 'em," Augustus said. "I'll see you're let be. But we can't stay here. Game's skimpy and there's no telling who'll come along."

Lorena began to cry when she got on her horse. She could no longer control her tears. They were apt to come at any time, though, like talk, they did no good. Things happened, no matter how hard you cried.

"Now, Lorie, don't you fret no more than you have to," Augustus said. "We'll get over to where the cowboys are and then we'll be fine. You'll get to San Francisco yet."

Lorena had almost forgotten what San Francisco was. Then she remembered: a place with boats, where it was cool. It was where Jake had promised to take her. Jake had gone out of her mind so completely, while she was confused, that it was strange to think of him. It was like thinking of someone who had died.

"Where is Jake?" she asked.

"I don't know," Augustus said. "He wanted to come with me but I didn't want to put up with the scamp."

They rode until the afternoon, keeping close to the Canadian, which was high from the rains. Toward evening they topped a ridge and saw a surprising sight: four great herds of cattle, spread as far as one could see across the plain.

"River's stopped 'em," Augustus said. "They're all waiting for it to go down."

The cowboys were still a mile or more away, but Lorena began to shake at the sight of them. They were just more men.

"They won't hurt you, honey," Augustus said. "Likely they'll be more scared of you than you are of them. Most of them's probably forgot what a woman looks like."

Lorena fell back into her silence. She had nowhere else to go.

As they approached the nearest herd, a man galloped out to meet them.

"My lord, it's the man from Yale college, the one who read that Latin on my sign," Augustus said. "I recognize the horse. It's that nice bay we stole back from old Pedro just before he died."

Lorena didn't look at the man.

Wilbarger was as surprised as Augustus. He had seen two riders and supposed they were scouts for yet another herd. "By God, McCrae, you're a surprise," he said. "I thought you was three weeks behind me, and here you are attacking from the west. How far back is your herd, or do you have one?"

"As you can see, I ain't brought a cow," Augustus said. "Call may still have a herd of them if he ain't lost them or just turned them loose."

"If he would do that he's a fool, and he didn't act like a fool," Wilbarger said. "He wouldn't trade me that mare."

He tipped his hat to Lorena. "I don't believe I've met the young lady," he said.

"This is Miss Lorena Wood," Augustus said. "She had the misfortune to be abducted. Now I've abducted her back. We're short of grub and would like to purchase some if you have any to spare."

Wilbarger glanced once more at Lorena, who sat with her head down.

"I am not such a scoundrel as to sell grub," he said. "You're welcome to come to camp and eat with my tough bunch, if you can stand them."

"I doubt we could," Augustus said quietly. "We're both shy."

"Oh, I see," Wilbarger said, glancing at Lorena again. "I'm damn glad you don't have a herd. You'd think there'd be room enough for everybody on these plains, but as you can see, the view is crowding up. I was going to try a crossing today but I've decided to wait for morning."

He was silent a moment, considering the problem of their shyness.

"We're about to eat," he said. "It's a free country, so my advice to you would be to make camp where you choose. I'll borrow a pot from our cook and bring you some grub once you get settled."

"I'm much obliged," Augustus said. "Noticed a tree in these parts?"

"No, sir," Wilbarger said. "If there was a tree in these parts I'd be sitting under it."

They made camp on the plain. Wilbarger was as good as his word. In an hour he returned with a small pack mule. Besides an ample pot of beefsteak and beans he brought a small tent.

"I scarcely use this tent," Wilbarger said, dropping it by their campfire. "You're welcome to borrow it. The young lady might like a little privacy."

"I guess it's your training in Latin that's given you such good manners," Augustus remarked. "The sky's unpredictable and we would enjoy a tent."

"I also brought a bottle," Wilbarger said. "I seem to remember you're a drinking man."

As soon as the tent was up, Lorena went in. Gus spread her a pallet and she sat where she could watch him through the open flap. The men sat outside and drank.

"Had an easy trip?" Augustus asked.

"No, sir," Wilbarger said. "My foreman died, south of Fort Worth. I have another herd somewhere ahead of me, but I can't leave to go check on it. I don't know that I'll ever see it again, although I may."

"What'd he die of?" Augustus asked. "It's a healthy climate down that way."

"He died of a horse falling over backwards on him," Wilbarger said. "He *would* test the broncs."

"Foolish," Augustus said. "A grown man ought to have sense enough to seek gentle horses."

"Many don't," Wilbarger pointed out. "That mare Captain Call wouldn't trade me didn't look that gentle, yet he's a grown man."

"Grown, but not what you'd call normal," Augustus said. "I put it down to lack of education. If he'd been trained in Latin he'd most likely have let you have that horse."

"Do you consider yourself normal, then?" Wilbarger asked.

"Certainly," Augustus said. "I never met a soul in this world as normal as me."

"And yet here you sit, far out on the naked plain, with a shy woman you had to rescue," Wilbarger pointed out. "How many skunks did you have to kill in order to rescue her?"

"A passel," Augustus said. "I got the peons but the *jefe* got away. A bandit named Blue Duck, whom I'd advise you to give a wide berth unless you're skilled in battle."

"You think he's around? I've heard of the scamp."

"No, I think he's headed for the Purgatory River," Augustus said. "But then, I underestimated him once, which is why the lady got abducted. I'm out of practice when it comes to figuring out bandits."

"She's a little peaked, that girl," Wilbarger said. "You ought to take her back to Fort Worth. There's not much in the way of accommodations or medical care north of here."

"We'll ease along," Augustus said. "Where shall I return this tent?"

"I have business in Denver, later in the year," Wilbarger said. "That's if I live, of course. Send it over to Denver, if you have a chance. I don't use the dern thing much, but I might next winter, if I'm still out where it's windy."

"I'm enjoying this whiskey," Augustus said. "A man is foolish to give up the stable pleasure of life just to follow a bunch of shitting cattle."

"You have a point, and it's a point I've often taxed myself with," Wilbarger said. "If you're such a normal boy then how come you done it?"

"Unfinished business in Ogallala, Nebraska," Augustus said. "I'd hate to grow old without finishing it."

"I see," Wilbarger said. "Another shy lady who must have got abducted."

They drank until the bottle was empty.

"If you had two, I wish you'd brought two," Augustus said. "I need to get back in practice drinking."

"Well, if we don't get across that goddamn river tomorrow, I'll see if I can rustle up another one," Wilbarger said, standing up. "I seldom get conversation like yours. I can't figure out if I like it or not, but I will admit it's conversation, which is more than can be had in my camp."

He mounted his horse and was about to ride away.

"I'll send the cook over with some breakfast," he said. "By the way, you didn't cross the path of a young sheriff from Arkansas, did you? He's up this way somewhere, and I've been worried about him."

"You must be referring to July Johnson," Augustus said. "We left him four days ago. He was headed on north."

"Well, he had a funny crew with him. I was just a little uneasy," Wilbarger said. "I found him a likable man, but inexperienced."

"He's got more experience now," Augustus said. "Blue Duck killed his crew."

"Killed all three of them?" Wilbarger asked, startled. "I even offered that young boy a job."

"He should have took it," Augustus said. "We buried them west of here."

"That Duck must be a hard son of a bitch," Wilbarger said.

He sat on his horse a moment, looking into the night. "I had a feeling young Johnson was inexperienced," he said, and trotted off.

The next morning Wilbarger's old cook came over with some breakfast. It was a fine morning, the sun up and the plains well dried out. Augustus stepped out of the tent, but Lorena was content to look through the flaps.

"This is like living in a hotel, Lorie," Augustus said. "We got people toting us meals as fast as we can eat them."

At that point the cook got careless and the little pack mule took a kick at him which barely missed.

"He's getting tired of making this trip," the cook said.

"Or it could just be the company he's tired of," Augustus suggested. "I'd buy him if he was for sale. I've always got along with mules."

"This mule ain't for sale," the cook said, looking the camp over. "I wisht all I had to do was live in a tent."

Without further ado, he turned and went back.

When he was gone, Lorena came out and sat in the bright sun. While they ate, Wilbarger's cowboys began to move the herd toward the river.

"That Wilbarger is a curious man," Augustus said. "He's blunt-spoken, but I guess he'll do."

Before noon all the herds had crossed and the wagon and remuda of the last one was just moving out of sight to the north.

"We might as well cross while the crossing's good," Augustus said. "It could come another rain."

He folded the tent, which was awkward to carry on a horse. His horse didn't like it and tried to pitch, but Augustus finally got him settled down. The river had gone down some, and they crossed without difficulty and made camp on a long ridge about two miles to the north of it.

"Now then, we ought to be set," Augustus said, once he had the tent secured. "I imagine the boys will be along in a week or so."

Lorena didn't care if they never came along, but she was glad they had the tent. It was scarcely up before rain clouds boiled again out of the northwest.

"Let her rain, we're ready," Augustus said, taking the box of buttons from his saddlebag. "I guess it won't stop us from playing cards."

Wilbarger had thoughtfully let them have some coffee and a side of bacon, and with those provisions and the tent and the buttons, they passed a week. A little of the hollowness left Lorena's cheeks, and her bruises healed. She still slept close to Augustus at night and her eyes still followed him when he went out to move the horses or do some errand. Once or twice on pretty evenings they rode over to the river. Augustus had rigged a fishing line out of some coarse thread they had found in Adobe Walls. He bent a needle for a hook and used tadpoles for bait. But he caught no fish. Whenever he went to the river, he stripped off and bathed.

"Come in, Lorie," he said several times. "A bath won't hurt you."

Finally she did. She had not washed in a long time, and it felt good. Gus was sitting on a rock not far away, letting the sun dry him. The water was rapid, and she didn't wade in too deep. She was surprised to see how white her skin looked, once the dirt was all washed off. The sight of her own brown legs and white belly surprised her so that she began to cry. Once the crying started, she couldn't stop it—she cried as if she would never stop. Gus noticed and walked over to help her out of the river, for she was just standing there sobbing, the water up to her thighs.

Gus didn't reprimand her. "I 'spect the best thing is for you to cry it out, Lorie," he said. "You just remember, you got a long time to live."

"They shouldn't have took me," Lorena said, when she stopped crying. She got her rag of a dress and went back to the tent.

62

ONCE THEY HIT the Territory, Newt began to worry about Indians. He was not alone in his worrying. The Irishman had heard so much about scalping that he often tugged at his own hair as if to reassure himself that it wouldn't come off easily. Pea Eye, who spent most of his time sharpening his knife or making sure he had enough ammunition, was astonished that the Irishman had never seen a scalped person. During Pea's years as a Ranger they were always finding scalped settlers, and, for that matter, several of his friends had been scalped.

The Spettle boys, who were slowly becoming more talkative, confided in Newt that they would run away and go home if they weren't afraid of getting lost.

"But you have to drive the horses," Newt pointed out. "The Captain hired you."

"Didn't know we was coming where the Indians were," Bill Spettle said.

For all the talk, they saw neither Indians nor cowboys for days on end. They saw no one—just an occasional wolf or coyote. It seemed to Newt that the sky got bigger and the country emptier every day. There was nothing to see but grass and sky. The space was so empty that it was hard to imagine that there might ever be towns in it, or people.

The Irishman particularly found the huge emptiness disturbing. "I guess we left the people," he said often. Or, "When's the next people?"

Nobody was quite sure when to expect the next people. "It's too bad Gus ain't here," Pea Eye said. "Gus would know. He's an expert on where places is at."

"Why, there's nothing north of here," Dish said, surprised that anyone would think otherwise. "You have to go east a ways to get into the towns."

"I thought we was going to strike Ogallala," Needle reminded him.

"I don't say we won't," Dish said. "That's up to the Captain. But if it ain't no bigger than Dodge, it wouldn't take much to miss it."

Po Campo had become a great favorite with the men because of the tastiness of his cooking. He was friendly and kind to everyone, and yet, like the Captain, he kept apart. Po just did it in a different way. He might sing to them in his throaty voice, but he was a man of mystery, a strange man, walking all day behind the wagon, and at night whittling his little women. Soon each of the cowboys had been given one of the carvings.

"To remind you of your sisters," Po said.

A day and a half before they reached the Canadian the rains started again. At the sight of the great gray clouds forming in the west, morale immediately sank and the men untied their slickers, resigned to a long, cold, dangerous night.

The storm that struck them half a day from the Canadian was of a different intensity because of the lightning. By midafternoon, Newt, who was as usual with the drags, became conscious of rumblings and flashing far on the west. He saw

Deets conferring with the Captain, though it was hard to imagine what advice might help. They were out in the middle of the plain, far from any shelter.

All through the late afternoon lightning flickered in the west. As the sun was setting Newt saw something he had never seen: a bolt of lightning shot south to north, bisecting the setting sun. The bolt seemed to travel the whole length of the western horizon—the crack that came with it was so sharp that Newt almost expected to see the sun split in half, like a big red melon.

After that bolt, the clouds rolled down on the group like a huge black herd, snuffing out the afterglow in five minutes. The remuda became restless, and Newt rode over to help Pete Spettle, but a bolt of lightning struck so close by that his horse went into a violent fit of pitching and promptly threw him. He had kept a tight grip on the reins and the horse didn't break free, but Newt had a time calming him enough that he could remount. Claps of thunder were almost constant by then, and so loud that they made his head ring. The herd was stopped, the cowboys spread around it in as tight a ring as possible.

Just as Newt mounted, a bolt of lightning struck the edge of the herd not a hundred feet from where the Captain rode. A number of cattle instantly fell, as if clubbed by the same club. It was as if a portion of the wall of cattle had broken and fallen to earth like so many bricks.

A second later the cattle were running. They broke west in a mass and surged through the riders as if they weren't there, although Dish, the Captain and Deets were all trying to turn them. The rain came almost as the cattle began to move. Newt spurred and tried to reach the head of the herd, which was nearer him than anyone. He saw a long line of lightning curl down and strike, but the cattle didn't stop. He heard the clicking of thousands of horns as the cattle bumped one another. Again he saw the bluish light rolling on the tips of the cattle's horns, and was glad when the wall of rain came. He rushed to it with relief. Rain was just wet—it didn't scare him, and he knew that if it rained hard enough the lightning would finally stop.

The cattle ran for many miles, but soon the storm was to the east of them and he had only the rain and darkness to contend with. As he had done before, he plodded along much of the night beside the cattle. Occasionally he would hear the shout of another cowboy, but it was too dark and rainy to see anything. The length of such nights was a torment. A hundred times, or a thousand, he would look in what he thought was an easterly direction, hoping to see the grayness that meant dawn. But all directions were equally black for what seemed like twenty hours.

When dawn did come, it was a low and gloomy one, the sky heavily overcast. Newt, with Dish, the Irishman and Needle Nelson, was with a large portion of the herd, perhaps a thousand cattle. No one was quite sure where the rest of the herd was. The cattle were too tired to be troublesome, so Dish loped off to look and was gone what seemed like half a day. When he finally came back, Deets was with him. The main herd was six or seven miles east.

"How many did the lightning hit?" Newt asked, remembering the sight of the cattle falling dead.

"Thirteen," Dish said. "That ain't the worst, though. It kilt Bill Spettle. Knocked him right off his horse. They're burying him now."

Newt had been feeling very hungry, but the news took his appetite. He had been chatting with Bill Spettle not two hours before the storm began. Bill was beginning to be rather talkative, after hundreds of miles of silence.

"They say it turned him black," Dish remarked. "I didn't see it."

Newt was never to see where Bill Spettle was buried. When they rejoined the main herd it was on the move, the grave somewhere behind on the muddy plain. No one knew quite what to say to Pete Spettle, who had somehow held the remuda together all night. He was holding it together still, though he looked weary and stunned.

The men were all starving, so Call allowed them to stop for a quick feed, but only a quick one. It was looking like rain again. He knew the Canadian was near and he wanted to cross it before more rains came; otherwise they might be trapped for a week.

"Ain't we gonna rest?" Jasper asked, appalled that they were required to keep driving after such a night.

"We'll rest north of the river," Call said.

Deets had been sent to find a crossing, but came back almost before he had left. The Canadian was only four miles away, and there was a crossing that had obviously been used by many herds.

"We all gonna have to swim," he said, to Jasper's consternation.

"I just hope we don't have to swim it in a dern rainstorm," Dish said, looking at the heavy clouds.

"I don't see what difference it makes," Needle said. "It can get just so wet, and if you're swimming you're bound to be wet."

"It oughta quit raining, it's rained enough," Pea Eye said, but the heavens ignored him.

Call was more worried than he let on. They had already lost a boy that day— another boy hastily buried, who would never see his home again. He had no wish to risk any more, and yet the river had to be crossed. He loped up to look at the crossing and satisfied himself that it was safe. The river was high, but it wasn't a wide river—they wouldn't need to swim far.

He rode back to the herd. Many of the men had changed into their dry clothes while he was gone, a wasteful effort, with the river coming up.

"You best strip off when we get to the river or you'll just get those clothes wet too," Call said. "Wrap your clothes up good in your slickers so you'll have something dry to put on when we get across."

"Ride naked?" Jasper asked, shocked that such a thing would be required of him. Northern travel was proving even worse than he had thought it would be. Bill Spettle had been so stiffened when they found him that they had not been able to straighten him out properly—they had just wrapped him in a bedroll and stuck him in a hole.

"Well, I'd rather be naked a spell than to have to travel in wet duds, like we done all last night," Pea Eye said.

When they approached the river, the herd was held up so the men could strip off. It was so chilly that Newt got goosebumps all over his body when he undressed. He wrapped his clothes and tied them high on his saddle, even his boots. The sight of all the men riding naked would have been amusing if he hadn't been so tired and nervous about the crossing. Everyone looked white as a fish belly, except their hands and faces, which were brown.

"Good lord, we're a bunch of beauties," Dish said, surveying the crew. "Deets is the best-looking of the lot, at least he's one color. The rest of us is kind of brindled."

Nobody expected weather conditions to get worse, but it seemed that in plains weather there was always room for surprises. A squall blew up as they were starting the cattle into the water, and by the time Old Dog was across the twenty yards of swimming water, Dish on one side of him and Call on the other, the gray sky suddenly began to spit out little white pellets. Dish, who was out of the saddle, hanging onto his saddle strings as his horse swam, saw the first pellets plunking into the water and jerked with fear, for he assumed they were bullets. It was only when he looked up and had a small hailstone peck at his cheek that he realized what was happening.

Call, too, saw the hail begin to pepper the river. At first the stones were small, and he wasn't too worried, for he had seen fleeting hail squalls pass in five minutes.

But by the time he and Dish hit the north shore and regained their wet saddles, he realized it was more than a squall. Hailstones were hitting all around him, bouncing off his arms, his saddle, his horse—and they were getting larger by the minute. Dish came riding over, still naked, trying to shelter his face and head with one arm. Hailstones were falling everywhere, splashing into the river, bouncing off the backs of the cattle and plunking into the muddy banks.

"What will we do, Captain?" Dish asked. "They're getting bigger. Reckon they'll beat us to death?"

Call had never heard of anyone being killed by hailstones, but he had just taken a hard crack behind the ear from a stone the size of a pullet egg. Yet they couldn't stop. Two of the boys were in the river, swimming, and the cattle were still crossing.

"Get under your horse if it gets worse," he said. "Use your saddle for cover."

"This horse would kick me to death, if I was to try that," Dish said. He quickly unsaddled and used his saddle blanket for immediate shelter.

Newt didn't know what was happening when the first hailstones hit. When he saw the tiny white pellets bouncing on the grass he assumed he was at last seeing snow.

"Look, it's snowing," he said excitedly to Needle Nelson, who was near him.

"It ain't snow, it's hail," Needle said.

"I thought snow was white," Newt said, disappointed.

"They're both white," Needle said. "The difference is, hail is harder."

Within a few minutes, Newt was to find out just how hard. The sky began to rain balls of ice—small at first, but then not so small.

"By God, we better get in that river," Needle said. He had a large hat and was trying to hide under it, but the hailstones pounded his body.

Newt looked around for the wagon, but couldn't see it, the hail was so thick. Then he couldn't see Needle, either. He spurred hard and raced for the river, though he didn't know what he was supposed to do once he got there. As he ran for the river, he almost trampled Jasper, who had dismounted and made a kind of tent of his slicker and saddle—he was crouching under it in the mud.

It was hailing so thickly that when they did reach the river Mouse jumped off a six-foot bank, throwing Newt. Again, he managed to hang onto his reins, but he was naked, and hailstones were pounding all around him. When he stood up he happened to notice that Mouse made a kind of wall. By crouching close under him Newt avoided most of the hailstones—Mouse absorbed them. Mouse wasn't happy about it, but since he had taken it upon himself to jump off the bank, Newt didn't feel very sorry for him.

He crouched under the horse until the hailstorm subsided, which was not more than ten minutes after it began. The muddy banks of the Canadian were covered with hailstones, and so were the plains around them. The cattle and horses crunched through the hail as they walked. Isolated stones continued to plop down now and then, bouncing off the ones already there.

Newt saw that the cattle had crossed the wild Canadian, the river that had scared everybody, without much help from the cowboys, who were scattered here and there, naked, crouched under their saddles or, in some cases, their horses. It was a funny sight; Newt was so glad to be alive that suddenly he felt like laughing. Funniest of all was Pea Eye, who stood not thirty yards away, up to his neck in the river, with his hat on. He was just standing there calmly, waiting for the hail to stop.

"How come you got in the water?" Newt asked, when Pea waded out.

"It's fine protection," Pea said. "It can't hail through water."

It was amazing to Newt to see the plains, which had been mostly brown a few minutes before, turned mostly white.

The Irishman walked up leading his horse and kicking hailstones out of the way. He began to pick up the hailstones and throw them in the river. Soon several of the cowboys were doing it, seeing who could throw the farthest or make the hailstones skip across the water.

Then they saw a strange sight: Po Campo was gathering hailstones in a bucket, the two pigs following him like dogs.

"What do you reckon he expects to do with them?" Needle Nelson asked.

"I guess he'll stew 'em, probably," Pea said. "He's looking them over like he's picking peas."

"I wouldn't want to see this outfit naked tomorrow," Jasper said. "I guess we'll all be black and blue. One hit me on the elbow and I can't straighten my arm yet."

"You don't do much with it when you do straighten it," Bert remarked unsympathetically.

"Just 'cause he can't rope like you can don't mean he wouldn't like to use his arm," Pea Eye said. Everyone picked on Jasper, and once in a while Pea felt obliged to come to his defense. He swung onto his horse and froze before getting his other foot in the stirrup. He had happened to glance across the river and had spotted a horseman riding toward them. The crew on the north bank had their backs to the rider and hadn't seen him.

"Why, I swear, it's Gus," Pea Eye said. "He ain't dead at all."

They all looked, and saw the rider coming.

"How do you know it's him?" Bert wanted to know. "He's too far. It could be an Indian chief for all you know."

"I guess I know Gus," Pea said. "I wonder where he's been."

63

CALL AND DISH were just getting into their dry pants when Augustus came riding up. It was not until they heard the sound of his horse crushing the hailstones that they turned around. Call saw at once that Gus was riding a different horse from the one on which he had ridden off, but he himself looked fit.

"'I god, I never thought you boys would start working naked," Augustus said. "I guess the minute I left camp things went right to hell. You jaybirds look like you're scattered from here to Fort Worth."

"Well, the river was deep and we ain't overloaded with dry clothes," Call said. "What happened to you?"

"Nothing much," Augustus said. "I got here last week and decided there wasn't no sense in riding south. I'd just have to turn around and come back."

"Did you ever find Lorie?" Dish asked.

"Oh, sure," Augustus said. "I found her. She's probably sitting out in front of the tent right now watching you prance around naked."

At that Dish blushed and made haste to get the rest of his clothes on, though when Gus pointed out the tent to him he saw it was too far away for Lorie to have seen anything.

At that point several of the naked cowboys on the south bank plunged into the river and swam over, so excited by Gus's return that they forgot caution.

"I swear, Gus, we near give you up," Pea Eye said. "Did you catch the bandit?"

"No, but I hope I do someday," Augustus said. "I met plenty of his friends, but he slipped by me."

"Did you get to town or what?" Dish asked. "You didn't have no tent when you rode off."

"Mr. Wilbarger loaned me that tent," Augustus said. "Lorie's feeling shy and she needs a little privacy."

"We best get the wagon across," Call said. "We can listen to Gus's story later. You boys that ain't dressed go back and help."

The sun came out, and that plus Gus's arrival put the hands in a high mood. Even Jasper, normally so worried about rivers, forgot his fear and swam right back across the Canadian to help get the wagon. They all treated swimming the river like a frolic, though they had been anxious about it for a week. Before long they had the wagon across. They had put both pigs in it but the blue shoat jumped out and swam across.

"That's an independent pig," Augustus said. "I see you still got that old cook."

"Yes, his food's right tasty," Call said. "Is the girl all right?"

"She's had an ordeal but she's young," Augustus said. "She won't forget it, but she might outlive it."

"We're a long way from any place we could leave her," Call said.

"Oh, I have no intention of leaving her," Augustus said. "We've got Wilbarger's tent. We'll go along with you cowboys until we hit Nebraska."

"Then what?" Call asked.

"I don't know, we ain't there yet," Augustus said. "What's the word on Jake?"

"He was in Fort Worth when we passed by," Call said. "I guess he's mainly card playing."

"I met that sheriff that's after him," Augustus said. "He's ahead of us somewhere. His wife run off and Blue Duck killed his deputy and two youngsters who were traveling with him. He's got other things on his mind besides Jake."

"He's welcome to Jake, if he wants him," Call said. "I won't defend a man who lets a woman get stolen and just goes back to his cards."

"It was wisdom," Augustus said. "Blue Duck would have scattered Jake over two counties if he had run into him."

"I call it cowardice," Call said. "Why didn't you kill Blue Duck?"

"He's quick," Augustus said. "I couldn't follow him on this piece of soap I'm riding. Anyway, I had Lorie to consider."

"I hate to let a man like that get away," Call said.

"Go get him, Woodrow," Augustus said. "He's west of here, probably in Colorado. You go get him and I'll nurse these cows along until you get back. Now what's that old cook doing?"

They saw all the cowboys gathered around the wagon, which still dripped from its passage through the river.

"He likes to surprise the boys," Call said. "He's always coming up with something different."

They trotted over and saw that Po Campo had made the hailstones into a kind of candy, with the use of a little molasses. He dipped them in molasses and gave each of the hands one to lick.

"Well, *señor*," he said to Augustus, "I see you made it back in time for dessert."

"I made it back in time to see a bunch of naked waddies cross a river," Augustus said. "I thought you'd all turned Indian and was aiming to scalp Jasper. Where's young Bill Spettle? Has he gone into hiding?"

There was an awkward silence. Lippy, sitting on the wagon seat, stopped licking the hailstone he had been given.

"No, *señor*, he is buried," Po Campo said. "A victim of lightning."

"That's a pity," Augustus said. "He was young and had promise."

"It kilt thirteen head with one bolt," Pea Eye said. "You never seen such lightning, Gus."

"I seen it," Augustus said. "We had a little weather too."

Newt felt warm and happy, his clothes on and Mr. Gus back with the crew. The sky had cleared and the clouds that had caused the terrible hail were only a few wisps on the eastern horizon. In the bright sun, with the river crossed and the cattle grazing on the wet grass, and Lorena rescued, life seemed like a fine thing, though every once in a while he would remember Bill Spettle, buried in the mud a few miles back, or Sean O'Brien, way down on the Nueces—the warm sun and bright air had brought them no pleasure. Po Campo had given him a hailstone dipped in molasses and he sat licking it and feeling alternately happy and sad while the men got dressed and prepared to be cowboys again.

"Are there any more trees, or does this plain just go on to Canady?" Bert Borum asked.

"I wouldn't bet on trees for the next few months," Augustus said.

The men wondered about Lorena. Many still held her beauty in their minds. What had happened to her? What did she look like now? Hers was the most beauty many of them had seen, and now that she was near it shone fresh in memory and made them all the more anxious to see her.

Dish, especially, could not keep his eyes off the little tent. He longed for a glimpse of her and kept imagining that any minute she would step out of the tent and look his way. Surely she remembered him; perhaps she would even wave, and call him over.

Lorena knew the cowboys were near, but she didn't look out of the tent. Gus had assured her he would be back soon, and she trusted him—though sometimes when he was gone for an hour looking for game, she still got the shakes. Blue Duck wasn't dead. He might come back and get her again, if Gus didn't watch close. She remembered his face and the way he smiled when he kicked her. Gus was the only thing that kept the memories away, and sometimes they were so fresh and frightening that she wished she had died so her brain would stop working and just leave her in the quiet. But her brain wouldn't stop—only Gus could distract it with talk and card games. Only his presence relaxed her enough that she could sleep.

Now and then she peeped out and saw the wagon, with Gus standing by it. He was easy to spot because of his white hair. As long as she could spot him she didn't feel worried.

Call let the men camp—they had had a rough twenty-four hours. A big steer had crippled itself crossing the river. Bert roped it and Po Campo killed it efficiently with a sharp blow of an ax. He butchered it just as efficiently and soon had beefsteaks cooking. The smell reminded the men that they were famished—they went at the meat like wolves.

"A cow don't go far with this bunch," Augustus observed. "If you boys don't learn to curb your appetites you'll have eaten the whole dern herd before we strike the Powder River. It'll be a big joke on you, Call," he added.

"What will?" Call asked. His mind had been on Blue Duck.

"Think of it," Augustus said. "You start off to Montana with a bunch of cattle and some hungry hands. By the time you get there the hands will have et the cattle and you're back at nothing. Then the Cheyenne or the Sioux will wipe out the hands, and that'll leave you."

"What about yourself?" Call asked. "You're along."

"I'll have stopped and got married, probably," Augustus said. "It's time I started my family."

"Are you marrying Lorie, then, Gus?" Dish asked, in sudden panic. He was aware that Gus had saved Lorena from a bad fate and supposed she might be going to marry him in gratitude.

"No, Dish, I've someone else in mind," Augustus said. "Don't run your hopes up no flagpole, though. Lorie's apt to be skittish of men for the next few years."

"Hell, she always was," Needle observed. "I offered her good money twice and she looked right through me like I was a glass window or something."

"Well, you are skinny," Augustus said. "Plus you're too tall to suit a woman. Women would rather have runts, on the whole."

The remark struck the company as odd—why would women rather have runts? And how did Gus know such a thing? But then, it was a comforting remark too, for it was like Gus to say something none of them expected to hear. Those that had night guard would be able to amuse themselves with the remark for hours, considering the pros and cons of it and debating among themselves whether it could be true.

"Dern, I missed listening to you, Gus," Pea Eye said as Augustus was mounting to leave.

Call rode a little way out of camp with Augustus. A flock of cranes came in and settled on the banks of the river.

"This trip is hard on boys," Augustus said. "We've lost two already, and the young sheriff lost a boy and a girl."

They stopped for a smoke. In the distance the night guard was just going out to the herd.

"We should have stayed lawmen and left these boys at home," Augustus said. "Half of 'em will get drowned or hit by lightning before we hit Montana. We should have just gone ourselves and found some rough old town and civilized it. That's the way to make a reputation these days."

"I don't want a reputation," Call said. "I've had enough outlaws shoot at me. I'd rather have a ranch."

"Well, I got to admit I still like a fight," Augustus said. "They sharpen the wits. The only other thing that does that is talking to women, which is usually more dangerous."

"Now you've ended up the caretaker of that girl," Call said. "She ain't the woman you're after."

"Nope, she ain't," Augustus said. He had been pondering that point himself. Of course, for all he knew Clara was still a happily married woman and all his thinking about her no more than idle daydreams. He had long wanted to marry her, and yet life was continually slipping other women between her and him. It had happened with his wives, earlier.

"I wish you'd been married," he said to Call.

"Why?" Call asked.

"I'd like your thoughts on the subject, that's why," Augustus said. "Only you ain't got no experience, so you can't be no help."

"Well, I never come close," Call said. "I don't know why."

"No interest," Augustus said. "Also, you ain't never figured yourself out, and you don't like to take chances."

"I could argue that," Call said. "I've taken my share of chances, I guess."

"In battle, not in love," Augustus said. "Unless you want to call what you done with Maggie taking a chance."

"Why do you always want to talk about that?" Call said.

"Because it was as close as you ever came to doing something normal," Augustus said. "It's all I've got to work with. Here you've brought these cattle all this way, with all this inconvenience to me and everybody else, and you don't have no reason in this world to be doing it."

Call didn't answer. He sat smoking. The Irishman had begun to sing to the herd.

"Since you know so much about me, have you got any suggestions?" he asked.

"Certainly have," Augustus said. "Take these cattle over to the nearest cow town and sell 'em. Pay off whatever boys is still alive."

"Then what?"

"I'll go deal with the ladies for a while," Augustus said. "You take Pea and Deets and ride up the Purgatory River until you find Blue Duck. Then either you'll kill him or he'll kill all of you."

"What about the boy?" Call asked.

"Newt can go with me and learn to be a ladies' man," Augustus said. "You won't claim him anyway, and the last boy that got near Blue Duck had his head smashed in with a rifle butt."

"Nope," Call said. "I'm primed to see Montana. If we're the first ones there we can take our pick of the land."

"You take your pick," Augustus said. "I'm in the mood to travel. Once you boys get settled I may go to China, for all you know."

And with that he rode off. Call smoked a while, feeling odd and a little sad. Jake had proved a coward and would never be part of the old crew again. Of course, he hadn't been for ten years—the old crew was mostly a memory, though Pea and Deets were still there, and Gus, in his strange way. But it was all changing.

He saw the girl come out of the tent when Gus dismounted. She was just a shape in the twilight. Gus said she wouldn't talk much, not even to him. Call didn't intend to try her. He loped a mile or two to the west and put the mare on her lead rope. The sky overhead was still light and there was a little fingernail moon.

64

JAKE SPENT MOST of his days in a place called Bill's Saloon, a little clapboard place on the Trinity River bluffs. It was a two-story building. The whores took the top story and the gamblers and cowboys used the bottom. From the top floor there were usually cattle in sight trailing north, small herds and large. Once in a while a foreman came in for liquor and met Jake. When they found out he had been north to Montana, some tried to hire him, but Jake just laughed at them. The week after he left the Hat Creek herd had been a good week. He couldn't draw a bad card, and by the time the week was over he had a stake enough to last him a month or two.

"I believe I'll just stay," he told the foreman. "I like the view."

He also liked a long-legged whore named Sally Skull—at least that was what she called herself. She ran the whoring establishment for Bill Sloan, who owned the saloon. There were five girls but only three rooms, and with the herds coming through in such numbers the cowboys were in the place practically all the time. Sally had alarm clocks outside the rooms—she gave each man twenty minutes, after which the big alarm clocks went off with a sound like a firebell. When that happened, Sally would throw the door open and watch while the cowboys got dressed. Sally was skinny but tall, with short black hair. She was taller than all but a few of the cowboys, and the sight of her standing there unnerved most of the men so much they could hardly button their buttons. The majority of them were just boys, anyway, and not used to whorehouse customs and alarm clocks.

One or two of the bolder ones complained, but Sally was unimpressed and uncompromising.

"If you can't squirt your squirt in twenty minutes, you need a doctor, not a whore," she said.

Sally drank hard from the time she woke up until the time she passed out. She kept one of the three rooms for her own exclusive use—the one with a little porch off it. When Jake got tired of card playing he would come and sit with his feet propped up on the porch rail and watch the wagons move up and down the streets of Fort Worth. Once Sally had the alarm clocks set she would come in for a few minutes herself, with a whiskey glass, and help him watch. He had hit it off with her at once, and she let him sleep in her bed, but the bed and the privileges that went with it cost him ten dollars a day—a sum he readily agreed to, since he was on a winning streak. Once he had got his first ten dollars' worth, he felt free to discuss the arrangements.

"What if we don't do nothing but sleep?" he asked. "Is it still ten dollars?"

"Yep," Sally said.

"I can buy a dern bed for the night a sight cheaper than that," Jake pointed out.

"If it's got me in it, it ain't just a bed," Sally said. "Besides, you get to sit on the balcony all you want to, unless one of my good sweethearts is in town."

It turned out that Sally Skull had quite a number of good sweethearts, some of them so rank that Jake didn't see how she could stand them. She didn't mind mule skinners or buffalo hunters; in fact, she seemed to prefer them.

"Hell, I'm the only one of your customers that's taken a bath this year," Jake complained. "You could take up with bankers and lawyers, and the sheets wouldn't stink so."

"I like 'em muddy and bloody," Sally said. "I ain't nice, this ain't a nice place, and it ain't a nice life. I'd take a hog to bed if I could find one that walked on two legs."

Jake had seen hogs that kept cleaner than some of the men Sally Skull took upstairs, but something about her raw behavior stirred him, and he stayed with her and paid the daily ten dollars. The cowboys that came through were very poor cardplayers, so he could usually make his fee back in an hour. He tried other whores in other saloons, skinny ones and fat ones, but with them a time came when he would remember Lorena and immediately lose interest. Lorena was the most beautiful woman he had ever known, and her beauty grew in his memory. He thought of her often with a pang, but also with anger, for in his view it was entirely her own fault that she had been stolen. Whatever was happening to her, it was her punishment for stubbornness. She could easily have been living with him in a decent hotel in Austin or Fort Worth.

Sally Skull had bad teeth and a thin body with no particular beauties. Her long legs were skinny as a bird's, and she had nothing that could match Lorena's fine bosom. If anyone said a wrong word to her they got a tongue-lashing that would make the coarsest man blush. If one of her girls got too sweet on a cowboy, which could always happen in her profession, Sal promptly got rid of her, shoving her out the back door of the saloon into the dusty street. "Don't get in love around me," she would say. "Go do it in the alley if you want to give it away." Once she fired three girls in one day for lazing around with the boys. For the next week she serviced most of the customers herself.

Jake decided he was crazy for taking up with Sally—she lived too raw for him. Besides the drinking and the men, she also took powders of various kinds, which she bought from a druggist. She would take the powders and lay beside him wide-eyed, not saying a word for hours. Still, he would be awakened at dawn when she pulled the cork out of the whiskey bottle she kept by the bed. After a few swigs to wake herself up, she would always want him, no matter that she had serviced twenty cowboys the night before. Sally flared with the first light—he couldn't think what he liked about her, yet he couldn't deny her, either. She made a hundred dollars a day, or more, but spent most of it on her powders or on dresses, most of which she only wore once or twice.

When the Hat Creek outfit passed through, some of the men came in and said hello to Jake, but he froze them out. It was their fault that Lorena was lost, and he had no more use for them. But tales about him were told, and they soon got back to Sally Skull.

"Why'd you let that Indian get your whore?" she asked him bluntly.

"He was a tricky bandit," Jake said. "For all I know she may have liked him. She never liked me much."

Sally Skull had green eyes, which dilated when she took her powders. She looked at him like a mean cat that was about to pounce on a lizard. Though it was barely sunup they had already been at it, and the grimy sheets were a puddle of sweat.

"She never would mind," Jake said, wishing the Hat Creek outfit had kept their mouths shut.

"I wouldn't mind you either, Jake," Sally said. "I wish I could trade places with her."

"You what?" he asked, mightily startled.

"I've went with a nigger but never an Indian," she said. "I'd like to try one."

The news about the nigger was a shock to Jake. He knew Sal was wild, but hadn't supposed she was *that* wild. The look on her face frightened him a little.

"You know something else? I paid that nigger," she said. "I give him ten dollars to turn whore and then he never got to spend it."

"Why not?" Jake asked.

"He bragged and they hung him from a tree," Sally said. "Wrong thing to brag about in Georgia. Some of them wanted to hang me but they didn't have the guts to hang a woman. I just got run out of town."

That night there was trouble. A young foreman gave Sally some lip when she tried to rush him off, and she shot him in the shoulder with a derringer she kept under her pillow. He wasn't hurt much, but he complained, and the sheriff took Sally to jail and kept her. Jake tried to bail her out but the sheriff wouldn't take his money. "Leave her sit," he said. Only Sally did more than sit. She bribed one of the deputies into bringing her some powders. She looked a mess, but somehow it was the mess about her that men couldn't resist. Jake couldn't, himself—somehow she could bring him to it despite her teeth and her oniony smells and the rest. She brought the deputy to it, too, and then tried to grab his gun and break jail, although if she had waited, the sheriff would have let her out in a day or two. Somehow, in fighting over the one gun, she and the deputy managed to shoot each other fatally. They died together on the cell floor in a pool of blood, both half naked.

The deputy had nine children, and his death caused an uproar against whores and gamblers, so much so that Jake thought it prudent to leave town. He searched Sally's room before he left and found six hundred dollars in a hatbox; since Sally was dead and buried, he took it. The whores who were left were so scared that they hired a buggy and came with him over to Dallas, where they soon found work in another saloon.

In Dallas Jake won some money from a soldier who reported that he had met a deputy sheriff from Arkansas. The deputy was looking for the sheriff, and the sheriff was looking for a man who had killed his brother. The soldier had forgotten all the names and Jake didn't mention that he was the man being sought. The information made him nervous, though. The sheriff from Arkansas was evidently in Texas somewhere, and might show up any time.

While he was pondering what his next move might be, a hard-looking crew showed up in the saloon where he was playing. It consisted of three brothers— the Suggs brothers. Dan Suggs was the oldest and most talkative. The younger two, Ed and Roy, were sullen and restless, always watching the doors to see who might be coming in. Dan had no interest in doors, or any apparent concern other than a need to have his whiskey glass filled rather often. All three were scragglybearded men.

"Didn't you ranger?" Dan asked, when he heard Jake's name.

"I rangered some," Jake said.

"You run with Call and McCrae, didn't you?" Dan said. "I've never met Call or McCrae but I've heard they're hard men."

It irked Jake a little that those two had such reputations. It seemed to him that he had done about as much as they had, in the rangering days. After all, he was the man who had shot one of the most famous bandits on the border.

While they talked and played cards a little, Roy Suggs kept spitting tobacco on the barroom floor. It irked Ralph, the man who owned the bar. He brought over a spittoon and put it by Roy's chair, but Roy Suggs looked at him with a cold eye and continued to spit on the floor.

"Roy will spit where he pleases," Dan said, with a mean grin.

"Spoon, how'd you like to be a regulator?" he asked a little later. "I recall from stories I've heard that you can shoot a gun."

"What is a regulator?" Jake asked. "I've not heard the term."

"Folks up in Kansas are getting tired of these Texas cattle tramping in constantly," Dan said. "They want this trail-driving business regulated."

"Regulated how?"

"Well, taxed," Dan said. "People can't go on driving cattle just anywhere. If they want to cross certain rivers at certain crossings, they've got to pay for the privilege. If they won't pay in cash, then they've got to pay in cattle."

"Is it the law in Kansas, or what?" Jake asked.

"It ain't, but some folks think it ought to be," Dan said.

"Us folks, mainly," Roy said, spitting.

"I see," Jake said. "If Call and Gus try to take some cattle across one of them rivers you're regulating, then you stop 'em and tell them they have to pay? Is that how the scheme works?"

"That's it," Dan said.

"I'd like to see you tell Woodrow Call he has to pay you money to drive cattle across a river," Jake said. "I ain't a friend of the man—he's recently treated me poorly. But unless there's a law and you can show it to him, you won't be collecting no double eagles."

"Then he'll have to suffer the consequences," Dan said.

Jake laughed. "The consequences of that would be that somebody would have to dig your grave," he said. "If Call didn't shoot you, Gus would. They ain't used to taking orders from you regulators."

"By God, then they'll learn," Roy Suggs said.

"Maybe, but you won't teach them," Jake said. "You'd be sitting dead in your saddle if you tried it." Though he was annoyed with Call and Gus, it amused him that three scraggly bandits thought they could beat them.

Dan Suggs was not pleased with the conversation, either. "I thought you might be a man with some gumption," he said. "I see I was wrong."

"I can supply enough gumption," Jake said. "But I don't ride with inexperienced men. If you think you can ride up to Call and McCrae and collect money from 'em with a few threats, then you're too inexperienced for me."

Dan was silent for a bit. "Well, they're just one bunch," he said. "There are plenty of other herds on the trail."

"That's right," Jake said. "If I was you I'd try to regulate some of the ones that ain't been led by Texas Rangers."

Roy and Ed looked at him hostilely. They didn't like hearing it suggested that they weren't up to the job. But Dan Suggs was a cooler man. After they'd played some cards and worked through a bottle of whiskey he admitted that the regulating scheme was something he'd just thought up.

"My notion was that most cowboys can't fight," Dan said. "Hell, they're just boys. Them settlers up there can't fight, neither. A lot of them might pay us to keep the beeves out of their corn patches."

"They might, but it sounds like you're speculating," Jake said. "Before I leave this here easy life to go and get shot at I'd like a little better prospect to think about."

"How about robbing banks, if the regulating don't work out?" Dan asked bluntly. "You got any objections to robbing banks?"

"It would depend on the bank," Jake said. "I wouldn't enjoy it if there was too much law stacked up against me. I'd think you'd want to pick small towns."

They talked for several hours, Roy Suggs resolutely spitting tobacco on the floor. Dan Suggs pointed out that all the money seemed to be in Kansas. If they went up there and weren't too particular about what they did they ought to be able to latch onto some of it.

Jake found the Suggs brothers unattractive. They all had cold, mean eyes, and no great affection even for one another. Roy and Ed almost got into a gunfight over a hand of cards. He offered to get them whores, for he had stayed friendly with several of the girls who had come over from Fort Worth, but the Suggs brothers weren't interested. Drinking and card playing appealed to them more.

Had it not been for the threat of July Johnson somewhere around, he would have let the Suggs brothers head for Kansas without him. He was comfortable where he was, and had no appetite for hard riding and gunfighting. But Dallas wasn't far from Fort Smith, and July Johnson might arrive any time. That was an uncomfortable thought, so uncomfortable that three days later Jake found himself riding north with the three Suggs boys and a tall black man they called Frog Lip. Jake equipped himself with a new rifle before they left. He had made the Suggs brothers no promises, and as soon as he found a nice saloon in Kansas, he meant to let them go their way.

Frog Lip owned five guns of various calibers, and spent most of his time cleaning them. He was a fine marksman. The first day out he brought down a deer at a distance Jake would have considered impossible. Frog Lip seemed to take the shot for granted. Jake had the strong feeling that the black man's guns would soon be pointed at something besides deer, but he himself didn't plan to be around to see it.

65

JULY RODE FOR DAYS without seeing any person, or, for that matter, many signs of life except the hawks and buzzards circling in the blue prairie sky. Once he saw a wolf loping along a ridge, and at night he heard coyotes, but the only game he saw were jackrabbits, and it was mostly rabbit he ate.

He kept going north, reminding himself that it was a long way to any towns; but soon the unvarying emptiness of the country began to disturb him, and he was already disturbed enough by the deaths of the three people buried on the Canadian. He thought of them more or less all day. Waking in the gray dawn, he would have Roscoe's face in his mind; when he dreamed, it was of Roscoe and Joe and the young girl. Several times he cried at the thought of the finality of it. He had a longing to get them back in places they belonged: Fort Smith, in the case of Roscoe and Joe. He didn't know where the girl had belonged, though it wasn't in a grave on the Canadian.

What he was doing—indeed, his whole life—now seemed to him completely futile. He rode through the empty land without hope of anything, simply going on because he had to do something. As he went farther and farther onto the plains, he ceased to be able to imagine Fort Smith as a place where he might ever live and work again. What would he do if he did go back? Sit in the jail where he had worked with Roscoe? Or in the cabin where he had lived with Elmira?

July didn't see how things could get worse, since he had lost his wife and led three people to their deaths. But four days after he left Augustus, his horse went lame. Some small spiky cactus hidden by the tall prairie grass proved more deadly than a snake. A thorn worked its way far up into the horse's hoof. July had to tie the horse down to get the thorn out, and even then he was not sure he had got it all. They were three days north of the Cimarron when it happened. Water was scarce and the horse soon too lame to ride. He led the horse, taking it slow, hoping the hoof would get better, but it did no good. The horse was lamed and could put no weight on the hoof at all.

Finally, sadly feeling that he was parting with his last companion in life, July unsaddled the horse and shot him. He left his saddle but took his rifle and started walking east. The next day, from a ridge, he saw a great cloud of buzzards over the place where the horse lay. The sight made him cry.

He walked all day, hoping to cross a creek but finding none. He had a half canteen of water—not enough to get him back to the Cimarron. And he had nothing to eat. He made a dry camp and sat all night on his blanket, so wakeful he thought he would never sleep again. He sat for hours, watching the moon climb high amid the bright stars. He remembered the cold nights in their Arkansas cabin when he was a boy—how his mother piled quilts on top of him and his brothers, how

359

peaceful it seemed under the quilts. Then it seemed like sleep was one of the most wonderful things in life.

July wondered if perhaps the sleep of death would be as good, as comforting and warming, as his boyhood slumber. He had a rifle and a pistol—one pull of the trigger would bring him all the sleep he wanted. In his five years as a lawman he had never shot anyone, though he had a reputation as a dangerous fighter. It would be a joke on everyone if the only person he ever killed was himself. He had always assumed that people who killed themselves were cowards. His own uncle had done it in a painful way, by drinking lye. His uncle had been deep in debt.

Now, as he sat and watched the moon, killing himself merely seemed sensible. His life had been ruined—surprisingly, inexplicably, swiftly, but ruined for sure. He had made wrong choices all along, and it had cost three lives. Killing himself would put him at one with Roscoe, Janey, Joe—and the horse. They had started traveling together; it would be fitting that they all ended in the same place.

He began to think about which gun to use. The barrel of the rifle gleamed in the moonlight; the pistol was heavy in its holster. He took out the pistol and slowly turned the cylinder, listening to the heavy clicks. But he didn't put it to his head. He remembered Elmira. It seemed to him he had to find her, to tell her what had happened to her son. It was true she had never seemed fond of the boy—Elmira had never seemed fond of anyone—but Joe had been her son and she might want to know.

July thought all night. Knowing that he had only to raise the pistol eased his mind a little. He had better go and find Elmira first. He wanted to explain to her that he had never meant to do whatever had caused her to run off. Once that was done, he could go off with the pistol and join his dead.

The next morning he started walking, but he didn't feel the same. He felt like he no longer belonged to life. It would not have surprised him to see a cloud of buzzards circling over him. In spirit he had gone to visit Roscoe. He finished his water that night, having walked all day through the brown wavy grass. He tried a long shot at a deer but missed. The next morning he was awakened by the cawing of crows. He looked up to see several of them flapping overhead in the early grayness. He was tired from his long day's walk and didn't get up immediately. There was nothing to get up for but the bright sun and the shimmering plains. But he kept hearing the crows, cawing and quarreling not far away. When he stood up, he saw a little grove of low trees not two hundred yards away—they weren't much, but they were trees, and the crows were resting in them.

Among the trees he found a spring—just a trickle of a spring, but it had formed a shallow pool ten feet wide. A black snake was curled on a rock at the water's edge—it was probably what the crows were complaining about.

July spent the day by the spring. He drank, bathed, and soaked his dirty clothes, spreading them out on the grass to dry. While he rested, a big badger walked up to the spring and July shot him with his pistol. He had never eaten badger, but he ate this one and drank the spring water. Even better than food were the trees. Being in the shade again eased his spirit a little. He could look across the hot prairies for miles, from the comfort of his shade. The sun couldn't parch him while he was under the trees.

But he couldn't live forever on spring water and one badger. Besides, he had his chore to do. He waited until the cool of the evening and then set out again. The second day he crossed a wagon track coming from the south. It led him to a running creek, but he saw no wagon. The next day he saw a dust cloud, which turned out to be a small cow herd. The cowboys were mighty surprised to see a lone figure walking toward them from the west, and dumbfounded to learn that he was a sheriff from Arkansas.

"Did you come from California, or where?" the trail boss asked. He was an old white-mustached man named Johns, suspicious at first. Not many men came walking out of Texas. But July soon persuaded the old man to sell him a horse. It was the worst horse in the remuda, but it was a horse. July gave forty dollars for it. The Johns outfit had no saddle to spare, but they did give him directions. They tried to get him to stay the night with them—they had been on the trail six weeks and a stranger was a welcome novelty.

But once he was mounted, July felt a sense of hurry seize him. He ate with them, thanked them again, and left under a rising moon. Four days later, sore from riding bareback on the little sharp-spined bay, he trotted into Dodge City.

66

LONG BEFORE THEY STRUCK the Republican River, Elmira had begun to wonder if any of it was worth it. For two weeks, when they were on the open plain, it rained, hailed, lightning flashed. Everything she owned was wet, and she didn't like feeling like a muskrat, though it didn't bother Luke and Zwey. It was cold at night. She slept on wet blankets in the hard wagon and woke up feeling more tired than when she lay down. The plains turned soggy and the wagon bogged time after time. The hides smelled and the food was chancy. The wagon was rough, even when the going was good. She bounced around all day and felt sick to her stomach. If she lost the baby in such a place, she felt she would probably die.

It occurred to her that she had taken a hard route, just to escape July Johnson. Her own folly amused her: she had once thought of herself as smart—but look at where she was. If Dee Boot could see her he would laugh his head off. Dee loved to laugh about the absurd things people did for bad reasons. The fact that she had done it because she wanted to see him would only amuse him more. Dee would tell her she ought to have gone back to Dodge and asked one of the girls to get her work.

Instead, she was driving a mule wagon across northern Kansas. They had been lucky and seen no Indians, but that could always change. Besides, it soon developed that Luke was going to be as much trouble as an Indian. It was something she knew that Zwey hadn't noticed. Zwey treated her kindly, insofar as he treated her at all. Now that he had got her to come on a trip he seemed well content. She didn't have to do anything but be there, and he was surprised when she offered to cook, which she mainly did out of boredom and because Zwey and Luke were such dirty cooks she was afraid she would get poisoned if she didn't take that chore into her own hands. Zwey exhibited no lustful intentions at all—he seemed happy just to rest his eyes on her at the end of the day.

Luke, on the other hand, was a feisty little rabbit who lost no time in making his wants known. In the early morning he would stand and relieve himself in plain sight of her, grinning and looking at her while he did it. Zwey, who slept like a rock, never noticed this strange habit.

Luke was not easy to discourage. Soon he took a new tack, which was to persuade Zwey that when they hunted the two of them ought to hunt in separate directions. It was true that game was scarce, but that wasn't the reason Luke hunted by himself. All he was hunting was Elmira. As soon as he knew that Zwey was two or three miles from the wagon, he circled back and pressed his suit. He was direct about it, too. He would tie his horse to the wagon and climb right in with her. He put his arm around her and made crude suggestions.

"No," Elmira said. "I came with Zwey. He told me I wouldn't be bothered."

"What bother?" Luke asked.

"I'm going to have a baby," she said, hoping that would discourage him.

Luke looked at her belly. "Not for a while yet," he said. "This ain't gonna take no month. It probably won't take six minutes. I'll pay you. I won good money playing cards back at the Fort."

"No," Elmira said. "I'm afraid of Zwey."

She wasn't really, but it made a handy excuse. She was more afraid of Luke, who had mean eyes—there was something crazy in his looks. He also had a disgusting habit, which was that he liked to suck his own fingers. He would do it sitting by the fire at night—suck his fingers as if they were candy.

Luke kept climbing up on the wagon and putting his hands on her, but Elmira kept saying no. She dreamed of Dee occasionally, but other than that she had no interest in men. She thought about telling Zwey that Luke was bothering her, but Zwey was not an easy man to talk to. Anyway, it might start a fight, and Luke might win, in which case her goose would be cooked. Zwey was strong but slow, and Luke didn't look like a man who would fight fair.

So when Luke snuck back and climbed onto the wagon seat, Elmira possumed. She couldn't stop his hands entirely, but she made herself into a tight light little package and concentrated on driving the mules.

When Luke saw he wasn't going to change her mind with talk or the offer of money, he tried threats. Twice he cuffed her and once shoved her completely off the wagon seat. She fell hard and barely got out of way of the wagon wheel. Immediately she thought of the baby, but she didn't lose it. Luke cursed her and rode off and she climbed back up and drove the wagon.

The next day he threatened to kill Zwey if she didn't let him. "Zwey's dumb," he said. "He ain't no smarter than a buffalo. I'll shoot him while he sleeps."

"I'll tell him that," Elmira said. "Maybe he won't sleep. Maybe he'll kill you, while you're at it."

"What have you got against me?" Luke said. "I mostly treat you nice."

"You knocked me off the wagon," she said. "If that's nice treatment I'll pass."

"I only want a little," Luke said. "Only once. We're still a long ways from Nebraska. I can't go that long."

The next day he caught her off guard and shoved her back in the wagon by the hides. He was on her like a terrier, but she kicked and scratched, and before he could do anything the mules took fright and started to run away. Luke had to grab the reins with his pants half down, and when he did Elmira grabbed Zwey's extra rifle. When Luke got the mules stopped, he found a buffalo gun pointed at him.

Luke smiled his mean smile. "That gun would break your shoulder if you fired it," he said.

"Yes, and what would it do to you?" she said.

"When I get you you'll wish you'd give it to me," Luke said, flushing red with anger. He got on his horse and rode off.

Zwey came back well before sundown with a wild turkey he had managed to shoot. But Luke wasn't back. Elmira decided she might as well tell Zwey. She couldn't tolerate any more of Luke. Zwey was mildly puzzled that Luke wasn't there.

"I chased him off with the gun," Elmira said.

Zwey looked surprised. His mouth opened and the look spread up his big face. "With the gun?" he asked. "Why?"

"He tried to interfere with me," Elmira said. "He tries it nearly ever day, once you go off."

Zwey pondered that information for a time. They had made a mess of cooking the turkey, but at least it was something to eat. Zwey gnawed on a big drumstick while he pondered.

"Was it he tried to marry you?" he asked.

"You can call it that, if you like," she said. "He tries to do me. I want him to let be."

Zwey said nothing more until he had finished his drumstick. He cracked the bone with his teeth, sucked at the marrow a minute and then threw the bone into the darkness.

"I guess I better kill him if he's going to act that way," he said.

"You could take him with you when you hunt, like you used to," she said. "He couldn't pester me if he's with you."

She had hardly spoken when a shot rang out. It passed between the two of them and hit the turkey, knocking it off its stick into the ashes. They both scrambled for the cover of the wagon and waited. An hour later they were still waiting. There were no more shots, and Luke didn't appear.

"I wonder why he shot the turkey," Zwey said. "It was done dead."

"He didn't shoot the turkey, he missed you," Elmira suggested.

"Well, it tore up the turkey," he said, when they came out of cover and picked up the cold bird.

That night he slept under the wagon with a cocked pistol but there was no attack. They ate cold turkey for breakfast. Two days later Luke showed up, acting as if he'd never been away.

Elmira was apprehensive, fearing a fight then and there, but Zwey seemed to have forgotten the whole business. About the time Luke rode up they spotted two or three buffalo and immediately rode off to shoot them, leaving Elmira to drive the wagon. They came back after dark with three fresh hides, and seemed in good spirits. Luke scarcely looked at her. He and Zwey sat up late, cooking slices of buffalo liver. They were both as bloody as if they'd been skinned. Elmira hated the smell of blood and kept away from them as best she could.

The next morning, before good light, she woke up gagging at the blood smell and looked up to see Luke sitting astraddle of her. He was rubbing his bloody hands over her bosom. Her stomach heaved from the smell.

Luke was fumbling with her blanket, trying to get her uncovered. When he raised up to loosen his clothes Elmira rolled on her stomach, thinking that might stop him. It did annoy him. He bent over her and she felt his hot breath at her ear.

"You're no better than a bitch dog, we'll have it that way," he said. She squeezed her legs together as tightly as she could. Luke pinched her but she kept squeezing. Then he tried to wedge a knee between her legs but he wasn't strong enough. The next thing she knew Zwey was dragging Luke over the side of the wagon. Zwey was smiling, as if he were playing with a child. He lifted Luke and began to smash his head into the wagon wheel. He did it two or three times, smashing Luke into the iron rim, and then he dropped him as if he were deadwood. Zwey didn't really seem angry. He stood by the wagon, looking at Elmira. Luke had pulled her clothes half off.

"I wish he wouldn't act that way," Zwey said. "I won't have nobody to hunt with if I kill him."

He looked down at Luke, who was still breathing, though his head and face were a pulp.

"He just keeps wanting to marry you," Zwey said. "Looks like he'd quit it."

Luke did quit, at that point. He lay in the wagon for four days, trying to get his breath through his broken nose. One of his ears had been nearly scraped off on the wheel; his lips were smashed and several of his teeth broken. His face swelled to such a point that they couldn't tell at first if his jaw was broken, but it turned out it wasn't. The first day, he could barely mumble, but he did persuade Elmira to try and sew his ear back on. Zwey was for cutting it off, since it just hung by a bit of skin, but Elmira took pity on Luke and sewed on the ear. She made a bad job of it, mainly because Luke yelped and jerked every time she touched him with the needle. When she finished, the ear wasn't quite in its right place; it set a little lower than the other and she had pulled the threads a little too tight, so that it didn't have quite the right shape. But at least it was on his head.

Zwey laughed about the fight as if he and Luke had just been two boys playing, although Luke's nose was bent sideways. Then Luke developed a fever and got chills. He rolled around in the wagon moaning and sweating. They had no medicine and could do nothing for him. He looked bad, his face swollen and black. It was strange, Elmira thought, that he would bring such punishment on himself just because he wanted to interfere with her.

There was no more danger of that. When Luke's fever broke, he was so weak he could barely turn over. Zwey went off and hunted, as he had been doing, and Elmira drove the wagon. Twice she got the wagon stuck in a creek and had to wait until Zwey found her and pulled it out. He seemed as strong as either of the mules.

They had not seen one soul since leaving the Fort. Once she thought she saw an Indian watching her from a little ridge, but it turned out to be an antelope.

It was two weeks before Luke could get out of the wagon. All that time Elmira brought him his food and coaxed him to eat it. All the passion seemed to have been beaten out of him. But he did say once, watching Zwey, "I'll kill him someday."

"You shouldn't have missed that shot you had," Elmira said, thinking to tease him.

"What shot?" he asked.

She told him about the shot that hit the turkey, and Luke shook his head.

"I never shot no turkey," he said. "I was thinking to ride off and leave you but I changed my mind."

"Who shot it then?" she asked. Luke had no answer.

She reported this to Zwey but he had forgotten the incident—he wasn't very interested.

After that, though, she grew afraid of the nights—whoever had shot the turkey might still be out there. She huddled in the wagon, scared, and spent her days wishing they would come to Ogallala.

67

ALL THROUGH THE TERRITORY, Newt kept expecting to see Indians—the prospect was all the cowboys talked about. Dish claimed there were all manner of Indians in the Territory, and that some of them were far from whipped. The claim upset Pea Eye, who liked to believe that his Indian-fighting days were over.

"They ain't supposed to fight us no more," he said. "Gus claims the government paid 'em to stop."

"Yes, but whoever heard of an Indian doing what he was supposed to do?" Lippy said. "Maybe some of them consider that they wasn't paid enough."

"What would you know?" Jasper inquired. "When did you ever see an Indian?"

"I seen plenty," Lippy informed him. "What do you think made this hole in my stomach? An Apache Indian made that hole."

"Apache?" Dish said. "Where did you find an Apache?"

"West of Santa Fe," Lippy said. "I traded in them parts, you know. That's where I learned to play the piano."

"I wouldn't be surprised if you forget how before we come to a place that's got one," Pea Eye said. He found himself more and more depressed by the prospect of endless plains. Normally, in his traveling days, he had ridden through one kind of country for a while and then come to another kind of country. It had even been true on the trail drive: first there had been brush, then the limestone hills, then some different brush, and then the plains. But after that there had just been more and more plains, and no end in sight that he could see. Once or twice he asked Deets how soon they could expect to come to the end of them, for Deets was the acknowledged expert on distances, but this time Deets had to admit he was stumped. He didn't know how long the plains went on. "Over a thousand, I guess," he said.

"A thousand miles?" Pea said. "We'll all get old and grow beards before we get that far."

Jasper pointed out to him that at an average of fifteen miles a day it would only take them about two months to get a thousand miles. Thinking of it in terms of months proved more comforting than thinking of it in terms of miles, so Pea tried that for a while.

"When will it be a month up?" he asked Po Campo one night. Po was another much-relied-on source of information.

"Don't worry about months," Po Campo said. "Months won't bother you. I'm more worried about it being dry."

"Lord, it ain't been dry yet," Pea said. "It's rained aplenty."

"I know," Po said. "But we may come to a place where it will forget to rain."

He had long since won the affection of Gus's pigs. The shoat followed him around everywhere. It had grown tall and skinny. It annoyed Augustus that the pigs had shown so little fidelity; when he came to the camp and noticed the shoat sleeping right beside Po Campo's workplace, he was apt to make tart remarks. The fact that many of the men had come to regard Po Campo as an oracle also annoyed Augustus.

"Po, you're too short to see far, but I hear you can tell fortunes," he said one morning when he had ridden over for breakfast.

"I can tell some fortunes," Po allowed. "I don't know if I can tell yours."

"I don't want nobody to tell mine," Jasper said. "I might find out that I'm going to drown in the Republican River."

"I'd like to know mine," Augustus said. "I've had mine told a few times by old black women in New Orleans, and they always say the same thing."

"Probably they tell you that you'll never be rich and you'll never be poor," Po said, whipping at his scrambled eggs.

"That's right," Augustus said. "It's a boring fortune. Besides, I can look in my pocket and tell that much myself. I ain't rich and I ain't poor, exactly."

"What more would you like to know about your fortune?" Po Campo inquired politely.

"How many more times I'm likely to marry," Augustus said. "That's the only interesting question, ain't it? Which river I drown in don't matter to me. That's Jasper's interest. I'd just like to know my matrimonial prospects."

"Spit," Po said. "Spit in the wagon here."

Augustus walked over to the wagon and spat on the boards. The day before, Po Campo had caught six prairie-chicken hatchlings, for some reason, and they were running around in the wagon bed, chirping. Po came over and looked for a moment at Augustus's expectoration.

"No more wives for you," he said immediately, and turned back to his eggs.

"That's disappointing," Augustus said. "I've only had two wives so far, and neither of them lived long. I figured I was due one more."

"You don't really want another wife," Po said. "You are like me, a free man. The sky is your wife."

"Well, I've got a dry one then," Augustus said, looking up at the cloudless sky.

The shoat stood on its hind legs and put its front hooves on the side of the wagon. It was trying to see the hatchlings.

"I'd have turned you into bacon long since if I'd have known you were going to be so fickle," Augustus said.

"Can you tell stuff about a feller from looking at his spit?" Pea Eye asked. He had heard of fortune-tellers, but thought they usually did it with cards.

"Yes," Po Campo said, but he didn't explain.

Just as they were about to cross into Kansas, some Indians showed up. There were only five of them, and they came so quietly that nobody noticed them at first. Newt was on the drags. When the dust let up for a moment he looked over and saw the Captain talking to a small group of riders. At first he supposed them to be cowboys from another herd. He didn't think about them being Indians until the Captain came trotting over with them. "Take him," the Captain said, pointing to a steer with a split hoof who was hobbling along in the rear.

By the time it registered that they were really Indians, they had already cut off the steer and were driving it away, as the Captain sat and watched. Newt was almost afraid to look at them, but when he did he was surprised at how thin and poor they looked. The old man who was their leader was just skin and bones. He rode near enough for Newt to see that one of his eyes was milky white. The other Indians were young. Their ponies were as thin as they were. They had no saddles, just saddle blankets, and only one had a gun, an old carbine. The Indians boxed the steer out of the herd as skillfully as any cowboys and soon had him headed across the empty plain. The old man raised his hand to the Captain as they left, and the Captain returned the gesture.

That night there was much talk about the event.

"Why, they didn't look scary," Jimmy Rainey said. "I reckon we could have whipped them easy enough."

Po Campo chuckled. "They weren't here to fight," he said. "They're just hungry. When they're fighting they look different."

"That's right," Lippy said. "It don't take but a second for one to shoot a hole in your stomach. It happened to me."

Call had formed the habit of riding over with Augustus every night as he took Lorena her supper. Augustus usually camped about a mile from the herd, so it gave them a few minutes to talk. Augustus had not seen the Indians, but he had heard about the gift of the beef.

"I guess you're getting mellow in your old age," he said. "Now you're feeding Indians."

"They were just Wichitas," Call said, "and they were hungry. That steer couldn't have kept up anyway. Besides, I knew the old man," he added. "Remember old Bacon Rind?—or that's what we called him, anyway."

"Yes, he was never a fighter," Augustus said. "I'm surprised he's still alive."

"He fed us buffalo once," Call said. "It was only fair he should have a beef."

They were fifty yards from the tent, so Call drew rein. He couldn't see the girl, but he took care not to come too close. Augustus said she was spooked.

"Look how blue it is toward the sunset," Augustus said. "I've heard about what they call the Blue Mounds. I guess those must be them."

The prairie was rolling, and there were humplike rises to the north as far as they could see. Though the sky was still bright yellow with afterglow, the mounds ahead did have a bluish electric look, almost as if blue lightning had condensed over their tops.

In the dawn the Blue Mounds shimmered to the north. Augustus usually came out of the tent early so he could see the sunrise. Lorena had stopped having so many nightmares and she slept heavily, so heavily that it was hard to get her awake in the mornings. Augustus never rushed her. She had regained her appetite and put on flesh, and it seemed to him her sleeping late was healthy. The grass was wet with dew, so he sat on his saddle blanket watching Dish Boggett point the cattle into the blue distances. Dish always swung the point as close to the tent as he dared, hoping for a glimpse of Lorena, but it was a hope seldom rewarded.

When Lorena awoke and came out of the tent the herd was almost out of sight, though Lippy and the wagon were not far away. Po Campo and the two pigs were walking along looking at things, a hundred yards ahead of the wagon.

Augustus made room for Lorena on the blanket and she sat down without a word, watching the strange little man walk along with the pigs. As the sun rose, the blueness to the north diminished, and it could be seen that the mounds were just low brown hills.

"It must be that wavy grass that gives it the blue look—or else it's the air," Augustus said.

Lorena didn't say anything. She felt so sleepy that she could hardly sit up, and after a moment she leaned against Gus and shut her eyes. He put his arms around her. His arms were warm and the sun on her face was warm. Sleep had pulled at her so much lately that it seemed she was never fully awake, but it didn't matter so long as Gus was there to talk to her and sleep close beside her. If he was there she could let go and slide into sleep. He didn't mind. Often she would rest in his arms, while he held forth, talking almost to himself, for she only half heard. Only when she thought of coming to a town did she feel worried. She stayed in her sleeps as long as she could, so as not to have to worry about the towns.

Augustus stroked her hair as she lay against him. He was thinking how strange life was, that he and Lorena were sitting on a saddle blanket on the south edge of Kansas, watching Call's cattle herd disappear to the north.

One little shot during a card game in Arkansas had started things happening—things he couldn't see the end of. The shot had ended up killing more than a dentist. Sean O'Brien, Bill Spettle, and the three people who were traveling with July Johnson had lost their lives so far, and Montana nowhere in sight.

"He ought to have taken his hanging," Augustus said out loud.

Actually, Jake couldn't fairly be blamed for any of the deaths, though he could be blamed for Lorena's troubles, which were worth a hanging by Augustus's reckoning.

"Who ought?" Lorena asked. Her eyes were open but she still rested her head against Augustus's chest.

"Jake," he said. "Look at all the bad that happened since he showed up."

"He wanted to take me to town," Lorena said. "I wouldn't go. I didn't want no towns.

"I still don't want no towns," she said a little later, beginning to tremble at the thought of all the men that would be in them.

Augustus held her close and didn't try to discuss it with her. Soon she stopped trembling. Two big hawks were skimming the surface of the prairie, not far away.

"Look at them birds," Augustus said. "I'd give a passel if I could fly like that."

Lorena had an uneasy thought in her mind. Gus was holding her in his arms, as he had every day and night since he had rescued her. Yet he had not approached her, had never mentioned it. She understood it was kindness—he was letting her get well. She didn't want him to approach her, never would want any man to again. And yet it troubled her. She knew what men wanted with her. It wasn't just a bedfellow. If Gus had stopped wanting her, what did that mean? Would he take her to a town someday and say goodbye?

"My goodness, Lorie, you smell fresh as dew," he said, sniffing her hair. "It's a miracle you can keep fresh out in these raw parts."

One button had come off his shirt, and a few tufts of the white hair on his chest were sticking out. She wanted to say something, but she was afraid to. She tried to poke the little white chest hairs back under his shirt.

Augustus laughed at the tidy way she did it. "I know I'm a shameful sight," he said. "It's all Call's fault. He wouldn't let me bring my tailor on this trip."

Lorena was silent, but fear was building up in her. Gus had become too important to her. It was disturbing to think that he might leave her someday. She wanted to make sure of him, but she didn't know how to do it. After all, he had already told her there was a woman in Ogallala. She began to tremble again from her sudden fear.

"What's the matter?" he asked. "Here it is, a beautiful morning, and you're sitting here shaking."

She was afraid to speak but began to cry.

"Lorie, we're an honest pair," he said. "Why don't you tell me why you're so upset?"

He seemed so friendly that it eased her mind a little. "You can have a poke," she said. "If you want one. I wouldn't charge you."

Augustus smiled. "That's neighborly of you," he said. "But why should a beauty like you drop her price? You ought to raise it, for you're getting more beautiful than ever. I ain't never seen nothing wrong with paying a toll to beauty."

"You can have one if you want one," she said, trembling still.

"What if I want five or six?" he asked, rubbing her neck with his warm hand. It relieved her—he was still the same. She could see it in his eyes.

"The truth is you want to stay clear of such doings for a while," Augustus said. "That's natural. You best take your time."

"It won't matter how much time," she said, and began to cry again. Gus held her.

"I'm glad we didn't break camp," he said. "There's a rough cloud to the north. We'd be in for a drenching. I bet them cowboys is already floating."

It suited her that it was going to rain and they would stay longer. She didn't like being too close to the cowboys. It was more restful just being with Gus. When he was there it was easier not to think of the things that had happened.

For some reason Gus was still watching the cloud, which seemed to her no worse-looking than many another cloud. But he was studying it intently.

"That's a dern funny cloud," he said.

"I don't care if it rains," Lorena said. "We got the tent."

"The funny part is, I can hear it," Augustus said. "I never heard a cloud make a noise like that before."

Lorena listened. It seemed she did hear something, but it was a long way off, and faint.

"Maybe it's the wind getting up," she said.

Augustus was listening. "It don't sound like no wind I ever heard," he said, standing up. The horses were looking at the cloud, too. They were acting nervous. The sound the brown cloud made had become a little louder, but was still far away and indefinable.

Suddenly Augustus realized what it was. "Good lord," he said. "It's grasshoppers, Lorie. I've heard they came in clouds out on the plains, and there's the proof. It's a cloud of grasshoppers."

The horses were grazing on long lead ropes. There were no trees to tie the ropes to, so he had loosened a heavy block of soil and put the lead ropes under it.

Usually that was sufficient, for the horses weren't troublesome. But now they were rolling their eyes and jerking at the ropes. Augustus grabbed the ropes—he would have to hold them himself.

Lorena watched the cloud, which came down on them faster than any rain cloud. She could plainly hear the hum of millions of insects. The cloud covered the plain in front of them from the ground far up in the air. It was blotting out the ground as if a cover were being pulled over it.

"Get in the tent," Augustus said. He was holding the terrified horses. "Get in and pile whatever you can around the bottom to keep 'em out."

Lorena ran in, and before Augustus could follow, grasshoppers covered the canvas, every inch. Augustus had fifty on his hat, though he tried to knock them off outside the tent, and more on his clothes. He backed in, hanging to the lead ropes as the horses tried to break free.

"Pull the flaps," he said, and Lorena did. Soon there was just the hole the two ropes fed through. It was dim and dark in the tent, as more and more grasshoppers covered the canvas—insects on top of insects. The hum they made as they spread over the prairie grass was so loud Lorena had to grit her teeth. As the tent got darker, she began to cry and shake—it was just more trouble and more fear, this life.

"It's all right, honey, it's just bugs," Augustus said. "Hang onto me and we'll be fine. I don't think bugs will eat canvas when they've got all this grass."

Lorena put her arms around him and shut her eyes. Augustus peeked out and saw that every inch of the lead ropes were covered with grasshoppers.

"Well, that old cook of Call's that likes to fry bugs will be happy, at least," he said. "He can fry up a damn wagonful tonight."

=====

When the cloud of grasshoppers hit the Hat Creek outfit, they were on a totally open plain and could do nothing but watch it come, in terror and astonishment. Lippy sat on the wagon seat, his mouth hanging open.

"Is them grasshoppers?" he asked.

"Yes, but shut your mouth unless you want to choke on them," Po Campo said. He promptly crawled in the wagon and pulled his hat down and his serape close around him.

The cowboys who saw the cloud while on horseback were mostly terrified. Dish Boggett came racing back to the Captain, who sat with Deets, watching the cloud come.

"Captain, what'll we do?" he asked. "There's millions of them. What'll we do?"

"Live through it," Call said. "That's all we can do."

"It's the plague," Deets said. "Ain't it in the Bible?"

"Well, that was locusts," Call said.

Deets looked in wonderment as the insects swirled toward them, a storm of bugs that filled the sky and covered the land. Though he was a little frightened, it was more the mystery of it that affected him. Where did they come from, where would they go? The sunshine glinted strangely off the millions of insects.

"Maybe the Indians sent 'em," he said.

"More likely they ate the Indians," Call said. "The Indians and everything else."

Newt's first fear when the cloud hit was that he would suffocate. In a second the grasshoppers covered every inch of his hands, his face, his clothes, his saddle. A hundred were stuck in Mouse's mane. Newt was afraid to draw breath for fear he'd suck them into his mouth and nose. The air was so dense with them that he couldn't see the cattle and could barely see the ground. At every step Mouse crunched them underfoot. The whirring they made was so loud he felt he could have screamed and not been heard, although Pea Eye and Ben Rainey were both within yards. Newt ducked his head into the crook of his arm for protection. Mouse suddenly broke into a run, which meant the cattle were running, but Newt didn't look up. He feared to look, afraid the grasshoppers would scratch his eyes. As he and Mouse raced, he felt the insects beating against him. It was a relief to find he could breathe.

Then Mouse began to buck and twist, trying to rid himself of some of the grasshoppers, and almost ridding himself of Newt in the process. Newt clung to the saddle horn, afraid that if he were thrown the grasshoppers would smother him. From the way the ground shook he knew the cattle were running. Mouse soon stopped bucking and ran too. When Newt risked a glimpse, all he saw was millions of fluttering bugs. Even as he raced they clung to his shirt. When he tried to change his reins from one hand to another he closed his hand on several grasshoppers and almost dropped his rein. It would have been a comfort if he could have seen at least one cowboy, but he couldn't. In that regard, running through a bug cloud wasn't much different than running in rain: he was alone and miserable, not knowing what his fate might be.

And, as in the rainstorms, his misery increased to a pitch and then was gradually replaced by fatigue and resignation. The sky had turned to grasshoppers—it seemed that simple. The other day it had turned to hailstones, now it was grasshoppers. All he could do was try and endure it—you couldn't shoot grasshoppers. Finally the cattle slowed, and Mouse slowed, and Newt just plodded along, occasionally wiping the grasshoppers off the front of his shirt when they got two or three layers deep. He had no idea how long a grasshopper storm might last.

In this case it lasted for hours. Newt mainly hoped it wouldn't go on all night. If he had to ride through grasshoppers all day and then all night, he felt he'd just give up. It was already fairly dark from the cloud they made, though it was only midday.

Finally, like all other storms, the grasshopper storm did end. The air cleared—there were still thousands of grasshoppers fluttering around in it, but thousands were better than millions. The ground was still covered with them, and Mouse still mashed them when he walked, but at least Newt could see a little distance, though what he saw wasn't very cheering. He was totally alone with fifty or sixty cattle. He had no idea where the main herd might be, or where anything might be. Dozens of grasshoppers still clung to his shirt and to Mouse's mane, and he could hear them stirring in the grass, eating what little of it was left. Most of it had been chewed off to the roots.

He gave Mouse his head, hoping he would have some notion of where the wagon might be, but Mouse seemed as lost as he was. The cattle were walking listlessly, worn out from their run. A few of them tried to stop and graze, but there was nothing left to graze on except grasshoppers.

There was a rise a mile or two to the north, and Newt rode over to it. To his vast relief, he saw several riders coming and waved his hat to make sure they saw him. The hoppers had nibbled on his clothes, and he felt lucky not to be naked.

He went back to get the cattle, and when he glanced again at the boys, they looked funny. They didn't have hats. A second later he realized why: they were

Indians, all of them. Newt felt so scared he went weak. He hated life on the plains. One minute it was pretty, then a cloud of grasshoppers came, and now Indians. The worst of it was that he was alone. It was always happening, and he felt convinced it was Mouse's fault. Somehow he could never stay with the rest of the boys when there was a run. He had to wander off by himself. This time the results were serious, for the five Indians were only fifty yards away. He felt he ought to pull his gun, but he knew he couldn't shoot well enough to kill five of them—anyhow, the Captain hadn't shot when the old chief with the milky eye had asked for a beef. Maybe they were friendly.

Indeed, that proved the case, although they were rather smelly and a little too familiar to suit Newt. They smelled like the lard Bolivar had used on his hair. They crowded right around him, several of them talking to him in words he couldn't understand. All of them were armed with old rifles. The rifles looked in bad repair, but they would have sufficed to kill him if that had been what the Indians wanted to do. Newt was sure they would want the cattle, for they were as skinny as the first bunch of Indians.

He began to try and work out in his mind how many he could let them have without risking dishonor. If they wanted them all, of course, he would just have to fight and be killed, for he could never face the Captain if he had been responsible for the loss of fifty head. But if they could be bought off with two or three, that was different.

Sure enough, a little, short Indian began to point at the cattle. He jabbered a lot, and Newt assumed he was saying he wanted them all.

"*No sabe,*" he said, thinking maybe some of the Indians knew Mexican. But the little short Indian just kept jabbering and pointing west. Newt didn't know what to make of that. Meanwhile the others crowded around, not being mean exactly, but being familiar, fingering his hat and his rope and his quirt, and generally making it difficult for him to think clearly. One even lifted his pistol out of its holster, and Newt's heart nearly stopped. He expected to be shot with his own gun and felt foolish for allowing it to be taken so easily. But the Indians merely passed it around for comment and then stuck it back in the holster. Newt smiled at them, relieved. If they would give him his gun back, they couldn't mean to harm him.

But he shook his head when they pointed at the cattle. He thought they wanted to take the cattle and go west. When he shook his head, it caused a big laugh. The Indians seemed to think everything he did was pretty comical. They jabbered and pointed to the west, laughing, and then, to his dismay, three of them began to whoop at the cattle and got them started west. It seemed they were just going to take them. Newt felt sick with confusion. He knew the point had been reached when he ought to draw his pistol and try to stop it, but he couldn't seem to do it. The fact that the Indians were laughing and seemed friendly made it difficult. How do you shoot people who were laughing? Maybe the Captain could have, but the Captain wasn't there.

The Indians motioned for him to come with them, and, very reluctantly, Newt went. He felt he ought to make a break for it, go find the cowboys and get them to help him reclaim the sixty head. Of course the Indians might shoot him if he ran, but what really stopped him was the fact that he had no idea where the rest of the boys were. He might just charge off and be lost for good.

So, with a sinking heart, he slowly followed the five Indians and the cattle. At least he wasn't deserting by doing that. He was still with the cattle, for what it was worth.

Before he had gone a mile or two he wished he had thought of another alternative. The plains had always seemed empty, and somehow, with the grass chewed off and him captured by Indians, they seemed even more empty. He began to remember all the stories he had heard about how tricky Indians were and decided these were just laughing to trick him. Probably they had a camp nearby, and when they got there they might stop laughing and butcher him and the cattle both. The surprising thing was how young they were. None of them looked any older than Ben Rainey.

Then they rode over a ridge so low it hardly seemed like a ridge, and there was the herd and the cowboys too. They were two or three miles away, but it was them—he could even see the wagon. Instead of stealing him, the Indians had just been keeping him from getting lost, for he had been angling off in the wrong direction. He realized then that the young Indians were laughing because he was so dumb he didn't even know which way his own cattle were. He didn't blame them. Now that he was safe, he felt like laughing too. He wanted to thank the Indians, but he didn't know their words. All he could do was smile at them.

Then Dish Boggett and Soupy Jones rode over to help him hurry the cattle along. Their clothes had little holes in them where the grasshoppers had nibbled through.

"It's a good thing they found you, we ain't had time to look," Soupy said. "If we'd gone on north, it would be sixty miles to water, the Indians say. Most of these cattle wouldn't make no sixty miles."

"Nor most of these men, either," Dish said.

"Did the grasshoppers hurt anybody?" Newt asked, still amazed that such a thing could happen.

"No, but they ruint my Sunday shirt," Soupy said. "Jasper's horse spooked and he got thrown and claims his collarbone might be broken, but Deets and Po don't think so."

"I hope Lorie didn't suffer," Dish said. "Their horses could have spooked. They might be afoot and a long way from grub."

"I suppose you'd like to go check on their safety?" Soupy said.

"Somebody ought," Dish said.

"Ask the Captain," Soupy said. "I expect he'll want to assign you the chore."

Dish thought otherwise. Already the Captain was looking at him as if he expected him to rush back to the point, although the cattle were moving along fine.

"You ask him, Newt," Dish said.

"Newt?" Soupy said. "Why, Newt was just lost himself. If he went looking for Gus he'd just be lost again."

"Ask him, Newt," Dish said again, with such intensity that Newt knew he had to do it. He knew it meant Dish trusted him a lot to ask such a thing of him.

The Captain was talking in sign to ten or twelve young Indians. Then the Indians went over to the herd and cut out three beeves. Newt rode over, feeling foolish. He didn't want to ask the Captain, but on the other hand he couldn't ignore Dish's request.

"Do you think I ought to go check on Mr. Gus?" Newt asked. "The boys think they might be in trouble." Call noticed how nervous the boy seemed and sensed that somebody had put him up to asking the question.

"No, we better all drive," he said. "Gus had a tent. I imagine he's happy as a badger. They're probably just sitting there playing cards."

It was what he had expected, but Newt still felt chastened as he turned back to the drags. He felt he would never learn to say the right thing to the Captain.

68

ALMOST AT ONCE, before the group even got out of Texas, Jake had cause to regret that he had ever agreed to ride with the Suggs brothers. The first night he camped with them, not thirty miles north of Dallas, he heard talk that frightened him. The boys were discussing two outlaws who were in jail in Fort Worth, waiting to hang, and Dan Suggs claimed it was July Johnson who had brought them in. The robbers had put out the story that July was traveling with a young girl who could throw rocks better than most men could shoot.

"I'd like to see her throw rocks better than Frog can shoot," Roy Suggs said. "I guess Frog could cool her off."

Frog Lip didn't say much. He was a black man, but Jake didn't notice anyone giving him many orders. Little Eddie Suggs cooked the supper, such as it was, while Frog Lip sat idle, not even chopping wood for the fire. The horse he rode was the best in the group, a white gelding. It was unusual to see a bandit who used a white horse, for it made him stand out in a group. Frog Lip evidently didn't care.

"We oughta go get them boys out of jail," Roy Suggs said. "They might make good regulators."

"If a girl and one sheriff can take 'em. I wouldn't want 'em," Dan Suggs said. "Besides, I had some trouble with Jim once, myself. I'd go watch him hang, if I had time, damn him."

Their talk, it seemed, was mostly of killing. Even little Eddie, the youngest, claimed to have killed three men, two nesters and a Mexican. The rest of the outfit didn't mention numbers, but Jake had no doubt that he was riding with accomplished killers. Dan Suggs seemed to hate everybody he knew—he spoke in the vilest language of everyone, but his particular hatred was cowboys. He had trailed a herd once and not done well with it, and it had left him resentful of those with better luck.

"I'd like to steal a whole goddamn herd and sell it," Dan said.

"There ain't but five of us," Eddie pointed out. "It takes more than five to drive cattle."

Dan Suggs had a mean glint in his eye. He had made the remark idly, but once he thought about it, it seemed to make a great deal of sense. "We could hire a little more help," he said.

"I remember that time we tried to drive cattle," Roy said. "The Indians run off half of them, and we all nearly drowned in them rivers. Why try it again?"

"You ain't heard the plan, so shut up," Dan said, with a touch of anger. "What we done wrong the first time was doing it honest. I'm through with honest. It's every man for himself in this country, and that's the way I like it. There ain't much law and mostly it can be outrun."

"Whose herd would you steal?" Jake asked.

374

"Oh, the closest one to Dodge," Dan said. "Find some herd that's just about there and steal it, maybe a day or two shy of the towns. Then we could just drive it in and sell it and be gone. We'd get all the money and none of the work."

"What about the boys who drove it all that way?" Jake asked. "They might not want to give up their profits that easy."

"We'd plant 'em," Dan said. "Shoot them and sell their cattle, and be long gone before anyone ever missed them."

"What if one run off and didn't get planted?" Roy said. "It don't take but one to tell the story, and then we'd have a posse to fight."

"Frog's got a fast horse," Dan said. "He could run down any man who escaped."

"I'd rather rob banks, myself," little Eddie said. "Then you got the money right in your hands. You don't have to sell no cows."

"Well, you're lazy, Ed," Dan said, looking at his brother as if he were mad enough to shoot him. In fact, the Suggs brothers seemed to live on the edge of fratricidal warfare.

"What do you boys know of this Blue Duck?" Jake asked, mainly to change the subject.

"We know to let him be," Dan said. "Frog don't care for him."

"Why not?"

"Stole my horse," Frog Lip said. He didn't elaborate. They were passing a whiskey bottle around and he took his turn as if he were a white man. Whiskey had no effect on any of them except little Eddie, who turned red-eyed and wobbly after five or six turns.

Jake drank liberally, for he felt uncomfortable. He had not meant to slip into such rough company and was worried, for now that he had slipped in, he could see that it wasn't going to be any too easy to slip back out. After all, he had heard them discuss killing a whole crew of cowboys, calculating the killings as casually as they might pick ticks off a dog. He had been in much questionable company in his life, but the Suggs brothers weren't questionable. They were just hard. Moreover, the silent black man, Frog, had a very fast horse. Escaping them would need some care. He knew they didn't trust him. Their eyes were cold when they looked his way. He resolved to be very careful and make no move that might antagonize them until the situation was in his favor, which it wouldn't be until they got into the Kansas towns. With a crowd around, he might slip away.

Besides that, killing could always work two ways. Gus was fond of saying that even the meanest bad man could always run into someone meaner and quicker. Dan Suggs could easily meet a violent end, in which case the others might not care who stayed or went.

The next day they rode on to Doan's Store, on the banks of the Red River, and stopped to buy whiskey and consider their route. A trail herd was crossing the river a mile or more to the west.

"There's one we could steal, right there," little Eddie said.

"That one's barely in the Territory," Dan said. "We'd have to follow it for a month, and I ain't in the mood."

"I say we head for Arkansas first," Roy said. "We could rob a bank or two."

Jake was not listening to the palaver very closely. A party of nesters—four wagons of them—had stopped at the store, buying supplies. They were farmers, and they had left Missouri and were planning to try out Texas. Most of the menfolk were inside the store buying supplies, though some were repairing wagon wheels or shoeing horses. Most of the womenfolk were starved-looking creatures in bonnets, but one of them was neither starved nor in a bonnet. She was a girl of about seventeen with long black hair. She sat on the seat of one of the wagons, barefoot, waiting for her folks to finish shopping.

To Jake she looked like a beauty. It occurred to him that beauties were his real calling, if he had one, and he wondered what could have possessed him to start out with a rough bunch like the Suggses, when there were beauties right there in Texas that he hadn't even met, including the one on the wagon seat. He watched her for a while and, since her folks hadn't reappeared, decided he might just stroll over and have a word with her. Already he felt a yearning for woman's talk, and he had only been gone from Dallas a little more than a day.

He had been lounging in the shade of the store, but he stood up and carefully dusted his pants.

"Are you fixing to go to church, or what?" Dan Suggs asked.

"No, but I fancy a word or two with that black-haired gal sitting there on the wagon," Jake said. "I've never talked to a woman from Missouri. I figure I might like it."

"Why wouldn't they talk like any other gals?" Roy wondered.

"I heard you was a ladies' man," Dan said, as if it were a condemnation of some sort.

"You met me in a whorehouse, why would you doubt it?" Jake said, tired of the little man's biting tone. "If I like that gal maybe I'll elope with her," he said, just to remind everyone that he was still his own man.

The closer he got to the girl, the better he liked her looks. She had fine features, and her thin, worn-out dress concealed a swelling young bosom. She realized Jake was coming her way, which agitated her a little. She looked off, pretending not to notice him.

At close range she looked younger, perhaps only fifteen or sixteen. Probably she had scarcely even had beaux, or if she had, they would only have been farm boys with no knowledge of the world. She had a curling upper lip, which he liked—it indicated she had some spirit. If she had been a whore, he would have contracted with her for a week, just on the strength of that lip and the curve of her bosom. But she was just a barefoot girl sitting on a wagon, with dust on her bare feet.

"Hello, miss," he said, when he walked up. "Going far?"

The young girl met his eye, though he could see that she was agitated that he had spoken to her.

"My name's Jake Spoon," he said. "What's yours?"

"Lou," she said, not much more than whispering the information. He did like the way her upper lip curved, and was about to say more, but before he could get the words out something slammed him in the back and his face was in the dirt. He hit the ground so hard he busted his lip.

He rolled over, wondering if somehow one of the mules had got in a kick—it wouldn't have been the first time he was surprised by a mule. But when he looked up and blinked the dust out of his eyes he saw an angry old man with a long sandy beard standing over him, gripping a ten-gauge shotgun. It was the shotgun that had knocked him down—the old fool had whacked him across the shoulder blades with it. The man must have been standing behind the wagon.

Jake's head was ringing, and he couldn't see good, though he could tell the old man was gripping the shotgun like a club—he wasn't planning to shoot. Jake got to his knees and waited until he caught his wind.

"You git," the old man said. "Don't be talking to my wife."

Jake looked up in surprise—he had assumed the old man must be her father. Though certainly a brusque greeting, it was not much more than he would have expected from a father—fathers had always been touchy when he attempted to talk to their daughters. But the girl on the wagon seat was already a wife. He looked at her again, surprised that such a fresh pullet would be married to a man who looked to be in his seventies, at least. The girl just sat there, pretty as ever, watching the scene without expression.

That Jake had deigned to look at her again infuriated the farmer more, and he drew back the shotgun to deliver another blow.

"Hold on, mister," Jake said. One lick he might let pass, but not two. Besides, the ten-gauge was a heavy gun, and used as a club it could break a shoulder, or do worse.

When Jake spoke, the old man hesitated a second—he even glanced at the girl on the wagon seat. But at the sight of her he drew back his lips in a snarl and raised the shotgun again.

Before he could strike the second blow, Jake shot him. It surprised him as much as it did the nester, for he was not aware of having pulled his gun. The bullet caught the nester in the breast and knocked him back against the wagon. He dropped the shotgun, and as he was sliding to the ground, Jake shot again, the second shot as much a surprise to him as the first. It was as if his arm and his gun were acting on their own. But the second shot also hit the old nester in the breast. He slid to the ground and rolled partly under the wagon on top of his own shotgun.

"He never needed to hit me," Jake said to the girl. He expected her to scream, but she didn't. The shooting seemed not to have registered with her yet. Jake glanced at the nester and saw that he was stone dead, a big bloodstain on his gray work shirt. A line of blood ran down the stock of the shotgun he lay across.

Then nesters began to boil out of Doan's Store—it seemed there were twenty or thirty of them. Jake felt discouraged by the sight, for it reminded him of how people had boiled out of the saloons in Fort Smith when they discovered Benny Johnson lying dead in the mud. Now another man was lying dead, and it was just as much an accident: if the old nester had just announced himself politely as the girl's husband, Jake would have tipped his hat and walked off. But the old man had whacked him and offered to do it again—he had only shot to protect himself.

This time he was up against twenty or thirty nesters. They were grouped in front of the store as if puzzled by the situation. Jake put his gun back in its holster and looked at the girl once more.

"Tell 'em I had to do it," he said. "That old man might have cracked my skull with that gun."

Then he turned and walked back toward the Suggs brothers. He looked back once at the girl, and she smiled at him—a smile that was to puzzle him whenever he thought about it. She had not even got down from the wagon to see if her husband was dead—yet she gave him that smile, though by that time the nesters were all around the wagon.

The Suggs boys were already mounted. Little Eddie handed Jake his rein.

"I guess that's the end of that romance," Dan Suggs said.

"Dern, I just asked her name," Jake said. "I never knowed she was married."

The nesters were all grouped around the body. The girl still sat on the wagon seat.

"Let's cross the river," Dan Suggs said. "It's that or hire you a lawyer, and I say, why waste the money?"

"That store don't sell lawyers anyway," Roy Suggs remarked.

Jake mounted, but he was reluctant to leave. It occurred to him that if he went back to the nesters he might bluff his way out of it. After all, it had been self-defense—even dirt farmers from Missouri could understand that. The nesters were looking their way, but none of them were offering to fight. If he turned and rode into the Territory, he would be carrying two killings against his name. In neither case had he meant to kill, or even known the man he killed. It was just more bad luck—noticing a pretty girl on a wagon seat was where it started in this case.

But the law wouldn't look at it like that, of course. If he rode across the river with a hard bunch like the Suggses he would be an outlaw, whereas if he stayed, the nesters might try to hang him or at least try to jail him in Fort Worth or Dallas. If that happened, he'd soon be on trial for one accident or another.

It was a poor set of choices, it seemed to him, but when the Suggs brothers rode off he followed, and in fifteen minutes was across the Red River. Once he looked back and could still see the wagons grouped around the little store. He remembered the girl's last smile—yet he had killed a man before he had even seen her smile. The nesters made no pursuit.

"Them punkin' rollers," Dan Suggs said contemptuously. "If they was to follow we'd thin them out in a hurry."

Jake fell into a gloom—it seemed he could do nothing right. He hardly asked for more in life than a clean saloon to gamble in and a pretty whore to sleep with, that and a little whiskey to drink. He had no desire to be shooting people—even during his years in the Rangers he seldom actually drew aim at anyone, although he cheerfully threw off shots in the direction of the enemy. He certainly didn't consider himself a killer: in battle, Call and Gus were capable of killing ten to his one.

And yet, now Call and Gus were respectable cattlemen, looked up to everywhere they went, and he was riding with a gang of hardened outlaws who didn't care who they killed. Somehow he had slipped out of the respectable life. He had never been a churchgoer, but until recently he had had no reason to fear the law.

The Suggs brothers kept plenty of whiskey on hand, and Jake began to avail himself of it. He stayed half drunk most of the time as they rode north. Even though he had killed a man in plain sight of them, the Suggses didn't treat him with any new respect. Of course, they didn't offer one another much respect either. Dan and Roy both poured scorn on little Eddie if he slipped up in his chores or made a remark they disagreed with. The only man of the company who escaped their scorn was Frog Lip—they seldom spoke to him, and he seldom spoke, but everyone knew he was there.

They rode through the Territory without incident, frequently seeing cattle herds on the move but always swinging around them. Dan Suggs had an old pair of spyglasses he had brought back from the war, and once in a while he would stand up in his stirrups and look one of the cattle outfits over to see if they contained enemies of his, or any cowboys he recognized.

Jake watched the herds too, for he still had hope of escaping from the situation he was in. Rude as Call and Gus had treated him, they were still his *compañeros.* If he spotted the Hat Creek outfit he had it in mind to sneak off and rejoin them. Even though he had made another mistake, the boys wouldn't know about it and the news might never reach Montana. He would even cowboy, if he had to—it beat taking his chances with the Suggses.

He was careful not to give his feelings away though—he never inquired about the herds, and if the subject of Call and McCrae came up he made it plain that he harbored a grudge against them and would not be sorry to see them come to grief.

When they got up into Kansas they began to see the occasional settler, sod-house nesters, mostly. Jake hardly thought any of them could have enough money to be worth the trouble of robbing, but the younger Suggs brothers were all for trying them.

"I thought we was gonna regulate the settlers," Roy said one night. "What are we waiting for?"

"A nester that's got something besides a milk cow and a pile of buffalo chips," Dan Suggs said. "I'm looking for a rich one."

"If one was rich, he wouldn't be living in a hole dug out of a hill up here in Kansas," Jake said. "I slept in one of those soddies once—so much dirt leaked out of the roof during the night that I woke up dern near buried."

"That don't mean some of them couldn't have some gold," little Eddie said. "I'd like to practice regulating a little so I'd have the hang of it when we do strike the rich ones."

"All we aim to let you do is watch, anyway," Dan said. "It don't take no practice to watch."

"I've shot a nester," little Eddie reminded him. "Shot two. If they don't pay up, I might make it three."

"The object is to scare them out of their money, not shoot them," Dan said. "You shoot too many and pretty soon you've got the law after you. We want to get rich, not get hung."

"He's too young to know what he's talking about," Roy said.

"Well, I won't shoot them then, I'll just scare them," little Eddie said.

"No, that's Frog Lip's job, scaring them punkin'-eaters," Dan said. "He'll scare them a sight worse than you will."

The next day Frog Lip got his chance. They saw a man plowing beside a team of big horses. A woman and a small boy were carrying buffalo chips in a wheelbarrow and piling them beside a low sod house that was dug into a slope. Two milk cows grazed nearby.

"He can afford them big horses," Roy pointed out. "Maybe he's got money."

Dan had been about to ride past, and Jake hoped he would. He still hoped they'd hit Dodge before the Suggs boys did any regulating. He might get free of them in Dodge. Two accidents wouldn't necessarily brand him for life, but if he traveled much farther with a gun outfit like the Suggses, he couldn't expect a peaceful old age—or any old age, probably.

But Dan decided, on a whim, to go rob the farmer, if he had anything worth being robbed of.

"They usually hide their money in the chimney," he said. "Either that or they bury it in the orchard, though I don't see no orchard."

Frog Lip kept an extra pistol in his saddlebags. As they approached the farmer he got it out and stuck it in his belt.

The farmer was plowing a shallow furrow through the tough prairie grass. Seeing the riders approach, he stopped. He was a middle-aged man with a curly black beard, thoroughly sweated from his work. His wife and son watched the Suggses approach. Their wheelbarrow was nearly full of buffalo chips.

"Well, I guess you can expect a fine crop along about July, if the damn Texas cattle don't come along and eat it all up," Dan said.

The man nodded in a friendly way, as if he agreed with the sentiment.

"We're here to see you reap what you sow," Dan went on. "It'll cost you forty dollars gold, but we'll deal with the herds when they show up and your crops won't be disturbed."

"No speaken English," the man said, still smiling and nodding in a friendly way.

"Oh, hell, a damn German," Dan said. "I figured this was a waste of time. Round up the woman and the sprout, Frog. Maybe this old Dutchman married an American gal."

Frog Lip loped over and drove the woman and the boy near the farmer; he rode so close to them that if they had fallen his horse would have stepped on them. He had taken the pistol out of his belt, but he didn't need it. The woman and the boy were terrified, and the farmer too. He put his arms around his wife and child, and they all stood there, crying.

"Look at them blubber," little Eddie said. "I never seen such cowards."

"Will you shut your damn mouth?" Dan said. "Why wouldn't they be scared? I would be, in their place. But I'd like to get the woman hushed long enough to see if she can talk English."

The woman either couldn't or wouldn't. She didn't utter a word in any language. She was tall and skinny, and she just stood there by her husband, crying. It was plain all three of them expected to be killed.

Dan repeated his request for money, and only the boy looked as if he understood it. He stopped crying for a minute.

"That's it, sonny, it's only cash we want," Dan said. "Tell your pa to pay us and we'll help him guard his crops."

Jake hardly expected a scared boy to believe that, but the boy did stop crying. He spoke to his father in the old tongue, and the man, whose face ran with tears, composed himself a little and jabbered at the boy.

The boy turned and ran lickety-split for the sod house.

"Go with him and see what you can find, boys," Dan said. "Me and Jake can ride herd on the family, I guess. They don't look too violent."

Ten minutes later the boy came racing back, crying again, and Frog Lip and the two younger Suggses followed. They had an old leather wallet with them, which Roy Suggs threw to Dan. It had two small gold pieces in it.

"Why, this ain't but four dollars," Dan said. "Did you look good?"

"Yeah, we tore up the chimney and opened all the trunks," Roy said. "That purse was under the pallet they sleep on. They don't have a dern thing worth taking besides that."

"Four dollars to see 'em through," Dan said. "That won't help 'em much, we might as well take it." He took the two gold pieces and tossed the worn leather purse back at the man's feet.

"Let's go," he said.

Jake was glad to see it come to no worse than that, but as they were riding away Frog Lip turned and loped over to the milk cows.

"What's he aim to do, shoot the milk cows?" little Eddie asked; for Frog Lip had his pistol in his hand.

"I didn't ask him and he didn't say," Dan replied.

Frog Lip rode up beside the cows and fired a couple of shots into the air. When the cows started a lumbering run, he skillfully turned them up the slope and chased them right onto the roof of the sod house. The sod on the roof had grass still on it and looked not unlike the prairie. The cows took a few steps onto the roof and then their forequarters disappeared, as if they had fallen into a hole. Then their hindquarters disappeared too. Frog Lip reined in his horse and watched as both cows fell through the roof of the sod house. A minute later one came squeezing out the small door, and the other followed. Both cows trotted back to where they had been grazing.

"That Frog," Dan Suggs said. "I guess he just wanted to ventilate the house a little."

"All we got was four dollars," little Eddie said.

"Well, it was your idea," Dan said. "You wanted the practice, and you got it."

"He's mad because he didn't get to shoot nobody," Roy said. "He thinks he's a shooter."

"Well, this is a gun outfit, ain't it?" little Eddie said. "We ain't cowboys, so what are we then?"

"Travelers," Dan said. "Right now we're traveling to Kansas, looking for what we can find."

Frog Lip rejoined them as silently as he had left. Despite himself Jake could not conquer his fear of the man. Frog Lip had never said anything hostile to him, or even looked his way on the whole trip, and yet Jake felt a sort of apprehension whenever he even rode close to the man. In all his travels in the west he had met few men who gave off such a sense of danger. Even Indians didn't—although of course there had been few occasions when he had ridden close to an Indian.

"I wonder if them soddies will get that roof fixed before the next rain?" Dan Suggs said. "If they had had a little more cash, Frog might have left them alone."

Frog Lip didn't comment.

69

IT TOOK JULY only a day or two to determine that Elmira was not in Dodge City. The town was a shock to him, for almost every woman in it seemed to be a whore and almost every business a saloon. He kept trying to tell himself he shouldn't be surprised, for he had heard for years that Kansas towns were wild. In Missouri, where he had gone to testify at the trial, there was much talk of Kansas. People in Missouri seemed to consider that they had gotten rid of all their riffraff to the cow towns. July quickly concluded that they were right. There might be rough elements in Missouri, but what struck him in Kansas was the absence of any elements that weren't rough. Of course there were a few stores and a livery stable or two in Dodge—even a hotel of sorts, though the whores were in and out of the hotel so much that it seemed more like a whorehouse. Gamblers were thick in the saloons and he had never seen a place where as many people went armed.

The first thing July did was buy a decent horse. He went to the post office, for he felt he owed Fort Smith an explanation as to why he had not come back. For some reason he felt a surge of optimism as he walked down the street to the post office. Now that he had survived the plains it seemed possible that he could find Ellie after all. He had lost all interest in catching Jake Spoon; he just wanted to find his wife and go home. If Peach didn't like it—and she wouldn't—she would just have to lump it. If Ellie wasn't in Dodge she would probably be in Abilene. He would soon catch up with her.

But to his surprise, the minute he stepped inside the door of the post office his optimism gave way in a flash to bitter depression. In trying to think of what he would say in his letter he remembered all that had happened. Roscoe was dead, Joe was dead, the girl was dead, and Ellie not found—maybe she too was dead. All he had to report was death and failure. At the thought of poor Roscoe, gutted and left under a little pile of rocks on the prairie, his eyes filled with tears and he had to turn and walk back out the door to keep from embarrassing himself.

He walked along the dusty street for a few minutes, wiping the tears out of his eyes with his shirtsleeve. One or two men observed him curiously. It was obvious that he was upset, but no one said anything to him. He remembered walking into the post office in Fort Worth and getting the letter that told him about Ellie. Since then, it had all been puzzlement and pain. He felt that in most ways it would have been better if he had died on the plains with the rest of them. He was tired of wandering and looking.

But he hadn't died, and eventually he turned and went back to the post office, which was empty except for an elderly clerk with a white mustache.

"Well, you're back," the clerk said. "That was you a while ago, wasn't it?"

"That was me," July admitted.

He bought an envelope, a stamp and a couple of sheets of writing paper, and the clerk, who seemed kindly, loaned him a pencil to write with.

"You can write it right here at the window," the clerk said. "We're not doing much business today."

July started, and then, to his embarrassment, began to cry again. His memories were too sad, his hopes too thin. To have to say things on paper seemed a terrible task, for it stirred the memories.

"I guess somebody died and you've got to write their folks, is that it?" the clerk said.

"Yes," July said. "Only two of them didn't have no folks." He vaguely remembered that Roscoe had a few brothers, but none of them lived around Fort Smith or had been heard of in years. He wiped his eyes on his shirtsleeve again, reflecting that he had cried more in the last few weeks than he had in his whole life up to that point.

After standing there staring at the paper for a few minutes, he finally wrote a brief letter, addressed to Peach:

Dear Peach,

Roscoe Brown was killed by a bad outlaw, so was Joe. A girl named Janey was also kilt, I don't know much about her, Roscoe said he met her in the woods.

I don't know when I will be back—the folks can hire another sheriff if they want to, somebody has to look after the town.

YOUR BROTHER-IN-LAW
JULY JOHNSON

He had already pretty well convinced himself that Elmira was not in Dodge City, for he had been in every public place in town and had not seen her. But since the old clerk seemed kindly, he thought he might as well ask. Maybe she had come in to mail a letter at some point.

"I'm looking for a woman named Elmira," he said. "She's got brown hair and she ain't very big."

"Ellie?" the clerk said. "Why, I ain't seen Ellie in two or three years. Seems like I heard she moved to Abilene."

"That's her," July said, encouraged again all of a sudden. Ellie had been living in Abilene before she moved to St. Jo, where he had found her. "I thought she might have come back," he added.

"No, ain't seen her," the clerk said. "But you might ask Jennie, up at the third saloon. She and Elmira used to be thick once. I think they even married the same man, if you want to call it married."

"Oh, Mr. Boot?" July asked.

"Yes, Dee Boot, the scoundrel," the clerk said.

"How could he be married to the two of them?" July asked, not sure he wanted the information but unable to stop talking to a man who could tell him something about Ellie.

"Why, Dee Boot would bed down with a possum, if the possum was female. He was a cutter with the ladies."

"Didn't he die of smallpox?" July asked.

The clerk shook his head. "Not so far as I know," he said. "He's up in Ogallala or Deadwood or somewhere, where there's lots of whores and not too much law. I imagine he's got five or six whores in his string right now. Of course he could have died, but he's my nephew and I ain't heard no news to that effect."

"Thank you for the loan of the pencil," July said. He turned and walked out. He went straight to the livery stable and got his new horse, whose name was Pete. If Elmira wasn't in Dodge she might be in Abilene, so he might as well start. But he didn't start. He rode halfway out of town and then went back to the third saloon from the post office and inquired about the woman named Jennie. They said she had moved to another bar, up the street—a cowboy was even kind enough to point out the bar. A herd had been sold that morning and was being loaded onto boxcars. July rode over and watched the work a while—slow work and made slower by the cattle's long horns, which kept getting tangled with one another as the cattle were being forced up the narrow loading chute. The cowboys yelled and popped their quirts, and the horses behaved expertly, but despite that, it seemed to take a long time to fill a boxcar.

Still, July liked the look of the cowboys—he always had, even when they got a little rowdy, as they sometimes did in Fort Smith. They were young and friendly and seemed not to have a care in the world. They rode as if they were grown to their horses. Their teamwork when the cattle misbehaved and tried to break out was interesting to see. He saw a cowboy rope a running steer by the horns and then cleverly trip it so that the steer fell heavily. When the animal rose, it showed no more fight and was soon loaded.

After watching the loading for a while he went back to the saloon where the woman named Jennie was said to work. He inquired for her at the bar, and the bartender, a skinny runt, said she was busy and asked if he wanted a whiskey. July seldom drank whiskey but he said yes, to be courteous, mainly. If he was taking up space in a bar he ought to pay for it, he figured. So he took the whiskey and sipped it until it was gone, and then took another. Soon he was feeling heavy, as if it would be difficult to walk fast if he had to, but in fact he didn't have to. Women came and went in the saloon, but the bartender who poured the whiskeys kept assuring him that Jennie would be down any minute. July kept drinking. It seemed to him that he was taking on weight in a hurry. He felt that just getting out of his chair would be more than he could do, he felt so heavy.

The bartender kept bringing whiskeys and it seemed to July he must be running up quite a bill, but it didn't worry him. Occasionally a cowboy would pass by, his spurs jingling. Some of them gave July a look, but none of them spoke to him. It was comfortable to sit in the saloon—as sheriff, he had usually avoided them unless he had business in one. It had always puzzled him how some men could spend their days just sitting in a saloon, drinking, but now it was beginning to seem less puzzling. It was restful, and the heavy feeling that came with the drinking was a relief to him, in a way. For the last few weeks he had been struggling to do things which were beyond his powers—he knew he was supposed to keep trying, even if he wasn't succeeding, but it was pleasant not to try for a little while.

Then he looked up and saw a woman standing by the table—she was skinny, like Elmira, and had stringy black hair.

"Let's get going, cowboy," she said. "You can't do nothing sitting there."

"Get going where?" he asked, taken by surprise. No one had ever called him "cowboy" before, but it was a natural mistake. He had taken off his sheriff's star for a few days—a precaution he often took in a strange town.

"I'm Jennie," she said. "Sam said you were looking for me, or have I got the wrong cowboy?"

"Oh," July said, embarrassed. He had even forgotten he was waiting for someone named Jennie.

"We could get going, even if you ain't the right cowboy," Jennie said. "If you can afford that much whiskey you can afford me. You could even buy me a drink if you felt polite."

July had never in his life bought a woman a drink, or even sat with a woman who liked to drink. Any other time such an invitation would have shocked him, but in this case it just made him feel that his manners weren't all they should be. Jennie had huge brown eyes, too large for her thin face. She was looking at him impatiently.

"Yes, have a drink," he said. "I'm running up a bill."

Jennie sat down and waved at the bartender, who immediately appeared with a bottle. "This one's drinking like a fish," he said cheerfully. "I guess it's been a long, dry trail."

July suddenly remembered why he was waiting to see the girl named Jennie. "Did you know Ellie?" he asked. "I heard you knowed her."

It was Jennie's turn to be surprised. Elmira had been her best friend for three years, and she hardly expected a drunken young cowboy to mention her name.

"You mean Ellie Tims?" she asked.

"Yes," July said. "That's the Ellie. I was hoping you had news of her. I don't know where she is."

"Well, she moved to Missouri," Jennie said. "Then we heard she married a sheriff from Arkansas, but I didn't put no stock in that kind of rumor. I can't imagine Ellie staying married to no sheriff."

"She didn't," July said. "She run off while I was chasing Jake Spoon, and I got three people killed since I started looking for her."

Jennie looked at the young man more closely. She had noticed right off that he was drunk, but drunks were an everyday sight and she had not looked close. The man seemed very young, which is why she had taken him for a cowboy. They were mostly just boys. But this man didn't have the look of a cowboy once she looked close. He had a solemn face and sad eyes, the saddest she had looked into for a while. On the basis of the eyes he was an unlikely man for Ellie to have married—Ellie liked her laughs. But then people often did unlikely things.

"Are you a sheriff?" she asked, sipping the whiskey Sam had poured.

"I was," July said. "I'm most likely going to have to give it up."

"Why do that?" Jennie asked.

"I ain't a good fighter," July said. "I can crack a drunk on the head and get him to jail, but I ain't really a good fighter. When we rode into that camp, the man with me killed six or seven men and I never killed a one. I went off and left Roscoe and the others and they got killed before I could get back. It was only Jake Spoon I went to catch, but I made a mess of it. I don't want to be a sheriff now."

He had not expected such words to rush out—he had suddenly lost control of his speech somehow.

Jennie had not expected it either. She sipped her whiskey and watched him.

"They say Ellie left on a whiskey boat," July said. "I don't know why she would have done it, but that's what they say. Roscoe thought a bear might have got her, but they didn't see no tracks."

"What's your name?" Jennie asked.

"July Johnson," he said, glad that she was no longer looking at him quite so impatiently.

"It sounds like Ellie to me," Jennie said. "When Ellie gets enough of a place, she jumps in the first wagon and goes. I remember when she went to Abilene I didn't have no idea she was even thinking of leaving, and then, before it was even time to go to work, she had paid some mule skinners to take her, and she was gone."

"I got to find her," July said simply.

"You come to the wrong town, mister," Jennie said. "She ain't in Dodge."

"Well, then I'll have to keep looking," July said.

He thought of the empty plains, which it seemed to him he had been lucky to get across. There seemed only the smallest chance that Ellie would have been so lucky.

"I fear she's dead," he said.

"She's hunting Dee, I'd say," Jennie said. "Did you know Dee?"

"Why, no," July said. "I was told he died of smallpox."

Jennie chuckled. "Dee ain't dead," she said. "He's in Ogallala. There's a gambler sitting right over there who seen him not two months ago."

"Where?" July asked, and Jennie pointed to a pudgy man in a white shirt and black coat who sat alone at a table, shuffling cards.

"That's Webster Witter," Jennie said. "He keeps up with Dee Boot. I used to but I quit."

"Why?" July asked. He sensed that it was a rather loose-tongued question, but the fact was, his tongue was out of control and behaving ever more loosely.

"It's like trying to keep up with a tumbleweed," Jennie said. "Dee wears out one town and then he's off to another. I ain't that way. I like to settle in. I been here in Dodge five years already and I guess this is where I'll stay."

"I don't know why she married me," July said. "I ain't got any idea about it."

Jennie looked at him for a bit. "Do you always drink like this?" she asked.

"No, I seldom drink," July said. "Though I do like toddy in the winter."

Jennie looked at him a while. "You ought to stop worrying about Ellie, mister," she said. "No man's ever been able to stop Ellie for long, not even Dee."

"She married me," July said. He felt he had to insist on that point.

"Well, I married Dee once, myself," Jennie said. "I just did it because he was good-looking. That and the fact that I was mad at somebody else. Ellie and me are a lot alike," she added.

July just looked at her sadly. Jennie sighed. She had not expected to encounter such misery in the middle of the afternoon.

"You're right good-looking," she said. "I expect that explains it. If I were you I'd start getting over it."

"I got to find her," July said. "I got to tell her about little Joe. He got killed on the Canadian."

"She oughtn't to had him," Jeannie said. "I told her not to. I wouldn't have one for anything. I've had offers, too."

July drank two more whiskeys but had little more to say.

"Well, the bar's getting rich but I ain't," Jennie said. "Don't you want a little fun, to take your mind off it?"

It seemed to July that he was not so much sitting in the chair as floating in it. The world seemed kind of watery to him, but it was all right because he was easily able to float.

Jennie giggled, looking at him. "You sure are drunk, Mister Johnson," she said. "Let's go have a little fun. I always liked stealing Ellie's boys and here I've got a chance to steal her husband."

The way she giggled made July feel happy suddenly. He had not heard a woman giggle in a long time. Ellie never giggled. So he got up and followed Jennie up the stairs, walking carefully so as not to embarrass himself. He got upstairs all right, but before they could get to Jennie's room he began to feel wrong. His stomach began to float higher than he was. It began to float right out of his mouth.

Jennie had kept a close eye on him, and she quickly guided him to the outside stairs. July knelt down on the little landing and vomited over the edge. The next thing he knew he was lying flat on the landing, still vomiting. From time to time he quit vomiting and just lay there, but then he would start again, his body heaving upward like a bucking horse. He held to the rail of the landing with one hand so he wouldn't accidentally heave himself over. It was a bright day, the Kansas sun beating down, but July felt like he was in darkness. Cowboys rode up and down the street below him—once in a while one would hear him vomiting and look up and laugh. Wagons went by, and the drivers didn't even look up. Once, while he was resting two cowboys stopped and looked at him.

"I guess we ought to rope him and drag him to the graveyard," one said. "He looks dead to me."

"Hell, I wish all I had to do was lay on them stairs and vomit," the other cowboy said. "It beats loading them longhorns."

July lay face down for a long time. The heaves finally diminished, but from time to time he raised his head and spat over the edge, to clear his throat. It was nearly sundown before he felt like sitting up, and then it was only to sit with his back against the building. He was high enough that he could see over the main street and the cattle pens and west to where the sun was setting, far off on the plain. It was setting behind a large herd of cattle being held a mile or two from town. There were thousands of cattle, but only a few cowboys holding them—he could see the other cowboys racing for town. The dust their running horses kicked up was turned golden by the sun. No doubt they were just off the trail and couldn't wait for a taste of Dodge—the very taste he had just vomited up. The last sunlight filtered through the settling dust behind the cowboys' horses.

July sat where he was until the afterglow was just a pale line on the western horizon. The white moon shone on the railroad ties that snaked out of town to the east. He felt too weak to stand up, and he sat listening to the sounds of laughter that came from the saloon behind him.

When he finally stood up he was indecisive. He didn't know if he should go in and thank Jennie, or just slip away and continue the search for Elmira. He had an urge to just ride on out into the dark country. He didn't feel right in a town any-more. The crowds of happy cowboys just made him feel more lonesome some-how. On the plains, with nobody in sight, he wasn't reminded so often of how cut off he felt.

He decided, though, that politeness required him to at least say goodbye to Jennie. As he stepped back in the door, a cowboy came out of her room, looking cheerful, and went clumping down the stairs. A moment later Jennie came out too. She didn't notice July standing there. To his astonishment she stopped and lifted her skirts, so that he saw her thin legs, and more. There was a smear of something on one thigh and she hastily wet her fingers with a little spit and wiped it off. Just then she noticed July, who wished he had not bothered to come through the door. He had never seen a woman do such an intimate thing and the shock was so strong he thought his stomach might float up again.

When Jennie saw him she was not very embarrassed. She giggled again and lowered her skirts. "Well, you got a free look but I won't count it," she said. "I guess you didn't die."

"No," July said.

Jennie looked closely at him as if to make sure he was all right. She had a poor complexion, but he liked her frank brown eyes.

"What about the fun?" she said. "You lost out this afternoon."

"Oh," July said, "I'm not much fun."

"I guess you wouldn't be, after vomiting up your stomach," Jennie said. "I can't wait, though, mister. Three herds came in today, and there's a line of cowboys waiting to fall in love with me." She looked down the stairs; the noise from the saloon was loud.

"It's what I did with Ellie," July said. Meeting her friend Jennie had made his life clearer to him, suddenly. He was as simple as the cowboys—he had fallen in love with a whore.

Jennie looked at him a moment. She had come out of her room briskly, pre-pared for more business, but something in July's eyes slowed her down. She had never seen eyes with so much sadness in them—to look at him made her heart drop a little.

"Ellie was tired of this business," she said. "It was the buffalo hunters made her decide to quit. I guess you just come along at the right time."

"Yes," July said.

They were silent, looking at one another, Jennie reluctant to go down into the well of noise, July not ready to go out the door and head for the livery stable.

"Don't you want to quit?" he asked.

"Why, are you going to fall in love with me too?" Jennie asked, in her frank way.

July knew he could if he wasn't careful. He was so lonely, and he didn't have much control.

"Don't you want to quit?" he asked again.

Jennie shook her head. "I like to see the boys coming in," she said. "People are always coming in, here in Dodge. The cowboys are nicer than the buffalo hunters, but even the buffalo hunters was people."

She thought a moment. "I couldn't sit around in a house all day," she said. "If someone was ever to marry me I expect I'd run off, too. The time I get blue is the winter—there ain't no people coming in."

July thought of Ellie, sitting in the cabin loft all day, dangling her legs—no people came in at all except him and Joe, and Roscoe once in a while when they caught a catfish. Hearing Jennie talk put his life with Ellie in a very different light.

"You ought to go on back home," Jennie said. "Even if you catch her it won't do no good."

July feared it wouldn't, but he didn't want to go back. He just stood there. Something in his manner made Jennie suddenly impatient.

"I got to go," she said. "If you ever do find Ellie, tell her I still got that blue dress she gave me. If she ever wants it back she'll have to write."

July nodded. Jennie gave him a final look, half pitying, half exasperated, and hurried on down the stairs.

July felt sad when she left. He had the feeling that an opportunity had been missed, though he didn't know what kind of opportunity. The streets were full of cowboys going from one saloon to the next. There were horses tied to every hitch rail.

He went to the livery stable and saddled his new horse. The old man who ran the stable was sitting with his back against a barrel of horseshoe nails, drinking now and then from a jug he had between his legs. July paid him, but the old man didn't stand up.

"Which outfit are you with?" the old man asked.

"I'm with myself," July said.

"Oh," the man said. "A small outfit. This is a funny time of night to be starting out, ain't it?"

"I guess it is," July said, but he started anyway.

70

O NCE THEY GOT WEST, beyond the line of the grasshopper plague, the herd found good grass, the skies stayed clear for nearly two weeks, and the drive went the smoothest it had gone. The cattle settled down and moved north toward the Arkansas without stampedes or other incidents, except for one—a freak accident that cost Newt his favorite horse, Mouse.

Newt wasn't even riding Mouse when the accident occurred. He had traded mounts for the day with Ben Rainey. The day's work was over and Ben had ridden into the herd with Call's permission to cut out a beef for the cook. He rode up to a little bridled cow, meaning to take her yearling calf, and while he was easing the calf away from her the cow turned mean suddenly and hooked Mouse right back of the girth. She was a small cow with unusually sharp horns, and her thrust was so violent that Mouse's hindquarters were lifted off the ground. Ben Rainey was thrown, and had to scramble to keep from being hooked himself. Soupy Jones saw it happen. He loped in and soon turned the mad cow, but the damage was done. Mouse was spurting blood like a fountain from his abdomen.

"Get Deets," Soupy said. Deets was the best horse doctor in the outfit, though Po Campo was also good. Both men came over to look at the wound and both shook their heads. Newt, on the other side of the herd, saw people waving at him, and loped over. When he saw Mouse gushing blood he felt faint, from the shock.

"I don't know what went wrong with her," Ben Rainey said, feeling guilty. "I wasn't doin' nothing to her. She just hooked the horse. Next thing I knew she was after me. She has them little sharp twisty horns."

Mouse's hind legs were quivering.

"Well, you better put him down," Call said, looking at Newt. "He's finished."

Newt was about to take the reins when Dish Boggett intervened. "Oh, now, Captain," he said quietly, "a feller oughtn't to have to shoot his own horse when there's others around that can do it as well." And without another word he led the bleeding horse a hundred yards away and shot him. He came back, carrying the saddle. Newt was very grateful—he knew he would have had a hard time shooting Mouse.

"I wish now we'd never traded," Ben Rainey said. "I never thought anything would happen."

That night there was much discussion of the dangers of handling cattle. Everyone agreed there were dangers, but no one had ever heard of a small cow hooking a horse under the girth before and killing it. Newt traded shifts with the Irishman and then traded again with his replacement, four hours later. He wanted to be in the dark, where people couldn't see him cry. Mouse had never behaved like other horses, and now he had even found a unique way to die. Newt had had him for eight years and felt his loss so keenly that for the first time on the drive he wished it wouldn't get light so soon.

But the sun came up beautifully, and he knew he would have to go into breakfast. He rubbed the tear streaks off his face as best he could and was about to head
for the wagon when he saw Mr. Gus standing outside his little tent, waving at him.
Newt rode over. As he passed the open flap of the tent he saw Lorena sitting on a
pallet just inside. Her hair was loose around her shoulders and she looked very
beautiful.

Augustus had made a fire of buffalo chips and was complaining about it. "Dern,
I hate to cook with shit," he said. "I hear you lost your pony."

"Yes. Ben was riding him. It wasn't his fault, though," Newt said.

"Get down and drink a cup of coffee to cut the grief," Augustus said.

As he was drinking the coffee, Lorena came out of the tent. To Newt's surprise, she smiled at him—she didn't say anything, but she smiled. It was such a
joy that he immediately started feeling better. All the way from Texas he had
been worrying secretly that Lorena would blame him for her kidnap. After all,
he had been supposed to watch her the night she got taken. But she obviously
bore him no grudge. She stood in front of the tent, looking at the beautiful
morning.

"I've got so I like this looking far," she said. Augustus handed her a cup of coffee and she held it in both hands, the smoke drifting in front of her face. Newt was
sure he had never seen anyone as beautiful as her—that he was getting to share
breakfast with her was like a miracle. Dish or any of the other boys would give
their spurs and saddles to be doing what he was doing.

She sat down in front of the tent and blew on her coffee until it was cool
enough to drink. Newt drank his and felt a lot better. Poor Mouse was lost, but it
was a wonderful day, and he was enjoying the rare privilege of having breakfast
with Mr. Gus and Lorena. Across the plain they could see the herd, strung out to
the north. The wagon and the remuda were a mile behind them. Po Campo, a tiny
dot on the plain, walked well behind the wagon.

"That old cook is a sight," Augustus said. "I guess he plans to walk all the way to
Canada."

"He likes to watch the grass," Newt explained. "He's always finding stuff. He'll
cook most anything he picks up."

"Does he cook grass?" Lorena asked, interested. She had never seen Po Campo
close up but was intrigued by the sight of the tiny figure walking day after day
across the great plain.

"No, but he cooks things like grasshoppers once in a while," Newt said.

Lorena laughed—a delightful sound to Newt.

As she blew on her coffee, she looked at Gus. She had spent many hours looking at him since he had rescued her. It was comfortable traveling with him, for he
never got angry or scolded her, as other men had. In the weeks when she trembled and cried, he had expressed no impatience and made no demands. She had
become so used to him that she had begun to hope the trip would last longer. It
had become simple and even pleasant for her. No one bothered her at all, and it
was nice to ride along in the early summer sun, looking at the miles and miles of
waving grass. Gus talked and talked. Some of what he said was interesting and
some of it wasn't, but it was reassuring that he liked to talk to her.

It was enough of a life, and better than any she had had before. But she could
not forget the other woman Gus had mentioned. The other woman was the one
thing he didn't talk about. She didn't ask, of course, but she couldn't forget, either.
She dreaded the day when they would come to the town where the other woman

lived, for then the simple life might end. It wouldn't if she could help it, though. She meant to fight for it. She had decided to tell Gus she would marry him before they got to the town.

Never before had she given any thought to marrying a man. It had not seemed a likely thing. She had had enough of the kind of men who came into the saloons. Some of them wanted to marry her, of course—young cowboys, mostly. But she didn't take that seriously. Gus was different. He had never said he wanted to marry her, but he was handier than most at complimenting her on her beauty. He complimented her still, almost every day, telling her she was the most beautiful woman on the plains. They got along well; they didn't quarrel. To her, it all said that he might want to marry her, when they stopped. She was glad he had waved the boy over for breakfast. The boy was harmless, even rather sweet and likable. If she was friendly to the boy, it might make Gus think better of her as a wife-to-be. Though he had still not approached her, she felt him stirring when they slept close at night, and she meant to see that he did approach her before they got to Ogallala. She meant to do what she could to make him forget the other woman.

When Newt rode back to the herd he practically floated over the ground, he felt so happy. The death of Mouse was forgotten in the pleasure of remembering Lorena. She had smiled at him as he was mounting to leave.

It was not lost on the cowboys that Newt had secured a rare invitation. As he loped back to the drags, many heads were turned his way. But the drive had started, and no one got much of a chance to question him until that evening, when they were all getting their grub.

Dish, the friend who had relieved him of the burden of killing his own horse, was the most curious.

"Did you get to see Lorie?" Dish asked point-blank. He still felt such love for Lorie that even speaking her name caused him to feel weak sometimes.

"I seen her, she was drinking coffee," Newt said.

"Yes, she always took coffee in the morning," Lippy said, demonstrating a familiarity with Lorena's habits that offended Dish at once.

"Yes, and I'm sure you spied on her every opportunity you got," he said hotly.

"It didn't take no spying, she took it right in the saloon," Lippy said. "It was watch or go blind."

He was aware, as all the hands were, that Dish was mighty in love, but Dish was not the first cowboy to fall in love with a whore, and Lippy didn't feel he had to make too many concessions to the situation.

"Dish don't allow low types like us the right even to look at the girl," Jasper remarked. He had met with nothing but rejection at the hands of Lorena, and was still bitter about it.

"I bet Newt got a good look," Soupy said. "Newt's getting to an age to have an eye for the damsels."

Newt kept silent, embarrassed. He would have liked to brag a little about his visit, perhaps even repeat one of the remarks Lorena had made, but he was aware that he couldn't do so without causing Dish Boggett to feel bad that it wasn't him who had got the visit.

"Is Lorie still pretty or has all this traveling ruint her looks?" Needle Nelson asked.

"As if it could," Dish said angrily.

"She's real pretty still," Newt said. "Mr. Gus did most of the talking."

"Oh, Gus always does the most of it," Pea Eye said. "If they'd just pitch their tent a little closer, we could all hear it. Gus has a loud voice."

"I wouldn't care to listen," Dish said. It rankled him continually that Gus had all of Lorena's company, day after day.

"I never seen such a jealous bug as you are, Dish," Jasper said.

Call had eaten quickly and left with Deets—the Arkansas was only a few miles away and he wanted to have a look at the crossing. They loped up to the river through the long prairie dusk and sat on the riverbank awhile. Even in the moonlight they could see that the current was strong.

"I've always heard the Arkansas was swift," Call said. "Did you try it?"

"Oh yes," Deets said. "It took me down aways."

"It comes out of the same mountains as the Rio Grande," Call said. "Just a different side."

"Reckon we'll ever get back, Captain?" Deets asked. He had not planned to ask, but at mention of the Rio Grande he felt a sudden homesickness. He had been back and forth across the Rio Grande for so many years that it made him sad to think he might never see it again. The Rio Grande was shallow and warm, and no trouble to cross, whereas the farther north they went, the colder and swifter the rivers became.

Call was surprised by the question. "Why, some of the boys will be going back, I guess," he said. "I doubt that I'll return myself," he added, and hoped that Deets wouldn't want to go either. He relied on Deets too much. None of the other hands had his judgment.

Deets said no more about it, but his heart was heavy with a longing for Texas.

Call looked up the river toward Colorado. "That dern bandit's up there somewhere," he said. "I wish Gus had got him."

Deets could tell by the grim way the Captain was looking toward the mountains that he wished he could go after the man. Pursuit was what he and the Captain did best, and now he was wishing he could pursue Blue Duck.

Thinking to turn the Captain's mind from the outlaw, Deets mentioned something he had considered keeping to himself. It was something he had noticed the day before while scouting to the east a few miles.

"Wouldn't be surprised if Mr. Jake is around," he said.

"Jake?" Call asked. "Why would he be around?"

"Might not be him, but his horse is around," Deets said. "I crossed the track yesterday. It was that pacing horse he come home on."

"I'll swear," Call said. "Are you sure about the horse?"

"Oh, yes," Deets said. "I know the track. Four other horses with him. I guess Mr. Jake could have sold the horse."

"I doubt he would," Call said. "Jake likes a pacer."

He thought the information over as they trotted back toward the herd. He had meant it when he told Gus he wanted no more to do with Jake Spoon. Jake had only come back to Lonesome Dove to use them for support, and no doubt he would try to do it again if he got in trouble. This time it would probably be worse trouble, too. Once a man like Jake—who had got by on dash and little else all his life—started sliding, he might slide faster and faster.

"Oh, well," Call said, "we ain't far from Dodge. He may just be looking for a summer of gambling. Keep your eye out, though," he added. "If you strike his track again, let me know."

Deets went on back to camp, but Call stopped a mile away and staked his mare. He considered riding over to see Gus and passing on the news, but decided it could wait until morning. News of Jake might disturb the girl. If he was right, and Jake was just headed for Dodge, there was nothing to worry about.

He sat up much of the night, listening to the Irishman sing to the cattle. As he was listening, a skunk walked between him and the mare. It nosed along, stopping now and then to scratch at the dirt. Call sat still and the skunk soon went on its way. The Hell Bitch paid it no mind. She went on quietly grazing.

71

"I'LL BE GLAD to get to Dodge," Jake said. "I'd like a bath and a whore. And a good barber to shave me. There's a barber there named Sandy that I fancy, if nobody ain't shot him."

"You'll know tomorrow, I guess," Dan Suggs said. "I've never liked barbers myself."

"Dan don't even like whores," Roy Suggs said. "Dan's hard to please."

Jake was cheered by the thought that Dodge was so close. He was tired of the empty prairie and the sullen Suggses, and was looking forward to jolly company and some good card games. He had every intention of wiggling loose from the Suggses in Dodge. Gambling might be his ticket. He could win a lot of money and tell them he'd had enough of the roving life. They didn't own him, after all.

It was a sunny day, and Jake rode along happily. Sometimes he got a lucky feeling—the feeling that he was meant for riches and beautiful women and that nothing could keep him down for long. The lucky feeling came to him as he rode, and the main part of it was his sense that he was about to get free of the Suggs brothers. They were hard men, and he had made a bad choice in riding with them, but nothing very terrible had come of it, and they were almost to Dodge. It seemed to him he had slid into bad luck in Arkansas the day he accidentally shot the dentist, and now he was about to slide out of it in Kansas and resume the kind of enjoyable life he felt he deserved. Frog Lip was riding just in front of him, and he felt how nice it would be not to have to consort with such a man again. Frog Lip rode along silently, as he had the whole trip, but there was menace in his silence, and Jake was ready for lighter company—a whore, particularly. There were sure to be plenty of them in Dodge.

In the afternoon, though, Dan Suggs, the man who was hard to please, saw something he liked: a herd of about twenty-five horses being driven south by three men. He rode over to a ridge and inspected the horses through his spyglasses. When he came back he had a pleased look on his face. At the sight of it Jake immediately lost his lucky feeling.

"It's old Wilbarger," Dan said. "He's just got two hands with him."

"Why, I've heard of him," Jake said. "We returned some of his horses to him, out of Mexico. Pedro Flores had them. I never met Wilbarger myself."

"I've met him, the son of a bitch," Dan said. "I rode for him once."

"Where's he goin' with them horses, back to Texas?" Roy asked.

"He's probably sold his lead herd in Dodge and has got another bunch or two headed for Denver. He's taking his boys some fresh mounts."

Wilbarger and his horses were soon out of sight, but Dan Suggs made no move to resume the trip to Dodge.

"I guess Dan's feeling bloody," Roy said, observing his brother.

"I thought Wilbarger was rough," little Eddie said.

"He is, but so am I," Dan Suggs said. "I never liked the man. I see no reason why we shouldn't have them horses."

Roy Suggs was not greatly pleased by his brother's behavior. "Have 'em and do what with 'em?" he asked. "We can't sell 'em in Dodge if Wilbarger's just been there."

"Dodge ain't the only town in Kansas," Dan said. "We can sell 'em in Abilene."

With no further discussion, he turned and rode southwest at a slow trot. His brothers followed. Jake sat for a moment, his lucky feeling gone and a sense of dread in its place. He thought maybe the Suggs brothers would forget him and he could ride on to Dodge, but then he saw Frog Lip looking at him. The black man was impassive.

"You coming?" he asked—the first time on the whole trip that he had spoken to Jake directly. There was an insolence in his voice that caused Jake to flare up for a moment despite himself.

"I guess if you watch you'll find out," Jake said, bitter that the man would address him so.

Frog Lip just looked at him, neither smiling nor frowning. The insolence of the look was so great that for a moment Jake contemplated gunplay. He wanted to shoot the look off the black man's face. But instead he touched his horse lightly with the spurs and followed the Suggs brothers across the plain. He felt angry— the barber and the whore he had been looking forward to had been put off. Soon he heard the black man's horse fall in behind him.

Dan Suggs traveled at a leisurely pace; they didn't see Wilbarger or his horses again that day. When they spotted a spring with a few low trees growing by it, Dan even stopped for a nap.

"You don't want to steal horses in the daytime," he remarked when he awoke. "It works better at night. That way you can put it off on Indians, if you're lucky."

"We better pull the shoes off these horses then," Roy Suggs said. "Indians don't use horseshoes much."

"You're a stickler for details, ain't you?" Dan said. "Who's gonna track us?" He lay back in the shade and put his hat over his eyes.

"Wilbarger might, if he's so rough," little Eddie said.

Dan Suggs just chuckled.

"Hell, I thought we come up here to rob banks and regulate settlers," Jake said. "I don't remember hiring on to steal horses. Stealing horses is a hanging crime, as I recall."

"I never seen such a bunch of young ladies," Dan said. "Everything's a hanging crime up here in Kansas. They ain't got around to making too many laws."

"That may be," Jake said. "Horse stealing don't happen to be my line of work."

"You're young, you can learn a new line of work," Dan said, raising up on an elbow. "And if you'd rather not learn, we can leave you here dead on the ground. I won't tolerate a shirker." With that he put his hat back over his face and went to sleep.

Jake knew he was trapped. He could not fight four men. The Suggs brothers all took naps, but Frog Lip sat by the spring all afternoon, cleaning his guns.

Late in the afternoon Dan Suggs got up and took a piss by the spring. Then he lay down on his belly and had a long drink of water. When he got up, he mounted his horse and rode off, without a word to anyone. His brothers quickly mounted and followed him, and Jake had no choice but to do the same. Frog Lip, as usual, brought up the rear.

"Dan's feeling real bloody," little Eddie said.

"Well, he gets that way," Roy said. "I hope you don't expect me to preach him a sermon."

"He don't want them horses," little Eddie said. "He wants to kill that man."

"I doubt he'll turn down free horses, once he has them," Roy said.

Jake felt bitter that the day had turned so bad. It was his bad luck again—he couldn't seem to beat it. If Wilbarger had been traveling even half a mile further west, they would never have seen him and his horses, and they would be in Dodge, enjoying the comforts of the town. On that vast plain, spotting three men and some horses was a mere accident—as much a matter of luck as the bullet that killed Benny Johnson. Yet both had happened. It was enough to make a man a pessimist, that such things had started occurring regularly.

They soon struck Wilbarger's trail and followed it west through the sunset and the long dusk. The trail led northwest toward the Arkansas, easy to follow even in the twilight. Dan Suggs never slowed. They struck the river and swam it by moonlight. Jake hated to ride sopping wet, but was offered no choice, for Dan Suggs didn't pause. Nobody said a word when they came to the river; nobody said one afterward. The moon was well over in the west before Dan Suggs drew rein.

"Go find them, Frog," he said. "I doubt they're far."

"Do I shoot or not?" the black man asked.

"Hell, no, don't shoot," Dan said. "Do you think I'd ride all this way and swim a river just to miss the fun? Come on back when you find 'em."

Frog Lip was back in a few minutes.

"We nearly rode into them," he said. "They're close."

Dan Suggs had been smoking, but he quickly put his smoke out and dismounted.

"You hold the horses," he said to little Eddie. "Come on once you hear the shooting."

"I can shoot as good as Roy," little Eddie protested.

"Hell, Roy couldn't hit his foot if it was nailed to a tree," Dan said. "Anyway, we're gonna let Jake shoot them—he's the man with the reputation."

He took the rifle and walked off. Jake and the others followed. There was no sign of a campfire, no sign of anything but plains and darkness. Though Frog Lip had said the men were close, it seemed to Jake they walked a long time. He didn't see the horses until he almost bumped into one. For a moment he thought of trying to grab a horse and run away bareback. The commotion would warn Wilbarger, and maybe one or two of the Suggs boys would get shot. But the horse quickly stepped away from him and the moment passed. He drew his pistol, not knowing what else to do. They had found the horses, but he didn't know where the camp was. Frog Lip was near him, watching, Jake supposed.

When the first shot came, he didn't know who fired it, though he saw a flash from a rifle barrel. It seemed so far away that he almost felt it must be another battle. Then gunfire flared just in front of him, too much to be produced by three men, it seemed. So much shooting panicked him for a second and he fired twice into the darkness, with no idea of what he might be shooting at. He heard gunfire behind him—it was Frog Lip shooting. He began to sense running figures, although it was not clear to him who they were. Then there were five or six shots close together, like sudden thunder, and the sound of a running horse. Jake could see almost nothing— once in a while he would think he saw a man, but he couldn't be sure.

"Frog, did you get him?" he heard Dan Suggs ask.

"No, he got me, damn him," he heard the black man say.

"I swear I put three into him but he made it to that horse anyway," Dan said. "You alive, Roy?"

"I'm alive," Roy Suggs said, from back near the horse herd.

"Well, what are you doing over there?" Dan wanted to know. "The damn fight was over here."

"We want the horses, don't we?" Roy asked, anger in his voice.

"I wanted that goddamn Wilbarger worse," Dan said. "What about you, Spoon?"

"Not hurt," Jake said.

"Hell, you and Roy might as well have stayed in Dodge, for all the good you are in the dark," Dan said.

Jake didn't answer. He was just glad he had not been forced to shoot anybody. It seemed ridiculous, attacking men in the dark. Even Indians waited until sunup. He took some hope from the fact that Frog Lip claimed to have been hit, though how anybody knew where to shoot was a mystery to him.

"Where's that goddamn kid?" Dan asked. "I told him to bring them horses. Old Wilbarger's getting away. Where'd you get hit, Frog?"

Frog Lip didn't answer.

"Goddamn the old son of a bitch," Dan said. "I guess he's killed Frog. Go get Eddie, Roy."

"You told him to come, I guess he'll come," Roy said.

"You best go get him unless you think you're bulletproof," Dan said in a deadly voice.

"I ain't going if Wilbarger's out there," Roy said. "You won't shoot me neither— I'm your brother."

There were two more shots, so close that Jake jumped.

"Did I get you?" Dan asked.

"No, and don't shoot no more," Roy said, in a surprised voice. "Why would you shoot at me?"

"There ain't nobody else around to shoot at except Jake, and you know his reputation," Dan said sarcastically.

They heard horses coming. "Boys?" little Eddie called out.

"No, mostly girls here tonight," Dan said. "Are you waiting for election day or what? Bring the goddamn horses."

Little Eddie brought them. The dawn was behind him, very faint but coming. Soon it was possible to make out the results of the battle. Wilbarger's two men were dead, still in their blankets. One was Chick, the little weasel Jake remembered seeing the morning they brought the horses in from Mexico. He had been hit in the neck by a rifle bullet, Frog Lip's, Dan said. The bullet had practically torn his head loose from his body—the corpse reminded Jake of a dead rabbit, perhaps because Chick had rabbitlike teeth, exposed now in a stiff grimace.

The other dead man was just a boy, probably Wilbarger's wrangler.

Of Wilbarger himself, there was no sign.

"I know I put three into him," Dan Suggs said. "He must have slept with the damn reins in his hand or he'd have never got to his horse."

Frog Lip lay on the ground, still gripping his rifle. His eyes were wide open and he was breathing as heavily as a horse after a long run. His wound was in the groin—his pants were wet with blood. The rising sun shone in his face, which was bearded with sweat.

"Who shot Frog?" little Eddie asked in surprise.

"Why, that damn Wilbarger, who else?" Dan said. He had no more than glanced at Frog Lip—he was scanning the plains with his spyglass, hoping to catch a glimpse of the cowman. But the plains were empty.

"I never thought anybody would get Frog," little Eddie said, unnerved by what he saw.

Dan Suggs was snarling with frustration. He glared at his brothers as if they were solely responsible for Wilbarger's escape.

"You boys ought to go home and teach school," he said. "It's all you're good for."

"What did you expect me to do?" Roy asked. "I can't see in the dark."

Dan walked over and looked down at Frog Lip. He ignored his brothers. He knelt down and pulled the Negro's bloodstained shirt loose from his pants, exposing the wound. After a second he stood up.

"Frog, I guess this was your unlucky day," he said. "I guess we better just shoot you."

Frog Lip didn't answer. He didn't move or even blink his eyes.

"Shoot him and let's go," Dan said, looking at little Eddie.

"Shoot Frog?" little Eddie said, as if he had not heard quite right.

"Yes, Frog's the one with the slug in his gut," Dan said. "He's the one that needs to finish up dying. Shoot him and let's ride."

"I hate to shoot Frog," little Eddie said in a dazed tone.

"I guess we'll just leave him for the buzzards then, if you're so squeamish," Dan said. He removed the rifle from the Negro's hand and took the big pistol out of his belt.

"Ain't you gonna let him keep his guns?" Roy asked.

"Nope," Dan said. "He won't need 'em, but we might."

With that he mounted and rode over to look at the horse herd they had captured.

"You shoot him, Roy," little Eddie said. "I hate to."

"No, Dan's mad at me anyway," Roy said. "If I do something he ordered you to do, I'll be the one shot."

With that he mounted and rode off too. Jake walked over to his horse, feeling that it had been a black day when he met the Suggses.

"Would you like to shoot him, Jake?" little Eddie asked. "I've known him all my life."

"I wouldn't care to," Jake said. He remembered how insolent Frog Lip had been only the day before, and how he had wanted to shoot him then. It had been a rapid turnabout. The man lay on the ground, dying of a cruel wound, and none of the men he rode with even wanted to put him out of his misery.

"Well, damn," little Eddie said. "Nobody's much help."

He shrugged, drew his gun, and without another word walked over and shot Frog Lip in the head. The body jerked, and that was that.

"Get his money," Dan Suggs yelled. "I forgot to."

Little Eddie went through the dead man's bloody pockets before he mounted.

Jake had supposed they might try to go after Wilbarger, since he was wounded, but Dan Suggs turned the horse herd north.

"Ain't we going after that man?" Roy asked.

"I couldn't track an elephant and neither could you," Dan said. "Frog was our tracker. I shot Wilbarger three times, I expect he'll die."

"I thought we was going to Abilene," little Eddie said. "Abilene ain't this way."

Dan sneered at his brother. "I wish Wilbarger had shot you instead of Frog," he said. "Frog was a damn sight better hand."

Jake thought maybe he had seen the last of the killing. He felt it could be worse. The shooting had all been in pitch-darkness. Wilbarger hadn't seen him. He couldn't be connected with the raid. It was luck, of a sort. If he could just get free of the Suggses, he wouldn't be in such hopeless trouble.

As he rode along, trailing the twenty-five horses, he decided the best thing for him would be to leave the west. He could travel over to St. Louis and catch a boat down to New Orleans, or even go east to New York. Both of them were fine towns for gamblers, or so he had heard. In either one he could be safe and could pursue the kind of life he enjoyed. Looking back on it, it seemed to him that he had been remarkably lucky to survive as long as he had in such a rough place, where killing was an everyday affair. No man's luck lasted forever, and the very fact that he had fallen in with the Suggses suggested that his was about exhausted.

He resolved to bend his wits to getting out while the getting was possible. The death of Frog Lip made the task easier, for, as Dan said, Frog Lip was the only tracker in the crowd. If he could just manage to get a good jump, somehow, he might get away. And if he did he wouldn't stop until he hit the Mississippi.

With his mind made up, he felt cheerful—it always gave a man a lift to escape death. It was a beautiful sunny day and he was alive to see it. With any luck at all, he had seen the end of the trouble.

His good mood lasted two hours, and then something occurred which turned it sour. It seemed as if the world was deserted except for them and the horses, and then to his surprise he saw a tent. It was staked under a single tree, directly ahead of them. Near the tent, two men were plowing with four mules. Dan Suggs was riding ahead of the horse herd, and Jake saw him lope off toward the settlers. He didn't think much about it—he was watching the tent to see if any women were around. Then he heard the faint pop of a shot and looked up to see one of the settlers fall. The other man was standing there, no gun in his hand, nothing. He stood as if paralyzed, and in a second Dan Suggs shot him too. Then he trotted over to the tent, got off his horse and went inside.

Jake hardly knew what to think. He had just seen two men shot in the space of seconds. He had no idea why. By the time he got near the tent Dan Suggs had drug a little trunk outside and was rifling it. He pitched the clothes which were in the trunk out on the grass. His brothers rode over to join the fun, and were soon holding up various garments, to see if they fit. Jake rode over too, feeling nervous. Dan Suggs was clearly in a killing mood. Both farmers lay dead on the grass near their mule team, which was quietly grazing. Both had bullet holes in their foreheads. Dan had shot them at point-blank range.

"Well, they didn't have much but a watch," Dan said, holding up a fine-looking silver pocket watch. "I guess I'll take the watch."

His brothers found nothing of comparable value, although they searched the tent thoroughly. While they were looking, Dan started a fire with some coal oil he had found and made some coffee.

"I tell you, let's hang 'em," he said, strolling over to look at the dead men. Both were in their forties, and both had scraggly beards.

Roy Suggs looked puzzled. "Why would you want to hang them?" he asked. "They're already dead."

"I know, but it's a shame to waste that tree," Dan said. "It's the only tree around. What's a tree good for if not to hang somebody from?"

The thought made little Eddie giggle, a nervous giggle.

"Dan, you beat all," he said. "I never heard of hanging dead men."

Nonetheless Dan meant it. He put ropes around both the dead men's necks and had his brothers drag them to the tree and hoist them up. It was not a large tree, and the dead men's feet were only a few inches off the ground. Jake was not called on to help, and he didn't.

When the men were hung, twisting at the end of the ropes, Dan Suggs stood back to study the effect, and evidently didn't like it. His brothers were watching him nervously—it was plain from his face that he was still in an angry mood.

"These goddamn sodbusters," he said. "I hate their guts and livers."

"Well, that's fine, Dan," Roy said. "They're dead enough."

"No, they ain't," Dan said. "A goddamn sodbuster can never be dead enough to suit me."

With that he went over and got the can of coal oil he had used to start the fire. He began to splash it on the hanged men's clothes.

"What's that for?" little Eddie asked. "You've already shot 'em and hung 'em."

"Yes, and now I intend to burn them," Dan said. "Any objections from you schoolteachers?" He looked at all three of them, challenge in his angry eyes. No one said a word. Jake felt sickened by what was happening, but he didn't try and stop it. Dan Suggs was crazy, there was no doubt of that, but his craziness didn't affect his aim. The only way to stop him would be to kill him, a risky business in broad daylight.

Little Eddie giggled his nervous giggle again as he watched his brother set the dead men's clothes on fire. Even with the coal oil it wasn't easy—Dan had to splash them several times before he got their clothes wet enough to blaze. But finally he did, and the clothes flared up. It was a terrible sight. Jake thought he wouldn't look, but despite himself he did. The men's sweaty clothes were burned right off them, and their scraggly beards seared. A few rags of clothes fell off beneath their feet. The men's pants burned off, leaving their belts and a few shreds of cloth around their waists.

"Dan, you beat all," little Eddie repeated several times. He giggled often—he was unnerved. Roy Suggs methodically tore the tent apart and poked through all the men's meager belongings, hoping to find valuables.

"They didn't have nothing," he said. "I don't know why you even bothered to kill them."

"It was their unlucky day, same as it was Frog's," Dan said. "We'll miss Frog, the man could shoot. I wish I had that damn Wilbarger here, I'd cook him good."

After drinking some more coffee, Dan Suggs mounted up. The two farmers, the trunks of their bodies blackened, still hung from the tree.

"Don't you intend to bury them?" Jake asked. "Somebody's gonna find them, you know, and it could be the law."

Dan Suggs just laughed. "I'd like to see the law that could take me," he said. "No man in Kansas could manage it, and anyway I fancy seeing Nebraska."

He turned to his brothers, who were dispiritedly raking through the settlers' clothes, still hoping to find something worth taking.

"Get them mules, boys," Dan said. "No sense in leaving good mules."

With that he rode off.

"He's bloody today," Roy said, going over to the mules. "If we run into any more sodbusters, it's too bad for them."

Jake's happy mood was gone, though the day was as sunny as ever. It was clear to him that his only hope was to escape the Suggses as soon as possible. Dan Suggs could wake up feeling bloody any day, and the next time there might be no sodbusters around to absorb his fury, in which case things could turn really grim. He trotted along all day, well back from the horse herd, trying to forget the two blackened bodies, whose shoes had still been smoldering when they left.

72

DEETS FOUND WILBARGER by backtracking his horse. The horse, with dried blood on the saddle and crusted in its mane, was waiting for them on the north bank of the Arkansas. Several times, as they were bringing the cattle to the crossing, the horse started to swim over to them, but turned back. Deets crossed first, ahead of Old Dog, and recognized the horse even before he hit the bank. It was the big bay Wilbarger had ridden into Lonesome Dove several months before.

He rode up and caught the horse easily—but then, what looked to be a simple cattle crossing turned out to be anything but simple. Dish Boggett's horse, which had crossed many rivers calmly and easily, took fright in midstream and very nearly drowned Dish. The horse went crazy in the water, and if Dish hadn't been a strong swimmer, would have pawed him under. Even then it might have happened if Deets had not dashed back into the water and fought the horse off long enough for Dish to get ashore.

The trouble opened a gap in the line of cowboys and some three hundred cattle veered off and began to swim straight downstream. The line of cattle broke, and in no time there were pockets of cattle here and there, swimming down the Arkansas, paying no attention to the riders who tried to turn them. Newt got caught beside such a bunch, and after swimming two hundred yards downstream with them, ended up on the same bank he had started out on.

Eventually the herd split into five or six groups. Augustus came over to help, but there was not much he could do. Most of the cattle went back to the south bank, but quite a few swam far downstream.

"Looks like your herd's floating away, Woodrow," Augustus said.

"I know, I'm surprised that it ain't hailing or shooting lightning bolts at us," Call said. Though the scattering was annoying, he was not seriously disturbed, for the river was fairly shallow and the banks rather low where they were crossing. It would only take a little more time to restart the cattle that had gone back to the south bank. Fortunately no cattle were bogged, and this time no cowboys drowned.

"Good lord," Augustus said, as Deets came up leading the bay. "Where's Mister Wilbarger, that he could afford to let his horse run loose?"

"Dead, I fear," Call said. "Look at the blood on that horse's mane."

"Hell, I liked Wilbarger," Augustus said. "I'd be right sorry if he's dead. I'll go have a look."

"Who'll watch the girl while you're gone?" Call asked.

Augustus stopped. "You're right," he said. "It might make her uneasy if I just ride off. Maybe Deets better go have the look."

"It could be Indians, you know," Call said. "I think you better move her a little closer to the wagon."

Deets didn't come back until midafternoon, by which time the herd was a few miles north of the Arkansas.

"I doubt cattle has ever et this grass," Augustus said. "I doubt anyone's trailed cattle this far west of Dodge. Buffalo is probably all that's et it."

Call's mind was on Wilbarger, a resourceful man if ever he had seen one. If such a man had got caught, then there could well be serious trouble waiting for them.

"You're supposed to be able to smell Indians," he said to Augustus. "Do you smell any?"

"No," Augustus said. "I just smell a lot of cowshit. I expect my smeller will be ruined forever before this trip is over by smelling so much cowshit."

"It don't mention buffalo in the Bible," Augustus remarked.

"Well, why should it?" Call said.

"It might be that a buffalo is a kind of ox, only browner," Augustus said. "Ox are mentioned in the Bible."

"What got you on the Bible?" Call asked.

"Boredom," Augustus said. "Religious controversy is better than none."

"If there's mad Indians around, you may get more controversy than you bargained for," Call said.

Lorena heard the remark—she was riding behind them. Mention of Indians brought back memories and made her nervous.

Finally they saw Deets, coming along the river from the southeast. It was clear from the dried sweat on his horse that he had ridden hard.

"They didn't get Deets, whoever they are," Augustus said.

"I found the man," Deets said, drawing rein. "He's shot."

"Dead?" Call asked.

"Dying, I 'spect," Deets said. "I couldn't move him. He's hit three times."

"How far away?"

"About ten miles," Deets said. "I got him propped up, but I couldn't bring him."

"Did he say much?" Augustus asked.

"He wants to see you, if you're not too busy," Deets said. "He said if you were busy don't make the trip."

"Why would I be that busy?" Augustus asked.

Deets looked at him. "He's real polite, that gentleman," he said. "I guess he thinks he might be dead before you get there."

"Oh, I see—the man don't want to put nobody out," Augustus said. "I'll go anyway. I admire his conversation."

"Change horses," Call said to Deets, and Deets loped off. He was trying to decide who they ought to take, and finally decided just to take Pea Eye, Deets and the boy. The boy could watch the horses, if there was trouble. It meant leaving the herd, but there was no help for it. There was good grazing and the herd looked peaceful. Dish and the rest of the crew ought to be about to handle it.

"Was it Indians got him?" he asked, when Deets returned.

Deets shook his head. "White men," he said. "Horsethieves."

"Oh," Call said. "Murdering horsethieves, at that." But it relieved his mind, for horsethieves wouldn't attack an outfit as large as theirs.

Augustus dropped back to explain matters to Lorena. She looked at him with worry in her eyes.

"Now, Lorie, you relax," he said. "It wasn't Indians, after all."

"What was it then?" she asked.

"The man who loaned us this tent got shot," he said. "He's in a bad way, it appears. We're going to see if we can help him."

"How long will it take?" Lorena asked. It was already late afternoon—it meant a night without Gus, and she had not had to face one since he rescued her.

"I don't know, honey," he said. "A few days, maybe, if we go after the horsethieves that shot him. If there's a chance to get them we'll try. Call won't let a horsethief off, and he's right."

"I'll go," Lorena said. "I can keep up. We don't need the tent."

"No," Augustus said. "You stay with the wagon—you'll be perfectly safe. I'll ask Dish to look after you."

Lorena began to shake. Maybe Gus was doing it because he was tired of her. Maybe he would never come back. He might slip off and find the woman in Nebraska.

To her surprise, Gus read her mind. He smiled his devilish smile at her. "I ain't running for the bushes, if that's what you think," he said.

"There ain't no bushes," she pointed out. "I just don't want you to go, Gus."

"I got to," Augustus said. "A man's dying and he asked for me. We're kind of friends, and think what would have happened when the grasshoppers hit if we hadn't had this tent to hide in. I'll be back, and I'll see that Dish looks after you in the meantime."

"Why him?" she asked. "I don't need him. Just tell him to leave me be."

"Dish is the best hand," Augustus said. "Just because he's in love with you don't mean he couldn't be helpful if a storm blew up or something. It ain't his fault he's in love with you. He's smitten, and that's all there is to it."

"I don't care about him," Lorena said. "I want you to come back."

"I will, honey," he said, checking the loads in his rifle.

Dish could hardly believe his luck when Augustus told him to take Lorena her meals and look after her. The thought that he would be allowed to go over to the tent made him a little dizzy.

"Do you think she'll speak to me?" he asked, looking at the tent. Lorena had gone inside and pulled the flaps, though it was hot.

"Not today," Augustus said. "Today she's feeling sulky. If I was you I'd sing to her."

"Sing to Lorie?" Dish said, incredulous. "Why, I'd be so scared I'd choke."

"Well, if you require timid women there's not much I can do for you," Augustus said. "Just keep a good guard at night and see she don't get kidnapped."

Call hated to leave the herd, and most of the cowboys hated it that he was leaving. Though it was midsummer, the skies clear, and the plains seemingly peaceful, most of the hands looked worried as the little group prepared to leave. They sat around worrying, all but Po Campo, who was singing quietly in his raspy voice as he made supper. Even Lippy was unnerved. He was modest in some matters and had just returned from walking a mile, in order to relieve his bowels in private.

"If you see any bushes, bring one back with you," he said to the mounted men. "If we had a bush or two I wouldn't have to walk so far just to do my business."

"I don't know why you're so modest," Augustus said. "Go over and squat behind a cow. You got a hole in your stomach anyway."

"I wish we'd brought the pia-ner," Lippy said. "A little pia-ner music would go good right now."

Call put Dish in charge of the outfit, meaning that he suddenly had two heavy responsibilities—Lorena and the herd. It left him subdued, just thinking about it. If anything should happen to the girl or the herd he'd never be able to hold up his head again.

"Ease 'em along," Call told Dish. "Bert can scout ahead and make sure there's water."

If Dish felt subdued, Newt felt nothing but pride to have been selected for the trip. He could tell some of the other hands were envious, particularly the Rainey boys, but it was the Captain's order, and no one dared say a word. When he saw the Captain put two boxes of rifle shells into his saddlebag he felt even prouder, for it meant he might be expected to fight. The Captain must have decided he was grown, to bring him on such a trip. After all, only the original Hat Creek outfit— the Captain and Mr. Gus, Pea and Deets—were going along, and now he was included. Every few minutes, as they rode east, he put his hand on his pistol to reassure himself that it was still there.

They got back to Wilbarger a little after sundown, before the plains had begun to lose the long twilight. He had reached the Arkansas before collapsing, and lay under the shade of the bank on a blanket Deets had left him. He was too weak to do more than raise his head when they rode up; even that exhausted him.

"Well, you just keep turning up," he said to Augustus, with a wan smile. "I've been lying here trying not to bleed on this good blanket your man left me."

Augustus stooped to examine him and saw at once there was no hope.

"I've bled so much already I expect I'm white as snow," Wilbarger said. "I'm a dern mess. I took one in the lung and another seems to have ruint my hip. The third was just a flesh wound."

"I don't think we can do anything about the lung," Call said.

Wilbarger smiled. "No, and neither could a Boston surgeon," he said.

He raised his head again. "Still riding that mare, I see," he said. "If I could have talked you out of her I probably wouldn't be lying here shot. She'd have smelled the damn horsethieves. I do think she's a beauty."

"How many were there?" Call asked. "Or could you get a count?"

"I expect it was Dan Suggs and his two brothers, and a bad nigger they ride with," Wilbarger said. "I think I hit the nigger."

"I don't know the Suggses," Call said.

"They're well known around Fort Worth for being murdering rascals," Wilbarger said. "I never expected to be fool enough to let them murder *me*. It's humbling. I lived through the worst war ever fought and then got killed by a damn sneaking horsethief. That galls me, I tell you."

"Any of us can oversleep," Augustus said quietly. "If you was to lie quiet that lung might heal."

"No sir, not likely," Wilbarger said. "I saw too many lung-shot boys when we were fighting the Rebs to expect that to happen. I'd rather just enjoy a little more conversation."

He turned his eyes toward the Hell Bitch and smiled—the sight of her seemed to cheer him more than anything.

"I do admire that mare," he said. "I want you to keep that mean plug of mine for your troubles. He's not brilliant, but he's sturdy."

He lay back and was quiet for a while, as the dusk deepened.

"I was born on the Hudson, you know," he said, a little later. "I fully expected to die on it, but I guess the dern Arkansas will have to do."

"I wish you'd stop talking about your own death," Augustus said in a joking tone. "It ain't genteel."

Wilbarger looked at him and chuckled, a chuckle that brought up blood. "Why, it's because I ain't genteel that I'm bleeding to death beside the Arkansas," he said. "I could have been a lawyer, like my brother, and be in New York right now, eating oysters."

He didn't speak again until after it was full dark. Newt stood over with the horses, trying not to cry. He had scarcely known Mr. Wilbarger, and had found him blunt at first, but the fact that he was lying there on a bloody blanket dying so calmly affected him more than he had thought it would. The emptiness of the plains as they darkened was so immense that that affected him too, and a sadness grew in him until tears began to spill from his eyes. Captain Call and Mr. Gus sat by the dying man. Deets was on the riverbank, a hundred yards away, keeping watch. And Pea Eye stood with Newt, by the horses, thinking his own thoughts.

"How long will it take him to die?" Newt asked, feeling he couldn't bear such a strain for a whole night.

"I've seen boys linger for days," Pea Eye said quietly—he had always thought it impolite to talk about a man's death within his hearing. Gus's joke had shocked him a little.

"But then sometimes they just go," he added. "Go when they're ready, or even if they ain't. This man's lost so much blood he might go over pretty soon."

Call and Augustus knew there was nothing to do but wait, so they sat beside Wilbarger's pallet, saying little. Two hours passed with no sound but Wilbarger's faint breathing.

Then, to Call's surprise, Wilbarger's hand reached out and clutched him for a moment.

"Let's shake, for the favors you've done me," Wilbarger said weakly. When Call had given him a handshake, Wilbarger reached for Augustus, who shook his hand in turn.

"McCrae, I'll give you credit for having written a damn amusing sign," he said. "I've laughed about that sign many a time, and laughing's a pleasure. I've got two good books in my saddlebags. One's Mister Milton and the other's a Virgil. I want you to have them. The Virgil might improve your Latin."

"I admit it's rusty," Augustus said. "I'll apply myself, and many thanks."

"To tell the truth, I can't read it either," Wilbarger said. "I could once, but I lost it. I just like to look at it on the page. It reminds me of the Hudson, and my schooling and all. Now and then I catch a word."

He coughed up a lot of blood and both Call and Augustus thought it was over, but it wasn't. Wilbarger was still breathing, though faintly. Call went over and told Pea Eye and Newt to start digging the grave—he wanted to get started after the horsethieves as soon as it was light enough to track. Restless, he walked over and helped Deets keep watch.

To Augustus's surprise, Wilbarger raised his head. He had heard the digging. "Your friend's efficient, ain't he?" he said.

"Efficient," Augustus agreed. "He likes to chase horsethieves too. Seems like we're always having to get your horses back, Wilbarger. Where do you want 'em delivered this time?"

"Oh, hell, sell 'em," Wilbarger said, in shaky tones. "I'm done with the cow business, finally. Send the money to my brother, John Wilbarger, Fifty Broadway, New York City."

He coughed again. "Keep the tent," he said. "How's the shy young lady?"

"She's improved," Augustus said.

"I wish we'd met sooner, McCrae," Wilbarger said. "I enjoy your conversation. I hope you'll bury my man Chick and that boy that was with us. I wish now I'd never hired that boy."

"We'll tend to it," Augustus said.

An hour later, Wilbarger was still breathing. Augustus stepped away for a minute, to relieve himself, and when he came back Wilbarger had rolled off the blanket and was dead. Augustus rolled him on his back and tied him in the blanket. Call was down by the river, smoking and waiting. He looked up when Augustus approached.

"He's gone," Augustus said.

"All right," Call said.

"He said he was traveling with a man and a boy," Augustus said.

"Let's go, then," Call said, standing up. "We won't have to backtrack him, we can just look for the buzzards."

Augustus was troubled by the fact that he could find nothing with which to mark Wilbarger's grave—the plains and the riverbank were bare. He gave up and came to the grave just as Pea Eye and Deets were covering the man with dirt.

"If he had a family and they cared to look, they'd never find him," Augustus said.

"Well, I can't help it," Call said.

"I know something," Deets said, and to everyone's surprise mounted and loped off. A few minutes later he came loping back, with the skull of a cow buffalo. "I seen the bones," he said.

"It's better than nothing," Augustus said as he sat the skull on the grave. Of course, it wasn't much better than nothing—a coyote would probably just come along and drag the skull off, and Wilbarger too.

Deets had found Wilbarger's rifle, and offered it to Augustus.

"Give it to Newt," Augustus said. "I got a rifle."

Newt took the gun. He had always wanted a rifle, but at the moment he couldn't feel excited. It was such a strain, people always dying. He had a headache, and wanted to cry or be sick or go to sleep—he didn't know which. It was such a strain that he almost wished he had been left with the wagon, although being selected to go had been his greatest pride only a few hours before.

Augustus, riding beside him, noticed the boy's downcast look. "Feeling poorly?" he asked.

Newt didn't know what to say. He was surprised that Mr. Gus had even noticed him.

"You've been on too many burying parties," Augustus said. "Old Wilbarger had a sense of humor. He'd laugh right out loud if he knew he had the skull of a buffalo cow for a grave marker. Probably the only man who ever went to Yale College who was buried under a buffalo skull."

How he died hadn't been funny, Newt thought.

"It's all right, though," Augustus said. "It's mostly bones we're riding over, anyway. Why, think of all the buffalo that have died on these plains. Buffalo and other critters too. And the Indians have been here forever; their bones are down there in the earth. I'm told that over in the Old Country you can't dig six feet without uncovering skulls and leg bones and such. People have been living there since the beginning, and their bones have kinda filled up the ground. It's interesting to think about, all the bones in the ground. But it's just fellow creatures, it's nothing to shy from."

It was such a startling thought—that under him, beneath the long grass, were millions of bones—that Newt stopped feeling so strained. He rode beside Mr. Gus, thinking about it, the rest of the night.

73

AS SOON AS HE HAD the herd well settled, Dish decided to see if there was anything he could do for Lorena. It had been months since the afternoon in Lonesome Dove when he had got so drunk, and in all that time he had not even spoken to her. He was out of practice—in fact, had never been in practice, though that was not his fault. He would cheerfully have talked to Lorena all day and all night, but she didn't want it and they had never exchanged more than a few words. His heart was beating hard, and he felt more fearful than if he were about to swim a swift river, as he approached her tent.

Gus had set up the tent before he left, but it was supper time, so Dish got a plate of beef for Lorena's supper. He took his responsibilities so seriously that he had tried to pick out the best piece, in the process holding up the line and irritating the crew, none of whom were the least impressed with his responsibilities.

"That gal don't need beefsteak, she can just eat you if she's hungry, Dish," Jasper said. "I expect you'd make about three good bites for a woman like her."

Dish flared up at Jasper's insulting tone, but he had the plate in his hand and was in no position to fight.

"I'll settle you when I come back, Jasper," he said. "You've provoked me once too often."

"Hell, you better run for the border, then, Jas," Soupy Jones said. "With a top hand like Dish after you, you won't stand a chance."

Dish had to mount holding the plate, which was awkward, but no one offered to help.

"Why don't you walk?" Po Campo suggested. "The tent is not very far."

That was true, but Dish preferred to ride, which he did, managing not to spill any of Lorena's food. She was sitting just inside the tent, with the flaps open.

"I've come with some food," Dish said, still on his horse.

"I'm not hungry," Lorena said. "I'll wait till Gus gets back."

It seemed to Dish that she was as grudging in her tone as ever. He felt foolish sitting on a horse holding a plate of beefsteak, so he dismounted.

"Gus is after them horsethieves," he said. "He might not be back for a day or two. I'm supposed to look after you."

"Send Newt," Lorena said.

"Well, he went, too," Dish said.

Lorena came out of the tent for a moment and took the plate. Dish was paralyzed to be so close to her after so many months. She went right back into the tent. "You don't need to stay," she said. "I'll be all right."

"I'll help you with the tent in the morning," he said. "Captain said we're to ease on north."

Lorena didn't answer. She closed the flaps of the tent.

Dish walked back toward the campfire, but he stopped about halfway and staked his horse. He didn't want to go back to camp, even to eat, for he would just have to box Jasper Fant if he did. It was full dusk, but to his irritation Lippy spotted him and came walking over.

"Did you get a good look at her, Dish?" Lippy asked.

"Why, yes," Dish said. "I delivered her supper, if you don't mind."

"Is she still as beautiful?" Lippy asked, remembering their days together at the Dry Bean, when she had come down toward noon every day. He and Xavier would both wait for her and would feel better just watching her walk down the stairs.

"Why, yes," Dish said, not wanting to discuss it, though at least Lippy had spoken respectfully.

"Well, that Gus, he would end up with her," Lippy said. "Gus is too sly for the girls."

"I'd like to know what you mean by that," Dish said.

"I seen him trick her once," Lippy said, remembering the extraordinary wager he had witnessed. "He offered to cut the cards for a poke and he won. Then he paid her fifty dollars anyway. And he paid me ten not to tell Jake. He didn't pay me nothing not to tell *you*, though, Dish," Lippy added. It occurred to him suddenly that Gus might consider that they had breached their bargain.

"Fifty dollars?" Dish said, genuinely astonished. He had never heard of such extravagance in his life. "Did he actually pay it?"

"Well, he give me the ten," Lippy said. "I imagine he give Lorie the fifty, too. Gus ain't cheap, he's just crazy."

Dish remembered the night before he had hired on with the Hat Creek outfit, when Gus had lent him two dollars for the same purpose on which he had apparently spent fifty. There was no figuring the man out.

"You oughtn't to blabbed," he told Lippy.

"I ain't told nobody else," Lippy said, realizing himself that he shouldn't have blabbed.

Lippy soon went back to the wagon, subdued by his own indiscretion, but not before assuring Dish that the story would go no further.

Dish unsaddled his horse and got his bedroll. He lay on the blanket all night, his head on his saddle, thinking of Lorie, wondering if his chance with her would ever come.

The Kansas sky was thickly seeded with stars. He listened to the Irishman sing the sad songs that seemed to soothe the cattle. He spent the whole night thinking about the woman in the tent nearby, imagining things that might happen when they finally came to Montana and were through with the trail. He didn't sleep, or want to sleep, for there was no telling when he would get a chance to spend another night close to her. His horse grazed nearby on the good grass, which grew wet with dew as the morning came.

Dish saddled a little before sunup and rode out to look at the herd, which was perfectly peaceful. Then he went to the wagon, ignoring Jasper and Soupy, who were as insolent as ever. He wanted to teach them both a lesson, but couldn't afford the time. The herd had to be set moving, and somebody would have to hold the point. It was a ticklish problem, for he couldn't hold the point and help Lorie too. He fixed a plate for Lorena and just grabbed a hunk of bacon for himself.

"Why, look at him, he's taking her breakfast," Jasper said. "Dish, you're so good at toting food, you ought to work in a hotel."

Dish ignored this sally and walked over to the tent with the plate of food. He was hoping she would be in a talking mood. All night, as he had lain awake, he had thought of things he might say to her, things that would make her see how much he loved her or convince her how happy he could make her. If he could just get her talking for five minutes he might have the opportunity to change everything.

But when he walked up to the tent, Lorena was already standing outside it, buttoning her shirt. She turned and he stopped and blushed, fearful that he had ruined everything by approaching at the wrong time. All the speeches he had practiced in the night left him at once.

"I brought your breakfast," he said.

Lorena saw that he was embarrassed, although she had only had the top button to go on her shirt. It was just a second of awkwardness, but it brought back memories of her old life and reminded her how it had once pleased her to embarrass men. They might pay her, but they could never really get their money's worth, for being embarrassed. She had only to look them in the eye for it to happen—it was her revenge. It didn't work on Gus, but there were precious few like Gus.

"I'll take down the tent while you eat," Dish said.

Lorena sat on her saddle and ate. It took Dish only a few minutes to roll up the tent and carry it to the wagon. Then he came back and saddled her horse for her.

"I've got to ride the point," he said. "Just follow along with the wagon. Lippy and the cook will look after you. If you need anything, send for me."

"I need Gus," Lorena said. "I wish he hadn't left. Do you think he'll come back?"

"Oh, why, of course he will," Dish said. It was the friendliest she had ever talked to him, though it was about Gus.

"I get shaky," she said. "Gus knows why. I hope he gets back tonight."

"It depends on how big a start the horsethieves had," Dish said.

The day passed, and there was no sign of Gus. Lorena rode close to the wagon. Every few minutes Lippy turned and looked back at her as if he had never seen her before. Almost every time he did, he tipped his hat, which was even filthier than it had been when he worked in the saloon. Lorena didn't acknowledge him—she remembered how he had always tried to look up her skirts when she came downstairs. She just rode along, watching the horizon to see if she could spot Gus returning. The horizon shimmered so that it would have been hard to see Gus in any case.

They crossed a little creek about noon. There were a few scraggly bushes growing along the line of the creek. Lorena didn't pay them much attention, but Po Campo did. When the herd had moved on, he came walking over to her, his sack half full of wild plums.

"These plums are sweet," he said, handing her a few.

She dismounted and ate the plums, which indeed were sweet. Then she walked over and washed her face in the creek. The water was green and cold.

"Snow water," Po Campo said.

"I don't see no snow," she said.

"It comes from up there," Po Campo said, pointing west. "From those mountains you can't see."

Lorena looked but could only see the brown plain. She ate a few more of the wild plums.

"I've been finding onions," Po said. "That's good. I'll put them in the beans."

I wish you'd find Gus, she thought, but of course that was impossible. They rode into the dusk, but Gus did not return. Soon after the herd was bedded, Dish came and unrolled the little tent. He could tell from Lorena's face that she was sad. She had unsaddled, and she sat by her saddle in the grass. It pained him to see her look so alone and so tired. He tried to think of something to say that might cheer her up, but words had deserted him again. They always seemed to desert him just when he needed them most.

"I guess those horsethieves had a big start on them," he said.

"He could be dead," Lorena said.

"No, not Gus," Dish said. "He's had lots of experience with horsethieves. Besides, he's got the Captain with him. They're expert fighters."

Lorena knew that. She had seen Gus kill the Kiowas and the buffalo hunters. But it didn't ease her fears. She would have to lie in the tent all night, worrying. A bullet could hit anyone, she knew—even Gus. If he didn't come back, she would have no hope of protection.

"Well, I'll always help, if you'll let me," Dish said. "I'll do about anything for you, Lorie."

Lorena knew that already, but she didn't want him to do anything for her. She didn't answer, and she didn't eat, either. She went into the tent and lay awake all night while Dish Boggett sat nearby, keeping watch. It seemed to him he had never felt so lonely. The mere fact that she was so close, and yet they were separate, made the loneliness keener. When he had just thrown his blanket down with the boys, he didn't imagine her so much, and he could sleep. Now she was just a few yards away—he could have crept up to the tent and heard her breathing. And yet it seemed he would never be able to eliminate those few yards. In some way Lorie would always be as distant from him as the Kansas stars. At times he felt that he had almost rather not be in love with her, for it brought him no peace. What was the use of it, if it was only going to be so painful? And yet, she had spoken to him in a friendly voice only that day. He couldn't give up while there was a chance.

He lay awake all night with his head on his saddle, thinking of Lorie—not sleeping, nor even wanting to.

74

WHEN THEY FOUND Wilbarger's man Chick and the boy who had been traveling with them, there wasn't much left to bury. The coyotes and buzzards had
had a full day at them. As they rode toward the little knoll where the buzzards
swarmed, they passed a fat old badger carrying a human hand—a black hand at
that. Newt was stunned—he assumed they would shoot the badger and get the
hand back so it could be buried, but no one seemed concerned that the badger
had someone's hand.

"He had a hand," he pointed out to Pea Eye.

"Well, whoever it was won't be using it no more, and that old badger had to
work for it with all them dern buzzards around," Pea Eye said. "A hand is mostly
just bone, anyway."

Newt didn't see what that had to do with it—it was still a human hand.

"Yes, that's interesting," Augustus said. "That old badger made a good snatch
and got himself a few bones. But the ground will get his bones too, in a year or
two. It's like I told you last night, son. The earth is mostly just a boneyard.

"But pretty in the sunlight," he added.

It was a fine, bright day, but Newt didn't feel fine. He wanted to go catch up
with the badger and shoot him, but he didn't. There seemed to be hundreds of
buzzards on the knoll. Suddenly a big coyote ran right out of the midst of them,
carrying something—Newt couldn't see what.

"I guess the buzzards outnumber the coyotes in these parts," Augustus said.
"Usually the buzzards have to wait until they get through."

When they rode up on the knoll, the smell hit them. A few of the buzzards flew
off, but many stood their ground defiantly, even continuing to feed. Captain Call
drew rein, but Augustus rode up to them and shot two with his pistol. The rest
reluctantly flew off.

"You like to eat, see how you like being eaten," he said to the dead buzzards.
"There's that bad black man. Wilbarger did get him."

The smell suddenly got to Newt—he dismounted and was sick. Pea Eye dug a
shallow grave with a little shovel they had brought. They rolled the remains in the
grave and covered them, while the buzzards watched. Many stood on the prairie,
like a black army, while others circled in the sky. Deets went off to study the
thieves' tracks. Newt had vomited so hard that he felt lightheaded, but even so, he
noticed that Deets didn't look happy when he returned.

"How many are we up against?" Call asked.

"Four," Deets said. "Just four."

"Hell, there's five of us," Augustus said. "There's less than one apiece of the
horsethieves, so what are you so down about?"

Deets pointed to a horse track. "Mr. Jake is with them," he said. "That's his track."

410

They all looked at the track for a moment.

"Well, they're horsethieves and murderers," Augustus reminded them. "They could have stolen Jake's horse—they could have even murdered him for it."

Deets was silent. They could speculate all they wanted—he knew. A different man would have resulted in a different track. Mr. Jake tended to ride slightly sideways in the saddle, which the track showed. It was not just his horse—it was him.

The news hit Call hard. He had stopped expecting anything of Jake Spoon, and had supposed they would travel different routes for the rest of their lives. Jake would gamble and whore—he always had. No one expected any better of him, but no one had expected any worse, either. Jake hadn't the nerve to lead a criminal life, in Call's estimation. But there was his track, beside the tracks of three killers.

"Well, I hope you're wrong," he said to Deets.

Deets was silent. So, for once, was Augustus. If Jake was with the killers, then there was no hope for him.

"I wish he'd had the sense to stay with Lorie," Augustus said. "She might have aggravated him some, but she wouldn't have led him to this."

"It's his dern laziness," Call said. "Jake just kind of drifts. Any wind can blow him."

He touched the mare and rode on—he didn't need Deets in order to follow the tracks of nearly thirty horses. He put the mare into a slow lope, a gait she could hold all day if necessary.

Newt rode beside Pea Eye, who appeared to be solemn too. "Do you think it's Jake?" Newt asked.

"I can't read a dern track," Pea Eye said. "Never could. But Deets can read 'em easier than I could read a newspaper. I guess it's Jake. It'd be a pity if it's us that has to hang him," he added, a little later.

"We couldn't," Newt said, startled. It had not dawned on him that Jake could have put himself in that bad a position.

Pea Eye looked at him, an unhappy expression on his face. It was unusual for Pea to change expressions. Usually he just looked puzzled.

"The Captain would hang you, if he caught you with a stolen horse," Pea Eye said. "So would Gus."

A few hours later they came upon the dead settlers, still hanging, shreds of charred clothes clinging to their bodies. A coyote was tugging at the foot of one of them, trying to pull the body down. It ran when the party approached. Newt wanted to be sick again, but had nothing in his stomach. He had never expected to see anything more awful than the buzzard-torn bodies they had buried that morning, and yet it was still the same day and already there was a worse sight. It seemed the farther they went through the plains, the worse things got.

"Those boys are bad ones, whoever they are," Augustus said. "Hung those poor bastards and burned them too."

Call had ridden in for a closer look. "No," he said. "Shot 'em, then hung 'em, then burned them."

They cut the men down and buried them in one grave.

"Hell, gravediggers could make a fortune in these parts," Augustus said. "Pea, you ought to buy you a bigger spade and go in business."

"No, I'll pass, Gus," Pea Eye said mildly. "I'd rather dig wells."

Call was thinking of Jake—that a man who had ridden with them so long could let such a thing happen. Of course he was outnumbered, but it was no excuse. He could have fought or run, once he saw the caliber of his companions.

Deets had ridden on, to evaluate the trail. They overtook him a few hours later. His face was sad.

"They're close," he said. "Stopped at a creek."

"Probably stopped to baptize one another," Augustus said. "Did you see 'em, or just smell 'em?"

"I seen 'em," Deets said. "Four men."

"What about Jake?" Call asked.

"He's one," Deets said.

"Are they just watering the stock, or have they camped?" Call wanted to know.

"They're camped," Deets said. "They killed somebody in a wagon and he had whiskey."

"More work for the gravediggers," Augustus said, checking his rifle. "We better go challenge them before they wipe out Kansas."

Pea Eye and Newt were left with the horses. Deets led Call and Augustus on foot for a mile. They crept up the crest of a ridge and saw Wilbarger's horses grazing three or four miles away on the rolling prairie. Between them and the horse herd was a steep banked creek. A small wagon was stopped on the near bank, and four men were lounging on their saddle blankets. One of the men was Jake Spoon. The corpse of the man who had been driving the wagon lay some fifty yards away. The men on the blankets were amusing themselves by shooting their pistols at the buzzards that attempted to approach the corpse. One man, annoyed at missing with his pistol, picked up a rifle and knocked over a buzzard.

"They're cocky, I'd say," Call said. "They don't even have a guard."

"Well, they've killed the whole population of this part of the country except us, and we're just wandering through," Augustus said.

"Let's wait awhile," Call said. "When they're good and drunk we'll come along the creek bed and surprise 'em."

Augustus watched for a few minutes. "I hope Jake makes a fight," he said.

"He can't fight, and you know it," Call said.

"The point is, I'd rather shoot him than hang him," Augustus said.

"I wouldn't relish hanging him," Call said. "But there he is."

He walked back and explained the situation to Pea Eye and Newt. There was nothing they need do except bring the horses fast when they heard shooting.

"Jake with them?" Pea Eye asked.

"He's there," Call said. "It's a bad situation, but he put himself in it."

They waited until late afternoon, when the sun was angling down toward the horizon. Then, walking a wide circle to the east, they struck the creek a mile below where the men were camped and walked quietly up the creek bed. The banks were high and made a perfect shelter. They saw three horses watering at the creek, and Call feared the animals would give them away, but the horses were not alarmed.

Soon they heard the faint talk of the men—they were still lounging on their saddle blankets.

Call, in the lead, crept a little closer.

"Let's stay the night," he heard a man say. "I'm too full of liquor to be chousing horses in the dark."

"It'll sober you up," another voice said. "It's cooler traveling at night."

"Why travel?" the first man said. "Some more wagons might come along and we could rob 'em. It's easier than banks."

"Eddie, you're as lazy as Jake," the second voice said. "Neither one of you pulls your weight in this outfit."

"I'd have to be quick to beat you at killing people, Dan," little Eddie said.

Call and Augustus looked at one another. Dan Suggs was the name Wilbarger had mentioned—he had called his killers accurately.

Jake was lying on his saddle blanket feeling drunk and depressed. Dan Suggs had shot the old man driving the wagon at a hundred yards' distance, without even speaking to him. Dan had been hiding in the trees along the creek, so the old man died without even suspecting that he was in danger. He only had about thirty dollars on him, but he had four jugs of whiskey, and they were divided equally, although Dan claimed he ought to have two for doing the shooting. Jake had been drinking steadily, hoping he would get so drunk the Suggses would just go off and leave him. But he knew they wouldn't. For one thing, he had eight hundred dollars on him, won in poker games in Fort Worth, and if Dan Suggs didn't know it, he certainly suspected it. They wouldn't leave him without robbing him, or rob him without killing him, so for the time being his hope was to ride along and not rile Dan.

He had been lying flat down, for he felt very weary, but he raised up on his elbow to take another swig from the jug, and he and little Eddie saw the three men at the same moment: three men with leveled rifles, standing on the riverbank with the sun at a blinding angle right behind them. Jake had taken off his gun belt—he couldn't rest comfortably with it on. Little Eddie had his pistol on and grabbed for it, but a rifle cracked and a bullet took him in the shoulder and kicked him back off the saddle blanket.

Dan and Roy Suggs were sitting with their backs to the creek, each with a jug between their legs. They were caught cold, their rifles propped on their saddles well out of reach.

"Sit still, boys," Call said, as soon as the crack of the shot died. Deets, who had the best angle, had shot little Eddie.

Dan Suggs leaped to his feet and turned to see the bright sun glinting on three rifle barrels.

"Who are you?" he asked. "We're horse traders, so hold your damn fire."

He realized it would be suicide to draw and decided a bluff was his best chance, though the shock, plus the whiskey he had just drunk, made him unsteady for a moment. It was a moment too long, for a black man with a rifle stepped behind him and lifted his pistol. Roy Suggs was sitting where he was, his mouth open, too surprised even to move. Little Eddie lay flat on his back, stunned by his shoulder wound.

Augustus took little Eddie's pistol as he stepped over him, and in a moment had Roy's. Deets got the rifles. Call kept his gun trained right on Dan Suggs, who, because of the sun, still could not see clearly whom he faced.

Deets, with a downcast look, picked up Jake's gun belt.

"Why, Deets, do you think I'd shoot you?" Jake asked, though he knew too well where he stood, and if he had moved quicker would have shot, whatever the cost. A clean bullet was better than a scratchy rope, and his old partners could shoot clean when they wanted to.

Deets, without answering, removed the rifle from Jake's saddle scabbard.

"Get your boots off, boys," Call said, coming closer.

"Goddamned if we will," Dan Suggs said, his anger rising. "Didn't you hear me? I told you we were horse traders."

"We're more persuaded by that dead fellow over there," Augustus said. "He says you're murderers. And Mr. Wilbarger's good horses says you're horsethieves to boot."

"Hell, you don't know what you're talking about," Dan Suggs said. He was genuinely furious at having been taken without a shot, and he used his anger to try and carry the bluff.

"I bought these horses from Wilbarger," he said. "I gave him thirty dollars apiece."

"You're a black liar," Augustus said calmly. "Take off your boots, like Captain Call said. It's time to collect the boot guns."

Dan Suggs stood quivering, for it galled him to be caught and galled him more to be coolly given orders, even if it was Augustus McCrae who was giving them. Besides, he had a derringer in his right boot, and knew it was his last hope. One of his brothers was shot and the other too drunk and too stunned to take in what was happening.

"I'll be damned if I'll go barefoot for you or any man," Dan said.

Augustus drew his big dragoon Colt and jammed the barrel into Dan's stomach.

"You can keep your socks, if you're that refined," he said.

Call quickly knelt behind Dan Suggs and got the derringer.

"Just ask Jake if we didn't buy these horses," Dan said. "Jake's a friend of yours, ain't he?"

"Did you buy that old man?" Call asked. "Did you buy them two farmers you burned? Did you buy Wilbarger and his man and that boy?"

Little Eddie sat up. When he saw that his shirt was drenched with blood, his face went white. "I'm bleeding, Dan," he said.

Jake looked at Call and Augustus, hoping one or the other of them would show some sign of concern, but neither would even look at him. Call covered Roy Suggs while Deets tied his hands with his own saddle strings. Augustus stood calmly, the barrel of the big Colt still stuck into Dan Suggs's stomach. Dan's face was twitching. Jake could see he longed to go for his gun—only he had no gun. Jake thought Dan might go anyway, his whole frame was quivering so. He might go, even if it meant getting shot at point-blank range.

"This gun leaves a hole the size of a tunnel, Mr. Suggs," Augustus said. "If you'd like to land in hell with a tunnel through you, just try me."

Dan quivered, his eyes popping with hatred. When Deets came over with some rawhide strings he snarled at him, baring his teeth. "Don't you tie me, nigger boy," he said. "I'll not forget you if you do."

"You're dying to try it, ain't you?" Augustus said. "Go on. Try it. See what you look like with a tunnel through your ribs."

Dan held back, though he shook and snarled, while Deets tied him securely.

"Tie Jake," Call said, when Dan was secure. Augustus grinned and put the Colt back in its holster.

"I guess you ain't as hard as you talk, Mr. Suggs," he said.

"You sneaking son of a bitch, who do you think you are?" Dan said.

"Deets don't need to tie me," Jake said. For a moment his spirits rose, just from the sound of Gus's voice. It was Call and Gus, his old *compañeros*. It was just a matter of making them realize what an accident it had been, him riding with the Suggs. It was just that they had happened by the saloon just as he was deciding to leave. If he could just get his head clear of the whiskey he could soon explain it all.

Little Eddie could not believe that he was shot and his brother Dan tied up. He was white and trembling. He looked at Dan in disbelief.

"You said there wasn't a man in Kansas that could take you, Dan," Eddie said. "Why didn't you fight?"

Augustus went over and knelt by little Eddie, tearing his shirt so he could look at the wound.

"You oughtn't to listened to your big brother, son," he said. "He was plumb easy to catch. This is just a flesh wound—the bullet went right through."

Call went over to Jake. Deets seemed hesitant to tie him, but Call nodded and covered Jake with his rifle while Deets tied his hands. As he was doing it Pea Eye and Newt came over the hill with the horses.

"Call, he don't need to tie me," Jake said. "I ain't done nothing. I just fell in with these boys to get through the Territory. I was aiming to leave them first chance I got."

Call saw that Jake was so drunk he could barely sit up.

"You should have made a chance a little sooner, Jake," Augustus said. "A man that will go along with six killings is making his escape a little slow."

"I had to wait for a chance, Gus," Jake said. "You can't just trot off from Dan Suggs."

"You shut your damn mouth, Spoon," Dan Suggs said. "These friends of yours are no more than rank outlaws. I don't see no badges on them. They got their damn gall, taking us to jail."

Pea Eye and Newt stopped and dismounted. Newt saw that Jake was tied like the rest.

"Saddle these men's horses," Call said to the boy. Then he walked off toward the nearest trees.

"Where's he going?" Roy Suggs asked, finding his voice at last.

"Gone to pick a tree to hang you from, son," Augustus said mildly. He turned to Dan Suggs, who looked at him with his teeth bared in a snarl. "I don't know what makes you think we'd tote you all the way to a jail," Gus said.

"I tell you we bought them horses!" Dan said.

"Oh, drop your bluff," Augustus said. "I buried Wilbarger myself, not to mention his two cowboys. We buried them farmers and we'll bury that body over there. I imagine it's all your doings, too. Your brothers don't look so rough, and Jake ain't normally a killer."

Augustus looked at Jake, who was still sitting down. "What's the story on that one, Jake?" he asked.

"Why, I merely said hello to a girl," Jake said. "I didn't know she was anybody's wife, and the old bastard knocked me down with a shotgun. He was gonna do worse, too. It was only self-defense. No jury will hang you for self-defense."

Augustus was silent. Jake got to his feet awkwardly, for his hands were tied behind him. He looked at Pea Eye, who was standing quietly with Deets.

"Pea, you know me," Jake said. "You know I ain't no killer. Old Deets knows it too. You boys wouldn't want to hang a friend, I hope."

"I've done a many a thing I didn't want to do, Jake," Pea Eye said.

Jake walked over to Augustus. "I ain't no criminal, Gus," he said. "Dan's the only one that done anything. He shot that old man over there, and he killed them farmers. He shot Wilbarger and his men. Me and the other boys have killed nobody."

"We'll hang him for the killings and the rest of you for the horse theft, then," Augustus said. "Out in these parts the punishment's the same, as you well know.

"Ride with an outlaw, die with him," he added. "I admit it's a harsh code. But you rode on the other side long enough to know how it works. I'm sorry you crossed the line, though."

Jake's momentary optimism had passed, and he felt tired and despairing. He would have liked a good bed in a whorehouse and a nice night's sleep.

"I never seen no line, Gus," he said. "I was just trying to get to Kansas without getting scalped."

Newt had saddled the men's horses. Call came back and took the ropes off the four saddles.

"We're lucky to have caught 'em by the trees," he said. Newt felt numb from all that he had seen.

"Have we got to hang Jake too?" he asked. "He was my ma's friend."

Call was surprised by the remark. Newt was surprised too—it had just popped out. He remembered how jolly Jake had been, then—it was mainly on Jake's visits that he had heard his mother laugh. It puzzled him how the years could have moved so, to bring them from such happy times to the moment at hand.

"Yes, he's guilty with the rest of them," Call said. "Any judge would hang him."

He walked on, and Newt put his cheek for a moment against the warm neck of the horse he had just saddled. The warmth made him want to cry. His mother had been warm too, in the years when they first knew Jake. But he couldn't bring any of it back, and Jake was standing not twenty yards away, weaving from drink, his hands tied, sad-looking. Newt choked back his feelings and led the horses over.

The men had to be helped onto the horses because of the way their hands were tied. Little Eddie had lost a lot of blood and was so weak he could barely keep his seat.

"I'll lead yours, Jake," Newt said, hoping Jake would realize he meant it as a friendly gesture. Jake had several days' stubble on his face and looked dirty and tired; his eyes had a dull look in them, as if he merely wanted to go to sleep.

Call took the rein of Dan Suggs's horse, just in case Dan tried something—though there was little he could try. Augustus walked behind and Pea Eye led the other two horses. Deets went ahead to fix the nooses—he was good with knots.

"Dan, ain't you gonna fight?" little Eddie kept asking. He had never seen his brother tied up and could not quite believe it. That Dan had been outsmarted and taken without a battle shocked him more than the fact that he himself was about to be hung.

"Shut up, you damn whining pup," Dan said. "If you'd been standing guard this wouldn't have happened."

"You never told him to," Roy Suggs said. He too was in a daze, the result of shock and whiskey, but it annoyed him that Dan would try to put the blame on little Eddie.

"Well, do I have to do everything?" Dan said. He was watching, hoping to get Call to relax a minute—he meant to kick the horse and try to run over him. It might startle everyone long enough that he could jump the horse down into the creek bed, where he would be hard to hit. He had said what he had merely to distract the crowd, but it didn't work. Call kept the horse under tight control and in no time they came to the tree with the four dangling nooses.

It took a while for Deets to fix the knots to his satisfaction. The twilight began to deepen into dusk.

Jake tried to get his mind to work, but it wouldn't snap to. He had the feeling that there ought to be something he could say that would move Call or Gus on his behalf. It made him proud that the two of them had caught Dan Suggs so easily, although it had brought him to a hard fix. Still, it cut Dan Suggs down to size. Jake tried to think back over his years of rangering—to try and think of a debt he could call in, or a memory that might move the boys—but his brain seemed to be asleep. He could think of nothing. The only one who seemed to care was the boy Newt—Maggie's boy, Jake remembered. She had fat legs, but she was always friendly, Maggie. Of all the whores he had known, she was the easiest to get along with. The thought crossed his mind that he ought to have married her and not gone rambling. If he had, he wouldn't be in such a fix. But he felt little fear; just an overpowering fatigue. Life had slipped out of line. It was unfair, it was too bad, but he couldn't find the energy to fight it any longer.

Deets finally got the nooses done. He mounted and rode behind each man, to carefully set the knots. Little Eddie submitted quietly, but Dan Suggs shook his head and struggled like a wildcat when Deets came to him.

"Nigger boy, don't you get near me," he said. "I won't be hung by no black nigger."

Call and Augustus had to grab his arms and hold him steady. Dan dug his chin into his chest, so that Deets had to grab his hair and pull his head back to get the rope around his neck.

"You're a fool, Suggs," Augustus said. "You don't appreciate a professional when you see one. Men Deets hangs don't have to dance on the rope, like some I've seen."

"You're yellowbellies, both of you, or you would have fought me fair," Dan Suggs said, glaring down at him. "I'll fight you yet, barehanded, if you'll just let me down. I'll fight the both of you right now, and this nigger boy too."

"You'd do better to say goodbye to your brothers," Call said. "I expect you got them into this."

"They're not worth a red piss and neither are you," Dan said.

"I'll say this for you, Suggs, you're the kind of son of a bitch it's a pleasure to hang," Augustus said. "If guff's all you can talk, go talk it to the devil."

He gave Dan Suggs's horse a whack with a coiled rope and the horse jumped out from under him. When Dan's horse jumped, little Eddie's bolted too, and in a moment the two men were both swinging dead from the limb.

Roy Suggs looked pained. A brother dangled on either side of him. "I ought to have been second," he said. "Little Eddie was the youngest."

"You're right and I'm sorry," Augustus said. "I never meant to scare that boy's horse."

"That horse never had no sense," Roy Suggs remarked. "If I was little Eddie I would have got rid of him long ago."

"I guess he waited too long to make the change," Augustus said. "Are you about ready, sir?"

"Guess so, since the boys are dead," Roy Suggs said. "Right or wrong, they're my brothers."

"It's damn bad luck, having a big brother like Dan Suggs, I'd say," Augustus said.

He walked over to Jake and put a hand on his leg for a moment.

"Jake, you might like to know that I got Lorie back," he said.

"Who?" Jake asked. He felt very dull, and for a second the name meant nothing to him. Then he remembered the young blond whore who had been so much trouble. She had put him off several times.

"Why, Lorie—have you had so many beauties that you've forgotten?" Augustus said. "That damn outlaw took her away."

To Jake it seemed as remote as his rangering days—he could barely get his mind back to it. Call walked over. Now that they were about it he felt a keen

sorrow. Jake had ridden the river with them and been the life of the camp once—
not the steadiest boy in the troop, but lively and friendly to a fault.

"Well, it'll soon be dark," he said. "I'm sorry it's us, Jake—I wish it had fallen to
somebody else."

Jake grinned. Something in the way Call said it amused him, and for a second
he regained a bit of his old dash.

"Hell, don't worry about it, boys," he said. "I'd a damn sight rather be hung by
my friends than by a bunch of strangers. The thing is, I never meant no harm," he
added. "I didn't know they was such a gun outfit."

He looked down at Pea Eye and Deets, and at the boy. Everyone was silent,
even Gus, who held the coiled rope. They were all looking at him, but it seemed
no one could speak. For a moment, Jake felt good. He was back with his old *compañeros,* at least—those boys who had haunted his dreams. Straying off from
them had been his worst mistake.

"Well, *adiós,* boys," he said. "I hope you won't hold it against me."

He waited a moment, but Augustus seemed dumbstruck, holding the rope.

Jake looked down again and saw the glint of tears in the boy's eyes. Little Newt
cared for him, at least.

"Newt, why don't you take this pony?" he said, looking at the boy. "He's a
pacer—you won't find no easier gait. And the rest of you boys divide what money's
in my pocket."

He smiled at the thought of how surprised they would be when they saw how
much he had—it was that lucky week in Fort Worth he had to thank for it.

"All right, Jake, many thanks," Newt said, his voice cracking.

Before he got the thanks out, Jake Spoon had quickly spurred his pacing horse
high back in the flanks with both spurs. The rope squeaked against the bark of the
limb. Augustus stepped over and caught the swinging body and held it still.

"I swear," Pea Eye said. "He didn't wait for you, Gus."

"Nope, he died fine," Augustus said. "Go dig him a grave, will you, Pea?"

They buried Jake Spoon by moonlight on the slope above the creek and, after
some discussion, cut down Roy Suggs and little Eddie, plus the old man Dan
Suggs had killed, a drummer named Collins with a wagonful of patent medicines.
There was a good lantern in the wagon, which, besides the medicines, contained
four white rabbits in a cage. The old man had run a medicine show, evidently, and
did a little magic. The wagon contained a lot of cheaply printed circulars which
advertised the show.

"Headed for Denver, I guess," Call said.

Dan Suggs they left hanging. Augustus took one of the circulars and wrote
"Dan Suggs, Man Burner and Horse Thief" on the back of it. He rode over and
pinned the sign to Dan Suggs's shirt.

"That way if a lawman comes looking for him he'll know he can quit the
search," Augustus said.

They rounded up Wilbarger's horses and unhitched the two mules that had
been pulling the little wagon. Augustus wanted to take the white rabbits, but the
cage was awkward to carry. Finally Deets put two in his saddlebags, and Augustus
took the other two. He also sampled the patent medicines and took several bottles of it.

"What do you think it will cure, Gus?" Pea Eye asked.

"Sobriety, if you guzzle enough of it," Augustus said. "I expect it's just whiskey
and syrup."

The wagon itself was in such poor repair that they decided to leave it sit. Call broke up the tailgate and made a little marker for Jake's grave, scratching his name on it with a pocketknife by the light of the old man's lantern. He hammered the marker into the loose-packed dirt with the blunt side of a hatchet they had found in the wagon. Augustus trotted over, bringing Call his mare.

"I'm tired of justice, ain't you?" he asked.

"Well, I wish he hadn't got so careless about his company," Call said. "It was that that cost him."

"Life works out peculiar," Augustus said. "If he hadn't talked you into making this trip, we wouldn't have had to hang him today. He could be sitting down in Lonesome Dove, playing cards with Wanz."

"On the other hand, it was gambling brought him down," Call said. "That's what started it."

Deets and Pea Eye and Newt held the little horse herd. Newt was leading the horse Jake had left him. He didn't know if it was right to get on him so soon after Jake's death.

"You can ride the pacing pony," Deets said. "Mister Jake meant you to have it."

"What will I do with his saddle?" Newt asked. "He didn't say anything about the saddle."

"It's better than that old singletree of yours," Pea Eye said. "Take it—Jake's through with it."

"Don't neither of you want it?" Newt asked. It bothered him to take it, for Jake hadn't mentioned it.

"Oh, no," Deets said. "Saddle goes with the horse, I guess."

Nervous and a little reluctant, Newt got on Jake's horse. The stirrups were too long for him, but Deets got down and quickly adjusted them. As he was finishing the lacing, Call and Augustus rode by. Deets took the bridle off Newt's other horse and turned him, still saddled, into the horse herd. No one seemed to have anything to say.

They started Wilbarger's horses west across the dark prairie in the direction the cattle should be. Captain Call led, Augustus and Deets rode to the sides, and Pea Eye and Newt brought up the rear. Newt had to admit that Jake's horse had a beautiful smooth gait, but even so he wished he hadn't changed horses—not so soon. It seemed wrong to be enjoying Jake's horse, and his fine saddle too, after what had happened. But he was tired, so tired he didn't even feel the sadness for very long. Soon his head dropped and he sat on the pacing gelding, sound asleep. Pea Eye noticed and trotted close beside him so he could catch the weary boy if he started to fall off.

PART III

75

CLARA WAS MILKING A MARE when Sally, her oldest girl, came racing down to the lots.

"Somebody's coming, Ma," Sally said, excitement in her face. Sally was ten years old and sociable—she loved visitors.

The young mare had dropped her foal early and the colt was too weak to stand up, which was why she was milking. The colt would suck milk off a rag, and Clara was determined to save it if she could. When Sally ran up, the mare flinched, causing Clara to squirt a stream of milk along her own arm.

"Haven't I told you to *walk* up to horses?" Clara said. She stood up and wiped the milk off her dripping arm.

"I'm sorry, Ma," Sally said, more excited than sorry. "See, there's a wagon coming."

Then Betsey, only seven, came flying out of the house, her brown hair streaming, and raced down to the corrals. Betsey liked company as much as her sister.

"Who's coming?" she asked.

The wagon was barely visible coming along the Platte from the west.

"I thought I told you girls to churn," Clara said. "Seems like all you do is hang out the window watching for travelers."

Of course, no one could blame them, for company was rare. They lived twenty miles from town, and a bad town at that—Ogallala. If they went in, it was usually for church, but they seldom made the trip. Their company mostly consisted of men who came to trade horses with Bob, her husband, and now that he was injured, few came. They had just as many horses—more, in fact—and Clara knew more about them than Bob had ever learned, but there were few men disposed to bargain with a woman, and Clara was not disposed to give their horses away. When she named a price she meant it, but usually men got their backs up and wouldn't buy.

"I expect they're just buffalo hunters," Clara said, watching the distant wagon creep over the brown plains. "You girls won't learn much from them, unless you're interested in learning how to spit tobacco."

"I ain't," Betsey said.

"You aren't, you mean," Sally said. "I thought all the buffalo were dead—how come they still hunt them?"

"Because people are slow learners, like your sister," Clara said, grinning at Betsey to mitigate the criticism.

"Are you gonna invite them for the night?" Sally asked. "Want me to kill a hen?"

"Not just yet, they may not be in the mood to stop," Clara said. "Besides, you and I don't agree about hens. You might kill one of the ones I like."

"Mother, they're just to eat," Sally said.

423

"Nope. I keep those hens to talk to me when I'm lonesome," Clara said. "I'll only eat the ones who can't make good conversation." Betsey wrinkled up her nose, amused by the comment. "Oh, Ma," she said, "hens don't talk."

"They talk," Clara said. "You just don't understand hen talk. I'm an old hen myself and it makes good sense to me."

"You ain't old, Ma," Sally said.

"That wagon won't be here for an hour," Clara said. "Go see about your pa. His fever comes up in the afternoon. Wet a rag and wipe his face."

Both girls stood looking at her silently. They hated to go into the sickroom. Both of them had bright-blue eyes, their legacy from Bob, but their hair was like hers and they were built like her, even to the knobby knees. Bob had been kicked in the head by a mustang he was determined to break, against Clara's advice. She had seen it happen—he had the mare snubbed to a post with a heavy rope and only turned his back on her for a second. But the mare struck with her front feet, quick as a snake. Bob had bent over to pick up another rope and the kick had caught him right back of the ear. The crack had sounded like a shot. The mare pawed him three or four times before Clara could reach him and drag him out of the way, but those blows had been minor. The kick behind the ear had almost killed him. They had been so sure he would die that they even dug the grave, up on the knoll east of the house where their three boys were buried: Jim and Jeff and Johnny, the three deaths Clara felt had turned her heart to stone: she hoped for stone, anyway, for stone wouldn't suffer from such losses.

Bob, though, hadn't died—neither had he recovered. His eyes were open, but he could neither speak nor move. He could swallow soup, if his head was tilted a certain way, and it was chicken broth that had kept him alive the three months since his accident. He simply lay staring up with his large blue eyes, feverish sometimes but mostly as still as if he were dead. He was a large man, over two hundred pounds, and it took all her strength to move him and clean him every day—he had no control over bowels or bladder. Day after day Clara removed the soiled bedclothes, stuffing them in a washtub she filled beforehand from the cistern. She never let the girls see or help her with the operation; she supposed Bob would die in time, and she didn't want his daughters to feel disgust for him, if she could prevent it. She only sent them in once a day to bathe his face, hoping that the sight of them would bring him out of his state.

"Is Daddy going to die?" Betsey often asked. She had been only one when Johnny, her last brother, had died, and had no memories of death, just a great curiosity about it.

"I don't know, Betsey," Clara said. "I don't know at all. I hope not."

"Well, but can't he ever talk again?" Sally asked. "His eyes are open, why can't he talk?"

"His head is hurt," Clara said. "It's hurt on the inside. Maybe it'll heal, if we take care of him, and then he can talk again."

"Do you think he can hear the piano when I play?" Betsey asked.

"Just go and bathe his face, please. I don't know what he can hear," she said. She felt as if a flood of tears might come at any moment, and she didn't want the girls to see them. The piano, over which she and Bob had argued for two years, had come the week before his accident—it had been her victory, but a sad one. She had ordered it all the way from St. Louis, and it had been woefully out of tune when it finally came, but there was a Frenchman who played the piano in a saloon in town who tuned it for her for five dollars. And although she assumed it was a whorehouse he played the piano in, she hired him at the big fee of two dollars a week to ride out and give her daughters lessons.

The Frenchman's name was Jules. He was really a French-Canadian who had been a trader on the Red River of the North and had gone broke when smallpox hit the tribes. He had wandered down through the Dakotas to Ogallala and turned to music for a living. He loved to come out and teach the girls—he said they reminded him of the cousins he had once played with in his grandmother's house in Montreal. He wore a black coat, when he came, and waxed his mustache. Both girls thought he was the most refined man they had ever seen, and he was.

Clara had bought the piano with money saved all those years from the sale of her parents' little business in Texas. She had never let Bob use the money—another bone of contention between them. She wanted it for her children, so when the time came they could be sent away to school and not have to spend their whole youth in such a raw, lonely place. The first of the money she spent was on the two-story frame house they had built three years before, after nearly fifteen years of life in the sod house Bob had dug for her on a slope above the Platte. Clara had always hated the sod house—hated the dirt that seeped down on her bedclothes, year after year. It was dust that caused her firstborn, Jim, to cough virtually from his birth until he died a year later. In the mornings Clara would walk down and wash her hair in the icy waters of the Platte, and yet by supper time, if she happened to scratch her head, her fingernails would fill with dirt that had seeped down during the day. For some reason, no matter where she moved her bed, the roof would trickle dirt right onto it. She tacked muslin, and finally canvas, on the ceiling over the bed but nothing stopped the dirt for long. It sifted through. It seemed to her that all her children had been conceived in dust clouds, dust rising from the bedclothes or sifting down from the ceiling. Centipedes and other bugs loved the roof; day after day they crawled down the walls, to end up in her stewpots or her skillets or the trunks where she stored her clothes.

"I'd rather live in a tepee, like an Indian," she told Bob many times. "I'd be cleaner. When it got dirty we could burn it."

The idea had shocked Bob, a conventional man if there ever was one. He could not believe he had married a woman who wanted to live like an Indian. He worked hard to give her a respectable life, and yet she said things like that—and meant them. And she stubbornly kept her own money, year after year—for the children's education, she said, although one by one the three boys died long before they were old enough to be sent anywhere. The last two lived long enough for Clara to teach them to read. She had read them Walter Scott's *Ivanhoe* when Jeff and Johnny were six and seven, respectively. Then the next winter both boys had died of pneumonia within a month of one another. It was a terrible winter, the ground frozen so deep there was no way to dig a grave. They had had to put the boys in the little kindling shed, wrapped tightly in wagon sheets, until winter let up enough that they could be buried. Many days Bob would come home from delivering horses to the Army—his main customer—to find Clara sitting in the icy shed by the two small bodies, tears frozen on her cheeks so hard that he would have to heat water and bathe the ice from her face. He tried to point out to her that she mustn't do it—the weather was below zero, and the wind swept endlessly along the Platte. She could freeze to death, sitting in the kindling shed. If only I would, Clara thought—I'd be with my boys.

But she didn't freeze, and Jeff and Johnny had been buried beside Jim, and despite her resolve never to lay herself open to such heartbreak again, she had the girls, neither of whom had ever had more than a cold. Bob couldn't believe his own bad luck; he longed for a strong boy or two to help him with the stock.

And yet he loved the girls in his unspeaking way. His love mostly came out in awkwardness, for their delicacy frightened him. He was continually warning them about their health and trying to keep them wrapped up. Their recklessness almost stopped his heart at times—they were the kind of girls who would run out in the snow barefoot if they chose. He feared for them, and also feared the effect on his wife if one of them should die. Impervious to weather himself, he came to dread the winters for fear winter would take the rest of his family. Yet the girls proved as strong as their mother, whereas the boys had all been weak. It made no sense to Bob, and he was hoping if they could only have another boy, he would turn into the helper he needed.

The only hand they had was an old Mexican cowboy named Cholo. The old man was wiry and strong, despite his age, and stayed mainly because of his devotion to Clara. It was Cholo, and not her husband, who taught her to love horses and to understand them. Cholo had pointed out to her at once that her husband would never break the mustang mare; he had urged her to persuade Bob to sell the mare unbroken, or else let her go. Though Bob had been a horse trader all his adult life, he had no real skill with horses. If they disobeyed him, he beat them— Clara had often turned her back in disgust from the sight of her husband beating a horse, for she knew it was his incompetence, not the horse's, that was to blame for whatever incident had provoked the beating. Bob could not contain his violence when angered by a horse.

With her, it was different. He had never raised a hand to her, though she provoked him often, and deeply. Perhaps it was because he had never quite believed that she would marry him, or never quite understood why she had. The shadow of Augustus McCrae had hung over their courtship; Bob had never known why she chose him over the famous Ranger, or over any of the other men she could have had. In her day she had been the most sought-after girl in Texas, and yet she had married him, and followed him to the Nebraska plains, and stayed and worked beside him. It was hard country for women, Bob knew that. Women died, went crazy or left. The wife of their nearest neighbor, Maude Jones, had killed herself with a shotgun one morning, leaving a note which merely said, "Can't stand listening to this wind no more." Maude had had a husband and four children, but had killed herself anyway. For a time, Clara had taken in the children, until their grandparents in Missouri came for them. Len Jones, Maude's husband, soon drank himself into poverty. He fell out of his wagon drunk one night and froze to death not two hundred yards from a saloon.

Clara had lived, and stayed, though she had a look in her gray eyes that frightened Bob every time he saw it. He didn't really know what the look meant, but to him it meant she might leave if he didn't watch out. When they first came to Nebraska, he had had the drinking habit. Ogallala was hardly even a town then; there were few neighbors, and almost no socials. The Indians were a dire threat, though Clara didn't seem to fear them. If they had company, it was usually soldiers—the soldiers drank, and so did he. Clara didn't like it. One night he got pretty drunk, and when he got up in the morning she had that look in her eye. She made him breakfast, but then she looked at him coldly and lay down a threat. "I want you to stop drinking," she said. "You've been drunk three times this week. I won't live here and get dirt in my hair for the love of a drunkard."

It was the only threat she ever had to make. Bob spent the day worrying, looking at the bleak plains and wondering what he would do in such a place without her. He never touched whiskey again. The jug he had been working on sat in the cupboard for years, until Clara finally mixed it with sorghum molasses and used it for cough medicine.

They had few quarrels, most of them about money. Clara was a good wife and worked hard; she never did anything untoward or unrespectable, and yet the fact that she had that Texas money made Bob uneasy. She wouldn't give it up or let him use it, no matter how poor they were. Not that she spent it on herself—Clara spent nothing on herself, except for the books she ordered or the magazines she took. She kept the money for her children, she said—but Bob could never be sure she wasn't keeping it so she could leave if she took a notion. He knew it was foolish—Clara would leave, money or no money, if she decided to go—but he couldn't get the idea out of his mind. She wouldn't even use the money on the house, although she had wanted the house, and they had had to haul the timber two hundred miles. Of course, he had prospered in the horse business, mainly because of the Army trade; he could afford to build her a house. But he still resented her money. She told him it was only for the girls' education—and yet she did things with it that he didn't expect. The winter before she had bought Cholo a buffalo coat, an action which shocked Bob. He had never heard of a married woman buying a Mexican cowboy an expensive coat. Then there was the piano. She had ordered that too, although it cost two hundred dollars and another forty to transport. And yet he had to admit he loved to see his girls sitting at the piano, trying to learn their fingering. And the buffalo coat had saved Cholo's life when he was trapped in an April blizzard up on the Dismal River. Clara got her way, and her way often turned out to make sense—and yet Bob more and more felt that her way skipped him, somehow. She didn't neglect him in any way that he could put his finger on, and the girls loved him, but there were many times when he felt left out of the life of his own family. He would never have said that to Clara—he was not good with words, and seldom spoke unless he was spoken to, unless it was about business. Watching his wife, he often felt lonely. Clara seemed to sense it and would usually come and try to be especially nice to him, or to get him laughing at something the girls had done—and yet he still felt lonely, even in their bed.

Now Bob lay in that bed all day, staring his empty stare. They had moved the bed near the window so that he would get the summer breezes and could look out if he liked and watch his horses grazing on the plain, or the hawks circling, or whatever little sights there might be. But Bob never turned his head, and no one knew if he felt the breezes. Clara had taken to sleeping on a little cot. The house had a small upper porch and she moved the cot out there in good weather. Often she lay awake, listening, half expecting Bob to come back to himself and call her. More often what happened was that he fouled himself; and instead of hearing him she would smell him. Even so, she was glad it happened at night so she could change him without the girls seeing.

It seemed to her, after a month of it, that she was carrying Bob away with those sheets; he had already lost much weight and every morning seemed a little thinner to her. The large body that had lain beside her so many nights, that had warmed her in the icy nights, that had covered her those many times through the years and given her five children, was dribbling away as offal, and there was nothing she could do about it. The doctors in Ogallala said Bob's skull was fractured;

you couldn't put a splint on a skull; probably he'd die. And yet he wasn't dead. Often when she was cleaning him, bathing his soiled loins and thighs with warm water, the stem of life between his legs would raise itself, growing as if a fractured skull meant nothing to it. Clara cried at the sight—what it meant to her was that Bob still hoped for a boy. He couldn't talk or turn himself, and he would never beat another horse, most likely, but he still wanted a boy. The stem let her know it, night after night, when all she came in to do was clean the stains from a dying body. She would roll Bob on his side and hold him there for a while, for his back and legs were developing terrible bedsores. She was afraid to turn him on his belly for fear he might suffocate, but she would hold him on his side for an hour, sometimes napping as she held him. Then she would roll him back and cover him and go back to her cot, often to lie awake half the night, looking at the prairies, sad beyond tears at the ways of things. There Bob lay, barely alive, his ribs showing more every morning, still wanting a boy. I could do it, she thought—would it save him if I did? I could go through it one more time—the pregnancy, the fear, the sore nipples, the worry—and maybe it would be a boy. Though she had borne five children, she sometimes felt barren, lying on her cot at night. She felt she was ignoring her husband's last wish—that if she had any generosity she would do it for him. How could she lie night after night and ignore the strange, mute urgings of a dying man, one who had never been anything but kind to her, in his clumsy way. Bob, dying, still wanted her to make a little Bob. Sometimes in the long silent nights she felt she must be going crazy to think about such things, in such a way. And yet she came to dread having to go to him at night; it became as hard as anything she had had to do in her marriage. It was so hard that at times she wished Bob would go on and die, if he couldn't get well. The truth was, she didn't want another child, particularly not another boy. Somehow she felt confident she could keep her girls alive—but she lacked that confidence where boys were concerned. She remembered too well the days of icy terror and restless pain as she listened to Jim cough his way to death. She remembered her hatred of, and helplessness before, the fevers that had taken Jeff and Johnny. Not again, she thought—I won't live that again, even for you, Bob. The memory of the fear that had torn her as her children approached death was the most vivid of her life: she could remember the coughings, the painful breathing. She never wanted to listen helplessly to such again.

Besides, Bob wasn't really alive, even then—his eyes never flickered. It was only reflex that enabled him to swallow the soup she fed him. That his rod still seemed to live when she bathed him, that, too, was reflex, an obscene joke that life was playing on the two of them. It raised no feelings of tenderness in her, just a feeling of disgust at the cruelties of existence. It seemed to mock her, to make her feel that she was cheating Bob of something, though it was not easy to say what. She had married him, followed him, fed him, worked beside him, borne his children— and yet even as she changed his sheets she felt there was a selfishness in her that she had never mastered. Something had been held back—what it was, considering all that she had done, was hard to say. But she felt it anyway, fair judgment or not, and lay awake on her cot through half the night, tense with self-reproach.

In the mornings she lay wrapped in a quilt until the smell of Cholo's coffee waked her. She had fallen into the habit of letting Cholo make the coffee, mainly because he was better at it than she was. She would lie in her quilt, watching the mists float over the Platte, until one or both of the girls tiptoed out. They always tiptoed, as if they might wake their father, though his eyes were as wide open as ever.

"Ma, ain't you up?" Sally would say. "We been up awhile."

"Wanta gather the eggs?" Betsey asked. It was her favorite chore but she preferred to do it with her mother—some of the hens were irritable with Betsey and would peck her if she tried to slide an egg out from under them, whereas they would never peck Clara.

"I'd rather gather you two," Clara said, pulling both girls onto the cot with her. With the sunlight flooding the wide plain, and both her two girls in bed with her, it was hard to feel as bad about herself as she had felt alone in the night.

"Don't you wanta get up?" Sally asked. She had more of her father in her than Betsey had, and it bothered her a little to see her mother lazing in bed with the sun up. It seemed to her a little wrong—at least, her father had often complained about it.

"Oh, shush," Clara said. "The sun's just been up five minutes."

She reflected that perhaps that was what she had held back—she had never become proficient at early rising, despite all the practice she'd had. She had got up dutifully and made breakfast for Bob and whatever hands happened to be there, but she was not at her best, and the breakfasts seldom arrived on the table in the orderly fashion that Bob expected. It was a relief to her when he went away on horse-trading expeditions and she could sleep late, or just lie in bed thinking and reading the magazines she ordered from the East or from England.

The ladies' magazines had stories and parts of novels in them, in many of which were ladies who led lives so different from hers that she felt she might as well be on another planet. She liked Thackeray's ladies better than Dickens's, and George Eliot's best of all—but it was a frustration that the mail came so seldom. Sometimes she would have to wait for two or three months for her *Blackwoods,* wondering all the time what was happening to the people in the stories. Reading stories by all the women, not only George Eliot, but Mrs. Gore and Mrs. Gaskell and Charlotte Yonge, she sometimes had a longing to do what those women did—write stories. But those women lived in cities or towns and had many friends and relatives nearby. It discouraged her to look out the window at the empty plains and reflect that even if she had the eloquence to write, and the time, she had nothing to write about. With Maude Jones dead, she seldom saw another woman, and had no relatives near except her husband and her children. There was an aunt in Cincinnati, but they only exchanged letters once or twice a year. Her characters would have to be the horses and the hens, if she ever wrote, for the menfolk that came by weren't interesting enough to put in books, it seemed to her. None of them were capable of the kind of talk men managed in English novels.

She longed, sometimes, to talk to a person who actually wrote stories and had them printed in magazines. It interested her to speculate how it was done: whether they used people they knew, or just made people up. Once she had even ordered some big writing tablets, thinking she might try it anyway, even if she didn't know how, but that was in the hopeful years before her boys died. With all the work that had to be done she never actually sat down and tried to write anything—and then the boys died and her feeling changed. Once the sight of the writing tablets had made her hopeful, but after those deaths it ceased to matter. The tablets were just another reproach to her, something willful she had wanted. She burned the tablets one day, trembling with anger and pain, as if the paper and not the weather had been somehow responsible for the deaths of her boys. And, for a time, she stopped reading the magazines. The stories in them seemed hateful to her: how could people talk that way and spend their time going to balls and parties, when children died and had to be buried?

But a few years passed, and Clara went back to the stories in the magazines. She loved to read aloud, and she read snatches of them to her daughters as soon as they were big enough to listen. Bob didn't particularly like it, but he tolerated it. No other woman he knew read as much as his wife, and he thought it might be the cause of certain of her vanities: the care she took with her hair, for instance, washing it every day and brushing it. To him it seemed a waste—hair was just hair.

As Clara watched the wagon the girls had spotted drawing closer, she saw Cholo come riding in with two mares who were ready to foal. Cholo had seen the wagon too, and had come to look after her. He was a cautious old man, as puzzled by Clara as he was devoted to her. It was her recklessness that disturbed him. She was respectful of dangerous horses, but seemed to have no fear at all of dangerous men. She laughed when Cholo tried to counsel her. She was not even afraid of Indians, though Cholo had showed her the scars of the arrow wounds he had suffered.

Now he penned the mares and loped over to be sure she wasn't threatened by whoever was coming in the wagon. They kept a shotgun in the saddle shed, but Clara only used it to kill snakes, and she only killed snakes because they were always stealing her eggs. At times the hens seemed to her almost more trouble than they were worth, for they had to be protected constantly from coyotes, skunks, badgers, even hawks and eagles.

"I don't see but two men, Cholo," Clara said, watching the wagon.

"Two men is two too many if they are bad men," Cholo said.

"Bad men would have a better team," Clara said. "Find any colts?" Cholo shook his head. His hair was white—Clara had never been able to get his age out of him, but she imagined he was seventy-five at least, perhaps eighty. At night by the fire, with the work done, Cholo wove horsehair lariats. Clara loved to watch the way his fingers worked. When a horse died or had to be killed, Cholo always saved its mane and tail for his ropes. He could weave them of rawhide too, and once had made one for her of buckskin, although she didn't rope. Bob had been puzzled by the gift—"Clara couldn't rope a post," he said—but Clara was not puzzled at all. She had been very pleased. It was a beautiful gift; Cholo had the finest manners. She knew he appreciated her as she appreciated him. That was the year she bought him the coat. Sometimes, reading her magazines, she would look up and see Cholo weaving a rope and imagine that if she ever did try to write a story she would write it about him. It would be very different from any of the stories she read in the English magazines. Cholo was not much like an English gentleman, but it was his gentleness and skill with horses, in contrast to Bob's incompetence, that made her want badly to encourage him to stay with them. He talked little, which would be a problem if she put him in a story—the people in the stories she read seemed to talk a great deal. He had been stolen as a child by Comanches and had gradually worked his way north, traded from one tribe to another, until he had escaped one day during a battle. Though he was an old man and had lived among Indians and whites his whole life, he still preferred to speak Spanish. Clara knew a little from her girlhood in Texas, and tried to speak it with him. At the sound of the Spanish words his wrinkled face would light up with happiness. Clara persuaded him to teach her girls. Cholo couldn't read, but he was a good teacher anyway—he loved the girls and would take them on rides, pointing at things and giving them their Spanish names.

Soon all the mares in the corral were pricking their ears and watching the approaching wagon. A big man in a coat heavier than Cholo's rode beside it on a little brown horse that looked as if it would drop if it had to carry him much farther. A man with a badly scarred face rode on the wagon seat, beside a woman who was heavy with child. The woman drove the team. All three looked so blank with exhaustion that even the sight of people, after what must have been a long journey, didn't excite them much. A few buffalo hides were piled in the wagon. Cholo watched the travelers carefully, but they didn't seem to pose a threat. The woman drew rein and looked down at them as if dazed.

"Are we to Nebraska yet?" she asked.

"Yes," Clara said. "It's nearly twenty miles to town. Won't you get down and rest?"

"Do you know Dee Boot?" the woman said. "I'm looking for him."

"*Sí—pistolero,*" Cholo said quietly. He did most of their shopping and knew practically everyone in Ogallala.

Elmira heard the word, and knew what it meant, but she didn't care what anybody called Dee—the fact that he was nearby was all that mattered. If Dee was near, it meant that she was safe and could soon be rid of Luke and Big Zwey, and not have to ride on the jolting wagon seat all day or be scared all night that they would run into Indians at the last minute.

"Get down—at least you'll want to water your stock," Clara said. "You're welcome to stay the night, if you like. You can easily make town tomorrow. I'd say you all could use a rest."

"What town would that be?" Luke asked, easing down from the wagon seat. He had twisted a leg several days before, running to try and get a better shot at an antelope—it was all he could do to walk.

Elmira didn't want to stop, even when told that it was still over half a day to Ogallala, but Zwey had already dismounted and unhitched the horses. I wish I could get to Dee, she thought—but then decided one more day wouldn't matter. She got slowly down from the wagon seat.

"Come on up to the house," Clara said. "I'll have the girls draw some water. I guess you've come a ways."

"Arkansas," Elmira said. The house didn't look very far away, but as they walked toward it, it seemed to wobble in her vision.

"My goodness, that is a ways," Clara said. "I lived in Texas once." Then she turned and saw that the woman was sitting on the ground. Before Clara could reach her she had toppled sideways and lay face up on the trail that led from the house to the barn.

Clara was not too alarmed. Just tired, she thought. A journey all the way from Arkansas, in a wagon like that, would wear anybody out. She fanned the woman's face for a while but it did no good. Cholo had seen the woman fall and he ran to her, but the big man lifted the woman as easily as if she were a child and carried her to the house.

"I didn't get your name, or her name either," Clara said.

The big man just looked at her silently. Is he mute? Clara thought. But later the man with the scarred face came to the house and said no, the big man just didn't talk much. "Name's Zwey," he said. "Big Zwey. I'm Luke. I got my face bunged up coming, and now I hurt this dern leg. Her name's Elmira."

"And she's a friend of Mr. Boot?" Clara asked. They put Elmira in bed but she hadn't yet opened her eyes.

"Don't know about that, she's married to a sheriff," Luke said. He felt uncomfortable in the house after so many days outside, and soon went out again to sit on the wagon with Zwey. He happened to look up and see two young girls peering at him from an open window. He wondered where the man was, for surely the good-looking woman he had talked to couldn't be married to the old Mexican.

That night she asked if they would like to come in and eat supper. Zwey wouldn't—he was too shy—so the woman brought their suppers out and they ate in the wagon.

The girls were disappointed at that turn of events. They seldom had company and wanted a better look at the men.

"Make 'em come in, Ma," Sally whispered. She was particularly fascinated by the one with the scarred face.

"I can't just order men around," Clara said. "Anyway, you've met buffalo hunters before. Smelled them too. These don't smell much different from any of the others."

"One of them's big," Betsey observed. "Is he the lady's husband?"

"I don't think so, and don't be a busybody," Clara said. "She's worn out. Maybe tomorrow she'll feel like talking."

But the girls were to hear Elmira's voice long before morning. The men sitting in the wagon heard it too—long screams that raked the prairie night for hours.

Once again, Clara had reason to be glad of Cholo, who was as good with women as he was with horses. Difficult births didn't frighten him as they did most men, and many women. Elmira's was difficult, too—the exhausting journey over the plains had left her too weak for the task at hand. She fainted many times during the night. Clara could do nothing about it except bathe her face with cool water from the cistern. When day came, Elmira was too weak to scream. Clara was worried—the woman had lost too much blood.

"Momma, Daddy's sick, he smells bad," Sally said, peeking for a moment into the sickroom. The girls had slept downstairs on pallets, so as to be farther from the screams.

"Just leave him be, I'll take care of him," Clara said.

"But he's sick—he smells bad," Sally repeated. Her eyes were fearful.

"He's alive—life don't always smell nice," Clara said. "Go make us some breakfast and take some to those men. They must be hungry."

A few minutes later, Elmira fainted again.

"She's too weak," Cholo said.

"Poor thing," Clara said. "I would be too, if I came that far. That baby isn't going to wait for her to get strong."

"No, it's going to kill her," Cholo said.

"Well then, save it, at least," Clara said, feeling so downcast suddenly that she left the room. She got a water bucket and walked out of the house, meaning to get some water for Bob. It was a beautiful morning, light touching the farthest edges of the plains. Clara noticed the beauty and thought it strange that she could still respond to it, tired as she was and with two people dying in her house—perhaps three. But she loved the fine light of the prairie mornings; it had resurrected her spirits time after time though the years, when it seemed that dirt and cold and death would crush her. Just to see the light spreading like that, far on toward Wyoming, was her joy. It seemed to put energy into her, make her want to do things.

And the thing she wanted most to do was plant flowers—flowers that might bloom in the light. She did plant them, ordering bulbs and seeds from the East.

The light brought them up, and then the wind tore them from her. Worse than the dirt she hated the wind. The dirt she could hold her own with, sweeping it away each morning, but the wind was endless and fierce. It renewed itself again and again, curling out of the north to take her flowers from her, petal by petal, until nothing remained but the sad stalks. Clara kept on planting anyway, hiding the flowers in the most protected spots she could find. The wind always found them too, in time, but sometimes the blooms lasted a few days before the petals were blown away. It was a battle she wouldn't give up on: every winter she read seed catalogues with the girls and described to them the flowers they would have when spring came.

Coming back with the bucket from the cistern she noticed the two dirty, silent men sitting on the wagon—she had walked past them without a thought on her way to the well.

"Is it born yet?" Luke asked.

"Not yet," Clara said. "She's too tired to help much."

The large man followed her with his eyes but said nothing.

"You've got too much fire in that stove, you'll burn everything," Clara said, when she saw how the girls were progressing with breakfast.

"Oh, Ma, we can cook," Sally said. She loved to get her mother out of the kitchen—then she could boss her younger sister around.

"Is that woman real sick?" Betsey asked. "Why does she yell so much?"

"She's working at a hard task," Clara said. "You better not burn that porridge, because I want some."

She carried the bucket up to the bedroom, pulled the smelly sheets out from under Bob, and washed him. Bob stared straight up, as he always did. Usually she warmed the water but this morning she hadn't taken the time. It was cold and raised goosebumps on his legs. His big ribs seemed to stick out more every day. She had forgotten to bring fresh sheets—it was a constant problem, keeping fresh sheets—so she covered him with a blanket and walked out on her porch for a minute. She heard Elmira begin to moan, again and again. She ought to go relieve Cholo, she knew, but she didn't rush. The birth might take another day. Everything took longer than it should, or else went too quick. Her sons' lives had been whipped away like a breath, while her husband had lain motionless for two months and still wasn't dead. It was wearying, trying to adjust to all the paces life required.

After she had stood for a moment on the cool porch, she went down the hall, just in time to hold Elmira down and watch Cholo ease a baby boy from her bloodied loins.

The baby looked dead, and Elmira looked as if she were dying—but in fact both lived. Cholo held the little boy close to his face and blew on it, until finally the child moved and began to cry, a thin sound not much stronger than the squeak of a mouse. Elmira had passed out, but she was breathing.

Clara went downstairs to heat some water and saw that the girls had taken breakfast to the two men. They were standing around while the men ate, not to be denied the novelty of conversation, even if only with two buffalo hunters, one of whom wouldn't talk. It made her want to cry, suddenly, that her children were so devoid of playmates that they would hang around two sullen men just for the excitement of company. She heated the water and let the girls be. Probably the men would go on soon, though Luke seemed to be talking to the girls happily. Maybe he was as lonesome as they were.

When she went up with the hot water Elmira was awake, her eyes wide open. She was pale, almost bloodless, no color in her cheeks at all.

"It's a miracle you got here," Clara said. "If you'd had that baby down on the plains I doubt either one of you would have lived."

The old Mexican had wrapped the infant in a flannel robe and brought it to Elmira to see, but Elmira didn't look at it. She didn't speak and she wouldn't look.

She didn't want the baby. Maybe it'll die, she thought. Dee won't want it either.

Clara saw the woman turn her eyes away. Without a word she took the infant from Cholo and walked downstairs with it, out into the sunlight. The girls still stood by the wagon, though the men had eaten. She shielded the baby's eyes with the robe and carried it over to the group.

"Oh, Ma," Betsey said—she had never seen a newborn child. "What's its name?"

"The lady's too tired to worry about naming it just now," Clara said. "It's a boy, though."

"It's lucky we got here, ain't it?" Luke said. "Me and Zwey would have had no idea what to do."

"Yes, it's lucky," Clara said.

Big Zwey stared at the baby silently for a time. "It's red, Luke," he said finally. "I guess it's an Indian."

Clara laughed. "It's no Indian," she said. "Babies mostly are red."

"Can I hold it?" Sally asked. "I held Betsey, I know how."

Clara let her take the child. Cholo had come downstairs and was standing at the back porch, a cup of coffee in his hand.

"Zwey wants to get to town," Luke said. "Can Ellie go yet?"

"Oh, no," Clara said. "She's had a bad time and she's weak. It would kill her to travel today. She'll need to rest for about a week. Maybe you could come back for her, or else we could bring her in our little wagon when she gets well."

But Zwey refused to leave. Ellie had wanted to get to town, he remembered, and he was determined to wait until she could go. He sat in the shade of the wagon all day and taught the two young girls how to play mumblety-peg. Clara looked out at them occasionally from the upper windows—there seemed no harm in the man. Luke, bored, had ridden off with Cholo to check the mares.

When Clara took the child in to nurse, she began to see that Elmira didn't want it. She turned her wide eyes away when Clara brought it near. The infant was whimpering and hungry.

"Ma'am, it's got to nurse," Clara said. Elmira made no objection when the baby was put to her breast, but the business was difficult. At first no milk would come—Clara began to fear the baby would weaken and die before it could even be fed. Finally it nursed a little but the milk didn't satisfy it—an hour later it was crying in hunger again.

Thin milk, Clara thought—and no wonder, for the woman probably hadn't eaten a decent meal in months. She refused to look at the baby, even when it took her breast. Clara had to hold it and encourage it, rubbing its little lips with milk.

"They say you're married to a sheriff," Clara said, thinking conversation might help. The man might be the cause of her flight, she thought. She probably didn't want him in the first place, and hadn't asked for this child.

Elmira didn't answer. She didn't want to talk to this woman. Her breasts were so full they hurt; she didn't care that the baby took the milk, she just didn't want to look at it. She wanted to get up and make Zwey take her to town, to Dee, but she knew she couldn't do it yet. Her legs were so weak she could hardly move them on the bed. She would never get downstairs unless she crawled.

Clara looked at Elmira for a moment and held her peace. It was not a great surprise for her that the woman didn't want the baby. She hadn't wanted Sally, out of fear that she would die. The woman must have her own fears—after all, she had traveled for months across the plains with two buffalo hunters. Perhaps she was fleeing a man, perhaps looking for a man, perhaps just running—there was no point in pressing questions, for the woman might not know herself why she ran.

Besides, Clara remembered the immense fatigue that had seized her when Betsey was born. Though the last, Betsey had been the most difficult of her births, and when it was over she could not lift her head for three hours. To speak took an immense effort—and Elmira had had a harder time than she had. Best just to let her rest. When her strength came back she might not be so ill-disposed toward the child.

Clara took the baby downstairs and had the girls watch him while she went outside and killed a pullet. Big Zwey watched silently from the wagon as she quickly wrung the chicken's neck and plucked and cleaned it.

"It takes a mess of chicken soup to run this household these days," she said, bringing the chicken back in. They had some broth left and she heated a little and took it to Elmira. She was startled to find Elmira on her feet, staring out the window.

"Goodness, you best lay down," Clara said. "You've lost blood—we've got to build you up."

Elmira obeyed passively. She allowed Clara to feed her a few spoonfuls of the soup.

"How far's town?" she asked.

"Too far for you to walk, or ride either," Clara said. "That town isn't going to run away. Can't you just rest for a day or two?"

Elmira didn't answer. The old man had said Dee was a *pistolero*. Though she didn't care what Dee was, as long as she could find him, the news worried her. Somebody might shoot him before she arrived. He might leave, might have already left. She couldn't stand the thought. The future had shrunk to one fact: Dee Boot. If she couldn't find him she meant to kill herself.

Clara tried several times during the day to get Elmira interested in the little boy, but with no success. Elmira allowed it to nurse, but that was not successful, either. The milk was so weak that the baby would only sleep an hour and then be hungry again. Her girls wanted to know why the baby cried so much. "He's hungry," Clara said.

"I can milk the cow early," Sally said. "We can give him some of that milk."

"We may have to," Clara said. "We'll have to boil it first." It'll be too rich for him and the colic will probably kill him, she thought. She carried the helpless little creature herself most of the day, rocking him in her arms and whispering to him. From being red, he had gone to pale, and he was a small baby, not five pounds, she guessed. She herself was very tired, and as the evening drew on and the sun fell she found herself in a very uneven temper—scolding the girls harshly for their loudness one minute, going out on her porch with the baby, almost in tears herself, another. Perhaps it's best that it dies, she doesn't want it, she thought, and then the next moment the baby's eyes would open for a second and her heart would fill. Then she would reproach herself for her own callousness.

When night fell she went in and lit a lamp in the room where Elmira lay. Clara, seeing that her eyes were open, started to take the baby to her. But once again Elmira turned her head away.

"What's your husband's name?" Clara asked.

"I'm looking for Dee Boot," Elmira said. She didn't want to say July's name. The baby was whimpering but she didn't care. It was July's and she didn't want to have anything to do with anything of July's.

Clara got the infant to nurse a little and then took it up to her own room, to lie down awhile. She knew it wouldn't sleep long, but she herself had to sleep and was afraid to trust it with its mother yet.

At some point she heard the baby whimpering but she was too tired to rise. In the back of her mind she knew that she had to get up and feed Bob but the desire to sleep was too heavy—she couldn't make herself move.

Then she felt a hand on her shoulder and saw Cholo kneeling by the bed.

"What's the matter?" Clara asked.

"They leave," Cholo said.

Clara jumped up and ran into the room where Elmira had been—sure enough, she was gone. She went to the window and could see the wagon, north of the corrals. Behind her she could hear the baby crying.

"*Señora,* I couldn't stop them," Cholo said.

"I doubt they'll stop just because you ask, and we don't need any gunfights," Clara said.

"Let 'em go. If she lives, she might come back. Did you milk?"

Cholo nodded.

"I wish we had a goat," Clara said. "I've heard goat's milk is better for babies than cow's milk. If you see any goats next time you go to town, let's buy a couple."

Then she grew a little embarrassed. Sometimes she talked to Cholo as if he were her husband, and not Bob. She went downstairs, made a fire in the cookstove and began to boil some milk. When it was boiled, she took it up and gave the baby a little, dipping a cotton rag in the milk and letting the baby suck it. It was a slow method and took patience. The child was too weak to work at it, but she knew if she didn't persist the baby would only get weaker and die. So she kept on, dribbling milk into its mouth even when it grew too tired to suck on the rag.

"I know this is slow," she whispered to it. When the baby had taken all it would, she got up to walk it. It was a nice moonlight night and she went out on her porch for a while. The baby was asleep, tucked against her breast. You could be worse off, she thought, looking at it. Your mother had pretty good sense—she waited to have you until she got to where there were people who'll look after you.

Then she remembered that she had not fed Bob. She took the baby down to the kitchen and heated the chicken broth. "Think of the work I'd save if everything didn't have to be hot," she said to the infant, who slept on.

She laid it at the foot of Bob's bed while she fed her husband, tilting his head so he could swallow. It was strange to her that he could swallow when he couldn't even close his eyes. He was a big man with a big head—every time she fed him her wrist ached from supporting his head.

"I guess we got us a boy, Bob," she said. The doctors had told her to talk to him—they thought it might make a difference, but Clara found that the only difference was that she got depressed. The depressing aspect of it was that it reminded her too clearly of their years together, for she had liked to chatter, and Bob never talked. She had talked at him for years and got no answers. He only spoke if money was concerned. She would talk for two hours and he would never utter a sentence. So far as conversation went, the marriage was no different than it had ever been—it was just easier for her to have her way about money, something that also struck her as sad.

She picked the baby up and held it to her bosom—the thought was in her head that if he saw her with a child it might make a difference. Bob might see it, think it was theirs. It might startle him into life again.

It was unnatural, she knew, for a mother to leave her child a day after it was born. Of course, children were endless work. They came when you didn't want them and had needs you didn't always want to meet. Worst of all, they died no matter how much you loved them—the death of her own had frozen the hope inside her harder than the wintry ground. Her hopes had frozen hard and she vowed to keep it that way, and yet she hadn't: the hopes thawed. She had hopes for her girls, and might even come to have them for the baby at her bosom, child of another mother. Weak as it was, and slim though its chances, she liked holding the child to her. I stole you, she thought. I got you and I didn't even have to go through the pain. Your mother's a fool not to want you, but she's smart to realize you wouldn't have much of a chance with her and those buffalo hunters.

It wasn't smartness, though, she thought—the woman just didn't care.

She looked down at Bob and saw that the baby had made no difference. He lay as he had, nothing left to him but need. Suddenly Clara felt angry that the man had been fool enough to think he could break that mare, when both she and Cholo had warned him to leave her alone. It made her angry at herself, to have lived so long with a horse trader who had no more savvy than that.

Yet there he was, his eyes staring upward, as helpless as the baby. She put the child down again and fed Bob soup until her wrist got tired from holding his head. Then she lay Bob's head back on his pillow, and ate the rest of the chicken soup herself.

76

BIG ZWEY WAS WORRIED that Elmira had left the baby. When she came out to the wagon, she didn't have it. "Hitch the team and let's go," she said, and that was all she said. He did it, but he felt confused.

"Ain't we gonna take the baby?" he asked shyly, just before they left.

Elmira didn't answer. She had no breath to answer with, she was so tired. Walking downstairs and out to the wagon had taken all her strength. Zwey had to lift her into the wagon, at that, and she sat propped against the buffalo skins, too tired even to care about the smell. She was so tired that she felt like she wasn't there. She couldn't even tell Zwey to start—Luke had to do it.

"Let's go, Zwey," he said. "She don't want the baby."

Zwey started the wagon, and they were soon out of sight of the house, but he was bothered. He kept looking back at Ellie, propped against the buffalo skins, her eyes wide open. Why didn't she want her baby? It was a puzzle. He had never understood the whole business, but he knew mothers took care of babies, just as husbands took care of wives. In his eyes he had married Ellie, and he intended to take good care of her. He felt he was her husband. They had come all that way together in the wagon. Luke had tried to marry her too, but Zwey had soon stopped that, and Luke had been behaving a lot better since.

Luke had tied his horse beside the wagon, and he rode on the wagon seat beside Zwey, who kept looking around to see if Ellie was asleep. She wasn't moving, but her eyes were still wide open.

"What are you looking at?" Luke asked.

"I wisht she'd brought the baby," Zwey said. "I always wanted us to have one."

The way he said it struck Luke as curious. It was almost as if Zwey thought the baby was his.

"Why would you care? It ain't yours," Luke said, to scotch that suspicion. Even if Zwey had got up his nerve to approach Ellie, which he doubted, they hadn't been on the road long enough to make a baby.

"We're married," Zwey answered. "I guess it's ours."

A suspicion dawned on Luke which was even more curious—the suspicion that Zwey didn't even understand about men and women. They had spent days around the buffalo herds when the bulls and cows were mating, and yet Zwey had evidently never connected such goings-on with humans. Luke remembered that Zwey never went with whores. He mainly just watched the wagon when the other hunters went to town. Zwey had always been considered the dumbest of the dumb, but Luke knew that none of the hunters had suspected him of being that dumb. That much dumbness was hard to believe—Luke wanted to make sure he hadn't misunderstood.

"Now, wait a minute, Zwey," he said. "Why do you think that baby was yours?"

Zwey was silent a long time. Luke was smiling, as he did when he wanted to make fun of him. It didn't ordinarily much bother him that Luke made fun of him, but he didn't want him to make fun about the baby. He didn't want Luke to talk about it. It was painful enough that she had had it and then gone off and left it. He decided not to answer.

"What's the matter with you, Zwey?" Luke said. "You and Ellie ain't really married. You ain't married to somebody just because she comes on a trip with you."

Zwey began to feel very sad—it might be true, what Luke said. Yet he liked to think that he and Ellie were married.

"Well, we are," he said finally.

Luke began to laugh. He turned to Ellie, who was still sitting with her back against the skins.

"He thinks that baby's his," Luke said. "He really thinks it's his. I guess he thinks all he had to do was look at you to make it happen."

Then Luke laughed a long time. Zwey felt sad, but he didn't say any more. Luke could always find something to laugh at him about.

Elmira began to feel cold. She started to shiver and reached for the pile of blankets in the wagon, but she was too weak even to untangle the blankets.

"Help me, boys," she said. "I'm real cold."

Zwey immediately handed the reins to Luke and went back to help cover her up. It was a warm night, but Ellie was still shivering. He put the blankets on her, but she didn't stop shivering. On the wagon seat, Luke would laugh from time to time when he thought of Zwey's baby. Before they had gone five miles, Ellie was delirious. She huddled in the blankets, talking to herself, mostly about the man called Dee Boot. Her look was so wild that Zwey became frightened. Once his hand happened to brush her and her skin was as hot as if the sun were burning down on her.

"Luke, she's got a fever," Zwey said.

"I ain't a doctor," Luke said. "We shouldn't have left that house."

Zwey bathed her face with water, but it was like putting water on a stove, she was so hot. Zwey didn't know what to do. A person so hot could die. He had seen much death, and very often it came with fever. He didn't understand why she had had the baby if it was only going to make her so sick. While he was bathing her face, she sat up straight and looked at him, her eyes wide.

"Dee, is that you?" she asked. "Where have you been?" Then she fell back against the skins.

Luke drove as fast as he could, but it was still a long road. The sky was light in the east when they finally found a wagon track and pulled into Ogallala.

The town was not large—just a long street of saloons and stores, and a few shacks on the slope north of the Platte. One of the saloons was still open. Three cowboys were lounging around outside, getting ready to mount up and go back to work. The two who were soberest were laughing at the third because he was so drunk he was trying to mount his horse from the wrong side.

"Hell, Joe's fixing to get on backwards," one said. They were not much interested in the fact that a wagon had pulled up. The drunk cowboy slipped and fell in the street. The other cowboys found that hilarious, one laughing so hard that he had to go over by the saloon and vomit.

"Where's the doctor live?" Luke asked the soberest cowboy. "We got a sick woman here."

At that the cowboys all stopped and stared. All they could see was Ellie's hair. The rest of her was covered with blankets.

"Where'd she come from?" one asked.

"Arkansas," Luke said. "Where's the doctor?"

Ellie had dropped into a fevered doze. She opened her eyes and saw the buildings. It must be the town where Dee was. She began to shove off the blankets.

"Do you know Dee Boot?" she asked the cowboys. "I come to find Dee Boot."

The cowboys stared at her as if they hadn't heard. Her hair was long and tangled, and she was wearing a nightdress. A huge buffalo hunter sat beside her.

"Ma'am, Dee Boot is in jail," one of the cowboys said politely. "It's that building over there."

Light was just filtering into the street between the shadowed buildings.

"Where's the doctor?" Luke asked again.

"I don't know if there is one," the cowboy said. "We just got here last night. I know about Boot because they were talking about him in the saloon."

Ellie began to try and climb over the side of the wagon. "Help me, Zwey," she said. "I wanta see Dee." She got one leg over the side board of the wagon and suddenly began to feel weak again. She clung to the board, trembling.

"Help me, Zwey," she said again.

Zwey lifted her out of the wagon as if she were a doll. Elmira took two steps and stopped. She knew she would fall if she tried another step, and yet Dee Boot was just across the street. Once she saw Dee she felt she could start getting well.

Zwey stood beside her, big as one of the horses the cowboys rode.

"Carry me over," she said.

Zwey felt afraid. He had never carried a woman, much less Ellie. He felt he might break her, if he wasn't careful. But she was looking at him and he felt he had to try. He lifted her in his arms and found again that she was light as a doll. She smelled different from anything he had ever carried, too. Mostly he had just carried skins, or carcasses of game.

As he was carrying her, a man came out of the jail and stepped around the corner of the building. It proved to be a deputy sheriff—his name was Leon—going out to relieve himself. He was startled to see a huge man standing there with a tiny woman in a nightgown in his arms. Nothing so surprising had happened in his whole tenure as deputy. It stopped him in his tracks.

"I want to see Dee Boot," the woman said, her voice just a whisper.

"Dee Boot?" Leon said, startled. "Well, we got him, all right, but I doubt he's up."

"I'm his wife," Ellie said.

That was another surprise. "Didn't know he was even married," Leon said.

Leon was watching the buffalo hunter, who was very large. It occurred to him that the couple might have come to try and break Dee Boot out of jail.

"I'm his wife, I want to see Dee," the woman said. "Zwey don't have to come."

"Dee can probably hear you, he's right in this cell," Leon said, pointing to a small barred window on the side of the jail.

"Carry me over, Zwey," Elmira said, and Zwey obeyed.

The window was tiny and the cell still mostly dark, but Elmira could make out a man lying on a little bare bunk. He had his arm over his eyes and at first she doubted it was Dee—if so, he had put on weight, which wouldn't be like Dee. He prided himself on being slim and quick.

"Dee," she said. "Dee, it's me." Her voice was the merest whisper, and the man didn't awake. Ellie felt angry—here she had come such a distance, and she had found him, yet she couldn't make him hear.

"Say something to him, Zwey," she whispered. "Your voice is louder."

Zwey was at a loss. He had never met Dee Boot and had no idea what to say to him. The task embarrassed him a little.

"Don't know nothing to say," he said.

Fortunately it didn't matter. The deputy had gone back in and he woke Dee Boot himself.

"Wake up, Boot," he said. "You got visitors."

The sleeping man immediately sprang up with a wild look. Ellie saw that it was him, although he hardly looked like the dapper man she remembered. He glanced at the window fearfully, then just stood and stared.

"Who's that?" he asked.

"Why, it's your wife," Leon said.

Dee came to the window—it was just two steps. Ellie saw that he had not shaved in several days—another surprise. Dee was particular about barbering and had always had the best barber in town come and shave him every morning. The eyes that she had remembered almost every day of the long trip—Dee's merry eyes—now just looked scared and sad.

"It's me, Dee," she said.

Dee just stared at her and at the large man holding her in his arms. Ellie realized he might have the wrong idea about Zwey, although he had never been particularly the jealous type.

"It's just Zwey," she whispered. "Him and Luke brought me in the wagon."

"There ain't nobody else?" Dee said, coming close to the bars and trying to peer out.

Ellie didn't know what was wrong. He could see it was her, and yet he hardly looked at her. He seemed scared, and his hair had little pieces of cotton ticking in it from a tear in the thin mattress he slept on. The scruffy growth of whiskers made him seem a lot older than she had remembered him.

"It's just me," Elmira whispered. She was beginning to feel scared—she felt so weak she could hardly hold her eyes open, and she wanted more than anything to talk to Dee. She didn't want to faint before they had their talk, and yet she was afraid she might.

"I left July," she said. "I couldn't do it. All I could think of was you, the whole time. I should have gone with you and not even tried it. I took a whiskey boat and then Zwey and Luke brought me in the wagon. I had a baby but I left it. I been coming back to you as quick as I could, Dee."

Dee kept trying to peer around them, as if he was sure there were more people than he could see. Finally he stopped trying, and looked at her. She was hoping for the old smile, but Dee didn't have it in him to smile.

"They're gonna hang me, Ellie," he said. "That's why I jumped up—I been expecting lynchers."

Elmira couldn't believe it. Dee had never done anything wrong—not wrong enough to make people hang him. He gambled and flirted, but those weren't hanging crimes.

"Why, Dee?" she asked.

Dee shrugged. "Killed a boy," he said. "I was just trying to scare him and he jumped the wrong way."

Ellie felt confused. She had never even heard of Dee Boot shooting a gun. He carried one, like all men did, but he never ever practiced with it that she knew. Why would he try to scare a boy?

"Was he aggravating you, or what?" she asked.

Dee shrugged again. "It was a settler's boy," he said. "Some cowmen hired me to run the settlers out. Most of them will run if you shoot over their heads a time or two. This one just moved the wrong way."

"We'll get you out," Elmira said. "Zwey and Luke will help me."

Dee looked at the big man holding Ellie. He did look big enough to pull the little jail apart—but of course he couldn't do it while he was holding a sick woman.

"I'm due to hang next Friday, but they may come lynch me first," Dee said.

Zwey felt something wet on his arms. Ellie was so light he didn't mind holding her. The sun was up and they could see into the cell a little better. Zwey didn't know why he felt so wet. He shifted Ellie a little and saw to his shock that the wetness was blood.

"She's bleeding," he said.

Dee looked out and saw that blood was dripping off Ellie's nightdress.

"Get her to the Doc," Dee said. "Leon knows where he lives."

Dee began to yell for the deputy and soon Leon came running around the jail. Elmira didn't want to go. She wanted to stay and talk to Dee, assure him that it would be all right, they would get him out. She would never let them hang Dee

Boot. She looked in at him, but she couldn't talk anymore. She couldn't say the things she wanted to say. She tried, but no words came out. Her eyes wanted to close, and no matter how hard she tried to keep them open and look at Dee, they kept trying to close. She tried to see Dee again, as Zwey was carrying her away, but Dee's face was lost in a patch of sunlight. The sun shone brightly against the wall of the jail and Dee's face was lost in the light. Then, despite herself, her head fell back against Zwey's arm and all she could see was the sky.

77

IT SEEMED TO JULY that he was nearly as cursed as Job when it came to catching Elmira. Despite his caution, he kept having accidents and setbacks of a kind that had never happened at home in Fort Smith. Three days out of Dodge, the new horse he had bought, which turned out not to be well-broken, fell and crippled himself trying to throw a hobble. July waited a day, hoping it wasn't as bad as he thought it was—but the next day he saw it was even worse. It hardly seemed possible to lose two horses on one trip, when he had never lost a horse before in his life, but it was a fact he had to face.

With that fact went another: he wasn't likely to get another horse unless he went back to Dodge. North of him there was only the plains, until he came to the Platte River—a long walk. July hated to double back on himself, but he had no choice. It was as if Dodge City was some kind of magnet, letting him go and then sucking him back. He shot the second horse, just as he had shot the first one, hid his saddle and went back. He walked grimly, trying to keep his mind off the fact that Ellie was getting farther and farther away all the time.

He swam the Arkansas River when he came to it, walked into town in wet clothes, bought another horse, and left again within the hour. The old horse trader was half drunk and eager to bargain, but July cut him short.

"You ain't getting anywhere very fast, are you, young feller?" the old man said, chuckling. July thought it an unnecessary remark. He went right back across the river.

All during the trip he had been haunted by the memory of something that had happened in Fort Smith several years before. One of the nicest men in town, a cotton merchant, had gone to Memphis on a business trip, only to have his wife take sick while he was gone. They tried to send a telegram to notify the man, but he was on his way back and the telegram never got delivered. The man's name was John Fisher. As he rode back into Fort Smith, John Fisher saw a burying party out behind the church. Being a neighborly man, he had ridden over to see who had died, and the people had all stopped, stricken, for they were burying his wife. July had been helping to cover the coffin. He never forgot the look on John Fisher's face when he realized he was a day late—his wife had died the afternoon before his return. Though a healthy man, John Fisher only lived another year himself. If he ran into someone on the street who had seen his wife on her sickbed he always asked, "Do you think Jane might have lived if I'd got back sooner?" Everyone told him no, you couldn't have done a thing, but John Fisher didn't believe them.

July had no reason to think that Elmira was sick, but he had so much worry that he hated every delay. Fortunately the new horse was strong, a good traveler. July pushed him hard, taking his own rest when he felt the horse needed it. He watched the horse closely, knowing that he couldn't afford to lose him. He only had two dollars left, plus some coffee, bacon and his rifle. He hoped to kill an antelope, but could not hit one. Mostly he lived on bacon.

Near the Republican River he had his second piece of bad luck. He had camped on a little bluff, exhausted, and after hobbling the horse, fell asleep like a stone. He didn't sleep well. In the night he felt a stinging in his leg but was too heavy with sleep to care—red ants had gotten him several times.

When he awoke it was to severe pain and a right leg so swollen that he had to cut his pants open to see what was wrong. When he did, he saw fang marks, just above his knee. A snake must have crawled near him in the night, and in his thrashing he had turned over and scared it. He had heard no rattle, but it might have been a young snake, or had its rattle broken off.

At first he was very scared. He had been bitten in the night—the poison had had several hours in which to work. It was already too late to cut the bite and try to drain the poison. He had no medicines and could do nothing for himself. He grew lightheaded and assumed he was dying. From the bluff he could see far north across the Republican, almost to Nebraska, he supposed. It was terribly bad luck, to be snakebit almost in sight of where he needed to be. He didn't even have much water, for with the river so close he had let himself run low.

There was no shade on the bluff. He covered his face with his hat and lay back against his saddle, sweating, and ashamed of his own carelessness. He grew delirious and in his delirium would have long talks with Roscoe. He could see Roscoe's face as plain as day. Roscoe didn't seem to blame him for the fact that he was dead. If he himself was soon going to be dead, too, it might not matter so much.

July didn't die. His leg felt terrible, though. In the night came a rainstorm and he could do nothing but huddle under his saddle blanket. His teeth began to chatter and he couldn't stop them. He almost wished he could go on and die, it was so uncomfortable.

But in the morning the sun was hot, he soon dried out. He felt weak, but he didn't feel as if he were dying. Mainly he had to avoid looking at his leg. It looked so bad he didn't know what to think. If a doctor saw it he could probably just cut it off and be done with it. When he tried to bend it even a little, a terrible pain shot through him—yet he had to get down to the river or else die of thirst, even though it had just rained. He had been too sick to try and catch any of the rainwater.

That afternoon he stood up, but he couldn't touch his right foot to the ground. He managed to belly over the horse and get down to the river. It was three days before he had the strength to go back and get the saddle. The effort of getting to the river had exhausted him so much he could barely undo a button. Early one morning he shot a large crane with his pistol, and the meat put a little strength in him. His leg had not returned to normal, but it had not fallen off either. He could put a little weight on it, but not much.

Five days after the snake bit him, July saddled up and rode across the Republican River. Since leaving Dodge he had not seen one person. He worried about Indians—wounded as he was, he would have been easy prey—and yet finally he grew so lonesome that he would have been glad to see an Indian or two. He began to wonder if there were any people at all in the north.

As he neared Nebraska, the plains took on a browner look. Though he was fairly sure now he wasn't going to die, he kept having spells of lightheadedness in which his vision wavered and he tended to run off at the mouth. At night he would wake and find himself in the middle of a conversation with Roscoe—it embarrassed him, though no one was around to hear.

But he kept on. Streams became a little more plentiful and he ceased to worry too much about water. Once he thought he saw riders, far in the distance, but when he went toward them they turned out to be two buffalo, standing on the prairie as if they were lost. July started to shoot one, but it was more meat than he needed, and if he killed one the other buffalo would be as alone as he was. He passed on and that night killed a big prairie chicken with a rock.

Three days later he saw the Platte, winding between low brown slopes. He soon hit a good wagon track and followed it west.

About noon he saw a lone frame house standing a half mile south of the Platte. There were corrals and a few sheds near it, and a sizable horse herd grazing in sight of the house. July felt like crying—it meant he wasn't lost anymore. No one would build a frame house unless there was a town somewhere near. Being alone on the prairie for so many weeks had made him realize how much he liked being in towns, though when he thought about all that he had been through, he didn't feel he had much hope of finding Ellie there. How could a woman come across such distances?

As he approached the house an old man appeared to the north, riding out of the Platte, his horse dripping water. July saw there were more horses north of the river. The old man had white hair and seemed to be a Mexican. He rode with a rifle held lightly across his saddle. July didn't want to appear unfriendly. He stopped to wait.

The old man looked mainly at his leg. July had forgotten how ugly it looked—he had even forgotten it was still yellowish and almost bare, for he had cut his pants leg off when the leg was so swollen.

"Is it bad?" the old man asked in English. July was glad for the English.

"Not as bad as it was," July said. "Is Ogallala near here?"

"Twenty miles," the old man said. "I'm Cholo. Come to the house. You must be hungry."

July didn't argue. He had almost forgotten that people sat at tables, in houses, to eat. He had lived so long on half-cooked bacon, or half-cooked game, that he had become shy at the thought of sitting at a proper table. He didn't look proper, he knew.

As he approached the house he suddenly heard shrieks of laughter, and a little girl flew around the corner of the house, another slightly older girl in hot pursuit. The girl in the lead ran on to one of the sheds between the house and the corral and tried to hide in it, but her sister caught her before she could get inside, and they tussled and shrieked. The older girl was trying to put something down the younger girl's neck, and she finally succeeded, at which point the younger girl began to hop up and down while the older one ran off, laughing.

As the two men rode up, a woman appeared on the back steps of the house. She wore a gray smock and an apron and had an infant in her arms. She was clearly out of temper, for she yelled something at the two girls, who stopped their shrieking, looked at one another and slowly approached the house. The infant the woman held was crying fretfully, though, at that, making less noise than the girls. The woman addressed herself to the older girl, who made some excuse, and the younger girl, in her own defense, pointed back toward the shed. The woman listened a minute and began to talk rapidly, giving her daughters what for, July supposed.

To see a woman so suddenly, after so much time alone, made him very nervous—particularly since the woman was so out of temper. But as they drew closer he found that, out of temper or not, he couldn't stop looking at her. Her eyes flashed as she lectured her daughters, neither of whom was taking the lecture silently—both were trying to talk back but the mother didn't pause to listen. She had abundant brown hair tucked into a bun at the back of her neck, though the bun had partly come loose.

The old Mexican seemed not the least disturbed by the argument in progress. In fact, he seemed amused by it, and he rode up and got off his horse as if nothing were happening.

"But she put a grasshopper down my neck," the younger girl said. "I hate her."

"I don't care who hates who," the woman said. "I was up with this baby all night—you know how colicky he is. You don't have to scream right under my window—looks like there be room on this prairie for you to scream without doing it under my window. All we got here is room."

"It was a grasshopper," the little girl insisted.

"Well, is it the first one you've ever seen?" the woman asked. "You'll have more to worry about than grasshoppers if you wake this baby again."

The woman was rather thin, but anger put color in her cheeks. The girls finally were subdued and the woman looked up and saw him, lifting her chin with a bit of belligerence, as though she might have to tie into him too. Then she saw his discolored leg, and her look changed. She had gray eyes and she turned them on him with sudden gravity.

"Get down, *señor*," the old man said.

The girls looked around and became aware for the first time that a stranger had come. They instantly stopped fidgeting and stood like statues.

The woman smiled. She seemed to have switched from anger to amusement.

"Hello, I'm Clara," she said. "Pardon the commotion. We're a loud bunch. Get down, sir. You're welcome."

July had not spoken in so long, except for the few words he had said to Cholo and his ravings to Roscoe Brown, that his voice came out cracked. "Thank you, I wouldn't want to trouble you," he said.

Clara laughed. "You don't look strong enough to trouble nobody around here," she said. "We grow our own troubles—it would be a novelty to have some we ain't already used to. These are my daughters, Sally and Betsey."

July nodded to the girls and got off his horse. After a ride his leg stiffened and he had to hobble over to the porch. The baby was still fretting. The woman rocked it in her arms as she watched July hobble.

"Snake bit him," Cholo observed.

"I guess I rolled into it at night," July said. "I never even seen it. Just woke up with a yellow leg."

"Well, if you've lived this long I expect you have nothing to fear," Clara said. "We'll get some food in you. The way sick people have been turning up lately, I sometimes think we oughta go out of the horse business and open a hospital. Come on in the house—you girls set him a place."

The old man helped him up the steps and into the roomy kitchen. Clara was poking the fire in the cookstove, the baby still held in one arm.

"If you'd like a wash first, I'll have the girls draw some water," Clara said. "I didn't get your name."

"I'm July Johnson," July said. "I come from Arkansas."

Clara almost dropped the poker. The girls had told her the little scarfaced man had said the woman they were with was married to a sheriff named Johnson, from Arkansas. She hadn't given the story much credence—the woman didn't strike her as the marrying type. Besides, the little man had whispered something to the effect that the big buffalo hunter considered himself married to her. The girls thought it mighty exciting, having a woman in the house who was married to two men. And if that wasn't complicated enough, the woman herself claimed to be married to Dee Boot, the gunfighter they had hung last week. Cholo had been in town when the hanging took place and reported that the hanging had gone smoothly.

Clara looked more closely at the man standing in her kitchen. He was very thin and in a kind of daze—probably couldn't quite believe that he was still alive after such a journey. She had felt that way herself upon arriving in Ogallala after her trip over the plains with Bob, and she hadn't been snakebit or had any particular adventures.

But if he was married to the woman, the baby drooling on her bosom might be his. Clara felt a flash of annoyance, most of it with herself. She had already grown attached to the baby. She liked to lie in bed with him and watch him try to work his tiny hands. He would peer at her for long stretches, frowning, as if trying to figure life out. But when Clara laughed at him and gave him her finger to hold he would stop frowning and gurgle happily. Apart from the colic, he seemed to be a healthy baby. She knew the mother was probably still in Ogallala, and that she ought to take the child into town and see if the woman had had a change of heart and wanted her son, but she kept putting it off. It would be discouraging to have to give him up—she told herself if the mother didn't want him bad enough to come and get him, then the mother was too foolish to have him. She reminded herself it was time she got out of the habit of babies. She wouldn't be likely to get any more, and she knew she ought to figure out another way to keep herself amused. But she did like babies. Few things were as likely to cheer her up.

She had never seriously supposed a father would turn up, and yet only three weeks had passed and one had, standing in her kitchen, dirty, tired, and with a badly discolored leg.

Clara poked the fire a time or two more, trying to adjust to the surprise. Then she turned and looked at July.

"Mr. Johnson," she said, "are you looking for your wife, by any chance?"

July almost fell over from surprise. "Yes, her name is Ellie—Elmira," he said. "How'd you ever know?"

He began to tremble. Clara came over, took his arm and led him to a chair. The girls were standing in the doorway, watching every move.

"I been looking for Ellie all the way," July said. "I didn't even know she come this way. She's not a large woman, I was afraid she might have died. Have you seen her?"

"Yes," Clara said. "She stopped here for the night about three weeks ago in the company of two buffalo hunters."

To July it seemed too much of a miracle—that with the whole plains to cross he and Ellie would strike the same house. The woman, who was watching him intently, seemed to read his mind.

"We get a lot of travelers," she said, as though he hadn't spoken. "Situating this place right here was one of the smartest things my husband ever did. Anyone coming along the Platte who might need a horse isn't going to miss us. We're on the only road. If we hadn't located on this road, we'd have been starved out long ago."

"It seems . . ." July said, and he couldn't finish. It was all he had hoped for, to be able to find her someday. He had risked and lost three lives to do it, and though Ellie wasn't right there, surely she was in town. He began to tremble and then to cry—he couldn't help it. His hopes were to be answered after all.

Silently Clara handed him a rough dish towel. She scowled fiercely at the girls until they backed off. She followed them out the back door to give the man a moment to collect himself.

"Why's he crying?" Betsey asked.

"He's just unnerved—he's come along a long way and I imagine he had stopped expecting to make it," Clara said.

"But he's a man," Sally said. Their father had never cried, as far as she knew.

"Men have tears in them too, same as you," Clara said. "Go draw some water. I think we might offer him a bath."

She went back in. July had not quite gained control of himself. He was too shaken with relief. The baby, now in a good mood, was mouthing its own fingers and rolling its eyes up to her. Might as well tell the man, she thought. She pulled out a chair and sat down at the table.

"Mr. Johnson, I guess I've got another piece of news for you," Clara said. She looked from the baby's face to his, seeking resemblances. It seemed to her the foreheads were the same, and though the child had little hair, the little was the same color as July's. He was not a bad-looking man, just gaunt from his travels, and dirty. She had a notion to make him shave, when he had rested, so she could compare his face with the baby's. He could use Bob's razor. One week ago she had stropped it and shaved Bob.

July looked at her as she fiddled with the baby. The tears had left him feeling empty, but his gratitude to the woman just for being there and treating him kindly was so great that he felt he might cry again if he tried to speak. The woman seemed too beautiful and too kind to be true. It was clear she was older—she had fine wrinkles around her mouth—but her skin was still soft and her face, as she wiggled the baby's little hand with one finger, was very beautiful. The thought of more news troubled him a little, though—probably one of Elmira's companions had stolen something or made some mischief.

"If that woman was your wife, I guess this child is yours," Clara said. "She had it the night she was here. Then she left. She was very anxious to get to town. I don't believe she realized what a fine boy she had. We all took to him right away around this place."

July had not really looked at the baby. He had supposed it belonged to Clara—she had said her name was Clara. She was watching him closely with her kind gray eyes. But what she said seemed so unlikely that he couldn't really credit it. Elmira had said nothing to him about wanting a baby, or planning to have one, or anything. To him, so tired he could hardly sit straight, it just meant another mystery. Maybe it explained why Elmira ran away—though it didn't to him. As for the little boy, wiggling in Clara's lap, he didn't know what to think. The notion that he had a son was too big a notion. His mind wouldn't really approach it. The thought made him feel lost again, as he had felt out on the plains.

Clara saw that he was past dealing with it for the moment.

"I'm sorry, Mr. Johnson," she said, immediately getting up. "I should be cooking instead of worrying you with things you're too tired to deal with. You eat and go rest. This boy will still be here—we can discuss it tomorrow."

July didn't answer, but he felt he was remiss. Not only was Clara going to a lot of trouble to feed him, she was taking care of a baby that might be his. He tried to think of things he might do or say, but nothing came to mind. Clara went cheerfully about the cooking, holding the baby in her arms most of the time but occasionally plunking him on the table for a minute if she needed both hands for the work.

"Just catch him if he starts to roll," she said. "That's all I ask."

She fed July beefsteak and potatoes and peas. July felt he would be too tired to eat, and yet at the smell of the food his appetite returned and he ate every bite.

"I made Bob build me a windbreak," she said. "I watched my gardens blow away for ten or twelve years and I finally got tired of it."

July looked at her questioningly.

"Bob's my husband," she said. "He's injured. We don't hold out too much hope for him."

She had strained and heated a little milk, and while July ate she fed the baby, using a big nipple she had fixed over a fruit jar.

"We use this nipple for the colts," she said. "Sometimes the mares don't have their milk at first. It's a good thing this boy's got a big mouth."

The child was sucking greedily on the nipple, which was quite large, it seemed to July.

"I've been calling him Martin," Clara said. "Since he's yours, you may want to change it. I think Martin is a nice name for a man. A man named Martin could be a judge, or maybe go into politics. My girls fancy the name too."

"I don't guess he's mine," July said. "Ellie never mentioned anything about it."

Clara laughed. It surprised him. "Had you been married long?" she asked.

"About six months," July said. "When she left."

"Oh, well, you were newlyweds then," Clara said. "She might have been put out with you and decided not to tell you."

"She had another boy, Joe," July said. "He went with me when I went after Jake Spoon. Only Joe got killed on the plains. Ellie don't know it yet."

"Did you say Jake Spoon?" Clara said. "I know Jake. We courted once. I saw him in Ogallala about a year ago but the woman he was with didn't like my looks so we didn't talk much. Why were you after Jake?"

July could barely remember it all, it seemed to have happened so long ago.

"Jake was gambling and a fight got started," he said. "Jake shot off a buffalo gun and the bullet went through the wall and killed my brother. I was out of town at the time. Peach, my sister-in-law, wanted me to go after Jake. I wish now I hadn't."

"It sounds accidental to me," Clara said. "Though I know that's no consolation to your family. Jake was no killer."

"Well, I didn't catch him anyway," July said. "Elmira ran off and Roscoe come and told me. Now Roscoe's dead too. I don't guess it could be my baby."

Clara was still studying the two faces, the little one and the gaunt, tired one. It interested her, what came across from parent to child.

"When did your wife run off?" she asked.

"Oh, it's been over four months," July said. "A long time."

Clara chuckled. "Mr. Johnson, I don't think arithmetic's your strong suit," she said. "I think this is young Mr. Johnson you're looking at. I had that figured out, even without the dates, but the dates jibe pretty well."

July didn't know what to say. Clara seemed delighted with her conclusion, but he didn't feel anything at all. It was just a puzzle.

"I guess I'm awful," Clara said. "Any kind of company affects me this way. I shouldn't be bothering you when you're so tired. The girls are drawing water. You have a bath. You can sleep in their room—it's a good bed."

Later, when he had bathed and fallen into a sleep so deep that he didn't even turn over for several hours, Clara brought the baby in and peeked at July. He hadn't shaved, but at least he had washed. Cleaned of dirt he looked very young, only a few years older than her oldest boy would have been had he lived.

Then she went to look at Bob for a moment—an ugly ooze had been seeping onto his pillow. The stitches in his head had been removed but underneath the wound seemed hot. It might be a new infection. Clara cleaned it as best she could, and took the baby out on her little porch.

"Well, Martin, your pa showed up," she said, grinning at the baby. "It's a good thing we got a house right on the road. I wonder what your pa will think of us when he gets his wits together."

The baby waved a hand in the warm air. Down at the lots, the girls were watching Cholo work with a two-year-old filly.

Clara looked at the baby and offered it her finger. "We don't much care what your pa thinks of us, do we, Martin?" she said. "We already know what we think of him."

78

LORENA WAS SITTING in her tent when Gus returned. She had been sitting there hoping he wasn't dead. It was an unreasoning fear she had, that Gus might die. He had only been gone three days, but it seemed longer to her. The cowboys didn't bother her, but she was uneasy anyway. Dish Boggett set up her tent at night and stayed close by, but it meant nothing to her. Gus was the only man she wanted to look after her.

Then, before it was quite dark, she heard horses and looked out to see Gus riding toward her. She was so glad she wanted to run out to him, but Dish Boggett was nearby, trimming his horse's feet, so she kept still.

"She's just fine, Gus," Dish said, when Gus dismounted. "I looked after her as best I could."

"I'm much obliged," Augustus said.

"She won't hardly even look at me," Dish said. He said it mildly, but he didn't feel it mildly. Lorena's indifference pained him more than anything he had ever experienced.

"Did you catch the horsethieves?" he asked.

"We did, but not before they murdered Wilbarger and four other people," Augustus said.

"Hang 'em?"

"Yes, hung them all, including Jake Spoon."

"Well, I'll swear," Dish said, shocked. "I didn't like the man but I never figured him for a killer."

"He wasn't a killer," Augustus said. "Jake liked a joke and didn't like to work. I've got exactly the same failings. It's lucky I ain't been hung."

He pulled the saddle off his tired horse. The horse lay down and had a good roll, scratching its sweaty back.

"Howdy do, miss," Augustus said, opening the tent. "Give me a hug."

Lorena did. It made her blush that he just asked, like that.

"If hugs are to be had for the asking, what about kisses?" Augustus asked.

Lorena turned her face up—the feel of his whiskers made her want to cry, and she held him as tight as she could.

"I wish we'd brought a bathtub on this trip," Augustus said, grinning. "I'm so dirty it's like kissing a groundhog."

Later, he went to the chuck wagon and brought back some supper. They ate outside the tent. In the distance the Irishman was singing. Gus told her about Jake, but Lorena felt little. Jake hadn't come to find her. For days she had hoped he would, but when he didn't, and her hope died, the memory of Jake died with it. When she listened to Gus talk about him it was as if he were talking about a man she hadn't known. She had a stronger memory of Xavier Wanz. Sometimes she dreamed of Xavier, standing with his dishrag in the Dry Bean. She remembered how he had cried the morning she left, how he'd offered to take her to Galveston.

But she didn't remember Jake particularly. He had faded into all the other men who had come and gone. He had got a thorn in his hand, she remembered that, but she didn't remember much else. She didn't much care that he was dead—he wasn't a good man, like Gus.

What scared her was all the death. Now that she had found Gus, it was very frightening to her to think that he might die. She didn't want to be without him. Yet that very night she dreamed that he had died and she couldn't find the body. When she came out of the dream and heard him breathing, she clung so tightly to him that he woke up. It was very hot and her clinging made them sweaty.

"What scared you?" Augustus asked.

"I dreamed you died," Lorena said. "I'm sorry I woke you."

Augustus sat up. "Don't fret," he said. "I need to go water the grass, anyway."

He went out, made water, and stood in the moonlight awhile, cooling off. There was no breeze in the tent, so Lorena came out too.

"It's a good thing this grass don't depend on me," Augustus said. "There's a lot more of it than I can get watered."

They were on a plain of grass so huge that it was hard to imagine there was a world beyond it. The herd, and themselves, were like a dot, surrounded by endless grass. Lorena had come to like the space—it was a relief after her years of being crowded in a little saloon.

Gus was staring at the moon and scratching himself. "I keep thinking we'll see the mountains," he said. "I grew up in mountains, you know. Tennessee. I hear them Rockies are a lot higher than the Smokies. They say they have snow on top of them the year round, which you won't find in Tennessee."

He sat down in the grass. "Let's sit out," he said. "We can nap in the morning. It will scandalize Call."

"Why does he go off at night?" Lorena asked.

"He goes off to be by himself," Augustus said. "Woodrow ain't a sociable man."

Lorena remembered her other worry, the woman in Nebraska. "When will we get there, Gus?" she asked. "Nebraska, I mean."

"I ain't sure," he said. "Nebraska's north of the Republican River, which we ain't come to yet. It might take us three weeks yet."

Lorena felt a dread she couldn't get rid of. She might lose him to the woman. The strange trembling started—it was beyond her control. Gus put his arms around her to make it stop.

"Well, it's natural to worry," he said. "This is a chancy life. What's the main thing that worries you?"

"I'm feared you'll die," Lorena said.

Augustus chuckled. "Dern right, I'll die," he said. "What else worries you?"

"I'm feared you'll marry that woman," she said.

"I doubt it," Augustus said. "That woman had two or three chances to marry me already, and she didn't take them. She's an independent type, like you used to be."

That was so, Lorena reflected. She had been quite independent, but now all she could think of was keeping Gus. She wasn't ashamed, though. He was worth keeping.

"It's funny humans take to the daylight so," he said. "Lots of animals would rather work at night."

Lorena wanted him to want her. She knew he did want her, but he had done nothing. She didn't care about it, but if she could be sure that he still wanted her, then the dread of losing him might go away.

"Let's go in," she whispered, hoping he'd know what she meant. He immediately turned to her with a grin.

"My, my," he said. "Times do change. I remember when I had to cheat at cards to get a poke. We don't have to go in that old hot tent. I'll drag the bedding out here."

Lorena didn't care that the cowboys might see, or who might see. Gus had become her only concern. The rest of the world could watch out. But Gus merely hugged her and gave her a kiss. Then he held her tight all night, and when the sun woke her the herd was already gone.

"Did anybody see us?" she asked.

"If they did they're lucky," Augustus said. "They won't get too many chances to see such beauties as us."

He laughed and got up to make the coffee.

79

NEWT COULDN'T GET JAKE out of his mind—how he had smiled at the end and given him his horse. He rode the horse every third day and liked his gait so much that he soon became his favorite horse. Jake hadn't told him what the horse's name was, which worried Newt. A horse needed a name.

Jake's hanging had happened so quickly that it was hard to remember—it was like a terrible dream, of the kind you can only remember parts of. He remembered the shock it had been to see Jake with his hands tied, sitting on his horse with a noose around his neck. He remembered how tired Jake looked, too tired even to care that he was going to be hung. Also, nobody talked much. There should have been some discussion, it seemed to Newt. Jake might have had a good excuse for being there, but nobody even asked him for it.

Not only had no one talked at the hanging, no one had talked since, either. Captain Call kept well to himself, riding far from the herd all day and sleeping apart at night. Mr. Gus stayed back with Lorena, only showing up at mealtimes. Deets was very quiet when he was around, and he wasn't around much—he spent his days scouting far ahead of the herd, which was traveling easily. The Texas bull had assumed the lead position, passing Old Dog almost every day and only giving up the lead to go snort around the tails of whatever cows interested him. He had lost none of his belligerence. Dish, who rode the point, had come to hate him even more than Needle Nelson did.

"I don't know why we don't cut him," Dish said. "It's only a matter of time before he kills one of us."

"If he kills me he'll die with me," Needle said grimly.

Of course, all the hands were curious about Jake. They asked endless questions. The fact that the farmers had been burned puzzled them. "Do you think they was trying to make people think Indians did it?" Jasper asked.

"No, Dan Suggs just did it because he felt like it," Pea Eye said. "What's more, he hung 'em after they were already dead. Shot 'em, hung 'em, and *then* burned 'em."

"He must have been a hard case, that Dan," Jasper said. "I seen him once. He had them little squint eyes."

"I'm glad he never squinted them at me, if that's the way he behaves to white men," Needle said. "What was Jake doing with an outfit like that?"

"If you ask my opinion, that whore that Gus has got was Jake's downfall," Bert Borum volunteered.

"You can keep your damn opinion to yourself, if that's what you think," Dish said. He was as touchy as ever where Lorena was concerned.

"Just because you're in love with a whore don't mean I can't express my opinion," Bert countered.

"You can express it and I can knock your dern teeth down your throat for you," Dish said. "Lorie didn't make Jake Spoon into no criminal."

Bert had always considered that Dish had been awarded the top-hand position unfairly, and he was not about to put up with such insolence from him. He took his gun belt off, and Dish did the same. They squared off, but didn't immediately proceed to fisticuffs. Each walked cautiously around the other, watching for an opening—their cautiousness provoked much jocularity in the onlookers.

"Look at them priss around," Needle Nelson said. "I used to have a rooster I'd match against either one of them."

"It'll be winter before they hit the first lick at this rate," Jasper said.

Dish finally leaped at Bert, but instead of boxing, the two men grappled and were soon rolling on the ground, neither gaining much of an advantage. Call had seen the men square off, and he loped over. When he got there they were rolling on the ground, both red in the face but doing one another no harm. He rode the Hell Bitch right up to them, and when they saw him they both stopped. He had it in his mind to dress them down, but the fact that the other hands were laughing at their ineffectual combat was probably all that was needed. Anyway, the men were natural rivals in ability and could be expected to puff up at some point. He turned and rode back out of camp without saying a word to them.

When he saw him go, Newt's heart sank. The Captain said less and less to him, or to anyone. Newt felt more and more of a need for somebody to talk about Jake. He had been the Captain's friend, and Mr. Gus's. It didn't seem right that he could be killed and buried, and no more said.

It was Deets, finally, who understood and helped. Deets was good at mending things, and one night as he was mending Newt's bridle Newt said what was on his mind. "I wish we could at least have taken him to jail," Newt said.

"They'd hang him too," Deets said. "I 'spect he'd rather us did it."

"I wish we hadn't even come," Newt said. "It's just too many people dying. I didn't think we'd ever kill Jake. It wasn't like an accident.

"If he didn't kill anybody, then it wasn't fair," he added.

"Well, there was the horses, too," Deets said.

"He only liked pacers," Newt said. "He wouldn't be bothered to steal horses as long as he had one to ride. Just being along didn't make him a horsethief."

"It do to the Captain," Deets said. "It do to Mr. Gus."

"They didn't even talk to him," Newt said bitterly. "They just hung him. They didn't even act like they were sorry."

"They sorry," Deets said. "Saying won't change it. He's gone, don't worry about him. He's gone to the peaceful place."

He put his hand for a moment on Newt's shoulder. "You need to rest your mind," he said. "Don't worry about the sleepers."

How do you stop? Newt wondered. It wasn't a thing he could forget. Pea Eye mentioned it as he would mention the weather, something natural that just happened and was over. Only for Newt it wasn't over. Every day it would rise in his mind and stay there until something distracted him.

Newt didn't know it, but Call, too, lived almost constantly with the thought of Jake Spoon. He felt half sick from thinking about it. He couldn't concentrate on the work at hand, and often if spoken to he wouldn't respond. He wanted somehow to move time backwards to a point where Jake could have been saved. Many times, in his thoughts, he managed to save Jake, usually by having made him stay with the herd. As the herd approached the Republican, Call's thoughts were back on the Brazos, where Jake had been allowed to go astray.

At night, alone, he grew bitter at himself for indulging in such pointless thoughts. It was like the business with Maggie that Gus harped on so. His mind tried to change it, have it different, but those too were pointless thoughts. Things thought and things said didn't make much difference and with Gus spending all his time with the woman there was very little said anyway. Sometimes Gus would come over and ride with him for a few miles, but they didn't discuss Jake Spoon. As such things went, it had been simple. He could remember hangings that had been harder: once they had to hang a boy for something his father had made him do.

When they sighted the Republican River Gus was with him. From a distance it didn't seem like much of a river. "That's the one that got the Pumphrey boy, ain't it?" Augustus said. "Hope it don't get none of us, we're a skinny outfit as it is."

"We wouldn't be if you did any work," Call said. "Are you going to leave her in Ogallala or what?"

"Are you talking about Lorie or this mare I'm riding?" Augustus asked. "If it's Lorie, it wouldn't kill you to use her name."

"I don't see that it matters," Call said, though even as he said it he remembered that it had seemed to matter to Maggie—she had wanted to hear him say her name.

"You've got a name," Augustus said. "Don't it matter to you, whether people use it?"

"Not much," Call said.

"No, I guess it wouldn't," Augustus said. "You're so sure you're right it doesn't matter to you whether people talk to you at all. I'm glad I've been wrong enough to keep in practice."

"Why would you want to keep in practice being wrong?" Call asked. "I'd think it would be something you'd try to avoid."

"You can't avoid it, you've got to learn to handle it," Augustus said. "If you only come face to face with your own mistakes once or twice in your life it's bound to be extra painful. I face mine every day—that way they ain't usually much worse than a dry shave."

"Anyway, I hope you leave her," Call said. "We might get in the Indians before we get to Montana."

"I'll have to see," Augustus said. "We've grown attached. I won't leave her unless I'm sure she's in good hands."

"Are you aiming to marry?"

"I could do worse," Augustus said. "I've done worse twice, in fact. However, matrimony's a big step and we ain't discussed it."

"Of course, you ain't seen the other one yet," Call said.

"That one's got a name too—Clara," Augustus pointed out. "You are determined not to use names for females. I'm surprised you even named your mare."

"Pea Eye named her," Call said. It was true. Pea Eye had done it the first time she bit him.

That afternoon they swam the Republican without losing an animal. At supper afterward, Jasper Fant's spirits were high—he had built up an unreasoning fear of the Republican River and felt that once he crossed it he could count on living practically forever. He felt so good he even danced an impromptu jig.

"You've missed your calling, Jasper," Augustus said, highly amused by this display. "You ought to try dancing in whorehouses—you might pick up a favor or two that you otherwise couldn't afford."

"Reckon the Captain will let us go to town once we get to Nebraska?" Needle asked. "It seems like a long time since there's been a town."

"If he don't, I think I'll marry a heifer," Bert said.

Po Campo sat with his back against a wagon wheel, jingling his tambourine.

"It's going to get dry," he said.

"Fine," Soupy replied. "I got wet enough down about the Red to last me forever."

"It's better to be wet than dry," Po Campo said. Usually cheerful, he had fallen into a somber mood.

"It ain't if you drown," Pea Eye observed.

"There won't be much to cook when it gets dry," Po said.

Newt and the Rainey boys had begun to talk of whores. Surely the Captain would let them go to town with the rest of the crew when they hit Ogallala. The puzzling thing was how much a whore might cost. The talk around the wagon was never very specific on that score. The Rainey boys were constantly tallying up their wages and trying to calculate whether they would be sufficient. What made it complicated was that they had played cards for credit the whole way north. The older hands had done the same, and the debts were complicated. As the arrival in Ogallala began to dominate their thoughts almost entirely, the question of cash was constantly discussed, and many debts discounted on the promise of actual money.

"What if they don't pay us here?" the pessimistic Needle asked one night. "We signed on for Montana, we might not get no wages in Nebraska."

"Oh, the Captain will pay us," Dish said. Despite his attachment to Lorena he was becoming as excited as the rest about going to town.

"Why would he?" Lippy asked. "He don't care whether you have a whore or not, Dish."

That sentiment struck everyone as almost undoubtedly true, and established a general worry. By the time they crossed the Stinking Water the worry had become so oppressive that many hands could think of nothing else. Finally a delegation, headed by Jasper, approached Augustus on the subject. They surrounded him one morning when he came for breakfast and expressed their fear.

Augustus had a big laugh when he figured out what was bothering them. "Why, you girls," he said. "All you want is orgies."

"No, it's whores we want," Jasper said, a little irritated. "It's fine for you to laugh, you got Lorie."

"Yes, but what's good for me ain't necessarily good for the weak-minded," Augustus said.

However, the next day he passed the word that everyone would be paid half wages in Ogallala. Call was not enthusiastic but the men had worked well and he couldn't oppose giving them a day in town.

As soon as they heard the ruling, spirits improved, all except Po Campo's. He continued to insist that it would be dry.

80

WHEN ELMIRA'S FEVER finally broke she was so weak she could barely turn her head on the pillow. The first thing she saw was Zwey, looking in the window of the doctor's little house. It was raining, but Zwey stood there in his buffalo coat, looking in at her.

The next day he was still there, and the next. She wanted to call out to him to see if he had news of Dee, but she was too weak. Her voice was just a whisper. The doctor who tended her, a short man with a red beard, seemed not much healthier than she was. He coughed so hard that sometimes he would have to set her medicine down to keep from spilling it. His name was Patrick Arandel, and his hands shook after each coughing fit. But he had taken her in and tended her almost constantly for the first week, expecting all the time that she would die.

"He's as loyal as any dog," he whispered to her, when she was well enough to understand conversation. For a while she had just stared back at him without comprehension when he spoke to her. He meant Zwey, of course.

"I couldn't even get the man to go away and eat," the doctor told her. "I live on tea, myself, but he's a big man. Tea won't keep him going. I guess he asked me a thousand times if you were going to live."

The doctor sat in a little thin frame chair by her bed and gave her medicine by the spoonful. "It's to build you up," he said. "You didn't hardly have no blood in you when you got here."

Elmira wished there was a window shade so she couldn't see Zwey staring at her. He stared for hours. She could feel his eyes on her, but she was too weak to turn her head away. Luke seemed to be gone—at least he never showed up.

"Where's Dee?" she whispered, when her voice came back a little. The doctor didn't hear her, she said it so faint, but he happened to notice her lips move. She had to say it again.

"Dee Boot?" she whispered.

"Oh, did you follow that story?" the doctor said. "Hung him right on schedule about a week after they brought you in. Buried him in Boot Hill. It's a good joke on him, since his name was Boot. He killed a nine-year-old boy, he won't be missed around here."

Elmira shut her eyes, hoping she could be dead. From then on she spat out her medicine, letting it dribble onto the gown the doctor had given her. He didn't understand at first.

"Sick to your stomach?" he said. "That's natural. We'll try soup."

He tried soup and she spat that out too for a day, but she was too weak to fight the doctor, who was almost as patient as Zwey. They kept her jailed with their patience, when all she wanted to do was die. Dee was gone, after she had come such a way and found him. She hated Zwey and Luke for bringing her to the

456

doctor—surely she would have died right on the street if they hadn't. The last thing she wanted to do was get well and have to live—but days passed, and the doctor sat in the little chair, feeding her soup, and Zwey stared in the window, even though she wouldn't look.

Even not looking, she could smell Zwey. It was hot summer, and the doctor left the window open all day. She could hear horses going by on the street and smell Zwey standing there only a few feet from her. Flies bothered her—the doctor asked if she wanted Zwey to come in, for he would be only too happy to sit and shoo the flies, but Elmira didn't answer. If Dee was dead, she was through with talk.

It occurred to her one night that she could ask Zwey to shoot her. He would give her a gun, of course, but she didn't think she had the strength to pull the trigger. Better to ask him to shoot her. That would solve it, and they wouldn't do much to Zwey if he told them he killed her at her own request.

Just thinking of such a simple solution seemed to ease her mind a bit—she could have Zwey shoot her. And yet, days passed and she got so she could sit up in bed, and she didn't do it. Her mind kept going back to the spot of sunlight where Dee's face had vanished. His face had just faded into the sunlight. She couldn't stop thinking of it—in dreams she would see it so clearly that she would wake up, to the sound of Zwey's snoring. He slept outside her window, with his back to the wall of the house—his snores were so loud a person might have thought a bull was sleeping there.

"What went with Luke?" she asked him one day.

"Went to Santa Fe," Zwey said. It had been a month since she had spoken to him. He thought probably she never would again.

"Hired on with some traders," he said. "Come all this way and then headed back."

"I guess your child didn't live," the doctor said one day. "I wouldn't have expected it to, out on the prairie, with you having such a close call."

Elmira didn't answer. She remembered her breasts hurting, that was all. She had forgotten the child, the woman with the two daughters, the big house. Maybe the baby was dead. Then she remembered July, and Arkansas, and a lot that she had forgotten. It was just as well forgotten: none of it mattered compared to Dee. It was all past, well past. Some day she would have Zwey shoot her and she wouldn't have to think about things anymore.

But she put it off, and in time got well enough to walk. She didn't go far, just to the door, to get a chamber pot or put one out of the room—the heat made the smells worse. Even Zwey had finally taken off his buffalo coat—he stood at the window in an old shirt, with holes worn in it so that the thick hairs of his chest poked through.

The doctor never asked her about money. Though she had gotten better, he hadn't. She could hear him coughing through the wall, and sometimes saw him spit into a handkerchief. His hands trembled badly, and he always smelled of whiskey. It troubled her that he didn't ask her for money. She had always been one to pay her way. Finally she mentioned it. She knew Zwey would go to work and get money for her if she asked him to.

"You'll have to let me know what I owe," she said, but Patrick Arandel just shook his head.

"I came here to get away from money," he said. "Did it, too. I got away from it, and it ain't easy to get away from money."

Elmira didn't mention it again. If he wanted to be paid, he could mention it—she had tried.

Then one day, with no warning from anyone, the door to her room opened and July walked in. Zwey was standing at the window when it happened. July's face seemed thinner.

"I found you, Ellie," he said, and there were tears in his eyes. Zwey was watching, but because of the shadows she didn't know if he could see that July was crying.

Elmira looked away. She didn't know what to do. Mainly she regretted that she had not had Zwey shoot her. Now July had found her. He had not come all the way in the room, but he was standing there, with the door half open, waiting for her to ask him in.

She didn't ask him in, didn't speak. It seemed she would always have bad luck, if he could come all that way across the plains and still find her.

Finally July came in the room and closed the door.

"The doctor says you're strong enough to talk," July said, wiping his eyes on his shirtsleeve. "You don't have to talk, though. You just lie there and get well. I won't stay very long. I just wanted you to know I came."

Elmira looked at him once and then looked at the wall. Well, you're a fool, she thought. You ought not to have followed. You ought to just told folks I was dead.

"I got one piece of bad news," July said, and his eyes filled up again. "It's real bad, and it's my fault. Joe got killed, him and Roscoe and a girl. An outlaw killed them. I ought to have stayed with them, but I don't know if it would have come out different if I had."

You wouldn't be here telling me, anyway, Elmira thought.

The news about Joe didn't touch her. She had never thought much about Joe. He had come when she had other things to worry about and she had never got in the habit of worrying about him. He gave her less trouble than July, though. At least he had sense enough to figure out she didn't want to be bothered with him, and had let her alone. If he was dead, that was that. She didn't remember him well—he hadn't talked much. He had just run out of luck on the plains. It might have happened to her, and she wished it had.

"Ellie, the baby's fine," July said. "I didn't even know it was ours, that's the funny thing. I seen Clara holding it and I had no notion it was ours. She named him Martin, if that's all right with you."

"I guess we got our own family now," July added. His heart was sinking so that his voice almost failed, for Ellie had not turned her head or given much more than a momentary sign of recognition. She hadn't spoken. He wanted to think it was just her weakness, but he knew it was more than that. She wasn't happy that he had found her. She didn't care about the baby—didn't even care that Joe was dead. Her face had not changed expression since the first look of surprise.

And all the while the large man with the holes in his shirt stood at the window silently, looking in. He was one of the buffalo hunters, July supposed. The doctor had spoken well of the man, mentioning how loyal he was to Elmira. But July didn't understand why he was standing there, and his heart was sinking because Ellie wouldn't look at him. He had come such a way, too. But she wouldn't, and he didn't think it was just because she was sick.

"We'll bring the baby in whenever you want it," July said. "I can rent a room till you're better. He's a strong baby. Clara says it won't hurt him a bit to come in. They've got a little wagon."

Elmira waited. If she didn't talk, sooner or later he would leave.

His voice was shaky. He sat down in the chair the doctor usually sat in, by the bedside. After a moment he took one of her hands. Zwey was still looking in. July only held her hand for a moment. He dropped it and stood up.

"I'll check every few days, Ellie," he said. "The doctor can send for me if you need me."

He paused. In the face of her silence, he didn't know what to say. She sat propped up against the pillow, silent—it was almost as if she were dead. It reminded him of times in Arkansas, times in the loft when he felt as if he were with someone who wasn't there. When he had found out she was alive and at the doctor's in Ogallala, he had gone off behind Clara's saddle shed and wept for an hour from relief. After all the worry and doubt, he had found her.

But now, in a minute, the relief was gone, and he was reminded of all her difficulties, how nothing he did pleased her, not even finding her in Ogallala. He didn't know what more to do or say. She had married him and carried his child, and yet she wouldn't turn her head to look at him.

Maybe it's too soon, he thought, as he stumbled, in a daze of pain and worry, out of the doctor's house. The big man was there watching.

"I'm much obliged for all the help you've given Ellie," he said. "I'll pay you back for any expense."

Zwey said nothing, and July walked away to get his horse.

Ellie saw him ride past the window. She got up and watched him until he was out of sight. Zwey stood watching, too.

"Zwey," Elmira said. "Get the wagon. I want to go."

Zwey was surprised. He had got used to her being in the bed in the doctor's house. He liked standing in the warm sun, watching her. She was so pretty in the bed.

"Ain't you sick?" he asked.

"No, get the wagon," she said. "I want to go today."

"Go which way?" he asked.

"Go," Elmira said. "Go away from here. I don't care where. Over to St. Louis will do."

"I don't know the way to St. Louis," Zwey said.

"Oh, get the wagon, we'll find the way," she said. "There's a road, I guess." She was out of patience with men. They were great ones for asking questions. Even Zwey asked them, and he could barely talk.

Zwey did as he was told. The doctor was gone, treating a farmer who had broken his hip. Elmira thought about leaving him a note, but didn't. The doctor was smart, he would figure out soon enough that she was gone. And before the sun set they left Ogallala, going east. Elmira rode in the wagon on a buffalo skin. Zwey drove. His horse was hitched to the rear of the wagon. She had asked him to take her, which made him proud. Luke had tried to confuse him, but now Luke was gone, and the man who came to see Elmira had been left behind. She had asked *him* to take her, not the other man. It must mean that they were married, just as he had hoped. She didn't say much to him, but she had asked him to take her, and that knowledge made him feel happy. He would take her anywhere she asked.

The only troublesome thought he had was the result of something the man at the livery stable said. He had been a dried-up little fellow, smaller than Luke. He had asked which way they were going and Zwey pointed east—he knew St. Louis was east.

"You might as well leave your scalps, then," the man said. "Have 'em sent by mail, once you get there."

"Why?" Zwey asked, puzzled. He had never heard of anyone sending a scalp in the mail.

"Because of the Sioux," the man said.

"We never saw no Indians, the whole way from Texas," Zwey remarked.

"You might not see the Sioux, either," the man said. "But they'll see you. You're a damn fool to take a woman east of here."

Zwey mentioned it to Elmira while he was helping her into the wagon.

"There might be Indians that way," he said.

"I don't care," Elmira said. "Let's go."

Many nights on the trail from Texas she had lain awake, in terror of Indians. They saw none, but the fear stayed with her all the way to Nebraska. She had heard too many stories.

Now she didn't care. The sickness had changed her—that and the death of Dee. She had lost the fear. A few miles from town they stopped and camped. She lay awake in the wagon much of the night. Zwey slept on the ground, snoring, his rifle held tightly in his big hands. She wasn't sleepy, but she wasn't afraid, either. It was cloudy, and the plains were very dark. Anything could come out of the darkness—Indians, bandits, snakes. The doctor had claimed there were panthers. All she heard was the wind, rustling the grass. Her only worry was that July might follow. He had followed all the way from Texas—he might follow again. Maybe Zwey would kill him if he followed. It was peculiar that she disliked July so, but she did. If he didn't leave her alone she would have Zwey kill him.

Zwey woke early. The man at the livery stable had worried him. He had been in three Indian fights, but each time he had several men with him. Now it was just he who would have to do all the fighting, if it came to that. He wished Luke hadn't been so quick to rush off to Santa Fe. Luke didn't always behave right, but he was a good shot. The livery-stable man acted as if they were as good as dead. It was morning, and they weren't dead, but Zwey felt worried. He felt perhaps he had not explained things well to Ellie.

"It's them Ogallala Sioux," he said, looking in the wagon at her. It was a warm morning, and she had thrown off the blankets. "He said the Army had them all stirred up," he added.

"I'll stir you up if you don't quit blabbing to me about Indians," Elmira said. "I told you yesterday. I want to get gone a good ways before July shows up in town again."

Her eyes flashed when she spoke, as they had before she got sick. Ashamed to have angered her, Zwey began to stir the fire under the coffeepot.

81

WHEN JULY CAME BACK FROM TOWN he was so depressed he couldn't
speak. Clara had asked him to do a few errands, but the visit with Elmira troubled
him so that he had forgotten them. Even after he got back to the ranch he didn't
remember that he had been asked to do anything.

Clara saw at once that he had sustained some blow. When she saw him come
back without even the mail, it had been on her tongue to say something about
his poor memory. She and the girls hungered for the magazines and catalogues
that came in the mail, and it was a disappointment to have someone ride right
past the post office and not pick them up. But July looked so low that she
refrained from speaking. At the supper table she tried several times to get a
word or two out of him, but he just sat there, scarcely even touching his food.
He had been ravenous since coming off the plains—so whatever the blow was,
it was serious.

She knew he was a man who was grateful for any kindness; she had shown him
several, and she showed him another by holding her tongue and giving him time
to get past whatever had happened in town. But there was something about his
silent, sunken manner that irritated her.

"Everything's gloomy," Betsey said. Betsey was quick to pick up moods.

"Yep," Clara said. She was holding the baby, who was babbling and gumming
his fist.

"It's a good thing we got Martin here," she said. "He's the only man we got who
can still talk."

"He don't talk," Sally said. "That ain't talk."

"Well, it's sound, at least," Clara said.

"I think you're mean," Sally said. She was quick to attack mother and sister
alike. "Daddy's sick, or he'd talk."

"All right," Clara said. "I'll take that back." In fact, she could remember a thousand meals when Bob hadn't said a word.

"I think you're mean," Sally repeated, not satisfied.

"Yes, and you're my equal," Clara said, looking at her daughter.

July realized it all had something to do with him, but he couldn't get his mind
on it. He carried his plate to the sink and thanked Clara for the meal. Then he
went out on the front porch, glad it was a dark night. He felt he would cry. It was
puzzling; he didn't know what to do. He had never heard of a wife doing any of
the things Elmira had done. He sat on the steps of the porch, sadder and more
bewildered than he had been even on the night when he got back to the river and
discovered the three bodies. There was nothing to do about death, but Elmira was
alive. He had to do something—he just didn't know what.

The girls came out and chattered behind him for a while, but he paid them no mind. He had a headache and thought he ought to lie down, except that lying down usually made his headaches worse.

Clara came out, still holding the baby, and sat in a rocker. "You seem to be feeling poorly, Mister Johnson," she said.

"Just call me July," he said.

"I'll be happy to," she said. "You can drop the Mrs., too. I think we know one another well enough for first names now."

July didn't think he knew her very well, but he didn't say it. He didn't think he knew any woman.

"I need to ask you a favor," she said. "Could you help me turn my husband, or are you feeling too poorly?"

He would help her, of course. Several times he had helped her with her husband. The man had lost so much weight that July could simply lift him while Clara changed the bedding. The first time it bothered him a good deal, for the man never closed his eyes. That night he worried about what the man might think— another man coming in with his wife. Clara was businesslike about it, telling him what to do when he was slow. July wondered if the man was listening, and what he was thinking, in case he was.

Clara handed him a lantern and they went inside. She left the baby with the girls for a minute. Clara stopped at the door of her bedroom and listened before going in.

"Every time I come I expect he'll have stopped breathing," she said. "I always stop and listen."

The man was breathing, though. July lifted him and Clara removed the sheets.

"Dern it, I forgot the water," she said, going to the door. "Sally, bring up the bucket," she yelled, and in a little while the girl appeared with it.

"Betsey's going to let the baby fall off the bed," she said. "She don't know how to hold it."

"Well, she better learn," Clara said. "You girls quit fighting over that baby."

July felt embarrassed, holding the sick, naked man while his wife sponged him with warm water. It seemed very improper to him. Clara seemed to understand how he felt and made the bed quickly.

"It's just nurse work, Mister Johnson," she said. "I tried keeping clothes on him, but it's no good. The poor man can't control himself."

She stopped and looked at him. "I forgot I was supposed to call you July," she said.

July felt that his head would burst. He didn't care what she called him. It hurt so that he could hardly walk straight on the stairs. He bumped into the door at the foot of the stairs. Above them, the baby was squalling.

Clara was about to go and see to the baby, but when she saw July stumble into the door she changed her mind. He went back out on the porch and sank on the steps, as if at the end of his strength. Clara reached down and put her palm against his forehead, which caused him to jump as if he had been struck.

"My goodness, you're shy as a colt," she said. "I thought you might be feverish, but you ain't."

"It's just my head," he said.

"You need a cool rag, then," she said.

She went back into the house and got a rag and a little water. She made him let her bathe his forehead and temples. He had to admit the cool water felt good.

"Thank you," he said.

"Oh, you don't have to thank me for a washrag," Clara said. "I'm not much of a nurse. It's one of my failings. I'm too impatient. I'll give a person a week or two, and then if they don't improve I'd just about as soon they'd die.

"Not children," she added, a little later. "I ain't that harsh with children. I'd rather have them sick five years than to lose one. It's just my observation that nursing don't do that much good. People get well if they're able, or else they die."

They were silent for several minutes.

"Did you find your wife?" Clara asked. "It ain't my business, I know, but I'll ask you anyway."

"Yes," July said. "She was at the doctor's."

"She must not have been very glad to see you," Clara said.

July wished she would leave him alone. She had taken him in and fed him, saved his wife and cared for his child, and yet he did wish she would just leave him alone. He felt so weak himself that if he hadn't been braced against the porch railing he might have rolled off the steps. He had nothing to say and nothing to offer. And yet there was something tireless in Clara that never seemed to stop. His head hurt so he felt like shooting himself, the baby was squalling overhead, and yet she would ask questions.

"I guess she's still sick," he said. "She didn't say much."

"Did she want the baby?"

"She didn't say," July said.

"Did she ask any questions about it at all?"

"No," July admitted. "She never said a word."

The baby had stopped crying. They heard a horse splash out of the river—Cholo was coming in late. Even with no moon they could see his white hair as he trotted to the corrals.

"July, I know you're tired," Clara said. "I expect you're heartsick. I'm going to say a terrible thing to you. I used to be ladylike, but Nebraska's made me blunt. I don't think that woman wants you or the baby either. I don't know what she does want, but she left that baby without even looking at it."

"She must have been addled," July said. "She had a hard trip."

Clara sighed. "She had a hard trip, but she wasn't addled," she said. "Not every woman wants every child, and plenty of wives don't want the husbands they took.

"It's your child and her child," she added. "But I don't think she wants it, and if she means to prove me wrong she better do it soon."

July didn't know what she meant and didn't really care. He felt too low to pay any attention.

"I like young things," Clara said. "Babies and young horses. I get attached real quick. They don't have to be mine."

She paused. She knew he wished she'd shut up, but she was determined to say what was on her mind.

"I'm getting attached to Martin," she said. "He ain't mine, but he ain't your wife's anymore, either. Young things mainly belong to themselves. How they grow up depends on who gets attached to them. I'll take Martin, if she don't, or you don't."

"But your husband's sick," July said. Why would the woman want a baby to care for when she had two girls to manage and a big horse outfit to run?

"My husband's dying," Clara said. "But whether he's dead or alive, I'll still raise that child."

"I don't know what to do," July said. "It's been so long since I done anything right that I can't remember it. I don't know if I'll ever get Ellie back to Fort Smith. They might even have hired a new sheriff by now."

"Finding a job's the least of your problems," Clara said. "I'll give you a job, if you want one. Cholo's been doing Bob's work and his too, and he can't keep it up forever."

"I always lived in Arkansas," July said. It had never occurred to him that he might settle anywhere else.

Clara laughed. "Go to bed," she said. "I've worried you enough for one night."

He went, but the next morning at breakfast he didn't look much better or feel much better. He would scarcely talk to the girls, both of whom doted on him. Clara sent them off to gather eggs so she could have a word or two more with July in private.

"Did you understand what I said last night, about raising Martin?" she asked.

July hadn't. He wished she would just be quiet. He had no idea what to do next, and hadn't since he left Fort Smith many months ago. At moments, what he wanted was just to go home. Let Ellie go, if she didn't want to be his wife. Let Clara have the baby, if she wanted him so much. He had once felt competent being a sheriff—maybe if he went back and stuck to it he would someday feel competent again. He didn't know how much longer he could stand to feel such a failure.

"If your wife don't want Martin, do you have a mother or sisters that would want to raise him?" Clara asked. "The point is, I don't want to keep him a year or two and then give him up. If I have to give him up I'd rather do it soon."

"No, Ma's dead," July said. "I just had brothers."

"I've lost three boys," Clara said. "I don't want to lose another to a woman who keeps changing her mind."

"I'll ask her," July said. "I'll go back in a day or two. Maybe she'll be feeling better."

But he found he couldn't stand it to wait—he had to see her again, even if she wouldn't look at him. At least he could look at her and know he had found her after all. Maybe, if he was patient, she would change.

He saddled and rode to town. But when he got to the doctor's no one was there at all. The room Ellie had been in was empty, the big man no longer to be found.

By asking around, he found the doctor, who was delivering a baby in one of the whorehouses.

"She's left," the doctor said. "I came home yesterday and she was gone. She didn't leave a note."

"But she was sick," July said.

"Only unhappy," Patrick Arandel said. He felt sorry for the young man. Five idle young whores were listening to the conversation, while one of their friends lay in labor in the next room.

"She took it hard when they hung that killer," he added. "That and the childbirth nearly killed her. I thought she *would* die—she ran one of the highest fevers I've ever seen. It's a good sign that she left. It means she's decided to live a little longer."

The man at the livery stable shook his head when July asked which way they went.

"The wrong way," he said. "If they get past them Sioux they're lucky people."

July felt frantic. He had not even brought his rifle to town, or his bedroll or any-thing. They had a day's start, though they were traveling in a wagon and would have to move slow. Still, he would lose another half day going back to the ranch to get his gear. He was tempted to follow with just his pistol, and he even rode to the east end of town. But there were the vast, endless plains. They had almost swallowed him once.

He turned back, racing for the ranch. He wore the horse half down, and he remembered it was a borrowed horse, so he slowed up. By the time he got back to Clara's he was not racing at all. He seemed to have no strength, and his head hurt again. He was barely able to unsaddle; instead of going right to the house, he sat down behind the saddle shed and wept. Why would Ellie keep leaving? What was he supposed to do? Didn't she know about the Indians? It seemed he would have to chase her forever, and yet catching her did no good.

When he stood up, he saw Clara. She had been on her way back from the garden with a basket of vegetables. It was hot, and she had rolled the sleeves up on her dress. Her arms were thin and yet strong, as if they were all bone.

"Did she leave?" Clara asked.

July nodded. He didn't want to talk.

"Come help me shuck this corn," Clara said. "The roasting ears are about gone. I get so hungry for them during the winter, I could eat a dozen."

She went on toward the house, carrying her heavy garden basket. When she didn't hear his footsteps, she looked back at him. July wiped his face and followed her to the house.

82

THE NEXT MORNING, when he managed to get up, July came into the kitchen to find Cholo sharpening a thin-bladed knife. The baby lay on the table, kicking his bare feet, and Clara, wearing a man's hat, was giving the two girls instructions.

"Don't feed him just because he hollers," she said. "Feed him when it's time."

She looked at July, who felt embarrassed. He was not sick, and yet he felt as weak as if he had had a long fever. A plate with some cold eggs on it and a bit of bacon sat on the table—his breakfast, no doubt. Being the last one up made him feel a burden.

Cholo stood up. It was clear he and Clara were contemplating some work. July knew he ought to offer to help, but his legs would barely carry him to the table. He couldn't understand it. He had long since been over his jaundice, and yet he had no strength.

"We've got to geld some horses," Clara said. "We've put it off too long, hoping Bob would get back on his feet."

"I hate it when you do that," Sally said.

"You'd hate it worse if we had a bunch of studs running around here," Clara said. "One of them might crack your head just like that mustang cracked your father's."

She paused by the table a minute and tickled one of the baby's feet.

"I'd like to help," July said.

"You don't look that vigorous," she said.

"I'm not sick," July said. "I must have slept too hard."

"I expect you did something too hard," she said. "Stay and make conversation with these girls. That's harder work than gelding horses."

July liked the girls, though he had not said much to them. They seemed fine girls to him, always chattering. Mostly they fought over who got to tend the baby.

Clara and Cholo left and July slowly ate his breakfast, feeling guilty. Then he remembered what had happened—Ellie was gone, into Indian country. He had to go after her as soon as he ate. The baby, still on the table, gurgled at him. July had scarcely looked at it, though it seemed a good baby. Clara wanted it, the girls fought over it, and yet Ellie had left it. Thinking about it made him more confused.

After breakfast he got his rifle, but instead of leaving, he walked down to the lots. Every now and then he heard the squeal of a young horse. Walking, he didn't feel quite so weak, and it occurred to him that he ought to try and be some help—he could start after Ellie later.

It was hot, and the young horses were kicking up dust in the lots. To his surprise, he saw that Clara was doing the cutting, while the old man held the ropes. It was hard work—the horses were strong, and they badly needed another man. July quickly climbed into the lots and helped the old man anchor the hind legs of a quivering young bay.

Clara paused a moment, wiping the sweat off her forehead with her shirttail. Her hands were bloody.

"Shouldn't one of us do it?" July asked.

"No," Cholo said. "She is better."

"Bob taught me," Clara said. "We didn't have any help when we first came here. I wasn't strong enough to hold the horses so I got stuck with the messier job."

They gelded fifteen young horses and left them in the pen where they could be watched. July had stopped feeling weak, but even so it was a wonder to him how hard Clara and the old man worked. They didn't stop to rest until the job was done, by which time they were all soaked with sweat. Clara splashed water out of the horse trough to wash her hands and forearms, and immediately started for the house.

"I hope those worthless girls have been cooking," she said. "I've built an appetite."

"Do you know anything about the Indian situation?" July asked.

"I know Red Cloud," Clara said. "Bob was good to him. They lived on our horses that hard winter we had four years ago—they couldn't find buffalo."

"I've heard they're dangerous," July said.

"Yes," Clara said. "Red Cloud's fed up. Bob treated them fair and we've never had to fear them. I was more scared as a girl. The Comanches would come right into Austin and take children. I always dreamed they'd get me and I'd have red babies."

July had never felt so irresolute. He ought to go, and yet he didn't. Though he had worked hard, he had little appetite, and after the meal spent more time cleaning his gun than was really necessary.

When he finished, he sat the rifle against the porch railing, telling himself that he would get up and leave. But before he could get up, Clara walked out on the porch with no warning at all and put the baby into his hands. She practically dropped the child into his lap, an act July felt was very reckless. He had to catch him.

"That's a good sign," Clara said. "At least you'd catch him if somebody threw him off a roof."

The baby stared at July with wide eyes, as surprised, evidently, as he was. July looked at Clara, who seemed angry.

"I think it's time you took a look at him," she said. "He's your boy. He might come to like you, in which case he'll bring you more happiness than that woman ever will. He needs you a sight more than she does, too."

July felt scared he would do something wrong with the baby. He also was a little scared of Clara.

"I don't know anything about babies," he said.

"No, and you've never lived any place but Arkansas," Clara said. "But you ain't stupid and you ain't nailed down. You can live other places and you can learn about children—people dumber than you learn about them."

Again, July felt belabored by the tireless thing in Clara. Ellie might not look at him, but she didn't pursue him relentlessly with words, as Clara did.

"Stay here," she said. "Do you hear me? Stay here! Martin needs a pa and I could use a good hand. If you go trailing after that woman, either the Indians will kill you or that buffalo hunter will, or you'll just get lost and starve. It's a miracle you made it this far. You don't know the plains and I don't believe you know your wife, either. How long did you know her before you married?"

July tried to remember. The trial in Missouri had lasted three days, but he had met Ellie nearly a week before that.

"Two weeks, I guess," he said.

"That's short acquaintance," Clara said. "The smartest man alive can't learn much about a woman in two weeks."

"Well, she wanted to marry," July said. It was all he could remember about it. Ellie had made it clear she wanted to marry.

"That could have been another way of saying she wanted a change of scene," Clara said. "People get a hankering to quit what they're doing. They think they want to try something else. I do it myself. Half the time I think I'd like to pack up these girls and go live with my aunt in Richmond, Virginia."

"What would you do there?" July asked.

"I might write books," Clara said. "I've a hankering to try it. But then it'll come a pretty morning and I see the horses grazing and think how I'd miss them. So I doubt I'll get off to Richmond."

Just then the baby began to cry, squirming in his hands. July looked at Clara, but she made no effort to take the baby. July didn't know what to do. He was afraid he might drop the child, who twisted in his hands like a rabbit and yelled so loud he turned red as a beet.

"Is he sick?" July asked.

"No, he's fine," Clara said. "Maybe he's telling you off for ignoring him all this time. I wouldn't blame him."

With that she turned and went back in the house, leaving him with the baby, who at once began to cry even harder. July hoped one of the girls would come out and help, but neither seemed to be around. It seemed very irresponsible of Clara to simply leave him with the child. He felt again that she was not a very helpful woman. But then Ellie hadn't been helpful, either.

He was afraid to stand up with the baby squirming so—he might drop him. So he sat, wondering why in the world people wanted children. How could anyone know what a baby wanted, or what to do for them?

But, as abruptly as he had started, the baby stopped crying. He whimpered a time or two, stuck his fist in his mouth, and then simply stared at July again as he had at first. July was so relieved that he scarcely moved.

"Talk to him a little," Clara said. She stood in the door behind him.

"What do you say?"

She made a snort of disgust. "Introduce yourself, if you can't think of nothing else," she said. "Or sing him a song. He's sociable. He likes a little talk."

July looked at the baby, but couldn't think of a song.

"Can't you even hum?" Clara asked, as if it were a crime that he had not immediately started singing.

July remembered a saloon song he had always liked: "Lorena." He tried humming a little of it. The baby, who had been wiggling, stopped at once and looked at him solemnly. July felt silly humming, but since it calmed the baby, he kept on. He was holding the baby almost at arm's length.

"Put him against your shoulder," Clara said. "You don't have to hold him like that—he ain't a newspaper."

July tried it. The baby soon wet his shirt with slobbers, but he wasn't crying. July continued to hum "Lorena."

Then, to his relief, Clara took the baby.

"That's progress," she said. "Rome wasn't built in a day."

Dusk came and July didn't leave. He sat on the porch, his rifle across his lap, trying to make up his mind to go. He knew he ought to. However difficult she was, Ellie was still his wife. She might be in danger, and it was his duty to try and save her. If he didn't go, he would be giving up forever. He might never even know if she had lived or died. He didn't want to be the kind of man who would just let his wife blow out of his life like a weed. And yet that was what he was doing. He felt too tired to do otherwise. Even if the Indians didn't get him, or them, even if he didn't get lost on the plains, he might just find her, in some other room, and have her turn her face away again. Then what? She could go on running, and he would go on chasing, until something really bad happened.

When Clara came out again to call him to supper, he felt worn out from thinking. He almost flinched when he heard Clara's step, for he had a feeling she was ill-disposed toward him and might have something sharp to say. Again he was wrong. She walked down the steps and paused to watch three cranes flying across the sunset, along the silver path of the Platte.

"Ain't they great birds?" she said quietly. "I wonder which I'd miss most, them or the horses, if I was to move away."

July didn't suppose she would move away. She seemed so much of the place that it didn't seem likely.

After watching the birds, she looked at him as if just noticing that he was still there.

"Are you willing to stay?" she asked.

July had rather she hadn't asked—rather it had been something that just happened. He didn't feel he had made a decision—and yet he hadn't left.

"I guess I oughtn't to chase her," he said finally. "I guess I ought to let her be."

"It doesn't do to sacrifice for people unless they want you to," Clara said. "It's just a waste."

"Ma, it's getting cold," Betsey said from the doorway.

"I was just enjoying the summer for a minute," Clara said.

"Well, you're always telling us how much you hate to serve cold food," Betsey said.

Clara looked at her daughter for a moment and then went up the steps.

"Come on, July," she said. "These girls mean to see that we keep up our standards."

He put the rifle back in the saddle scabbard and followed her into the house.

83

AS THE HERD wound across the brown prairies toward the Platte, whoring became the only thing the men could talk about. Of course, they always liked to talk about it, but there had been sections of the drive when they occasionally mentioned other things—the weather, cards, the personalities of horses, trials and tribulations of the past. After Jake's death they had talked a good deal about the vagaries of justice, and what might cause a pleasant man to go bad. Once in a while they might talk about their families, although that usually ended with everyone getting homesick. Though a popular subject, it was tricky to handle.

By the time they were within a week of Ogallala, all subjects other than whoring were judged to be superfluous. Newt and the Rainey boys were rather surprised. They were interested in whoring too, in a vague sort of way, but listening to the grown men talk at night, or during almost any stop, they concluded there must be more to whoring than they had imagined. Getting to visit a whore quickly came to seem the most exciting prospect life had to offer.

"What if the Captain don't even want to stop in Ogallala?" Lippy asked, one night. "He ain't much of a stopper."

"Nobody's asking *him* to stop," Needle said. "He can keep driving, if he's a mind. We're the ones need to stop."

"I don't guess he likes whores," Lippy said. "He didn't come in the saloon much, that I remember."

Jasper was impatient with Lippy's pessimism. Any suggestion that they might not get to visit Ogallala was extremely upsetting to him.

"Can't you shut up?" he said. "We don't care what the Captain does. We just want to be let off."

Po Campo was also likely to dampen the discussion, once he was free from his cooking chores.

"I think you should all go to the barber and forget these whores," he added. "They will just take your money, and what will you get for it?"

"Something nice," Needle said.

"A haircut will last you a month, but what you get from the whores will only last a moment," Po remarked. "Unless she gives you something you don't want."

From the heated responses that ensued, Newt gathered that whores sometimes were not simply givers of pleasure. Diseases apparently sometimes resulted, although no one was very specific about them.

Po Campo was unshakable. He kept plugging for the barbershop over the whorehouse.

"If you think I'd rather have a haircut than a whore you're crazy as a June bug," Jasper said.

Newt and the Raineys left the more abstruse questions to others and spent most of their time trying to reckon the economics of a visit to town. The summer days were long and slow, the herd placid, the heat intense. Just having Ogallala to think about made the time pass quicker.

Occasionally one of the Raineys would ride over by Newt to offer some new speculation. "Soupy says they take off their clothes," Ben Rainey said, one day.

Newt had once seen a Mexican girl who had pulled up her skirt to wade in the Rio Grande. She wore nothing under the skirt. When she noticed he was watching she merely giggled. Often, after that, he had slipped down to the river when nothing much was happening, hoping to see her cross again. But he never had; that one glimpse was all he had to go on when it came to naked women. He had run it through his mind so many times it was hardly useful.

"I guess that costs a bunch," he said.

"'Bout a month's wages," Jimmy Rainey speculated.

Late one afternoon Deets rode in to report that the Platte was only ten miles ahead. Everyone in camp let out a whoop.

"By God, I wonder which way town is," Soupy said. "I'm ready to go."

Call knew the men were boiling to get to town. Though he had brought happy news, Deets himself seemed subdued. He had not been himself since Jake's hanging.

"You feeling poorly?" Call asked.

"Don't like this north," Deets said.

"It's good grazing country," Call remarked.

"Don't like it," Deets said. "The light's too thin."

Deets had a faraway look in his eye. It puzzled Call. The man had been cheerful through far harder times. Now Call would often see him sitting on his horse, looking south, across the long miles they had come. At breakfast, sometimes, Call would catch him staring into the fire the way old animals stared before they died—as if looking across into the other place. The look in Deets's eyes unsettled Call so much that he mentioned it to Augustus. He rode over to the tent one evening. Gus was sitting on a saddle blanket, barefoot, trimming his corns with a sharp pocketknife. The woman was not in sight, but Call stopped a good distance from the tent so as not to disturb her.

"If you want to talk to me you'll have to come a little closer," Augustus said. "I ain't walking that far barefooted."

Call dismounted and walked over to him. "I don't know what's the matter with Deets," he said.

"Well, Deets is sensitive," Augustus said. "Probably you hurt his feelings in your blunt way."

"I didn't hurt his feelings," Call said. "I always try to be especially good to Deets. He's the best man we got."

"Best man we've ever had," Augustus said. "Maybe he's sick."

"No," Call said.

"I hope he ain't planning to leave us," Augustus said. "I doubt the rest of us could even find the water holes."

"He says he don't like the north," Call said. "That's all he'll say."

"I hear we strike the Platte tomorrow," Augustus said. "All the boys are ready to go off and catch social diseases."

"I know it," Call said. "I'd just as soon miss this town, but we do need supplies."

"Let them boys go off and hurrah a little," Augustus said. "It might be their last chance."

"Why would it be their last chance?"

"Old Deets might know something," Augustus said. "Since he's so sensitive. We might all get killed by Indians in the next week or two."

"I doubt that," Call said. "You ain't much more cheerful than he is."

"No," Augustus said. He knew they were not far from Clara's house, a fact which made Lorena extremely nervous.

"What will you do with me?" she had asked. "Leave me in the tent when you go see her?"

"No, ma'am," he said. "I'll take you along and introduce you properly. You ain't just baggage, you know. Clara probably don't see another woman once a month. She'll be happy for feminine conversation."

"She may know what I am, though," Lorena said.

"Yes, she'll know you're a human being," Augustus said. "You don't have to duck your head to nobody. Half the women in this country probably started out like you did, working in saloons."

"She didn't," Lorena said. "I bet she was always a lady. That's why you wanted to marry her."

Augustus chuckled. "A lady can slice your jugular as quick as a Comanche," he said. "Clara's got a sharp tongue. She's tomahawked me many a time in the past."

"I'll be afraid to meet her, then," Lorena said. "I'll be afraid of what she'll say."

"Oh, she'll be polite to you," Augustus assured her. "I'm the one that will have to watch my step."

But no matter what he said, he couldn't soothe the girl's agitation. She felt she would lose him, and that was that. She offered her body—it was all she knew to do. Something in the manner of the offer saddened him, though he accepted it. In their embraces she seemed to feel, for a moment, that he loved her; yet soon afterward she would grow sad again.

"You're worrying yourself into a sweat for nothing," he said. "Clara's husband will probably live to be ninety-six, and anyway she and I probably ain't got no use for one another now. I ain't got the energy for Clara. I doubt I ever did."

At night, when she finally slept, he would sit in the tent, pondering it all. He could see the campfire. Whatever boys weren't night herding would be standing around it, swapping jokes. Probably all of them envied him, for he had a woman and they didn't. He envied them back, for they were carefree and he wasn't. Once started, love couldn't easily be stopped. He had started it with Lorie, and it might never be stopped. He would be lucky to get again such easy pleasures as the men enjoyed, sitting around a campfire swapping jokes. Though he felt deeply fond of Lorena, he could also feel a yearning to be loose again and have nothing to do but win at cards.

The next morning he left Lorena for a bit and fell in with Deets.

"Deets, have you ever spent much time wanting what you know you can't have?" he asked, figuring to get the conversation off to a brisk start.

"'Spect I've had a good life," Deets said. "Captain paid me a fair wage. Ain't been sick but twice, and one time was when I got shot over by the river."

"That ain't an answer to the question I asked," Augustus said.

"Wantin' takes too much time," Deets said. "I'd rather be working."

"Yes, but what would you have, if you could have what you really want, right now?"

Deets trotted along for a bit before he answered. "Be back on the river," he said.

"Hell, the Rio Grande ain't the only river," Augustus commented, but before they could continue the discussion they saw a group of riders come over a ridge, far to the north. Augustus saw at once that they were soldiers.

"'I god, we've found the cavalry, at least," he said.

There were nearly forty soldiers. The ponies in the remuda began to nicker at the sight of so many strange horses. Call and Augustus loped out and met them a half mile away, for the herd was looking restive at the sight of the riders.

The leader of the troop was a small man with a gray mustache, who wore a Captain's bars. He seemed irritated at the sight of the herd. It was soon plain that he was drunk.

Beside him rode a large man in greasy buckskins, clearly a scout. He was bearded and had a wad of tobacco in his jaw.

"I'm Captain Weaver and this is Dixon, our scout," the Captain said. "Where the hell do you men think you're taking these cattle?"

"We thought we were headed for Montana," Augustus said lightly. "Where are we, Illinois?"

Call was irritated with Gus. He would make a joke.

"No, but you'll wish you were if Red Cloud finds you," Captain Weaver said. "You're in the middle of an Indian war, that's where you are."

"Why in hell would anybody think they wanted to take cattle to Montana?" Dixon, the scout, said. He had an insolent look.

"We thought it would be a good place to sit back and watch 'em shit," Augustus said. Insolence was apt to bring out the comic in him, as Call knew too well.

"We've heard there are wonderful pastures in Montana," Call said, hoping to correct the bad impression Gus was giving.

"There may be, but you cowpokes won't live to see them," Dixon said.

"Oh, well," Augustus said, "we wasn't always cowpokes. We put in some twenty years fighting Comanches in the state of Texas. Don't these Indians up here fall off their horses like other Indians when you put a bullet or two in them?"

"Some do and some just keep coming," Captain Weaver said. "I didn't come over here to talk all morning. Have you men seen any sign?"

"Our scout didn't mention any," Call said, waving to Deets.

"Oh, you've got a nigger for a scout," Dixon said. "No wonder you're lost."

"We ain't lost," Call said, annoyed suddenly, "and that black man could track you across the coals of hell."

"And bring you back on a pitchfork, if we asked him to," Augustus added.

"What makes you think you can say things like that to us?" Captain Weaver said, flushing with anger.

"Ain't it still a free country?" Augustus asked. "Who asked you to ride up and insult our scout?"

Deets came loping up and Call asked him if he had seen any Indian sign.

"None between here and the river," Deets said.

A pale-looking young lieutenant suddenly spoke up.

"I thought they went east," he said.

"*We* went east," Weaver said. "Where do you think we've been for the last week?"

"Maybe they went farther and faster," Augustus said. "Indians usually do. From the looks of those nags you're riding they could probably outrun you on foot."

"You're a damn impertinent man," Weaver said. "Those Indians killed a buffalo hunter and a woman, two days ago. Three weeks ago they wiped out a family southeast of here. If you see them you'll wish you'd kept your damn beeves in Texas."

"Let's go," Call said, abruptly turning his horse.

"We need horses," Captain Weaver said. "Ours are about ridden down."

"Ain't that what I said that you thought was so impertinent?" Augustus remarked.

"I see you've got extras," Weaver said. "We'll take 'em. There's a man who sells horses west of Ogallala. You can buy some more there and send the Army a bill."

"No, thanks," Call said. "We like the ones we've got."

"I wasn't asking," Weaver said. "I'm requisitioning your horses."

Augustus laughed. Call didn't. He saw that the man was serious.

"We need 'em," Dixon said. "We've got to protect this frontier."

Augustus laughed again. "Who have you protected lately?" he asked. "All you've told us about are people you didn't protect."

"I'm tired of talking," Weaver said. "Go get the horses, Jim. Take a couple of men and pick out good ones."

"You can't have any horses," Call said. "You have no authority to requisition stock from us."

"By God, I'll have those horses or I'll have your hides," Weaver said. "Go get 'em, Jim."

The young lieutenant looked very nervous, but he turned as if to ride over to the herd.

"Hold on, son, the argument ain't over," Augustus said.

"You'd defy an officer of the U.S. Army?" Weaver asked.

"You're as close to that horse trader in Ogallala as we are," Call pointed out.

"Yes, but we're going the other way," Weaver said.

"You were headed this way when you spotted us," Augustus said. "When'd you change your mind?"

Dixon, the big scout, was listening to the conversation with contempt in his expression. The contempt was as much for Weaver as for them.

Captain Weaver turned to the young man. "I gave you an order. These men are all bluff. They're just cowboys. Go get the horses."

As the young man passed, Augustus reached down and caught his bridle.

"If you want them horses, why don't you go get 'em?" he said. "You're the Captain."

"I call this treason," Weaver said. "You men can be hung for treason."

Call had been looking over the rest of the troop. Throughout his career in the Rangers he had been bothered by how sluggishly the cavalry performed, and the troop he saw watching the proceedings looked more sluggish than most. Half the men had gone to sleep in their saddles the moment the column stopped, and the horses all looked as if they needed a month off on good grass.

"How far is Ogallala?" Call asked.

"I'm not interested in Ogallala," Weaver said. "I'm interested in Red Cloud."

"We don't know this Red Cloud," Augustus said. "But if he's much of a war chief you better hope you don't catch him. I doubt an Indian would even consent to eat them ponies you're riding. I never saw a worse-mounted bunch of men."

"Well, we've been out ten days, and it's none of your concern," Weaver said, trembling with indignation. Although Augustus was doing most of the talking, it was Call whom he looked at with hatred.

"Let's go," Call said. "This is pointless talk." He saw that the little Captain was keyed up to the point where it wouldn't take much to provoke him into an explosion.

"Jim, get them horses," Weaver said.

"No," Call said. "You can't have our horses. And I'll give you some advice, too. Your troop's exhausted. If you was to find Indians you'd be the one's massacred, most likely. You don't just need fresh horses, you need fresh men."

"What I don't need is advice from a goddamn cowboy," Weaver said.

"We've fought Comanches and Kiowas and Mexican bandits for twenty years and we're still here," Call said. "You'd do well to listen."

"If I see you in town I'll box your goddamn ears," Dixon said, addressing himself to Call.

Call ignored the man. He turned and started to ride away. Augustus released the young lieutenant's bridle.

"Leave me that nigger," Weaver said. "I've heard they can smell Indians. They're just red niggers, anyway."

"No," Call said. "I'd be afraid you'd mistreat him."

They went to the wagon. When they turned to look, the cavalry troop was still sitting there.

"Reckon they'll charge?" Augustus asked.

"Charge a cow herd?" Call said. "I wouldn't think so. Weaver's mad, but not that mad."

They waited, but the cavalry merely sat on the ridge for a few minutes and then turned and rode away.

84

THAT AFTERNOON they crossed the Platte River just east of Ogallala and turned the herd northwest. From the slopes north of the river they saw the little collection of shacks and frame buildings that made up the town. The cowboys were so entranced by the sight that they could hardly keep their minds on their business long enough to drive the cattle to a good bed-ground.

Call tried to caution them a little, mentioning that there were said to be Indians on the rampage, but the men scarcely heard him. Even Dish Boggett was in a fever to go. Call let six men go in first: Dish, Soupy, Bert, Jasper, Needle and the

Irishman. They all put on fresh shirts and raced away as if a hundred Comanches were after them.

Augustus, setting up his tent, stopped a moment to watch them run. The cowboys whooped and waved their hats as they raced.

"Look at 'em go, Lorie," Augustus said. "Can't wait to get to town."

Lorena was uninterested. She had only one thing on her mind.

"When are you going to see her?" she asked.

"Oh, tomorrow will do," Augustus said. "We'll both go."

"I'll stay here," Lorena said. "I'd be too scared of what you'd say."

Her hands were shaking at the thought of the woman, but she helped Gus peg the tent.

"I've a mind to go to Ogallala myself," Augustus said. "Would you like to come?"

"Why do you want to?" she asked.

"Well, it's a town, of sorts," he said. "I've a mind to do something civilized, like eat dinner in a restaurant. If that's asking too much, I could at least go in a barroom and drink a glass of whiskey.

"Come with me," he added. "They've probably got a store or two. We could buy you some clothes."

Lorena considered it. She had been wearing men's clothes since Gus rescued her. There hadn't been any place to buy any others. She would need a dress if she went with Gus to see the woman. But she didn't know if she really wanted to go see her—although she had built up a good deal of curiosity about her. Lots of curiosity, but more fear. It was a strange life, just staying in the tent and talking to no one but Gus, but she was used to it. The thought of town frightened her almost as much as the thought of the woman.

"Do you want a whore or what?" she asked, when she saw him getting ready to go to town.

"Why would I want a whore, when I've got you?" he asked. "You womenfolk have got strange minds. What I'd mainly like to do is sit in a chair and drink whiskey. I wouldn't mind a hand or two of cards either."

"You want that other woman, and you've got me," Lorena said. "You could want us both and a whore too, I guess. Go get one if you want—I don't care."

She almost hoped he would. It would strengthen her case against the other woman.

"Come with me," Augustus said. "I'll buy you some new dresses."

"Just buy me one yourself," Lorena said. "Buy one you like."

"But I don't know your size," he said. "Why are you so shy of towns? There ain't a soul in that town who's ever met you."

She wouldn't go, so he gave up asking her and went himself, stopping at the wagon a minute to make sure Po Campo would take her her food. Call was there, looking restless. Since most of the experienced hands were gone, he had decided to stay with the herd and buy supplies tomorrow once some of them got back.

The herd was grazing peacefully on the rolling slopes. The hands who were left, boys mostly, looked melancholy at the thought of the opportunities they were missing.

"Come ride to town with me," Augustus said to Call. "This place is quiet as a church on Monday. I'll buy you a meal and we can sit and talk philosophy."

"No, I'll stay," Call said. "I don't know a philosophy."

"Your philosophy is to worry too much," Augustus said. "Jake would have gone with me quick enough if we hadn't hung him."

"Damn it, he brought it on himself," Call said.

"I know that, but when I spot a town I remember what a fine companion he was around supper time," Augustus said.

He loped the five or six miles to Ogallala, feeling rather strange, for it had just hit him how much he did miss Jake Spoon. Many a time, returning from a scout on the Brazos, they had raced into Austin together and divided the night between whiskey, cards and women. Clara and Call would both be stiff with them for a week after such a carouse; Clara, if anything, softened slower than Call.

Now Jake was gone and Clara near. It seemed to him he might be wise not to go see her—just trail on into Montana and let the past be past. No woman had affected his heart in the way she had. The memory was so sweet he was almost afraid to threaten it by seeing what Clara had become. She might have become a tyrant—she had that potential, even as a girl. Or she might have become merely a worked-out, worn-down pioneer woman, her beauty gone and her spirit tamed. He might look at her and not feel a thing—in which case he would lose something he treasured. On the other hand, he might look at her and feel all that he had felt in their younger days—in which case riding off and leaving her wouldn't be very easy.

Then there was Lorena. In the last weeks she had proved sweeter than any woman he had known—more responsive than his wives, kinder than Clara. Her beauty had flowered again—the cowboys were always thinking of excuses to ride within twenty or thirty yards of them, so they could get a glimpse of it. He ought to consider himself lucky, he knew—everyone in the outfit, with the possible exception of Call, considered him lucky. He ought to let the past keep its glow and not try to mix it with what he had in the present.

But then he knew he could not simply ride by Clara, whatever the threat of turmoil or disappointment. Of all the women he knew, she had meant the most; and was the one person in his life he felt he had missed, in some ways.

He remembered what she had said when she told him she was going to marry Bob—that she would want his friendship for her daughters. He would at least go and offer it; besides, it would be interesting to see if the girls were like their mother.

To his surprise, he didn't enjoy the visit to Ogallala very much. He hit the dry-goods store just as the owner was closing and persuaded him to reopen long enough for him to buy Lorie a mass of clothes. He bought everything from petticoats to dresses, a hat, and also a warm coat, for they were sure to strike cool weather in Montana. He even bought himself a black frock coat worthy of a preacher, and a silk string tie. The merchant soon was in no mood to close; he offered Augustus muffs and gloves and felt-lined boots and other oddities. In the end he had such a purchase that he couldn't even consider carrying it—they would have to come in tomorrow and pick it up in the wagon, though he did wrap up a few things in case Lorie wanted to wear them to Clara's. He bought her combs and brushes and a mirror—women liked to see themselves, he knew, and Lorena hadn't had the opportunity since Fort Worth.

The one hotel was easy to find, but the restaurant in it was a smoky little room with no charm and only one diner, a somber man with mutton-chop whiskers. Augustus decided he would prefer a cheerful bar, but that proved not easy to find.

He went into one that had a huge rack of elk horns over the door and a clientele consisting mostly of mule skinners who hauled freight for the Army. None of the Hat Creek outfit was there, though he had seen a couple of their horses tied outside. They had probably gone straight to the whorehouse next door, he concluded.

He ordered a bottle and a glass, but the boisterous mule skinners made so much racket he couldn't enjoy his drinking. A middle-aged gambler with a thin mustache and a greasy cravat soon spotted him and came over.

"You look like a man who could tolerate a game of cards," the gambler said. "My name is Shaw."

"Two-handed gambling don't interest me," Augustus said. "Anyway, it's too rackety in here. It's hard work just getting drunk when things are this loud."

"This ain't the only whiskey joint in town," Mr. Shaw said. "Maybe we could find one that's quiet enough for you."

Just then a girl walked in, painted and powdered. Several of the mule skinners whooped at her, but she came over to where Augustus sat. She was skinny and could hardly have been more than seventeen.

"Now, Nellie, leave us be," the gambler said. "We were about to go have a game."

Before the girl could answer, one of the mule skinners at the next table toppled backwards in his chair. He had gone to sleep with the chair tilted back, and he fell to the floor, to the amusement of his peers. The fall did not wake him—he sprawled on the saloon floor, dead drunk.

"Oh, go along, Shaw," the girl said. "There ain't but two of you. What kind of game would that be?"

"I made that point myself," Augustus said.

A bartender came over, got the drunk man by the collar and drug him out the door.

"Wanta go next door, Mister?" Nellie asked.

The gambler, to Augustus's surprise, suddenly cuffed the girl—it was not a hard blow, but it surprised and embarrassed her.

"Now, here," Augustus said. "There's no excuse for that. The young lady was talking perfectly polite."

"She ain't a lady, she's a tart, and I won't have her interfering with our pleasure," the gambler said.

Augustus stood up and pulled out a chair for Nellie.

"Sit down, miss," he said. Then he turned to the gambler. "You scoot," he said. "I don't gamble with men who mistreat women."

The gambler had a ferretlike expression. He ignored Augustus and glared at the girl. "What have I told you?" he said. "You'll get a beating you won't forget if you interfere with me again."

The girl trembled and seemed on the verge of tears.

"I won't have a slut interrupting my play," the gambler said.

Augustus hit the man in the chest so hard that he was knocked back onto the next table, amid three or four mule skinners. The mule skinners looked up in surprise—the gambler had the wind knocked out of him so thoroughly that he waved his arms in the air, his mouth open, afraid he would die before he could draw another breath.

Augustus paid him no more attention. The girl, after a moment, sat down, though she kept glancing nervously toward the gambler. A big mule skinner shoved him unceremoniously off the table, and he was now on his hands and knees, still trying to get his breath.

"He ain't hurt," Augustus assured the girl. "Would you like a sip of whiskey?"

"Yeah," the girl said, and when the bartender brought a glass, quaffed the whiskey Augustus poured her. She couldn't keep her eyes off the gambler, though. He had managed to breathe again, and was standing by the bar, holding his chest.

"Have you had trouble with that fellow before?" Augustus asked.

"He's Rosie's husband," Nellie said. "Rosie is the woman I work for. They don't get along. Rosie sends me out, and he runs me off."

She tried to recover from her fright and to look alluring, but the attempt was so pathetic that it saddened Augustus. She looked like a frightened young girl.

"Rosie ain't nice to work for," she said. "Do you want to go next door? I got to do something quick. If Shaw complains she'll whup me. Rosie's meaner than Shaw."

"I'd say you need to change bosses," Augustus said. As soon as he put more whiskey in her glass, the girl quaffed it.

"There ain't but one other madam, and she's just as bad," Nellie said. "You sure you won't come next door? I got to find a customer."

"I guess you better bribe that gambler, if that's the situation," Augustus said. "Give him five and Rosie five and keep the rest for yourself." He handed her twenty dollars.

The girl looked surprised, but took the money and quaffed another whiskey. Then she went up to the bar and had the bartender change the money for her. Soon she was talking to Shaw as if nothing had happened. Depressed, Gus bought a bottle to take with him and left town.

The moon was full and the prairie shadowy. Pea Eye was attempting to sing to the cattle, but his voice was nothing to compare to the Irishman's.

To his surprise, Augustus saw that Lorena was sitting outside the tent. Usually she stayed inside. When he dismounted, he bent to touch her and found that her cheek was wet—she had been sitting there crying.

"Why, Lorie, what's the matter?" he asked.

"I'm afraid of her," she said simply. Her voice sounded thick with discouragement. "I'm afraid she'll take you."

Augustus didn't try to reason with her. What she felt was past reason. He had caused it by talking too freely about the woman he had once loved. He unsaddled and sat down beside her on the grass.

"I thought you went to her," she said. "I didn't believe you went to town."

"Ain't the moon beautiful?" he said. "These plains seem like fine country under a full moon."

Lorena didn't look up. She wasn't interested in the moon. She only wanted it to be settled about the woman. If Gus was going to leave, she wanted to know it, although she couldn't imagine a life if that happened.

"Did you ever like to sing?" he asked, trying to get her to talk about something else.

She didn't answer.

"I think it must be a fine gift, singing," he said. "If I could sing like the Irishman, I would just ride around singing all day. I might get a job in a barroom, like Lippy used to have."

Lorena didn't want to talk to him. She hated the way she felt. Better if something happens and kills us both, she thought. At least I wouldn't have to be alone.

85

NEWT, THE RAINEY BOYS and Pea Eye got to go into town the next after-noon. The fact that the first group drug back in ones and twos, looking horrible, in no way discouraged them. Jasper Fant had vomited all over his horse on the ride out, too beaten to dismount or even to lean over.

"You are a sorry sight," Po Campo said sternly, when Jasper rode in. "I told you it would be that way. Now all your money is gone and all you feel is pain."

Jasper didn't comment.

Needle Nelson and Soupy Jones rode in next—they looked no different from Jasper, but at least their horses were clean.

"It's a good thing there's no more towns," Needle said when he dismounted. "I don't think I'd survive another town."

"If that's the best Nebraska can do, I pass," Soupy said.

After hearing all the reports, which merely confirmed his suspicions, Po Campo was reluctant to let Augustus borrow the wagon.

"Towns are full of thieves," he argued. "Somebody might steal it."

"If they do, they'll have to steal it with me sitting in it," Augustus said. "I'd like to see the thief who could manage that."

He had promised Lippy a ride to town. Lippy had grown homesick for his old profession and hoped at least to hear some piano music on his visit.

Call decided to ride in and help with the provisioning. He was trying to make an inventory of things they needed, and the fact that Po Campo was in a cranky, uncooperative mood didn't make things any easier.

"It's summertime," Po said. "We don't need much. Buy a water barrel and we'll fill it in the river. It is going to get very dry."

"What makes you think it's going to get dry?" Augustus asked.

"It will get dry," Po Campo insisted. "We will be drinking horses' blood if we're not lucky."

"I think I must have drunk some last night," Jasper said. "I never got sick enough to puke on my horse before."

Newt and the other boys raced to town, leaving Pea Eye far behind, but once they got there they felt somewhat at a loss as to what to do first. For an hour or two they merely walked up and down the one long street, looking at the people. None of them had actually been in a building in such a while that they felt shy about going in one. They stared in the window of a big hardware store, but didn't go in. The street itself seemed lively enough—there were plenty of soldiers in sight, and men driving wagons, and even a few Indians. Of whores they saw none: the few women on the street were just matrons, doing their shopping.

The town abounded in saloons, of course, but at first the boys were too spooked to go in one. Probably they would be looked at, because of their age, and anyway they didn't have funds for drinking. What little they had must be saved for whores—at least that was their intention. But the fourth or fifth time they passed the big general store their intentions wavered, and they all slipped in for a look at the merchandise. They stared at the guns: buffalo rifles and pistols with long blue barrels, and far beyond their means. All they came out with was a sack of horehound candy. Since it was the first candy any of them had had in months, it tasted wonderful. They sat down in the shade and promptly ate the whole sack.

"I wish the Captain would fill the wagon with it," Ben Rainey said. The opportunity existed, for Augustus was just driving up to the dry-goods store in the wagon, and the Captain rode beside him on the Hell Bitch.

"Why, he won't let us fill it with candy," Jimmy Rainey said. Nonetheless, feeling bolder and more experienced, they went back in the store and bought two more sacks.

"Let's save one for Montana," Newt said. "There might not be no more towns." But his cautions fell on deaf ears. Pete Spettle and the others consumed their share of the candy with dispatch.

While they were finishing it they saw Dish Boggett come walking around the side of a saloon across the street.

"Let's ask him where the whores are," Ben suggested. "I doubt we can find any by ourselves."

They caught up with Dish by the livery stable. He didn't look to be in high spirits, but at least he was walking straight, which was more than could be said for the men who had returned to camp.

"What are you sprouts doing in town?" he asked.

"We want a whore," Ben said.

"Go around to the back of that saloon, then," Dish said. "You'll find plenty."

Dish now rode a fine little mare he called Sugar. In disposition, she was the opposite of the Hell Bitch. She was almost like a pet. Dish would take tidbits from his plate and feed them to her by hand. He claimed she had the best night vision of any horse he had ever seen—in all their stampedes she had never stepped in a hole.

He delighted in her so much that he always gave her a brushing before he saddled her, keeping a little horse brush in his saddlebag just for that purpose.

"How much do they cost?" Jimmy Rainey asked, referring to the whores. The thought that some were only a few steps away made them all a little nervous.

"It depends on how long you intend to stay upstairs," Dish said. "I met a nice one named Mary, but they ain't all like her. There's one they call the Buffalo Heifer— somebody would have to offer me a month's wages before I'd get near her, but I expect she'd do for you sprouts. You can't expect top quality your first time off."

As they were talking, a party of some half-dozen soldiers came riding up the street, led by the big scout, Dixon.

"There come them soldiers again," Newt said.

Dish hardly glanced at the soldiers. "I guess the rest of them got lost." He had brushed Sugar and was just preparing to saddle her when the scout and the soldiers suddenly trotted over their way.

Newt felt nervous—he knew there had almost been serious trouble with the soldiers. He glanced at the Captain and Mr. Gus, who were loading a water barrel into the wagon. Evidently they had decided to take Po Campo's advice.

Dixon, who looked ungodly big to Newt, rode his black gelding practically on top of Dish Boggett before he stopped. Dish, cool as ice, put the saddle blanket on the mare and paid him no mind.

"How much for the filly?" Dixon asked. "She's got a stylish look."

"Not for sale," Dish said, reaching down for his saddle.

As he stooped, Dixon leaned over him and spat a stream of tobacco juice on the back of Dish's neck. The brown juice hit Dish at the hairline and dripped down under the collar of his loose shirt.

Dish straightened up and put his hand to his neck. When he saw the tobacco juice his face flushed.

"You dern cowboys are too fond of your horses," Dixon said. "I'm fair tired of being told your ponies ain't for sale."

"This one ain't, for damn sure, and anyway you won't be in no shape to ride when I get through with you," Dish said, barely controlling his voice. "I'd hate to think I'd let a man spit on me and then ride off."

Dixon spat again. This time, since Dish was facing him, the juice hit him square in the breast. Dixon and the soldiers all laughed.

"Are you going to dismount or will you require me to come and drag you off that pile of soap bones you're riding?" Dish asked, meeting the big man's eye.

"Well, ain't you a tomcat," Dixon said, grinning. He spat at Dish again, but Dish ducked the stream of tobacco juice and leaped for the man. He meant to knock the scout off the other side of the horse, but Dixon was too strong and too quick. Though no one had seen it, he held a long-barreled pistol in his off hand, and when Dish grappled with him he used it like a club, hitting Dish twice in the head with the butt.

To Newt's horror, Dish crumpled without a sound—he slid down the side of Dixon's horse and flopped on his back on the ground. Blood poured from a gash over his ear, staining his dark hair. His hat fell off and Newt picked it up, not knowing what else to do.

Dixon stuffed his pistol back in its holster. He spat once more at Dish and reached to take the filly's reins. He reached down, undid the girth, and dumped Dish's saddle on the ground.

"That'll teach you to sass me, cowboy," he said. Then he glanced at the boys. "He can send the bill for this mare to the U.S. Army," Dixon said. "That is if he ever remembers there was a mare, when he wakes up."

Newt was all but paralyzed with worry. He had seen the pistol butt strike Dish twice, and for all he knew Dish was dead. It had happened so quickly that Ben Rainey still had his hands in the sack of candy.

All Newt knew was that the man mustn't be allowed to take Dish's horse. When Dixon turned to trot away, he grabbed the bridle bit and hung on. Sugar, pulled two different ways, tried to rear, almost lifting Newt off the ground. But he hung on.

Dixon tried to jerk the horse loose, but Newt had both hands on the bit now and wouldn't let go.

"Damn, these cowboys are pests," Dixon said. "Even the pups."

The soldier next to him had a rawhide quirt hanging from his saddle horn. Dixon reached over and got it, and without another word rode close to the mare and began to lash Newt with it.

Pete Spettle, anger in his face, leaped in and tried to get the quirt, but Dixon backhanded him and Pete went down—it turned out his nose was broken.

Newt tried to hunker close to the mare. At first Dixon was mainly quirting his hands, to make him turn loose, but when that was unsuccessful he began to hit Newt wherever he could catch him. One whistling blow cut his ear. He tried to duck his head, but Sugar was scared and kept turning, exposing him to the quirt.

Dixon began to whip him on the neck and shoulders. Newt shut his eyes and clung to the bit. Once he glanced at Dixon and saw the man smiling—he had cruel eyes, like a boar pig's. Then he ducked, for Dixon attempted to cut him across the face. The blow hit Sugar instead, causing the horse to rear and squeal.

It was the squeal that caught Call's attention. After loading the heavy oak water barrel, he and Augustus had stepped back into the store a minute. Augustus was contemplating buying a lighter pistol to replace the big Colt he carried, but he decided against it. He carried out some of the things he had bought for Lorena, and Call took a sack of flour. They heard the horse squeal while they were still in the store, and came out to see Dixon quirting Newt, as Dish Boggett's mare turned round and round. Two cowboys lay on the ground, one of them Dish.

"I thought that son of a bitch was a bad one," Augustus said. He pitched the goods in the wagon and drew his pistol.

Call dropped the sack of flour onto the tailgate and quickly swung onto the Hell Bitch.

"Don't shoot him," he said. "Just watch the soldiers."

He saw Dixon again savagely quirt the boy across the back of the neck, and anger flooded him, of a kind he had not felt in many years. He put spurs to the Hell Bitch and she raced down the street and burst through the surprised soldiers. Dixon, intent on his quirting, was the last to see Call, who made no attempt to check the Hell Bitch. Dixon tried to jerk his mount out of the way at the last minute, but his nervous mount merely turned into the charge and the two horses collided. Call kept his seat and the Hell Bitch kept her feet, but Dixon's horse went down, throwing him hard in the process. Sugar nearly trampled Newt, trying to get out of the melee. Dixon's horse struggled to its feet practically underneath Sugar. There was dust everywhere.

Dixon sprang up, not hurt by the fall, but disoriented. When he turned, Call had dismounted and was running at him. He didn't look large, and Dixon was puzzled that the man would charge him that way. He reached for his pistol, not realizing he still had the quirt looped around his wrist. The quirt interfered with his draw and Call ran right into him, just as his horse had run into Dixon's horse. Dixon was knocked down again, and when he turned his head to look up he saw a boot coming at his eye.

"You wouldn't," he said, meaning to tell the man not to kick, but the boot hit his face before he could get his words out.

The six soldiers, watching, were too astonished to move. The small-seeming cowman kicked Dixon so hard in the face that it seemed his head would fly off. Then the man stood over Dixon, who spat out blood and teeth. When Dixon struggled to his feet, the smaller man immediately knocked him down again and then ground his face into the dirt with a boot.

"He's gonna kill him," one soldier said, his face going white. "He's gonna kill Dixon."

Newt thought so too. He had never seen such a look of fury as was on the Captain's face when he attacked the big scout. It was clear that Dixon, though larger, had no chance. Dixon never landed a blow, or even tried one. Newt felt he might get sick just seeing the way the Captain punished the man.

Dish Boggett sat up, holding his head, and saw Captain Call dragging the big scout by his buckskin shirt. The fight had carried a few yards down the street to a blacksmith shop with a big anvil sitting in front of it. To Dish's astonishment, the Captain straddled Dixon and started banging his head against the anvil.

"He'll kill him," he said out loud, forgetting that a few moments before he too had wanted to kill the scout.

Then he saw Augustus run over, mount the Hell Bitch, and take down Call's rope.

Augustus trotted the few steps to the blacksmith shop and dropped a loop over Call's shoulders. Then he turned the horse away, took a wrap around the saddle horn, and began to ride up the street. Call wouldn't turn loose of Dixon at first. He hung on and dragged him a few feet from the anvil. But Augustus kept the rope tight and held the horse in a walk. Finally Call let the man drop, though he turned with a black, wild look and started for whoever had roped him, not realizing who the man was. The skin was torn completely off his knuckles from the blows he had dealt Dixon, but he was lost in his anger and his only thought was to get the next assailant. It was in him to kill—he didn't know if Dixon was dead, but he would make sure of the next man.

"Woodrow," Augustus said sharply, as Call was about to leap for him.

Call heard his name and saw his mare. Augustus walked toward him, loosening the rope. Call recognized him and stopped. He turned to look at the six soldiers, all on their horses nearby, silent and white-faced. He took a step toward them, and threw the rope off his shoulders.

"Woodrow!" Augustus said again. He took out his big Colt, thinking he might have to hit Call to stop him from going for the soldiers. But Call stopped. For a moment, nothing moved.

Augustus dismounted and looped the rope over the saddle horn. Call was still standing in the street, getting his breath. Augustus walked over to the soldiers.

"Get your man and go," he said quietly.

Dixon lay by the anvil. He had not moved.

"Reckon he's dead?" a sergeant asked.

"If he ain't, he's lucky," Augustus said.

Call walked down the street and picked up his hat, which had fallen off. The soldiers rode slowly past him. Two dismounted and began to try to load Dixon on his horse. Finally all six dismounted—the man was so heavy it took all of them to get him up and draped over his horse. Call watched. At the sight of Dixon, his anger threatened to rise again. If the man moved, Call was ready to go for him again.

But Dixon didn't move. He hung over his horse, blood dripping off his head and face into the dust. The soldiers mounted and slowly led the horse away.

Call looked and saw Dish Boggett sitting on the ground by his saddle. He walked slowly over to him—Dish had a gash behind his ear.

"Are you much hurt?" he asked.

"No, Captain," Dish said. "Guess I'm too hardheaded."

Call looked at Newt. There were welts beginning to form on his neck and one of his cheeks. A little blood showed in a cut on his ear. Newt was still tightly gripping Sugar's bit, a fact which Dish noticed for the first time. He stood up.

"You hurt?" Call asked the boy.

"No, sir," Newt said. "He just quirted me a little. I wasn't gonna let him have Dish's horse."

"Well, you can let her go now," Dish said. "He's gone. I'm much obliged to you for what you did, Newt."

Newt had gripped the bit so tightly that it was painful to let go. It had cut deep creases in his palms, and he seemed to have squeezed the blood out of his fingers. But he turned the mare loose. Dish took the reins and patted her on the neck.

Augustus walked over and stooped down by Pete Spettle, who was blowing frothy blood out of his broken nose.

"I better take you to the doctor," Augustus said.

"Don't want no doc," Pete said.

"'I god, this is a hardheaded lot," Augustus said, walking over to Ben Rainey. He took the candy sack and helped himself to a piece. "Hardly a one of you will take good advice."

Call mounted the Hell Bitch, slowly re-coiling his rope. Several townspeople had witnessed the fight. Most were still standing there, watching the man on the gray mare.

When he had his rope fixed again, Call rode over to Augustus. "Will you bring the grub?" he asked.

"Yep," Augustus said. "I'll bring it."

Call saw that everyone was looking at him, the hands and cowboys and towns-people alike. The anger had drained out of him, leaving him feeling tired. He didn't remember the fight, particularly, but people were looking at him as if they were stunned. He felt he should make some explanation, though it seemed to him a simple situation.

"I hate a man that talks rude," he said. "I won't tolerate it."

With that he turned and rode out of town. The people watching kept quiet. Rough as the place was, accustomed as they all were to sudden death, they felt they had seen something extraordinary, something they would rather not have seen.

"My lord, Gus," Dish said, as he watched the Captain leave. Like the others, he was awed by the fury he had seen erupt in the Captain. He had seen men fight many times, but not like that. Though he himself hated Dixon, it was still disturb-ing to see him destroyed—not even with a gun, either.

"Have you ever seen him like that before?" he asked Augustus.

"Once," Augustus said. "He killed a Mexican bandit that way once before I could stop it. The Mexican had cut up three white people, but that wasn't what prompted it. The man scorned Call."

He took another piece of candy. "It don't do to scorn W. F. Call," he said.

"Was it me?" Newt asked, feeling that maybe he should have managed things better. "Was it just that he was quirting me?"

"That was part of it," Augustus said. "Call don't know himself what the rest of it was."

"Why, he'd have killed that man, if you hadn't roped him," Dish said. "He would have killed anybody. Anybody!"

Augustus, eating his candy, did not dispute it.

86

IT WAS BECAUSE of the fight that the boys ended up amid the whores. Dish saddled and left, and Augustus finished loading the wagon and started out of town. When he turned the wagon around, Newt and the Raineys were talking to Pea Eye, who had been up the street getting barbered and had missed the fight. Pea Eye had so much toilet water on that Augustus could smell him from ten feet away. He and the boys were standing around the bloody anvil and the boys were explaining the matter to him. Pea didn't seem particularly surprised.

"Well, he's a fighter, the Captain," he said mildly. "He'll box 'em if they get him riled."

"Box?" Ben Rainey said. "He didn't box. He run over the man with a horse and then near kicked his head off when he had him laying on the ground."

"Oh, that's boxing, to the Captain," Pea Eye said.

Augustus stopped the wagon. "You boys aim to linger around here?" he asked.

The boys looked at one another. The fight had startled them so that they had more or less forgotten their plans—not that they had many.

"Well, it's our only chance to see the town," Newt said, thinking Augustus was going to tell them to go back to the wagon.

That was not Augustus's intention. He had four ten-dollar gold pieces in his pocket, which he had intended to slip the boys on the sly. With Call gone, that was unnecessary. He flipped one to Newt, then handed them to each of the other boys.

"This is a bonus," Augustus said. "It's hard to enjoy a metropolis like this if you've got nothing but your hands in your pockets."

"Hell, if you're giving away money, give me some, Gus," Pea Eye said.

"No, you'd just spend it on barbers," Augustus said. "These boys will put it to better use. They deserve a frolic before we set out to the far north."

He popped the team with the reins and rode out of town, thinking how young the boys were. Age had never mattered to him much. He felt that, if anything, he himself had gained in ability as the years went by. Yet he became a little wistful, thinking of the boys. However he might best them, he could never stand again where they stood, ready to go into a whorehouse for the first time. The world of women was about to open to them. Of course, if a whorehouse in Ogallala was the door they had to go through, some would be scared back to the safety of the wagon and the cowboys. But some wouldn't.

The boys stood around the blacksmith's shop, talking about the money Augustus had given them. In a flash, all the calculating they had done for the last few weeks was rendered unnecessary. They had means right in their hands. It was a dizzying feeling, and a little frightening.

"Ten dollars is enough for a whore, ain't it?" Ben Rainey asked Pea Eye.

"Ain't priced none lately," Pea Eye said. It irked him that he had gone to the barbershop at the wrong time and missed the fight.

"Why not, Pea?" Newt asked. He was curious. All the other hands had rushed in, to the whores. Even Dish had done it, and Dish was said to be in love with Lorena. Yet Pea was unaffected by the clamor—even around the campfire he kept quiet when the talk was of women. Pea was one of Newt's oldest friends, and it was important to know what Pea felt on the subject.

But Pea was not forthcoming. "Oh, I mostly just stay with the wagon," he said, which was no answer at all. Indeed, while they were standing around getting used to having money to spend, Pea got his horse and rode off. Except for Lippy and the Irishman, they were the only members of the Hat Creek outfit left in town.

Still, none of the boys felt bold enough just to go up the back stairs, as Dish had instructed them. It was decided to find Lippy, who was known to be a frequenter of whores.

They found him standing outside a saloon looking very disappointed. "There's only one pia-ner in this town, and it's broke," he said. "A mule skinner busted it. I rode all this way in and ain't got to hear a note."

"What do you do about whores?" Jimmy Rainey asked. He felt he couldn't bear much more frustration.

"Why, that's a dumb question," Lippy said. "You do like the bull does with the heifer, only frontways, if you want to."

Instead of clarifying matters, that only made them more obscure, at least to Newt. His sense of the mechanics of whoring was vague at best. Now Lippy was suggesting that there was more than one method, which was not helpful to someone who had yet to practice any method.

"Yeah, but do you just ask?" he inquired. "We don't know how much it costs."

"Oh, that varies from gal to gal, or madam to madam," Lippy said. "Gus gave Lorena fifty dollars once, but that price is way out of line."

Then he realized he had just revealed something he was not supposed to tell, and to boys too. Boys were not reliable when it came to keeping secrets.

"I oughtn't to tolt that," he said. "Gus threatened to shoot another hole in my stomach if I did."

"We won't tell," Newt assured him.

"Yes, you will," Lippy said. He was depressed anyway, because of the piano situation. He loved music and had felt sure he would get to play a little, or at least listen to some, in Ogallala. Yet the best he had done so far was a bartender with a harmonica, and he couldn't play that very well. Now he had really messed up and told Gus's secret.

Then, in a flash of inspiration, it occurred to him that the best way out of that tight spot was to get the boys drunk. They were young and not used to drinking. Get them drunk enough and they might forget Ogallala entirely, or even Nebraska. They certainly would not be likely to remember his chance remark. He saw that the strongest thing they had treated themselves to so far was horehound candy.

"Of course you boys are way too sober to be visiting whores," he said. "You've got to beer up a little before you attempt the ladies."

"Why?" Newt asked. Though he knew whores were often to be found in saloons, he wasn't aware that being drunk was required of their customers.

"Oh, yeah, them girls is apt to be rank," Lippy assured them. "Hell, they wallow around with buffalo hunters and such like. You want to have plenty of alcohol in you before you slip up on one. Otherwise you'll start to take a leak some morning and your pecker will come right off in your hand."

That was startling information. The boys looked at one another.

"Mine better not," Pete Spettle said darkly. He was not enjoying himself in town so far, apart from the miracle of being handed ten dollars by Gus.

"Why, that's a leg pull," Jimmy Rainey said. "How could one come off?"

"Oh, well, if it don't come plumb off it'll drip worse than my stomach," Lippy said. "You boys oughtn't to doubt me. I was living with whores before any of you sprouted."

"How do we get the beer?" Newt asked. He was almost as intrigued by the thought of beer as by the thought of whores. He had never quite dared go in a saloon for fear the Captain would walk in and find him.

"Oh, I'll get you the beer," Lippy said. "Got any cash?"

The boys looked at one another, reluctant to reveal the extent of their riches lest Lippy try to exploit them in some way. Fortunately they had nearly three dollars over and above what Gus had given them.

They shook out the small change and handed it to Lippy. They knew that drinking was something required of all real cowboys, and they were hot to try it.

"Will this get much?" Newt asked.

"Hell, will a frog hop?" Lippy said. "I can get you plenty of beer and a bottle of whiskey to chase it."

Lippy was as good as his word. In ten minutes he was back with plenty of beer and a quart of whiskey. He had a twinkle in his eyes, but the boys were all so excited by the prospect of drinking that they didn't notice. Lippy gave them the liquor and immediately started up the street.

"Where are you going?" Newt asked.

"The barber says there's a drummer with an accordion staying in the hotel," Lippy said. "If he ain't too attached to the accordion, I might buy it. We could make some fine music back at the wagon if we had an accordion to play."

"You oughta buy a new hat," Jimmy Rainey said boldly, for Lippy was still wearing the disgraceful bowler he had worn in Lonesome Dove.

"That hat looks like it was et by a heifer that had the green slobbers," Newt said, feeling proud of his wit. Lippy was out of hearing by then, so the wit was wasted.

The beer wasn't, however. Feeling that it was not appropriate to drink right out on the main street, the boys took their liquor around to the back of the livery stable and fell to. At first they sipped cautiously, finding the beer rather bitter. But the more they drank, the less bothered they were by the bitter taste.

"Let's sample the whiskey," Ben Rainey suggested. The suggestion was immediately adopted. After the cool beer, the whiskey tasted like liquid fire, and its effects were just as immediate as fire. By the time he had three long swigs of the whiskey Newt felt that the world had suddenly changed. The sun had been sinking rapidly as they drank, but a few swallows of whiskey seemed to stop everything. They sat down with their backs against the wall of the livery stable and watched the sun hang there, red and beautiful, over the brown prairie. Newt felt it might be hours before it disappeared. He swigged a couple of bottles of beer and felt himself getting lighter. In fact, he felt so light he had to put his hands on the ground every once in a while—he felt like as if he might float away. He might float up to where the sun was hanging. It was amazing that a few swallows of liquid could produce such a sensation. It was silly, but after a while he felt like lying down and hugging his stomach and hugging the earth, to make sure he didn't float off.

Young Jimmy Rainey turned out to have no stomach for liquor at all. He started vomiting almost as soon as he started drinking. Pete Spettle drank freely, but only looked darker and more depressed, whereas Ben Rainey enjoyed the liquor hugely and guzzled considerably more than his share.

In no time, it seemed, they had finished off the beer. Somehow the sun had slipped on down while no one was looking, and the afterglow was dying. Stars were already out, and the four of them were just sitting behind a livery stable, drunk, and no closer to the whores than they had been when they first came to town.

Newt decided it wouldn't do. He stood up and found that he didn't float off—though when he tried to walk he found it no simple matter to put his feet down one after the other. It irritated him a bit, for he had never experienced any trouble in walking before and felt a resentment against his feet for behaving so peculiarly.

Still, he could make progress, in some fashion, and he started boldly for the back stairs of the saloon.

"I'm gonna meet one, at least," he said. He kept walking, fearing that if he stopped the whole project might slide to a halt. The others picked themselves up and began to follow, Ben Rainey bringing the whiskey bottle. This was unnecessary, because it was empty.

Newt made the stairs with no trouble and clomped right on up them. He had not really meant to seize the lead, and his heart was in his throat. He felt delicately balanced, as if his stomach might be in his throat too, if he didn't proceed carefully.

The stairs had seemed long and steep from the bottom, but in a second he found himself standing at the top. The door was slightly ajar and he saw that someone was there. All he could see was a large shape.

Then, before he could speak, he saw a woman with almost no clothes on come out of a room behind the shape. The woman's legs were naked, a sight so startling that Newt couldn't believe he was seeing it.

"Who is it, Buf?" the girl with the naked legs asked.

"I guess the cat's got his tongue," the shape said in a husky voice. "He ain't introduced himself."

"I'm Newt," he said, feeling uncertain suddenly about the whole enterprise.

The other boys were just making their way up the stairs.

The shape—it was a woman, too—stepped half out the door and surveyed the group on the stairs. She was a large woman and she smelled rather like Pea Eye had after he came out of the barbershop. Newt saw to his astonishment that her legs were naked too.

"It's a troop of little fellers," she said to her companion in the hall. "They must have just let out school."

"They better get on in here while we ain't busy, then," her friend said. "That is, if they can afford it."

"Oh, we got money," Newt volunteered. "We come up with a herd and we just got paid."

"I didn't know cowboys come this young," the big woman said. "Show me the money."

Newt pulled out his gold piece and the woman leaned in the hall to look at it under the light.

"I take it all back," she said to her friend. "It's a bunch of rich cattlemen."

Newt noticed that she didn't give him back his gold piece, but he didn't feel he ought to say anything. Maybe it cost ten dollars just to get in the door of a place where women went naked.

The large woman held the door open and he went past her, taking care not to stumble, for his feet were feeling more and more untrustworthy. The other boys sidled in after him. They found themselves standing in a bare hall, being stared at by the two women.

"This is Mary and I'm Buf," the large woman said. Her ample bosom seemed to Newt to be about to burst out of the gown she wore. In the light it was clear that she was not very old herself—but she was large. The other girl, by comparison, seemed thin as a rail.

"This one's paid," Buf said, putting a hand casually on Newt's shoulder. "I hope you other fellows are as rich as he is, otherwise you're welcome to pile back down those stairs."

The Rainey boys immediately produced their money, but Pete Spettle held back. He put his hand in his pocket, but instead of bringing out his money he brought his hand out empty, and turned for the door without a word. They heard him clump back down the stairs.

"These two look like brothers," Buf said, quickly sizing up the Rainey boys.

"You take 'em, Buf," Mary said. "I'll take the one that come in first."

"Well, maybe you will and maybe you won't," Buf said. "I seen him first, I oughta have dibs."

Newt almost began to wish he had followed the example of Pete Spettle. It was a hot night, and close in the hall. He felt he might be sick. Also, from listening to the conversation he realized they were the two whores Dish had described. The big one was the Buffalo Heifer, and the other one was the one Dish said treated him nice. The Buffalo Heifer still had her large hand on his shoulder as she looked the group over. She had a black tooth right in front of her mouth. Her large body seemed to give off waves of heat, like a stove, and the toilet water she wore was so strong it made him queasy.

"We got the whole night to get through," Mary said. "We can't waste too much of it on these tadpoles." She took Ben Rainey's hand and quickly led him into a little room off the hall.

"Mary gets the fidgets if something ain't happening every minute," Buf said. "Come on, Newt."

Jimmy Rainey didn't like being left in the hall all by himself.

"Who do I do?" he asked plaintively.

"Just stand there like a post," Buf said. "Mary's quick, especially with tadpoles. She'll get you in a minute." Jimmy stood where he was, looking forlorn.

She led Newt into a small room with nothing much in it but an iron bedstead and a small washbasin on a tiny stand. A small unlit coal-oil lamp with no shade over the wick sat on a windowsill. The window was open and the rim of the prairie still red, as if a line of coals had been spread along it.

"Come far?" Buf asked in a husky voice.

"Yes, ma'am, from Texas," Newt said.

"Well, skin them pants off, Texas," she said, and to his astonishment, unbuttoned three buttons on the front of her gown and pitched it on the bed. She stood before him naked and, since he was too startled to move, reached down and unbuckled his pants.

"The problem with cowboys is all the time it takes to get their boots off," she confided, as she was unbuttoning his pants. "I don't get paid for watching cowboys wrestle with their dern boots, so I just leave the sheets off the bed. If they can't shuck 'em quick, they have to do it with them on."

Meanwhile she had unbuttoned his pants and reached for his peter, which, once it was freed, met her halfway at least. Newt couldn't get over how large she was—she would easily make two of him.

"I doubt you've had a chance to get much, but it won't hurt to check," she said.

She led him to the window and lit the coal-oil lamp. The movement of her large breasts threw strange shadows on the wall. To Newt's surprise she poured a little water on his peter. Then she lathered her hands with a bar of coarse soap and soaped him so vigorously that before he could stop himself he squirted right at her.

He was horrified, sure that what he had done was a dreadful breach of decorum, far worse than not being able to get his boots off quickly. Of course he had seen boys jerk at themselves, and he had done it plenty, but having a woman use soap and warm water on it brought matters to a head much quicker than was usual.

Buf merely chuckled, exposing her black tooth.

"I forgot you tadpoles are so randy you can't tolerate a soaping," she said, wiping him off on a piece of sacking.

She walked over to the bed and lay back on the cornshuck mattress, which crackled in protest. "Come on, try it," she said. "You might have another load yet."

"Should I take my boots off first?" Newt said, feeling hopelessly inexperienced and afraid of making another mistake.

"Naw, quick as you are, it ain't worth the effort," Buf said, scratching herself indelicately. "You got a pretty good one on, still."

He knelt between her thighs and she grasped him and tried to pull him in, but he was too far away.

"Flop over here, you ain't gonna do no good down there at the foot of the bed," she said. "You spent ten dollars, you oughta at least try. Some girls would charge you ten just to soap you up, but Mary and me, we're fair."

Newt allowed himself to be directed and made entrance, but then to his embarrassment he slipped out. He tried to reinsert himself but couldn't find the spot. Buf's belly was huge and slippery. Newt got dizzy again and felt himself sliding off it. Again he had the sensation that he might fall off the earth, and he grasped her arms to stop himself.

The Buffalo Heifer was unperturbed by his wigglings.

"You'll have to come back next time you draw your wages," she said. "Pull up your pants and send in that other tadpole."

As Newt got off the bed, he remembered Lorena suddenly. This was what she had done during all those months at the Dry Bean, with any man who had drawn his wages. He felt a terrible regret that he hadn't had the ten dollars then. Though the Buffalo Heifer had not been unfriendly, he would far rather have had Lorena soap him up—though he knew he probably wouldn't have had the nerve to go in, if it had been Lorena.

"Is it just the two of you?" he asked, buttoning his pants. He had built up a certain curiosity about Mary, and despite all his embarrassments decided he might try to visit her if he ever got another ten.

"Me and Mary," Buf said. "I get the ones that like 'em fat, and she gets the one's that like 'em skinny. And if it's a feller who likes 'em either way it's just a matter of who ain't busy at the time."

She was still lying naked on the bed.

"I'll go get Jimmy," he said. When he opened the door, Jimmy was not more than a foot away. Probably he had been listening, which Newt resented, but in the dim hall Jimmy looked too sick to be mad at.

"Your turn," Newt said. Jimmy went in, and Newt clumped down the stairs and found Pete Spettle waiting at the bottom.

"Why'd you leave?" Newt asked.

"Told Ma I'd save my money," Pete said.

"I wish we had some more beer," Newt said. Though his experience with the Buffalo Heifer had been mostly embarrassing as it was happening, he did not feel disappointed. Only the fact that he was down to a quarter in cash kept him from going back in and trying his luck with Mary. For all the peculiarity of what was happening, it was powerfully interesting. The fact that it cost ten dollars hardly mattered to him, but it turned out that he was the only one who took that attitude. Ben Rainey came down the stairs just behind him, complaining about how over-priced the experience was.

"I doubt it took a minute, once she got me washed," he said.

Jimmy Rainey soon followed, and was totally silent about his own experience. He was not over his upset stomach and kept falling behind to vomit as they walked around town looking for Lippy.

"Hell, whores make a sight more than cowboys," Ben kept saying—it seemed to trouble him a good deal. "We don't make but thirty dollars a month and them two made thirty dollars off us in about three minutes. It would have been forty if Pete hadn't backed out."

To Newt such an argument seemed wide of the point. What the whores sold was unique. The fact that it exceeded top-hand wages didn't matter. He decided he would probably be as big a whore as Jake and Mr. Gus when he grew up and had money to spend.

They found Lippy by the sound of the accordion, which he had managed to purchase but had not exactly learned to play. He was sitting on the steps of the saloon with the big rack of elkhorns over it, trying to squeeze out "Buffalo Gal" to an audience of one mule skinner and Allen O'Brien. The Irishman was wincing at Lippy's fumbling efforts.

"He'll never get the hang of it," the mule skinner said. "It sounds like a dern mule whinnying."

"I just bought this accordion," Lippy said. "I'll learn to play it by the time we hit Montany."

"Yeah, and if them Sioux catch you you'll be squealing worse than that music box," the mule skinner said.

Allen O'Brien kindly bought the boys each a beer. Though it was well after dark, people were still milling in the streets of Ogallala. At one point they heard gunshots, but no one cared to go investigate.

One beer was sufficient to make Jimmy Rainey start vomiting all over again. As they were riding back to the herd, Newt felt a little sad—there was no telling when he would get the chance to visit another whorehouse.

He was riding along wishing he had another ten dollars when something spooked their horses—they never knew what, although Pete Spettle thought he might have glimpsed a panther. At any rate, Newt and Ben were thrown before they knew what was happening, and Pete and Jimmy were carried off into the darkness by their frightened mounts.

"What if it was Indians?" Ben suggested, when they picked themselves up.

It was bright moonlight and they could see no Indians, but both drew their pistols anyway, just in case, and crouched down together as they listened to the depressing sound of their horses running away.

There was nothing for it but for them to walk to camp on foot, their pistols ready—too ready, really, for Ben almost shot his brother when Jimmy finally came back to see about them.

"Where's Pete?" Newt asked, but Jimmy didn't know.

Jimmy's horse would ride double, but not triple, so Newt had to walk the last two miles, annoyed with himself for not having kept a grip on the reins. It was the second time he had been put afoot on the drive, and he was sure everyone would comment on it the next day.

But when he arrived, his horse was grazing with the rest of the remuda, and only Po Campo was awake to take notice. Po seemed to sleep little. Whenever anyone came in from a watch he was usually up, slicing beef or freshening his coffee.

"Have you had a good walk?" he asked, offering Newt a piece of cold meat. Newt took it but discovered once he sat down that he was too tired to eat. He went to sleep with a hunk of beef still in his hand.

87

CLARA WAS UPSTAIRS when she saw the four riders. She had just cleaned her husband—the baby was downstairs with the girls. She happened to glance out a window and see them, but they were still far away, on the north side of the Platte. Any approaching rider was something to pay attention to in that country. In the first years the sight of any rider scared her and made her look to see where Bob was, or be sure a rifle was handy. Indians had been known to dress in white men's clothes to disarm unwary settlers, and there were plenty of white men in the Territory who were just as dangerous as Indians. If she was alone, the sight of any rider caused her a moment of terror.

But through the years they had been so lucky with visitors that Clara had gradually ceased to jump and take fright at the sight of a rider on the horizon. Their tragedies had come from weather and sickness, not attackers. But the habit of looking close had not left her, and she turned with a clean sheet in one hand and watched out her window as the horsemen dipped off the far slopes and disappeared behind the brush along the river.

Something about the riders struck her. Over the years she had acquired a good eye for horses, and also for horsemen. Something about the men coming from the north struck a key in her memory, but struck it so weakly that she only paused for a moment to wonder who it could be. She finished her task and then washed her face, for the dust was blowing and she had gotten gritty coming back from the lots. It was the kind of dust that seemed to sift through your clothes. She contemplated changing blouses, but if she did that, the next thing she knew she would be taking baths in the morning and changing clothes three times a day like a fine lady, and she didn't have that many clothes, or consider herself that fine. So she made do with a face wash and forgot about the riders. July and Cholo were both working the lots and would no doubt notice them too. Probably it was just a few Army men wanting to buy horses. Red Cloud was harrying them hard, and every week two or three Army men would show up wanting horses.

It was one of those who had brought July the news about his wife, although of course the soldier didn't know it was July's wife when he talked about finding the corpses of the woman and the buffalo hunter. Clara had been washing clothes and hadn't heard the story, but when she went down to the lots a little later she knew something was wrong. July stood by the fence, white as a sheet.

"Are you sick?" she asked. Cholo had ridden off with the soldier to look at some stock.

"No, ma'am," he said, in a voice she could barely hear. At times, to her intense irritation, he called her "ma'am," usually when he was too upset to think.

"It's Ellie," he added. "That soldier said the Indians killed a woman and a buffalo hunter about sixty miles east of town. I have no doubt it was her. They were traveling that way."

"Come on up to the house," she said. He was almost too weak to walk and was worthless for several days, faint with grief over a woman who had done nothing but run away from him or abuse him almost from the day they married.

The girls were devoted to July by this time, and they nursed him constantly, bringing him bowls of soup and arguing with one another over the privilege of serving him. Clara let them, though she herself felt more irritated than not by the man's foolishness. The girls couldn't understand her attitude and said so.

"His wife got butchered up, Ma!" Betsey protested.

"I know that," Clara said.

"You look so stern," Sally said. "Don't you like July?"

"I like July a lot," Clara said.

"He thinks you're mad at him," Betsey said.

"Why would he care?" Clara said, with a little smile. "He's got the two of you to pamper him. You're both nicer than I've ever been."

"We want you to like him," Betsey said. She was the more direct of the two.

"I told you I like him," Clara said. "I know people ain't smart and often love those who don't care for them. Up to a point, I'm tolerant of that. Then past a point, I'm not tolerant of it. I think it's a sickness to grieve too much for those who never cared a fig for you."

Both of the girls were silent for a time.

"You remember that," Clara said. "Do your best, if you happen to love a fool. You'll have my sympathy. Some folks will preach that it's a woman's duty never to quit, once you make a bond with a man. I say that's folly. A bond has to work two ways. If a man don't hold up his end, there comes a time to quit."

She sat down at the table and faced the girls. July was outside, well out of hearing. "July don't want to face up to the fact that his wife never loved him," she said.

"She *ought* to have loved him," Sally said.

"Ought don't count for as much as a gnat, when you're talking about love," Clara said. "She didn't. You seen her. She didn't even care for Martin. We've already given July and Martin more love than that poor woman ever gave them. I don't say that to condemn her. I know she had her troubles, and I doubt she was often in her right mind. I'm sorry she had no more control of herself to run off from her husband and child and get killed."

She stopped, to let the girls work on the various questions a little. It interested her which they would pick as the main point.

"We want July to stay," Betsey said finally. "You'll just make him run off, being so stern, and then he'll get butchered up too."

"You think I'm that bad?" Clara asked, with a smile.

"You're pretty bad," Betsey said.

Clara laughed. "You'll be just as bad, if you don't reform," she said. "I got a right to my feelings too, you know. We're doing a nice job of taking care of July Johnson. It just gripes me that he let himself be tromped on and can't even figure out that it wasn't right, and that he didn't like it."

"Can't you just be patient?" Sally said. "You're patient with Daddy."

"Daddy got his head kicked," Clara said. "He can't help how he is."

"Did he keep his bond?" Betsey asked.

"Yes, for sixteen years," Clara said. "Although I never liked his drinking."

"I wish he'd get well," Sally said. She had been her father's favorite and grieved over him the most.

"Ain't he going to die?" Betsey asked.

"I fear he will," Clara said. She had been careful not to let that notion take hold of the girls, but she wondered if she was wrong. Bob wasn't getting better, and wasn't likely to.

Sally started to cry, and Clara put her arms around her.

"Anyway, we have July," Betsey said.

"If I don't run him off," Clara said.

"You just better not!" Betsey said, eyes flashing.

"He might get bored and leave of his own accord," Clara volunteered.

"How could he get bored? There's lots to do," Sally said.

"Don't be so stern with him, Ma," Betsey pleaded. "We don't want him to leave."

"It won't hurt the man to learn a thing or two," Clara said. "If he plans to stay here he'd better start learning how to treat women."

"He treats *us* fine," Sally pointed out.

"You ain't women yet," Clara said. "I'm the only one around here, and he better spruce up if he wants to keep on my good side."

====

July soon returned to work, but his demeanor had not greatly improved. He had little humor in him and could not be teased successfully, which was an irritant to Clara. She had always loved to tease and considered it an irony of her life that she was often drawn to men who didn't recognize teasing even when she was inflicting it on them. Bob had never responded to teasing, or even noticed it, and her powers in that line had slowly rusted from lack of practice. Of course she teased the girls, but it was not the same as having a grown man to work on—she had often felt like pinching Bob for being so stolid. July was no better—in fact, he and Bob were cut from the same mold, a strong but unimaginative mold.

When she came down from washing her face, she heard talk from the back and stopped dead on the stairs, for there was no doubt who was talking. The chord of memory that had been weakly struck by the sight of the horsemen resounded through her suddenly like an organ note. No sound in the world could have made her happier, for she heard the voice of Augustus McCrae, a voice like no other. He sounded exactly as he always had—hearing his voice so unexpectedly after sixteen years caused her eyes to fill. The sound took the years away. She stood on the stairs in momentary agitation, uncertain for a second as to when it was, or where she was, so much did it remind her of other times when Augustus would show up unexpectedly, and she, in her little room over the store, would hear him talking to her parents.

Only now he was talking to her girls. Clara regretted not changing blouses—Gus had always appreciated her appearance. She walked on down the stairs and looked out the kitchen window. Sure enough, Gus was standing there, in front of his horse, talking to Betsey and Sally. Woodrow Call sat beside him, still mounted, and beside Call, on a bay horse, was a young blond woman wearing men's clothes. A good-looking boy on a brown mare was the last of the group.

Clara noted that Gus had already charmed the girls—July Johnson would be lucky to get another bowl of soup out of them as long as Gus was around.

She stood at the window a minute studying him. To her he seemed not much older. His hair had already turned white when he was young. He had always made her feel keen, Gus—his appetite for talk matched hers. She stood for a moment in the kitchen doorway, a smile on her lips. Just seeing him made her feel keen. She was in the shadows and he had not seen her. Then she took a step or two and Augustus looked around. Their eyes met and he smiled.

"Well, pretty as ever," he said.

To the huge astonishment of her girls, Clara walked straight off the porch and into the stranger's arms. She had a look in her eyes that they had never seen, and she raised her face to the stranger and kissed him right on the mouth, an action so startling and so unexpected that both girls remembered the moment for the rest of their lives.

Newt was so surprised that he scarcely knew where to look.

When Clara kissed him, Lorena looked down, nothing but despair in her heart. There the woman was, Gus loved her, and she herself was lost. She should have stayed in the tent and not come to see it—yet she had wanted to come. Now that she had, she would have given anything to be somewhere else, but of course it was too late. When she looked up again she saw that Clara had stepped back a bit and was looking at Gus, her face shining with happiness. She had thin arms and large hands, Lorena noticed. Two men were walking up from the lots, having seen the crowd.

"Well, introduce your friends, Gus," Clara said. She had a hand on his arm, and walked with him over to the horses.

"Oh, you know Woodrow," Augustus said.

"How do you do?" Call said, feeling at a loss.

"This is Miss Lorena Wood," Augustus said, reaching up to help her dismount. "She's come a far piece with us. All the way from Lonesome Dove, in fact. And this young gentleman is Newt."

"Newt who?" Clara asked.

"Newt Dobbs," Augustus said, after a pause.

"Hello, Miss Wood," Clara said. To Lorena's surprise she seemed quite friendly—far more so than most women were to her.

"I don't know whether to envy you or pity you, Miss Wood," Clara said. "Riding all that way with Mr. McCrae, I mean. I know he's entertaining, but that much entertainment could break a person for life."

Then Clara laughed, a happy laugh—she was amused that Augustus had seen fit to arrive with a woman, that she had stunned her girls by kissing him, and that Woodrow Call, a man she had always disliked and considered scarcely more inter-esting than a stump, had been able to think of nothing better to say to her after sixteen years than "How do you do?" It added up to a lively time, in her book, and she felt she had been in Nebraska long enough to deserve a little liveliness.

She saw that the young woman was very frightened of her. She had dismounted but kept her eyes cast down. July and Cholo walked up just at that time, July with a look of surprise on his face.

"Why, Sheriff Johnson," Augustus said. "I guess, as they say, it's a small world."

"Just to you, Gus, you've met everybody in it now, I'm sure," Clara said. She glanced at July, who so far hadn't spoken. He was watching her and it struck her that it might be because she was still holding Gus's arm. It made Clara want to laugh again. In minutes, the arrival of Gus McCrae had mixed up everyone, just as it usually had in the past. It had always been a peculiarity of her friendship with Augustus. Nobody had ever been able to figure out whether she was in love with him or not. Her parents had puzzled over the question for years—it had replaced Bible arguments as their staple of conversation. Even when she had accepted Bob, Gus's presence in her life confused most people, for she had soon demonstrated that she had no intention of giving him up just because she was planning to marry. The situation had been made the more amusing by the fact that Bob himself worshipped Gus, and would probably have thought it odd that she had chosen him over Gus if he had been sharp enough to figure out that she could have had Gus if she'd wanted him.

It had been one-sided adoration, though, for Gus considered Bob one of the dullest men alive, and often said so. "Why are you marrying that dullard?" he asked her often.

"He suits me," she said. "Two racehorses like us would never get along. I'd want to be in the lead, and so would you."

"I never thought you'd marry a man with nothing to say," he said.

"Talk ain't everything," she said—words she had often remembered with rue during years when Bob scarcely seemed to utter two words a month.

Now Gus was back, and had instantly captured her girls—that was clear. Betsey and Sally were fascinated, if embarrassed, that this white-haired man had ridden up and kissed their mother.

"Where's Robert?" Augustus asked, to be polite.

"Upstairs, sick," Clara said. "A horse kicked him in the head. It's a bad wound."

For a second, remembering the silent man upstairs, she thought how unfair life was. Bob was slipping away, and yet that knowledge couldn't quell her happiness at the sight of Gus and his friends. It was a lovely summer day, too—a fine day for a social occasion.

"You girls go catch three pullets," she said. "I imagine Miss Wood is tired of eating beefsteak. It's such a fair day, we might want to picnic a little later."

"Oh, Ma, let's do," Sally said. She loved picnics.

Clara would have liked a few words with Augustus alone, but that would have to wait until things settled down a little, she saw. Miss Wood mostly kept her eyes down and said nothing, but when she raised them it was always to look at Gus. Clara took them into the kitchen and left them a moment, for she heard the baby.

"Now, see, all your worrying was for nothing," Augustus whispered to Lorena. "She's got a young child."

Lorena held her peace. The woman seemed kind—she had even offered her a bath—but she still felt frightened. What she wanted was to be on the trail again with Gus. Her mind kept looking ahead to when the visit would be over and she would have Gus alone again. Then she would feel less frightened.

Clara soon came down, a baby in her arms.

"It's July's son," she said, handing the baby to Gus as if it were a package.

"Well, what do I want with it?" Augustus asked. He had seldom held a baby in his arms and was somewhat discommoded.

"Just hold him or give him to Miss Wood," Clara said. "I can't hold him and cook too."

Call, July and Cholo had walked off to the lots, for Call wanted to buy a few horses and anyway didn't care to sit in a kitchen and try to make conversation.

It amused Lorena that Gus had got stuck with the baby. Somehow it made things more relaxed that the woman would just hand him to Gus that way. She stopped feeling quite so nervous, and she watched the baby chew on his fat little fist.

"If this is Sheriff Johnson's child, whereabouts is his wife?" Augustus asked.

"Dead," Clara said. "She stopped here with two buffalo hunters, had the child and left. July showed up two weeks later, half dead from worry."

"So you adopted them both," Augustus said. "You was always one to grab."

"Listen to him," Clara said. "Hasn't seen me in sixteen years, and he feels free to criticize.

"It's mainly Martin that I wanted," she continued. "As life goes on I got less and less use for grown men."

Lorena smiled in spite of herself. There was something amusing about the sassy way Clara talked. It was no wonder Gus admired her, for he liked to talk a lot himself.

"Let me hold him," she said, reaching for the baby. Augustus was glad to hand the baby over. He had been watching Clara and didn't enjoy having to divert his attention to a wiggly baby. It was the same old Clara, so far as spirit went, though her body had changed. She was fuller in the bosom, thinner in the face. The real change was in her hands. As a girl she had had delicate hands, with long fingers and tiny wrists. Now it was her hands that drew his eyes: the work she had done had swollen and strengthened them; they seemed as large at the joints as a man's. She was peeling potatoes with them and handled a knife as deftly as a trapper. Her hands were no longer as beautiful, but they were arresting: the hands of a formidable woman, perhaps too formidable.

Though he had only glanced at her hands, Clara picked up the glance, displaying her old habit of being able to read his mind.

"That's right, Gus," she said. "I've coarsened a little, but this country will take your bloom."

"It didn't take your bloom," he said, wanting her to know how glad he was that she was in so many ways her old self, the self he remembered with such pleasure.

Clara smiled and paused a minute to tickle the baby. She smiled, too, at Newt, who blushed, not used to ladies' smiles. The girls kept looking at him.

"You'll have to pardon us, Miss Wood," she said. "Gus and I were old sweethearts. It's a miracle both of us are still alive, considering the lives we've led. We've got to make up for a lot of lost time, if you'll excuse us."

Lorena found she didn't mind, not nearly so much as she had thought she would even a few minutes earlier. It was pleasant to sit in the kitchen and hold the baby. Even hearing Clara josh with Gus was pleasant.

"So what happened to Mr. Johnson's wife, once she left?" Augustus asked.

"She was looking for an old boyfriend," Clara said. "He was a killer who got hung while she was recovering from having the baby. July went and saw her but she wouldn't have anything to do with him. She and one of the buffalo hunters traveled on, and the Sioux killed her. You watch close, or they'll get you too," she added.

"I guess no Indian would dare bother you," Augustus said. "They know they wouldn't stand a chance."

"We kept some of them alive the last few winters, once the buffalo were gone," Clara said. "Bob gives them old horses. Horse meat's better than nothing."

She put a little milk in the baby's bottle and showed Lorena how to feed him. The baby stared up solemnly at Lorena as he drank.

"He's taken with you, Miss Wood," Clara said. "He's never seen a blonde, I guess."

The baby took a sneezing fit and Lorena was afraid she had done something wrong, but Clara merely laughed at her anxiety and the child soon settled down.

A little later, while Clara was frying the chicken, Call came up from the lots. He wanted to buy some horses and had found some to his liking, but neither Cholo nor July would make the deal. They had shown him the horses readily enough, but informed him that Clara made all the deals. It seemed irregular to him: two grown men right there, and yet he was forced to do business with a woman.

"I was told you're the horse trader," he said.

"Yes," Clara said. "I'm the horse trader. You girls finish this chicken and I'll see what Captain Call has picked out."

She looked again at the boy who had blushed when she smiled at him. He was saying something to Sally and didn't notice her look. To her eye he was the spitting image of Captain Call, built the same way, and with the same movements. So why is your name Dobbs? she wondered.

On their way to the lots Call tried to think of something to say, but he was at a loss. "You have a pretty ranch," he said finally. "I hope we do as well in Montana."

"I just hope you get there alive," Clara said. "You ought to settle around here and wait five years. I imagine Montana will be safer by then. It ain't safe now."

"We're set on being the first there," Call said. "It can't be no rougher than Texas used to be."

Clara set such a stiff price for her horses that Call was tempted to balk. He felt sure he would have done better with her husband, if he had been up and about. There was something uncompromising in Clara's look when she named the prices. It was as if she dared him to bargain. He had bargained over many a horse in his day, but never with a woman. He felt shy. Worse, he felt she didn't like him, though so far as he could remember he had never given her any reason to take offense. He studied the situation in silence for several minutes—so long that Clara grew impatient.

Newt had followed them, thinking the Captain might need him to help with the horses if he bought some. He could see that the Captain was mighty put out with the woman. It surprised him that she didn't seem to care. When the Captain was put out with the men, they cared, but the woman just stood there, her brown hair blowing, not caring in the least and not giving an inch. It was shocking: he had never expected to see anyone stand up to the Captain, except maybe Mr. Gus.

"I'm neglecting my guests," Clara said. "There's no telling when I'll get to see Gus McCrae again. You take all the time you want to think it over."

Newt was even more shocked. The Captain didn't say a word. It was almost as if the woman had issued him an order.

The woman turned, and as she did, she looked at Newt. Before he could drop his eyes she had caught him looking at her in turn. He felt greatly embarrassed, but to his surprise Clara smiled again, a friendly smile that vanished when she turned back to the Captain.

"Well, it's a stiff price, but they're good horses," Call said, wondering how the men could bring themselves to work for such a testy woman.

Then he remembered that the younger man had been the sheriff chasing Jake. "You come from Arkansas, don't you?" he asked.

"Fort Smith," July said.

"We hung your man for you," Call said. "He fell in with a bad bunch. We caught them up in Kansas."

For a second, July didn't remember what he was talking about. It seemed a life ago that he had left Fort Smith in pursuit of Jake Spoon. He had long since ceased to give the man any thought. The news that he was dead did not affect him.

"I doubt I would have caught him myself," July said. "I had horse trouble, up around Dodge."

When Clara got back to the house she was in high color. The way Call had stood there silently, not even asking a question or making an offer, just waiting for her to come down on the price, struck her as arrogant. The more she thought about it, the less hospitable she felt toward the man.

"I can't say that I'm fond of your partner," she said to Augustus. He had talked the girls out of some chicken gizzards and was eating them off a plate.

"He ain't skilled with the ladies," Augustus said, amused that she was angry. As long as she wasn't angry at him, it just made her the better-looking.

"Ma, shall we take buttermilk?" Betsey asked. She and Sally had changed dresses without their mother's permission, and were so excited by the prospect of a picnic that they could hardly keep still.

"Yes, today we feast," Clara said. "I asked Cholo to hitch the little wagon. One of you go change that baby, he's rather fragrant."

"I'll help," Lorena said. It surprised Augustus, but she went off upstairs with the girls. Clara stood listening as their footsteps went up the stairs. Then she turned her deep-gray eyes on Augustus.

"She's hardly older than my daughters," Clara said.

"Don't you be scolding me," he said. "It ain't my fault you went off and got married."

"If I'd married you, you would have left me for somebody younger and stupider long before now, I imagine," Clara said. To his surprise she came over and stood near him for a moment, putting one of her large, strong hands on his shoulder.

"I like your girl," she said. "What I don't like is that you spent all these years with Woodrow Call. I detest that man and it rankles that he got so much of you and I got so little. I think I had the better claim."

Augustus was taken aback. The anger in her was in her eyes again, this time directed at him.

"Where have you been for the last fifteen years?" she asked.

"Lonesome Dove, mostly," he said. "I wrote you three letters."

"I got them," she said. "And what did you accomplish in all that time?"

"Drank a lot of whiskey," Augustus said.

Clara nodded and went back to packing the picnic basket. "If that was all you accomplished you could have done it in Ogallala and been a friend to me," she said. "I lost three boys, Gus. I needed a friend."

"You ought to wrote me that, then," he said. "I didn't know."

Clara's mouth tightened. "I hope I meet a man sometime in my life who can figure such things out," she said. "I wrote you but I tore up the letters. I figured if you didn't come of your own accord you wouldn't be no good to me anyway."

"Well, you was married," he said, not knowing why he bothered to argue.

"I was never so married but what I could have managed a friend," she said. "I want you to look at Bob before you go. The poor man's laid up there for two months, wasting away."

The anger had died out of her eyes. She came and sat down in a chair, looking at him in the intent way she had, as if reading in his face the events of the fifteen years he had spent away from her.

"Where'd you get Miss Wood?" she asked.

"She's been in Lonesome Dove a while," he said.

"Doing what?"

"Doing what she could, but don't you hold it against her," he said.

Clara looked at him coolly. "I don't judge women that harsh," she said. "I might have done the same under some circumstances."

"I doubt it," he said.

"Yes, but you don't know as much about women as you like to think you do," Clara said. "You're overrated in that regard."

"By God, you're sassy," Augustus said.

Clara just smiled, her old beguiling smile. "I'm honest," she said. "To most men, that's sassy."

"Well, it might interest you to know that Lorie started this trip with your old friend Jake Spoon," Augustus said. "He was his usual careless self and let her get kidnapped by a real rough man."

"Oh, so you rescued her?" Clara said. "No wonder she worships you. What happened to Jake?"

"He met a bad end," Augustus said. "We hung him. He was with a gang of murderers."

Clara didn't flinch at the news. She heard the girls coming back down the stairs. Lorena was carrying the baby. Clara stood up so Lorena could sit. The baby's eyes followed her.

"Betsey, go find July and the men and ask them if they want to wash up before we go," she said.

"I doubt you can get Woodrow Call to go to your picnic," Augustus said. "He'll be wanting to get back to work."

But Call went. He had come back to the house, still trying to think of a way to talk Clara down on the horses, only to find the girls loading a small wagon, Lorena holding a baby, and Gus carrying a crock of buttermilk.

"Could you drive for us, Captain?" Clara asked, handing him the reins to the little mule team before he could answer. With such a crowd there watching he couldn't muster a protest, and he drove the little wagon three miles west on the Platte to a place where there were a few small cottonwoods.

"It ain't as nice as our place on the Guadalupe, Gus, but it's the best we can do," Clara said.

"Oh, your orchard, you mean," Augustus said.

Clara looked puzzled for a moment—she had forgotten that that was what they called the picnic spot on the Guadalupe.

The day remained fair, and the picnic was a great success for everyone except Captain Call and July Johnson, both of whom felt awkward and merely waited for it to be over. The girls tried to get July to wade in the Platte, but he resisted solemnly. Newt waded, and then Lorena, rolling up her pants, and Lorena and Betsey walked far downstream, out of sight of the party. The baby dozed in the shade, while Clara and Augustus bantered. The sixteen-year gap in their communications proved no hindrance at all. Then Augustus rolled up *his* pants and waded with the girls, while Clara and Lorena watched. All the food was consumed, Call drinking about half the buttermilk himself. He had always loved buttermilk and had not had any for a long time.

"You don't plan on returning to Arkansas, Mr. Johnson?" he asked.

"I don't know that I will," July said. In fact, he had given no thought to his future at all.

Augustus ate most of the fried chicken and marveled at how comfortable Lorena seemed to be. She liked the girls, and seeing her with them reminded him that she was not much more than a girl herself, despite her experiences. He knew that she had been advanced too quickly into life, though perhaps not so far to yet enjoy a bit of girlhood.

When it came time to go back to the ranch he helped Lorie into the wagon with the girls, and he and Clara walked behind. Newt, who had enjoyed the picnic mightily, fell into conversation with Sally and rode beside the wagon. Lorena didn't seem concerned—she and Betsey had taken to one another at once, and were chatting happily.

"You should leave that girl here," Clara said, startling Augustus. He had been thinking the same thing.

"I doubt she'd stay," he said.

"If you stay out of it she might," Clara said. "I'll ask her. You have no business taking a girl like that into Montana. She might not survive."

"In some ways she ain't so young," he said.

"I like her," Clara said, ignoring him. "I expect you'll marry her and I'll have to watch you have five or six babies in your old age. I guess I'd be annoyed, but I could live with it. Don't take her up to Montana. She'll either die or get killed, or else she'll age before her time, like I have."

"I can't tell that you've aged much," Augustus said.

"You've just been around me one day," Clara said. "There's certain things I can still do and certain things I'm finished with."

"What things are you finished with?" he asked.

"You'd find out if you stayed around me much," Clara said.

"I notice you've taken a fancy to young Mr. Johnson," Augustus said. "I expect if I did stay around he'd beat me out."

"He's nearly as dull as Woodrow Call, but he's nicer," Clara said. "He'll do what he's told, mostly, and I've come to appreciate that quality in a man. I could never count on you to do what you're told."

"So do you aim to marry him?"

"No, that's one of the things I'm through with," Clara said. "Of course I ain't quite—poor Bob ain't dead. But if he passes away, I'm through with it."

Clara smiled. Augustus chuckled. "I hope you ain't contemplating an irregular situation," he said.

Clara smiled. "What's irregular about having a boarder?" she asked. "Lots of widows take boarders. Anyway, he likes my girls better than he likes me. He might be ready to marry again by the time Sally's of age."

At that moment Sally was chattering away to young Newt, who was getting his first taste of conversation with a sprightly young lady.

"Who's his mother?" Clara asked. She liked the boy's looks, and also his manners. "I never knew Call was prone to ladies," she added.

"Oh, Woodrow ain't," Augustus said. "He can barely stand to be within fifty yards of you."

"I know that," Clara said. "He's been stiff all day because I won't bargain away my horses. My price is my price. But that boy's his, and don't you tell me he ain't. They walk alike, they stand alike, and they look alike."

"I expect you're right," Augustus said.

"Yes, I'm right," Clara said. "You ain't answered my question."

"His mother was a woman named Maggie," he said. "She was a whore. She died when Newt was six."

"I like that boy," Clara said. "I'd keep *him* too, if I got the chance. He's about the age my Jimmy would be, if Jimmy had lived."

"Newt's a fine boy," Augustus said.

"It's a miracle, ain't it, when one grows up nice," Clara said. "He's got a quiet way, that boy. I like that. It's surprising to find gentle behavior when his father is Captain Call."

"Oh, Newt don't know Call's his father," Augustus said. "I expect he's heard hints, but he don't know it."

"And Call don't claim him, when anybody can see it?" Clara said, shocked. "I never had much opinion of Call, and now I have less."

"Call don't like to admit mistakes," Augustus said. "It's his way."

"What mistake?" Clara said. "I wouldn't call it a mistake if I raised a boy that nice. My Jimmy had wildness in him. I couldn't handle him, though he died when he was eight. I expect he'd have ended like Jake. Now where'd it come from? I ain't wild, and Bob ain't wild."

"I don't know," Augustus said.

"Well, I had two sweet ones, though," Clara said. "My last one, Johnny, was the sweetest. I ain't been the same since that child died. It's a wonder the girls aren't worse-behaved than they are. I don't consider that I've ever had the proper feeling for them. It went out of me that winter I lost Jeff and Johnny."

They walked in silence for a while.

"Why don't you tell that boy who his pa is?" Clara said. "I'd do it, if he was around here long. He should know who his pa is. He's got to wonder."

"I always thought Call would work up to it, eventually," Augustus said. "I still think so."

"I don't," Clara said.

A big gray wolf loped up out of the riverbed, looked at them for a moment, and loped on.

Ahead, the baby was fretting, and the girls and Lorena were trying to shush it.

When they got back to the ranch, Call gave in and told Clara he'd pay her price for the horses. He didn't like it, but he couldn't stay around there forever, and her horses were in far better condition than the nags he had looked at in Ogallala.

"Fine, go help him, boys," Clara said. Cholo and July went off to help. Newt was helping the girls carry the remains of the picnic in.

He was sorry they were leaving. Sally had been telling him all she planned to do when she grew up. She was going East to school and then planned to play the piano professionally, she said. That seemed unusual to Newt. The only musician he knew was Lippy, and he couldn't imagine Sally doing what Lippy did. But he enjoyed listening to her talk about her future life.

As he was coming down the steps, Clara stopped him. She put an arm across his shoulder and walked him to his horse. No woman had ever done such a thing with him.

"Newt, we've enjoyed having you," Clara said. "I want you to know that if Montana don't suit you, you can just head back here. I'll give you all the work you can stand."

"I'd like to," Newt said. He meant it. Since meeting the girls and seeing the ranch, he had begun to wonder why they were taking the herd so far. It seemed to him Nebraska had plenty of room.

For most of the trip Newt had supposed that nothing could be better than being allowed to be a cowboy, but now that they had got to Nebraska, his thinking was changing. Between the Buffalo Heifer and the other whores in Ogallala and Clara's spirited daughters, he had begun to see that a world with women in it could be even more interesting. The taste he had of that world seemed all too brief. Though he had been more or less scared of Clara all day, and was still a little scared of her, there was something powerfully appealing about her, too.

"Thank you for the picnic," he said. "I never went on one before."

Something in the boy touched Clara. Boys had always touched her—far more than girls. This one had a lonely look in his eye although he also had a quick smile.

"Come back when you can, we'll go on many more," she said. "I believe Sally's taken a fancy to you."

Newt didn't know what to say to that. He got on his horse. "I expect I better go help, ma'am," he said.

"If you get to choose one of my horses, choose that little sorrel with the star on his forehead," Clara said. "He's the best of that bunch."

"Oh, I imagine Dish will get the first pick," Newt said. "Dish is our top hand."

"Well, I don't want Dish to have him," Clara said. "I want you to have him. Come on."

She started for the lots and made straight for Call.

"Captain," she said, "there's a three-year-old sorrel gelding with a white star on his forehead in this lot you bought. I want to give that horse to Newt, so don't let anyone have him. You can deduct him from the price."

"Give it to him?" Call asked, surprised. Newt, who overheard, was surprised too. The woman who drove such a hard bargain wanted to give him a horse.

"Yes, I'm making him a gift," Clara said. "I'd feel better knowing Newt was well mounted, if you're really going to take him to Montana." With that she went back to the house.

Call looked at the boy. "Why'd she do that?" he asked. Of course it was fine for the boy to have the horse—it saved fifty dollars.

"I don't know," Newt said.

"That's the whole trouble with women," Call said, as if to himself. "They do things that don't make sense. She wouldn't give a nickel on the rest of them horses. Most horse traders would have taken off a dollar just to help the deal."

88

AFTER CALL AND NEWT LEFT with the horses, Clara lit a lantern and took Augustus up to the room where her husband lay. Lorena sat at the kitchen table with the girls, playing draughts. July watched, but could not be persuaded to take part in the game. Even Betsey, his favorite, couldn't persuade him, and Betsey could usually get July to do anything she wanted him to do. Lorena's presence made him shy. He enjoyed sitting and looking at her in the lamplight, though. It seemed to him he had never seen anyone so beautiful. He had only seen her before on that dreadful morning on the plains when he had had to bury Roscoe, Joe and Janey, and had been too stricken to notice her. Then she had been bruised and thin from her treatment by Blue Duck and the Kiowas. Now she was neither bruised nor thin.

Clara and Augustus sat for an hour in the room where Bob lay. Augustus found it difficult to get used to the fact that the man's eyes were open. Clara had ceased to care, or even notice.

"He's been that way two months," she said. "I guess he sees some, but I don't think he hears."

"It reminds me of old Tom Mustard," Augustus said. "He rangered with us when we started the troop. His horse went over a cutbank on the salt fork of the Brazos one night and fell on him. Broke his back. Tom never moved a muscle after that, but his eyes were open when we found him. We started back to Austin with Tom on a travois, but he died a week later. He never closed his eyes in all that time, that I know of."

"I wish Bob would go," Clara said. "He's no use to himself like this. All Bob liked to do was work, and now he can't."

They walked out on the little upper porch, where it was cooler. "Why'd you come up here, Gus?" she asked. "You ain't a cowboy."

"The truth is, I was hoping to find you a widow," he said. "I didn't miss by much, either."

Clara was amused that her old beau would be so blunt. "You missed by years," she said. "I'm a bony old woman now and you're a deceiving man, anyway. You always were a deceiving man. I think the best thing would be for you to leave me your bride to be and I'll see if I can give her some polish."

"I never meant to get in the position I'm in, to be truthful," Augustus said.

"No, but you like it, now that you're in it," Clara said, taking his hand. "She's got nearly as high an opinion of you as you have of yourself, Gus. I could never match it. I know your character too well. She's younger and prettier, which is always a consideration with you men."

Augustus had forgotten how fond she was of goading him. Even with a dying husband in the next room, she was capable of it. The only chance with Clara was to be as bold as she was. He looked at her, and was thinking of kissing her.

Clara saw the look and was startled by it. Although she kissed her girls every day and lavished kisses on the baby, it had been years since she had been kissed by a man. Bob would occasionally kiss her cheek if he had returned from a trip—otherwise kissing played no part in his view of married love. Looking off the porch, with Augustus standing near her, Clara felt sad. She mainly had snatched kisses from her courtship, with Gus or Jake, twenty years before, to remember.

She looked at Gus again, wondering if he would really be so bold or so foolish. He didn't move to kiss her, but he still stood close and looked into her face.

"The older the violin, the sweeter the music," he said with a smile.

"That proves you're a deceiving man, if you think that," she said. "You've had a long ride for nothing, I guess."

"Why, no," he said. "It's happiness to see you."

Clara felt a sudden irritation. "Do you think you can have us both?" she said. "My husband isn't dead. I haven't seen you in sixteen years. I've mostly raised children and horses during those years. Three of the children died, and plenty of the horses. It took all the romance out of me, if romance is what you were hoping for. I read about it in my magazines but I left it behind for myself when I left Austin."

"Don't you regret it?" Augustus asked.

"Oh, well," Clara said, "yes and no. I'm too strong for the normal man and too jealous once my feelings get started. I'm surprised you dare bring another woman into my house."

"I thought you liked her," he said.

"I do like her," Clara said. "I mind you doing it, though. Don't you understand the facts of nature yet? She's younger and prettier."

"It happened accidentally, like I mentioned," Augustus said.

"I never noticed you having such accidents with ugly girls," Clara said. "I don't care how it happened. You've been my dream, Gus. I used to think about you two or three hours a day."

"I wish you'd wrote, then," he said.

"I didn't want you here," she said. "I needed the dreams. I knew you for a rake and a rambler but it was sweet to pretend you only loved me."

"I do only love you, Clara," he said. "I've grown right fond of Lorie, but it ain't like this feeling I have for you."

"Well, she loves you," Clara said. "It would destroy her if I was to have you. Don't you know that?"

"Yes, I know that," Augustus said, thinking there would never again be such a woman as the one who looked at him with anger in her face.

"Would you destroy her, then, if I said stay?" Clara asked.

"I expect so," Augustus said.

"That ain't an answer."

"Yes, you know I would," he said. "I'd smother Bob for you and send Lorie to perdition."

Clara sighed, and her anger wore out with the sigh.

"Such talk," she said. "Bob'll die when he can manage it, and I'll see what I can do for your bride. It's just her beauty that set me off. I was always the youngest and prettiest, and now I'm not."

"You're mighty pretty, and anyway pretty ain't everything," he said.

"Where men like you are concerned it's ninety-nine percent," she said. "You ain't had time to look at me close. I ain't the prettiest anymore. The prettiest is downstairs."

"I'd still like a kiss," he said.

A tickle of amusement took her. He saw her smile and took it for encouragement. When he bent forward the result was so bland that after a moment Clara drew back her head and laughed.

"You've ridden a long way for some pretty weak courting," she said, but she felt better. Gus looked rather hangdog at his failure—one of the few times she had ever seen him look that way.

"You beat any woman I ever saw for taking the starch out of a man," he said, a little perplexed. Despite all the complications, he felt his old love for her returning with its old power. So much feeling flooded him, just looking at her, that he felt shaky. It was a puzzle to him that such a thing could happen, for it was true she had become rather bony and her face had thinned too much, and certainly she was as taxing as a woman could be. And yet the feeling made him shaky.

"Think I'm rough, Gus?" she asked with a smile.

"I ain't been scorched by lightning, but I doubt it could be hotter than being scorched by you," he said.

"Still think you'd have been up to being married to me?"

"I don't know," he said truthfully.

Clara laughed and took his arm to lead him downstairs.

"What about the young sheriff?" he asked, stopping her. He was unwilling to end their privacy so soon.

"What sheriff?"

"Why, July Johnson," he said. "It seems you've adopted him."

"I mainly wanted the baby, but I guess it's only fair to keep the father too," she said.

"Keep him and do what with him?"

"What do you care?" Clara said. "You're engaged. You can ride all over the country with a pretty girl, I guess I can be allowed a man. I'd forgotten how jealous you were. You were jealous of Jake and I did little more than flirt with Jake."

"To hear him talk, you did," Augustus said.

"Neither of us will hear him talk again," Clara said. "And I won't marry again."

"What makes you so sure?"

"I don't have enough respect for men," she said. "I've found very few who are honest, and you ain't one of the few."

"I'm about half honest," Augustus said.

"That's right," she said, and led him on downstairs.

To his surprise, Clara simply walked into the kitchen and invited Lorena to stay with them while the herd went on to Montana.

"We could use your help and you'd be more than welcome," she said. "Montana's no place for a lady."

Lorena blushed when she said it—no one had ever applied the word "lady" to her before. She knew she didn't deserve it. She wasn't a lady like Clara. She had never even met a lady like Clara, and in the space of a day had come to admire her more than she had ever admired anyone excepting Gus. Clara had shown her nothing but courtesy and had made her welcome in her house, whereas other respectable women had always shunned her because of the way she lived.

Sitting in the kitchen with the girls and the baby, Lorena felt happy in a way that was new to her. It stirred in her distant memories of the days she had spent in her grandmother's house in Mobile when she was four. Her grandmother's house had been like Clara's—she had gone there only once that she could remember. Her grandmother had put her in a soft bed, the softest she had ever slept in, and sung songs to her while she went to sleep. It was her happiest memory, one she treasured so, that in her years of traveling she grew almost afraid to remember it—someday she might try to remember it and find it gone. She was very afraid of losing her one good, warm memory. If she lost that, she felt she might be too sad to go on.

But in Clara's house she wasn't afraid to remember her grandmother, and the softness of the bed. Clara's house was the kind of house she thought she might live in someday—at least she had hoped to when she was little. But when her parents sickened and died, she lost hope of living in such a house. Mosby's home had been nothing like it, and then she had started living in hotels or little rooms. She slowly stopped thinking of nice houses and the things that went with them, such as little girls and babies.

So when Clara came downstairs and asked her to stay, it felt like being given back something—something that had been lost so long that she had ceased to think about it. Just before Clara and Gus came in, the girls had been nagging her to teach them how to sew. Lorena could sew fairly well. The girls complained that their mother never took the time to teach them. Their mother, about whom they were full of gripes, was more interested in horses than in sewing.

The girls were not at all surprised when Clara asked Lorena to stay.

"Oh, do," Sally said. "We could learn to sew if you would."

"We could sew new dresses, we never get any," Betsey said.

Lorena looked at Gus. He seemed flustered, and he seldom was flustered. She thought he might be bothered by the thought of her staying.

"Would you come back, Gus?" she asked. It seemed all right to ask him in front of Clara and the girls. Clara, after issuing the invitation, had started making coffee.

Augustus saw that she wanted to stay. If asked that morning if such a thing could occur, he would have said it was impossible. Lorena had clung to him since the rescue. But being at Clara's, even for so short a space, had changed her. She had refused to go to Ogallala, and was frightened of the thought of going into a store, but she wasn't frightened of Clara.

"I sure will come back," he said, smiling. "A ladies' man like me could hardly be expected to resist such a passel of ladies."

"Good, that's settled, but I warn you, Lorie, these girls will wear you down," Clara said. "You may wish you were back in a cow camp before it's all over. I'm going to turn them over to you, you know. All they want to do is quarrel with me, and I'm tired of it. You can argue with them, and I'll break horses."

After the coffee, Clara made the girls go to bed, and tactfully went up herself, so that Augustus and Lorena could have a moment alone. She saw that Augustus was a little shocked that she had so easily persuaded the girl away from his side.

Lorena felt embarrassed—she had not expected to be asked to stay, or to want to, and yet both things had happened. She was afraid at first that Gus might have his feelings hurt. She looked at him a little fearfully, hard put to explain the strange desire she had to stay at Clara's. Only that morning she had been resolved to stay with Gus at all costs.

"I'll go if you want, Gus," she said. "But it's so nice here, and they're friendly."

"I'm happy for you to stay," Augustus said. "You'll be a help to Clara, and you'll enjoy those girls. You've spent time enough in that dirty tent of Wilbarger's. Winter's said to be hard in Montana, too."

"I didn't think I'd want to stay," Lorena admitted. "I never thought about it till she asked. Don't you still want to marry her, Gus?"

"No," Augustus lied.

"I don't see why you wouldn't," she said. Now that she knew Clara a little, it seemed perfectly natural that Gus would want to marry her.

"Well, time's changed us," he said, feeling very uneasy in the conversation. Lorena was looking at him solemnly. He had had women look at him solemnly before and it always made him uncomfortable—it meant they were primed to detect any lies.

"I don't think nobody could change you, Gus," she said. "Maybe you'll want to marry her when you come back."

"Why, I'll be coming back to *you*, Lorie," Augustus said. "Of course, by then you might change, too. You might not want me."

"Why wouldn't I?"

"Because you'll have discovered there's more to the world than me," he said. "You'll find that there are others that treat you decent."

What he said caused Lorena to feel confused. Since the rescue, life had been simple: it had been just Gus. With him gone it might change, and when he came back it might have changed so much that it would never be simple again.

Yet when it had been simple, she had always worried that Gus didn't want it. Maybe he was just being kind. She didn't know—didn't know what things meant, or didn't mean. She had never expected to find, in the whole world, a place where someone would *ask* her to stay—even in her dreams of San Francisco no one had ever asked her to stay. She had seldom even spoken to a woman in her years in Lonesome Dove, and had no expectation that one would speak to her. The fact that Clara had volunteered made everything seem different.

"Can't you wait till morning to leave?" she asked.

"No, I'm going as soon as I can saddle up," Augustus said. "It takes willpower to leave a houseful of ladies just to ride along with some scraggly cowhands. I better do it now, if I'm going to."

Clara came downstairs to see him off; she held the baby, who was colicky and wakeful. They went outside with Augustus, Lorena feeling trembly, not sure of what she was doing. Cholo was going with him to Ogallala to bring back all the clothes he had bought her.

Clara devoted five minutes to trying to persuade him to settle somewhere on the Platte. "There's cheap land not three days' ride from here," she pointed out. "You could have the whole north part of this state if you wanted it. Why go to Montana?"

"Well, that's where we started for," he said. "Me and Call have always liked to get where we started for, even if it don't make a damn bit of sense."

"It don't, and I wish I knew of some way to divorce you from that man," Clara said. "He ain't worth it, Gus. Besides, the Montana Indians can outfight you."

"You bought these here Indians off with horses," he said. "Maybe we can buy those in Montana off with beef."

"It bothers me," Clara said. "You ain't a cattleman. Why do you want to be so stubborn? You've come far enough. You could settle around here and be some use to me and Lorie."

It amused Augustus that his Lorie had been adopted as an ally by his old love. The old love and the new stood by his horse's head, neither of them looking quite calm. Clara, in fact, was getting angry; Lorena looked sad. He hugged them both and gave them each a kiss.

"We've heard Montana's the last place that ain't settled," Augustus said. "I'd like to see one more place that ain't settled before I get decrepit and have to take up the rocking chair."

"You call Nebraska settled?" Clara asked.

"Well, you're here," he said. "It won't last long. Pretty soon it'll be nothing but schoolhouses."

With that he mounted, tipped his hat to them and turned toward the Platte.

The two women stood where they were until the sound of hoofbeats faded. Lorena felt wrong. Part of her felt she should have gone with him, to look after him. But she knew that was foolish: Gus, if anyone, could look after himself.

She was dry-eyed and felt blank, but Clara cried, tears born of vexation, long affection and regret.

"He was always stubborn like that," she said, attempting to control herself.

"He left so quick," Lorena said. "Do you think I should have gone? I don't know what's best."

"No. I'm glad you stayed," Clara said. "You've had enough rough living—not that it can't be rough around here. But it won't be as rough as Montana."

She put her arm around the girl as they turned toward the house.

"Come on in," she said. "I'll show you where to sleep. We've got a nice little room that might suit you."

89

WHEN AUGUSTUS RETURNED without Lorena, Dish Boggett felt deeply unhappy. It shocked him that Gus would leave her. Though he had been constantly jealous while she was traveling with Gus, at least she was there. In the evening he would often see her sitting outside the tent. He dreamed about her often—once had even dreamed that she was sleeping near him. In the dream she was so beautiful that he ached when he woke up. That Gus had seen fit to leave her on the Platte made him terribly irritable.

Newt was happy with his new horse, which he named Candy. It was the first real gift he had ever been given in his life, and he talked to anyone who would listen of the wonderful woman on the Platte who knew how to break horses and conduct picnics too. His enthusiasm soon caused the other hands to be jealous, for they had accomplished nothing except a drunk in Ogallala, and had missed the nice picnic and the girls.

Though confident that he had done the right thing in leaving Lorena, Augustus soon found that he missed her more than he had expected to. He missed Clara, too, and for a few days was in a surly mood. He had grown accustomed to sleeping late and sitting outside the tent with Lorena in the mornings. Alone on the long plain, with no cowboys to disturb her, she was a beautiful companion, whereas the cowboys who gathered around Po Campo's cookfire every morning were far from beautiful, in his view.

It was high summer, the days blazing hot almost until the sun touched the horizon. The cattle were mulish and hard to move, stopping whenever possible to graze, or simply to stand. For several days they trailed west along the Platte, but when the river curved south, toward Colorado, Call pointed the herd northwest.

Po Campo hated to leave the river. The morning they left it he lingered behind so long with the wagon that the herd was completely out of sight. Lippy, who rode on the wagon, found this fact alarming. After all, they were in Indian country, and there was nothing to keep a few Indians from nipping in and taking their scalps.

"What are we waiting on?" Lippy asked. "We're three miles behind already."

Po Campo stood by the water's edge, looking across the Platte to the south. He was thinking of his dead sons, killed by Blue Duck on the Canadian. He didn't think often of his sons, but when he did, a feeling of sadness filled him, a feeling so heavy that it was an effort for him to move. Thinking of them in their graves in New Mexico made him feel disloyal, made him feel that he should have shot himself and been buried with them, for was it not the duty of a parent to stay with the children? But he had left, first to go south and kill his faithless wife, and now to the north, while Blue Duck, the killer, still rode free on the *llano*—unless someone had killed him, which Po Campo doubted. Lippy's fears about Indians did not move him—the sight of flowing water moved him, stirring feelings in him which, though sad, were deep feelings. They made him want to sing his saddest songs.

He finally turned and plodded after the herd, Lippy following at a slow walk in the wagon. But Po Campo felt they were wrong to leave the river. He became moody and ceased to have pride in his cooking, and if the cowboys complained he said nothing. Also, he grew stingy with water, which irritated the cowboys, who came in parched and dusty, dying for a drink. Po Campo would only give them a dipperful each.

"You will wish you had this water when you drink your own piss," he said to Jasper one evening.

"I ain't planning on drinking my own piss or anybody else's, either," Jasper said.

"You have not been very thirsty then," Po said. "I once drank the urine of a mule. It kept me alive."

"Well, it couldn't taste much worse than that Ogallala beer," Needle observed. "My tongue's been peeling ever since we was there."

"It ain't what you drink that causes your tongue to peel," Augustus said. "That's the result of who you bedded down with."

The remark caused much apprehension among the men, and they were apprehensive anyway, mainly because everyone they met in Ogallala assured them they were dead men if they tried to go to Montana. As they edged into Wyoming the country grew bleaker—the grass was no longer as luxuriant as it had been in Kansas and Nebraska. To the north were sandy slopes where the grass only grew in tufts. Deets ranged far ahead during the day, looking for water. He always found it, but the streams grew smaller and the water more alkaline. "Near as bad as the Pecos," Augustus said.

Call seemed only mildly concerned about the increasing dryness. Indeed, Call was cheerful, easier on the men than was his wont. He seemed relaxed and almost at ease with himself.

"Have you cheered up because I left Lorie behind?" Augustus asked as they were riding together one morning. Far to the south they saw a black line of mountains. To the north there was only the dusty plain.

"That was your business," Call said. "I didn't tell you to leave her behind, though I'm sure it's the best thing."

"I think we ought to have listened to our cook," Augustus said. "It's looking droughty to me."

"If we can make Powder River I guess we'll be all right," Call said.

"What if Jake lied to us?" Augustus said. "What if Montana ain't the paradise he said it was? We'll have come a hell of a way for nothing."

"I want to see it," Call said. "We'll be the first to graze cattle on it. Don't that interest you?"

"Not much," Augustus said. "I've watched these goddamn cattle graze all I want to."

The next day Deets came back from his scout looking worried. "Dry as a bone, Captain," he said.

"How far did you go?"

"Twenty miles and more," Deets said.

The plain ahead was white with heat. Of course, the cattle could make twenty miles, though it would be better to wait a day and drive them at night.

"I was told if we went straight west we'd strike Salt Creek and could follow it to the Powder," Call said. "It can't be too far."

"It don't take much to be too far, in this heat," Augustus said.

"Try going due north," Call said.

Deets changed horses and left. It was well after dark when he reappeared. Call stopped the herd, and the men lounged around the wagon, playing cards. While they played, the Texas bull milled through the cows, now and then mounting one. Augustus kept one eye on his cards and one eye on the bull, keeping a loose count of his winnings and of the bull's.

"That's six he's had since we started playing," he said. "That sucker's got more stamina than me."

"More opportunity, too," Allen O'Brien observed. He had adjusted quite well to the cowboy life, but he still could not forget Ireland. When he thought of his little wife he would break into tears of homesickness, and the songs he sung to the cattle would often remind him of her.

When Deets returned it was to report that there was no water to the north. "No antelope, Captain," he said. The plains of western Nebraska had been spotted with them.

"I'll have a look in the morning," Call said. "You rest, Deets."

He found he couldn't sleep, and rose at three to saddle the Hell Bitch. Po Campo was up, stirring the coals of his cookfire, but Call only took a cup of coffee.

"Have you been up here before?" he asked. The old cook's wanderings had been a subject of much speculation among the men. Po Campo was always letting slip tantalizing bits of information. Once, for example, he had described the great gorge of the Columbia River. Again, he had casually mentioned Jim Bridger.

"No," Po Campo said. "I don't know this country. But I'll tell you this, it is dry. Water your horse before you leave."

Call thought the old man rather patronizing—he knew enough to water a horse before setting off into a desert.

"Don't wait supper," he said.

All day he rode west, and the country around him grew more bleak. Not fit for sheep, Call thought. Not hardly fit for lizards—in fact, a small gray lizard was the only life he saw all day. That night he made a dry camp in sandy country where the dirt was light-colored, almost white. He supposed he had come some sixty miles and could not imagine that the herd would make it that far, although the Hell Bitch seemed unaffected. He slept for a few hours and went on, arriving just after sunup on the banks of Salt Creek. It was not running, but there was adequate water in scattered shallow pools. The water was not good, but it was water. The trouble was, the herd was nearly eighty miles back—a four-day drive under normal conditions; and in this case the miles were entirely waterless, which wouldn't make for normal conditions.

Call rested the mare and let her have a good roll. Then he started back and rode almost straight through, only stopping once for two hours' rest. He arrived in camp at midmorning to find most of the hands still playing cards.

When he unsaddled the mare, one of Augustus's pigs grunted at him. Both of them were lying under the wagon, sharing the shade with Lippy, who was sound asleep. The shoat was a large pig now, but travel had kept him thin. Call felt it was slightly absurd having pigs along on a cattle drive, but they had proven good foragers as well as good swimmers. They got across the rivers without any help.

Augustus was oiling his rifle. "How far did you ride that horse?" he asked.

"To the next water and back," Call said. "Did you ever see a horse like her? She ain't even tired."

"How far is it to water?" Augustus asked.

"About eighty miles," Call said. "What do you think?"

"I ain't give it no thought at all, so far," Augustus said.

"We can't just sit here," Call said.

"Oh, we could," Augustus said. "We could have stopped pretty much anywhere along the way. It's only your stubbornness kept us going this long. I guess it'll be interesting to see if it can get us the next eighty miles."

Call got a plate and ate a big meal. He expected Po Campo to say something about their predicament, but the old cook merely dished out the food and said nothing. Deets was helping Pea Eye trim one of his horse's feet, a task Pea Eye had never been good at.

"Find the water, Captain?" Deets asked, smiling.

"I found it, 'bout eighty miles away," Call said.

"That's far," Pea Eye said.

They had stopped the cattle at the last stream that Deets had found, and now Call walked down it a way to think things over. He saw a gray wolf. It seemed to him to be the same wolf they had seen in Nebraska, after the picnic, but he told himself that was foolish speculation. A gray wolf wouldn't follow a cattle herd.

Deets finished trimming the horse's hooves and wiped the sweat off his face with his shirtsleeve. Pea Eye stood silently nearby. Though the two of them had soldiered together for most of their lives, they had never really had a conversation. It had seemed unnecessary. They exchanged information, and that was about it. Pea, indeed, had always been a little doubtful of the propriety of talking to Negroes, although he liked and respected Deets and was grateful to him now for trimming the horse's feet. He knew Deets was a great deal more competent than he was in many areas—tracking, for example. He knew that if it had not been for Deets's skill in finding water they might have all starved years before in campaigns on the *llano*. He knew, too, that Deets had risked his life a number of times to save his, and yet, standing there side by side, the only thing he could think of to talk about was the Captain's great love for the Hell Bitch.

"Well, he's mighty fond of that horse," he said. "And she might kill him yet."

"She ain't gonna kill the Captain," Deets said. He had the sad sense that things were not right. It seemed they were going to go north forever, and he couldn't think why. Life had been orderly and peaceful in Texas. He himself had particularly enjoyed his periodic trips to San Antonio to deposit money. Texas had always been their country, and it was a puzzle to him why they were going to a country that would probably be so wild there wouldn't even be banks to take money to.

"We way up here and it ain't our country," he said, looking at Pea. That was the heart of it—best to stay in your own country and not go wandering off where you didn't know the rivers or the water holes.

"Now up here, it's gonna be cold," he added, as if that were proof enough of the folly of their trip.

"Well, I hope we get there before the rivers start icing," Pea said. "I always worry about that thin ice."

With that he turned away, and the lengthy conversation was over.

By midafternoon Call came back from his walk and decided they would go ahead. It was go ahead or go back, and he didn't mean to go back. It wasn't rational to think of driving cattle over eighty waterless miles, but he had learned in his years of tracking Indians that things which seemed impossible often weren't. They only became so if one thought about them too much so that fear took over. The thing to do was go. Some of the cattle might not make it, but then, he had never expected to reach Montana with every head.

He told the cowboys to push the cattle and horses onto water and hold them there.

Without saying a word, Augustus walked over, took off his clothes, and had a long bath in the little stream. The cowboys holding the herd could see him sitting in the shallow water, now and then splashing some of his long white hair.

"Sometimes I think Gus is crazy," Soupy Jones said. "Why is he sitting in the water?"

"Maybe he's fishing," Dish Boggett said facetiously. He had no opinion of Soupy Jones and saw no reason why Gus shouldn't bathe if he wanted to.

Augustus came walking back to the wagon with his hair dripping.

"It looks like sandy times ahead," he said. "Call, you got too much of the prophet in you. You're always trying to lead us into the deserts."

"Well, there's water there," Call said. "I seen it. If we can get them close enough that they can smell it, they'll go. How far do you think a cow can smell water?"

"Not no eighty miles," Augustus said.

They started the herd two hours before sundown and drove all night through the barren country. The hands had made night drives before and were glad to be traveling in the cool. Most of them expected, though, that Call would stop for breakfast, but he didn't. He rode ahead of the herd and kept on going. Some of the hands were beginning to feel empty. They kept looking hopefully for a sign that Call might slacken and let Po Campo feed them—but Call didn't slacken. They kept the cattle moving until midday, by which time some of the weaker cattle were already lagging well behind. The leaders were tired and acting fractious.

Finally Call did stop. "We'll rest a little until it starts to get cool," he said. "Then we'll drive all night again. That ought to put us close."

He wasn't sure, though. For all their effort, they had covered only some thirty-five or forty miles. It would be touch and go.

Late that afternoon, while the cowboys were lying around resting, a wind sprang up from the west. From the first, it was as hot as if it were blowing over coals. By the time Call was ready to start the herd again, the wind had risen and they faced a full-fledged sandstorm. It blew so hard that the cattle were reluctant to face it.

Newt, with the Rainey boys, was holding the drags, as usual. The wind howled across the flat plain, and the sand seemed to sing as it skimmed the ground. Newt found that looking into the wind blinded him almost instantly. He mostly ducked his head and kept his eyes shut. The horses didn't like the sand either. They began to duck and jump around, irritated at being forced into such a wind.

"This is bad luck," Augustus said to Call. He adjusted his bandana over his nose and he pulled his hat down as far as it would go.

"We can't stop here," Call said. "We ain't but halfway to water."

"Yes, and some of them will still be halfway when this blows itself out," Augustus said.

Call helped Lippy and the cook tie down everything on the wagon. Lippy, who hated wind, looked frightened; Po Campo said nothing.

"You better ride tonight," Call said to Po Campo. "If you try to walk you might get lost."

"We all might get lost tonight," Po Campo said. He took an old ax handle that he sometimes used as a cane and walked, but at least he consented to walk right with the wagon.

None of the men—no strangers to sandstorms—could remember such a sunset. The sun was like a dying coal, ringed with black long before it neared the horizon. After it set, the rim of the earth was blood-red for a few minutes, then the red was streaked with black. The afterglow was quickly snuffed out by the sand. Jasper Fant wished for the thousandth time that he had stayed in Texas. Dish Boggett was troubled by the sensation that there was a kind of river of sand flowing above his head. When he looked up in the eerie twilight, he seemed to see it, as if somehow the world had turned over and the road that ought to be beneath his feet was now over his head. If the wind stopped, he felt, the sand river would fall and bury him.

Call told them to keep as close to the cattle as possible and to keep the cattle moving. Any cattle that wandered far would probably starve to death.

Augustus thought the order foolish. "The only way to keep this herd together would be to string a rope around them—and we ain't got that much rope," he said.

Shortly after dark he was proven right. None of the animals wanted to go into the wind. It quickly became necessary for the cowboys to cover their horses' eyes with jackets or shirts; and despite the hands' precautions, little strings of cattle began to stray. Newt tried unsuccessfully to turn back two bunches, but the cattle paid him no mind, even when he bumped them with his horse. Finally he let them go, feeling guilty as he did it but not guilty enough to risk getting lost himself. He knew if he lost the herd he was probably done for; he knew it was a long way to water and he might not be able to find it, even though he was riding the good sorrel that Clara had given him.

Call felt sick with worry—the sandstorm was the worst possible luck, for it slowed down the herd and sapped the animals' strength just when they needed all they had just to reach the water. And yet there was nothing he could do about it. He tried to tie an old shirt around the Hell Bitch's eyes, but she shook him off so vigorously that he finally let it go.

At the height of the storm it seemed as if the herd might split into fragments. It was hard to see ten feet, and little bunches of cattle broke off unnoticed and slipped past the cowboys. Deets, more confident of his ability to find his way around than most, rode well west of the herd, turning back cattle whenever he found any. But it finally became pitch-dark, and even Deets could do nothing.

Augustus rode through the storm with a certain indifference, thinking of the two women he had just left. He took no interest in the straying cattle. That was Call's affair. He felt he himself deserved to be in the middle of a sandstorm on the Wyoming plain for being such a fool as to leave the women. Not a man to feel guilty, he was merely annoyed at himself for what he considered a misjudgment.

To Call's great relief, the storm blew itself out in three hours. The wind gradually died and the sand lay under their feet again instead of peppering them. The moon was soon visible, and the sky filled with bright stars. It would not be possible to judge how many cattle had strayed until the morning, but at least the main herd was still under their control.

But the storm and the long drive the day before had taken its toll in energy. By dawn, half the men were asleep in their saddles. They wanted to stop, but again Call pushed on; he knew they had lost ground, and was not going to stop just because the men were sleepy. All morning he rode through the herd, encouraging the men to push the cattle. He was not sure how far they had come, but he knew they still had a full day to go. Lack of water was beginning to tell on the horses, and the weaker cattle were barely stumbling along.

Deets alone brought back most of the strayed bunches, none of which had strayed very far. The plain was so vast and flat that the cattle were visible for miles, at least to Augustus and Deets, the eyesight champions.

"There's a bunch you missed," Augustus said, pointing to the northwest. Deets looked, nodded, and rode away. Jasper Fant looked and saw nothing but heat waves and blue sky. "I guess I need spectacles," he said. "I can't see nothing but nothing."

"Weak brains breed weak eyesight," Augustus said.

"We all got weak brains or we wouldn't be here," Soupy said sourly. He had grown noticeably more discontented in recent weeks—no one knew why.

Finally at noon Call stopped. The effort to move the drags was wearing out the horses. When the cowboys got to the wagon, most of them took a cup of water and dropped sound asleep on the ground, not bothering with bedrolls or even saddle blankets. Po Campo rationed the water carefully, giving each man only three swallows. Newt felt that he could have drunk a thousand swallows. He had never tasted anything so delicious. He had never supposed plain water could be so desirable. He remembered all the times he had carelessly drunk his fill. If he ever got another chance, he meant to enjoy it more.

Call let them rest three hours and then told them to get their best mounts. Some of the cattle were so weak the cowboys had to dismount, pull their tails and shout at them to get them up. Call knew that if they didn't make it on the next push, they would have to abandon the cattle in order to save the horses. Even after their rest, many of the cattle had their tongues hanging out. They were mulish, reluctant to move, but after much effort on the part of the exhausted men, the drive was started again.

Through the late afternoon and far into the night the cattle stumbled over the plain, the weaker cattle falling farther and farther behind. By daybreak the herd was strung out to a distance of more than five miles, most of the men plodding along as listlessly as the cattle. The day was as hot as any they remembered from south Texas—the distances that had spawned yesterday's wind refused to yield even a breeze, and it seemed to the men that the last moisture in their bodies was pouring out as sweat. They all yearned for evening and looked at the sun constantly, but the sun seemed as immobile as if suspended by a wire.

Toward midday many of the cattle began to turn back toward the water they had left two days before. Newt, struggling with a bunch, nearly got knocked off his horse by three steers that walked right into him. He noticed, to his shock, that the cattle didn't seem to see him—they were stumbling along, white-eyed. Appalled, he rode over to the Captain.

"Captain, they're going blind," he said.

Call looked grim. "It ain't real blindness," he said. "They get that way when they're real thirsty. They'll try to go back to the last water."

He told the men to forget the weaker cattle and try to keep the stronger ones moving.

"We ought to make the water by night," he said.

"If we make night," Augustus said.

"We can't just stop and die," Call said.

"I don't intend to," Augustus said. "But some of the men might. That Irishman is delirious. He ain't used to such dry country."

Indeed the terrible heat had driven Allen O'Brien out of his head. Now and then he would try to sing, though his tongue was swollen and his lips cracked.

"You don't need to sing," Call said.

Allen O'Brien looked at him angrily. "I need to cry, but I've got no tears," he said. "This goddamn country has burned up my tears."

Call had been awake for over three days, and he began to feel confused himself. He knew water couldn't be much farther, but, all the same, fatigue made him doubtful. Perhaps it had been a hundred miles rather than eighty. They would never make it, if so. He tried to remember, searching his mind for details that would suggest how far the river might be, but there were precious few landmarks on the dry plain, and the harder he concentrated the more his mind seemed to slip. He was riding the Hell Bitch, but for long moments he imagined he was riding old Ben again—a mule he had relied on frequently during his campaigning on the *llano*. Ben had had an infallible sense of direction and a fine nose for water. He wasn't fast but he was sure. At the time, some men had scoffed at him for riding a mule, but Call ignored them. The stakes were life or death, and Ben was the most reliable animal he had ever seen, if far from the prettiest.

The men had had the last of Po Campo's water that morning, barely enough to wet their tongues. Po Campo doled it out with severity, careful to see that no one got more than his share. Though the old man had walked the whole distance, using his ax-handle cane, he seemed not particularly tired.

Call, though, was so tired he felt his mind slipping. Try as he might, he couldn't stay awake. Once he slept for a few steps, then jerked awake, convinced he was fighting again the battle of Fort Phantom Hill. He looked around for Indians, but saw only the thirst-blinded cattle, their long tongues hanging out, their breath rasping. His mind slipped again, and when he awoke next it was dark. The Hell Bitch was trotting. When he opened his eyes he saw the Texas bull trot past him. He reached for his reins, but they were not there. His hands were empty. Then, to his amazement, he saw that Deets had taken his reins and was leading the Hell Bitch.

No one had ever led his horse before. Call felt embarrassed. "Here, I'm awake," he said, his voice just a whisper.

Deets stopped and gave him his reins. "Didn't want you to fall and get left, Captain," he said. "The water ain't far now."

That was evident from the quickened pace of the cattle, from the way the horses began to prick their ears. Call tried to shake the sleep off, but it was as if he were stuck in it. He could see, but it took a great effort to move, and he wasn't immediately able to resume command.

Augustus loped up, seemingly fresh. "We better get everybody to the front," he said. "We'll need to try and spread them when they hit the water. Otherwise they'll all pile into the first mudhole and tromple themselves."

Most of the cattle were too weak to run, but they broke into a trot. Call finally shook the sleep off and helped Dish and Deets and Augustus split the herd. They were only partially successful. The cattle were moving like a blind army, the scent of water in their nostrils. Fortunately they hit the river above where Call had hit it, and there was more water. The cattle spread of their own accord.

Call had not recovered from his embarrassment at having been led. Yet he knew Deets had done the right thing. He had still been dreaming of Ben and that hot day at Phantom Hill, and if he had slipped off his horse he might just have laid there and slept. But it was the first time in his life he had not been able to last through a task in command of his wits, and it bothered him.

All during the night and the next day, cattle straggled into the river, some of them cattle Call had supposed would merely become carcasses, rotting on the trail. Yet a day on the water worked wonders for them. Augustus and Dish made counts, once the stragglers stopped coming, and it appeared they had only lost six head.

The Irishman spent most of the day sitting in a puddle in Salt Creek, recovering from his delirium. He could not remember having been delirious and grew angry when the others kidded him about it. Newt, who had planned to drink all day once he got to water, soon found that he couldn't drink any more. He devoted his leisure to complicated games of mumblety-peg with the Rainey boys.

Deets went on a scout and reported that the country to the west didn't improve—grass was as scarce as water in that direction. Far to the north they could see the outlines of mountains, and there was much talk about which mountains they were.

"Why, the Rocky Mountains," Augustus said.

"Will we have to climb them?" Jasper asked. He had survived rivers and drought, but did not look forward to climbing mountains.

"No," Call said. "We'll go north, up the Powder River, right into Montana."

"How many days will it take now?" Newt asked. He had almost forgotten that Montana was a real place that they might get to someday.

"I expect three weeks or a little more and we might hit the Yellowstone," Call said.

"The Yellowstone already?" Dish Boggett said. It was the last river—or at least the last river anyone knew much about. At mention of it the whole camp fell silent, looking at the mountains.

90

THEY RESTED ON the Salt for two days, giving the animals and men plenty of time to recover. The men spent much of their time speculating about what lay on beyond the mountains, and how long it would take to get there.

Call slept a distance out of camp, as was his habit. He knew the men were in a good mood, for he could hear them singing most of the night. Now that he had the leisure to sleep, he found he couldn't, much. He had always thought his energies equal to any situation, but he had begun to have doubts. A tiredness clung to his bones, but not a tiredness that produced sleep. He felt played out, and wished they were already in Montana. There were only a few hundred miles left, but it seemed farther to him than all the distance they had come.

Trotting back into camp one morning he saw there was excitement around the cook fire. Several of the men were holding rifles. The sight surprised him, for it had seemed a peaceful night.

"Twelve horses are gone, Captain," Dish Boggett said. "Indians got 'em."

Deets was looking hangdog, and the Spettle boy could only shake his head. Neither of them had heard a thing, they said.

"Well, you boys was singing opry loud enough to wake the deaf," Augustus remarked. "I guess it was just their charity that they didn't take the whole herd. Nobody would have noticed."

Call was vexed. He had been awake almost all night and had had no suspicion of Indians. All his years of trying to stay prepared hadn't helped. "They must have been good with horses," he said.

Deets felt it was mainly his fault, since it was his job to watch for Indian sign. He had always had a good ear for Indians, but he had sat by the wagon, listening to the singing, and had heard nothing.

"They came on foot, Captain," he said. He had found their tracks, at least.

"That was bold," Call said. "But they ain't on foot now."

He decided to take only Augustus and Deets, though that left the camp without a really competent Indian fighter, in case the raid was a feint. On the other hand, whoever took the horses might have a good deal of help nearby. If it became necessary to take on an Indian camp, three men were about the minimum that could expect to succeed.

Ten minutes later the three men were ready to go. Call was well aware that they were leaving a camp full of scared men.

Augustus laughed at the sight. "You boys will get the drizzles if you don't relax," he said.

"If they got the dern horses they might decide to come back and get us," Jasper Fant pointed out. "They got Custer, didn't they? And he fought Indians his whole life."

Call was more worried about the grass situation. It was too sparse to support the herd for long.

"Graze 'em upriver," he said. "Start tomorrow if we ain't back, but don't push 'em. Just let 'em graze along. You'll make the Powder in a few days."

Newt felt very nervous when he saw the three men ride off. It was Lippy's fault that he felt so nervous—all morning Lippy had done nothing but talk about how it felt to be scalped. Lippy hadn't been scalped, and couldn't possibly know, but that didn't keep him from talking and scaring everybody.

The horsethieves had gone southwest. Call thought that with luck they might catch them within a day, but in that he was disappointed. The country grew more barren as they rode, and the only sign of life was an occasional buzzard and many, many rattlesnakes.

"If we was to settle around here we'd have to start a snake ranch," Augustus said.

They rested only a little while at night, and by midmorning of the next day were a hundred miles from the herd, with no results in sight.

"Hell, they'll be to the Wind River before we catch them," Augustus said. "I've always heard the Wind River country was worse than the Pecos country, when it comes to being dry."

"We're better mounted than they are," Call said. "We'll catch them."

It was another long day, though, before they closed the gap.

"You sure this is worth it for twelve horses?" Augustus asked. "This is the poorest dern country I ever saw. A chigger would starve to death out here."

Indeed, the land was bleak, the surface sometimes streaked with salt. There were ocher-colored ridges here and there, completely free of grass.

"We can't start putting up with horse theft," Call said.

Deets was ranging ahead, and in the afternoon they saw him coming back. The simmering heat waves made him appear larger than he was.

"Camp's up ahead," he said. "They're in a draw, with a little water."

"How many?" Call asked.

"Didn't get no count," Deets said. "Not many. Couldn't be many and live out here."

"I say we wait for night and steal the nags back," Augustus said. "It's too hot to fight. Steal 'em back and let the red man chase the white for a while."

"If we wait for night we might lose half the horses," Call said. "They'll probably post a better guard than we had."

"I don't want to argue with you in this heat," Augustus said. "If you want to go now, okay. We'll just ride in and massacre them."

"Didn't see many men," Deets said. "Mostly women and children. They're real poor, Captain."

"What do you mean, real poor?"

"Means they're starving," Deets said. "They done cut up one horse."

"My God," Augustus said. "You mean they stole them horses for meat?"

That proved to be the case. They carefully approached the draw where the camp was and saw the whole little tribe gathered around the dead horse. There were only some twenty Indians, mostly women, children and old men. Call saw only two braves who looked to be of fighting age, and they were no more than boys. The Indians had pulled the dead horse's guts out and were hacking them into slices and eating them. Usually there were dogs around an Indian camp, but there were no dogs around this time.

"I guess these ain't the mighty plains Indians we've been hearing about," Augustus said. The whole little tribe was almost silent, each person concentrating on eating. They were all thin. Two old women were cutting meat off the haunch, meaning to dry it, and two young men, probably the ones who had stolen the horses, had caught another and were preparing to cut its throat. To prevent this, Call drew his pistol and fired into the air.

"Oh, let's go," Augustus said. "We don't want to be shooting these people, although it would probably be a mercy. I don't think they even have guns."

"I didn't shoot nobody," Call said. "But they're our horses."

At the shot the whole tribe looked up, stunned. One of the young men grabbed an old single-shot rifle but didn't fire. It seemed to be the only firearm the tribe possessed. Call fired in the air again, to scare them away from the horse, and succeeded better than he had expected to. Those who had been eating got to their feet, some with sections of gut still in their hands, and fled toward the four small ragged tepees that stood up the draw. The young man with the gun retreated too, helping one of the older women. She was bloody from the feast.

"They were just having a picnic," Augustus said. "We had a picnic the other day without nobody shooting at us."

"We can leave them two or three horses," Call said. "I just don't want to lose that sorrel they were about to kill."

In the tribe's flight a child had been forgotten—a little boy barely old enough to walk. He stood near the neck of the dead horse, crying, trying to find his mother. The tribe huddled in front of the tepees, silent. The only sound, for a moment, was the sound of the child's crying.

"He blind," Deets said.

Augustus saw that it was true. The child couldn't see where he was going, and a second later tripped over a pile of bloody horse guts, falling into them.

Deets, who was closest to the dead horse, walked over and picked the child up. The little blind boy kept wailing.

"Hush now," Deets said. "You a mess. You done rolled in all that blood."

At that moment there was a wild yell from the tepees and Deets looked up to see one of the young braves rushing toward him. He was the one who had picked up the rifle, but he had discarded the rifle and was charging with an old lance, crying his battle cry. Deets held out the baby and smiled—the young man, no older than Newt, didn't need to cry any battle cry. Deets kept holding the baby out toward the tribe and smiling, trusting that the young brave would realize he was friendly. The young man didn't need his lance—he could just take the squalling baby back to its mother.

Call and Augustus thought too that the young man would probably stop once he saw that Deets meant no harm. If not, Deets could whop him—Deets was a good hand-to-hand fighter.

It was only at the last second that they both realized that the Indian wasn't going to stop. His charge was desperate, and he didn't notice that Deets was friendly. He closed at a run.

"Shoot him, Deets!" Call yelled, raising his own gun.

Deets saw, too, at the last second, that the boy wasn't going to stop. The young warrior wasn't blind, but the look in his eyes was as unseeing as the baby's. He was still screaming a war cry—it was unnerving in the stillness—and his eyes were filled with hate. The old lance just looked silly. Deets held the baby out again, thinking the boy hadn't understood.

"Here, take him, I just helping him up," he said. Only then he saw it was too late—the young man couldn't stop coming and couldn't stop hating, either. His eyes were wild with hatred. Deets felt a deep regret that he should be hated so by this thin boy when he meant no harm. He tried to sidestep, hoping to gain a moment so he could set the baby down and wrestle with the Indian and maybe calm him.

But when Deets turned, the boy thrust the lance straight into his side and up into his chest.

Call and Augustus shot almost at the same time—the boy died with his hands still on the lance. They ran down to Deets, who still had the baby in his hands, although he had over a foot of lance inside him.

"Would you take him, Captain?" Deets asked, handing Call the child. "I don't want to sit him back in all that blood."

Then Deets dropped to his knees. He noticed with surprise that the young Indian was near him, already dead. For a moment he feared that somehow he had killed him, but then he saw that his own gun was still holstered. It must have been the Captain, or Mr. Gus. That was a sad thing, that the boy had had to die just because he couldn't understand that they were friendly. It was one more regret— probably the boy had just been so hungry he couldn't think straight.

Then he realized that he was on his knees and tried to get up, but Mr. Gus put a hand on his shoulder and asked him to wait.

"No, you don't have to get up yet, Deets," Augustus said. "Just rest a minute."

Deets noticed the handle of the lance protruding from his side. He knew the dead boy had put it there, but he felt nothing. The Captain stood in front of him, awkwardly holding the Indian baby. Deets looked at the Captain sadly. He hoped that now the Captain would see that he had been right to feel worried about leaving Texas. It was a mistake, coming into other people's country. It only disturbed them and led to things like the dead boy. People wouldn't understand, wouldn't know that they were friendly.

It would have been so much better to stay where they had lived, by the old river. Deets felt a longing to be back, to sit in the corrals at night and wonder about the moon. Many a time he had dozed off, wondering about the moon, whether the Indians had managed to get on it. Sometimes he dreamed he was on it himself—a foolish dream. But the thought made him sleepy, and with one more look of regret at the dead boy who hadn't understood that he meant no harm, he carefully lay down on his side. Mr. Gus knelt beside him. For a moment Deets thought he was going to try to pull the lance out, but all he did was steady it so the handle wouldn't quiver.

"Where's little Newt?" Deets asked.

"Well, Newt didn't come, Deets," Augustus said. "He's with the boys."

Then it seemed to Deets that something was happening to Mr. Gus's head. It had grown larger. He couldn't see it all well. It was as if he were looking through water—as if he had come back to the old river and were lying on the bottom, looking at Mr. Gus through the shallow brown water. Mr. Gus's head had grown larger, was floating off. It was rising toward the sky like the moon. He could barely see it and then couldn't see it at all, but the waters parted for a moment and he saw a blade or two of grass, close to his eye; then to his relief the brown waters came back and covered him again, deep this time and warm.

"Can't you take that lance out?" Call asked. He didn't know what to do with the baby, and there Deets lay dying.

"I will in a minute, Call," Augustus said. "Just let him be dead for a minute."

"Is he dead already?" Call asked. Though he knew from long experience that such things happened quickly, he could not accept it in Deets's case. "I guess it went to the heart," he added pointlessly.

Augustus didn't answer. He was resting for a moment, wondering if he could get the lance out or if he should just break it off or what. If he pulled it out he might bring half of Deets out with it. Of course Deets was dead—in a way, it didn't matter. Yet it did—if there was one thing he didn't want to do, it was tear Deets up.

"Can't you give that squalling baby to the women?" he asked. "Just set it down over there and maybe they'll come and get it."

Call took a few steps toward the huddled Indians, holding out the baby. None of the Indians moved. He went a few more steps and set the baby on the ground. When he turned back he saw Augustus put a foot against Deets's side and try to remove the lance, which did not budge.

Augustus gave up and sat down beside the dead man. "I can't do this today, Deets," he said. "Somebody else will have to do it if it gets done."

Call also knelt down by Deets's body. He could not get over his surprise. Though he had seen hundreds of surprising things in battle, this was the most shocking. An Indian boy who probably hadn't been fifteen years old had run up to Deets and killed him.

It must have shocked Augustus just as much, because he didn't have anything to say.

"I guess it's our fault," Call said. "We should have shot sooner."

"I don't want to start thinking about all the things we should have done for this man," Augustus said. "If you've got the strength to ride, let's get out of here."

They managed to break the lance off so it wouldn't wave in the air, and loaded Deets's body on his horse. While Augustus was tying the body securely, Call rounded up the horses. The Indians watched him silently. He changed his mind and cut off three of the horses that were of little account anyway. He rode over to the Indians.

"You better tie them three," he said. "Otherwise they'll follow us."

"I doubt they speak English, Woodrow," Augustus said. "I imagine they speak Ute. Anyway, we killed their best warrior; they're done for now unless they find some better country. Three horses won't last them through the winter."

He looked around at the parched country, the naked ridges where the earth had split from drought. The ridges were varicolored, smudged with red and salt-white splotches, as if the fluids of the earth had leaked out through the cracks.

"Montana better not be nothing like this," he said. "If it is, I'm going back and dig up that goddamn Jake Spoon and scatter his bones."

They rode all night, all the next day and into the following night. Augustus just rode, his mind mostly blank, but Call was sick with self-reproach. All his talk of being ready, all his preparation—and then he had just walked up to an Indian camp and let Josh Deets get killed. He had known better. They all knew better. He had known men killed by Indian boys no older than ten, and by old Indian women who looked as if they could barely walk. Any Indian might kill you: that was the first law of the Rangers. And yet they had just walked in, and now Josh Deets was gone. He had never called the man by his first name, but now he remembered Gus's foolish sign and how Deets had been troubled by it. Deets had finally concluded that his first name was Josh—that was the way he would think of him from then on, Call decided. He had been Josh Deets. It deepened his sense of reproach that, only a few days before, Josh Deets had been so thoughtful as to lead his horse through the sandstorm, recognizing that he himself was played out.

Then he had stood there with a rifle in his hands and let the man be killed. They had all concluded the Indians were too starved down to do anything. It was a mistake he would never forgive himself.

"I think he knowed it was coming," Augustus said, to Call's surprise, as they rode through the cracked valleys toward the Salt Creek.

"What do you mean, knowed it?" Call asked. "He didn't know it. It was just that one boy who showed any fight."

"I think he knowed it," Augustus said. "He just stood there waiting."

"He had that baby in his hands," Call reminded him.

"He could have dropped that baby," Augustus said.

They came back the second night to where the herd had been, only to find it gone. Josh Deets had begun to smell.

"We could bury him here," Augustus said.

Call looked around at the empty range.

"We ain't gonna find no churchyard, if that's what you're looking for," Augustus said.

"Let's take him on," Call said. "The men will want to pay their respects. I imagine we can catch them tonight."

They caught the herd not long before dawn. Dish Boggett was the night herder who saw them coming. He was very relieved, for with both of them gone, the herd had been his responsibility. Since he didn't know the country, it was a heavy responsibility, and he had been hoping the bosses would get back soon. When he saw them he felt a little proud of himself, for he had kept the cattle on grass and had moved them along nicely.

"Mornin', Captain," he said. Then he noticed that something was wrong. There were three horses, not counting the stolen ones, but only two riders. There was something on the third horse, but it wasn't a rider. It was only a body.

"Who's that, Gus?" he asked, startled.

"It's what's left of Deets," Augustus said. "I hope the cook's awake." After feeling nothing for two days, he had begun to feel hungry.

Newt had taken the middle watch and was sleeping soundly when dawn broke. He was using his saddle for a pillow and had covered himself with a saddle blanket as the nights had begun to be quite cool.

The sound of voices reached him. One belonged to the Captain, the other to Mr. Gus. Po Campo's voice could be heard, too, and Dish Boggett said something. Newt opened his eyes a moment and saw they were all kneeling by something on the ground. Maybe they had killed an antelope. He was very drowsy and wanted to go back to sleep. He closed his eyes again, then opened them. It wasn't an antelope. He sat up and saw that Po Campo was kneeling down, twisting on something. Someone had been hurt and Po was trying to pull a stob of some kind out of his body. He was straining hard, but the stob wouldn't come out. He stopped trying, and Dish, who had been holding the wounded man down, turned away suddenly, white and sick.

When Dish moved, Newt saw Deets. He was in the process of yawning when he saw him. Instead of springing up, he lay back down and pulled his blanket tighter. He opened his eyes and looked, and then shut them tightly. He felt angry at the men for having talked so loud that they had awakened him. He wished they would all die, if that was the best they could do. He wanted to go back to sleep. He wanted it to be one of those dreams that you wake up from just as the dream gets bad. He felt that was probably what it was. When he opened his eyes again he wouldn't see Deets's body lying on the wagon sheet a few yards away.

Yet it didn't work. He couldn't go back to sleep, and when he sat up the body was there—though if it hadn't been black he might not have known it was Deets.

He looked and saw that Pea Eye knelt on the other side of the body, looking dazed. Far away, toward the river, he saw the Captain and Lippy, digging. Mr. Gus sat by himself, near the cook fire, eating. The three horses had been unsaddled but no one had returned them to the remuda. They grazed nearby. Most of the hands stood in a group near Deets's feet, just looking as Po Campo worked.

Finally Po Campo gave up. "Better to bury him with it," he said. "I would have liked to see that boy. The lance went all the way to his collarbone. It went through the heart."

Newt sat in his blankets, feeling alone. No one noticed him or spoke to him. No one explained Deets's death. Newt began to cry, but no one noticed that either. The sun had risen, and everyone was busy with what they were doing, Mr. Gus eating, the Captain and Lippy digging the grave. Soupy Jones was repairing a stirrup and talking in subdued tones to Bert Borum. Newt sat and cried, wondering if Deets knew anything about what was going on. The Irishman and Needle and the Rainey boys held the herd. It was a beautiful morning, too—mountains seemed closer. Newt wondered if Deets knew about any of it. He didn't look at the corpse again, but he wondered if Deets had kept on knowing, somehow. He felt he did. He felt that if anyone was taking any notice of him, it was probably Deets, who had always been his friend. It was only the thought that Deets was still knowing him, somehow, that kept him from feeling totally alone.

Even so, the Deets who had walked around and smiled and been kind to him day after day, through the years—that Deets was dead. Newt sat on his blankets and cried until he was afraid he would never stop. No one seemed to notice. No one said anything to him as preparations for burying Deets went on.

Pea Eye didn't cry, but he was so shaken he went weak in the legs.

"Well, my lord," he said, from time to time. "My lord." An Indian boy had killed him, the Captain said. Deets was still wearing a pair of the old patchy quilt pants that he had favored for so long. Pea Eye scarcely knew what to think. He and Deets had been the main hired help on the Hat Creek outfit ever since there had been a Hat Creek outfit. Now it was down to him. It would mean a lot more chores for him, undoubtedly, for the Captain only trusted the two of them with certain chores. He remembered that he and Deets had had a pretty good conversation once. He had been vaguely planning to have another one with him if the chance came along. Of course that was off, now. Pea Eye went over and leaned against a wagon wheel, wishing he could stop feeling weak in the legs.

The other hands were somber. Soupy Jones and Bert Borum, who didn't feel it appropriate for white men to talk much to niggers, exchanged the view that nevertheless this one had been uncommonly decent. Needle Nelson offered to help dig the grave, for Deets had been the man who finally turned the Texas bull the day the bull got after him. Dish Boggett hadn't said much to Deets, either, but he had often been cheered, from his position on the point, to see Deets come riding back through the heat waves. It meant he was on course, and that water was somewhere near. Dish wished he had said more to the man at some point.

Lippy offered to help with the grave-digging, and Call let him. It was the task that usually got assigned to Deets himself, grave-digging. Call had laid many a *compañero* in graves Josh Deets had dug, including, most recently, Jake Spoon. Lippy was not a good digger—in fact, he was mostly in the way, but Call tolerated him. Lippy also talked constantly, saying nothing. They were digging on a little rise, north of the juncture of where Salt Creek joined the Powder River.

Augustus wrapped Deets carefully in a piece of wagon sheet and tied the sheet around him with heavy cord.

"A shroud for a journey," Augustus said.

No one else said anything. They loaded Deets in the wagon. Newt finally got out of his blanket, though he was almost blind from crying.

Po Campo led the team down to the grave and Deets was put in and quickly covered. The Irishman, unasked, began to sing a song of mourning so sad that all the cowboys at once began to cry, even the Spettle boy, who had not shed a tear when his own brother was buried.

Augustus turned and walked away. "I hate funerals," he said. "Particularly this one."

"At the rate we're dropping off, there won't be many of us left by the time we get to Montana," Lippy said, as they were all walking back to camp.

They expected to start the herd that day, as Captain Call had never been known to linger. But this time he did. He came back from the grave, got a big hammer and knocked a board loose from the side of the wagon. He didn't explain what he was doing to anyone, and the look on his face discouraged anyone from asking. He took the board and carried it down to the grave. The rest of the day he sat alone by Deets's grave, carving something into it with his knife. The sun flashed on his knife, and the cowhands watched in puzzlement. They just didn't know what it could be that would take the Captain so long.

"He had a short name," Lippy observed.

"It wasn't his full name," Newt pointed out. He had stopped crying but he felt empty.

"What was the other one then?" Jasper asked.

"It was Josh."

"Well, I swear," Jasper said. "That's a fine name. Starts with a J, like mine. We could have been calling him that all the time, if we'd known."

Then they heard the sound of the hammer—it was the big hammer that they used for straightening the rims of the wagon wheels. Captain Call was hammering the long board deep into the dirt by the grave.

Augustus, who had sat by himself most of the day, walked over and squatted down by Newt, who sat a little way apart. He had been afraid he would start crying again and wanted a little privacy.

"Let's go see what he wrote for old Deets," Augustus said. "I've seen your father bury many a man, but I never saw him take this kind of pains."

Newt hadn't really been listening. He had just been sitting there, feeling numb. When he heard Augustus mention his father, the words sank into the numbness for a minute and didn't affect him.

Then they did. "My what?" Newt asked.

"Your father," Augustus said. "Your pa."

Newt thought it an odd time for Mr. Gus to make a joke. The Captain wasn't his pa. Perhaps Mr. Gus had been so affected by Deets's death that he had gone a little crazy. Newt stood up. He thought it best just to ignore the remark—he didn't want to embarrass Mr. Gus at such a time. The Captain was still hammering, driving the long board into the hard ground.

They walked down to the grave. Call had finished his hammering and stood resting. Two or three of the cowboys trailed back to the grave, a little tentative, not sure they were invited.

Captain Call had carved the words deeply into the rough board so that the wind and sand couldn't quickly rub them out.

JOSH DEETS

SERVED WITH ME 30 YEARS. FOUGHT IN 21 ENGAGEMENTS WITH THE
COMMANCHE AND KIOWA. CHERFUL IN ALL WEATHERS, NEVER SHERKED
A TASK. SPLENDID BEHAVIOUR.

The cowboys came down one by one and looked at it in silence. Po Campo
crossed himself. Augustus took something out of his pocket. It was the medal the
Governor of Texas had given him for service on the border during the hard war
years. Call had one too. The medal had a green ribbon on it, but the color had
mostly faded out. Augustus made a loop of the ribbon and put the loop over the
grave board and tied it tightly. Captain Call had walked away to put up the hammer. Augustus followed. Lippy, who had not cried all day, suddenly began to sob,
tears running into his loose lip.

"I do wish I'd just stayed in Lonesome Dove," he said, when he stopped crying.

91

THEY TRAILED THE HERD up the Powder River, whose water none of the
cowboys liked. A few complained of stomach cramps and others said the water
affected their bowel movements. Jasper Fant in particular had taken to watching
his own droppings closely. They were coming out almost white, when any came
out at all. It seemed an ominous sign.

"I've met ladies that wasn't as finicky as you, Jasper," Augustus said, but he
didn't bother to tease Jasper very hard. The whole camp was subdued by Deets's
death. They were not missing Deets so much, most of them, as wondering what
fate awaited them in the north.

When they crossed the Powder they could see the Bighorn Mountains looming
to the west—not really close, but close enough that anyone could see the snow on
top of them. The nights began to be cold, and many of the hands began to regret
the fact that they had not bought better coats in Ogallala when they had the
opportunity.

The discussions around the campfire began to focus mainly on storms. Many of
the hands had experienced plains northers and the occasional ice storm, but they
were south Texas cowhands and had seldom seen snow. A few talked of loping
over to the mountains to examine the snow at close range and see what it was like.

Newt had always been interested in snow, and looked at the mountains often,
but in the weeks following Deets's death he found it difficult to care much about
anything, even snow. He didn't pay much attention to the talk of storms, and
didn't really care if they all froze, herd and hands together.

Occasionally the strange remark Mr. Gus had made came back to him. He didn't know what to make of it—the clear meaning had been that Captain Call was his father. It didn't make sense to Newt. If the Captain had been his father, surely he would have mentioned it at some point in the last seventeen years.

At other times the question would have excited him, but under the circumstances he felt too dull to care much. Set beside the fact that Deets was gone, it didn't seem to matter greatly.

Anyway, if Newt had wanted to question the Captain about it, he would have had a hard time catching him. The Captain took Deets's job and spent his days ranging far ahead. Usually he only rode back to the herd about dark, to guide them to a bed-ground. Once during the day he had come back in a high lope to report that he had crossed the tracks of about forty Indians. The Indians had been heading northwest, the same direction they were heading.

For the next few days everyone was tense, expecting Indian attack. Several men took alarm at the sight of what turned out to be sagebrush or low bushes. No one could sleep at night, and even those hands who were not on guard spent much of the night checking and rechecking their ammunition. The Irishman was afraid to sing on night duty for fear of leading the Indians straight to them. In fact, night herding became highly unpopular with everyone, and instead of gambling for money men began to gamble over who took what watch. The midnight watch was the most unpopular. No one wanted to leave the campfire: the men who came in from the watches did so with profound relief, and the men who went out assumed they were going to their deaths. Some almost cried. Needle Nelson trembled so that he could barely get his foot in his stirrup. Jasper Fant sometimes even got off and walked when he was on the far side of the herd, reasoning that the Indians would be less likely to spot him if he was on foot.

But a week passed and they saw no Indians. The men relaxed a little. Antelope became more common, and twice they saw small groups of buffalo. Once the remuda took fright in the night; the next morning Call found the tracks of a cougar.

The country began to change slightly for the better. The grass improved, and occasionally there were clumps of trees and bushes along the river bed. It was still hot in the afternoon, but the mornings were crisp.

Finally Call decided to leave the valley of the Powder. He felt the threat of drought was over. The grass was thick and wavy and there were plenty of streams. Not long after leaving the Powder, they crossed Crazy Woman Creek. Every day it seemed there was more snow on the mountains. Traveling became comparatively easy, and the cattle regained most of the flesh they had lost on the hard drive.

Almost daily, from then on, Call saw Indian sign, but no Indians. It bothered him a little. He had fought Indians long enough not to underrate them, but neither did he exaggerate their capacities. Talk of Indians was never accurate, in his view. It always made them seem worse or better than they were. He preferred to judge the northern Indians with his own eyes, but in this case the Indians didn't oblige him.

"We're driving three thousand cattle," Call said. "They're bound to notice us."

"They ain't expecting cattle," Augustus said. "There's never been cattle here before. They're probably just out hunting, trying to lay in enough meat to last them the winter."

"I guess we'll meet soon enough," Call said.

"If not too soon. They may come biling out of them hills and wipe us out any day. Then they'd have enough meat to last the winter. They'd be rich Indians, and we'd be dead fools."

"Fools for doing what?" Call asked. "This country's looking better all the time."

"Fools for living the lives we've lived," Augustus said.

"I've enjoyed mine," Call said. "What was wrong with yours?"

"I should have married again," Augustus said. "Two wives ain't very many. Solomon beat me by several hundred, although I've got the same equipment he had. I could have managed eight or ten at least. I don't know why I stuck with this scraggly old crew."

"Because you didn't have to work, I guess," Call said. "You sat around, and we worked."

"I was working in my head, you see," Augustus said. "I was trying to figure out life. If I'd had a couple more fat women to lay around with I might have figured out the puzzle."

"I never understood why you didn't stay in Tennessee, if your family was rich," Call said.

"Well, it was tame, that's why," Augustus said. "I didn't want to be a doctor or a lawyer, and there wasn't nothing else to do in those parts. I'd rather go outlaw than be a doctor or a lawyer."

The next day, as they were trailing along a little stream that branched off Crazy Woman Creek, Dish Boggett's horse suddenly threw up its head and bolted. Dish was surprised and embarrassed. It had been a peaceful morning, and he was half asleep when he discovered he was in a runaway, headed back for the wagon. He sawed on the reins with all his might but the bit seemed to make no difference to the horse.

The cattle began to turn too, all except the Texas bull, who let out a loud bellow.

Call saw the runaway without seeing what caused it at first. He and Augustus were riding along together, discussing how far west they ought to go before angling north again.

"Reckon that horse ate loco weed or what?" Call asked, spurring up to go help hold the cattle. He almost went over the mare's neck, for he leaned forward, expecting her to break into a lope, and the mare stopped dead. It was a shock, for she had been quite obedient lately and had tried no tricks.

"Call, look," Augustus said.

There was a thicket of low trees along the creek, and a large, orangish-brown animal had just come out of the thicket.

"My lord, it's a grizzly," Call said.

Augustus didn't have time to reply, for his horse suddenly began to buck. All the cowhands were having trouble with their mounts. The horses were turning and running as if they meant to run back to Texas. Augustus, riding a horse that hadn't bucked in several years, was almost thrown.

Instead of fleeing, most of the cattle turned and looked at the bear. The Texas bull stood all by himself in front of the herd.

Call drew his rifle and tried to urge the Hell Bitch a little closer, but had no luck. She moved, but she moved sideways, always keeping her eyes fixed on the bear, though it was a good hundred and fifty yards away. No matter how he spurred her, the mare sidestepped, as if there were an invisible line on the prairie that she would not cross.

"Damnation, there goes the grub," Augustus said. He had managed to subdue his mount.

Call looked and saw that the mules were dashing off back toward the Powder, Lippy sawing futilely on the reins and bouncing a foot off the wagon seat from time to time.

"Captain, it's a bear," Dish Boggett said. He had managed to turn his horse in a wide circle, but he couldn't stop him and he yelled the words as he raced past.

There was confusion everywhere. The remuda was running south, carrying the Spettle boy along with it. Two or three of the men had been thrown and their mounts were fleeing south. The thrown cowhands, expecting to die any minute, though they had no idea what was attacking, crept around with their pistols drawn.

"I expect they'll start shooting one another right off," Augustus said. "They'll mistake one another for outlaws if they ain't stopped."

"Go stop them," Call said. He could do nothing except watch the bear and hold the mare more or less in place. So far, the bear had done nothing except stand on its hind legs and sniff the air. It was a very large bear, though; to Call it looked larger than a buffalo.

"Hell, I don't care if they shoot at one another," Augustus said. "None of them can hit anything. I doubt we'll lose many."

He studied the bear for a time. The bear was not making any trouble, but he apparently had no intention of moving either. "I doubt that bear has ever seen a brindle bull before," Augustus said. "He's a mite surprised, and you can't blame him."

"Dern, that's a bit big bear," Call said.

"Yes, and he put the whole outfit to flight just by walking up out of the creek," Augustus said.

Indeed, the Hat Creek outfit was in disarray, the wagon and the remuda still fleeing south, half the hands thrown and the other half fighting their horses. The cattle hadn't run yet, but they were nervous. Newt had been thrown sky-high off the sorrel Clara had given him and had landed painfully on his tailbone. He started to limp back to the wagon, only to discover that the wagon was gone. All that was left of it was Po Campo, who looked puzzled. He was too short to see over the cattle and had no idea there was a bear around.

"Is it Indians?" Newt asked. He had not yet seen the bear either.

"I don't know what it is," Po Campo said. "But it's something mules don't like."

Only the two pigs were relatively undisturbed. A sack of potatoes had bounced out of the fleeing wagon and the pigs were calmly eating them, grunting now and then with satisfaction.

The Texas bull was the only animal directly facing the bear. The bull let out a challenging bellow and began to paw the earth. He took a few steps forward and pawed the earth again, throwing clouds of dust above his back.

"You don't think that little bull is fool enough to charge that bear, do you?" Augustus asked. "Charging Needle Nelson is one thing. That bear'll turn him wrong side out."

"Well, if you want to go rope that bull and lead him to the barn, help yourself," Call said. "I can't do nothing with this horse."

The bull trotted forward another few steps and stopped again. He was no more than thirty or forty yards from the bear. The bear dropped on all fours, watching the bull. He growled a rough, throaty growl that caused a hundred or so cattle to scatter and run back a short distance. They stopped again to watch. The bull bellowed and slung a string of slobber over his back. He was hot and angry. He pawed the earth again, then lowered his head and charged the bear.

To the amazement of all who saw it, the bear batted the Texas bull aside. He rose on his hind legs again, dealt the bull a swipe with his forepaw that knocked the bull off its feet. The bull was up in a second and charged the bear again—this time it seemed the bear almost skinned him. He hit the bull on the shoulder and ripped a capelike piece of skin loose on his back, but despite that, the bull managed to drive into the bear and thrust a horn into his flank. The bear roared and dug his teeth into the bull's neck, but the bull was still moving, and soon bear and bull were rolling over and over in the dust, the bull's bellows and the bear's roar so loud that the cattle did panic and begin to run. The Hell Bitch danced backward, and Augustus's horse began to pitch again and threw him, though Augustus held the rein and managed to get his rifle out of the scabbard before the horse broke free and fled. Then Call found himself thrown too; the Hell Bitch, catlike, had simply doubled out from under him.

It came at an inopportune moment too, for the bull and the bear, twisting like cats, had left the creek bank and were moving in the direction of the herd, although the dust the battle raised was so thick no one could see who had the advantage. It seemed to Call, when he looked, that the bull was being ripped to pieces by the bear's teeth and claws, but at least once the bull knocked the bear backward and got a horn into him again.

"Reckon we ought to shoot?" Augustus said. "Hell, this outfit will run clean back to the Red River if this keeps up."

"If you shoot, you might hit the bull," Call said. "Then we'd have to fight the bear ourselves, and I ain't sure we can stop him. That's a pretty mad bear."

Po Campo came up, holding his shotgun, Newt a few steps behind him. Most of the men had been thrown and were watching the battle tensely, clutching their guns.

The sounds the two animals made were so frightening that they made the men want to run. Jasper Fant wanted badly to run—he just didn't want to run alone. Now and then he would see the bear's head, teeth bared, or his great claws slashing; now and then he would see the bull seem to turn to bunched muscle as he tried to force the bear backward. Both were bleeding, and in the heat the blood smell was so strong that Newt almost gagged.

Then it stopped. Everyone expected to see the bull down—but the bull wasn't down. Neither was the bear. They broke apart, circling one another in the dust. Everyone prepared to pour bullets into the bear if he should charge their way, but the bear didn't charge. He snarled at the bull, the bull answering with a slobbery bellow. The bull turned back toward the herd, then stopped and faced the bear. The bear rose on his hind legs again, still snarling—one side was soaked with blood. To the men, the bear seemed to tower over them, although fifty yards away. In a minute he dropped back on all fours, roared once more at the bull, and disappeared into the brush along the creek.

"Captain, can we go after him?" Soupy Jones said, clutching his rifle.

"Go after him on what?" Augustus asked. "Have you gone daft, Soupy? You want to chase a grizzly bear on foot, after what you've seen? You wouldn't even make one good bite for that bear."

The bear had crossed the stream and was ambling along lazily across the open plain.

Despite Augustus's cautions, as soon as the men could catch their horses, five of them, including Dish Boggett, Soupy, Bert, the Irishman and Needle Nelson, raced after the bear, still visible though a mile or more away. They began to fire long before they were in range, and the bear loped toward the mountains. An hour later the men returned, their horses run down, but with no bear trophies.

"We hit him but he was faster than we thought," Soupy explained. "He got in some trees up toward the hills."

"We'll get the next one," Bert predicted.

"Hell, if he was in the trees, you should have gone in and tapped him with your pistol butt," Augustus said. "That would probably have tamed him."

"Well, the horses wouldn't go in them trees," Soupy explained.

"I didn't want to either," Allen O'Brien admitted. "If we had gone in the trees we might not have come out."

The mules had run three miles before stopping, but because the plain was fairly smooth, the wagon was undamaged. The same could not be said for Lippy, who had bounced so hard at one point that he had bitten his tongue nearly in two. The tongue bled for hours, little streams of blood spilling over his long lip. The remuda was eventually rounded up, as well as the cattle.

When the Texas bull calmed down enough so that it was possible to approach him, his wounds seemed so extensive that Call at first considered shooting him. He had only one eye, the other having been raked out, and the skin had been ripped off his neck and hung like a blanket over one shoulder. There was a deep gash in his flank and a claw wound running almost the whole length of his back. One horn had been broken off at the skull as if with a sledgehammer. Yet the bull still pawed the earth and bellowed when the cowboys rode too close.

"It seems a pity to shoot him," Augustus said. "He fought a draw with a grizzly. Not many critters can say that."

"He can't walk to Montana with half his skin hanging off his shoulders," Call pointed out. "The flies will get on that wound and he'll die anyway."

Po Campo walked to within fifty feet of the bull and looked at him.

"I can sew him up," he said. "He might live. Somebody catch him for me."

"Yes, rope him, Dish," Augustus said. "It's your job. You're our top hand."

Dish had to do it or be embarrassed by his failure for the rest of the trip. His horse didn't want to go near the bull, and he missed two throws from nervousness and expected to be killed himself if he did catch the animal. But he finally got a rope over the bull's head and slowed him until four more ropes could be thrown on him.

Even then, it was all they could do to throw the bull, and it took Po Campo over two hours to sew the huge flap of skin back in place. When it was necessary to turn the bull from one side to another, it took virtually the whole crew, plus five horses and ropes, to keep him from getting up again. Then, when the bull did roll, he nearly rolled on Needle Nelson, who hated him anyway and didn't approve of all the doctoring. When the bull nearly rolled on him Needle retreated to the wagon and refused to come near him again. "I was rooting for the bear," he said. "A bull like that is going to get somebody sooner or later, and it might be me."

The next day the bull was so sore he could barely hobble, and Call feared the doctoring had been in vain. The bull fell so far behind the herd that they decided to leave him. He fell several miles behind in the course of the day. Call kept looking back, expecting to see buzzards in the sky—if the bull finally dropped, they would feast.

But he saw no buzzards, and a week after the fight the bull was in the herd again. No one had seen him return, but one morning he was there. He had only one horn and one eye, and Po Campo's sewing job was somewhat uneven, the folds of skin having separated in two or three places—but the bull was ornery as ever, bellowing at the cowboys when they came too close. He resumed his habit of keeping well to the front of the herd. His wounds only made him more irascible; the hands gave him a wide berth.

As a result of the battle, night herding became even more unpopular. Where there was one grizzly bear, there could be others. The men who had been worrying constantly about Indians began to worry about bears. Those who had chased the wounded bear horseback could not stop talking about how fast he had moved. Though he had only seemed to be loping along, he had easily run off and left them. "There ain't a horse in this outfit that bear couldn't catch, if he wanted to," Dish contended.

The observation worried Jasper Fant so much that he lost his appetite and his ability to sleep. He lay awake in his blankets for three nights, clutching his gun—and when he couldn't avoid night herding he felt such anxiety that he usually threw up whatever he ate. He would have quit the outfit, but that would only mean crossing hundreds of miles of bear-infested prairie alone, a prospect he couldn't face. He decided if he ever got to a town where there was a railroad, he would take a train, no matter where it was going.

Pea Eye, too, found the prospect of bears disturbing. "If we strike any more, let's all shoot at once," he suggested to the men repeatedly. "I guess if enough of us hit one it'd fall," he always added. But no one seemed convinced, and no one bothered to reply.

92

WHEN SALLY AND BETSEY asked her questions about her past, Lorena was perplexed. They were just girls—she couldn't tell them the truth. They both idolized her and made much of her adventure in crossing the prairies. Betsey had a lively curiosity and could ask about a hundred questions an hour. Sally was more reserved and often chided her sister for prying into Lorena's affairs.

"She don't have to tell you about her whole life," Sally would protest. "Maybe she can't remember. I can only remember back to when I was three."

"What happened when you was three?" Lorena asked.

"That old turkey pecked me," Sally said. "A wolf got him and I'm glad."

Clara overheard part of the conversation. "I'm getting some more turkeys pretty soon," she said. "Lorie's so good with the poultry, I think we might raise a few."

The poultry chores had been assigned to Lorena—mainly just feeding the twenty-five or thirty hens and gathering the eggs. At first it seemed that such a small household couldn't possibly need so many eggs, and yet they absorbed them effortlessly. July Johnson was a big egg eater, and Clara, who had a ferocious sweet tooth, used them in the cakes she was always making. She made so many cakes that everyone got tired of them except her.

"I got to have sweets, at least," Clara said, eating a piece of cake before she went to bed, or again while she was cooking breakfast. "Sweets make up for a lot."

It didn't seem to Lorena that Clara had that much that needed making up for. She mostly did what she pleased, and what she pleased usually had to do with horses. Housework didn't interest her, and washing, in particular, didn't interest her. That became Lorena's job too, though the girls helped her. They asked questions all the time they worked, and Lorena just gave them whatever answers came into her head—few of them true answers. She didn't know if the answers fooled them—the girls were smart. Sometimes she knew she didn't fool them.

"Are you gonna marry that man?" Betsey asked one day. "He's already got white hair."

"That's no reason not to marry him," Sally said.

"It is, too," Betsey insisted. "If he's got white hair he could die any time."

Lorena found that she didn't think about Gus all that much. She was glad she had stayed at Clara's. For almost the first time in her life she had a decent bed in a clean room and tasteful meals and people around who were kind to her. She liked having a whole room to herself, alone. Of course, she had had a room in Lonesome Dove, but it hadn't been the same. Men could come into that room—letting them in was a condition of having it. But she didn't have to let anyone into her room in Clara's house, though often she did let Betsey, who suffered from nightmares, into it. One night Betsey stumbled in, crying—Clara was out of the house, taking one of the strange walks she liked to take. Lorena was surprised and offered to go find Clara, but Betsey wasn't listening. She came into the bed like a small animal and snuggled into Lorena's arms. Lorena let her stay the night, and from then on, when Betsey had a nightmare, she came to Lorena's room and Lorena soothed her.

Only now and then did she miss Gus, though then she missed him with a painful ache and felt almost desperate to see him. At such times she felt cowardly for not having gone with him, though, of course, he himself had urged her to stay. She didn't miss the rest of it at all—the cowboys watching her and thinking things about her, the hot tent, the unpredictable storms and the fleas and mosquitoes that were always there.

She didn't miss the fear, either—the fear that someday Gus would be off somewhere and Blue Duck would come back. What had happened had been bad enough, but she knew if he ever got her again it would be worse. Fearing him and missing Gus were mixed together, for Gus was the only person who could protect her from him.

Unlike the girls, Clara seldom asked her any questions. Lorena came to wish that she would. For a while she had an urge to apologize to Clara for not having always been able to be a lady. It still seemed to her a miracle that she had been allowed to stay in Clara's house and be one of the family. She looked for it to go bad in some way, but it didn't go bad. The only thing that changed was that Clara spent more and more time with the horses, and less and less time in the house.

"You came at a good time," she said one day as Lorena was coming in from feeding the hens. It was a task Lorena enjoyed—she liked the way the hens chirped and complained.

"How's that?" Lorena asked.

"I nagged Bob to build this house, and I don't really care about a house," Clara said. "We needed it for the girls, but that wasn't why I built it. I just wanted to nag him into it and I did. The main reason was he wouldn't let me work with the horses, although I'm better with them than he ever was. But he didn't think it fitting—so I thought. All right then, Bob, build me a house. But I'd rather be down with the horses, and now there's nothing to stop me."

Two weeks later, Bob died in the night. Clara went in in the morning to change him, and found him dead. He looked exactly as he had: he just was no longer breathing. He weighed so little by then that she could lift him. Having long concluded that he would die, she had had Cholo bring a pine coffin from town. He had brought it in at night and hidden it from the girls. It was ready.

Clara closed Bob's eyes and sat with her memories for an hour. The girls were downstairs now, pestering Lorena and eating. Now and then she could hear their laughter.

They were happy girls; they laughed often. It pleased Clara to hear them. She wondered if Bob could hear his two lively daughters laughing, as he lay dying. She wondered if it helped, if it made up in any way for her bad tempers and the deaths of the three boys. He had counted so on those boys—they would be his help, boys. Bob had never talked much, but the one thing he did talk about was how much they would get done once the boys got big enough to do their part of the work. Often, just hearing him describe the fences they would build, or the barns, or the cattle they would buy, Clara felt out of sorts—it made her feel very distant from Bob that he saw their boys mainly as hired hands that he wouldn't have to pay. He sees them different, she thought. For her part, she just liked to have them there. She liked to look at them as they sat around the table, liked to watch them swimming and frolicking in the river, liked to sit by them sometimes when they slept, listening to them breathe. Yet they had died, and both she and Bob lost what they loved—Bob his dreams of future work with his sons, she the immediate pleasure of having sons to look at, to touch, to scold and tease and kiss.

It struck her that endings were never as you would expect them to be. She had thought she would be relieved when Bob finally died. She hadn't felt he was part of their life anymore, and yet, now that he was gone, she knew he had been. A silent part, an uncomfortable part, but still there, still her husband, still the girls' father. He had been changed, but not removed.

Now he had gone where her boys had gone. As well as she knew the boys, as much as she loved them, time had robbed her of them. At times she found herself mixing details and events up, not in big ways but in small. In dreams she saw her sons' faces, and when she awoke could not remember which son she had dreamed about. She wondered if she would dream of Bob, and what she would remember if she thought of him in ten years. Their marriage had had few high spots. She had often been happy during it, but not because of anything Bob did. She had had more happiness from horses than from her husband, though he had been a decent husband, better than most women had, from what she could judge.

She didn't cry, but merely felt a wish, now he was gone, that she could somehow escape dealing with the tiresome formalities of death. Someone would have to go for a preacher; there would have to be some kind of funeral. They had no close neighbors, but the two or three closest would still feel they had to come, bring food, pay their respects.

She covered Bob with a clean sheet and went downstairs. Lorena was teaching the girls to play cards. They were playing poker for buttons. Clara stood in the shadows, wishing she didn't have to interrupt their fun. Why interrupt it for a death that couldn't be helped? And yet death was not something you could ignore. It had its weight. It was a dead man lying upstairs, not a man who was sick. It seemed to her she had better not form the practice of ignoring death. If she tried it, death would find a way to answer back—it would take another of her loved ones, to remind her to respect it.

So she walked into the room. Betsey had just won a hand. She whooped, for she loved to beat her sister. She was a beautiful child, with curls that would drive men mad some day. "I won the pot, Ma," she said, and then saw by the grave set of Clara's face that something was wrong.

"Good," Clara said. "A good cardplayer is just what this family needs. Now I have to tell you something sad. Your father's dead."

"Oh, he ain't!" Sally said.

"Honey, he died just now," Clara said.

Sally ran to her, but Betsey turned to Lorena, who was nearer. Lorena was surprised, but she put her arms around the child.

"Could you go get July?" Clara asked Lorena, when the girls had calmed a bit.

July now lived in a little room attached to the saddle shed. It wouldn't do when winter came, but for summer it was all right. He had never felt comfortable in the house with Clara and the girls, and since Lorena had come he felt even more uncomfortable. Lorena seldom spoke to him, and Clara mainly discussed horses, or other ranch problems, yet he felt nervous in their company. Day to day, he felt it was wrong to have taken the job with Clara. Sometimes he felt a strong longing to be back in his old job in Fort Smith, even if Roscoe was no longer alive to be his deputy.

But he had a son now, a baby he saw every day at supper and breakfast. His son was the darling of the ranch. The women and girls passed Martin around as if he belonged to them all; Lorena had developed a rapport with him and took the main responsibility for him when Clara was off with the horses. The baby was happy, and no wonder, with two women and two girls to spoil him. July could hardly imagine what the women would do if he tried to take the baby and raise him in Arkansas. Anyway, such a plan was not feasible.

So he stayed on and did his work, neither truly content nor bitterly discontented. He still dreamed of Elmira and felt an aching sadness when he thought about her.

Despite that ache, the thing that made July least comfortable of all was that he knew he was in love with Clara. The feeling had started even before he knew Elmira was dead, and it grew even when he knew he ought to be grieving for Elmira. He felt guilty about it, he felt hopeless about it, but it was true. At night he thought of her, and imagined her in her room, in her gown. At breakfast and supper he watched her, whenever he thought he could do so without her noticing. He had many opportunities, too, for she seemed to have ceased taking any notice of him at all. He had the sense that she had become disappointed in him, though he didn't know why. And when she did look at him it frightened him. Occasionally, when he caught Clara looking at him, he almost flinched, for he did not imagine that he could hide anything from her. She was too smart—he had the sense that she could figure out anything. Her eyes were mysterious to him—often she seemed to be amused by him, at other times irritated. Sometimes her eyes seemed to pierce him, as if she had decided to read his thoughts as she would read a book. And then, in a moment, she would lift her head and ignore him, as if he were a book she had glanced through and found too uninteresting for further perusal.

And she was married. Her husband lay sick above their heads, which made his love seem all the more hopeless. But it didn't stop the longing he felt for her. In his daydreams he fell to reinventing the past, imagining that he had married Clara instead of Elmira. He gave himself a very different marriage. Clara wouldn't sit in the loft with her feet dangling all day. She wouldn't have run off on a whiskey boat. Probably she wouldn't have cared that Jake Spoon shot Benny. He imagined them raising horses and children together.

Of course, they had begun to do just that—raise horses and children together. But the reality was far different from the daydream. They weren't together. He could not go into her room at night and talk to her. He knew that if he could, he probably wouldn't be able to think of much to say, or if he did and said something stupid, Clara would answer sharply. Still he longed for it and lay awake at night in his little shed, thinking of her.

He was doing that when Lorena came to tell him Bob was dead. Hearing the footsteps, he had the hope that it was Clara, and he pictured her face in his mind, not stern and impersonal, as it often was when she was directing some work, but soft and smiling, as it might be if she were playing with Martin at the dinner table.

He opened the door and saw to his surprise that it was Lorena.

"He died," Lorena said.

"Who?" July asked absently.

"Her husband," Lorena said.

Then she's free, July thought. He couldn't feel sad.

"Well, I guess it's for the best," he said. "The man wasn't getting no better."

Lorena noticed that he sounded happier than she had heard him sound since she arrived at the ranch. She knew exactly what it meant. She had often seen him looking at Clara with helpless love in his eyes. She herself didn't care one way or the other about July Johnson, but the dumb quality of his love annoyed her. Many men had looked at her that way, and she was not flattered by it. They wanted to pretend, such men, that they were different, that she was different, and that what might happen between them would be different than it would ever be. They wanted to pretend that they wanted pretty dresses and smiles, when what they really wanted was for her to lay down under them. That was the real wish beneath all the pretty wishes men had. And when she *was* under them, they could look down and pretend something pretty was happening, but she would look up and only see a dumb face above her, strained, dishonest and anything but pretty.

"She wants you to bring the coffin," she said to July, watching him. Let Clara worry about the man. Watching him only made her long for Gus. He gave things that no one else could give. He wasn't dumb, and he didn't pretend that he wanted smiles when he wanted a poke.

They put the coffin in the front room, and July carried the frail corpse downstairs and put him in the coffin. Then, on Clara's instructions, he rode off to inform the few neighbors and to find a preacher. Clara and Lorena and the girls sat with the body all night, while Cholo dug a grave on the ridge above the barn where the boys were buried. Betsey slept most of the night in Lorena's arms—Clara thought it nice that she had taken to the young woman so.

At dawn Clara went out and took Cholo some coffee. He had finished digging and was sitting on the mound of earth that would soon cover Bob. Walking toward the ridge in the early sunlight, Clara had the momentary sense that they were all watching her, the boys and Bob. The vision lasted a second; it was Cholo who was watching her. It was windy, and the grass waved over the graves of her three boys—four now, she felt. In memory Bob seemed like a boy to her also. He had a boyish innocence and kept it to the end, despite the strains of work and marriage in a rough place. It often irritated her, that innocence of his. She had felt it to be laziness—it left her alone to do the thinking, which she resented. Yet she had loved it, too. He had never been a knowing man in the way that Gus was knowing, or even Jake Spoon. When she decided to marry Bob, Jake, who was a hothead, grew red in the face and proceeded to throw a fit. It disturbed him terribly that she had chosen someone he thought was dumb. Gus had been better behaved, if no less puzzled. She remembered how it pleased her to thwart them—to make them realize that her measure was different from theirs. "I'll always know where he is," she told Gus. It was the only explanation she ever offered.

Now, indeed, she would know where he was.

Cholo was watching her to see if she was hurt. He loved Clara completely and tried in small ways to make life easier for her, although he had concluded long before that she wasn't seeking ease. Often in the morning when she came down to the lots she would be somber and would stand by the fence for an hour, not saying a word to anyone. Other times there would be something working in her that scared the horses. He thought of Clara as like the clouds. Sometimes the small black clouds would pour out of the north; they seemed to roll over and over as they swept across the sky, like tumbleweeds. On some mornings things rolled inside Clara, and made her tense and snappish. She could do nothing with the horses on days like that. They became as she was, and Cholo would try gently to persuade her that it was not a good day to do the work. Other days, her spirit was quiet and calm and the horses felt that too. Those were the days they made progress training them.

Clara had brought two cups. She was very glad to be out of the house. She poured Cholo his coffee and then poured some for herself. She sat down on the mound of dirt beside him and looked into the open grave.

"Sometimes it seems like grave-digging is all we do," she said. "But that's wrong. I guess if we lived in a big town it wouldn't seem that way. I guess in New York there are so many people you don't notice the dying so much. People come faster than they go. Out here it shows more when people go—especially when it's your people."

"Mister Bob, he didn't know mares," Cholo said, remembering that ignorance had been his downfall.

"Nope," Clara said. "He didn't know mares."

They sat quietly for a while, drinking coffee. Watching Clara, Cholo felt sad. He did not believe she had ever been happy. Always her eyes seemed to be looking for something that wasn't there. She might look pleased for a time, watching her daughters or watching some young horse, but then the rolling would start inside her again and the pleased look would give way to one that was sad.

"What do you think happens when you die?" she asked, surprising him. Cholo shrugged. He had seen much death, but had not thought much about it. Time enough to think about it when it happened.

"Not too much," he said. "You're just dead."

"Maybe it ain't as big a change as we think," Clara said. "Maybe you just stay around near where you lived. Near your family, or wherever you was happiest. Only you're just a spirit, and you don't have the troubles the living have."

A minute later she shook her head, and stood up. "I guess that's silly," she said, and started back to the house.

That afternoon July came back with a minister. The two nearest neighbors came—German families. Clara had seen more of the men than of the women— the men would come to buy horses and stay for a meal. She almost regretted having notified them. Why should they interrupt their work just to see Bob put in the ground? They sang two hymns, the Germans singing loudly in poor English. Mrs. Jensch, the wife of one of the German farmers, weighed over three hundred pounds. The girls had a hard time not staring at her. The buggy she rode in tilted far to one side under her weight. The minister was invited to stay the night and got rather drunk after supper—he was known to drink too much, when he got the chance. His name was the Reverend Spinnow and he had a large purple birthmark under one ear. A widower, he was easily excited by the presence of women. He was writing a book on prophecy and rattled on about it as they all sat in the living room. Soon both Clara and Lorena felt like choking him.

"Will you be thinking of moving into town now, Mrs. Allen?" the Reverend asked hopefully. It was worth the inconvenience of a funeral way out in the country to sit with two women for a while.

"No, we'll be staying right here," Clara said.

July and Cholo carried out the mattress Bob had died on—it needed a good airing. Betsey cried a long time that night and Lorena went up to be with her. It was better than listening to a minister go on about prophecy.

The baby was colicky and Clara rocked him while the minister drank. July came in and asked if there was anything else she needed him to do.

"No," Clara said, but July sat down anyway. He felt he should offer to rock his son, but knew the baby would just cry louder if he took him away from Clara. The minister finally fell asleep on the sofa and then, to their surprise, rolled off on the floor and began to snore loudly.

"Do you want me to carry him out?" July asked, hoping to feel useful. "He could sleep in a wagon just as well."

"Let him lie," Clara said, thinking it had been an odd day. "I doubt it's the first time he's slept on a floor, and anyway he isn't your lookout."

She knew July was in love with her and was irritated that he was so awkward about it. He was as innocent as Bob, but she didn't feel moved to patience, in July's case. She would save her patience for his son, who slept at her breast, whimpering now and then. Soon she got up with the baby and went to her room, leaving July sitting silently in a chair while the drunken minister snored on the floor.

Once upstairs she called Sally. Sally had not cried much. When she came into Clara's room she looked drawn. Almost immediately she began to sob. Clara put the baby down and held her daughter.

"Oh, I'm so bad," Sally said, when she could talk. "I wanted Daddy to die. I didn't like it that he just lay up there with his eyes open. It was like he was a spook. Only now I wish he hadn't died."

"Hush," Clara said. "You ain't bad. I wanted him to die too."

"And now you wish he hadn't, Ma?" Sally asked.

"I wish he had been more careful around horses, is what I wish," Clara said.

93

AS THE HERD and the Hat Creek outfit slowly rode into Montana out of the barren Wyoming plain, it seemed to all of them that they were leaving behind not only heat and drought, but ugliness and danger too. Instead of being chalky and covered with tough sage, the rolling plains were covered with tall grass and a sprinkling of yellow flowers. The roll of the plains got longer; the heat shimmers they had looked through all summer gave way to cool air, crisp in the mornings and cold at night. They rode for days beside the Bighorn Mountains, whose peaks were sometimes hidden in cloud.

The coolness of the air seemed to improve the men's eyesight—they fell to speculating about how many miles they could see. The plains stretched north before them. They saw plenty of game, mainly deer and antelope. Once they saw a large herd of elk, and twice small groups of buffalo. They saw no more bears, but bears were seldom far from their thoughts.

The cowboys had lived for months under the great bowl of the sky, and yet the Montana skies seemed deeper than the skies of Texas or Nebraska. Their depth and blueness robbed even the sun of its harsh force—it seemed smaller, in the vastness, and the whole sky no longer turned white at noon as it had in the lower plains. Always, somewhere to the north, there was a swath of blueness, with white clouds floating in it like petals in a pond.

Call had scarcely spoken since the death of Deets, but the beauty of the high prairies, the abundance of game, the coolness of the mornings finally raised his spirits. It was plain that Jake Spoon, who had been wrong about most things, had been right about Montana. It was a cattleman's paradise, and they were the only cattlemen in it. The grassy plains seemed limitless, stretching north. It was strange that they had seen no Indians, though. Often he mentioned this to Augustus.

"Custer didn't see them either," Augustus pointed out. "Not till he was caught. Now that we're here, do you plan to stop, or will we just keep going north till we get into the polar bears?"

"I plan to stop, but not yet," Call said. "We ain't crossed the Yellowstone. I like the thought of having the first ranch north of the Yellowstone."

"But you ain't a rancher," Augustus said.

"I guess I am now."

"No, you're a fighter," Augustus said. "We should have left these damn cows down in Texas. You used them as an excuse to come up here, when you ain't interested in them and didn't need an excuse anyway. I think we oughta just give them to the Indians when the Indians show up."

"Give the Indians three thousand cattle?" Call said, amazed at the notions his friend had. "Why do that?"

"Because then we'd be shut of them," Augustus said. "We could follow our noses, for a change, instead of following their asses. Ain't you bored?"

"I don't think like you do," Call said. "They're ours. We got 'em. I don't plan on giving them to anybody."

"I miss Texas and I miss whiskey," Augustus said. "Now here we are in Montana and there's no telling what will become of us."

"Miles City's up here somewhere," Call said. "You can buy whiskey."

"Yes, but I'll have to drink it indoors," Augustus complained. "It's cool up here."

As if to confirm his remark, the very next day an early storm blew out of the Bighorns. An icy wind came up and snow fell in the night. The men on night herd wrapped blankets around themselves to keep warm. A thin snow covered the plains in the morning, to the amazement of everyone. The Spettle boy was so astonished to wake and see it that he refused to come out of his blankets at first, afraid of what might happen. He lay wide-eyed, looking at the whiteness. Only when he saw the other hands tramping in it without ill effect did he get up.

Newt had been curious about snow all the way north, but he had lost his jacket somewhere in Kansas, and now that snow had actually fallen he felt too cold to enjoy it. All he wanted was to be warm again. He had taken his boots off when he lay down to sleep, and the snow had melted on his feet, getting his socks wet. His boots were a tight fit, and it was almost impossible to get them on over wet socks. He went over to the fire barefoot, hoping to dry his socks, but so many of the cowboys were huddled around the fire that he couldn't get a place at first.

Pea Eye had scooped up a handful of snow and was eating it. The Rainey boys had made snowballs, but all the cowboys were stiff and cold and looked threatening, so the Raineys merely threw the snowballs at one another.

"This snow tastes like hail, except that it's soft," Pea Eye observed.

The sun came out just then and shone so brightly on the white plains that some of the men had to shield their eyes. Newt finally got a place by the fire, but by then the Captain was anxious to move on and he didn't get to dry his socks. He tried to pull his boots on but had no luck until Po Campo noticed his difficulty and came over with a little flour, which he sprinkled in the boots.

"This will help," he said, and he was right, though getting the boots on still wasn't easy.

The sun soon melted the thin snow, and for the next week the days were hot again. Po Campo walked all day behind the wagon, followed by the pigs, who bored through the tall grass like moles—a sight that amused the cowboys, although Augustus worried that the pigs might stray off.

"We ought to let them ride in the wagon," he suggested to Call.

"I don't see why."

"Well, they've made history," Augustus pointed out.

"When?" Call asked. "I didn't notice."

"Why, they're the first pigs to walk all the way from Texas to Montana," Augustus said. "That's quite a feat for a pig."

"What will it get them?" Call inquired. "Eaten by a bear if they ain't careful, or eaten by us if they are. They've had a long walk for nothing."

"Yes, and the same's likely true for us," Augustus said, irritated that his friend wasn't more appreciative of pigs.

With Deets dead, Augustus and Call alternated the scouting duties. One day Augustus asked Newt to ride along with him, much to Newt's surprise. In the morning they saw a grizzly, but the bear was far upwind and didn't scent them. It was a beautiful day—no clouds in the sky. Augustus rode with his big rifle propped across the saddle—he was in the highest of spirits. They rode ahead of the herd some fifteen miles or more, and yet when they stopped to look back they could still see the cattle, tiny black dots in the middle of the plain, with the southern horizon still far behind them.

"I never thought to see so far," Newt said.

"Ain't it something," Augustus said with a grin. "This is rare country, this Montana. We're a lucky bunch. There ain't nothing better than this—though you don't have to tell your pa I said it."

Newt had decided it must be one of Mr. Gus's many jokes, making out that the Captain was his pa.

"I like to keep Woodrow feeling that he's caused a peck of trouble," Augustus said. "I don't want him to get sassy. But I wouldn't have missed coming up here. I can't think of nothing better than riding a fine horse into a new country. It's exactly what I was meant for, and Woodrow too."

"Do you think we'll see Indians?" Newt asked.

"You bet," Augustus said. "We might all get killed this afternoon, for all I know. That's the wild for you—it's got its dangers, which is part of the beauty. 'Course the Indians have had this land forever. To them it's precious because it's old. To us it's exciting because it's new."

Newt noticed that Mr. Gus had a keen look in his eye. His white hair was long, almost to his shoulders. There seemed to be no one who could enjoy himself like Mr. Gus.

"Now there's women, of course," Augustus said. "I do cotton to them. But I ain't found the one yet who could hold me back from a chance like this. Women are persistent creatures, and will try to nail you down. But if you just dance on off, you'll usually find them close to the spot where you left them—most of 'em."

"Do you really know who my pa is?" Newt asked. Mr. Gus was being so friendly, he felt he could ask.

"Oh, Woodrow Call is your pa, son," Augustus said, as if it were a matter of casual knowledge.

For the first time Newt felt it might be true, although extremely puzzling. "Well, he never mentioned it," he pointed out. Just being told such news didn't settle much. In fact it just made new problems, for if the Captain was his father, then why hadn't he mentioned it?

"It's a subtle problem," Augustus said.

Newt didn't find that a helpful answer, mainly because he didn't know what subtle meant. "Looks like he'd mention it," he said softly. He didn't want to criticize the Captain, especially not to Mr. Gus, the only man who *did* criticize the Captain.

"It wouldn't be his way, to mention it," Augustus said. "Woodrow don't mention nothing he can keep from mentioning. You couldn't call him a mentioner."

Newt found it very puzzling. If the Captain was his father, then he must have known his mother, but he had never mentioned that either. He could remember times when he had daydreamed that the Captain was his father and would take him on long trips.

Now, in a way, the daydream had come true. The Captain had taken him on a long trip. But instead of feeling proud and happy, he felt let down and confused. If it was true, why had everybody been such a long time mentioning it? Deets had never mentioned it. Pea Eye had never mentioned it. Worst of all, his mother had never mentioned it. He had been young when she died, but not too young to remember something so important. He could still remember some of the songs she had sung to him—he could have remembered who his father was. It didn't make sense, and he rode beside Mr. Gus for several miles, puzzling about it silently.

"Did you ask me along just to tell me?" Newt asked finally.

"Yep," Augustus admitted.

Newt knew he ought to thank him, but he didn't feel in the mood to thank anybody. The information just seemed to make his whole life more puzzling. It spoiled every good thing he had felt, for most of his life—not only about his mother, but about the Captain, and about the Hat Creek outfit as a whole.

"I know it's tardy news," Augustus said. "Since Woodrow ain't a mentioner, I thought I'd tell you. You never know what might happen."

"I wish I'd known sooner," Newt said—it was the one thing he was sure of.

"Yes, I expect you do," Augustus said. "I ought to have discussed it sooner, but it was really Woodrow's place to tell you and I kept hoping he'd do it, though I knew he wouldn't."

"Is it that he don't like me?" Newt asked. He felt a longing to be back in Texas. The news, coming when it did, had spoiled Montana.

"No," Augustus said. "What you have to understand is that Woodrow Call is a peculiar man. He likes to think that things are a certain way. He likes to think everybody does their duty, especially him. He likes to think people live for duty— I don't know what started him thinking that way. He ain't dumb. He knows perfectly well people don't live for duty. But he won't admit it about anybody if he can help it, and he especially won't admit it about himself."

Newt saw that Mr. Gus was laboring to explain it to him, but it was no good. So far as he could tell, the Captain *did* live for duty. What did that have to do with the Captain being his father?

"Woodrow don't like to admit that he's like the rest of us," Augustus said, seeing the boy's perplexity.

"He ain't," Newt said. That was obvious. The Captain never behaved like other people.

"He ain't, that's true," Augustus said. "But he had a chance to be once. He turned his back on it, and now he ain't about to admit that he made the wrong choice. He'd as soon kill himself. He's got to keep trying to be the way he thinks he is, and he's got to make out that he was always that way—it's why he ain't owned up to being your pa."

Soon they turned and headed back toward the herd.

"It's funny," Augustus said. "I knew my pa. He was a gentleman. He didn't do much but raise horses and hounds and drink whiskey. He never hit me a lick in my life, nor even raised his voice to me. He drank whiskey every night and disappointed my mother, but both my sisters doted on him like he was the only man. In fact one of them's an old maid to this day because she doted on Dad.

"But he never interested me, Dad," he went on. "I lit out from that place when I was thirteen years old, and I ain't stopped yet. I didn't care one way or the other for Dad. I just seen that horses and hounds would get boring if you tried to make 'em a life. I 'spect I'd have wrecked every marriage in the county if I'd stayed in Tennessee. Or else have got killed in a duel."

Newt knew Mr. Gus was trying to be kind, but he wasn't listening. Much of his life he had wondered who his father was and where he might be. He felt it would be a relief to know. But now he knew, and it wasn't a relief. There was something in it that thrilled him—he was Captain Call's son—but more that felt sad. He was glad when Mr. Gus put the horses in a lope—he didn't have to think as much. They loped along over the grassy plains toward the cattle in the far distance. The cattle looked tiny as ants.

94

THE MEN BEGAN TO TALK of the Yellowstone River as if it were the place where the world ended—or, at least, the place where the drive would end. In their thinking it had taken on a magical quality, partly because no one really knew anything about it. Jasper Fant had somehow picked up the rumor that the Yellowstone was the size of the Mississippi, and as deep. All the way north everyone had been trying to convince Jasper that it didn't really make any difference how deep a river was, once it got deep enough to swim a horse, but Jasper felt the argument violated common sense. The deeper the river, the more dangerous— that was axiomatic to him. He had heard about something called undercurrents, which could suck you down. The deeper the river, the farther down you could be sucked, and Jasper had a profound fear of being sucked down. Particularly he didn't want to be sucked down in the Yellowstone, and had made himself a pair of rude floats from some empty lard buckets, just in case the Yellowstone really did turn out to be as deep as the Mississippi.

"I didn't come all this way just to drown in the last dern river," Jasper said.

"It ain't the last," Augustus said. "Montana don't stop at the Yellowstone. The Missouri's up there somewhere, and it's a whale of a river."

"Well, I don't aim to cross it," Jasper said. It seemed to him he had spent half the trip imagining how it would be to be sucked down into a deep river, and he wanted it understood that he was only willing to take so many chances.

"I guess you'll cross it if the Captain wants to keep going," Dish said. Jasper's river fears grated on everybody's nerves. Nobody liked crossing rivers, but it didn't help to talk about the dangers constantly for three thousand miles.

"Well, Jake talked of a Milk River, and one called the Marais," Augustus said.

"Looks like you'd be satisfied," Jasper said. "Ain't we traveled enough? I'd like to step into a saloon in good old Fort Worth, myself. I'd like to see my home again while my folks are still alive."

"Why, that ain't the plan," Augustus said. "We're up here to start a ranch. Home and hearth don't interest us. We hired you men for life. You ought to have said goodbye to the old folks before you left."

"What are we going to do, now that we're here?" Lippy asked. The question was on everyone's minds. Usually when a cattle drive ended the men just turned around and went back to Texas, but then most drives stopped in Kansas, which seemed close to home compared to where they were now. Many of them harbored secret doubts about their ability to navigate a successful return to Texas. Of course, they knew the direction, but they would have to make the trip in winter, and the Indians that hadn't been troublesome on the way north might want to fight as they went south.

"I like a town," Lippy added. "It don't have to be St. Louis, just a town. As long as it has a saloon or two I can get by. But I wasn't meant to live out in the open during the winter."

Call knew the men were wondering, but he wasn't ready to stop. Jake had said some of the most beautiful land was far to the north, near Canada. It would be a pity to stop and make a choice before they had looked around thoroughly.

He contemplated leaving the men and going on a long look around himself, north of Yellowstone, but decided against it, mainly because of Indians. Things looked peaceful, but that didn't mean they would stay peaceful. There could easily be a bad fight, and he didn't want to be gone if one came.

Finally he decided to send Augustus. "I hate to give you the first look, but somebody's got to look," he said. "Would you want to go?"

"Oh, sure," Augustus said. "I'd be happy to get away from all this tedious conversation. Maybe I'll trot through this Miles City community and see if anyone stocks champagne."

"Take the look around first, if you can be bothered," Call said. "I doubt the main street of Miles City would make a good ranch, and I doubt you'll get any farther, once you spot a saloon. We need to find a place and get some shelters built before winter hits. Take a man with you, in case you get into trouble," Call suggested.

"I can get myself out of trouble," Augustus said. "But if I have to lead some quaking spirit like Jasper Fant it'll slow me down. None of these cowpokes is exactly wilderness hands. We buried the last reliable man down on the Powder, remember?"

"I remember," Call said.

"You don't want to make too many mistakes in this part of the country," Augustus said. "You'll end up bearshit."

"Take Pea," Call said. "Pea can follow orders."

"Yes, that's what he can do," Augustus said. "I guess I'll take him, though he won't provide much conversation."

Pea Eye was not enthusiastic about going on a scout with Gus, but since the Captain told him to, he tied his bedroll on his saddle and got ready. Other than securing his bedroll, his preparations consisted mainly of sharpening his knife. One thing Pea Eye firmly believed was that it was foolish to start on a trip without a sharp knife. Inevitably on a trip there were things that needed cutting or skinning or trimming. Once his knife was sharp, Pea Eye was ready, more or less. He knew he wouldn't get much relaxation on the trip because he was traveling with Gus, and Gus talked all the time. It was hard to relax when he had to be constantly listening. Besides, Gus was always asking questions which were hard to understand, much less answer.

It was a breezy morning when they started out—a dark cloud bank had formed in the northwest, and the men were talking of snow.

"I said way back in Lonesome Dove we'd be crossing the dern Yellowstone on the ice if we didn't get started," Jasper reminded them. "Now all this time has passed, and I may be right."

"Even if you was right, you'd be wrong, Jasper," Augustus said, as he stuffed an extra box or two of ammunition into his saddlebags.

"I'd like to know why, Gus," Jasper said, annoyed that Gus was always singling him out for criticism.

"I'll explain it when I get back," Augustus said. "Come on, Pea, let's go see if we can find Canada."

They loped off, watched by the whole camp. The crew had been made melancholy by the approaching clouds. Po Campo had wandered off looking for roots.

Augustus and Pea Eye passed him nearly a mile from camp. "Po, you're a rambler," Augustus said. "What do you expect to find on this old plain?"

"Wild onions," Po Campo said. "I'd like an onion."

"I'd like a jug of bourbon whiskey, myself," Augustus said. "I wonder which one of us will get his wish."

"*Adios,*" Po Campo said.

A day and a half later the two scouts rode over a grassy bluff and saw the Yellowstone River, a few miles away. Fifty or sixty buffalo were watering when they rode up. At the sight of the horsemen the buffalo scattered. The cloud bank had blown away and the blue sky was clear for as far as one could see. The river was swift but not deep—Augustus paused in his crossing and leaned down, drinking from his cupped hands. The water was cold.

"Sweet water, but it don't compare with bourbon whiskey," he said.

"Jasper won't need them floats," Pea Eye remarked.

"He might," Augustus said. "He might fall off his horse if he gets real nervous. Let's chase the buffalo for a while."

"Why?" Pea asked. Po Campo had packed them plenty of meat. He couldn't imagine why Gus would bother with buffalo. They were cumbersome to skin, and he and Gus had no need for so much meat.

Nonetheless, it was follow or be left, for Augustus had loped off after the buffalo, who had only run about a mile. He soon put them to flight again and raced along beside them, riding close to the herd. Pea Eye, caught by surprise, was left far behind in the race. He kept expecting to hear Gus's big rifle, but he didn't, and after a run of about two miles came upon Gus sitting peacefully on a little rise. The buffalo were still running, two or three miles ahead.

"Kill any?" Pea asked.

"No, I wasn't hunting," Augustus said.

"Did you just want to run 'em off, or what?" Pea asked. As usual, Gus's behavior was a complete puzzle.

"Pea, you ain't got your grip on the point," Augustus said. "I just wanted to chase a buffalo once more. I won't have the chance much longer, and nobody else will either, because there won't be no buffalo to chase. It's a grand sport too."

"Them bulls can hook you," Pea Eye reminded him. "Remember old Barlow? A buffalo bull hooked his horse and the horse fell on Barlow and broke his hip."

"Barlow was a slow thinker," Augustus observed. "He just loped along and got hooked."

"A slow walker, too, once his hip got broke," Pea Eye said. "I wonder what happened to Barlow."

"I think he migrated to Seguin, or somewhere over in there," Augustus said. "Married a fat widow and had a passel of offspring. You ought to have done the same, but here you are in Montana."

"Well, I'd hate not to be a bachelor," Pea Eye said.

"Just because it's all you know don't mean it's all you'd enjoy," Augustus said. "You had a chance at a fine widow right there in Lonesome Dove, as I recall."

Pea Eye was sorry the subject of widows had come up. He had nearly forgotten the Widow Cole and the day he had helped her take the washing off the line. He didn't know why he hadn't forgotten it completely—he surely had forgotten more important things. Yet there it was, and from time to time it shoved into his brain. If he had married some widow his brain would probably have been so full of such things that he would have no time to think, or even to keep his knife sharp.

"Ever meet any of the mountain men?" Augustus asked. "They got up in here and took the beavers."

"Well, I met old Kit," Pea Eye said. "You ought to remember. You was there."

"Yes, I remember," Augustus said. "I never thought much of Kit Carson."

"Why, what was wrong with Kit Carson?" Pea Eye asked. "They say he could track anything."

"Kit was vain," Augustus said. "I won't tolerate vanity in a man, though I will in a woman. If I had gone north in my youth I might have got to be a mountain man, but I took to riverboating instead. The whores on them riverboats in my day barely wore enough clothes to pad a crutch."

As they rode north they saw more buffalo, mostly small bunches of twenty or thirty. The third day north of the Yellowstone they killed a crippled buffalo calf and dined on its liver. In the morning, when they left, there were a number of buzzards and two or three prairie wolves hanging around, waiting for them to leave the carcass.

It was a beautiful morning, crisp for an hour or two and then sunny and warm. The country rolled on to the north, as it had for thousands of miles, brown in the distance, the prairie grass waving in the breeze.

"Lord, how much land does the Captain want?" Pea Eye asked. "Looks like this country around here would be good enough for anybody."

"Plenty would settle for it, you're right," Augustus said. "Call might himself. But let's just go on for a day or two more. We ain't struck the Milk River yet."

"Does it run milk?" Pea Eye asked.

"Now think a minute, Pea," Augustus said. "How could it run milk when there ain't no cows up here yet?"

"Why did they call it the Milk, then? Milk is milk."

"Crazy is crazy, too," Augustus said. "That's what I'll be before long from listening to you. Crazy."

"Well, Jasper's mind might break if he don't stop worrying about them rivers," Pea Eye allowed. "I expect the rest of us will keep our wits."

Augustus laughed heartily at the notion of the Hat Creek outfit keeping its wits. "It's true they could be kept in a thimble," he said, "but who brought a thimble?"

There was a little rise to the west, and Augustus loped over to it to see what the land looked like in that direction. Pea trotted along north, as he had been doing, not paying much attention. Gus was always loping off to test the view, as he called it, and Pea didn't feel obliged to follow him every time.

Then Pea heard the sound of a running horse and looked for Gus, supposing he had jumped another little bunch of buffalo. What he saw froze him instantly in place. Gus was racing down the little slope he had just gone up, with at least twenty mounted Indians hot on his heels. He must have ridden right into them. The Indians were shooting both guns and arrows. A bullet cut the grass ahead of Pea and he yanked out his rifle and popped a shot back at the Indians before whirling his horse and fleeing. Gus and he had crossed a good-sized creek less than an hour back, with some trees along it and some weeds and shrubbery in the creek bed. He assumed Gus must be racing for that, since it was the only shelter on the wide prairie. Even as he started, Pea saw five or six Indians veer toward him. He swerved over to join Gus, who had two arrows in his leg. Gus was flailing his horse with his rifle barrel and the horse was running full out.

Fortunately the Indians were poorly mounted—their horses were no match for the Hat Creek horses, and the two men soon widened the gap between them and their pursuers. They were out of range of arrows, and of bullets too, Pea hoped, but he had hardly hoped it when a bullet stung him just above the shoulder blade. But the creek was only three or four miles ahead. If they could make it there would be time enough to worry about wounds.

Gus was trying to pull the arrows out of his leg as he rode, but he was having no luck.

They saw the curve of the little creek from two miles away and angled for the nearest juncture. The Indians had fallen nearly a quarter of a mile back, but were still coming. When they struck the creek Augustus raced along the bank until he found a spot where the weeds and brush were thickest. Then he jumped his horse off the bank and grabbed his saddlebags.

"Get all the ammunition you can," he said. "We're in for a shooting match. And tie the horses in the best cover you can find, or they'll shoot 'em. This is long country to be afoot in."

Then he hobbled to the bank, wishing he had time to cut the two arrows out of his leg. But if they were poisoned it was already too late, and if he didn't do some fine shooting it wouldn't matter anyway because the Indians would overrun them.

Pea heard the big Henry rifle begin to roar as he dragged the sweating horses into the thickest part of the underbrush. It was thick but low, and he didn't think there was much chance for the horses. He yanked the saddlebags and bedrolls off both horses and was hiding them under the bank when Gus stopped firing for a moment.

"Get my saddle," he said. "I'll show you a trick."

Then he began to fire again. Evidently he had turned the Indians, or they would already have been in the creek bed. Pea dutifully got the saddle.

When he got back Gus was reloading. Pea peeped over the bank and saw the Indians, stopped some distance away. Many of them had dismounted and were standing behind their horses, using them as shields.

"How many'd you kill?" he asked.

"Not but three," Augustus said. "This is a smart bunch we're up against. They seen right off a rush would cost them dear."

Pea Eye watched the Indians for a while. They weren't yelling, and they didn't seem excited.

"I don't see what's so smart about them," he said. "They're just standing there."

"Yes, but they're out of range," Augustus said. "They're hoping to tempt me to waste ammunition."

Augustus propped the saddle on the bank in such a way that he could shoot under it and be that much safer if the Indians shot back. He then proceeded to shoot six times, rapidly. Five of the Indians horses dropped, and a sixth ran squealing over the prairie—it fell several hundred yards away. The Indians fired several shots in reply, their bullets slicing harmlessly into the underbrush.

The party of Indians then split. Several Indians went north of them, several south, and eight or ten stayed where they were.

"Well, we're practically surrounded," Augustus said. "I don't expect we'll hear any more from them till dark."

"I'd hate to wait around here till dark," Pea Eye said.

"Did you know you're shot?" Augustus asked.

Pea had forgotten it. Sure enough, the front of his shirt was soaked with blood. He took it off and Augustus examined the wound, which was clean. The bullet had gone right through.

They turned their attention to the arrows in Augustus's left leg. Augustus twisted at them whenever he got a moment. One arrow he soon got out, but the other wouldn't budge.

"This one's in deep," he said. "That brave wasn't more than twenty yards away when he let fly. I think it's worked under the bone, but it ain't poisoned. If it was I'd be feeling it by now."

Pea had a try at removing the arrow, while Gus gritted his teeth and held his leg steady with both hands. The arrow wouldn't budge. It wouldn't even turn, though Pea Eye twisted hard enough to cause a stream of blood to flow down Gus's leg.

As they were working with the arrow there was a sudden terrified squeal from the horses. Augustus hobbled over, drawing his pistol, and saw that both horses were down, their throats cut, their blood very bright on the green weeds and bushes.

"Stay back, Pea," he said, crouching. The Indian that had killed the horses was there somewhere, in the underbrush, but he couldn't see him.

"Watch to the north, Pea," he said. "I don't think these boys want to stay around here till dark, either."

He quickly wiped the sweat from his forehead. Keeping a bush directly in front of him he edged very slowly to the bank, just high enough that he could see the tops of the weeds and underbrush. Then he waited. Once the dying horses finally stopped thrashing, it was very still. Augustus regretted that his preoccupation with the arrows had made him so lax that he had failed to protect the horses. It put them in a ticklish spot. It was over a hundred miles back to the Yellowstone and in all likelihood the herd hadn't even got there yet.

He kept his eyes focused on the tops of the underbrush. It was perfectly windless in the creek bottom, and if the underbrush moved it would be because someone moved it. His big pistol was cocked. He didn't move, and time stretched out. Minutes passed. Augustus carefully kept the sweat wiped out of his eyes, concentrating on keeping his focus. The silence seemed to ring, it was so absolute. There were no flies buzzing yet, no birds flying, nothing. He would have bet the Indian was not twenty yards away from him, and yet he had no inkling of precisely where he was.

"Ain't you coming back, Gus?" Pea Eye asked, after several minutes.

Augustus didn't answer. He watched the tops of the weeds, patiently. It was no time for hurry, much less for conversation. Patience was an Indian virtue. He, himself, didn't have it in day-to-day life, but he could summon it when it seemed essential. Then he heard a movement behind him, and glanced around quickly, to see if Pea had suddenly decided to take a stroll. When he did he saw the edge of a rifle extending an inch or two from the weeds, pointed not at himself but at Pea. He immediately fired twice into the weeds and an Indian flopped over as a fish might flop.

A second later, as the echo of the gun died, he heard a click a few yards to his right. He whirled and fired at it. A moment later the underbrush began to shake as if a huge snake were wriggling through it. Augustus ran into the weeds and saw the wounded Indian trying to crawl away. He at once shot him in the back of the head, and didn't stop to turn him over. Backing out of the weeds, he stepped on the pistol that had misfired, an old cap-and-ball gun. He stuck it in his belt and hurried back to Pea, who looked white. He had sense enough to realize he had just almost been shot. Augustus glanced at the other dead Indian, a fat boy of maybe seventeen. His rifle was an old Sharps carbine, which Augustus threw to Pea.

"We gotta move," he said. "This cover's working against us. But for luck we'd both be dead now already. What we need is a stretch with a steep bank and no cover."

They worked their way upstream, carrying the saddle, saddlebags and guns, for nearly a mile, hugging the bank. Augustus was limping badly but didn't stop to worry about it. Finally they came to a bend in the creek, where the bank was sheer and about ten feet high. The creek bottom was nearly bare of foliage.

"Let's dig," Augustus said, and began to work with his knife to create a shallow cave under the bank. They worked furiously for half an hour until both were drenched with sweat and covered with dirt. Augustus used the stock of the Indian boy's carbine as a rude shovel and tried to shape the dirt they raked out into low breastworks on either side of the cave. They watched as best they could, but saw no Indians.

"Maybe they gave up," Pea Eye said. "You kilt five so far."

"Five reasons why they won't give up," Augustus said. "They'll fight for their dead, since they expect to meet them agin. Ain't you learned that by now?"

Pea Eye could not be sure that he had learned anything about Indians except that he was scared of them, and he had learned that long before he ever saw one. The digging was hard work, but they didn't dare stop. The Indians might show up at any time.

"Which Indians is these we're fighting?" he asked.

"They didn't introduce themselves, Pea," Augustus said. "It might be written on these arrows. I'm going to be one-legged if we don't get this other arrow out pretty soon."

No sooner had he said it than it began to rain arrows, all arching over the south bank of the creek. "Crawl in," Augustus said. He and Pea scrunched back into the cave and stacked the saddlebags in front of them. Many of the arrows went over the creek bed entirely and into the prairie on the other side. A few stuck in the earthworks they had thrown up, and one or two fell in the water.

"They're just hoping to get lucky," Augustus said. "If my dern leg was better I'd sneak over to the other side of the creek and whittle down the odds a little more."

The shower of arrows soon stopped, but the two men stayed in the cave, taking no chances.

"I've got to push this arrow on through," Augustus said. "I may pass out, and if I do, I better do it now. When it gets dark we'll both need to be watching."

He stopped talking and listened. He put his finger to his lips so Pea Eye would be quiet. Someone was on the bank above them—at least one Indian, maybe more. He motioned to Pea to have his pistol ready, in case the Indians tried to rush them. Augustus was hoping for a rush, confident that with the two of them shooting they could decimate the Indians to such an extent that the survivors might leave. If the Indians couldn't be discouraged and driven off, then the situation was serious. They had no horses, the herd was more than a hundred miles away, and he was crippled. They could follow the creek down to the Yellowstone and perhaps strike Miles City, but it would be a slow trip for him to make crippled. Given his choice of gambles, he would prefer a fight. They might even be able to catch one of the Indian horses.

But the rush never came. Whoever was above them left. The creek bank on their side was already in shadow. Augustus uncocked his pistol and stretched his leg out again. He knew better than to put off anything to do with wounds, so he grasped the arrow and began to push it on through his leg. The pain was severe and caused a cold sweat to break out but at least the arrow moved.

"My lord, Gus, you're shot too," Pea Eye said. When Augustus bent over to twist the arrow, Pea noticed that the back of his shirt, down low near his belt, was caked with blood. The dirt from their diggings had covered it, but there was no doubt that it was blood.

"One wound at a time," Augustus said. It took both hands to move the arrow. The skin on his leg began to bulge.

"Cut," he said to Pea. "Pretend I'm snake-bit."

Pea went white. He hated even looking at wounds. The thought of cutting Gus made him want to be sick, but the fact that he had a sharp knife helped. He barely touched the skin and the cut was made. The bloody tip of the arrow poked through. Gus shoved the tip on out and then fainted. Pea Eye had to pull the arrow on through. It was as hard as pulling a bolt out of a board, but he got it out.

Then he felt deeply frightened. If the Indians came now, they were lost, he felt sure. He cocked his pistol and Gus's, and held them both at the ready until his hands grew tired. His head was throbbing. He laid the guns down and wet Gus's forehead from the water bag, hoping Gus would revive. If the Indians came, he would have to shoot quick, and his best shooting had always been done slowly. He liked to take a fine aim. It seemed Gus would never revive. Pea Eye thought he might be dying, although he could hear him breathing.

Finally Gus opened his eyes. His breathing was ragged but he reached over and took his pistol back as if he had just awakened from a refreshing nap. Then to Pea Eye's amazement he crawled out of the cave, hobbled down to the water's edge, and dug in the mud with his knife. He came back with a handful of mud the size of a cannonball.

"Montana mud," he said. "I ain't happy about this wound. Maybe this mud will cool it off."

He covered his wound with mud and offered Pea some. "It's free mud," he said. "Take some." Then he felt behind him, trying to judge the wound in his back that Pea had drawn attention to. "It wasn't a bullet," he concluded. "I could feel a bullet. It was probably another arrow, only it jiggled out during that run."

The twilight was deepening, the creek bed in shadow, though the upper sky was still light.

"I'll watch west and you watch east," Augustus said. Almost as soon as he finished speaking a shot hit the cave bank just above their heads, causing dirt to shower down. Augustus looked down the creek and saw two horsemen cross it, too far away to make accurate targets in the dusk.

"I guess we're fairly surrounded," he said. "Some downstream and some upstream."

"I don't see why we didn't stay in Texas," Pea Eye said. "The Indians was mostly whipped down there."

"Well, this is just bad luck we're having," Augustus said. "We just run into a little bunch of fighters. I imagine they're about as scarce as the buffalo."

"Reckon we can hold 'em off until the Captain comes and looks for us?" Pea asked.

"Yes, if I don't get sick from this leg," Augustus said. "This leg don't feel right. If it don't heal you may have to go for help."

The thought frightened Pea Eye badly. Go for help, when Gus had just said they were surrounded? Go and be scalped, was what that was an invitation to.

"I 'spect they'd catch me if I tried that," Pea said. "Maybe the Captain will figure out that we're in trouble and hurry on up here."

"He won't miss us for another week," Augustus said. "I don't fancy squatting here by this creek for a week."

A few minutes later they heard a loud, strange cry from the east. It was an Indian war cry. Another came from the west, and several from the far bank of the river. The evening would be still and peaceful for a few minutes and then the war cries would start again. Pea had never approved of the way Indians yelled when they fought—it upset his nerves. This yelling was no exception. Some of the cries were so piercing that he wanted to hold his ears.

Augustus, however, listened with appreciation. The war cries continued for an hour. In a lull, Augustus cupped his hands and let out a long, loud cry himself. He kept it up until he ran out of breath. Pea Eye had never heard Augustus yell like that and hardly knew what to make of it. It sounded exactly like a Comanche war cry.

The Indians surrounding them apparently didn't know what to make of it either. When Gus stopped yelling, they did too.

"I was just thanking them for the concert," Augustus said. "Remember that old Comanche that went blind and used to hang around the Fort? He taught me that. I doubt they've ever heard Comanche up in these parts. It might spook them a little."

"Reckon they'll sneak up in the dark?" Pea asked. That was his lifelong worry—being snuck up on in the dark by an Indian.

"I doubt it," Augustus said. "The eyesight of your average Indian is overrated. They spend too much time in them smoky tepees. The bulk of them can't see in the dark no better than we can, if as well. So it's a big chance for them, sneaking up on sharpshooters like us."

"Well, I ain't a sharpshooter," Pea Eye said. "I need to take a good aim or else I miss."

"You're near as depressing as Jasper Fant," Augustus said.

No Indians came in the night, and Augustus was glad of that. He began to feel feverish and was afraid of taking a chill. He had to cover himself with saddle blankets, though he kept his gun hand free and managed to stay awake most of the night—unlike Pea, who snored beside him, as deeply asleep as if he were in a feather bed.

By morning Augustus had a high fever. Though his leg worried him most, he also had pain in his side. He decided he had been wrong in his first analysis, and that he did have a bullet wound there, after all. The fever had him feeling weak.

While he was waiting, pistol cocked, to see if the Indians would try to rush them, he heard thunder. Within half an hour lightning was striking all around them, and thunder crashing.

"Oh, dern," Pea Eye said. "Now I guess we'll get lightning-struck."

"Go back to sleep, if all you can do is be pessimistic," Augustus said. "I smell rain, which is a blessing. Indians mostly don't like to fight in the wet. Only white men are dumb enough just to keep on fighting no matter what the weather is like."

"We've fought Indians in the wet," Pea Eye said.

"Yes, but it was us forced it on *them*," Augustus said. "They'd rather do battle on sunny days, which is only sensible."

"Here they're probably gonna kill us, and you take up for them," Pea Eye said. He had never understood Gus and never would, even if the Indians didn't kill them.

"I'm an admirer of good sense wherever I find it," Augustus said.

"I hope you find some today, then, and get us out of this," Pea said.

Then it began to rain in earnest. It rained so hard that it became impossible to see, or even talk. A muddy stream began to pour off the bank, only inches in front of them. The rain struck so hard it reminded Pea of driving nails. Usually such freshets were short-lived, but this one wasn't. It seemed to rain for hours, and was still raining when dawn came, though not as hard. Alarmingly, to Pea, the creek had become a river, more than deep enough to swim a horse. It rose so that it was only two or three yards in from where they were scrunched into the cave, and it soon washed away their crude breastworks.

And it was still raining. It was cold, too, though fortunately they had a good overhang and were fairly dry. Gus had drug the bedrolls in before the rain started.

Pea was shocked to see that Gus didn't look himself. His face was drawn and his hands unsteady. He was chewing on some jerky he had pulled out of a saddlebag, but it seemed he barely had the strength to eat.

"Are you poorly?" Pea asked.

"I should have got that arrow out sooner," Augustus said. "This leg's gonna give me problems." He handed Pea some jerky and they sat in silence for a while, watching the brown flood sweep past them.

"Hell, a frog could have waded that creek yesterday," Pea said. "Now look at it. It's still raining, too. We may get drowned instead of scalped. It's a good thing Jasper ain't here," he added. "He's mighty afraid of water."

"Actually, this flood is an opportunity for you," Augustus said. "If we can last the day, you might swim past them tonight and get away."

"Well, but that wouldn't be right," Pea Eye said. "I wouldn't want just to leave you sitting here."

"I won't be sitting, I'll be floating, if this keeps up," Augustus said. "The good aspect of it is that it might cool off these Indians. They might go back to their families and let us be."

"I'd still hate to leave you, even so," Pea said.

"You can't carry me to the herd, and I doubt I can walk it," Augustus said. "I'm running such a fever I'm apt to go out of my head any time. You'll probably have to trot back and bring some of the boys, or maybe the wagon. Then I can ride back in style."

The thought struck Pea Eye for the first time that Gus might die. He had no color, and he was shaking. It had never been suggested that Gus might die. Of course, he knew any man could die. Pea himself had seen many die. Yet it was a condition he had never associated with Gus McCrae, or with the Captain either. They were not normal men, as he understood normal, and he had never reckoned with the possibility that either of them might die. Now, when he looked at Gus and saw his pallor and his shakes, the thought came into his mind and wouldn't leave. Gus might die. Pea knew at once that he had to do everything possible to prevent it. If he went back to the wagon and reported that Gus was dead, there was no telling what the Captain would say.

Yet he didn't know exactly what he could do. They had no medicine, it was raining fits, the Indians had them surrounded, and they were a hundred miles or more from the Hat Creek outfit.

"It's a soggy situation, I admit," Augustus said, as if reading Pea Eye's thoughts. "But it ain't fatal yet. I could hold out here for a few days. Call could make it back to this creek in one ride on that feisty mare of his. Best thing for you to do would be just to travel at night. If you walk around in the daytime, some of these red boys might spot you and you'd have about the chance of a rabbit. I guess you could make it to the Yellowstone in three nights, though, and they ought to be there by then."

Pea Eye dreaded the prospect. He hated night travel, and it would be worse afoot. He began to hope that maybe the rain had discouraged the Indians, but that hope only lasted an hour. Three times during the day the Indians fired on them. They shot from downriver, and Gus opened up on them at once. They were so respectful of his gun that their bullets only splattered uselessly in the mud, or else hit the water and ricocheted off with a whine. Gus looked so weak and shaky that Pea Eye wondered if he could still shoot accurately, but the question was answered later in the day when an Indian tried to shoot them from the opposite bank, using a little rain squall as cover. He got off his shot, which hit one of the saddles; then Gus shot him as he turned to crawl away. The shot caused the Indian to straighten up, and Gus shot him again. The second bullet seemed to suck the Indian backward—he toppled off the bank and rolled into the water. He was not dead; he tried to swim, so Gus shot him again. A minute or two later he floated past them face down.

"I expect he would have drowned," Pea Eye said, thinking it wasteful of Gus to shoot the man three times.

"He might have, or he might have lived to cut off your nuts," Augustus said.

There were no more attacks that day, but there was no doubt that the Indians were still there. Before sundown they raised their war cries again. This time Augustus didn't answer.

The day had never been bright, but it seemed to linger. There was a long, rainy dusk, so long that it made Pea Eye feel gloomy. It was cramped in the cave. He longed to stretch his legs, and then made the foolish mistake of saying so to Gus.

"Wait till it's full dark," Augustus said. "Then you can stretch 'em."

"What if I get lost?" Pea Eye said. "I ain't never been in this country."

"Go south," Augustus said. "That's all you have to remember. If you mess up and go north, a polar bear will eat you."

"Yes, and a grizzly bear might if I go south," Pea Eye said with some bitterness. "Either way I'd be dead."

He regretted that Gus had mentioned bears. Bears had been preying on his mind since the Texas bull had had his great fight. It struck him that things were tough up here in the north. It had taken Gus three shots to kill a small Indian. How many shots would it take to kill a grizzly bear?

"Well, you ought to start, Pea," Augustus said finally. It had been dark for over an hour, and the Indians were silent.

"That dern water looks cold," Pea Eye said. "I was never one for cold baths."

"Well, I'm sorry we didn't bring a bathtub and a cook-stove," Augustus said. "If we had we could heat some water for you, but as it is you'll just have to rough it. The rain's stopped. The creek could start going down any time, and the more water in it the better for you. Get out in the middle and pretend you're a muskrat."

Pea Eye was half a mind not to go. He had never disobeyed an order in his life, but this time he was sorely tempted, and it was not just the cold swim or the chancy trek that made him hesitate. It was leaving Gus. Gus was close to being out of his head. If he went on out of his head the Indians would have a good chance to get him. He sat for a while, trying to think of some argument that would make Gus let him stay with him.

"Maybe we could both swim out," he said. "I know you're crippled, but you could lean on me once we started walking."

"Pea, go," Augustus said. "I ain't getting well, I'm getting sicker. If you want to help, go get Captain Call. Have him lope up here with an extra horse and tote me over to Miles City."

Pea Eye got ready with a heavy heart. It all seemed wrong, and none of it would have happened if they'd just stayed in Texas.

"Just take your rifle," Augustus said. "A pistol won't do you no good if you have to stop one of them bears. Besides, I'll need both pistols—any fighting that happens here will be close-range work."

"I can't swim and hold a dern rifle, Gus," Pea Eye said.

"Stick it through your belt and down your pants leg," Augustus said. "You can float downstream, you won't actually have to swim much."

Pea Eye took off his boots and his shirt and made a bundle of them. Then he did as Gus ordered and stuck his rifle through his belt. He stuffed some jerky in one boot for provisions. All he needed to do was leave, but it was hard.

"Now go on, Pea," Augustus said. "Go get the Captain, and don't worry about me. Don't let the Indians catch you, whatever you do."

Gus reached out a hand and Pea Eye realized he was offering a handshake. Pea Eye shook his hand, feeling terribly sad.

"Gus, I never thought I'd be leaving you," he said.

"Well, you are, though," Augustus said. "Trod carefully."

It was then that the conviction struck Pea Eye that he would never see Gus alive again. Mainly what they were into was just another Indian fight, and all of those had inconveniences. But Gus had never sustained a wound before that Pea could remember. The arrows and bullets that had missed him so many times had finally found him.

After the handshake, Gus treated him as if he were already gone. He didn't offer any messages or say another word. Pea Eye wanted to say something else, but couldn't think what. Feeling very disconsolate, he waded into the cold water. It was far colder than he had supposed. His legs at once felt numb. He looked back once and could dimly see the cave, but not Gus.

As soon as he reached swimming depth, he forgot Gus and everything else, due to a fear of drowning. The icy water pushed him under at once. Floating wasn't as easy as Gus had made it seem. The rifle was a big problem. Stuck in his pants leg, it seemed to weigh like lead. Also, he had no experience in such fast water. Several times he got swept over to the side of the creek and almost got tangled in the underbrush that the rushing water covered.

Worse than that, he almost immediately lost the little bundle of boots and pants, shirt, all his provisions and part of his ammunition. He had reached down with one hand to try and move the rifle a little higher up on his leg, and the water sucked the bundle away and swept it far ahead of him. Pea Eye began to realize he was going to drown unless he did better than he was doing. The water pushed him under several times. He wanted badly to climb up the bank but was by no means sure he was past the Indians. Gus said to go down at least a mile, and he wasn't sure he had gone that far. The water had a suck to it that he had constantly to fight against; to his horror he felt it sucking his pants off. He had been so disconsolate when he walked into the river that he had not buckled his belt tightly. He had nothing much in the way of hips, and the water sucked his pants down past them. The rifle sight was gouging him in the leg. He grabbed the rifle, but then went under. The dragging pants, with the rifle in one leg, were drowning him. He began to try frantically to get them off, so as to have the free use of his legs. He wanted to cuss Gus for having suggested sticking the rifle in his pants leg. He could never get it out in time to shoot an Indian, if one appeared, and it was causing him terrible aggravation. He fought to the surface again, went under, and when he came up wanted to yell for help, and then remembered there would be no one around to hear him but Indians. Then his leg was almost jerked off—he had been swept close to the bank and the dragging gun had caught in some underbrush. The bank was only a few feet away and he tried to claw over to it, but that didn't work. While he was struggling, the pants came off and he was swept down the river backwards. One minute he could see the south bank of the river, and the next minute all he could see was water. Twice he opened his mouth to suck in air and sucked in water instead, some of which came back out his nose. His legs and feet were so numb from the cold water that he couldn't feel them.

He never remembered getting out of the water, but somehow he did, for when he next took note of things he was laying in the mud, his feet still in the water. He was stark naked and the mud was cold, so he pulled himself up and laboriously climbed the bank. It was only eight or ten feet high, but it was slippery.

When he got up, he wanted to lay in the grass and go to sleep, but he was awake enough to think about his situation, and thinking soon made him wakeful. He hadn't drowned, but he was naked, unarmed, without food, and something like a hundred miles from the Hat Creek wagon. He didn't know the country and was up against some tough Indians who did. Gus was sick and maybe dying somewhere upriver. It would be daylight in a few hours and the danger from Indians would increase.

Pea Eye at once started walking as fast as he could. Though it had stopped raining, it was still cloudy, and he could not see one star or the moon or, for that matter, anything either on heaven or earth. The awful thought struck him that, rolling around and around in the water, he might even have confused north and south and crawled up the wrong bank. He might be walking north, in which case he was as good as dead, but he couldn't stop to worry about it. He had to move. He had lost his pack and his gun in the river, and as soon as the river sank to being a normal stream again, they would all be lying in the creek bed, in plain sight. If the Indians found them they would know he was gone, and that Gus was alone, which would make things hot for Gus. If they were in a tracking mood it would also make things hot for him. They had horses and could run him down in a matter of hours. The faster he traveled, the better chance he had.

After he had thought about it for a while, Pea was profoundly glad the night was so dark. He wished it could stay dark forever, or at least until he pulled in sight of the herd. When he thought of all the perils he was exposed to, it was all he could do to keep from running. He remembered vividly all the things Indians did to white men. In his rangering days he had helped bury several men who had had such things done to them, and memories of those charred and gouged corpses was with him in the darkness. With him too, and just as terrifying, was the memory of the great orange bear who had nearly ripped the Texas bull wide open. He remembered how fast the bear had gone when they tried to chase it on horseback. If such a bear spotted him he felt he would probably just lie down and give up.

The darkness didn't last. The only blessing the light brought was that Pea Eye caught a glimpse of the north star as the clouds were breaking. He knew, at least, that he was going in the right direction. The sun soon came up, and he remembered Gus's warning not to travel in the daytime. Pea Eye decided to ignore it. For one thing, he was on an absolutely open plain, where there was no good place to hide. He might as well be moving as sitting.

When he looked ahead he felt very discouraged, for the country seemed endless. It seemed to him he could see almost a hundred miles—just empty country, and he had to walk it. He had never been an advocate of walking, and coming up the trail horseback had given him even less affection for it. He had never bargained for doing so much walking, especially barefoot. Before he had gone more than a few miles his feet were cut and sore. The plains looked grassy and smooth, but there were rocks scattered here and there, and he stepped on a goodly number of them.

Also, it embarrassed him that he was naked. Of course, there was no one around to see him, but he could see himself, and it was disconcerting. The Captain would be mighty surprised to see him come tramping up naked; the boys would undoubtedly think it hilarious and would kid him about it for weeks.

At first the nakedness worried him almost as much as his sore feet, but before he had walked half a day his feet hurt so much that he had stopped caring whether he was naked, or even alive. He had to wade two little creeks, and he got into some thorny underbrush in one of them. Soon every step was painful, but he knew he had to keep walking or he would never find the boys. Every time he looked back, he expected to see either Indians or a bear. By evening he was just stumbling along. He found a good patch of high grass and weeds and lay down to sleep for a while.

He woke up bitterly cold to find it was snowing. A squall had blown in. Pea Eye heard a strange sound and took a minute to realize it was his own chattering teeth. His feet were so sore he could scarcely walk on them, and the snow didn't help. It was a wet snow, melting almost as it fell, but that didn't make it much more comfortable.

Somehow he hobbled south all night. The snow soon stopped, but his feet were very cold and every time he stepped on a rock in the dark they hurt so he could hardly keep from crying out. He felt very weak and empty and knew he wasn't making very good time. He bitterly regretted not having hung onto some of the jerky, or his rifle, or something. Gus would think him a fine fool if he found out he had lost everything before he even got clear of the creek.

In his weariness, he even forgot for a time that Gus had been left in the little cave. Several times he spoke to Gus as he stumbled along—mainly asking directions. For a time he felt Gus was just ahead, leading the way. Or was it Deets? Pea Eye felt confused. Whoever it was wouldn't speak to him, and yet he continued to ask questions. He took comfort in thinking Gus or Deets was there. They were the best scouts. They would lead him in.

When the second day dawned, Pea Eye stopped to rest. He realized no one was with him, unless it was ghosts. But then, it might *be* ghosts. Gus might be dead by then, and Deets was, for sure. Maybe one of them, having nothing to do, had decided to float along ahead of him, guiding him to the Yellowstone.

When he looked at his feet, it seemed to him that he might make almost as good time crawling or walking on his hands. His feet were swollen to twice their size, besides being cut here and there. Yet they were the only feet he had, and after dozing for an hour in the sun, he got up and hobbled on. He was very hungry and wished he had paid more attention to Po Campo, who could find things to eat just by walking along looking. Pea tried to look, but he saw nothing but grass and weeds. Fortunately he struck several small creeks and had plenty of water. Once he even managed to sluice some minnows up on dry land. They wiggled and flopped and were hard to catch, and of course they only made a few bites, but they were better than nothing.

His biggest piece of luck came late that day when he was able to knock over a big prairie chicken with a rock. He only broke the bird's wing and had to chase it through the grass a long way, but the bird tired before he did, and he finally caught it, skinned it and ate it raw. He rested three hours and then hobbled on through another night.

The third morning he could barely make himself move. His feet were worse than ever, the plains ahead still endless and empty. His eyes ached from looking so hard for the line of the Yellowstone, but he still couldn't see it.

It was the emptiness that discouraged him most. He had almost stopped worrying about Indians and bears. What he worried about was being lost. He knew by the stars he was still going south, but south where? Maybe he had veered east of the herd, or west of it, so that no one would spot him. Maybe he had already passed them, in which case there was little hope. The snows would just come and freeze him, or else he would starve.

He lay until midmorning, unable to decide what to do. For a time he thought the best plan might be just to sit. There were supposed to be soldiers in Montana, somewhere. If he sat long enough, maybe some would find him.

Finally, though, he got up and stumbled on. The soldiers would only find his bones, if they found anything. It was a blazing day, so hot it made him feel annoyed at Montana weather. What kind of country was it where you could get frostbite one night and sunburn two days later? He saw a couple of prairie dogs and wasted an hour trying to get one with a rock. But the prairie dogs were smarter than prairie chickens, and he never came close.

He stumbled on, feeling that the sun would burn off what skin he had left. Several times during the afternoon he fell. He grew lightheaded and felt as if he were floating. Then his swollen feet would refuse to work, and instead of floating he would fall. Once he came to lying flat on his back in the grass, the sun burning into his eyes. He scrambled up and looked around, feeling that the herd might have walked right past him when he slept. He tried very hard to walk a straight line south, but his legs were so weak that he kept wobbling off course.

"Dern you, walk straight," he said. The sound of his own cracked voice startled him out of his fury.

Then he felt embarrassed. A man who would cuss his own legs just because they were weak was peculiar, he knew. He got the floating feeling again, so strong that he felt frightened. He felt he might be going to float right out of his own body. He wondered if he was dying, if that was how it felt. He had never heard of anyone dying while they were just walking along, but then dying was something he knew little about. He would take a few steps and then feel himself begin to rise out of his own body, which frightened him so that he stumbled and fell. He didn't want to stand up again, and he began to crawl, looking up now and then to see if the herd was in sight. He felt he couldn't live another night so alone and hungry. He would die in the grass like some beaten animal.

Then it grew dark, and he wanted to cry with disappointment. He had walked long enough—surely it was time the boys showed up. Once it was full dark, he stopped and listened. He felt the herd might be close, and if he listened maybe he would hear the Irishman singing. He heard no singing, but when he got up and tried to stumble on, he felt the presence of his guide again. This time he knew it was Deets. He couldn't see him because it was dark, and of course Deets was dark, but he lost the floating feeling and walked easier, though he was a little scared. He didn't know what the rules were with people who were dead. He would have liked to say something but felt he shouldn't. Deets might go away and leave him to stumble along in the dark if he said anything. Maybe travel was no trouble for the dead—Pea didn't know. It was a considerable trouble for him. He walked slow, for he didn't like to fall, but he walked on all night.

Two hours after sunup the next day, Dish Boggett, who had been sent off to do a little scouting, thought he saw a figure, far to the north. At first he couldn't tell if it was a man or an antelope. If it was a man, it was an Indian, he imagined, and he raced back to the herd and got the Captain, who had been shoeing the mare— always an arduous task. She hated anyone to handle her feet and had to be securely snubbed before she would submit to it.

Fortunately Call was finished, and he rode back with Dish, to look for the man. There was no sign of him at first, but Dish had a good eye for country and knew where he had seen him. Call privately supposed it had only been an antelope, but he wanted to check. They had crossed the Yellowstone the day before—the men and all the stock had got across safely. Jasper Fant was in his best mood of the trip, having survived all the rivers after all.

"There he is," Dish said suddenly. "If it ain't Pea."

Dish was almost stunned with surprise. Pea was no longer walking. He was sitting down in the grass, naked, nodding his head as if in conversation with somebody. When he heard them he looked around, as if not particularly surprised, but when they dismounted there were tears in his eyes.

"Howdy, Captain," Pea Eye said, embarrassed by his own emotion. "You just missed Deets, I guess."

Call saw that Pea Eye was wounded and out of his head. There was blood on his chest from a shoulder wound, the sun had blotched his body, and his feet were swollen the size of a cow's bladder and cut to shreds.

"Is Gus dead?" Call asked, afraid to hear the answer. Though he knew Gus's penchant for trouble, it was a shock to see Pea Eye in such a state.

Pea Eye had been thinking of Deets, who had kindly walked him through the night. He was embarrassed to be naked, and he found it hard to turn his mind back to where he could deal with the question the Captain had asked him.

"The creek's up, it's why I lost my clothes," he said.

Call untied his slicker from his saddle and covered Pea Eye with it. Pea Eye immediately felt better. He tried to button the slicker so his dingus wouldn't show, but his fingers shook and Dish Boggett finally did it for him.

"Is Gus dead?" Call asked again.

Pea Eye let his mind turn slowly. Then he remembered that Gus had been sitting with two guns in his hands, not saying a word, when he waded into the river. He had had that bad wound in his leg.

"The creek was up when I left him," Pea Eye said. "I had to swim down past the Indians and I lost all my gear. Gus kept my pistol."

"Where was this?" Call asked.

"Up north, Captain," Pea Eye said. "We dug a cave in a riverbank. That's all I know."

"But he wasn't dead when you left him?"

"No, he sent me off," Pea said. "He said he wanted you to lope on up there and help him with those Indians."

Dish Boggett could not adjust to the fact that Pea Eye was naked and all scarred up. They had had such a peaceful time of it that he had lost the sense that they were in dangerous country.

"What was that about Deets?" he asked.

"Helped me," Pea said simply. "Are we going after Gus, Captain? We had a hard time getting one of them arrows out and his leg was giving him pain."

"You're going to the wagon," Call said. "You need some grub. How many Indians were there?"

Pea tried to think. "A bunch jumped us," he said. "About twenty, I guess. Gus shot a few."

Call and Dish had to lift him; all strength seemed to have left him, now that he knew he was safe. Dish had to hold him on his horse as they rode back, for Pea Eye had so little strength he could not even grip the saddle horn.

The crew, which had been in high spirits and drunk on their own celebrity—for weren't they the first men to bring a Texas herd across the Yellowstone?—sobered up immediately when they saw the condition Pea Eye was in.

"Why, hello, boys," Pea said, when he was helped off the horse. They all gathered around to greet him, and Bert and Needle Nelson helped him down. Po Campo had some coffee ready. Pea reached out for a cup, once they had him propped against the wagon, but his hands were too shaky to hold it. Po fed him a little with a spoon, and between one sip and the next, Pea slid from his position and passed out. He collapsed so quickly that no one even caught him.

"Is he dead?" Newt asked, anxious.

"No, just tuckered out," Call said.

He was filling his saddlebags with ammunition, glad that he had got new shoes on the mare.

"He said Deets helped him," Dish Boggett said. The way Pea said it had unnerved him. Deets was dead and buried, back on the Powder River.

Call didn't answer. He was pondering the question of whether to take a man with him.

"I guess he was out of his head," Dish said. "I guess that explains it."

Po Campo smiled. "The dead can help us if we let them, and if they want to," he said.

Jasper Fant, delighted not to be among the dead, looked at Po severely. "Ain't none ever helped me except my own pa," he said.

"How'd he help you?" Needle asked.

"Left me twenty dollars in his will. I bought this saddle with it and I been a cowboy ever since."

"You call yourself one, you mean," Soupy Jones said. He had poor relations with Jasper as a result of a dispute over cards.

"I'm here, ain't I?" Jasper said. "Just because you lost that hand don't mean I can't cow."

"Oh, shut your trap, Jasper," Dish said. He had had enough of Jasper and Soupy and felt that the whole question of Pea and Deets had been treated too brusquely. After all, the first words Pea had said was that they had just missed Deets. Dish didn't want to admit it, but he had been scared of ghosts all his life, and didn't like to think that any were wandering around. It would just make night herding more nerve-racking, even if the ghost in question was one that might be friendly to him.

Then someone noticed that Captain Call was leaving. He took an extra rifle from the wagon and got the slicker that he had lent Pea, covering Pea with a blanket.

"Just move the stock on north," he said. "Be alert. I'm going to get Gus."

The thought of him leaving sent a ripple of apprehension through the camp. Though independent to a man in some respects, the outfit was happier in all respects when Captain Call was around. Or if not the Captain, then Gus. Only a few hours earlier, they had felt cocky enough to take on an army. After all, they were the conquerors of the Yellowstone. But now, watching the Captain catch a horse for Gus to ride back on, they all felt daunted. The vast plain was beautiful, but it had reduced Pea Eye to a scarred wreck. And the Indians had Gus holed up somewhere. They might kill him and the Captain too. All men were mortal, and they felt particularly so. A thousand Indians might come by nightfall. The Indians might fall on them as they had fallen on Custer.

Call had no time to soothe the men with elaborate instructions. If Gus was badly wounded, he would weaken rapidly, and every hour counted. Arriving ten minutes too late would be as bad as ten days, or a year, for that matter. Besides, the almost beseeching way the men looked at him was irritating. Sometimes they acted as if they would forget how to breathe if he or Gus wasn't there to show them. They were all resourceful men—he knew that, if they didn't—and yet at certain times they became like children, wanting to be led. All his adult life, he had consented to lead, and yet occasionally, when the men seemed particularly dumbstruck, he wondered why he had done it.

He and Augustus had discussed the question of leadership many times.

"It ain't complicated," Augustus maintained. "Most men doubt their own abilities. You don't. It's no wonder they want to keep you around. It keeps them from having to worry about failure all the time."

"They ain't failures, most of them," Call pointed out. "They can do perfectly well for themselves."

Augustus chuckled. "You work too hard," he said. "It puts most men to shame. They figure out they can't keep up, and it's just a step or two from that to feeling that they can't do nothing much unless you're around to get them started.

"It don't take on me, which is lucky," he added. "I don't care how hard you work, or where you go."

"I'd like to see something that could put you to shame," Call said.

"My pecker's done it a few times," Augustus said.

Call wondered what he meant by that, but didn't ask.

When he was packed, he mounted at once, and rode over to Dish Boggett. "You're in charge," he said. "Trail on north. I'll be back when I can."

Dish paled at the thought of so much responsibility. He had enough worries as it was, what with Pea Eye talking of ghosts.

The Captain looked angry, which made the men better reconciled to the fact that he was leaving. All of them feared his angers. But once he left, before he and the mare were even out of sight, their mood of relief changed back to one of apprehension.

Jasper Fant, so cheerful only an hour before, sank the fastest. "Good lord," he said. "Here we are in Montana and there's Indians and bears and it's winter coming on and the Captain and Gus both off somewhere. I'll be surprised if we don't get massacred."

For once Soupy Jones didn't have a word to say.

95

AUGUSTUS KEPT HIS PISTOL COCKED ALL NIGHT, once Pea Eye left. He watched the surface of the river closely, for the trick he hoped might work for Pea could also work for the Indians. They might put a log in the water and float down on him, using the log for cover. He tried to look and listen closely, a task not helped by the fact that he was shaking and feverish.

He expected the Indians to come sliding out of the water like big snakes, right in front of him, but none came, and as his fever mounted he began to mumble. From time to time he was half aware that he was delirious, but there was nothing he could do about it, and anyway he preferred the delirium to the tedium of waiting for the Indians to attack. One minute he would be trying to watch the black water, the next he would be back at Clara's. At times he saw her face vividly.

The dawn broke sunny. Bad as he felt, Augustus still enjoyed seeing the sun. It helped clear his head and stirred him to thoughts of escape. He was sick of the little cold cave under the riverbank. He had thought to wait there for Call, but the more he considered, the more he felt it to be a bad plan. Call's arrival was days away, and dependent on Pea getting through. If Pea didn't get through—and the chances were good that he wouldn't—then Call might not even start to look for him for another week.

As a student of wounds, he knew just by looking at his leg that he was in trouble. The leg was yellowish, with black streaks striping the yellow. Blood poisoning was a possibility. He knew that if he didn't get medical attention within the next few days his chances were slim. Even waiting for nightfall might be folly.

If the Indians caught him in the open, his chances would be equally slim, of course, but it took no deliberation to know that if he had to choose, and he did, he would prefer the active to the passive course.

As soon as the sun was well up he eased out of the cave and stood up. The bad leg throbbed. Even to touch his toes to the ground hurt. The waters were rapidly receding. Fifty yards to the east, a game trail led up the creek bank. Augustus decided to use the carbine he had taken off the Indian boy as a crutch. He cut the stirrups off the saddle and lashed one over each end of the rifle, then padded one end of his rude crutch with a piece of saddle leather. He stuffed one pistol under his belt, holstered the other, took his rifle and a pocketful of jerky, and hobbled across along the bank to the animal trail.

He edged cautiously out of the riverbed, but saw no Indians. The broad plain was empty for miles. The Indians had left. Augustus wasted no time in speculation. He started at once, hobbling southeast toward Miles City. He hoped he had not more than thirty or forty miles to go before he struck the town.

He was not used to the crutch and he made poor time. When occasionally he forgot and set his bad foot to the ground, the pain was almost enough to make him pass out. He was weak, and had to stop every hour or so to rest. In the hot sun, sweat poured out of him, though he felt cold and feared a chill. Two or three miles from where he started, he crossed the tracks of a sizable herd of buffalo—they were probably the reason the Indians had left. With winter coming, buffalo were more important to the warriors than two white men, though probably they meant to return and finish off the whites once the hunt was over.

All day he persevered, dragging himself along. He stopped less frequently, because he found it hard to get started once he stopped. Rest was seductive, made more so by his tendency to improve the situation through imagination. Maybe the herd had moved north faster than he calculated. Maybe Call would show up the next day and save him the painful business of dragging along with his crutch.

Yet he hated waiting almost as much as he hated the traveling. His habit had been to go and meet whatever needed to be met, not to wait idly for what might approach.

What was approaching now was death, he knew. He had faced it before and overridden its motion with his own. To sit and wait for it gave it too many advantages. He had seen many men die of wounds, and had watched the turning of their spirits from active desire to live to indifference. With a bad wound, the moment indifference took over, life began to subside. Few men rose out of it: most lost all impulse toward activity and ended by offering death at least a half-hearted welcome.

Augustus didn't intend to do that, so he struggled on. When he took his rests he took them standing up, leaning on the crutch. It took less will to get started if one was standing up.

He hobbled over the plain through the long afternoon and twilight, finally collapsing sometime in the night. His hand slipped off the crutch and he felt it falling from him. In stooping to reach for it, he fell face down, unconscious before he hit the ground. In his dreams he was with Lorena, in the tent on the hot Kansas plains. He longed for her to cool him somehow, touch him with her cool hand, but though she smiled, she didn't cool him. The world had become red, as though the sun had swollen and absorbed it. He felt as if he were lying on the surface of the red sun as it looked at sunset when it sank into the plain.

When he got his eyes open the sun was white, not red, and directly above him. He heard a spitting sound, such as a human would make, and his hand went to the pistol at his belt, thinking the Indians had come. But when he turned his head, it was a white man he saw: a very old, small white man in patched buckskins. The old man had a tobacco-stained beard and a bowie knife in his hand. A spotted horse grazed nearby. The old man was just squatting there, watching. Augustus kept his hand on his gun, but didn't draw it—he didn't know if he had the strength to draw it.

"Them was Blood Indians," the old man said. "It beats all that they didn't get you. You got enough of them."

"Five is all," Augustus said, raising himself to a sitting position. He didn't like to talk lying down.

"Seven I heard," the old man said. "I get along with the Bloods and the Blackfeet too. Bought lots of beaver from them in the beaverin' days."

"I'm Augustus McCrae," Augustus said.

"Hugh Auld," the visitor said. "Down Miles City they call me Old Hugh, although I doubt I'm eighty yet."

"Was you meaning to stab me with that knife?" Augustus asked. "I'd rather not shoot you unnecessarily."

Old Hugh grinned and spat again. "I was about to have a go at cutting off that rotten leg of yours," he said. "Before you come to, I was. That leg's ruint, but I might have a hell of a time cutting through the bone without no saw. Besides, you might have woke up and give me trouble."

"'Spect I would have," Augustus said, looking at the leg. It was no longer black-striped—just black.

"We got to take it off," Old Hugh said. "If that rot gets in the other leg you'll lose both of them."

Augustus knew the old man was right in everything he said. The leg was rotting, but a bowie knife was no instrument for taking it off.

"How far is Miles City?" he asked. "I guess they've got a sawbones there."

"Two, last time I went to town," Old Hugh said. "Both drunkards."

"You forgot to inform me of the distance," Augustus said.

"Forty miles and a fraction," Hugh said. "I don't believe you could have walked it."

Augustus used the crutch to pull himself up. "I might fool you," he said, though it was just pride talking. He knew quite well he couldn't have walked it. Just getting to his feet left him nauseous.

"Where'd you come from, stranger?" the old man asked. He rose to his feet but did not exactly straighten up. His back was bent. To Augustus he seemed scarcely five feet tall.

"I was setting a deadfall and let it fall on me," Old Hugh explained cheerfully. "Some Blood warriors found me. They thought it was funny, but my back never did straighten out."

"We all have misfortunes," Augustus said. "Could I borrow your horse?"

"Take it, only don't kick him," Old Hugh said. "If you kick him he'll buck. I'll follow along as best I can in case you fall off."

He led the spotted horse over and helped Augustus mount. Augustus thought he might pass out, but managed not to. He looked at Old Hugh.

"You sure you get along with these Indians?" he asked. "I'd be embarrassed if you came to any trouble on my account."

"I won't," Old Hugh said. "They're off stuffing themselves with fresh buffalo meat. I was invited to join 'em but I think I'll poke along after you, even though I don't know where you come from."

"A little fart of a town called Lonesome Dove," Augustus said. "It's in south Texas, on the Rio Grande."

"Dern," the old man said, clearly impressed by the information. "You're a traveling son of a bitch, ain't you?"

"Does this horse have a name?" Augustus asked. "I might need to speak to him."

"I been calling him Custer," Old Hugh said. "I done a little scouting for the General once."

Augustus paused a minute, looking down at the old trapper. "I got one more favor to ask you," he said. "Tie me on. I ain't got strength enough to mount again if I should fall."

The old man was surprised. "I guess you've learned some tricks, with all your traveling," he said. He fixed a rawhide loop around Augustus's waist and made it tight to the cantle.

"Let's go, Custer," Augustus said, giving the horse rein and remembering not to kick him.

Five hours later, as the sun was setting, he nudged the exhausted horse over a slope north of the Yellowstone and saw the little town of Miles City four or five miles to the east.

When he got to town it was nearly dark. He stopped in front of what appeared to be a saloon but found he could not dismount. Then he remembered that he was tied on. He couldn't untie the knots in the rawhide, but managed to draw his pistol and fire in the air. The first shot seemed to go unnoticed, but when he fired twice more several men came to the door of the saloon and looked at him.

"That's Old Hugh's horse," one said in a sullen voice, as if he suspected Augustus of horse theft.

"Yes, Mr. Auld was kind enough to loan him to me," Augustus said, staring the man down. "I've a ruined leg and would appreciate it if someone would locate me a medical man quick."

The men walked out and came around the horse. When they saw the leg, one whistled.

"What done that?" he asked.

"An arrow," Augustus said.

"Who are you, sir?" the oldest of the men asked, more respectfully.

"Augustus McCrae, Captain in the Texas Rangers," Augustus said. "One of you gentlemen will need to help me with these knots."

They hurried to help, but before they could get him off the horse the red water washed over his eyes again. The spotted horse named Custer didn't like so many men around him. He tried to bite one of them, then bucked twice, throwing Augustus, who had just been untied, into the street. Two of the men tried to catch the horse but he easily outran them and raced back out of town.

96

AUGUSTUS FLOATED in the red water. Sometimes he saw faces, heard voices, saw more faces. He saw Bolivar and Lippy, his two wives, his three sisters. He saw men long dead whom he had rangered with, saw Pedro Flores and Pea Eye and a redheaded whore he had taken up with for a month in his riverboating days. He sloshed helplessly back and forth, as if something were churning the water.

When the redness receded and he opened his eyes again, he heard a piano playing in the distance. He was in bed in a small hot room. Through the open window he could see the great Montana prairie. Looking around, he noticed a small fat man dozing in a chair nearby. The man wore a black frock coat sprinkled with dandruff. A bottle of whiskey and an old bowler hat nearly as disreputable as Lippy's sat on a small bureau. The fat man was snoring peacefully.

Feeling considerable pain, Augustus looked down and saw that his left leg was gone. The stump had been bandaged, but the bandage was leaking. Blood seeped through it, though it was a thick bandage.

"If you're the sawbones, wake up and stop this drip," Augustus said. He felt irritable and sad, and wished the whiskey bottle were in reach.

The little fat man jerked as if poked with a fork, and opened his eyes. His cheeks were red-streaked—from excessive drinking, Augustus supposed. He put both hands on his head as if surprised that it was still there.

"And pass the whiskey, if you can spare any," Augustus added. "I hope you ain't thrown my leg away."

The doctor jerked again, as if every statement pricked him.

"You've got a mighty healthy voice for a sick man," the doctor said. "In this room, such a voice is a tight fit."

"Well, it's the only voice I got," Augustus said.

The doctor put his hands to his temple again. "It strikes my temples like a tenpound hammer," he said. "Though I'm sorry to complain. The truth is I don't feel well myself."

"You probably drink too much," Augustus said. "If you'll hand me the bottle I'll reduce your temptations."

The doctor did, but not before taking a swig. Augustus took several while the doctor shuffled around and stood looking out the window. Across the street the piano was still playing.

"That girl plays beautifully," the doctor said. "They say she studied music in Philadelphia when she was younger."

"How old is she now?" Augustus asked. "Maybe I'll send her a bouquet."

The doctor smiled. "It's plain you're a man of spirit," he said. "That's good. I'm afraid you've a few fractuosities yet to endure."

"A few what?" Augustus asked. "You better introduce yourself before you start talking Latin."

"Dr. Mobley," the man said. "Joseph C. Mobley, to be precise. The C stands for Cincinnatus."

"More Latin, I guess," Augustus said. "Explain that first bunch of Latin you talked."

"I mean we've got to take off that other leg," Dr. Mobley said. "I should have done it while you were out, but frankly, getting the left leg off exhausted me."

"It's a good thing," Augustus said. "If you'd hacked off my right leg, you'd be the one who was out. I need that right leg."

His gun belt was hanging over a chair nearby, and he reached out and took his pistol from the holster.

The doctor looked around, reaching out his hand for the whiskey bottle. Augustus gave it to him and he took a long drink and handed it back.

"I understand your attachment to your own appendages," he said, opening the bandage. He winced when he looked at the wound, but kept working. "I don't want to cut your other leg off bad enough to get shot in the process. However, you'll die if you don't reconsider. That's a plain fact."

"Go buy me some more whiskey," Augustus said. "There's money in my pants. Is that girl playing the piano a whore?"

"Yes, her name is Dora," the doctor said. "Consumptive, I'm afraid. She'll never see Philadelphia again." He began to wrap the leg in a clean bandage.

Augustus suddenly grew faint. "Give her twenty dollars out of my pants and tell her to keep playing," he said. "And shove this bed a little closer to the window— it's stuffy in here."

The doctor managed to shove the bed over near the window, but the effort tired him so that he sat back down in the chair where he had been dozing.

Augustus recovered a little. He watched the doctor a moment. "Physician, heal thyself, ain't that what they say?" he remarked.

Dr. Mobley chuckled unhappily. "That's what they say," he said. He breathed heavily for a time, and then stood up.

"I'll go get the whiskey," he said. "While I'm about it, I'd advise you to take a sober look at your prospects. If you persist in your attachment to your right leg it'll be the last opportunity you have to take a sober look at anything."

"Don't forget to tip that girl," Augustus said. "Hurry back with my whiskey and bring a glass."

Dr. Mobley turned at the door. "We should operate today," he said. "Within the hour, in fact, although we could wait long enough for you to get thoroughly drunk, if that would help. There's men enough around here to hold you down, and I think I could have that leg off in fifteen minutes."

"You ain't getting that leg," Augustus said. "I might could get by without the one, but I can't without both."

"I assure you the alternative is gloomy," Dr. Mobley said. "Why close your own case? You've a taste for music and you seem to have funds. Why not spend the next few years listening to whores play the piano?"

"You said the girl was dying," Augustus said. "Just go get the whiskey."

Dr. Mobley returned a little later with two bottles of whiskey and a glass. A young giant of a man, so tall he had to stoop to get in the room, followed him.

"This is Jim," Dr. Mobley said nervously. "He's offered to sit with you while I go make my rounds."

Augustus cocked his pistol and leveled it at the young man. "Get out, Jim," he said. "I don't need company."

Jim left immediately—so immediately that he forgot to stoop and bumped his head on the door frame. Dr. Mobley looked even more nervous. He moved the bureau a little nearer the bed and sat both bottles within Augustus's reach.

"That was rude," he said.

"Listen," Augustus said. "You can't have this leg, and if you're thinking of over- powering me you have to calculate on losing about half the town. I can shoot straight when I'm drunk, too."

"I only want to save your life," Dr. Mobley said, taking a drink from the first bottle before pouring Augustus a glassful.

"It's my worry, mainly," Augustus said. "You stated your case, but the jury went against you. Jury of one. Did you pay the whore?"

"I did," Dr. Mobley said. "Since you refuse company, you'll have to drink alone. I have to go deliver a child into this unhappy world."

"It's a fine world, though rich in hardships at times," Augustus said.

"You won't need to worry about hardships much longer if you insist on keeping that leg," Dr. Mobley said somewhat pettishly.

"I guess you don't care much for stubborn customers, do you?"

"No, they irk me," Dr. Mobley said. "You might have lived, but now you'll die. Your reasoning escapes me."

"Well, I'll pay your bill right now," Augustus said. "My reasoning ain't your concern."

"Are you a man of property?" the doctor asked.

"I've funds in a bank in San Antonio," Augustus said. "Also I own half a cattle herd. It ought to be north of the Yellowstone by now."

"I brought pen and ink," the doctor said. "If I were you I'd make your will while you're still sober."

Augustus drank all afternoon and did not use the pen or ink. Once, when the music stopped, he looked out the window and saw a skinny pockmarked girl in a black dress standing in the street looking up at him curiously. He waved but could not be sure she saw him. He took another twenty-dollar gold piece from his pants pocket and sailed it out the window toward her. It landed in the street, to the puzzlement of the girl. She walked over and picked up the gold piece, looking up.

"It's yours, for the music," Augustus said loudly. The pockmarked girl smiled, picked up the money and went back into the saloon. In a minute, Augustus heard the piano again.

A little later his fever rose. He felt hungry, though, and banged on the floor with his pistol until a timid-looking little bartender with a walrus mustache as good as Dish Boggett's opened the door.

"Is beefsteak to be had in this town?" Augustus asked.

"No, but I can get you venison," the bartender said. He was as good as his word. Augustus ate and then vomited in a brass spittoon. His leg was as black as the one that had been lost. He went back to the whiskey and from time to time recovered the misty feeling that he had always been so fond of—the feeling that reminded him of Tennessee mornings. He wished for a woman's company and thought of having someone ask the pockmarked girl if she would come and sit a while. But there was no one to ask, and in time he lost the impulse.

In the night, sweating heavily, he awoke to a familiar step. W. F. Call stepped into the room and set a lantern on the bureau.

"Well, slow but sure," Augustus said, feeling relieved.

"Not too dern slow," Call said. "We just found Pea Eye yesterday."

He turned back the covers and looked at Augustus's leg. Dr. Mobley was also in the room. Call stood looking at the black leg a minute. Its meaning was clear enough.

"I did plead with him, Captain," Dr. Mobley said. "I told him it should come off. I regret now that I didn't take it when we took the other."

"You should have," Call said bluntly. "I would have known to do that, and I ain't a medical man."

"Don't berate the man, Woodrow," Augustus said. "If I had waked up with no legs, I would have shot the first man I saw, and Dr. Joseph C. Mobley was the first man I saw."

"Leaving you a gun was another mistake," Call said. "But I guess he didn't know you as well as I do."

He looked at the leg again, and at the doctor. "We could try it now," he said. "He's always been strong. He might still live."

Augustus immediately cocked the pistol. "You don't boss me, Woodrow," he said. "I'm the one man you don't boss. You also don't boss most of the women, but that don't concern us now."

"I wouldn't think you'd shoot me for trying to save your life," Call said quietly. Augustus looked sweaty and unsteady, but the range was short.

"Not to kill," Augustus said. "But I'll promise to disable you if you don't let me be about this leg."

"I never took you for a suicide, Gus," Call said. "Men have gotten by without legs. Lots of 'em lost legs in the war. You don't like to do nothing but sit on the porch and drink whiskey anyway. It don't take legs to do that."

"No, I also like to walk around to the springhouse once in a while, to see if my jug's cooled proper," Augustus said. "Or I might want to kick a pig if one aggravates me."

Call saw that it was pointless unless he wanted to risk a fight. Gus had not uncocked the pistol either. Call looked at the doctor to see what he thought.

"I wouldn't bother him now," the doctor said. "It's much too late. I suppose I'm to blame for not outwitting him. He was brought to me unconscious, or I might have figured out what a testy character he is."

Augustus smiled. "Would you bring Captain Call a glass, and some of that venison?" he said. "I imagine he's hungry."

Call wasn't ready to give up, although he felt it was probably hopeless. "You got those two women, back in Nebraska," he pointed out. "Those women would race to take care of you."

"Clara's got one invalid already, and she's bored with him," Augustus said. "Lorie would look after me but it would be a sorry life for her."

"Not as sorry as the one you rescued her from," Call reminded him.

"You don't get the point, Woodrow," Augustus said. "I've walked the earth in my pride all these years. If that's lost, then let the rest be lost with it. There's certain things my vanity won't abide."

"That's all it is, too," Call said bitterly. "Your goddamn vanity." He had expected to find Gus wounded, but not to find him dying. The sight affected him so much that he felt weak, of a sudden. When the doctor left the room, he sat down in a chair and took off his hat. He looked at Gus for a long time, trying to think of some argument he might use, but Gus was Gus, and he knew no argument would be of any use. None ever had been. He could either fight him and take off the leg if he won, or else sit and watch him die. The doctor seemed convinced he would die now in any case, though doctors could be wrong in such matters.

He tried to gird himself for a fight—Gus might miss, or not even shoot, though both were doubtful—but his own weakness held him in the chair. He was trembling and didn't know why.

"Woodrow, I wish you'd relax," Augustus said. "You can't save me, and it would be a pity if we fought at this stage. I might kill you accidentally and them boys would sit out on the plains and freeze."

Call didn't answer. He felt tired and old and sad. He had pressed the mare all day and all night, had easily found the river where the battle took place, recovered Pea Eye's rifle and even his boots and shirt, found Gus's saddle, and raced for Miles City. He had risked ruining the Hell Bitch—he hadn't, though she was tired—and still he had arrived too late. Gus would die, and all he could do was keep a death watch.

The bartender brought a plate of venison, but he had no appetite. He accepted a glass of whiskey, though, and then another. They had no effect.

"I hope you won't become a drunkard over this," Augustus said.

"I won't," Call said. "You can uncock that pistol. If you want to die, go ahead."

Augustus laughed. "You act like you hold it against me," he said.

"I do," Call said. "You got a good head, if you'd use it. A man with a good head can be useful."

"Doing what, braiding ropes?" Augustus asked. "Not my style, Captain."

"Your goddamn style is your downfall, and it's a wonder it didn't come sooner. Any special funeral?"

"Yes, I've been thinking of that," Augustus said. "I've a big favor to ask you, and one more to do you."

"What favor?"

"The favor I want from you will be my favor to you," Augustus said. "I want to be buried in Clara's orchard."

"In Nebraska?" Call asked, surprised. "I didn't see no orchard."

Augustus chuckled. "Not in Nebraska," he said. "In Texas. By that little grove of live oaks on the south Guadalupe. Remember, we stopped by there a minute?"

"My God," Call said, thinking his friend must be delirious. "You want me to haul you to *Texas?* We just got to Montana."

"I know where you just got," Augustus said. "My burial can wait a spell. I got nothing against wintering in Montana. Just pack me in salt or charcoal or what you will. I'll keep well enough and you can make the trip in the spring. You'll be a rich cattle king by then and might need a restful trip."

Call looked at his friend closely. Augustus looked sober and reasonably serious.

"To *Texas?*" he repeated.

"Yes, that's my favor to you," Augustus said. "It's the kind of job you was made for, that nobody else could do or even try. Now that the country is about settled, I don't know how you'll keep busy, Woodrow. But if you'll do this for me you'll be all right for another year, I guess."

"You're one of a kind, Gus," Call said, sighing. "We'll all miss you."

"Even you, Woodrow?" Augustus asked.

"Yes, me," Call said. "Why not me?"

"I take it back, Woodrow," Augustus said. "I have no doubt you'll miss me. You'll probably die of boredom this winter and I'll never get to Clara's orchard."

"Why do you call it that?"

"We had picnics there," Augustus said. "I took to calling it that. It pleased Clara. I could please her oftener in those days."

"Well, but is that any reason to go so far to be buried?" Call said. "She'd allow you a grave in Nebraska, I'm sure."

"Yes, but we had our happiness in Texas," Augustus said. "It was my best happiness, too. If you're too lazy to take me to Texas, then just throw me out the window and be done with it." He spoke with vehemence. "She's got her family in Nebraska," Augustus added, more quietly. "I don't want to lie there with that dumb horse trader she married."

"This would make a story if there was anybody to tell it," Call said. "You want me to carry your body three thousand miles because you used to go picnicking with a girl on the Guadalupe River?"

"That, plus I want to see if you can do it," Augustus said.

"But you won't know if I do it," Call said. "I reckon I'll do it, since you've asked."

He said no more, and soon noticed that Augustus was dozing. He pulled his chair closer to the window. It was a cool night, but the lamp made the little room stuffy. He blew it out—there was a little moonlight. He tried to doze, but couldn't for a time. Then he did doze and woke to find Augustus wide awake, burning with fever. Call lit the lamp but could do nothing for him.

"That was the Musselshell River, where you holed up," he said. "I met that old trapper and he told me. We may take him with us to scout, since he knows the country."

"I wish I had some better whiskey," Augustus said. "This is a cheap product."

"Well, the saloon's closed, probably," Call said.

"I doubt they got better, open or closed," Augustus said. "I have a few more instructions, if you're ready to hear them."

"Why, fine," Call said. "I suppose now you've decided you'd rather be buried at the South Pole."

"No, but do stop in Nebraska a night and let the women know," Augustus said. "I'm leaving my half of the herd to Lorie, and don't you dispute with me about it. Just see she gets what money's coming to her. I'll leave you a note to hand her, and one for Clara."

"I'll pass them on," Call said.

"I told Newt you was his pa," Augustus said.

"Well, you oughtn't to," Call said.

"I oughtn't to have *had* to, but you never got around to it, so I did," Augustus said. "All you can do about it now is shoot me, which would be a blessing. I feel mighty poorly, and embarrassed to boot."

"Why embarrassed?" Call asked.

"Imagine getting killed by an arrow in this day and age," Augustus said. "It's ridiculous, especially since they shot at us fifty times with modern weapons and did no harm."

"You always was careless," Call said. "Pea said you rode over a hill and right into them. I've warned you about that very thing a thousand times. There's better ways to approach a hill."

"Yes, but I like being free on the earth," Augustus said. "I'll cross the hills where I please."

He paused a minute. "I hope you won't mistreat Newt," he said.

"Have I ever mistreated him?" Call asked.

"Yes, always," Augustus said. "I admit it's practically your only sin, but it's a big one. You ought to do better by that boy. He's the only son you'll ever have—I'd bet my wad on that—though I guess it's possible you'll take to women in your old age."

"No, I won't," Call said. "They don't like me. I never recall mistreating that boy."

"Not naming him is mistreatment," Augustus said. "Give him your name, and you'll have a son you can be proud of. And Newt will know you're his pa."

"I don't know that myself," Call said.

"I know it and you know it," Augustus said. "You're worse than me. I'm stubborn about legs, but what about you? Women are goddamn right not to like you. You don't want to admit you ever needed one of them, even for a moment's pleasure. Though you're human, and you did need one once—but you don't want to need nothing you can't get for yourself."

Call didn't answer. It seemed wrong to quarrel while Gus was dying. Always over the same thing too. That one thing, after all they had done together.

Gus slept through the morning, fitful and feverish. Call didn't expect him to wake. He didn't leave the room. He was finally eating the plate of cold venison when Gus came to his senses briefly.

"Do you want me to do anything about them Indians?" Call asked.

"Which Indians?" Augustus asked, wondering what his friend could be talking about. Call's cheeks looked drawn, as though he hadn't eaten for days, though he was eating even as he asked the question.

"Those that shot the arrows into you," Call said.

"Oh, no, Woodrow," Augustus said. "We won more than our share with the natives. They didn't invite us here, you know. We got no call to be vengeful. You start that and I'll spoil your appetite."

"I don't have much, anyway," Call said.

"Didn't I stick that sign in the wagon, that one I made in Lonesome Dove that upset Deets so much at first?" Augustus asked.

"Upset me too," Call said. "It was a peculiar sign. It's on the wagon."

"I consider it my masterpiece, that and the fact that I've kept you from not getting no worse for so long," Augustus said. "Take the sign back and stick it over my grave."

"Have you wrote them notes for the women yet?" Call asked. "I won't know what to say to them, you see."

"Dern, I forgot, and my two favorite women, too," Augustus said. "Get me some paper."

The doctor had brought in a tablet for Augustus to write his will on. Augustus drew himself up and slowly wrote two notes.

"Dangerous to write to two women at the same time," he said. "Especially when I'm this lightheaded. I might not be as particular in my sentiments as women expect a fellow to be."

But he wrote on. Then Call saw his hand drop and thought he was dead. He wasn't, but he was too weak to fold the second note. Call folded it for him.

"Woodrow, quite a party," Augustus said.

"What?" Call asked.

Augustus was looking out the window. "Look there at Montana," he said. "It's fine and fresh, and now we've come and it'll soon be ruint, like my legs."

Then he turned his head back to Call. "I near forgot," he said. "Give my saddle to Pea Eye. I cut his up to brace my crutch, and I wouldn't want him to think ill of me."

"Well, he don't, Gus," Call said.

But Augustus had closed his eyes. He saw a mist, red at first but then as silvery as the morning mists in the valleys of Tennessee.

Call sat by the bed, hoping he would open his eyes again. He could hear Gus breathing. The sun set, and Call moved back to the chair, listening to his friend's ragged breath. He tried to remain alert, but he was tired. Some time later the doctor came in with a lamp. Call noticed blood dripping off the sheet onto the floor.

"That bed's full of blood and your friend's dead," the doctor said.

Call felt bad for having dozed. He saw that one of Gus's notes to the women was still on the bed. There was blood on it, but not much. Call wiped the note carefully on his pants leg before going downstairs.

97

WHEN CALL TOLD Dr. Mobley that Gus wanted to be transported to Texas to be buried, the little doctor merely smiled.

"People have their whimsies," he said. "Your friend was a crazy patient. I imagine we'd have quarreled if he'd lived."

"I imagine," Call said. "But I intend to honor the wish."

"We'll pack him in charcoal and salt," the doctor said. "It'll take a barrel or two. Luckily there's a good salt lick not far from here."

"I may need to leave him all winter," Call said. "Is there a place I could store him?"

"My harness shed would do fine," the doctor said. "It's well ventilated, and he'll keep better in the cool. Do you want his other leg?"

"Well, where is it?" Call asked, startled.

"Oh, I've got it," the doctor said. "Contrary as he was, he might have asked me to sew it back on. It's a rotten old thing."

Call went outside and walked down the empty street to the livery stable. The doctor had told him to rest and had offered to locate the undertaker himself.

The Hell Bitch looked up when he came into the livery stable, where he had put her. He felt an impulse to saddle her and ride out into the country, but weariness overcame him and he threw his bedroll on some straw and lay down. He couldn't sleep, though. He regretted not trying harder to save Gus. He should have disarmed him at once and seen that the other leg was amputated. Of course, Gus might have shot him, but he felt he should have taken the risk.

It seemed he only dozed a minute when the sun streamed into the livery stable. Call didn't welcome the day. All he had to think about were mistakes, it seemed—mistakes and death. His old rangering gang was gone, only Pea Eye left, of all of them. Jake was dead in Kansas, Deets in Wyoming, and now Gus in Montana.

An old man named Gill owned the livery stable. He had rheumatism and walked slowly and with a limp. But he was a kindly old man, with a rusty beard and one milky eye. He came limping in not long after Call woke up.

"I guess you need a coffin," the old man said. "Get Joe Veitenheimer, he'll make you a good one."

"It will have to be sturdy," Call said.

"I know," the old man said. "That's all the talk is in this town today, about the feller who wants to be hauled all the way to Texas to be stuck in the ground."

"He considered it his home," Call said, seeing no reason to go into the part about the picnics.

"My attitude is, why not, if he can find someone to tote him," old man Gill said. "I'd be buried in Georgia, if I could have my way, but it's a far piece to Georgia and nobody's gonna tote me. So I'll be buried up here in this cold," he added. "I don't like this cold. Of course, they say when you're dead the temperature don't concern you, but who knows the truth on that?"

"I don't," Call said.

"People got opinions, that's all they've got," the old man grumbled. "If somebody was to go and come back, now that's an opinion I'd listen to."

The old man forked the Hell Bitch a little hay. When he stood watching her eat, the mare snaked out her neck and tried to bite him, causing the old man to stumble backward and nearly stumble over his own pitchfork.

"Dern, she ain't very grateful," he said. "Struck at me like a snake, and I just fed her. Typical female. My wife done exactly the same a hunnert times. Buried her in Missouri, where it's considerable warmer."

Call found the carpenter and ordered a coffin. Then he borrowed a wagon and team and a big scoop shovel from a drunken man at the hardware store. It struck him that the citizenry of Miles City seemed to drink liquor day and night. Half the town was drunk at dawn.

"The lick's about six miles north," the hardware-store man said. "You can find it by the game trails."

Sure enough, several antelope were at the salt lick, and he saw the tracks of buffalo and elk. He worked up a sweat scooping the salt into the wagon.

When he got back to town the undertaker had finished with Gus. The undertaker was a tall man, with the shakes—his whole body trembled, even when he was standing still. "It's a nervous disease," he said. "I took it when I was young, and had it ever since. I put extra fluid in your friend, since I understand he'll be aboveground for a while."

"Yes, until next summer," Call said.

"I don't know how he'll do," the undertaker said. "If he weren't a human you could smoke him, like a ham."

"I'll try salt and charcoal," Call said.

When the coffin was ready, Call bought a fine bandana to cover Gus's face with. Dr. Mobley brought in the leg he had removed, wrapped in some burlap and soaked in formaldehyde to cover the smell. A bartender and the blacksmith helped pack the charcoal in. Call felt very awkward, though everyone was relaxed and cheerful. Once Gus was well covered, they filled the coffin to the top with salt and nailed it shut. Call gave the extra salt to the drunk at the hardware store to compensate him a little for the use of his wagon. They carried the coffin around and put it in the doctor's harness shed on top of two empty barrels.

"That'll do fine," Dr. Mobley said. "He'll be there, and if you change your mind about the trip, we'll just bury him. He'll have lots of company here. We've got more people in the cemetery already than we've got in the town."

Call didn't like the implication. He looked at the doctor sternly. "Why would I change my mind?" he asked.

The doctor had been nipping at a flask of whiskey during the packing, and was fairly drunk. "Dying people get foolish," he said. "They forget they won't be alive to appreciate the things they ask people to do for them. People make any kind of promise, but when they realize it's a dead creature they made the promise to, they usually squirm a little and then forget the whole business. It's human nature."

"I'm told I don't have a human nature," Call said. "How much do I owe you?"

"Nothing," the doctor said. "The deceased paid me himself."

"I'll get him in the spring," Call said.

When he got back to the livery stable he found old man Gill drinking from a jug. It reminded him of Gus, for the old man would hook one finger through the loop of the jug and throw back his head and drink. He was sitting in the wheelbarrow, his pitchfork across his lap, glaring at the Hell Bitch.

"Next time you come, why don't you just catch a grizzly bear and ride him in?" Gill said. "I'd rather stable a grizzly than this mare."

"She bite you or what?"

"No, but she's biding her time," the old man said. "Take her away so I can relax. I ain't been drunk this early in several years, and it's just from having her around."

"We're leaving," Call said.

"Now, why would you keep a creature like that?" the old man said, once Call had her saddled.

"Because I like to be horseback when I'm horseback," Call said.

Old man Gill was not persuaded. "Hope you like to be dead when you're dead, then," he said. "I reckon she's deadlier than a cobra."

"I reckon you talk too much," Call said, feeling more and more that he didn't care for Miles City.

He found the old trapper, Hugh Auld, sitting in front of the drygoods store. It was a cloudy day and a cool wind blew. The wind had a wintry feel, though it had been hot the day before. Call knew they didn't have long before winter, and his men were poorly equipped.

"Can you drive a wagon?" he asked old Hugh.

"Yes, I can whip a mule as good as anybody else," Hugh said.

Call bought supplies—not only coats and overshoes and gloves but building supplies as well. He managed to rent the wagon he had carried the salt in, promising to return it when possible.

"You're restless," Old Hugh said. "You go on. I'll creep along in this wagon and catch you north of the Musselshell."

Call rode back toward the herd, but at a fairly slow pace. In the afternoon he stopped and sat for several hours by a little stream. Ordinarily he would have felt guilty for not heading back to the boys right away, but Gus's death had changed that. Gus was not a person he had expected to outlive; now that he had, much was different. Gus had always been lucky—everybody said so, and he said so himself. Only Gus's luck ran out. Jake's had run out, Deets's had run out; both deaths were unexpected, both sad, terribly sad, but Call believed them. He had seen them both with his own eyes. And, believing in the deaths, he had put them behind him.

He had seen Gus die, too—or seen him dying, at least—but it seemed he hadn't started believing it. Gus had left, and that was final, but Call felt too confused even to feel sad. Gus had been so much himself to the end that he wouldn't let even his death be an occasion—it had just felt like one of their many arguments that normally would be resumed in a few days.

This time it wouldn't be resumed, and Call found he couldn't adjust to the change. He felt so alone that he didn't really want to go back to the outfit. The herd and the men no longer seemed to have anything to do with him. Nothing had anything to do with him, unless it was the mare. For his part he would just as soon have ridden around Montana alone until the Indians jumped him, too. It wasn't that he even missed Gus yet all that much. Only yesterday they had talked, as they had talked for thirty years.

Call felt some resentment, as he almost always had when thinking of his friend. Gus had died and left the world without taking him with him, so that once again he was left to do the work. He had always done the work—only he suddenly no longer believed in the work. Gus had tricked him out of his belief, as easily as if cheating at cards. All his work, and it hadn't saved anyone, or slowed the moment of their going by a minute.

Finally, as night fell, he mounted and rode on, not anxious to get anywhere, but tired of sitting. He rode on, his mind a blank, until the next afternoon, when he spotted the herd.

The cattle were spread for three miles over the great plain, grazing peacefully along. No sooner had the hands spotted him than Dish and Needle Nelson came racing over. Both looked scared.

"Captain, we seen some Indians," Dish said. "There was a bunch of them but they didn't attack us yet."

"What did they do?" Call asked.

"Just sat on a hill and watched us," Needle Nelson said. "We were going to give them two of these slow beeves if they'd ask, but they didn't ask."

"How many in the bunch?"

"We didn't count," Dish said. "But it was a bunch."

"Women and children with them?" Call asked.

"Oh yes, a passel," Needle said.

"They seldom drag their womenfolk into battle," Call said. "Probably Crow. I'm told the Crow are peaceful."

"Did you find Gus?" Dish asked. "Pea can't talk about nothing else."

"I found him. He's dead," Call said.

The men were turning their horses to go back to the herd. They stopped as if frozen.

"Gus is dead?" Needle Nelson asked.

Call nodded. He knew he would have to tell the story, but didn't want to have to tell it a dozen times. He trotted on over to the wagon, which Lippy was driving. Pea Eye sat in the back end, resting. He was still barefoot, though Call saw at once that his feet were better. When he saw Call riding in alone he looked worried.

"Did they carry him off, Captain?" he asked.

"No, he made it to Miles City," Call said. "But he had blood poisoning in both legs from those arrows, and he died day before yesterday."

"Well, I swear," Pea Eye said, "I wished he hadn't."

"I got away and Gus died," he added sadly. "Wouldn't you figure it'd be the other way around?"

"I would if I had to make odds," Jasper Fant said. He was close by and had loped over in time to hear.

Newt heard the facts from Dish, who soon rode around the herd, telling the boys. Many of them loped into the wagon to get more details, but Newt didn't. He felt like he had the morning he saw Deets dead—like turning away. If he never went to the wagon, he would never have to hear any more. He cried all afternoon, riding as far back on the drags as he could get. For once he was grateful for the dust the herd raised.

It seemed to him it would have been better if the Indians had ridden in and killed them all—having it happen one at a time was too much to bear, and it was happening to the best people too. The ones who teased him and made sport of him, like Bert and Soupy, were happy as pigs. Even Pea Eye had nearly died, and except for the Captain and himself, Pea was the last one left of the old Hat Creek outfit.

All the men were annoyed with Captain Call because he told of Gus's dying brusquely, got himself a little food and rode away to be alone, as he always did in the evening. His account was pregnant with mysteries, and the men spent all night discussing them. Why had Gus refused to have the other leg amputated, in the face of plain warnings?

"I knew a spry little fellow from Virginia who could go nearly as fast on crutches as I can on my own legs," Lippy reported. "He had two crutches, and once he got his rhythm he could skip along."

"Gus could have made a cart and got him a billygoat to pull it," Bert Borum suggested.

"Or a donkey," Needle said.

"Or his dern pigs, if they're so smart," Soupy said. Both pigs were under the wagon. Pea Eye, who slept in the wagon, had to listen to their grunts and snores all night.

Only the Irishman seemed sympathetic to Gus's stance. "Why, it would only have left half of him," he said. "Who wants to be half of himself?"

"No, half would be about the hips," Jasper calculated. "Half would be your nuts and all. Just your legs ain't half."

Dish Boggett took no part in the conversation. He felt sad about Gus. He remembered that Gus had once lent him money to visit Lorena, and this memory lent another tone to his sadness. He had supposed Gus would go back and visit Lorena, but now, clearly, he couldn't. She was there in Nebraska, waiting for Gus, who would never come.

Into his sadness came a hope that when the drive was over he could draw his wages and go back and win Lorena, after all. He could still remember her face as she sat in front of the little tent on the Kansas plains. How he had envied Gus, for Lorena would smile at Gus, but she had never smiled at him. Now Gus was dead, and Dish determined to mention to the Captain that he wanted to draw his wages and leave as soon as the drive was finished.

Lippy broke down and cried a time or two, thinking of Gus. To him, the mysterious part was why Gus wanted to be taken to Texas.

"All that way to Texas," Lippy kept saying. "He must have been drunk."

"I never seen Gus too drunk to know what he meant," Pea Eye said. He, too, was very sad. It seemed to him it would have been better if he could have persuaded Gus to come with him.

"All that way to Texas," Lippy kept saying. "I wager the Captain won't do it."

"I'll take that wager," Dish said. "He and Gus rangered together."

"And me too," Pea Eye said sadly. "I rangered with them."

"Gus won't be much but a skeleton, if the Captain does do it," Jasper said. "I wouldn't do it. I'd get to thinking of ghosts and ride off in a hole."

At the mention of ghosts, Dish got up and left the campfire. He couldn't abide the thought of any more ghosts. If Deets and Gus were both roaming around, one might approach him, and he didn't like the thought. The very notion made him white, and he pitched his bedroll as close to the wagon as he could get.

The other men continued to talk of Augustus's strange request.

"Why Texas beats me," Soupy said. "I always heard he was from Tennessee."

"I wonder what he'd have to say about being dead?" Needle said. "Gus always had something to say about everything."

Po Campo began to jingle his tambourine lightly, and the Irishman whistled sadly.

"He never collected all that money he won from us at cards," Bert remembered. "That's the bright side of the matter."

"Oh, dern," Pea Eye said, feeling so sorrowful that he wanted to die himself. No one had to ask him what he was derning about.

98

OLD HUGH AULD soon replaced Augustus as the main talker in the Hat Creek outfit. He caught up with the herd, with his wagonload of coats and supplies, near the Missouri, which they crossed near Fort Benton. The soldiers at the tiny outpost were as surprised to see the cowboys as if they were men from another planet. The commander, a lanky major named Court, could scarcely believe his eyes when he looked up and saw the herd spread out over the plain. When told that most of the cattle had been gathered below the Mexican border he was astonished, but not too astonished to buy two hundred head. Buffalo were scarce, and the fort not well provisioned.

Call was short with Major Court. He had been short with everyone since Gus's death. Everyone wondered when he would stop going north, but no one dared ask. There had been several light snows, and when they crossed the Missouri, it was so cold that the men built a huge fire on the north bank to warm up. Jasper Fant came near to realizing his lifelong fear of drowning when his horse spooked at a beaver and shook him off into the icy water. Fortunately Ben Rainey caught him and pulled him ashore. Jasper was blue with cold; even though they covered him with blankets and got him to the fire, it was a while before he could be convinced that he was alive.

"Why, you could have waded out," Old Hugh said, astonished that a man would be frightened over such a little thing as a soaking. "If you think this water's cold now, try setting a few beaver traps around February," he added, thinking it would help the man put things in perspective.

Jasper couldn't speak for an hour. Most of the men had long since grown bored with his drowning fears, and they left him to dry out his clothes as best he could. That night, when he was warm enough to be bitter, Jasper vowed to spend the rest of his life north of the Missouri rather than cross such a stream again. Also, he had developed an immediate resentment against beavers and angered Old Hugh several times on the trip north by firing at them recklessly with his pistol if he saw some in a pond.

"Them's *beaver*," Old Hugh kept saying. "You trap beaver, you don't shoot 'em. A bullet will ruin the pelt and the pelt's the whole point."

"Well, I hate the little toothy sons of bitches," Jasper said. "The pelts be damned."

Call kept riding northwest until even Old Hugh began to be worried. The great line of the Rockies was clear to the west. Though Old Hugh was the scout, it was Call who rode on ahead. Once in a while Old Hugh might point out a landmark, but he was shy about offering advice. Call made it clear that he didn't want advice.

Though accustomed to his silences, none of the men could remember him being *that* silent. For days he didn't utter a word—he merely came in and got his food and left again. Several of the men became convinced that he didn't mean to stop—that he would lead them north into the snows and they would all freeze.

The day after they crossed the Marais, Old Dog disappeared. From being a lead steer, he had drifted back to the drags and usually trailed a mile or two behind the herd. Always he was there in the morning, but one morning he wasn't. Newt and the Raineys, still in charge of the drags, went back to look for him and saw two grizzlies making a meal of the old steer. At the sight of the bears their horses bolted and raced back to the herd. Their fear instantly communicated itself to all the animals and the herd and remuda stampeded. Several cowboys got thrown, including Newt, but no one was hurt, though it took an afternoon to gather the scattered herd.

A few days later they finally came to the Milk River. It was a crisp fall day, and most of the men were wearing their new coats. The slopes of the mountains to the west were covered with snow.

"That's the last one," Old Hugh said. "You go much north of that river and you're in Canada."

Call left the herd to graze and rode east alone for a day. The country was beautiful, with plenty of grass and timber enough in the creek bottoms for building a house and corrals. He came across scattered buffalo, including one large herd. He saw plentiful Indian sign, but no Indians. It was cold but brilliantly sunny. He felt that the whole top of the Montana territory was empty except for the buffalo, the Indians and the Hat Creek outfit. He knew it was time to stop and get a house of some kind built before a blizzard caught them. He knew one could come any time. He himself paid no attention to weather, and didn't care, but there were the men to think of. It was too late for most of them to go back to Texas that fall. Like it or not, they were going to be wintering in Montana.

That night, camping alone, he dreamed of Gus. Frequently he woke up to hear Gus's voice, so real he looked around expecting to see him. Sometimes he would scarcely fall asleep before he dreamed of Gus, and it was even beginning to happen in the daytime if he rode along not paying much attention to his surroundings. Gus dead invaded his thoughts as readily as he had when he was alive. Usually he came to josh and tease, much as he had in life. "Just because you've got to the top of the country, you don't have to stop," he said, in one dream. "Turn east and keep going until you hit Chicago."

Call didn't want to turn east, but neither did he particularly want to stop. Gus's death, and the ones before it, had caused him to lose his sense of purpose to such an extent that he scarcely cared from one day to the next what he was doing. He kept on going north because it had become a habit. But they had reached the Milk River and winter was coming, so he had to break the habit or else lose most of the men and probably the cattle too.

He found a creek with a good stand of sheltering timber and decided it would do for a headquarters, but he felt no eagerness for the tasks ahead. Work, the one thing that had always belonged to him, no longer seemed to matter. He did it because there was nothing else to do, not because he felt the need. Some days he felt so little interest in the herd and the men that he could simply have ridden off and left them to make the best of things. The old sense of being responsible for their well-being had left him so completely that he often wondered how he could ever have felt it so strongly. The way they looked at him in the morning, as they waited for orders, irritated him more and more. Why should grown men wait for orders every day, after coming three thousand miles?

Frequently he gave no orders—merely ate his breakfast and rode off, leaving them with puzzled expressions on their faces. An hour later, when he looked back, he would see that they were following, and that, too, irritated him. Sometimes he felt he would prefer to look back and see the plains empty, all the followers and cattle vanished.

But nothing like that happened, and when he had settled on a headquarters, he told the men to drive the cattle east for a day and then let them graze at will. The drive was over. The ranch would lie between the Milk and the Missouri. He would file on the land in the spring.

"What about them of us that want to go back to Texas?" Dish Boggett asked.

Call was surprised. Until then no one had suggested going back to Texas.

"It's late in the year," he said. "You'd be better advised to wait and go in the spring."

Dish looked at him stubbornly. "I didn't hire on for no winter in Montana," he said. "I guess if I could have my wages I'd take my chances."

"Well, you're needed for the building," Call said, reluctant to lose him. Dish looked as if he stood ready to ride south then and there. "Once that's done any can go that wants," Call added.

Dish Boggett felt angry. He hadn't hired on to carpenter either. His first work for the Hat Creek outfit had been well-digging, and his last would be swinging an ax, it appeared. Neither was work fit for a cowhand, and he was on the verge of demanding his wages and standing up for his rights as a free man—but the Captain's look dissuaded him, and the next morning, when they started the herd east along the Milk, he took the point for the last time. With Old Dog dead, the Texas bull was frequently in the forefront of the drive. He looked ugly, for his wound had been sewn up unevenly, and being one-eyed and one-horned had made him even more irascible. He would often turn and attack anyone who approached him on his blind side. Several men had narrowly escaped disaster, and only the fact that Captain Call favored the bull had kept them from shooting him.

Dish resolved that as soon as the building was done he would go like a streak for Nebraska. The thought that a stranger might come along and win Lorie before he could get back was a torment to him—but it made him one of the more vigorous members of the logging crew once the building got started. Most of the other members of the crew, Jasper and Needle particularly, were less vigorous, and they irritated Dish by taking frequent breaks, leaving him to chop alone. They would sit around smoking, keeping a close watch for bears, while Dish flailed away, the sound of the striking ax echoing far across the valley of the Milk River.

Before the work had been in progress a week, an event occurred which changed the men's attitudes dramatically. The event was a blizzard, which howled out of the north for three days. Only the fact that Call had seen to it that ample firewood had been cut saved the outfit. The men had never known or imagined such cold. They built two large fires and huddled between them, feeding them logs, freezing on the side not closest to the fire. The first day there was no visibility at all—the men could not even to go the horses without the risk of being lost in the swirling snow.

"It's worse than a sandstorm," Needle said.

"Yes, and colder too," Jasper said. "I've got my feet practically in the fire and my dern toes are still frozen."

Dish found to his annoyance that his own breath caused his mustache to freeze, something he would not have imagined could happen. The men put on all the clothes they had and were still terribly cold. When the storm blew out and the sun reappeared, the cold refused to leave. In fact, it got colder, and formed such a hard crust on the snow that the men slipped and fell just going a few feet to the wagon.

Only Po Campo seemed to thrive in the weather. He still relied largely on his serape, plus an old scarf he had found somewhere, and he annoyed the men by nagging them to go shoot a bear. His theory was that bear meat would help them get used to the weather. Even if it didn't, a bearskin might come in handy.

"Yes, and them dern bears probably think a little man meat would come in handy," Soupy observed.

Pea Eye, the tallest man in the group, had developed a new fear, which was that he would be swallowed up in a snowdrift. He had always worried about quicksand, and now he was in a place where all he could see, for miles around, was a colder version of quicksand.

"If it was to cover you up, I reckon you'd freeze," he said, over and over, until the men were tired of hearing it. Most of the men were tired of hearing one another say anything—the complaints characteristic of each had come to bore them thoroughly as a group.

Newt found that he had no urge either to talk or listen, but he did have an urge to stay warm, and he spent as much time by the fire as he honorably could. The only parts of his body that he was still conscious of were his hands, feet and ears, all of which were dreadfully cold. When the storm abated and they rode out to check the cattle he tied an old flannel shirt over his ears and they still felt frozen.

The livestock weathered the storm fairly well, although some of the cattle had drifted far south and had to be pushed back toward the Milk.

Even so, within ten days of the blizzard, a sizable rough log house had been built, complete with fireplace and chimney, both the work of Po Campo. He took advantage of a few days' thaw to make a great quantity of mud bricks, all of which froze hard with the next freeze. The roof had hardly been on the cabin a day when the next blizzard hit. This time, though, the men were comparatively warm.

To their amazement, Captain Call refused to live in the house. He set up the old tent of Wilbarger's in a sheltered spot on the creek, and spent his nights in it, sometimes building a small fire in front of it.

Every morning, the men expected to come out and find him frozen; instead, he came in every morning and found them sleeping too late, reluctant to leave their blankets for the chill.

But there were still corrals to build, and a smokehouse, and improvements on the cabin. Call saw that the men stayed at work while he himself did most of the checking on the livestock, sometimes taking Newt with him on his rounds. He killed several buffalo and taught Newt how to quarter them.

Old Hugh Auld came and went at will on his spotted pony. Though he talked constantly while he was with the crew, he often developed what he called lonesome feelings and disappeared for ten days at a time. Once in a prolonged warm spell he came racing in excitely and informed Call that there was a herd of wild horses grazing only twenty miles to the south.

Since the Hat Creek remuda was not in the best of shape, Call decided to go see about the horses. They had a great stroke of luck and caught them in a box canyon only fifteen miles from the headquarters. The horses were smallish, but still fat from a summer's grazing. Bert Borum, the best roper in the outfit, caught eighteen of the horses and they were brought back, hobbled, to the remuda.

True to his word, Dish Boggett drew his wages and left the day after they caught the wild horses. Call had assumed the blizzards would have taught the young man the folly of leaving, and was annoyed when Dish asked for his pay.

"It's no time to be traveling in country you don't know," Call said.

"I pointed that herd the whole way up here," Dish said stubbornly. "I guess I can find my way back. Besides, I got a coat."

Call had little money on him, but he had arranged for credit in the little bank in Miles City and he wrote Dish out an order for his wages, using the bottom of a frying pan to rest his tablet on. It was just after breakfast and a number of the hands were watching. There had been a light snowfall the night before and the plains were white for miles around.

"Dern, we might as well hold the funeral right now," Soupy said. "He won't even make it to the Yellowstone, much less to Nebraska."

"It's that whore," Jasper said. "He's in a hurry to get back before somebody beats his time."

Dish reddened and whirled on Jasper. "She ain't a whore," he said. "You take that back or I'll box your dern ears."

Jasper was appalled at the challenge. His feet were cold and he knew he couldn't cut much of a figure in a fight with Dish. His hands were cold too—they were usually cold—and the thought of having to strike someone with a hard head with one of them was not pleasant.

"Well, I meant she was in her younger days," Jasper said. "I don't know what she does for a living now."

Dish stalked off in a cold silent fury. He had resented many of the men throughout the whole trip because of their casual talk about Lorie and saw no reason for elaborate goodbyes. Po Campo hung him with so many provisions that he could scarcely mount.

Dish thought them unnecessary. "I got a rifle," he reminded Po. "There's plenty of game."

"You may not want to hunt in the blizzards," Po Campo said.

Before Dish left, Call told him to take an extra horse. Dish had mainly ridden Sugar all the way north and planned to ride him all the way back, but Call insisted that he take a little buckskin for insurance.

"A horse can always go lame," he said.

All the men were standing around, disturbed that Dish was leaving. Newt felt like crying. Leavings and dyings felt a lot alike.

Dish, too, at the last moment, felt a powerful ache inside him at the thought of leaving the bunch. Though most of the hands were disgraceful, rude and incompetent, they were still his *compañeros*. He liked young Newt and enjoyed teasing Jasper. He even had a sneaking fondness for Lippy, who had appointed himself cook's helper and seldom got far from the big fireplace.

But Dish had gone too far to stop. He had no fear at all of the dangers. He had to go see Lorena, and that was that. He mounted and took the lead rope of the little buckskin.

Pea Eye, who had been off near the lots trying to loosen his bowels—the main effect of Montana had been to constipate him—missed the preparations for leave-taking. He had been in a sorrowful mood ever since the report had come back on Gus, and the sight of Dish ready to ride off upset him all over again. "Well, I swear, Dish," he said. Tears welled in his eyes and he could say no more. Several of the men were disturbed by the sight, fearing that they might behave no better. Dish shook hands quickly all around.

"So long, boys," he said. "Look for me south of the Brazos if you ever get home." Then he touched Sugar with his spurs and was soon only a black speck on the snow.

Call had debated giving him the letters Gus had written to the women, but thought better of it. If Dish was lost, and probably he would be, the letters would be lost too, and they were Gus's last words. Better to keep them and deliver them himself—though the thought didn't cheer him.

Sitting in his tent that night, he pondered the change in himself. He had let the young man override his warning and leave. He could have ordered him to stay and put a little more of himself into the order, as he often had at times when men were unruly. Dish had been determined, but not determined enough to buck a forceful command. As Captain he had given such commands many times and never had one failed to be obeyed.

But in this case he lacked the interest. When it came time to summon the force, he hadn't. He admired Dish Boggett, who indeed had held a true point for three thousand miles; he had also often proved himself the best man to break a stampede. But Call had let him go, and didn't really care. He knew that he wouldn't care if they all went, excepting Pea and the boy. He had no impulse to lead the men another step.

The next day, since the weather continued pretty, he decided to go to Fort Benton himself. Major Court had indicated that the Army might frequently need beef if the winter got bad and the tribes fared poorly. After all, he had come to Montana in the hope of selling cattle. Once the news reached Texas that they had made the drive, others would soon follow, probably by next fall, and it was well to establish good connections with the Army, the only buyer in the Territory who might want beef.

It was during the Captain's absence that Newt discovered a talent for breaking horses. Ben Rainey, an excellent rider, had been assigned the task of breaking the mustangs, but on the very first day of work a strong black horse threw him into a tree and broke his arm. Po Campo set the bone, but Ben declared he had had enough of bucking broncs. He meant to apply for another job when the Captain returned. Newt had been on wood detail, dragging dead timbers up from the creek and helping Pea Eye and Pete Spettle split them. He told Ben Rainey he would have a try at the black, and he rode him to a standstill, to the surprise of everyone, including himself.

Of course he knew that riding a horse through a bucking spell represented just a small part of a horse's education. They had to be gentled enough that it wouldn't be necessary to tie them down to saddle them. They had to be taught to rein, and, if possible, to take an interest in cattle.

When the Captain returned a week later with an order for three hundred beeves to be delivered to Fort Benton by Christmas, Newt was in the little sapling corral they had built, working with a hammer-headed bay. He looked nervously at the Captain, expecting to be reprimanded for changing jobs, but Call merely sat on the Hell Bitch and watched. Newt tried to ignore the fact that he was there— he didn't want to get nervous and upset the bay. He had discovered that if he talked a lot and was soothing in what he said it had a good effect on the horse he was working with. He murmured to the bay while the Captain watched. Finally Call dismounted and unsaddled. It pleased him to see the quiet way the boy worked. He had never been one for talk when there was work to be done—it was his big point of difference with Gus, who could do nothing without talking. He was glad the boy was inclined to his way. When they drove the beeves to Fort Benton he took Newt and two other men with him.

That winter there were several such trips—not merely to Fort Benton but to Fort Buford as well. Once when they arrived at Fort Benton the Army had just trailed in a bunch of raw, half-broken horses from the south. When they brought in beeves, the fort was always full of Indians, and there was much bargaining over how the beeves would be divided between the Major and an old Blackfoot chief the soldiers call Saw, because of the sharpness of his features. Some Blood Indians were there too on this occasion, and Call felt angry—he knew he was seeing some of the warriors who had killed Gus. When the Indians left he felt like tracking them and revenging his friend—though he didn't know which braves had done it. He held back, but it made him uneasy to leave an attack unanswered.

The Major found out that Newt was good at breaking horses and asked Call if he would mind leaving the boy at the fort for a few weeks to rough out the new string of horses. Call didn't want to, but the Major had dealt with him on fair terms and he didn't feel he could refuse the request, particularly since there was not much to do back at ranch headquarters. They spent their time making improvements on the log house, starting a barn and checking the cattle after the frequent storms. Most of the men spent their spare time hunting, and had already brought in more buffalo and elk meat than could be eaten in a winter.

So Call agreed, and Newt stayed at the fort a month, breaking horses. The weather improved. It was cold, but the days were often fine and sunny. Newt's only scare came when he took a strong sorrel gelding out of the fort for his first ride and the horse took the bit between his teeth and raced out onto the Missouri ice. When the horse hit the ice he slipped and, though he crashed through the ice, fortunately they were in shallow water and Newt was able to struggle out and lead the horse out too. A few soldiers coming in with a load of wood helped him get dry. Newt knew it would have been a different story if the horse had made it to the center of the river before breaking through the ice.

After that, when he took his raw mounts out for a ride, he turned them away from the river as soon as he left the fort.

99

JULY JOHNSON PROPOSED to Clara in the first week of the new year. He had been trying to stop himself from doing just that for months, and then he did it one day when, at her request, he brought in a sack of potatoes. It had been very cold and the potatoes were frozen—Clara wanted them in the warm kitchen to thaw. His son Martin was crawling on the kitchen floor when he came in and Clara was stirring batter for one of the cakes she couldn't live without. As soon as he sat the frozen potatoes on the table, he did it. "Would you ever marry me?" was the way he put it, and immediately felt a terrible fool for having uttered the words. In the months he had worked for her their relations had been unchanged, and he supposed she would think him drunk or out of his head for raising such a thought.

Instead, Clara did a thing that amazed him—she stuck a finger in the sweet cake batter and held her hand out to him, as if he were just supposed to eat the glob of uncooked cake right off her finger.

"Have a taste, July," she said. "I think I've overdone the cinnamon."

July decided she must not have heard his question. He wondered if she were merely trying to be polite. Though he knew he should have been glad she hadn't heard it, he felt ready to say it again, and was about to when Clara stopped him with a look.

"You don't have to repeat yourself," she said. "I heard you. Do you want to give me an opinion on this cinnamon or not?"

July felt awkward and embarrassed. He hadn't meant to ask such a question just then—and yet the question would be asked. He didn't know what to do about the cake batter, but didn't feel it proper just to lean over and eat it off her finger. He reached out and took as much of it as he could on one of his own fingers before he sampled it.

"Tastes fine," he said, but Clara looked annoyed, or scornful, or somehow displeased. He could never tell what her looks meant—all he registered was how uncomfortable they made him.

"I don't think you're much of a judge of sweets," Clara said, heat in her tone but a coldness in her gray eyes.

She ate the rest of the batter off her own finger and went back to stirring the cake. A minute later Lorena walked into the room and picked up the baby. July was hoping she would take the baby out of the kitchen, but instead she sat down at the table and began to sing to him. Then, to make matters worse, both girls came in and began to make over the baby too. Martin was laughing and trying to grab a spoon away from one of the girls. Clara looked at July again, and the look made him feel a fool. He didn't get an answer to his question and soon had to go back to doing his chores.

That night he wondered if he ought to leave. He could not stay around Clara without nursing hopes, and yet he could detect no sign that she cared about him. Sometimes he thought she did, but when he thought it over he always concluded that he had just been imagining things. Her remarks to him generally had a stinging quality, but he would often not realize he had been stung until after she left the scene. Working together in the lots, which they did whenever the weather was decent, she often lectured him on his behavior with the horses. She didn't feel he paid close attention to them. July was at a loss to know how anyone could pay close attention to a horse when she was around, and yet the more his eyes turned to her the worse he did with the horses and the more disgusted she grew. His eyes would turn to her, though. She had taken to wearing her husband's old coat and overshoes, both much too big for her. She wouldn't wear gloves—she claimed the horses didn't like it—and her large bony hands often got so cold she would have to stick them under the coat for a few minutes to warm them. She wore a variety of caps that she had ordered from somewhere—apparently she liked caps as much as she liked cake. None of them were particularly suited to a Nebraska winter. Her favorite one was an old Army cap Cholo had picked up on the plains somewhere. Sometimes Clara would tie a wool scarf over it to keep her ears warm, but usually the scarf came untied in the course of working with the horses, so that when they walked back up for a meal her hair was usually spilling over the collar of the big coat. Yet July couldn't stop his eyes from feasting on her. He thought she was wonderfully beautiful, so beautiful that merely to walk with her from the lots to the house, when she was in a good mood, was enough to make him give up for another month all thought of leaving. He told himself that just being able to work with her was enough. And yet, it wasn't—which is why the question finally forced itself out.

He was miserable all night, for she hadn't answered the question. But he had spoken the words and revealed what he wanted. He supposed she would think worse of him than she already did, once she thought it over.

It was three days before they were alone again. Some soldiers needing horses showed up, and Clara asked them to spend the night. Then Martin got a bad cough and developed a high fever. Cholo was sent to bring the doctor. Clara spent most of the day sitting with the baby, who coughed with every breath. She tried every remedy she knew, with no effect. Martin couldn't sleep for coughing. July went into the sickroom from time to time, feeling awkward and helpless. The boy was his child, and yet he didn't know what to do. He felt in the way. Clara sat in a straight chair, holding the child. He asked in the morning if there was anything special she wanted him to do and she shook her head. The child's sickness had driven out all other concerns. When July came back that evening, Clara was still sitting. Martin was too weak by then to cough very hard, but his breath was a rasp and his fever still high. Clara was impassive, rocking the baby's cradle, but not looking at him.

"I guess the doctor will be getting here soon," July said uncertainly.

"The doctor might have been gone in the other direction," Clara said. "This will be over before he gets here. He'll have had the ride for nothing."

"You mean the baby's dying?" July asked.

"I mean he'll either die or get well before the doctor comes," Clara said, standing up. "I've done all I can. The rest is up to Martin."

Clara looked at him and then, to his shock, walked over and put her head against his chest. She put her arms around him and held him tightly. It was so surprising that July almost lost his balance. He put his arms around her to steady himself. Clara didn't raise her head for what seemed like minutes. He could feel her body trembling and could smell her hair.

Then she stepped back from him as abruptly as she had come to him, though she caught one of his hands and held it a moment. Her cheeks were wet with tears.

"I hate it when a child is sick," she said. "I loathe it. I get too scared. It's like . . ." She stopped a minute to wipe the tears off her cheeks. "It's like there's something doesn't want me to get a boy raised," Clara said, her voice cracking.

July lay awake all night, remembering how it felt to have her take his hand. Her fingers had twined for a moment in his before she let go. It had seemed she needed him, else she wouldn't have squeezed so. It made him so excited that he couldn't sleep, yet when he went back upstairs in the morning and stepped into the sickroom, Clara was distant, though it was a fine sunny day and the baby's fever was down. His breath still rattled, but he was asleep.

"I could bring you up some coffee," July said.

"No, thanks, I know my way to the kitchen well enough," she said, standing up. This time she neither hugged him nor took his hand; she walked past him without a look. All he could do was follow her downstairs. Lorena and the girls had already made breakfast and Cholo came in to eat. July didn't feel hungry. The fact that Clara was displeased took his appetite away. He tried to think why she might be displeased, but could come up with no reasons. He sat numbly through breakfast and went out the door feeling that it would be hard to get his mind on work. He needed to repair the wheel of the big wagon, which had cracked somehow.

Before he could even get the wheel off, he saw Clara coming toward the tool shed. Though it was sunny, it was also very cold—her breath made little clouds. July was afraid the baby might have taken a turn for the worse, but that was not it. Clara was very angry.

"You'd do better to talk to me when I'm mad," she said, with no preamble. There were points of red in her cheeks.

"I'm no talker, I guess," July said.

"You're not much of anything, but you could be," she said. "I know you're smart, because Martin is, and he didn't get it all from your poor wife. But a fence post is more useful generally than you are."

July took it as a criticism of his work, which he felt he had done scrupulously.

"I've nearly got this wheel fixed," he said.

"July, I'm not talking about chores," she said. "I'm talking about me. I sat there all night in that room with your baby. Where were you?"

July had been thinking that he probably should have offered to sit with her. Of course, now it was too late. He wanted to explain that he was too shy just to come into a room where she was, particularly a bedroom, unless she asked him. Even coming into the kitchen, if she was alone, was not something he did casually. But he didn't know how to explain all the cautions she prompted in him.

"I wish now I had," he said.

Clara's eyes were flashing. "I told you how sickness frightens me," she said. "The only times I've ever wished I could die is when I've had to sit and watch a child suffer."

She was twisting one hand in the other. July, seeing that she was shivering, took off his coat and held it out to her, but Clara ignored the offer.

"I sit there alone," she said. "I don't want the girls to be there because I don't want them to get death too much in their minds. I sit there and I think, I'm alone, and I can't help this child. If it wants to die I can't stop it. I can love it until I bleed and it won't stop it. I hope it won't die. I hope it can grow up and have its time. I know how I'll feel if it does die, how long it'll take me to care if I draw breath, much less about cooking and the girls and all the things you have to do if you're alive."

Clara paused. In the lots a sorrel stallion whinnied. He was her favorite, but this day she appeared not to hear him.

"I know if I lose one more child I'll never care again," she said. "I won't. Nothing will make any difference to me again if I lose one more. It'll ruin me, and that'll ruin my girls. I'll never buy another horse, or cook another meal, or take another man. I'll starve, or else I'll go crazy and welcome it. Or I'll kill the doctor for not coming, or you for not sitting with me, or something. If you want to marry me, why don't you come and sit?"

July realized then that he had managed to do a terrible thing, though all he had done was go to his room in the ordinary way. It startled him to hear Clara say she could kill him over such a thing as that, but he knew from her look that it wasn't just talk.

"Would you ever marry me?" he asked. "You never said."

"No, and I'm not about to say now," Clara said. "Ask me in a year."

"Why in a year?"

"Because you deserve to suffer for a year," Clara said. "I suffered a year's worth just last night, and I guess you were lying at your ease, dreaming of our wedding night."

July had no reply. He had never known a woman who spoke so boldly. He looked at her through the fog of their breath, wishing she would at least take the coat. The cold made goosebumps on her wrists.

"I thought you were a sheriff once," Clara said. The stallion whinnied again, and, still watching July, she waved at the horse. He had the eyes of a sweet but bewildered boy in the body of a sturdy man. She wanted the sturdiness close to her, but was irritated by the bewilderment.

"Oh, I was a sheriff," he said.

"Didn't you ever give orders, then?" she said.

"Well, I told Roscoe when to clean the jail," July said.

"It ain't much, but it's more than we hear from you around here," Clara said. "Try telling me when to clean something, just for practice, once in a while. At least I'd get to hear a sound out of your throat."

Again, she refused the coat, though it was clear to him that she was in a somewhat better temper. She went over and rubbed the stallion's neck for ten minutes before going back to the house.

Then the other man, Dish Boggett, had to come, bringing the news that Augustus McCrae was dead. He had picked his way along the Platte River in a January blizzard. Both his horses were exhausted, but Dish himself seemed no worse for wear. He treated blizzards as a matter-of-fact occurrence.

It seemed to July that Clara took an instant liking to Dish Boggett, and he couldn't help feeling resentful, although he soon perceived that Dish had come to court Lorena, not Clara. Lorena had hardly spoken since she learned that Gus was dead. Clara immediately offered Dish a job—it was a hard winter and they were always behind. The colts would start coming soon, and they would be farther behind, so of course it was only sensible to hire another man, but July hated it. He had grown used to working with Clara and Cholo, and he had a hard time adjusting to Dish. Part of it was that Dish was twice as competent with horses as he was himself, and everyone immediately recognized Dish's value. Clara was soon asking Dish to do things with the horses that she had once let July do. July was more and more left with the kind of chores that a boy could handle.

To make matters worse, Dish Boggett was standoffish and made no attempt to make friends with him. Dish knew many card games and could even play charades, so he was a great hit with the girls. Many a night through the long winter, July sat against a wall, feeling left out, while Clara, Dish and the girls played games at the big kitchen table.

Dish tried every way he could to draw Lorena into some of the games, but the most Lorena would do was sit in the room. She sat silently, not watching, while July sat just as silently. He could not help but wish that Dish Boggett had got lost in Wyoming or had somehow gone on to Texas. Hardly a day passed without him seeing what he thought were signs that Clara was taken with the man. Sooner or later, when Dish gave up on Lorena, he would be bound to notice. July felt helpless—there was nothing he could do about it. Sometimes he sat near Lorena, feeling that he had more in common with her than with anyone else at the ranch. She loved a dead man, he a woman who hardly noticed him. But whatever they had in common didn't cause Lorena to so much as look his way. Lorena looked more beautiful than ever, but it was a grave beauty since news of the death had come. Only the young girl, Betsey, who loved Lorena completely, could occasionally bring a spark of life to her eyes. If Betsey was ill, Lorena nursed her tirelessly, taking her into her own bed and singing to her. They read stories together, Betsey doing the reading. Lorena could only piece out a few words—the sisters planned to teach her reading, but knew it would have to wait until she felt better.

Even Sally, usually so jealous of any attention her sister got, respected the fact that Betsey and Lorena were especially close. She would let off teasing Betsey if Lorena looked at her in a certain way.

Clara felt no terrible stab of grief when the news of Gus's death came. The years had kept them too separate. It had been a tremendous joy to see him when he visited—to realize that he still loved her, and that she still enjoyed him. She liked his tolerance and his humor, and felt an amused pride in the thought that he still put her above other women, despite all the years since they had first courted.

Often she sat out on her upper porch at night, wrapped in Bob's huge coat. She liked the bitter cold, a cold that seemed to dim the stars. Reflecting, she decided there had been something in what she and Gus had felt that needed separation. At close quarters she felt she would have struggled bitterly with him. Even during his brief visit she felt the struggle might start, and if it did start, gentler souls, such as July and Lorena, might have been destroyed.

In the dark nights on the ice-encrusted porch she occasionally felt a cold tear on her cheek. In Gus she had lost her ultimate ally, and felt that much more alone, but she had none of the tired despair she had felt when her children died.

Now there was July Johnson, a man whose love was nearly mute. Not only was he inept where feelings were concerned, he was also a dolt with horses. Loving horses as she did, Clara was hard put to know why she could even consider settling in with a man who was no better with them than Bob had been. Of course, the settling-in process was hardly complete, and Clara was in no hurry that it should be. Closer relations would probably only increase her impatience with him.

It amused her that he was so jealous of Dish, who, though friendly, companionable and an excellent hand, was not interested in her at all. His love for Lorena

leaped out of every look he cast in her direction, although not one of them pene-
trated Lorena's iron grief. Clara herself didn't try to touch or change Lorena's
grief—it was like Martin's fever: either it would kill her or it wouldn't. Clara would
not have been surprised by a gunshot if it had come from Lorena's room. She
knew the girl felt what she had felt when her boys died: unrelievable grief. In
those times, the well-meaning efforts of Bob or the neighbors to cheer her up had
merely affronted her. She hadn't wanted to live, particularly not cheerfully. Kindly
people told her that the living must live. *I don't, if my boys can't,* she wanted to
say to them. Yet the kindly people were right; she came slowly back to enjoyment
and one day would even find herself making a cake again and eating it with relish.

Watching Lorena, as she sat blank with grief every day, scarcely stirring unless
Betsey urged her to, Clara felt helpless. Lorena would either live or die, and Clara
felt it might be die. Lorena's only tie to life was Betsey. She didn't care for sweets
or men or horses; her only experience with happiness had been Gus. The handsome young cowboy who sent her countless looks of love meant nothing to her.
Pleasure had no hold on Lorena—she had known little of it, and Clara didn't
count on its drawing her back to life. The young cowboy would be doomed to find
his love blocked by Gus in death even as it had been in life. Betsey had a better
chance of saving Lorena than Dish. Betsey worried about her constantly and tried
to get her mother to do something.

"I can't make Mr. McCrae alive again, which is all she wants," Clara said. "What
do you think I can do?"

"Make her not so sad," Betsey pleaded.

"Nobody can do that," Clara said. "I can't even make you not sad when you're sad."

Yet one day she did try. She came upon Lorie standing in the hall, her hair
uncombed. She had the look of a beaten dog. Clara stopped and hugged her, as
suddenly as she had hugged July Johnson. In him her hug had stirred a fever of
hope; in Lorena it stirred nothing.

"I guess you wish you'd gone with him," Clara said. "It would have given you a
little more time."

Lorena looked surprised—it was the one thing she had been thinking since the
news came.

"I should have," she said.

"No," Clara said. "You would have had a little more time, I grant you, but now
you'd be stuck in Montana with a bunch of men who don't care that you loved
Gus. They'd want you to love them. Dish wants it so much that he rode to you
through the blizzards."

The thought of Dish merely made Lorena feel cold. "He wasted his time,"
she said.

"I know that, but don't expect him to realize it," Clara said.

"He bought me once, when I was a whore," Lorena said, surprised at the word
on her tongue. She had never used it before.

"And Gus didn't?" Clara said.

Lorena was silent. Of course Gus had. She wondered if Clara would ask her to
leave, knowing what she had been.

"Dish loved you and took the only way he had to get your attention," Clara said.

"He didn't get my attention," Lorena said. "He didn't get anything."

"And Gus did the same and got everything," Clara said. "Gus was lucky and
Dish isn't."

"I ain't either," Lorena said.

Clara offered no advice. A few days later, when she was sewing, Lorena came and stood in front of her. She looked no better. "Why did you ask me to stay, when it was you Gus loved?" she asked. "Why didn't you ask him to stay? If you had he'd be alive."

Clara shook her head. "He loved us both," she said, "but Gus would never miss an adventure. Not for you or me or any other woman. No one could have kept him home. He was a rake and a rambler, though you'd have kept him longer than I could have."

Lorena didn't believe it. She remembered how often Gus had talked of Clara. Of course it no longer mattered—nothing like that mattered anymore, and yet she couldn't keep her mind from turning to it.

"It ain't so," she said. She had used her voice so little that it sounded weak.

"It *is* so," Clara said. "You're more beautiful and less bossy. When I told Gus I was marrying Bob, all those years ago, he looked relieved. He tried to act disappointed, but he was relieved. I've never forgot it. And he had proposed to me thirty times at least. But he saw it would be a struggle if he won me, and he didn't want it."

Clara was silent for a moment, looking into the other woman's eyes.

"Bob was too dumb to realize there'd be a struggle," Clara said. "Half the time he didn't notice it even when he was in it. So mainly I had the struggle with myself.

"It's been lonely," she added.

She thought the conversation a good sign. Maybe Lorie was going to come out of it. But it was the last conversation they had for months. Lorena lived through the winter in silence, only speaking to Betsey, who remained as loyal as ever.

Dish Boggett remained loyal too, although Lorena gave him no encouragement. He spent more and more time playing cards with Sally, whose bright girlish chatter he had come to like. Every day he tried his best with Lorena, but he had begun to feel hopeless. She would not even speak to him, no matter how sweetly he asked. She met everything he said with silence—the same silence she had had in Lonesome Dove, only deeper. He told himself that if the situation didn't improve by the spring he would go to Texas and try to forget her.

Yet when spring came Dish told Clara he would be glad to stay and help her with the colts.

100

IT CAME TO RANKLE CALL that Gus had left his half of the cattle herd to the woman. The woman was down in Nebraska. She was not there helping. Of course, if she had been there helping, there would have been trouble, but that didn't lessen the aggravation of what Gus had done. He could simply have given her money—he had money. As it was, every time Call sold a bunch of stock to the Army he had to put aside half the money for a woman he had never approved of, who might, for all any of them knew, have already forgotten Gus and married someone else, or even gone back to being a whore.

Still, Call had halved the money. However aggravating it was, Gus had meant it, and he would do it, though when he went back with the body he planned to see if he could at least buy her out. He didn't like the thought of being in partnership with a woman, much less a whore—although he conceded that she might have reformed.

He lived in the tent all winter, keeping the men working but taking little interest in the result. Sometimes he hunted, taking the Hell Bitch and riding off onto the plains. He always killed game but was not much interested in the hunt. He went because he no longer felt comfortable around the men. The Indians had not bothered them, and the men did well enough by themselves. Soupy Jones had assumed the top-hand role, once Dish left, and flourished in it. The other men did well too, although there was some grumbling and many small disputes. Hugh Auld and Po Campo became friends and often tramped off together for a day or two so Hugh could show Po Campo some pond where there were still beaver, or some other interesting place he knew about. Lippy, starved for music, played the accordion and spent nearly the whole winter trying to make a fiddle from a shoebox. The instrument yielded a powerful screeching sound, but none of the cowboys were ready to admit that the sound was music.

At Christmas, hungering for pork, they killed Gus's pigs. The most surprising development was that Jasper Fant learned to cook. He took it up mainly out of boredom, but, tutored by Po Campo, his progress was so rapid that when Po Campo went off with Old Hugh the cuisine didn't suffer.

In the early spring, while the weather was still chancy, fifteen horses disappeared one night. It was only by luck that the theft was discovered, for in such a place at such a time horsethieves were the last thing they were expecting. Call had taken the precaution of going with Old Hugh to two or three of the nearest Indian camps to meet the chiefs and do the usual diplomacy, in the hope of preventing the sort of surprise encounter that had proven deadly for Gus. The visits made him sad, for the Indians were not belligerent and it was apparent that Gus had merely struck the wrong bunch at the wrong time, in the wrong manner. It was a depressing irony, for Gus had always been one to preach diplomacy with the red man and over the years had engaged in many councils that Call himself thought pointless. Gus had talked to many a warrior that Call would merely have shot, and yet had got killed in a place where most of the Indians were happy to talk, particularly to a man who owned an endless supply of beef.

But Call noticed on the visits that, in the main, the Indians had better horses than he did, and he had even arranged a trade with the Blackfeet: fifty beeves for ten horses. The negotiations had required Old Hugh to talk for two days and had left him hoarse.

Thus, when the Spettle boy came in to report the horses gone, Call was surprised. Where would a horsethief come from, and where would one go?

Still, a fact was a fact: the horses were gone. Call took Pea, Newt, Needle Nelson, and Old Hugh, and went in pursuit. He soon ruled out Indians, for the thieves were traveling too slow, and had even stopped to camp not thirty miles from their headquarters, which Indians with stolen horses would never have been foolish enough to do. It was soon plain that they were only chasing two men. They crossed into Canada on the second day and caught the thieves on the third, surprising them at breakfast. They were a shaky old man with a dirty gray beard and a strapping boy about Newt's age. The old man had a single-shot buffalo gun, and the boy a cap-and-ball pistol. The boy was cooking venison and the old man propped against his saddle muttering over a Bible when Call walked in with his pistol drawn. The boy, though big as an ox, began to tremble when he saw the five men with guns.

"I tolt you, Pa," he said. "Now we're caught."

The old man, who had a jug beside his saddle, was clearly drunk, and seemed scarcely conscious of what was occurring.

"Why, I'm a minister of the Lord," he said. "Don't point your dern guns at me, we're just having breakfast. This is my boy, Tom."

Call disarmed the two, which only took a second. The fifteen horses were grazing in plain sight not a hundred yards from the camp.

"We didn't know they were your horses," the boy said, quivering with fright. "We thought they were Indian horses."

"They're all branded," Call said. "You could see that, unless you're blind."

"Not blind and not sinners, either," the old man said, getting to his feet. He was so drunk he couldn't walk straight.

"Well, you're horsethieves, and that's a sin in my book," Call said. "Where do you people come from?"

"From God, man," the old fellow said.

"Where on earth, I meant," Call said, feeling weary. He wondered what had possessed a minister and a boy to run off their horses, each plainly branded. It struck him as a stupid and pointless crime, for they were driving the horses north, where there were no towns and no ranches. It was clear the two were poor, and the old man out of his head. Call could tell the hands were glum at the prospect of hanging such a pair, and he himself didn't relish it, but they were horsethieves and he felt he had no choice. His own distaste for the prospect caused him to make a mistake—he didn't immediately tie the old man, who seemed so weak he could hardly stand. He was not too weak, though, to snatch up a hatchet and strike a blow at Needle that would have killed him had not Needle jerked back—as it was, the blade of the hatchet tore a bad cut in his arm. Call shot the old man before he could strike again. The boy took off running across the open prairie. He was easily caught, of course, but by the time he was tied and led back the old man was dead. The boy sat down in the thin snow and wept.

"He was all right until Ma died and Sister died," he said. "We were in a wagon train. Then he just went daft and said we had to go off by ourselves. I didn't want to."

"I wish he hadn't taken our horses," Call said.

The boy was trembling and crying. "Don't hang me, mister," he said. "I never stole in my life. I told him to leave them horses, but he said they were horses the Indians had already stole.

"I'll work for you," the boy added. "I can blacksmith. I worked two years at a forge back in Missouri, before we left."

Call knew there was not a decent tree in miles. It would be a hardship on them to ride along with the boy for a day in order to hang him. Besides, they needed a blacksmith. As for the boy's story, maybe it was true and maybe it wasn't. The old man had appeared to be mad, but Call had seen many thieves act that way in hopes that it would save them.

"Pa said he'd shoot me if I didn't help," the boy said.

Call didn't believe him. He had been about to cut the boy loose, but he didn't. He put him on one of the stolen horses, and they started back.

Newt felt sick at the thought of what would happen. He didn't want to see another person hang.

"You ask him," he said to Pea.

"Ask him what?" Pea said.

"Not to hang him," Newt said.

"He'll hang him," Pea said. "He hung Jake, didn't he?"

"His pa made him do it," Newt said.

"Maybe," Pea said. "And maybe he's just a dern horsethief."

When they came to a good tree, Call rode on, all the way to the Hat Creek headquarters. Once there, he cut the boy loose.

"You can work," he said.

For ten days the big boy was the friendliest person in the outfit. He shoed all the horses, cut wood, did every chore he was asked to do and some that he wasn't. He chattered constantly and tried his best to be friendly, and yet no one really liked him. Even Newt didn't really like him. Tom stood too close to him, when he talked, and he talked all the time. His large face was always sweaty, even on the coldest days. Even Po Campo didn't like him, and gave him food grudgingly.

Then, before dawn one morning Call caught Big Tom, as they called him, saddling a horse and preparing to ride off. He had four of the men's wallets on him, stolen so smoothly that none of the men had even missed them. He had also taken the best saddle in the outfit, which belonged to Bert Borum.

Call had been expecting the move for two or three days and had made Pea Eye help him watch. Big Tom tried to make a dash for it, and Call shot him off his horse. Cowboys ran out of their house in their long johns, at the shot. Even wounded, the boy proved full of fight—Call had to rap him with the barrel of his Henry before he could be tied. This time he was summarily hung, though he wept again and begged for mercy.

"It's wasted on horsethieves," Call said, before kicking the boy's horse out from under him. None of the men said a word.

"Should have hung him in the first place, although he did shoe them horses," Pea Eye commented later.

Call had begun to think of Gus, and the promise he had made. It would soon be spring, and he would have to be going if he were to keep the promise, which of course he must. Yet the ranch had barely been started, and it was hard to know who to leave in command. The question had been in his mind all winter. There seemed to be no grave danger from Indians or anything else. Who would best keep things going? Soupy was excellent when set a task, but had no initiative and was unused to planning. The men were all independent to a fault and constantly on the verge of fist fights because they fancied that someone had attempted to put himself above them in some way. Pea Eye was clearly the senior man, but Pea Eye had contentedly taken orders for thirty years; to expect him to suddenly start giving them was to expect the impossible.

Call thought often of Newt. He watched him with increasing pride all winter. The boy was the only one left in the crew whom he enjoyed being with. The boy's skill and persistence with horses pleased him. He knew it would be chancy to leave a seventeen-year-old boy in charge of a group of grown men—yet he himself had led men at that age, and that had been in rougher times. He liked the way the boy went about his work without complaint. He had filled out physically during the year and could work all day energetically and accomplish more than most of the men.

Once, watching the boy cross a corral after having worked with one of the mustangs, Pea Eye said innocently, "Why, Captain, little Newt walks just like you."

Call flinched, but Pea Eye didn't notice—Pea Eye was no noticer, as Augustus had often said.

That night, sitting in Wilbarger's little tent, Call remembered the remark. He also remembered Gus's efforts to talk to him about the boy. With Gus pressing him, it was his nature to resist, but with Gus gone he didn't find it so distasteful to consider that the boy was his son. He had certainly gone to his mother, hateful as the memory was. Maggie, of course, had not been hateful—it was the strange need she induced in him that he disliked to remember.

He started taking the boy with him on every trip he made to the forts, not merely to familiarize him with the country but to let him participate in the selling and trading. Once, as a test, he sent Pea and the boy and the Raineys to Fort Benton with a sizable bunch of cattle, stipulating that the boy was to handle the details of the sale and bring home the money. Newt did well, as well as he himself could have done. He delivered the cattle safely, sold them for a fair amount and brought the money home.

It didn't sit well with Soupy Jones that Newt was being given such authority. It seemed to Soupy that he should have taken the cattle, and possibly received a commission, in his capacity as top hand. Soupy was rude to Newt from time to time, and Newt ignored him as best he could. Call did nothing, but two weeks later he let it be known that he was preparing to send the boy to the fort again—at which point Soupy boiled over. He took it as a slight and said he would draw his wages and go if that was how things were going to be.

Call promptly paid him his wages, much to Soupy's astonishment. He had never imagined such an outcome. "Why, Captain, I don't want to leave," he said plaintively. "I got nothing to go to back down south."

"Then give me back the money and behave yourself," Call said. "I decide who'll do what around here."

"I know, Captain," Soupy said. He was aware that he had chosen a bad moment to make his scene—right after breakfast, with many of the hands standing around.

"If you have other complaints, I'm listening," Call said. "You seem to be mad at Newt."

The words made the hairs stand up on the back of Newt's neck. It was the first time he could ever remember the Captain having spoken his name.

"Well, no, I ain't," Soupy said. "He's a fair hand, but it don't seem right a fair hand should be put over a top hand unless there's a reason."

"He's young and needs the training—you don't. That's the reason," Call said. "If I tell you to take orders from him you will, or else leave. They'll be my orders, at second hand."

Soupy reddened at the disgusting thought of taking orders from a boy. He stuffed his wages in his pocket, planning to leave, but an hour's contemplation caused him to mellow and he gave Call back the wages. That night, though, he suddenly stuck out a foot and tripped Newt, when Newt walked past with a plateful of food. Newt fell on his face but he rose and flung himself on Soupy in a second, so angry at the insult that he even held his own for a few licks, until Soupy could bring his weight and experience into play—after which Newt got thoroughly pounded, so thoroughly that he was not aware when the fight stopped. He was sitting on the ground spitting blood, and Soupy had walked away. Call had expected the fight and watched impassively, pleased that the boy had fought so hard. Winning would have been beyond his powers.

The battle won Soupy no friends; he had assumed so many airs once Dish left that he had few friends anyway, whereas Newt was popular. Reaction was so unfavorable that a few days later Soupy drew his wages again and left, taking Bert with him. They had concluded they could make Texas, if they went together.

Call was worried for a few weeks about being shorthanded, but then three young men he had seen at the fort decided to quit soldiering and try their hand at ranching. All three were from Kentucky. They were inept at first but industrious. Then two genuine cowboys showed up; lured all the way north from Miles City by the news that there was a ranch on the Milk. They had given up cowboying for mule skinning the year before and concluded they had made a bad mistake. Then a tall boy named Jim wandered in alone. He had been with a wagon train but had lost interest in getting to Oregon.

Soon, instead of being short-handed, Call found that he had almost more men than he needed. He decided to start the branding early. Several hundred calves had been born since they left Texas; many were yearlings, and a struggle to brand. A few of the men questioned the necessity, since they were the only cattle outfit in the Territory, but Call knew that would soon change. Others would come.

The roundup took ten days. The cattle had spread themselves wide over the range between the Milk and the Missouri in their foraging during the winter. Then the branding took a week. At first the men enjoyed the activity, competing with one another to see who could throw the largest animals the quickest. There was also much disagreement over who should get to rope and who should work on foot. Newt improved so rapidly as a roper that he was soon sharing that task with Needle Nelson, the only one of the original crew skilled with a lariat.

With the branding ended, and the spring grass spiking through the thin May snows, Call knew the time had come for him to fulfill his promise to his old friend. It was awkward—indeed, it seemed absurd—to have to tote a six-months-old corpse to Texas, but there it was.

Yet May wore on and June approached, and still he had not gone. The snows had melted, all down the plains, he imagined, and yet something held him. It wasn't work. There were plenty of men to do the work—they had even had to turn away three or four men who came looking to hire on. Many times Call spent much of the afternoon watching Newt work with the new batch of horses they had bought on a recent trip to the fort. It was work he himself had never been particularly good at—he had always lacked the patience. He let the boy alone and never made suggestions. He liked to watch the boy with the horses; it had become a keen pleasure. If a cowboy came over and tried to talk to him while he was watching he usually simply ignored the man until he went away. He wanted to watch the boy and not be bothered. It could only be for a few days, he knew. It was a long piece to Texas and back. Sometimes he wondered if he would even come back. The ranch was started, and the dangers so far had been less than he feared. He felt sometimes that he had no more to do. He felt much older than anyone he knew. Gus had seemed young even when he was dying, and yet Call felt old. His interest in work had not returned. It was only when he was watching the boy with the horses that he felt himself.

In those hours he would lose himself in memory of other times, of other men who had lived with horses, who had broken them, ridden them, died on them. He felt proud of the boy, and with it, anguish that their beginnings had been as they had. It could not be changed, though. He thought he might speak of it sometime, as Gus had wanted him to, and yet he said nothing. He couldn't. If he happened to be alone with the boy, his words went away. At the thought of speaking about it a tightness came into his throat, as if a hand had seized it. Anyway, what could a few words change? They couldn't change the years.

Newt was puzzled at first when the Captain began watching him with the horses. At first he was nervous—he felt the Captain might be watching because he was doing something that needed correcting. But the afternoons passed, and the Captain merely watched, sometimes sitting there for hours, even if it turned wet or squally. Newt came to expect him. He came to feel that the Captain enjoyed watching. Because of the way the Captain had been behaving, giving him more and more of the responsibility for the work, Newt came to feel that Mr. Gus must have been right. The Captain might be his father. On some afternoons, with the Captain there by the corrals watching, he felt almost sure of it, and began to expect that the Captain would tell him soon. He began to listen—waiting to be told, his hope always growing. Even when the Captain didn't speak, Newt still felt proud when he saw him come to watch him work.

For two weeks, through the spring evenings, Newt was very happy. He had never expected to share such a time with the Captain, and he hoped the Captain would speak to him soon and explain all that had puzzled him for so long.

One night toward the end of May, Call couldn't sleep. He sat in front of the tent all night, thinking of the boy, and Gus, and the trip he had to make. That morning, after breakfast, he called Newt aside. For a moment he couldn't speak—the hand had seized his throat again. The boy stood waiting, not impatient. Call was annoyed with himself for his strange behavior, and he eventually found his voice.

"I have to take Gus back," he said. "I guess I'll be gone a year. You'll have to be the range boss. Pea will help you, and the rest are mostly reliable, though I think that Irishman is homesick and might go home."

Newt didn't know what to say. He looked at the Captain.

"That woman gets half the money when you sell stock," Call said. "It was Gus's request. You can bank it for her in Miles City. I'll tell her it's there when I see her."

Newt could hardly believe he would be made boss over the men. He expected more orders, but the Captain turned away.

Later in the morning, he and Pea Eye and Needle were riding the banks of the Milk, seeing if any cattle were bogged. They were always bogging. Getting them out was hard, muddy work, but it had to be done; if it rained, the river might rise in the night and drown the bogged animals.

The day was cold and blowy. Newt had to wade out into the mud three times to lift the hind ends of the bogged yearlings, while Needle roped the animals by the head and drug them out. Newt scraped the mud off his legs as best he could, put his pants back on, and was getting ready to turn back toward headquarters when he saw the Captain riding toward them. He was riding the Hell Bitch and leading Greasy, the big mule that had come with them all the way from Texas, and a rangy dun named Jerry, the mount he preferred after the Hell Bitch. Augustus's old sign was tied to the pack mule.

"I guess the Captain's going," Pea Eye said. "He's taking old Greasy and an extra horse."

Newt felt his spirits sink. He knew the Captain had to leave, and yet he hoped he wouldn't—not for another few days anyway.

Call rode up to the three men, dismounted and, to everyone's surprise unsaddled the Hell Bitch and put the saddle on Jerry. Then he led the Hell Bitch over to where Newt stood.

"See how your saddle fits her," Call said.

Newt was so surprised he could only look at the Captain in silence. He thought he must have misunderstood. No one but the Captain had ridden the mare since the Hat Creek outfit had acquired her.

"Do what?" he asked finally.

"Put your saddle on her," Call said. He felt tired and was finding it difficult to speak. He felt at any moment he might choke.

"I doubt she'd like it," Newt said, looking at the mare, who pointed her ears at him as if she knew what had been said. But the Captain didn't take back the order, so he unsaddled the little sorrel he had been riding, the one Clara had given him, and carried his saddle over to the mare. Call held the bridle while Newt saddled her. Then he handed Newt the reins and went over and took his big Henry out of its scabbard. He removed the Winchester from the boy's saddle and stuck the Henry in his saddle scabbard. It wasn't a perfect fit, but it would do.

"You'll need it for them big bears," he said.

When he turned back to look at the boy the choking feeling almost overcame him. He decided he would tell the boy he was his son, as Gus had wanted him to. He thought they would ride away a little distance, so they could speak in private.

And yet, when he looked at Newt, standing there in the cold wind, with Canada behind him, Call found he couldn't speak at all. It was as if his whole life had suddenly lodged in his throat, a raw bite he could neither spit out nor swallow. He had once seen a Ranger choke to death on a tough bite of buffalo meat, and he felt that he was choking, too—choking on himself. He felt he had failed in all he had tried to be: the good boy standing there was evidence of it. The shame he felt was so strong it stopped the words in his throat. Night after night, sitting in front of Wilbarger's tent, he had struggled with thoughts so bitter that he had not even felt the Montana cold. All his life he had preached honesty to his men and had summarily discharged those who were not capable of it, though they had mostly only lied about duties neglected or orders sloppily executed. He himself was far worse, for he had been dishonest about his own son, who stood not ten feet away, holding the reins of the Hell Bitch.

Call thought he might yet say it, even if the men were there to hear. He trembled from the effort, and his trembling and the look on his face caused great consternation in Pea Eye, who had never known the Captain to be at a loss for words.

The Captain would ride up and give an order, and that was that—but now he merely stood looking at Newt, a jerking in his throat.

Looking at the Captain, Newt began to feel sadder than he had ever felt in his life. Just go on, he wanted to say. Go on, if it's that hard. He didn't want the Captain to go on, of course. He felt too young; he didn't want to be left with it all. He felt he couldn't bear what was happening, it was so surprising. Five minutes before, he had been pulling a yearling out of a bog. Now the Captain had given him his horse and his gun, and stood with a look of suffering on his face. Even Sean O'Brien, dying of a dozen snakebites, had not shown so much pain. Go on, then, Newt thought. Just let it be. It's been this way always. Let it be, Captain.

Call walked the few steps to the boy and squeezed his arm so hard Newt thought his fingers had pinched the bone. Then he turned and tried to mount the dun. He had to try for the stirrup three times before he could mount. He wished he had died on the Musselshell with Gus. It would have been easier than knowing he could not be honest. His own son stood there—surely, it was true; after doubting it for years, his own mind told him over and over that it was true—yet he couldn't call him a son. His honesty was lost, had long been lost, and he only wanted to leave.

When he mounted, the feeling loosened a bit and he fell back into the habit he had vowed to discard—the habit of leading.

"There's two heifers bogged yet," he said. "They're half a mile downstream. You better go get them."

Then he rode over and shook Pea Eye's hand. Pea Eye was so astonished he couldn't close his mouth. Gus had never shaken his hand until the last minute, and now the Captain was shaking it too.

"Help Newt," Call said. "He'll need a steady man, and you qualify if anybody ever did."

He raised his hand to Needle Nelson and turned his horse.

"So long, boys," he said.

But he looked again at Newt. The boy looked so lonesome that he was reminded of his own father, who had never been comfortable with people. His father had fallen drunk out of a barn loft in Mississippi and broken his neck. Call remembered the watch that had been passed on to him, an old pocket watch with a thin gold case. He had carried it since he was a boy. He raised up in his stirrups, took it out of his pocket and handed it to Newt.

"It was my pa's," he said, and turned and left.

"Dern, Newt," Pea Eye said, more astonished than he had ever been in his life. "He gave you his horse and his gun and that watch. He acts like you're his kin."

"No, I ain't kin to nobody in this world," Newt said bitterly. "I don't want to be. I won't be."

Despair in his heart, he mounted the Hell Bitch as if he had ridden her for years, and turned downstream. He felt he never wanted to hope for anything again, and yet no more than a minute later the strange hope struck him that the Captain might have turned back. He might have forgotten something—perhaps an order he had meant to give. Even that he would have welcomed. It felt so lonely to think of the Captain being gone. But when he turned to look, the Captain was merely a speck on the long plain. He was gone, and things would never be as Newt had hoped—never. Somehow it had been too hard for the Captain, and he had left.

Pea Eye and Needle followed Newt silently. Pea Eye felt old and frightened. In a few minutes the whole ground of his life had shifted, and he felt stricken with foreboding. For thirty years the Captain had been there to give orders, and frequently the orders had kept them alive. He had always been with the Captain, and yet now he wasn't. He couldn't understand why the Captain had given Newt the horse, the gun and the watch. The business of the ax, and what he had heard when retrieving it, was forgotten—it had puzzled him so long that it had finally just slipped from his mind.

"Well, here we are," he said wearily. "I guess we'll just have to do the work."

The Texas bull was standing a hundred yards or so away with a small group of cows. When the riders drew near, he began to bellow and paw the earth. It irritated him if he saw several riders together, though he had not charged anyone lately.

"I'll tell you one thing, I may shoot that bull yet," Needle said. "I've put up with that son of a bitch about long enough. The Captain may like him, but I don't."

Newt heard the talk, but didn't speak. He knew the Captain had left him with too much, but he didn't say it. He would have to try and do the work, even if he no longer cared.

Feeling that it was pointless, but acting from force of habit, they pulled the two stuck heifers from the Milk River mud.

101

IN MILES CITY, Call found that the storage of Augustus's remains had been bungled. Something had broken into the shed and knocked the coffin off the barrels. In the doctor's opinion it had probably been a wolverine, or possibly a cougar. The coffin had splintered and the varmint had run off with the amputated leg. The mistake wasn't discovered until after a blizzard had passed through, so of course the leg had not been recovered.

The look on Call's face, when he heard the news, was so grim it made the doctor extremely nervous.

"We've mostly kept him," he said, avoiding Call's eye. "I had him repacked. He had done lost that leg before he died anyway."

"It was in the coffin when I left here," Call said. He didn't care to discuss the matter with the man. Instead, he found the carpenter who had built the coffin in the first place and had him reinforce it with strong planks. The result was a heavy piece of work.

By luck, the same day, Call saw a buggy for sale. It was old but it looked sturdy enough, and he bought it. The next day he had the coffin covered in canvas and lashed to the seat. The buggy hood was in tatters, so he tore it off. Greasy, the mule, was used to pulling the wagon and hardly noticed the buggy, it was so light. They left Miles City on a morning when it had turned unseasonably cold—so cold that the sun only cast a pale light through the frigid clouds. Call knew it was dangerous to go off with only two animals, but he felt like taking his chances.

The weather improved the next day and he rode for a time beside a hundred or so Crow Indians who were traveling south. The Crow were friendly, and their old chief, a dried-up little man with a great appetite for tobacco and talk, tried to get Call to camp with them. They were all interested in the fact that he was traveling with a coffin and asked him many questions about the man inside it.

"We traveled together," Call said. He did not want to talk about Gus with the old man, or anyone. He wanted to get on, but he was cordial and rode with the Crow because he felt that if he were discourteous some of the young bucks might try to make sport with him farther south, when he was out of range of the old chief's protection.

Once he struck Wyoming, he rode for eleven days without seeing a soul. The buggy held up well, but Greasy lost flesh from the pace Call kept up. The coffin got some bad jolts crossing the gullies near the Powder River, but the reinforcements held it together.

The first people he saw, as he approached Nebraska, were five young Indians who had gotten liquor somewhere. When they saw he was carrying a dead man they let him alone, though they were too drunk to hunt successfully and begged him for food. None of them looked to be eighteen, and their horses were poor. Call started to refuse, but then he reflected that they were just boys. He offered them food if they would give up their liquor, but at that they grew quarrelsome. One drew an old pistol and acted as if he might fire at him, but Call ignored the threat, and they were soon gone.

He regretted that he had to take Gus to the women, but felt it was part of his obligation to deliver the notes Gus had written when he was dying. The Platte was so full of ducks and geese that he heard their gabbling all day, though he rode a mile from the river.

He thought often of the men he had left up on the Milk, and of the boy. He had not expected the parting to go as it had, and could not get his mind off it. For several hundred miles, down through Montana and Wyoming, he left them all over again in his mind, day after day. He imagined many times that he had said things he had not said, and, from concentrating on it too much as he traveled down the plains, he began to grow confused. He missed being able to sit at the corrals and watch Newt work with the horses. He wondered if the boy was handling the Hell Bitch well and if any more men had left the ranch.

Then, before he had scarcely reined in at Clara's house, where he found Dish Boggett breaking horses with the young sheriff from Arkansas, the woman began a quarrel with him. She had acquired some small shrubs somehow and was out planting them, bareheaded and in overshoes, when he arrived.

"So you're doing it, are you, Mr. Call?" Clara said, when she saw him. She had a look of scorn in her eyes, which puzzled him, since he was merely carrying out the request of the man who had loved her for so long. Of course Dish had told her that Gus wanted his body taken to Texas.

"Well, he asked, and I said I'd do it," Call said, wondering why she disliked him so. He had just dismounted.

"Gus was crazy and you're foolish to drag a corpse that far," Clara said bluntly. "Bury him here and go back to your son and your men. They need you. Gus can rest with my boys."

Call flinched when she said the word "son," as if she had never had a doubt that Newt was his. He himself had once been a man of firm opinion, but now it seemed to him that he knew almost nothing, whereas the words Clara flung at him were hard as rocks.

"I told him that very thing," Call said. "I told him you'd likely want him here."

"I've always kept Gus where I wanted him, Mr. Call," Clara said. "I kept him in my memory for sixteen years. Now we're just talking of burying his body. Take him to the ridge and I'll have July and Dish get a grave dug."

"Well, it wasn't what he asked of me," Call said, avoiding her eyes. "It seems that picnic spot you had in Texas is where he wanted to lay."

"Gus was a fine fool," Clara said. "He was foolish for me or any other girl who would have him for a while. Because it was me he thought of, dying, is no reason to tote his bones all the way to Texas."

"It was because you picnicked in the place," Call said, confused by her anger. He would have thought a woman would feel complimented by such a request, but Clara clearly didn't take it that way.

"Yes, I remember our picnics," she said. "We mostly quarreled. He wanted what I wouldn't give. I wanted what he didn't have. That was a long time ago, before my boys died."

Tears came to her eyes when she said it, as they always did when the thought of her boys struck her. She was aware that she was being anything but hospitable, and that the man didn't understand what she said. She scarcely knew what she meant herself—she just knew that the sight of Woodrow Call aroused in her an unreasoning hate and disgust.

"He wrote you," Call said, remembering why he had come. "There's a letter for you and one for her. He left her his half of our cattle." He untied his saddlebag and brought out the two notes, handing them to Clara.

"I would have sent them with Dish but he left in the winter and there was no knowing if he'd get through," Call said.

"But you always get through, don't you, Captain?" Clara said, with a look so hard that Call turned aside from it and stood by the horses, tired. He was ready to agree with her that Gus had been foolish to make such a request of him.

Then he turned and saw Clara walk over to Greasy, the mule. She stroked the mule along his neck and spoke to him softly before breaking into sobs. She hid her face against the mule, who stood as if planted, though normally he was a rather skittish animal. But he stood while Clara sobbed against his side. Then, taking the notes and not looking at Call, she hurried into the house.

From the lots, Dish and July were watching. Dish felt a little queasy, seeing Gus's coffin. He had not gotten over his nervousness about the dead. It seemed to him quick burial was the best way to slow their ghosts.

July, of course, had heard all about Gus McCrae's death, and his strange request, but had not quite believed it. Now it had turned out to be true. He remembered that Gus had ridden down with him on the Kiowa campfire and killed every single man, while he himself had not been able to pull a trigger. Now the same man, dead a whole winter, had turned up in Nebraska. It was something out of the ordinary, of that he felt sure.

"I knowed the Captain would do it," Dish said. "I bet them boys up on the Milk are good and skeert, now he's gone."

"I hear it's hard winters up there," July said—not that they were easy in Nebraska.

The Captain, as if distracted, walked a little way toward the lots and then stopped. Dish walked out to greet him, followed by July, and was shocked by the change in the man. The Captain looked like an old man—he had little flesh on his face and his beard and mustache were sprinkled with gray.

"Why, Captain, it's fine to see you," Dish said. "How are them northern boys doing?"

Call shook Dish's hand, then July's. "We wintered without losing a man, or much stock either," he said, very tired.

Then he saw that Dish was looking beyond him. He turned and saw that the blond woman had come out of the house. She walked to the buggy and stood by the coffin. Clara's two daughters followed her out on the back porch, a toddling child between them. The girls didn't follow Lorena to the buggy. They watched a minute and then guided the child back in the house.

Dish Boggett would have given anything to be able to go to Lorena, but he knew he couldn't. Instead he led the Captain back down to the lots and tried to interest him in the horses. But the Captain's mind was elsewhere.

When the plains darkened and they went in to supper, Lorena still stood by the wagon. The meal was eaten in silence, except for little Martin's fretting. He was used to being the center of gay attention and couldn't understand why no one laughed when he flung his spoon down, or why no one sang to him, or offered him sweets.

"Oughtn't we to go get Lorie?" Dish asked, at one point, anguished that she was left to stand alone in the darkness.

Clara didn't answer. The girls had cooked the meal, and she directed the serving with only a glance now and then. Watching Woodrow Call awkwardly handling his fork caused her to repent a little of her harshness when he arrived, but she didn't apologize. She had stopped expecting July to contribute to the conversation, but she resented his silence nevertheless. Once Martin spat out a bite of perfectly good food and Clara looked at him sharply and said "You behave," in a tone that instantly put a stop to his fretting. Martin opened his mouth to cry but thought better of it and chewed miserably on his spoon until the meal was finished.

After supper the men went out of the house to smoke, all glad to escape the company of the silent woman. Even Betsey and Sally, accustomed to chattering through supper, competing for the men's attention, were subdued by their mother's silence, and merely attended to serving.

After supper Clara went to her bedroom. Gus's letter lay on her bureau, unread. She lit her lamp and picked it up, scratching at the dried blood that stained one corner of the folded sheet. "I ought not to read this," she said, aloud. "I don't like the notion of words from the dead."

"What, Momma?" Betsey asked. She had come upstairs with Martin and had overheard.

"Nothing, Betsey," Clara said. "Just a crazy woman talking to herself."

"Martin acts like he's got a stomachache," Betsey complained. "You didn't have to look so mean at him, Ma."

Clara turned for a moment. "I won't have him spitting out food," she said. "The reason men are awful is because some woman has spoiled them. Martin's going to learn manners if he learns nothing else."

"I don't think men are awful," Betsey said. "Dish ain't."

"Let me be, Betsey," Clara said. "Put Martin to bed."

She opened the letter—just a few words in a scrawling hand:

DEAR CLARA—

I would be obliged if you'd look after Lorie. I fear she'll take this hard.

I'm down to one leg now and this life is fading fast, so I can't say more. Good luck to you and your gals, I hope you do well with the horses.

GUS

Clara went out on her porch and sat, twisting her hands, for an hour. She could see that the men were below, still smoking, but they were silent. It's too much death, she thought. Why does it keep coming to me?

The dark heavens gave no answer, and after a while she got up and went downstairs and out to Lorena, who still stood by the buggy, where she had been from the time Call arrived.

"Do you want me to read you this letter?" she said, knowing the girl couldn't read. "It's bad handwriting."

Lorena held the letter tightly in her hand. "No, I'll just keep it," she said. "He put my name on it. I can read that. I'll just keep it."

She didn't want Clara to see the letter. It was hers from Gus. What the words were didn't matter.

Clara stood with her for a bit and went back in.

The moon rose late, and when it did the men walked to the little shack by the lots where they slept. The old Mexican was coughing. Later Lorena heard the Captain get his bedroll and walk away with it. She was glad when the lights went out in the house and the men were all gone. It made it easier to believe Gus knew she was there.

They'll all forget you—they got their doings, she thought. But I won't, Gus. Whenever it comes morning or night, I'll think of you. You come and got me away from him. She can forget and they can forget, but I won't, never, Gus.

The next morning Lorena still stood by the buggy. The men scarcely knew what to think about it. Call was perplexed. Clara made breakfast as silently as she had presided over supper. They could all look out the window and see the blond girl standing like a statue by the buggy, the letter from Augustus clutched in her hand.

"For that girl's sake I wish you'd forget your promise, Mister Call," Clara said finally.

"I can't forget no promise to a friend," Call said. "Though I do agree it's foolish and told him so myself."

"People lose their minds over things like this," Clara said. "Gus was all to that girl. Who'll help me, if she loses hers?"

Dish wanted to say that he would, but couldn't get the words out. The sight of Lorie, standing in grief, made him so unhappy that he wished he'd never set foot in the town of Lonesome Dove. Yet he loved her, though he could not approach her.

Clara saw that it was hopeless to hammer at Call. He would go unless she shot him. His face was set, and only the fact that the girl stood by the buggy had kept him from leaving already. It angered her that Gus had been so perverse as to extract such a promise. There was no proportion in it—being drug three thousand miles to be buried at a picnic site. Probably he had been delirious and would have withdrawn the request at once if he had been allowed a lucid moment. What angered her most was Gus's selfishness in regard to Call's son. He had been a sweet boy with lonesome eyes, polite. He was the kind of boy she would have given anything to raise, and here, for a romantic whim, Gus had seen to it that father and son were separated.

It seemed so wrong to her, and raised such anger in her, that for a moment she was almost tempted to shoot Call, just to thwart Gus. Not kill, but shoot him enough to keep him down until Gus could be buried and the folly checked.

Then, between one minute and the next, Lorena crumpled to the ground, unconscious. Clara knew it was only a faint, but the men had to carry her in and upstairs. Clara shooed them out as soon as she could, and put Betsey to watching her. By that time Captain Call had mounted and hitched the brown mule to the buggy and mounted his horse. He was ready to go.

Clara walked out to try once more. Dish and July were shaking hands with Call, but they beat an immediate retreat when they saw her coming.

"I put it to you once more, in the plainest terms, Mr. Call," Clara said. "A live son is more important than a dead friend Can you understand that?"

"A promise is a promise," Call said.

"A promise is words—a son is a life," Clara said. "A *life*, Mr. Call. I was better fit to raise boys than you've ever been, and yet I lost three. I tell you no promise is worth leaving that boy up there, as you have. Does he know he's your son?"

"I suppose he does—I give him my horse," Call said, feeling that it was hell to have her, of all women, talk to him about the matter.

"Your horse but not your name?" Clara said. "You haven't even given him your name?"

"I put more value on the horse," Call said, turning the dun. He rode off, but Clara, terrible in her anger, strode beside him.

"I'll write him," she said. "I'll see he gets your name if I have to carry the letter to Montana myself. And I'll tell you another thing: I'm sorry you and Gus McCrae ever met. All you two done was ruin one another, not to mention those close to you. Another reason I didn't marry him was because I didn't want to fight you for him every day of my life. You men and your promises: they're just excuses to do what you plan to do anyway, which is leave. You think you've always done right—that's your ugly pride, Mr. Call. But you never did right and it would be a sad woman that needed anything from you. You're a vain coward, for all your fighting. I despised you then, for what you were, and I despise you now, for what you're doing."

Clara could not check her bitterness—even now, she knew, the man thought he was doing the right thing. She strode beside the horse, pouring out her contempt, until Call put the mule and the dun into a trot, the buggy, with the coffin on it, squeaking as it bounced over the rough plain.

102

S O C A P T A I N C A L L turned back down the rivers, cut by the quirt of Clara's contempt and seared with the burn of his own regret. For a week, down from the Platte and across the Republican, he could not forget what she said: that he had never done right, that he and Gus had ruined one another, that he was a coward, that she would take a letter to the boy. He had gone through life feeling that he had known what should be done, and now a woman flung it at him that he hadn't. He found that he could not easily forget a word Clara said. He could only trail the buggy down the lonely plains, her words stinging in his heart and head.

Before he reached Kansas, word had filtered ahead of him that a man was carrying a body home to Texas. The plain was filled with herds, for it was full summer. Cowboys spread the word, soldiers spread it. Several times he met trappers, coming east from the Rockies, or buffalo hunters who were finding no buffalo. The Indians heard—Pawnee and Arapahoe and Ogallala Sioux. Sometimes he would ride past parties of braves, their horses fat on spring grass, come to watch his journey. Some were curious enough to approach him, even to question him. Why did he not bury the *compañero?* Was he a holy man whose spirit must have a special place?

No, Call answered. Not a holy man. Beyond that he couldn't explain. He had come to feel that Augustus had probably been out of his mind at the end, though he hadn't looked it, and that *he* had been out of his mind to make the promise he had.

In one week in Kansas he ran into eight cattle herds—he would no sooner pass one than he encountered another. The only advantage to him was that the trail bosses were generous with wire and pliers. The Miles City buggy had been patched so many times that it was mostly wire by then, Call felt. He knew it would never make Texas, but he determined to keep going as long as he could—what he would do when it finally fell apart he didn't know.

Finally he was asked about Augustus and the purpose of his journey so many times that he couldn't tolerate it. He turned west into Colorado, meaning to skirt the main cattle trails. He was tired of meeting people. His only moments of peace came late in the day when he was too tired to think and was just bouncing along with Gus.

He rode through Denver, remembering that he had never sent Wilbarger's brother the telegram he had promised, notifying him of Wilbarger's death. It had been a year and he felt he owed Wilbarger that consideration, though he soon regretted coming into the town, a noisy place filled with miners and cattlemen. The sight of the buggy with the coffin excited such general curiosity that by the time he was out of the telegraph office a crowd had gathered. Call had scarcely walked out the door when an undertaker in a black hat and a blue bow tie approached him.

"Mister, you ain't nowhere near the graveyard," the man said. He had even waxed his mustache and was altogether too shiny for Call's taste.

"I wasn't looking for it," Call said, mounting. People were touching the coffin as if they had the right.

"We give a nice ten-dollar funeral," the undertaker said. "You could just leave the fellow with me and come pick out the gravestone at your leisure. Of course the gravestone's extra."

"Not in the market," Call said.

"Who is it, mister?" a boy asked.

"His name was McCrae," Call said.

He was glad to put the town behind him, and thereafter took to driving at night to avoid people, though it was harder on the buggy, for he couldn't always see the bumps.

One night he felt the country was too rough for evening travel so he camped by the Purgatoire River, or Picketwire, as the cowboys called it. He heard the sound of an approaching horse and wearily picked up his rifle. It was only one horse. Dusk had not quite settled into night, and he could see the rider coming—a big man. The horse turned out to be a red mule and the big man Charles Goodnight. Call had known the famous cattleman since the Fifties, and they had ridden together a few times in the Frontier Regiment, before he and Gus were sent to the border. Call had never taken to the man—Goodnight was indifferent to authority, or at least unlikely to put any above his own—but he could not deny that the man had uncommon ability. Goodnight rode up to the campfire but did not dismount.

"I like to keep up with who's traveling the country," he said. "I admit I did not expect it to be you."

"You're welcome to coffee," Call said.

"I don't take much else at night," he added.

"Hell, if I didn't take some grub in at night I'd starve," Goodnight said. "Usually too busy to eat breakfast."

"You're welcome to get down then," Call said.

"No, I'm too busy to do that either," Goodnight said. "I've got interests in Pueblo. Besides, I was never a man to sit around and gossip.

"I reckon that's McCrae," he said, glancing at the coffin on the buggy.

"That's him," Call said, dreading the questions that seemed to be inevitable.

"I owe him a debt for cleaning out that mangy bunch on the Canadian," Goodnight said. "I'd have soon had to do it myself, if he hadn't."

"Well, he's past collecting debts," Call said. "Anyway he let that dern killer get away."

"No shame to McCrae," Goodnight said. "I let the son of a bitch get away myself, and more than once, but a luckier man caught him. He butchered two families in the Bosque Redondo, and as he was leaving a deputy sheriff made a lucky shot and crippled his horse. They ran him down and mean to hang him in Santa Rosa next week. If you spur up you can see it."

"Well, I swear," Call said. "You going?"

"No," Goodnight said. "I don't attend hangings, although I've presided over some, of the homegrown sort. This is the longest conversation I've had in ten years. Goodbye."

Call took the buggy over Raton Pass and edged down into the great New Mexican plain. Though he had seen nothing but plains for a year, he was still struck by the immense reach of land that lay before him. To the north, there was still snow on the peaks of the Sangre de Cristo. He hurried to Santa Rosa, risking further damage to the wagon, only to discover that the hanging had been put back a week.

Everyone in the Territory wanted to see Blue Duck hanged, it seemed. The little town was full of cowhands, with women and children sleeping in wagons. There was much argument, most of it in favor of hanging Blue Duck instantly lest he escape. Parties were constantly forming to present petitions to the sheriff, or else storm the jail, but the latter were unenthusiastic. Blue Duck had ranged the *llano* for so long, and butchered and raped and stolen so often, that superstitions had formed around him. Some, particularly women, felt he couldn't die, and that their lives would never be safe.

Call took the opportunity to have a blacksmith completely rebuild the buggy. The blacksmith had lots of wagons to work on and took three days to get around to the buggy, but he let Call store the coffin in his back room, since it was attracting attention.

The only thing to do in town besides drink was to admire the new courthouse, three stories high and with a gallows at the top, from which Blue Duck would be hung. The courthouse had fine glass windows and polished floors.

Two days before the hanging was to take place, Call decided to go see the prisoner. He had already met the deputy who had crippled Blue Duck's horse. The man, whose name was Decker, was fat and stone drunk, leading Call to suspect that Goodnight had been right—the shot had been lucky. But every man in the Territory had insisted on buying the deputy a drink since then; perhaps he had been capable of sobriety before he became a hero. He was easily moved to sobs at the memory of his exploit, which he had recounted so many times that he was hoarse.

The sheriff, a balding man named Owensby, had of course heard of Call and was eager to show him the prisoner. The jail had only three cells, and Blue Duck was in the middle one, which had no window. The others had been cleared, minor culprits having simply been turned loose in order to lessen the chances that Blue Duck might somehow contrive an escape.

The minute Call saw the man he knew it was unlikely. Blue Duck had been shot in the shoulder and leg, and had a greasy rag wound around his forehead, covering another wound. Call had never seen a man so draped in chains. He was handcuffed; each leg was heavily chained; and the chains draped around his torso were bolted to the wall. Two deputies with Winchesters kept constant watch. Despite the chains and bars, Call judged that both were scared to death.

Blue Duck himself seemed indifferent to the furor outside. He was leaning back against the wall, his eyes half closed, when Call came in.

"What's he doing?" Sheriff Owensby asked. Despite all the precautions, he was so nervous that he had not been able to keep food down since the prisoner was brought in.

"Ain't doin' much," one deputy said. "What can he do?"

"Well, it's been said he can escape from any jail," the sheriff reminded them. "We got to watch him close."

"Only way to watch him closer is to go in with him, and I'll quit before I'll do that," the other deputy said.

Blue Duck opened his slumbrous eyes a fraction wider and looked at Call.

"I hear you brought your stinkin' old friend to my hanging," Blue Duck said, his low, heavy voice startling the deputies and the sheriff too.

"Just luck," Call said.

"I should have caught him and cooked him when I had the chance," Blue Duck said.

"He would have killed you," Call said, annoyed by the man's insolent tone. "Or I would have, if need be."

Blue Duck smiled. "I raped women and stole children and burned houses and shot men and run off horses and killed cattle and robbed who I pleased, all over your territory, ever since you been a law," he said. "And you never even had a good look at me until today. I don't reckon you would have killed me."

Sheriff Owensby reddened, embarrassed that the man would insult a famous Ranger, but there was little he could do about it. Call knew there was truth in what Blue Duck said, and merely stood looking at the man, who was larger than he had supposed. His head was huge and his eyes cold as snake's eyes.

"I despise all you fine-haired sons of bitches," Blue Duck said. "You Rangers. I expect I'll kill a passel of you yet."

"I doubt it," Call said. "Not unless you can fly."

Blue Duck smiled a cold smile. "I *can* fly," he said. "An old woman taught me. And if you care to wait, you'll see me."

"I'll wait," Call said.

On the day of the hanging the square in front of the courthouse was packed with spectators. Call had to tie his animals over a hundred yards away—he wanted to get started as soon as the hanging was over. He worked his way to the front of the crowd and watched as Blue Duck was moved from the jail to the courthouse in a small wagon under heavy escort. Call thought it likely somebody would be killed accidentally before it was over, since all the deputies were so scared they had their rifles on cock. Blue Duck was as heavily chained as ever and still had the greasy rag tied around his head wound. He was led into the courthouse and up the stairs. The hangman was making last-minute improvements on the hangrope and Call was looking off, thinking he saw a man who had once served under him in the crowd, when he heard a scream and a sudden shattering of glass. He looked up and the hair on his neck rose, for Blue Duck was flying through the air in his chains. It seemed to Call the man's cold smile was fixed on him as he fell: he had managed to dive through one of the long glass windows on the third floor—and not alone, either. He had grabbed Deputy Decker with his handcuffed hands and pulled him out too. Both fell to the stony ground right in front of the courthouse. Blue Duck hit right on his head, while the Deputy had fallen backwards, like a man pushed out of a hayloft. Blue Duck didn't move after he hit, but the deputy squirmed and cried. Tinkling glass fell about the two men.

The crowd was too stunned to move. Sheriff Owensby stood high above them, looking out the window, mortified that he had allowed hundreds of people to be cheated of a hanging.

Call walked out alone and knelt by the two men. Finally a few others joined him. Blue Duck was stone dead, his eyes wide open, the cruel smile still on his lips. Decker was broken to bits and spitting blood already—he wouldn't last long.

"I guess that old woman didn't teach you well enough," Call said to the outlaw.

Owensby ran down the stairs and insisted that they carry Blue Duck up and string him from the gallows. "By God, I said he'd hang, and he'll hang," he said. Many of the spectators were so afraid of the outlaw that they wouldn't touch him, even dead. Six men who were too drunk to be spooked finally carried him up and left him dangling above the crowd.

Call thought it a silly waste of work, though he supposed the sheriff had politics to think of.

He himself could not forget that Blue Duck had smiled at him in the moment that he flew. As he walked through the crowd he heard a woman say she had seen Blue Duck's eyes move as he lay on the ground. Even with the man hanging from a gallows, the people were priming themselves to believe he hadn't died. Probably half the crimes committed on the *llano* in the next ten years would be laid to Blue Duck.

As Call was getting into his wagon, a newspaperman ran up, a red-headed boy scarcely twenty years old, white with excitement at what he had just seen.

"Captain Call?" he asked. "I write for the Denver paper. They pointed you out to me. Can I speak to you for a minute?"

Call mounted the dun and caught the mule's lead rope. "I have to ride," he said. "It's still a ways to Texas."

He started to go, but the boy would not give up. He strode beside the dun, talking, much as Clara had, except that the boy was merely excited. Call thought it strange that two people on one trip would follow him off.

"But, Captain," the boy said. "They say you were the most famous Ranger. They say you've carried Captain McCrae three thousand miles just to bury him. They say you started the first ranch in Montana. My boss will fire me if I don't talk to you. They say you're a man of vision."

"Yes, a hell of a vision," Call said. He was forced to put spurs to the dun to get away from the boy, who stood scribbling on a pad.

It was a dry year, the grass of the *llano* brown, the long plain shimmering with mirages. Call followed the Pecos, down through Bosque Redondo and south through New Mexico. He knew it was dangerous—in such a year, Indians might follow the river too. But he feared the drought worse. At night lightning flickered high above the plains; thunder rumbled but no rain fell. The days were dull and hot, and he saw no one—just an occasional antelope. His animals were tiring, and so was he. He tried driving at night but had to give it up—too often he would nod off, and once came within an ace of smashing a buggy wheel. The coffin was sprung from so much bouncing and began to leak a fine trail of salt.

A day above Horsehead Crossing, as he was plodding along half asleep in the still afternoon, he felt something hit him and immediately put his hand to his side. It came away bloody, although he had not seen an Indian or even heard a gunshot. As he turned to race for the river he glimpsed a short brown man rising from behind a large yucca plant. Call didn't know how badly he was shot, or how many Indians he was up against. He went off the bank too fast and the buggy crashed against a big rock at the water's edge. It splintered and turned over, the coffin underneath it. Call glanced back and saw only four Indians. He dismounted, snuck north along the river for a hundred yards, and was able to shoot one of the four. He crossed the river and waited all day and all night, but never saw the other three again. His wound felt minor, though the bullet was somewhere in him, and would have to stay until he made Austin, he knew.

The narrow-channeled Pecos was running and the coffin was underwater. Call finally cut it loose, and with the help of Greasy dragged it from the mud. He knew he was in a fine fix, for it was still five hundred miles to the south Guadalupe and the buggy was ruined. For all he knew, more Indians might arrive at any moment, which meant that he had to work looking over his shoulder. He managed to drag the coffin over, but it was a sorry, muddy affair by the time he was done. Also, the Pecos water scalded his innards and drained his strength.

Call knew he could never drag the coffin all the way to Austin—he himself would be lucky to get across the bleached, waterless land to the Colorado or the San Saba. On the other hand he had no intention of leaving Gus, now that he had brought him so far. He broke open the coffin and rewrapped his friend's remains in the tarp he had been using for a bed cover on wet nights—there were few of those to worry about. Then he lashed the bundle to Gus's sign, itself well weathered, with most of the lettering worn off. He cut down a small salt-cedar and made a crude axle, fixing the sign between the two buggy wheels. It was more travois than buggy, but it moved. He felt his wound a trifle less every day, though he knew it had been a small-bore bullet that hit him. A larger bore and he would be down and probably dead.

Several times he thought he glimpsed Indians slipping over a ridge or behind distant yucca, but could never be sure. Soon he felt feverish and began to distrust his own eyesight. In the shining mirages ahead he thought he saw horsemen, who never appeared. Once he thought he saw Deets, and another time Blue Duck. He decided his reason must be going and began to blame Gus for it all. Gus had spent a lifetime trying to get him into situations that confused him, and had finally succeeded.

"You done this," he said aloud several times. "Jake started me off, but you was the one sent me back across here."

His water ran out the third day. The mule and the dun chewed on the greasewood bushes or what sage there was, but both were weakening. Call longed for the Kiowa mare. He wished he had given the boy his name and kept the mare.

Then Greasy, the mule, stopped—he had decided to die. Call had to use the dun to pull the travois. Greasy didn't bother following them.

Call supposed the dun would die too, but the horse walked on to the Colorado. After that, there was little more to fear, although his wound festered somewhat, and leaked. It reminded him of Lippy—often his eyes would fill when he thought of the boys left up north.

By the time he finally rode onto the little hill with the live oaks above the Guadalupe, the sign was about gone. The Latin motto, of which Augustus had been so proud, being at the bottom, had long since been broken off. The part about the pigs was gone, and the part about what they rented and sold, and Deets's name as well. Most of Pea Eye's name had flaked off, and his own also. Call hoped to save the plank where Gus had written his own name, but the rope he had tied the body with had rubbed out most of the lettering. In fact, the sign was not much more than a collection of splinters, two of which Call got in his hand as he was untying Gus. Only the top of the sign, the part that said "Hat Creek Cattle Company and Livery Emporium" was still readable.

Call dug the grave with a little hand shovel. In his condition it took most of a day; at one point he grew so weak that he sat down in the grave to rest, sweat pouring off him—if there had been anyone else to shovel he would have been inclined to be buried there himself. But he pulled himself up and finished the work and lowered Augustus in.

"There," he said. "This will teach me to be more careful about what I promise."

He used the plank with "Hat Creek Cattle Company and Livery Emporium" on it as a crossbar, tying it to a long mesquite stick, which he drove into the ground with a big rock. While he was tying the crossbar tight with two saddle strings, a wagon with settlers in it came along the ridge. They were a young couple, with two or three children peeking shyly around them, narrow-faced as young possums. The young man was fair and the sun had blistered him beet-red; his young wife had a bonnet pulled close about her face. It was clear that the grave marker puzzled them. The young man stopped the wagon and stared at it. Not having seen him put Augustus under, they were not sure whether they were looking at a grave, or just a sign.

"Where is this Hat Creek outfit, mister?" the young man asked.

"Buried, what ain't in Montana," Call said. He knew it wasn't helpful, but he was in no mood for conversation.

"Dern, I was hoping to come to a place with a blacksmith," the young man said. Then he noticed that Call walked stiffly, and saw that he was wounded.

"Can we help you, mister?" the young man asked.

"Much obliged," Call said. "I've only a short way to go."

The young settlers moved down the ridge toward San Antonio. Call walked down to the little pool, meaning to rest a few minutes. He fell into a heavy sleep and didn't wake until dawn. The business of the sign worried him, one more evidence of Augustus's ability to vex well beyond the grave. If one young man supposed it meant there was a livery stable nearby, others would do the same. People might be inconvenienced for days, wandering through the limestone hills, trying to find a company who were mostly ghosts.

Besides, Augustus's name wasn't on the sign, though it was his grave. No one might ever realize that it *was* his grave. Call walked back up the hill and got out his knife, thinking he might carve the name on the other side of the board, but the old board was so dry and splintery that he felt he might destroy it altogether if he worked on it much. Finally he just scratched A.M. on the other side of the board. It wasn't much, and it wouldn't last, he knew. Somebody would just get irritated at not finding the livery stable and bust the sign up anyway. In any case, Gus was where he had decided he wanted to be, and they had both known many fine men who lay in unmarked graves.

Call remembered he had told the young couple that he only had a short way to travel. It showed that his mind was probably going, for he had no place in particular to travel at all. Worn out, and with a festering wound, he was in no shape to turn back for Montana, and Jerry, the dun, could never have made the trip, even if he himself could have. He didn't know that he wanted to go back, for that matter. He had never felt that he had any home on the earth anyway. He remembered riding to Texas in a wagon when just a boy—his parents were already dead. Since then it had been mostly roaming, the years in Lonesome Dove apart.

Call turned south toward San Antonio, thinking he might find a doctor. But when he came to the town he turned and went around it, spooked at the thought of all the people. He didn't want to go among such a lot of people with his mind so shaky. He rode the weary dun on south, feeling that he might just as well go to Lonesome Dove as anywhere.

Crossing the green Nueces, he remembered the snakes and the Irish boy. He knew he ought to go by and find the widow Spettle to tell her she had one less son, but decided the bad news could wait. It had already waited a year, unless she had gotten it from one of the returning cowhands.

He rode the dun into Lonesome Dove late on a day in August, only to be startled by the harsh clanging of the dinner bell, the one Bolivar had loved to beat with the broken crowbar. The sound made him feel that he rode through a land of ghosts. He felt lost in his mind and wondered if all the boys would be there when he got home.

But when he trotted through the chaparral toward the Hat Creek barn, he saw that it was old Bolivar himself, beating the same bell with the same piece of crowbar. The old man's hair was white and his serape filthier than ever.

When Bolivar looked up and saw the Captain riding out of the sunset, he dropped the piece of crowbar, narrowly missing his foot. His return to Mexico had been a trial and a disappointment. His girls were married and gone, his wife unrelenting in her anger at his years of neglect. Her tongue was like a saw and the look in her eyes made him feel bad. So he had left her one day forever, and walked to Lonesome Dove, living in the house the gringos had abandoned. He sharpened knives to earn a living, which for himself was merely coffee and frijoles. He slept on the cookstove; rats had chewed up the old beds. He grew lonely, and could not remember who he had been. Still, every evening, he took the broken crowbar and beat the bell—the sound rang through the town and across the Rio Grande.

When Call dismounted and dropped his reins old Bolivar walked over, trembling, a look of disbelief on his face. "Oh, *Capitán, Capitán,*" he said, and began to blubber. Tears of relief rolled down his rough cheeks. He clutched at Call's arms, as if he were worn out and might fall.

"That's all right, Bol," Call said. He lead the shaking man to the house, which was all shambles and filth, spiderwebs and rat shit everywhere. Bol shuffled around and heated coffee, and Call stood on the front porch and drank a cup. Looking down the street, he was surprised to see that the town didn't look the same. Something wasn't there that had been. At first he couldn't place what, and he thought it might be the dust or his erratic vision, but then he remembered the Dry Bean. It was the saloon that seemed to be gone.

Call took the dun down to the roofless barn and unsaddled him. The stone watering trough was full of water, clear water, but there was not much to feed the horse. Call turned him out to graze and watched while he took a long roll.

Then, curious to know if the saloon was really gone, he walked across the dry bed of Hat Creek and into the main street.

He had no sooner turned into the street than he saw a one-legged man coming toward him through the dusk. Why, Gus? he thought, not knowing for a second if he were with the living or the dead. He remembered sitting in the grave on the Guadalupe, and for a moment could not remember climbing out.

But the one-legged man only turned out to be Dillard Brawley, the barber who had ruined his voice screeching the time he and Gus had had to take off his leg.

For his part, Dillard Brawley was so surprised to see Captain Call standing in the street that he almost dropped the few perch he had managed to catch in the river. In the growing dark he had to step close to see it was the Captain—there was only a little light left.

"Why, Captain," Dillard said in his hoarse whisper, "did you and the boys finally get back?"

"Not the boys," Call said. "Just me. What happened to the saloon?"

He could see that he had been right—the general store was still there, but the Dry Bean was gone.

"Burnt," Dillard whispered. "Burnt near a year ago."

"What started the fire?" Call asked.

"Wanz started it. Burnt up in it, too. Locked himself in that whore's room and wouldn't come out."

"Well, I swear," Call said.

"The pi-aner burnt up with him," Dillard said. "Made the church folks mad. They thought if he was gonna roast himself he ought to have at least rolled the pi-aner out the door. They've had to sing hymns to a fiddle ever since."

Call walked over and stood where the saloon had been. There was nothing left but pale ashes and a few charred boards.

"When she left, Wanz couldn't stand it," Dillard said. "He sat in her room a month and then he burnt it."

"Who?" Call asked, looking at the ashes.

"The woman," Dillard whispered. "The woman. They say he missed that whore."

LEAVING CHEYENNE

*To Jo,
for her gallantry and her integrity,
with my love*

My foot's in the stirrup,
My pony won't stand;
Goodbye, old partner,
I'm leaving Cheyenne.

*The Cheyenne of this book is that part of the cowboy's day's circle
which is earliest and best: his blood's country and his heart's
pastureland.*

L. M.

PART ONE

The Blood's Country

South of my days' circle,
  part of my blood's country,
rises that tableland . . . clean, lean,
hungry country. . . .

I know it dark against the stars,
  the high lean country,
full of old stories that still go walking in my sleep.

—Judith Wright,
from *South of My Days*

1

WHEN I WOKE UP Dad was standing by the bed shaking my foot. I opened my eyes, but he never stopped shaking it. He shook it like it was a fence post and he was testing it to see if it was in the ground solid enough. All my life that's the way he'd wake me up—I hated it like poison. Once I offered to set a glass of water by the bed, so he could pour that over me in the mornings and wake me up, but Dad wouldn't do it. I set the water out for him six or seven times, and he just let it sit and shook my foot anyway. Sometimes though, if he was thirsty, he'd drink the water first.

"Get up from there," he said. "If you're big enough to vote, you don't need to sleep past daylight. You do the chores today. I'm gonna trot off down in the pasture and look around. One of them scrawny heifers might have calved, for all I know."

And off he went, as usual. The last time Dad done the chores was when I was twelve years old, and the only reason he done them then was because I had let the ax slip and cut my foot nearly off. I never did know what he done down in the pasture every morning; by the time I could get the horses fed and the milking done, he'd be back.

For once though I was kinda glad he woke me up. It was election day, and my sly friend Johnny had worked it around somehow so that he and Molly got to watch the ballot box during the first shift. There was supposed to be at least two people to a shift. What he figured was that nobody would be there to vote till after dinner, so he could do a little courting with Molly on the government's time. Only I didn't intend to let him get away with it. I never liked to see a man cheat on the government.

===

I done the chores a little too quick. By six-thirty I didn't have a thing left to do, and I knew there wasn't any use getting to the schoolhouse before about eight o'clock. It was just over on Idiot Ridge, about a ten-minute ride. If there's one thing I can't do at all, it's wait. So I got a rag and polished the saddle a little, and that was a mistake. It was a pleasure to polish a saddle like that; the mistake was that Dad walked in and caught me.

"You needn't jump," he said. "And you needn't try to hide it. I found it day before yesterday anyhow. It's a nice saddle. Why ain't you been using it?"

I had put the saddle under a tarp, way back in the dark end of an empty oatbin. But you couldn't hide nothing from Dad.

"Because it ain't mine," I said.

"Hell it ain't," he said, a little surprised. "What'd you do, steal it?"

623

"You aggravate the piss out of me," I said. "I never stole a penny in my life, and you know it."

"Plenty's waited longer than you to start. Whose is it then?"

"Didn't you see the name plate?" I said. "It's sterling silver, looks like you'd have noticed it. I had this saddle made for Johnny, and I just haven't got around to giving it to him yet."

For once Dad was flabbergasted. I knew he would be, but I didn't see no sense in lying to him.

"Giving it to him?" he said. "You're giving a hundred-and-fifty-dollar saddle to a thirty-dollar-a-month cowboy. That wouldn't make sense to a crazy man. And it sure don't to me."

"Well, I can't help it, Dad," I said. "Johnny did me a big favor, which I ain't at liberty to talk about. Nobody ever did me that much favor before, and I may live to be older than you without nobody doing me that much favor agin. Johnny never owned a quality piece of equipment his whole life. I had the money and I just thought I'd get him something he could use. There's nothing wrong with that."

Dad had real black eyes, and when he wanted to look fierce he didn't look it halfway. He looked fierce then.

"Giving a saddle like that to a McCloud is like pinning a diamond stud pin on a goat's ass," he said. "Favor or no favor. And besides, whatever money you had come from me."

"Johnny ain't sorry," I said. "Being poor don't make him no-count. I worked plenty hard for the money I spent on this saddle, and if you think I'm overpaid, hire you another hand."

"Settle down," he said. "I ain't gonna whip you, you're too old. Let's go outside. You can polish his saddle some other time."

We went out and stood by the water trough and looked at the cattle grazing down in the Field pasture, just this side of the River. I washed the saddlesoap off my hands.

"Ain't this a good ranch?" Dad said. "I put a lot of work and a lot of years into it, but by god I've got it all back in money and satisfaction."

"Go on and bawl me out," I said. "I've got some pretty urgent business to get to this morning."

"You sure have," he said. "You've got to rush over to the schoolhouse and see if you can keep your good friend Johnny from getting in Miss Molly's pants. If you can keep him out, you figure you'll eventually get in. Well, suppose you just sit here and listen about five minutes. You might learn something."

"I don't like the way you talk about my friends," I said.

"Pity," he said. "I'm gonna have to leave this ranch to you some day; now I want you to get to taking that serious. I ain't mad about the saddle. But you took off and left, right in the middle of the calving season. You never gave me no warning or nothing, and you took that McCloud kid with you. And you've never said one word to me about where you've been or why. That don't add up to very sensible behavior, and I ain't too happy about leaving this ranch to somebody who ain't sensible, I don't care what kin he is to me."

"Well, I'm sorry as I can be, and you know it," I said. "But there ain't nothing I can tell you about that. I just had to leave."

He set there and looked off down the pasture. Dad was getting quite a bit of age on him.

"Nobody ever did me favor enough in my entire life for me to waste two hundred dollars on them," he said. "I guess by the time I'm dead ten years you'll have thrown away what I spent fifty years making. Old age is a worthless damn thing."

"Oh, hush," I said. "By the time I've run this ranch for ten years it's liable to be twice the size it is now."

"Yeah and I'm liable to flap my arms and take off from here and fly like a buzzard any minute now," he said. "That sure is a good saddle. I'll tell you one thing, Johnny McCloud ain't no favorite of mine."

"Well, you ain't no favorite of his either, that I know of," I said. I went and put the tarp back over the saddle, and Dad went up to the house to eat.

==

Of course things never worked like I planned. Dad had found a sick yearling that morning, but he never took time to doctor it himself, so I had to catch a horse and go hunt it up and doctor it before I could go to the voting place. It was after nine o'clock when I got there, and Johnny and Molly had been there since eight. I hated it so bad I could taste it.

They were sitting on the schoolhouse steps when I loped up. She was letting Johnny hold her hand, and they were both grinning. Oh me, Molly looked pretty. She had on a blue and white polka-dot dress, and her long black hair was whipping around in the wind. There wasn't another soul around. Johnny was looking wild and reckless, so no telling what had went on. Molly was just a sucker when it come to Johnny.

"Look who's here," he said. "What happened, you ain't but an hour early? Where's your friend Ikey?"

"I been working," I said. "Hello, Molly." I knew he'd bring Ikey up, but I didn't intend to talk about it. Ikey was a nigger, but he was a nigger that could vote, and he was supposed to be partners with me to watch the voting box. Molly had already promised she would stay awhile with me after Johnny's shift was up, so what I had to do was figure out a way to get rid of Ikey quick. Johnny knew just what I was up to, of course, but it wasn't gonna do him any good.

"Get down," Molly said. She grinned at me, as sweet as ever, but Johnny still had ahold of her hand, and she never made him turn loose.

I couldn't think of too much to say, so I took my horse over and tied him to a mesquite. I went in and was going to vote, but they had been so busy spooning around they hadn't even unpacked the ballots, and I had to do it. I never voted though, I forgot about it. I don't think I voted in that election at all. Molly had finally got her hand loose, and when she stood up we all went over to the cistern and got a drink.

"What's that I smell on you, Gid?" Johnny said. "Smells like screwworm dope. You ought to taken a bath before you come to work for the government."

"You don't smell like no prairie flower yourself," I said. "Been trapping any skunks lately?" When Johnny was just a boy the McClouds had had to sell skunk hides to keep going. They wasn't the only ones, of course, but Johnny hated skunks worse than anything. His folks had finally got better off, but they still just had a little two-section place.

"Not lately," he said, but it kinda irritated him.

Molly, she never taken sides when me and Johnny argued. She would just stand there and grin her pretty, friendly grin, and curl a loop of her hair around one finger. She was pretty as a picture when she done that.

It didn't seem like I'd been there no time when Ikey come. He had an old brown mule that was about half-cripple; he rode the mule bareback wherever he went. We seen Ikey coming and Johnny began to grin. He always had some trick to play on Ikey, and most of them were funny.

"Looky there," he said. "Here he comes, riding that three-legged mule. I tell you what, Gid, some day let's saw that crippled leg off. That way it won't drag and slow Ikey down."

"You hush that," Molly said. "How'd you like to have one of your legs sawed off?"

"I might like it," he said. "You want to saw one off for me?"

"That's no way to talk. Make him hush, Gid." She sidled over toward me just a little bit.

Johnny just looked that much more devilish.

"What he needs is his damn head sawed off," I said. "That's the only kind of sawing that would do him any good."

Ikey arrived about then, and got off his mule. "Good mornin', Mis' Molly," he said. "Mornin', Mistuh Johnny, mornin', Mistuh Gid." The thing that worried me about Ikey was that he was so proud of being good enough to watch a ballot box like the white folks that he probably wasn't going to be in too big a hurry to leave. But I figured I could persuade him.

"Morning, Ikey," Johnny said. "Whyn't you shoot that pore old mule and put him out of his misery?"

I had to grin at that. Ikey was as surprised as if Johnny had asked him to shoot his wife. He thought he had one of the best mules in the country.

"Shoot dis mule?" he said, looking at it real close. "Den how'd I get aroun'?"

"Don't pay any attention to him," Molly said. "He's crazy. Come on in and vote, Ikey."

I was all for that, so I went in and fixed him up a ballot. I thought if we made a big enough thing of him voting Ikey might be satisfied and go on home.

"Boy, this is a big election," I said. "They say every vote is gonna be important. Think it over good, Ikey. Don't be in too big a hurry."

"Naw, don't excite Ikey," Johnny said. "He might stab himself with that pencil. It ain't worth the trouble, Ikey. The man with the most money's gonna get it anyway. It always turns out that way."

"It don't, do it?" Molly said. She never liked to hear anybody run down politics. I guess it was because her old man had been commissioner for our precinct one year; everybody criticized him so she had to take up for him twice as hard as she usually done. He was the most thieving commissioner there ever was, besides the most lazy, and Molly knew it. She just never would admit it, to herself or nobody else. Her daddy didn't get elected because he was the man with the most money; he got elected because he was the man with the most whiskey to give away. There weren't but twelve people in the precinct able to vote, and he gave ever one of them a jug of whiskey and still only won by one vote. The man that was running against him was too decent to vote for himself, and Old Man Taylor wasn't, so he won it. Afterward he got hold of the ballots and found out who voted against him and went around and got his jugs back from those. I know that's true, because one of the ones that voted against him was Dad, and the jug was damn sure all he got back. I guess Molly was the only person in the world who ever liked that old man.

Ikey, though, he never paid any attention to what we were saying to him. He was set up so he could just pay attention to one thing at a time, and right then he was paying attention to voting. He got out his spectacles that he was so proud of and polished them on his pants leg and put them on and adjusted them so he could see over them. It's a damn cinch he couldn't see through them. It would have been like looking through a pair of stovelids. After he got them set so they wouldn't interfere with his vision, he began to read the ballot. That took so long that me and Johnny had to go off behind the schoolhouse to pee before he got through. We left Molly there to help Ikey read.

"You sneaky bastard," I said, when we got out. "How long was you'all over here before I come?"

"Why, I'm ashamed of myself about that," he said. "Don't you think I've got a pretty girl, though?"

"I think Molly's a pretty girl, all right," I said, "but you ain't got her by a long shot. Why don't you take after Mabel Peters, anyway?"

"Why, Mabel's crazy about you," he said. "Watch where you're pissing. You get it on these gabardine pants and your name's mud. I mean it."

Actually I just splattered a little on his boots. "It's about time you were going home, ain't it?"

"Why, yes," he said. "I'll go get Molly."

He went, but he never got her. I went too. She walked out the door with him and he had her hand agin, but she must have told him she had promised to stay awhile with me. He didn't look too cheerful. I went on in to help Ikey.

He was sitting there licking his pencil, and after he'd done that about five minutes, he voted.

"Good lord," I said. "I just remembered something. I was supposed to cut a big patch of cuckleburrs today. Down on the River. Dad's been after me about that for two weeks."

"Well then, why don't you go cut them?" Johnny said. "I'll stay here and do your turn at the voting box. You just go right ahead."

"Oh no," I said. "I wouldn't want nobody to do that. That's my responsibility."

"Don't worry so much," Molly said. I guess she was so sweet it never occurred to her what I was really worrying about. It damn sure occurred to Johnny.

"He better worry," he said. "I wouldn't want Mr. Fry mad at me. I think his best chance is just to forget about this voting and go do his work."

"Well," I said. "Since you're so anxious to help, I wonder if you'd like to lope off down there and cut them for me. It wouldn't take more than four hours."

That got into his quick. "Hell no, I wouldn't like to," he said. "I'm a cowboy, I ain't no damn cuckleburr chopper."

"Well, Ikey, what all do you have to do today?" I said. "Maybe I can hire you to do it. I'll give you two dollars, and you don't need to worry about watching this voting. Miss Molly's gonna stay here a little while and she'll be glad to do your part for you."

Ikey didn't give any argument at all. I wasn't much expecting him to: his normal wage was about a quarter a day.

"I'll cut 'em an' be glad," he said. "I'll jus' be glad." I gave him the two dollars and that settled it. That much money was such a shock to him that he couldn't hardly get it in his pocketbook. Then he folded up his ballot real slow and careful and looked kinda sad about having to drop it in the box. One thing about him, he really liked to vote. Then he got up and put away his spectacles.

"Well, I'll go cut 'em, Mistuh Gid," he said. "I sho enjoyed de elecshun day, Miss Molly. I hope we have anothuh one soon as we can."

Molly kinda laughed. "We will," she said. "We'll have one in November. You be careful, Ikey. Don't chop off your foot, and don't get on no snakes."

Ikey got on his mule and went off. Johnny just grinned and winked at Molly. It was hard to get his goat.

"I wish I was well off enough to hire my dirty work done," he said. "But I ain't that lucky. I always have to do my own."

"I never noticed you doing much," I said. "Besides, I felt sorry for Ikey. I'd like to see him get himself a better mule."

"If that ain't a lie I never heard one," he said. "Ikey's gonna spend that money on whiskey, and you knew it before you gave it to him. And you'll probably talk him out of three-quarters of that. You can't fool me."

"Why, Gid, I heard you quit drinking," Molly said. "I didn't know you started agin."

"I haven't," I said. "Johnny's just spoofing you."

"Well, I got to be going," Johnny said. He'd done all the damage he dared do. "Don't you all take no bribes under five dollars."

That made Molly mad, so he was smart to leave. She was kinda patriotic, and never liked to hear people hint about crooked government. It was because her old man was so crooked himself.

Anyway, Johnny got on his horse and loped off, and there we were. It was about ten o'clock, and I didn't figure we much needed to worry about anybody coming to vote before dinnertime. Voting is the kind of thing most people like to put off as long as they can.

I looked at Molly, and she was looking at me and grinning. I guess she knew good and well what I was up to, rushing Ikey off.

"Well, Mr. Fry," she said. "You sure was in a big hurry to chase everybody off. That wasn't very sociable."

"I ain't very sociable with crowds," I said. "Specially not crowds with Johnny in them." I kinda reached for her hand, but I missed. She laughed and stepped out the schoolhouse door. The wind begin whipping her hair up around her face.

"You're grabby," she said. "Grabby Mr. Fry."

"Don't call me that," I said. "And don't put on thataway. Let's go around to the cistern."

"Okay," she said, "let's do. Only you're so unsociable. I might just better go home."

I got her hand after all and squeezed it and she squeezed back.

"I'm a lot more sociable where you're concerned," I said.

I got my big slicker off my saddle and spread it out by the cistern so we could sit down without the grass and the chiggers eating us up. We got on the shady side and leaned up against the rocks and just set there. It was right on the hill, high enough that we could see anybody coming a long time before they would notice us. Molly let me put my arm around her, and she kind of slumped against me, and talked about this and that. I mostly listened. After a while my arm went to sleep, but I didn't dare move. Her hair was in my face. She must have washed it that morning, because it was real clean and I could still barely smell the vinegar she rinsed it in.

"It's a nice day for election," she said. "Look at the way the grass waves. I bet we can see nearly all over the county from here."

I kept wishing she'd turn her face around, but she wouldn't do it.

"Gid-ing-ton," she said, "what are you doing back there where I can't see you?" She called me that sometimes; she thought Gid was too short a name. I was agreeable.

"Don't you wish I'd turn my face around, so you could kiss me?" she said. "Now don't you?"

"I could stand it," I said. "You won't, though."

"You think I should let a boy kiss me on election day?" she said, and then she turned around anyway, and let me. Some of her hair was between me and her mouth; I didn't care. Only after a while she began to giggle and squirm.

"Let me fix it," she said. "Who wants to kiss hair?" She sat up and turned her back, and all I could see was black hair and her polka dot dress. Then she rolled over on the slicker and propped up on her elbows.

"Let's quit," she said. "Let's just talk. What if Johnny was to come back?"

"What if? It ain't none of his business what we do."

"He thinks it is, though." I made her let me kiss her again, but she kept giggling and wouldn't get serious about it. "Johnny thinks it's all his business," she said. "He keeps asking me all about us."

"Well, he can just cut it out," I said. "I'm not going to put up with much more of him. You're my girl now, ain't you?"

"Am I?" she said, looking up at me through her hair, half-grinning and half-serious. "I think I'm too silly for you."

"No you ain't. Why, I'm worse that way than you are."

"No you ain't," she said, and she wasn't kidding. "You're not even as silly as Johnny, and he's not as silly as me. Eddie's the only one who is."

"If you mean he's the only one who's dumb, you're right," I said. I hated that sorry Eddie. "At least I'm a little smart. I'm smart enough to know you're the prettiest girl there is."

I made her let me kiss her agin, and finally it shut her up and she got real quiet and sweet. Once you get Molly quiet she's the warmest, sweetest girl in the world.

"I still think you're my girl," I said.

"Maybe I am," she said. "Lay down here and hush."

She hugged me real tight, and just about that time we heard Ikey's mule. I could tell that mule a quarter of a mile away.

"Damn it all," I said. "Ikey's coming back. I'd like to wring Johnny's neck. I know damn good and well he put him up to it."

"Let's just lay here," she said. "Let's don't get up. Maybe if Ikey sees us he'll go on away. Or we could run hide."

"No," I said. "Damn Johnny anyway. I'll get even with him. I don't want Ikey to see us, and it's silly to hide. I ain't gonna do that."

She got up and I folded the slicker.

"Brush the grass off my dress," she said. "I got off the slicker."

She turned her back and I brushed her off. She didn't really look mad, and she put her arm around me and let me hold her hand even while Ikey was coming up. But she kept looking off across the pasture, off down Idiot Ridge.

"Where did you get that dress?" I said. "It's awful pretty, Molly."

"I made it. Thank you." She looked up then and seen I had grass on my cheek, and she brushed it off with her hand. "You just ain't very silly, are you?" she said.

2

JOHNNY NEVER WOULD ADMIT he sent Ikey back; he was too stubborn. But I knew he was the one responsible. I finally got Ikey sent off agin, but it was too late. Ikey wasn't hardly out of sight the second time before Dad come, of all people.

Dad made out like he come to vote, but he never: he just come to see what I was doing. He knew I was there with Molly, and he just thought he'd come and spy a little. I hated it like poison when he did something like that. Molly, she never minded. She always took up for Dad, and I guess he liked her for it; he always treated her like she was the prize of the world. Except when I got to talking about marrying her—then he got mad.

"Don't be a damn fool and marry young," he said. "Specially not to no poor woman. Work about thirty more years and make you lots of money. Then go off somewhere and marry a rich widow. Don't never marry somebody who's as broke and ignorant as you are; marry somebody who knows a little about it. Then you might have a chance to enjoy yourself a little."

That was Dad for you. I didn't pay him much mind. He never could understand that he wasn't me.

What I knew was that Johnny McCloud had two things coming: one was a good saddle, and the other was a good whipping. I guess he thought I had a whipping coming too, because he started it all.

About a week after election day, Old Man Ashtoe, the feller Johnny was cowboying for, sent him up to Henrietta with a little bunch of cattle he wanted delivered. Johnny delivered the cattle, all right, but then he bought some whiskey from somebody and got drunk and insulted a deputy sheriff or two and got put in jail. Soon as he got home Old Man Ashtoe fired him, and Johnny was so broke he had to take a job with a harvesting crew. The first day he worked with them was the day they were finishing up harvesting our oats. Dad had me out helping them, of course.

"Ain't this hell?" Johnny said, when we were going out that afternoon for another big load of shocks. "A cowboy oughtn't to do work like this. This here's clodhopper work. It's a kind of disgrace, ain't it to you?"

"Not to me," I said. "I don't have no choice about it. It's a real disgrace where you're concerned, though. If you'd have behaved right, you could be horseback right now."

"I never asked for no sermons," he said, grinning at me. "You've got just as much oatseed in your hair as I have. Where you want to work, on the wagon or on the ground?"

"On the wagon," I said. "You're such a good hand with a pitchfork, I don't want you to get out of practice."

We worked for about an hour, I guess. He threw the shocks up to me with his fork, and I stacked them on the wagon. The wagon was stacked up pretty high.

"I just need eight or ten more," I said. "Let's hurry, then we can take a rest."

He stuck his fork in a big shock, and I noticed him stop to look at it pretty close. I figured there was a rattlesnake under it; we had killed five or six that day. Oat-shocks were a great place for rattlesnakes, because so many rats lived under them.

It was awful hot, and I started to take my gloves off to wipe my face. Then Johnny picked up the shock and got ready to heave. I seen it coming and reached out to catch it, but just before I got my hands on it this big snake head came right up between my hands and hissed in my face. It scared the piss out of me and I went to running backward for all I was worth, but the shock kept right on coming till it looked like the snake was going to fall right on my face. I kicked like hell and went off the wagon backward, fighting with my hands to keep the snake out of my lap. I never seen where it went, because I hit the ground like I had fallen off a cloud. I never rolled an inch. In a little while I heard a lot of people laughing and one of them was Johnny. I looked around and Johnny and three or four of the harvesters were about to bust their guts laughing. Then I seen the snake sliding off the wagon wheel: it was an old brown bullsnake was all. It was mad, too, but not no madder than I was. I had to lay back down; I was seeing spots before my eyes.

"We better help him up," one of them said. "He might have busted something."

"Hell no, he'll be up in a minute," Johnny said. "You better get back to work or you'll be the one with something busted."

I propped up on my elbows and looked at him. "You're a damn bastard," I said. "What if that had been a rattlesnake?"

"It couldn't have scared you any worse," he said. "Besides, I seen what it was."

"Well, you better take a good look at the world," I said, getting up on my hands and knees. "You won't be able to see much when I get through with you."

"Goodness me," he said. "Maybe that'll teach you not to fiddle with my girl."

I was beginning to feel the blood coming back from wherever it went to when I seen that snake. Johnny was standing about ten feet away, leaning against the wagon wheel and grinning.

"She's no such a thing your girl," I said.

Then I went for him, and we had it out right there. I nearly got the best of him right off, but then I got to missing every time I swung at him. I guess the fall had thrown off my aim. Pretty soon I got tired and he did too, but we just kept standing there, pounding the piss out of one another. Finally we both stopped for a minute.

"When you've had enough, say calf rope," I said. "I don't want to put you in no hospital."

"Calf rope, your ass," he said. "You're going to bleed to death if we don't quit."

"Hell," I said. "My nose always bleeds in the summertime."

"Let's quit anyway," he said. "Get a drink of water. You quit first."

"Nope."

"Then we'll just have to stand here till you drop," he said. "I never seen such a stubborn bastard."

We might have stood there till dark, I don't know. Finally the boss harvester noticed us and came over.

"Damn boys," he said, "why don't you fight with the pitchforks next time? There won't be so much blood that way."

"He started it," I said.

"Load the wagon," he said. "You can fight some more tonight if you want to."

So I wiped off a little blood and Johnny got his pitchfork, and we finished making up the load. He never threw up no more snakes, either. Finally we got all the oats we could haul and went to the barn. Johnny rode on the seat with me.

"Shit-fire," he said. "I'm quitting this job. I ain't no damn clodhopper, and I ain't gonna let no fat-ass like that give me orders."

"What are you gonna do for money when you quit?" I asked.

"I been thinking about that," he said. "You know what, Gid, I think I'll go to the Panhandle. This here country ain't no place for a cowboy. It's all right if you got your own ranch, like you have, but if you ain't, it's no good. I'd like to go up on the plains, where them big ranches are, and do some real cowboying. I'm tired of sitting around here listening to my old man bitch at me. I think I'll just strike out."

"I wouldn't mind going with you," I said. "Hell, working for Dad's worse than being a hired hand. He thinks he has to tell me ever move to make."

"Then let's go," he said. He was excited about it. But I knew I never would be able to get away from Dad. There was too much that needed doing around the place that he couldn't do. Besides, we had done been gone two months, to that hospital. I pulled the wagon over in the shade of the barn, and we got down.

"Let's go over to the horse trough," I said. "Wash this blood off." I figured if he was going off to punch cattle, I had better give him his saddle. Even if I was still mad at him.

"Well, you coming with me?" he said. Then he bent over and ducked his head plumb under the water and came up shaking it like a wet dog.

"I don't reckon so," I said. "I guess I got too much to do here."

"Too much cowboying or too much courting, which one?"

"You better watch out," I said. "I ain't going to take no more off you today."

He slapped his hat back on without even drying his hair. "Hell, I ain't eager to go off and leave Molly, either," he said. "But a man's got to get out and see a little of the world in his life. I guess they'll be some pretty sweet girls up there."

"Not that sweet," I said. "Let's unload the hay."

"I may not go after all," he said.

But stacking those damn itchy oats in the hot oatbin almost got us down. I guess we was both weak from the fight.

"Oh hell," he said, when we finished. "Piss on this. This here'll kill a good cowboy in a week. It takes weak-minded bastards to stand this kind of work. I'm quitting."

"I don't blame you," I said, and I didn't. It would be the real life, up on the plains, with all those big ranches and cow outfits. I just couldn't manage it, though.

"Come around here," I said. "I got something for you."

We went around in the hallway of the barn, and I drug out the saddle. He never knew what to make of it.

"That's a beauty," he said. "Whose is it?"

"Yours," I said. "I thought you ought to have it for going up to the hospital with me and taking care of me all that time. If you're going off to cowboy, you'll get some use out of this."

"Why, my god," he said. "You don't mean it! Why, ain't it a beauty. That's as nice a saddle as I ever seen."

"Yeah, it ought to last you a long time."

"Well damn, sure much obliged, Gid," he said, feeling of the leather. "This here's something to be proud of. I never had nothing this well made in my life."

"Let's try it out," I said. "It's too late to haul oats today."

We caught a couple of horses and went for a ride. I never saw Johnny so tickled over anything, or so excited. He rode it awhile and then I rode it awhile, and it rode like a rocking chair. It was a little creaky and new, but he would ride that out of it in a hurry.

We got back to the barn just in time to start the evening chores. Dad was out fiddling around in the lots, watching the milk-pen calves.

"Well, this settles it," Johnny said. "I ain't wasting a saddle like this on this part of the country. I think I'll leave in a day or two. Sure wish you'd go with me."

"Can't make it," I said. "You better wait till them eyes get better. Ain't nobody going to hire a blind man."

"Blind, my ass," he said. "What about your nose?"

"It ain't very bad squashed. It'll straighten out."

Dad finally come poddling over and looked at the saddle some.

"Well, I see you boys been beating on one another," he said. "Too bad neither one of you had any sense to beat into the other one."

"Oh, we wasn't out for blood," Johnny said. Dad got a big laugh when he told him about me reaching out for the snake. Johnny could tell things so they sounded a whole lot funnier than they were.

"What do you think about my new saddle, Mr. Fry?" Johnny asked.

Dad just grunted. "I think it's a better one than I ever had," he said. "And I'm four times your age and several times your smart." He walked off toward the house. Johnny winked at me and I grinned. Dad never got Johnny's goat quite, and it tickled me.

———

Two days later Johnny rode to Henrietta and pitched his saddle in the caboose and took the train north. That left me and Molly with the country to ourselves, but I was kinda sorry to see old Johnny go. He was a good buddy even if he was a smart aleck, and I felt lonesome whenever he wasn't around.

3

I GUESS DAD had been hoping I'd change my mind and keep the new saddle for myself. When Johnny actually took off and left the country with it, it put Dad in such a bad humor he never got over it for a month. And when he was in a bad humor he could think up a million mean jobs for me to do. I spent the last part of July and the whole damn month of August digging corner postholes and cleaning out sewer lines and cutting devil's claws and plowing. I hated the plowing the worst. And all the time I was down in the field, eating dust and yanking on the damn contrary mules, Johnny was up on the plains, riding his new saddle and living like a cowboy should. I got so tired of thinking about it that one day I just come right out and told Dad I was pretty much in the notion to go up there too.

"The hell you will," he said. We were riding one of the River pastures, looking for screwworms, and Dad rode up on a hill and stopped his horse long enough to tell me off.

"You'll just stay right where you are," he said. "And if I tell you to plow, by god, you plow."

"But I ain't no damn farmer," I said. "Why don't you hire your farming done? Why do I have to waste my time doing it?"

"I am hiring it done, and you're the one I'm hiring," he said. "Why pay somebody else to do something we can do ourselves? That ain't no way to get rich."

"I see a few cattle down toward the southwest corner," I said. "What makes you think I want to be rich anyway?"

"Because I bred you," he said. "I know damn well I couldn't breed a boy with so little sense as to want to be poor. You got enough sense to know it's better to be rich than poor, ain't you?"

"That ain't what the Bible says," I said.

He just looked at me. "I ain't responsible for what the Bible says," he said. "If it says that, it's wrong. And I never asked you for no preaching, either. I know there's fools in the world who say poverty is holy, but you let them go without shoes some cold winter, like I did when I was a kid, and then see how holy they think it is. Being poor just makes people little and mean, most of the time. It's a damn degrading thing."

"All right," I said. "Hold your horses. I don't want to be poor. But you can not want to be poor and still not care whether you're rich or not."

"Yes, and them's the kind of people that never accomplish nothing," he said. "They're just damn mediocre. If you're gonna try at all, you ought to try for something big."

"Well, I'll never get nothing big from plowing that wornout field."

"You might," he said. "You might plow up a diamond, you don't know. I count twenty cattle in that corner."

"I just counted eighteen. Let's go get them."

"I ain't finished telling you what's good for you yet. Now you got the itch to go up on the plains and cowboy, just because Johnny McCloud's up there. Now I'll tell you about Johnny McCloud. He's a good cowhand and he ain't scared of nothing, I'll admit that. But that's the limitation of him, right there. He'll never be nothing but a damn good cowhand. When he dies he'll own just what he's got on and what he's inherited. And that saddle you gave him, if he don't lose it in a poker game first. He'll fiddle around his whole life working for wages, and never accomplish a damn thing."

"That don't make him bad," I said.

"Course not. It don't make him bad at all. I've known a lot of fellers like him, and some of them I liked a lot. The point is, you ain't like that. You've got too much of me in you. Punching somebody else's cows never would satisfy you. But you might waste a lot of time before you figure that out. The man that gets the farthest is the man that wastes the least time and the least energy he possibly can. You ain't old enough to know that yet, but I am. If you can just learn to listen to me, you'll save yourself a lot of misery."

"I guess you know everything in the world, don't you?" I said. "I don't guess you was ever known to be wrong, was you?"

"Oh yes. I've been wrong. I've been wrong more times than most people have been right. But that ain't no significance. I've also done forgot more than most people ever know.

"But anyhow," he said, "it don't take much sense to figure out that you and Johnny are two different kinds of people. Let's go look at them cattle."

We doctored a few worms, and was riding home down the lane, late in the afternoon. It was close to sundown, and Dad had worn down a little around the edges.

"Gid," he said, "now there's no need for you to go around feeling sorry for yourself for two months just because you have to plow an oat field once in a while. Before you're my age you'll have had all the cowboying you need. A man that's training himself to run a ranch has got to be able to do all kinds of things."

"You can say all you want to," I said. "I still wish I'd gone to the Panhandle. I ain't training to be no oat planter. I intend to enjoy my life."

"If that ain't a fine ambition," he said. "Why, any damn fool can enjoy himself. What makes you think life's supposed to be enjoyed anyhow?"

"Well," I said, "if you ain't supposed to enjoy it, what are you supposed to do with it?"

"Fight it. Fight the hell out of it." And then he got to talking about the cattle and the screwworms, and about how dry it was. He said he'd like to build some new tanks if he thought he'd have the pleasure of living long enough to see them full; we didn't argue no more. In a way I wanted to go, and in a way I didn't. Old as Dad was getting, and as much work as there was to do, I wouldn't have been too happy about going off and leaving him. There would be too many times when I'd have to think about him making the rounds by himself, and that would have spoiled the fun. When it come right down to it, Dad and I got along pretty well. All that time I was in the hospital I kept thinking about him home working, and it bothered me worse than the stuff itself. Johnny and me *was* different that way. His dad was just as old and had about as much to do, but it never bothered Johnny to go off and leave him. Course Johnny's mother was still alive, but he just figured his dad could take care of himself.

"If I did stay home it wouldn't make no difference," he said. "Daddy would be out working himself to death anyway, only he'd be working me to death along with him. I can't see no profit in that."

He was right, I guess. It's just all in the way you feel about a thing like that. Me being home never slowed Dad down either, but at least if I was there I didn't have to fight no guilty conscience.

═══

One good thing about having old Johnny out of the country was that I didn't have to watch Molly so close all the time. I knew there wasn't nobody besides me and him she cared much about; not unless you wanted to count Eddie White, and I never. Eddie was a shiftless old boy about my age; he worked around the oil patch whenever he felt like working, and when he didn't he hung around Thalia playing dominos or running his hounds. He was too no-count for a girl like Molly to pay much attention to. I think she just mentioned him once in a while to keep me and Johnny uneasy.

I guess the best time me and her had all the time Johnny was gone was the day I took her fishing. We had shipped a carload of calves to Fort Worth just to try out the market, and Dad had gone with them, to sit around the stockyards a day or two and watch them sell. When Dad took a big vacation like that he always come back wanting to do all the work in sight in the first half-hour, so I thought I better take me a little time off while I had the chance.

It was late September then—a nice warm day, but not too warm. We had had our first little norther about four days before; it cooled things off to where they were just about right. I waited around the house till nine or ten o'clock, then caught my horse and rode across the west pasture and up the hill to the Taylor place.

Old Man Taylor was there of course. He was sitting on the cellar, sharpening his pocketknife and drinking his morning whiskey. He was a terrifying sight. Along his cheeks his beard was white, but all of it that was underneath his mouth was a kind of muddy yellow from all the tobacco juice and whiskey he had dripped on it.

"Clean your feet before you come in this yard," he said. "I don't want none of your damn cowshit in my yard."

That would have been funny if he hadn't said it in such a mean voice. His yard looked like a slaughterhouse anyway. The old man done everything he had to do in the yard, and it showed it: there were bones and chicken heads and empty whiskey jugs and junk iron and baling wire and old shoes and pieces of plank and mule harness and horse turds and slop buckets, and I don't know what all else scattered everywhere. Molly said she tried to clean the yard up once in a while, but the old man wouldn't let her: anything that was there, he said, was there because he might need it. The miracle of it was that such a sweet, nice girl like Molly could have grown up in such a nasty place.

I scraped my feet on the fence wire and the old man never said another word to me.

Molly was in the living room, trying to kill a stinging lizard that had run in one of the woodboxes. She was dressed like a boy, in an old shirt and a pair of pants that had belonged to one of her brothers; they had all left home. But she looked like a girl; I wanted to grab her right there and kiss her, but if the old man had come in there would have been hell to pay.

"Let's go fishing," I said.

"Guess what?" she said, grinning and looking happy. "I got a postcard from Johnny last week. Want to see it?"

"No, I don't want to see it," I said. "I want to go fishing with you. Now do you want to go or don't you?"

"Yes," she said, "let's go right now. I just thought you might like to read Johnny's card. He mentioned you in it too."

I did want to read it, but I wasn't going to admit that to Molly. No telling what an idiot like Johnny would write on a postcard.

"Your dad don't look in too good a humor," I said.

"Get the poles out of the smokehouse and I'll wrap up some bait," she said. "Dad won't bother us. He likes catfish for supper."

I got the poles and propped them against the fence and went down and saddled Molly's horse. The old man was still drinking and sharpening his knife; he never even looked up. In a minute Molly came out with a lunch sack and a bait sack. She went up to the old man and hugged him a little with one arm and whispered to him and kissed him on one cheek and then come on out to me. She really liked that old bugger—it always surprised me to see it. He looked up at the lunch sack, but he didn't say anything.

"Want to go to a tank or to the River?" I said.

"Let's go to the big tank," she said. "South of the hill, in you'all's place."

It was my favorite tank too, but it was better for courting than for fishing. I never caught nothing there. There was a lot of Bermuda grass around it, though, and shade trees and nice places to sit.

Molly was riding a little gray horse her old man had cheated a feller out of two years before. I was riding old Denver; we named him that because his momma come from Colorado. We loped nearly all the way to our fence before we pulled up. I let Molly go in front of me. Her hair was flying all over the place, and her shirttail come out. She rode good though. There wasn't no cattle around the tank when we got there, and not a ripple on the water, except once in a while when some dragonfly would light on the tank for a minute. We used liver for bait, and I put enough on the hooks to last awhile and stuck the poles in the mud. Molly sat down on the Bermuda grass, in the shade, and I sat down by her and held her hand. We were all set to fish.

It was about a perfect day. The sky was clear, and the sun felt warm like summer while the air felt cool like fall. We lolled around on the Bermuda grass and courted and ate lunch and fished all day. We caught three fish too, two croppies and one nice little cat; I guess we could have caught more if we had tried. We got a lot of nibbles, but Molly was so good to be with that day that I quit paying attention to them. I held her down and told her it was just turtles gnawing at the bait. She knew how inconvenient it was to catch turtles.

Sometime in the early afternoon, when we were over under the big shade trees and not even pretending to fish, I finally asked Molly to marry me for the first time. There wasn't much grass under the trees, and we were laying on the slicker. We had been kissing a good deal and she seemed to like me so much that I didn't see why not to ask her. I was crazy about her.

"Molly," I said, "say, Molly. We're sweethearts anyway, why don't we go on and get married? Wouldn't that be the best thing to do? I sure would like to marry you."

She kinda grinned to herself and wouldn't look at me.

"Don't you want to at all?" I said. "You're the one for me, I know that for sure."

"You're my favorite," she said, and sat up and kissed me. "Gid-ing-ton. But what in the world would we do married?"

"Why, what everybody else does, I guess. We ain't so different."

"Maybe you ain't," she said, "but I am. I don't want to get into all that stuff yet. It ain't near as much fun as things like we're doing today."

"How do you know?" I said. "You ain't been married. It might be more fun."

She got kinda mad. "Don't tell me that," she said. "I don't want to marry you or nobody else. Girls who get married just to do a lot of things with boys ain't very nice. I don't like it. I'd just as soon do all those things and not be married, and I mean it. I ain't gonna marry till I have to because of having a baby, and I mean that too. And I wish I didn't even have to then."

Well, that shocked me as much as anything I ever heard, Molly saying that. It was just like her though. She never cared what people thought about her. I guess she never thought she was very respectable anyway, growing up with the daddy she had. I knew a lot of people around Thalia who didn't think she was nice, either, but they didn't mean anything to me.

"Honey, don't talk that way," I said. "I'm crazy about you and I just want you for a wife, that's all."

She looked sorry then, but she looked kinda wild, too, and we lay there and hugged one another for a long time before she would talk agin at all.

"I'm crazy about you too, Gid," she said, hugging my neck. "You're the best to me of anybody. But I ain't going to marry, I mean it. I'll do anything you want me to but that. I'll do everything else if you want me to right now," and when I kissed her she was trembling like a leaf. But we never managed it, somehow: it was my fault. I guess I was too surprised at Molly, and I couldn't quit thinking about it. She practically took her shirt off and that was something, but I couldn't quit thinking about it, and I knew it wasn't right, so I made her quit.

"Now we got to quit," I said. "You know it, Molly. Why can't we get married?"

Then she got real cool and mad at me, but I was pretty mad too, and I didn't back down.

"Let's go swimming, Gid," she said. "It's so hot. Then we can talk about it some more." She was cool as ice when she said that.

"You hush," I said. "There ain't no use in you teasing me, and you know it. I ain't no damn kid. We got nothing to go swimming in, so how can we go?"

"We got skin," she said. "I didn't know you was such a scardy-cat. Why do you want to get married if you're scared of girls?"

"Now listen, Molly," I said. "I told you to quit teasing me and you better do it before I shake the hell out of you. I'm sorry. But I ain't scared of you. I just know what's right and what ain't, and you ain't gonna talk me out of it just because you're mad. And if you don't like it, you can just stay mad."

"Don't ask me to marry you any more," she said, only she wasn't mad then, she was kind of quiet. "Get off my shirt, honey. You're too sober, I never could get along with you. You didn't know I was like this, did you?"

I grabbed her and made her let me hold her, even if she didn't want me to.

"I may be too sober," I said. "I guess I am. But I'm not going to get stampeded into doing something crazy even if we do both want to. You got to be a little careful about some things."

"Okay," she said. "You done said that. Shut up about it. Let's fish or ride or do something. I'm tired of sitting here being so careful. I guess you're so careful you won't even want to hold hands with me no more, will you?"

But after a while she got in a good humor again and we walked around the dam and rode horses some and finally went home about five o'clock, just when the shadows were beginning to stretch out. The old man was gone when we got there and I cleaned the fish for her. She cooked them and made biscuits and gravy and we each ate one of the croppie, bones or no bones. We left the catfish for the old man.

After supper we went out on the porch and swung in her porch swing and she was real warm and sweet again and we kissed all we wanted to. I don't guess things could have been any nicer, except that I had already begin to feel mad at myself for not taking better advantage of the afternoon. But she acted like she'd forgot about it. She teased me a little about Johnny.

"I know why you don't come see me as much any more," she said. "It's because Johnny's gone. You don't really care much about me, do you? You just like to spite Johnny."

She was wrong about that and we both knew it, but it was true that I got a little extra kick out of being with Molly when Johnny was around to notice it. It would have probably been the same with him if he'd been in my place.

I made up with her for the afternoon, only she wouldn't hear a word about marrying. I had to drop that for a while, but I didn't care. She gave me a big kiss just before I got on my horse and held on to my hand until I had to turn loose and ride away. And she stood on the hill and watched me go.

Later I got awful mad at myself for being such a sissy down at the tank. I must have been either scared to death or crazy, I couldn't figure which. At least we could have gone swimming, that wouldn't have been no great crime. The more I thought about it the worse it got, and it was all I could do to keep from riding back over that night. But I figured the old man would be back, so I never.

I guess I always did think things over too much, at least where Molly was concerned. She was a special girl. Johnny, he would have done it and then thought it over later, but I always did the thinking first. The next time I got the chance I decided I would try his way.

But things never worked out too good. Dad rode in the next morning with about a month's work lined up to do, and I had to stay mad at myself all the time I was doing it. By the time things loosened up enough that I could get back over to see Molly, why it was the middle of October and Johnny was home agin, so I had him to worry about. If there was one thing I learned that day, it was not to miss no opportunities. I just wish learning it had done me a little more good.

4

I GUESS it was being so mad at myself over Molly that caused me to run off one night and court Mabel Peters. I knew at the time I didn't have no business doing it. In the first place it was on a Friday night, and I never got off work till after dark, and I knew I would have to start agin before sunup. And it was nearly six miles over to Mabel's house; I could have gone over and seen Molly with a lot less trouble. But I was still kind of ashamed of the way I acted around Molly; I didn't want to see her that night. Mabel wasn't the kind of a girl I could get excited about in no permanent way, but every once in a while she was the kind I could get real excited about in a temporary way. Her folks were so poor and they lived so far off from everybody that none of the boys courted Mabel much. She was right pretty in a neat, timid kind of way, but she never had no real boy friends, and I knew she was so anxious for a sweetheart she would do most anything. So I wasn't very proud of the reasons I went to see her, but I went, anyway.

Mabel's ma and pa were pretty old and usually went to bed early; except for one or two of the younger kids, Mabel was nearly always up by herself. I rode up to the yard gate in the dark and sat on my horse till the dogs kind of quieted down. One thing I hated about visiting the Peterses was them barking dogs. There must have been six or eight; I never knew Old Man Peters to keep no less. In a minute Mabel came out and stood in the door.

"Who's that out there?" she said.

"It's just me, Mabel," I said. "I'd get down but I'm afraid these dogs would eat me."

"Gid?" she said. "Hush up, Pete, hush that." I guess Pete was the boss dog, because he went running over to her, and in a minute they all quieted down. Then I got off my horse and tied him to their mailbox.

"Have you been to supper?" she said. "Come on in and I'll fix you some."

But I never let her get me in the house. Their little old house always nearly suffocated me. It was an old chickenhouse, was what it was; Old Man Peters had just kinda rebuilt it. It never had but four little tight rooms, and they were so small and squeezed up and had such low ceilings that I couldn't hardly breathe when I was inside. I don't see how they lived through the summertime; it would have been like living in an oven.

Mabel knew I didn't like it, too, and it always embarrassed her. She wanted me to come and see her, but then when I did come she didn't have no nice place where we could go, and that preyed on her mind. Mabel was awful pretty in the face; I was just kinda awkward around her because it took me twenty or thirty minutes each time to get over feeling sorry for her. She'd worked and wanted her whole life, and she always looked like she'd do just anything for somebody who'd give her the chance to have some fun.

"Aren't you going to come in awhile?" she said. "We can't just stand out here on the steps."

"No," I said. "I feel like moving around, how about you? I thought you might like to take a little walk with me. It's such a bright moonlight night we wouldn't need no lantern." That was true. The moon was big and white that night, sailing up over the pastures.

The Peterses' house didn't have a porch, just front steps and back steps, because it was propped up on bricks, but Old Man Peters kept his wagon back behind the barn and I figured that would be our destination. It was a good big Studebaker wagon, and he kept his wagon sheet in it.

Mabel was agreeable enough to the walk.

"That'd be nice, Gid," she said. "Where will we walk?"

"Just here and there." She grabbed my hand herself and held on to me tight. I guess she was afraid of snakes. She walked so close to me I was afraid to move my feet for fear of stepping on her. I went dumb then; I could have kicked myself. I couldn't think of one thing to say. And I was a little snake-shy myself; nobody's very anxious to get rattlesnake-bit. But Mabel didn't mind the quiet; she walked along sort of humming to herself.

"It's sure nice to see somebody," she said. "I swear Ma and Pa have been about to bore me plumb to death."

"Dad bores me a good deal sometimes too," I said. I was beginning to get a little excited from her walking so close to me that way. I never could understand how a little thing like Mabel could get me so excited, but she sure could. She was so thin you wouldn't even notice her if she was standing sideways to you, but once she got near you she sure did make herself felt. We sashayed around by the post-pile a time or two and the pigpen once or twice and then I sidled over toward the wagon. I didn't need to sidle. When I asked her if she wanted to sit down awhile she just nodded, and it wasn't two minutes till we were kissing like old sweethearts. Mabel never pulled back a time; it was always me. At first I was kind of wishing it was Molly that was there, but then I quit caring so much, and I guess we'd have done the whole works without no conversation or nothing if I hadn't made the mistake of stopping to ask.

"You can if you want to, Gid," she whispered. "I don't care. And then we can get married and start having babies. That's what I've always wanted to do. You'll be the best husband in the world."

She just barely whispered that in my ear, but it hit me like a bucket of ice water.

"Goodness, we can't do that, Mabel," I said. "Dad would raise too much Cain, and your dad too. Let's go ahead anyway."

She didn't get mad, or say a word back to me, and she kissed me a whole lot more, but it never meant anything then. She had put on all the brakes. I was so mad at her I could have stomped her for a minute, but she kept on acting sweet and happy and never seemed to notice. She did notice, though; she was just too sly to let on. That was the big difference in her and Molly. Molly was wild, but she was warm, and she wasn't sly. Mabel wasn't really a bit wild, but she was really cold and sly. Mabel's little brain was cold as an icicle.

You couldn't guess that from the way she acted in the wagon. She cuddled up with me on the wagon sheet just as long as I wanted to stay, and I did stay a good while, hoping she would change her mind. But she wouldn't change her mind any more than the moon would change its direction. She sure did want to get married.

Finally I helped her out of the wagon and we walked back to the house. She never talked at all; she knew she couldn't do any good talking. But she kept close to me; I practically had to crawl out from under her to get on my horse.

It was just when I was about to ride away that she began to look real sorry. She had one hand on my ankle, and I was afraid she was fixing to cry.

"Come back to see me," she said. "I get awful bored around here, and I don't like for nobody to come to see me but you." And before I could get away, I was feeling sorry for her agin. I decided on the way home I would have to come back and give her another try. It had been worth it anyway.

Only next morning I wasn't so sure. I hadn't been asleep but two or three hours when Dad came in and started shaking my damn foot to wake me up. That was sure a long day.

5

JOHNNY GOT BACK from the Panhandle on a Sunday night and went to work for us on Monday morning. He rode over about breakfast time, to see how I was doing, I guess. It was branding season and we were getting in some new cattle, so when Dad got back from his morning ride he asked Johnny if he wanted to go to work on a day basis, and Johnny said he did.

"And when I say work, I mean work," Dad said. "I ain't gonna squander no dollar a day for you to sit on your butt."

"I ain't never run from no work yet," Johnny said. "Of course there's some kinds I'd rather do than others. But you're probably that way about it too, aren't you, Mr. Fry?"

Dad grunted. He didn't like much conversation out of Johnny. "The kind I like best is none," he said.

=====

I thought working up on the big ranches might have given Johnny a little responsibility, but it never. He was just as wild and crazy as he'd always been. One thing I noticed, though, he must have done a lot of riding. His new saddle was broken in to where it was comfortable as could be. He let me ride it a time or two, and I liked the way it rode.

He asked me right off if I had been taking good care of his girl.

"Mabel, you mean?" I said. "You bet, ever chance I get."

"Much obliged," he said. "Only she wasn't really the one I meant. I don't guess you know who that would be?"

"I don't guess. Not unless it's Annie Eldenfelder."

We carried on and kidded one another a lot. I was glad to see Johnny get back, really. Things were a good bit snappier with him around.

=====

He hadn't been working for us a week when me and him got into a real scrape with Molly's dad. We never meant to, either, because we both knew how she felt about him, and getting into a scrape with him was the best way in the world to get crosswise with her. But sometimes you don't have much control over what happens to you.

A couple of our yearling steers had crawled through a busted water gap into Old Man Taylor's pasture. Dad seen their tracks going through when he was out on his early morning lookaround, and when he got back to the house he sent me and Johnny over there to get them out. Which wasn't no trouble to do. We found them with the old man's milk cows and drove the whole bunch down to our gate and roped a yearling apiece and drug them through the gate where they belonged. It was still early then, and chilly, with mist hanging over the ground nearly high as a horse's belly. We was glad for a little action to warm us up.

It was when we were going to fix the water gap that we got in trouble. The first thing we done wrong was to ride down toward the creek on the Taylor side of the fence. We knew the old man would raise hell about that if he caught us, but we did it anyway, just to spite him. Then Johnny spotted a coyote. He loped through the fence about a hundred yards ahead of us, and Johnny said he saw him squat down in the grass and stop.

"Hell, let's rope that sonofabitch," he said. "I ain't never roped a coyote, have you?"

"Naw," I said. "Reckon we can catch him?" But I was already making me a loop. I had always wanted to rope one, and I figured this was my chance. Johnny, he couldn't throw his rope in the creek, so I never worried about him catching it. He made a loop big enough for a dinosaur to go through.

"I tell you now," he said. "I can't see him, but he's right over there between them two big bunches of chaparral. Let's sneak up on this side of him, so he can't dodge back through the fence. That way we can chase him clear to the north side if we need to. He ain't gonna sit forever, so when we get past that third post let's charge hell out of him. You ready?"

"He's practically roped," I said. "If you miss your first loop, haze him over my way so I can get a good throw."

We held our ponies down to a slow walk till we got past the post: then we jobbed the spurs to them and away we went, holding up our ropes and yelling like mad. I lost my hat before we even seen the coyote, and Johnny lost his a minute later. In about two seconds we was to the chaparral and up Mr. Coyote come; he jumped plumb over the bushes and it looked for a while like he was running along on top of the mist, two feet off the ground. Me and Johnny was right on his ass, and Johnny was done swinging. I swung to the side to give him room. Johnny had a damn good roping horse, he run right up by the coyote and leaned over, so all Johnny had to do was drop on the loop, but Johnny threw too late and missed about twenty feet, only this throw turned the coyote and it cut right under my horse while I was running full speed. I yanked to the right and went to spurring for all I was worth. Old Denver turned on about fifteen cents and was after the coyote agin before Johnny even got pulled up. By then we hit a strip of mesquite brush and I thought we had lost him, but then I decided to ride like hell and try to chase him through the brush and out into the clearing by the Taylor horse tank, so I could get my throw. Into the brush we went, with me about twenty yards behind the coyote and Johnny somewhere back of me. I ducked and spurred and the mesquite limbs flew. Only if Johnny couldn't rope, boy he could ride. By the time we were past the middle of the brush he went by me on the left just a-flying, waving his rope and his horse jumping trees and bushes and limbs busting like crazy. The coyote was still ahead though, sailing along on top of the mist. I spurred a little harder and we all three hit the clearing about the same time. In a second we were at the tank. I beat the coyote to the water about two steps and turned him over the dam, and Johnny was right there to keep him from ducking back so he went over the dam and down on the other side and I went right over with him and threw while we were still half in the air: caught him clean as a whistle. Old Denver fell then and nobody could blame him; I went rolling off to one side and the coyote to the other. But when we all got up we had a big dog coyote on the end of the rope.

"Good throw, by god," Johnny said. "I thought you was gonna turn a flip off that dam."

"It's a wonder I didn't," I said. I was too out of breath to say much. Johnny got his rope on the coyote too, and we had him where he couldn't do any harm.

"I wish Dad was here," I said. "I bet he never roped one." One thing I could do, and that was rope.

We were about to knock the coyote in the head and get the ears so we could collect our bounty when Old Man Taylor walked up on the tank dam from the other side. He had his .10-gauge shotgun in one hand and a couple of dead squirrels in the other—probably they were going to be Molly's breakfast. When he got up closer I seen his beard was wet, so I guess he had him a whiskey jug hid off in a stump somewhere.

"Goddam you boys," he said, "Goddam trespassers. What are you little sonsofbitches doing on my place?"

We never said a word, but we didn't like it. People can't just come up and cuss you without you getting mad.

"Well, the cat got your tongues?" he said. "Answer me when I ask you something. Didn't your folks teach you no manners?"

"We had to come over and get a couple of our yearlings and fix the water gap on the river," I said. "Then we accidentally run on to this coyote and roped him. That's all, Mr. Taylor."

"Oh you did, did you?" he said. Boy he looked mad. "Young farts ought to have your asses kicked."

We were getting about all we could stand of it, but we didn't know quite what to do. For one thing, we still had the coyote on the ropes, and the old man noticed it.

"Turn that coyote loose," he said. "That there's my own coyote anyway. I don't ever want to catch you roping my coyotes agin. Turn the sonofabitch loose."

That was the silliest thing I ever heard of, claiming that coyote.

"No sir," I said. "We caught him coming out of our pasture, and we'll just have to take him back." I thought I could be just as silly as he was.

"Oh you are, are you?" he said, stuffing his squirrels in his hip pocket. "Now what about you, little McCloud? You get down and turn that coyote loose."

Johnny was half-tickled by it all.

"No sir," he said. "I would, only I'm scared to. I'm kind of a coward when it comes to getting one of my hands bit off."

The old man got madder and madder, but he shut up and just stared at us. That's when I really got uneasy, and I don't know where it would have gone if Dad hadn't rode up about that time. For once in my life I was glad to see Dad. Old Man Taylor was just crazy enough to have shot us.

I guess Dad had missed me and Johnny and come to see what kind of mischief we was in. When Dad was impatient to work it never took him long to miss a person. He rode up like there wasn't nothing unusual about the gathering at all.

"I see you boys been fiddling around," he said. "I thought I told you to come on home when you got them yearlings out. How are you today, Cletus?"

"No damn good," the old man said. "Looky what them boys done. I wisht you'd make them turn that coyote loose. I don't like boys roping coyotes of mine."

Crazy old fart.

"Aw, you didn't look close enough, Cletus," Dad said. "That's my coyote. See that earmark I put on him. Hell, I never even knowed he was out. It's lucky these boys found him. Once your coyotes get off in the brush they're hard to find."

I was flabbergasted and so was Old Man Taylor. Johnny was just tickled. We all looked, and sure enough the coyote did have a piece of his ear missing. And I don't know yet whether Dad was really responsible for it being gone or not. I imagine it was just chewed off in a fight, but you can't tell about Dad. Old Man Taylor like to swallowed his Adam's apple.

"How do you mark your coyotes, Cletus?" Dad asked, solemn as a judge. "I never noticed. If you'll show me, I'll have these boys run what they find of yours back in your pasture."

But Old Man Taylor was a pretty sly old bastard himself—you couldn't hem him up for long. He walked over and grabbed the coyote by the snout and looked at his ear.

"By god, it is yours," he said. "I come off without my spectacles this morning.

"Say," he said. "I like the looks of this coyote, Adam. How much will you take for him?"

That even surprised Dad, only he never much let on. He got out his plug and cut himself off some tobacco; then he offered the plug to Old Man Taylor and he cut off a bigger chew than Dad's. All the time Dad was thinking it over. I bet he thought it was funny as hell.

"Oh, I don't know, Cletus," he said. "I ain't been watching the market too close. I'd have to get about three dollars for him, I guess."

"By god, that's fair," the old man said, and I'll be damned if he didn't take out his pocketbook and pull three one-dollar bills out of it and hand them to Dad. Dad folded them together and stuck them in his shirt pocket. That was a dollar more than the ears would bring in bounty money.

"Good trade," the old man said. "Wonder if them boys would help me a minute, Adam. I might as well earmark him while I got him caught."

"Sure," Dad said. "You boys get down and help Mr. Taylor mark that coyote."

The old man stood back and opened his pocketknife, and there wasn't nothing for it but for us to do the dangerous work. I went up one rope and Johnny up the other, and we managed to get his snout without being bit too bad. I muzzled him with my piggin string and we threw him down and hogtied him with Johnny's. Then the old man cropped his ear and the job was done.

"Much obliged, boys," he said. "Now I'll know the bastard next time I see him."

"Can I borrow your piggin strings and just leave him tied awhile?" he asked, real friendly. "Tame him up a little. After a while I'll send that girl of mine and get her to lead him up to the house. She ain't got a damn thing else to do."

The thought of Molly having to drag that coyote to the house made me fighting mad. But Dad was ready to go.

"Let's get home, boys," he said. "We got all them calves to brand. Much obliged, Cletus. Take care of yourself. Hope he makes you a good coyote."

"Oh yeah," the old man said. "He'll do."

===

"Well, that was a damn good trade," Dad said. "Three dollars always comes in handy."

"Hell, we caught him," I said. "We ought to get a little of it."

We come to the gate and Dad stopped and waited for one of us to get down and open it. Johnny did.

"Oh you think so, do you?" Dad said. "Well, I don't. He was my coyote to begin with. All you done was rope him. If you was to rope one of my calves, that wouldn't make it yours, would it?"

"What made him yours?" I said. "You wasn't serious about that earmark business, was you?"

He just kept riding and never answered.

"Shit-fire," Johnny said. "I believe I'll quit, Mr. Fry. I better go back and untie that coyote before Molly has to come drag him to the house. I don't want her fiddling with that big bastard. He might bite her hand off."

"I'm with you," I said. "Let's turn him loose. We can get back in plenty of time to do the branding."

"The hell you will," Dad said. "I just got you boys out of one scrape and I ain't got time to get you out of another. Cletus is just waiting for one of you to come back so he can get that extra dollar out of your hide. He'd get it too, don't think he wouldn't."

"Dollar," I said. "You made three."

"Yeah, but Cletus will get two back when he sells them ears to the county. Why, he ain't gonna keep no coyotes. He just spent that money to keep from backing down."

Me and Johnny couldn't hardly believe it.

"You mean a poor man like him would spend three dollars just for that?" I said.

"Who's a poor man?" Dad said. "Cletus Taylor ain't poor. He's just tight. Just because he don't spend money don't mean he ain't got any. I don't spend much myself, and that's one reason I got so much more than most people."

"Well," Johnny said, "if I was a man and I had money, I believe I'd at least buy myself and my daughter some decent clothes to wear. I wouldn't go around dressed disgraceful. I believe I'd spend a little of it enjoying life."

"Most young fools would," Dad said. "That's why most young fools are broke."

Me and Johnny shut up. There was no use arguing with Dad. And he was right about one thing. Just as we crossed the Ridge we heard the .10-gauge go KLA-BOOM, like a damn cannon.

"One less coyote," Dad said. "And that many more frying chickens I'll get to eat next spring. I'm glad you boys have finally learned to rope."

6

OLD MAN TAYLOR got his damn revenge anyhow, only he took it out on Molly instead of us. I could have killed him for it.

Two nights after the coyote roping they were having a big harvest-time square dance over in Thalia. It was about the biggest dance or get-together they had between the Fourth of July and Christmas, and I had an agreement with Molly that me and her would go. I asked her the day we went fishing, while Johnny was still up in the Panhandle. He was mad enough to bite himself when he found out I had done asked her. He ended up having to take Mabel Peters, and it served him right.

Anyway, I got all spruced up and was going to use Dad's buggy. I drove over to Molly's just about dark, and I was sure excited. I didn't care too much about the dance, but the thought of getting to ride all that way with Molly sitting by me was something to be excited about.

But when I got to Molly's the house was completely dark. It surprised the devil out of me. There wasn't no light on of no kind. For a minute I thought Johnny must have pulled some kind of sneak and taken her off already. I didn't know what to think. It was a still, pretty night, and not a sound to be heard. Finally I hitched the horses and walked across the yard and up on the porch. Still not a sound. I hesitated a minute before I knocked on the door—I decided her old devil of a daddy was hiding in there someplace, waiting to jump out and give me hell about the coyote. I walked around on the porch for a few minutes, hoping somebody inside the house would finally hear me and say something. Molly could have lain down to take a little nap and rest up for the dance.

But nobody said nothing.

"Hell-fire," I said, finally, and went up and knocked on the door good and loud.

"I can't go tonight, Gid," Molly said, and it like to scared me to death. She had been standing just inside the door all the time, but off to one side of the screen, so I couldn't see her.

"You'll have to go on without me," she said. "I ain't feeling good."

"My goodness, Molly, you scared the daylights out of me. Why don't you turn on some kind of light."

"I don't want to," she said, and her voice was trembling. "I just want to be in the dark, Gid." And then it was real quiet, and I knew she was standing there crying, even if I couldn't see her. Molly cried the quietest, she never made a sound at all. Then I heard her move off in the dark and bump into a table or something and run down the hall, and things were quiet agin. The only sound I could hear was the windmill creaking.

I didn't know what to make of it. Something was bothering her pretty bad for her not even to ask me in. One thing I knew, I wasn't going to no dance without her. She could forget about that.

But that didn't solve the problem of what to do. I had to get to talk to her, and the only way to do that was to go in the damn dark house and find her. I wished I had had enough sense to ask her if her dad was there. If she was the only one home, I was all right. But I could just imagine that old man, standing in the living room with a club, waiting for me. The more I thought about it, the madder it made me. I remembered how he had cussed me and Johnny when he found us with that coyote. Finally I opened the screen door and doubled up my fists and clobbered on in. About three steps inside I stopped and crouched over, watching for him.

But he didn't come. If somebody had come in with a light, I would have looked silly as hell. Pretty soon I knew damn well he wasn't there. Molly wouldn't have let me walk into no bad situation without warning me. And the old man wouldn't have waited for me to come in: he would have come out. Besides, if he had been there I would have smelled him, he was such a fragrant old bastard.

So I went on down the hall to Molly's room and didn't give the old man another thought. Sure enough she was in on her bed, crying. The moonlight was coming through the window. I went over and sat down on the edge of the old creaky bed and put my hand on her arm.

"Now, honey," I said, "don't lay there taking on. Turn over and tell me where you hurt and I'll see if I can find some medicine." It was strange, because Molly wasn't the kind that went around being sick.

She wouldn't answer me, though, and for a few minutes I just had to sit there, holding her the best she would let me. She moved over under my arm and acted like she was glad to have me there, but she wouldn't look up. She wasn't crying loud, but she sure wasn't happy.

In a little while I fumbled around and found some matches and lit the lamp. The minute I had the light on I seen what it was all about. Her face and throat and the front of her dress was all wet from tears, but the trouble was, she had a black eye. It wasn't a bad one. In fact it kind of made her look prettier or older, in a way, but you could tell she had one. I knew who done it, too.

"Don't you say a word against my daddy," she said. "I know what you're think-ing. He wouldn't have done it if I hadn't been so mean."

That was a lie, but I never said a word.

"I sure am sorry about it," I said in a minute. "But it ain't bad, Molly. It ain't no reason to stay in the dark all the time. By tomorrow you won't even be able to tell it."

I wanted to cuss the worthless old bastard good, but that would have just messed things up.

"I know it, Gid," and the tears were pouring out of her eyes. I sat down and hugged her again. "But the dance is just tonight," she said. "And you're all dressed up and look so nice, you ought to go on. I had my dress all fixed, too. I'd been looking forward to it for I don't know how long. Why does it have to happen at such a bad time?"

I could see how it was a pretty big disappointment. To a girl, especially. Molly never got to go places very often. In fact, it was just very very seldom that she went any place. When you come right down to it, she didn't like much being as cooped up as Mabel Peters, only there was so much more of Molly to coop up.

"Now hush, sugar," I said. "It ain't such a great calamity. This ain't the only dance there'll ever be. We'll get to go to plenty more."

"No we won't," she said. "I don't care." She pulled up the counterpane and wiped her face, but there was still a little puddle of tears in the hollow of her neck. She looked at me kinda mad and I got out my handkerchief and wiped her throat. She was so pretty, black eye or not.

"I wish there never would be another one," she said. "Then I wouldn't have to be so disappointed. I know I won't get to go, even if there's a hundred dances. I guess I'm just too mean."

"Oh hush that up," I said. "You ain't mean, and you ain't hurt, either. We can have just as much fun right here as we could have at the dance."

"But I don't want to stay here. I stay here all the time, Gid. I wanted to go where there were a lot of people having fun."

"Okay," I said, "let's go. It ain't late. That little old shadow on your eye ain't no reason to stay home."

But that just made her cry more. I never knew girls had so much crying in them. Missing that dance didn't amount to a hill-of-beans in the long run, but Molly acted like her heart was broken.

"Now you hush," I said. "This is a silly damn way for you to act. If you want to go, why get up and dry your face and let's go. Hell, by the time we get there every-body will be so drunk they wouldn't notice if you had three black eyes. And if you don't want to go, why hush anyway, and let's go in the living room and pop some popcorn or something. Crying all night won't do any good."

Finally she did hush and just lay back against me. I held her until I was sure she had calmed down.

"That's better," I said. "Have you decided yet?"

"We'll just have to stay here," she said. "I don't want to go to the dance unless I can go looking nice, and I can't do that with this eye. Besides, my dress is all wet. But you ought to go. Just think of all the girls you could dance with."

"I don't know," I said. "Me and you may dance a little ourselves, before the night is over. Johnny can take care of all them other girls."

"He said he wouldn't. When I told him I had already promised you, he said he intended to go to the dance drunk and not dance a single time, just to spite me."

"Sounds like him," I said. "But what he says and what he does are two different things. You know that, don't you?"

"Not when it comes to me, they ain't," she said.

"Where's your dad tonight, anyway?"

"He was out of whiskey and had to go to Henrietta. He may not be back for two or three days."

"Let's go in the living room then," I said.

===

We did, but we never popped no popcorn. I had had a big supper anyway. We built a big fire in the fireplace; it was the only light we had. Molly started to the kitchen to get something and I caught her in my arms and swung her around a time or two and kissed her.

"Now ain't this dancing?" I said. "Ain't this better'n dancing in a big crowd, anyway? If you ask me, that black eye is the nicest thing about you tonight."

"I wish you'd take off that scratchy necktie," she said. "It's about to rub a raw place on me."

"Boy, I will," I said. "It was choking me anyway." I took it off, and my wool coat too. But I never let Molly get to the kitchen.

"Now let's dance," I said. "Just us two. Let's round dance. You hum the music."

She put her head on my chest and hummed a little bit of some song. I hugged her against me real tight and we moved around the living room floor, in the shadows of the fire. "Let's just imagine the music, Gid," she said. "I can't remember what I'm humming half the time."

"I ain't got that much imagination," I said, but we kept dancing anyway; we danced real slow. Molly's hair had a good smell. I got to wanting to kiss more than I wanted to dance, so I stopped and made her tilt her face up and let me. We stood there so long I expected the sun would be coming up. But it was still dark and shadowy.

"I want to make up to you for the other day," I said. "I sure do love you."

She kept standing there against me with her eyes shut, and didn't say anything, but when I kissed her agin she seemed real glad.

"It's okay then? If I make it up to you tonight? I've been worrying about it a lot."

"Yes, I want you to," she said, "but let's stand here a little while longer. Let's not think about anything."

So we stood there and kissed some more and got closer and closer together and finally moved on down the hall to Molly's room, where we had been at first. When we got there I remembered something and left her for a minute and went and latched the screen doors. I went back and she was crying.

She grabbed me and I held her tight. "Where did you go?" she said. "You never needed to leave me and go nowhere."

"Just to latch the doors," I said.

She got fighting mad all of a sudden. I had to hold her to keep her from hitting me. "Don't ever leave me like that agin," she said. "I don't care if the doors are latched or not. Next time you leave me, just keep going." And she actually bit me, she was so mad or hurt or something. I almost shoved her down I was so surprised. But I held her in the middle of the floor till she got real quiet and we were close together and kissed a long time agin. I never wanted to leave her, that's for sure. What I couldn't figure was, how I was going to get my boots off without stopping the kissing for a minute.

"Let's sit down, Molly. These new boots are killing me."

"Poor Gid," she said. "Here, sit on the bed. I'll help you take them off."

And in a minute she had, and I was holding her agin. Then I accidentally tore her pretty dress. I thought that would cook my goose, but it never. She put her hand on my neck and kissed me. I started to tell her I was sorry but her mouth kept stopping me. "Don't talk no more," she said, "don't you say another word tonight."

=====

I was the first one awake. I guess I expected Dad to be shaking my foot. But there was just Molly; she was lovely. In a minute she woke up too and yawned and saw me and giggled and snuggled over and kissed me. It was purely delicious. Only I had begun to realize that Dad's buggy and horses were still hitched outside, and that it was past daylight and he was wondering where I was.

"Good god," I said. "Dad'll skin me alive. I ought to woken up and gone home."

"Scardy-cat," she said. "Let's stay here all day. That will show them they ain't the boss of us. I'd like to stay right here, where it's nice and warm and just us, wouldn't you? Can we?"

"Oh lord, I'd like to too," I said. "But Dad is the boss of me, I guess. I better skedaddle."

"Well, I wish we could stay," she said. Then she sat up and grinned, without no covers or nothing. "But I'll cook you some hot biscuits, anyway." And in a minute she had kissed me and crawled over and got out of bed. She was poking around in a drawer looking for some Levis, with just her behind pointed at me.

If it didn't bother her, I didn't see why it ought to bother me. I loved her and I didn't figure I'd have too much trouble persuading her to marry me, after we'd spent the night. Only when I looked down at the bedsheets I couldn't figure it out.

"Hey, sweetie," I said. "Ain't you normal? I thought you was supposed to bleed all over the place."

"Why, didn't you know no better than that?" she said, turning around and grinning at me. She had a pair of Levis in her hand, but she hadn't put them on. "You're the funniest boy, Gid." The morning light was coming in on her through the windows; she pulled on a shirt and never buttoned it, and her hair was down over her shoulders. I thought she was the prettiest thing I had ever seen.

"You didn't have to worry," she said, innocent as daylight. "You only bleed like that the first time."

I was absolutely flabbergasted.

7

I T M A D E M E pretty down in the mouth, finding out that I wasn't the first feller
ever to spend a night with Molly. I couldn't think straight for a while, I was so
upset. But there wasn't much I could say about it, because she got up just happy
as a lark, and not the least bit down in the dumps about anything. She fed me
some awful good biscuits for breakfast, too. But I never enjoyed my food. All I
could think about was wanting to get married to her as soon as I could.

Of course Dad raked me over the coals when I finally got home. He seen me
unhitching the buggy, and here he came.

"Well, at least you ain't eloped with her," he said, looking at the buggy to see
how scratched up it was. "But I bet it wasn't because you didn't try. Your good
buddy Johnny's been down there digging postholes for three hours. Get on down
there and help him."

"He ain't my good buddy," I said. "I guess I can change clothes before I go,
can't I?"

"I'd just as soon you worked in them you got on," Dad said. "If you dirty them
up, you won't be running around so much at night." And I had been out two
nights in a month, and one of them he never knew about.

Johnny, he was sweating his whiskey out. But I wasn't in no mood to sympathize
with him.

"Where you been?" he said. "Why wasn't you'all at the dance? Hell, I waited for
you till one o'clock."

"We got lost and never made it. How'd you and your sweetheart Mabel get along?"

He leaned on his diggers a minute. "Why, she'd be a darling if she wasn't such a
bitch," he said. "I had to run backward all night to keep her from proposing to me."

He would have chattered all day if I had let him, but I grabbed my diggers and
walked off a hundred yards or so and went to digging. I wasn't in a talking mood.

——

Well, I thought about it and thought about it, and I couldn't come to no decision.
It had to be Johnny that done it, but he never acted the least bit guilty about it,
and Molly never either, so I had no way of knowing. The only thing that made me
doubt it was Johnny was him not bragging about it. He just naturally bragged a little if he had done anything to brag about. Anyhow, I didn't think it was right for
two fellers to have spent the night with a sweet girl like Molly and not either one
of them have married her. The more I thought about it, the surer I was about that,
and something had to be done about it. If Johnny had been there first, then he
ought to have the first chance at marrying her, and if he didn't want to, why I
damn sure did. And the way I seen it, Molly could have her choice of me and him,

but that was all the choice there was to it. She couldn't go running around single much longer, that was for sure.

All the same, I couldn't help being mad at myself, because I kept wanting to go right back over and spend another night. And I would have, too, if her damned old man had ever left agin; I snuck over several times to check, but he was always there. I hadn't forgot about him giving her that black eye, either.

Finally me and Johnny had it out about her, when we were going to Fort Worth, of all places. About the middle of November, Dad decided to ship the rest of his calves, but he didn't want to go along and fool with them, so he sent me and Johnny.

"I guess I'm a damn fool for sending two idiots when I could just send one," he said. "But maybe if I send two, one will be sober enough to look after the cattle part of the time. I want you boys back here on Sunday, and I don't want you to give them cattle away. If you see any yearling steers worth the money, you might buy me about a hundred of them and bring 'em home with you."

Of course it was the biggest lark in the world to me and Johnny. We struck out early one morning, with a norther blowing cold as hell, and drove the cattle to Henrietta and put them on the railroad cars for Fort Worth about night that same day.

"Them cattle are safe," Johnny said. "Let's go wet our whistles. My damn throat's full of dust."

Mine was too, and we bought some whiskey and went to washing out the dust. About that time we went into a little honkytonk there by the railroad yards and run into the deputy sheriff that had arrested Johnny the last time he was in Henrietta. Only he wasn't a deputy no more and was a good bit drunker than we was, and had two of his drinking buddies with him. Johnny asked me if I'd back him up, and I said sure, so he went over and called the feller a sonofabitch and the other feller called him one back and they went outside and had a fist fight in the street. Me and the other fellers went too, but we didn't fight. The ex-deputy bloodied Johnny's nose, but I think Johnny had the best of the fight.

"That'll show you, you bastard," Johnny said. "Next time just try and arrest me."

"Sonofabitch," the man said. "Want me to whip you good?"

That was funny, because they had already fought for fifteen minutes. Me and Johnny walked over to the pens and climbed around on the cars awhile, and the cattle looked all right to us, so we went to the caboose and went to sleep. Sometime during the night the train come and hooked onto the cars and off we went, I don't know just when. The caboose was awful bouncy, and it woke me up about Decatur. Johnny was sitting up holding his jaw; I guess it had bounced against the floor. There wasn't but one other passenger, a damn greasy oilfield hand, who looked like he'd got on the train about Burkburnett. He was asleep on the bench.

"Hell, let's go outside," Johnny said. "I can't sleep in this rickety bastard. Let's go out and look at the country awhile."

"I'm ready," I said.

We put on our jackets and walked out on the little porch of a thing at the tail-end of the caboose. It was a clear, starry night, but cold as hell. The norther was still blowing, and we was getting it right in our faces. We set down with our backs to the door of the caboose and watched the country go by in the dark.

"I sure like riding trains," Johnny said. "Lots faster than going some place ahorseback."

I watched the rails come out from under the car, and they didn't seem to be coming so fast. But they came awful steady; I kept halfway looking for them to end, and they never did. We went through some little old town, I never have known the name of it, and all it had in it was grain elevators. It was the most grain elevators I knew of this side of Kansas. We could see the shapes of them in the moonlight. It was real exciting to be going someplace.

"This here's where they make all the oatmeal," Johnny said. "Boy, I'm glad I ain't no farmer. There ain't nothing that can compare with a cowboy's life, if you ask me. You don't have to worry about a damn thing."

"It just depends," I said. "What if you own the ranch you're working on? Then you got to worry about making money and taking care of the cattle and all that kind of thing."

"Then you ain't a cowboy, you're a rancher," he said. "I never said I wanted to be a rancher. Damn, I wish I'd brought my sheepskin coat. I didn't figure it would get this cold in November."

"It's because we're moving so fast." My ears were getting numb, but it was a lot nicer ride out on the end than in that bouncy caboose.

"What you ought to do," he said, "is to forget all that ranching. And forget about marrying, too. Then one of these days we could go up on the plains and really have us a time. When the ranch gets to be yours, you can sell it and not have it worrying you all your life."

"That's just like you," I said. "You ain't got no more responsibility than a monkey. That ain't no way to amount to nothing."

"Responsibility ain't no valuable thing to have, necessarily," he said. "Listen at you. It depends on what you want to amount to. I want to amount to a good cowboy."

"Talking about marrying," I said, "that reminds me of something I've been meaning to talk to you about. Something pretty serious. I guess I got to admit you got first claims on Molly, but what I want to know is, do you really intend to marry her or not? One of us has got to, that's for sure, and if you ain't going to, I am."

He looked at me like I was crazy. Finally he laughed, but he was kind of uncertain about it.

"You needn't snicker," I said. "I found out all about it. I know you laid up with her. I done it too, of course, but you was the first, so she's really your responsibility. Now one of us has got to do something."

"I believe you're serious," he said. "And I know you're crazy. What in the world are you talking about?"

"It's simple as mud," I said. "You sweet-talked Molly into letting you spend the night with her. Okay. Hell, I don't blame you, I done it too. Anybody would want to. Only the first one has the most responsibility. It ain't no way to do a good-hearted girl like Molly, and you know it. Now is it?"

"Why, you beat all I ever seen," he said. "After being in that whorehouse and all that mess we went through in Kansas getting you cured, and you still sit there and talk like a damn preacher."

"Now you better watch it, or you'll get a real fight, Johnny," I said. "I ain't talking like no preacher. I'm just talking about doing what's right about Molly."

"I wasn't meaning her," he said. "I was talking about you. She's as nice as they come, I wasn't calling her no whore. But you ain't no more of a lily-white boy than I am."

"I know it," I said. "I just want to get this settled. It's been bothering me for two weeks."

"What I'm trying to get you to understand, there ain't nothing to settle. Molly ain't done nothing to be ashamed of. We've always treated her nice and she likes both of us. You're just ashamed of something that ain't shameful."

"Maybe so," I said, "but I'm pretty crazy about her, and I imagine you are too. But one of us ought to take care of her, and it'll be a shame if one of us don't, that's all I meant to say. You was first, so you get the first chance."

"But that ain't even right, Gid," he said. "I wasn't first, no such thing. I always figured you was first. You was, and you know it. So why try to put the blame on me. I wouldn't do a thing like that to you."

That confused me. "The hell you wasn't first," I said. "Molly told me herself— she wasn't thinking what she was saying, I guess—that I wasn't the first one. Why are you trying to get out of it if you ain't ashamed?"

"Because I wasn't first," he said. "If you wasn't, then somebody else was. Not you nor me. Hell, I never stayed with her a time till last summer. When did you start?"

"The night of that harvest dance," I said. It flabbergasted us both. We never said a word for about fifteen miles, I guess. My ears like to froze off.

"Well, I guess we caught her," he said, finally. "I swear. I always figured it had been you. I wonder who the hell it was."

"It can't be just anybody," I said. "She's too sweet a girl. Who have we over-looked?"

"Aw hell," he said. "We ought to thought of it sooner. It must have been that damn Eddie."

"Not that worthless bastard, I can't believe that." But I remembered one time she said he was the only one silly enough for her. I guess she meant it.

"He's the very one," Johnny said. "He ought to have the shit kicked out of him. What business does he have fiddling around with Molly anyway? That hound-running sonofabitch has probably got fleas plumb up to his middle."

"Yeah, that shit-ass," I said. "Evertime I see him he's greasy to the elbows. What would she want to take up with somebody like that for?"

"Aw, Molly's crazy," he said. He didn't sound too happy, and I wasn't, either. Neither of us could stand that goddamn Eddie. "She don't think like other girls," he said. "Her trouble is, she's too nice. She's lived with that no-count bastard of a daddy so long she can't tell worthless people from them that's got something to them."

"That's about it. That old man's the cause of it all."

"I guess she figures she don't have no chance of being a nice girl anyway, grow-ing up around him. That's probably why she took up with Eddie."

"Maybe there's somebody else," I said. "I'd rather it be nearly anybody than him."

But we couldn't think of another soul.

"Anyhow," Johnny said, "now you see that neither one of us has got to marry her. We don't need to have no guilty conscience. If he done it first, he's the one ought to marry her."

That shocked me worse than anything he'd said the whole night. "My god," I said. "You think I'd sit by and watch Molly marry a worthless sonofabitch like him. Why he ain't got nothing but a few hound dogs and a pair of roughnecking boots. He'd just drag her to one oil patch after another all her life."

"Serve her right, by god," he said. "She oughtn't to taken up with him in the first place."

"I know," I said. "But it don't make no difference. I'll just marry her anyway, even if I am third man. I ain't going to let her marry Eddie."

"Looky there," he said. "Ain't that a sight? I never knowed we was this close."

I looked, and there were the lights of Fort Worth. You never saw so many lights in your life. It was hard to imagine living in a place that big, but it sure was exciting to see all the lights at once. The train blew its whistle.

"That's cowtown," Johnny said.

"It's too early for anybody to be up," I said. "I wonder what they need with so many lights."

"I guess they just leave them lit so jackasses like us can tell when we're coming to a real town."

We stood up and looked, and pretty soon there were houses all around us and we went back in the caboose awhile, to warm up. The oil-fielder was still asleep. We decided he was drunk.

"I tell you what," Johnny said. We took off his shoes real careful and hid them over in a corner and got his shoelaces and tied his ankles together with them. We left a little play in the laces, but we tied about a dozen real hard knots and then spit on them to make them slippery.

"It'll take him a solid hour to get loose," Johnny said.

"It serves him right. It's what he gets for being an oilfielder." We thought that was a pretty funny trick.

Pretty soon the train slowed down and stopped at the stockyards, and then the fun stopped too, for a while. We didn't know up from down about the stockyards, or what we were supposed to do or nothing, and we got out and stood around in the cold and the dark for about an hour, waiting to unload the cattle. There were a lot of stockyards fellers moving around with lanterns and punchpoles, and a lot of railroad men too, but they never said nothing to us and we didn't bother them.

"Hell, maybe we ought to ask somebody," I said finally. "What if the train goes on and takes our stock with it?"

"I don't know," Johnny said. "My damn hands are froze. I hate to bother any of these men, don't you?"

I hated to too, so we stood awhile longer. Then the train blew its whistle, and that scared us enough that we found a Mexican and asked him. But he only knew Mexican and we only knew white man, so we finally had to ask one of the stockyards men.

"Goddamn, boys, you'all look about frozen," he said. We told him our problem, and, by god, if they hadn't already unloaded our cattle and taken them to a pen way off across the yards. We had been so cold we never noticed and had got by the wrong railroad car, one full of cattle that was going on to the slaughterhouse.

"Well, I guess we can go get a hotel room, can't we?" Johnny said.

"Not till we find them cattle," I said. "What if somebody tried to mix them with another bunch? Dad would have a fit."

So we struck off across the yards looking for them, and just had an awful time. We had to crawl over about a hundred fences, and we couldn't see well enough to tell if any of the bunches of cattle were ours or not. There must have been a thousand bunches of cattle, each one in a different pen. Finally by mistake we got in a pen with a couple of damn boar hogs. We didn't even see them and thought the pen was empty till we got about halfway across it and heard one grunt as he come for us.

"Goddamn," Johnny said. "Run." We took off and hadn't taken two steps till another hog jumped up in front of us. He squealed and come at us too, but we jumped him before he got to his feet good and hit the fence and went up it.

"Shit," Johnny said, "you can look for them cattle if you want to. I'm going to the hotel. I ain't no hog fighter."

The old boars were grunting and squealing around below us like they really wanted blood. I wasn't a hog fighter either.

"Goddammit," I said. "They oughtn't to taken them cattle out of the cars without asking me. I'm the one responsible for them, ain't I? Now I guess they're lost."

"Well, if they are, we just won't go home," Johnny said. "We can work around here for a few days and then catch a train up north. If them cattle are lost, I don't never want to see Archer County agin."

We finally found our way out of the yards and went through the big Exchange building. On the other side of it was the street. We walked down it and came to a lot of honkytonks and hotels; the honkytonks were closed, and the hotels didn't look too lively, but we finally come to one called the Longhorn, and an old feller came out dripping chewing tobacco on the rug and gave us a room for fifty cents apiece. I was worried about the cattle. I figured if I had lost them, I better go farther away than the Panhandle. I better go at least to Canada.

Johnny, though, he wasn't worrying; they wasn't his cattle.

"Me for some shut-eye," he said. "I wonder if that roughneck ever woke up."

It was an awful small, bare room we got, without no bathroom and with one of the littlest beds you ever saw.

"You mean we paid fifty cents apiece just to get a little old bed like that?" I said. "Hell, I slept in a bigger bed than that when I was a baby."

Johnny could sleep anywhere; he pulled off his boots and lay down. "Which you want," he said, "top or bottom? There ain't room enough for sideways."

But I thought I'd look at the street a minute, and when I let the windowshade up I seen it was daylight.

"Why, it's morning," I said. "Get up and let's go look for those cattle."

But he was done asleep and I went on without him. I figured I could do as well by myself anyway.

═══

When I got back to the yards things looked a lot more cheerful; the sun was up and the cattle were bawling and people were charging around everywhere. They had big wide planks nailed on top of the fences, so you could just walk around above the pens and see the cattle without having to get down in the cowshit. I found my cattle in about ten minutes, and was I relieved. There was even a feller with them filling up the hayrack with hay. Them yards was really run right. The hay feller turned out to be a sourpuss.

"Howdy," I said. "I sure am glad to see those cattle."

"You're the Fry boy, ain't you?" he said.

"Gideon Fry. I'm glad to meet you."

"Why'd the hell you sleep so late?" he said. "You done missed two good chances to sell these cattle already. Your dad, now, he was always out at the yards by daybreak."

I never cared much to take a chewing out from an old fat hay hauler in a corduroy cap, so I asked him which way the buyers went. He got up on the fence and pointed one out to me, way across the yards. He bought for Swift & Armour, it turned out. I went over and introduced myself, and I'll be damned if he didn't buy the cattle right there, for a dime a pound. He took me right on in the Exchange building after the cattle were weighed and gave me a check. So that was that. I was so surprised I felt lightheaded; I had expected a hell of a day's work selling them cattle. It was just an hour after sunup and they were already sold.

There was a little lunch counter over in one corner of the big rotunda of the Exchange building, and I went over and bought myself a cup of coffee and set down with it. I just set there, feeling good, drinking the hot coffee; I felt like I could handle anything.

By then it was seven o'clock on a Monday morning, and the floor of the Exchange building was swirling with people. There was a big blackboard over on one wall and two men were at it all the time with chalk and erasers, marking up reports of prices and the number of cattle and whatnot at all the other big markets, Chicago and Kansas City and Omaha and I don't remember where else. The big cattlemen were stomping around the lobby, making deals and ordering people around. You could tell them right off from the just plain cowboys, even if they dressed alike. The cattlemen were the ones giving orders and acting like Dad acts, and the cowboys were taking orders and going off every which way to carry them out. I heard one feller, he was standing about ten feet from me, make a deal for over a hundred thousand dollars' worth of cattle, and he was just standing there drinking coffee, like me. Watching them big operators made an impression on me. They acted like what they were doing was important, and they did things like they meant them. Nobody was ordering them around, like Dad done me and Johnny. They was their own bosses—they weren't nasty about it, you could just tell. I guess it was independence. Anyhow, I went and got another cup of good strong hot coffee and set down to think about it. Dad had probably been right about me. Johnny, he could go off and cowboy if he wanted to; I might enjoy going along for a while, but it just wouldn't suit me for long. I wanted to amount to what all them big boys amounted to.

In a little while I went down the street a few doors and had breakfast at a little café. I started to go get Johnny, but I decided I might as well let him sleep. I felt like I'd wasted too much time in my life, and that cattle money was burning my pocket. There was all them cattle out in the yards, just waiting for somebody to buy them and make money on them. I intended to go make a little.

So I went back and spent the day on the yards. I kept expecting Johnny, but he never come, and I didn't have time to go get him. I had over eight thousand dollars of Dad's money when I started buying and trading and fooling around. Right off I bought a little bunch of steers and sold them not an hour later for a dollar a hundred profit. Boy, I felt like I was on the way. Only then a damn scoundrel from South Texas sold me another bunch too high. I guess I was tired or something and didn't look at them good. It was the ruination of me. I had made six hundred dollars on my first little deal and I figured I'd make that much more on the steers. Then I could buy some real good steers to take home to Dad, and I would still have made money. But, by god, if the last bunch wasn't the worst bunch of cattle I ever bought in my life. When I finally took time to really look them over, I seen how sorry they was, full of pinkeyes and foul foots and crisps of one kind and another; looking at them from up above had fooled me. I spent all afternoon trying to sell them: I didn't dare go home with them. Finally I sold them back to the bastard I bought them from, at a four dollar a hundred loss. I lost twelve hundred dollars right there. During the afternoon I did buy some good steers and arranged to ship them to Henrietta, but that didn't make up for the twelve hundred dollars. It was just gone. I seen right then I was going to have to pay better attention if I was ever going to make a cattleman. Only I just gave up for that day. Losing that money kinda made me sick. I wanted to whip that South Texas bastard, but I didn't have a legitimate reason to. He had skinned me fair and square. It just left a bad taste in my mouth.

About an hour before dark I went through the Exchange building and walked on back to the Longhorn Hotel. It was getting cold agin, and I felt sleepy and lonesome and plumb depressed with the world. Who I really wanted to see right then was Molly, in the worst way. Fort Worth didn't look like a very cheerful place any more. In fact, when I looked at it close, it looked like the dustiest, ugliest place I'd ever seen, except that town in Kansas where the hospital was. I would have given another twelve hundred dollars to have been back home, eating supper with Molly and listening to her talk.

But I wasn't there, and I had lost the money, and that was all there was to it. I sure did feel blue. I went up the stairs to our room, intending to get Johnny up so I could lay down and sleep, but when I opened the door I seen he wasn't there. And it was such a cold lonesome ugly little old bare room that I didn't feel like going to sleep in it, even if I was about to drop. The bed never had nothing on it but a little thin green counterpane anyway, and that wouldn't have kept a midget warm.

So I went back down stairs and out on the street. The street lights were done on, and they made the town look yellow and full of shadows. I figured Johnny was at the nearest honkytonk, but he wasn't; I had to go in eight or ten before I found him. Finally I seen him, way back in a bar, sitting at a table with some old feller I didn't know. They couldn't hardly see one another for the beer bottles stacked in front of them. Then I recognized the feller he was with: I had heard Dad tell about him. His name was Sam, and he was kind of a stockyards beggar, I guess; he had one real leg and one pegleg, and he wore a boot on the peg just like he did on the real foot. In his younger days he had been a cowboy on some big ranch and had got his leg pinched off between two boxcars, loading cattle one day. Johnny looked in high spirits.

"Hello, partner," he said. "Where you been all day? I had me a good nap."

"I stayed out on the yards and traded a little," I said. "Wish I hadn't. A sonofabitch got the best of me and I lost a lot of Dad's money. I don't know what I'm going to do now."

"Drink a beer and don't brood," he said. "Hell, don't never brood. Sam can show us where and we'll go lose our virginity; then we can go home plumb busted."

"I can show you, sonny," Sam said. "Call that waitress over here. I'm strangling of thirst."

The waitress was a big fat woman in a red skirt; she was too ugly to look at if you could help it. I drank a couple of bottles right quick, but they didn't improve my spirits none.

"I wished you'd have come out there," I said to Johnny. "I needed you. What kind of a hand are you, anyway?"

"One with sense," he said. "And I ain't drunk, either, so quit frowning at me. I wouldn't get drunk before you did; it wouldn't be polite. Hell, if I had come out the way I was feeling today, we might have lost everything and really been up shit creek."

"I lost enough for both of us," I said. "Goddamn the luck."

"That's what I say, sonny," Sam said. "Goddamn the luck. I been saying that for years. Call that waitress over here, I could stand a little more beer, couldn't you'all?"

We stood a hell of a lot more of it. I don't guess we left the place till ten or eleven o'clock, and by that time the table top was full of beer bottles and we had set so many on the floor we were practically surrounded. We left a little alley for the waitress to come through, between me and where Sam was laying. He had slid off on the floor and went to sleep earlier in the evening and was stretched out nice and comfortable with his pegleg boot propped up on one rung of the chair. They had tried to drag him out, but me and Johnny made them let him alone. He had so much of our beer in him, me and Johnny felt like we ought to protect him. We would have fought like hell if anybody had grabbed him.

About that time, it was funny as hell: we both drank so much beer we got so we couldn't taste it. I don't know whether it was being tired or what, but it got so it didn't taste like beer, it tasted like real good water. And we were both awful thirsty, so we just kept pouring it down and ever now and then peeing some of it out.

"This is the best damn beerwater I ever drank," Johnny said. "How's yours taste?"

"Fine," I said. "Just fine. It goes down like twelve hundred dollars."

"Quit that damn brooding," he said, standing up all of a sudden. "Let's go to the whorehouse so you won't brood. Let old Sam sleep, we can find it. He don't need no pussy anyhow."

"Let him sleep," I said. "He don't need none."

I got up too, but then I fell down. I guess I stepped on a damn beer bottle; anyway, down I went. I fell right in about a hundred bottles, and Johnny he reached down meaning to help me and he fell too and there we were, rolling around in the bottles. At first I wanted to cuss, but then we both got tickled; it was kind of fun to lay there knocking empty bottles over, and we just sort of rolled and laughed and knocked the bottles every which way till I happened to notice we wasn't inside no more. It was colder and there wasn't any bottles and we were laying behind somebody's damn automobile.

"Hell, they threw us out," I said. "Did they throw you out too?"

He was up on his hands and knees laughing like mad. "Hell yes, can't you see me? They threw us both out."

"Want to go attack them?" I said. "Get back in the bottles?"

"Naw. Let's find the whorehouse."

I had forgot about that. Then the next thing this fat streetcar man was shaking me. "You boys need to sleep, go to a damn hotel," he said. "I've carried you far enough."

We were standing on a brick street, not very far from the courthouse, and the norther was blowing right down the street at us. Brother, it was cold.

"There's the courthouse," Johnny said. "Want to go there?"

"No," I said. "There ain't no whores in the courthouse, you damn fool."

"Might be some in jail," he said.

"I guess so," I said.

Then we ran into a damn drunk and he took us right to the whorehouse. He was so drunk he couldn't walk straight; he walked all over the street.

In the house there was a nice-looking redhead and I was going to be friendliest with her, only when we come in she said, "Here come two cowshits," and that made us so mad we didn't go near her. The carpet was so deep it confused me; my boots didn't make no noise; I thought I was barefoot.

Johnny just about fell over the banister going upstairs.

The girl in my room was blond-headed, and I seen her turning back the counterpane on a big white bed. I watched her do that awhile and then I noticed we were laying on the bed and I didn't have my pants with me, just my socks and shirt. But she didn't have nothing on at all and she was getting out of the bed instead of in it; I seen her big floppy fanny going across the room and then she hiked up one leg and washed herself at a little dishpan of a thing.

"That was real nice, sweetheart," she said. "Now be a darling and help me make up this bed."

"We ain't through already, are we?" I said.

"Why sure, sugar," she said. "Can't you tell by your equipment?"

I wished then I hadn't drunk all that beer. Johnny was done downstairs when I got there and we went out.

"How do you feel?" I said.

"Horny," he said.

"Let's catch that streetcar, I'm about to freeze."

====

Of course we missed the train we was supposed to catch, so the new cattle got to Henrietta about twelve hours earlier than we did. That shrunk them a little. It was dark when we got there; we spent all night and till nine-thirty the next morning driving them home. We kept getting in thickets all night and like to froze to death, too; both of us looked like Ned when we finally got the cattle home and penned. Dad was in the barn loft when we penned them, and he come down and looked them over.

"Well, they ain't the worst cattle I ever seen," he said. "How'd the other cattle sell?"

"Good," I said. "Only I never got home with all the money. I got to cattle-trading and made a little money and let a damn feller skin me and lost all that and twelve hundred dollars besides. Maybe I can work it out in a few years."

I expected him to blow up, but he just kept walking around, inspecting the cattle.

"Got you in a little trading practice, did you?" he said. "Good. You may learn yet."

And he put us right to work, branding the new stock. I was so surprised at Dad that I never even minded the work. Dad was one man I never learned to predict.

8

IT TOOK US till past the middle of November to recuperate from the trip to Fort Worth. Johnny, he swore off beer drinking forever, but his forevers usually just lasted about a week, and this one wasn't no exception. I couldn't enjoy myself much for worrying about when Dad was going to come down on me about the twelve hundred dollars. He just seemed to forget it, and Dad wasn't the kind to forget that much money.

One pretty warm fall day we worked like hell dipping cattle and hadn't much more than got to bed when somebody come riding up to the back gate just a-screaming. I jumped up and grabbed my pants and run out; Dad was down there. It was one of Mabel Peters' little brothers.

"Daddy says come tell you our house is on fire," he said. "Grandma burned it up."

We took his word for it. Dad yanked the kid off the horse and told me to take it and get on over there, he would follow and bring the kid in the wagon. So I grabbed a Levi jacket off the back porch and went.

When I got there it was just a nice campfire left; an old chickenhouse don't take long to burn. The Peterses were all out in the yard, squatting around patting the dogs and crying: it was the only time in my life I ever saw that family all in one place, and I was surprised at how many of them there was. Six kids younger than Mabel, her momma and dad, and her grandma.

"Well, she's gone, Momma," the old man said. "Now we'll just have to trust in the Lord."

The grandma was taking on the worst; she had started the fire. She was about ninety-five. One of the boys said she had sloshed some kerosene out of a lamp onto the tablecloth. Mabel's mother was hysterical because she missed the boy they had sent to our place and thought he was burned up in the fire. There wasn't any fire fighting to do at all, and it was pretty miserable standing there watching the Peterses try to figure out what they had to go on living with. The old man had run out on the back porch and took out the milk strainer; it probably wouldn't have burned anyway. One of the boys had grabbed a Montgomery Ward catalogue and let the Bible burn, and Mabel had brought out a dish of pecans that was sitting on the new chair. The chair was the only new thing in the house, but nobody ever thought of grabbing it, and the two littlest boys had already eaten about half the pecans.

"Well, son," the old man said, coming over to me, "we're burned out."

"Dad's coming," I said. Then I went over and got Mabel and made her squat down close enough to the fire that she could at least keep warm. She was barefoot and never had on very warm clothes.

Pretty soon people that had seen the fire began to come. Dad was the last one there, but he had filled the wagon up with quilts, coffeepots and stuff to eat, so he done the most good once he come. We raked off a little of the fire and made some coffee, and gave each of the Peterses a quilt.

"Ain't it a mess, Gid?" Mabel said. Her teeth were chattering. "Now's when I wish I was married," she said, looking at me; the fire lit up her thin little face. She was pretty as could be in the face.

"If I was married," she said, "it wouldn't be so bad. We could all go over to my husband's house and live."

That about made my teeth chatter. I felt sorry for the Peterses, but nobody would have wanted all them kids and old folks swarming into their house.

"I wisht I'd got the chair," she said, starting to cry again. "Why didn't I get the chair? Instead of the pecans."

Dad told Mr. Peters that if his family would all get in the wagon and wrap up real good in the quilts, I would drive them to Thalia. Mrs. Peters had a sister there, and they could stay with her a day or two, whether they liked it or not.

Everybody went home and Dad caught one of the Peterses' mules and went home himself, and I started down the road to Thalia with the biggest wagonload of sad people you ever saw. A norther had come up; I didn't have on a shirt under my jacket, and like to froze. All the Peterses went to sleep, but about halfway into town Mabel woke up and came up on the seat by me. She let me have a little of her quilt.

"We're much obliged to you, Gid," she said. "You're the nicest one that came tonight.

"Some of these days I'll marry you and make it all up to you," she said. "You see if I don't."

I started to tell her that I didn't want her to get her hopes up, but she squirmed over and kissed me and was like that all the rest of the way to Thalia. I could barely drive. It livened up the ride a whole lot.

"You remember what I said," she said, when we were coming into town. Her face was all white and excited, and neither one of us was particularly cold any more.

I got the job of going in and waking up Mrs. Peters' sister. Everybody else was afraid of the dog, but I beat him off with the wagon whip. When the lights came on all the Peterses climbed out and clobbered into the living room, looking like some Indian nation in all their quilts. The lady took them in, and I got ahold of two quilts and started back. Before I could get off, Mabel ran out and wrapped around me for about ten minutes. "Come and see me," she said. "I'll get awful lonesome in here."

═══

After that, the Peterses had a real hard time of it. The sister kept them a week, and then they moved into the firehouse, and finally ended up back at the place living in their barn. People scraped up for them and gave them preserves and bacon and old clothes and a little money to get started on. But the old man never had the energy to start, and the boy had the energy but not enough sense. They were the poorest folks in the country, and Mabel felt disgraced. Finally they all left but her and went to some little town in Arkansas, where they had kinfolks. Mabel got a job in a grocery store and a room in a widow's house and stayed and tried to make herself well thought of. But she was still the poorest of the poor, and it was a long time before she got over it enough to have any prosperous boy friends.

9

AS MUCH AS I worked around Dad, it looked like I would have been able to figure him out. A man as set in his ways as he was ought to have been more predictable. But he could always keep about a jump ahead of me.

We had three fair rains in October and a damn good slow three-inch rain the second week in November, and all our country looked good. We had more grass than we had cattle for, and it didn't look like it would be too hard a winter. I figured

Dad would stock some more calves; that would have been the logical thing for a cattleman to do. One morning he sent Johnny off to check the water gaps, and told me to hitch up the wagon, we were going to Thalia. That was okay with me.

"Well," he said, once we were started, "I think I'll let you plant a little wheat this year. See what kind of a wheat farmer you are. Thought we'd buy some seed today.

"And don't go getting red in the face," he said. I was. "You ain't got no say-so about it, so just keep your mouth shut. I got the damn toothache this morning anyway."

"A toothache ain't got a damn thing to do with it," I said. "If you ask me."

"I never asked you. What I mean is, I can't stand no long conversation with my tooth hurting this way."

I got all nervous. It's terrible to be in a wagon when you get mad; you can't make it go no faster or anything. You just have to poke along when you feel like whipping and spurring.

"Well, I don't intend to do no farming," I said. "Your tooth can stand that much. You're crazy anyway. We ought to be buying cattle.

"Knock hell out of that mule," he said. "Keep him out of the ditch. He don't need to graze all the time.

"I figure it's gonna get dry," he said. "We've got some dry years coming. We might need this grass next summer more than we need it now, so I ain't gonna stock very heavy. It won't hurt you to try a little farming."

I began to get the Panhandle on my mind when he said that. It would take something drastic to bring Dad to his senses about me. Maybe if I run off for a little while it would do it.

We got to Thalia and got the wheat seed, and while I was loading it and fooling around the feed store trying to bargain with the feller for half a load of cottonseed hulls, Dad went up and got the doctor to pull his tooth for him. It must have had roots plumb down to the collarbone, because Dad spit blood all the way home.

"That was three dollars throwed away," he said. "Next time one wears out you can pull it."

"Okay," I said. "I'll do it for two and a half and save you the trip besides."

"I wish it would quit coming these damn cold northers," he said. "My blood's getting thin."

We didn't say much going home till we got to the place where the road went over Idiot Ridge. When we got there we could see the Taylor place across the long flat on the other hill, and off to the west of us we could see the Peterses' barn.

"Which one of them damn girls do you reckon you'll marry?" Dad said. "We may as well thrash that out while we're thrashing."

He beat all. "Why, I may not marry at all," I said. "I can't see that it's too much of your business, anyway."

"Oh, I guess it is. I was just curious as to which kind of trouble you mean to get yourself into."

"Well, if I marry either one it will damn sure be Molly," I said. "You couldn't get me to marry Mabel with a thirty-thirty."

"That so," he said, spitting. "He said not to, but I think I'll chew a little tobacco. I'm bleeding to death through the head."

So the rest of the way he spit blood and tobacco juice, instead of just blood.

"Okay," he said. "Mabel ain't the kind of girl you want; she's just the kind of girl that wants you. Molly, she don't want you."

"She damn sure does," I said. It made me mad. "What makes you think you know so much about her? Me and her get along real well."

"Oh, of course," he said. "I never meant to say you didn't. But you ain't gonna catch her, and your buddy Johnny ain't either, that's plain as day. And it's a damn good thing. She'd run you ragged if you did."

"How'd we get to talking about this, anyway?" I said. "I may not even marry. But if I do, it'll be Molly."

"Don't make no bets," he said. "And don't be sorry if you don't. If you stay loose from her, she'll make you the best kind of friend you can have. If you do marry her, you'll have ninety-nine kinds of misery. And you remember I told you that. A woman is a wonderful thing, goddamn them, but a man oughtn't to marry one unless he just absolutely has to have some kids. There's no other excuse."

"Well, you married, didn't you? You survived it, didn't you?"

"Yes," he said, "but your mother didn't. And I'm surprised I did. It like to done for us both."

"Anyhow, you're wrong about Molly," I said. "I can tell you that."

He kinda grinned at me. "You might tell me the time of day," he said, "if you had a better watch than mine. That's about all you can tell me. Of course if you marry the Peters girl, that'll be hell too, but at least you won't lost no friend."

"I swear I can't talk to you," I said. "You don't no more know me than the man in the moon. You think you know everything about me and you don't really know a damn thing."

"You're probably right," he said. "Maybe I'll improve." He got tickled at something and set there popping the reins on the mules and laughing to himself for the next mile or two.

"Did you mean you think I ought to marry Mabel instead of Molly?" I said. "I'm just curious."

"Oh no," he said. "I told you already I didn't want you to marry till you were forty or fifty years old. By then you might have enough judgment to marry right. Only I can see already you ain't gonna have enough judgment to last that long. I just mentioned it to see how much you knew about yourself."

"I'm sure you know more about me than I do," I said.

Dad sighed. "People are the hardest animals in the world to raise," he said. "And it's because nobody ever got them to breeding right in the first place."

"You don't breed people," I said.

"No, and it's a damn pity," he said. "I can take me a bull and get him with just the right cows at just the right time, and I won't have to worry much about the calf crop. But the chances of anybody getting the right man anywhere near the right woman are as slim as chances get. That's why I don't mind so bad being old. If I was young agin, I'd probably mess up even worse than I did."

Dad said that in a pretty sad way. It bothered me to hear him.

"That's a pessimistic damn thing to say," I said. "Why, I think life's a damn sight more fun than that."

"You ain't lived one," he said. Then he told me how much work we were going to get done that winter.

10

DAD KEPT ME SO BUSY with one thing and another that it was after the first of December before I got over to Molly's to ask her to go to the Christmas dance with me. One afternoon I got off early, though. Dad decided it was going to come a storm, and he wanted to leave the cattle alone till it was over. Johnny never come to work that day anyway; his old man had kept him home to help him kill their hogs. Dad said he didn't need me, so I saddled up and got my sheepskin coat and rode over to the Taylors'. It was cloudy and cold and looked sleety back in the northwest. I seen a big flock of geese going over. I hated the wintertime; it sure made the cow-work mean.

Molly was hanging out clothes when I rode up. She had on an old red flannel shirt and a pair of overalls and was actually barefooted out in that cold. I guess it was a habit. The Taylor kids hardly ever put on shoes before Christmas, and they had them off agin by Washington's birthday. She looked as pretty as ever. When I walked up she put her hand on the back of my neck, and it was cold from the wet clothes.

"Don't you hope it snows?" she said.

I kissed her right quick and made her let me help her hang up clothes. It was so cold they practically froze while we were getting them over the clothesline. There were scraps of burned tow sack floating around the yard, so I figured the old man had let the windmill freeze and Molly had had to thaw out the pipes.

Molly's cheeks were red and her hair all blowy, but she didn't seem to mind the weather. "Dad said he might kill a goose," she said. "If he does, maybe you can come over and eat some of it."

"Maybe I'll kill one myself," I said. "Let's go inside for a while."

I got the bushel basket the clothes had been in, and she caught me by the hand and led me in the house. The kitchen was nice. It was so warm the windows were fogged over. Molly had made some cookies that morning, and we sat down at the kitchen table and ate them.

"It's about time you came," she said. "I been missing you so much." She reached her foot under the table and kicked me with her toes.

"Dad's been working the daylights out of me. By the time I get loose from him I ain't fit company for a pretty young lady."

"I guess I could stand you," she said. "Ain't these good cookies? I feel so good today now that you showed up."

I pulled my chair around by hers, so we could sit close together. I decided I would start taking more afternoons off.

"Johnny comes by a lot," she said. "He said you'all had a pretty big time in Fort Worth. I wouldn't mind seeing Fort Worth sometimes."

"Maybe we'll go there on our honeymoon," I said.

She looked at me, half-grinning and half-serious; part of what was in her eyes was mischief and part of it wasn't. She had my hand in both of hers.

"I told you about that once," she said. "I don't intend to get married till I'm going to have a baby."

"Oh, now hush," I said. "That's silly. We'll get married by next summer, I don't care what you say."

She shook her head and thought about it to herself for a while, and wouldn't look at me.

"Anyway, don't go getting no black eyes week after next," I said. "We don't want to miss another big dance."

"I'm sorry about that, Gid," she said. "I knew that was why you come over. I already told somebody else I'd go with him."

That knocked a hole in my spirits. But when I thought about it a minute, it didn't surprise me. Johnny rode within two miles of her place every day; it was no wonder he'd asked her.

"Well, I guess he deserves to take you to one dance," I said. "Anyway I'll get to dance with you a lot. Johnny won't care about that."

"Oh, it wasn't Johnny," she said. "He asked me a long time ago. I promised Eddie I wouldn't go to dances with anybody but him any more."

I didn't have no idea what to say to that. I couldn't believe it.

"Are you plumb crazy?" I said. I started to bawl her out, but I seen she was sitting there about ready to cry. I held up.

"Well, has he asked you to this dance?" I said. "I haven't seen him lately. He may not be in this part of the country."

"No." She didn't let herself cry, but her eyes spilled over once. "I guess he's in Oklahoma," she said. "He ain't been here in a month. But I promised him anyway."

"But, sweetheart," I said. "He may not even be back in time for the dance. You don't want to miss it, do you?"

"No," she said. "You know I don't. But he told me not to go unless he was here to take me. So I better not."

"That beats anything in the damn world," I said. "I ought to spank you right here. What kind of a feller is he? That ain't no way to treat a girl." But I hugged her anyway, and her face was all wet against my neck.

"He's not any count," I said. "You know that, Molly."

"Sometimes I wish I hadn't promised him," she said. "But I did. You're my favorite."

We set in the kitchen for a long time, kissing and not talking much. She wouldn't say another word about Eddie or the dance. I didn't care. It was a comfortable time, and I didn't think much about the dance.

"Stay for supper with me," she said. "We butchered the milkpen calf, so we can have beef. Dad may not be coming home today, I don't know."

So I decided to stay, and I meant to make it all night if she'd let me. I milked and done her chores for her and chopped enough wood to last her through the cold spell. I even put my horse in the barn. Then we ate and got real cheerful. We found some popcorn and went in the living room to pop it in the fireplace. The living room was neat, so I knew the old man hadn't been there for a while. When he was around it was always full of junk and whiskey jugs.

"Wouldn't you like to get away from here?" I said. We were sitting on the floor close to the fire. Molly had unbuttoned her shirt a little and I was watching the firelight on her throat and chest.

"Why no," she said. "I couldn't leave here. This is where I intend to live. Anyhow, who'd look after Dad?"

We salted the popcorn and buttered it and ate it, and when Molly kissed me after that she tasted like warm butter and salt; I'll always remember that.

"I sure do like you," she said. "You can come stay with me anytime you want to, you know that, don't you? It doesn't make any difference about the dances."

She lay down with her head in my lap, and I looked down at her.

"I sure do like you too. But it makes a difference to me. You're the one I want and I don't want no other fellers around you."

She grinned and sat up and gave me one of those butter-and-salt kisses. The firelight lit up our faces. And just that minute we heard the back door kick in and the old man stomped into the kitchen. We heard him stamping around trying to get his overshoes off.

It made us both so sad at first we didn't even move. Then we sat up, and by the time he came into the room we were eating popcorn, just as innocent as you please.

"We're in here," she said. "It's Gid and me."

"Oh it is is it?" he said. He turned and went back to the kitchen and we heard him getting a glass out of the cabinet. When he came back he had a glass of whiskey in one hand and his bottle in the other. It was the first time I ever saw him drink out of a glass. He still had on his big sheepskin coat and his old dirty plaid cap, with the earflaps still pulled down over his ears and tied under his chin. He didn't look in too good a mood; it kinda scared me, actually. I kept on eating popcorn.

"Go get some firewood," he said. "It's a goddamn cold night."

I didn't know whether he was talking to me or Molly, but I got up and went to the woodpile and got an armful of wood.

"Put it over here," he said. So I dumped it right by his chair and he took his gloves off and picked out a chunk and leaned over and pitched it in the fire. Sparks and ashes flew everywhere, and Molly had to jump to keep them from getting on her. It made me mad.

"Good way to catch the house on fire," I said. "Let me do it for you, Mr. Taylor."

"Hell no," he said. He sat the glass down on one side of the chair and drank out of the bottle. I never did see him drink out of the glass agin.

"All right," I said. I didn't want no argument with him. "It's dangerous though."

"Danger-rus, my ass," he said, grinning at Molly like he was fixing to tell her some big joke. "This here's my house anyway, if I want to burn it down then by god I'll burn it down. Never asked you nohow. Get on out of here and go home. Who asked you over here in the first place?"

"He's just visiting a little," Molly said. "He ain't doing any harm, Daddy." She said it kinda timidly.

He gave her a hard look. "I never asked you to take up for him," he said. "A little licking wouldn't hurt you, sister. You ain't fixed my supper, so what are you sitting here for?"

She looked hurt and sad: I think she was really scared to death of him and didn't know it herself. She picked up the popcorn bowl and went to the kitchen without saying another thing.

I stood up and put on my coat and went over to the fire to warm my hands a minute.

"Get away from there," he said. "Don't stand between me and the fire, don't you know better than that? A little licking wouldn't hurt you none either, you damn coyote roper."

I didn't see why I needed to take any more off an old surly bastard like him.

"You ain't gonna lick me," I said. "You're too drunk."

He grinned, but it was a pretty mean grin.

"And quit trying to court my girl," he said. "I'd chop her in two with an ax before I'd let a feller like you have her."

"You're so damn tough my teeth chatter," I said. "I'm a good notion to stuff you up this fireplace right now."

That was the first time in my life I ever said anything bad to a person older than I was. It scared me a little, but the old man just took another drink.

"You're a little piss-ant," he said. After that he just stared at the fire, and I left him to his bottle.

Molly was in the kitchen crying and stirring stuff on the stove.

"Don't argue with Daddy agin," she said. "Please don't, Gid. I won't like you any more if you do."

I went up behind her and hugged her. "Yes you will," I said. "I sure hate to go off and leave you tonight, you know that, don't you?"

She turned loose of the frying pan a minute and turned around and kissed me, but we were both uneasy because the old man was so close by.

"You're my girl," I said. "You're the only one I'm ever going to have." I let her go then and started to leave, but she shoved the frying pan off the fire right quick and went out the back door with me, into the cold. And she still didn't have no more clothes on than she had that morning.

"I'll go help you get your horse," she said. "Dad's done forgot about supper, and he won't think of it till I remind him."

I hugged her up against me as close as I could. "What made him so mad?" I said. "I wasn't doing anything wrong."

"Hush," she said. "Don't talk about Dad. I don't want you putting the blame on him."

I shut up, but it still seemed an awful way for a girl's daddy to act.

"I don't think he'll lick me tonight," she said. "He was just talking." Molly was funny. She didn't seem to realize there was much wrong with him licking her.

The wind was singing down off the plains cold as ice, and by the time we got to the barn, Molly was about froze. I made her take my sheepskin while I caught the horse and saddled him. We lit the barn lantern and she held it so I could see what I was doing; even so the barn was mostly shadows and the horse didn't like it. When I got through I set the lantern down and rubbed her hands to get them warm.

"You'll probably take pneumonia," I said. "You ain't got many brains to be so sweet."

She put her cold hands on my neck. "I just came out so you could kiss me goodnight," she said. "It ain't much fun in the kitchen when somebody else is around."

I did, and it was funny: she was so cold on the outside and so warm underneath it all. Molly was always the warmest girl I knew. I blew out the lantern and led her and the horse out into the cold. I put her in the saddle in front of me, where I could hold her. The moon was up, and the little thin cold clouds were whipping across it, going south.

"I'd hate to be the moon," she said.

At the yard gate I got down and helped her off. But I held her up against the horse for a minute, so he could warm her on one side and me on the other.

"Come on to the dance with me," I said. "If Eddie bothers you about it, I'll stop him."

She kissed me for a long time then, and kept changing from one foot to the other. I guess they were about to freeze. Then she pulled back and looked at me.

"You ain't the only kind of good person," she said. "How do you know you're any better than him?"

"The same way you know it," I said. "Only you won't admit it. Come on and go with me."

"I can't, honey," she said. "I'd done promised. But I'm so glad you come over. Come back and see me a lot, Gid."

"You'll see a world of me before it's over," I said. "That's a promise I can make."

She held my hand even after I was on the horse; then we remembered she had on my jacket and she took it off and gave it to me.

"Now get on in before you freeze," I said. "I'll see you pretty soon."

"I wish you could stay," she said. "I hate to see you go off. You're liable to freeze."

But she's the one who would have frozen, if I hadn't turned and ridden off. I don't think she wanted to go back in very bad. I know I sure did hate to leave. I rode off about twenty steps and stopped to button my coat. "Don't get lost," Molly said.

"Go in, honey," I said. "It's awful cold." I guess she just grinned, I don't know. The last time I looked she was still standing there by the fence, with the wind blowing around her.

11

JOHNNY AND ME talked it over and decided we would go to the dance anyway, and not take no girls. Neither one of us wanted to take anybody but Molly.

"Course I might take Mabel home," Johnny said. "If she comes. But I ain't going to take her both ways."

"She won't go home with you," I said. "Mabel's got more pride than that."

Neither of us could understand why Molly would make a promise like that to a no-count like Eddie. But we knew it had to be stopped.

"I think we better whip him," Johnny said. "You and me can fight over her in our own good time."

"Naw, we better not fight him," I said. "That would just make her feel sorry for him. I guess that's why she goes with him anyway. I'll just tell him to stay away from her."

"He won't pay a damn bit of attention to you," he said. "Hell, I don't pay much attention to you myself."

At least it was a pretty night for a Christmas dance, and not too cold. When we crossed Onion Creek we both got the real dancing spirit, and we loped the rest of the way into town. But we sure weren't the first ones there. Half the horses and buggies in the country were hitched outside the dancehall, and there were even quite a few automobiles.

I wanted an automobile myself, but Dad was too tight to buy one. Johnny said he wouldn't have one of the things.

We came in right in the middle of a square dance and didn't have any way to get in on it, so we stood around patting our feet. The hall was nearly full, and the people were stomping and drinking a lot of eggnog and having a real good time.

"There they are," I said.

Molly was dancing in a set just across the floor from us. Her black hair was flying around her shoulders, and she looked her rosiest. Eddie had on his rough-necking boots, so you could hear him all over the hall when his feet hit the floor. He wasn't dressed up or nothing, and he looked like he was already drunk. It made me so damn jealous I could hardly stand still. Once when him and Molly met to do-ce-do he swung down and kissed her big before he went to the next girl; she never seemed to mind. I guess she was having such a big time being away from home that she forgot herself.

"Why do you reckon all these old folks want to get out there and dance?" Johnny said. "It's just making a spectacle of themselves, if you ask me."

I thought so too. The whole town was there. All the little kids were running around screaming and chasing one another and talking about what they were going to get for Christmas; their mommas and poppas weren't paying any attention to them at all. Everybody that could move danced. Fat ones and skinny ones and ugly ones and pretty ones. Of course there were a few bachelors off in the refreshment room, emptying the eggnog bowl and talking about the war, but there wasn't over a dozen of them. I even seen a preacher dance one set, and that was a pretty rare sight.

"I think I'll partake of a little eggnog," Johnny said. "Then we'll see what we can do about Molly."

I let him go. I didn't intend to drink much myself till after the dancing was over. I had a hard enough time dancing as it was.

When the set was over I started across to Molly, but it was crowded on the floor, and of course about fifty people stopped me to shake hands and ask how I was and wish me Merry Christmas and ask how Dad was and how the cattle were and all that, so that they started a round dance before I could get over to her, and Eddie hugged her up and was dancing with her. It made me so mad I could have bitten myself. I didn't see how she could breathe he was holding her so tight.

I was right on the spot when that dance was over, though. Johnny was across the hall, talking to Mabel and some feller she was with. Eddie was grinning and red in the face and his cowlick was falling down in his eyes. He was in an awful good humor.

"Howdy, cowpuncher," he said, "dance with my girl awhile. I got to have me a drink. This dancehall is hot." He handed me Molly's hand and went outside; I guess he had him a bottle somewhere.

"Merry Christmas, Gid," Molly said. "I'm glad you'all finally got here. Guess what? Eddie's bought him a car."

I never asked her the story on it; it made me blue enough just to hear it. It was just the kind of thing that crazy bastard would do. He never owned a shirt in his life that didn't have fifteen patches on it, neither. We found out later he got the car secondhand for forty-five dollars. I guess he made the money roughnecking.

The next one was a round dance too, and we danced real slow. Molly had on a dark blue dress, and she had little tiny shadows under her eyes, like she hadn't been getting enough sleep. Her neck smelled like lavender. But her breath smelled a little like whiskey; I guess Eddie got her to take a drink. I wanted to say a lot of things to her, but she laid her head on my shoulder, and we didn't talk. Then I let Johnny dance one with her; I told him it was his Christmas present. I danced one with Mabel; she talked a blue streak.

After that I got to dance a good square dance with Molly, and that was fun. Eddie come in in the middle of it, but he had to sit down and wait. I figured I would give up on it for the night and get drunk myself. As I was leading Molly off the floor I told her I had her a Christmas present.

"Let me come over and get it," she said. "Dad hasn't been in too good a mood lately."

Eddie grabbed her and hugged her; he was about five degrees drunker than he had been. Johnny was getting drunk too; he spent most of his time with Mabel.

"Old Josh is going to take her home," he said. "I asked. But she said I could come by later and she'd make me some hot choclate. You know how I am about hot choclate."

I went in and took after the eggnog pretty heavy. I liked to sit and listen to fiddle music, so I sat down by the refreshment table and listened to "Sally Goodin," and "Four Little Ladies," and "The Texas Star" and all the others.

Then all of a sudden Molly run in and squatted down by me and whispered in my ear. I seen she was crying.

"Go stop them, Gid," she said. "It's such a nice dance; I don't want them to fight. Eddie gets so mean. Tell Johnny I won't never like him agin if he fights."

"What happened?" I said. "I been drinking too much. Where'd they go?"

"Outside," she said. "Go stop them, Gid."

Most of the people still seemed to be dancing and having a good time. Usually when there was a fight a lot of the men would go out and watch.

"They went off behind the cars," she said.

When I stood up I didn't feel so drunk. "I doubt if I can stop them," I said. "But I'll try."

The cold air felt real good after the dancehall, and my head felt clearer. Sure enough, they were over behind the cars. I guess they had already fought a little, because Johnny had a nosebleed. It didn't mean much; I think his nose bleeds just from excitement. Six or eight of the bachelors were standing around watching; they had turned some car lights on, so everybody could see better.

Eddie had one fist doubled up and his arm drawn back, and Johnny was just standing there watching him; he had his thumbs hooked in his pockets. Johnny was drunk as a bat; they both were.

"You're a damn oil-field hound-running coward," Johnny said. Johnny looked happy about it all; he never minded fighting. But Eddie was serious about it; he kept his fist doubled up. Eddie was a coward, that's why I wouldn't have wanted to fight him; somebody that's scared of you can really be dangerous. Johnny never noticed things like that.

I started to say something to Johnny, but decided not to. They were going to fight anyway. Eddie kept standing there, holding back his fist and sneering that mean sneer of his, and all of a sudden Johnny made a run at him and they went to the ground. Johnny was a quick bastard when he started. They went to rolling and bumping on the ground, each one trying to get a choke hold and neither one doing the other much damage.

"Hell, them boys ain't fighting," a man said. "They're just wallowing on the ground. Get up from there and fight, boys, if you're gonna fight."

They did, and that was Johnny's mistake. Eddie got him off balance and knocked him down and went to pounding on him. Then Johnny nearly got up agin and Eddie jumped on him and began to pound him against an automobile.

"Now that's fighting," the feller said.

I was getting nervous. It looked like we were going to be disgraced. Johnny couldn't get his balance, and Eddie kept pouring it on. Finally he got Johnny down agin, only he didn't go down with him. He stood back with his fist doubled up. I guess he thought he had won, because he kinda laughed.

"You goddamn cowpunchers, you can't fight," he said. "Hell, it takes a rough-neck to fight."

And that was Eddie's mistake, thinking Johnny McCloud would quit fighting just because he was beat on a little. I knew damn well Johnny wasn't done with the fight because his eyes were open; Johnny never quit nothing while he still had his eyes open. I guess he was resting. Eddie sneered and Johnny come up and stayed up. Eddie tried to kick him back down, but Johnny got the leg and set Eddie down himself. And while he had his leg he managed to yank off one of the roughneck-ing boots and he threw it out in the darkness as far as he could throw. Then he run Eddie against an automobile. They were out of the light then; I don't know exactly what happened. Somehow Johnny got Eddie up on the hood of a car and shoved him clear off on the other side. He ran around the car right quick and we did too, but the show was over. Eddie was holding his neck and spiting and wouldn't get up or say anything; I think he had bitten his tongue when he hit. Besides the sher-iff came out about that time.

"These boys ain't hurting one another, are they?" he said.

"Naw, they're just fighting, Gus," a feller said. "I guess they're about done."

Eddie stood up, but him and Johnny were both too tired to say much. I motioned at Johnny to keep quiet but he didn't see me. The sheriff didn't mind fighting, but he couldn't stand nasty talking.

"So you leave her alone," Johnny said. "You horse's butt you."

Eddie walked off to look for his shoe, and the sheriff turned around and took hold of Johnny's arm.

"I don't like that filthy language," the sheriff said. "Who started this fight anyway?"

"I did, by god," Johnny said. "And by god I finished it, too. And I'd whip you too if you didn't have that damn badge on."

That was just the kind of crazy thing Johnny would say. The sheriff started off with him. "Taking the Lord's name in vain is one thing I won't stand for," he said. "Not even at Christmastime. What if a lady had heard you say that?" And off they went.

"Don't think that Gus won't arrest them," the feller said. "He won't stand for no goddamn cussing, and I don't blame him."

"No, but you know something," another feller said, "he'll never get elected in this damn county agin. That's just how goddamn sorry people are getting."

I danced a round dance with Molly and told her it was okay.

"They wasn't neither one hurt," I said. "Eddie will be back when he finds his shoe. I guess I better take Johnny's horse up to the jail and see if I can talk the sheriff into letting him out."

Molly felt a little better when she was satisfied there was nobody killed.

"I wish I could take you home," I said. "Even if he has got an automobile."

"It makes me mad the way you talk about Eddie," she said. "Working in the oil field ain't no crime, is it?"

"No, and you're too sweet to argue with." We walked off the floor and I got my coat.

"I hope they let Johnny go," she said. "Tell him to come and see me when he can. I'm sorry he got in trouble on my account."

She wouldn't go outside with me, even for a minute—afraid she would bump into Eddie, I guess—but I made her promise to come over and help us with the hog-killing, the next week. I figured I could give her her Christmas present then. I sure did hate to leave her at the dance.

===

The sheriff of course wouldn't let Johnny go. I guess Johnny cussed him all the way to the jail. He was a funny sheriff. He never got mad and he never got tickled, either.

"That boy talks too nasty," he said. "I ain't gonna have that nasty talk around where there's ladies. Why, that would be a disgrace to the county."

"I know it," I said. I thought I better agree with him. "If you'll let me have him, I'll take him out of town quick, so there won't be no danger."

"No, I'll keep him tonight," he said. "Just put his horse in the barn. Be a good lesson to a boy like that. Besides, I want to give him a good talking to before I let him go, and he's done asleep."

So I went on home, eighteen miles by myself.

12

THE WEDNESDAY before Christmas, Dad decided it would be a good time to kill the hogs. We had four big shoats to butcher; more hog meat than me and Dad could have eaten in two years. Dad had done made arrangements to sell three of the carcasses, though; the fellers he sold them to came over to help us. Dad had gone over special and asked Molly to come cook for the crew, and Johnny was there, of course, mostly just getting in the way. When you took Johnny off of his horse he was the worst hand in the world.

Me and him did the actual killing, shooting, and sticking, while Dad and the other men built the fires and got the water ready. Dad, he wouldn't have wallowed around in the hogpen mud for half the pork in Texas. Johnny worked the gun and I worked the butcher knife, and we laid them low. Then we got our horses and drug the carcasses up to the fire one at a time.

Johnny bitched around so much while we were scraping the carcasses that Dad finally sent him off down in the River pasture to drive in a yearling he thought was getting sick. Actually Dad must have liked Johnny; he let him get away with a damn sight more than I ever got away with.

About nine-thirty Molly come riding up; she had on her red mackinaw. Just seeing her made me feel so good I could have jumped six feet. I never realized how lonesome I stayed till I got close to Molly. Not even then. When I realized it was when I had been close to her and one of us was leaving. Then for a day or two the world would look twice as bad as it really was.

I took her down to the barn and put her horse where ours wouldn't kick hell out of him. I got her back in the hallway, out of sight, and gave her a kiss.

"Silly," she said. "Who ever heard of kissing in the morning?"

She wouldn't let me hold her hand when we got outside because she was afraid everybody would tease us. She was right; they would have.

It was a good day. We got the hogs butchered without no trouble, and Molly cooked a big dinner and everybody enjoyed it and complimented her on it, and that made her feel good. Johnny even made it back in time to eat; for once he showed pretty good manners. In the afternoon we made soap and cracklins and the other fellers loaded their pork and went home. It was nearly suppertime before we got all the kettles cleaned, so Molly decided to stay and fix supper, too. Johnny went on home. Dad gave him a quarter of pork for a Christmas bonus and he told us all Merry Christmas and went off with it tied to his saddle. Watching him leave made me blue for a minute; it was strange. I knew right then he'd never get Molly to marry him, only for a minute I wished he could have. It would have been nice for him if he could have.

"Well, we done a good day's work," Dad said. "Let's go inside where it's warm. I could stand some supper."

We went in and the kitchen was nice and warm. The lamps were lit. Me and Dad sat at the table and watched Molly working around the sink and around the stove, not paying us much mind; it was a treat for us just to watch. Me and Dad had batched for nine years, and we thought we got along pretty well, but having Molly in the kitchen eating supper made the way we usually done it seem pretty flat and dull. The house was just so much fuller with her in it. I guess Dad felt it too.

"Sure do appreciate your coming over to cook," he said. "This here'll beat Christmas."

Molly turned and looked at him a minute; she had a pan of biscuits in one hand and a gravy bowl in the other, and I don't think she even heard him. She just smiled and went on cooking, and Dad never repeated it. He was looking too tired, Dad was. He hadn't been feeling too good. I didn't think. Course he never said a word about it.

Molly fed us beef and beans and biscuits and gravy and pie, and we ate plenty of it. I couldn't take my eyes off her, and I couldn't keep from wishing I could get her to marry me. Then we could have her around all the time. She sat down at the other end of the table and drank her coffee, not saying anything but perfectly content. We were all quiet, but it was a real easy quiet.

Finally Dad got up and said he had to go to bed. He offered to pay Molly something, but of course she wouldn't take nothing. So he gave her a quarter of pork and some cracklins and told me to ride home with her to see that she got there all right.

Then it was just me and her in the kitchen.

"Let's go over to my house, Gid," she said. "Dad's gone to Wichita. You and him won't bother one another tonight."

"Okay," I said.

When we got there we built up the fire in the fireplace and sat in front of it a long time. I gave Molly her Christmas present, but I wouldn't let her open it, and we sat there not talking much or kissing much or anything, just resting together. Then she leaned forward and took some pins loose and shook down her long hair and lay back against me so the firelight shone on her face and eyes and mouth. I was half-sick, I loved her so much and was so excited by her. In a minute I was all wrapped around her. She wanted to go in the bedroom, and pulled her shirttail out as we went down the hall. It was cold as ice until we had been under the covers for a while, and then it got toasty warm and only Molly's fingers were cold. And there wasn't no old man to worry about, so we could go ahead. Only I was so excited about her I didn't do no good; I don't guess I knew enough about what I was doing.

"Oh hell," I said. "Dammit. I wouldn't blame you for marrying somebody else."

"Be still and hush," she said, and kissed me.

"I don't see why you put up with me," I said.

"You're my favorite," she said. "You ain't done nothing wrong. You just enjoy me a whole lot, I can tell that. And that's what I want you to do. Go to sleep, sugar."

And I did: it was the best sleeping in the world. When I woke up I could hardly believe I'd slept so good. Molly was still asleep and I was holding her. It was pure enjoyment. Finally I woke her up because having her asleep made me feel lonesome. We hugged and talked awhile. But she wouldn't say she'd marry me.

"That would be wrong," she said. "I don't love you that way." And then she leaned over and looked me right in the face, with her hair touching my chest. "But you love me that way, don't you?" she said, as if she had never thought of it before. "You do love me that way, Gid," she said. "That's going to be so sad. I don't love anybody that way." And she lay with her face tucked into my neck a long time, so I could feel her breath on my Adam's apple.

About daybreak we got up and had a real good breakfast and were cheerful as we'd ever been. I went home and worked and was all right that day. But the next day when I woke up I was so lonesome for her I was sick. All I could see that day was her face leaning over me, and her hair.

13

IT DIDN'T SEEM like I was going to be able to stand not having Molly around more of the time. Every time I thought about her I got bluer and bluer. And if that wasn't trouble enough, Dad had me farming. It was a warm January and looked like it was going to be warm all winter. Johnny was doing most of the cow-work, and Dad was just mostly piddling around; he still wasn't feeling good. So for four days in a row I had to go down and follow them worthless mules around that worthless field, thinking about Molly all the time and wondering when I'd get to see her.

Then one Monday about the middle of the morning Johnny come through the field on his way to the League pasture. He was jogging along looking pretty discouraged, and I waved at him to come over. I was tired of kicking clods around anyway, and he got off his horse and we set by the plow awhile.

"Don't you get tired of this?" he said.

"Naw, I love it," I said. "I'd like to do this for the rest of my life. What are you so down in the dumps about?"

"Oh, Molly, I guess. I wish I wasn't so damn sweet on her. Hell, I oughtn't to be. She don't care nothing about me. At least not like I want her to. She just ain't got no sense."

"She's got the wrong kind of sense," I said. "Anyhow, what's she done now?"

"Nothing she hasn't done before," he said, looking real sour. "I rode all the way over there to visit her last night and the first thing I saw was Eddie's damn automobile. I never even went in."

"See 'em?"

"I looked through the kitchen window. He was sitting there eating vinegar cobbler and she was waiting on him just like he owned the place."

That made me plain sick. We sat there for about ten minutes, neither one of us saying a word. I couldn't think of one hopeful thing.

"Shit on the world," I said. "Let's go someplace. I'll be damned if I'll plow my legs off while she cooks cobbler for somebody like Eddie. Let's just go to the Panhandle and show them all."

"All right," he said. "You going to leave the plow here?"

==

I did. I rode in on one mule and unharnessed. Dad was up at the house, sitting by the fireplace trying to shave a corn off his toe. He looked pretty tired, but I wasn't in no mood to sympathize.

"Dad," I said, "things are just going wrong. I've had enough of this country. Me and Johnny are going up on the plains for a little while. I hope you can hire you a little help."

676

"Going, are you?" he said. "That oil-fielder running you off?"

"Not by a damn sight," I said. "I'm sorry to leave you."

"Oh, I guess I can do the work," he said. "I always have."

I seen he wasn't gonna act nice, so I didn't say any more to him.

"Let me hear from you now and then," was the last thing he said.

So we rode to Henrietta that night and arranged with an old boy to take the horses back to Archer County for us. We got good and drunk, and along about midnight we caught the train north. Our spirits weren't too good, but we were the only passengers, and we each got a bench and went to sleep. I dreamed that Dad was out terracing in the moonlight. When I woke up Johnny was still asleep and I had a headache, so I went out on the porch of the caboose. I guess we were about to Childress then; anyhow we were on the plains. The cold air kind of cleared my head. It was exciting to see all that country stretched out around me, but I felt pretty sad, too. I was split: I was glad to be where I was, and yet I wanted to be where I had just left. Looking down the rails, I couldn't help but think of the people at home, Dad and Molly mostly.

Thinking about them, I got lonesome, and went in and woke Johnny up. We stayed awake the rest of the night, talking about all the different big outfits we could work for. It would be the JAs most likely, or maybe the Matadors, depending on where we decided to go from Amarillo. We had about fifteen dollars apiece, cash money, and our saddles and saddle blankets, so we felt pretty well off.

We got off the train at the big brick station in Amarillo, and it was like getting off at the North Pole. The wind whistled down those big streets like the town belonged to it, and the people were just renters it was letting stay.

"Goddamn," Johnny said. "I never realized it was this cold up north in the wintertime."

We got a hotel room and decided to take the day to look around. Only the hotel room was so toasty and warm we stretched out and slept till almost six o'clock. When we went outside the lights were on and the streets were plumb empty, like the wind had blown everybody away. We found some saloons, though, and the people were in them.

"Let's celebrate before we go to work," I said.

He was agreeable, and boy did we celebrate. I wished we'd eaten supper first. I guess around home we never drank enough to keep in shape. We found some girls, too, even if they wasn't no raving beauties. We would have kept them for the night but they said our hotel was too respectable for them. They wouldn't take us to their places, so we went back to the saloons and drank some more and did without.

When we finally got back to the room we agreed we'd have to get up at four o'clock and look for a job. Boy, it was a bad night. If the hotel hadn't had a bathtub, we would have ruined the place. I brought up a good gallon, myself, before morning, and I wasn't nothing to Johnny. He made twice as many trips as I did. About the time it got light I seen him on his way to the bathroom agin, only he was crawling.

"What are you doing crawling?" I said. "Can't you even walk?"

"I might could," he said, and crawled on in anyway. I thought that was pretty funny.

"Hell, I can at least walk," I said. He was in asleep on the bathroom floor.

We never made it up at four, but we did get downstairs by about six-thirty. I had got emptied out and was feeling okay, but Johnny wasn't. I made him eat some breakfast, though, and he kept it down.

"That'll make you good as new," I said.

"I'll never be that good agin," he said.

By the time we got our hotel bills paid it was after sunup. The wind was still cold as ice.

"How much money you got?" I said.

"Oh, few dollars," he said. "Enough to last."

But, by god, when we counted, we had three dollars between us. Where the rest of it went I'll never know.

"We better go to Clarendon," he said. "That's the place to get jobs. Hell, we'll be broke by supper."

So we got railroad tickets to Clarendon; they cost a dollar apiece. Johnny went to sleep right off, but I sat up and looked out the window. That old plains country sure did look cold and gray to me, and I wasn't so sure I liked it. We ought to have waited till springtime to leave home. But still, it was a good feeling to be loose like we were; it was a kind of adventure, in a way, and it didn't too much matter about the cold. It mattered more about Molly and Dad. I was just glad Johnny was along. It wouldn't have been much fun by myself. I couldn't figure out what had happened to all our money.

They put us off in Clarendon about one o'clock. Johnny was all refreshed, and we turned up our collars and went walking down the street to see the town. It would have been a nice walk if it hadn't been for carrying the saddles.

I guess we were lucky; the first thing we struck was a horse auction. They were auctioning off a couple of hundred broncs some fellers had driven in from New Mexico. A lot of cattlemen were there. After we watched the bidding awhile we saw a funny-looking old man who didn't look like he could be very important, so we asked him if he knew where two cowpunchers could get a job. He was pretty friendly.

"You boys cowpunchers?" he said. "What else can you do? Can either one of you ride broncs?" He was a grizzly old feller and didn't have but half an ear on one side of his head.

"Both of us can," Johnny said. Which was a damn lie; he couldn't ride a bronc if all four of its feet were hobbled. He was an awful good hand on a horse, but he wasn't no hand to make a horse, so I contradicted him.

"I can ride broncs and he can do everything else," I said.

"My name's Grinsom," he said. "I could use a couple of hands myself. I'm gonna have a bunch of horses to drive home when this is over, and then somebody's gonna have to break them, I damn sure ain't. You boys come along and I'll try you for a week. I'll give you a dollar apiece to give these broncs a good ride, and if we get along with one another it'll be fifteen a month and bunk and board. That suit you?"

It didn't seem no great amount of money to me, and I couldn't figure a little dried-up feller like Mr. Grinsom owning much of a ranch, but Johnny thought it was fine, so we hired on. It turned out Mr. Grinsom owned thirty-eight thousand acres. He bought nineteen broncs and offered me and Johnny our pick of them to ride to the ranch.

Since Johnny had spoke up about being a bronc rider, that was pretty funny. He got throwed four times on the way to the ranch. I only got thrown once, and that was an accident. I was looking around and not paying enough attention to what I was doing.

"You ain't gonna break no broncs that way," Mr. Grinsom said to him, after the fourth buck-off.

Johnny was about half-crippled by then, and too mad to lie. "Hell no, I ain't no damn bronc rider," he said. "Gid can break these horses; he likes that kind of stuff. I'm a cowboy. I like to ride a horse that already knows something, so I can get work done. You keep me a week, and if I don't turn out to be the best hand you got by then, why by god just fire me."

Mr. Grinsom got tickled. He had pretty much of a sense of humor, at least about some things.

"My boys may give you a little competition," he said.

===

It turned out he really meant *his* boys, too. He had a big fat good-natured wife and seven grown sons. He had two hired hands, too, but he never worked them half as hard as he worked his own boys. All the boys' names started with J: Jimmy, Johnny, Jerry, Joe, Jakey, Jay, and Jordman. I never could tell them apart, but they were nice enough old boys. They had a great big bunkhouse, and me and Johnny and the two hired hands and the seven boys all slept in it. We ate supper at the big house, and Mrs. Grinsom explained to us that after they'd had the fourth boy it had got too noisy in the house and they'd put them out in the bunkhouse with the cowboys when they got big enough to get around. I don't know where all the noise went; the only words I ever heard them say were: "Thank you for the supper, Momma, it sure was good." Each one of them said that to Mrs. Grinsom after their meals.

Me and Johnny thought it was a pretty strange family. But the other two cowboys, one's name was Ed and the other's name was Malonus, they *really* thought so. They were so glad to have new hands around that wasn't in the family that they just about hugged us.

===

The next morning the old man asked me if I really wanted to break the horses. I said for a dollar apiece, like he offered, I'd give them a good first ride.

"How many do you want to ride a day?" he said.

"Oh, I ought to be done with them by three o'clock," I said. "There ain't but eighteen left. I rode one yesterday."

He acted like he didn't believe me. He sent Johnny off with the boys and the other hands and stayed around the lots all day, doing little chores and watching me out of the corner of his eye.

I didn't care. I felt real good that morning. The cold didn't even bother me. I made a good strong hackamore and went after them broncs. By dinnertime I only liked six being done with them, and I got the six in another three hours. I even saddled up a few of the worst ones and rode them agin, just so the old man would really get his money's worth. By that time he was sitting on the fence. I bet he chewed a whole plug of tobacco that afternoon. When I got done and turned them out in the horse pasture, he walked off to the house without saying a word. But I didn't care about that, either. I had been throwed seven times and was stiff and sore as hell, but I felt like a million dollars. I felt like I could have ridden fifty horses if I'd just had somebody to do the saddling for me.

That night the old man did a strange thing. He paid me at the supper table.

"By god," he said, after supper. "Now, Mother, make these boys be quiet." None of the boys had made a sound anyway. "I want you all to notice," he said. "This here's one feller that can do the job. He rode eighteen wild horses today, I seen him myself. And one yesterday." I was real embarrassed. The old man got up and stomped off to the bedroom and came back jingling a sack full of money. "I'll pay you right here," he said. "It might put some ambition into these boys of mine." And he counted me out nineteen dollars, mostly in silver money. There wasn't a sound in the room but the money clinking. Even after I gathered it up and put it in my pockets, there still wasn't a sound. Later that night Ed told me the old man never paid the boys atall, just give them a dollar apiece at Christmastime. That didn't surprise me much. Mr. Grinsom wasn't the first tight feller I'd ever seen.

We worked pretty good for about a week. Me and Johnny never had no trouble matching the other hands; by the time the week was over Johnny wasn't in no danger of getting fired. The old man was funny. He treated us like friends and his own boys like hound dogs.

But there were two things I couldn't get over: one was making nineteen dollars in one day, and the other was being homesick. If I could make nineteen dollars in one day, I was stupid to work a whole month for fifteen. And besides, I remembered the time in Fort Worth when I'd made four hundred in about two hours. Cowboying was fun, but it wasn't near enough fun to make fifteen dollars a month worth while. I knew I could beat that.

The homesickness was the worst part of it, though. I didn't mind the work, and I didn't mind the company; I didn't mind the country, or even the cold weather. I just minded feeling like I wasn't where I belonged. Home was where I belonged, but tell that to Johnny and he would have laughed like hell. He didn't feel like he belonged to any certain place, and I did. He was born not five miles from where I was, too. When you came right down to it, Dad was right: me and him was a lot different. I couldn't get over thinking about Dad and Molly and the country and the ranch, the things I knew. The things that were mine. It wasn't that I liked being in Archer County so much—sometimes I hated it. But I was just tied up with it; whatever happened there was happening to me, even if I wasn't there to see it. The country might not be very nice and the people might be onery; but it was my country and my people, and no other country was; no other people, either. You do better staying with what's your own, even if it's hard. Johnny carried his with him; I didn't. If you don't stick with a place, you don't have it very long.

Me and Johnny argued for ten days. I just plain wanted to go back, and he just plain didn't. I got so I couldn't sleep; I would wake up and lie awake for hours. Then one Saturday, Johnny was in Clarendon and run into a man who had a ranch out near the New Mexico line; he wanted a cowboy or two to look after it through the winter; it was so dull he couldn't stand the winter there himself. He offered double what we were getting, and said besides he had a pretty little Indian woman who would stay out and do the cooking. So Johnny hired on for both of us, but he told the man we had two more weeks to go for Grinsom. I told him right off I wasn't going any farther west or north, but he thought I'd change my mind. Then on a Tuesday, Mr. Grinsom sent us out in one of his big pastures to look for sicklings—that was all he had for us to do—and I just decided I was through. I pulled up and stopped.

"Hell with it," I said. "I'm going to Archer County. There ain't no use in me loafing around here any longer."

We turned our backs to the wind and watched it whipping across the high open flats. He tried to talk me out of it. "Don't do nothing rash," he said. "Wait till we get on the new job. Think of that Indian woman."

"You go on out there," I said. "I don't want to spend no winter in New Mexico. What would I want with an Indian woman when Molly's just three miles from home?"

"Yes, but Molly's crazy," he said.

"I never stopped to argue," I said. "You coming or staying?"

He hunched his neck down into his collar and frowned. "I hate to see you miss a good winter," he said. "What'll I do for company if that woman don't talk English?"

But he was staying. "There ain't as much at home for me as there is for you," he said. "This here's more the life for me."

And I was crazy enough to want to stay with him, even when I knew I was going home. We were pretty good buddies.

"Well, I hate to run off and leave you," I said. "But I got to go. You'll be coming home next summer, won't you?"

"Oh sure," he said. "I just don't feel like going that direction right now, Gid. I hate to be stuck off out here with no company, though."

"Well, write me once in a while," I said. "I believe I'll lope on back. I might could get to Amarillo tonight."

"Say hello to the country for me," he said. "Give old Molly a big kiss and tell her she's still my girl."

"I'll sure do it," I said. "Don't let no crazy horse fall on you."

"Oh hell," he said. "Won't nothing hurt me unless I freeze to death. You watch out yourself."

I guess we should have shook hands, but we never. He kinda nodded, and turned and tucked his head down and trotted off into the wind, headed north. I set there a minute, watching him cross the windy pasture. Then I loped back to the ranch, gave notice, and talked the old man into loaning me a horse to ride to Clarendon.

"Why you running off?" he said. "To dull? I may buy some more broncs in a week or two."

"Oh no," I said. "I just guess I'll go run my own ranch."

It was a pretty lonesome trip home. I had to wait till way after dark for a train out of Clarendon, and was the only one on it, then, so I didn't have a soul to talk to. I never slept a wink all night, I was too excited about going home. Only I wisht old Johnny had come; train riding was dull without him. I got off in Wichita Falls about ten the next morning and found a man with a wagon going to Thalia. We drove in about an hour before dark, and the first person I saw was Mabel Peters, coming out of the dry goods store where she worked.

"Why, if it ain't Gid," she said. She had put on a little flesh and was dressed nice and looked real cheerful. In spite of all I could do, she made me go home and have supper with her at the boardinghouse. All the boarders were there, so she didn't dare ask me up to her room, but she followed me out on the porch after supper and hung on to me for an hour, she was so glad to see me. She asked me four or five times if I would come back and see her.

It was so late when I left Mabel that I had trouble finding anybody to borrow a horse from, but I finally got one and rode home. I was practically sick at my stomach I was so glad to be going home. It was good to ride over some familiar country. I even went by Molly's, but there wasn't no light; I sat on my horse by the back fence a minute, thinking about her.

Our place was dark too. When I got in the first thing I did was tiptoe down the hall to Dad's door, to listen a minute. He was snoring like he always did. Once I heard him cough and hawrk. I was glad he was asleep. I guess I was afraid I would find him out in the moonlight, plowing that old oat field.

14

THE MORNING AFTER I got home I remember Dad came in my room real early, but he never woke me up. I was about half-awake and I seen him standing inside the door. But I guess he figured I needed the rest, because he went on out and I stayed in bed till nine o'clock.

When I finally got dressed and outside he was down at the lots filling up the hayracks. It was a cold morning, with a big frost on the ground.

"Well, how's the Panhandle?" he said. "I guess you got rich quicker than I thought you would, or else you went broke quicker. Which was it?"

"Aw, I just got homesick," I said. "How's ever thing here?"

"Run down and wore out," he said. "Specially me. Why don't you get the horses up? A couple of them need their shoes pulled off, and I ain't had the energy."

Dad sure looked bad. He hadn't hired no help at all; I knew he wouldn't. But he wasn't lying when he said he was worn out. He didn't have much flesh on him any more, and he had been a big fleshy man. When I first got home I thought it was from working too hard, but it wasn't. He was just sick; he didn't have no wind any more, nor much grip in his hands. But he wouldn't go to a doctor for love nor money.

I felt real bad about having gone off and left him so long. I know it wouldn't have made any difference to his health if I had stayed, but it would have made some difference to me.

"Hell, you ought to go see a doctor, Dad," I told him. "You probably just need some kind of pep-up medicine. Why do you want to be so contrary?"

"I ain't contrary," he said. "I just don't want to pay no doctor to tell me what I already know. There ain't no medicine for old age."

"You're just tight," I said. "You oughtn't to let a few dollars stand between you and your health."

"I am tight," he said. "I'm rich, too."

"You don't live like it," I said.

"No, because I want to stay rich. The best way in the world to get poor is to start living rich."

I couldn't do a damn thing with him. He kept on working, day in and day out, warm or cold. And the thing was he wasn't much help any more, only he didn't seem to notice it. I was doing nine-tenths of the work, and it kept me busy and worn out and tired. It was just miserable old hard cold work, no fun to it, like loading cake and hay and feeding cattle and building fence and all kinds of winter work like that. I'd been home three weeks before I ever seen Molly.

But then she come over to see me one day and cooked us supper, and I guess she seen right off how Dad was. I think it worried her, but she was real cheerful that day and never mentioned it to me. But she started coming over two or three times a week and cooking for us. Sometimes she even got there in time to ride a pasture with me, or help me with the chores. It was real good of her to come; I was crazier about her than I had ever been. I was pretty lonesome anyway, and worn out and worried about Dad, and it was awful nice to have somebody warm like Molly to be with once in a while. But no matter what I said or how I said it, she wouldn't marry me.

"I know you want me to, Gid," she said. "But it might be bad if I did. You might be sorry you ever asked me," she said.

"That ain't true," I said. "I wouldn't be."

She thought a minute, and grinned, but a sad grin. "Then I might be," she said. "That would be just as bad."

One night after Dad had gone upstairs to bed we sat by the fireplace awhile, and we got to talking about him. Molly was the best person there ever was for sitting by the fire with. Every time she came over we got off by ourselves a little while, and those were about the only times I got unwound.

"You better make him go to the doctor," she said. "If you don't, I think he's going to get real sick."

"He's too damn contrary," I said. "He just won't go."

"Don't talk bad about him," she said. "He's a real good man. He treats me better than anybody I know, you included." I don't know what that had to do with it, but it was true. Dad always let Molly know he thought she was about tops.

"I don't reckon he'll die," I said. "You don't, do you?"

She hugged me then. "He might, Gid," she said. "He's just getting sicker and sicker."

I thought that over for a while and it really scared me. I couldn't imagine Dad not being around to give the orders. Even sick he was just as active as he could be, and never missed a thing. It was hard to think of Dad being any other way than alive.

"Dad couldn't keep still long enough to die," I said. Neither one of us thought it was funny, though.

"I sure am glad my dad's healthy," she said. "I guess he'll live to be a hundred. If he was to die, I think I'd just plain go crazy."

"I don't guess anybody lasts forever," I said. "Funny thing, I've always been sure Dad would outlive me. I just never thought of it any other way."

We sat for a long time, thinking about it. But I couldn't believe it would happen. I guess I knew it had to sometime, but I just couldn't believe it. Not even in my brain.

"Well, if he'd just quit working and set around and rest up a little," I said. "I think he'd get all right. He stays on the go too much."

She shook her head. "That ain't his trouble. I think that's good for him. If your dad had to die, I'd want him to do it working, wouldn't you? Just to go on working till it happens. That's all he loves to do. If he was to sit around in a rocking chair, he'd get to feeling useless, and that'd be worse than being tired."

I kissed her and we sat on the couch for another hour or so. I meant to ride her home, but I was too tired, and she wouldn't let me.

"Much obliged," I said. "Come back whenever you can. We sure are glad to see you."

"Why, I enjoy it, Gid," she said. "Next time Dad goes off I'll come over." When she rode off into the wind it reminded me of Johnny, up there on the plains. I missed having him around.

Life is just a hard, mean business, sometimes. Here we were worrying about my dad, and three days after we had that conversation Molly's own dad staggered into his smokehouse drunk, looking for some whiskey, and picked up a jug of lye by mistake and drank a big swallow of it and it killed him. He never even got out of the smokehouse. Eddie and one of his cronies was over there at the time; he had been drinking with the old man, and he went out and found him. It was a windy, dusty evening. And the first thing Molly said to me when I got there was, "Well, Gid, my poor old daddy never lived to be a hundred after all." And she just about did go crazy that night.

It was the end of any respect I ever had for Eddie White. I guess he was just scared of dead people. Anyhow he sent his damn oil-field crony over in the car to tell us. Dad had gone to bed, and I didn't wake him. I left a note on the kitchen table, where he'd see it in the morning. And then I saddled up and got over there on the run, and when I got there Eddie and his buddie were just driving away. I don't know where they were going in such a hurry, but they left Molly by herself with her dad, and there wasn't no excuse for that, drunk or not. I rushed in and she was in the kitchen, bawling her head off—she didn't even know Eddie was gone; the old man was dumped on a bed in his bedroom, with just a quilt thrown over him. I never mentioned Eddie and she never either; maybe she was so torn up she forgot he had been there.

She wanted me to do something for her daddy, clean him up a little; but she didn't want to go in the room with me and I didn't want to leave her by herself for fear she'd get to taking on agin. I made her drink some coffee, and I got a towel and wiped her face and kinda dried her eyes, and then we washed the dishes. There was a lot to wash; I guess she had cooked supper for Eddie and his friend. Washing them calmed her down some. When we had the kitchen good and clean I made her hold the lamp while I went in and straightened the old man out the best I could. He looked terrible, and I didn't know a thing about what I was doing, but I got his boots off anyway, and got him wiped up some and laid out and covered up neater than he had been. It was a mistake for Molly to come; it made her sick at her stomach. She vomited in the bedroom first, and then I carried her to the bathroom and held her head while she finished emptying her stomach. She was awfully white and shaky. I walked her down to the bedroom and made her take her clothes off and put her nightgown on and get in bed, and she laid there and cried while I went back and cleaned up in the bathroom and the other bedroom. Then I left the lamp on the kitchen table and got in bed with her. She thought some people might come; she thought Eddie must have gone to tell some, when she remembered him. But I didn't expect him to tell a soul that night, and he didn't.

"But what will I do, Gid?" she said. "You know I can't do without Dad."

"Hush, sugar," I said. "Let me just hug you tight. Let's don't talk for a while."

And I did hold her. For maybe half an hour her eyes were wide open and she was stiff in the bed, but then she got warm and relaxed and her eyes shut and she was asleep. I stayed awake just about all night, holding her, and she never moved or turned over till morning. She was lucky to be able to sleep, I thought. She was so helpless, in a way. And when it got light and she woke up I was watching her and still holding her. I saw just as plain as day when she remembered what had happened, and I thought she would get bad again, but she never. She looked real serious and then she pulled my head down and kissed me and got up and put up her hair standing by the bed, and she never cried at all until later that morning, when Dad and the other people begin to come.

15

DAD FINALLY DID go to a doctor, in fact he went to five of them, but he had been right all along. They never done him no good. One of them kept him in the hospital for two weeks, though, and that threw ever bit of the ranch work on me. It was around the first of April before I got Johnny off a letter, and then I never said much.

DEAR JONATHAN:

I know you love that name so much I thought I would just use it on you.

Well, how was the winter up there? I guess you have got a family of half-breed kids by now, or did that deal ever turn out? Let me know, I am sure curious.

I guess the big news down here is about Molly's old man. He drunk lye last month and died, it was awful hard on Molly but I think she is over the worst of it now. She is getting sweeter all the time, and I mean it, I think I am going to get her in the notion of marrying me one of these days, then when you come back you will really know what you've missed. But I guess you will bring your Indian sweetheart home, so you won't mind too much.

Eddie is acting sorrier than ever, I may have to fight him yet.

Well, I wish you would come home, we could sure put you to work, we might even give you a raise. Our steers wintered good but the calf crop is pretty puny. If we don't get some rain the grass will all play out by June.

I guess that's all the news I know of. If you see Old Man Grinsom, say hello for me and ask him if he thinks I can ride or not. I have got a new sorrel horse by the way, he can foxtrot like nobody's business but he ain't no cowhorse yet. He's just a four-year-old though. I give thirty-five dollars for him.

Write me sometime and send me the news from New Mexico.

YOUR FRIEND,
GID

I guess old Johnny must have been sitting at the table with his pencil licked when he got my letter, because I got one from him in less than a week's time.

DEAR GID:

I would use the rest of your name too, but I ain't the kind that has to get even with ever mean trick that's played on me.

Well, this is the life for me, and I don't mean maybe. This place I'm at is the rancho grandy for sure, there ain't no damn mesquite to get in your way, but I do kinda wish it had a few more windbreaks in it. It like to blown us all away in Feb. and March, them was just fall breezes you got when you was up here. Jelly, she made a big wool bandanna to keep my neck warm.

Jelly ain't her real name, but that's what the boss called her so I use it too. He wasn't kidding when he said she was pretty. Boy I never would have made it through the winter without her.

Well, tell Molly I'm awful sorry about her trouble. I'm just sorry for her, I ain't gonna miss the old bastard personally, are you? I wish I had been there though.

If you do fight Eddie, don't let him get the first lick. Get the first one yourself, with a two-by-four if one's handy.

I ain't losing no sleep over you and her getting married, I know she ain't that far gone.

We had quite a bit of snow in early March, never had much before that. It's all the moisture we've had. This here ain't a very big ranch, really, and it's a good thing because there's just me to take care of it. The coyotes have got six calves so far, I even seen one Lobo but didn't get a shot at him. There ain't a decent horse on the place.

Well, write me agin. I like to hear the news. I may come home one of these days if I don't get lost in the sandstorms. Tell Molly I'll be seeing her.

YOUR FRIEND,
JOHNNY

16

WE HAD A GOOD RAIN in early February, and it looked like that would be the last we'd ever have. We never had a sprinkle in March, and by the middle of April the pastures were looking like they usually looked in July. It never helped Dad's disposition, or mine either. We had to feed the cattle, and it was such hard, hot work Dad just couldn't do it. Between the dry weather and Dad being sick, I wasn't in a very good humor.

One morning I run into Eddie. I was down in the River pasture, feeding. The cattle could hear me well enough, but it was hot and they didn't want to come to the wagon. I hollered around for an hour and only got sixty-five or seventy. I was just about to go ahead and feed them when three damn floppy-eared turd hounds come loping up through the brush, barking like hell. The cattle took off in about ten different directions. I got down and chunked the dogs and went on and got most of the cattle back together agin, and I'll be damned if the dogs didn't come up and run them off agin. My horse was tied to the back of the wagon, so I got on him and took my rope down and went after some dogs. I didn't rope them, but I whipped the shit out of two of them. The other one was too much of a dodger. When I was trotting back to the wagon, coiling my rope, I seen Eddie slouching across the flat. I might have known they was his dogs; nobody but him had time to run hounds that time of year. He had on an old khaki jumper and some patched pants and some roughnecking boots and looked like he hadn't seen a razor in about ten days. Both of us were mad.

But I didn't start off unfriendly. "Howdy, Ed," I said.

"Goddammit, Fry, that ain't no way to treat dogs," he said. "No telling where they are now. I been looking for them all morning, and now I got it to do over agin."

"I'd been after these cattle they run off a good while, myself," I said. "I guess the dogs will come home when they get hungry, won't they?"

"But maybe I don't want them home," he said. "I might want to hunt some more."

"Listen here," I said. "I don't give a plugged nickel what you want, if you're asking me. But what I want is for you and them dogs to get out of this pasture. And the next time they scare off cattle of mine they ain't gonna get off so easy. Next time they're gonna get the shit drug out of them."

"I'm a notion to whip your butt, right now," he said.

I got off my horse.

"Have at it," I said. "I hope you brought your lunch. You may need it before you're through."

"Aw, hell no," he said. "Then I'd have to carry you to the hospital. But let me tell you, you got one coming. Write it down in your little book."

"Don't wait till I get too old," I said.

"Another thing," he said. "Stay the hell away from my wife. I don't even want to see you on her place."

"Stay away from your what?" I said.

"My wife!" he said. "Just leave her the hell alone."

It was like lightning had hit me, only not fast lightning but a real slow bolt that slid all the way down me. By the time it got to my feet I was plumb numb. I couldn't have said boo.

"Why, you look surprised," he said. "I guess that shows you, now don't it. You and your long-legged buddy, too. Hell, we been married three weeks, and she's a real dilly. Me and her we really take after one another. I never had a woman so crazy about me.

"Well, ain't you gonna congratulate me?" He winked and grinned.

I got back on my horse and went on back to the wagon, and he went off after his dogs. A good many of the cattle had come back, and I fed them.

——

That afternoon I went out with the posthole diggers and the wire stretchers, but I didn't do no fencing. I went down to the far tank and sat under a big shade tree, watching the mockingbirds and the kildeers fly around. There were a lot of bubbles on top of the water; I should have fished. I just couldn't understand Molly doing it. I wouldn't have cared if lightning *had* struck me. There didn't seem no reason left to work or nothing. I got to wondering if I would ever see her agin, and I couldn't think what I'd say if I did. There wasn't no clouds to look at, just water and sky, so I watched the water awhile and then I watched the sky. I didn't do much thinking; I just sat there feeling tight and sick. About sundown I rode home. Dad noticed there wasn't no dirt on my diggers, but he was tired too, and he never said nothing about it. We had cold steak and cold potatoes for supper, and I made the coffee too weak. It wasn't such a good supper.

17

IT LOOKED LIKE the world was going completely to pot. Dad was getting worse instead of better, and three or four days after I found out about Molly I got another letter from Johnny.

DEAR GID:

Well, I've got so much time to kill now, I thought I would write you agin. I have been in a real scrape, it's what I get for riding sorry horses, I ought to know better. I was off riding line and my horse buggered at a damn skunk and off I went, only I got caught in my rope and he drug me about half a mile. I guess I am the most skinned-up person you ever saw. Besides, my hip was broke, and I was about ten miles from home; it was a pretty hard crawl, I tell you for sure, I was out lost all one night. If it had been cold the coyotes would have ate me by now.

Jelly she got me into town and now they got me cemented up so I can't turn over. It's pretty tiresome, so don't ever break no hips if you can help it.

The horse come in, so I ain't lost the saddle.

These doctors are no-count, they give me a lot of trouble. I guess it will be June before I'm worth anything agin.

Wish you was up here, we could play some cards and talk over old times. Write me when you get time and let me know all about Molly and your dad and what's happening down that way. I ain't had much news lately.

YOUR FRIEND,
JOHNNY

So he wasn't having no luck, either. I didn't know what to write him, all the news was so bad. I wished I could have gone up and stayed with him like he done with me, but it just couldn't be managed. Finally I wrote him a note.

DEAR JOHNNY:

We are all sorry to hear about your trouble, that's a cowboy's life. I would come and stay, only Dad's pretty sick now and there ain't nobody but me to run the ranch.

Molly has married Eddie, I guess that's the end of that. I haven't seen her. He is too sorry to talk about.

We haven't had no rain, either.

I wish you would come on home when you get well, we could sure use a good hand.

YOUR FRIEND,
GID

Dad was looking low. I would have given anything to talk to Molly about it, but the times when I could talk to her were over and gone. I did go in and see Mabel Peters a time or two. She was a nice old girl, but she wasn't much help. She was after me to marry her, and I was half a mind to. I didn't see how I could be no worse off than I was. At least we'd have somebody to do the cooking and the housework. I wanted to hire somebody, but Dad wouldn't let me.

"Hell no," he said. "A hired woman would get the best of me in no time. We'll just get along by ourselves."

One day me and him drove a little bunch of cattle down to the League pasture. On the way back we stopped on the Ridge and talked and rested awhile. It was a pretty day. The mesquite was leafed out, and everything smelled like spring. Dad had got down to pull up a devil's claw, and said he didn't feel like getting back up right then; we sat under a post oak and talked. I had got where I liked to talk to Dad; it had taken me a long time. From where we were sitting we could look off west and see halfway across the county, to the little ridges above Onion Creek, where Dad's land ended.

"I got a good ranch," he said. "That's one thing that cheers me up. The best land in the county."

He was right, I guess. To me it didn't seem like much consolation.

"The nice thing is that I'm a damn sight nearer worn out than this country. I'd hate to get old in a worn-out country."

"You ain't worn out," I said. "You're just damn pessimistic. If you'd stay in the hospital awhile, you'd get well."

He didn't say nothing for a minute.

"Well, it's too bad she married him," he said, looking across the country. "She'll make a good one. But just let me tell you something, son, a woman's love is like the morning dew, it's just as apt to settle on a horse turd as it is on a rose. So you better just get over it."

"Aw, I ain't hurt much," I said. "Why in the world did she want to marry a bastard like that? It just don't figure."

"Well, she's got a lot of sense when it comes to taking care of herself," he said. "A lot more than you have. She'll make it."

"Why, she ain't got no sense, when it comes to taking care of herself," I said.

Sitting on the ground, you could smell the spring coming right up through the grass and into the breeze. It was sad Dad felt so awful at such a pretty time of year.

"It's my fault you don't have more," he said. "You've always had me to give you orders. I never put you on your own enough. She's been on her own since she could walk.

"But there's no use in you sitting on your butt sulking," he said. "Sulking never made a dime nor kept a friend."

"We better get on home," I said.

By the time we got to the barn it was late evening, and the last of the sun was shining on the weathervanes above the barn. Dad was tired. He drank some buttermilk and went to bed. He had seemed a little bit worried about me.

"Anyhow you're stubborn," he said. "Stubbornness will get a feller through a lot of mean places."

———

The next morning he never woke me up, and there was a note lying on the table when I come down.

DEAR GID:

Miserable night. There's no profit in putting up with this.

I think I'll go out on the hill and turn my horses free, or did you ever know that song? It's an old one.

Take good care of the ranch, it's a dilly, and don't trust ever damn fool that comes up the road. Always work outside when you can, it's the healthiest thing.

Tell Miss Molly I appreciated her coming and helping us, just tell her much obliged until she is better paid.

Well, this is the longest letter I've written in ten years, it is too long. Be sure and get that windmill fixed, I guess you had better put in some new sucker rod.

YOUR DAD

The rifle wasn't in the closet, so I knew that was that, and I sat down and held my head. I wisht old Johnny had been there, or Molly, but they wasn't. Directly I went outside and turned off the windmill and went on down to the barn and hitched the wagon and put the wagon sheet in it and headed off across the hill. He was right on the west side; he had on a clean khaki shirt and Levis and had taken his hat off and was laying on his back on the grass. Once I seen him I wasn't so scared, for some reason. He just looked natural, like Dad, and comfortable. I put him in the wagon and took him up to the house and laid him on the couch in the living room and got a counterpane to cover him with. It was worse in that cool darkish dusty old living room than it had been out in the sunshine. I hated to be the one to start treating Dad like a dead person. It was a long time before he seemed dead to me. For three months after that I would wonder in the morning why he hadn't come to wake me up.

I guess Dad had been better known than I thought; there was a big funeral and a lot of talk about what a pioneer he had been. It never done him much good, or me either. The worst of it all was seeing Molly. After I went into town to the undertaker a lot of people came out to visit me and bring stuff to eat. Molly, she came too, and brought a cake, and it was so awkward I got a headache from it. I knew she was remembering when her dad died and wishing she could really help me, but she couldn't. All those people were there trying to cheer me up, and it just made me bluer. Every once in a while I would see Molly looking at me from across the room, and she would be crying and looking so sad I wished I could have gone over and hugged her and told her it was okay. Finally I did talk to her just a minute.

"Molly," I said. "One of the last things Dad did was tell me to thank you for helping us last winter. He sure appreciated it."

"I hope you'll come and see me sometime, Gid," she said. "When all of this is over." Right after that she left. I seen her at the funeral, but just at a distance. Eddie was even there. I guess old Johnny was the only one that wasn't. I wrote him a card and told him a little about it, but he never answered. In September, after he was back, we had a kind of little funeral ourselves: we took Dad's old white saddlehorse that he called Snowman out on the hill and let him loose in the pasture; nobody ever rode him agin. We left Dad's saddle hanging in the harness shed. Sometimes when I'm doing the chores early in the mornings, I wonder if Dad and that old pony aren't still out there, maybe, slipping around through the misty pastures and checking up on the new calves.

18

ONE AFTERNOON about ten days after Dad died I decided I ought to look over the ranch. Of course I had been over every inch of it a hundred times, but it had been Dad's ranch then, and not mine. It was a nice sunny day, with a few white clouds in the sky, and not too hot; the week Dad killed himself we had a two-inch rain—it was just his luck to miss it—and the country looked wonderful. We had lots of grass, and the weeds weren't too bad yet. Dad had about ten thousand acres; he had had the whole county to pick from, and he picked careful. There was a creek to the southeast and a creek to the northwest, and the River down the middle, so if there was water anywhere in the country, we had it. And of course he had built good tanks. I saddled old Denver and started off east, through the Dale pasture and rode down our east fence plumb to the southeast corner; then I cut back across Westfork and rode west between it and the river, winding through the brush till I got nearly to the west side and then turned north and rode up on the hill in the south pasture and rested awhile. The whole south end of our land was brushy, mesquite and post oak mixed; the farther north you went, the more mesquite and the less post oak. Dad said when he first saw the country there wasn't a mesquite tree anywhere, or a prickly pear. Then I crossed the River and rode northwest till I hit Onion Creek, and turned and came back southeast agin along the top of Idiot Ridge. There wasn't no mesquite on the Ridge; it hadn't got that far north. The north end of our land was still prairie, but you could look south off the Ridge and see the brush coming. Our headquarters sits southeast of the Ridge, on a long hill. Finally I rode back through the League pasture to the barn and turned old Denver loose. I sat on the lot fence awhile, resting and thinking. It was about an hour before sundown, and I didn't much want to go up to the house, since there wasn't nobody there. At least the milkpen calves were a little company.

For a day or two after Dad died I had actually been in the mood to sell the place, just dump it, and go where I wouldn't have to be reminded of Dad all the time, or of Molly. But I got over wanting to do that. For one thing, I got so I liked being reminded of Dad. Of course I didn't like to think of Molly and Eddie, but it would have been pretty yellow-bellied to let them run me out of the country. Most of the time I hadn't paid much attention to the country; Dad had done that. But what I saw that afternoon looked pretty good to me.

I didn't think no more about moving; but even staying took a lot of thinking about. One thing for sure, I wasn't no solitary owl. I couldn't stay on the place by myself; in about a month I would have been dead of lonesomeness. So I figured the best thing to do was marry Mabel. She was the best girl left in the county, and I figured I could get along with her okay. She would be so grateful to me just for marrying her that she shouldn't fuss none for about fifteen years.

Then if Johnny ever come back, I could hire him to help me run the place. I wanted to buy some new land if I could; I didn't intend to stop with what I'd inherited; that would have been pure laziness. Of course Mabel and Johnny wasn't too fond of one another, but I figured that would iron out once me and her was married and he quit trying to get in her pants.

I sat on the fence and never even noticed sundown. I happened to notice the moon's reflection in the milklot water trough. The house looked so lonesome I just didn't go in, I caught old Denver and rode to Thalia without even eating supper.

===

When I stepped up on the boardinghouse porch I could see Mabel hadn't gone to bed. She was sitting in her chair, patching a quilt. I felt sorry for her. When I knocked she had to put on a bathrobe before she let me in.

"Why, come in, Gid," she said. "I was just thinking about you."

"You look kinda blue," she said. "Want some hot chocolate?"

I said no. Her bedroom was neat as a pin.

"I guess I am a little down in the dumps," I said. "You want to sit out on the porch awhile? It's a real warm night."

"Okay," she said.

We got in the glider and rocked, and she snuggled up against me, warm as a hot-water bottle. We seen the moon, way up there, and I wondered if its reflection was still down at the ranch, in the water trough.

"Honey, let's get married," I said. "I'm sick of this living alone."

"Why, I am too," she said, and she squeezed my hand right hard.

I hugged her and kissed her and stood up, thinking she'd go in and get her clothes on, so we could wake up the J.P. and get it done and go on home, but boy she fooled me. I never seen her run backward so quick.

"Why, I couldn't hold my head up if I got married that way," she said. "What are you thinking about?"

She talked like it would take us two weeks, just to get married. I never knew she was that silly about things before. She wouldn't even let me spend the night with her. I ended up having to pay fifty cents to spend the night in the damn hotel.

=====

But I didn't back out. There wasn't nothing to be gained from that; not that I knew of. Only I told her the next morning that I wasn't going to wait around no two weeks, I had too many other things to do. She said I'd have to at least ride back to the ranch and get my good clothes; I had just come in like I was. So I done it. While I was gone she quit her job and packed her suitcases. And when I got back to town I hunted up a feller I knew and just bought me an automobile. I figured if Eddie White could afford one, I could too. He showed me how to drive it and I got it to the rooming house and put Mabel's stuff in it. Then we walked over to the Methodist preacher's house. It was a pretty day and Mabel was dolled up like a hundred dollars; I had on a wool suit and was about to cook. Anyway, the preacher called his wife in to witness, and he married us. I gave him three dollars. Mabel hung on my arm all the way back to the rooming house, and I guess everybody in town knew what we'd done. I sure was hot and embarrassed, but Mabel didn't even want me to take my coat off till we got out of town. It took a lot of wrassling to get that damn car home, no better roads than there were; I wisht a hundred times I'd never bought it. But we finally made it, and I yanked the car stopped by the back gate.

"Well, here we are," I said. "Man and wife." And I started to get her stuff out of the rumbleseat.

"Gid, you ought to be ashamed, ain't you going to help me down?" she said. "I see I'll have to do a little work on you." And she never wasted no time starting.

19

THE FIRST MONTH we were married, I don't think we saw a living soul but one another. I guess I must have run into a few other people, here and there, but I sure didn't say much to them, and I didn't give them the chance to say much to me. If there was one thing I didn't feel like putting up with, it was jokes about newlyweds. Just being one was joke enough.

Of course, it really wasn't that Mabel was so bad herself. She was a good person, a real good person, I guess, and she damn sure wasn't lazy or anything like that. She did her work, and she looked after me a damn sight better than I had been looking after myself. And there was a many a time when I was awful glad to have her around.

Still, it never changed the facts, and the facts was that I had done an awful ignorant thing. When I first realized just *how* ignorant, I was flat embarrassed for myself. A ten-year-old kid could have showed as much judgment as I showed. I guess Dad had been right when he said I didn't know anything about taking care of myself.

Mabel was a big surprise to me, of course. I thought I knew her to a T before I ever went in to marry her. I hadn't been married to her two weeks before I knew that a blind idiot could have found out more about her than I managed to. For one thing, she was a lot prouder of herself than I thought she was, and for another, a lot less proud of me. I soon found out that she didn't consider me no particular prize, but I had better be sure and let her know that I considered her one. She seen herself as the belle of the county; nobody was going to talk her out of that view. I soon gave up trying; she could see herself any way she wanted to.

It come down to two things: the first was that Mabel just wasn't a very generous person. I guess she never had anything to learn to be generous with. For every nickel's worth of her she put out, she wanted a dollar's worth of me. And got it, too.

The second thing was that I was still crazy about Molly. What few little times I'd been with her meant more to me than a lifetime with Mabel could have. I had feeling for Molly, and didn't for Mabel. And Mabel had none for me.

It wasn't very long before I was hanging around the lots till dark for a plumb different reason. It used to be I didn't want to go to the house because nobody was there; pretty soon I was working late because I didn't know what to do at the house when I got there. I seen the moon in the water trough many a time, and I seen it in the sky, and if one thing was for sure, it was that the moon didn't care. What I did didn't make no difference to it, or to nothing, or to nobody, I felt like. I did get a card from Johnny, but I didn't have the guts to answer it.

I never was bluer than I was that first month. If a feller has to be lonesome, he's better off being lonesome alone. But I'd kicked that advantage away forever, and there was no use sulking about it. It was done and that was final; I would just have to make the best of it. Only it didn't look like a very good best.

It reminded me of something Old Man Grinsom had said one time; it was the day we first run into him in Clarendon. Just to make conversation I asked him how long he had been in the Panhandle.

"Since '93," he said. "I come here with nothing but a fiddle and a hard on. I've still got the fiddle." And when we seen them seven boys we knew where the other went. My case was a little different. I got married with a ranch and the other, and I still had them both. And to be right honest, I guess it served me right.

20

IT WAS LATE APRIL when we married, and May was the month we stayed by ourselves. By June I knew I had to do a little better than that for myself, some-way. I was getting where I didn't even enjoy my work. One morning I had to fix a little fence on the northwest side, and when I got that done I decided it was time I went and checked up on my neighbors. The closest one was Molly.

When I rode past her barn I didn't see no automobile, and that was a great relief. It took so much nerve to get me there I would have hated to have to ride away agin. But Molly, she was there, out in the back yard hanging the washing on the line. There was a good breeze, and the sheets were flapping, so she didn't notice me riding up. She looked like the same old Molly, only more so, wearing Levis and an old cotton shirt with the shirttail out; she had a clothespin in her mouth and three or four more in the shirt pocket. Her shirttail was damp in front, where the sheets had flopped against her. And her hair was loose, hanging down her back and getting in face now and then; I seen her brush it out of the way with one hand. I thought she just looked lovely.

I got off and tied old Willy to a mesquite tree; then I walked into the yard and stopped behind her, at the windmill. I didn't know if I could talk.

"Hello, neighbor," I said. "How are you getting along?"

She turned around with a tablecloth in her hands; I thought she was going to cry. She had those little dark places under her eyes. She dropped the wet table-cloth in the grass, and I went over to pick it up.

"My, Gid," she said. "You scared me."

For some reason I was real embarrassed; I squatted down and picked up the wet tablecloth and was going to try and wipe the grass off it. But Molly squatted down too and put one of her wet hands on my neck, and then there was her face and she kissed me. I shivered clear through. But her face against mine was as warm as sunshine, and I had to sit down in the grass and hug her.

"Now ain't this some way for old married folks to be acting?" I said.

She grinned, but it was just half a grin, really, and her mouth quivered.

"It's nice, though," she said. "I'm so glad to see you. Let's go in the house."

I helped her up and put my arm around her; we let the tablecloth and the clothespins lie where they fell. I asked her if she wanted to finish hanging out the washing, and she shook her head.

"No, but let's sit on the cellar awhile," she said. "It's too pretty to go in; I just don't like to sit on the dewy grass."

The cellar was stone, and the sun had warmed it up. She held one of my hands.

"Where's Eddie?" I said.

"Just relax," she said. She knew what I was thinking. "He's gone to Oklahoma, working in the oil fields."

"Good lord," I said. "He's a strange feller. I don't see how he can stand to go off and leave somebody like you."

She snickered. "That's because you ain't Eddie. He ain't the married kind. He'd go crazy if he couldn't get off and run around."

I wanted to ask her why in the hell she married him, then, but I bit my tongue and didn't.

Molly was in the sweetest, happiest mood. She kept glancing at me and smiling and she rubbed my hand between hers.

"Well, I'm just so glad to see you," she said, and in a minute turned around and kissed me. I held onto her for a long time, and then I figured I better tell her something for her own good. Only she knew what was on my mind agin.

"Don't be so scared," she said. "That's no way to make me happy. It's just us here, you know."

"I know," I said. "And you're the sweetest woman I ever had hold of, I don't mind saying that. But now listen. We got to get something straight. I'm married and you're married, and I ain't the shy old kid I used to be."

"Good," she said, grinning. "What's shy got to do with it?" She reached up and pulled a thread off my shirt collar and rubbed my neck with her hand.

"It's got a lot," I said. "This kissing and hugging is just inviting it. The state I'm in, it's whole hog or nothing."

"That's so nice," she said. "One thing I've always hoped is that you'd come over here some day ready to be whole hog in love with me. I hoped sooner or later you would."

That just flabbergasted me.

"Honey, good lord," I said. "I been whole hog in love with you for the last ten years. Maybe more. Surely you know that."

She looked me in the eye for a long time, a little sad, with one corner of her mouth turned up just a little. "I know you think so," she said. "But you haven't, Gid. You ain't even this morning, yet."

"Well, what do you mean, whole hog?" I said. It seemed to me, looking at her with her face so close to mine, that it was impossible to love a person more than I loved her, and the way she sent that cool look up at me made me mad. I could have hated her. It was a bad feeling; I felt myself getting mad, and I didn't want to.

"I mean just you loving me," she said. "And nothin' else. Just pure me and pure you. But you're always thinking about Johnny or Eddie or your ranch or your dad or what people will think, or what's right and what's wrong, something like that. Or else you're thinking about yourself, and how much you like me. Or else you just want to get me in bed. Or else you just like to think about having me for a girl. That ain't loving nobody much. I can tell that."

"Why, goddamn you," I said. "That's some way for you to talk." I was thinking about her marrying Eddie.

"That's the way I've always talked to you, darling," she said. "You ain't thinking about me, you're thinking about Eddie." She reached up her hand to my cheek and smiled, but I was too mad then to care; it was like my blood vessels had busted. I yanked her back across the cellar, I seen later where it skinned her leg, and held her down and kissed her. It's a wonder she didn't get fever blisters. And for a long time we stayed that way, and she kissed back, only I knew it wasn't working somehow, it wasn't convincing her of anything. I let up and looked at her: she felt warm but she still looked cool, and there was a terrible strain inside me; I didn't know what to do or how.

"Molly, what do I have to do?" I said. "You drive me half-crazy, don't you know that?"

"I wish I could drive you all the way," she said, holding my hand against her chest. I could feel her breathing.

"I didn't know you were like that," I said. "Why do you want to hurt me that way?"

"Oh, Gid," she said, and tears come in her eyes, "I don't want to hurt you. I just want you to turn loose of yourself for a minute, so you can hold *me*. That's the only thing I want."

She got upset then and cried and I was ashamed of myself for getting mad. At the same time I was still mad. I didn't see how she could go marry Eddie and then expect much of me. But I didn't want her sad.

"I just don't guess I know how to do that," I said. "If I did I would."

She sat up and wiped away the tears and smiled at me, her cheeks still wet. "I know you don't," she said. "But maybe I can show you."

She took me in the house then, and it was nice and cool and shady, after the sunshine. I made her let me put some iodine on the big skinned place on her leg; it burned like the devil. I felt silly, to have done a rough thing like that. But Molly never mentioned it. I was all nervous and tense and jumpy and nearly sick, and she kind of loved it all out of me, like a fever. I was so upset that for a long time after we had done it I couldn't go to sleep or be still in the bed, but she stayed with me, I remember her face, and I finally did sleep and slept good. When I woke up the afternoon sun was pouring in the windows and the room was hot. Molly was still with me and was holding my hand against her chest. She had thrown all the covers back.

"You're a good sleeper once you get to sleep," she said. "You slept four hours without even turning over."

I pulled her down so my face was right against hers. "I'm not going to let you go," I said. "I'm going to give you everything I've got to give; you're the only person that's worth it. I don't know why you wanted to take up with somebody worthless like me agin, but it's too late for you now."

She swung her head back to get her hair out of her eyes, and it fell all over my face. I lay for a hour, I guess, smelling her and listening to her breath; I could tell she was pleased about something. She was a mystery to me, but I was glad I had finally pleased her someway. After a while the sun moved and the sunlight came right on the bed, so we were laying in a shaft of it, with a million little dustmotes in the air above us. Things looked lovely and funny for a change.

"I swear you smell like a gourd, Molly," I said. "I never noticed that before."

"Maybe I never smelled that way before," she said. "I'm starving, you stay here and let me get us something to eat."

I was pretty hungry too. Only not hungry enough to get up; I never felt so good and lazy in my life. Maybe I would just stay there in Molly's bed for a month or two. That would have set people on their ears. Molly crawled out and wound up her hair, standing by the bed with the sunlight across her stomach.

"You're a shapely hussy," I said.

She snickered and pulled on her Levis. I must have dozed off agin for a little while. When I opened my eyes she was sitting on the bed cross-legged, with just her Levis on, eating a piece of cornbread and drinking buttermilk. There was some for me, with a couple of pieces of cold chicken, sitting on a chair by the bed. It wasn't there long. When we finished there were cornbread crumbs all over the bed and Molly had buttermilk on her upper lip. I wiped it off with a corner of the sheet. I wanted her to lay down agin, but there were so many cornbread crumbs in the bed that it wouldn't do, so we both got up and I put on my pants and we went in the living room and sat on the couch and hugged and talked awhile.

"When I come over here today I was going to ask you a lot of questions," I said. "Like why you married him, and all that. But I've just about forgot the questions, and I don't guess I really care about the ones I remember. What do you reckon caused that?"

"Me, I guess," she said. She was eating a piece of stick candy she had found somewhere, and was slouched back against my arm without nothing on but her pants, just as relaxed as she could be, and in a perfect humor. She wouldn't let me have any of the candy, but when I kissed her now and then I got her taste and the candy's too.

"One thing I do want to settle, Molly. What do you want to do about these people we're married to? Do you want us to go off somewhere or anything like that?"

"Do you want to go?" she said.

"No," I said. "That's kind of against my style."

"I'm glad," she said. "Because I wouldn't go. Right here in this house is where I always want to live."

We got a quilt and stretched out together on the living room floor and stayed there till plumb dark. I just couldn't quite get my mind made up to go home, and she didn't hurry me.

"Gid, I'm ready to have a baby now," she said. "I'm convinced you'll make a good daddy."

"Good lord," I said, sitting up. It was all shadowy in the room; she rested her head against my chest. We sure didn't get very far from one another that day. I guess she had been as lonesome as me.

"You're a strange woman," I said. "How come you don't want your husband for its daddy?"

"Oh, Gid," she said, "he wouldn't make no good daddy. Not as good a one as you.

"You don't really care, do you?" she said, looking up at me. I could barely see her eyes, but her voice was real serious. "I mean if me and you have a baby. Of course I'll let on it's Eddie's, just you and me and the baby will know."

I thought about it a long time. Here I was married to Mabel and her to Eddie. It was strange to think of a baby coming out of Molly, but I knew one thing, if one did I wanted it to be mine.

"No, I don't care, sweetheart. I'd like for you to if you want to."

She curled around me. "I knew you'd come to me sometime," she said. And that was all we said that day. After a while I got up and dressed to go, and she walked out to my horse with me. We stood there awhile, looking at the Milky Way and the Big Dipper and all the rest of the summer stars. Finally I got on.

"I'll just get over when I can," I said. "Okay? I probably can't stay this long ever time. I sure will miss you."

"Okay," she said. "Me too."

I rode on home by moonlight; it was bright enough I seen a big old coyote loping into the brush ahead of me. I should have been thinking about a story for Mabel, I guess, but I was thinking about Molly instead, and what a tender sort of person she was. And yet she had something fierce in her, like Dad had in him. I saw her agin, all the ways she'd looked that day, hanging up clothes in the morning, with her shirttail out, and sitting on the couch that evening, without no shirttail atall. She had the most changing kind of face, for it always to be the same one. Riding across the League I run into Dad's old horse, and he nickered. I sure did miss Dad.

21

IT WAS JUST AMAZING how seeing Molly ever once in awhile improved things for me. I begin to kinda take an interest in life agin. And I never seen a whole lot of her, either—I hardly ever got over more than once a week. Lots of time I was too busy, and other times, when I did ride over, I'd see Eddie's car and have to go back. There wasn't no sense aggravating him. But it didn't bother me too much if I missed seeing her one occasion or another. I knew that if I was a little patient, there would be a time when we could get together. Those times were worth the wait. Molly was awful good to me.

═══

And good for me, too. In the meantime, between visits to her, I had the ranch to run, and Mabel to live with, and I began to see that I had better get busy and try to do a little better job of both than I had been doing. It wasn't fair to Dad and Mabel not to.

At first I was pretty worried that Mabel would find out I was courting somebody else, but that was just because I still didn't know Mabel too well. In those days she was so proud of herself I couldn't have convinced her I was in love with somebody else if I'd come right out and told her. Which I didn't. I was fond of Mabel, and a little sad for her, but not as torn up about marrying her as I had been. And I made her a pretty decent husband too. I got to understanding her a lot better as time went on. We never was much of a delight to one another, I had to admit that, but I know I treated her better after I took up with Molly. Mabel was just a combination of proud and scared; she never had anything, and she always thought she was entitled to everything. It made me blue that I couldn't be more wholehearted with her, but I just couldn't. She wasn't the one. But anyway, she kept such a close eye on herself all the time that she hardly noticed me. She didn't have much notion of what was going on with me, and a good thing she didn't. After I got over my first blueness and began to treat her about half-nice, she thought I was plumb crazy about her.

"Well, I see you're beginning to learn how to treat a lady," she said one night. It was after supper, and we were sitting on the porch. I had complimented her on her cobbler, or something like that.

"I guess I ain't had much practice," I said.

"Well, you can get a lot on me," she said. "And don't think I won't tell you when you make a mistake. I ain't bashful about that." She scooted a little closer to me on the step.

I put my arm around her and hugged her and never said a word. It was dark, and we could hear an old hoot owl hooting somewhere in the pastures to the east. There wasn't no moon that night, but there was a good breeze from the southeast, and the country smelled good. We done had lilac in the yard. Life always seemed so complicated in the evenings. Mabel seemed perfectly happy, and I was sitting with my arm around her, about two-thirds melancholy. "Let's go in, honey," I said, "before the mosquitoes get to biting." "Well, you've got to kiss me first," she said. I did, and then we went inside and lit the lamps.

22

EARLY IN JUNE I spent a hell of a day. Mabel woke up in a bossy mood and practically chased me out of the house, so I done the chores and doctored a few sicklings and then decided I'd go to Antelope. That was where we got our mail, then, and I thought while I was there I'd hire somebody to come up and thrash my wheat. We had a pretty fair wheat crop and I was ready to get it thrashed; it was the last farm produce I ever intended to raise.

I rode old Dirtdobber that day, and I guess that was a mistake. He was the oldest horse on the place, and I never rode him nowhere except to get the mail. I think he was twenty-three years old. When I got to Antelope I tied him up and gave him a good rest, while I talked with the boys a little. I found an old boy with a thresher, said he'd be up after my wheat the next day. While I was fiddling around it come up a real mean-looking cloud in the northwest, and I figured then I'd do good to get home without getting wet. Besides which, the Montgomery Ward catalogue had come that day, and it was so much extra weight I didn't know if old Dirt would be able to carry it. He was particular about weight.

But I stuck the catalogue in my saddle pouch, and we headed out. If it rained like it looked like it aimed to, that old boy wouldn't have to bother about my wheat. But I was wrong about the rain, it never rained five drops. What it did was hail.

And I mean hailed. It started out the size of plums and moved up to pullet eggs, and before it was done there was hailstones on the ground bigger than anything our old turkeys ever hatched. Course me and Dirt were right out in the open when it started, and getting him to run was out of the question. I tried holding the catalogue over my head, and dropped it in about two minutes. Finally we got to a little old half-grown post oak, and I figured that was the best protection we would find. I unsaddled right quick and crawled under Dirt and then under the saddle too, and scrunched down tight. The first thing Dirt did was try to piss on me, but I wasn't worried about that, I was worried about my skull. I jobbed him a time or two to cut him off and damned if the old sonofabitch didn't jerk loose and step right on my hip and run off. So far as I was concerned it could hail him to death; I wasn't going after him. I got on the downwind side of the tree and hid as much of me as I could under the saddle, and stayed put. At least none of the big ones hit my head. My saddle got dents in it that never did come out. It hailed for a solid hour. Finally I didn't have to worry so much, I reached out and raked me up a kind of igloo and was pretty cozy. I had one less worry anyway, and that was the damn wheat crop.

When it quit the country looked like it was under a snowstorm. The sun came out in a little while and started melting it off, but some of the big piles didn't melt for two or three days. I was in a hell of a shape; Dirt had about halfway squashed my hip. I could hobble along, but carrying the saddle and blanket I couldn't make no time, particularly over that slippery hail. I guess Dirt had weathered it all right; I seen him about half a mile away, poking along toward home. "You old bastard," I said, "wait till I catch you." But all I could do was hobble on over to the Elden-felders', they was a Dutch family that lived about half a mile away. I hated to run the risk of getting dogbit—they had about fifty damn mean turd hounds—but it was the only place in hobbling distance. However, it turned out all right. They fed me a little rotten cowmeat and sent their big old dumb girl Annie to haul me home. A lot of the boys thought it was smart to get in Annie's pants, because she was willing and about a half-idiot, but I never fooled with her. She seemed kind of pathetic to me. The creek was up, so that was as far as she got me, but I gave her a dollar. "Bye-bye," she said. It's a wonder she could drive the wagon. I waded the creek and went on home. My hip was beginning to unsquash a little by then.

Old Dirt was in the barn when I got there, trying to kick in the door to the oatbin. The old fart had so many knots on him I didn't have the heart not to feed him.

But when I got to the house I wished I was back outside in the hailstorm. The ten or fifteen broken windowlights hadn't improved Mabel's humor. I was thinking I might get a good hip rub, but I could have staggered in on two wooden legs and she wouldn't have cared. I didn't see no signs of supper, and I guess I said the wrong thing.

"Hello," I said. "What's for supper, hail soup?"

"I'll hail soup you," she said, "going off and leaving me in a storm like that. Where you been all afternoon?"

"Well, I been coming home," I said. "It wasn't a very quick trip, I'll admit."

"I bet you was," she said. "I bet you was sitting down in the Antelope domino hall, losing some of your inherited money."

I let that pass.

"Where's the mail?" she said.

"Wasn't none but the catalogue, and I lost that in the hail. I guess we'll have to get them to send us another one."

She got so mad it tickled me.

"What kind of a husband are you?" she said. "We'll do no such thing. You just saddle up and trot back and find it; I want to do some ordering out of that catalogue before it gets too old."

"Why, you're crazy," I said. "Hell, it's beat to pieces by now, anyway. I imagine we can borrow one."

"We ain't going to borrow nothing," she said. "You go get it. You lost it."

I tried to grab her and hug her, hoping it would get her in a better humor, but she just stomped out to the bedroom, and I let her go. I got the milk bucket and milked, and when I got back, no sign of her. I cooked myself some bacon and eggs and ate supper. Then I washed the dishes, and still no Mabel. I went in the living room and did some figuring in my little daybook; I was thinking of buying three sections of land that joined us on the northwest.

About nine o'clock I heard her, and she came in in her bathrobe and nightgown, looking like she'd had a good nap. She was a shapely woman, too, when you caught her looking just right.

"Hi," I said, and she set down on my lap and kissed me and seemed fairly friendly.

"Where's the catalogue?" she said.

"Good lord," I said. "Ain't you forgot that yet? It's right where I dropped it, and that's where it's going to stay, as far as I'm concerned."

"Well, I knew you was ignorant but I never thought you was lazy," she said, and she jumped off my lap and went out the back door just boohooing. I would have swore she was crazy.

But I went out to get her; I didn't want her to run around barefooted and get on a snake. That would really aggravate her. When I came out on the backsteps she ran down in the storm cellar. It was pitch dark down there, and I went over an stood on the steps.

"Now, Mabel, come on out of there," I said. "There's no use in you taking on so over a damn catalogue. You'll get on a stinging lizard down there if you ain't careful."

"I hope I do," she said. "I hope they sting me to death, so I won't have to live with you."

I started down, and damned if she didn't grab a jar of peach pickles off the shelf and threw it; I heard it hit the steps below me and break. Then she threw two more, just whatever she happened to grab.

I thought what the hell, there wasn't no use in provoking her to ruin all the preserves.

"Okay," I said, "sleep down there if that's how silly you are." She didn't say nothing, so I went in and went to bed. There was a cot in the cellar, and it was a warm night; I didn't figure it would do her any harm.

Only I couldn't sleep worth a flip. I went back out twice more to try and persuade her, and all it did was cost me preserves. The last time I went was about three-thirty, and I just sat down in the kitchen and read the almanac till it got light. Then I went down in the cellar, and she was curled up on the cot asleep, peaceable as a baby. But the cellar steps looked like a cyclone had hit a jelly factory. I went in to cook breakfast, and I heard her hollering at me. So I went out.

"No, I ain't gone after the catalogue yet," I said.

"Could you carry me up these steps?" she said. "I'm barefooted and I'm afraid I'll cut my foot off on all this broken glass."

"No, I'm afraid to carry you, I might drop you and break your precious butt." I went and got a basket and a broom and the ashes shovel and cleaned up the mess, while she sat on the cot and watched. Then she came in and made coffee and never said another word about it. And for a day or two, she was sweet as pie.

23

ONE MORNING early in July a damn horse kicked a hole in the water trough, and while I was down patching it, getting wet up to my ears, I looked up and seen a horseback rider loping across the Ridge toward the barn. By god, if it wasn't Johnny, he'd come home, and he was riding the prettiest little sorrel gelding you ever saw. He called him Jack-a-Diamonds.

"Well, by god," I said, standing up to shake his hand. "Where'd you get that horse?"

"Bought him off a feller," he said. "How you been?"

"Oh, fair," I said. "How long you been home?"

"Since last night."

"You're walking just like a normal feller. You don't look crippled."

"I finally growed back together," he said. "This country sure looks good to me."

"Well, we had four inches of rain in May. Course we had that hail."

"Heard about that. See it smashed hell out of your wheat."

"What I get for raising it," I said. "Tie up your horse and stay awhile, I got to patch this water trough."

"I'll help you," he said, and he did. If he hadn't I wouldn't have got the damn thing patched by dinnertime. While we worked he told me a million funny stories; he was the same old Johnny. I was sure glad to see him back.

=

That night, of all things, me and him and Molly went coon hunting, and had a hilarious time. Johnny's dad had a new coon dog he was proud of and Johnny wanted some excitement, so he asked me if I wanted to go with him to try the dog out. I said sure, and after supper I told Mabel where I was going and met Johnny on the Ridge. We decided to go over and see if Eddie was home, and if he wasn't to take Molly. She was there by herself, peeling potatoes in the kitchen, and she put on an old pair of boots and was ready in a minute. Johnny had brought the dog with him across his saddle, and we all struck off toward the creek, walking. It was a hot night with plenty of moon, but we took a lantern anyway.

"I hope we don't get snake-bit," Molly said. She had been bit once and was afraid of snakes. Sure enough we killed three rattlers that night, but we didn't have any close calls.

We hadn't been out thirty minutes when the dog treed a big old fat coon in a live-oak tree. I didn't much want to kill him, because we'd have to lug him around all night, but we went ahead and done it. After that we got pretty excited, and the dog soon struck another trail. Johnny had the lantern and the gun, and I had the coon in one hand and Molly's hand in the other, so I could help her through the brush.

"I like this," she said. "I'm glad you'all came by."

Then the dog treed in the shaft of an old hollow oak, and from the squealing we heard it was a momma coon and two or three little ones. We never brought an ax, but the old tree was just barely standing, and me and Johnny pushed it over. Only no coons come running out.

"Now what?" Molly said.

"I'll stomp it open, I guess," Johnny said. About the time he said it the momma coon went scooting out the open end of the tree, right between Molly's legs. She jumped about three feet. I had the gun and couldn't shoot for Molly, so it was up to the dog, and he let the old momma get plumb away. He was a good dog for treeing, but he wasn't worth a shit for fighting. She got in the creek and he didn't have the backbone to go in after her.

"Don't you all kill the little ones," Molly said. "I want one for a pet."

"Sure," Johnny said.

We blocked up the open end and then Johnny stomped a hole in the old rotten wood. One little coon jumped right out into the dog's mouth, and that was all for him. I got down on my hands and knees and managed to grab another one by the neck and drag him out. He was nearly half-grown though, and I sure needed something to tie him with. Baling wire was what I needed, but that's the way, when you need baling wire you can't find it and when you don't need it you're tangled up in it.

"Do you think you can gentle him?" I said, holding him out so Molly could see.

"Probably not," Molly said.

Then Johnny yelled. He had kept his foot in the stomp hole, so the other little coon couldn't run out, only he discovered that his foot was stuck. I wasn't very worried.

"Pull your boot off," I said. "Or sit down or something."

"Hell no," he said. "If I was to sit down wrong, I'd break this hip agin and be laid up in the hospital another three months. My heel's stuck. See if you can stomp more hole."

Molly and me thought it was funny; we stood there and laughed. Only I didn't laugh long. The little coon that was in the log decided it was time to come out, and he did, right up Johnny's leg. Johnny yanked backward and fell aspraddling. The coon went right over him and off, and the dog never seen it. I got so tickled I forgot I was holding anything, and the little coon I had whipped around and bit clear through the palm of my hand. When he turned me loose I was glad to do the same for him. I howled like a banshee.

So Molly didn't get no pet, and we went home with just one and a half coons and a cowardly dog, but we had fun anyhow. When we got to Molly's she bandaged my hand and we sat up in the kitchen, eating all the stray food and talking over old times. We were all in high spirits and Johnny told us a lot of stories about life on the plains. Finally me and him slept awhile on her living room floor, and about sunup she came in in her nightgown and bathrobe and woke us up and cooked the best breakfast I ever ate. We did her chores for her and about six o'clock rode off toward home, with Molly standing by the yard gate with a milk bucket in one hand, watching us go.

There was a big dew that morning, and the country looked as green and sparkly as it ever had in July. We stopped our horses on the Ridge and talked about the grass and the cattle for a while.

"Well, are you home to stay?" I said. "Did you quit your job?"

"Yep, I'm here for good," he said. "You need a hand?"

"Boy, you bet," I said. "If you want a job you can start today. And live in our bunkhouse and we'll board you if you want to."

"Fine with me if it's okay with Mabel," he said.

I said it was. We hadn't said two words about her.

"Course you might be ready to go in business for yourself," I said. "I wouldn't want to stand in your way if you do."

"I am in business," he said. "The cowboying business. You can have the ranching business; I don't want no part of it."

"Okay," I said.

"I'll go home and tell my old man and get my stuff," he said. "See you after while."

And him and old Jack-a-Diamonds went off along the Ridge west in a long easy lope, neither one of them carrying a care in the world. I just about envied Johnny, but I didn't quite. He was the most carefree, but I thought I had a few more good things than he had. I meant to swap him out of his horse, though. The sun was drying up the dew, so I got rid of Molly's bandage and went on home and ate another breakfast.

24

JOHNNY SURE MADE a good hand. Me and him got things done in a day that I would have fiddled around with a week if I had been by myself. Besides, he was enjoyable to work with. At least most times. Sometimes he was the most aggravating feller I knew. Ever once in a while he acted like he still intended to try and court Molly some, but I didn't figure he'd get very far with that.

=

Having him to do the cow-work left me more time to get ambitious, and the land bug began to bite me pretty bad. I had already decided that land was something I'd never have enough of. So one day I buckled on my spurs and rode to Wichita to the bank and borrowed enough money to buy them three sections that joined me on the northwest. They were a good place to start extending. I had a deed drawn up and took it with me for the other feller to sign, and started home.

I rode hard that afternoon; the automobile was broke down or I would have gone in it. The weather was terrible—it was late August—and I didn't need no thermometer to tell me it was over a hundred degrees. When I crossed the Taylor place I decided to take the deed up and show it to Molly. I was proud of that deed, and I already knew Eddie wasn't there; I had looked that morning.

Molly was, though, ever inch of her, and she couldn't have looked better to me if she'd been Lily Langtry. I knocked at the back door and went on in, and she was just turning away from the stove. She had been putting up the last of her garden stuff.

"You're about as hot as I am," I said.

"I'm glad you come," she said. "Let's sit down and cool off."

I drank a couple of dippers of water out of the water bucket. She sat down at the table and I offered her a dipper full.

"I believe I will," she said, and she took the dipper and tilted her head back and drank. She had really been working: the arms of her shirt were sweated halfway down her side, and the tip ends of hair around her neck were wet. Her old shirt was plastered to her stomach. But she looked like the real thing to me; when she took the dipper down I leaned over and kissed her and she reached up to put her hands behind my head, so the dipper dripped water on my shoulder.

"You know why I'm glad you come?" she said. "I've been saving something to show you."

I grinned; I sure felt good. "What have you got I ain't already seen?" I said.

"This, Gid," she said, standing up. She grinned to herself and pulled the ends of her shirttail up and stuck her stomach out at me. It didn't look much bigger than it ever had, but it looked a little, and I got the message. Besides she grabbed me and hugged me.

"Don't that make you glad?" she said. "We've got one started. That makes me so proud. It's just what I've been wanting."

I didn't know what to say. It was okay with me, but I wasn't wildly happy about it, like she was. I was more excited about the deed.

"Why sure, Molly," I said, "if it's what you been wanting. And it's ours for sure?"

"It's ours for sure."

There was nothing else *to* say. She was happy enough to faint; she just sort of slid on me.

"Well, sugar," I said, after it was too late for it to have done any good, "I don't know about all this. You're so excited about it, we want to be careful and not jar it loose."

"This bed's just a puddle of sweat," she said, crawling over me. "I'll get some water and sprinkle us, so we'll be cooler." She brought in the dipper and sprinkled the sheets with me in them, and then sat down by me and caught my hand.

"It won't jar loose," she said. "I'm so glad the first one is yours. I wouldn't have wanted anybody else's to be the first."

"Honey, you're an awful strange woman," I said. "There ain't another like you in the world."

"That's okay," she said.

"See how this stretches the elastic," she said, sticking out her stomach agin when she started dressing. She had just got into her underpants.

"I thought it was supposed to make women less exciting," I said. "It sure hasn't you."

She flopped back on the bed and laughed a big one. I liked the way Molly laughed. "These sheets are still nice and cool," she said. I was done half-dressed but I lay back down a minute and grinned and kissed her.

"And you're my honey," she said. In a minute we got up and dressed. I showed her the deed, but it didn't impress her a snap's worth. But I must have impressed her a little; she wouldn't hardly turn loose of me that day.

"Gid, have you got time to see what's wrong with my windmill?" she said. "It just barely has been drawing lately."

"Sure, come on out with me," I said.

"I'll be out in a minute," she said. "I want to pin up this old hot hair." She raised her arms to pin it.

I got a pair of pliers and a couple of wrenches out of her tool box and climbed to the top of the pipe. It was just the sucker rod loose, and I tightened it in two minutes. But I didn't climb down, I rested a minute on the crossbars while I waited for Molly to come out. Dad was the only thing missing in life; I hated it that he had missed such a good year for cattle; it was just the kind of year he had always waited for. From where I sat I could see my new land.

I had my hand on the top of the pipe, and the damn rod went down and mashed my finger before I noticed. I damn near fell off, but caught myself. I had a blood blister to suck, and a big one. Some grayish clouds were building up in the north-west, so we might get rain.

Molly stepped out on the back porch, buttoning her shirt, with her hair pinned up high in a knot and her neck looking cool.

"Come on down," she said. "I'll get a crick in my neck looking up there."

"I'm surveying my new land," I said. "Except for your place I own everything west of here that I can see."

"You and your land," she said, "you ain't getting mine. Come on down here to me." She was shading her eyes and looking up.

So I climbed down. "I like to pinched my finger off," I said. "I better get on home before I get in more trouble."

She took my mashed finger and put it in her mouth and wet it; the finger still stung but I didn't much want to go home.

"You're supposed to kiss it," I said, "not slobber on it."

"I can't feel him yet," she said. "I ought to pretty soon."

"One of these days I'll repipe your windmill," I said, and then I remembered Eddie. Molly looked a lot thinner with her hair up on her head; it made her look cool and tender.

"I see you ain't interested in babies," she said. "Come with me to milk. It's cool enough now."

I got the bucket. The old brindle cow was already in the lot, waiting.

"Want me to milk?"

"No, she don't like strangers. You'd have to hobble her." So I put the feed in the stall and old Brindle went in. Molly got out her milking stool from under the trough and set down on it and went to milking. The old cow was an easy milker, but she kept switching her tail at flies and hitting Molly in the face. I got tickled.

"Here," I said. "I'll hold her tail." The old cow never noticed.

"If she ever steps on your foot you'll learn to wear shoes," I said. I squatted down by her and put my free hand on the back of her neck, where her skin was cool. I slipped my hand on under her shirt and rubbed her back and belly a little; a trickle of sweat slid along her ribs from her armpit.

"I wish I understood you," I said. "I never know just what you want from me. You'll make a good milker yourself." I felt in front and she grinned.

"I just want your loving and a little less conversation," she said.

We left old Brindle in the lot, eating prairie hay. I carried the milk bucket and she put her arm around my middle; we walked up to where my horse was tied. I set the milk bucket over in the yard and came back and kissed her bye. She poked her belly against me, but I got on my horse anyway, and she stood there grinning, fiddling with her shirttails.

"Aw, I'm glad, Molly," I said. "I just got this new land on my mind. I better go, I'm getting lonesome for you and I ain't even left yet."

"I guess I know what's good," she said. "Say hello to Mabel."

"I will, you say hello to Eddie." It was a kind of joke. If either of us actually did, it was her; she was just that crazy.

"If I come by agin in a day or two, will you chase me off?" I said.

"That's one thing I've never been guilty of," she said. The little barn swallows come out and begin to flitter around, and she looked up at them. "I love the cool of the evening," she said.

I loped across the hill and left her standing by the fence, fiddling with her shirt-tails. It was strange riding off from Molly; I never done it in my life that I didn't want to turn and go back a dozen times before I got out of sight. She always stood right where you left her, as long as she could see you. I remembered her in the kitchen that afternoon, all sweaty and loving, drinking the dipper of water and her throat wet. I felt like Molly was just as permanent as my land. Old Denver wanted to tear out for the barn, but I held him to a lope and we got to the lots just as the sun was going down behind the Ridge.

PART TWO

Ruin Hath Taught Me

Ruin hath taught me thus to ruminate,
That Time will come and take my love away.

—SHAKESPEARE,
Sonnet 64

1

JOHNNY CAME IN one afternoon and caught me crying. I had been listening to Kate Smith.

"My god, cheer up, Molly," he said. "You're going to ruin the oilcloth."

"Sit down," I said. "I know it's silly." I got up and poured him a cup of coffee, and he blew on it awhile and didn't say anything, and finally he reached over and squeezed one of my hands.

"Now look, quit this stuff," he said. "It's a beautiful day. You ought to be out making a garden instead of sitting in here like this. What brought it on?"

"Oh, the radio," I said. "Listening to Kate Smith. Ever time I do that I get blue." And not because of her, because of the songs. "God bless A-mer-ica, land that I love . . ."—she always sang that. I just wanted the war over and my boys home. My boy home.

"Aw, quit listening to all this patriotic stuff," he said. "It's just depressing. And it don't do no good."

"You make me mad," I said. "It wouldn't hurt you to be a little more patriotic. You ain't gonna cheer me up talking that way. I just wish we knew something definite about Joe."

He rubbed my hand and drank his coffee.

"Well, I do too, honey," he said. "He was my boy too. But imagine he's dead; be better for us to face it. Missing over a year. We can't just sit here and quit."

He made me get up and go outside with him, and he was right, it was a real pretty day. Being outside cheered me up. We sat on the cellar awhile and he took his hat off and put his arm around me.

"I knew you'd smile sooner or later," he said.

"Look how tall my corn's getting," I said. "Three more weeks and I can cook you some roasting ears. Where's your boss today?"

"He's off trying to buy him another ranch for me to take care of," he said. "Gids plain land-crazy."

"Well, you just let him go ahead." Johnny was always trying to slow Gid down. "Everybody's some kind of crazy." It was so clear we could see half the county. May was usually my favorite month.

"What kind of crazy are you?" Johnny said.

"Just plain crazy," I said. "I haven't got enough brains to be any other kind." Then he leaned over and kissed me; I figured he was getting about ready to. He'd had it in his mind ever since he came in.

"Well, Molly, I'm woman-crazy," he said, holding my shoulders and grinning his old reckless grin. He tickled me. I couldn't help loving Johnny, even when I wasn't much in the mood for him. Even when he was acting the soberest there was something about him that was like a boy; he never lost it, and it was one of the nicest things about him; when he was around I could have a boy and a man in the same person. Not like Gid at all—Gid never had been a boy; I guess his dad never gave him the chance. And that was why Jimmy was so much harder for me to raise than Joe. I never had any trouble handling Johnny and Joe.

"You want to help me tie up my tomato plants?" I said. "I might as well do that today."

"Well, now, you might as well not, either," he said. "I'd like to be treated like company for once, not like a damn hired hand. If I'm going to have to work, it had just as well be for Gid. He pays me."

"Pardon me," I said. "You was the one that mentioned gardening."

"Yeah, but you had the war blues then. Actually, why I'm here, I came a-courting." He kissed me agin; he was so funny.

"Why yes, honey, I'll marry you," I said when he quit. "Just let me go get my pocketbook so we can pay the preacher."

That always embarrassed him, even if he knew I was kidding. If there was ever a bachelor, it was Johnny McCloud.

"Aw hush," he said. "I'd just as soon marry an alligator."

It really got off with Johnny when I mentioned marrying; I should have quit doing it. I guess Gid kidded him about it all the time, and he was probably ashamed of himself for not wanting to marry me. If he had ever really asked me, I could have really turned him down, and he wouldn't have felt that way any more. I wouldn't have married agin anyhow; Eddie was enough husband for me. At least not Johnny. Gid I might have. But that was a different story.

"Well, I guess the tomatoes won't get tied up," I said, and took his arm. I wasn't too eager to go in the house with him then—for one thing, it was so pretty outside—but he was eager to go with me, so it was okay. I was the only woman Johnny had ever been able to count on, and I usually tried to give him what he needed—it wouldn't have been very loving of me not to.

He had a big ugly-looking blue spot on his hip where he said a horse had pitched him off against a tree stump, and I went in the pantry and got the liniment and made him lay back down while I rubbed some on it.

"You're sure nice to me," he said. "I'd have probably been a cripple years ago if it hadn't been for you."

"It don't take much to rub on liniment," I said. "You could have done that much already if you weren't so careless of yourself."

"It's so much more pleasant when you do it," he said. "You can rub my back a little if you just insist."

That was another difference in Johnny and Gid. Once Johnny got in a bed, no matter for what reason, he'd think of excuses to stay there for hours on end. Gid was just the opposite. You practically had to tie him down to keep him in bed ten minutes. I had been trying to break him of it for nearly twenty years; I hadn't made no progress, and in fact I'd lost ground. When we were both younger I could entice him to relax once in a while, but the older we got the less luck I had. Mostly, I guess, it was because Gid had so much energy he couldn't hardly stay still; but partly it was because he was ashamed of himself for being there in the first place, especially if it was in the daytime. At night he wasn't as bad, but then I never got to see much of him at night.

Not Johnny. He could lay around and enjoy himself for hours.

"Say, Molly," he said. He was lying there watching me; he was such a watcher it tickled me sometimes. "What'll you take to patch my britches pocket before I get them back on? I'm afraid I'll lose my billfold and all them valuables in it."

"I may not have any blue thread," I said.

"That's all right, I ain't particular."

I put my brassière on and patched them for him, while he dozed. His clothes were always just on the verge of being worn out; I think he just wore that kind when he visited me so there would be something for me to patch. I watched him sleep. Joe had his features to a T, and his eyes, and his recklessness; if he hadn't had the recklessness he wouldn't have got in no bomber crew to begin with. But that pleased Johnny. One day after Joe had already been reported missing, Johnny told me he'd rather have a dead hero for a son than a live coward.

"I'd rather have Joe than either one," I said, and I don't think he knew what I meant. Men don't think like women, or maybe it's that they don't feel the same kind of feelings. Gid had said practically the same thing to me when Jimmy got sent to the Pacific. And the boys were the same way, I guess. Joe actually enjoyed living over in England and flying in the bomber. I guess he had a million girl friends over there; I was always afraid he'd marry one of those English girls and bring her home to Texas and not know what to do with her. In his letters he never mentioned things like that. "How's the place, Momma?" or "What's Gid and Johnny doing?" or "Momma, I sure do miss your cooking, these army chefs sure can't cook like you. Why don't you send me some cookies?" Letters like that. Joe was the liveliest kid in the world, and the best natured. I waited till he was sixteen to tell him Johnny was his dad—it had bothered Jim so much when he found out Gid was his. But it tickled Joe flat to death. I imagine he pretty well suspected it anyway, but when he grinned at the news I cried for half an hour I was so relieved. I doubt Johnny and him ever talked about it. They usually just talked about horses and ballplaying and rodeos, things they were interested in. They probably never even mentioned it. Things like that just didn't worry Joe like they did Jimmy.

Johnny was sound asleep. He was woman-crazy all right, at least where I was concerned, and he tickled me the way he let me know it. But he wasn't as crazy as he had been. One time years before he had come charging into the kitchen in such a hurry that he hadn't even seen me and knocked me flat on my back—it scared Jimmy to death. I guess the time was coming when Johnny wouldn't barge in on me in the afternoons, and I would miss that, mood or no mood. I put the needle in the pincushion and got back in bed and made him turn over so I could lay against him, under one of his arms. I never did doze off, I just lay and looked out the window and counted Johnny's pulse once in a while, for the fun of it. It looked like a cloud was building up in the south. Ever once in a while Johnny would grunt like a hog, just one grunt, and then be quiet agin. One time straightening out his leg he scratched me, so I jumped; he was the worst in the world about toenails. Once I gave him a pair of clippers and he kept them about two days and broke them trying to cut a piece of baling wire. The arm I was holding had his watch on it, and when it got to be six o'clock I got up right quiet and put on my dress and cooked supper. Steak and gravy and black-eyed peas was about all we had, but I had a few fresh onions from the garden, and Johnny loved fresh onions.

When I went back to the bedroom the room was full of shadows, except for the one west window where the last of the sunlight was coming in. I sat down on the bed and gave Johnny a shake.

"Get up if you want any supper," I said.

He opened his eyes and stretched. "Aw hell, you're done dressed," he said, and grinned.

"You heard me," I said.

"We ain't wrestled in a long time," he said. "You want to?"

"Not specially," I said. "I've lost my girlish strength."

"You never had none, you was just awful wiggly," he said.

I went on and set the table and he stomped around dressing and washing up for ten minutes before he ever showed himself in the kitchen.

"Boy, where'd you get them onions?" he said. "Have you milked?"

"No," I said. "You can milk while I wash the dishes."

"These dishes won't need washing," he said, and they didn't much.

He went to the barn with me but I did the milking. He let the cow in and made conversation, but milking was a little beneath his dignity. Gid would grab ahold and do anything, but Johnny was finicky about the things he worked at. A lot of that rubbed off on Joe, only I never let Joe get away with it. One time I sent him out to hoe goatheads, and when I went out to see about him he was playing with a stick horse and hadn't hoed a lick.

"What are you doing?" I said. "I thought I sent you out here with a hoe."

He had really worked his nerve up by that time. "Momma, go to hell," he said. "I'm riding. Cowboys don't hoe."

"I'll cowboy you, sonny," I said, and I did. Johnny, he laughed about the whole thing and just made Joe worse, so the next time he came loving up to me I told him a thing or two. "Go court your horse," I said, "cowboys don't fool around with girls."

"Aw, honey, now you ain't mad at me," he said, but he didn't get nowhere that day.

When I finished the milking Johnny opened the gate so old Muley could go out, and I started to the house with the milk bucket. He came up and put his arm around me and made me slosh some milk out on my foot, so I gave him the bucket to carry.

"I never was no hand at milking," he said. "Think of the time it's saved me."

The only time I ever got Johnny to do chores was the winter after Eddie got killed, when I come down with the flu so bad. Gid and him took turns with my chores until I got over it. Both the boys had it too.

It was a warm, pretty evening. I strained the milk and Johnny poured himself some coffee. I got a jar of plum preserves and opened it for him; he loved to drink coffee and eat plum preserves. After he had spit about a hundred seeds into his coffee saucer I took the jar away from him and put it back in the icebox.

"It's a wonder you haven't took sugar diabetes, as much sweet stuff as you eat," I said.

"It's a wonder I haven't tooken something worse than that from associating with old widow women like you," he said.

I walked over behind him and squeezed his neck a little. "I always get old after supper," I said. "In the afternoon I'm still young and pretty."

"I've noticed that," he said. "I wonder why it is."

We sat around a while and then he put his hat on and we walked out to the back gate. There were plenty of stars showing, but there was a good bit of lightning back in the west.

"Well, I guess Gid's bought him another five sections by now," he said. "It's all I can do to keep him from working me to death. You'd think a man forty-seven years old would begin to slow down."

"Gid got a late start," I said. "He didn't really catch hold till after his dad died."

"He's making up for it."

"Tell him to come and see me," I said. "I don't get to see too much of him since they moved to town." And when he did come by he was in such a hurry I didn't get to talk to him long.

"He comes by often enough without me telling him to," Johnny said. "I'd just as soon not encourage the competition."

"How are him and Mabel making it?" I said.

"Oh, they're having trouble, Molly. But when ain't they? At least now they got a house big enough that they can kinda keep out of one another's way."

"I'm sorry," I said. "Gid deserves better."

"I think so too," he said.

"We never heard the news tonight. I forgot about it."

"We didn't miss nothing," he said. "You keep up with this war stuff too close."

"Well, you're an American," I said. "Don't you want to know what's happening?"

"Not particularly," he said. "When the Japs or the Germans cross the county line, then I'll be interested."

I didn't say no more; it was a sore spot with us. There was no changing Johnny. But I think he was sorry he said it, because he knew it made me blue.

"I 'pologize, honey," he said, patting my arm. "I didn't mean to hurt your feelings. Sure enjoyed the meal."

"I'm glad," I said. I kissed him on the cheek and he got in the pickup and started off. Then he stopped and leaned out the window.

"Much obliged for patching them pants," he said.

"You're welcome." He bounced on across the hill, hitting all the bumps. I could see the taillights bouncing. Johnny was a sorry driver and so was Gid. Joe and Jimmy could drive circles around either one of their dads. I stood by the fence until the taillights went out of sight. It seemed like I'd spent a lot of my life watching Gid or Johnny or one of the boys drive off across the hill. That was all right. I enjoyed being there where they could find me if they took a notion to come back—and they always had. After I watched the clouds awhile I decided it wasn't stormy looking enough to worry, so I went in and went to bed.

2

IT WASN'T BUT A few nights after that that it come a real bad cloud. Just before I went to bed I stepped outside to look around, and it was as pretty a night as anybody could want—I could see ever star in the Milky Way. I went back in and read a piece or two in the *Reader's Digest* and went to sleep. When I woke up the wind was blowing a gale and the limbs of the old sycamore tree were thrashing against the roof. I got out of bed and made sure the windows were all down, and then went out on the back porch to see if I could tell anything about the cloud.

The wind was out of the southwest and just about took my nightgown off. That was too much wind to sleep under, so I went back to the bedroom and got my bathrobe and a pillow. There was a cot with several quilts on it already made up in the storm cellar; I had learned long ago to have things like that ready.

I sat down at the radio a minute and tried to get a weather report, but all I got was static. Anyway, the way the sycamore thrashed was weather report enough. I put an apple in my pocket, in case I got hungry, and shut the back door good when I went out. Just as I stepped off the porch the big raindrops began to splatter me; there was an awful wind, and a big old tumbleweed came swooshing across the yard from the south and bounced right into me. In the dark I never seen it coming, and it scared me, and stung a little, but I got loose from it and went on to the cellar and shut the door after me. The sandstone steps felt cool on my feet; it was pitch dark. I had a kerosene lantern sitting on a table, but before I could work my way over to it I stumped my toe on an old pressure cooker that was sitting on the floor. I never could remember to throw it away, and I stumped my toe on it practically ever time I went to the cellar. From down there I could still hear the wind singing, but it didn't sound dangerous; nothing sounded dangerous from down in the cellar. I lit the lantern and looked through the quilts to be sure there wasn't no stinging lizard in them. The cellar was clean, and there never had been many stinging lizards down there, but it never hurt to look; not near as much as it hurt to get stung. Then I blew out the lantern and snuggled down in the quilts and ate my apple. It was a nice sweet one and smelled fresh, like it had just come off the tree that day.

When I got done I dropped the core under the cot. I had such a good taste in my mouth; it was one thing I liked about apples. Lately I had got so I always belched peaches, so I didn't eat them much, except in homemade ice cream. I felt nice and cozy and relaxed snuggled in the quilts, and I wasn't too worried about the storm. Where cyclones were concerned I was awful lucky. One time one went right between the house and the barn, and all it done was turn Dad's old wagon over; it never even hurt the chickenhouse.

I thought I would doze right off to sleep, but I didn't. I lay there wide awake. It began to rain real hard; I heard it beating against the tin door of the cellar. After I lay there thirty minutes or an hour I knew I was going to get real blue before the night was over, and in a little while I began to cry. I didn't even try to stop myself. At first I was just barely sniffing, but then all my feelings rushed up to my chest and my head and I heard myself crying over the rain on the door. I was crying so hard I thought I had fallen off the cot; when I was coughing and trying to get my breath I pulled back one of the quilts and felt the canvas with my hand, so I hadn't fallen. My breasts just felt like empty sacks. I turned the pillow over on the dry side and cried some more hard crying, and finally I quit and pushed the pillow off the cot and lay on my stomach with my head on my arms. I was all upset and knew I wouldn't go to sleep, but I didn't feel any more like I was going to die.

There was no cure for being upset that way; I just had to grit my teeth and wait for the feelings to die down. Being lonesome itself was just part of it—mostly I couldn't stand not having anybody to do for. I never was happy when I just had myself to do for, or even when I had somebody else wanting to do for me. That was nice, but that wasn't the main point about loving, at least not with me. The main point was having somebody I could let my feelings out on. And I couldn't do that very well at a distance, I needed to have somebody right around close, so I could touch them and cook for them and do little things like that. It was always men or boys, with me. I never knew a woman I cared for—not even Ma. Men need a lot of things they don't even know about themselves, and most of them they can't get nowhere but from women. It was easy to do for them, most of the time, and it made me feel so comfortable. A lot of times it wasn't easy, of course, but it still felt better to try. With Johnny and Joe it was easy; they were just alike and needed exactly the same kind of handling. With Gid it was sometimes awful hard because Gid was too honest; he never would fool himself or let nobody else fool him, even if it was for his own good. I tried it enough times to know it couldn't be done, especially if he was having hard times with Mabel. It had nearly always been hard with Dad, and with Eddie, and it was hardest of all with Jimmy, who was just Gid times two. At least Dad and Eddie liked themselves, even if they didn't like me, and I could figure out what to do from that. But Jimmy, he never liked himself or me, and that made life hell for him. And he hadn't changed. Wherever he was, over there in the Pacific, he was wishing he was somebody else's son besides me. I never even put my hand on Jimmy, not even on his arm, after he found out that Gid was his daddy, and that I was still letting Gid and Johnny get in bed with me. Only I wasn't letting them come, I was wanting them to: Jimmy didn't know that, or didn't understand it, but if he had he would have just hated me more. I blame some of Jimmy's troubles on religion, but I can't blame them all on it; I have to blame most of them on myself. If I had married Gid instead of Eddie, Jim might have been a happy boy. But if that had happened, Eddie would have killed Gid, or Gid and Johnny would have fell apart, and there might not have even been a Joe. I don't know that I done very wrong. But I know that Jimmy's miserable; some of the time I am too. Four men and two boys were what I'd had for a life, and laying there on the cot I could picture every one of them, plain as day. But there wasn't a one of them I could get my arms around, and right then, that was what I wanted; I would rather have been blind and had the touch than like I was, with just the picture.

Everybody gets hard nights, though, I guess. It wasn't the first time I'd ever felt sick with my feelings, and I wasn't girl enough to think it would be the last. When you lay around feeling cut off from folks, crazy things go through your mind. I would see men's hands and faces and other parts of them, sometimes even their stomachs, Eddie's or Johnny's, or Gid's. Probably if I had gone on and married Johnny, it would have been good for both of us, but he wouldn't have done it, even if I had really wanted to. He was too responsibility-shy. Besides it would have made Gid feel terrible; he had wanted to marry me all his life.

Once I almost decided to marry Gid—I guess I was just jealous of Mabel. We were in my bedroom.

"If you've got the guts to quit her, I'll marry you," I said. "If you don't, I wish you'd quit wishing out loud."

That was when Gid was having terrible times at home, and when I said that he looked like he was about to split in two.

"Honey, you know it ain't a matter of guts," he said. "If I didn't have that much guts, I wouldn't be here now. But I don't believe in divorcement—it ain't right. If Mabel wants to do it, she can. I ain't going to."

"If it was conscience, you wouldn't be here," I said. "So I still think it's guts." I talked awful to Gid sometimes; I don't know why he didn't choke me. I would nearly drive him crazy.

"Well, let's just be quiet for a little while," he said. "Honey, I got to go in fifteen or twenty minutes."

That made me feel terrible, and I pulled him over to me. We had some rough times, me and Gid, a lot rougher than any I ever had with Johnny. Or with Eddie either. Nothing was rough with Johnny, and when things were bad with me and Eddie it was just because he plain enjoyed being rough and mean to women; I was hardly ever hard on him like I was on Gid. Sometimes I hated Gid, and I never felt that strong about Eddie one way or the other.

After I had cried enough, and thought about things enough, I finally did go to sleep. It wasn't good sleeping—I felt like I had fever, but I guess I would have slept all morning if Gid hadn't been good enough to come by and see about me. First thing I knew someone was banging on the cellar door. Down where I was it was still pitch dark.

"I'm down here," I said. "You can open the door."

Bright sunlight fell on the steps and across the foot of the cot, and I seen Gid's old boots on the top step and knew it was him.

"Well, thank goodness," he said. "Can I come on down? I was scared you'd blown plumb away." He took another step, so I could see about to his knees.

I sat up and pushed the hair back out of my face. "My lord," I said, "I've overslept. What time is it, Gid? I bet the milk cow thinks she's forgot."

"Oh, it's not too late," he said. "About seven. I can get them chores for you. Can I come down?"

"Please come on down here," I said, pulling the quilts up around my middle. "Did the house blow away?" He came on down the steps, I seen his legs and his belly—he was getting a little bulge—and then all of him, standing there kinda grinning at me but looking like he had been worried. Gid was always my favorite; sometimes when I seen him the delight would shoot right through me, as sharp sometimes as a sting.

"Well, Molly, I sure was worried about you," he said. "I heard on the five o'clock weather report there was two tornadoes sighted out this way."

"Oh, sit down here," I said. "I'm all right." And when he sat down on the cot I couldn't keep from hugging him. He hadn't shaved that morning, and I felt the bristles on his face against my neck and his arms squeezing my sides; it made me feel good clear to the bottom. He was tense and tight as a drum. Gid always came to me tense. I held him and rubbed my hand on his neck and down his back, and in about two minutes he kind of sighed and let things loosen inside him.

"I don't know what I'd do if you was to blow away," he said.

"Hush," I said. "I won't." I made enough room on the cot that he could lay down by me; it wasn't comfortable, but for a few minutes it was okay; I felt like myself agin. Then Gid got embarrassed that I would think he came for bedroom stuff—as many times as he had come for that he still got embarrassed if he thought I knew it—and he sat up.

"Well, I never meant to come out here and go back to bed," he said, picking his hat up off the floor.

"I guess you're the silliest man alive," I said. "Maybe that's why I love you so much. When you were young I didn't think you were silly at all."

I got up too and slipped my bathrobe on and we went up the steps and outside. The yard grass was wet and cool against my bare feet, but it was a clear day, and the sun was drying things up fast. I guess it was the latest I'd slept in two or three years. There were a lot of broken limbs and leaves and tumbleweeds in the yard, and it had blown a few shingles off the roof, but I didn't see any serious damage. Gid went around the house, inspecting everything, but I felt too good to worry about wind damage; I stood by the cellar, yawning and stretching the kinks out of myself, soaking up the sun. Gid went in the house and got the milk bucket and came and stood by me a minute. He had a look on his face that meant he really wanted to spend the day with me but wanted to do fifty other things too.

"I'll go milk," he said. "I never ate breakfast in town, I could eat with you. I got a million things to do today."

I rubbed my head against his neck; it embarrassed him a little.

"Go on and milk," I said. "I'll get breakfast. But you needn't be planning on rushing off."

"I got to, Molly," he said. "I just wish I didn't."

I went in and cooked a big breakfast, eggs and bacon and biscuits and gravy, and pretty soon he came in with the milk. We sat down and ate.

"What do you hear from Jimmy?" he said, while we were drinking coffee.

"Nothing." And that was all he said during breakfast. I knew he was getting up his nerve to leave.

"Well, that was a good breakfast," he said, pushing back his chair. "I hate to eat and run, but I guess I better. I got many a mile to make today."

"Don't leave this morning, Gid," I said. "Just stay around here."

When I came right out and asked him, flat like that, he had to at least look at me. He was too honest just to dodge behind his hat.

"You need me to help you do something?" he said.

I could have slapped him for saying that. I needed him to help me live. "No," I said. "I just like to be around you."

It was like I had run a needle into his quick. He shoved his hands in his pockets and shook his head. He didn't say anything, and I sipped my coffee.

"I'm glad you do," he said, finally. "I'd like to stay a month. But you know what I'm up against. I've got a few more obligations than you have."

I felt miserable for being so hard on him, but I got harder in spite of it.

"Okay," I said. "Come back next time there's a storm."

"Aw, now be fair," he said, and I could tell he was trembling. "I got things I *have* to do; I'm a husband. Can't you understand that?"

"I understand you ain't going to stay," I said. "It's pretty plain what you don't want to do." Before I could finish saying it he had stepped over and yanked me out of the chair so quick I didn't even see his hand, grabbed my hair and yanked my head back so tears sprang out of my eyes, and my face was about two inches from his. But after he held me that way a minute his hands began to tremble.

"I'm sorry, Gid," I said, and we walked outside together and stood in the yard.

"I'm the most worthless white man alive," he said. "I'll stay a week."

"No, honey, go on and work," I said.

"You got some gloves? We might as well patch up them old corrals of yours."

We went down to the barn and he got out the tools, and we spent the whole morning patching on the lots, putting a new board in here and there and resting with one another and doing odds and ends and talking. We just piddled, and enjoyed it. Then I fixed him a big dinner and about two o'clock hugged him and sent him on. He was thinking about taking me in the bedroom but I didn't encourage him; if he had that day, he would have been down on himself for a month and wouldn't have come to see me all that time. If we held off, he'd be back in a day or two, when he felt easier, and it would be better for him. Gid was a complicated person, but I had been studying him a long time, and I knew his twists. We had given one another a lot of good times, of one kind or another, since that summer I got pregnant with Jimmy. That seemed an awful long time ago. I guess the times we spent together, the good ones, not the bad ones—there were enough of them, too—were the best times either one of us ever had.

Three days later, about the middle of the afternoon, Gid came back over. I had been working in the henhouse all day and was sweated down, but I was still glad to see him. I wiped off my face and took him right in the house.

3

ONE DAY about the middle of June a man from up around Vernon came by and wanted to sell me some alfalfa hay. I hadn't bought any alfalfa in three years and it sounded cheap enough, so I told him to go ahead and bring me ten ton; he said he'd be there with it the next day.

That afternoon about three o'clock I put on my overalls and got the hull fork and climbed up to see what I could do about cleaning out the loft. I didn't want the men to have to do it when they got there with the hay. It was a pretty hot day for that time of the year. I turned on the faucet at the water trough and washed my face and got a big drink before I climbed up. Working in the loft was like working in an oven.

I opened the loft doors at both ends, so there would be a little ventilation. There was plenty to do, I seen that. The loft probably hadn't been cleaned out since Dad built the barn. The wastage and chaff from all the hay we'd put up was about shin deep, all over the loft, and it was full of all kinds of mess that Dad had left around and I never had bothered: bailing wire and hay hooks and buckets and whatnot. I got to poking around, and there was every kind of nest you could imagine in the old loose, dry hay. Rats' nests and mice nests and cats' nests and barn owls' nests and possum nests and probably even a skunk nest or two, if skunks can climb. Many a time, in the winter, I would go up in the loft and find a big old momma possum curled up in the hay, snoozing where it was warm.

There were fifteen or twenty rotten bales of leftover hay that wasn't good enough to feed, so the first thing I did was get a hay hook and drag those over and shove them out the north loft door; that way the milk cows could find them and eat what they wanted of them. I left one bale, to sit on.

Moving the bales was work itself, and when I got done I could feel the sweat dripping down my legs and down my sides. I drug my sitting bale over by the south door where I could get some breeze, and rested a while. From the loft I could see way off south, to where Gid's fence line ran across Idiot Ridge. I wisht I could see more of Gid. I missed him when I didn't get to see him regular; but I guess he came over ever time his conscience would let him. I never had been able to talk Gid out of his conscience, or love him out of it, either; I had tried both ways. Me and Gid were in a situation where neither one of us could completely win, and I used to wonder why we let ourselves get that way. Maybe we didn't—I don't know that there are situations where you can completely win. Not where you can completely win something important.

A lot of medium-sized thunderheads were blowing around in the sky, so that patches of shadow would come over the pastures and sometimes right up to the barn. Then the clouds would go on north, and it would be bright and sunny till another bunch came along. When I had rested enough I got up and took the hull fork and went to raking the wastage out the loft door. The old stuff was so matted down that it made hard raking. I was always scaring out rats; most of them run along the rafters till they found a hole and went down into the saddlehouse or the oatbin. When Jimmy and Joe were little boys they used to take their rat terrier up in the loft and let him kill rats; it was how we lost that dog, actually. One day he ran a big rat out the loft door and went right out after it. The dog broke his neck and the rat got away. Joe come running up to the house, screaming; he was just heartbroken. It was the first time anything he loved had died. I picked Joe up and ran down to the barn and Jimmy had already carried the dog over by the post pile and was digging a hole to bury him. He was crying, but he wasn't hysterical. He had had one dog die of a rattlesnake bite. Joe couldn't understand why he was putting Scooter in the ground.

"We don't want the buzzards to eat him," Jimmy said, but Joe didn't know what a buzzard was. He had crying fits for three weeks after that.

I had raked out the east side pretty thorough and was trying to make a start in the northwest corner when my fork struck something that made a glassy sound, and, of all things, I fished up one of Dad's old whiskey jugs. It surprised the daylights out of me. No telling how long it had been back in that corner. It was still corked, and had whiskey sloshing around in it. Nobody had touched it since the day Dad set it in the corner.

I laid my hull fork down and picked up the jug and went back to my sitting bale. I felt real strange. Picking up the jug brought Dad back to me, and it gave me the weak trembles. Dad's beard and his hat pulled down over his eyes. When I pulled out the stopper and put my nose to the mouth of the jug, the strong whiskey fumes went right up my nostrils and made my eyes water. His eyes and his eyebrows and skinned-up hands and yellow fingernails and two broken-off teeth and the gray hair under his hat, around his ears. The whiskey smell was Dad's smell: I never got close to him in my life that I didn't smell it. The night Eddie and Wart brought him in out of the smokehouse they didn't even pull off his boots; Gid had to do it after he came.

For a while I sat by the bale, just holding the jug. It was brown, that thick glass kind. The outside was dusty, but the dust hadn't got through the stopper; it hadn't even rotted much. If I had drunk the whiskey, it would have made my tongue numb in a second. Twice in my life Dad had made me drink whiskey, and it scalded my throat both times. The first time I was just a little girl, three or four years old, and Johnny and his dad came over. The men were drinking. I don't know why they did it, but they caught us kids and made us each take a swallow of whiskey out of a tin cup. We cried and then ran off down to the pigpen together, me and Johnny; that was the day we got to be friends. That night Dad got me on his lap and teased me. "How'd you like that likker?" he said. "You want a little more? You can have some if you want it." Momma had done gone to bed. I hugged his neck big so he wouldn't make me drink any more.

The other time was years later, three or four years before he died. I had slipped off somewhere with Eddie while Dad was gone to Henrietta. Dad got back first, and when Eddie and me seen the wagon we knew he'd be mad. Eddie wouldn't come in with me; he let me off at the barn.

"Hell, he's your dad," he said. "You can handle him better than I can."

But I couldn't, really. When I went in the kitchen and told Dad where I'd been, he grabbed me and like to whipped the pants off me with his razor strap.

"When I leave you at home," he said, "I want to find you here when I come back."

My feelings were hurt and I hurt from the whipping too and wanted to go to bed, but Dad felt lonesome and sorry for himself and he made me sit up till midnight, keeping him company. We sat at the kitchen table and he poured me a big glass of straight whiskey and told me not to drink it too fast and not to leave till I drank every drop of it. I vomited half the night.

There was only one time in my life when I ever drank whiskey of my own accord, and that was the afternoon Eddie told me he wanted me to miscarry Jimmy. He didn't know I was pregnant by Gid, either; he thought it was by him. I cried and argued and argued with him about it.

"Shut up arguing," he said. "I told you before we started all this I never intended to have no kids. All the time I was growing up I had them little brothers and sisters of mine under my feet constantly, and I don't intend to fiddle with no more kids. They're just trouble. You should never have let it happen. If you don't get rid of it yourself, I'll take you to a man who'll get rid of it for you."

"What kind of a man is that?" I said. "And how do you know about him?"

"I done rung the bell a time or two before, in my life," he said. "It cost me fifty dollars, both times, but that's a damn sight cheaper than raising a goddamn kid. If you're smart though, you can save us that fifty dollars. Go horseback riding a lot."

"No, I want to have him, Eddie," I said. "I won't have any more, but I want to have this one." I was crazy about Gid in those days; he was all I could think about.

"I told you what you better do," he said, finishing his beans. "And you better do it, if you don't want no operation. Because I'll take you if I have to drag you, you can believe that, can't you?"

I could believe it. Eddie was just like Dad when it came to doing what he made his mind up to do. The only way to stop either one of them was to be stronger than they were, and I never was that strong, at least not physically. Once in a while I could stop them another way.

That afternoon I cried and cried. I could already feel Jimmy kick against my belly. Then I got one of Eddie's whiskey bottles and kept mixing it with water and drinking it till I guess I got drunk. My head felt like it had smoke in it, and everything in the house looked funny. I decided I would try to get Gid to run away with me, and if he wouldn't, I'd run away myself. I had fourteen dollars of Dad's money that Eddie had never found. I figured I would catch a train to Amarillo; that was where Gid and Johnny went when they ran away. I guess I was crazy. I changed clothes three or four times that afternoon, trying to decide what to wear to go see Gid. And I never had that many clothes; I changed into some twice. When Eddie came in I just had on an old cotton slip and was down on my hands and knees fishing under the sink trying to find a tow sack or something to use for a suitcase. I must have been drunk; I never knew Eddie was in the house till I felt his hips jammed against my behind and his hand around my middle. But I knew it was his hand; nobody's hand behaved like Eddie's.

"I'm glad I got me a wife that goes around half-naked," he said. "That's the most exciting kind."

I was crazy, I didn't even know what he was saying. "Eddie, have you seen a sack?" I said. "I need a good big sack." For a while he wouldn't even let me back out from under the sink; I couldn't even raise my head.

"Sack, my eye," he said. "You don't need no sack, sugardoll," and his hand gave me fits and he got to wanting to kiss me; then he let me out. I couldn't get it out of my head that I was leaving; I wouldn't even know he was kissing me till he would quit for a minute. I had to vomit a lot that day too. When Eddie woke up he told me I could have the baby.

"I learned something today," he said. "It's more fun wallowing around with you when you're pregnant. I never knew that before. I wonder why it is?"

I was feeling so bad the news didn't penetrate to me till later.

"I guess it must be the tilt," he said. "The tilt's a lot better this way. I hope it keeps on improving, I like to have something to look forward to."

I guess it did, because it was him wallowing that made me start with Jimmy, when the time came. I never even tried to get him to quit; that wouldn't have worked with Eddie. The day the baby was born he left and didn't come home for three months, and that meant that Gid could come every day or two. I was happy. And Eddie liking the tilt so good made things a lot easier when Johnny got me pregnant agin, three years later. Otherwise Eddie would have either beat me to death or left me, then and there. Or both. If there was one thing Eddie never had much of, it was patience with me.

And Dad never either. Smelling the whiskey made me think of things about Dad that I hadn't thought of in years. He always felt the worst when he was the nearest sober; I guess it just took whiskey to make life look good to him.

One of the worst times I ever had with Dad in my life was the afternoon he told me and Richard about the facts of life. It was four or five years after Momma died; I was about seventeen. Except for one trip to town when I was a little girl, I had never been farther away from home than the schoolhouse. Eddie wasn't even in the country then, and since we were all too big for school, I didn't see Gid or Johnny more than a few times a year. Once in a while they would stop at the windmill for a drink of water. I had never even thought of having a boy friend—my brothers were the only boys I really knew.

And it was the same way with the boys—none of them ever had a girl friend till after they run away from home. Richard never, I'm sure; he only went to the schoolhouse two years. Me and Mary Margaret were the only girls he ever saw, and him and Mary Margaret fought like cats and dogs.

One evening I was rolling the flour to cook the supper biscuits, and Dad came in and sat down at the table. It was March or April, and the sand had been blowing; Dad's hair was full of grit, and he sat at the table and scratched his head. He never said a word to me. I started to ask him if he wanted me to give him a haircut; I gave all the haircuts my family had, as long as I had a family. Except for one burr haircut Joe got while he was in high school; it made me mad because he snaked around so about it.

But Dad didn't want one. He was in a strange kind of mood, and I didn't bother him. I was getting ready to grease the biscuit pan when Dad went to the back door and yelled at Richard. In a minute Richard slouched in.

"Just leave them biscuits awhile," Dad said. "Come back here with Richard and me." They went off down the hall, and I wiped some grease off my thumb and followed them. They had gone into Daddy's bedroom and it was the biggest mess in the world. Dad never even let me make the bed.

"Shut the door," Dad said. He sat down on his bed and pushed back his hat. He sat there about ten minutes, just thinking, and I wanted to get back to my biscuits.

"What did you want, Daddy?" I said. Me and Richard were just standing there. Except Richard wasn't impatient. He never was.

"I guess Richard's old enough for me to show him a few things," he said. Neither one of us had any idea what he was talking about. Finally he grinned at Richard.

"Take your pants off," Dad said. It didn't surprise Richard; I guess he thought he was going to get a whipping, was all; he took off his overalls. It had been cold and he still had on his long johns.

"My god them's dirty underwear," Dad said. "Take them off too."

"Aw, it's cold," Richard said, but he started unbuttoning, anyway. In those days me and Richard and Mary Margaret all slept in the same bed—just Shep got to sleep by himself—and I had seen Richard pee a million times, so he never thought of being embarrassed just because of me. I was just a little bit embarrassed—not so much that as worried, because Dad was acting so strange. Richard was cold-natured and got goose bumps all over his legs.

"Now, Molly, get your clothes off a minute," Dad said.

I had been about to giggle at Richard's goose bumps, but that surprised me. "Why do I have to?" I said. I knew better than that. Dad looked at me for the first time since he'd come in.

"The next time you ask me why when I tell you to do something, you'll get a real tanning," he said. But he wasn't mad, he was just warning.

"What all did you say take off?" I said.

He was cutting himself some tobacco then. "Ever stitch," he said. "I need to show Richard about women, and you're the only one around. Hurry up."

That was the first time I ever felt funny being around a boy. I took my pants and shirt off, but I sure did want to keep my underwear.

"I'm cold too," I said. "Ain't this enough, Daddy?"

"I'm gonna warm you in a minute," he said. "I told you what to take off."

I still had on long johns too, only the legs were cut out of mine. I went ahead and took them off and stood there naked, holding my underwear in front of me. Dad never looked at me, but I felt awfully embarrassed; it was a strange feeling. Then Dad noticed I was holding my underwear and he snatched it out of my hands and threw it down on the floor. That made it worse.

"All right, now, Richard, looky there," Dad said, nodding at me. "That's how they look." Then he looked me up and down himself, a real long look. "Molly's a real pretty gal," he said. "You're lucky to get to see such a pretty one. She's a damn sight prettier than her momma ever was."

"What am I supposed to look at?" Richard said. "All I see is Molly, and I know her anyway." If it had been anybody but Richard, I would have been even worse embarrassed. There wasn't no harm to Richard.

Dad laughed. "You ain't looking good," he said. "Come up here by her and squat down where you can see. See where that hair's growing on her?"

I didn't know what to do with my hands. I knew Dad didn't want me to cover myself up with them. Finally I held them behind me. Richard had squatted down by me and was really looking.

"Oh yeah, that's where she pees," he said. "I see that. Why's all that hair grow there? It's on me, too, but not as much."

"That's to make it hard to get into," Dad said. "The thing to remember about it is that's where you make babies, right up in that crack."

"It don't look like a big enough place," Richard said. "I'm still cold without my pants."

"Stand up here," Dad said. "You can just stay cold. You ain't much of a boy, anyhow. Make him stiffen up, Molly, so I can tell him how it works."

I knew what he meant, or thought I did, and I didn't move. I didn't want to touch Richard.

"Take ahold of him," Dad said. "He don't know the first thing."

"No, I don't want to," I said. "Richard don't want me to, either. He understands it, he's seen the bulls."

"You're the contrariest damn girl I ever saw," Dad said. "Do like I told you."

Richard's was hanging there, about arm's length away, but I knew I wasn't going to touch it, not even because Dad said to. In a minute I started to cry, and tears were running down my chest and stomach.

"I'll give you something to cry about," Dad said, and stomped out. I knew he was going after the razor strap, and I couldn't think of anything to do. I just stood there crying. But the minute Dad left Richard's got stiff. When Dad got back it still was. Richard and me were both surprised.

"Well, did she help you?" Dad said, when he seen it.

"Naw, it just done it by itself," Richard said. "I'm sorry. I never meant for it to." He was as embarrassed as me.

"Why, hell," Dad said, "that's what I've been trying to get you to do. Now you see, when it's like that it fits the crack in Molly. And most of the time it makes a baby, so you got to be careful where you shove it."

"You mean if you don't put it in you don't have no babies? Then why do people have babies anyway?" Richard said. Richard had a hard time understanding it. But I did too. I just stood there wishing it was over.

"Because it feels so good when it's up in there," Dad said. "You'll feel it some day."

Richard perked up at that; he loved to feel good. "Oh," he said. "Then can I try it with Molly right now? I'd like to know just how it does feel."

Dad hit him across the behind with the razor strap.

"No, and get your pants on and get out of here," he said. "I've shown you all you need to see. You don't never do it with your sister; not never. And you better remember that."

I reached to pick up my underwear, but Dad shoved me back away from it.

"I'm going to have a little talk with you," he said, and Richard left.

"Why didn't you do what I told you to?" he said.

I tried to think of a good answer, but I couldn't. I didn't know why, actually.

"I don't know, Daddy," I said.

"Do you want me to whip you with this razor strap?" he said, standing up.

I shook my head. But I knew he was going to.

"If I brought that boy back and told you to do it agin, would you mind me this time?" he asked.

I thought about that a long time. From the way Dad looked I knew about all I could do was take up for myself. Besides, I didn't want to touch Richard.

"No, I wouldn't," I said, "I sure wouldn't."

"I'll make you think wouldn't," he said, and I got the worst whipping he ever gave me. But I never did say I would, and he finally quit. He would always quit if I took up for myself long enough. Sometimes it was real hard to do, and it was hard then.

==

Of course Richard was a pest after that. Dad had got his curiosity aroused, and he soon forgot the part about not doing it with his sister. He pestered me for two solid years. But he wasn't no danger; he was just a nuisance. I could always fight Richard off.

Dad always expected his kids to mind him without asking no questions, and whenever I got in trouble it was always for not minding, or for asking questions first. But I still thought he was an awful good daddy, and that's what Johnny and Gid could never understand. They never liked Dad; neither did Eddie. But all they seen was his rough side. Dad never went around making over me, but I could tell he liked the way I fixed things and took care of him. It used to make me blue that I was the only one he had to love him. Momma and him wasn't suited for one another; Dad was rougher on her than he was on any of us. The boys all hated him because he worked them so hard, and Mary Margaret couldn't stand him.

Him and Eddie did manage to tolerate one another, I guess because they both liked to drink whiskey. Likker was the only thing Dad ever gave away; mostly because he liked company when he drank. And Eddie liked free likker. He took advantage of Dad that way.

Once Dad even told me that if I got married, to marry Eddie.

"He ain't much count," he said. "But at least, by god, he'll treat you like a wife ought to be treated. He won't pussyfoot around with you, I'll tell you that."

That may have been part of the reason I married Eddie. We hadn't never been considered respectable, and he hadn't either. Eddie and Dad were a lot alike; they never tried to get ahead like most men do. They spent their time trying to enjoy themselves, and a lot of the time they were miserable anyway. All Eddie's folks were living in Arkansas, and he never had a soul to look after him or take up for him.

I had liked Johnny ever since I knew him, but I never took marrying him serious. He wasn't the marrying kind, and we both knew it. So it was between Gid and Eddie. I liked Gid better, and there were times when I stayed upset for days, trying to make up my mind to marry him. Sometimes I wanted to so bad I could taste it. But I thought Eddie needed a wife the worst—I was dead wrong about that. And then I thought I was too wild and bad ever to suit Gid; I was afraid if I married Gid everything I did would disgust him—and I was dead wrong about that. I married Eddie, and everything I did disgusted *him,* and nothing I did ever made Gid stop caring for me. I'm more like Gid, in the long run, than I am like Dad or Eddie, but I was years and years finding that out.

I wasn't just sorry for Eddie, either; I was crazy about him sometimes. I was just crazy about him, about the way his hair was always shaggy and curly on the back of his neck. That may have been what I liked best about Eddie; it may have been why I married him, silly as that is. He never got a haircut and I was always dying to put my hand on the back of his neck.

==

But thinking about old times never got no loft cleaned out. I finally stoppered the bottle and got up, and then I pushed the sitting bale out the loft door so I wouldn't be tempted to sit down and daydream no more. It was four-thirty or so, and cooling off, and by the time I got the west side of the loft raked it was six or after, and milking time. I stood in the loft door and wiped the sweat off my neck and face with my shirttail and watched the milk cow come up. When I got down I hung the jug on a nail in the saddle shed, with the whiskey still in it. It was good and aged, there wasn't no use pouring it out. While I was milking Johnny drove up in his pickup and I talked him into staying for supper with me. He wasn't very hard to persuade.

4

I HADN'T GOT A CAR till 1941. Besides being expensive and dangerous, I thought they was just plain ugly. I couldn't understand why so many people took such an interest in them. Both the boys were big car-lovers, of course: the first hundred dollars Jimmy ever made he spent on an old rattletrap Hupmobile. He run it for three years and sold it to Joe for fifty. From that time on they were both on the road constantly, going somewhere. I just let them go. Them driving didn't worry me like me driving. They grew up in a time when cars were the thing, and they knew enough about them to handle them okay.

After I had driven two years I got so I could wrestle the car to town and back without any serious danger, unless the road was slick or I met somebody in a nar-row place. Gid and Johnny had taken me to Wichita and advised me when I bought the car. It was a Ford, a black one. We looked at about fifty, and it was the one Gid said I ought to get. I was enjoying the company, and I didn't care. Johnny was in a hi-larious mood that day.

"I wisht you'd get that red convertible," he said. "A widow like you needs a car like that to haul her boy friends in."

"I wouldn't mind it," I said. "I think I'd like one open, so I could climb out if I needed to."

"You'd need to if I was with you," he said. We had stopped to drink coffee and Johnny had drunk beer instead. It was old watery café coffee, so I wisht I'd drunk beer too. I was feeling good that day. We all were.

Gid was solemn as a judge though until we got the car bought. Spending that much money, even if it wasn't his, always made Gid sober. Just to tease him I made them take me around to the Cadillac place, and I even got out and went in. They had the nicest salesman we met, too; I would have just as soon bought one of his cars. But Gid rushed me off.

"Whew, I'm glad to get out of there," he said. "He'd have sold you a limousine in another ten minutes."

"Well, I guess if I had wanted it I'd have bought it," I said. "It's my money, you know."

"I know," he said. "But it won't be long."

After we bought the Ford he loosened up a lot and we went to a big cafeteria and ate lunch. Johnny cut up with all the waitresses; it's a wonder they let us stay. Gid was just cutting up with me.

"Well, we got that done, we can enjoy ourselves," he said.

After dinner they flipped a coin to see who would drive me home in the new car, and Gid won. Johnny didn't care. He took off in Gid's car, and I bet he went right to some beer joint and tanked up.

Gid had on new boots and a new gray shirt that day, and he looked fine and handsome. He was just getting rich then; anyway he had a lot of confidence in himself. It was before Mabel made him move to town.

"Well, since we're here," he said, "let's just make a holiday of it. You want to go to a picture show?"

"I guess so," I said, "I'm just with you."

So we went and he bought some popcorn and we sat right in the middle of the theater, and Gid put his arm on the seat behind me, so that when I leaned back I could feel it against my shoulders and neck. It was such a comfortable feeling, and once in a while he would put his hand against my neck or my hair. Nobody else made me feel comfortable that way. I don't remember what the picture was, or what it was about. I never can remember picture shows; most of them are so silly, anyway. When we came out of the dark show the sun was so bright I could hardly see, and he had to practically lead me down the street to the car. It was a shiny, new-smelling car then; after I'd hauled chicken feed in it for a month or two it smelled different.

Gid drove, and we rode out of Wichita toward Scotland, into the open country. I took off my neck scarf and unpinned my hair; the bobby pins were hurting my head. It was nice to get out in the country agin; so far as I was concerned, Wichita Falls was the ugliest place on the earth.

"Drives like a good car," Gid said. "Just stiff. You bounce it over them old dirt roads awhile and it'll get broke in."

"It better be good," I said. "I intend for it to last me the rest of my life."

My hair itched from being pinned up all morning, and I combed it out while Gid drove home. It was early fall. The boys had both volunteered in August, and they were still in boot camp. After that Jimmy got sent to New Jersey and Joe to California. All the way across the country from one another.

"Well, I guess the boys are doing okay," I said. "The worst thing they've complained about is the cooking."

"Oh, have you heard from both of them?" Gid said.

"No, just from Joe." We were past Scotland, over in the dairy-farming country; I began to notice milk cows grazing in the pastures. "But he said Jimmy didn't like the cooking either."

Gid was looking blue.

"Don't get depressed, honey," I said. "We've had such a good day. There's nothing we can do about him now."

"Well, I wish we could think of something," he said. "I wish we could make it up to Jimmy someway, whatever we done wrong."

Gid's little girl Sarah was six years old then, and Jimmy had been on his mind a lot longer than she had. She was a cute little girl, but you could sure see her mother in her.

"You know we can't," I said. "We'd have to do over our whole lives. We just have to hope he'll outgrow hating us for it."

"Oh, he don't hate us, I don't guess, does he?" Gid said. He couldn't stand to think that. I had lived with Jimmy, and got so I could stand it long ago.

"Oh yes," I said. "He does. I'm just surprised he hasn't killed us."

"The army might change him," he said. "He might be a little more tolerant when he comes back."

I was looking at my comb. There were some hairs stuck in it, and the sun through the windshield was turning them golden. I was wondering how I would have been if I had been a blond; even worse, I guess.

"It won't change Jimmy," I said. "Any more than it would have changed you. We could have changed him if anybody could, and we didn't."

I had begun to cry. He wanted me to scoot over by the wheel, but I wouldn't do it. I sat by the door till after we turned off on the dirt road, and all Gid could do was pat me on the knee with his hand and try to watch the road.

When we got about a mile off the highway, out with the pastures on both sides of us and no cars anywhere, he stopped and pulled on the emergency brake—it squeaked, and it still squeaks—and took out his handkerchief and moved over by me and wiped my face. I took his hat off and laid it in the back seat; he done had some gray in his temples.

"You oughtn't to cry," he said. His handkerchief was plumb damp; I took it and put it in my purse, so I could wash and iron it for him. I looked out the window when he hugged me. I had my knees up in the seat, and he pulled back my skirt a little and rubbed his hand down the calf of my leg.

"If it was Mabel, she'd have on stockings," was all he said.

In a little while he drove on and I scooted over by him and finished combing out my hair. It was such a pretty afternoon, so cool and sharp and clear.

When we got home I let Gid know I wanted him to come in with me, but he was ashamed from thinking about Jimmy, and wouldn't do it. Gid's car was there and Johnny's pickup was gone, so he had beat us home.

"You don't have to go," I said. "Nobody will come."

But he stood on the back porch and kissed me and wouldn't come in the house. It was me he was ashamed of, someway. He wasn't very often, but when he was it hurt me like a nail.

"You can stay," I said.

"I know I can," he said. "But, Molly, I better not."

I turned and walked off from him, into the cold house; one of the few times in my life I walked away from Gid like that. I guess he left; when I came out to milk he was gone. It made me feel terrible, because I knew he was mad at himself and in the awfulest misery, but there was nothing I could do about it but wait till he came to see me again. It was two months, two of the worst ones I ever spent. But he came back, and I made it up to him. Then for maybe six months he came every day or two.

━━

The night we got the car, though, Johnny came, and for once in his life he wished he'd stayed away. I was sick of myself and sick of everybody that night, and it was a lot more than Johnny could handle. I would wake him up and say terrible things to him. Finally he got his clothes and left. In three or four days I went over and found him and apologized, and it was all right.

Who needed to have been there that night was Eddie. He would have really thought I was nasty if he could have spent that one with me. I would have run him off too, or else he would have laid me out with a poker. Maybe that was what I tried to provoke Johnny into doing. Eddie might have done it; he wasn't scared of being mean.

═══

Of all the boys and men I loved, Jimmy was the one I completely lost. His eyes and the way he went about things was Gid to a T; everybody knew it, and that made it worse. Eddie was dead before Jimmy got big enough for it to show, so it never bothered him. Actually it didn't bother Gid too much; he was proud of Jimmy, and couldn't help showing it. Mabel thought I was so trashy anyway, she was probably glad to have Jimmy and Joe for proof.

But it broke Jimmy. He was too smart to try and fool. Maybe the boys made fun of him—he and Joe both had lots of fights. Joe never minded them. Jimmy did. Jimmy was crazy about me till he was eight years old. Then he wasn't sure about me from then till he was thirteen. When he was thirteen I told him Gid was his daddy; then he was sure about me, and he hated me. He had been the most loving little boy; for eight years I couldn't turn around without him being around my neck, and when the coin turned he was just that hard a hater.

When he was ten or eleven his teachers at school started him going to church. There was a man teacher that liked Jimmy a lot—his name was Mr. Bracey—and for a long time he drove out ever Sunday and got Jimmy and took him to church and Sunday school, and then brought him home. He never even asked to take Joe—it was always Jimmy—but Joe didn't care. He probably wasn't in a church five times his entire life. And in the long run, Mr. Bracey done Jimmy more good than harm. I never was mad at him, even after Jimmy told me what he done. I never told Gid about it.

But it was the church people that really turned Jimmy into a hater; the more he took to religion, the more he turned against me.

When I told him Gid was his daddy, he didn't bat an eye. We were sitting at the table.

"I'm never going to call him Daddy, though," he said.

"I didn't mean for you to. I just wanted to tell you."

"I'm not ever going to call him anything," he said, and he didn't. Gid tried his best to get Jimmy friendly with him; he offered to take him cowboying and fishing and lots of places, but Jimmy wouldn't go. When he was real little he idolized Gid, but after he found out, Mr. Bracey was the only daddy he had.

Jimmy was the only person I ever saw I couldn't have a little effect on. Even Dad I could help a little, and even Eddie. But I might have been a stone so far as Jimmy was concerned.

He had friends, though. Him and Joe were always close brothers, in spite of being so different, and Jimmy had plenty of other friends, too. He went out for all the teams, mostly just to keep from coming home and doing chores, but he made them all. They tell me he was an awful good player; the whole town bragged on him. He was twice as good as Joe; he went out too, but he never took it seriously, and was just medium. I never went to any of the games Jimmy was in, because I knew he didn't want me too. I did see Joe play a few times.

Jimmy and me only talked about things once. He had been off to a religious camp one summer and they convinced him he was going to be a preacher. I didn't have much to say about it—I kept thinking about how much his grandaddy would have said. Gid didn't like it, but he never said a word about it. Johnny kidded Jim a little, but it was all right. Jimmy liked Johnny in spite of himself, and Johnny's kidding never made him mad.

But one Sunday night Jim come in from church. I guess he was eighteen or nineteen then, and I was sitting in the kitchen shelling peas. It was summertime, and I got up and fixed him a glass of iced tea. He tolerated me enough to drink it. I guess his resistance was down that night; he started asking me questions.

"Have you ever been to church in your life?" he said. "I just want to know."

"Oh yes," I said. "I used to go to camp meetings."

"Don't you like it in the Lord's house?" he said, looking at me through Gid's very eyes.

I didn't know what to say, except no, because I didn't, really.

He kinda looked down his nose.

"The minister says I ought to bring you to church so he could try and save you," he said. "But I don't think I will. You wouldn't go anyway."

I tried to grin, but it was hard. "No, I wouldn't go," I said.

"Molly, you don't believe in salvation, do you?" he said. Once in a while he called me just by my name, I guess to hurt me. He didn't like to call me Mother. But I couldn't stand him calling me Molly, as if he were just my friend.

"Jimmy, if you can't call me Mother don't call me anything," I said. "I mean that. Honor your father and mother, ain't that in the Bible?"

He didn't say a word; looked at the sugar in the bottom of his tea glass. His forelock fell down in his eyes and I kept wanting to reach out with my hand and brush it back out of his face.

"I don't guess I do believe in church salvation," I said.

I went on snapping the little peas and shelling the big ones, and he sat across from me a long time without saying a word. When I looked up from my fingers he looked me in the eye. He was like Gid; he always looked you in the eye when he hurt you.

"You committed adultery and fornication," he said. "That's about as bad as a woman can get." When he said it, though, he sucked at the corner of his mouth, and looked like a little boy trying not to cry.

"You don't know how ashamed I am of you, Momma," he said. "I'm so ashamed of you I can't tell you."

I let the peas alone. "You're telling me, Jim," I said. I would have given the best touches of my life to have been able to hold Jimmy then. I probably would have died right there if it would have taken what was bothering him away, but I knew nothing that easy would happen. He couldn't say any more, and I was choked up so I couldn't talk. We just sat.

"Fornication and adultery is what you did, Momma," he said.

I guess what he wanted was for me to deny it, to tell him I hadn't really done neither one, and that everything the preacher said about me was wrong. I sat the peas on the table.

"Jimmy, those are just two words to me," I said. "Even if they do come out of the Bible."

"But you did them," he said. "In this house we're living in, too."

"I wasn't saying I didn't," I said. "And I wasn't saying I'm good. I guess I'm terrible. But words is one thing and loving a man is another thing; that's all I can say about it." And that was true. The words didn't describe what I had lived with Gid, or with Johnny, at all; they didn't describe what we had felt. But Jimmy hadn't felt it, so I couldn't tell him that and make him understand.

"There's such a thing as right and wrong," he said. Like his daddy used to say.

"I guess so," I said. He wanted me to argue, and I just couldn't. I felt too bad and worn out. I wanted to cry and never shed a tear.

He finally got up and went to the door. "Yes, but there is," he said. "And if you live unrighteous, you'll end up turning on a spit in hell." He sounded like a little hurt boy trying to convince himself. It was silly to think of turning on a spit the way I felt; I couldn't be seared no worse than I was. In a little while I went on and shelled the peas.

Him and Joe left for boot camp about two weeks apart. Johnny and me took Joe to the train in Wichita, and I would have taken Jimmy, but he wouldn't let me. He hitchhiked, and he walked the three miles over to the highway, too; he wouldn't even let us take him that far. When he was out on the front porch ready to go I gave him twenty dollars but I didn't try to kiss him. He said good-by and walked out of the yard and off across the pasture without ever looking back. Just before he went over the Ridge he shifted his suitcase to the other hand.

I sent him a lot of cakes and cookies. He probably wouldn't like them, but maybe his buddies would.

5

WHEN I STARTED THINKING about Jimmy I always ended up thinking about Eddie. One morning out gathering the eggs I got him on my mind. It was funny, and Jimmy never would have understood it, but if I really done them two things he accused me of, I done them with Eddie, and he was the one I was married to.

I guess it really was the way the hair on the back of his neck was so shaggy that I liked best about him. A lot of times I felt completely crazy when I was around him, and I didn't care what I did. That's why he never liked me very well and was mean to me. He wanted somebody that acted real respectable to play like they was his wife while he went on and did what he pleased.

But I guess it was a good thing I married him. I read in the paper about these sex fiends who are always killing people because they can't get enough woman, and it wouldn't have taken very much of a push to make Eddie one of those. In fact, when he would be after me three or four times a day I thought he was one, and I told him so. It made him so mad he would almost choke me, because he thought I was to blame. He thought I was always stirring him up on purpose. And I did once in a while; but not no four times a day. He didn't really like me very much.

"You're a nasty bitch," he used to say. He said it so many times it finally quit bothering me. And the less I let things like that bother me, the meaner he got.

Lots of times when one of his hounds was in heat he'd grab me and drag me out in the back yard and make me watch while all the dogs fooled around with her. I soon quit fighting that too; it didn't bother me that much to have to watch. I don't guess it really bothered me at all.

"Looky there, sweetie," he said. "Why, she's just like you, ain't she? Just the same. What do you think about that sight?"

I wouldn't answer, or wouldn't say much. "It's just dogs breeding; it ain't too unusual," I said. Once in a while he would be fiddling around with me and make me mad.

"Well, honey," I said one time, "I didn't know you like to watch so much. I feel sorry for you. Let's go in and move the mirror over by the bed, so you can watch us." I knew how to take up for myself where Eddie was concerned.

What I said surprised him, but he couldn't back out. "All right, by god, let's do," he said. We went in and moved the mirror. I liked to drove him crazy that day. Eddie had to feel that he was the most exciting man that ever went in me, and when I didn't let him feel that way, he squirmed. That day we moved the mirror I lay there and laughed and giggled at him for fifteen minutes, and I could have been a feather pillow for all the good he was doing. He knew it, too. Every time he looked in the mirror I was grinning at him. I guess that was one of the times I hated him because I had married him instead of Gid. That was the time he squeezed my hand so hard he broke my next to littlest finger.

"I'm tired of your goddamn laughing, let's see you cry a little," he said, and squeezed it. But I wouldn't cry, either, I just looked at him, and he got up and dressed and went to Oklahoma and was gone six weeks. About the time he came back I got pregnant with Jimmy.

Our times weren't always bad though, mine and Eddie's. I was only mean to him four or five times, when I couldn't help it. He would come in sometimes when I was washing dishes and grin at me and untie my apron and stand there behind me, fiddling with my hair or rubbing my neck or back or sides or front till I would finally turn around and kiss him, and leave soap on his shirt.

I never seen but one of his girl friends; she was a redhead. She was at his funeral, and she came in with Eddie's sister Lorine. Lorine didn't mind letting me know that the redhead was the girl Eddie ought to have married. They never brought Eddie home after he was killed; he was buried in Chickisha, Oklahoma, where Lorine lived. I went up there on a train; it was the longest trip I ever made in my life; it was right in February, cold and rainy. Eddie looked nice. I didn't think the redheaded girl was too pretty, and she didn't act very kind. I rode all night on the train, back to Henrietta; it was a pretty sad trip for me. I kept seeing my face in the train windows; I couldn't see out at all. It was hard for me to believe Eddie was dead; I kept thinking I would feel his hands on me agin. When I got off the train in Henrietta it was after sunup, and Johnny and the boys were there waiting; I had left them with him, and they stayed in a little hotel; it was the first time the boys had ever been away from home. Johnny looked tired—I guess they had run him ragged—but I was so glad to see him. When they saw me the boys were too timid to say anything, but Johnny came up and put his hand on my fore-head; his hand was so cool.

"Molly, you've got fever, honey," he said. "You've worried yourself sick."

"I sure don't like to travel," I said. I squatted down so the boys would see I wasn't mad at them, and they came and hugged my neck. Johnny bought them some doughnuts for breakfast; they hadn't ever had any before. Neither had I, I don't guess. While we ate he fixed the tarp over the wagon; it was drizzling rain. We had plenty of quilts and he fixed us a good pallet and me and the boys curled up and slept nearly all the way home. The boys were just worn out from missing me. They didn't let me out of their sight for days. Just before we got home I woke up and got on the seat with Johnny. He tried to make me wrap up, but the misty rain felt good. When we seen the house up on the hill, I cried till we got to it. That night I woke up in the bed and Johnny was asleep and snoring, with his arm around me. I kept imagining Eddie, but it would never be Eddie agin. I cried till the hairs on Johnny's arm were all wet, but he never did wake up.

===

I had the eggs gathered and was changing the chickens' water when Gid and Johnny drove up in Gid's car. They never got out, but sat by the back gate with the motor running, watching me. I knew they wouldn't be staying no time, or they would already be out of the car and in the kitchen, so I went on and fixed the water. Gid was in a hurry somewhere and Johnny had just managed to stall him a little while by coming by to say hello to me.

"Boy, I'm sure having a scrumptious dinner today," I said, when I did get over to the car. Gid still had his gloves on and his hand on the steering wheel.

"Well, I hope you've got a big appetite, so you can eat it all," he said. "We've got two days' work to do before dinnertime. How are you?"

"Except for being short of company, I'm fine," I said. "You look awful prosperous today."

"Hell, he is," Johnny said. "Who wouldn't be, hiring cheap help like me?"

I walked around to his side.

"That was dangerous," he said. "Didn't you know Gid had his foot on the foot-feed? He might have run right over you."

"I ain't that bad," Gid said.

"I should have gone around behind," I said.

"No, you should have climbed over. He's just as apt to back up as he is to go forward."

They kidded with me a minute and said they would see me in a day or two; then they left. I got a little blue, because I knew some day I would have to show Gid the letter from Jimmy. It would nearly kill him. But the war would be over some day, and there wasn't much hope of getting out of it.

===

Gid never understood much about sex stuff, or at least I didn't think he did. Maybe I didn't understand it, or was wrong about it. I guess we were just raised different. Except for that one time with Richard, Dad never mentioned it—and then he hadn't been talking to me, anyway. Momma died when I was still pretty young, but she wouldn't have said anything about sex if I had got up one morning with triplets. It just wasn't nothing Momma would have talked about. Whatever ideas us kids had about it, we come up with on our own. I guess I just didn't have the background for thinking it was especially wrong; by the time I was eighteen or nineteen I would just as soon have had a baby as not.

Gid and Johnny were the boys I started out liking, and they weren't really go-getters in that respect. I guess their folks had thrown a scare into them. Then

Eddie came along, and he knew just exactly what he was after and how to go about getting it. I didn't have no idea atall how to stop him, or even that I was supposed to stop him. Besides, Eddie was exciting. But I hadn't seen him five times when he got me down where I couldn't get up, and then it wasn't exciting, it was just plain hurting. I yelled to beat the band. It didn't matter to Eddie. And he hurt me every time, for six months or a year; I couldn't see why a woman would ever want anybody to do her that way. But then I kinda begin to see one reason why: it was because a man needed it, and had it all tangled up with his pride, so that it was a sure way of helping him or hurting him, whichever you wanted to do. I hadn't been doing nothing atall for Eddie; just letting him have a good time. He was really nasty about it and I thought I'd quit him. Only before I did I started getting where I enjoyed it as much as he did; then I got so I enjoyed it more than he did. And that's when he quit caring anything about me: because he didn't want me to like it—not for my sake—he just wanted me not to be able to help liking it if it was him doing it. But of course I could help it, and by that time anyway Gid and Johnny had got a whole lot bolder, and I seen where it could really do wonderful things for a man if a woman cared to take a few pains with him.

I guess for a while I must have been pretty exciting to Eddie. It was after Joe was born that he completely quit caring about me. He still fooled around with me a lot, but he quit paying any attention to whether I liked it or not. He done what he pleased, and when he got done he stopped. One day I was just laying there watching him, and he said so.

"Well, there ain't but so much peaches and cream in any one bowl," he said.

"That's right," I said. "And when they're all eaten up you don't have nothing left but a dirty dish."

I think Eddie just married me to show up Johnny and Gid.

=====

Gid was just the opposite of Eddie. He thought I was nice and pure and he was nasty and bad—it shocked him to death to find out he wasn't my first boy. He just couldn't believe sex was right. I don't guess he left my bedroom five times in his life that he wasn't ashamed of himself—in spite of all I done. I had to be careful where I touched him or he would jump like he was electrocuted. But he was the thoughtfulest man I knew, and took the most interest in me. He just wasn't able to understand that I loved him and wanted him to enjoy himself—he got it in his head, but he never got it in his bones.

Old Johnny did though. He had more pure talent for enjoying himself than Gid and Eddie put together. He could enjoy himself and pat me on the shoulder and sleep for a week, and I loved that about him. The right or wrong of it seldom entered Johnny's mind.

=====

I always wished I had known Gid's daddy better. I think he could have straightened me out on a lot of things that it took me years to learn by myself. He had the highest standards of any man I ever knew—to this day Gid worries because he can't live up to those standards of his dad's.

One evening three or four months before he died me and him had a little talk. We were sitting at his kitchen table; Gid was out doing chores. I went over there a few times and cooked supper; they had had to batch for so long I felt sorry for them. Mr. Fry was in pain a lot of the time. I think he liked me, but I was always a little scared of him.

"Well," he said. "Some have to take and some have to give, and a very few can do both. I was always just a taker, but I was damn particular about what I took, and that's important."

"Why, Mr. Fry," I said. "Look at all you've give Gid."

"Oh yeah," he said. "A good ranch he ain't old enough to want and a lot of advice he ain't constructed to use.

"Them biscuits smell good," he said. "Let's get a head start on old Gid."

He buttered himself four biscuits. But I still had my mind on what he said.

"I don't guess I've ever done much of either one," I said.

"Aw hell," he said. "You could take a million dollars' worth, if you would. But instead you'll give out twice that much to sorry bastards that don't deserve it. And they won't put much back. I'm glad you and Gid won't marry. You'd smother him in sweetweed and he'd loaf the rest of his life. Misery makes a man work."

I was embarrassed, and he went on and ate his biscuits.

"Anyway, it ain't hurt your cooking," he said, and he looked up and gave me one of the longest looks I ever had in my life. I remembered that look a hundred times, whenever Gid or Jimmy looked at me across a table; they both had Mr. Fry's eyes.

"Molly, if I was just ten years younger I'd take your whole two million myself," he said. "The rest of the pack could go hungry. Gid would probably be the first one starved."

I couldn't say a word. My legs trembled, and I was glad they were under the table. I was looking at his hands. Finally he took a match out of his pocket and whittled it into a toothpick. I thought when I seen him in his coffin that if he had been ten years younger he would probably have done just what he said.

6

ON THE LAST DAY of July I went into town to get some groceries and my mail, and to buy a war bond. Old Washington at the feed store had some new kind of chicken feed he wanted to sell me, and I stood around there talking to him about one thing and another till the middle of the morning. I never did buy the feed; I had more eggs than I knew what to do with anyway. I bought the war bond though—it was about the only patriotic thing I knew to do. When the war started they made me a plane spotter and gave me a lot of materials on what to look for, but no airplanes ever came over except the oil company's Piper cub, flying the pipelines. Once in a while a big one would go over at night, but I couldn't tell anything about it.

I stopped in the drugstore a minute and drank a four hundred, and then went
to the post office. My *Good Housekeeping* had come, and a new *Reader's Digest,*
and the rest of the box was full of sale circulars of one kind and another. When I
pulled all them out, the letter dropped on the floor. I threw all the circulars in a
wastebasket before I picked it up. Then I went over to the counter and opened it
and read it, and my mouth felt dry, it felt like my lips were chapped. People kept
going by me to get their mail; I don't know who; they were just like shadows.
Finally Old Man Berdeau, the postmaster, came out and tacked some kind of
notice on the bulletin board, and then he came over to me and offered me his
handkerchief. I didn't think I was crying, but I was.

"I'm mighty sorry, Mrs. White," he said. "I guess they're going to get all the
boys before it's over."

It was a month before I remembered to give him back his handkerchief. I
walked out and started to look for Gid. I knew he had built a new house on the
west side of town. On what they called Silk Stocking Avenue; he said they ought
to call it Mortgage Row. People in cars kept stopping and offering me rides. I
don't know what I said to them. I knew the house by Gid's car setting in front of
it; then I seen him way at the back, digging postholes; he was putting up some
kind of pen. He looked so surprised when I came running up to him; I put my face
against his chest, so I couldn't see anything. I could smell the starch on his shirt
and the sweat under his arms when he put them around me.

"They killed my last old boy," I said.

"Molly, would you like to go in?" I looked at his house a minute, it was a big ugly
brick house.

"Let's go home," I said.

He took me to his car and put me in the front seat. "I've got to go in a minute,"
he said. I was hoping he wouldn't bring Mabel out, and he didn't. We went off.

"Stop at the post office a minute," I said. "I left my magazines." He went in and
got them; Mr. Berdeau had put them up.

When we crossed Onion Creek I scooted over by him. "What's life going to
leave me?" I said. And when we stopped at the back gate I noticed the car wasn't
there. It was still parked at the post office, with the groceries in it.

I didn't really see Gid till we were sitting at the kitchen table. I had drunk my
coffee but his was getting cold in the cup, and I reached out and put my hand on
his wrist. When I saw the look in his eye I was ashamed of myself for being so
selfish.

"Drink your coffee," I said.

And I quit grieving for Jimmy; it was strange to feel myself quitting, but I
couldn't have cried any more right then if I had wanted to. I didn't really think
about him agin that day, and when I did the next day it was not me losing Jimmy
I thought about, it was Jimmy losing his life and never getting to have it.

Gid was there with me, at the table; I had never in my life been able to think of
two men at a time. One would always crowd the other out.

"Stay here tonight," I said.

That afternoon we sat on the porch, in the glider, and Gid talked more than he
ever had in his life. He told me about his business, and his trouble with Mabel,
and a lot of other things. It was a hot day, and we could see the heat waves rising
off the pastures. I had a hold of one of Gid's arms.

"We're the ones should have got married," he said, during the afternoon. I
didn't say anything. I never did like to think about how much better things might
have turned out if we hadn't acted like we did. We *did* act like we did, and some

bad things happened, but others would have happened if we had acted some other way.

We did the chores and I cooked us a little supper and we turned on the lights and sat in the living room, and there wasn't much to do.

"Let's play dominos," I said. So we got out the card table and the dominos and played for three or four hours; neither one of us was sleepy. I got a lot of good hands and won more games than Gid.

"Domino," he said, and I laid down my hand and shuffled for a long time. Gid had asked to see the one letter Jimmy wrote, and I had lied about it and said it was lost. Actually I had hidden it in a shoebox. I felt dry inside and out when I lied to Gid—he was so trusting and it was so easy to do. And part of me wanted to show him the letter; if I had he never could have left me again. But thank God I didn't.

"Well," he said. "Maybe you'll locate it one of these days. We can't do nothing staying up."

It was hot that night; no breeze at all. I told Gid he ought to take his undershirt off, but he didn't. He went right off to sleep. I got up three or four times during the night to sprinkle the sheets with water. I couldn't get cool; I was dripping sweat. Once Gid woke up and raised up on his elbows a minute and seen I was awake.

"We've covered a lot of miles together, haven't we?" he said, and then went back to sleep. He always slept on his stomach. We had covered a lot of miles together—and we had covered a lot when we weren't together, too, I thought. Tomorrow night I would just have the moon and an empty bed. I put my hand on his neck and there was sweat in the little wrinkles of his skin.

I guess I slept a little; Gid was pulling on his Levis when I woke up.

"I'll go get the chores," he said. "You stay here and rest."

"I can stay in bed the rest of my life, if I want to," I said. And I got up and cooked while he tended the animals. We didn't have much to say that morning. I went in to town with him so I could get my car. When we got to the post office I leaned over and kissed his cheek.

"Many thanks for staying," I said.

"Why, Molly?" he said. "He was the only son we'll ever have."

As soon as I got home I went to the hall closet and got the letter out of the shoebox and took it to the trash barrel and read it agin.

DEAR MOLLY:

This is just a note to tell you I won't be home after the war, so don't you'all look for me. If I never see Texas agin it will be too soon, as there are lots of other parts of the world I like better.

Joe wrote me that you was afraid I would marry some Filipino girl and bring her home without telling you. Don't worry, I am not going to marry no girl, Filipino or otherwise. I'm not very religious no more, this war has caused that, and I don't take after girls any more, I take after men. I have a friend who is rich, and I mean rich, he says if I will stay with him I will never have to work a day, so I am going to. I guess we will live in Los Angeles if we don't get killed.

JIMMY

I hope his rich friend loved him. He was a cruel boy, but I guess I had it all coming. After I burned the letter I went and got the basket and gathered yesterday's eggs.

7

I GUESS GID told Johnny, because he came over right after dinner, that day that I burned the letter. I was glad to see him; he was just the one I was in a mood for. We sat on the glider awhile too.

"Did you see Gid?" I said. "How did you think he looked?"

He kinda grinned. "He's taking it hard," he said, "because he decided not to work this afternoon. That's unusual. The last time Gid took an afternoon off was the day Sarah was born."

"It could have been worse," I said. And in two minutes I had told him about the letter. Telling him didn't make me feel any better—it just made me feel disloyal to Jimmy. But I had to tell it.

"That's terrible," Johnny said. But the surprising thing was, Johnny was in a good mood. He tried to act solemn and sad, but he just wasn't—Jimmy had never been close to him. Once in a while he would grin to himself about something.

And I guess I was a bad mother to the end, because I began to feel good too. It was such a relief, somehow, that Johnny wasn't really sad. Johnny could still sit there and enjoy life—I guess I had thought everybody would stop enjoying it forever because my sons were dead.

"You know what I'd like to do this afternoon?" he said. "I'd like to gather up a pretty woman like you and go fish that big tank in the southwest corner. We ain't fished that tank in nearly a year."

"That's right," I said. "It was last September, wasn't it, that we went down there?"

"Well, you're the pretty woman I had in mind," he said. "Do you want to go?"

"Did you know I'm forty-three years old?" I said. "That's about too old to be thinking about pretty."

"Why, I'm older than that, and I think about it all the time," he said. "Besides, I know a lot of young pullets that ain't thirty yet who'd trade looks with you this afternoon."

"It's because I've had you to keep me fresh," I said, and I smiled too. It felt good to really smile.

"I'll get us some worms," he said. "You get your fishing clothes on."

I packed the old picnic box with some bacon and eggs and potatoes and the coffeepot and part of a mincemeat pie I had left over in the icebox. I thought we might just stay out and have supper by the tank if we felt like it.

"Well, I didn't know we was going camping," he said, when he saw me putting the box in his pickup.

"I just put in a skillet and some stuff to eat in case we don't catch nothing," I said. "I thought we might have a fish fry and do a little night fishin'."

"I got enough worms to catch half the fish in the ocean," he said. "Look at them big fat grubs." We put the poles in, and a few quilts to sit on, and left.

===

The tank was still as a mirror, and the fish weren't biting much. "I guess they don't want to risk getting yanked up in this heat," Johnny said. We spread the quilts at the south corner of the tank dam, under three cottonwood trees. The trees made pretty good shade.

And Johnny couldn't resist shade. Before we'd been there an hour he was sound asleep on the quilts, and I was left to do the fishing. I didn't mind. We just had three poles, and they weren't much trouble to watch. In the summertime I usually did my sewing while we fished. Johnny's shirt had a rip in the shoulder, and I sewed it up and patched one of his socks while he slept. The tank and the country around it were just as still: there wasn't even enough breeze to stir the cottonwoods. I watched the water and sewed and fished a little, and couldn't keep much on my mind. Since Jimmy was dead, I could imagine that we had been closer than we were, and I let myself make up a lot of little scenes that never happened, where we were having fun together. Later I got to believing a few of them. I made up that Gid and I had married, and one fall he and Jimmy and me went to Dallas to the Fair. I never had been to the Fair, but Jimmy and Joe both went once, and Joe tried to bring me home some cotton candy; he didn't have much luck. Johnny slept two hours and I only caught four fish worth keeping: three nice little cat and one good-sized perch. I quit on worms and tried a little bacon for bait, but had no luck. I was feeling too lazy to go catch grasshoppers. When fish don't bite you might as well leave them alone.

About five I woke Johnny up, because I knew when he slept too long he always felt sour and sluggish.

"Supper ready?" he said.

"I just do the catching," I said. "You get to do the cleaning."

"I believe I'll swim a little, first," he said. "You want to come in?"

I didn't think it would fit too well with the day, for me to go in, so I said I would just dunk my feet. Johnny and I swum together a lot in the summertime, usually. I sat on the dam and cooled my feet down by the four fish, and he swum the tank a time or two and came out spluttering. He looked so cool I wished I had swum after all.

"Let's have a little target practice," he said, and he got his twenty-two out of the pickup and threw three cowchips out in the water and we shot at them till we had used up a box of shells. I had shot that gun so much I could shoot it nearly as well as he could.

===

Then we dug out a little place not too far from the water, and I laid the fire and got out the supper stuff while he cleaned the fish. The sun was easing on down and it turned the water gold when you looked across it. Five of my old cows came to drink on the other side of the tank and stood and looked across at us and bawled. I guess they were hoping I had a little cowfeed for them, but they never came on around. I greased the skillet and cooked the fish and some of the bacon and made the coffee, and we put the potatoes where they would bake. I had forgot to bring any pepper, but it was a pretty good supper, anyway. The sun went into the mesquites, over west of us, and just a few streaks of light got through and struck the water. Then it was gone and there was just the afterglow, and the killdees and bullbats were swooping down over the water.

"You ever eat a killdee?" Johnny said. "They don't make two mouthfuls." We seen some crows going to roost. The dam's shadow began to stretch across the water.

"My potato didn't get quite done," I said.

"Now if you ask me," he said, "this is the good life." He was leaning back on one elbow drinking his second cup of coffee.

"It is good," I said. "I wish the boys could have lived some of it."

"They did, some of it," he said. "At least Joe did. I reckon old Jim was the one missed out."

"Reckon they'll ever find Jody?" I said.

"No, I don't imagine."

Mine would just be scattered, I guess. Dad was buried in Decatur, where his ma had lived, and Eddie was in Chickisha. I forget the name of the place where they buried Jim, and Joe was nobody knew where. I felt calm and rested, but pretty sad.

Johnny moved over by me. "What would you think if I was to steal a kiss from a pretty forty-three-year-old woman who's lost her boys?" he said. "She can cook the best fish I ever ate."

That was a funny speech, coming from Johnny. His voice kinda trembled. I smiled and leaned back against him.

"I guess you would just be kissing her because you feel sorry for her," I said.

"I guess that wouldn't have nothing at all to do with it," he said.

We kissed once and sat by the tank listening to the bullfrogs. There wasn't much moon that night, just a little sliver. We heard a snake get a frog, and the frog squeaked a long time. That sound always made me wince. Johnny turned on the pickup lights so we could gather up the stuff.

When we got to the house he helped me get the stuff in, and I figured he would stay all night. But he kissed me agin at the back gate, and went on.

"Aw, I'm too rambunctious," he said, when I asked him why. "You got too much on your mind to have me around. I'll be over in a night or two."

"Well, I hope so," I said. I hadn't had a bath in three days, so I went in and took one. The bed was empty and there wasn't no moon either, but I went right to sleep. I guess Johnny knew I was completely worn out.

8

ONE DAY the last of August I cleaned out the cellar. I had preserves and canned goods in there going back ten years or more. Some of it I had put up when the boys were little and we were real poor; I thought we had better keep as much stuff on hand as we could, in case of a hard winter. But I put up so much we never could use it all, and ever year we would wind up a little farther ahead of ourselves. Half of it had probably spoiled. I was the only one left, and I knew I couldn't ever eat half of the good stuff, much less the bad. What looked bad I threw away, and what looked good I stacked in the smokehouse, so I could get Johnny to haul it into Thalia and give it to some poor folks there.

After I got the stuff sorted I set what was left of the jars off on the floor, so I could wash the shelves. Even as cool as the cellar was, it was a hot, dusty job. About halfway through I climbed out and started to the house to get a drink, and there was Gid, standing in the yard waiting for me. He looked all tense.

"Why, hello," I said. "How long have you been standing out here in the sun?" It was only the second time he had been by since the day we heard about Jimmy.

"Just a few minutes," he said. "You look like you been working."

"Cleaning out the cellar," I said. "Can you stay for dinner?"

"I don't imagine," he said. "I just wanted to talk to you a little while."

But that was just what he thought he wanted, I knew that the minute I seen him. Gid had come to me keyed up like that too many times for me not to know what he was needing. I wisht I hadn't been so hot and dusty.

"Well, come on in," I said. "I'll at least get some ice tea down you while we talk."

But I didn't have no intention of fixing him any. I knew Gid too well. If I made him sit around and talk when he didn't want to talk, he would just get self-conscious, and get ashamed of himself, and that would spoil things for him before he ever touched me. The only way with Gid was to keep him from having to face what was on his mind until he was already in the bed. When I could manage that, he loved it. He loved it as much as Eddie or more; but it was just very seldom that he could let himself go.

When we went into the kitchen he was walking right behind me, and I turned real quick so that he ran right up against me. He kissed me without thinking, and I knew I had him for once, so I could forget it too. I wisht I could have gone to the bathroom and washed off a little of the dust, but it didn't really matter. Gid was loose, and that was the main thing; unless he was, neither of us could be.

I slept awhile—I didn't usually—and when I woke up Gid was sitting by me on the bed, washing my face and neck with a washrag.

"You had dust on your eyelids," he said. "I didn't mean to wake you up."

"I'm sweaty," I said. "Let me get some ice tea, I already got some made."

I went and got two glasses and brought them back to the bedroom. He was still sitting on the edge of the bed holding the washrag, but he had put his pants on.

And he had the saddest look on his face. I didn't know why; I felt so happy. I handed him his tea and crawled back on the bed.

"What's the matter, hon?" I said.

He pitched the washrag on the bedside table and didn't say anything for a minute. He squeezed one of my feet.

"I was just thinking about you," he said. "I guess I'm still crazy in love with you, after all these years. What I come out here for today was to tell you I wasn't going to do this any more. I guess I'm sad because it was our last time."

"Oh now," I said. I smiled, but it hurt my stomach, and I wanted to grab him and hold him. Gid had never said anything like that before, and I knew the instant he said it that he meant it, and that he would stick by it. And I knew I oughtn't to say a word: the more I said, the more we would lose. But I loved him, so I fought anyway.

"Well, it just about kills me when I think of it," he said. "But it has just got to be that way, Molly."

I waited a minute. "Gid," I said, "it ain't one bit of my business, but I've always wanted to ask you, and I might just as well. Do you and Mabel ever do this?"

He kinda twisted his mouth. "Oh yes, of course," he said. "Three or four times a year, I guess. But Mabel don't have nothing to do with what I just said."

"Well, Gid," I said. "That ain't very much. If she don't care to give it and I do, what's the harm in letting me? Why make it hard on both of us? Don't you know I need to be able to give somebody a little something?"

He didn't say anything; he still had one hand on my foot.

"Are you ashamed of me, too?" I said.

"Ashamed of you 'too'?" he said. "Who's good enough to be ashamed of you?"

"Jimmy was ashamed of me," I said. I didn't feel happy at all, any more.

"Who I'm ashamed of is us," he said. "The both of us. And Jimmy's part of the reason I made up my mind like I have."

"Why is it you're ashamed and I'm not?" I said. "Am I just sorry? I always thought really caring about a person made a difference in what was right and wrong."

"I don't know," he said. "I was raised to believe that what we done is wrong. The Bible says it's wrong. The churches say it's wrong. The law says it's wrong. And I've always believed it was wrong—except when we did it. But any no-count bastard can get around something that way. Lots of people think stealing's wrong, except when it's them stealing. But if this here's wrong, it's wrong when we do it too, now ain't it?"

My leg was trembling, I knew I had come to the wall, and I don't know why I even argued, but I had to.

"Gid, I'm just me," I said. "I ain't the law, and I ain't the church. All I say is, if it's wrong, then let's go ahead and have the guts to be wrong. We can't but go to hell for it, and that would be better than doing without you."

"We could do a lot worse than that," he said, and he put his head in his hands. "We could have another Jimmy. You ain't too old. And I've got a little girl now that's got to be thought of too. We ruined one child's life and we could ruin another. That's worse than any going to hell."

There wasn't one word I could say to that.

"Molly, you could marry Johnny," he said. "He's always loved you too."

"Johnny don't want to marry," I said. "And I don't either. You know you've always been my mainstay."

"Then why did you marry that sorry bastard you married?" he said. He'd been wanting to say it twenty years. "Why didn't you marry me? It's just about ruined my life, Molly!"

It *had* just about ruined his life, and I was to blame. And Jimmy's too, and I was to blame for that. And Gid was going to quit me. That was the way.

"I wish I knew what all was involved in this loving somebody," he said. "Mostly a lot of damn heartbreak, I know that."

"I know we've done at least a little something that was good," I said. "Please don't quit me, Gid."

"Oh, I'll be by," he said, "whenever I can risk it."

That was what finally made me cry. "Well, good-by then, damn you," I said, "because you can't ever risk it, not even if I am forty-three. I've liked it, even if you haven't, and I ain't ashamed of it, even if you are."

"What about Jimmy?" he said.

"Jimmy's dead. You quitting me won't make nothing up to him."

"Molly, it ain't quitting," he said. "We got to do it. Don't you know this is killing me? I never quit nothing in my life."

"If you can think of a prettier word for it, fine," I said. "You're the one that has clothes on."

Things were just a blur, but I reached out for him and he got up and put his shirt on. "I don't have much pride where you're concerned," I said, but he left, and I laid on the bed and cried for a long time.

9

GID KEPT HIS WORD. I knew he would. He never loosened the reins on himself agin. It was over ten years before he ever touched me, and then it was just a pat on the shoulder.

Right after he quit me I couldn't stand to think he would actually make it stick. I was determined I'd bring him back the next time I saw him, whatever it cost me, or him. I knew I could make him come back; I had ways I had never had to use.

But I didn't lay eyes on him for two months, and when he finally did come I knew in five minutes that I wouldn't do what I had planned to do. It was October when he came; I was in the kitchen; and he knocked and came in with a coyote puppy. He had brought me one or two to raise before that.

"Well, I killed his momma, Molly," he said. "You want to raise him?"

"Of course," I said. "I'll get him a box."

And when we had the puppy fixed I walked to the gate with him. Only I stopped inside the fence and didn't go to the car, the way I usually did.

It would have been easy to have touched Gid, that day; he was just starving for somebody to. But it wouldn't have been loving him much to have tricked him into doing something he had suffered so much to quit doing. And the two months had really told on Gid, I guess worse than they had on me. If he really wanted to quit that bad, I thought I would do better to help him keep his word. If he broke it, it would just be that much more agony for him. But I don't know; never will know. The way he looked before he drove off, I think he was wanting me to help him break his word. Those things are awful complicated. Or more likely it was both he wanted: me, on the one hand, and to do what he thought was right on the other. I never will know which one he wanted the most. I don't imagine he knew himself. But when he drove off and I went back in, I thought he had sure been right about the heartbreak.

=====

That last day, when he asked me why I married Eddie instead of him, I didn't have no answer for him. I thought about it a lot after that—too much, I guess—but I never came up with an answer for myself, either. Not one I could be sure was right. There may not have been no one answer, but if there was, I didn't know it. I guess that said something pretty bad about me, that I didn't know why I married who I did. I knew an awful lot of little things about myself, what I liked to eat and smell and do. And I knew some bigger things than that—about giving and taking, and the things Mr. Fry had talked about the one time we talked. But marrying Eddie may have been the most important thing, for all of us, that I ever did. I didn't know why I done it, and I don't know what good it would have done me if I had. Knowing wouldn't have made it any less done.

For a month or so after Gid quit me, I like to have run Johnny ragged. He came over a lot. Sometimes I wouldn't let him in ten feet of me, and other times I went to the other extreme. I wasn't in very good control of myself. Finally one night at the supper table he brought it up.

"Well, I guess I better tell you off, Molly," he said. "You been getting me mixed up with Gid, lately, and it's about to get me down. You know me and him are different fellers. It ain't fair to me for you to pretend I'm him."

I was so ashamed I couldn't say a word. We sat for several minutes.

"You're right," I said finally. "I'm sorry, Johnny. Don't hold that against me, will you?"

"Of course not," he said. "Now that you've quit. I couldn't hold anything against such a good cook."

"Gid's changed his way of thinking about me," I said. "I guess you knew that. It made me pretty miserable."

"Not as miserable as it made him," he said. "I've been thinking he'd probably kill himself. But since he's made it this long, I guess he'll probably survive."

I let him know I appreciated his patience, and his finally speaking up. It made me feel a lot better after he had. I felt calm for the first time since Gid left the bedroom that day.

"Now see," Johnny said. "Me and you may not kill nobody over one another, but we're comfortable. We've always been comfortable, and I want us to keep on being that way."

"I don't know," I said. "I might kill a person or two for you. It would depend on who." That made him feel good. He knew I probably meant it.

But I guess Gid was still heavy on my mind, because I had to talk about it.

"Johnny," I said. "What do you think about this we do? Is it right or is it wrong?"

"Well, it's enjoyable," he said. "I ain't gonna bother to look no farther than that."

But that wasn't answered enough, just then.

"You quit worrying," he said. "That's the kind of thing Gid has to worry about. There's no need in you worrying about it too."

"But you know I've done it with him, too," I said. "Do you think it's wrong for me to do it with both of you all these years?"

"Of course not," he said. "Gid's even more crazy about you than I am, and he deserves a little enjoyment too. Only he's so crazy he reasons himself out of it.

"After all, we raised a son," he said. "And a good one. You and Gid had bad luck with yours, but that's life. The stars were just set wrong for Jim. I never lost a night's sleep in my life from being ashamed, and I don't intend to start."

"You're right about it," I said. "In a way, you are. I never lost much sleep over it, either, not till lately. I just wish Gid agreed with us."

"Oh no," he said. "That wouldn't be Gid. Somebody's got to take an interest in the right and wrong of things."

All the same I would always miss Gid, even if Johnny was right.

About nine o'clock I woke up and he was pulling on his boots.

"You ain't leaving tonight, are you?" I said.

"Oh, of all the stupid things," he said. "I left my damn milk cows in the lot; I just now remembered. If I don't go turn them out, there's no telling what they'll get into. I hate to leave."

"Oh, it's all right if that's all it is," I said. I got up and put on my nightgown and got a flashlight and walked out to his pickup with him.

"I guess you'll be barefooted the day you die," he said.

He had just half-thrown his clothes on; one of his sleeves was flopping, and I made him wait till I buttoned it at the wrist.

"You come back when you can," I said. "Now that I'm straightened out on who you are."

"Don't you worry," he said. "You won't hardly know I ain't living here."

It was a beautiful warm night and I walked around to the porch and sat on the glider awhile, in just my nightgown. I didn't feel very sleepy; I heard a coyote, back off toward the Ridge. The moon was just rising; it was full, and I sat and watched it, a big old gold harvest moon, barely up above the pastures. My hair was down, but I didn't have no comb, and I didn't feel like going in the house. While I sat there my menfolk begin rising with the moon, moving over the pastures, over the porch, over the yard. Dad and Eddie, they was drunk, had whiskey on their breath. Jimmy was looking away from me, thinking of school. Joe, he was laughing, and Johnny was lazing along, grinning about something. But Gid was looking at my face, and wishing he could put his hands on my hair.

PART THREE

Go Turn My Horses Free

But, Lord Christ! whan that it remembreth me
Upon my yowthe, and on me jolitee,
It tickleth me aboute myn herte roote.
Unto this day it dooth myn herte boote
That I have had my world as in my tyme.
But age, allas! that al wole envenyme
Hath me biraft my beautee and my pith.
Lat go, farewel! the devel go therewith!
The flour is goon, ther is namoore to telle;
The bren, as I best kan, now moste I selle. . . .

—The Wife of Bath

Oh lay my spurs upon my breast, my rope
*   and old saddle tree,*
And while the boys are lowering me to rest,
*   go turn my horses free.*

—TEDDY BLUE,
from *We Pointed Them North*

1

I HAD JUST dropped a post in a hole and was tamping the dirt around it with my shovel handle when I looked up and seen Gid hot-footin' it for the lots. He never said a word to me—he just struck out. Well sir, I thought, we'll both go. I knew he had some cold beer on ice in the water can, and I thought I'd help him siphon off a little. When I got there he was plopped down in the shade of his new GMC pickup, swigging on the first can. I opened me one and sat down and rested my back against the rear wheel and settled in to listen. Gid had pitched his hat on the running board and set his beer can down between his legs, so he'd have both hands free to wave. I seen the sun had blistered his old bald noggin agin, right through the straw hat. He had the hailstorm on his mind. Molly had come out that morning and argued with us a little about the fence line, and for some reason arguments with Molly always made Gid think of that hail.

"I'd been over at Antelope, getting the mail," he said. "Old Dirtdobber thought the cloud was just threatening, but I knew better. You can't fool me when it comes to hail."

"Hell no," I said. "Nothing simple as weather could fool you."

"The Montgomery Ward catalogue had come that day," he said. "I yanked it out of my saddle pouch, and then I took down my lariat rope. 'Run, you old bastard,' I said, and I keewawed him between the ears with that rope. It broke him into a lope he was so surprised."

"Watch out, Gid," I said. "You're going to knock that can of beer over if you don't."

But he didn't give a shit for beer when he got to talking. Gid never started talking till he was sixty years old, and then he never stopped. That hailstorm hit Thalia in the spring of 1924, and Gid hadn't forgotten it yet. None of the old-timers had—in the long run it done more damage to the people than it done to the windowlights or the wheat crops. I guess the worst was Old Man Hurshel Monroe getting his skull cracked outside the door of the bank. They say Beulah Monroe found the hailstone that conked him and kept it home in the icebox for nearly ten years, till one of her grandkids ate it for an allday sucker. I've heard that so many times I probably even believe it myself.

"We made it to a little mesquite tree," he said. "Old Dirt was slowing down."

"I guess so," I said. "What a man gets for riding a twenty-two-year-old horse."

"So I got down and yanked the saddle off. Uuuups . . . !"

"I knew you'd spill it sooner or later," I said. "Half a can of good beer nobody gets to drink."

"You wasn't gonna get to drink it nohow," he said. "What difference does it make to you?"

"Your beer all right," I admitted. "Why open it if you ain't gonna drink it?"

"Why buy it if I ain't gonna open it?" he said, reaching in the water can for another one.

"Here," I said. "Let me pour this one out for you so it won't interrupt your story."

"Just shut up," he said. "I've emptied two cans of beer to your one."

"Why sure," I said. "In the first place you're older than me. And in the second place, I've always had to drink my cans. I never been able to afford just to pour them out."

He stopped and swigged beer till there wasn't much left in the new can. "If you worked as smart as you talked, you'd have something to show for your long life," he said. That was Gid—he thought my working for wages was a disgrace. But I got my pleasure out of doing what I wanted to, not out of owning no damn mesquite and prickly pear. I told him that a hundred times, but he never did understand it.

"I figured old Dirt would stand," he said. "So I crawled under him and scrunched up under the saddle." He kept wiping his face with his shirt sleeve, and I knew the sweat was stinging his old nose, where it had blistered and peeled. "Shore hot," he said.

"Finish your story. It'll be sundown before we get back to work."

"About the time I got under the saddle I heard water falling on it. I thought it must have quit hailing and gone to raining, and then I smelled it, and it didn't smell like no rain water I ever smelled. I peeped out to one side and saw some of it trickling along the ground, and it didn't look like no rain water I ever saw. It was still hailing to beat the dickens, and all I could do was sit there thinking about it. Finally I raised up and jobbed him in the stomach with the saddle horn. 'Damn you,' I said. 'You could have waited a minute.' "

"Haw," I said. "That's pretty good. I'd have paid money to have seen that."

"I wouldn't laugh, if I was you," he said. "It wasn't nothing to be ashamed of."

"No, but it ain't much to brag about, either," I said.

He waved his beercan in my face. "You better not talk," he said. "Where was you when we had that storm? At least I was home where I belonged. I wasn't off in New Mexico living with no Indian woman."

"Neither was I," I said. "I knew you'd drag that in. I can tell what you're going to say before you even say it. For the nine hundredth time, I wasn't off in no New Mexico. I was right near Baileyboro, Texas. And I wasn't where no horse could weewee on me, that's for damn sure."

"Not on me! On the saddle!" Gid was very particular about that point.

"It's too hot to listen to you explain." Actually, when they had that storm, I had done been busted up in my horsewreck and was in the hospital. I wasn't even living with Jelly.

"When I jobbed him, he kicked me," Gid said, and he looked kinda sad, remembering. Contrary as he was, I could feel sorry for Gid sometimes. He was getting old, and he wouldn't admit it. Middle of July, hot as a firecracker, and the old fart wouldn't stretch out and rest for love nor money. Telling them old stories, getting himself in a stir, remembering them. I wish I could have talked some sense into him, sat him down and told him, "Now goddamnit, Gid, you're getting about old enough to slow down. It won't hurt you to take a little rest in the afternoons." But when it come right down to saying it, I just let him go. Making him mad would have done more damage than the advice was worth. Besides, I kinda got a kick out of hearing the stories agin myself.

"Put your hat on, Gid," I said. "You'll go off and forget it and take a sunstroke."

"That was the first time Dirt had kicked in ten years," he said.

"It surprised me. And then he run off."

"Did you cuss him?" I said.

"Yeah, but it didn't do no good."

"Why no, that don't surprise me," I said. "It don't do no good when you yell at me, either."

"Yeah, but you ain't a horse," he said.

"That's all right. Neither one of us can understand you when you yell. You don't talk plain."

"Bullshit," he said. "If you'd just get you one of them little invisible hearing aids, you could hear fine. Nobody's going to blame you for getting old."

Gid was the worst about that kind of remark I ever saw. "Who said anything about old?" I said. "You splutter when you yell; maybe it's them false teeth, I don't know. And the next time I wish you'd buy Pearl if you're going to buy beer. You let this get a little warm and it tastes like horsepiss."

He threw his beer can on the pile we were building up by the loading chute. "You know, Johnny, we're going to have to haul them cans off, one of these days," he said. "Cattle will get to where they won't load with all them tin cans shining at them."

I chunked one on the pile myself. It's nice to have a pile to throw a beercan at. A man can see he's been accomplishing something. "Leave them cans where they are," I said. "The pile's just now getting big enough it's easy to hit. Besides, we ain't gonna load no cattle recently."

"That's about the size of it," he said. And that can pile is still right where it was. We never got around to hauling it off, and I'm glad. It's kind of a monument.

"When are we going to get to work?" I said.

He had to strike five matches to get his stogie lit, and then it went right out. He just bought them to chew, anyway.

"Looks like you'd be willing to rest," he said. "I try to ease up on you in the heat of the day and you go to rearing and tearing. You have to sit on an old bugger like you to keep him from killing himself. I guess you just want to prove you can still work."

"Blame it on me," I said. "I'm handy."

"Now if you were able to work in weather like this, it'd be different. I seen you get the weak trembles yesterday, digging that corner posthole."

"It was hot yesterday," I had to admit. "Anybody that works hard can get too hot."

"Sure, sure," he said.

"Don't be sure, suring me," I said. "You had the weaves yourself a dozen times. You just had the crowbar to prop up on or you'd have gone down fifteen times."

"Aw," he said, "that's just your imagination. The sweat drips on my bifocals and I stumble once in a while, that's all."

"Of course," I said. "That must be it. That's why you're going to have that operation next month. Sweat's what does it."

"Making fun of a sick man," he said. "Let me finish my story."

I knew that story like a good preacher knows the Bible, but I listened anyway. I liked to hear what new lies Gid would put in.

"What happened," he said, "was old Dirt squashed my hip when he ran over me."

"No wonder you're so bunged up nowadays," I said. "You ought to have taken better care of yourself when you were young."

"There's a blister bug on your hat," he said. "You better get him before he gets you. What do you mean bunged up? I've got a crick or two, but I ain't feeble."

I caught the brim of my hat and flipped the blister bug halfway across the lot. "Them sonofabitches are going to take this country," I said.

"Yeah, them and the mesquite. And the government. I hope I ain't alive to see it."

"You won't be," I said. "The country ain't that far gone."

"Then it don't like much," he said. "Ten more years like this and it will strain a man to make an honest living in this country." He flipped about four inches of stogie over toward the can pile.

"It strains the ones that make an honest living now," I said, "but that don't affect the majority. What was the matter with that cigar?"

"Nothing. Good cigar. That little piece I threw away wasn't worth lighting."

"Kiss my butt," I said. "I guess if you laid down a dollar and they give you two bits change, you'd let it lay, like it wasn't worth keeping."

"That's right," he said. "It ain't worth keeping. Won't buy nothing."

"Now, Gid," I said. "Think a minute. That's a hamburger you'd be throwing away. That's five Peanut Patties."

"Think yourself," he said. "Who want's a goddamn Peanut Pattie anyway, much less five of them? You'd think a man your age would get over craving candy."

"Nothing wrong with Peanut Patties. They stick to your ribs." Everybody hurrahed me about my sweet tooth. But I've craved candy all my life, and I don't believe in doing without something just because a bunch of idiots thinks it's silly. Delaware Punch is another thing I like.

"And anyway we're letting the cool part of the day go to waste," I said. "I guess it'll be a hundred and ten tomorrow."

"We ain't gonna work tomorrow," he said. "I promised Susie I'd take her to see *Snow White*." Then he went back to his story. "I don't know how I survived," he said. "Finally the hail was piled up around me and the saddle like it was an igloo, I remember that."

I reached in and got my pocketknife and slipped the boot off my right foot. "You're gonna talk till suppertime I might as well trim my corns," I said.

"Poor bastard," he said. "I guess a man's feet give out first."

"Not mine," I said. "I've had sense enough not to use mine much. I just got a few corns."

"Mabel talked me into having Susie a pair of little boots made," he said. "Made outa javelina skin. Shore purty."

"I bet," I said. "And probably didn't cost over five times what they were worth. What'd you want to spend money on that javelina skin for?"

"Soft. Don't hurt a kid's feet so much."

"That's the way the whip pops," I said. "The first pair of shoes I ever bought felt like they was made out of tin."

"Mine did too," he said. "No wonder we're both cripples."

"What'd you do when it quit hailing?"

"Stood up," he said. "When I looked around I seen I wasn't but just across the peach orchard from the Eldenfelders' house. So I got me a limb for a crutch and hopscotched across the orchard."

"A man's taking his life in his hands, going up to a Dutchman's house on one leg," I said. "It's a wonder the dogs didn't rip you up."

"I thought about that," he said. "We was near neighbors, and the dogs knew me a little, else I wouldn't have gone up at all. I picked me up a pocketful of big hails, just in case."

"Just in case what? You couldn't hit a dog with a hailstone in fifteen throws."

"I don't know," he said. "I could always chunk good and straight. Remember the time we played that baseball game in Thalia and I chunked that Methodist preacher they had playing second base. I chunked him good enough."

"Yeah," I said. "By god I do remember. I remember he got you down and beat hell out of you after the ballgame, too. You didn't chunk him hard enough."

"He surprised me," he said. "Got in the first lick. I didn't figure a preacher would hit a man without warning him."

"A preacher's got that much sense," I said. "He may not have much more." And there's a sad end to that story. The preacher waited a year or two and got in a hell of a last lick—he was the one married Gid and Mabel.

"Anyhow I didn't need the hails," he said. "The dogs come charging out all right, thirty or forty of them, but that little bitty old rat terrier they used to have was the only one actually went for my legs. The rest just stood around growling and showing their teeth."

"By god now, that took nerve," I said. "If you'd a fell, there wouldn't have even been a belt buckle left. I might not have ragged you so hard all these years if I had seen that. I admire a man with the kind of backbone you showed."

"Just shut up," he said. "I limped on to the house. That rat terrier give me hell, too. I meant to come over some day when the folks were gone and kick the shit out of that dog, but the coyotes got him first. Finally the old man heard the commotion and came out on the porch. He thought it was funny, me fighting that rat terrier with my peach limb. 'Get up steps,' he said. 'Dead cow's for dinner.' Only I didn't find out what he meant till it was too late."

"Find out whose cow it was, you mean?"

"Naw, how long it had been dead. I thought it tasted all right for Dutchman's cooking. So did old Wolf. 'Good-cow,' he said. 'Dead mit de lightnin' vee days ven we find her.' "

"Poison you?"

"No, it didn't hurt me. Wasn't as spoiled as some of the stuff you buy in grocery stores nowadays."

"Was Bartle home then?" I asked. I remember Bartle Eldenfelder; he was a fighting demon.

Gid had to stop and laugh when I mentioned Bartle. "No, he was gone," he said. "That bastard." He had to wipe the laugh tears off his cheeks. "Frank Scott come by my place one morning and said he was going to whip Bartle for dancing with his wife. I told him I hoped he'd eaten a big breakfast—it just made him madder."

"Who won?" I said. I had underestimated Frank Scott's fighting ability once myself.

"Bartle whipped him right off. Frank came dragging back by bleeding like a stuck hog. Said Bartle hit him with a hoe handle."

"That was about the time his wife left him, I guess. She told everybody Frank hit her with a hoe handle, but nobody believed her, neither." But if he never, he should have. She was too pretty for her own good, and a whole lot too pretty for Frank's. Once I was taking her out the door at a dance and met Frank coming in. If he hadn't taken time to hit her first, I would have got whipped worse than I did.

"Anyhow, that's the story," he said. "After I ate the rotten cow Annie hitched up the wagon and took me home. I had to wade the creek."

"Okay now," I said. "It's what you and Annie did before you waded the creek that I been waiting all this time to hear. Just tell that."

Gid grinned a little. "I swear you got a filthy mind," he said.

"No, I just like to know the feller I'm working for. If I'm working for a sex maniac, I want to know about it."

"That ain't it," he said. "You just got the damn nostalgia. You wish you was young enough to have a shot at Annie agin yourself."

"You damn right I am," I said. "And kiss my butt. I was better off then than I am now, it don't take no college degree to know that."

"Maybe you were and maybe you weren't," he said. "I know one thing, them times were hard. You couldn't drag me back."

I just snorted. "Okay," I said. "How about if I could show you Molly, looking like she looked in 1924. I don't guess that would tempt you none."

That hit him right on the sore spot; I knew it would. I stood up and brushed the dirt off my pants.

"Well, that might change my mind all right," he said.

I was sorry I said it. I could remember how she looked in 1924 myself.

"You want me to bring the water can?" I said.

"Naw, we ain't gonna work very long. Take a big drink."

We started back down the fence row, with him a little in the lead. I stumbled and like to fell; memories had kept me from seeing the ground.

"She could make my mouth water," I said.

"I'd just as soon not think about it," he said. "I'll be glad when I get that operation. My kidneys shore do ache."

"You don't reckon Molly will really get upset about the way we run this fence, do you?"

"I don't think so," he said. "But then I never could predict Molly very well. Anything that's connected with her dad she's touchy about."

When we got to the working place, Gid began to tamp the posts and I began to dig. The damn ground was so hard it took me half a dozen licks to get through the top crust, and then the sandrock started. I don't know how long we worked, but after a while I looked up and seen the old red sun sitting right on top of Squaw Mountain, ten miles away. That brought her back too. When we were young it was an awful good picnicking place—there was supposed to be an Indian woman buried there, and me and Molly spent many an afternoon looking for her grave. Squaw Mountain was where the rattlesnake bit her. It wasn't even coiled but it got her right in the fat part of her calf. She shut her eyes when I got ready to cut around the bite; I barely had the nerve to do it. "If you don't I won't be your girl," she said, and I went ahead. While I was working the tourniquet she kissed me. "I'm still your girl," she said. I had the devil of a time getting her home.

"She's going down, Gid," I said. "Let's quit."

He leaned on his tamping bar a minute, looking at the sun. He was so hot he was sweating on the ears. "One more hole," he said. I dug it and he dropped the post in and tamped it while I took my sweaty shirttail out so the evening cool would get to my belly.

"That's a day," he said. He dropped the tamping bar and stood there leaning on the post, panting a little and glaring at me.

"What's the matter?" I said. "Wasn't that hole deep enough?"

He snorted through his nose. "You never have believed how bad that hailstorm was," he said. "Out in New Mexico, living with an Indian woman. Your old man never made a bushel of wheat that year."

"So what," I said. "He knew about hail when he decided to plant the stuff in the first place." But I guess I should have been sorry where it concerned Dad. The hailstorm turned Dad back into a poor man, and that turned him into a drunkard. But I guess if the hail hadn't, something else would have.

Gid picked up the crowbar and I shouldered my diggers, and we started back up the fence row.

"Nearly seven o'clock," I said. "Too many hours for an old-timer like you to work. You ain't no wild coyote any more."

"You're no young stud yourself," he said.

We made it to the lots and pitched our fencing stuff in the back of the pickup. Gid flipped a coin to see which one of us would drive, and he won. He was an expert coin flipper, or else the luckiest man alive. He never had to drive over once a month.

"Don't run over that rock," he said, after we started off.

"You just settle down," I said. "I'm driving this vehicle, now. Tomorrow, is it, you're taking your granddaughter to the picture show?"

"Tomorrow," he said. "*Snow White.* Get you in a good game of dominos."

I drove out of the pastures and onto the highway. "Pretty sundown," Gid said. "Looky how the sky's lit up. Looks like somebody set the world on fire."

"It wasn't neither one of us that done it," I said. But the sky was awful bright, over west of Thalia. The whole west side of the sky was orange and red.

"I wish we had time to go by and see Molly," he said. "Maybe we can day after tomorrow."

2

THREE DAYS LATER, I met Gid on the road. He never showed up in the morning, so after I ate my dinner I decided I'd go in to the domino hall and play a little. I didn't figure he was coming; but I just shouldn't have figured. Before I got halfway to town I seen his car, about two hills up the road, coming like sixty: I knew right then I'd made the trip for nothing.

Usually, when I met him on the road, he'd come flying over some hill and get nearly by me before he even seen the pickup, much less recognized it. I'd get to watch him go skidding by, cussing and talking to himself. I always just stopped my vehicle and waited: there wasn't no sense in both of us trying to back up in a narrow road, no better than either one of us could drive. Gid would grind into reverse and back he'd come, leaning out the window and spitting cigar and backing as fast as a six-cylinder Chevvy would back. Usually he would swerve off in the bar ditch a time or two, and run over a beer bottle or an old railroad tie somebody had thrown out to get rid of. Most of the time the damage wasn't serious. Some times were worse than others.

It had rained that morning, and I met him right at the top of the hill by Jamison Williams' boat pasture. The old claytop hill was a little slippery. Gid went somewhere down the south side of the hill getting stopped. I kept one foot on the clutch and the other on the brake and sat there on my side of the hill, waiting. In a minute I heard the gears grind, and then I seen the back end of the Chevvy come over the hill. I saw right off it was coming in a sight too fast and too far to the west, so I pushed in on my clutch and rolled on down out of the way. It looked like what happened was Gid's hands were sweaty and slipped off the wheel. Anyhow, the Chevvy went into a slide and came sideslipping down the hill and kinda bounced the bar ditch and went through Jamison's fence and made a little dido and came back through another part of the fence and headed for the road agin. Only by then it was slowed too much to bounce the ditch, and it hit the soft dirt and turned over.

Well, when I seen that I jumped out of the pickup and ran over and yanked open the first door I came to and helped Gid out. The glove compartment had come open and he was practically buried in maps and beer openers and pliers and old envelopes; he kept that glove compartment about as full as Fibber McGee kept his hall closet.

"Are you hurt, Gid?" I said. The only thing I could see was a big skinned place on his nose. It didn't look deep, but the blood was dripping on his new gray shirt. "Is your nose broke?" I said.

"No, goddamnit!" he said. "Get to hell away if you can't do nothing but stand there asking questions."

"You must have bumped the windshield," I said.

"Hell, I bumped the whole damn roof," he said.

"Don't talk," I said. "Sit down here a minute. You was just in a wreck, don't you realize that?"

But he went walking up the hill, bending over so his nose wouldn't drip on his shirt. He acted like he was going on to the ranch, afoot. "Hey," I said. "Don't go walking off that way. Your insides may be hurt."

"I lost my cigar coming down here somewheres," he said. "I just got it lit and I don't intend to let it go to waste." Now if that wasn't consistent. I sat down on the Chevvy and he went on and found his cigar and came back.

"Get up from there," he said. "Get the pickup and chain and we'll drag this sonofabitch out."

I got up and looked around, and if it wasn't just my luck. When I jumped out of my pickup I plumb forgot about it and the bastard had rolled off in the east bar ditch and stuck itself tight as a wedge. Gid was moderately mad when he seen he had two vehicles not fifty feet apart that wouldn't neither one budge.

"Shit," he said. "Looks like you could have taken time to stop that pickup, Johnny. I guess if I was chasing a herd of cattle and my horse fell, you'd just bail off and let the horses and cattle go."

"I might," I admitted. "There ain't much telling what I'll do." A kid would have known better than to leave that pickup out of gear.

"I thought I heard you yell at me when you went through the fence," I said. "That's what made me in such a big hurry."

"Aw, you got to do something when you're running over a fence," he said. "I just yelled to be yelling. What do you think I'm paying you for?"

"Damned if I know," I said. "I haven't worked for you but thirty-eight years, you ain't had time yet to tell me what you wanted me to do."

"Well, it's not for driving into the domino parlor every day, that's for sure," he said.

"I thought I better come in and get the news," I said. "The country could have gone to war, for all I knowed."

"You got a radio," he said.

"Yes, but when I turn it on I don't get nothing but music or static. And most of the time I'd rather listen to the static."

"Okay," he said. "Don't stand out there in the road arguing with me all day. Let's dig her out."

"Which one?" I said.

"Yours. It wouldn't do no good to dig mine, it would still be wrong side up when we got it dug."

"Dig her out yourself, by god," I said. I thought the car wreck must have driven him out of his mind. "Why, there's a tractor at the Henrys', not two mile away. I can go get it and be back before we could get the shovel sharp."

"Dig her out, by god," he said. "I don't intend to borrow from the Henrys."

But just then a hundred or so of Jamison Williams' goats came out of a post-oak thicket and made for the hole in the fence. When Gid seen them coming it sobered him a minute.

"Run," he said. "Let's stop up them holes or them bastards will be all over the country and we'll have to round them up."

And by god they would. Goats could hide in weeds and badger holes where it would take you a week to find one, much less a hundred.

"Get your rope," he said. "Maybe we can string it between the posts."

"I've seen eight wire fences that couldn't stop a goat," I said. "What good do you think a lariat rope would do?"

"Okay," he said. "You take the north hole and I'll take the south."

"Take it and do what with it?" I said. "You don't mean patch it, do you?"

"Goddamn, Johnny," he said. "Ain't you got any initiation at all! Have I got to tell you ever move to make?"

"If you mean go-ahead, I don't guess I got any," I said. "You whipped that out of me long ago."

He went trotting over to the south hole, no faster than I could walk. I guess he thought he was running. I walked on to my hole and stood there.

"Wave your hands and yell," he said.

"Gid," I said. "Why don't you try out for the Olympics? You were really picking them up and laying them down. I'd hate to think what would happen if something got after you someplace where there wasn't nothing to climb."

But he was mad enough to bite somebody, and I was the only one handy, so I shut up. We made what noise we could, and it kept the most of them from just walking right on through. But the old Chevvy had cut a pretty wide dido, and there was about thirty yards of fence between me and him. It wasn't exactly hole, but it wasn't no goat fence, either. Gid was yelling like the Choctaw nation, but one old billy went right on through. I thought Gid might call up an ambulance or the volunteer firemen, though. The old billy stood in the road blatting and trying to get the rest to follow him.

"Chunk that sonofabitch," Gid yelled. I couldn't find nothing to throw but a clod, and I missed with it. Gid was farther up the hill, where there was more sand-rock, and he begin giving the old goat hell. Only about the fourth throw he led him too much and the sandrock went sailing right on through the rear window of the pickup and rattled around in the cab.

"Goddamn," he said. "Of all the places you could have stopped that pickup."

"Of all the places you could have thrown that rock," I said. "If it broke that bottle of screwworm dope I had sitting in the seat, I'm quitting you for good. I don't intend to ride along smelling that stuff for the rest of my life."

About then the rest of the goats decided to move. They spread out and come for the fence like a covey of quail. We did our best to turn them, but there wasn't no way, short of actually grabbing hold. I wasn't in the mood to wrestle no

Jamison Williams goat, so I stood there and tried to get a count on the ones that went through.

Gid gave up the hardest of any man I ever saw. He grabbed a nannie and fought her around and got her turned and then let her go and grabbed an old billy. The minute he did the nannie whipped around like a bobcat and jumped the bar ditch and run down the road a ways and jumped the off bar ditch and went on through the barbed-wire fence into the brush and was gone. Gid and the old billy went to the ground. It looked like Gid was getting the worst of it, only sometimes Gid had more stubbornness to him than a billy goat. A lot more, actually. It ain't no exaggeration to say he was the stubbornest man I ever knew, except his dad. It ain't no miscompliment, either. He was determined that at least one goat was going to stay in Jamison's pasture, and by god one did. We tied him with our belts, and Gid sat on him.

Gid sure did look worn out. He looked so old all of a sudden it worried me. His hat had got mashed in the struggle and was laying off to one side; he leaned over to reach for it and the old goat hunched and over Gid went, on his face. It wasn't particularly funny, and I reached down to help him up, but he wouldn't move.

"I'll just stay down awhile," he said. "I ain't no good when I'm up noways. I can't even stay on a tied-down goat."

I remembered the time, up on the plains, when Gid had ridden eighteen wild horses in one day. Falling off the goat was a real comedown. He sat there on the ground, wiping his skint nose on his shirt sleeve. I handed him his hat.

"And take this handkerchief, too," I said. "You'll get infected wiping that nose on your shirt."

"Don't give a damn if I do," he said.

"Maybe it won't be so bad," I said. "Maybe Jamison's got those goats trained to come to a horn."

"Aw, you couldn't call them up with an elephant horn," he said.

I never knew there was such a thing as an elephant horn, but I didn't say so. I squatted down on my hunkers. The old billy thought he was plumb to the high and lonesome, since he'd got rid of Gid, and he went hunching along the ground on one side.

"If I had the money, I'd just buy them goats," Gid said. "Then we could let them go, and anybody found one would be welcome to it."

"We'll get 'em a few at a time," I said. "Jamison oughtn't to be in no hurry."

Jamison was the slowest white man either of us had ever seen, and pretty near the most worthless. He kept him a little herd of sorry Mississippi cows, that he let run loose on the road in the summertime. Ever evening his old lady and his boys would have to get out and gather them up. I've seen them many a time, moving the herd, Jamison poking along behind in his old blue Dodge, and Judith and the boys driving the cattle down the road afoot.

"Oh hell," Gid said. "He's slow, but he ain't dumb. He'll figure out how much to charge us for this fence. If you had just stayed home a few more minutes, all this never would have happened."

"No, nor if you had started a few minutes sooner. Same difference. If you could drive worth a shit it wouldn't have happened anyway. Whoever heard of a grown man letting his car get out of control that way?"

"I have," he said. "It happens all the time."

I noticed he kept rubbing his elbow, like something was wrong with it. Finally I asked him about it.

"Why nothing's wrong with it," he said, and then he looked at it and winced. He rolled up his sleeve and it looked like a rattlesnake had struck him; his elbow was the size of a grapefruit. I guess the blood vessels in it had burst; it was about the color of an old inner tube.

"That beats all," I said. "Wrestling with a damn goat and your arm nearly knocked off. Look how black it's getting."

"It's that damn steering wheel knob," he said. "It's as dangerous as a snake. I seen it whipping around at me when I first lost holt of the wheel, but I thought I got out of its way. Reckon my arm's broke."

I figured so. He had done broke that arm three times. One time a whirlwind blew him off the barn roof, and one time a little mean Hereford bull knocked him down. Once I think he even broke it slamming a pickup door on himself.

"I hear a car," I said. "I'll flag them down and they can run you into a hospital. You better get it X-rayed. I'll stay here and dig that pickup out." Actually I meant to go on up to the Henrys' and get that tractor.

But Gid wouldn't even get up and walk out to the road. I never seen a man turn down as much good advice as he done.

"Let them go," he said. "I'll rest a minute, and help you dig."

"No sir," I said. "That arm needs tending to."

I went out to the road. And of all the people to be coming along just then, it had to be Molly. I knowed it was her before I even seen the car; she always went in to sell her eggs on Friday. And sure enough, it was her old Ford, the only car she'd ever had. We were humiliated for sure, one wrecked and one stuck, and I just turned my back to the road. As proud and contrary as Gid was, he wouldn't ride in with her if his jugular vein was cut.

———

The way she drove, I thought she might go by without seeing us. The driver's seat on her old car was sunk in, and she had to drive with her chin way up in order to see at all. Usually she never looked to the sides of the road. Actually, I don't know that she did see us. She may have smelled us. Anyway, she threw the skids to the Ford, and if the hill had been about one degree slicker there would have been three cars in the ditch instead of two. I wish she had stuck it—it would have evened things up. Her and Gid was ever bit as bad a driver as one another; the only difference was that when Molly got in a tight place she slowed down, and when Gid got in one he speeded up. Anything fancy was out of their category.

But by pure luck she got stopped all right. Gid was still sitting there, feeling of his arm, and the old billy had hunched and floundered about thirty yards away. Molly had on her sunbonnet and her blue milking overalls, and an old pair of men's overshoes that had belonged to me at one time, so she didn't exactly look like Lily Langtry. But she would be a good-looking woman the day she died; she always kept enough of her looks to make me remember how much she had when she had them all. She stood there in the road, taking her own good time looking the situation over. She shoved Gid's car with her foot, to see if it would shake, and then she studied the car tracks on the hill awhile, trying to make out what happened.

Gid couldn't stand the wait. "Come on over here," he said. "We ain't ashamed to admit we had a wreck. We'll tell you all about it."

But she walked off up the hill a little ways, trying to get it settled for herself.

"Look at her," he said. "Hog on ice. She's too independent for her own good. Somebody needs to take Molly down a notch or two."

"I could spit on two fellers who've been trying it for forty years," I said.

"Yes, and I've accomplished it," he said, "and I'll accomplish it agin."

"I never knowed you was such an optimist," I said.

In a minute she came stepping across the bar ditch. She looked perfectly peaceful: it was the way she usually looked. Lots of times I'd go by her place and find her sitting at the kitchen table, looking rich as cream. Life had took different on Molly than it had on me and Gid. She rested her hands on her hips and looked down at him a minute before she said anything. She had tipped her bonnet off, and her hair was blowing around her face. It was getting a sprinkle of gray, but it was still mostly black, and as long and pretty as it had ever been.

"Well, you sure skinned your nose," she said. "You look like you had an accident." Gid snorted.

"Oh no, it wasn't no accident," I said. "We set out on purpose to see who could make the biggest idiot of himself."

"It's hard to say who won," she said, grinning at me.

"I don't want a word out of you," Gid said. "As many times as I've pulled you out of ditches and off culverts."

"I know it," she said. "I don't claim to be a good driver. But I'm going to town after while, and what are you going to do?"

"Sit here till my nose scabs over," he said. "I don't intend to walk a dripping blood."

"Aw, get your hook and chain," she said. "I can pull the pickup out."

He had just been waiting for her to offer so he wouldn't need to ask.

"If you think your old hoopey can do it, we'll sure be glad to let you try," he said. He reached out a hand for me to pull him up, but when I took it and pulled he bellered like a bull. He had stretched out his sore arm before he thought, and I had to ease him back. Molly squatted down and rolled his sleeve back up and had a look at the elbow. He tried to wave her away with his good hand, but she paid it no mind.

"Quit flapping that hand in my face," she said. "You look snake-bit." His arm was hurting so he couldn't talk, but he held up his good arm and I got him to his feet.

"Let's go," he said. "You get the chain and she can pull you out." He wouldn't look at Molly; he was afraid she was going to take him up to her place and doctor him awhile. And before I had time to move he went across the road to the pickup and began fishing around for the chain himself.

Molly grinned. "He never will learn," she said, "and I'm glad. You better go find that chain if you can. He's liable to drop it on his foot and be down agin."

"I wish he would. If he had an arm and a leg out of commission, we could slow him down enough that he wouldn't really hurt himself."

I went over to the pickup to see what I could do. Gid had about half the stuff under the seat slung out on the road.

"Get out of the way," I said. "A one-armed man ain't got no business trying to handle a chain."

The chain was tricky to get out once you found it. It was between the hydraulic jack and a big pipe wrench that had got wedged in so tight a couple of years before that we couldn't move it. I had to be awful careful about moving that jack: with the slightest excuse it would have wedged itself, and the chain would have been gone for good. Damn the man that invented pickup seats anyway: you can't get nothing under them without skinning your knuckles, and then you can't get it back out if you do get it in. Gid was grumbling because I'd pushed him out of the way.

"That's how it is," he said. "I pay a fortune in wages, and then I'm the one gets ordered around."

I had managed to ease the jack past the seat brace, and I finally captured the chain. Molly came up about that time and Gid shut up like a terrapin shell.

"I wonder where all those goats will go," she said. "They were strung out clear back to the bridge."

"I hope the sonofabitches starve to death," he said. He had given up trying to do anything and was leaning against the fender. "I hope the creek gets up tonight and drowns ever one of them. A man that would own a goat would own a hound dog—they ain't no worse."

"Why, I think goats are okay," she said. "They probably make Jamison good money."

They went on that way, having a nice friendly dispute to settle their nerves, and I drug out the chain. Then I gathered up all the stuff Gid had drug out and stuffed what I could of it back. I was just getting ready to hook on the chain when I seen Jamison Williams coming over the hill riding his old fat blue horse.

"Looky yonder," I said. "Get your checkbook ready."

"Damn you," he said. "If you wasn't so slow, we'd be in town by now."

"He's riding old Blue-ass," I said. "We could outrun him on foot."

Molly got tickled, but she tried not to show it.

"Why Jamison won't hurt you," she said. "I've never seen him mad."

"Oh no," Gid said. "I ain't scared of him hurting me. It's his ideas I'm scared of. He'll have some crazy idea about how much that old rotted-out fence is worth to fix. You watch and see."

"Don't let yourself panic," I said. "Think up a good story to tell him. Say a hit-and-run driver knocked you through that fence."

"Naw," he said, "what's the use? Jamison's too dumb to lie to. It'll be all he can do to understand the truth."

Actually, Jamison managed that without much strain. He rode straight up to the hole and slid off old Blue-ass and came right over to Gid, sticking out his hand. Jamison was foolish about shaking hands. He tipped his hat to Molly and came and shook hands with me before he ever said a word.

"By god, Gideon," he said. "I see you run through my fence. These roads are slick, would you say?"

"A little slick," Gid said. When he was in a tight corner he got mighty scarce with his conversation.

"Well, Gid," Jamison said, "I wonder how long it will take you and Johnny to bring them goats back in? Judith don't like for them goats to run loose on the road." Which was a lie. Judith Jamison never cared. In fact, she might have been glad.

"Depends," Gid said. "How much are they worth to you, Jamison, by the head?"

"Well, you know, Gid," Jamison said. "You know how I knew them goats was out. By god, if that old one-eyed billy didn't come right up in the yard and butt that littlest boy of mine. He butted that boy good and hard and was after the dogs."

"Goodness," Molly said. "Why, they looked so gentle. You wouldn't think they'd hurt anybody."

"That's what I told my wife," he said. "It's too bad she can't shoot no better. She would shoot that good dog before she hit the goat."

"Probably should have used the shotgun," Gid said. "Rifles are a little hard."

"Well, you know, Gid, it was the ten-gauge she used. I don't know whether her shoulder's broke or not. I guess the doc can X-ray it when we take the boy in. He would butt him through the garden fence."

"These roads are pretty slick, Jamison," Gid said. "If I was you, I'd wait till they dried up a little before I went in. A man can get off in the ditch and wreck his car before he knows what's happening to him."

"I guess forty dollars apiece for them goats," Jamison said. "They got to be drenched if I keep them, and they ain't due to wool till September."

He tipped his hat to Molly agin and went over and began to climb on old Blue-ass. I watched that, because Jamison Williams getting on a horse was a sight not many people got to see. Jamison was a little short fart; he led old Blue over to Gid's car and got up the car so he'd have elevation and got on from there. Gid didn't get much kick out of that performance. He was in a fairly solemn mood.

"Forty *apiece?*" he said. He was trying to let on he thought that was too high.

"Why, you could have them for that, Gid," Jamison said. "There was eighty-six of them. If you don't want to buy them, you and Johnny just feel free to bring them in any time and leave them in the pen. Judith and the boys can take them back to the pasture after they milk." We found out later it was Judith's collarbone that broke. I guess we ought to be glad she didn't shoot one of the children.

"We'll get them back tomorrow," Gid said. "And I'll get a crew out to fix your fence. Shore sorry all this happened. Send me them doctor bills."

"Well, Gid, such is life," Jamison said. "By god, this rain did us good. Just leave the goats in the pen. We don't mind helping our neighbors, me and the wife."

"Okay. You'll all come to see us," Gid said.

"Sure, sure. Go, Blue. By god, I hope that boy's stopped bleeding when I get home."

He turned old Blue-ass toward the barn, and off they went.

"Ain't that a sight?" Gid said.

"Get in and back her up, Molly," I said. "This chain ain't very long."

===

It didn't take long to get the pickup out, once I got her hitched to it. It's just a wonder she didn't pull it in two.

"Now you got about ten feet of slack," I said. "Go slow till the chain gets tight. Then give her hell."

"You reckon she can do it?" Gid said.

"You just stand back so the mud won't splatter on you," she said.

She gunned that old Ford like it was a B-36. I just braced myself; I knew what she was going to do. Directly off she went, and it like to popped my head off when she hit the end of the chain. But we sure came out of the mud. Gid gave a jump for the running board, but he wasn't close enough, so he got left. I went to honking for her to stop: the road was still so slick I was afraid to tap my brakes. I just sat loose in the seat and got ready to jump if it come to that. There wasn't no limit to how reckless Molly could drive. Once I was riding with her when she turned over a trailer with two sows and eleven shoats in it; a Greyhound bus passed us and honked. "He never needed to honk at me," she said. It took me half a day to gather those squealing bastards up.

For a change, I was lucky. We came to a corner, and when we got around it she felt a little jerk on the chain and remembered me. I was out of the pickup and had the chain unhooked before we quit rolling good.

"I'll be," she said. "I guess we left Gid."

"He's coming down the road." I hadn't looked, but I knew Gid that well. I was fixing to back up for him when I heard him holler.

"Just hold on," he said. "If you was to back up you'd run over me." He was red in the face as an old turkey gobbler.

"What's the matter with you?" he said to Molly. "I wish you'd been tied to a tree."

"You didn't need to walk," she said. He didn't bother Molly. "Now git in this car. We won't go to town, we'll just go back to my place. I want to work on this arm a little." She slipped up and got him by his sore arm, so he couldn't pull back, and led him right on over to the Ford without another word said. He knew better than to fool with her when she had the advantage. We stopped at the wreck a minute, so he could fish out a box of cigars. I bet it blistered him a little to have her drive him up the hill he'd just slid down.

===

Molly was still living on the old Taylor place, where she had lived her whole life. It was on a hill—some say the highest place in the county—and you could see it for miles and miles around. The first time I ever saw Molly was on that place; she was carrying a jug of the old man's whiskey up the cellar steps. It was the first time I had ever been visiting anywhere. All my folks were blonds, and I never will forget how surprised I was to see them black-headed Taylor kids. Pa and the old man sat on the back steps and drank whiskey out of the same jug for half an hour, and then they chased me and Molly down and made us drink a little. We cried and run off down to the pigpen together and made some mud pies out of the pigwallow and ate them, to get the whiskey taste out of our mouths. When we went back the old man thought of some more devilment: he sat a bucket on the fence and said he'd give me a dime if I'd shoot it off with his old twelve-gauge shotgun. I didn't know what a dime was, but I was crazy about guns. Pa steadied it for me, so I don't guess I caught the whole kick, but I caught enough. I missed the bucket, too, so the old man wouldn't give me the dime: I never found out what one was till two years later. Molly took up for me and led me down in the cellar and showed me the still.

And she stayed right there and done all of her living right up on that hill. I guess she just never saw no reason to move around. Her old man and old lady were dead before she married Eddie, and all the other kids had left home. Eddie never had nothing but a pack of turd hounds and a pair of roughnecking boots from the day he was born till the day he fell off the derrick; their getting married was just a matter of finding a justice of the peace who was sober enough to talk. But it's still strange to think of her spending her whole life there on her hill. One night when we were younger and were laying up together, I was awake listening to the wind rattle the windowpanes, and I asked her about it.

"Ain't you curious to see the world at all?" I said.

"No," she said. "I'm doing just as much living right here and now as I could anywhere." And she hugged me and we went back to sleep.

Probably, in the long run, she was right. She done her share up on that hill. She was born there, and went to school what little she went over in the Idiot Ridge schoolhouse. The flu killed the old lady in 1918; the old man drank lye. Her oldest brother Shep, I don't know what became of him. Mary Margaret married a store clerk, and Rich got caught stealing saddles and sent to the pen; Molly said once he was out, but he never came our way. Eddie fell off that oil rig, and then the Germans got Joe and the Japs got Jimmy. All that time Molly stayed there and went on. Sometimes I wonder what will become of the old Taylor place when Molly and the rest of us are gone. I can't imagine that hill without her. But I guess there ain't nothing that don't come to an end sometime.

When we got there she took us in the kitchen and fed us peach cobbler and coffee. Gid was quiet as a mouse. After a while she went out in the smokehouse and brought in some kerosene for him to soak his arm in.

He perked right up. "Oh, is that all?" he said. He couldn't get his sleeve up fast enough. I guess he thought she went after the dehorning saw.

"Yell if she gets too rough," I said. "I got to go outside. Smelling that kerosene ain't good for a healthy man."

I went out back and sat on the steps. You could see way off west, across Molly's land and a lot of Gid's. Her back bedroom was a nice place to wake up. The clouds to the west were peeling away like layers of gauze, and it wasn't long before the sun was shining on the wet mesquite. I could hear her and Gid talking through the screen door. It was childish, but it made me feel left out. I knew all about it. Old as they was, Gid was still halfway talking about leaving Mabel and coming to live with Molly, and she was halfway encouraging it. And it would have been a good thing for Gid and her both, I guess; it just made me feel a little left out. We had both hung around her so long. Course Gid ought to left Mabel. Living with her thirty years was no judgment, in my book. But she had a grandkid to hold over him. I got up and walked around to the garden, to see how the tomatoes and the roasting ears were holding out. I seen I was going to have to make it around for supper a little more often, if I was going to beat the blister bugs to what there was. Molly kind of expected me for supper anyway, a lot of times.

When I came out of the garden the sun was so bright that I went around to the front of the house, where the shade was. In a little while Gid come out on the porch; he had about half a bedsheet wrapped around his arm, and he was grinning like a possum.

"I'm as good as new," he said.

Molly came out with three big glasses of buttermilk and a plate of cold cornbread. Nobody had much to say, so we sat quiet for a change, eating cornbread and buttermilk. Once in a while the conversation would kinda settle; I guess we were all thinking about old times. Finally I looked around and Molly and Gid were staring off across the pastures, not seeing anything.

"What time is it?" I said. They both jumped.

Gid fished out his pocket watch, but it was stopped.

"Shadows are pretty long," Molly said.

"Time we got on," he said.

"Aw, you all stay for supper. I've got some fresh black-eyed peas shelled. We'll dress a fryer."

"I guess we can't," Gid said, sounding a little gloomy. He set his empty buttermilk glass down on the tray. His nose still looked raw and stingy.

Molly walked out in the yard and began to pick on the lilac bushes. "I don't see why you all don't just sit a few more minutes," she said. "Supper won't take no time."

"We'll have to put it off till some other time," Gid said. "We're much obliged."

"I don't want your much obliged," she said, kinda snappy. "I want you to eat with me."

Then we walked around the house and stood by the cellar a minute, the cellar Old Man Taylor had built. The sun was down and it was clouding up agin over in the northwest.

Gid said let's go and Molly tried one more time to get us to stay. She walked out to the pickup with us, looking down in the dumps. Gid bragged on her bandage a little, to try and perk her up.

"You all come by and see me," she said.

"I'll be by," I said. "I might even get back tonight."

"I wish you would, if it ain't out of your way. I'll keep something on the stove."

"No, don't go to no trouble," I said. "No sense in you waiting up special. I might not get by till eleven o'clock, I don't know."

"Okay," she said. "Do as you please."

We told her good-by and I drove on out through the cattle guard, into the lane. Molly was still standing by her windmill, watching the world, or maybe just watching us.

==

"She's getting lonesome in her old age," he said.

"Tell me where to go," I said. "I don't want to get blamed for taking you some-place wrong." He never had found out I wasn't no mind reader. Once when we was younger and got drunk I took him to a rodeo in Newcastle and it turned out he had paid his entry fee in one in Waurika, Oklahoma, a hundred and fifty miles the other way.

"Just take me home," he said. He was blue; he always got blue in the late evenings—had been for years. If I had to face Mabel, I wouldn't have had no fondness for sundown, either.

"Molly's been lonesome a good while," I said. "Her independent talk don't fool me."

"We're the only ones that ever go and see her," he said. "Wonder why she don't like womenfolk."

"Same reason I don't. They're silly as hens, all of them except her."

He turned it over in his mind for a while. It wasn't quite dark good, but all the lights were on in Thalia. Ever time we topped a hill I seen them flashing. The shower had cooled things off and the country smelled nice and green. Being in wrecks made Gid thoughtful.

"Molly's had a lot," he said.

"Yes," I said. "But I wouldn't call it no whopping success of a life."

"She's made mistakes," he said. "So have I and so have you."

"At least I ain't made the same ones over and over agin," I said.

"Why not? You might as well make them you're used to as to make new ones all the time. It don't do no more damage."

"Anyhow," he said, "I wish she wasn't lonesome."

We drove through Thalia. Two or three cars were parked in front of the picture show, and a couple more outside the domino hall.

"Television's got the picture show business," he said.

"No wonder. They quit making good shows. The last one I seen that was any count was *Red River.*"

"Good night," he said, "that was years ago."

"So were a lot of good things," I said. Six or eight kids were scuffling and fighting on the courthouse lawn, under the mulberry trees.

"You don't keep up," he said. "*Shane* was made since then. So was *The Searchers.*"

"Them was so-so," I said. "All the good movie stars are getting too old."

"I wish I had the energy them kids have," he said.

"You'd waste it," I said. "Just like they're doing."

We passed the drive-in eating place, and it looked like 90 percent of the cars in town were there. "Them things are what makes the money," I said.

"I know it," he said. "I hate a drive-in. Them jukeboxes are awful."

"Susie'll be right there in a few years," I said. "Right in the middle of it."

"I guess so," he said. "I reckon so."

I pulled up in his driveway and stopped. Gid opened the door, but he kept sitting there.

"How'll we get those goddamn goats?" he said.

"I favor a thirty-thirty," I said. "The ammunition's cheap."

"But the goats ain't. We'll just get out there about daybreak and get them ourselves."

"I knew you'd decide on the hardest way."

"If you stop at the domino hall," he said, "tell Charlie Starton to get his wrecker and go get that car. You might show him where it is." What he meant was, be damn sure I didn't let that car sit out there all night.

"Okay," I said. "See you when it gets light. Any special horse? You got one that's good on goats?"

"Bring me any one you can catch," he said.

He was out, still holding to the car door. I began to back up. The only way to get loose from him was to drive loose. When I swung into the street my headlights shone on him, standing outside his door cleaning his boots.

Charlie Starton was standing on the sidewalk in front of the domino hall, smoking a cigar.

"What's the matter with Gid?" he said. "Can't he drive?"

I never cared to stand around having no conversation with Charlie Starton.

"His reflexes don't work too fast," I said. "Are you coming or ain't you?"

When there was money involved Charlie's reflexes worked awful fast. He followed me right out and winched up the car. I turned in at Molly's, but it was past ten, and she had gone to bed; I hated that. I hated to see Molly lonesome, and I had been counting on some cold supper besides. But it wasn't no go. I went home and fed the chickens and ate me a bowl of Post Toasties and went to bed.

3

ABOUT TWO WEEKS LATER we met Molly at the feed store one morning. It was August then, and the country was drying up, so Gid wanted to feed his old cows a little. I was in town early and we thought we'd be the first customers, but Molly's old Ford was sitting by the loading platform.

"She's getting her chicken feed," I said.

Gid looked a little nervous. Him and her might have been having arguments. I didn't know.

Her and the feed-store hands were sitting in the back of the store on the sacks of dogfood, drinking coffee. Samuel Houston was petting his old mangy dog and telling a big windy. He didn't own the feed store, he just foremanned it: His boy T.I. and a crew of Mexicans did what little work got done.

Molly looked up and said hello to us, but Samuel H. never broke his stride.

"He caught me about two miles this side of the stop sign," he said. "Come walking up to the car with a big gun on his hip and a badge on his chest. 'I'd like to see your driver's license,' he said, like it was a friendly conversation. 'I'd like to see your funeral notice, you sonofabitch,' I said. 'Now, mister, don't use that foul language,' he said. 'What are you going to tell the judge when you have to show him this ticket?' 'I guess, by god, I'll tell him I run a goddamn stop sign,' I said. 'Now give it here, I got to get this feed unloaded this morning.' "

"Why, I'd have stomped that mother into the pavement," T.I. said. "Where he needed to be stomped." He might have, too. Once at a medicine show T.I. won what they said was a genuine white Mormon wife, only it turned out to be a genuine White Rock Hen. He stomped a little that night. His real name was Texas Independence.

"Why, hello, Gid," Samuel Houston said, "have you seen my dog? This here's the smartest dog I ever raised, and I call him Billie Sol. He can suck the eggs right out from under the hens without them ever noticing."

Gid just looked impatient. "I hate to bother you fellers," he said. "But if it ain't too much trouble, I'd like about a dozen sacks of cottonseed cake."

The three Mexicans got the biggest laugh out of that. They led such easy lives sitting around that percolator, I guess they could get a big laugh out of anything.

"Oh, it's no trouble," Samuel H. said. "No trouble atall. That's what we're in business for. Sit down and help yourself to some coffee."

"No thank you," Gid said. "I believe we'll get the cake and get on. The longer we wait the hotter it will get."

"Then, by god, why go? A man can get too hot out working, if he ain't careful. It'll be cool agin this afternoon."

"Oh, sit down a minute," Molly said. "I got a favor to ask you."

But Gid was having a stubborn fit; he kept standing up fidgeting. Finally I got tired of standing and sat down.

"We'd sure like to get on," Gid said. "Maybe me and Johnny could just load the feed ourselves, if you'd show us where it is."

"Why sure, Gid," Samuel Houston said. "It's right over there in the corner. Just feel right at home. Show him where that cottonseed cake is, T.I."

T.I. yawned like he had just got up. "Sure," he said. "Why don't you let these boys help you pitch it in the truck? They don't mind."

I knew it would eventually come down to me helping load it. Gid would have soon handled a rattlesnake as a sack of cattle feed. He never lifted one except in emergencies. But as soon as I stood up and moved, the Mexicans grabbed the sacks and had the feed loaded in a minute and a half. And as soon as Gid saw that, he was perfectly happy to stay awhile; he felt like things were getting done.

Only he said the exact wrong thing, and Molly thought he said it to her.

"That's the stuff," he said. "We can get going in a minute now and get some work done. I wasn't raised lazy, like most people."

I don't know what possessed him to say it; maybe it was being nervous. And I don't know what possessed Molly to take it wrong; he never meant to aim it at her. But she sat her cup down and gave him the strangest hurt look.

The elevator boss drove up then, and Samuel and T.I. and the Mexicans jumped to get to work. Just us three stayed there, and it was real quiet. I tried my hardest to think of some conversation to kinda pass it all over, and I know Gid did too, but we couldn't come up with much. It was plain silly, but it was awkward as hell; five minutes of it would have made me sick.

But it never lasted over two. Molly broke down crying; I knew she would. "That wasn't a very nice thing to say to me, Gid," she said. She bent over with her head between her knees and we could only see her hair, and her head shaking. Then all of a sudden she straightened up and looked right at me. "Well, aren't you going to take up for me?" she said, and went to crying agin.

I didn't know what to say. None of it made sense. I guess she took it as something against her dad—she always tried to fool herself about him. Gid never could appreciate how hard some people worked to fool themselves.

She cried hard when she cried, but it didn't last too long. Gid was just flabbergasted. In a minute her back got still, and she looked up. The tears were dripping everywhere, but she was kinda calm agin, and nobody would have believed she had been so upset. I went over and filled her coffee cup and handed it to her. "Thank you," she said. She rested her elbows on her knees and bent over, sipping coffee, with the tears running off the corner of her mouth and dripping right in the cup. Gid couldn't stand it—he got up and fished out his handkerchief.

"Here, don't ruin that good coffee," he said.

She took it and kinda grinned at him. "What am I going to do with myself?" she said.

"Why, I'm terribly sorry, Molly," he said. "I never meant a thing by that remark."

"Oh, I know you didn't," she said. "It's silly. I don't know why some things upset me so. You ain't to blame."

But he was, really. At least he sure thought he was. We sat for about five minutes, all of us a little bit worried, drinking our coffee.

"I thought of something while I was crying," Molly said. "I hadn't thought of it in years. It was when all of us kids were at home, when we still used blackstrap molasses for all our sweetening. Daddy went in to Thalia and bought the winter groceries one day." She stopped and looked out the feedstore door, at the hot, dusty street and the houses of Thalia on the other side of it, with television aerials sticking up on their roofs like I don't know what. She looked like she was looking through a telescope at something as far away as the moon. And I guess they was about that far away, them days. It takes a long memory to sit on a bunch of dogfeed sacks and call up Old Man Cletus Taylor riding off to Thalia in a wagon. I bet he had a whiskey jug on the seat beside him, too.

"When he come back, just before sundown," she said, "he had a big barrel of sorghum molasses sitting in the front of the wagon. Him and Shep went to unloading the flour and stuff, and the rest of us kids stood there looking at that syrup barrel. I couldn't hardly imagine that much syrup. It was the sweets for the whole winter. Pretty soon Dad and Shep came back and walked the barrel to the back of the wagon, so they could lift it down." Her talking quavered a little. "I never did know how it happened," she said, "but anyway, when they were lifting it out of the wagon, one of them lost his grip and it fell and busted open on the ground. The molasses stood by itself, just a second, and then it all spread out and began to run down the hill toward the chickenhouse. We all just stood there; we couldn't move for a minute. The first was when Richard stuck his toe in it. It ran real slow, and ants and doodlebugs got caught in it. There wasn't no way to scoop it up. Then we all begin to cry. Mary Margaret took it the worst. She held her breath and ran all the way around the house before anybody could catch her to pound her on the back; then she went over and began to bang her head on the cellar door. She was the worst to hold her breath and bang her head I ever saw. Even Shep was crying. Richard was the only one that showed good sense. He squatted down and stuck his finger in it and kept licking it up that way till after dark. I couldn't believe it. Nothing had hurt me that bad before. After a while Richard put a horned toad in it, and it got stuck. I went in the house and got in one of the woodboxes and wouldn't come out till after supper. Shep and Daddy argued over whose fault it was till Shep just finally left home, and Daddy stayed down in the cellar drinking whiskey nearly that whole winter."

"My god," Gid said. "That was a tragedy."

"Nothing will ever make me forget watching that sorghum run downhill," she said.

"What was that favor you wanted to ask?" Gid said.

"Oh, Old Roanie got out in the big pasture the other day," she said. "I can't get her back." Roanie was her milk cow. She was a wild old bitch.

"We'll come right on and get her," he said, standing up. Molly put up her coffee cup and got in her car, and we got in the pickup. "You drive," he said.

"Don't worry," I said. "This pickup is the only means of transportation I have. I ain't anxious to let you under the wheel."

"I wish we didn't have to get that cow in," he said. "We just barely will have time to do the feeding."

"I'm glad to do it today," I said. "Another day or two and you'll be gone to have your operation, and I'd have to do it by myself."

"Molly needs to be married," he said. "She ain't able to run that place by herself. I never meant to get her so upset this morning."

"She's too touchy sometimes," I said.

"I had heard that molasses story before," he said. "That was awful. I can imagine just how them kids felt."

When we got to Molly's house she was just going in the back door. Had her mind on dinner. I went on down to the barn. Gid was out before I got stopped.

"Let's pen the old hussy and eat dinner and go," he said. "Which one you want, Chester or Matt?" Molly named her horses after *Gunsmoke*.

"Chester, I guess," I said.

"Goddamn," he said, trying to saddle up. "This old bastard's so big around it's like trying to saddle a whiskey keg."

He didn't get no sympathy from me. I had reared back to throw my saddle on and heaved and Chester had got one of his big front feet on the girt. It like to broke my back. I dropped the saddle, too.

"Well, I've shot my wad," I said, "I never will get up strength for another throw."

Gid got a big laugh out of it.

And at that the horses was easier than the cow. She was standing right in plain sight, down by the salt lick. The sight cheered Gid up.

"Well, looky there," he said. "This won't take no time. I was afraid the old bitch would be off in the mesquite somewhere."

"She may be yet," I said. "I can remember cattle closer to the gate than she is that ended up getting away. How about Mick and Big Shitty?" They were two old outlaw steers Gid had owned for about ten years. We chased them up and down Onion Creek all one summer and finally tricked them into the lot with some hay. We kept Mick, too. But Gid got careless and Big Shitty ran over him and a water trough and tore up three fences and got plumb away.

"Aw, she's just an old milk cow," he said. "You sickle around behind her thataway."

I did. Old Chester loped about as graceful as a roadgrader. At first old Roanie came along fine; actually, I just don't think she had noticed us. I think she just thought it was Chester and Matt by themselves. Molly just sooked her afoot; she might not have never seen men on horses before.

But when she figured things out, the race was on. She had her head down and her bag swinging from side to side, and she was covering country. I was closest and I whipped up: I knew if I let her get in the brush, it would be my fault from the conception to the resurrection. Chester had no idea what it was all about, but he done his best. We barely got her turned before she hit the brush; then she struck out south, just as fast, and Gid and Matt struck out to head her agin. It was the funniest sight I ever seen. Old Matt didn't no more care about that cow than if she was the moon, and when it come time to stop and turn her he just went right on into the brush. The brush went to popping and the cuss words come a-flying back. But I took in after Roanie; I didn't have no time to worry about Gid. Actually, she turned out to have about twice as much speed as Chester, and I was just hoping she'd stop for the south fence when I seen Gid and Matt come flying out of the brush ahead of me, hot on her trail. Them thorny thickets hadn't helped Gid's disposition, I knew that; he didn't have his hat any more, or all his shirt. But he had his rope down. Nobody in their right mind would try to rope off a plowhorse, but Gid would rope an elephant off a Shetland if he took a notion. He was whopping old Matt with the rope about every two steps, and Matt was going to the races. Gid came roaring over a little knoll, swinging his rope and yelling, and pretty soon he let fly and caught him a cow. It was where his troubles began. Any horse with a grain of brains would have stopped when Gid threw the rope: Matt wasn't in that category. Gid reared back on the reins—he seen his fix immediately—but Matt went right on. I guess he seen the old cow when he run by her, but he sure never dreamed him and her were connected. She was just landscape to him. Roanie got a big surprise. One minute she was headed for the high and lonesome, and the next minute Matt had got to the end of the rope and she was tearing up the land like a plow. Gid, he was just a spectator, but his sympathies were all with the cow. Finally Matt figured out he was dragging an anchor. When I rode up all three of them were panting.

"She's caught now," I said. One of her horns was broke, and her front leg stuck out sideways, about as useful as a dishrag.

"Why can't nothing go right?" he said. Not "Why can't I do nothing right?" And if I had done it, it would have been "What in the goddamn hell did you mean pulling a stunt like that?"

"One consolation," I said. "We won't never have to get her up agin."

But Gid was too blue to rag.

"Nobody's fault," I said.

"No, but I'll get blamed," he said. "And I'll furnish the new cow."

"Oh no," I said. "Molly wouldn't want you to do that. We were just being neighbors. Accidents happen sometimes."

"Mostly to me," he said. "Let's go. She'll stay till we get back."

"She won't be hard to track if she don't," I said. "Where did you lose your hat?"

His hand flew up to his head, and he turned a shade bluer. He hadn't missed it till then. Me and Chester sat on the hill and waited while he went and found it.

====

Of course Molly was as nice as she could be about it. If it fazed her at all, it didn't show. She had meat and beans and gravy on the table when we got there, and some roasting ears steaming in a big bowl. Sweat was dripping off the ice-tea glasses.

"I hate to lose her," she said. "But she was wild as a wolf anyway. I had to hobble her all the time." She wouldn't hear of Gid furnishing her another cow, and she wouldn't even let us go down and kill the old hussy for her. Gid was out of the talking mood, so we ate and loaded our saddles and left. Molly was standing on her back porch tying her sunbonnet strings when we left.

"I shore hate that," Gid said.

I knew he would have to get over it in his own time, so I never said nothing. Nobody could talk Gid out of feeling bad. When something happened to get his mind off things a minute he was all right, and along came one of Jamison Williams' kids to do it. He was running right down the road.

"My god, ain't he running," Gid said. "Take to the ditch, he don't see us. Get out of his way and let him go."

But when he got even with us the boy stopped right quick and went to crying. He stood there in the road crying, picking one foot and then the other out of the hot sand and cooling it against his trousers leg.

"Nelson drowned in the horse trough," he said. "Just now."

We grabbed him and went. Judith was sitting in the porch rocker, rocking and crying and hugging the boy so tight he couldn't have breathed if he had been in perfect health. "Oh St. Peter," she said, "he's drowned and gone." Gid jerked the kid away from her and turned him upside down, and I ran to the back yard and kicked the rain barrel over and got it around there. Me and Gid squeezed the boy over it till about half the horse trough ran out of his mouth, and finally he came to. Gid carried him back and gave him to Judith; she was still hysterical. I don't think she ever knew it was us that drained him; she might have thought it was St. Peter. Anyhow, we went on.

"What a day," he said.

When we got to the ranch it was done too late to feed. I unloaded the twelve sacks of feed while Gid was trying to make up his mind what to do.

"I don't never get nothing done any more," he said. "These old pens need rebuilding. And that damn fencing ain't finished. Why does a man even try?"

"I've often wondered," I said.

"Well, you damn sure don't ever accomplish nothing if you don't try," he said. "Let's sit down in the shade here a minute."

"Some people get rich without trying," I said. "Look at Pearl Twass. She used to go in the bushes with just about anybody, and now she drives around in a big Chrysler and sends her kids off to fancy schools."

"Yeah, but that's just rich," he said. "That's just diamonds on a dog's ass."

"Maybe so. But Pearl don't go in the bushes so cheap any more."

"Now I got to organize," he said. "Before I go to the hospital. Wisht I never had agreed to this damn operation. No telling how long it will tie me up."

"I thought it was just a standard operation for kidney trouble," I said. "Like grinding your valves."

"Oh it is," he said. "But you never know. I'm pessimistic, I guess."

"Well, don't worry about the ranch," I said. "I've taken care of it for thirty-eight years. I won't lay down on the job now."

"That's what worries me," he said. "How well you've taken care of things. That's why nothing on this whole outfit works like it ought to."

"No, it's because you're too tight to buy good equipment," I said.

"Anyhow," he said, "and be that as it may, I'm going to draw you up enough orders to last you till I get back."

"Glad to have them," I said. "Then I'll at least know what not to do."

He wet his pencil and went to figuring, and I whittled some. The big white thunderheads were bouncing along on the south wind like tumbleweeds and the lot was a little dusty.

"I guess this will hold you for a while," he said, handing me four or five pages out of the little book. "I wrote them down so you wouldn't forget any. Don't lose them."

I gave them the once-over. "The first thing I need to do is lose these here," I said. "I ain't got no crew of Mexicans working for me."

"Just a few little chores," he said.

"I want to straighten one thing out," I said. "When Mabel took you off on that boat trip, I had a little trouble with your brother-in-law Willy. Now if he shows up this time trying to tell me what to do, he's liable to get his feelings hurt." Willy was the state representative from our district, and a fat-ass politician if there ever was one. Every year he'd show up at the town baseball games, passing out little old scrawny peaches. Once he offered me one. "You ain't too old to vote," he said. "I will be before I vote for you," I said. He shut up like I'd poured him full of alum.

"I never told you about him coming out," I said. "I didn't see no sense in embarrassing you."

"Well, by god, I like that," he said. "Willy trying to give you orders?"

"Just trying to get me to quit," I said. "Him and Mabel still think I'm a bad influence on you."

"That fat bastard," he said. "It's no wonder to me he'd try something like that."

"It ain't to me neither," I said. "I just wanted to tell you, so you wouldn't be surprised if he shows up at the hospital to tell you how nasty I was to him."

"I wouldn't care if you drowned him," he said. "Damn I wish Mabel wouldn't scheme around like that—she's behind it. Seems like the older I get, the less I know for sure."

"Well, don't lose no sleep over Willy," I said. "I just wanted to mention it."

"Just don't let him make you mad enough to quit," he said. He was so gloomy all of a sudden; he was practically planning his own funeral.

"I like that," I said. "We been friends sixty-five years. You don't think a fat-ass like Willy could run me off, do you?"

"Course not," he said. "I'm sorry."

We didn't say anything for a while.

"Molly takes her age pretty well," he said then, out of the blue. "I'm half a notion to quit Mabel and go live with her yet. I might have a few years' peace. If I live over this operation, I might just do it. You don't need to tell nobody though."

"Oh, I won't," I said, and he looked at me pretty close.

"Would that bother you much?" he said. "If I was to move in with Molly? I hadn't really thought about it from your angle."

"Why, it wouldn't bother me a bit," I said. "I think it would be good for both of you. Besides serving Mabel and Willy right." The part about it not bothering me was a plain lie, and he knew it; I kept whittling on my stick and didn't look at him.

"I guess it would though," he said, kinda sad. "We've kinda split her, haven't we? Anyhow it's just one of my crazy ideas. I doubt she'd want to do it anyway."

We sat there an hour, watching it get dark, and didn't say another word. He sure was lonesome for Molly. I was too. And neither one of us had the other fooled.

4

I WAS SURE RIGHT about Willy coming. About a week after Gid went to the hospital I was out one morning doctoring some puny calves, and I seen Gid's big Oldsmobile driving up to the lot. Willy got out and came toward me like I was the President. He was peeling off the glove on his handshaking hand.

"Put her there, Johnny," he said. "By god, it's been some time."

"I got screwworm dope on my hands," I said. "What can I do for you, Willy?"

"Oh, not a thing, not a thing," he said. "I was just in town staying with Mabel while Gid's in such a bad way. I thought I'd run out and see if I could be any help. To tell the truth, I could use the exercise."

"Aw, I've seen worse overweight men than you," I said. "One or two."

Actually he was just a fat tub of lard.

"Well, whatever you need doing, just show me. I wasn't raised on a dry-land farm for nothing."

"You wasn't?" I said. "I thought it was being raised on nothing on a dry-land farm was what caused you to go into politics. Or was it because you couldn't *raise* nothing?" I just came right out and got insulting when I talked to Willy. I didn't have no time to fool around.

"It's just like Mabel says," he said. "You don't try to get along with people. I came all the way out here at my own expense to see if I could be of some help, and you insult my ancestry."

"Get off the goddamn soapbox," I said. "There ain't no voters around. You know damn well whose expense you come out on—Gid's. It's just a pity he didn't throw away his car keys and cancel his charge accounts before he went in."

"Now you listen, McCloud," he said. "My sister and I have had about enough of you."

"Listen yourself," I said. "I've had a damn sight too much of you and your sister. Now you see this jar of screwworm dope? It's the blackest, shittiest-smelling stuff they ever put in a bottle. Unless you want about half a bottle on the front of that white shirt of yours, you better get in that car and skedaddle." I started around the feed trough, holding my bottle ready to throw. I would have thrown, too, if he'd opened his mouth, but he never. That's one quick way to get rid of a politician.

===

Only the next day I ran into him agin, and he had me at a disadvantage. I had just stepped out of the domino hall.

"Well, I see you been working hard today," he said, "looking after my sister's interests."

"No, I been playing dominos all afternoon," I said. "If it's any of your business."

"Mabel's business is my business," he said. "And you're working partly for her. So I guess we ought to talk."

"My checks are signed Gideon Fry," I said. "He's the one I work for."

"That's why we need to talk," he said. "Of course you haven't seen Gideon since the operation. If you had interest enough to go see him, you'd know he won't be in any shape to give orders for a long time."

"Hell, he don't have to be in very good shape to give orders," I said. "Besides, I'm going to see him day after tomorrow."

"Well he's a very sick man," he said. "The doctors have told him he'll have to quit work completely. Now what do you think of that?"

"It don't surprise me," I said. "They're always telling him something like that. But he ain't quit yet, and even if he had I wouldn't take no orders from you or Mabel. You can take your orders and put them where the monkey put the peanut."

And that ended conversation number two.

===

That one worried me just a little, though. On my way home that afternoon I stopped by Molly's. She met me at the back gate.

"I was hoping you'd come by today," she said. "I've been wanting to talk to you."

"You know, I talk a lot better when I'm full," I said.

She grinned. We had black-eyed peas and turnip greens and beef for supper. And I had about half of a custard pie and the better part of a pot of coffee.

"I've got to get the weeds mowed around my barn," she said. "I nearly stepped on a snake yesterday."

"One nearly stepped on me today," I said. "He was a political snake."

"Willy Peters," she said. "I was down to see Gid yesterday."

"I was hoping you'd been," I said. "How was he?"

She looked a little worried, too. "He was still a little dopey," she said. "I never got to stay but about ten minutes."

"Willy said they told him to quit work," I said.

"Oh, they told him that ten years ago," she said. "They just tell him that on general principles. One of the nurses told me they found some kind of little old tumor, but she didn't know if it was malignant or not. I think Mabel was in the building somewhere, what made them run me off so quick. I hated to leave."

"Well, I'll be down and see him tomorrow," I said. "Maybe we'll get to talk awhile. Let's go out on the porch."

The chairs were done out there; we went out and sat down. It was dark and we sat quiet awhile, enjoying the south breeze. The white clouds were rolling over, and the moon was done up. I wished old Gid could have been there with us—he would have enjoyed the cool. I could just barely see Molly, rocking in the dark. I reached out and patted her hand.

"What ever become of that old glider?" I said. "Tonight would be a nice night to swing a little."

"Good lord," she said. "I gave it to some high-school kids who come out hunting scrap iron. I wish I had it back."

"Want to ask you something," I said. "Just out of curiosity. Gid mentioned to me once that he was kinda thinking about leaving Mabel and moving out here with you. You'all ever decide about it?"

Molly sighed and didn't say anything for a while.

"Oh, we've talked about it a lot, Johnny," she said. "But we haven't decided. Gid hates to lose little Susie. Besides, I don't know, they may take him off to the Mayo Clinic now."

"I'd make a bet they don't do that," I said.

"Well, I just wish he'd come on out here where he'd have a little peace," she said. "He's done without it all his life. I believe I could take better care of him than he's been getting."

"Well, I just wondered how you felt about it," I said.

"I guess it will come down to whether he likes me better than he does Susie," Molly said. "He's got such a conscience, you know. You got to convince him something's right or he won't touch it. Or else you got to trick him someway."

"Why hell, tricking him's twice the easiest," I said. "I can trick him nine times an hour, but I never have been able to convince him of nothing."

We sat there watching the night till almost ten o'clock. The whippoorwills were calling all over the ridge.

"Bedtime for me," I said.

She walked to the pickup with me and told me to tell Gid hello for her. "Glad you came by," she said. "Come a little oftener."

She was standing by the running board, and I reached out and patted her shoulder. When I drove off I remembered a lot of the times when we was younger and I'd stayed the night. It wasn't that I wasn't welcome no more, either. We were just different. Use to we could chase around and have fun doing nearly anything. Now we both just got yawny. It seemed plain sad.

5

I HAD WONDERFUL LUCK at the hospital—Mabel and Willy had already left for the day, and Gid hadn't had no sedative. He had his bed cranked up so he could see out the window and watch the traffic. I knew the minute I seen him he wasn't in no danger.

"Country getting dry?" he asked. He was white as a bleached sheet, but he didn't seem weak. At least his voice wasn't.

"Some," I said.

"What do you mean, some?" he said. I could see he was primed for a long conversation.

"Just some," I said. "A rain wouldn't do no harm, but then I've seen it a damn sight dryer. We had a good shower down on the River country the day you went in."

"Just an inch, Molly said," he said. "That's already burned up."

"Now just back up," I said. "You've been lying here half-unconscious in an air-conditioned room for ten days, and you're trying to tell me how hot and dry it is?"

"I got eyes," he said. "I can see that lawn out there. They water it ever day and it's still dry.

"How's the cattle?" he said.

"They all died of blackleg and a whirlwind blew the windmill over," I said. "How's that for calamity? When you coming home?"

"Be out in two days," he said. "Don't tell nobody though. They think they're gonna keep me two more weeks." Gid was a great one for walking out of hospitals; he'd done it four or five times in his life.

"Glad to hear it," I said.

"Willy's been driving me crazy," he said. "Been bothering you?"

"Not much. I chased him off with some #62 screwworm dope. That the right tactic?"

"It'll do till I get out," he said.

"Molly said they want you to ease up," I said.

"Hell, don't they always?" he said. "If doctors had their way, the whole world would be sitting on its butt. But I'll tell you a secret. This is the last hospital I ever intend to go in. If I get to hurting too bad to live, by god I'll shoot myself, like Dad done. He had the right slant on this business, that's for sure."

"I better give you my present," I said. I had picked him up a good smooth cedar whittling stick, and I handed it to him. I didn't figure he'd hurt nobody with it. Once I give him a stockwhip, and the doctors and nurses like to ate me up. They figured he had weapons enough as it was.

But the stick tickled him to death. "Many thanks," he said. "Looks like a dandy." About that time the door opened and a little red-headed doctor popped in.

"Well, how's the patient?" he said. We didn't say anything, and he went over and checked the charts. I knew he had come to run me out.

"Now you're coming along fine," he said. "How would it be if this gentleman left, so you could take a little nap?" He said it just a little timidly; I guess he had already had a run-in with Gid.

"It wouldn't be worth a damn," Gid said, popping the stick on the sheet.

"Well, you know a sick man needs lots of rest," the doctor said. He wasn't Gid's regular man. "I'm sure this gentleman wouldn't mind leaving."

"What do you know about me?" I said. "I might not leave for love nor money."

"Get out of here," Gid said. "I've got some business to talk with this man. I'll sleep when I get sleepy, like I've done all my life."

"Hospital rules," the doctor said. "If he won't leave, we'll have to show him out."

"That'll be fine," I said. "Just bring a few pretty nurses to help you."

"You old cowboys seem to think the world revolves around you," he said. "We'll see about this." And he left; he was plenty mad.

Gid was popping his stick against the sheet.

"That makes me just mad enough to leave," he said. "Two days or no two days." I didn't say a word. He looked out the window for a while.

"Bring the pickup around the side," he said. "I've had my craw full."

And twenty minutes later me and him was on the road to Thalia, and everybody but the FBI was after us. The doctors and nurses acted like it was Judgment Day. But Gid didn't pay them any mind. That Wichita hospital was nothing to the one he walked out of in Galveston one time. That time he chartered a private airplane and had himself flown home. I guess having money is right convenient sometimes.

"Now I guess you'll die," I said. "Only I'll get the blame for killing you, instead of the doctors."

"Oh, I'm all right," he said. "I'll have to be careful of my side for a while."

"Take you home?"

"Yeah, I reckon."

We drove about fifteen miles and he was feeling a little sore.

"No, by god, take me to Molly's," he said. "If I go home, they'll just knock me out and haul me back to the hospital. Take me out there. The doctor can come and see me, and you and her can help me fight off the ambulance drivers."

"Okay," I said. "Once you get strong enough to take care of yourself, I can cart you in to town."

"You know, I may never get that strong," he said. "Won't this surprise Molly?"

Myself, I figured that question was settled, if he didn't die before I got him out there. I figured he'd stay right there the rest of his life. Where that left me, I couldn't tell.

6

GETTING GID OUT tickled us all. I came up the hill to Molly's honking, so I guess she thought the war was on agin. Coming over those country roads had bounced Gid up enough that I think for a while he was kinda wishing he had stayed where he was; but Molly ran out and we helped him in the house and got him installed in the big south bedroom, where he caught every breeze there was, and he picked up pretty quick. Molly asked him what she could get him, and he said fresh tomatoes, so she sliced him up a bunch fresh from the garden and brought them in to him. He ate tomatoes and drank coffee till he got his spirits back. Late that afternoon his regular doctor showed up and tried to get him to go back, but Gid wouldn't do it. The doctor had to come out and see about him every day for a while.

Just getting away from the hospital done Gid a world of good. There was a day or two when he didn't feel too spry, but in the long run he got better a lot quicker. Molly fed him good and watched after him and made him sleep a lot, and he didn't have Mabel or Willy always worrying him.

Of course I had a big run-in with Willy. I had been at the filling station, drinking a Delaware Punch. All the boys got a big laugh out of hearing about Gid. Then I ran into Willy on the sidewalk, and he motioned with his hand for me to stop.

"Willy, don't be waving me down," I said. "I ain't no motorcar."

"I guess you realize what a serious thing you done," he said. "Taking Gid out of everybody's reach."

"Whose reach?" I said. "The doctor was just out this morning and said he was improving fast."

"Well, out of the reach of the people who love him," he said. "Anyhow, when's he coming back?"

"When he gets ready, I guess," I said. "He told me yesterday he was going to start fencing agin next week. Does that ease your mind?"

"Not a bit," he said. "You know he ain't to work."

"Oh sure," I said. "I know it. But I ain't agile enough to stop him, are you?"

"Well, I just wanted to warn you," he said. "Just don't you get crosswise with the law. I got some friends who are judges."

"You'll probably need them," I said, and he left.

====

Molly and Gid enjoyed hearing about it. Gid was propped up in bed eating ice cream.

"I wish there was some way to run him out of the country," I said. "That's the damn trouble with democracy. You got to wait around and vote, and then the people are so stupid they put the scroungy sonsofbitches back in office."

778

"I don't like to hear that kind of talk," Molly said. She was democracy-crazy.

Gid handed Molly his ice-cream dish. "Uum," he said. "This is mighty nice. Only I got to get up from here and start getting a few things accomplished."

Molly frowned, but he never noticed; he was already planning. I knew right then he wouldn't be in bed much longer.

Molly done wonders, though. She fought him and argued with him and domi-noed him and ice-creamed him and kept him down another week. She was work-ing so hard keeping Gid down she was about to get down herself.

I didn't know what they had decided about him staying and living there. Molly wanted him to, that was plain as day, and I guess they must have talked about it. But never while I was there, which wasn't too often. Running the ranch kept me busy all day, and usually I got over about suppertime to see how the invalid was doing. The nights weren't too hot, and we all sat around on the porch and talked.

———

Then one morning it come to a head. I was over helping Molly set up an owl trap in her chickenyard. We worked on it about an hour and looked up and seen Gid coming out the back door, all dressed and carrying his suitcase. Molly was just crushed; I guess she thought he was going to stay for good.

"Now where's he fixing to go?" she said. "He don't have to go nowhere."

I was kinda wishing I wasn't nowhere around.

But she grabbed my wrist before he got to us. "Listen," she said. "Now if I can't talk him out of going, you be sure and see he takes it easy on his work. Will you do that for me?"

"Of course I will," I said.

Gid had put his gear in the pickup, and he came over, looking proud of himself. "Owl trouble," he said. "Can I help?"

Molly was all over him. "You sure can," she said, "you can go in out of this hot sun and get back in bed and stay there. That would help me a whole lot."

But Gid put up his bluff.

"Can't," he said. "I've got to get to working."

And we stood there. I kept on working on the trap. Molly was trembling and about to cry, I could tell. But Gid was determined.

"Don't think I ain't much obliged to you," he said. "But I've got to go to work, Molly."

She looked at me kinda funny. It was really tearing her. I was surprised to see she still had those terrible strong feelings, at her age. I never had felt things that hard, at any age.

"All right, go to work," she said. "But, honey, you don't have to leave, you can go to work and come back."

She had never called him honey in public, in all the years I'd known her, either. I was trembling a little too, from just watching, and I don't know what held Gid up.

"Yes I have, Molly," he said. "For right now, anyway. Just running off from a hospital like that ain't the right way to settle anything."

She was crying then, but neither one of us quite dared touch her.

"There never will be a way right enough for you," she said.

He said maybe there would. "And much obliged agin, for taking care of me."

I guess she thought Gid was sort of leaving her for the last time. "You're mighty welcome, Gid," she said. "God bless you." And she turned and went to the house, crying and snuffling.

"We better go if we're going," I said.

It upset Gid a good bit too. We were pretty quiet, driving to town.

"I wish I could have thought of a nicer way to leave," he said. "I hate to upset Molly."

"Well, Gid," I said. "My god, you ought to stay out there with her, if you want to. It's about time you pleased yourself a little, if you're ever going to. Or it looks that way to me."

"Well, I want to," he said. "And I may do it. In fact, I guess I intend to do it. But you can't just go off and do something like that on the spur of the moment, without making no arrangements. There's a right way and a wrong."

"And you're the only man alive that can tell them apart," I said. "Or maybe just the only one that bothers to try."

When I let him out at his house he told me to buy a keg of steeples. He said he'd be out Monday and we'd start steepling the fence. I never stopped by Molly's, going home. I couldn't think what I would say to her.

7

IT WAS A GOOD THING I got the steeples, because Monday morning he was there before I got the milk strained. I stayed about that far behind the rest of the day.

"Are you ready?" he said.

"I'm bound to be readier than you are," I said. "I'm well, anyway."

"Shut up and let's go," he said. I sat the milk in the icebox and got my steepling hatchet. I had soaked it in water all night so the head wouldn't fly off and kill Gid.

The wires were done stretched; I had done that; so all we had to do was steeple. We didn't waste no time. I got off from him a hundred yards or so, and we started in. I guess I steepled forty or fifty posts before I thought to look around, and Gid wasn't nowhere in sight. It scared the sense out of me: I thought he'd passed out. I started running back up the fence row, but I wasn't used to running and I thought I was gonna collapse. If he hadn't of hollered, I'd have passed him right by. He wasn't over fifty yards from where he started steepling. There was a little shady shrub oak tree there and he was sitting under it fanning himself with his hat. I never saw a man so wet with sweat in my whole life.

"I didn't know you could run so fast," he said. "Where's the fire?"

"By god," I said, trying to get my breath. "It looks like it's underneath you." I had to sit down and get my breath.

"I just came out here to rest," he said. "I was getting too hot."

"My god, Gid," I said. "If you're sweating like that already, what you better do is sickle in to town and rest on some nice cool bed. It ain't good for a man in your shape to get that hot."

"Oh, I'm all right," he said. "You're more give out than me, just from that run."

"I may be out of breath," I said. "But I ain't sweated down from steepling no ten or fifteen posts."

"It was more like a hundred and fifty, the way my arm feels," he said. "But it's just sweat. Must have been them drugs they gave me. I never sweated this much before."

"Hell of a note," I said. "Why don't you let me hire a Mexican or two, to finish this fence? They work a lot cheaper than doctors."

"I never asked for no advice," he said. "I guess I know when I'm able to work and when I'm not."

"I doubt very seriously that you do," I said. "But I can't do much about it."

"You can get to steepling," he said.

And that was the way it went, the rest of the week. Gid couldn't work but thirty minutes at a time without having to rest, but he wouldn't quit. The whole week he was just up and down. I finally just let him alone about it. I guess he just had so much sweat to get out of his system. After we finished the fencing we spent a week spraying the cattle and getting them shaped up. He finally got where he could work an hour or two at a stretch, but he wasn't the hand he used to be.

=====

I asked him once if he'd been by to see Molly, and he said he had. Mabel was off on a vacation in Colorado and had Sarah and Susie with her, so Gid was batching. I imagine he seen Molly a lot. I never asked him what they decided about living together, and he never said. I knew he wouldn't do nothing till Mabel got back; that would make him feel too sneaky. He didn't much want to talk about it, and I couldn't blame him particularly, so very little was ever said.

=====

One morning he came out looking kinda blue—he had got it into his head to fix the windmill that day. It was the mill on the old Fry place, where I was living. I had used it for years and years, without no particular trouble except a worn-out sucker rod now and then. But he had done ordered a new set of pipes and a new running barrel, and everything: a man was going to bring them out from town that morning. It looked like a hell of a hard day's work, and I tried to head him off.

"Just think a minute, Gid," I said. "It's the first of September. In another month it'll be cool, and that mill won't be half as hard to fix."

"I know it'll be a little hot," he said. "But we'll just fix it anyway, while we got the time. We might be doing something else in another month. Let's go get the sucker rod out."

The sucker rod in itself wasn't much of a job, and we had it out in no time. The job was going to be lifting that old pipe out and lowering the new pipe in. I never had been much of a pipe hand, and the old stuff was corroded at the joints. It had been in long enough to be petrified.

While we were waiting for the man with the pipe to come, we sat in the shade of the waterhouse and told some old windmilling stories we saved up for days like that. I had had an uncle get killed on a windmill, and I was scared of them as I was of a rattlesnake. I told Gid about it.

"It was a steel mill," I said. "Lightning struck it while he was up working on it. Electrocuted him."

"They're dangerous," he said. "If it's a wooden mill, the dam frames are apt to break and let you fall. Remember Clarence Fierson? He got his neck broke falling off one."

"Yeah, I remember," I said. "Went around with his neck in a brace for years. Lucky at that."

Pretty soon the pipe man came and the hard work began. It was all we could do to carry the new pipe over to the windmill where we needed it. Gid got as hot as a pistol, and I wasn't cool, myself.

"I don't believe we better fool with this stuff," I said. "You'll strain your operation, lifting this shit. I can barely hold out myself."

"You want to work on the mill or on the ground?" he said.

"I'm trying to think what will be the best for you. If you get up there you'll get dizzy and fall, and if you stay down here you'll get all the heavy lifting."

"Shut up about me," he said. "I ain't collapsed yet, and I been windmilling all my life. You stay down here."

He began to unscrew this and unscrew that, and in a little while it was too late to back out, we done had the thing torn into. We spent the rest of the morning unscrewing the old rotten pipe and lifting it out.

When dinner time came we were both give out. I went in the house and fried us a little steak and made some tea, and for dinner we had steak and bread and about a gallon of iced tea apiece. We were too tired to tell any windmill stories, too. Gid flopped down on the living room couch, and I got me a pillow and stretched out on the floor. We couldn't get ourselves moving agin till two o'clock.

"Godamighty," I said, when I finally sat up. "I sure hate to go back out there."

"Yeah, them pipes will be hot," he said. "Hot and heavy."

"I can't figure you out," I said. "As much money as you got, and you're still fighting a goddamn windmill. Why do you do it, Gid?"

"Sometimes I wonder myself," he said.

We got up and went back to work. The sun was just a blur in the sky it was so hot, and the new pipes would fry an egg. It was all we could do to keep ahold of them, gloves or no gloves, and we had to cut threads in three or four joints. That took half the afternoon. Then Gid got back up in the mill and we raised the pipe and let it down in the well, a foot at a time. Once Gid lost his grip and I thought the whole shebang would go to the bottom, but I managed to slow it with my pipe wrench till he could get another hold. Finally we got the pipe run and he came down to rest. We were both wringing wet.

"Well, we're nearly done," I said. "It'll be cool in another hour. I'm kinda glad we done her, now."

"Me too," he said, mopping his face. "One thing about it, when we get this bastard fixed this time, me and you oughtn't to have to ever lay a hand on it agin. It ought to last at least twenty-five years."

"So ought we," I said. "We might get to fix it agin. We're better windmillers than I thought we were."

"A man has to be experienced like us before he has enough know-how to fix one of these things."

"Watch out now," I said. "I fixed a lot of them while I was getting the experience, and you did too. Besides, it wasn't the know-how I was worried about, it was the do-how. Two weeks ago you were flat of your back eating soup."

"Laying around in bed's what like to ruined me," he said.

We put the sucker rod in, but it lacked about a foot coming up to where it was supposed to connect. So we had to go down to the barn and get another piece and replace it. The barn was beginning to make a shadow and the big heat was over for the day. Gid went up and made the connection and came back.

"Turn her on," he said. "I want to see the water run."

I turned the mill loose and a little south breeze caught the wheel. Pretty soon the old rusty water began to pour out of the hydrant, and we stood there waiting for the stream to get clear. It was still an hour to sundown, but we were two tired cowboys, I don't mind to admit. Gid was squatted down watching the water run, and I was propped up against a standard with my shirttail out, letting my belly cool. Pretty soon the rusty water washed out and the water came out of the faucet good and cold and clear. Gid stuck his mouth to the faucet and drank awhile, and then caught his breath and drank some more.

"Be careful you don't founder," I said, "drinking so much cold water."

"Sure good water," he said, leaning back on his heels. "I remember when me and Dad had that well dug. It sure has been a good well."

Then we heard water splashing behind us. We looked up and seen it was the overhead pipe, the one that went to the storage tank. We had forgot to connect it.

"I'll get it," I said. "Just take a second."

"No, go on and get you a drink," he said. "I left my pliers up there anyway."

"You're the derrick hand," I said, and went to drinking. I took about three good cool swallows and heard him yell: he had just hit the ground. I guess he lost his grip, or else his foot slipped, but he couldn't have been over three or four feet up the ladder when it happened. It didn't look like he hit very hard, either, and I seen him start to get right up, he even got his hand on a rung. Then he hesitated, and I thought one of his legs might be broke.

"Wait, Gid," I said.

I got to him and eased him down on one elbow and he never acted the least bit hurt or wild, but I don't believe he recognized me at all.

"Well, boys, he threw me agin," he said. "I'll ride him yet."

It made the hair stand up on the back of my neck for a minute. But I wasn't really worried. I thought he was just out of his senses for a minute. He had gone out of his head that way several times. He tried to get up but I held him.

"Let me up, boys," he said. "I ain't hurt."

"Okay, now, Gid," I said. "Just lay a minute and get your breath."

He minded me. "That bastard threw me, Johnny," he said. He had quit fighting to get up and lay there, looking real weak. I think that scared me the most.

"Here," I said. "Where do you think you are? You just fell off the ladder a couple of feet. That you're talking about was a long time ago."

I knew just exactly what he was thinking. When we was young there was a horse called Old Missouri, that everybody tried to ride. Dad owned him, God knows why. One day he threw Gid six times. He never threw me but once, because I never tried to ride him but one time. But there never was a horse that Gid couldn't wear down eventually, and he finally got so he could stay on Old Missouri.

"I've been throwed harder," he said.

He went on like that for a while, and I didn't try to stop him. I figured he'd come out of it in a few minutes. But he looked weak as a fish, and I finally decided to take him on it—getting him in the car was a real job. I stretched him out on the back seat and went back and turned off the faucet at the windmill. Gid's doctor was in Wichita, but I struck for Thalia, it was closer. I started out slow, trying to miss the bumps, but I finally let that go and concentrated on speed.

When I come to the highway I stopped a minute and Gid opened his eyes and looked at me. He seemed perfectly sensible.

"What you reckon Molly's doing?" he said. "I must be slipping." Then he went off agin. "Sounds like I hear a train," he said. "Let's me and you go to the Panhandle. I'm tired of this country."

It made me sad to hear him talk that way, when it was forty years too late and him out of his mind. I begin to let the hammer down on his old Chevvy.

And then, by god, he come completely out of it. "That goddamn old windmill," he said. "Did you turn it off?"

"Last thing I did," I said.

"Well, it won't take long to make that connection," he said. "My damn side hurts. I wish I'd woke up a little sooner, I'd had you take me over to Molly's, I ain't sick enough to go to town. Maybe this time I'd have sense enough to stay there where I belong. Why don't you just take me back? I'd kinda like to see her."

"Aw, we better let a doc look at you first," I said. "I can run you out there tonight or in the morning."

Then he looked out the window, I guess: he said what he always said when he looked at the country in that part of the summertime: "The country's too dry, I sure do wish it would rain. My grass is just about gone."

I didn't say nothing to that, but I was relieved he was back in his senses. I was trying to pass a Dutchman; he was pulling a load of hay.

"Oh me, Johnny," Gid said. "Ain't this been a hell of a time?"

"It sure has, Gid," I said. The sun was near enough down to be right in my eyes, and I needed all my concentration just to drive. I thought Gid said something else, to me, to Molly, to somebody, and then he didn't say no more and I was hoping he had dozed off to sleep. But when I caught the red light by the courthouse in Thalia, and had to stop, I looked back at him and knew right then that Gideon Fry was dead.

8

AT THE CLINIC they said he couldn't have been dead over ten minutes, or maybe fifteen. But I guess to Gid ten minutes was just as final as ten years. A bloodclot done it, they said. Some people blamed me for bumping him over them old roads. But I don't think it would have made any difference. I couldn't have gone off and left him there on the grass by the windmill, while I drove twenty-five miles in and the doctor drove twenty-five miles back. The doctor at the clinic said the fall had started internal bleeding.

The meanest, hardest part of it all, for me, was going off that night and leaving Gid at the hospital. They wheeled him away somewhere on a stretcher, and when I asked the doctor what I could do, he said, "Nothing." I called Buck, Gid's son-in-law, and he told me which funeral home to have Gid sent to; I asked him if he knew where Mabel was, and he give me her hotel number in Colorado Springs. When I got her I said, "Well, Mabel, I've got some pretty bad news for you." "What's happened to him?" she said. "He fell off a windmill," I said. "The fall never hurt him but it caused a bloodclot and the bloodclot killed him, Mabel. He died about an hour ago." "The Lord help us," she said. "Are you sure? What am I going to do?" They said she got hysterical after she hung up.

After that, things was kind of out of my hands; there wasn't no reason for me to stay. But I couldn't hardly go. It didn't seem right to just go off and leave him there. I kept wondering which jobs around the ranch he wanted me to get done in the next day or two. But I finally seen there wasn't nothing I could do but go. None of the hospital people paid any attention to me, and I hated the smell of the place.

====

I drove out to Molly's then, and broke it to her. She came out in the yard to meet me, it was done way after dark, and I told her about it and she cried, there by the yard gate. She was awful broke up. After a while we went over to the ranch and she drove Gid's car back to town for me and I followed in the pickup. We left it at Buck's. When we got back to Molly's she had quit crying for a little while.

"Well, come on in, let's make some coffee," she said. "You'll stay here with me tonight, won't you?"

"Of course," I said.

It was a sure sad night for us, but we didn't say fifteen words. We drank a good bit of coffee.

"You know, the night we got the word about Jimmy, me and Gid played dominos," she said.

"You want to play some tonight?" I said.

"Oh lord no," she said. "I'd rather not."

It was the first time I'd spent a whole night with Molly in three or four years, maybe longer than that. She went in the bathroom and put on her white nightgown and I got in bed. I held her hand and we both lay there awake for an hour and a half, on our backs. Once in a while Molly sniffled, but she wasn't crying much.

"Well, he was some feller," I said. "I don't expect to ever see another like him. You know that saddle he gave me? That's the most expensive saddle ever made in the Thalia saddle shop. Me and him had a big fight the day he give it to me. Over you, I guess."

I guess it was worse for Molly. Him and her had associated so much there, in the house, right there in that same bedroom we was in, there was no telling what all she was remembering. I guess he was all over the room, for her.

"Gid was my favorite," she said. I finally went to sleep, I don't know whether she did or not.

===

In the morning, when I woke up, an unusual thing happened. I had turned over during the night and I had my arm across Molly's middle and my face was in her hair. When I got my eyes open she was looking right square at me. There were dark circles under her eyes, but she had just the trace of a grin on her face. For a minute I didn't know why, and then I noticed myself. As old as I was, too, and on a morning like that. And Molly had done noticed, that's why she was watching me. At first I was plumb embarrassed.

"Well, I swear," I said. I didn't know what else to say.

But she grinned, and squeezed my hand. "That's the first time I've ever seen you embarrassed," she said. "I've had to wait sixty-two years."

"Well, it ain't because of that," I said. "You've caused that many a time. You've stayed too pretty. It's because of Gid I'm embarrassed."

"I don't want you to be," she said. "That's nature, she ain't no respecter. I don't want you to be embarrassed even if we're a hundred years old." Then she grinned a sad grin; for a minute she reminded me of herself when she was twenty years old. "And you better not waste it, either," she said.

"You're an unusual woman," I said, rubbing her side. "Only it ain't much to waste. If old Gid can't, then by god I won't neither, how's that?"

"About as foolish as something he'd say," she said. "Only thank god you won't stick to it like he did." And she rolled over and hugged me and cried for an hour, at least. I had to get up and hunt a box of Kleenex.

9

A WEEK AFTER THE FUNERAL I stopped by Molly's house; she never heard the car come up. She was out in the garden, and I walked around the house and stood by the gate a minute, watching her. The garden was just about gone. When I walked out she was down on her knees, pulling onions and putting them in her apron.

"You're getting a little deaf," I said. "A person could sneak up on you."

She grinned, happy and jolly as could be. "Hold these onions for me," she said.

"Let's go sit in the kitchen, where it's cool and there's something to eat," I said.

But she took me to the porch, instead. "You can eat here, what there is," she said. "Cold potato pie is all there is, and you don't like it. I didn't figure you'd come tonight."

"I just like two kinds of pie," I said. "Hot and cold. Go get me some."

We ate a little pie and rocked awhile and she brought out some coffee.

"Well, I'm all packed," I said. "I guess I'll move tomorrow." They had fired me, of course—I was going back to the old McCloud place, three mile off. It wasn't a very long move.

"They didn't allow you much time," she said.

"Aw yeah," I said. "They said no hurry. But it don't take much time to move what little I got."

We talked a little while, about Gid and the will and one thing and another. Gid had left me the old pickup and a thousand acres of land—he couldn't stand for me not to increase my holdings by at least that much. So I was set pretty for my old age—I done had two sections I inherited from Dad. That thousand acres sure burned Mabel and Willy; they thought the pickup would have been enough. He just left Molly his dad's old pocket watch. I guess he knew Mabel would have gone to court if he had left her anything more. Molly was plenty satisfied.

After a while the new moon came up, about the size of a basketball, and the conversation petered out. I could see Molly's face, and she looked tired. I was too. I gave her my pieplate to take in the house, and when she came back we walked around to the pickup together. The moon was so bright we could see the chickens roosting on the chickenhouse.

I had something big on my mind and I didn't know how to get it up. It just seemed like I better ask Molly to marry me, for the sake of all our old times, but I didn't know whether she'd much want to, and I didn't even know if I much wanted to, we got along so well like we were. Finally I came out with it; I was standing with my arm around her.

"Well, Molly, what would you think about us marrying?" I said.

"I'd think we ain't the kind, honey," she said, "but thank you a whole lot for asking."

It was kind of a sad relief. "It's a damn strange time for me to do it," I said. "I could have asked you forty years ago."

"We lived them pretty good," she said. "It ain't as important a question as a lot of people think."

"Don't you miss Gid?" I said. "I never thought I'd miss such a contrary so-and-so so much."

"Oh yes," she said.

"Molly, just for curiosity," I said. "Do you think you and him would have taken up together for good, if he had lived?"

She put one of her hands in my hip pocket and pulled out my handkerchief to see if it was clean. She had to smell it. This one wasn't, and she kept it so she could wash it.

"We'd decided to," she said. "I guess we decided about thirty times. And I think in about another year I would have got his conscience quiet enough and his nerve worked up so he could have come out and stayed."

We thought about it a minute.

"You know I think he worried about you as much as he did Mabel," she said. "He kept saying it wouldn't be fair to you if he moved out here." She gave me a long look. "I got sick of him wanting to be so fair to you," she said, "and I even got sick of you being around for him to worry about. You may have noticed."

"No," I said. "But I imagine it's true."

"Johnny, when it came to him, I just never cared to be fair," she said.

"I don't blame you none."

When I got in the pickup she leaned in and kissed me on the cheek. "I'll take you in to a ballgame one of these cool nights," I said.

"I wish you would," she said. "I ain't been to a half a dozen games since Joe quit playing."

I started to drive off, but she had ahold of my arm. "I'll have a better supper tomorrow night," she said. "Just because we ain't marrying don't mean you're free to miss a night. You're welcome here every night, all night, when you feel like putting up with me."

"I'll be here in time to carve the beef," I said, and drove off. I felt pretty blue driving down the hill, and kinda wished I had stayed that night. But sometimes you can't get around being lonesome for a while.

———

I took my time driving home on those old bumpy roads. When I got back to the house I put the pickup in the garage and shut the doors. I had me some Delaware Punches in the icebox and I got one and went out on the screened-in porch. Over at Molly's I had been a little sleepy, but the drive had woke me up.

The porch was cool, and the night was real quiet. I set my Punch bottle down and stepped out in the yard to take a leak. I could hear an oil rig working way over in the Dale, but except for that and a few crickets the night was perfectly still. When I got through I didn't much want to go in, so I walked around the old Fry place for a while, watching that white moon circling out over Gid's pastures. It was strange how I never knowed till Gid died just how used to him I was.

"You old so-and-so," I said. "You wouldn't listen. I offered to go up and fix that thing, but no sir, you had to do it yourself."

"Aw, you couldn't have fixed it if you'd a gone," he said. "You never was no hand with pipe."

"Hell no, a cowboy ain't supposed to be," I said.

"That's all right. Who made the fortune, and who worked for wages all his life?"

"You might have made the fortune," I said. "But I'd just like to know what good it did you. Working like a Turk. Which one of us was satisfied?"

"Hell, that's easy," he said. "Neither one. We neither one married her, did we?"

Talking to myself. Gid was off in the Great Perhaps. I looked around at the house and down toward the barn. One man's whoop is another man's holler, anyhow. At least Gid was stubborn about it. I remembered one election day, when I gave him hell. Me and Molly had the first shift. The bloom was really on the peach, as far as she was concerned. She wore a blue dress with white dots on it and never wore nothing on her hair. About two weeks before that I had got to spend my first whole night with her. We was there an hour by ourselves, and kissed and walked around and had the best time: I pumped my hat full of water so she could get a drink. Then Gid come and talked her into staying with him after I was supposed to leave. Only he had old Ikey for a partner and had to scheme around someway to get rid of him, I don't remember how he finally done it. It tickled me. He thought he'd have Molly to himself for two hours or so. I left about the time Ikey did and circled around and intercepted him; he was riding that old crippled mule. "Ikey, you ought to be ashamed of yourself," I said. "Living in a free country where they let you vote. And the first time the government gives you a little job you let somebody send you off on some damn errand. If you know what's good for you, you'll turn that mule around and get back up there where you belong." I broke me off a good-sized mesquite limb and handed it to him. "See if you can get that mule in locomotion," I said. I guess he thought I intended to use it on him. "Yes suh, Mistuh Johnny," he said. "I sure get back. I didn't inten' to leave in de fust place." So poor Gid got about twenty minutes. I guess it was kinda mean, really—nobody gets enough chances at the wild and sweet. But he would have done the same thing. There's just two things about it that I really regret. One was not being there to see the look on Gid's face when he heard that crippled mule clomping up, and the other is forgetting to bring a Kodak that morning, so I could have got a picture of Molly while she was sitting in her blue and white dress on the schoolhouse steps.

THE LAST PICTURE SHOW

The Last Picture Show
is lovingly dedicated to my home town.

1

SOMETIMES SONNY FELT like he was the only human creature in the town. It was a bad feeling, and it usually came on him in the mornings early, when the streets were completely empty, the way they were one Saturday morning in late November. The night before Sonny had played his last game of football for Thalia High School, but it wasn't that that made him feel so strange and alone. It was just the look of the town.

There was only one car parked on the courthouse square—the night watchman's old white Nash. A cold norther was singing in off the plains, swirling long ribbons of dust down Main Street, the only street in Thalia with businesses on it. Sonny's pickup was a '41 Chevrolet, not at its best on cold mornings. In front of the picture show it coughed out and had to be choked for a while, but then it started again and jerked its way to the red light, blowing out spumes of white exhaust that the wind whipped away.

At the red light he started to turn south toward the all-night café, but when he looked north to see if anyone was coming he turned that way instead. No one at all was coming but he saw his young friend Billy, headed out. He had his broom and was sweeping right down the middle of the highway into the gusting wind. Billy lived at the poolhall with Sam the Lion, and sweeping was all he really knew how to do. The only trouble was that he overdid it. He swept out the poolhall in the mornings, the café in the afternoons, and the picture show at night, and always, unless someone specifically told him to stop, he just kept sweeping, down the sidewalk, on through the town, sometimes one way and sometimes another, sweeping happily on until someone noticed him and brought him back to the poolhall.

Sonny drove up beside him and honked. Billy quit sweeping at once and got in the pickup. He was a stocky boy, not very smart, but perfectly friendly; picking him up made Sonny feel less lonesome. If Billy was out the poolhall must be open, and when the poolhall was open he was never lonesome. One of the nice things about living in Thalia was that the poolhall often opened by 6:30 or 7 A.M., the reason being that Sam the Lion, who owned it, was a very bad sleeper.

Sonny drove to the hall and parked and took Billy's broom so he wouldn't go sweeping off again. The air was so dry and dusty it made the nostrils sting and the two boys hustled inside. Sam the Lion was up, all right, brushing one of the snooker tables. He was an old man, but big and heavy, with a mane of white hair; cold weather made his feet swell and he wore his old sheepskin house shoes to work in in the wintertime. He was expecting the boys and barely gave them a glance.

Once they were inside, Sonny let Billy have the broom again and Billy immediately went over to the gas stove to warm himself. While he warmed he leaned on the broom and licked a piece of green pool chalk. Sam the Lion didn't particularly care that Billy licked chalk all the time; it was cheap enough nourishment, he said. Sonny got himself a package of Cheese Crisps and made room for himself at the stove, turning Billy's cap around backward for friendship's sake. It was an old green baseball cap some lady had given Billy three or four summers before.

"Cold in here, Sam," Sonny said. "It's nearly as cold in here as it is outside."

"Not as windy, though," Sam replied. "I'm surprised you had the nerve to come in this mornin', after the beatin' you all took. Anybody ever tell you boys about blockin'? Or tacklin'?"

Sonny ate his Cheese Crisps, unabashed. Crowell, the visiting team, had tromped Thalia 28 to 6. It had been a little embarrassing for Coach Popper, but that was because the local Quarterback Club had been so sure Thalia was finally going to win a District Crown that they had literally jumped the gun and presented the coach with a new .12 gauge Marlin under-over at the homecoming game two weeks before. The coach was quite a hunter. Two of Crowell's four touchdowns had been run over Sonny's guard position, but he felt quite calm about it all. Four years of playing for Thalia had inured him to defeat, and so far as he was concerned the Quarterback Club had been foolishly optimistic.

Besides, he could not see that he had much to gain by helping the coach get new shotguns, the coach being a man of most uncertain temper. He had already shot at Sonny once in his life, and with a new under-over he might not miss.

"Where's your buddy?" Sam asked.

"Not in yet," Sonny said. That was Duane, Sonny's best friend, who besides being an All-Conference fullback, roughnecked the midnight tower with a local drilling crew.

"Duane's gonna work himself into an early grave," Sam the Lion said. "He oughtn't to play a football game and then go out and work all night on top of it. He made half the yardage we made."

"Well, that never tired him out," Sonny said, going to get another package of Cheese Crisps.

Sam the Lion started to cough, and the coughing got away from him, as it often did. His whole body shook; he couldn't stop. Finally he had to stagger back to the washroom and take a drink of water and a swig of cough medicine to get it under control.

"Suckin' in too much chalk dust," he said when he came back. Billy hardly noticed, but Sonny felt a little uneasy. He didn't like to be reminded that Sam the Lion was not as young or as healthy as he once had been. Sam the Lion was the man who took care of things, particularly of boys, and Sonny did not like to think that he might die. The reason Sam was so especially good to boys was that he himself had had three sons, none of whom lived to be eighteen. The first was killed when Sam was still a rancher: he and his son were trying to drive a herd of yearlings across the Little Wichita River one day when it was up, and the boy had been knocked loose from his horse, pawed under, and drowned. A few years later, after Sam had gone into the oil business, a gas explosion knocked his second son off a derrick. He fell over fifty feet and was dead before they got him to town. Sam sold his oil holdings and put in the first Ford agency in Thalia, and his youngest son was run over by a deputy sheriff. His wife lost her mind and spent her last ten years rocking in a rocking chair. Sam drank a lot, quit going to church, and was said to be loose with women, even married women.

He began to come out of it when he bought the picture show, or so people said. He got lots of comedies and serials and Westerns and the kids came as often as they could talk their parents into letting them. Then Sam bought the poolhall and the all-night café and he perked up more and more.

No one really knew why he was called Sam the Lion. Some thought it was because he hated barbers and always went around with a shaggy head of hair. Others thought it was because he had been such a hell-raising cowboy when he was young, but Sonny found that a little hard to believe. He had seen Sam mad only once, and that was one Fourth of July when Duane stuck a Roman candle in the pocket of one of the snooker tables and set it off. When it finally quit shooting, Sam grabbed the pisspot and chased Duane out, meaning to sling it at him. He slung it, but Duane was too quick. Joe Bob Blanton, the Methodist preacher's son, happened to be standing on the sidewalk wishing he was allowed to go in and shoot pool, and he was the one that got drenched. The boys all got a big laugh but Sam the Lion was embarrassed about it and cleaned Joe Bob off as best he could.

When he was thoroughly warm Sonny got one of the brushes and began to brush the eight-ball tables. Sam went over and looked disgustedly at the two nickels Sonny had left for the Cheese Crisps.

"You'll never get nowhere, Sonny," he said. "You've already spent a dime today and you ain't even had a decent breakfast. Billy, you might get the other side of the hall swept out, son."

While the boys worked Sam stood by the stove and warmed his aching feet. He wished Sonny weren't so reckless economically, but there was nothing he could do about it. Billy was less of a problem, partly because he was so dumb. Billy's real father was an old railroad man who had worked in Thalia for a short time just before the war; his mother was a deaf and dumb girl who had no people except an aunt. The old man cornered the girl in the balcony of the picture show one night and begat Billy. The sheriff saw to it that the old man married the girl, but she died when Billy was born and he was raised by the family of Mexicans who helped the old man keep the railroad track repaired. After the war the hauling petered out and the track was taken up. The old man left and got a job bumping cars on a stockyards track in Oklahoma, leaving Billy with the Mexicans. They hung around for several more years, piling prickly pear and grubbing mesquite, but then a man from Plainview talked them into moving out there to pick cotton. They snuck off one morning and left Billy sitting on the curb in front of the picture show.

From then on, Sam the Lion took care of him. Billy learned to sweep, and he kept all three of Sam's places swept out; in return he got his keep and also, every single night, he got to watch the picture show. He always sat in the balcony, his broom at his side; for years he saw every show that came to Thalia, and so far as anyone knew, he liked them all. He was never known to leave while the screen was lit.

"You workin' today?" Sam asked, noticing that Sonny was taking his time brushing the eight-ball table.

"The truck's being greased," Sonny said. On weekends, and sometimes weeknights too, he drove a butane truck for Frank Fartley of Fartley Butane and Propane. He didn't make as much money as his friend Duane made roughnecking, but the work was easier.

Just as Sam the Lion was about to get back to the subject of the football game they all heard a familiar sound and paused to listen. Abilene was coming into town in his Mercury. Abilene was the driller Duane worked for. He had spent a lot of money souping up the Mercury, and in Thalia the sound of his exhausts was as unmistakable as the sound of the wind.

"Well, we barely got 'em clean in time," Sam said. Abilene not only had the best car in the country, he also shot the best stick of pool. Drilling and pool shooting

were things he did so well that no one could decide which was his true vocation
and which his avocation. Some mornings he went home and cleaned up before he
came to the poolhall—he liked to be clean and well dressed when he gambled—
but if it was too early for any of the nine-ball players to be up he would often stop
and practice in his drilling clothes.

The Mercury stopped in front of the poolhall and Sam went over and got Abilene's ivory-banded cue out of the padlocked rack and laid it on the counter for
him. When the door opened the wind sliced inside ahead of the man. Abilene had
on sunglasses and the heavy green coveralls he wore to protect his clothes from
the oil-field grease; as soon as he was in he unzipped the coveralls and hung them
on a nail Sam had fixed for him. His blue wool shirt and gabardine pants were
creased and trim.

"Mornin'," Sam said.

"Mornin'," Abilene replied, handing Sam his expensive-looking sunglasses. He
once had a pair fall out of his pocket and break when he was bending over to pick
up a piece of pool chalk; after that he always had Sam put the sunglasses in a
drawer for him. Though he was the poolhall's best customer, he and Sam the Lion
had almost nothing to say to one another. Abilene paid Sam two hundred and fifty
dollars a year for a private key to the poolhall, so he could come in and practice
any time he wanted to. Often Sonny would come in from some long butane run at
two or three o'clock in the morning and see that Abilene was in the poolhall, practicing. The garage where the butane truck was kept was right across the street
from the poolhall and sometimes Sonny would walk across and stand by one of
the windows watching Abilene shoot. No one ever tried to go in when Abilene was
in the poolhall alone.

"Let's shoot one, Sonny," Abilene said. "I feel like a little snooker before
breakfast."

Sonny was taken by surprise. He knew he would not even be good competition
for Abilene, but he went and got a cue anyway. It did not occur to him to turn
down the invitation. Abilene shot first and ran thirty points off the break.

"Duane didn't go to sleep on you last night, did he?" Sonny asked, feeling that
he ought at least to make conversation.

"No, the breeze kept us awake," Abilene replied. That was their conversation.
Sonny only got to shoot four times; for the most part he just stood back and
watched Abilene move gracefully around the green table, easing in his shots with
the ivory-banded cue. He won the game by 175 points.

"You shoot pool about like you play football," he said, when the game was over.

Sonny ignored the insult and pitched a quarter on the felt to pay for the game.
Abilene insulted everybody, young and old alike, and Sonny was not obliged to
take it personally. Sam the Lion came over to rack the balls.

"I hope they hurry and get that truck greased," he said. "The way your fortune's
sinking you'll be bankrupt before you get out of here."

"What'd our bet come to, Sam," Abilene asked casually. He busted the fresh
rack and started shooting red balls. Sam grinned at Sonny and went over to the
cash register and got five ten-dollar bills. He laid them on the side of the snooker
table and when Abilene noticed them he took a money clip out of his pocket and
put the fifty dollars in it.

"It's what I get for bettin' on my hometown ball club," Sam said. "I ought to
have better sense."

"It wouldn't hurt if you had a better home town," Abilene said.

Sam always bet on the boys, thinking it would make them feel good, but the strategy seldom worked because they almost always lost. Most of them only trained when they felt like it, and that was not very often. The few who did train were handicapped by their intense dislike of Coach Popper. Sonny was not alone in considering the coach a horse's ass, but the school board liked the coach and never considered firing him: he was a man's man, and he worked cheap. They saw no reason to hire a better coach until a better bunch of boys came along, and there was no telling when that would be. Sam the Lion went loyally on losing money, while Abilene, who invariably bet against Thalia, cleared about a thousand dollars a season from Sam and others like him.

While Sam and Sonny were idly watching Abilene practice, Billy swept quietly down the other side of the poolhall and on out the door. The cold wind that came through the door when Billy went out woke them up. "Go get him, Sonny," Sam said. "Make him put his broom up for a while."

Billy hadn't had time to get far; he was just three doors away, in front of what once had been the Thalia Pontiac Agency. He was calmly sweeping north, into the cold wind. All his floor-sweep had already blown away, but he was quite content to sweep at the curling ribbons of sand that the wind blew past him. A time or two in his life he had swept all the way to the Thalia city limits sign before anyone had noticed him.

When Sonny stepped out of the poolhall the black pickup that the roughnecks used was stopped at the red light. The light changed and the pickup passed the courthouse and slowed a moment at the corner by the poolhall, so Duane could jump out. He was a tall boy with curly black hair. Because he was a fullback and a roughneck he held himself a little stiffly. He had on Levi's and a Levi's jacket with the collar turned up. Sonny pointed at Billy and he and Duane each grabbed one of Billy's arms and hustled him back down the sidewalk into the warming poolhall. Sam took the broom and put it up on a shelf where Billy couldn't reach it.

"Let's go eat, buddy," Duane said, knowing that Sonny had put off having breakfast until he came.

Sam the Lion looked Duane over carefully to see if he could detect any symptoms of overwork, but Duane was in his usual Saturday morning good humor, and if there were such symptoms they didn't show.

"If you boys are going to the café, take this change for me," Sam said, pitching Sonny the dark green coin sack that he used to tote change from one of his establishments to the other. Sonny caught it and the boys hurried out and jogged down the street two blocks to the café, tucking their heads down so the wind wouldn't take their breath. "Boy, I froze my ass last night," Duane grunted, as they ran.

The café was a little one-story red building, so deliciously warm inside that all the windows were steamed over. Penny, the daytime waitress, was in the kitchen frying eggs for a couple of truck drivers, so Sonny set the change sack on the cash register. There was no sign of old Marston, the cook. The boys counted their money and found they had only eighty cents between them.

"I had to shoot Abilene a game of snooker," Sonny explained. "If it hadn't been for that I'd have a quarter more."

"We got enough," Duane said. They were always short of money on Saturday morning, but they were paid Saturday afternoon, so it was no calamity. They ordered eggs and sausage and flipped to see who got what—by the end of the week they often ended up splitting meals. Sonny got the sausage and Duane the eggs.

While Penny was counting the new change into the cash register old Marston came dragging in. He looked as though he had just frozen out of a bar ditch somewhere, and Penny was on him instantly.

"Where you been, you old fart?" she yelled. "I done had to cook ten orders and you know I ain't no cook."

"I swear, Penny," Marston said. "I just forgot to set my alarm clock last night."

"You're a lying old sot if I ever saw one," Penny said. "I ought to douse you under the hydrant a time or two, maybe you wouldn't stink of whiskey so much."

Marston slipped by her and had his apron on in a minute. Penny was a 185-pound redhead, not given to idle threats. She was Church of Christ and didn't mind calling a sinner a sinner. Five years before she had accidentally gotten pregnant before she was engaged; the whole town knew about it and Penny got a lot of backhanded sympathy. The ladies of the community thought it was just awful for a girl that fat to get pregnant. Once married, she discovered she didn't much like her husband, and that made her harder to get along with in general. On Wednesday nights, when the Church of Christ held its prayer meetings and shouting contests anybody who happened to be within half a mile of the church could hear what Penny thought about wickedness; it was old Marston's misfortune to hear it every morning, and at considerably closer range. He only worked to drink, and the thought of being doused under a hydrant made him so shaky he could barely turn the eggs.

Sonny and Duane winked at him to cheer him up, and gave Penny the finger when she wasn't looking. They also managed to indicate that they were broke, so Marston would put a couple of extra slices of toast on the order. The boys gave him a ride to the county-line liquor store once a week, and in return he helped out with extra food when their money was low.

"How we gonna work it tonight?" Duane asked. He and Sonny owned the Chevrolet pickup jointly, and because there were two of them and only one pickup their Saturday night dating was a little complicated.

"We might as well wait and see," Sonny replied, looking disgustedly at the grape jelly Marston had put on the plate. He hated grape jelly, and the café never seemed to have any other kind.

"If I have to make a delivery to Ranger this afternoon there won't be no problem," he added. "You just take the pickup. If I get back in time I can meet Charlene at the picture show."

"Okay," Duane said, glad to get that off his mind. Sonny never got the pickup first on Saturday night and Duane always felt slightly guilty about it but not quite guilty enough to change anything.

The problem was that he was going with Jacy Farrow, whose folks were rich enough to make them unenthusiastic about her going with a poor boy like Duane. He and Jacy couldn't use her car because her father, Gene Farrow, made a point of driving by the picture show every Saturday night to see that Jacy's car was parked out front. They were able to get around that easily enough by sneaking out the back of the show and going somewhere in the pickup, but that arrangement created something of a courting problem for Sonny, who went with a girl named Charlene Duggs. Charlene had to be home by eleven thirty, and if Duane and Jacy kept the pickup tied up until almost eleven, it didn't allow Sonny much time in which to make out.

Sonny had assured Duane time and time again that he didn't particularly care, but Duane remained secretly uneasy. His uneasiness really stemmed from the fact that he was going with Jacy, the prettiest, most desirable girl in town, while Sonny was only going with Charlene Duggs, a mediocre date by any standard. Occasionally the two couples double-dated, but that was really harder on Sonny than no date at all. With all four of them squeezed up in the cab of the pickup it was impossible for him to ignore the fact that Jacy was several times as desirable as Charlene. Even if it was totally dark, her perfume smelled better. For days after such a date Sonny had very disloyal fantasies involving himself and Jacy, and after an hour's sloppy necking with Charlene even the fantasy that he was kissing Jacy had a dangerous power. Charlene kissed convulsively, as if she had just swallowed a golf ball and was trying to force it back up.

Of course Sonny had often considered breaking up with Charlene, but there weren't many girls in the town and the only unattached girl who was any prettier than Charlene was an unusually prudish sophomore. Charlene would let Sonny do anything he wanted to above the waist; it was only as time wore on that he had begun to realize that there really wasn't much of permanent interest to do in that zone. As the weeks went by, Sonny observed that Jacy seemed to become more and more delightful, passionate, inventive, while by contrast Charlene just seemed more of a slug.

When the boys finished eating and paid their check they had a nickel left. Duane was going home to bed, so Sonny kept the nickel; he could buy himself a Butterfinger for lunch. Outside the air was still cold and dusty and gray clouds were blowing south off the High Plains.

Duane took the pickup and went to the rooming house where the two of them had roomed since their sophomore year. People thought it a little strange, because each had a parent alive, but the boys liked it. Sonny's father ran the local domino parlor and lived in a room at the little hotel, and Duane's mother didn't really have much more room. His grandmother was still alive and living with his mother in their two-room house; his mother took in laundry, so the house was pretty full. The boys were actually rather proud that they lived in a rooming house and paid their own rent; most of the boys with real homes envied the two their freedom. Nobody envied them Old Lady Malone, of course, but she owned the rooming house and couldn't be helped. She was nosy, dipped snuff, had a compulsion about turning off fires, and was afflicted with one of the most persistent cases of diarrhea on record. The one bathroom was so badly aired that the boys frequently performed their morning toilet in the rest room of the Texaco filling station.

After Sonny got his delivery orders he jogged up the street to the filling station to get the truck, an old green International. The seat springs had about worn through the padding, and most of the rubber was gone from the footpedals. Still, it ran, and Sonny gunned it a few times and struck out for Megargel, a town even smaller than Thalia. Out in the open country the norther gusted strongly across the highway, making the truck hard to hold. Once in a while a big ragweed would shake loose from the barbed-wire fences and skitter across the road, only to catch again in the barbed-wire fence on the other side. The dry grass in the pastures was gray-brown, and the leafless winter mesquite gray-black. A few Hereford yearlings wandered dispiritedly into the wind, the only signs of life; there was really nothing between Thalia and Megargel but thirty miles of lonesome country. Except for a few sandscraped ranch houses there was nothing to see but a long succession of low brown ridges, with the wind singing over them. It occurred to Sonny that perhaps people called them "blue northers" because it was so hard not to get blue when one was blowing. He regretted that he had not asked Billy to ride along with him on the morning deliveries. Billy was no talker, but he was company, and with nobody at all on the road or in the cab Sonny sometimes got the funny feeling that he was driving the old truck around and around in a completely empty place.

2

SONNY'S NEXT DELIVERY after Megargel was in Scotland, a farming community fifty miles in the opposite direction. As luck would have it he arrived at the farm where the butane was needed while the farmer and his family were in town doing their weekly shopping. The butane tank was in their backyard, and so were nine dogs, six of them chows.

Besides the chows, which were all brown and ill-tempered, there was a German shepherd, a rat terrier, and a subdued black cocker that the farmer had given his kids for a Christmas present. When Sonny approached the yard gate the chows leapt and snarled and tried to bite through the wire. It seemed very unlikely that he could bluff them, but he stood outside the gate for several minutes getting up his nerve to try. While he was standing there five little teal flew off a stock tank north of the house and angled south over the yard. The sight of them made Sonny long for a shotgun of his own, and some ammunition money; all his life he had hunted with borrowed guns. The longer he stood at the gate the more certain he became that the dogs could not be bluffed, and he finally turned and walked back to the truck, a little depressed. He had never owned a shotgun, and he had never found a yardful of dogs that he could intimidate, at least not around Scotland. He sat in the truck for almost an hour, enjoying fantasies of himself carrying Jacy Farrow past dozens of sullen but respectful chows.

Just before noon the farmer came driving up, his red GMC pickup loaded with groceries, kids, and a fat-ankled wife. Some of the kids looked meaner than the dogs.

"Hell, you should just 'a gone on in," the farmer said cheerfully. "Them dogs don't bite many people."

Like so many Saturdays, it was a long work day; when Sonny rattled back into Thalia after his last delivery it was almost 10 P.M. He found his boss, Frank Fartley, in the poolhall shooting his usual comical Saturday night eight-ball game. The reason it was comical was because Mr. Fartley's cigar was cocked at such an angle that there was always a small dense cloud of white smoke between his eye and the cue ball. He tried to compensate for not being able to see the cue ball by lunging madly with his cue at a spot where he thought it was, a style of play that made Sam the Lion terribly nervous because it was not only hard on the felt but also extremely dangerous to unwatchful kibitzers, one or two of whom had been rather seriously speared. When Sonny came in Frank stopped lunging long enough to give him his check, and Sonny immediately got Sam the Lion to cash it. Abilene was there, dressed in a dark brown pearl-buttoned shirt and gray slacks; he was shooting nine-ball at five dollars a game with Lester Marlow, his usual Saturday night opponent.

Lester was a wealthy boy from Wichita Falls who came to Thalia often. Ostensibly, his purpose in coming was to screw Jacy Farrow, but his suit was not progressing too well and the real reason he kept coming was because losing large sums of money to Abilene gave him a certain local prestige. It was very important to Lester that he do *something* big, and since losing was a lot easier than winning, he contented himself with losing big.

Sonny had watched the two shoot so many times that it held no interest for him, so he took his week's wages and walked across the dark courthouse lawn to the picture show. Jacy's white Ford convertible was parked out front, where it always was on Saturday night. The movie that night was called *Storm Warning,* and the posterboards held pictures of Doris Day, Ronald Reagan, Steve Cochran, and Ginger Rogers. It was past 10 P.M., and Miss Mosey, who sold tickets, had already closed the window; Sonny found her in the lobby, cleaning out the popcorn machine. She was a thin little old lady with such bad eyesight and hearing that she sometimes had to walk halfway down the aisle to tell whether the comedy or the newsreel was on.

"My goodness, Frank oughtn't to work you so late on weekends," she said. "You done missed the comedy so you don't need to give me but thirty cents."

Sonny thanked her and bought a package of Doublemint gum before he went into the show. Very few people ever came to the late feature; there were not more than twenty in the whole theater. As soon as his eyes adjusted Sonny determined that Jacy and Duane were still out parking; Charlene Duggs was sitting about halfway down the aisle with her little sister Marlene. Sonny walked down the aisle and tapped her on the shoulder, and the two girls scooted over a seat.

"I decided you had a wreck," Charlene said, not bothering to whisper. She smelled like powder and toilet water.

"You two want some chewin' gum?" Sonny offered, holding out the package. The girls each instantly took a stick and popped the gum into their mouths almost simultaneously. They never had any gum money themselves and were both great moochers. Their father, Royce Duggs, ran a dinky little one-man garage out on the highway; most of his work was done on pickups and tractors, and money was tight. The girls would not have been able to afford the toilet water either, but their mother, Beulah Duggs, had a secret passion for it and bought it with money that Royce Duggs thought was going for the girls' school lunches. The three of them could only get away with using it on Saturday night when Royce was customarily too drunk to be able to smell.

After the feature had been playing for a few minutes Sonny and Charlene got up and moved back into one of the corners. It made Sonny nervous to sit with Charlene and Marlene both. Even though Charlene was a senior and Marlene just a sophomore, the two looked so much alike that he was afraid he might accidentally start holding hands with the wrong one. Back in the corner, he held Charlene's hand and they smooched a little, but not much. Sonny really wanted to see the movie, and it was easy for him to hold his passion down. Charlene had not got all the sweetness out of the stick of Doublemint and didn't want to take it out of her mouth just to kiss Sonny, but after a few minutes she changed her mind, took it out, and stuck it under the arm of her seat. It seemed to her that Sonny looked a little bit like Steve Cochran, and she began to kiss him energetically, squirming and pressing herself against his knee. Sonny returned the kiss, but with somewhat muted interest. He wanted to keep at least one eye on the screen, so if Ginger Rogers decided to take her clothes off he wouldn't miss it. The posters outside indicated she at least got down to her slip at one point. Besides, Charlene was always getting worked up in picture shows; at first Sonny had thought her fits of cinematic passion very encouraging, until he discovered it was practically impossible to get her worked up *except* in picture shows.

The movies were Charlene's life, as she was fond of saying. She spent most of her afternoons hanging around the little beauty shop where her mother worked, reading movie magazines, and she always referred to movie stars by their first names. Once when an aunt gave her a dollar for her birthday she went down to the variety store and bought two fifty-cent portraits to sit on her dresser: one was of June Allyson and the other Van Johnson. Marlene copied Charlene's passions as exactly as possible, but when the same aunt gave *her* a dollar the variety store's stock of portraits was low and she had to make do with Esther Williams and Mickey Rooney. Charlene kidded her mercilessly about the latter, and took to sleeping with Van Johnson under her pillow because she was afraid Marlene might mutilate him out of envy.

After a few minutes of squirming alternately against the seat arm and Sonny's knee, lost in visions of Steve Cochran, Charlene abruptly relaxed and sat back. She languidly returned the chewing gum to her mouth, and for a while they watched the movie in silence. Then she remembered a matter she had been intending to bring up.

"Guess what?" she said. "We been going steady a year tonight. You should have got me something for an anniversary present."

Sonny had been contentedly watching Ginger Rogers, waiting for the slip scene. Charlene's remark took him by surprise.

"Well, you can have another stick of gum," he said. "That's all I've got on me."

"Okay, and I'll take a dollar, too," Charlene said. "It cost that much for me and Marlene to come to the show, and I don't want to pay my own way on my anniversary."

Sonny handed her the package of chewing gum, but not the dollar. Normally he expected to pay Charlene's way to the show, but he saw no reason at all why he should spend fifty cents on Marlene. While he was thinking out the ethics of the matter the exit door opened down to the right of the screen and Duane and Jacy slipped in, their arms around one another. They came back and sat down by Sonny and Charlene.

"Hi you all, what are you doin' back here in the dark?" Jacy whispered gaily. Her pretty mouth was a little numb from two hours of virtually uninterrupted kissing. As soon as it seemed polite, she and Duane started kissing again and set-tled into an osculatory doze that lasted through the final reel of the movie. Char-lene began nervously popping her finger joints, something she did whenever Jacy came around. Sonny tried to concentrate on the screen, but it was hard. Jacy and Duane kept right on kissing, even when the movie ended and the lights came on. They didn't break their clinch until Billy came down from the balcony with his broom, and began to sweep.

"Sure was a short show," Jacy said, turning to grin at Sonny. Her nose wrinkled delightfully when she grinned. She shook her head so that her straight blond hair would hang more smoothly against her neck. Duane's hair was tousled, but when Jacy playfully tried to comb it he yawned and shook her off. She put on fresh lipstick and they all got up and went outside.

Miss Mosey had taken the *Storm Warning* posters down and was gallantly trying to tack up the posters for Sunday's show, which was *Francis Goes to the Army.* The wind whipped around the corners of the old building, making the posters flop. Miss Mosey's fingers were so cold she could barely hold the tacks, so the boys helped her finish while the girls shivered on the curb. Marlene was shivering on the curb too, waiting for Sonny to drop her off at the Duggses'. Duane walked Jacy to her convertible and kissed her good-night a time or two, then came gloomily to the pickup, depressed at the thought of how long it was until Saturday night came again.

When they had taken Marlene home and dropped Duane at the rooming house, Sonny and Charlene drove back to town so they could find out what time it was from the clock in the jewelry store window. As usual, it was almost time for Charlene to go home.

"Oh, let's go on to the lake," she said. "I guess I can be a few minutes late tonight, since it's my anniversary."

"I never saw anything like that Jacy and Duane," she said. "Kissing in the picture show after the lights go on. That's pretty bad if you ask me. One of these days Mrs. Farrow's gonna catch 'em an' that'll be the end of that romance."

Sonny drove on to the city lake without saying anything, but the remark depressed him. So far as he was concerned Jacy and Duane knew true love and would surely manage to get married and be happy. What depressed him was that it had just become clear to him that Charlene really wanted to go with Duane, just as he himself really wanted to go with Jacy.

As soon as the pickup stopped Charlene moved over against him. "Crack your window and leave the heater on," she said. "It's still too cold in here for me."

Sonny tried to shrug off his depression by beginning the little routine they always went through when they parked: first he would kiss Charlene for about ten minutes; then she would let him take off her brassiere and play with her breasts; finally, when he tried to move on to other things she would quickly scoot back across the seat, put the bra back on, and make him take her home. Sometimes she indulged in an engulfing kiss or two on the doorstep, knowing that she could fling herself inside the house if a perilously high wave of passion threatened to sweep over her.

After the proper amount of kissing Sonny deftly unhooked her bra. This was the signal for Charlene to draw her arms from the sleeves of her sweater and slip out of the straps. Sonny hung the bra on the rear-view mirror. So long as the proprieties were observed, Charlene liked being felt; she obligingly slipped her sweater up around her neck.

"Eeh, your hands are like ice," she said, sucking in her breath. Despite the heater the cab was cold enough to make her nipples crinkle. The wind had blown all the clouds away, but the moon was thin and dim and the choppy lake lay in darkness. When Sonny moved his hand the little dash-light threw patches of shadow over Charlene's stocky torso.

In a few minutes it became apparent that the cab was warming up faster than either Sonny or Charlene. He idly held one of her breasts in his hand, but it might have been an apple someone had given him just when he was least hungry.

"Hey," Charlene said suddenly, noticing. "What's the matter with you? You act half asleep."

Sonny was disconcerted. He was not sure what was wrong. It did not occur to him that he was bored. After all, he had Charlene's breast in his hand, and in Thalia it was generally agreed that the one thing that was never boring was feeling a girl's breasts. Grasping for straws, Sonny tried moving his hand downward, but it soon got entangled in Charlene's pudgy fingers.

"Quit, quit," she said, leaning her head back in expectation of a passionate kiss.

"But this is our anniversary," Sonny said. "Let's do something different."

Charlene grimly kept his hand at navel level, infuriated that he should think he really had license to go lower. That was plainly unfair, because he hadn't even given her a present. She scooted back toward her side of the cab and snatched her brassiere off the mirror.

"What are you trying to do, Sonny, get me pregnant?" she asked indignantly.

Sonny was stunned by the thought. "My lord," he said. "It was just my hand."

"Yeah, and one thing leads to another," she complained, struggling to catch the top hook of her bra. "Momma told me how that old stuff works."

Sonny reached over and hooked the hook for her, but he was more depressed than ever. It was obvious to him that it was a disgrace not to be going with someone prettier than Charlene, or if not prettier, at least someone more likable. The problem was how to break up with her and get his football jacket back.

"Well, you needn't to get mad," he said finally. "After so long a time I get tired of doing the same thing, and you do too. You wasn't no livelier than me."

"That's because you ain't good lookin' enough," she said coldly. "You ain't even got a ducktail. Why should I let you fiddle around and get me pregnant? We'll have plenty of time for that old stuff when we decide to get engaged."

Sonny twirled the knob of his steering wheel and looked out at the cold scudding water. He kept wanting to say something really nasty to Charlene, but he restrained himself. Charlene tucked her sweater back into her skirt and combed angrily at her brownish blond hair. Her mother had given her a permanent the day before and her hair was as stiff as wire.

"Let's go home," she said. "I'm done late anyway. Some anniversary."

Sonny backed the pickup around and started for the little cluster of yellow lights that was Thalia. The lake was only a couple of miles out.

"Charlene, if you feel that way I'd just as soon break up," he said. "I don't want to spoil no more anniversaries for you."

Charlene was surprised, but she recovered quickly. "That's the way nice girls get treated in this town," she said, proud to be a martyr to virtue.

"I knew you wasn't dependable," she added, taking the football jacket and laying it on the seat between them. "Boys that act like you do never are. That jacket's got a hole in the pocket, but you needn't ask me to sew it up. And you can give me back my pictures. I don't want you showin' 'em to a lot of other boys and tellin' them how hot I am."

Sonny stopped the pickup in front of her house and fished in his billfold for the three or four snapshots Charlene had given him. One of them, taken at a swimming pool in Wichita Falls, had been taken the summer before. Charlene was in a bathing suit. When she gave Sonny the picture she had taken a ballpoint pen and written on the back of the snapshot, "Look What Legs!", hoping he would show it to Duane. The photograph showed clearly that her legs were short and fat, but in spite of it she managed to think of herself as possessing gazellelike slimness. Sonny laid the pictures on top of the football jacket, and Charlene scooped them up.

"Well, good-night," Sonny said. "I ain't got no hard feelings if you don't."

Charlene got out, but then she bethought herself of something and held the pickup door open a moment. "Don't you try to go with Marlene," she said. "Marlene's young, and she's a good Christian girl. If you try to go with her I'll tell my Daddy what a wolf you was with me and he'll stomp the you-know-what out of you."

"You was pretty glad to let me do what little I did," Sonny said, angered. "You just mind your own business and let Marlene mind hers."

Charlene gave him a last ill-tempered look. "If you've given me one of those diseases you'll be sorry," she said.

She could cheerfully have stabbed Sonny with an ice pick, but instead, to impress Marlene, she went in the house, woke her up, and cried for half the night about her blighted romance. She told Marlene Sonny had forced her to fondle him indecently.

"What in the world did it look like?" Marlene asked, bug-eyed with startled envy.

"Oh, the awfulest thing you ever saw," Charlene assured her, smearing a thick coating of beauty cream on her face. "Ouuee, he was nasty. I hope you don't ever get involved with a man like that, honey—they make you old before your time. I bet I've aged a year, just tonight."

Later, when the lights were out, Marlene tried to figure on her fingers what month it would be when Charlene would be sent away in disgrace to Kizer, Arkansas, to have her baby. They had an aunt who lived in Kizer. Marlene was not exactly clear in her mind about how one went about getting pregnant, but she assumed that with such goings on Charlene must have. It was conceivable that her mother would make Charlene leave the picture of Van Johnson behind when she was sent away, and that thought cheered Marlene very much. In any case, it would be nice to have the bedroom to herself.

3

AFTER HE LET CHARLENE OUT Sonny drove back to town. He was amazed that breaking up with her had been so easy: all he felt was a strong sense of relief at having his football jacket back. It was the jacket he had earned in his junior year when he and Duane had been cocaptains, and it had "Cocaptain" stitched across the front in green thread. He was proud of it, and glad to have it safely out of Charlene's hands.

When he got back to the square it was midnight and the town looked just as deserted as it had looked that morning. The night watchman's old white Nash was parked where it always was, and the night watchman, a man named Andy Fanner, was asleep in the front seat, his heels propped on the dash. As usual, he had his motor running and his windows rolled up; the town thought Andy a very likely candidate for monoxide poisoning and expected any morning to find him a purplish corpse, but he slept comfortably through hundreds of winter nights with no apparent ill effects. Sonny didn't share the general worry: he had ridden in the Nash and knew there were holes enough in the floorboard to provide ample ventilation.

He drove to the all-night café and started in, but when he looked through the window he saw that his father, Frank Crawford, was sitting at the counter, sipping defensively at a cup of coffee and talking to Genevieve Morgan, the night waitress. His father liked Genevieve and Sonny liked her too, but they couldn't both talk to her at the same time so Sonny returned to the pickup and backed down the street to the square to wait for his father to come out. Waiting made him a little uneasy; somehow he couldn't help begrudging his father the nightly conversations with Genevieve. She was a shapely black-headed woman in her mid-thirties whose husband had been busted up in a rig accident almost a year before. He was not yet well enough to go back to the oil fields, and since they had two boys and were paying on a house, Genevieve had to go to work. The waitressing job was ten at night to six in the morning, and she didn't like it, but in Thalia there were not many jobs open at any hour. When she took over the night shift Sam's business had improved enormously: half the truckers and roughnecks and cowboys in that part of the country would hit the café at night, hoping to make out with Genevieve. She was beginning to thicken a bit at the waist, but she was still pretty, high-breasted, and long-legged; men accustomed to the droopy-hipped plod of most small town waitresses liked the way Genevieve carried herself. Sonny liked it himself and had as many fantasies about Genevieve as he had about Jacy Farrow.

He hadn't been parked long when he saw his father leave the café and come walking up the empty street toward the square, shivering and shaking. All he ever wore was summer slacks and a thin cotton jacket, too short at the wrists. Sonny felt briefly guilty for not offering him a ride to the hotel. He would have, but his father would only try to give him ten dollars and that would make them both nervous. It would not be worth it to either of them to get in a money argument that late at night. Money arguments often upset them for hours. Frank couldn't help offering it and Sonny couldn't help refusing to take it. Sonny did not want it, nor could he see how his father could possibly do without it, as high as his prescriptions were. Frank Crawford was not the town's only drug addict, but he was the one with the best excuse: he had been high-school principal in Thalia, until his car wreck. One night he was coming home from a high-school football game and sideswiped a cattle truck. Sonny's mother was killed and Frank was injured so badly that six operations failed to restore him to health. He couldn't stand the strain of teaching, tried to learn pharmacy and failed, and finally had to settle for the job at the domino hall. He got through life on prescriptions, but the prescriptions didn't make him feel any better about the fact that his son was living in a rooming house rather than in a proper home.

Sonny was a little afraid his father might spot the pickup, but Frank Crawford had his chin tucked down and the cold wind made his eyes water so badly that he hardly even saw the street. He passed under the blinking traffic light and went into the hotel, and Sonny quickly started the pickup and drove back to the café. Five soldiers had just come out and were standing around their car flipping quarters to see who drove the next stint. Their car had Kansas license plates and the boy who lost the toss looked depressed at the thought of how far there was to go.

When Sonny went in Genevieve was back in the kitchen cleaning off the grill. He sat down at the counter and tapped the countertop with a fifty-cent piece until she came out of the kitchen to see who the customer was.

"Surprise," he said. "I guess I'll have a cheeseburger to go to bed on."

"You would," Genevieve said, far from surprised. She went back to the kitchen and slapped a hamburger patty on her clean grill. When the burger was ready she carried it right past Sonny and set it down at one of the red leatherette booths. Then she got a glass of milk for him and a cup of coffee for herself.

"If you'll sit in that booth I'll keep you company," she said.

Sonny was quick to obey. The steam from her coffee rose between them as he ate his cheeseburger. The window by the booth was all fogged over, but the misted glass was cold to the touch, and the knowledge that the freezing wind was just outside made the booth seem all the cozier. Genevieve sat quietly, her hands on the coffee cup; the warmth against her palms was lovely, but it made her a little too nostalgic for all the winter nights she had spent at home, sleeping against her husband. Then her whole body had felt as warm and comfortable as her palms felt against the cup.

"Your dad was in a few minutes ago," she said, raising her arm to tuck a strand of black hair in place.

"Guess I just missed him," Sonny said quickly.

"Where'd you hide?" she asked, giving him a perceptive grin. Her teeth were a little uneven, but strong. Sonny pretended he hadn't understood her and tried to think of a way to change the subject. Charlene was the only thing that occurred to him.

"I guess you'll have to be my girl friend now," he said. "Me and Charlene broke up tonight."

"It was about time. I better take advantage of the situation while I can. Come on back in the kitchen and have a piece of pie while I do some dishwashing."

Sonny gladly went with her, but he was painfully aware that she was only joking about being his girl friend. He sat in a chair and ate a big piece of apricot pie while Genevieve attended to a sinkful of dishes. For a minute, lost in her work, she forgot Sonny completely and he felt free to watch her. Gallons of hot water poured into the sink and working over it soon had her sweating. Her cheeks and forehead shone with it; there were beads on her upper lip, and the armpits of her green uniform darkened. The errant strand of hair hung over her forehead when she bent to fish the knives and forks out of the water. As always, Sonny found himself strongly affected by her. Sweat, if it was Genevieve's, seemed a very intimate and feminine moisture. Even Jacy didn't affect him quite as strongly; beside Genevieve, Jacy seemed strangely diminished, and apparently Jacy knew it. She always made Duane take her to the drive-in rather than the café when they ate together.

When Genevieve finished her dishes she glanced over at Sonny and saw that he seemed rather melancholy.

"Honey, you shouldn't be down in the mouth about Charlene," she said. "You put up with her long enough. She didn't even have a good disposition."

"I ain't blue about her," Sonny said, handing her the pie dish.

When she asked him why he was blue, he shrugged, not knowing what to say. He was blue because he wanted her and knew he would never have her, but that wasn't something he could talk about. "There ain't nobody to go with in this town," he said finally. "Jacy's the only pretty girl in high school, and Duane's got her."

Genevieve squeezed out her gray dishrag. "I'd call that his tough luck," she said. "She'll bring him more misery than she'll ever be worth. She's just like her grandmother. Besides, I doubt Lois and Gene want her marrying a poor boy."

"What's the matter with them?" Sonny asked. "Why do they think everybody has to be rich?"

"Oh, I don't guess they do," Genevieve said. "I oughtn't to even talk about them. We were all good friends once. Gene and Dan roughnecked together when we first moved here and we all went to dances together. Lois' mother had disowned her and she and Gene were livin' in a little one-room place over the newspaper office. She couldn't even afford a flour-sack apron, much less a mink coat."

Genevieve untied her own apron, which was damp from having been pressed against the sink. She stared at the floor a moment, her look full of memory.

"I'll always have a soft spot for Lois," she said. "Lois is some woman. Gene just never could handle her. Since he started making his strikes we haven't seen much of one another. When folks get rich all of a sudden it makes them feel sort of guilty to be around folks who've stayed poor."

"I hate people like that," Sonny said.

Genevieve sighed and got herself a fresh apron. "You oughtn't to," she said. "It's perfectly natural. I've always wondered what would have happened if Dan had bought the rig and made the strikes. They offered that rig to Dan first. In fact, Gene Farrow tried to get Dan to go partners with him on it, but when it comes to money Dan Morgan never took a chance in his life. If we had made the money we might be just as touchy about it now as they are. It can change people, you know."

Sonny looked at her curiously. He could not imagine Genevieve rich.

"Do you wish you all had made it?" he asked.

"Oh sure," she said, smiling tiredly. "I wish we'd made it."

Sonny handed her a ten-dollar bill in payment for the cheeseburger.

"Your dad give you this?" she asked.

He shook his head. "I never take money from him if I can help it. He needs all he's got."

Genevieve frowned, and Sonny nervously began popping toothpicks out of the toothpick machine. "It wouldn't hurt you to take a little something from him once in a while," she said. "You're the only boy I know who won't even let his own father give him money."

But Sonny had his mind on other things. "I hear Dan's goin' back to work soon," he said. "I guess you'll be quittin' work before long."

Genevieve slapped at his hand to make him let the toothpicks alone, but she was touched by the question. Of all the boys who had crushes on her, Sonny was her favorite. Also, he had the worst crush, and was the most vulnerable. She watched a moment as he walked over to the brightly lit jukebox and stooped to catch his reflection in the shiny plastic dome. He got out his pocket comb and began to comb his brown hair. He was so young and so intent on himself that the sight of him made her feel good about life for a moment; she almost wanted to cry, and since her husband's accident that was something she only dared do in moments of optimism.

"Honey, we got four thousand dollars' worth of doctor bills to pay," she said finally. "I'll probably be making cheeseburgers for your grandkids."

Sonny shoved his comb back in his hip pocket. Four thousand dollars in debts was something he couldn't really imagine; it was a misfortune, of course, but somehow he felt lighter about things. He went back and got one more toothpick to show Genevieve he wasn't intimidated.

She ignored him and drew herself another cup of coffee. It was such a cold night that there probably wouldn't be any more customers until the bus came through at 3 A.M., and then it would only be the bus driver. The only time anyone ever got on or off in Thalia was when some soldierboy was coming home on leave or else going back to his base. The two hours before the bus came were the loneliest of the night.

"See you," Sonny said. "If I knew how to cook I'd stay and substitute for you."

Genevieve was idly peeling the polish off a fingernail, while her coffee cooled. "If you knew how to cook I'd let you," she said.

When he got within a block of the rooming house, Sonny killed his motor and let the pickup coast up to the curb. Sometimes just the sound of a pickup would waken Old Lady Malone. He tiptoed in, trying to miss all the squeaky boards. When Old Lady Malone woke up she always came slopping down the hall in her dead husband's house shoes to tell Sonny to be sure and turn out his fire. Then she frequently went in the bathroom and made bad smells for half an hour.

His room was discouragingly cold, and smelled dusty. Things always smelled dusty after the wind had been blowing for a day or two. He considered reading for a while, but there was nothing there to read except a couple of old *Reader's Digests* and a few sports magazines. He had read them all so many times he had them practically memorized.

That morning he hadn't bothered to make his bed and the quilts were all in a heap. He undressed and snuggled under the heap, his mind returning at once to Genevieve. Not Genevieve at the café, though—Genevieve naked, just out of her bath, with the ends of her black hair dampened and drops of water on her breasts. In a room so dry, with the dusty air chafing his nostrils, the thought of Genevieve dripping water was very exciting; but unfortunately the fantasy was disturbed by his feet poking out from under the ill-arranged covers into the cold air. For a moment he attempted to kick the covers straight but they were too tangled. He had to get up, turn on the light, and make the bed, all the while somewhat embarrassed by his own tumescence. Like most of his friends he went through life halfconvinced that the adults of Thalia would somehow detect even his most secret erections and put them down in the book against him. The chill of the room and his own nervousness were distracting, and by the time the quilts were spread right his only thought was to get under them and get warm. Before he could reestablish his picture of Genevieve naked he was asleep.

4

THE ONE REALLY NICE THING about high school in Thalia was that it gave everybody a chance to catch up on their sleep. Sonny and Duane habitually slept through their three study halls and were often able to do a considerable amount of sleeping in class. Working as hard as they did, school was the only thing that saved them. Occasionally they tried to stay awake in English class, but that was only because John Cecil, the teacher, was too nice a man to go to sleep on.

When they got to English class on Monday morning Jacy was already there, wearing a new blue blouse and looking fresh and cheerful. Mr. Cecil sat on his desk, and he also looked happy. He had on a brown suit and an old green tie that had been knotted so many times the edges were beginning to unravel. His wife Irene kept the family accounts and had decided the tie was good for one more year. She was a fat bossy woman and their two little girls took after her. Yet somehow, despite his family, Mr. Cecil managed to keep liking people. When he wasn't actually teaching he was always hauling a carload of kids somewhere, to a fair or a play or a concert. In the summertime he often hauled carloads of boys over to an irrigation ditch where they could swim. He didn't swim himself but he loved to sit on the bank and watch the boys.

"Well, I wonder what my chances are of interesting you kids in John Keats this morning," he said, when the class was settled.

"None at all," Duane said, and everybody laughed. Mr. Cecil laughed too—it was all in fun. The kids didn't hold it against him that he liked poetry, and he didn't hold it against them that they didn't. He read them whatever poetry he felt like reading, and they dozed or got other homework done and didn't interrupt. Once in a while he told good stories about the poets' lives; Lord Byron and all his mistresses interested the boys in the class a good deal. They agreed among themselves that Lord Byron must have been a great cocksman, but why he had bothered to write poetry they couldn't figure.

While Mr. Cecil was trying to decide what poetry to read that day Sonny got Joe Bob Blanton's algebra homework and began to copy it. For a year or two it had been necessary to threaten to whip Joe Bob before he would hand over his problems, but in time he began to want to be popular and handed them over willingly. That morning, to everyone's surprise, he held up his hand and got in an argument with Mr. Cecil over one of Keats's poems.

"I read the one about the nightingale," he said. "It didn't sound so good to me. It sounded like he wanted to be a nightingale, and I think it's silly of all these poets to want to be something besides what the Lord made them. It's criticizing the Lord."

Everybody snickered except Mr. Cecil. Joe Bob was sort of religion crazy, but nobody could blame him for it, considering the family he had. He was even a preacher himself, already: the summer before he had gone to church camp and got the call. Everybody figured Joe Bob had just done it to get a little extra attention from the girls at the church camp, but if that was it it sure backfired. So far as Brother Blanton was concerned the Lord's call was final: once you heard it you were a preacher forever. He started Joe Bob preaching sermons right away.

Mr. Cecil never quite knew what to do when Joe Bob got started. "Oh, I don't really think he wanted to be a nightingale, Joe Bob," he said. "Maybe he just wanted to be immortal."

Joe Bob was not satisfied with that either; he took out his pocket comb and slicked back his blond hair.

"All you have to do to be immortal is lead a good Christian life," he said. "Anybody can do it if they love the Lord, and you can't do it by writing poems anyway."

"Maybe not, maybe not," Mr. Cecil said, chuckling a little. "Here, now let me read you this."

He started reading the "Ode on a Grecian Urn," but the class was not listening. Joe Bob, having said his say, had lost interest in the whole matter and was doing his chemistry. Duane was catching a little nap, and Jacy was studying her mouth in a little mirror she kept behind her English book—she had been considering changing her lipstick shade but didn't want to do so hastily. Sonny looked out the window, and Mr. Cecil read peacefully on until the bell rang.

Civics class was next, a very popular class. Sonny and Duane had taken the precaution to sit in the back of the room, so they could cheat or sleep or do whatever they wanted to, but actually, in civics class, they could have done about as much if they had been sitting in the front row. Coach Popper taught civics—if what he did could be called teaching—and he could not have cared less what went on.

Not only was the coach the dumbest teacher in school, he was also the laziest. Three days out of four he would go to sleep in class while he was trying to figure out some paragraph in the textbook. He didn't even know the Pledge of Allegiance, and some of the kids at least knew that. When he went to sleep, he never woke up until the bell rang, and the kids did just as they pleased. Duane usually took a nap, and Joe Bob made a big point of reading the Bible. The only girl in class was a big ugly junior named Agnes Bean; the boys who didn't have anything else to do teased her. Leroy Malone, Old Lady Malone's grandson, sat right behind Agnes and kept the class amused by popping her brassiere strap against her back. Once he made her so mad popping the strap that Agnes reached under the desk, slipped off her brogan shoe, and turned and cold-cocked him with it before he could get his guard up. His nose bled all over his desk and he had to get up and sneak down to the rest room and hold wet towels on it until it stopped.

Another time, for meanness, the boys all ganged up on Joe Bob and stuck him out the window. They hung on to his ankles and let him dangle upside down a while, assuring him that if he yelled and woke up the coach they would drop him. Nobody was sure whether they really would have dropped him or not, but Joe Bob was sensible and kept quiet. The classroom was just on the second floor, so the fall might not have hurt him much even if they had dropped him.

After civics there was a study hall, and then lunch, a boring time. One year Duane and Jacy had been able to sneak off to the lake and court during lunch, but it was only because Lois Farrow was drinking unusually hard that year and wasn't watching her daughter too closely. Lois was the only woman in Thalia who drank and made no bones about it. That same year Gene Farrow gave a big barbecue out at a little ranch he owned, and all his employees were invited. Duane was roughnecking for Gene then and took Sonny along on his invitation. Lois was there in a low-necked yellow dress, drinking whiskey as fast as most of the rough-necks drank beer. She was also shooting craps with anyone who cared to shoot with her. That was the day that Abilene won over a thousand dollars shooting craps, six hundred of it from Lois and the other four hundred from Lester Mar-low, who was Jacy's official date. Lois thought Abilene cheated her and wanted Gene to fire him on the spot, but Gene wouldn't. She cussed them both out, got in her Cadillac, and started for town, but the steering wheel got away from her as the Cadillac was speeding up and she smashed into a mesquite tree. Lois just got out, gave everybody a good hard look, and started to town on foot. Nobody stopped her. Gene Farrow got drunk and Abilene kept gambling. While he was rolling dice with Lester, Duane took Jacy over behind some cars and in the excite-ment almost got her brassiere off. Sonny himself won $27 in a blackjack game, and he was not even an employee. That night somebody busted Lois' lip and blacked her eye; some thought Gene Farrow did it but others claimed it was Abi-lene. He had known the Farrows before they were rich, and he wasn't a man to put up with much name calling, and nobody but Lois would have had the guts to call him names in the first place; if there was anything in the world she was scared of nobody knew what it was. She was a tall, rangy blonde, still almost as slim as her daughter, and she was not in the habit of walking around anyone.

If you didn't have someone to sneak off and court with, all there was to do at lunchtime was play volleyball. The one alternative amusement was watching the Melly brothers, George and Ed, who ordinarily spent their lunch hour jacking off in the boys' rest room. The Melly boys lived on a broken-down farm in the west-ern part of the county, and had very few pleasures. Freshmen and sophomores got a kick out of watching them go at it, but it was really beneath the attention of seniors like Sonny and Duane.

As classes were being dismissed that afternoon Coach Popper announced that anyone interested in coming out for basketball should be in the gym in fifteen minutes. Basketball was not a big deal sport in Thalia; Sonny and Duane only went out because they were seniors and felt obligated. Also, the road trips were nice because the boys' and girls' teams rode on the same school bus. When all candidates were assembled in the boys' dressing room there turned out to be only nine boys there, not even enough for two teams. It was no real surprise: Thalia was generally conceded to have about the most miserable basketball team in the state. On a few spectacularly dismal occasions they had managed to lose games by over a hundred points.

The nine boys began to get into their jockey straps and shorts, and were rub-bing foot toughener on their feet when Coach Popper came in from the equip-ment room. He wore a green fatigue jacket that he had swiped from the army and he was dragging two big sacks of basketballs. He was big and he was proud of it: two hundred and thirty-five pounds, at least half of it gut.

As soon as he got to the dressing room he stopped and took a quick tally. His countenance darkened.

"Goddammit!" he said. "Ain't there but nine of you little farts? Forty-six boys in this high school, ain't but nine come out? If this ain't a piss-ignorant place to have to coach. Where's Joe Bob, anyhow? The least that little piss-ant can do is come out for basketball."

"He's home jackin' off," Leroy said. "Or else he's readin' the Bible. That's all he does, one or the other."

"You all take ten laps and get out there and shoot some free throws," the coach said. "I'm going down to the church and get him. He ain't worth a shit but he's easy to find and I ain't gonna drive all over this country looking for basketball players. I ain't gonna hold no practice unless we got at least two teams, either."

He hitched his pants up over his big, sagging belly and went out the door.

All but two or three of the boys ignored the ten-lap command and began shooting whatever kind of shots came into their heads. The only one who actually ran all ten laps was Bobby Logan, the most conscientious athlete in school. Bobby liked to stay in shape and always trained hard; he was smart, too, but he was such a nice kid that nobody held it against him. He was the coach's special favorite.

When the coach came back he had Joe Bob at his heels. By that time all the boys were throwing three-quarter court peg shots, like Ozark Ike in the comics. Balls were bouncing everywhere. Once in a game Sonny had seen an Indian boy from Durant, Oklahoma, actually make a three-quarter court peg shot in the last five seconds of play. It didn't really win the game for Durant, because they were already leading Thalia by about sixty-five points, but it impressed Sonny, and he resolved to start trying a few himself.

"Hey, quit chunkin' them balls, you little dumbasses," Coach Popper yelled. "Just for that we'll have some wind sprints."

Joe Bob was standing just behind the coach, combing his hair. The coach happened to turn around and the sight made him so mad he grabbed Joe Bob's comb and threw it up in the stands as high as he could. "Get your skinny ass suited out," he said. All the boys grinned when Joe Bob went into the dressing room because while the coach was gone they had mixed a little glue in with the foot toughener. If Joe Bob used any of the foot toughener he would probably have to keep his socks on for about three weeks.

The coach divided the boys into two teams and put them to running simple plays. He sat in a bridge chair with a blue towel around his neck and watched them, yelling from time to time. He had a little paper cup for his tobacco juice sitting by the chair. The loudest he yelled all afternoon was when a freshman who hadn't yet learned to dribble let a ball knock the cup over. They spent the last twenty minutes of practice running wind sprints up and down the gym. Joe Bob's feet were so badly blistered by that time that he had to hop the last two wind sprints on one leg. Some of the freshmen were no better off, and Coach Popper thought it was a hilarious sight.

"Tough it out, boys, tough it out," he yelled. "You got to be men like the rest of us, ain't none of you pretty enough to be women."

In the dressing room there was a great laugh when it turned out Joe Bob had used the foot toughener after all. The only reason he could get his socks off at all was that he had almost solid blisters and the blisters peeled loose a lot easier than the glue. When Coach Popper saw the sight he laughed till he cried. "You might try boilin' 'em off, Joe Bob," he said. "It wouldn't be no harder on your feet."

In fact, the coach made matters even worse for Joe Bob by horsing around and trying to grab his pecker.

"Look at that little worm there," he said, making a grab. "What kind of female you ever gonna get with that thing for bait, Joe? Wouldn't do for a six-year-old girl."

He kept laughing and grabbing, backing Joe Bob around the room until finally Joe Bob couldn't stand it anymore and ran to the showers with one sock still on.

"Another minute and I'd have had him bawling," the coach said jovially, sitting down to take off his tennis shoes.

It was all pretty funny, the boys thought, but when they came out of the shower something happened that wasn't so funny. Everybody was horsing around, popping towels and grabbing at one another's nuts, like they usually did after practice. Duane and Sonny and Bobby Logan were having a little three-way towel fight, and the trouble started when Duane caught Bobby a smacker on the hip. It was just a flat pop and didn't hurt Bobby at all, but the coach happened to be coming out of the shower about that time and for some reason it made him furious. He was naked except for a whistle around his neck, but he grabbed a towel and laid into Sonny and Duane. He let one fly at Duane that would have castrated him on the spot if it had landed. "I'll show you little fuckers some towel fightin'," he said. The boys were too surprised to fight back: they just retreated into a corner where there were benches and clothes hangers to block some of the coach's shots. His wet hair was down in his face and he was snorting and puffing like a mad boar hog.

In a minute or two he got over it, though, and threw the wet towel at Sonny. "No more goddamn towel fightin'," he said and went over and looked closely at Bobby Logan's hip. The freshmen were scared almost to death—one was so nervous he put his shoes on the wrong feet and wore them home that way, too scared to stop and change. The older boys had seen the coach flare up before and knew it was just a matter of surviving until he cooled off. The time he shot at Sonny it was because he thought Sonny had scared away a dove he was sneaking up on. Fortunately, Sonny was a hundred yards away and wasn't hit.

"I don't understand how Mrs. Popper's lasted," Duane said, as he was dressing.

"She ain't the healthiest looking woman in town," Sonny reminded him. Mrs. Popper's name was Ruth; she was a small woman, pretty but tired and nervous looking. No one saw much of her. At Christmastime she sometimes made Sonny and Duane cookies and brought them around. Sam the Lion had known her all her life and said that she had been lovely when she was young.

Jacy was waiting for the boys when they came out. "My folks are gone to Wichita," she said. "Let's go get a hamburger."

They got in the convertible and drove to the drive-in, a place called The Rat-Hole. The boys were starved and ordered two hamburgers apiece; while they were cooking, Jacy and Duane smooched a little and Sonny cleaned his fingernails and looked out the back window. About the time their order came Abilene drove up in his Mercury and parked beside them. They all waved at him and he nodded in reply, barely moving his head. He was drinking a can of beer.

"You need a haircut," Jacy said, putting her hand lightly on the back of Duane's neck. They were sitting very close together, and were feeding one another French fries when the Farrows' big blue Cadillac pulled in and parked beside them. Lois Farrow was driving. She had her sunglasses on, even though it was a cloudy day. Duane scooted back to his side of the car as quickly as he could, but the Farrows gave no indication that they even noticed him. In a minute Mrs. Farrow got out and walked around to Jacy's window.

"We're having supper at home tonight," she said. "As soon as the boys get through with their hamburgers you take them to town and get yourself home, you hear?"

Mrs. Farrow looked bored, even with her sunglasses on. For some reason Sonny felt scared of her, and so did Jacy and Duane. All three were nervous. Mrs. Farrow noticed Abilene sitting there and she calmly thumbed her nose at him. He gave her a finger in return and took another swallow of his beer. Lois went back to the Cadillac and the three kids hastily finished their meal, Jacy dripping tears of annoyance into her strawberry milk shake.

"She didn't have to look so hateful," Jacy said, sniffling. "I just wish my grandmother was alive. She'd see we got married even if we had to run away and do it."

5

AT THE FARROW SUPPER TABLE an hour later, Lois and Jacy politely ignored one another, while Gene made conversation with desperate good cheer. After supper, though, he gave up, watched Groucho Marx, and then got in bed and quickly drank himself to sleep. He just wasn't built to withstand the quality of tension Lois and Jacy could generate.

The one thing Lois envied Gene was his ability to drink himself to sleep quickly. He went to sleep on so little alcohol that he was never bothered with hangovers the next day, whereas Lois had to drink for hours before the liquor would turn her off. If she just had to sleep, she took pills.

When it was almost Jacy's bedtime Lois stopped at her door for a minute, knocked, and went in. Jacy had already showered and was sitting on the bed in pink pajamas, rubbing cleansing cream into her face. Occasionally, despite her precautions, Jacy got what she called a blemish, but she took great pains with her complexion and didn't have many.

"Go on, don't let me interrupt your facial," Lois said. She walked around the room, frowning. Almost every object in the room annoyed her; she couldn't decide whether Jacy simply had bad taste or had deliberately chosen ugly objects as a means of affronting her. There were five or six stuffed animals, all of which Duane had won for her at ball-throwing booths in the State Fair; they were grouped in one corner, around a large Mortimer Snerd doll, also a gift from Duane. One wall was mostly bulletin board, and every picture of Jacy or Duane that had ever appeared in the *Thalia Times* was tacked on it. In addition to the pictures there were football programs, photographs of Jacy as cheerleader (sophomore year) and as Football Queen (junior year), the menu of the junior dinner dance, the program of the junior play, and many other mementos. On the bedside table there was a framed picture of Duane, and on the wall, a framed picture of Jesus. Next to the picture of Duane was an alarm clock and a white zipper Bible, and on the other side of the bed was Jacy's pile of movie magazines, most of them with Debbie Reynolds on the cover. Debbie Reynolds was Jacy's ideal.

"Well, I guess you hate me tonight, right?" Lois said.

"Oh, Momma, you know I love you," Jacy said, wiping the cream off. "But I love Duane too, even if you don't like it."

"Like it? Liking it or disliking it hasn't entered my head, because I don't believe it. Who you love is your own pretty self and *what* you really love is knowing you're pretty—I'm sure he tells you how pretty you are all the time so I don't doubt you're fond of him. Even your grandmother learned that much about you. And you *are* pretty, you ought to enjoy it. I'd just sort of hate to see you marry Duane, though, because in about two months he'd quit flattering you and you wouldn't be rich anymore and life wouldn't be near as much fun for you as it is right now."

"But I don't care about money," Jacy said solemnly. "I don't care about it at all."

Lois sighed. "You're pretty stupid then," she said. "If you're that stupid you ought to go and marry him—it would be the cheapest way to educate you."

Jacy was so shocked at being called stupid that she didn't even cry. Her mother knew she made straight-A report cards!

"You married Daddy when he was poor," she said weakly. "He got rich so I don't see why Duane couldn't."

"I'll tell you why, beautiful," Lois said. "I scared your daddy into getting rich. He's so scared of me that for twenty years he's done nothing but run around trying to find things to please me. He's never found the right things but he made a million dollars looking."

"If Daddy could do it Duane could too," Jacy insisted, pouting.

"Not married to you, he couldn't," Lois said. "You're not scary enough. You'd be miserable poor but as long as you had somebody to hold your hand and tell you how pretty you are you'd make out."

"Well you're miserable and you're rich," Jacy countered. "I sure don't want to be like you."

"You sound exactly like your grandmother," Lois said, looking absently out the window. "There's not much danger you'll be like me. Have you ever slept with Duane?"

It was undoubtedly the most surprising conversation Jacy had ever had!

"Me?" she said. "You know I wouldn't do that, Momma."

"Well, you just as well," Lois said quietly, a little amused at herself and at life. She never had been able to resist shocking her mother; apparently it was going to be almost as difficult to resist shocking her daughter.

"Seriously," she added. "There's no reason you shouldn't have as much fun as you're capable of having. You can come with me to the doctor sometime and we'll arrange something so you won't have to worry about babies. You do have to be careful about that."

To Jacy what she was hearing was almost beyond belief.

"But Momma," she said. "It's a sin unless you're married, isn't it? I wouldn't want to do that."

"Oh, don't be so mealymouthed," Lois shouted. "Why am I even talking to you? I just thought if you slept with Duane a few times you'd find out there really isn't anything magic about him, and have yourself some fun to boot. Maybe then you'd realize that pretty things and pretty people are what you like in life and we can send you to a good school where you'll marry some good-looking kid with the wherewithal to give you a pleasant life."

"But I don't want to leave," Jacy said plaintively. "Why can't I just stay here and go to college in Wichita?"

"Because life's too damn hard here," Lois said. "The land's got too much power over you. Being rich here is a good way to go insane. Everything's flat and empty and there's nothing to do but spend money."

She walked over to Jacy's dresser and picked up the big fifty-dollar bottle of Chanel No. 5 that Gene had given his daughter the Christmas before.

"May I have some of your perfume?" she asked. "I suddenly feel like smelling good."

"Help yourself," Jacy said, suddenly wishing her mother were gone. "Don't you have any?"

"Yes, but this is right here, and I feel like smelling good right now. Do you ever feel like doing anything right now?"

She wet her palms and fingertips with perfume and placed her hands against her throat, then touched her fingers behind her ears. The cool scent was delicious. She dampened her hands again, touched her shoulders, and then stooped and ran her palms down the calves of her legs.

"That's lovely," she said. Almost at once the perfume made her feel less depressed, and when she looked at Jacy again she noticed how young she was. Jacy's hair was pulled back by a headband, and her face, clean of makeup, was so clearly a girl's face that Lois ceased to feel angry with her.

"This is the first time in months I've seen your eyelids," she said. "You should leave your face just like that—it would win you more. Makeup is just sort of a custom you've adopted. All you really need right now is an eyebrow pencil."

Jacy looked blank and sleepy and Lois knew her advice was wasted.

"Okay," she said. "I'll let you alone. I probably confused you tonight and I do hope so. If I could just confuse you it would be a start. The only really important thing I came in to tell you was that life is very monotonous. Things happen the same way over and over again. I think it's more monotonous in this part of the country than it is in other places, but I don't really know that—it may be monotonous everywhere. I'm sick of it, myself. Everything gets old if you do it often enough. I don't particularly care who you marry, but if you want to find out about monotony real quick just marry Duane."

With that she left and walked down the thickly carpeted hall to her bedroom. As she walked through the door she heard her husband snoring; the only light in the room was the tiny orange glow of the electric blanket control. Lois sat down on the bed and rubbed her calves wearily. To kill the morning she had gone to Wichita Falls and spent $150; to kill the afternoon she had had three drinks and several rubbers of bridge at the country club. It seemed unjust that after all that work she should still have the problem of how to kill the night. She got up and went out in the hall, where she could see her wristwatch. It was only a little after ten.

After considering a moment she went to the kitchen and got a whiskey glass out of the cabinet. Bourbon was her night drink. She picked up the wall phone and dialed the poolhall and Sam the Lion answered.

"Hi, friend," she said. "How are you?"

"Hi, honey," Sam said. "I'm winterin' fairly well. How about you?"

"Oh, I won't complain," Lois said. "I wish you'd come and see me sometime. Has your number one customer left for the night?"

"No, he's here shootin'," Sam said. "I'll let you talk to him as soon as he finishes his run. You come and see me, you got a car."

In a minute or so Abilene took the phone. "Yeah," he said.

"Hey. Feel like a night off?"

"Depends on the salary," he replied.

"Well, drill hard," she said. "You're better at oil wells anyway."

She took her bourbon into the den and switched the TV on. A Claudette Colbert movie was just starting. She pulled her bathrobe around her and settled back in Gene's big leather chair to watch. From time to time she rubbed her calves. When the third commercial came on she went back to the kitchen and refilled her whiskey glass.

6

AFTER CIVICS CLASS Tuesday morning Coach Popper stopped Sonny in the hall. There had been an assembly that morning and the coach had on a necktie, an article of dress he seldom wore.

"Like your tie, Coach," Sonny said jokingly. It was a bright orange necktie and it stuck out from under the coach's shirt collar in the back.

"Purty, ain't it," the coach said distractedly. "Need you to do somethin' for me. Ruth's been sick the last couple of days and needs somebody to drive her to Olney to the doctor. She's afraid they might drug her or something so she wouldn't be able to drive home. If you'll drive her down and back I'll get you out of your afternoon classes."

Sonny immediately accepted the offer. He was for anything that would get him out of algebra class. The Poppers' house was only a couple of blocks from school and as soon as he finished lunch he walked over. He looked through the doorpanes before he knocked and saw that Mrs. Popper was ready to go. She was sitting in the living room, her purse in her lap.

"Oh hello, Sonny, what do you want?" she asked, when she came to the door.

"Coach said you needed a driver," he said. "I thought he told you I was coming."

Mrs. Popper looked disappointed but she tried hard to hide it. "No, he didn't mention it," she said. "I thought he was going to drive me himself. I guess he just couldn't get off."

She handed Sonny the keychain and he went and got the car out of their garage. It was a black '53 Chevy. When Mrs. Popper got in she had a Kleenex in her hand and was daubing at her eyes with it. Sonny felt like he ought to say something to cheer her up, but he couldn't think of anything. The Chevy didn't have much pickup but it ran smoothly once they got on the road. The wind was rustling dust in the dry bar ditches beside the highway.

"I'm sorry to be all this trouble," Mrs. Popper said. "You're very nice to drive me."

"It sure beats sittin' through algebra," he said.

Mrs. Popper smiled, but neither of them spoke again, all the way to Olney. Sonny watched the road, only glancing at her occasionally; she was looking out the window at the gray pastures. Her hair was brown with just a few traces of gray, and she wore it long, almost shoulder length. There was something about her that was really pretty. She was a little too thin, and her skin was too fair for the country she lived in: wind and sun freckled her on her cheekbones and beneath her eyes. Just before they got to the clinic she opened her purse and got out her lipstick, but she just held it a minute and put it back in her purse without using any.

While she was with the doctor Sonny sat in the waiting room of the clinic, reading magazines. There were lots of copies of *Outdoor Life* around, with good hunting stories in them. The only trouble was that the people in the waiting room made him so gloomy he could hardly read. A shaky old man sat next to him on the green waiting-room couch. He had had his voicebox taken out and had a little screen where it ought to be; every third breath he wheezed so loud that Sonny couldn't concentrate on his reading. Then a little boy came over and spat his bubble gum in the pot of a rubber plant next to Sonny. It was a pink, wet hunk of bubble gum and Sonny kept wanting to cover it with dirt. Across the room from him there was a farmer and his wife with an old old lady between them. They were very nervous, and Sonny knew why because he had seen them there several times before: if they had to wait too long the old lady would start going to the bathroom right in her chair. It was very embarrassing, but then something about the waiting room was always embarrassing. When his father had still been getting regular shots Sonny had had to wait there often, and it hadn't changed a bit.

Finally the wheezing and the bubble gum and the old old lady got on his nerves so much that he went out and waited in the car. The coach was too tight to have a radio put in the car, so there was nothing to do but sit and look out the long empty street toward the west. Someone in a passing car threw out an empty ice-cream carton and the wind skittered it across the street to the far curb.

When Mrs. Popper finally came out she was walking so stiffly that Sonny thought they must have given her the drug after all; then when she got close he saw that she walked that way because she was crying. The wind blew her hair across her face and a few strands stuck to her wet cheek. She tried awkwardly to brush them back. Sonny got out and opened the door for her, wondering what he ought to do. He knew nothing at all about crying women.

He got in and drove back through Olney, thinking surely she would quit, but she didn't. She was not crying loudly, but she was crying.

"Would you like for me to take you to the hospital?" he asked. "I don't have to be back to school by any special time."

"Oh no," Mrs. Popper said, straightening up. She shook the tears out of her eyes so hard that two or three drops splattered on the dashboard. "I'm just scared," she said. "I have to have an operation tomorrow for a tumor in my breast."

The rest of the way home she sat quietly, but it wasn't really that she was just sitting, either. It seemed to Sonny that in some way she was pulling at him, trying to get him to say something to her. He would have been glad to say something to her, only he had no idea what to say. Even algebra class would have been better than what she was doing: nobody had ever pulled at him in such a strange way. It made him so nervous that he grew careless and let the car edge off the shoulder of the road. After that he concentrated very hard on his driving.

When they got to her house Sonny drove the car on into the garage. He got out, relieved that it was over, but Mrs. Potter kept sitting in the front seat as if she didn't know she was home or in her garage or anywhere. She wasn't crying, just sitting there. After a minute Sonny went around and opened the door for her.

"Oh," she said. "Thank you."

"Here's the car keys," Sonny said. "I guess I better go back to school."

"No, not yet," Ruth said. "If you can stand me for a few more minutes I'd like you to come in and have cookies and a Coke." She looked at him apologetically, but she didn't take the car keys.

Sonny knew he couldn't get out of going in. Somehow or other Mrs. Popper had got in control and he didn't know anything to do about it. Reluctantly he followed her through the back door and into the kitchen. The yellow kitchen linoleum was old and worn out.

"Just sit at the table," Mrs. Popper said. There was something wild in her face that made Sonny think of his father—when she smiled at him there was a pressure behind the smile, as if something inside her were trying to break through her skin.

"Would you like milk or a Coke?" she asked. "I'm really sorry I made you come in—you can go right now if you like. For a minute I was just scared to be alone."

Sonny said he would take a Coke. She got one, and set a plate of thin Nabisco cookies on the table with it. For a minute of two, watching him eat, she seemed to be getting all right, and then to his amazement and disgust she burst out crying again, loudly. She put her head in her arms and sobbed, her body shaking as if she had the heaves. Sonny was sure she must be crazy and he wanted to be away from her. He didn't even want to swallow the bite he had in his mouth. Mrs. Popper seemed to know what he was thinking; she looked up at him and tried to quit crying.

"You'll never forgive me, I know," she said. "You think I'm pitiable, you're disgusted. Go on away if you want to, you don't have to stay any longer."

"Thank you for the Coke," Sonny said hastily, taking her at her word. "Maybe you'll get to feeling better after your operation."

"Oh no, it's not the operation," she said, wiping her face with a yellow table napkin. "It's not the operation at all. The tumor probably won't be dangerous. It's just that thinking about it makes me so lonely I can't stand it."

"Well, I guess you'll be glad when basketball season is over," Sonny said, feeling a little more kindly toward her. "Coach probably doesn't get to stay home much during football and basketball season."

Mrs. Popper laid down her napkin and looked at Sonny as if she were seeing him for the first time. She quit crying and became completely calm. "My God," she said. "You don't know a thing about it, do you?"

Then she did a thing which he would never forget: she got up, came around the table, put out her hand, and traced her fingers down his jaw almost to his mouth. Her fingers were cool. She put her hand on his head for a minute, felt his hair against her palm and between her fingers, and then quickly reached down for one of his hands and pressed it against her cheek and throat. She held his hand there for a moment and then laid it back on the table as carefully as if it were a piece of china.

"I know I mustn't be that way," she said, and again it looked as if something were pushing at the inside of her skin. Sonny felt very confused, but no longer particularly scared or particularly anxious to get away. From the way she touched him and looked at him he knew she had thought about kissing him when she put her hand on his face. He didn't know what would have happened, because he had no idea how it would feel to kiss someone older than himself, someone who was married. But when he looked at Mrs. Popper's mouth he wished that she had gone ahead, or that he had done something. He was sure it would have been nice to kiss her, much nicer than it had been to kiss Charlene.

But Mrs. Popper went back to her own chair and looked at the splotch on the tablecloth her tears had made.

"Here I am wanting to tell you I'm sorry again," she said, smiling a little. "I know I've given you a bad afternoon. For ten seconds there I was ready to try and seduce you, if you know what that means. To tell you the honest truth, I don't know what it means myself. I've never seduced anyone and I've never been seduced, but I've always liked the word. I thought if I was ever going to find out what it meant it had better be now."

She sighed. "I don't guess you can imagine being seduced by the wife of your coach. I'm not so terribly pretty and I don't think you even like me. It probably wouldn't be best for you to be seduced by a forty-year-old woman you don't even like. Do you have a girl friend?"

"I did have," Sonny said. "We broke up last Saturday night."

"Why did you break up?" she asked. "Do you mind talking? I wish I wasn't so avid. You don't really have to answer my questions if you don't want to."

"I was going with Charlene Duggs," Sonny said. Something had changed; he felt more comfortable with Mrs. Popper than he had all afternoon. "Charlene thought I got fresh with her, but I never did, really. I guess the reason we broke up was because we didn't like one another much to begin with."

"I shouldn't be sad about it, if I were you," Ruth said. "I know Charlene and I don't think she's nearly nice enough for you. Even I would be better for you than she would."

She put her fingers to her temples and smoothed back her hair. "Besides, she must be a dumb creature, not to appreciate you. I can't even imagine how it would be to be young and have someone like you get fresh with me."

Sonny decided she really was a little crazy, but he liked her anyway. He even wanted to compliment her in some way, say something that would make her feel nice.

"I already like you better than I ever liked her," he said, wondering if it was a wrong thing to say.

Mrs. Popper's face lightened—she looked glad that he had said it. They were silent for a moment and Sonny finished his cookies and Coke. There was no longer a reason for him to stay, but he kept sitting, hoping that Mrs. Popper might want to come around the table again.

She knew that was why he was staying, too, and she did stand up, but not to come to him. She went to the sink and looked out the back window a moment before she spoke. She was not crying, but her face was sad. "Maybe you better go on to basketball practice," she said. He stood up and she walked with him to the front door.

"I see you feel you've missed a chance," Ruth said, when they were at the door. She looked at him frankly. "You see, I'm very confused, even if I look like I'm not. That's why you must go. I've got on a great many brakes right now—what I was thinking about a while ago is nothing I've ever done except with Herman, and for a long time I haven't even believed a man could want me that way. I don't know if I believe it now, even though I see you do. But then I think it isn't really *me* you want, it's only *that* . . . sex. Not that there's anything wrong with you wanting that, it's perfectly natural. . . ." She was talking faster and faster, but suddenly she stopped.

"You must really think I'm crazy," she said. "I am crazy I guess."

"Why's that?" Sonny asked.

"What?" Ruth said, caught by surprise.

"I mean why do you feel crazy? I guess I shouldn't be askin'."

"Of course you should," she said. "I was just surprised you had the nerve. The reason I'm so crazy is because nobody cares anything about me. I don't guess there's anybody I care much about, either. It's my own fault, though—I haven't had the guts to try and do anything about it. It took more guts for me to put my hand on your face than I ever thought I had, and even then I didn't have enough to go on."

She shut the screen door and they stood for a moment looking through the screen at one another. Sonny hated to leave; in some funny way he had come to like Mrs. Popper and he knew that the minute he left she would go in the house and cry again.

"Maybe I never will know what seduce means," she said quietly. "Thank you for putting up with me. You don't need to tell Herman about the operation. I'll tell him when he gets home."

Sonny was trying to think of something appropriate to say that would let her know that he really liked her, but he couldn't think of anything that didn't sound corny. Ruth noticed, and to spare him further embarrassment she shut the living-room door. When she heard his footsteps on the sidewalk she began to cry.

Basketball practice was so far along that Sonny didn't bother to suit out, but he did check in with the coach. Joe Bob and one of the freshmen had done something wrong and the coach was sitting on his bridge chair watching them run punishment laps.

"Come on, run 'em," the coach yelled. "Be men. I don't want no sissies on this team. Quit flapping your hands, Joe Bob, you look like a goddamn goose."

Sonny slipped his shoes off and took some free-throw practice with the rest of the team. He expected the coach to ask about Mrs. Popper, but he just sat on the bridge chair, chewing tobacco and occasionally scratching his balls. When he did ask, after practice, it was not exactly about Mrs. Popper—he wanted to know if the doctor had given her any prescription.

"I don't think so," Sonny said. "We didn't get any filled."

"Good," the coach said. "Damn doctors. Every time she goes over there they prescribe her ten dollars' worth of pills and they don't do a fuckin' bit of good. I tell her to take aspirin, that's all I ever take. If she's got a sore place she can rub a little analgesic balm on it—that's the best thing for soreness there is."

He didn't say so, but analgesic was also free. The school bought it by the case and the coach took what he needed.

"She wasn't feeling too good when I left her," Sonny said, thinking the coach might be worried enough to hurry on home. Instead, the news seemed merely to disgust him.

"Hell, women like to be sick," he said. He was on his way to the showers, but he stopped long enough to grab a cake of soap from a passing freshman. "Ruth had rather be sick than do anything. I could have bought a new deer rifle with what she's spent on pills just this last year, and I wish I had, by God. A good gun beats a woman any day."

7

"I GUESS SHE JUST COULDN'T get out of it," Sonny said, chalking his cue. It was Saturday night and Duane had just found out that Jacy wasn't going to be at the picture show that evening: she was going to a country club dance with Lester Marlow.

"She wasn't sheddin' no tears over the telephone," Duane said bitterly. "She may be getting to like country club dances, that's what worries me."

He was in such a terrible mood that the pool game wasn't much fun. Jerry Framingham, a friend of theirs who drove a cattle truck, was shooting with them; he had to truck a load of yearlings to Fort Worth that night and asked them to ride along with him, since neither of them had dates.

"We might as well," Duane said. "Be better than loafin' around here."

Sonny was agreeable. While Jerry went out in the country to pick up his load he and Duane walked over to the café to have supper. Sam the Lion was there, waiting for old Marston to bring out his nightly steak. Penny was still at work and Marston was hopping to get the orders out. Penny had taken to wearing orange lipstick.

The boys sat down with Sam the Lion and ordered chickenfried steaks. "Sam, how's the best way to get rich?" Duane asked.

"To be born rich," Sam said. "That's much the best way. Why?"

"I want to get that way. I want to get at least as rich as Lester Marlow."

"Well, of course," Sam said, buttering a cracker. "You're really too young to know what's good for you, though. Once you got rich you'd have to spend all your time staying rich, and that's hard thankless work. I tried it a while and quit, myself. If I can keep ten dollars ahead of the bills I'll be doin' all right."

"How much do you think Gene Farrow's worth?" Duane asked. "How rich would I have to get to be richer than him?"

"How much cash you got?" Sam asked.

"Fifty-two dollars right now. Fifty-one after we eat."

"Then cashwise I imagine you're as rich as Gene," Sam said, looking suspiciously at his salad. Marston was always sneaking cucumbers into his salads, against strict orders. Sam the Lion regarded cucumbers as a species of gourd and would not eat them.

"I doubt if Gene could lay his hands on fifty dollars tonight," he added.

Both boys were stunned. Everyone thought Gene Farrow was the richest man in town.

"Why Sam, he's bound to have lots of money," Duane said. "Mrs. Farrow's fur coat is supposed to be worth five thousand dollars."

"Probably is," Sam said. "That's five thousand he don't have in cash, though. He's got lots of trucks and equipment and oil leases, too, but it ain't cash and there's no way of tellin' how much of it's his and how much is the bank's."

He broke a biscuit in two and wiped his gravy bowl clean. "There ain't no sure-nuff rich people in this town now," he said. "I doubt there'll ever be any more. The oil fields are about to dry up and the cattle business looks like it's going to peter out. If I had to make a guess at who was the richest man in town I'd say Abilene. He may not own nothing but his car and his clothes, but I've never seen the day when he couldn't pull a thousand dollars out of his billfold. A man with a thousand dollars in his pocket is rich, for Thalia."

Duane cheered up suddenly and began to go after his steak with good appetite. "Well that's all good news," he said. "Maybe if the Farrows go broke they won't mind my marrying Jacy."

Sam grunted his disagreement. "Penny, bring me a dish of that cobbler," he said. "Apricot. Nope, Duane, you're wrong. I don't know about Lois, but if Gene was to even think he was going broke he wouldn't want you to get within a mile of that girl. There ain't nobody snootier than an oilman who's had to sell one of his Cadillacs."

"Aw, Sam, it's not him," Duane argued. "I get along with him all right. It's Mrs. Farrow who don't like me. I bet it's her fault Jacy's off with Lester tonight."

"Well, Lois has got a lot of judgment; maybe she's doin' you a favor," Sam said. "That little girl is goin' to be a hard one to please."

Talk like that made Duane huffy. "I please her well enough," he said. Sonny wished the meal were over. It was getting so Duane wanted to talk about Jacy half the time, and for some reason the conversations always left Sonny depressed.

Outside, after they had all finished, Sam the Lion slapped them on the shoulder. "Well, have fun in Cowtown," he said. "If I didn't have all these businesses to run I'd ride along with you. Ain't been to Fort Worth in fifteen years." The night was cold and sleety and he hobbled on back to the poolhall on his sore feet.

The boys walked over to the courthouse where they could wait out the wind. While they were waiting they saw Lester and Jacy drive by in Lester's Oldsmobile. Jacy wasn't sitting very close to him but as they passed under the street light the boys could see that she was laughing at something. Her hair was rolled up on her head in a fancy way.

"You don't need to look so blue about it," Sonny said. "This time next year you'll probably be married to her. Look at me, I ain't got no date either."

"Yeah, but you ain't in love," Duane said.

Finally Jerry's cattle truck screeched up to the stoplight, jam-packed with Hereford yearlings. When it stopped they all began to bawl and shove around and shit through the sideboards. The boys ran over and climbed up in the high cab—Jerry whanged the truck in gear and they were off.

"Break out the beer," Jerry said. "There's two six-packs there on the floor somewhere."

Sonny found an opener in the glove compartment. When he popped into a can the cold beer spewed all over him, its smell filling the cab. "The coach would have a shit fit if he knew we were breakin' trainin'," he said happily. For a moment Mrs. Popper crossed his mind—what would she be doing on a Saturday night?—but it was so much fun to be going down the road in a high, bouncy cattle truck that he soon forgot her. All he and Duane had to do was drink beer and watch the fence posts and the culverts whiz by; before the first six-pack was finished their troubles were forgotten and they were happily reminiscing about old times in Thalia High School, reliving all the ball games they had played and the fights and adventures they had had. Jerry Framingham enjoyed the conversation: most of the kids he had graduated with were in the army and he seldom had any company at all on his cattle hauls.

Sonny and Duane found that they were a little out of shape for beer drinking. By the time they reached Fort Worth they were both fairly drunk, and the anecdotes they were telling seemed so funny to them that it would sometimes take them three or four miles to quit laughing. One classic story simply broke them up: it was about the time they had persuaded Billy to come out for football, although he wasn't even enrolled in school. Billy knew nothing about football and hadn't thought it at all strange when they put his shoulder pads on backward, daubed foot toughener in his ears, and made him wear a jockey strap for a noseguard. When he trotted out on the field with his jockey strap on his nose the whole team had hysterics and Coach Popper laughed so hard he almost ruptured himself.

Jerry Framingham was not drunk and thus did not become uncontrollably amused when he heard such stories retold—in fact the boys' laughter seemed to irritate him a little. "You drunk bastards can't do anything but laugh," he said.

Jerry's turn came later, after they had unloaded the cattle. They were having a beer or two in a honky-tonk on North Main and Jerry talked them into putting up five dollars apiece toward a fifteen-dollar whore he knew about. They could all three have easily found five-dollar whores, but Jerry insisted on flipping to see who got the more expensive one, and he won the flips. The whore was in a dinky little North Main hotel. Sonny and Duane walked around outside, freezing their tails, while Jerry went up to have fun. They stepped inside a cheap dance hall a few minutes to warm up and watched a lot of sideburned stockyard hands dance their skinny girl friends around the room.

As soon as Jerry was done and they were back in the truck the boys went to sleep. Jerry was somewhat weakened himself and on the home side of Jacksboro he pulled the truck off the road and went to sleep himself. About four in the morning Sonny woke up, practically frozen to death. Jerry and Duane were both mashed on top of him, trying to keep warm, and the door handle was about to bore a hole in his back. The windshield was completely sleeted over. Sonny pushed around until he woke the others up and he and Jerry got out and scraped the sleet off the windshield with an old Levi jacket. While they were doing that Duane crawled over and vomited in the bar ditch. Coming back from Fort Worth was never as much fun as going.

While they had rolled around trying to sleep they had kicked the heater wires loose, so the rest of the trip home was miserably cold. The café looked like the most comfortable place in the world when they finally pulled in. Genevieve was sitting at the counter reading an old paperback of *Forever Amber* that everyone who worked at the café had read several times. When she saw what bad shape Sonny and Duane were in she put it away and fixed them some toast and coffee; as soon as they ate a little they dozed off and slept with their heads on the counter while she filled the coffee maker and got things ready for the morning business. Asleep they both had the tousled, helpless look of young children and she kept wanting to cover their shoulders with a tablecloth or something. When Marston came in she woke them up. She put on her heavy blue coat and the boys stumbled outside behind her, trying to keep their eyes open. The cold air snapped them out of it a little. Genevieve had an old gray Dodge that was hard to start and by the time she got it to kick off the boys were wide awake.

"What do you think about a woman that would make her daughter go with Lester Marlow?" Duane asked, remembering that he had a grievance.

"I don't know much about Lester, but if I had a daughter I don't know that I'd want her going with either one of you boys, the way you all cut up," she said, treating the whole matter lightly. She pulled up in front of their rooming house and raced her motor, so the old car wouldn't die.

The boys got out, thanked her, waved as the car pulled away, its exhaust white in the cold air. "Well, at least we got to go *somewhere*," Sonny said, picking up a beer can somebody had thrown out on the lawn. Fort Worth, after all, was a city, part of the big world, and he always came back from a trip there with the satisfying sense that he had traveled. They flipped to see who got the bathtub first and he won.

8

THE FIRST BASKETBALL GAME of the season was with Paducah, a town well over a hundred miles from Thalia. It was the longest trip of the year and usually the wildest: in Paducah they played basketball as if it were indoor football, and they had everything in their favor, including a gym so small that the out-of-bounds lines were painted on the walls. The Paducah boys were used to the gym and could run up the walls like lizards, but visiting teams, accustomed to normal-sized courts, had a hard time. Every year two or three Thalia players smashed into the walls and knocked themselves out.

This time it happened to Sonny, and in the very first minutes of play. Leroy Malone managed to trip the gangly Paducah center and while the center was sprawled on the floor Sonny ran right along his back, in pursuit of the ball. Just as he was about to grab it somebody tripped *him* and he hit the wall head first. The next thing he knew he was stretched out beside the bench and one of the freshmen players was squeezing a wet washrag on his forehead. Sonny tried to keep his eyes closed as long as he could—he knew Coach Popper would send him back into the game as soon as he regained consciousness. He feigned deep coma for about five minutes, but unfortunately the coach was experienced in such matters. He came over and lifted one of Sonny's eyelids and saw that he was awake.

"Possuming," he said. "I thought so. Get up and get your butt back in there. We're forty points behind and it ain't but the second quarter."

"I think I got a concussion," Sonny said, trying to look dangerously ill. "Maybe I ought to stay out a little while."

"Get up," the coach insisted. "We just quit football practice ten days ago, you ain't had time to get that out of shape. If you want to rest, by God go in there and foul out first. Knock the shit out of that forward two or three times—he's the one doin' all the scorin'. Hell, we come all this way, let's make a showing."

Sonny reluctantly got up and went back in. He managed three fouls before the half, but he was too weak to hit anybody very hard and none of the fouls was really satisfactory. The half-time score was Paducah 62 and Thalia 9. During the half the coach called them over for one of his little pep talks, this one very brief.

"You ten boys have got the shortest little peckers of any bunch of kids I've ever coached," he said sincerely. "By God, if you don't stomp some asses this next half I'll stomp a few tomorrow afternoon when we start practicing."

He scowled fiercely and strolled off to the concession stand to have some coffee.

In the second half things began to look really ominous. Sonny felt strangely lightheaded and went out on the floor not much caring what he did. Paducah defense had become virtually impenetrable: for one thing, they had started openly tackling whichever Thalia player had the ball. It seemed to Sonny that at last the time had come to shoot peg shots—there was not much chance of moving the ball down the court any other way. Whenever they tried, Paducah tackled them, tripped them, threw body blocks into them, or had the referee call fouls on them.

Actually, the refereeing was another very bad aspect of basketball in Paducah. Unusual as it was, Paducah had a male home economics teacher, a frail little man named Mr. Wean. The school board felt that teaching home ec was really too light a job for a man so they made Mr. Wean basketball referee. He had never managed to learn much about the game, but he was quite docile and called whatever the Paducah team told him to call. Also, he was in bad shape and couldn't possibly run up and down the court for forty-eight minutes. Instead of following the ball, he just stood on the center line and made all his calls from there.

After considering the matter for half a quarter or so Sonny concluded that peg shots were the only feasible tactic. He was simply too weak to dodge the blocks the Paducah boys were throwing. From then on, every time he got the ball he threw it at the backboard he was attacking. At the very worst it slowed down Paducah's scoring. The other Thalia players were quick to see the wisdom of such an offense and in five minutes they were all doing it. Whoever caught the throw-in after a Paducah score would immediately whirl and throw a full-court peg shot. The only one it didn't work for was Leroy Malone: the big Paducah center anticipated him, caught the ball, and threw a ten-yard peg shot right at Leroy's groin. It hurt so bad he later told Sonny he was unable to jack off for two weeks.

The groin shot drew such sustained applause from the Paducah bleachers that Sonny was angered. Mr. Wean had failed to see that it was a deliberate foul: indeed, Mr. Wean was seeing less and less all the time. Thalia's peg-shot offense confused him—he had to keep turning around and around to keep up with the ball. After a while this made him so dizzy that he simply stopped and stood facing the Thalia goal—most of the Paducah team was down there anyway, catching the peg shots and throwing them back. Mr. Wean felt that he had somehow got involved in a game of ante over, and he didn't like it. He had a fat wife and all he really wanted to do was stay in the home ec classroom and teach young, small-breasted girls how to make pies. Instead he was standing on the center line, sweating and wishing the quarter would end. Suddenly, Sonny had an irresistible urge to chunk somebody. He unleashed a flat, low peg shot that caught Mr. Wean squarely in the back of the head and sent him sprawling.

The Thalia bench, boys and girls alike, arose with shrieks and cheers, their jubilation all the more noticeable because of the moment of total silence in the

Paducah bleachers. The shot instantly made Sonny a celebrity, but it also scared hell out of him and his teammates who were on the floor at the time. They rushed over and tried to help Mr. Wean up, but his legs were like rubber. He had to be dragged off the floor. Paducah's assistant football coach was called in to referee the rest of the game—by the time he got his tennis shoes on, the hometown bleachers had recovered from their shock and were clamoring for Sonny's blood. He knew his only hope was to foul out immediately and get to the bench. While he was trying to decide on the safest way to foul, Coach Popper came to his rescue and took him out.

"Good lick," the coach said. "Nobody but a queer would teach home ec anyway."

From there on things were dismal for the Thalia five. Duane fouled out before the quarter ended, leaving no one but Joe Bob and the freshmen to play the fourth quarter. Paducah was ahead 88 to 14. Coach Popper got so mad at the freshmen that he couldn't see; he almost strangled himself tugging at the towel around his neck. He sent Sonny in again but Sonny quickly threw a couple of light body blocks and fouled out. That left Joe Bob and the freshmen to do the best they could. For the remainder of the game they never once managed to get the ball into their end of the court. As soon as they threw it in, the Paducah players took it away from them and made another goal. In five minutes the score was 110 to 14 and Coach Popper called time out. A huddle was in order.

"I tell you," the coach said philosophically, "let's just forget about winning and try to hold the score down. We're gonna get beat over a hundred points if we ain't careful. Oaks, you throw the ball into Joe Bob and Joe Bob, as soon as you get it lay down with it. That way they'll have to tie it up and jump for it every time. That'll slow 'em down a little."

The tactic worked fine the first time it was tried. Joe Bob swallowed the ball and Paducah had to tie it up to get possession. It took them about forty seconds to score. Thalia tried it again and three Paducah players gang-piled Joe Bob as he went down. He had to be carried off. The freshman who shot his free throw for him was so scared he barely got the ball halfway to the basket.

Joe Bob's injury left the four freshmen alone on the field for the last few minutes of the game. None of them wanted to swallow the ball and get gang-piled so they did what they could to cooperate with Paducah. The final score was 121 to 14.

"Well, hell, at least my B team got some experience," Coach Popper said. "Might as well look on the bright side. Let's go to the bus."

Basketball defeats weighed very lightly on the coach: football was the only sport that really counted. Ten minutes later he was flopped down in his bus seat, sound asleep.

The boys sat in a stupor for the first twenty miles or so, trying to get used to feeling safe again. Besides, Old Lady Fowler, the girls' coach, was still awake and they could not start to work on the girls until she dropped off. She went to sleep as they were pulling out of Vernon, and from there on it was dog-eat-dog.

The four little freshmen had no chance with the girls and had to get what amusement they could out of tormenting Joe Bob. They crowded him in a seat, took his underpants off, and threw them out the window. Joe Bob was too weak from the gang-piling to fight back, and he might not have bothered anyway. He lost so many pair of underwear that his mother bought them wholesale. He was the only boy on the team who wore his regulars, rather than a jockey strap: Brother Blanton wouldn't hear of him wearing anything so immodest.

"What if you got hurt and were taken to a hospital wearing a thing like that?" Brother Blanton said. "Our good name would be ruined."

Most of the kids had seen Joe Bob's underwear often enough to be thoroughly bored with it. The freshmen attracted no notice at all, and soon went to sleep.

Sonny started the return trip sitting by Leroy Malone, whose balls were so sore that the mere thought of girls made him writhe. After a little bargaining Sonny managed to switch with the kid in front of him, which put him next to the pretty but prudish sophomore he had had his eye on. Knocking Mr. Wean down gave him so much status that he was able to hold the girl's hand almost immediately. Martha Lou was her name. By the time they reached Electra she was willing to let him kiss her, but the results were pretty discouraging. Her teeth were clenched as tightly as if she had lockjaw, and even Sonny's status couldn't unlock them. His only reward was a taste of lipstick, in a flavor he didn't much care for.

The only real excitement on the bus ride home involved Jacy and Duane, the star couple. That was usually the case. None of the other kids excited one another much. There was a fat blonde named Vida May who would feel penises, but the teachers knew about her and made her sit so close to the front that it was dangerous to fool with her even when the teachers were asleep.

Jacy and Duane, as a matter of course, were sitting in the very back seat. Duane didn't like the back seat much because there was a little overhead light above it that the bus driver refused to turn off. The bus driver's name was Wilbur Tim and he wasn't about to trust any kids in a totally dark bus. One time years earlier his wife Jessie had found two prophylactics when she was sweeping out the bus, and it just about sent her into hysterics. She was the apprehensive type and went around for months worried sick that some nice little girl had got pregnant on her husband's bus. After that Wilbur installed the light.

It was a small bulb that didn't really give any light, just a nice orange glow. Jacy loved it and wouldn't sit anywhere else, despite Duane's protests. She thought the light was very romantic and suggestive: everyone in the bus could tell when the couple in the back seat were kissing or doing something sexy, but the light wasn't strong enough for them to see too clearly. Courting with Duane when all the kids on the school bus could watch gave Jacy a real thrill, and made her feel a little like a movie star: she could bring beauty and passion into the poor kids' lives.

Because Jacy enjoyed them so much, the kissing sessions in the back seat had become a sort of regular feature on basketball road trips. All the kids watched, even though it made them itchy and envious. Jacy, after all, was the prettiest girl in school and watching her get kissed and played with was something to do on the long drives home. The element that made it really exciting to everyone was the question of how far Jacy would go. Once Duane got started kissing he was completely indifferent to whether he had an audience or not: all he wanted was more. The dim light made it impossible to tell precisely how much more Jacy allowed: everyone caught shadowy glimpses, and occasionally a gasp or a little moan from Jacy indicated that Duane was making some headway at least, but no one ever knew how much or what kind.

Only Jacy and Duane knew that he was making a great deal of headway indeed. Jacy would kiss and play around any time, but she seldom got excited past the point of control unless she was on the school bus, where people were watching. Being in the public eye seemed to heighten the quality of every touch. On the bus seat she never had to feign passion—she was burning with it. It was easy for Duane to get his hands inside her loose uniform and touch her breasts, and she loved it. Also, since she was in shorts, it was easy for him to do even more abandoned things to her. She loved to have him slide his hands up the underside of her legs, and sometimes she would even get to the point where she wanted him to touch her crotch. It was a matter that took very delicate managing, but if Duane's hand were cupped against her at the right time so she could squeeze it with her legs, something nice would happen. That was not for the audience, however: she didn't want the kids to see that. When the moment came near she would try to get Duane to crowd her back in the corner, so they couldn't be seen so well. Sometimes it worked beautifully. The younger and more naïve kids were sure Duane went all the way; the juniors and seniors knew better, but felt he must be going a pretty significant distance, anyhow. Every trip added to Jacy's legend. The following day at school she would be on every tongue. Some of the girls said bitter things about her, but the boys took notice when she walked by. The only one seriously discommoded by bus-seat sessions was Duane, who frequently ached painfully by the time the bus reached home. He didn't like it, but he supposed such frustration was something he would simply have to bear until they were married.

Just before the bus got back to Thalia Coach Popper woke up and looked around. Most of the kids were asleep by that time, Jacy and Duane among them, but Jacy had gone to sleep with her legs across Duane's and when the coach saw that he was infuriated. It would put him in an awful spot if Lois Farrow somehow found out he had let her daughter go to sleep with her legs across Duane's. Gene Farrow was on the school board, and an incident like that could cost a coach his job. He stormed back and shook Jacy until she was awake enough to stumble down the aisle to the front seat, where she stayed the rest of the way home.

When all the kids had been delivered to their houses the coach got to thinking about it and began to cuss. There was no end to the trouble a couple of silly-ass kids might cause, particularly if one of them was Lois Farrow's daughter. Lois Farrow was the one person in Thalia who didn't give a damn for the fact that he was football coach.

Wilbur Tim dropped him off at his home, and he stomped inside, still angry. When he turned on the light in his bedroom closet it woke Ruth up. She had just had her breast operation a few days before and was still taking pain medicine. As he was taking off his shoes she sat up in bed.

"Herman, could you bring me a pain pill?" she asked. "It's hurting a little and I'm too groggy to get up."

"You sound goddamn wide awake to me," the coach said, fed up with women. "I bet if I let you you could lay there and talk for two hours. Get up and get your own pills, I ain't no pharmacist."

After a moment, Ruth did. She was dizzy and had to guide herself along the wall, holding her sore breast with one hand. She had washed that day and her white cotton nightgown smelled faintly of detergent. The coach ignored her and flopped on the bed. So far as he could tell, it had not been enough of an operation to make a fuss about. The scar on her breast was barely three inches long. He had cut himself worse than that many times, usually when he was hurrying through a barbed-wire fence to get to a covey of quail. The only thing that worried him about Ruth was the chance that they hadn't removed all the tumor and might have to operate again, in which case there would be no end to the expense. The cheapest and most sensible thing would have been for them to take the whole breast off while they were at it. The breast wasn't doing Ruth any good anyway, and if they had taken it all that would have been the end of the matter. He had told them so, too, but the doctor had ignored him and Ruth had gone off in another room and bawled. A woman like her would try the patience of a saint.

The next day at basketball practice the coach gave Duane a dressing down in front of the whole squad. He told him if he ever again so much as sat with Jacy on a basketball trip he would give him fifteen licks with a basketball shoe. A basketball shoe was the only thing the coach ever whipped boys with, but since he wore a size thirteen that was enough. He also told Duane to run fifty laps around the outside of the gym, and at that point Duane rebelled.

"I ain't runnin' no fifty laps all at one time," he said. "I'll do ten a day."

"You'll do fifty right now or check your suit in, by God," the coach said. "If you check it in you don't need to come out for track or baseball, neither. We can get along without you."

Duane went to the locker room, took his suit off, and left. It was just what the coach had hoped for. Any mess the boy got into with Jacy Farrow could no longer be laid at his door. It put him in such good spirits that he worked the boys until seven o'clock that night. The next day he commandeered a sophomore, and the team had ten players again.

9

IN THALIA, WINTER was always duller than summer, at least for the boys. In the winter it was too cold to sit around on the square and think up meanness to do—if they wanted to sit around they had to do it in the café, and that cost money. When the square became empty because of the cold, the town seemed emptier than ever.

A senior year was supposed to be exciting but with winter setting in Sonny's suddenly began to look very dull. When Duane quit basketball, the game became a sort of tiring chore that Sonny went on with because he didn't have a legitimate excuse to quit. Thalia lost every game by thirty points or more. Even teams that were as bad as they were beat them thirty points on sheer morale. No team had less in the way of morale than Thalia.

Besides that there was his work. It was an unusually cold winter, and the demand for butane was high. Often, after practice or after a game, Frank Fartley would be waiting for Sonny at the gym and Sonny would have to spend half the night driving over the dark, ice-rutted roads looking for a farmhouse with an empty butane tank. Sometimes he could only find them by the mailboxes, usually old-fashioned Sears and Roebuck models stuck on posts beside the road.

Sonny took to drinking coffee to stay awake, and Genevieve didn't approve. "You've got to get you another job," she told him one time. He had come stumbling into the café at two-thirty in the morning, half-frozen. The heater in the old International only worked about half the time.

The trouble was, there weren't any other jobs, and Genevieve was scarcely in a position to give that kind of advice. Her husband was not improving as rapidly as he had been—it looked like it would be summer before he got back to work. The strain had begun to tell on Genevieve: her uniform no longer fit so snugly at the shoulders, and often she was so tired she couldn't sleep even when she had the time.

Everybody seemed to have the winter doldrums, including Sam the Lion. He was taking daily naps for his heart condition and his cough was still just as bad. Duane's grandmother took the flu and was in the hospital two weeks; everyone expected it to carry her off but all it did was destroy what was left of her mind. Since he didn't have basketball to wear him out, Duane had taken to working a double shift. It was cold work, but it paid, and he could count on having Saturday nights off to spend with Jacy.

The strange conversation Jacy had had with her mother threw Jacy temporarily into a state of uncertainty. For a time she had been convinced that she knew exactly what her mother wanted of her, and exactly how to get around it; but since the conversation she hadn't been so sure. It seemed incredible that her mother would actually give her license to sleep with Duane. For a day or two she was rather tempted, just to see what sex felt like, but then she decided that would merely be walking into her mother's trap. Advice like that was bound to be a trap.

For a time the conversation had the effect of inhibiting Jacy drastically. After she and Duane had concluded they were in love she had taken to allowing him considerable freedom with her body. She had even let him feel inside her panties on a few occasions, but when her mother told her to go ahead and sleep with him she immediately put a stop to that. She felt she had to if she were going to protect their love from her mother's subtle treacheries. Besides, the only times she really enjoyed letting him touch her there was on the school bus.

She even tried to quit letting him take off her brassiere, but Duane complained so bitterly about the loss of that privilege that she finally let him start doing it again. There were a few awkward dates, but in time Jacy became rather proud of herself for the mature way she was handling the situation. She could let Duane kiss her and play with her breasts and yet remain quite cool about it all, protecting them from his passion and her own. Her mother was outwitted and Duane had as much fun as was good for him. Sometimes in church she felt a little like a martyr because of the effort it cost her to keep the two of them morally upright. Her grandmother would have approved if she had been alive and known about it—her grandmother had been a woman of virtue.

Besides, sexual intercourse was supposed to be painful at first, and she knew Duane wouldn't want to hurt her until it was absolutely necessary. There was a time and a place for everything, as her grandmother had always said.

The week before Christmas there was a big countywide dance held at the American Legion Hall, an annual affair that everybody looked forward to. About the only people that stayed away were the hardshell Baptists and a few of the smaller, eccentric denominations who, like the Baptists, believed that dancing was sinful. In the old days, before the church women of the town had organized, eggnog had been served at the dance, and the men who couldn't tolerate dilution brought their whiskey bottles inside and kept them in their coat pockets while they danced. But when the church women finally organized, they saw to it what drinking was done, was done outside.

This year Lester Marlow was one of the first people to arrive at the dance. He stood around the almost empty hall for an hour, practicing looking rakish and devil-may-care. Lester was temporarily a celebrity in Thalia by virtue of the fact that, only the night before, he had lost a record amount of money to Abilene in an all-night nine-ball game. He had come out the loser by some $820, winning only 11 of 181 games, but that fact did not dismay him at all. Instead he felt almost legendary for having lost so much, and as he strolled around the silent dance floor he continually adjusted the hang of his cashmere sports coat. He wanted to look like the sort of fellow who was ready to accept all risks. He had not bothered to bring a date, but had a plan involving Jacy that he meant to put into effect at the proper time.

Half an hour later, when Jacy drove up in her convertible, Lester was waiting at the curb, bourbon flask carelessly in hand.

"Why hi, Lester," Jacy said nervously. She knew Sonny and Duane would be coming along any minute.

"I hear you lost some money last night," she added. The sum *had* been impressive.

"Duane coming?" Lester asked at once. Jacy nodded. Any other time Lester would have taken the nod as final, but he had had enough whiskey to be able to set aside his normal caution.

"You know Bobby Sheen, in Wichita?" he asked. "He's going to have a midnight swimming party tonight in his indoor pool. A lot of kids from the club are going to be there. I guess you heard about the last one: his folks were gone to Miami and everybody swam naked. I was there and it was really something. I don't know what they'll do tonight, but his folks are gone again and it's probably going to be pretty wild. If you want to run over there with me after the dance, why don't you? Bobby has great parties."

Lester was smart enough to leave it at that. He rakishly took another sip of bourbon and went back into the dance. Just as he was walking away Sonny and Duane rattled up. They parked the pickup and immediately got in Jacy's car. Duane had noticed Lester talking to her and asked about it.

"Oh, he just wanted to tell me about losing all that money," Jacy said, a little on edge. She had been all primed to enjoy the dance, but Lester's invitation upset her timing a little and Duane came along before she could think things out.

In a few minutes Sonny got out of the car and went in the dance to see what Mr. and Mrs. Farrow were doing. They were on the sponsoring committee and Jacy felt she and Duane probably ought to go in separately unless her father was already drunk enough not to notice them.

While Sonny was reconnoitering Jacy made a quick decision: clearly she would have to go to the swimming party with Lester. It took a rich, fast crowd to go swimming naked, and Jacy always prided herself on belonging to the fastest crowd there was, moral or immoral. Indeed, for a rich, pretty girl like herself the most immoral thing imaginable would be to belong to a slow crowd. That would be wasting opportunities, and nothing was more immoral than waste.

Then too, when word got around that she had gone swimming naked with a lot of rich kids from Wichita Falls her legend would be secure for all time. No girl from Thalia had ever done anything like that.

It was clear that she had to go: the only problem was Duane. He had the night off and was expecting to devote it entirely to her—if she left him at eleven o'clock to go somewhere with Lester it would make him so mad he might even break up with her, and that was to be avoided. She quickly decided that her best bet would be to spend a couple of hours being extremely nice to him, so he would be too much in love with her to be mad when she left. If he was mad anyway she would have to blame it all on her mother—that always worked.

She turned to Duane and started to kiss him, but then stopped and looked at him fondly a moment. "I love you so much tonight," she said. "I wish we could stay together all night."

As soon as they settled into the kiss Jacy turned so that one of her breasts nudged Duane's hand. He was astonished, but not too astonished to take advantage of what was offered him. He pulled her brown sweater out of her skirt and slipped his hand beneath it. Her belly was warm but the brassiere was a cold barrier. It was frustrating to come up against the stiff, cold material when Jacy's warm breasts were just underneath. Duane had experienced that frustration many times before, but it was nothing Jacy usually cared to help him out with; anyway he could hardly expect her to undress right in front of the Legion Hall. Then Jacy broke the kiss with a soft sigh. "Wait a minute," she said. "I don't want to go in right now—let's get in the back seat a few minutes." As soon as they had she edged both her bra straps off her shoulders. Duane slipped the bra down a few inches and her breasts were free. She didn't seem to mind that the tight straps more or less imprisoned her arms. She kissed Duane lingeringly while he touched her breasts and nipples.

Sonny came out to report a minute or two later, meaning to tell the two that it was perfectly safe for them to come in together. Lois and Gene were at the other end of the hall, and both fairly tight besides. When he got to the car and saw what Jacy and Duane were doing, he hated to interrupt, but he wanted to let them know about Jacy's parents. Finally he rapped on the windshield a time or two and went hastily back inside.

Duane was annoyed that Sonny had even knocked. He was deliriously caressing Jacy's bosom, and gladly would have given up the dance for another hour with Jacy in her present mood. For her part, Jacy was quite ready to go in, though she was careful not to show it. The evening ahead would require delicate timing, and it would be unwise to allow Duane too many goodies right at the beginning. She straightened up and smiled at him, her arms still imprisoned by the bra straps.

"We better go in while we can," she said, turning so her back was toward him. "Would you put my bra back on? I can't manage it without taking off this sweater."

Her request was a perfect touch. She had never even used the word "bra" in Duane's presence before, and her willingness to let him put the garment on her added a quality of intimacy to the proceedings that more than compensated for the interruption. He reached under her sweater from behind and slipped the straps up over her slim shoulders—when her arms were free she raised them and let Duane put her breasts back in their cups. When he had the bra hooked he held her a moment, feeling very tender and protective.

A square dance was in progress as they entered the hall and Gene and Lois were dancing. All the men loved to square dance with Lois Farrow because if she was in a good mood she was tolerant of a little free-and-easy feeling around. She might be heavier at the waist than she had been once, but she was still a much prettier woman than most of the men saw at home, and they hovered around her.

During the course of the evening Jacy noticed that more people at the dance paid attention to her mother than to her—an annoying fact that she had never noticed before. Her mother was the belle of the ball, and she wasn't. She could tell by the men's faces that they found her mother very attractive, and the same men hardly noticed her at all. Lois was wearing a loose white dancing dress with a low neckline; her hair was combed out long and shook about her shoulders as she danced. Jacy noticed, too, that her mother was wearing some sort of very brief, fashionable bra. The men could see her breasts move as she danced. It wasn't that Lois' breasts were overly large or indecently exposed, exactly; it was just that they were shaped right and exposed just enough to excite the men in the hall. The more she saw the men watching her mother the more annoyed Jacy became. Not only were the respectable men like the bankers and the doctor watching her mother, but the unrespectables were, too: the farmers and oil-field hands and filling-station men. When her mother danced their faces lit up; when she danced they didn't even notice. It was very insulting. Jacy decided that the next day she would point out to her mother that highnecked dresses would be more becoming for a woman her age. She could say it had to do with facial structure and all that, but it might not work. Her mother knew a good bit about facial structure too.

Jacy was somewhat let down to discover that she had fewer admirers among the male community than she had supposed. A close count revealed that she had only two admirers who really counted: Lester and Duane. Sonny admired her extravagantly, but he had no money and had not been in the backfield, so he really just didn't count. Of course almost all the sweaty little sophomores admired her, but they counted even less than Sonny.

Since there was clearly nothing she could do about her mother, Jacy turned her attention back to the swimming party and guided Duane back to the farthest, darkest corner of the Legion Hall, where the couples most in love always danced. In that corner it was possible to dance very close, and an hour or so of really close dancing fitted in perfectly with Jacy's plan. She had known for a long time that boys had erections on dance floors, at least when they danced with her—apparently it was just one of the little commonplaces of life that pretty girls had to put up with. It had never occurred to her that such a phenomenon could be useful until she began laying plans to get away to the swimming party, when she concluded that the thing to do was make Duane simply delirious with love. If he were delirious, and convinced she was on the verge of giving herself to him, then he couldn't be too mad when she made ready to leave. The quickest way to convince him was by dancing as close as it was possible to dance; so grimly Jacy did it, pressing herself right against him. It was so creepy it almost set her teeth on edge, but the effect on Duane was very strong indeed.

"Let's sneak out to the car a minute," he said, his breath hot in her ear.

Jacy knew that wouldn't be sensible. Much better to hold out the promise of a brief trip to the car after she had his reaction to her leaving. Then if he just had to be pacified some way, she could let him put his hand inside her panties. After all, he *was* very sweet, and had given her a fifty-dollar wristwatch for Christmas.

"I'll go talk to Mother a minute," she said. "Maybe I can talk her into letting me stay out a little later tonight."

She left the dance floor and found her mother in the front foyer, but the circumstances were extremely surprising. Abilene had just come in the door and her mother was kissing him, right there in the Legion Hall. Not only was it a shock to Jacy, but even more of one to the short, pretty brunette Abilene had come in with. Lois was kissing him right on the mouth, and though he seemed a little flushed he was not trying to make her quit. Even when her mother broke the kiss she kept her hands locked around Abilene's neck.

"Merry Christmas," she said, glancing at the brunette, whom she had not noticed. The girl was angry, but she was shorter than Lois and much younger and didn't quite know what to do with her anger.

"Uh, this here's Jackie Lee French," Abilene said. "Jackie Lee, this is Lois Farrow, my boss's wife."

"Hello, Jackie," Lois said.

"I don't have to talk to her," Jackie Lee said, turning angrily to Abilene. "I think she's just awful. What do you mean kissin' her like that, I'm embarrassed to death. I ought to slap her face."

"You can't even reach it, honey," Lois said, smiling at her. "Is your name really French or is that just something you like to do?"

Jackie Lee was absolutely stunned. Her mouth fell open. Nobody had ever talked like that to her before—she was the star barmaid in the tavern where she worked, and all the cowboys and airmen treated her very much like a lady.

Abilene made an amused face and took Jackie Lee by the elbow. "I never come here to referee no fight," he said, moving toward the dance floor. Jackie Lee went with him, holding her butt in indignantly.

Lois snorted in amusement. "I know what I did wrong," she said. "You're supposed to have mistletoe." When she noticed Jacy she snorted again and went into the coatroom. She had a flask of bourbon in her coat pocket and took a neat nip, fishing in her purse for some Kleenex. The dancing had made her sweaty.

"My goodness, Mother," Jacy said, "you oughtn't to behave like that. What would Daddy say if he saw you?"

"Nothing," Lois replied. She took another nip and put the cap back on the flask. "He wouldn't say a damn thing and there's no reason he should. Kissing one another at Christmastime is a custom among civilized peoples. Besides, why are *you* lecturing *me?* What have you been doing back in that dark corner for the last hour, telling secrets?"

Jacy was taken aback. For a moment she couldn't think how to reply. "I was just coming to ask you something," she said finally. "Lester wants me to go with him to a swimming party in Wichita Falls. Is it okay if I go?"

"Sure," Lois said. "Have a good time. And let's you and me just leave one another alone so far as men are concerned, okay? We compete about enough things as it is."

After Lois went back to the dance floor Jacy decided her feelings were hurt and stayed in the coatroom, sniffling a little. It seemed to her her mother had no sense of responsibility at all, and it was very confusing. Then she grew angry, jerked the bourbon flask out of her mother's coat and took a tiny sip of whiskey in defiance. Like mother, like daughter, people would say if they saw her. She put the flask back and hurried in to Duane before the tears could dry on her cheeks. "Oh I'm just sick," she said. "Mother says I have to go to a swimming party with Lester. I can't get out of it now. It's all her fault and I could just kill her."

Ten minutes later she and Duane were in the front seat of the pickup, kissing. The pickup was parked in a darker place than the convertible. Duane had been furious and it had taken all Jacy's coaxing to get him out of the Legion Hall without some kind of scene taking place. Even when they got to the pickup he kept wanting to go back in and drag Lester out and fight him. Jacy quickly saw that she would have to go to desperate lengths to keep him with her. She sprawled across his lap, kissing him, and she didn't bother to cross her legs and trap his arms with her own, like she usually did. He could dimly make out her white, half-exposed legs in the dark cab. When he touched her lightly above the knee she didn't stop him. Wildly encouraged, he at once forgot Lester and leapt to the attack: he put his hand right on the warm slick band of silk that passed between her legs. She still didn't stop him! It was a miracle of generosity!

Jacy thought so too. She had never left herself quite so wide open before and she hoped Duane appreciated it. After a few nervous minutes of tracing his fingers delicately along the edges of her panties he got up enough nerve to slip his hand inside a leghole and touch the real place, which was surprisingly slippery. He had not really expected to arrive at that destination that evening and he was not quite sure what to do next. Jacy gave no clues. She quit kissing him and pressed her face tightly against his neck, not exactly sure if she liked what was happening or not. She was determined to go on with it a few minutes, though: it would never do to go to a naked swimming party in total ignorance of such matters. Once in a while Duane hit on the right spot and she couldn't help gasping and squirming a little, but most of the time he seemed to be fumbling around in a rather pointless way and that made her impatient. She went a little out of it for a few minutes, waiting for Duane to hit the right spot and quivering with pleasure when he did. It was not until he took his hand away and tried to lay her down on the seat that she realized she had pacified him quite enough. He was actually trying to get on top of her! It was terrible of him to try such a thing when her head wasn't completely clear—it was hard enough for her to finish the evening in the proper tone without him doing that.

"No, no, Duane, I've got to go," she said. "Lester will be coming any minute."

She struggled up, gave Duane a quick kiss to show she wasn't mad at him, and then got herself out of the pickup and into Lester's Oldsmobile. She wanted a minute or two to calm down before Lester came out—the dancing and the courting had left her wet with sweat, and she wasn't even sure but what she smelled.

To her great annoyance, Duane got out of the pickup, his hair all tousled, and stood right on the porch of the Legion Hall, obviously waiting for Lester. After all she had given him, it was infuriating! When Lester came out he bumped right into Duane and Duane grabbed him. They had words, that was clear, but Lester managed to shake loose and came on to the Olds. The sleeve of his sports coat was torn.

"What'd he say?" Jacy asked.

"God he's mad," Lester said, panting. He was visibly scared, but he did his best to make light of it. "He called me names, hoping I'd hit him."

"Oh, he's so silly," Jacy said. "I don't know what I'm going to do about him. He's just so crazy about me he doesn't have good sense."

"I'm not saying anything against Duane, but that's a roughneck for you," Lester said. "They never are very sophisticated about these things."

The farther he got from the scene the easier it was for Lester to believe he would have come out well in a fight with Duane. His emotions became mixed, and so did Jacy's. It occurred to her belatedly that it wouldn't have been so bad if Lester and Duane *had* fought over her. At the very least it would have taken a few people's minds off her mother.

They rode to Wichita in silence, each of them thinking out the kind of fight scene they wished had taken place. Lester imagined that he had fought to a standstill, contemptuous of pain, while Jacy saw it differently: Lester would win by dishonorable means, like kicking Duane in the groin, and she would weep on the sidelines. Then she would go and comfort Duane and drive away with him, contemptuous alike of money and parental displeasure, content to be ruined for love.

It seemed a pity to her that Lester hadn't had the guts to start the fight.

The Sheen home, where the party took place, was a two-story, twenty-room mansion near the Wichita Falls country club. When they drove up several sports cars were parked in the long curved drive.

"This may be the wildest thing yet," Lester said, smiling at Jacy a little nervously.

No one answered the doorbell, so they went on in. Lights were on and there were girls' coats and boys' coats and glasses and liquor bottles all around, but no people. A Dave Brubeck album was lying next to the phonograph.

Once they opened the basement area it was obvious from the yelling and splashing where everyone was.

"Yep, they're naked," Lester said when they arrived downstairs. He left Jacy in the ping-pong room a minute and peeked into the pool. She found the prospect of walking into a room full of naked city kids somewhat frightening, but she determined to do it and look delighted, whatever she might feel. She let Lester hold her hand when they walked in, and that was something she didn't permit very often.

At first it was not especially startling, because all the Wichita kids were in the water, having water fights and cutting up. You couldn't see what ordinarily you were not supposed to see. There were about six boys and six girls, most of them kids Jacy knew slightly from dances at the country club. One rather famous rich girl was there—her name was Annie-Annie and she was black-headed and notoriously wild. She was only seventeen and had been sleeping with boys for years. Her boy friend was Bobby Sheen, the kid whose parents owned the house. He was a very good-looking boy and had owned the first Ford Thunderbird in that part of the country.

"Hey, look," he yelled, when he saw Lester and Jacy. "New victims."

To Jacy's embarrassment all the kids immediately stopped their water fights and swam right over to the side of the pool where she and Lester were standing. Bobby Sheen made a big show of jumping out of the water and shaking Lester's hand, just as if he had been properly dressed.

"Hi, Jacy," he said, grinning and sluicing the water off his hair with one hand. "Glad you made it to the party. We're dressed informally, as you see."

That brought a big laugh from the kids in the pool, and Bobby cocked his leg in acknowledgment. Jacy laughed too, though a little thinly. She was trying not to look at Bobby's penis, or at anybody's penis.

Annie-Annie got out of the pool too and walked over to them. She was a tall, willowy girl, very graceful. Having her out of the water embarrassed Jacy almost as much as having Bobby out. Streams of water dripped off Annie-Annie's breasts and ran down her stomach into her black pubic hair. She didn't even bother to dry herself, and Jacy thought that most indecent. Letting drops of water shine in one's pubic hair was certainly not a ladylike thing to do.

"You two will have to join the club," Annie-Annie said. "We're the Senior Nudists, and we'll let you join if you want to."

"Sure," Lester said. "How much does it cost? I'll pay for both of us."

"Oh it doesn't cost money," Annie-Annie said, grinning and still dripping. "You just have to be initiated. You walk out on the diving board and take all your clothes off, while we watch. You all willing?"

"Sure," Lester said, not looking at Jacy. "We were just fixing to get undressed anyway."

When he asked Jacy if it was okay, she nodded. She didn't know what else to do. She certainly wasn't anxious to go out on the board and take her clothes off, but she couldn't very well stand around with them on while everybody else was naked.

"I'll go first," Lester said.

All the kids got out of the pool and sat on the edge, kicking their feet in the water. One little kid surprised Jacy no end. He was by far the youngest, littlest kid there; he had freckles and a burr haircut and looked about thirteen, and he had on a green diving mask. While they were all waiting for Lester to untie his shoes the kid walked right past Jacy to get a towel. What surprised Jacy was his penis, which stuck straight out. It wasn't very big or anything but it certainly was sticking out and Jacy thought it was just awful that he would walk around with it like that. A couple of the other girls giggled.

"That's my little brother Sandy," Bobby Sheen said. "Don't pay any attention to him—he's not in the club. He just likes to swim under water with his mask on and look at girls while he fiddles with himself. If he gooses you or anything tell me and I'll make him go to bed."

When Lester got out on the diving board, Jacy expected everybody to yell and whistle, but instead they just sat quietly on the side of the pool, watching. The room was so quiet that they could hear the gentle slap of water against the tile poolside. Lester had expected yelling too, and the silence unnerved him. He decided that speed was of the essence, and his disrobing was incredibly speedy. He peeled off his shirt, yanked down his pants and underwear at the same time, and in a second was in the water. Jacy was amazed at how quickly he did it. He swam over and pulled himself up on the side with the others, no longer the least embarrassed.

When Jacy saw how unselfconscious he had become she grew terribly annoyed with him for having gone first. If he had offered to let her be first, like a gentleman should have, she would be sitting calmly on the side and it would be over with. But everybody in the room was watching her and there was simply nothing to do but bluff it out.

"Goodness, I hope I don't fall off this thing," she said, when she got on the diving board. Diving boards always looked a lot higher up when you were on them.

"Sandy will fish you out if you do," Annie-Annie said.

Sure enough, that hideous little Sandy had slipped into the pool again and was swimming around like a frog about ten feet from the diving board. He had his mask on. Jacy decided she was with the most brazen bunch of kids she had ever seen, and she didn't like one of them.

She took her shoes off first, and then pulled her sweater off over her head. It was not as easy for her to undress fast as it had been for Lester. Once the sweater was off the question was whether she should take her skirt off first and then her bra and panties, or her bra off first and then her skirt and panties. She decided the skirt should come off first and she got out of it without looking up. It was embarrassing to have to reach back and unhook a bra in front of so many kids, but she had so much off already that she couldn't afford to dawdle. It seemed as though she had been out on the board about thirty minutes, as compared to five seconds for Lester. Once she got the bra off she started to yank her panties down and jump, but just as she bent over to slide them down Sandy frogged right under the board and peered up at her through his goggles. Jacy lost her balance and had to sit down very quickly to keep from falling in. At that all the kids burst out laughing and whistling and pointing at Sandy, who was becalmed just beneath her, his tiny little mast sticking up out of the water. It was plainly degrading. Angrily Jacy jerked the panties off her ankles and dropped them right on Sandy's mask.

Instantly the crowd became hers: they all began to laugh *at* Sandy, who frog kicked off toward the shallow end of the pool. Jacy let herself off the board and swam to the poolside to much acclaim—two boys helped her up on the side.

For an hour she swam and giggled, and the longer she stayed with them the more she came to like the crowd. They seemed like the wildest, most intelligent kids she had ever seen, and she determined then and there to throw in her lot with them. Before the night was over she could stand by the pool talking to some boy or other and feel perfectly at ease—the drops of water shining in her pubic hair soon ceased to disconcert her and began to seem rather becoming. At last she could even look at boys' penises without embarrassment.

Only one thing upset her: her new wristwatch, Duane's Christmas present. She had forgotten to take it off when she jumped into the pool. The kids all pooh-poohed her and told her not to worry so much about a fifty-dollar watch and she saw that they were right. It was just a wristwatch, and she could always make it up to Duane some other way.

10

JACY AND LESTER had not been gone from the dance ten minutes before word got around that they were going to a swimming party where everyone would be naked. The reason word got around so fast was that Lester told several of the younger kids about it just before he left. He told them he and Jacy were going to swim naked, just like everybody else. It was almost past belief, but when the kids saw him actually drive away with Jacy they instantly believed it and began to talk about it. Nothing wilder had ever been heard of in Thalia—it was even wilder than actually making out, because that was customarily done in the dark and nothing much could be seen.

In no time there were groups of excited boys standing around, speculating about the look of Jacy's breasts. They even had a hot argument over whether or not blond girls really had blond hair underneath their panties. Some of the younger, illiterate kids thought that all women had black hair in that particular place, but the better-read youths soon convinced them otherwise by reference to the panty-dropping scene in *I the Jury,* a book the local drugstore could never keep in stock.

The news about Lester and Jacy did not surprise Sonny much. He knew that any time Lester came to Thalia he was likely to end up taking Jacy somewhere, and since he had heard for years that Wichita kids were always having orgies it was only natural that sooner or later Lester would take Jacy to one. The worst thing about it was that it would depress Duane something fierce.

While he was waiting for Duane to get the news, Sonny wandered into the refreshment room. There had been a big table full of plates of cookies, with a huge bowl of punch for the kids and the grown-ups who didn't drink. All the punch was gone and the only cookies left were a few rubbery, inedible brownies. Empty paper cups were strewn all around and a lady in a black dress was bent over picking them up and putting them in a big wastebasket. It was Mrs. Popper. The school teachers' wives always fixed the refreshments for the Christmas dance, but somehow Sonny was surprised to bump into Mrs. Popper just then. Coach Popper never came to dances, and especially not to Saturday night dances. He would not have missed *Gunsmoke* for all the dances in Texas.

"Hello, Sonny," Mrs. Popper said. "Want to help me pick up these cups, since you're not dancing? I'm tired."

She looked tired, too—at least her face did. She was not wearing any makeup and had apparently just come down to do her part with the refreshments.

"Sure, be glad to," Sonny said, picking up a cup. The punch had been a sweet, grape mixture and the rims of the cups were sticky. Sonny gathered about twenty and went to drop them in the wastebasket.

"I guess you still haven't found a new girl friend, have you?" Mrs. Popper asked quietly. Sonny was very startled. He had forgotten she knew about his old girl friend.

"No ma'am, but I'm looking hard," he said.

"Are you?" Ruth said, even more quietly. "It seems to me that if you were really looking hard you might look at me."

Surprised, Sonny did look at her, and remembered that they had become a little fond of one another the afternoon he had driven her to the hospital. He remembered wishing they had kissed, and when he looked at her mouth he wished it again, a very strange wish to be having in the refreshment room of the Legion Hall, during the Christmas dance. But there was something fresh about Mrs. Popper's mouth, as if what was left of the softness and beauty she was said to have had as a girl still lingered there. Sonny was mute. Suddenly he wanted Mrs. Popper and he didn't have the slightest idea what to do about it. He was simply mute, and his silence filled Ruth with despair. She waited a moment, hoping he would say something; when he didn't she felt something slip out of line inside of her and she turned away, holding the wastebasket full of dirty cups. She was afraid she might cry. Sonny saw the look of sadness come in her face and realized he had to say something if he wanted anything to happen between them.

"I'll help you carry that out to the trash barrel," he said.

Then it was Ruth's turn to be mute—mute with relief. They went out the back door together and walked to the group of barrels at the edge of the alley. When they had dumped the cups into one of the barrels, Ruth hesitantly came close to Sonny and then came very close. Her cheek was warm against his throat, and he smelled the thin, clean smell of her perfume. For a minute they were too silent— Sonny looked over her head, beyond the town. Far across the pastures he saw the lights of an oil derrick, brighter than the cold winter stars. Suddenly Mrs. Popper lifted her head and they kissed. Their mouths didn't hit just right at first and she put her fingers gently on each side of his face and guided his mouth to hers. The touch of her cool fingers startled and excited him and he pulled her to him more tightly. Her breath was warm across his cheek. Near the end of the kiss she parted her lips and teeth for a moment and touched him once with her tongue. Then she took her mouth away and for several minutes pressed her lips lightly against his throat.

"You're not as scared as you were the first time I wanted to do this," she said.

It was true: Sonny didn't feel at all scared, though his legs were trembling just a little from excitement. He liked to feel Mrs. Popper's lips moving against his throat. This had been the first time in his life when kissing someone had been as pleasant as he imagined kissing should be. It was never that pleasant with Charlene.

"Maybe we're going to have something, after all," Ruth said. "Will you drive me to the hospital again next week, if I arrange for Herman to ask you?"

"You bet," Sonny said. "The sooner the better, as far as I'm concerned." He bent down to find her mouth and Ruth put her hands on his cheeks again. They kissed slowly and luxuriously. At first the kiss was as soft as the first one had been, but then Ruth discovered that Sonny had awakened and was thrusting at her, not so much with his mouth as with himself, wanting more of her. He kissed so hard her head was pushed back and when she opened her eyes for a moment she was looking straight up, toward the stars. Sonny tried to get even closer to her, pulling her against him with his arm. In years nothing had thrilled her so much or touched her so much as he did, simply by wanting her—the rush of her blood made her almost dizzy. She took his tongue into her mouth and touched it lightly for a second with her tongue and the edges of her teeth. Then she took her face away quickly, pressing it against his neck again.

"I'm going home now," she said. "This is no place to dawdle. Tuesday we'll do this more. I really want to do it more, don't you?"

"You bet," Sonny said, bending to kiss her neck. He didn't want to talk—what he wanted was more of the delicate, delicious sensations her mouth had given him. It seemed to him it might just be best if he said so.

"I want to kiss you one more time before you go home," he said.

"Goodness," Ruth said. "Okay." She lifted her hand and traced the edges of his lips with one finger before she kissed him. Again, when they kissed, he pressed against her with an insistence that thrilled Ruth: it was if he were trying to find her very center, her deepest place. While they were kissing, a car turned into the other end of the parking lot and the lights arced in their direction. It was simply some teenagers turning around, but it scared them and they broke apart immediately.

"In three days I'll see you," Ruth said, picking up the wastebasket.

Sonny felt it wouldn't do for him to follow her in, so he walked around the building and entered at the front door. When he came in Duane was standing by the coatroom, obviously furious. Leroy Malone and two or three other boys were standing there too.

"I guess you heard the news," Duane said. "My girl's gone swimming naked with Lester Marlow. That's about the damnedest thing I ever heard. It's enough to make a man go get drunk."

"I guess Mrs. Farrow forced her into it," Sonny said.

"Let's go get drunk," Leroy suggested. "I know where we can steal a couple of bottles of vodka—I saw a man put two in his car just a minute ago."

The suggestion had much appeal, and Sonny immediately seconded it. Getting drunk would be the only way to save Duane from a gloomy night, and besides he felt a good bit like getting drunk himself. Kissing Mrs. Popper had left him excited and confused.

Leroy swiped the vodka and the three of them drove to the poolhall, which generally stayed open until one or two o'clock on Saturday nights. A good many of the younger kids trailed up also, hoping to get a swallow or two of vodka.

They all bought Cokes and took them back to the john one at a time and spiked them. None of them were used to vodka and it was not long before it began to have an effect on their behavior, not to mention their pool shooting. They shot so badly that it took them thirty minutes to finish an eight-ball game.

"Boys, from the way you all are shootin' a feller would think you were drunk," Sam the Lion said innocently, breaking them all up.

Leroy Malone was very inventive when it came to pestering Billy, and when eight-ball began to get tiresome it occurred to him that it might be fun to get Billy drunk. He drew Sonny and Duane aside.

"Let's take Billy somewhere and get him drunk," he said. "Think how funny he'd be drunk."

The boys were not against it. Anything for mischief and adventure. They grabbed Billy and waltzed him outside. Several of the younger boys got wind of the plot and tagged along.

"We could go on down to the stockpens," Leroy suggested. "There's a blind heifer down there we could fuck. She belongs to my uncle. There's enough of us we could hold her down. It'd be as good a place as any to get Billy drunk."

The prospect of copulation with a blind heifer excited the younger boys almost to frenzy, but Duane and Sonny, being seniors, gave only tacit approval. They regarded such goings on without distaste, but were no longer as rabid about animals as they had been. Sensible youths, growing up in Thalia, soon learned to make do with what there was, and in the course of their adolescence both boys had frequently had recourse to bovine outlets. At that they were considered overfastidious by the farm youth of the area, who thought only dandies restricted themselves to cows and heifers. The farm kids did it with cows, mares, sheep, dogs, and whatever else they could catch. There were reports that a boy from Scotland did it with domesticated geese, but no one had ever actually witnessed it. It was common knowledge that the reason boys from the dairy farming communities were so reluctant to come out for football was because it put them home too late for the milking and caused them to miss regular connection with the milk cows.

Many of the town kids were also versatile and resourceful—the only difficulty was that they had access to a smaller and less varied animal population. Even so, one spindly sophomore whose father sold insurance had once been surprised in ecstatic union with a roan cocker spaniel, and a degraded youth from the north side of town got so desperate one day that he crawled into a neighbor's pig pen in broad daylight and did it with a sow.

"I say a blind heifer beats nothing," Leroy said, and no one actively disagreed with the sentiment. They all got in the pickup and headed for the stockpens, eight or nine of the younger boys shivering in the back.

The stockpens were a mile or two north of town, surrounded by mesquite. When they got there all the boys in the back piled out and went to locate the heifer, but Sonny and Duane stayed in the cab a minute and took a final drink of vodka to warm them up. They gave Billy a Coke that was about a third full of vodka and he drank it happily.

"We better slow him down," Duane said. "If he gets too drunk he may want a turn at the heifer. I doubt old Hank Malone would want an idiot screwin' his livestock."

Sonny got out, not saying anything. It bothered him when people called Billy an idiot. Billy didn't seem *that* much dumber than other people, and he was a lot friendlier than most.

When they got to the lots Leroy was sitting on the fence watching the younger kids chasing the scared, sightless heifer around the dark pen.

"They're after her," he said. "They'll get her in a minute."

The little heifer didn't weigh over three hundred pounds and in a few minutes the boys cornered her by the loading chute and wrestled her to the ground. She struggled for a while but finally gave it up and lay still. A freshman was sitting on her head and her frightened breath raised little puffs of dust from the sandy lot. Sonny, Duane, and Leroy got off the fence and went over to watch. Billy had climbed up on the fence, but he didn't know what was going on and just sat there sucking the empty Coke bottle.

"You boys are holding her wrong," Leroy said in a superior tone. "Ain't you ever fucked a heifer before? You little piss-ants must be virgins. Let her up on her knees."

The younger boys thought that was bitter news: the heifer had been trouble enough to get down. Leroy was a senior, however, and they respected his authority. When they let her up she almost got away, but there were nine of them and they managed to hang on and stop her.

It had come time to decide who went first, and the younger boys, nearing exhaustion just from holding the heifer, pressed for a decision. It would be one of the three seniors, of course.

"You all decide," one of them pleaded. "We can't hold her all night."

At that point Sonny surprised everyone, even himself, by suddenly withdrawing from the competition.

"You all help yourselves," he said hastily. "I drunk too much, I think I'm gonna have to puke."

It was the best excuse he could think of. When he agreed to come to the stockpens he supposed he would naturally be a participant, but the moment he saw the little blind heifer he knew he didn't want to. It had something to do with Mrs. Popper, though he was not certain just what. It didn't seem right to kiss Mrs. Popper and still fiddle around with heifers, blind or not blind. Not only did it not seem right: it no longer seemed like fun. Kissing Mrs. Popper even once was bound to be more fun than anything he could possibly do with the skinny, quivering little heifer. He suddenly felt like he had graduated, and it was an uneasy feeling. He knew Duane and the other boys would think it awfully strange of him not to take a turn, so to fool them he went off in the mesquites and pretended to be sick.

When he came back to the fence the orgy in the lot was in full progress. Duane was attacking the heifer, and Leroy, who had already finished, was helping hold. Two or three of the younger boys had their pants down and were parading lustfully around the lot. One sophomore was in something of a predicament because, by an unexpected stroke of luck, he had actually made out with a girl that night, a pig from Holliday who had come to the dance. As a consequence of that success the boy was feeling somewhat enervated and was attempting to restore himself by beating his member against a cold aluminum gate. When the freshmen started in on the heifer it was even more hilarious: many of them were too short to reach the target comfortably and had to struggle on tiptoe.

Then in the midst of it all the heifer finally broke loose and went dashing across the lot with one of the freshmen hanging furiously to her tail. Sonny was just as glad. Somehow it wasn't as exciting as it had been when he was a freshman.

"Look at ol' Billy takin' that in," Leroy said. "What we ought to do is buy him a piece. We could get the carhop for a dollar, if it was just Billy."

"Hell, if she's that cheap we ought to gone to her ourselves," Duane said. "I heard she was a five-dollar whore."

"Naw," Leroy said. "Anybody with five dollars can do better than Jimmie Sue. That heifer's got prettier legs than she has. She'd be okay for Billy, though. I've heard that idiots die when they're fifteen or sixteen—we oughtn't to sit around and let Billy die a virgin."

"I don't know if we ought to try anything like that," Sonny said. "What if it upset Billy and Sam the Lion found out about it? I'd just as soon not get crosswise with Sam."

"Aw don't be a chickenshit, Crawford," Leroy said. "It might do Billy good to get a little."

"Not if he gets it from Jimmie Sue it wouldn't," Sonny said, very ill at ease.

"You don't have to chip in if you're so stingy," Duane said. "Let's go on and get her."

Sonny quit arguing—he really didn't know how to argue against a whole crowd. He never had even wanted to before. They piled back in the pickup and he drove to the back entrance of the town's one little hotel. Leroy and Duane went up to make arrangements with Jimmie Sue Jones, the available girl, and Sonny sat in the cab with Billy, who was still sucking on the empty Coke bottle. It was almost the first time in Sonny's life that he had not been willing to go on and do whatever the crowd was doing. Before, it had always seemed like fun, whether it was getting drunk or screwing heifers, but he didn't think it would be any fun at all to make Billy do it with Jimmie Sue. Billy was in a perfectly peaceful mood, sucking on the bottle and glad to be along with all the boys, and it seemed a pity to disturb him.

In a minute the boys came out with Jimmie Sue, who was a sort of drive-in version of Penny, only dirtier. She had been car-hopping in Thalia for nine years and everyone in town was tired of her. She had been married once, to a mechanic with rat-tail sideburns, but he soon left her and went back to Bossier City, Louisiana, where he came from. The drive-in paid Jimmie Sue next to nothing and she seldom got tips, so she had to peddle herself when she could to make ends meet. She dyed her hair red and had no eyebrows except those she painted on in the morning, and she was so absentminded that sometimes she only painted on one eyebrow and went around like that all day. For Billy she didn't bother to paint on even one. When she got in the cab it immediately began to smell so oniony that Sonny had to roll his windows down. Jimmie Sue looked at Billy disgustedly.

"Why that thing's just a kid," she said. "You all oughtn't to woke me up for a thing like that. I ought to get at least two dollars."

"Hell no, you said a dollar and a half," Duane reminded her.

"Well, I'd just as soon it was an idiot as not," Jimmie Sue said, unpeeling a stick of chewing gum. "The only thing I draw the line at is Mixicans and niggers. I guess I told you about the time that nigger man in high heels stole my suitcase right out of the bus station, that time I went to Los Angeles. . . ."

It had been Jimmie Sue's one adventure. She saved her money and went to Los Angeles to work, but the very hour she arrived in the Los Angeles bus station a black man wearing high heels stole her suitcase and all her possessions. Jimmie Sue had never been so disappointed in all her life as she was with Los Angeles. She couldn't get a job and had to turn around and hitchhike back to Thalia, to keep from starving. Hitchhiking across the desert without any eyebrows proved a slow business, too. If it hadn't been for a carful of horny Mexicans she never would have got out of Needles, California, and bad as that was, Lordsburg, New Mexico, was worse. Tired of eating dust, she let a Negro pick her up. By the time she got back to Thalia she had nothing good to say about minority groups.

Billy looked at her with mild curiosity, but was obviously neither disturbed nor excited by her presence in the cab. Sonny drove back over the narrow, one-vehicle road that cut through the mesquite to the stockpens.

"You all just get that thing out while I get ready," Jimmie Sue said. "This ain't the ideal dressin' room."

Billy was happy to get out: he wondered if they were going to sit on the fence and watch the boys chase the cow again. To his surprise, no sooner was he out than six or seven of the boys grabbed him and unceremoniously threw him down on the cold hard ground. They took off his shoes, pants, and underwear. Groups of boys were always taking his pants off, and that alone wouldn't have bothered him. It was having them off so late at night and at the stockpens that puzzled him. Also his legs were cold.

"All right," Jimmie Sue said. "Let the stupid little thing in."

"Wait a minute," Duane said. "There's a flashlight there in the glove compartment. We want to show him where to go."

He got the flashlight and flashed it over Jimmie Sue, who was laying back in the pickup seat, as spraddle-legged as the narrow pickup would permit her to be. All the boys looked, and for a moment, paused in amazement. None of them had realized quite how fat Jimmy Sue was until the flashlight played over her huge hams and flabby stomach; nor had they considered how unappetizing the female anatomy could be when presented in its most unappealing light. They were all quiet for a moment, staring. It was only after they had looked for a while that they began to feel a little stirred up. Jimmie Sue was so ugly it was almost exciting—it was as if they were finally being shown the nasty things parents and preachers had always whispered about. It wasn't exactly what they had expected, because they persisted in thinking about it in terms of pretty girls, movie stars like Elizabeth Taylor, but it was precisely what they had been taught to expect, and after the shock wore off it was exciting.

"Shove that thing in here with me," Jimmie Sue said. "I never hired out for no peep show."

The boys shoved Billy in, more or less between Jimmie Sue's legs, and tried to shut the door. They couldn't get it completely shut but there were so many of them there was not much chance it would come open.

Billy grunted with surprise and tried to back out, but he was trapped.

"Why this is the dumbest thing I ever saw," Jimmie Sue said. "It don't even know what to do."

The boys flashed the light long enough to see that Jimmie Sue had managed to catch Billy with her legs, but she yelled at them to turn it off and they did. Apparently Billy got close enough to the object of it all that he caught on, because he stopped pushing backward and in a moment the pickup began to rock a little from side to side. Everybody yelled encouragement.

"Quit that yellin' and get hold of this thing," Jimmie Sue said irritably. "He ain't in."

The flashlight was brought into play again and it was discovered that Billy, cramped as he was, had completely missed his natural target and was poking energetically at a deep wrinkle in the folds of Jimmie Sue's stomach. Duane and Leroy laughed until they could barely stand up, but the younger kids were more fascinated than amused. None of them had ever seen so strange a sight, and they made no effort to correct Billy's aim. Jimmie Sue was getting madder by the minute.

Sonny stood by the rear end of the pickup, determined not to look. It wasn't that he thought Billy would mind him looking—it was just that he didn't really want to look. Jimmie Sue was uglier than Charlene, and the pickup would smell like onions for weeks.

"Why goddamn you, you little thing!" Jimmie Sue yelled furiously. "Now look what a mess you made!"

Sonny knew from the tone of her voice that it was time to get Billy out, so he hurried around to the door. The boys still had the flashlight on and were cackling and giggling: Billy had reached the end of his journey while still in the wrinkle, and Jimmie Sue was pounding at his face, trying to back him out of the pickup. Sonny managed to scatter the crowd enough to get the door open and help Billy out, but calming him down was something else. He was scared and confused and shivering, and Jimmie Sue had bloodied his nose. Sonny helped him get dressed and even found the empty Coke bottle for him, but Billy no longer wanted it.

"Well, now I know idiots is just as bad as Mixicans," Jimmie Sue said. "Don't you wake me up for that crazy thing no more. I wouldn't mess with him again for less than three-and-a-half."

By the time they got back to the poolhall the front of Billy's shirt was all covered with blood. Sonny couldn't get the nosebleed completely stopped. He knew Sam the Lion was going to be furious, and he didn't blame him: it was no way to treat Billy. He wished he had known how to stop the whole business, but the only possible way would have been to offer to fight if they didn't let Billy alone, and he couldn't very well offer to fight when his own best buddy was one of the crowd. If Lester and Jacy hadn't run off to the swimming party none of it would have ever happened.

As soon as the pickup stopped Billy jumped out and ran in the poolhall. It was officially closed, but they could all see Sam the Lion inside, reading a newspaper he had spread out on one of the tables. All he was really doing was waiting for Billy to come in. They lived in a plain little three-room apartment above the poolhall, and Sam never went to bed until Billy was in safe.

Billy ran right on past him, up the stairs, and Sam left his paper and followed him. The boys waited nervously outside, wondering if they would be able to narrate the episode in such a way that Sam the Lion would see the humor in it. Sonny knew they couldn't and waited miserably for Sam to come down, but the boys who thought they might strutted around on the sidewalk talking with great bravado. Duane was sleepy and lay down in the cab of the pickup and went to sleep. The boys could have left, but none of them really wanted to go home until Sam the Lion came down and bawled them out. His bawling them out would relieve their minds of whatever minor guilt feelings they had about Billy, and would leave them free to enjoy the celebrity of having participated in such an event.

Finally the light went out in the upstairs apartment and Sam the Lion came down. He opened the door and stood quietly a minute, looking at the boys. Sam the Lion was not the type who yelled and cussed about the pranks boys pulled. They could not see his face, but the light from the poolhall touched his white mane of hair.

"Who's got his underwear?" he asked, after a minute.

Sonny had them, and it put him on a terrible spot. He had been so anxious to get Billy back in his pants that he had forgotten to put the underwear on him—he picked them up later and stuffed them in his pocket. For a moment he was tempted to say nothing and pretend the underwear was lost—if he pulled them out and handed them over it would make him seem more of a participant than he had been. Sam didn't withdraw the question and the other boys began to look at Sonny nervously, so he took the underwear out of his pocket and awkwardly handed them over.

"When I was helpin' get his pants on I couldn't find them," he said. "I just forgot to hand them to him."

"Who went and bloodied his nose?"

"Jimmie Sue Jones," Leroy said. "We thought he was getting tired of being a virgin so we chipped in and bought him a piece. Jimmie Sue got mad about somethin' and gave him that nosebleed."

"Jimmie Sue?" Sam said, startled. "You what?" He had supposed it was just a simple case of the boys taking Billy's pants off, something that happened all the time. When he realized what Leroy said he was stunned, and sat down in the doorway of the poolhall.

Sonny became really worried. "Is Billy all right?" he asked. "We're sorry, Sam."

"He went to sleep," Sam said, a little absently. "Did he want to go with Jimmie Sue?"

"Not hardly," Leroy said. "He didn't even know what he was supposed to do."

Sam scratched his ankles for a minute and then stood up again. He didn't look particularly mad, just tired and discouraged.

"Boys, get on home," he said. "I'm done with all of you. I don't want to associate with you anymore and I don't want Billy to, either. Scaring an unfortunate creature like Billy when there ain't no reason to scare him is just plain trashy behavior. I've seen a lifetime of it and I'm tired of putting up with it. You can just stay out of this poolhall and out of my picture show and café too."

With that he closed and locked the door and went upstairs to bed. The boys were thunderstruck. They had been prepared for Sam to rage and storm and instead he had simply closed the door and locked them out. No one knew what to say. They stood on the cold sidewalk a minute, confused.

"We're his best customers," Leroy said. "He can't run us off, can he?"

Sonny and the other boys knew very well he could. It made Sonny feel a little sick. They all crawled back into the pickup and Sonny delivered them to their homes. Duane didn't fully wake up until they were back at the rooming house, and when Sonny told him what Sam the Lion had done he thought it was hilariously funny. Since he had been lying down and Sam had not seen him it was clear to Duane that he was not included in the banishment.

"Good thing I went to sleep when I did," he said. "I'd hate to have to eat at that drive-in all the time."

He went in and contentedly went back to sleep, but Sonny stayed awake and reread most of an old copy of *Outdoor Life*. Duane taking the news the way he had made the evening even more depressing, and it had been depressing enough as it was.

Kissing Mrs. Popper had been the only good thing that happened all night, and Sonny had no idea what would come of that. It occurred to him that at least it would be something exciting to think about in bed, so he turned the light off and tried it. Her face and the touch of her lips were fresh in his mind and it worked pretty well, though occasionally, before he finished, a few old images of Jacy and Genevieve slipped in. Jacking off was an old game, monotonous, but a good way to get to sleep when all else failed.

11

WHEN SONNY KISSED Mrs. Popper outside the Legion Hall it seemed to him that a whole spectrum of delicious experience lay suddenly within his grasp. No kisses had ever been so exciting and so full of promise, neither for him nor for Ruth. She felt as if she were finally about to discover something she had somehow missed discovering twenty years before. Neither of them foresaw any great difficulties, just the minor difficulty of keeping it all secret.

Both, in fact, were so excited that they longed to talk about it to someone, but that they couldn't do. In Thalia sex was just not talked about. Even Genevieve would go to considerable lengths to keep from calling a spade a spade. Everything acknowledged the existence of sex: babies were born now and then, and things to prevent them were sold at the drugstores and one or two of the filling stations. The men told dirty jokes and talked all the time about how they wished they had more pussy, but didn't really seem to bother many of them so long as the football team was doing well. The kids were told as little about sex as possible and spent most of their time trying to find out more. The boys speculated a lot among themselves and got the nature of the basic act straight when they were fairly young, but some of the girls were still in the dark about it when they graduated from high school. Many girls simply refused to believe that the things the boys peed out of could have any part in the creation of babies. They knew good and well that God wouldn't have wanted any arrangement of His to be *that* nasty.

The only thing everyone agreed on was that the act itself could only be earthly bliss. Once the obstacle of virginity was done away with, mutual ecstasy would be the invariable result. One or two of the bolder girls knew differently, but they didn't want to be thought freaks so they kept quiet about their difficulties.

When Sonny and Ruth met again, the Tuesday after the dance, they both expected things to be simple and wonderful, and they were both disappointed. For one thing, they both felt compelled to go through with the unnecessary trip to the doctor; both of them were nervous and tense and they rode to Olney in silence. The dusty air had given Ruth a sniffle, and Sonny could see the bluish shadows under her eyes. The wait in Olney was short, but on the way back they found themselves even more at a loss for conversation than they had been coming. Ruth could not imagine what had possessed her to think she could bring off such a thing as a love affair. They each concluded that they were not as appealing in the daylight as they had been in the dark, so they sat looking out their separate windows at their separate sides of the road. There was little in the leafless winter landscape to cheer them.

It was only when Sonny drove the Chevrolet into the dimness of the garage, with Herman's lawn tools and hedge shears hanging neatly on the walls, that they regained some hope. They both realized they were about to miss the chance they had been counting on. Sonny reached for Ruth's hand and she quickly scooted over toward him and they kissed. The kiss was awkward but warm and they didn't think of moving apart—for several minutes they let their mouths and faces touch.

Both would have been just as happy to stay in the garage all afternoon, but they felt obligated to complete the experience, and for that they had to go in the house, where things were not so good. The wallpaper in the bedroom was light green, and blotched in places. It was the bedroom where Ruth and Herman had spent virtually all their married nights: on one wall there was a plaque Herman had been given for taking a troop of Boy Scouts to the National Jubilee. Two or three copies of *High School Athletics* lay on the bedside table.

"Are you sure he won't come?" Sonny asked. The room seemed full of the coach.

"You know he won't," Ruth said. "He's just starting basketball practice."

She took his hand again and they kissed standing up. Neither of them really believed what she said: as they kissed both of them kept imagining the coach walking in. They were so conscious of him they hardly felt the kiss, but Ruth was determined to go on however dangerous it was, even if Herman did walk in.

They were unable to think of a smooth way to undress—it would have been better to do it while they were still kissing, but neither of them was expert enough for that. Ruth had on a dress and a slip, both of which had to come off over her head. Sonny could not even get her bra unhooked with the dress still on. Both of them wished for something to say, something that would break the tension, but neither could think of anything. Finally they simply broke apart and hurried about their own undressing. Ruth got her dress off, but when she bent to pull the slip over her head one of the straps caught on a bobby pin—for an awkward moment she could not get the slip loose. Her face was hidden in the silk. Sonny moved to help her, but just as he did she tore it loose and looked up at him with a wry smile, as if to comment on her awkwardness. They took their undergarments off at the same time, both of them choked with embarrassment. Ruth glanced at Sonny's body, curious and a little frightened. He was two or three steps away from her and for a moment they did not know how to get to one another. Sonny was too self-conscious about his erection to move. Finally, with another wry smile, Ruth sat down on the bed and he sat down with her. When she lifted her arms to embrace him he saw the small scar on her breast. They fell over in an embrace but in a moment scrambled up again: the room was cold and they needed to be under the covers.

When they were covered and warm they felt better and kissed again with pleasure. They were amazed at the feel of one another's skin, but in a minute or two they began to be nervous again. It seemed to them they must have been lying there kissing for half an hour at least. Ruth touched her hand to Sonny's throat and chest now and then, but other than that she didn't move. He felt very unsure: it occurred to him that perhaps his experience was inadequate. There might be some way of doing it that was especially suitable to ladies, some way he knew nothing about.

Ruth had her eyes closed and was waiting trustfully for a beautiful thing to happen to her. She knew that Herman knew nothing about the beautiful thing, or that if he did he had no interest in giving it to her. But she supposed Sonny would know: she would only have to wait and receive it. His body was very warm against her. It was only when she opened her eyes and looked at him that she remembered how young he was and realized he didn't know what to do.

"It's all right," she said, opening her legs. Sonny gratefully moved about her, but there was another long moment of awkwardness when they tried to join. Sonny was not absolutely sure of the target, and when he found it Ruth could not at first accommodate him easily. When he moved she gasped and Sonny's face was so close to hers that he could not tell whether she felt pain or pleasure. She said nothing, so he kept moving—in a moment it became easier and pleasure made him move faster and more surely.

For Ruth the discomfort was only momentary, but even once it ceased she could not manage to cross over into pleasure. The bed had begun to squeak. As Sonny moved more confidently it squeaked louder, and Ruth could not help hearing it. She would never have imagined it could squeak so loudly. Soon the squeaking drove all hope of pleasure from her mind. The noise made her fearful that someone outside the house might hear it; anyone walking on the sidewalk in front of the house could hear it, she was sure.

In a few moments she was near panic: she was convinced that everyone in Thalia could hear the squeaking bedsprings. If all the cars stopped, if the housewives came to their doors and listened, they could all hear the squeaking bed and would know what she was doing. It was a horrible bed; she felt it had betrayed her. No one could receive a beautiful thing with such a squeaking going on beneath her. She tried to lie very still, but Sonny's movement went on, and the sound was constant. Finally she began to cry, and when the tears dripped down her cheeks and wet Sonny's neck he realized that something was wrong after all. He raised his head and saw that Ruth's eyes were flooded with tears. She was ashamed that she had stopped him and quickly hooked her arm over his neck so he wouldn't raise up and see her face again. Sonny felt she must want him to stop but his body didn't want to and in a moment he went on, hearing the springs only as a faint background to his pleasure. Soon he finished and lay still upon her.

As soon as the squeaking stopped Ruth felt better. She kept her arms around Sonny, holding him so he could not see her face and now and then wiping the tears out of her eyes with the back of one hand. Once Sonny became still it was very pleasant to have his body upon hers—he was so warm and young, almost like a child. She had always wanted a child more than anything, but Herman wouldn't hear of it—he didn't want the expense. On the rare occasions when he took his pleasure of her he was always careful to wear a condom, even though they made Ruth's bladder hurt. Having Sonny upon her was very different, and deeply pleasant. She ran her hands up and down his back, and when she felt composed again lifted her arms so he could raise his head.

"I'm sorry I cried," she said. "I guess I was just scared."

"Aw, he isn't going to come," Sonny said, no longer worried. "They're runnin' plays right now, I bet."

"No, not scared of that," Ruth said, touching his mouth softly with her fingers. "I was scared I could never do this, I guess. I wanted to be wholehearted about it, but I wasn't."

She was silent a moment. "Do you know what it means to be heartbroken?" she said. "It means your heart isn't whole, so you can't really do anything wholeheartedly."

Sonny wanted to leave, but he didn't think he should, quite so soon. Mrs. Popper was sad, but at least she seemed calm and she kept touching him softly with her hands. He kissed her lightly and her cheeks were warm; then he stretched and drew the covers back a little, so he could see more of her body. She was very slim and smallbreasted, her arms a little too thin. When Ruth saw he was looking at her she grew frightened. She had never considered her body attractive, and she was afraid that if Sonny looked too long he would not want to be with her anymore. She turned on her side and curled toward him, her head on his thighs. Her shoulder bones stuck out, making her look even thinner. Sonny rubbed her back a minute and then got out of bed and quietly dressed. When he sat down on the edge of the bed to tell her good-bye she was on the verge of tears again.

"I was right the first time, wasn't I?" she said hopelessly. "I'm too old and ugly for a young man like you. I don't know how to do this anyway and maybe I'm too old to learn. I can't do anything without crying about it—how could you like me?"

"I like you," Sonny said awkwardly—actually he was not sure. All her crying upset him and made him nervous about himself, and she was certainly not as pretty as a movie star or as pretty as Jacy. Still, he did like her some. Since they hadn't got caught he had begun to feel elated about the whole thing. It was an adventure to have slept with somebody's wife. He didn't know if he would tell anybody or not, but it was sort of a feather in his cap, nonetheless.

Ruth sighed. "If you like me then you decide what to do about me," she said. "I'm not going to chase after you anymore. If you really like me you figure out how to come and see me—I sure don't want you to drive me to the doctor. I think right now you just like what you can do with me. That's fine, but now that you've found out women think you're good looking you'll probably want to go do it with somebody younger and prettier. I wouldn't blame you one bit."

Suddenly she wanted him to leave. She had become embarrassed about her body and didn't want him to see her naked anymore. She stayed curled up on the bed, her breasts and loins hidden from him.

"Track starts pretty soon," Sonny said. "I just won't go out. I can sneak up the alley and in the back door."

He sounded like he really wanted to, and Ruth changed back to hoping. What if he did only want her for sex? It was more than anyone else had ever wanted her for. Suddenly she felt like doing something a little wanton and she sat up and kissed him, her naked breasts against his shirt. Sonny liked that, and when he left he looked back through the doorway and saw her, still naked, bending over the bed to strip away the sheets. It would be well worth giving up track to come and see her, even though the coach would rage and storm at losing his only decent hurdler.

====

The second time Sonny came, Ruth wanted to tell him that the squeaking bedsprings bothered her, but she didn't quite have the nerve. She really wanted them to lie down on the floor, but she was afraid if she told Sonny he would think her depraved or something. She knew men were curious when it came to women's desires. Nothing revolted Herman more than to think that she was enjoying him that way. Once or twice in their marriage she had felt something good, but when she began to move or wiggle beneath him to make it feel even better it made Herman furious. "Lay still," he said. "What kind of woman do you think you are, anyway?" After that she lay still, and if she happened to feel something a little good she didn't let him know. Herman was so heavy that most of the time she just felt mashed.

She had not really expected Sonny to come again; when he slipped inside the back door she was filled with delight, and determined not to make any mistakes that might scare him away. They were both still very nervous, and the bedsprings bothered Ruth even more than they had the first time. They were almost too much. She felt something a little good but the springs kept her from concentrating on it; every time she felt it the grinding of the springs drove it away, and finally she simply endured them, waiting for the quiet lovely time when he was still, dozing on her body.

Sonny knew something was wrong because Ruth's body was cold and her arms and legs were tensed—she was trying to hold herself in such a way that the springs would be silent. She managed not to cry, but it took a long time for the tension to drain out of her—she was so tense that even the aftermath was not so enjoyable. Neither of them spoke—they simply had no words. Ruth was not sure she wanted him to come anymore; it was not working out at all like she had imagined. But when she felt a little better she began to stroke his back and to play with the shaggy hair at the back of his neck, and she decided she did want him again. Something about it was good, even if much was bad.

═══

On his third visit she gathered up her nerve and told him, as they were undressing, that the noise of the bedsprings bothered her. She asked if they could lie on a quilt on the floor. Sonny was mildly surprised, but it was okay with him. When Ruth saw that he didn't think it was wrong of her to want it all to be nice she was so relieved she couldn't speak. She walked to the hall closet, naked, and got an old blue quilt that she and Herman had quit using years ago.

They spread the quilt on the floor by the little gas stove and sat a moment watching the flicker of the blue gas flames as they touched one another. They still couldn't talk, but they had ceased to be nervous, and they quit trying to conceal their loins from one another. For Ruth the quiet was wonderful. All she could hear was Sonny's breath and her own and she knew no one in the street could hear them breathing. She realized too that Sonny was enjoying her keenly and that made her glad. He was in no hurry and Ruth had moments of pleasure that were stronger than any she had ever known before. She discovered that Sonny didn't mind at all if she moved: in fact, he liked it. She became excited enough that her breath was ragged, but it was all still new to her and she could not pull the moments of pleasure together into one that was complete. For her the beautiful time was still afterward. Sonny was still inside her when he went to sleep, and Ruth found that lovely. It was almost as if he were a child inside her, and she put her calves over his legs to keep him there. When he finally came out she slipped upward on the quilt so that his warm cheek was against one of her breasts. It was so lovely that she wanted it not to change. That day, for the first time, she was regretful when he had to leave.

═══

By the time Sonny had paid her a half-dozen visits he was everything to Ruth: he was what made the days worth confronting. The thought that he might quit coming filled her with terror. The thought of going back to the existence she had had before he came was too much to face.

Sonny allowed her to love him, though it was strange to him and he had to get used to it slowly. They were soon able to spend four or five hours a week on the old blue quilt. Ruth learned a great deal about Sonny and also a great deal about herself. After the first weeks she did nothing that would frighten him. She learned that he liked to be naked around her—it gave him a sense of adventure. She gladly let him, often mending his shirts or patching his pants after they had made love. She discovered that she had no particular modesty about her loins, only about her breasts, which seemed to her too small. Also she was afraid the small scar might disgust Sonny, since apparently it disgusted Herman. She took to wearing one of Herman's old hunting shirts while they talked. Sonny didn't like for her to wear anything while they were making love, but she always put it on afterward. She learned gradually how to play with him and how to tease him. One day she got a brush and comb and showed him a way to comb his hair that she felt was more becoming. Sonny was delighted. She would have liked to cut his hair for him, but there wouldn't have been time.

She soon made terms with lovemaking itself, though for a time they were not the best possible terms. She thought that once they relaxed with one another the beautiful thing would happen, the whole moment toward which all the sharp little individual moments tended. She had read about it, she expected it, she longed for it, and came very close to it, but it eluded her. For a week or two she was sure, every time, that it would happen. Once or twice she came so close that she was desperate for it to happen, and when she missed it after all her agitation was very intense. The violence of her excitement surprised Sonny and disturbed him a little: despite her weeping spells he thought of her as a quiet, rather timid woman. Her movements were sometimes so strong and unexpected that he was thrown off balance—once when she missed she was beside herself with disappointment. "Oh please," she said. "Please keep going." Sonny was already gone, but she continued to struggle against him until they were both soaked with sweat; he could not call himself back, and she gave up.

After that Sonny didn't come back for three days and Ruth was fearful she had ruined it all. When he did come she was so thrilled and relieved that she resolved not to seek the moment if it was going to put everything else in danger. If he would keep coming, keep wanting her, that would be enough. They sat on the blue quilt and she opened his shirt and rubbed his chest with her palm. When she looked past him, at the green wallpaper and Sears and Roebuck furniture she realized that she had lived for years in a room that was terribly drab.

Sonny was hesitant about making love, worried that he could cause Ruth disappointment again. "No, look," she said, taking his hand and kissing his palms and fingers. "Nothing was your fault. You have to remember that I've been lonely for a long time. Loneliness is like ice. After you've been lonely long enough you don't even realize you're cold, but you are. It's like I was a refrigerator that had never been defrosted at all—never. All these years the ice has just been getting thicker. You can't melt all that ice in a few days, I don't care how good a man you are. I didn't even realize it, like I didn't realize till just now how ugly this room is. I don't know, maybe at the center of me there's some ice that never will melt, maybe it's just been there too long. But you mustn't worry. You didn't put it there." She moved her hand up to his shoulders.

The talk of ice and refrigerators meant little to Sonny, but he was relieved that she wanted him to make love to her again. That day she was very warm and amenable, but much calmer—calmer than he had ever known her. He recognized that in a way she had withdrawn from the struggle, but his own pleasure was so strong that he merely felt grateful, not responsible. She saw to it that he didn't feel responsible, and for herself, had no difficulties except at the very end—then, for a wistful, regretful moment, she felt like crying.

=====

After that, for more than a month, she concentrated on making Sonny welcome. He came often, sometimes just to make love, sometimes staying to drink some hot chocolate or to let her mend his clothes. He tolerated the chocolate and the clothes mending, but Ruth knew very well that what they did on the quilt was what he really liked, what he enjoyed doing with her. It thrilled her that that, of all things, would be what made a person want to come and see her. She expected, almost from day to day, that he would tire of her, and when she saw him coming in the door wanting that same thing of her, she was always happy for a moment.

=====

Then, in March, things changed. Sonny came in one day and repeated a story about Coach Popper, one he had just heard. The week before the coach had taken the track boys to a meet in Fort Worth. Bobby Logan was sharing a room with the coach and in the middle of the night the coach mistook Bobby for Mrs. Popper and kissed him on the ear. All the boys thought that was pretty hilarious, and Sonny repeated the story to Ruth because he thought it might get her to talking about the coach a little. He could not help being curious about their life together. She told him that the coach seldom touched her, but Sonny could hardly believe that. The coach was so hairy and horny looking that the boys all supposed he kept after her all the time. Around the gym and the practice field the coach gave the impression that he was an inveterate woman chaser. "Find 'em, fool 'em, fuck 'em, and forget 'em," he was often heard to say. Sonny had the nagging feeling that the reason Ruth couldn't come with him was because the coach's tool was bigger and better. Time and again the coach had pointed out to one boy or another the ignominy of having an insufficient tool.

"Why hell yes, Joe Bob," he would say. "A feller can get along with false teeth and a glass eye and hearing aids and even a hook or a wooden leg if he has to, but there ain't no known substitute for a big dick. I guess you're just out of luck."

When he told Ruth about the ear-kissing incident he half expected her to be flattered that her husband would miss her so, but instead she looked miserable and forlorn. They had already finished lovemaking and she was so dispirited by the news that she neglected even to cover herself with the flannel shirt.

"I don't care," she said, tears seeping out of her eyes. "I don't care who he likes. If he wants to play around with little boys and they think it's funny why should I care? I just get tired of everybody thinking he's such a mighty man just because he coaches football. I'm the one they think is nothing, just his mousy wife, and they're right, I am mousy. I might not have been if I hadn't been ignored for twenty years. Now I'm forty and I don't have any children and I can't even do . . ." She sniffed. "I can't even do sex."

Sonny was stunned. He had never been so surprised.

"Why did you stay with him?" he asked finally. Then it was Ruth who was dumb. It was a question she had avoided for years.

"I wasn't brought up to leave a husband," she said in a small voice. "I guess that's why. Or maybe I was just scared to."

"But how did you come to marry him?" Sonny asked, still curious.

"Because my mother didn't like him, I guess," Ruth said. "I was fooled too. I was twenty years old and I thought hairy-chested football coaches were about it. I've paid for my own bad judgment."

There the conversation stalled—Ruth was too depressed to talk, and Sonny was confused. It seemed to him that Ruth must think the coach was queer or something, and the coach was the last man that anyone would accuse of such a thing. A few of the boys thought Mr. Cecil must be—they knew he got some kind of a kick out of watching them all swimming and horsing around naked at the irrigation ditch—but Mr. Cecil was much too much of a gentleman to do anything out of the ordinary, and nobody knew for sure about him. To suspect the coach of being that way was entirely too much—he didn't even mention the conversation to Duane. In fact, he had never told Duane he was sleeping with Mrs. Popper because he was afraid Duane would make fun of him for sleeping with an older woman.

It was that night, after that conversation, that things began to change for Ruth. She dreamed she was having a baby. She had had such dreams for years, but usually they were vague and fragmentary, but this one was vivid. It was not just a baby she had, though; it was Sonny. He was removed from between her legs, and afterward lay at her breast.

The next day Sonny came, and while they were spreading the blue quilt on the bedroom floor Ruth remembered the dream. It was very vivid in her mind as she undressed. She lay quietly, her eyes closed, as Sonny began, but almost before she knew it she became excited, so much so that she could not be still. She thought of the dream again, hoping the excitement would die before she became completely possessed by it, but instead of dying it became keener. Because of the dream, pleasure took her over: with her eyes shut she could pretend she was giving birth. Sonny was inside her but in truth she was bringing him out—it was that which excited her. She grabbed his hands and put them on her thighs, so that he would force them wider. She was filled with a strength that she had not suspected and held him with her thighs, just at the entrance, just connected, both of them struggling, until she was finally seized, rent by what she felt. Then she took Sonny back to her, her heart was pounding, her eyelids fluttering; she almost fainted with the relief of delivery. For half an hour she slept, not moving, and Sonny lay on top of her, not knowing if he dared move. He had no doubt that Ruth had broken through, but her success was as strange and almost as frightening as her failures. The strength she had called up amazed him: for minutes she had held him with just her thighs, his arms pinned to his sides so tightly he could not get one free. Yet, sleeping beneath him, she might have been a girl, so still and at peace she seemed.

When Ruth awakened she did not want Sonny to leave. She felt entirely comfortable, and she wanted to touch him, play with him, have his hand on her. After that, she never used the dream again, but she kept it in her mind as a safeguard, and even though she still sometimes missed, having the dream was a great reassurance.

In the weeks after Ruth's breakthrough the two of them became very close and comfortable. Once Sonny quit worrying about her response or lack of response, he found her much more pleasant to be with, and there were even afternoons when he visited her, not to make love but just to talk, hold hands, or watch television.

Only one problem arose, and that was one they had been expecting: the town knew about them. A couple of the housewives who lived along the alley compared notes, and in a few days the town knew. Sonny worried about it a lot, Ruth hardly at all.

"What do you think the coach would do if he found us?" Sonny asked one day. Ruth was sitting on the quilt combing her brown hair. She had decided to let her hair grow longer.

"Probably shoot us both," she said lightly. "He's always glad to have an excuse to use his deer rifle."

Sonny mused on that and decided she was right. "What do you think we ought to do about it?" he asked.

"I don't know," Ruth said, puckering her mouth at him happily. "Why don't we buy a new quilt? This one's about had it."

The next day she got one, for sentimental reasons also blue.

12

O N E   N I G H T   I N   M I D - M A R C H   Sonny woke up too early—around 3:30 A.M. The first thing that occurred to him was that Sam the Lion would be asleep. Sam the Lion had made his decree of banishment stick, and, though Sonny had endured it as best he could, he had about reached the point where he could endure it no longer. It occurred to him that if he got dressed and went down to the café Genevieve might let him sit and talk awhile. A cold March norther was blowing and the warm blankets were hard to leave, but the chances were he would have to leave them in an hour or so anyway, to make an early butane run.

Genevieve was sitting in one of the booths, reading an old issue of the *Ladies Home Journal*. To his immense relief she looked delighted to see him.

"Come on in here," she said. "I'm not going to throw any bottles at you."

"Could I have a cheeseburger?" he asked quickly. One of the worst parts of the penalty had been eating at the drive-in, where the cheeseburgers were half raw and the tomatoes soggy.

"You can have two if you want them," she said, and she made him two while he sat nervously in the booth. When she brought them in he swallowed the first one in only five or six bites.

"Quit eating so fast," Genevieve said. "You've lost weight. Even if it was a terrible thing to do to Billy, I'm on your side."

Sonny was grateful. "I couldn't talk them out of it," he said. "It was Leroy's idea."

"Where was Duane?" she asked.

It was a ticklish question. Duane had gone right on using the café and the pool-hall, just as if he hadn't been along. It was a sore spot with the other boys, and a few of them wanted to tell Sam the Lion about Duane's part in it. Thinking about it made Sonny uneasy.

"He was there," he admitted. "Just don't tell Sam."

"I figured he was," Genevieve said quietly. "He just didn't have the decency to own up and take his punishment. He probably got just as big a kick out of it as Leroy did."

Sonny was embarrassed and kept eating the cheeseburger. Nobody had ever criticized Duane in front of him before—for no reason that he could think of life was becoming more complicated.

"Well, I won't say no more about it," she said. "That's between you and him. But you've got to make up with Sam, that's for sure. I won't have you eating at that drive-in anymore. He misses you and he'll make it up if you do it right. He knows you too well to think you really went out of your way to upset Billy."

"How's Dan?" Sonny asked.

"Coming along. He's well enough to be contrary."

Sonny began to relax. The café was just the same: the jukebox, the booths, the high-school football schedule pinned on the wall. Genevieve cradled the coffee cup in her hand and stared at the frost-smoked windows.

"I've gotten into something else," Sonny said tentatively. She was the only person he could think of that he might be able to talk to.

"Got a new girl friend?" She grinned, and then she suddenly remembered the gossip. Until that moment she had not taken it at all seriously.

"I guess I have," Sonny said. "Not a girl friend, a lady friend. It's Mrs. Popper." He didn't know whether he was glad to have the secret out, and Genevieve was not sure at all that she was glad to have received it.

"Ruth Popper?" she said, amazed. "How do you mean, Sonny? Have you been flirtin' with her like you do with me, or is it different?"

"It's different," he said. "It's . . . like in a movie."

She saw that he was watching her face, dreadfully anxious to know what she thought about the news.

"I don't know what to think about you," she said. "Quit lookin' at me that way. This is an awful small town for that kind of carrying on, I can tell you that. You can't sneeze in this town without somebody offerin' you a handkerchief."

"Coach Popper don't care nothin' about her," Sonny said. "I don't see why he should care."

"He cares about himself, though—and about what people think of him. He owns a lot of guns, too."

Sonny looked so young and solemn and confused that after a moment it all amused her and she chuckled. He looked far too confused to be into anything wicked.

"All right," she said. "I won't say no more about it. You're a man of experience now, you don't need my advice anyway."

Sonny didn't know about advice, but he was glad to have her approval, however he could get it. He had some pie and chatted about lesser things until the streets outside were gray with a cold dawn. Genevieve got up to tend to the coffee maker.

"I better go on," Sonny said. "Sam's going to be coming any time."

"You stay," Genevieve said, not even turning around.

Sonny didn't like the idea, but he didn't have long to worry about it. In a few minutes the café door opened and Sam the Lion and Billy stepped inside. Sam had on his old plaid mackinaw, his khakis, and his house shoes. When he saw Sonny he opened his mouth to say something but Genevieve cut him off.

"Don't say a word," she said. "I won't have him eating at that drive-in no more. He can apologize like a civilized person and you can listen to him."

When Billy saw Sonny his face brightened and he went right over and sat down by him. He had forgotten all about the bad night, and didn't remember anything bad that Sonny had done. Sonny turned his baseball cap around backward for him.

"I'm sorry," Sonny said, when Sam the Lion came to the booth.

"Scoot over," Sam said, a little embarrassed. "If Billy can stand you I can too." He sat down by Sonny and ordered his sausage and eggs. Sonny was so relieved that he couldn't think of anything to say, and Sam the Lion was so relieved that he couldn't keep quiet. There was the basketball team to talk about, a disgraceful, hapless basketball team that hadn't come within thirty points of winning a game. Sam the Lion gave it hell, and continued giving it hell as the café filled, as the cowboys and the truckers came in, blowing on their cold hands. Soon smoke was rising from a dozen or more cups of Genevieve's coffee. Sam the Lion poured his in a saucer and went on talking while the two boys, not listening, happily ate their breakfasts.

13

IT WAS IN THE EARLY SPRING, when Sonny was really beginning to get in touch with Ruth, that Duane really began to get out of touch with Jacy. He forgave her for going to the nude swimming party in Wichita, but somehow they were never as comfortable with one another as they had been before that happened. The thing that bothered Duane most was that, instead of going to Wichita less and less, Jacy was going more and more. It got so he was lucky if he spent one Saturday night a month with her. Time after time she drove off to Wichita with Lester Marlow, always, she said, because her mother insisted. Duane raged and stormed, but he never quite got up the guts to have it out with Lois. Instead, he decided to concentrate on getting Jacy to marry him as soon as they graduated. He knew she had her application in to several fancy girls' schools, and he realized that if she got away to college he would have seen the last of her. His only chance was to marry her sometime during the summer, while she was still at home.

Jacy, however, had put aside all thought of marrying Duane. She had convinced herself that that would be a very selfish thing to do. Her parents, particularly her father, would never stand for it: he would have it annulled, Duane would lose his job and would probably be in the army before the summer was out. It would clearly be unfair of her to put Duane in such a position. If she sacrificed what she felt for him, he could keep his job and stay out of the army several months longer. It was the sort of thing he would thank her for someday.

The truth was, Jacy had been very strongly affected by the nude swimming party. Unknown to anyone but herself and Lester she had been back several times to exactly the same type of party. All the Saturday night trips were of her own arranging, but she told Duane they were her mother's doings. Duane was too naïve to understand her wanting to mix with kids like herself, kids who had money and lived recklessly. It would save everyone misery to let him think it was her mother's fault.

Jacy had begun to be very attracted to Bobby Sheen, the leader of the wild set. He was not especially handsome, but he combed his hair in a rakish fashion and he was always merry and lustful. It was rumored that he and Annie-Annie made love four times a week, sometimes in curious ways. He had an air of absolute confidence, as if he were ready for anything and could do anything that might be demanded of him. At first Jacy didn't give herself much of a chance with him, supposing that he and Annie-Annie would soon get married; but then she danced with him one night and took hope. He got erections while dancing with her, just like other boys did.

A week or so after that she thought it was really going to happen between Bobby and herself. After one of the naked swimming parties the boys and girls paired off and went to bed in various bedrooms of the huge Sheen house. Jacy had to share a bed with Lester Marlow, but that was all right; the first time it had happened she made it quite clear to Lester that sharing the bed was all she intended to do. Anything more intimate was out of the question. Lester had red pubic hair, which seemed to her ridiculous. After this particular party Lester and Jacy both went to sleep, as usual, but somebody woke Jacy up by kissing her. It was Bobby Sheen, and he didn't have any clothes on. When he saw she was wide awake he quietly motioned for her to follow him, and she did, trembling a little. Fortunately she had on some green pajamas, so it was not too immodest.

Bobby led her down the carpeted hall to an empty bedroom and the minute he got her through the door he unbuttoned her pajama top and began to play with her breasts. He was merry and confident about it all and it didn't occur to Jacy to stop him. There was a huge double bed in the room and once they got on it Bobby undressed her completely. Jacy was excited and decided to cast caution to the winds. She let him get between her legs and was prepared to let him go all the way, but he stopped wanting to. He started to and did something that hurt a little before he stopped, looking at her with disbelief.

"Are you a virgin?" he asked.

"I guess so," Jacy admitted miserably. "But I don't want to be."

Bobby made a face of mock-horror, as if he had discovered a leper in his bed.

"What a letdown," he said, but with his usual good cheer. "I'm sorry I woke you up. Why don't I give you the name of a gynecologist? There's no point in being messy on Momma and Daddy's bed."

"Okay," Jacy said, eager to be agreeable. She was not sure what having the name of such a person committed her to, but she was willing to try anything Bobby recommended. The look on his face made her realize that it was absolutely ridiculous for her to be a virgin: she was probably the only one in the whole house. That thought was so mortifying that she sat up and reached for her pajamas, prepared to go ignominiously back to bed. Bobby, however, was not all that discouraged.

"Don't run off," he said cheerfully. "I was just surprised. If you're not sleepy we can still play around a while."

Jacy was not sure what that involved either, but she dutifully lay back down. "What about Annie-Annie?" she asked.

"That bitch sleeps like a horse," Bobby said.

Jacy was quite shocked to discover all that "playing around" involved. Bobby Sheen knew amazing things to do, things she would not have put up with one second if it had been anyone other than him. As it was, she was determined not to show her ignorance and just let him do whatever he pleased. Him doing things was okay, but when he wanted her to do things to him she was so nervous and shaky that she got goose bumps all over. Bobby couldn't help giggling.

"Don't boys have cocks in that town you live in?" he asked, laughing.

Jacy was at a loss for an answer. For days she could not get the evening off her mind. It seemed to her she had come off very badly with Bobby. He didn't call her for any dates afterward, and every other boy who had ever been near her had promptly called her for dates. The only conclusion possible was that Bobby found her backward and country, and if there was anything she hated and loathed it was to be thought backward and country. It was clear that she was going to have to get rid of her virginity. She gave the matter much thought and came up with a plan that seemed to have multiple advantages. The week after graduation the senior class was going on what was called their senior trip. For four years the class had saved up money for it, and had given bake sales, conducted scrap iron drives, and done all sorts of other chores to make the money. They were going all the way to San Francisco and back on the bus and it would take every bit of the money they had made. She and Duane would thus be together practically all the time for a whole week, and it occurred to her that if she let Duane sleep with her sometime during the trip it would solve all kinds of problems. For one thing, it would *make* the senior trip. She and Duane would be regarded as extraordinarily daring, and all the kids would talk about them all the way home. Also, if she slept with Duane a time or two it would make it that much easier for her to break up with him after the senior trip was over. Duane would have something beautiful to remember, and he wouldn't be able to say she had promised him anything she hadn't delivered.

Then when she got back from the trip she would no longer be a virgin and could set about taking Bobby Sheen away from Annie-Annie. If she could get him in love with her before the summer was over she might forget about the girls' school and go to S.M.U., where Bobby was going. They might even pledge related fraternities.

The one flaw in the whole plan was Duane. It occurred to her that he might not want to break up with her even if she let him sleep with her before breaking the news. He was dead set on their getting married in the summer, and he was a very stubborn boy. She decided that the best thing to do would be to make an ally of Sonny—she knew Sonny would do anything she wanted him to if she played up to him the least little bit. If Duane got ugly and wouldn't quit trying to go with her she could then date Sonny a few times. Duane would never in his life excuse that.

The senior play was rehearsing at that time and Sonny and Jacy both had parts. In order to strengthen her hold over him Jacy started giving Sonny a ride home every night; often, at her suggestion, they would ride out to the lake and sit and talk a while before going home. Jacy mostly wanted to talk about Duane; about how much she wanted to marry him but how frightened she was that it would never work out, her parents being set against it like they were. Sonny tried to listen, but mostly he just looked. Jacy had a way of leaning forward so she could hook a finger inside her blouse and straighten her bra strap, a movement that always made him ache with desire. Even the flash of her white teeth as she popped her chewing gum—even that could cause discomfort. Once in a moment of emotion she reached out and they held hands for a little while. "I tell you I don't know what I would do if I didn't have you to talk to, Sonny," she said affectionately.

At such times Sonny could hardly keep from wishing that Duane and perhaps Ruth too were out of the picture. Jacy was everything he wanted. She had always seemed infinitely more desirable than Charlene or the other girls, but she had also begun to seem cool and simple and lovely in contrast to Ruth, who had begun to disturb him a good deal. Once Ruth found pleasure her need for him rapidly increased and her sensual appetite had become, if anything, stronger than his own. At first he had found it delightful—he had never imagined that he would ever in his life have as much sex as he wanted. By the time he had visited Ruth almost daily for a month he was forced to admit to himself that it might even be possible to have more than he wanted. Ruth lost all caution, all concern for what the townspeople might think. All she wanted was Sonny, and he began to feel strangely washed out and restless. He ceased to eat particularly much, or to sleep particularly well. Despite almost daily sex he had erotic dreams at night and would often wake up to find himself painfully engorged.

As he grew more tired and less certain of himself, Ruth seemed to grow fresher, more self-possessed, and more lovely, though it was only at odd, oblique moments, lying beside her or coming into her room, that he noticed that she was lovely. Instead of drooping about the house as she had once done she acquired grace and animation and moved about as active and lithe as a girl. She even repapered the bedroom, much to the coach's disgust.

Sonny found he could not keep a consistent feeling about her two days or even two hours in a row. At one moment, during lovemaking, seeing her become avid, sweaty, almost frenzied, he felt as he had the first day with her in the car, as if he were being pulled by some force stronger than his own. A few moments later, an hour later, he would see her, her face calmed, lit from within, her eyes wide and soft, and feel completely happy with her. He simply could not understand what had happened to her. When she touched him, drew him into her, it was not that she was trying to have him exactly—she was insisting that he have her. She was not saying "You're mine," she was saying "I'm yours," and that was almost more troubling. She was completely focused on him; the rest of her life had ceased to matter.

Her hair had grown longer, and he loved to smooth tendrils of it back behind her ears. But he wasn't sure that he wanted any person to be his: it made him too responsible.

"You're my love, I can't help it," she would say, if he brought the matter up. And she would go on brushing her hair, completely at peace with herself because of him.

One night he almost gave way to an impulse and spoke of Ruth to Jacy, but he didn't because he realized just in time that it would mean the end of his talks with Jacy. She wanted to talk about her problems, not his. Because of their talks she began to fill his fantasies again, and the fantasies made a fitful background to his afternoons with Ruth. Somehow he was sure that passion with Jacy would be more intense and yet less strained than it sometimes was with Ruth. With Jacy things would be sharper and better timed, and would never be blunted by anxiety or bad balance or anything.

To Ruth, that period of her life later seemed a little insane, but insane in a good way. She remembered little about it, just Sonny's person. Occasionally it occurred to her that people were probably talking, or that she ought to go to the store or somewhere, but none of those things seemed immediate. Sonny was the only thing immediate.

Later, when time was passing much more slowly, she told herself that she had not planned well—she had not thought to save anything. She had held nothing back for the morrow, but it was because she did not suppose she could afford to think about the morrow.

It was not until an evening in early May that the fact of a future was brought home to her. Sonny had come that afternoon, and all had gone well. Three hours later, while Herman was finishing his supper, Ruth went out into the backyard and began to take some clothes off the line. It was just dusk, a soft spring dusk, and as she was unpinning Herman's stiff, unironed khakis a car went by on the street. Idly curious, she glanced around to see who was passing and saw Sonny and Jacy, on their way to play practice in Jacy's convertible.

She only glimpsed them as the car passed between her house and the next, and all she saw really was the glint of spring sunset on Jacy's gold hair. She did not even see Sonny's face, did not know whether he looked happy or glum to be with Jacy, but the glimpse ruined her content. For a moment or two she had to hold onto the clothesline—it was as if she had been struck a numbing blow across her thighs. Her legs felt so unsteady that she could hardly move down the line to the next stiff pair of pants. Sonny had never mentioned Jacy to her: she had glimpsed the very beginning of something. Duane and Jacy might have broken up. As she dragged the sheets off the line she felt a sudden panic, silly but nonetheless terrifying. She was sure that Sonny was in love with Jacy and would never come to her house again. She would have wept, but the dread that seized her was too dry. It was as if she had suddenly been faced with her own end, an end too dry and commonplace to cry about. When all the clothes were piled in the basket she stood in the yard a minute, under the empty lines, her only comfort the soft evening air. She could not stand the thought of going into the tight, hot kitchen, where Herman was eating black-eyed peas, but the next moment a thought came to her and she grabbed the clothes basket and hurried in. Herman had finished the peas and was eating a bowlful of yellow canned peaches, one of his favorite desserts.

"Herman," she asked, "have Duane and Jacy broken up? I thought I saw her go by just now with someone else in the car."

The coach looked up with mild interest. "Hope so," he said. "Nothin' I'd like better than to see them two bust up. I might get a couple of good baseball games out of Duane if they would."

Ruth took heart and took out the ironing board and sprinkler bottle. Life came back into her legs; she decided the spasm of dread had been irrational. Even so, considering it calmly, it was clear that in time she was bound to be hurt, and badly so. She was twenty years older than him, and he would not keep wanting her forever. Sooner or later he would leave and she would have to get over him, but she was so relieved to know that it was going to be later—not for a week, at least, and perhaps not for a month or even a year—that she resolved not to care. As she ironed she indulged herself in the pleasant fantasy that she was in Sonny's room, doing the ironing for him. She nursed a strong secret wish to go to his room sometime, to be with him where he lived rather than where Herman lived.

The coach finished his peaches and lay on the couch for a couple of hours, watching television while Ruth finished ironing. When the late news came on he turned the set off: news bored him. He straggled lazily into the bedroom to undress, and found that Ruth was there ahead of him, sitting on the edge of the bed rubbing hand lotion into her hands. She had her shoes off and was barefooted. It seemed to the coach that she looked younger than a woman her age ought to look: her ankles were slim, and even her face looked young. He didn't know it, but she had managed to sustain her favorite fantasy all the way to the bedroom and was pretending to herself that she was undressing in Sonny's room. All the coach knew was that she irritated him. She went to the closet to hang up her dress and even the lightness of her walk irritated him. He sat down in the rocker to pull off his sweaty socks, remembering that she had mentioned Jacy and Duane.

"Who was it you seen with Jacy?" he asked, stirred by his dislike of the girl.

"I didn't get a good look at the boy," Ruth said, a little surprised. "It was Sonny Crawford I think."

The coach grunted. He stood up, emptied his pockets onto the dresser, and pitched his pants through the bathroom door in the general direction of the dirty-clothes hamper. It was a warm night and the room seemed a little close to him. He threw up a window and stood in front of it a minute, idly scratching his testicles and enjoying the nice south breeze.

After a minute he stretched out on the bed, but for some reason he couldn't get Jacy Farrow off his mind. It was little twats like her that ruined young athletes, so far as he was concerned. If it hadn't been for her, Duane would have come out for track and they might have won a track championship. As he lay on his back, still scratching himself, he thought how nice it would be to hump a little rich girl like her until she got so sick of it she would never want to see another boy, much less bother one. That would be a smart piece of coaching, but hard to bring off.

While his thoughts were running in that direction he happened to glance over and notice Ruth—or at least he noticed half of her. She was undressing behind the closet door, but the strong breeze had blown the door open a bit wider than usual and Ruth was half exposed, the line of the door bisecting her body. The coach saw one leg, one breast, one shoulder and the side of her head as she turned and reached into the closet to take her gown off the hook. Ordinarily the sight of Ruth's body gave him a feeling of mild distaste: his own mother had stood five-eleven and had worked just as hard as men worked nearly every day of her life. Nothing seemed more pathetic to him than a skinny woman, Ruth especially, but when he glanced at the closet he was not thinking of Ruth at all but of Jacy Farrow. He was thinking that if he ever got Jacy into the right corner he would pay back all the little pusses who had kept his boys stirred up over the years. The thought of administering such a lesson had him a little excited—his underwear developed a sizable hump. Ruth stepped out from behind the door, lowering the gown over her body, and the coach looked at her again. Something told him he would never get Jacy into the right corner, but Ruth was right there and she was just like a girl anyway. She had kept *him* stirred up at one time—if she hadn't he would have stayed a bachelor and had the money to take some real hunting trips. He could have gone to Alaska, even. She deserved a prod as much as Jacy; no woman who had done a proper day's work moved as lightly as she moved.

Ruth's mind was still elsewhere—she was unaware of the state her husband was in. It was not a state she had expected him to be in again. She sat down on the bed with her back to him and rubbed her calves a minute before stretching out. While she was sitting there the springs squeaked and Herman got out of bed; she supposed he had forgotten to go to the bathroom.

"Turn off the light in there, please, when you're done," she said. Light from the bathroom made a bright patch on the floor of the darkened bedroom.

Then she turned to lie down and noticed with a start that Herman was not headed for the bathroom at all. He was at the dresser, his underwear bulging out ludicrously. The sight stunned her, as it always had: all their married life Herman had announced his arousal by going to the dresser and rummaging in the sock drawer until he found the prophylactics. While she watched he found a package and strode into the bathroom to make himself ready.

She knew that she was supposed to use the time while he was in the bathroom to prepare herself for wifely service, but she suddenly felt as if her whole body had become stiff as a plank. She had been thinking how nice it would be to spend a whole night in Sonny's room, but when confronted with Herman's intention all thought seemed to leave her. She merely lay on the bed, not thinking at all.

When Herman came out he switched off the bathroom light, so that the bedroom was dark. He lay down heavily and without hesitation rolled himself onto Ruth, only to roll back a moment later, chagrined.

"What the hell?" he said. "You done asleep?"

In her paralysis Ruth had forgotten to do what she was supposed to do on such occasions: lift her nightgown and spread her legs. Those two actions were all that Herman required of her in the way of sexual cooperation. She raised her hips off the bed and pulled up the gown, and when he was satisfied that the obstruction had been removed the coach rolled back onto her and after a couple of badly aimed thrusts, made connection. Once he struck the place he went at it athletically.

Ruth clenched her fists at her sides. Her chest and abdomen felt crushed, but it crossed her mind that she had crushed herself. What was crushing her was the weight of all the food she had fed Herman through the years, all the steaks, all the black-eyed peas, all the canned peaches. It was particularly the canned peaches: she had never until that moment realized how much she hated them. It seemed to her that pyramids of cans of slimy peaches piled on her abdomen. After a moment the weight became intolerable and she moved a little, to try and ease it. She moved from side to side and stretched her legs, to try and escape it. Herman sweated easily and his sweat was already dripping down her ribs, but what bothered her was the weight of the cans. As she kept moving, trying to lighten the weight, she became aware of a distant pleasure. She began to writhe a little, in order to adjust the weight of the pyramid and intensify the pleasure—she flexed her legs and raised the lower part of her body a little, trying to get the weight right on the throbbing nerve.

Her movements annoyed the coach a great deal. When he started he had not even been thinking of her, but of Jacy, and thinking of Jacy had been very enjoyable. At first Ruth had acted perfectly decent, but just when it was getting nicest she began to writhe and wiggle and even started going up and down against him. The coach was too surprised and outraged to speak, and anyway he had got to the point where he needed to hold onto Jacy in his mind. He tried to beat Ruth down with his body, so she would be still again, but his efforts had the opposite effect: the harder he tried the more she moved. He couldn't slow her down at all, and he couldn't stop himself.

For a minute, with pounding heartbeats, they were running a hundred-yard dash with each other on equal terms. Neither knew how close the tape was, neither was sure of victory, but the coach crossed first. He recaptured Jacy for a second and desperately burst across, gasping with exhaustion and pleasure. Ruth was just at the turn. The weight was terribly sharp for a moment and then the coach's heavy surge burst the pyramid and left her gasping, free of all weight.

For his part the coach wanted badly to be gone on his side of the bed. Quickly he withdrew, but to his amazement and shame Ruth would not let him. She grasped him, put him back, would not have him leave, and he was too tired and surprised to fight. Except for the working of their lungs the two were still. In time, when their breath became quieter, the room was totally silent. The coach did not try again to withdraw, for fear he couldn't. When he did in the natural fashion he quickly rolled onto his side of the bed.

Ruth was away, in a misty, drowsy country, but even there she felt a little worried and a little sad. She had not meant it and could not understand how she had done it, given Herman something she thought was only for Sonny. It was as if her body had betrayed a trust and responded to the very man who had neglected it most. Perhaps she was not safe, not even from Herman. Hearing his exhausted breathing in her ear she had had a moment of sympathy for him as a person. She had felt for him a little bit. Perhaps she was no longer safe from anyone?

The coach knew good and well he wasn't safe. His body wanted to sleep, but his mind was far too agitated. He would never have imagined his own wife would grasp him: it was something worse than shameless. He didn't want to remain in the same bed with her and considered going to the couch. Still, Ruth was the one who had beslimed the bed: she ought to go. The messiness of the female body had never been more offensive to him. If he even moved his leg he touched a wet spot. Disgusted, he got up and went in the bathroom to clean himself. The bright light made him blink.

When he came back to the bed, Ruth was dozing. She knew he was offended, but it didn't touch her. She felt pleasantly sleepy and had overcome her mild distress at being suddenly accessible. If Herman was going to insist on his connubial rights, then all the better that she could finally enjoy it.

The coach stood over her in the dark, mad, but vaguely uneasy too. He had never dreamed Ruth had such wildness in her, and he was not sure how to get at her.

"Ain't you gonna change them sheets?" he asked sourly.

"Hum? No. Why?" she asked drowsily.

"Well by God," he said, walking distractedly around the bed. "You're a fine one, ain't you. If my mother was alive and knew how you acted she'd have your hide. I've always heard women got nasty in their old age but I never thought it would happen to no wife of mine."

"Didn't you like it, Herman?" Ruth asked, still sleepily. She was near enough asleep that she could be a little mean.

With a grunt the coach lay down and turned his back on her. Like it! It was a fine come-off. What could a man say to a damn woman?

14

KEEP AN EYE on them corks, Billy," Sam the Lion said, getting to his feet. "I've got to go water the grass a little."

The corks bobbed undisturbed in the brown water of a large stock tank, and Billy, also undisturbed, sat by the water's edge, watching them. Sonny was stretched out on his stomach in the Bermuda grass along the base of the tank dam. The May sun on his back was so warm that it made him drowsy, and he was almost asleep, content to leave Billy in full charge of the three fishing poles.

Sam the Lion took a long time to water the grass, but he finally came back, grumbling and buttoning his pants.

"Be nice to be able to piss," he said. "If I last another year I'll be dribblin' it on my shoes. I'd almost be willing to be young again if I could take a real piss. Looks like we ain't gonna catch much today."

"We never do," Sonny said. Once every year or two the pretty spring weather would tempt Sam the Lion to get out and, as he put it, get a little scenery. The rest of the time he was content to get his scenery from the pretty calendars the local foodstore put out.

When the urge for the outdoors came on him he would get Billy and the three fishing poles, enlist Sonny as a driver, and take the boys year after year to the same tank, perhaps the worst stocked fishing tank in the whole county. Once in a while they caught a perch or two, but always such undernourished specimens that old Marston refused to cook them.

"Hell, Sam, you wouldn't have nothing but two ounces of fried bones if I did cook them," he maintained.

Sam the Lion didn't much care, and neither did the boys. Billy loved to sit on the bank and watch the rings in the water or the dragonflies that skimmed along the surface. He was always surprised and a little disconcerted when Sam the Lion grabbed one of the poles and actually pulled up a fish. When he looked into the water he saw no fish, and he was never really sure where they came from.

After a while Sonny got tired of dozing and got up and walked along the tank dam a little way. It was a beautiful afternoon, a good day not to be doing anything—the sky was very blue and the pastures were green with spring grass and mesquite. In a moment he himself had the urge to water the grass in the way that Sam had, and he walked to the edge of the dam to do it. He felt warm and well and was faintly pleased by the spurt of his own water, even stretching himself a little to see if he could send a stream all the way to the foot of the dam. He didn't quite make it, but it was a high sloping dam and he came close enough to be fully content with his own range.

It was only as he turned around and was buttoning himself that he noticed that Sam the Lion had observed his little game. It embarrassed him just a little, but it did something much stranger to Sam the Lion. Sam began to snort, always a sign that something was affecting him powerfully, and then he began to laugh his loud, solid, rich laugh, something he did so rarely that both boys were startled. He sat by the water laughing, running his hands through his hair. Tears began to run down his face so freely that Sonny was not sure what was happening, whether Sam was laughing or crying. He pulled his handkerchief out of his hip pocket and began to wipe his face but no sooner had he done that than he burst out cussing and got up and stomped around furiously on the Bermuda grass.

"Goddammit! Goddammit!" he cursed. "I don't want to be old. It don't fit me!"

Then, seeing that the boys were scared, he became embarrassed and sat back down, still sniffing and snorting. He looked at the water and blew his nose and for a minute tried to pretend that nothing out of the ordinary had happened. But both boys continued to stare at him and he gave it up and tried to explain.

"I'll tell you what it was, son," he said, looking at Sonny a little ruefully. "Seein' you pissing off the dam reminded me of something. I used to own this land you know. It's been right at fifty years since the first time I watered a horse at this tank. Reason I always drag you all out here probably—I'm just as sentimental as anybody else when it comes to old times. What you reminded me of happened twenty years ago—I brought a young lady swimming here. It was after my boys were already dead, my wife had lost her mind. Me and this young lady were pretty crazy, I guess. She had all the spirit in the world, and we had some times. We come out here swimmin' one day without no bathin' suits and after we got out of the water I walked off up there to piss. She was always on the lookout for something funny and she offered to bet me a silver dollar I couldn't stand on the top of the dam and piss into the water. I took the bet and gave it a try but I never came no closer than you did. The lady's still got the silver dollar."

He was quiet, looking at the water.

Sonny had never known Sam the Lion except as an old man, and he was surprised and a little awed by the story. He wanted to ask who the woman was, but he didn't have the nerve.

"What became of the lady?" he asked.

"Oh, she growed up," Sam the Lion said, a tone of regret in his voice. "She was just a girl then, really."

"How come you never married her?"

"She was done married," Sam said gravely. "She and her husband were young and miserable with one another, but so many young married folks are that way that I figured they'd work out of it in time. I thought they'd get comfortable when they got a little older but it didn't turn out that way."

"Is growin' up always miserable?" Sonny said. "Nobody seems to enjoy it much."

"Oh, it ain't necessarily miserable," Sam replied. "About eighty per cent of the time, I guess."

They were silent again, Sam the Lion thinking of the lovely, spritely girl he had once led into the water, right there, where they were sitting.

"We ought to go to a real fishin' tank next year," Sam said finally. "It don't do to think about things like that too much. If she was here now I'd probably be crazy agin in about five minutes. Ain't that ridiculous?"

A half-hour later, when they had gathered up the gear and were on the way to town, he answered his own question.

"It ain't, really," he said. "Being crazy about a woman like her's always the right thing to do. Being a decrepit old bag of bones is what's ridiculous."

It had rained the week before and there were deep ruts in the dirt road. Sonny drove as carefully as he could, but Sam the Lion scratched his head and watched the speedometer nervously, convinced that they were proceeding at a reckless speed.

"Did you know about me and Mrs. Popper?" Sonny asked suddenly, feeling that if he was ever going to talk about it the time was at hand.

"Yeah, how is Ruth?" Sam asked. "I haven't had a close look at her in years."

"Sometimes she's okay," Sonny said. "Sometimes she doesn't seem to be too happy."

Sam snorted. "That's probably the understatement of the day," he said. "I figured her for a suicide ten years ago—people are always turning out to be tougher than I think they are."

"I don't exactly know what to do about her," Sonny said hopefully.

Sam the Lion laughed almost as loudly as he had on the tank dam.

"Don't look at me for advice," he said. "I never know exactly what to do about anybody, least of all women. You might stay with her and get some good out of her while you're growing up. Somebody ought to get some good out of Ruth."

They pulled onto the highway and in a few minutes the fenceposts were going by so fast that Sam the Lion could hardly see them. He breathed as little as possible until they hit the city limits sign—then Sonny slowed down and he relaxed.

"Say, was Duane along that night you all got Billy in the mess?" he asked. "I've been wondering about that lately."

Sonny was caught off guard and was completely at a loss to answer. He automatically started to lie, but because it was Sam the Lion the lie wouldn't come out. He decided it wouldn't hurt to tell the truth, but the truth wouldn't come out either. First the lie and then the truth stuck in his throat, and right in the same place.

"I see," Sam said. "Watch out, that's Old Lady Peters backing out of her driveway up there. She thinks it's still 1930 an' she's just as apt to back right in front of you as not."

He gripped the door handle tightly, prepared to leap out if necessary, but Sonny had seen the old lady blocks before he had and calmly, out of habit, swerved wide around her and coasted them safely up to the poolhall door.

15

THREE DAYS after the fishing trip, Duane got so frustrated that he beat up Lester Marlow. Jacy and Lester had gone to Wichita together three Saturday nights in a row, and Duane could stand it no longer.

"I don't care if it ain't Lester's fault," Duane told Sonny. "Maybe if he has a couple of front teeth missin' Mrs. Farrow won't be so anxious to have Jacy go with him."

Sam the Lion overheard the remark and gave a skeptical chuckle. "The only person who'll profit by that sort of reasonin' is Lester's dentist," he said. "Maybe Jacy likes to go with Lester."

That was an incredible thing to suggest. Duane and Sonny were both flabbergasted.

"You don't think she *wants* to go with that fart, do you?" Duane asked indignantly.

"Well, Lester ain't entirely unlikable," Sam replied, not at all flustered. "I don't know Jacy well enough to know what she wants, but you've been blaming her mother all this time for something that might not be her mother's fault. If I was you I'd investigate."

Duane stormed out of the poolhall, mad as he could be. He didn't want to investigate, he just wanted to whip Lester, and about midnight that night, as Lester was passing the courthouse, Duane waved him down. Sonny was the only other person to see it.

"I know you're mad," Lester said, as soon as he got out of the car, "but you needn't be. All I've done is take her to dances. I've never even kissed her."

It was a shameful admission, but true: Jacy gave Lester absolutely nothing in the way of intimacies. She didn't have to.

"You took her to a naked swimming party," Duane said. "Don't tell me you didn't kiss her."

"I didn't," Lester said, but at that point Duane hit him on the mouth. Lester swung a half-hearted blow in return and found himself sitting down—at least he found himself getting up, and he could only assume he had been knocked down first. The fight was well started and things were easier for him: he couldn't feel himself being hit, and after three or four more licks Duane bloodied his nose and stopped fighting.

"That's just a taste," he said. "Don't you take her anywhere else!"

Lester said nothing, and Duane and Sonny walked away. Not saying anything was something of a triumph, Lester thought. He had made no promises. He went across the street to the filling station and ran some water on his nose, thinking that in a way he had been ganged up on. Sonny had been there. It could even have been that he was not knocked down fairly—Sonny could have tripped him. On the way back to Wichita he concluded that Sonny probably did trip him, and instead of going to his home he drove out to a place on Holiday Creek where some of the wilder boys often gathered on Saturday nights. A lot of boys were there, sitting on the fenders of their cars drinking beer, and when they saw how bloody Lester was they were briefly impressed. What happened? they wanted to know.

"Couple of roughnecks beat me up," Lester said stoically. "You know, Crawford and Moore, over in Thalia. It was about Jacy Farrow. I would have done okay if one of them hadn't tripped me."

"Those motherfuckers," one of the boys said. "We ought to go over there and pile their asses."

"No," Lester said gallantly. "I don't want anybody fighting my fights."

"Aw, hell, it'd be somethin' to do," a boy said. "Besides we can get the Bunne brothers to do the fighting." The Bunne brothers were local Golden Gloves champions, a welterweight and a light-heavy. They enjoyed fighting, in the ring or out.

Lester didn't try again to discourage them, but for himself he decided it would be best not to go back to Thalia. The boys took that in stride—they didn't really like Lester much and were just as glad he stayed in Wichita. The nice thing about his getting beat up was that it gave them an excuse to drive to Thalia and watch a fight.

The Bunne brothers were located at a Pioneer drive-in, trying to make some girls in a green Pontiac. The welterweight was named Mickey, the light-heavy, Jack. They were glad to get a chance to go fighting: the girls were just a bunch of pimply virgins who had run off from a slumber party in Burkburnett. A couple of boys elected to stay and work on them, but that still left seven raring to go. They piled in a second-hand Mercury and headed for Thalia, driving about eighty-five and laughing and talking. Saturday night had taken a turn for the better.

After the fight with Lester, Sonny and Duane walked over to the café to have a cheeseburger. Duane really wanted sympathy, but Genevieve was not inclined to give him any.

"No sir," she said. "There wasn't any point in your bullyin' Lester—it ain't his fault you can't make your girl friend behave."

"You're as bad as Sam," Duane said bitterly. "Why Jacy would marry me tonight, if she had the chance."

Sonny got up and put a couple of nickels in the jukebox, hoping a little music would ease the tension. It didn't seem to help much, so after a few minutes the boys left and drove out to the Y, a fork in the road about five miles from town. The fork was on top of a hill, and when they got there they sat and looked across the flat at the cluster of lights that was Thalia. In the deep spring darkness the lights shone very clear. The windows of the pickup were down and they could smell the fresh smell of the pastures.

They only sat a few minutes, and then drove back to town. When they pulled up at the rooming house the Wichita boys were there, sitting on the fenders of the Mercury.

"There's the Bunne brothers," Duane said. "That damn Lester must have sent 'em."

Both of them were badly scared, but they didn't want the Wichita boys to know that so they got out as if nothing were wrong. For a moment no one said anything. Sonny nervously scraped his sole on the pavement and the sound was very loud in the still night.

Mickey Bunne came cockily over and broke the silence.

"Hear you men beat the piss out of Lester," he said.

"I beat the piss out of him," Duane said quickly. "Sonny wasn't involved."

"That ain't the way Lester tells it."

The other boys got off the fenders and began to edge around.

"He probably lied about it," Duane said. "I didn't hit him over five times, anyway. I told him to stop going with my girl."

Mickey moved a step closer. "He said you both whipped him."

"You don't really think it would take two of us to whip Lester, do you?" Sonny asked. "All he had was a bloody nose and a busted lip. If we'd both fought he wouldn't have been able to drive home, much less tell lies about it."

The Wichita boys were momentarily silent, even Mickey. What Sonny said was obviously true: it didn't take two people to whip Lester Marlow, and he hadn't been damaged much, anyway. Most of the boys didn't feel particularly unfriendly to Duane and Sonny, but that didn't matter. There had to be a fight. The Bunne brothers wouldn't go home without a fight. Fortunately Mickey Bunne was quick-witted and saw right away what tack to take.

"Who whipped him don't matter," he said. "We don't like you country boys tellin' us who to go with and who to leave alone. We like to screw country girls once in a while."

Duane was getting a little nervous. "I didn't tell him not to screw country girls," he said. "I told him not to bother Jacy. He can fuck the whole rest of this town for all I care—I'm just tired of him botherin' Jacy."

Mickey grinned. "Lester don't bother her," he said. "She laps it up. I seen her naked one time myself, out at Bobby Sheen's. She ain't bad lookin'. Who she really likes is Bobby Sheen—him and her played around all one night. I guess she's about as much ours as she is yours. I may want to go with her myself some time, you can't tell."

That was too much for Duane: he hit at Mickey, and the fight was on. It was not too bad for Duane, although Mickey beat him handily and knocked him down once. Duane was so mad he didn't really feel the pounding he took. He was fighting for his girl, after all. Sonny was the one who suffered most. He wasn't mad at all, and he wasn't fighting for anyone in particular. Besides that, he didn't like to fight and didn't know how, whereas Jack Bunne liked it and knew how very well. It made for a painful beating.

Fortunately the Bunne brothers knew when to quit. They were not looking for trouble, just for excitement. Sonny and Duane were both standing when they quit, although Sonny wanted very much to sit down. He had a pain in his ribs.

"Well let's go, men," one of the boys said. "The deputy sheriff's liable to come drivin' by."

"We ain't broke no laws," Jack Bunne said, not even winded, but the boys all went on and piled in the Mercury. They whooped and laughed as the car pulled away.

"Motherfuckers," Duane said wearily.

Sonny walked over and sat down on the curb. One of his ears was paining him severely, and he had caught at least a couple of hard licks in the rib cage. Duane came and sat down too. They were both too winded and depressed to say anything. It was enough just to sit. The town was very quiet. From the west, far out in the pastures, they heard some hounds, so far away that their braying sounded as thin as the yapping of puppies.

"Why don't we just take off an' go someplace," Duane said. "I'm sick of this town. You're the only friend I got here, except Jacy."

"You mean go and stay gone?" Sonny asked.

"No, just for a day or two. We could go to Mexico and get back by sometime Monday."

"Reckon the pickup would make it?" Sonny asked, welcoming the prospect.

They got out their billfolds and counted their money. Saturday had been payday, and between them they had almost a hundred dollars.

"We can make it on that," Duane said. "Let's go clean up."

A few minutes later Sonny vomited all over the bathroom, but once he got the mess cleaned up he felt much better. His ear was not throbbing so badly. They put on clean Levi's and shirts and doctored themselves with aspirin, convinced they would both survive. The pickup didn't have much gas in it and they had to stop in town and wake up Andy Fanner, who had a key to one of the gas stations.

"Why you boys or-tant to go all that way," Andy said cheerfully. "The water's buggy in Mexico."

"We'll just drink beer and tequila," Duane said.

"You need-ernt to tell me," Andy said sagely. "I been there. You get the clap you'll wish you hadn't drunk nothin'. Where you goin', Laredo?"

The boys looked at one another. They hadn't planned that far ahead; they were just going to Mexico.

"Which is the best place?" Sonny asked.

Andy wasn't positive and he didn't have a map, so they went back to the café and got one out of the glove compartment of Genevieve's old Dodge. They took it inside to read it.

"Good lord," Genevieve said, when she saw their skinned-up faces. They explained, and she sat down in a booth with them. "You all can just have the map," she said. "I ain't going far enough away that I need to worry about getting lost, I don't guess."

"Let's go all the way to Matamoros, since we're goin'," Duane suggested. "I've heard it's about the wildest."

"Matamoros suits me," Sonny said, gulping his coffee. They could hardly believe such an adventure was before them, and they wanted to get away before something happened to stop it.

Genevieve, however, was a little dubious. She followed them out to the pickup to see them off. The streets were empty, the streetlights shining palely. The stoplight blinked red and green all to itself.

"This pickup don't look so good," she said. The boys were so eager that it made her strangely sad. "Have either of you ever been that far away before?"

"Austin's the farthest I've been," Sonny said. It was the same with Duane, and Matamoros was almost twice as far as Austin. It made them all the more eager, but to their amazement Genevieve suddenly began to cry about something, right there on the street. Sonny had been just about to start the motor when she put her elbows on the pickup window and wiped away the tears with her hand. Both boys were stricken, afraid they were going to miss the trip after all.

"Why don't you boys take my car?" Genevieve sniffed. "You'll never make it in this old pickup."

They were astonished. It was an unprecedented offer. Women were clearly beyond all understanding.

"Naw, we better go in this one," Sonny told her softly. She was looking off down the street—he had never noticed before, but she seemed lonesome.

"We might wreck yours, an' then where would we be?" he added.

"Okay," Genevieve said, hardly paying attention. Something made her breasts ache. "Wait just a minute."

She went in the café and got a ten-dollar bill out of her purse. After she had wiped her eyes with a Kleenex she took the money outside and handed it to Sonny.

"Hide that somewhere," she said. "Use it when you don't have anything else to use. I'd like for you to get back in time for your graduation."

Both boys assured her that the money was quite unnecessary, but she pressed it on them anyway. "Sam's up there sitting on the curb," she said. "Guess he can't sleep. You might go say good-bye to him."

The boys were glad of anything that would prolong the ecstasy of departure a few more minutes. Sonny backed solemnly into the empty street and turned toward the poolhall. Sam the Lion was sitting on the curb, scratching his ankles. Sonny drove right up in front of him and leaned out the window.

"Better come go with us," he said. "We're headed for the Valley."

Astonished, Sam got up from the curb and came over to the pickup. He peered at the boys curiously.

"Going to the Valley tonight," he said. "My God." He was touched by the folly of youth and stood with his foot on the running board a moment.

"I guess the town can get along without us till Monday," Sonny said.

"I reckon," Sam said lightly. "If I was young enough to bounce that far I'd go with you. Need any money?"

"No. We got plenty."

"You can't tell," Sam said, fishing out his billfold. "Better take ten dollars for insurance. They say money kinda melts when you take it across a border."

The boys were too embarrassed to tell Sam that Genevieve had given them some already. They took the bill guiltily, anxious to be off. Sam stepped back to the curb and the boys waved and made a wide U-turn in the empty street. Genevieve was still outside the café and they waved at her too as they went by. She watched them, hugging her breasts. When they got to the stoplight it was red and they stopped, even though there wasn't another moving car within fifteen miles of them. The light winked green and the pickup turned the corner and sped out of sight.

Genevieve went over and kicked lightly at the front tire of her Dodge—to her the tire always looked low. The boys had made her remember what it was to be young. Once, before they had any kids, she and her husband Dan took off one weekend and drove to Raton, New Mexico. They stayed in a motel, lost twenty dollars at the horse races, made love six times in two days, and had dinner in the coffee shop of a fancy restaurant. She had even worn eye shadow. Romance might not last, but it was something while it did. She looked up the street and waved at Sam the Lion, but he was looking the other way and didn't notice her and she went back into the empty café, wishing for a few minutes that she was young again and free and could go rattling off across Texas toward the Rio Grande.

16

ALL DAY the boys alternated, one driving, the other sleeping, and by late evening they were in the Valley, driving between the green orange groves. It was amazing how different the world was, once the plains were left behind. In the Valley there were even palm trees. The sky was violet, and dusk lingered until they were almost to Matamoros. Every few miles they passed roadside groceries, lit with yellow light bulbs and crowded with tables piled high with corn and squash, cabbages and tomatoes.

"This is a crazy place," Duane said. "Who you reckon eats all that squash?"

They drove straight on through Brownsville and paid a fat, bored tollhouse keeper twenty cents so they could drive across the bridge. Below them was the Rio Grande, a river they had heard about all their lives. Its waters were mostly dark, touched only here and there by the yellow bridge lights. Several Mexican boys in ragged shirts were sitting on one of the guardrails, spitting into the water and chattering to one another.

A few blocks from the bridge they came to a stoplight on a pole, with four or five boys squatting by it. Apparently someone had run into the light pole because it was leaning away from the street at a forty-five-degree angle. As soon as Sonny stopped one of the boys ran out and jumped lightly onto the running board.

"Girl?" he said. "Boy's Town? Dirty movie?"

"Well, I guess," Sonny said. "I guess that's what we came for."

The boy quickly got in the cab and began to chatter directions in Tex-Mex—Sonny followed them as best he could. They soon left the boulevard and got into some of the narrowest streets the boys had ever seen. Barefooted kids and cats and dogs were playing in the street, night or no night, and they moved aside for the pickup very reluctantly. A smell of onions seemed to pervade the whole town, and the streets went every which direction. There were lots of intersections but no stop signs—apparently the right of way belonged to the driver with the most nerve. Sonny kept stopping at the intersections, but that was a reversal of local custom: most drivers beeped their horns and speeded up, hoping to dart through before anyone could hit them.

Mexico was more different from Thalia than either of the boys would have believed. The number of people who went about at night was amazing to them. In Thalia three or four boys on the courthouse square constituted a lively crowd, but the streets of Matamoros teemed with people. Groups of men stood on what, in Thalia, would have been sidewalks, children rushed about in the dust, and old men sat against buildings.

Their guide finally ordered them to stop in front of a dark lump that was apparently some sort of dwelling.

"This couldn't be no whorehouse," Duane said. "It ain't big enough to have a whore in it."

Not knowing what else to do, they got out and followed their guide to the door. A paunchy Mexican in his undershirt and khakis opened it and grunted at the guide. "Ees got movies," the boy said.

They all went inside, into a bedroom. Through an open doorway the boys could see an old woman stirring something in a pot, onions and tomatoes it smelled like. An old man with no shirt on and white hair on his chest sat at a table staring at some dominoes. Neither the old man nor old woman so much as glanced at the boys. There were two beds in the bedroom and on one of them three little Mexican boys were curled up, asleep. Sonny felt strange when he saw them. They looked very helpless, and he could not feel it was very polite for Duane and him to barge into their room. The paunchy man immediately brought up the subject of movies. "Ten dollars," he said. "Got all kinds."

He knelt and drew a tiny little projector out from under the bed and took several rolls of eight-millimeter film out of a little bureau. The boys looked uncomfortably at one another. They either had to pay and watch the movies or else refuse and leave, and since they had driven five hundred miles to see some wickedness it was pointless to refuse. Duane handed over a ten-dollar bill and the man stuffed it in his pocket and calmly began to clear one of the beds. He picked the sleeping boys up one at a time, carried them into the kitchen, and deposited them under the table where the old man sat. The little boys moaned a little and stirred in their sleep, but they didn't wake up. The paunchy man then put the projector on their bed and prepared to show the movies on a sheet hung against the opposite wall.

"I don't like this," Sonny said, appalled. "I never come all this way just to get some kids out of bed. If he ain't got a better place than this to show them I'd just as soon go on."

Duane was of the same mind, but when they tried to explain themselves, the guide and the projectionist both seemed puzzled.

"Ees okay," the guide said. "Sleepin' away." He gestured at the three little boys, all of whom were sound asleep on the dirt floor.

Sonny and Duane were stubborn. Even though the little boys were asleep, it wouldn't do: they couldn't enjoy a dirty movie so long as they were in sight of the displaced kids. Finally the projectionist shrugged, picked up the projector, and led them back through the hot kitchen and across an alley. The guide followed, carrying the film. Above them the sky was dark and the stars very bright.

They came to what seemed to be a sort of long outhouse, and when the guide knocked a thin, middle-aged man opened the door. He had only one leg, but no crutch, the room being so small that he could easily hop from one resting place to the next. As soon as they were all inside the guide informed the boys that it would cost them five dollars more because of the change of rooms: the one-legged man could not be put to the trouble of sitting through a pornographic movie for nothing. Sonny paid it and the projectionist plugged the projector into a light socket. An old American calendar hung on the door, a picture of a girl in mechanic's overalls on the front of it. The one-legged man simply turned the calendar around and they had a screen.

"You mean they're going to show it on the back of a calendar," Duane said. "For fifteen dollars?"

The light was turned off and the projector began to buzz—the title of the picture was *Man's Best Friend.* It was clearly an old picture, because the lady who came on the screen was dressed like ladies in Laurel and Hardy movies. The similarity was so strong that for a moment the boys expected Laurel and Hardy to come on the screen and do dirty things to her. As the plot unfolded the print became more and more scratchy and more and more faded; soon it was barely possible to tell that the figures on the screen were human. The boys leaned forward to get a better look and were amazed to discover that the figures on the screen *weren't* all human. One of the actors was a German shepherd dog.

"My God," Duane said.

They both immediately felt the trip was worthwhile, if only for the gossip value. Nobody in Thalia had ever seen a dog and a lady behaving that way: clearly it was the ultimate depravity, even more depraved than having congress with Negro whores. They were speechless. A man came on and replaced the dog, and then the dog came back on and he and the man teamed up. The projectionist and the guide chuckled with delight at this development, but the boys were too surprised to do anything but watch. The ugliness of it all held them spellbound. When it was over they walked to the pickup in silence, followed by the guide and the projectionist. The latter was making a sales pitch.

"Lots more reels," he said. "Got French, Gypsy, Chinese lesbians, all kinds. Five dollars a reel from now on."

The boys shook their heads. They wanted to get away and think. The guide shrugged and climbed in beside them and they drove away, leaving the fat man in the middle of the road.

"I hope he puts them kids back in bed," Sonny commented.

"Boy's Town now," the guide said happily. "Five hundred girls there. Clean, too."

They soon left the downtown area and bumped off toward the outskirts of Matamoros. A red Chevrolet with Texas license plates was just in front of them, throwing the white dust of the dirt road up into their headlights. Soon they saw Boy's Town, the neon lights from the larger cabarets winking red and green against the night. At first it looked like there were a hundred clubs, but after they drove around a while they saw that there were only fifteen or twenty big places, one on every corner. Between the corners were dark, unlit rows of cribs. The guide gestured contemptuously at the cribs and took them to a place called the Cabaret ZeeZee. When the boys parked, a fat policeman in khakis walked up and offered to open the door for them, but the guide chattered insultingly to him and he shrugged lazily and turned away.

The boys entered the cabaret timidly, expecting to be mobbed at once by whores or else slugged by Mexican gangsters, but neither thing happened. They were simply ignored. There was a large jukebox and a few couples dancing, but most of the people in the club were American boys, sitting around tables.

"The competition's gonna be worse here than it is in Thalia," Duane said. "We might as well get some beer."

They sat down at one of the tile-topped tables and waited several minutes before a waitress came over and got their order. She brought them the first Mexican beer they had ever tasted, and they drank the first bottles thirstily. In their tired, excited state the beer quickly took effect—before they knew it they had had five bottles apiece, and the fatigue of the trip seemed to be dropping away. A fat-faced girl in a green blouse came over, introduced herself as Juanita, and with no further preamble squeezed Sonny intimately through his blue jeans. He was amazed. Though responsive, he felt the evening would bring better things than Juanita, so he politely demurred. Juanita went around and squeezed Duane the same way, but got the same reply.

"Texas ees full of queers," she said, swishing her buttocks derogatorily as she walked away. The boys contemplated themselves over the beer bottles, wondering if they had been seriously insulted.

As the night wore on Sonny gradually set his mind on a slim, black-headed girl who spent most of her time on the dance floor, dancing with boys from Texas A & M. There were a good many boys from Texas A & M in the cabaret.

"I thought Aggies was all irresistible cocksmen," Duane said. "What's so many of them doing in a whorehouse?"

In time Sonny approached the girl, whose name was Maria. She cheerfully came to the table with him and downed three whiskeys while he was having a final beer. Between drinks she blew her warm, slightly sticky breath in his ear and squeezed him the way Juanita had.

"All night party?" she asked. "Jus' twenty-five dollars. We can leef right now."

It seemed ungallant to haggle with such a confident girl, so Sonny agreed. It turned out he owed eight dollars for the drinks, but it didn't seem gallant to haggle about that either. He paid, and Maria led him out the back door of the Cabaret ZeeZee into a very dark alley, where the only light was from the bright stars far above. The place she took him didn't even have a door, just a blue curtain with a light behind it. The room was extremely tiny. The one light bulb was in a socket on the wall and the bed was an old iron cot with a small mattress and a thin green bedspread.

In the room, Maria seemed less perky than she had in the club. She looked younger than she had inside. Sonny watched her unzip her dress—her back was brown and smooth, but when she turned to face him he was really surprised. Her breasts were heavy, her nipples large and purplish, and she was clearly pregnant. He had never seen a pregnant woman naked before, but he knew from the heavy bulge of her abdomen that she must be carrying a child. She tried to look at him with whorish gaiety, but somehow it didn't work: the smile was without life, and showed her gums. When he was undressed she splashed him with coolish water from a brown pitcher, and scrutinized him with such care that an old worry popped into his mind. Perhaps his equipment was too small? He had worried about that when he first began to go with Ruth, and had even tried to find out how large one's equipment was supposed to be, but the only two reference works in the high-school library were the *World Book* and the *Texas Almanac,* neither of which had anything helpful on penises. Gradually it had ceased to worry him, but with Maria he had begun to feel generally hesitant.

"But aren't you going to have a baby?" he asked, not sure that the question was proper.

Maria nodded. "Two already," she said, meaning to reassure him. Her heavy breasts and large grape-colored nipples were not at all congruous with her thin calves and girlish shoulders.

Sonny lay down with her on the cot, but he knew even before he began that somehow twenty-five dollars had been lost. He didn't want to stay in the room all night, or even very much of it.

Two minutes later it came home to him why Ruth had insisted they make love on the floor: the cot springs wailed and screamed, and the sound made him feel as though every move he made was sinful. He had driven five hundred miles to get away from Thalia, and the springs took him right back, made him feel exposed. Everyone in town would know that he had done it with a pregnant whore. Suddenly he ceased to care about the twenty-five dollars, or about anything; the fatigues of the long trip, down from the plains, through the hill country and the brush country, through Austin and San Antone, five hundred miles of it all pressed against the backs of his legs and up his body, too heavy to support. To Maria's amazement he simply stopped and went to sleep.

———

When he awoke, he was very hot. The green counterpane was soaked with his sweat. It was not until he had been awake a minute or two that he realized the sun was shining in his face. He was still in the room where Maria had brought him, but the room had no roof—the night before he had not even noticed. It was just an open crib.

He hurriedly got up and put on his clothes, his head aching. While he was tying his shoes he suddenly had to vomit, and barely made it past the blue curtain into the street. When he had finished vomiting and was kneeling in the white dust waiting for his strength to come back he heard a slow clop-clop and looked up to see a strange wagon rounding the corner into his part of the street. It was a water wagon, drawn by a decrepit brown mule and driven by an old man. The wagon was entirely filled by a large rubber water tank wrapped in ragged canvas; as the wagon moved the water sloshed out of the open tank and dripped down the sides of the wagon into the white dust. The old man wore a straw hat so old that it had turned brown. His grizzled whiskers were as white as Sam the Lion's hair. As he stopped the mule, three or four whores stepped out of their cribs with water pitchers in their hands. One passed right by Sonny, a heavy woman with a relaxed face and large white breasts that almost spilled out of her green robe. The whores were barefooted and seemed much happier than they had seemed the night before. They chattered like high-school girls and came lightly to the wagon to get their water. The old man spoke to them cheerfully, and when the first group had filled their pitchers he popped the mule lightly with the rein and proceeded up the street, the slow clop-clop of the mule's feet very loud in the still morning. When he passed where Sonny was kneeling the old man nodded to him kindly and gestured with a tin dipper he had in his hand. Sonny gratefully took a dipper of water from him, using it to wash the sour taste out of his mouth. The old man smiled at him sympathetically and said something in a philosophic tone, something which Sonny took to mean that life was a matter of ups and downs. He stayed where he was and watched the wagon until it rounded the next corner. As it moved slowly up the street the whores of Matamoros came out of their cribs, some of them combing their black hair, some with white bosoms uncovered, all with brown pitchers in their hands and coins for the old waterman.

Sonny found Duane asleep in the front seat of the pickup, his legs sticking out the window. Three little boys were playing in the road, trying to lead a dusty white goat across into a pasture of scraggly mesquite. The goat apparently wanted to go into the Cabaret ZeeZee. A depressed-looking spotted dog followed behind the boys and occasionally yapped discouragedly at the goat.

Duane was too bleary and sick to do more than grunt. His hair was plastered to his temples with sweat. "You drive," he said.

By some miracle Sonny managed to wind his way through Matamoros to the Rio Grande—in daylight the water in the river was green. The boys stood groggily under the customs shed for a few minutes, wondering why in the world they had been so foolish as to come all the way to Mexico. Thalia seemed an impossible distance away.

"I don't know if I can make it," Sonny said. "How much money we got?"

They found, to their dismay, that their money had somehow evaporated. They had four dollars between them. There was the money that Sam and Genevieve had given them, hidden in the seat springs, but they had not planned to use that.

"I guess we can pay them back in a week or two," Sonny said. "We'll have to use it."

When the customs men were through the boys got back in the pickup and drove slowly out of Brownsville, along the Valley highway. Heat waves shimmered above the green cabbage fields. Despite the sun and heat Duane soon went to sleep again and slept heavily, wallowing in his own sweat. Sonny drove automatically; he was depressed, but not exactly sleepy, and he paced himself from town to town, not daring to think any farther ahead than the next city limits sign.

Soon the thought of Ruth began to bother him. In retrospect it seemed incredibly foolish that he should drive a thousand miles to go to sleep on a pregnant girl's stomach, when any afternoon he could have a much better time with Ruth. The thought of her slim, familiar body and cool hands suddenly made him very horny and even more depressed with himself. It occurred to him that he might even be diseased, and he stopped in a filling station in Alice to inspect himself. Duane woke up and exhibited similar anxieties. For the rest of the day they stopped and peed every fifty miles, just to be sure they could.

There was money enough for gas, but not much for food, so they managed on Cokes, peanuts, and a couple of candy bars. Evening finally came, coolness with it, and the boys got a second wind. The trip ceased to seem like such a fiasco: after all, they had been to Mexico, visited whorehouses, seen dirty movies. In Thalia it would be regarded as a great adventure, and they could hardly wait to tell about it. The country around Thalia had never looked so good to them as it did when they came back into it, at four in the morning. The dark pastures, the farmhouses, the oil derricks and even the jackrabbits that went dashing across the road in front of them, all seemed comfortable, familiar, private even, part of what was theirs and no one else's. After the strangeness of Matamoros the lights of Thalia were especially reassuring.

Duane was driving when they pulled in. He whipped through the red light and turned toward the café. Genevieve would be glad to see they were safely back.

To their astonishment, the café was dark. No one at all was there. The café had never been closed, not even on Christmas, and the boys were stunned. Inside, one little light behind the counter shone on the aspirin, the coughdrops, the chewing gum, and cheap cigars.

"It ain't a holiday, is it?" Sonny said.

There was nothing to do but go over to the courthouse and wake up Andy Fanner—he would know what had happened.

Andy woke up hard, but they kept at him and he finally got out of the car and rubbed his stubbly jaw, trying to figure out what the boys wanted.

"Oh yeah, you all been gone, ain't you," he said. "Gone to Mexico. You don't know about it. Sam the Lion died yesterday mornin'."

"Died?" Sonny said. After a moment he walked over to the curb in front of the courthouse and sat down. The traffic light blinked red and green over the empty street. Andy came over to the curb too, yawning and rubbing the back of his neck.

"Yep," he said. "Quite a blow. Keeled over on one of the snooker tables. Had a stroke."

Soon it was dawn, a cool, dewy spring dawn that wet the courthouse grass and left a low white mist on the pastures for the sun to burn away. Andy sat on the fender of his Nash and told all about the death and how everybody had taken it, who had cried and who hadn't. "Good thing you all got back today, you'd 'a missed the funeral," he said. "How'd you find Mexico?" Sonny could not have told him; he had lost track of things and just wanted to sit on the curb and watch the traffic light change.

17

SONNY WAS EMBARRASSED that he didn't have a suit to wear to the funeral—all he had was a pair of slacks and a blue sports coat that was too short at the wrists. No one seemed to notice, though. The graveyard was on a rough, gravelly hill, where the wind was always blowing. Sonny was able to quit being embarrassed because of Mrs. Farrow, who cried all through the graveyard ceremonies. She stood at the edge of the crowd, the wind blowing her long hair, and her cheeks wet; when she walked back to her Cadillac to drive away she was still crying and wiping her eyes with her gloves.

It was because of her crying so much that Sonny learned she had been the woman who watched Sam the Lion piss off the tank dam. That night at the café Sonny asked Genevieve about it and she didn't hold back.

"Sam's gone and Lois never cared who knew," she said. "Everybody knew but Gene. She and Sam carried on for quite a while. Lois was just crazy about him. She would have married him, old as he was, but he wouldn't let her leave Gene."

A few weeks before Sonny would not have believed it, but the world had become so strange that he could believe anything. Genevieve was wiping the counter with a gray washrag.

"Sam was quite a man, you know," she said. "And Lois was just beautiful when she was young—I always envied her her looks. She was prettier than her daughter ever will be, and nine times as wild. She had more life than just about anybody in this town."

Sonny didn't tell her about the bet at the tank dam, but he thought about it a lot, just as he thought about many of the things Sam the Lion had done. Some of them were very strange things—the will he left, for instance. He left the poolhall to Sonny and Billy; he left the picture show to Old Lady Mosey and her nephew Junior Mosey, who was the projectionist; he left the café to Genevieve, five thousand dollars to the county swimming-pool fund, and strangest of all, a thousand dollars to Joe Bob Blanton. No one knew what to make of it, not even Joe Bob. People thought it was a damned outrage, but that was what the will said.

Two weeks after the funeral the seniors left for San Francisco, on their senior trip. Sonny was glad to go. It seemed to him he had jumped up and gone to Mexico on the spur of the moment and had never quite managed to get back to Thalia, really. The town had become strange to him, and he thought it might be easier to return to it from San Francisco.

The bus left Thalia at midnight and when dawn came was crossing the Pecos River, a dry winding rut cutting through the naked flats of West Texas. Most of the seniors had cut up all night and worn themselves out, but Sonny was awake, and just tired enough that his memory could do what it pleased. The sky was completely cloudless, a round white moon hanging in it. He had not thought of Sam the Lion much since the funeral—in Thalia it was no good thinking about him— but for some reason the bitter flats of the Pecos brought him to mind and Sonny remembered the way he used to slop around the poolhall in his house shoes, complaining about the ingrown toenail that had pained him for years. A bronc had stomped on his foot once, and the toenail had never recovered. Sam the Lion, the horsebreaker, pissing off the tank dam while Lois Farrow watched—it was too much to be thinking about on the way to San Francisco, and his eyes kept leaking tears all the way to Van Horn.

They got to San Francisco in the middle of the night and checked into an expensive cheap motel on Van Ness Avenue, not far from the bay. Duane and Jacy were full of secret plans about the Thing they were going to do, and all the boys were itching to go bowling or find whores. The first day there the room mothers kept them all herded together and saw to it that they rode a cable car, visited the Top of the Mark, and went across the Golden Gate bridge. All the Californians looked at them as if they were freaks, whereas it seemed to the kids it was the other way around. The room mothers were scandalized by the number of bars in the city and kept everyone in a tight group to protect them against lurking perverts.

The second day was unscheduled and most of the boys spent it on Market Street, looking at dirty magazines and talking to girls and sailors in the cheap sidewalk lunch counters. Sonny and three other boys wandered into a bar between Market and Mission and were met by a tall black-headed girl named Gloria who offered to let them take pictures of her naked. The bar itself was plastered with pictures of Gloria naked, a great inducement to photography. Unfortunately her fee for the privilege was twenty dollars and none of the boys could afford it.

The major event of the trip occurred on the afternoon of the second day in San Francisco when Jacy finally allowed Duane to seduce her. The girls were all supposed to accompany the room mothers to the De Young Museum that afternoon, but Jacy cleverly got out of it. She was rooming with an obliging little girl named Winnie Snips, and she got Winnie to tell the room mothers that she had taken to her bed with menstrual cramps. No one ever doubted the word of Winnie Snips. She was valedictorian, and just unpopular enough that she was glad to do anything anyone wanted of her.

After the girls and the room mothers left, Sonny stationed himself in the lobby of the motel so he could give the alarm if the party got back early. It was an ugly lobby full of postcard racks and it depressed him a little to sit in it. The only senior who bothered with postcards was Charlene Duggs who sent about a dozen a day to an airman boy friend of hers in Wichita Falls. She wanted everyone to know how much in love she was, but she didn't have much to say and just wrote "Gee, I miss you, Love and kisses, Charlene" on every card. When Sonny thought about Jacy he got even more depressed, but Duane was his friend and a scheme of such daring had to be supported.

As it turned out, Sonny's depression was nothing at all compared to the one Duane had to cope with in the seduction chamber upstairs. The glorious moment had arrived, and was going to be just perfect: they could even see the bay and a part of Alcatraz through the window. "I love you," Duane said, as soon as they had kissed a few times. "I love you too," Jacy said, breathing heavily. It was the way things were done. Then she let Duane take absolutely all her clothes off, something she had never done before. For some reason, being naked with him was different than being naked around a bunch of Wichita kids. She caught him looking right at the place between her legs, and that seemed rather discourteous. Still, there was no backing out, so she stretched out on the bed while Duane undressed. He had been in a state of anticipatory erection for at least half of the 1,800-mile drive, and could hardly wait to get his socks off. They kissed again for a moment, but both supposed speed to be of the essence and Duane soon rolled on top. Jacy sucked in her breath, preparing to be painfully devirginized. For a moment or two she did feel something that was hard and slightly painful, but it wasn't nearly as painful as she had expected it to be and in a moment it ceased to be hard at all and became flexible and rather wiggly. It certainly wasn't hurting her, but it wasn't going in, either. It sort of tickled, and kept sliding off into her public hair. Curiosity got the better of her and she opened her eyes. Duane had a very strange look on his face. He was horrified at himself, unable to believe his member should betray him—not then, of all times.

"What's wrong, honey?" Jacy asked, wiggling slightly. She couldn't stand to be tickled.

"Um," Duane said, a little choked. "I don't know."

He held himself above her, embarrassed to death but hoping beyond hope that his body would come to its senses and enable him to go on. He hoped for two or three long minutes, while Jacy offered her intimate of intimates, but his body continued to register complete indifference. Duane didn't have the faintest idea what to do: no emergency had ever been more unlooked for.

After a time Jacy felt a rising sense of exasperation.

"Well get off a minute," she said. "You might get tired and fall on me."

Duane complied, too disgraced to venture speech. He sat hopelessly on the edge of the bed, looking out at the bay. Jacy sat up and shrugged her hair back across her shoulders. Obviously they were faced with a crisis. The situation had to be salvaged or they would be the laughing stock of the class. Suddenly she felt furious with Duane. She looked with vexation at the offending organ.

"It was Mexico," she said. "I hate you. No tellin' what you got down there. I don't know why I ever went with you."

"I don't know what happened," Duane said glumly. He got up and crept reluctantly back into his clothes, but Jacy stalked about the room, indignantly naked and not giving a damn.

"What'll we say?" she said. "The whole class knows what we were going to do. I just want to cry. I think you're the meanest boy I ever saw and my mother was so right about you."

"I don't know what happened," Duane said again. He really didn't. He started for the door but Jacy stopped him.

"Don't go out there yet," she said. "We haven't had time to do it—Sonny would know. I don't want one soul to know."

Duane sat back down on the bed and Jacy went into the bathroom and cried a few real tears of anger. It seemed to her Duane had been a monster of thoughtlessness to put her in such a position. She didn't want to touch him again, ever, and it angered her to think she would have to go on pretending to be his sweetheart for the rest of the trip. It would never do to let the class think they had broken up over sex. In fact, she would have to be even more loving with him in public, so everyone would think they were having a warm, meaningful affair.

When she thought they had been in the room long enough she went out and told Duane to leave.

"You better not tell one soul, either," she said. "You just pretend it was wonderful. And wear your slacks when we go to supper tonight—I think we're going someplace nice."

She stood naked, hands on hips, conscious that her nudity embarrassed Duane a little, and thoroughly pleased that it did.

"Well, I'm sorry," he said again. "I don't know what happened."

"If you say that one more time I'll bite you," Jacy said.

When Winnie Snips and the other girls piled into the room an hour later, pale with curiosity, Jacy was sitting in a well-rumpled bed with only her pajama tops on, staring out at the bay. The evening fog was coming in.

"Oh gee," Winnie said. "Tell us about it, Jacy. What happened?"

Jacy looked languorously around at them, calm, replete, a little wasted even.

"I just can't describe it," she said. "I just can't describe it in words."

The very next day, to Duane's immense relief, the seduction happened after all. Jacy insisted he take her for a walk to show everyone how much they wanted to be alone, and while they were walking down Geary Street, holding hands in case anyone from the class should see them, Duane suddenly felt himself return. They were just outside a cheap hotel, and without hesitation he seized his chance.

"Come on," he said. He had Jacy in the lobby of the hotel before she even knew what he meant. An old lady in a blue-flowered silk bathrobe registered them without comment and took five dollars from Duane. In the creaky cage of an elevator he kissed Jacy hungrily and fondled her breast, conscious that all was still well below. Jacy was skeptical and didn't return the kiss, but there *was* something rather adventurous about being fondled in an elevator—Winnie Snips would faint if she heard of such a thing.

Their room was tiny, with green walls, an old-fashioned bed, and a narrow window that looked across Geary Street to a one-story nightclub with a dead neon sign outside. Duane wasted absolutely no time—he was taking no chances with himself. He was out of his clothes by the time the door closed, and he tugged Jacy toward the bed, pulling rudely at her skirt. She shrugged loose and went to the window to undress at her own pace.

"If you can't wait you can jump out this window," she said. "I don't think it will work anyway."

Duane was not certain it would either, and waited nervously. The room was chilly and Jacy had goose bumps on her breasts. As she lay down she looked at Duane casually—men were certainly strange. All she really expected was something tickly, but Duane surprised her horribly. He didn't tickle a bit, but instead he did something really painful. At first she was too startled to move, and then she yelled out loud. Someone in an adjoining room kicked the wall indignantly. "Quit, quit," she said—it was intolerable. Duane was much too thrilled to quit, but fortunately he didn't take long. Jacy was at her wit's end as it was.

She got gingerly out of bed, meaning to take a hot bath, and discovered that the little room didn't even have a bathroom in it, just a lavatory. "There must be one down the hall someplace," Duane said, but she wouldn't let him go look for it. She felt strange and wanted to leave. All the way back to the motel she kept glancing over her shoulder, expecting to see a trail of blood on the sidewalk behind her. Duane was walking happily along, infuriatingly proud of himself.

"Oh, quit prissing," Jacy said. "You needn't think I'm going to take you back just because of that. I don't think you did it right, anyway."

"Sure I did," Duane said, but he wasn't really positive, and he brooded about it during the remainder of the trip. They did it twice more, once in the motel in San Francisco and once in Flagstaff, Arizona, on the way home. Duane was confident he was doing it right, but for some reason Jacy didn't swoon with bliss. She only allowed it twice more because she thought Bobby Sheen would like it if she had a little more experience. The whole business was far from delightful, but she supposed that was probably because Duane was a roughneck. In Flagstaff it went on much too long and she got exasperated and told him off once and for all.

"You never will learn," she said. "I don't know why I went with you so long. I guess we have to keep on being sweethearts until we get home, but that's gonna be the end of it. We'll just have to think of something big to break up over."

Duane just couldn't understand it: he was more dejected and more in love than he ever had been. Jacy was bending over to slip her small breasts back into their brassiere cups; she had never looked more lovely, and he could not believe she was serious about breaking up. He tried to talk her out of it, but she went over to the motel dressing table and combed her hair thoroughly, looking at herself in the mirror and paying absolutely no attention to him.

The rest of the way home, across Arizona, New Mexico, Texas, he tried to think of ways to make her realize that they had to stay together. He was sure her disaffection would only be temporary. Jacy was thinking how glad she would be to get home. She had even decided there was no point in making a big production of breaking up: she was sick and tired of the seniors. As an audience they were not worth bothering about. When the bus finally pulled into Thalia late one June afternoon she didn't so much as tell Duane good-bye. She was tired and went right over to her parents' Cadillac while her father got her bags. Lois was watching her shrewdly.

"I see you got enough of him," she said quietly. "That's that."

"I'm just not interested in saying one word about it, if you don't mind," Jacy said.

Watching them drive away, Duane felt a little sick at his stomach. He realized Jacy had meant what she said: she was really done with him. It was very confusing to him because he had always thought you were supposed to get whoever you really loved. That was the way it worked in movies. It was all he could do to carry his suitcase to the pickup.

Sonny had merely endured the return trip, sitting in the back of the bus watching the desert go by. He had paid Duane and Jacy as little attention as possible, and it was not until he and Duane got in the pickup in Thalia that he noticed his friend was depressed.

"What's the matter?" he asked, surprised.

"Nothin'," Duane said.

Sonny knew better. "Well what is it?" he persisted. "You feel bad?"

For a moment Duane considered telling the truth, but then he decided not to. "I'm worn to a frazzle," he said. "That California's hard on a person."

They were living over the poolhall, Billy with them, though Genevieve had kept him while the seniors were gone. Returning to the poolhall was a little strange, particularly since Sam the Lion wasn't there. If he had been there they would have shot some pool and had a great time telling him all about the trip. It would have picked everyone's spirits up. As it was, the poolhall was quiet and empty, and there was not a great deal to do.

18

WHILE THE SENIORS were in California a great scandal rocked Thalia. All the mothers were agreed that it was the very worst thing that had ever happened in the town: John Cecil was fired from his teaching job for being a homosexual.

The scariest thing of all, the mothers thought, was that it was just by a happenstance that he was found out. If it hadn't been for Coach Popper's vigilance and his interest in the welfare of the children, nobody would have known about Mr. Cecil, and a whole generation of young innocents would have been exposed to corruption.

The gist of the matter was that Mr. Cecil had persuaded Bobby Logan to take a summer-school course in trigonometry, in Wichita Falls high school. Mr. Cecil was going to summer school himself, at the college there, so he drove Bobby over to his class every day. That seemingly innocent arrangement was enough to arouse the coach's suspicions. He had been planning to have Bobby work out in the gym every day during the summer, so he would be in good shape when football season came. It was a pleasure to work with a fine young athlete like Bobby, and when Bobby told him about the trigonometry class he was angered.

"Why goddamn," he said. "You mean you're gonna sit in a damn schoolhouse all summer when you could be workin' out? What kinda shit is that?"

Bobby was a little embarrassed. "I'll have to have trig to get in a good college," he said.

"Trig my ass," the coach said. "I can get you a scholarship anywhere and you won't need to know a fuckin' thing."

He raged on, but Bobby was determined, and that night, thinking it over, it came to the coach in a flash: Cecil was a queer.

He didn't say anything to Ruth about it because it wasn't a thing to talk to women about. The next morning he happened to be standing around the filling station and he mentioned his suspicion to some of the men. They were sitting on piles of old tires, chewing tobacco and discussing masculine matters, and all of them agreed with the coach right down the line.

"Hell yes," one said. "Whoever heard of a man teachin' English. That's a woman's job."

"Oughta see the school board about it," the coach said sternly. The idea got quick support.

"By God, if you don't I will," Andy Fanner said. "I got two boys in that school."

"Well, I tell you, men," the coach said, squaring his shoulders with purpose. "I hate to cost a man his job, but if there's anything I hate it's to see a goddamn homasexyul messing around with a bunch of young kids. I got too much respect for the teachin' profession to put up with that."

It turned out the coach didn't have to say a word to the school board. Some of the men went home and told their wives and the wives called the school board president even before they began to call one another. The school board president was a Pontiac salesman named Tom Todd. When Tom was fourteen years old he had been seduced one night at a family reunion by a male cousin from Jonesboro, Arkansas, and he had felt guilty about it ever since. He went right into action and that very night they got John Cecil before the board and fired him.

All Mr. Cecil could say was that he hadn't done anything to Bobby, or to anyone else. He was stunned and guilty looking though, and the board knew they had their man. They didn't question Bobby Logan because his father didn't want him to know what homosexuality was yet. If it had already happened to him his father preferred that he didn't realize it.

Mr. Cecil went home and tried to explain to his wife what a terrible mistake had been made. "Why I've never even touched one of my students," he said.

"Oh, they wouldn't have fired you if you hadn't," she said. Then she screamed and ran across to the neighbor's house and then screamed again and ran back and got the two girls. She didn't return that night, but the next morning she got some of her stuff and headed for Odessa in Mr. Cecil's car. Her sisters lived in Odessa.

Ruth Popper found out about it the night Mr. Cecil was fired. The coach was in an unusually good mood that night and was propped up in bed reading an old issue of *Sports Afield*—there was a fishing story in it he had read at least fifty times.

Ruth could not sleep with the light on, and was reading the *Reader's Digest*. She lay flat on her back, and Herman noticed.

"Prop up if you're gonna read," he said. "It ain't good for your eyes to read laying down."

She obediently tucked a pillow under her head, and as she did, noticed that Herman was looking at her in a very satisfied way. Suddenly, to her complete surprise, he reached under the cover and rubbed her in rough, husbandly fashion.

"I guess tonight there's a lot of women in this town glad they ain't in Irene Cecil's shoes," he said. "I feel awful sorry for Irene."

"Why?" Ruth asked. "I've always felt a little sorry for John."

"You would," the coach said, abruptly removing his hand. "I guess you'd like to be married to a queer. The school board fired him tonight. Me and some other fellers found out about him an' took some action. He'll never teach in this part of the country again."

Ruth didn't credit her hearing. "What did you say?" she asked.

"Why, didn't you know it, honey?" he said, gruffly condescending. "I could tell that feller was queer as a three-dollar bill—been thinking it for years. Reason I never spoke up sooner was because I never noticed him actually botherin' with any of the kids. When I saw he was after Bobby, I knew it was time to put a stop to it. That's one boy I don't intend to see messed up."

He farted gently into the sheets and went contentedly back to his fishing story.

Ruth wanted not to be there; not to be anywhere. She wanted to hug her knees with shame. Then gradually the shame was replaced by a dull, hot feeling inside her that soon filled her completely. Before she even recognized it as anger it had taken possession of her, and with no warning she swung her feet around in the bed and began to kick Herman furiously and as hard as she could. She kicked the magazine he held clear across the room and her bare heels caught him in the ribs and groin. The coach was so surprised he didn't know what to do. He tried to catch her ankles but he couldn't seem to and she continued to flail at him with her feet until he hastily got out and stood uncertainly by the bed, not sure what was happening to his wife.

"Here, now, here," he said. "You gone crazy? What's the matter with you?"

"You!" Ruth yelled, sitting up in bed. She was beside herself and meant to pursue him out of the house. "You're the matter," she said, her voice shaking. "You fat . . . you fat . . ." she didn't know what to call him. Looking around wildly, she saw the open bathroom door. "You fat turd!" she finished, a little lamely.

The two of them were both stunned. Quiet fell on the room. Ruth was panting, but since the coach had got beyond the range of her heels she had lost the urge to chase him. He would have liked to sit back down on the bed, but Ruth looked too strange and dangerous for him to risk it. He knew it would mean a fight if he got near her, so he stood where he was and scratched himself nervously. He would never have believed his own wife could look so dangerous.

"I never done nothin'," he said finally. "What if I did fart?" It was the only thing he could think of that might have made her mad.

"Oh, Herman," Ruth said. Her legs were trembling and all the strength had gone out of her.

"You got John Cecil fired."

"But he's a goddamn queer," the coach said righteously. "He needed it."

"Then how about you?" she said. "Who roomed with Bobby in Fort Worth, John or you? You think I don't know about things like that? Now you've ruined John's life."

The coach's mouth fell open. He felt tired and went over and sat down on the couch, fumbling with his undershirt.

"Why Ruth, you don't think nothin' like that," he said. "Nobody in this town would believe that. I'm the *football coach!*"

"Don't yell at me," she said. "I know what you are."

Herman looked at her solemnly. "I sure don't know what to think about a wife like you," he said, not at all belligerent.

"We're even," she said. "I don't know what to think about a husband like you, either. Marriage is a bad joke, isn't it."

She saw that she could rip him wide open if she said the right mean things, but she didn't really have the energy and it didn't seem worth doing.

"What are we going to do?" he asked.

"You're going to sleep on that couch from now on," she said, throwing his pillow across the room.

"Hell I am," the coach said, getting up. "Hell I am." But he picked up the pillow and stood holding it.

"You are," Ruth said, switching off the bedside light. "There's some sheets in the bathroom."

"Goddammit, I ain't gonna sleep on this couch," Herman said. "It's gonna take more than your kicking to keep me out of my own bed."

"I'll do whatever it takes," Ruth said. "Maybe I'll call the school board and get a few things off my chest."

Her calm voice infuriated the coach, but it frightened him, too. She was clearly an unstable woman. He felt like kicking hell out of her, but instead he went and got some sheets and made a bed on the couch, feeling like a martyr. She didn't deserve it, but the manly thing to do would be to give her a night to cool off. It seemed to him that his mother must have been the last good woman who had ever lived.

The next day Ruth went to see John Cecil, hoping to comfort him. It occurred to her that he might be hungry, so she took what was left of a banana-nut cake she had baked the day before and walked over to the Cecils' house. The porch was dusty and the morning paper lay in the flower bed where the newspaper boy had thrown it. John took a long time to answer her knock.

"Hello, John," she said. "Can I come in?"

He looked tired and a little sick, and she felt silly for bringing the rich cake. He had on a long-sleeved shirt with the sleeves rolled up unevenly.

"I'll just put this on the cabinet," she said awkwardly, moving past him with the cake. She got to the kitchen just in time to see a little pot of asparagus boil over— John had put too much water in the pot. "Oh, goodness," he said. She turned the burner off and he sponged off the stove. Curiously, the event seemed to lift his spirits a little.

"That's exactly the kind of bachelor I make," he said.

He pulled up a kitchen chair for Ruth to sit in and they looked at one another directly for the first time since she had entered.

"What are you going to do, John?" she asked. He seemed such a kind man, and she realized at that moment that they had lived three blocks apart for fifteen years without really becoming friends.

He shook his head, rubbing the back of his neck with both hands. "I'll just have to do what I can for Irene and the girls," he said. "I've got a friend who runs an Indian reservation in New Mexico—maybe he'll let me teach out there. If that don't work out I guess I can go back to Plainview and work in my brother's grocery store. When you've messed up your life the way I've messed up mine it doesn't much matter."

"But *you* didn't mess it up," Ruth said. "My husband messed it up. I'll never forgive him for it. If anybody needed to be fired for . . . what they fired you for, it was him."

John Cecil looked at her with astonishment. "Oh, you don't mean that, Ruth," he said, after a moment. "Why Herman's the football coach."

She saw that he didn't believe her, and knew that Herman had been right. Nobody, not even John Cecil, would believe her, and in truth she didn't even know for sure herself what Herman was. She just felt sad and uncertain and wanted to cry.

"But you've even got two kids," she said. "We don't have any kids, and we never will."

John chuckled. "It's kind of amazing to me that me and Irene had the girls," he said. "I guess it just don't take much enthusiasm for people to have two kids."

Suddenly Ruth wanted to be home, away from John Cecil. His sadness was so heavy that just being with him made her feel the weight, made her own limbs seem heavier. She made an excuse and left quickly, glad to be outside.

The next day John Cecil left Thalia for good, to go back to Plainview to his brother's grocery store. The job on the Indian reservation hadn't worked out.

When Sonny returned from the senior trip, Ruth and he discovered that they were famished for one another. The first afternoon he stayed so long that, while they were dressing, the coach's pickup drove into the driveway. It was something they had dreaded and been frightened of for months, but just then they felt so calm and comfortable with one another that they were not even scared. Besides, the coach customarily spent ten or fifteen minutes carefully putting away his fishing equipment. Sonny quietly finished dressing and went in the living room, so he could go out the front door as the coach came in the back. Ruth, wearing only her panties, folded the quilt and took it to the cedar chest in the hall closet, where it was kept. She was still a little excited, still a little warm. She picked up her dress and went into the living room—the late sun was filtering through the Venetian blinds and Sonny was peeping out of one window, watching the garage. Ruth came up behind him, slipped her arm around his waist and rubbed his stomach. When he realized she was still almost naked he turned with a smile and lifted her breasts. She put the dress on and Sonny buttoned it in back.

"I love you," she said. "You must treat me right from now on."

He didn't reply, but when they heard the back door open he kissed her lightly and walked blithely away, down the front sidewalk.

Herman was in the kitchen, poking around in the cabinet trying to find some Mercurochrome to put on a skinned hand. He could never find things like that when he needed them. Ruth stood in the door a moment, watching him fumble in the cabinet, and her mood was so good that she felt a moment of fondness for him. All he really needed of her was an occasional small kindness.

"I'll find that," she said. "How was fishing?"

For three weeks she continued to make his bed on the couch, and he accepted it, bewildered. Every night he thought he would think up a way to get his supremacy back, but every night the task proved too much for him and he decided it wouldn't hurt Ruth to have one more night to cool off.

In fact, he needed only to wait. Ruth found that she didn't like to sleep alone. She slept better with a body next to hers, even if it was Herman's. For a night or two she fought with herself, determined to keep the advantage she had gained, but she just felt more and more restless and decided finally that it was a silly way to keep an advantage. The next evening, when she was changing the pillowcases, she put Herman's pillow back on the bed. Without a word being said, he came too.

19

SUMMER SHAPED UP very well for Sonny, but very badly for Duane. The first thing Sonny did was quit his job with Frank Fartley. He then hired on as a roughneck with Gene Farrow. He liked driving the butane truck better, but doing it full time gave him no chance to be with Ruth, whereas if he rough-necked at night he could count on spending the whole afternoon with her. Coach Popper was away fishing almost every day. Ruth was becoming happier every day, and was a lot more fun to visit than she had been. She and Sonny both lived for the afternoons.

Duane, unfortunately, had no one to make his days worthwhile. True to her word, Jacy had cut him off cold. Once in a while he saw her driving through town, her sunglasses on, the top of her convertible down, her bare arms tanned from all the hours she spent lying around the country club pool in Wichita. Such glimpses made him ache with desire, but ache was about all he could do. He spent most of June futilely trying to get her to talk to him on the phone—usually she just hung up, but the few times she didn't hang up were even worse.

"Why don't you go back to Mexico," she said once. "I guess girls are just easier to please down there."

"Just go with me once more," he kept saying. "Just one more time. You can at least see me."

He was convinced that if he were actually in her presence for a few minutes all her craziness would go away and they could be in love again.

Jacy knew how he felt, and repeatedly refused to see him. The whole town knew he was desperate to get her back, which suited her fine. After a month had gone by she put a stop to the calls.

"You find somebody else to pester," she said. "I've got a new boy friend now and I can't be talking to you."

"Who?" Duane asked, confused. The blow was unexpected.

"Lester Marlow," Jacy said. "I guess I've just been wanting to go with Lester all along and didn't realize it."

Duane hung up, went downstairs, and threw three pool balls against the back wall of the building as hard as he could, knocking out three big hunks of plaster and scaring Old Man Parsons almost to death. Old Man Parsons was a retired hardware salesman who looked after the poolhall during the day.

That night Duane told Sonny that he was leaving town—he had already packed his suitcase.

"There's not a goddamn thing to stay for," he said. "I'm goin' to Midland. All the roughnecks say you can get a job out there anytime. Jacy's goin' with Lester, why not leave?"

Sonny had no answer. Late that night he and Duane and Genevieve had coffee and pie together and Duane caught the three o'clock bus out. The prospect of setting out into the world had already taken Duane's mind off his problem. He was speculating about what sort of wages he could draw in Midland. Sonny felt okay about it, figuring to see Duane back in Thalia as soon as Jacy got off to college. When they walked Duane to the bus in the warm summer night they all felt good. Sonny and Genevieve stood on the curb in front of the café and watched the bus pull out. Soon all they could see of it were the red taillights, far out beyond the city limits sign.

"Wouldn't mind goin' someplace myself," Sonny said.

"Well, Uncle Sam will see you get your chance," Genevieve said, stretching her arms.

Abilene's Mercury was parked in front of the poolhall. Sonny was ready to go home, but he hated to go through the poolhall while Abilene was practicing. Finally he went in and had another cup of coffee with Genevieve, waiting to hear the Mercury roar away.

When Jacy heard about Duane leaving town she was a little bit upset. His calls had not been all that annoying—sometimes when she was bored the calls picked her up a little. It was true that she had started going with Lester more or less officially, but it was certainly no deep love affair. She was getting ready to be deeply in love with Bobby Sheen, and she regarded Lester as a necessary stepping-stone. Only by going with someone in Bobby's circle could she keep herself constantly before his eyes, and she knew that if she kept herself constantly before his eyes he would soon realize that she was more beautiful than Annie-Annie. Jacy knew quite well that she was prettier than Annie-Annie, but at the same time it worried her a little than Annie-Annie always managed to look extremely sexy. The only thing Jacy could figure was that the sexy look was something Annie-Annie had acquired with experience, and there was certainly no reason why she couldn't get just as much experience as Annie-Annie had. Lester Marlow was exactly suitable for such a purpose: he adored Jacy and was completely manageable. She still thought red pubic hair was a little ridiculous, but some things had to be accepted if one was to become a woman of the world.

The Wichita kids called sexual intercourse "screwing," so Jacy took to calling it that too. Lester's parents were in Colorado for the summer, so she and Lester could screw whenever they wanted to—Lester was always willing and usually more or less able. In a week or so Jacy managed to become completely unshy about the whole business, and even worked out a sort of routine. She slept until noon, got up, ate some peanut butter, called Lester to see if he was home, put on shorts, sandals, a blouse, and her new sunglasses and drove to Wichita. The drive always made her sweat a little and it was pleasant to walk into Lester's big cool house. Lester would always be there looking slightly nervous.

"Hi," Jacy would say. "Want to screw?" That was the favored approach among the Bobby Sheen set. Lester wouldn't have dared not to want to, so Jacy would go up to his parents' bedroom, the room with the biggest, most comfortable bed. There she would peel off her clothes and wait for Lester to peel off his. The screwing itself was pretty athletic—Jacy had never been very big on athletics, but she knew good and well she could learn to screw if she put her mind to it. Fortunately, Lester had a good attitude: he would do exactly as directed. When they were finished they usually drove over to the country club and lay around the pool with Bobby Sheen and Annie-Annie and all the other kids, most of whom had been screwing too. One day Bobby Sheen offered to rub suntan oil on Jacy's back and legs and she knew she was making progress. He rubbed the oil on in a very sexy way, she thought.

From time to time it occurred to her that she had really run Duane off too soon. He wasn't quite as manageable as Lester, but he was really a good bit sexier, and she discovered that some of the girls thought there was something pretty romantic about sleeping with roughnecks. She could probably have got another month or so of good out of Duane, but that she hadn't didn't really worry her: Bobby Sheen was the main objective, and if for prestige reasons it became necessary to have a roughneck in love with her there was always Sonny. He was very available, and just as nice as Duane.

Once, just to show that she wasn't snobbish, she called Sonny up and invited him to have a hamburger with her. It was a pleasant summer evening in early July and they decided to drive to Wichita and eat. Jacy drove, her hair blowing across her face. She had on a white silk blouse with the ends tied together in a knot across her stomach—an inch or two of her midriff showed between blouse and shorts.

"Do you ever hear from Duane?" she asked, sighing. "I really feel bad about that."

"I had a postcard," Sonny said. "He's makin' three-twenty a month. Said he bought a car."

"Well, I guess I'll always be a little bit in love with Duane," Jacy said. "We just had too much against us. It wasn't easy having to be the one to break up."

Talking about it made Sonny uneasy. In fact, just riding with Jacy made him feel a little disloyal. He still thought of her as Duane's girl.

They ate hamburgers, drank milk shakes, and rode slowly back to Thalia, looking at the millions of summer stars. Jacy let Sonny out at the poolhall and went on home, realizing only after she got there that she had enjoyed the evening. Dating no one but Lester Marlow was really tiresome. Except for not being rich, Sonny was more her type of boy. The thought of screwing Lester one more time was utterly boring, but she didn't really feel like she could push things with Bobby Sheen. She decided that in a day or two she would call Sonny again and perhaps go to the lake with him to find out if she liked to kiss him. It would be nice once more to go with somebody she liked to kiss.

The very next day, Bobby Sheen seduced her. Annie-Annie had gone to Dallas to buy her college wardrobe, and Jacy had skipped Lester and gone straight to the club to swim. Bobby asked her if she wanted to go to his house to play some records and that was it. They spread towels over the seats of his MG and wore their wet bathing suits to the house. As soon as they were inside Bobby slipped her straps down so he could play with her breasts. Jacy tried to concentrate and do everything right but it was actually pretty arousing, screwing Bobby Sheen, and she couldn't keep her head clear. He was about five times as athletic as Lester and when she thought it over later she was pretty sure she came, which was what one was supposed to do. At any rate, she went to sleep and didn't wake up until six o'clock. She found Bobby downstairs. He had on Bermuda shorts and was eating a peanut butter sandwich while he watched the news on TV.

"Peanut butter?" he asked absently, when he noticed Jacy. She didn't want to eat, she wanted to sit in his lap, but she saw he was really watching the news and made herself refrain. They had come home in his car, she had no way to leave. During the commercial Bobby got up to fix himself another sandwich. "Oh, you're afoot, aren't you," he said. "As soon as the news is over I'll run you back to the club."

He was quite cheerful and relaxed, but Jacy was a little surprised that he didn't take on over her more than he did. For the next four or five days she hung around the club pool almost constantly, expecting to hear that Bobby and Annie-Annie had broken up; she was sure that as soon as that happened Bobby would call her for another date.

The next Sunday morning Jacy was in the kitchen peeling an orange when her mother came in from the bedroom to get more coffee. On Sunday mornings Lois always lay in bed and drank coffee until the coffee pot was empty. Gene was gone—he always spent Sunday morning inspecting his leases.

"Honey," Lois asked, "don't you know that Sheen boy in Wichita? Bobby Sheen?"

"I sure do," Jacy said. "Why?"

"He got married yesterday to some girl named Annie Martin," Lois said. "It's in the paper this morning. I knew I'd seen them around the club. They got married in Oklahoma a couple of days ago and it just now made the paper. You know her?"

Jacy walked into the bedroom and found the article. It was just a tiny article with no picture, the kind the paper always ran when kids of prominent families ran off and got married without their parents' consent.

When Lois came into the bedroom with her coffee, Jacy was sitting on the bed crying bitterly.

"He's the luh-ast one," she said. "I'll just be an ol' maid."

Lois set her coffee down and got her daughter a box of Kleenex. She had seldom seen Jacy so upset, and least of all over a boy. Her tears were ruining the newspaper, and since she hadn't finished reading it Lois gently pulled it away.

"Oh, honey," she said. "Don't cry like that. That's the way it is, you know. Win a few, lose a few. That's really the way it goes, all through life."

20

ABOUT A WEEK after Bobby Sheen got married, something totally unexpected happened to Jacy, and it was led up to by an event so startling that everyone in Thalia almost went mad with surprise. Joe Bob Blanton was arrested for rape!

It was one of those days when it seemed to Christian people that the Lord must have lost all patience with the town. It was a wonder he hadn't simply destroyed it by fire, like he had Sodom, and since the heat at midafternoon that day was 109 degrees He could easily have done so simply by making the sun a little hotter. A few degrees more and the grass would have flamed, the buildings begun to smoke, and the asphalt streets to melt and bubble.

Joe Bob didn't rape Jacy, of course, but the general confusion that followed his arrest made possible what did happen to her. Joe Bob didn't actually rape anybody, but very few would have believed that at the time.

"That poor kid's downfall started the day old man Blanton got the call to preach," Lois Farrow said, but she was the only one who took that view. No one else thought of blaming Brother Blanton for his son's disgrace, and still less did they think of blaming Coach Popper or the school board president or San Francisco or Esther Williams, the movie star. They were all quite willing to put the blame squarely on Joe Bob himself.

Joe Bob was a seventeen-year-old virgin. For years he had been tormented by lustful thoughts. When he was only fourteen Brother Blanton slipped into his room one night and caught him masturbating by flashlight over a picture of Esther Williams. Joe Bob had torn the picture out of a movie magazine one of their neighbors had thrown away. Of course Brother Blanton whipped him severely and disposed of the picture; he also told Joe Bob in no uncertain terms what the sequel of such actions would be.

"Joe Bob," he said, "have you ever been through the State Hospital in Wichita? The insane asylum?"

"No sir," Joe Bob said.

"Well, sometime I'll take you," Brother Blanton promised. "There are three or four hundred men over there, pitiful creatures, rotting away, no good to their families or to the Lord or anybody. I don't know about all of them, some of them may have come from broken homes or been alcoholics, but I'm sure most of those men are there because they did just what you were doing today. They abused themselves until their minds were destroyed. I don't want to scare you now. You're young, you haven't hurt yourself much, and the Lord will forgive you. I just want you to know what will happen if you keep on with this kind of filthiness. You understand, don't you?"

"Yes sir," Joe Bob said.

He understood, but he soon discovered he was just too weak to stop. He kept right on playing with himself, all through high school, in the face of certain insanity. His father hadn't told him how long it took for a mind to be destroyed, but he never doubted that his would be, sooner or later.

In the summer of his junior year, when he got the call to preach, he thought there still might be hope. If he preached, girls might like him, and if they did he might be able to overcome his vices and lead a normal life. The hope was very short-lived. The very night he preached his first sermon he succumbed to the vice again. Besides that, he found he did not really like to preach. He didn't have anything to say, and he soon decided he must have heard a false call: he could always get the Lord off his mind, but the only way he could get girls off his mind was by jacking off. In San Francisco he had been with the boys who wandered into the bar where Gloria was, and the thought of Gloria haunted him for weeks. By the time he got back home he had decided to resign himself to eventual insanity, and he ceased to make any effort to curb his self-abuse. If the Lord spared him until he got through college that would be enough to ask.

Joe Bob might have got through the summer all right if it had not been for the scandal caused by Mr. Cecil's dismissal. That set the town on its ear so that it made things hard for all sinners. The church ladies decided the time had come for some widespread soul-saving. If a homosexual was teaching English in high school, there was no telling what state of degeneracy the ordinary populace had fallen into. Ruth Popper herself was known to be sleeping with a high-school boy. They decided to have an All City Revival, and they didn't waste any money bringing in a slick traveling evangelist who would have charged them three hundred dollars. There were six active preachers in the town, plus Joe Bob and a few old ones that were retired, so the ladies decided to put aside denominational differences and make do with the native preaching stock.

Everybody but Joe Bob thought it was a fine idea. He didn't because it meant he would have to preach two sermons.

"Yes sir," Brother Blanton told him. "We've all got to get out there and preach our hearts out if we're going to get this town back on the right track."

Joe Bob agreed, but he was afraid he could preach his own heart completely out in just a minute or two. During the winter his ministerial flame had burned very low—he was not even confident that he himself was saved. He knew that he harbored hatred in his heart for about three-quarters of the boys of the town, and that was surely not a Christian attitude. He had no idea what he could say that might prompt anyone in the congregation to rededicate their life to Christ, and so far as he knew, getting people to rededicate their lives was the only point of a revival.

He worried about it for two weeks, and it turned out his worries were fully justified. Joe Bob had to preach the last sermon in the first go-round of preachers, which meant that he had to preach on a Thursday night, the worst possible night to preach. The first wave of revival spirit had had time to ebb, and the second wave had not yet begun to gather. The revival was held in the local baseball park under the lights, and when Joe Bob got up to preach there was just a sprinkle of a crowd, old faithfuls from all the churches in town, people so habituated to churchgoing that they never missed a sermon, no matter how dull. Joe Bob was dressed in his black wool suit, the only suit his father would let him preach in. The night was sweltering. For days Joe Bob had racked his brain, trying to come up with a sermon, but the only moral advice he could think of was that people ought to read the Bible more. That was his theme, and he sweated and stammered away at it for twenty minutes.

"When I say back to the Bible I don't mean just a chapter here and there," he tried. "I mean the *full* Gospel, the *whole* Bible, *all* of it! Ever bit!"

He kept working that point over desperately, hoping somebody, at least one person, would come down and rededicate his life. Finally, to his great relief, the Pender family got down out of the stands and came. It was not much of a triumph, because the Pender family rededicated their lives regularly, several times a year, but it was better than nothing. The Penders lived in a cabin down on Onion Creek where they shot squirrels and farmed sweet potatoes. Every two or three months, when things got boring, they came to church and rededicated their lives, hoping thereby to move the community to charity. They were a generally scruffy lot—in fact old man Elmer Pender spat tobacco juice right on home plate as Joe Bob was calling for the closing hymn.

Because of the Penders, the first sermon was not a total disgrace, but Joe Bob still had the second one to preach. That one was scheduled for a Saturday night, only one night before the revival was due to end. Hysteria would be at its height, and Joe Bob knew he would need something more potent than the Full Gospel to exhort on that night. On the next-to-last night of a revival it would be a black disgrace not to get twenty or thirty rededications.

All week he brooded about the final sermon. He knew good and well there was no way he could get out of it, and as the week wore on the only way he could get it off his mind was by abusing himself. By Saturday morning he was in a serious state. He stayed in his room until noon and abused himself twice. Then he talked his father into letting him use the family Plymouth, on the grounds that he needed to go off and commune with nature in order to get inspiration for his sermon. Nature that day was about as hot as the place Joe Bob was supposed to be saving people from. He drove out to the lake and sat staring at the water for a couple of hours, thinking how much he didn't want to preach that night. Finally he tired of staring at the bright sun-whitened water and drove into town to get a Coke. That move turned out to be his downfall.

The facts of it almost passed belief. Nobody in Thalia would have supposed that Joe Bob could get in so much trouble in Thalia, Texas, right in the middle of a hot Saturday afternoon. Sonny heard about it almost as soon as the news got out. The sheriff happened to be in the poolhall shooting a quiet game of snooker when Monroe, his skinny deputy, came bursting in, white as a sheet.

"Sheriff, Johnny Clarg's little girl has kinda been kidnapped," he said. "They seen the preacher's boy putting her in his car about an hour and a half ago, in front of the drugstore."

"What the hell?" the sheriff said, taking aim at a red ball. "Maybe Joe Bob gave her a ride home—be doing her a favor, hot as it is. Why should Joe Bob want to kidnap Molly Clarg?"

"Don't ask me," Monroe said. "She ain't at home, though. Miz Clarg's all upset—she's done looked everywhere for 'em. They was seen drivin' out of town toward Olney. Miz Clarg's afraid Joe Bob might be goin' to mo-lest her or something."

At that the sheriff quickly slapped his cue into a rack. He was getting beat anyway, and a sex crime called for immediate action.

"Some of you boys might come with us," he said. "If that's the way it is, no tellin' what we'll find."

In all, three cars set out on the search. Brother Blanton was in one, with his wife and some good church deacons. Mrs. Clarg was in another, with a deputy and some of her friends, and the sheriff and several men were in the lead car. Sonny was with the sheriff.

Fortunately, no particular searching was required. It was clear to everybody that Joe Bob had taken Molly out to an old lovers' lane, three or four miles south of town.

"Boys, I don't know what to think, but I fear the worst," the sheriff said, wiping his sweaty face on his shirt sleeve. He drove like sixty, roaring over the rattly cattle guards as if they weren't there. If they hadn't been lucky and encountered Joe Bob on an open stretch of dirt road the sheriff might well have plowed right into him and killed Molly and several other people. When they spotted him Joe Bob was on his way back to town, but he was coming reluctantly, at a speed of five miles an hour. He stopped instantly when he saw the three cars coming toward him.

The sheriff quickly got out of his car and rolled down the cuffs of his shirt sleeves, while Joe Bob sat in the Plymouth, looking miserable. Everyone but Brother Blanton and his wife got out of the cars and stood looking indecisively at the Plymouth. After a moment Mrs. Clarg became hysterical and ran over to the Plymouth and yanked Molly out. Molly was five, and had been sitting quietly in the front seat eating a lemon all-day sucker Joe Bob had given her. When her mother yanked her out everybody noticed that she didn't have her panties on.

"Get him, ain't you goin' to?" Mrs. Clarg cried. "He's the one done it, here's my little girl, why don't you get him. If my husband was here he'd kill him dead."

At that the sheriff and Monroe leaped in and pulled Joe Bob out of the car.

"What'd you do to that child?" the sheriff said. "We all know you done somethin'."

Joe Bob started to say something but he was too scared and nervous to get it out. Instead he collapsed, and they carried him to the sheriff's car and rushed him back to Thalia.

Sonny volunteered to drive the Blantons' Plymouth into town. Seeing Joe Bob so scared depressed him and he drove slowly. Molly Clarg's panties were lying in the car seat—no one had noticed them, but Sonny supposed they were evidence so he left them there. By the time he got back to town the poolhall was full of men, all of them talking about the crime. It was generally agreed that Johnny Clarg would go to the jailhouse and kill Joe Bob as soon as he came in off his rig.

Then Monroe came in with news that the doctor had said Joe Bob hadn't actually done anything to Molly. Apparently he had just given her the lemon all-day sucker as a bribe to get her to take her panties off, and that was all he had done. It was kind of a letdown.

"Never had the guts," Andy Fanner said. "Preacher's boy."

"Well, the sheriff figures he might have mo-lested her a little bit," Monroe said. "It stands to reason."

"I've thought for years the boy was that kind," Coach Popper said, when he found out about it.

At any rate, Joe Bob had found the one method available to him for getting out of his second revival sermon. He spent that night and many others in jail, but in a way, what *did* happen at the revival that night was his triumph. His disgrace made possible the greatest upsurge of religious feeling the town had ever known. Brother Blanton insisted on preaching his son's sermon, and what he said did it. He rose above calamity and got right out there on home plate to lay matters on the line.

"Good people," he said, "I guess today I've suffered about the worst shock that can come to a man of God. My own son sits in jail tonight, sick with corruption. This very afternoon he was caught in an act of carnal trespass, a thing so foul it's almost unspeakable. How that tears my heartstrings I can't say, but what I want you to know tonight is that I've come through. The Lord has held me up. I've not lost one bit of faith. As for Joe Bob, I've given him up to the Lord. I've prayed to the good Lord this very night that they'll send my boy to prison. Yes, to prison! Sometimes in this life things just don't work out, and I believe it is God's merciful will that Joe Bob go to suffer with the murderer and the thief. It will be a hard thing but a just thing, and I know Joe can count on God's help."

At that Brother Blanton broke down, stretched his arms to the crowd, and began to cry. "Oh, my friends," he said. "If only you would take heed from my trouble. If only you would listen and realize that Jesus Christ is the only answer. If only you would come down tonight, just come down and pray with me and let all of us rededicate our lives right now to the pure way, the righteous way. . . ."

The crowd was overcome by Brother Blanton's self-sacrifice. They flocked down, weeping and hugging one another, the women all slapping at their faces with damp powder puffs, trying to keep their makeup from running completely off. The Penders even came again, Elmer, Lee Harvey, and Mag, the three of them swept away by the general fervor.

There was one strange moment though, right at the start of the sermon: Lois Farrow walked out. As soon as Brother Blanton said he hoped Joe Bob would go to jail, Lois left the stands, got in the Cadillac, and drove away. A lot of tongues clicked—most people thought Lois needed saving worse than anyone in town. Even Brother Blanton felt a momentary irritation when he saw her leaving. Saving a soul as far gone as hers would have really gained him some heavenly credit.

What Lois did after she left was even more unusual: she went down to the jail and made Monroe let her play checkers with Joe Bob. It almost passed belief, but she sat right in the cell and played Joe Bob three games, two of which Joe Bob won. He was not feeling too bad, really. Getting out of the sermon had taken a big load off his mind.

Jacy stayed home from the revival and spent the evening watching television. While *Gunsmoke* was on, her Daddy and Abilene came in. She could hear them in the kitchen, drinking and talking about some drilling problem. After a while Abilene came into the room with a whiskey glass in his hand and stood looking at her.

"Hi," she said. "Where's Daddy?"

"Gone to bed."

"Want me to turn the TV off?" she asked. She was never quite sure what Abilene expected of her.

"Naw, I'm going to the poolhall soon as I finish this drink," he said, leaning against the doorjamb. She was in shorts and her legs were stretched out on Gene's footstool.

"Wish I could go to a poolhall," she said, with a small pout. "I've always wanted to. It's terrible the things girls aren't allowed to do."

"Why hell, come on," Abilene said. "No problem there. I'll show you the poolhall. I got my own key."

He had always thought of her as a prissy kid, but her legs convinced him he hadn't been watching close enough.

"Aren't there people there?" she asked.

"If there are they'll be upstairs asleep," he said. "They won't bother us."

"Okay, I will go then." She felt a little nervous, but she knew he would be irritated if she backed out. She stepped out into the night in front of him. Just getting in the Mercury was exciting: it was the most famous car in that part of the country, and the seat covers smelled of tobacco and beer. Abilene kept it very neat. There was nothing vulgar in it, no dice hanging from the rearview mirror, but there *was* something on the dashboard that fascinated Jacy. It was a tiny, expensive-looking statue of a naked woman. A magnet held it to the dashboard, and as the car moved the statue wiggled provocatively. The woman had a gold stomach and tiny little bloodstones for nipples. Jacy tried not to stare at her.

When they stopped in front of the poolhall Abilene took a comb from behind the sun visor and slicked his hair back a little. The building itself was very dark. Abilene went in first and turned on a little light behind the cash register; he looked at her so inscrutably that Jacy began to be nervous. After he locked the door he got his special cue out of its drawer.

He pulled the light string above one of the snooker tables and the fluorescent tubes blinked on and spread bright light over the green felt and the neat triangle of red balls. As Jacy watched, Abilene put the jointed cue together and glanced appreciatively down its polished length. The cue had an ivory band just below the tip. Jacy was fascinated. She had never been in such a male place before, and it was thrilling.

After he had carefully chalked his cue, Abilene took a white cue ball out of one of the pockets and rolled it slowly across the table. Then he nudged the ball gently with his cue and it went across the table and came back, right to the end of the cue. Abilene smiled, and Jacy came over and stood beside him, so that she could see better. He handled the cue as lovingly as if it were a part of his body.

"Can I see it a minute?" she asked.

Abilene held it out to her a little reluctantly, clearly unwilling to let it leave his hand. Jacy held it awkwardly, trying to sight along it as expertly as he had. When she leaned over the table and playfully attempted to shoot the cue ball Abilene stepped in and took the cue away.

"I don't let nobody shoot with this one," he said. "There's plenty of others to shoot with, if you just want to practice."

Jacy pouted a little, not really interested in the other cues. She sat down on a bench and watched Abilene as he got ready to shoot. She had never seen a man who was so absolutely sure of himself. He put the white cue ball in the center of the table, sighted quickly, and then with a quick hard thrust of his hips sent the white ball ramming into the tight triangle of red balls. There was a sharp crack, and the red balls scattered and rolled all over the table, a few of them bumping together with soft little clicks. Abilene began to shoot them into pockets, moving lightly and purposefully around the table. The cue was never still. Sometimes he held it up and rubbed a little more chalk onto the tip, or propped it briefly against his hip as he contemplated a shot, but most of the time he didn't contemplate, he just moved rapidly and smoothly from shot to shot.

Jacy began to bite a hangnail on her thumb. She had never seen anything like what she was seeing. Sometimes Abilene seemed to be teasing the red balls across the table, nudging the white ball softly and gently and barely easing the red ball into the pocket. Sometimes he was quick with one stroke and slow with the next, and sometimes, as if excited or annoyed, he suddenly shot a ball very hard, ramming it into a pocket with a quick disdainful thrust of the cue. The balls made a solid thonk when they were whammed into the pockets. Abilene was totally absorbed in the table full of balls, and Jacy became almost as absorbed in the lovely movements of the cue. When all the balls were gone Abilene racked them and quickly broke again. The hard crack of the cue ball affected Jacy strangely. She felt a trickle of sweat roll out of her armpit and down her ribs. She was vaguely aware that she wanted something, but she couldn't take her eyes off Abilene long enough to think what. He took his time with the second rack, moving around the table more slowly, now lifting the cue and dropping it, withdrawing it and shoving it forward, drawing out every stroke. Jacy was almost annoyed that he had forgotten her—she squirmed a little on the bench, feeling sweaty. She wanted to run and grab the cue away from him, so he would realize she was there. But she merely sat, and he kept shooting until only the cue ball and one red ball were left. That one he shot terribly hard, without caution, thonking it into one of the corner pockets. The sound made something happen in Jacy, something like what used to happen when she and Duane courted on the basketball trips.

Abilene must have known it happened. He laid the cue gently on the green felt and the next minute was kissing her, one hand rubbing her shorts. Jacy found she had no muscles left—she was limp, leaning back against the wall. But when he stepped back a little her hand followed and caught his wrist. Abilene shook her hand off and went and got an old pair of overalls that were hanging on a nail near the door of the poolhall. He turned off the light by the cash register and then carefully spread the overalls on the snooker table before he switched that light off too. When he came back to Jacy the hall was dark except for the rows of light coming through the south windows from the lampposts along the street.

"Come on, stand up," he said. When she did, he urged her out of her clothes, waiting impatiently, and when the clothes were strewn at her feet, he ran his hands down her sides, grinning a little, not at the thought of her but at the thought of her mother. "Be sure you got them overalls under you," he said, when he helped her up on the table.

In a moment he was above her and Jacy pressed her hands against the hard muscles of his arms, not sure of anything. Then he moved and she was sure again, sure it was hurting, sure he was too much. She stretched her arms above her head and caught her fingers in the corner pockets, sucking in her breath. She wanted to tell him to quit but he was ignoring her, and before she could tell him it changed; she was no longer hurting but she was still ignored. He was just going on, absorbed in himself, moving, nudging, thrusting—she was no more than an object. She wanted to protest that, but before she could she began to lose sight of herself, lose hold of herself. She was rolled this way and that, into feelings she hadn't known, hadn't expected, couldn't avoid. She lost all thought of doing anything, she was completely lost to herself. He played her out as recklessly as he had played the final ball, and when he did she scattered as the red balls had scattered when the white one struck them so hard. She spread out, diffused, almost unconscious. Abilene said nothing. Jacy didn't know anything until she realized he had left the table and was not touching her anymore.

In a minute she got up too and tried to find something of herself. It was all new, and it was going to be wonderful. Abilene was going to be in love with her, and he counted for more than Bobby Sheen or any of the boys at the club. The only thing that worried her was that he kept ignoring her. He didn't even help her find her clothes. But it was such a romantic situation, screwing in a poolhall, that surely being in love would follow. When they got back in the Mercury she tried to make him say something to her.

"What a night," she said. "I never thought anything like this would happen."

"Yeah," Abilene said. They pulled into the Farrow driveway and he glanced at her. She leaned over and kissed him but he turned his face away. Jacy got out, very puzzled, and walked across the yard. When she was halfway across, Abilene raced his motor and made his mufflers roar, so that anyone in the neighborhood who was awake would know what car was in the driveway. Then he backed out and left.

It was not until she stepped in the back door that Jacy realized her mother was home and would have heard the mufflers.

Lois did hear them—she was in the den in her bathrobe and slip, having a light drink and watching a Spencer Tracy movie on the Late Show. When she heard Abilene's car she got up and went to the kitchen, wondering what he wanted at that time of night. She had not even realized that Jacy was out until they met in the kitchen. Jacy's hair was tangled and she was barefooted, her slippers in her hand. She looked scared and very confused, and in a moment a couple of tears leaked out of her eyes—she had just realized that Abilene wasn't going to be in love with her at all. It was a terrible disappointment. She was too upset to keep quiet.

"Oh, he's awful," she said. "Why do you fool with him, Mama? Daddy's a nicer man than him, isn't he?"

Lois could only shake her head. She sat her glass down and with a Kleenex ruefully wiped Jacy's wet face. "He sure is, honey," she said. "Your daddy's a very nice man. I ought to have given Abilene hell, instead of him."

At that moment she didn't feel capable of giving anyone hell, or anything else, either. What Abilene had done hit hard, and her legs felt weak. She freshened her drink and went back to the den to sit down, but the movie was just a blur. For a minute she felt like crying, but she felt too insignificant to cry, too valueless. When she went back in to get another drink, Jacy was sitting morosely at the cabinet reading an article on lipsticks in an old fashion magazine.

"Go to bed, honey," Lois said. "Or come and watch television with me. Brooding's no good."

Jacy didn't feel like going to bed, so she obediently followed her mother into the den and they looked at Spencer Tracy for a while. In a few minutes Jacy began to cry again. She was sitting on the floor and she moved back against Lois' legs and put her face in her mother's lap. Lois stroked her hair.

"I don't know what I'm going to do," Jacy said, looking up. "What do *you* do about it, Mama? Life just isn't the way it's supposed to be at all."

"You're right," Lois said, smoothing back the hair on her daughter's temples. "It isn't the way it's supposed to be at all, but what I've done about it hasn't worked very well. Maybe we better work out something different for you."

21

HER DISAPPOINTMENT with Abilene left Jacy very depressed. It was only the middle of July and she couldn't leave for college for six weeks, but she just couldn't stand the idea of staying in Thalia that much longer. She had slept with two of the most interesting men in the whole area, and neither one of them had fallen in love with her or even shown any particular interest in sleeping with her again. Screwing in the poolhall had been wild while it lasted, but it was hardly going to keep her from rotting with boredom for the rest of the summer. It would have helped if she could have told somebody about it—if the story got out that she had slept with Abilene on a snooker table she would have been a legend in Thalia forever, but she couldn't think of any way to publicize it. Neither Abilene nor her mother were going to, that was for sure, so the whole thing was just wasted. It was disgusting.

The more she thought about matters the more annoyed she was at Duane for leaving town so soon. Things would not have looked quite so dull if he had stayed around. She was not about to start up again with Lester.

One morning while she and Lois were eating a listless breakfast, Jacy gave vent to her irritation.

"I'll be so glad to get to Dallas," she said, "I don't see how people keep livin' in this town. There's not one thing to do."

"Well, there is *one* thing to do," Lois said, chewing a section of orange. "The problem is finding a man to do it with who isn't either dull or obnoxious. Right now I guess Ruth Popper's got about as good a setup as anybody."

Jacy was amazed. "Ruth Popper," she said. "You mean you would like to do that with the coach, Mama? Why I think he's the most horrible man around here. He's even worse than Abilene."

"I didn't say anything about him," Lois said spitting the orange seeds into her hand. "I wouldn't let that tub of guts come within fifteen feet of me. Ruth's been sleeping with Sonny Crawford for about six months now, didn't you know? I don't know Sonny very well but he's reasonably good looking and he's young. If I didn't have anything better than Herman Popper, Sonny would look awfully good."

"What?" Jacy said. "Are you kidding me? Sonny sleeping with Mrs. Popper? Why that's the silliest thing I ever heard of. She's forty years old."

"So am I, honey," Lois said. "It's kind of an itchy age. You want the rest of this orange?"

Jacy was just flabbergasted—life was crazy. She didn't want the orange, and she didn't like the idea of Sonny sleeping with Mrs. Popper. That wouldn't do at all. She had always considered Mrs. Popper mousy, and besides Sonny had always wanted to go with her, not with someone forty years old. It was unflattering of him to sleep with Mrs. Popper.

It did end her boredom, though. She decided then and there that she would stop that romance and stop it good. She would go with Sonny for the rest of the summer, and he would never give Mrs. Popper another thought. He was reasonably good looking, like her mother said, and going with him wouldn't be too unpleasant. It would make August pass a lot quicker. Necking with him might even be fun, but she made up her mind right away that she wasn't going to let him screw her. She had had quite enough of that for one summer—it didn't really work out. She was nostalgic for the days when boys necked with her and wanted her desperately and didn't get her. That was better than actually screwing, somehow. When she got to college she could start screwing again and there it would probably be altogether great. Fraternity boys were gentlemen and would fall right in love with her when she let them screw her.

That very evening Jacy called Sonny and told him she was bored and lonesome; why didn't they go to Wichita and eat Mexican food? Sonny was eager, and the very thought of someone eager perked Jacy up. She took a long bath, shaved her legs and armpits, perfumed herself, and did her hair in an Italian way that made it look casually disarrayed. She wore a sleeveless dress and a sexy bra that left the tops of her breasts uncovered.

When Sonny went to pick her up he was not sure exactly what might happen. Jacy was relaxed and at ease and chattered away about one thing and another. They left Sonny's pickup in the Farrows' driveway and went in the convertible. One of Jacy's arms was stretched out on the top of the seat, almost touching Sonny's shoulder. Before they got to Wichita she scooted over next to him, close enough that he could smell her perfume. The wind whipped a few strands of her hair against his neck. On the way back, after the meal, she rested her arm lightly against his shoulder.

Sonny was in a quandary. He didn't know if he was still honor-bound to treat Jacy as Duane's girl, or if he could treat her as if she were free. Duane might decide to come back any time, but of course there was no guarantee that Jacy would go with him if he did. It was confusing, and having her so close to him made Sonny feel a little bit disloyal.

"Let's go to the lake," Jacy suggested, when they were back in Thalia. "I haven't been there in a long time."

It was exactly what Sonny wanted to do, but as he drove there his uneasiness increased. The thought of Ruth popped into his mind—they had seen each other that very afternoon, and had had an ardent, sweaty, good time. It was more sweaty than was usual because the Poppers' air conditioner had broken down and the coach had gone off fishing without fixing it. After their lovemaking Ruth and he had showered together, to cool off. He had stood behind her and watched the streams of water sluice off her shoulders, her back, her small hips. Driving to the lake, it occurred to him that in a way he was bound to Ruth, but with Jacy sitting close beside him, light-voiced, her hair fragrant, her arm cool, it was hard to keep Ruth in mind. He had wanted Jacy for years, and had fantasized just the sort of situation he was approaching. The lake was very still, but the crickets were singing and bullfrogs croaked loudly in the south channel, where the water was shallow.

For a moment, after stopping, Sonny sat still. Any move would put Jacy in his arms and involve him in two disloyalties, but Jacy was very close to him, so close that he could hear her breath, and soon he was unable to think about anything but her. When he turned, Jacy closed her eyes and they kissed for a long time.

She was delighted. It was thrilling to bestow oneself upon someone young and worshipful. It made her feel like a generous, experienced, worldly woman, and feeling that way did something for her that Abilene and Bobby couldn't do. It was the way life was supposed to be, and because it was so nice she rewarded Sonny with all the little amorous flourishes she could think of, nibbling his lower lip and now and then slipping her tongue into his mouth. She could not really believe all those stories about Mrs. Popper—he seemed too hesitant and inexperienced. She would be the one to teach him about love and passion. That thought excited her even more, and when his hand touched her bare throat she sat back and with a wanton shrug undid the front of her dress. She rested her head against the back of the seat and smiled at him when he lifted her breasts out of the shallow cups of the bra. To Sonny it seemed a little incredible that he was holding those particular soft breasts in his hands at last. He held them and fondled them for quite some time, and not only that night but almost every night for the following two weeks. Jacy's breasts were his, her mouth was his, indeed almost all of her was his. She shivered, smiled, kissed his fingers, nibbled at his throat, even let him touch her panties on occasion, but when he grew bold and began to want to go all the way, she diverted him with her mouth or her breasts and told him it wouldn't do.

"Not here," she said huskily. "I'm too old for screwing in cars. I like beds."

Sonny was surprised at her language, but encouraged. He suggested they go to Wichita and get a motel room, but Jacy quickly thought her way out of that.

"I would, but I'm afraid to right now," she said. "I think my folks are watchin' us. They know I don't want to go to college and they think we're goin' to run off and get married." Sonny was surprised, but not entirely persuaded and Jacy nuzzled at his ear. "We'll do it when it's safe," she said. "I don't like to be in a hurry."

Until that night it had never occurred to Sonny that he could marry Jacy, but the idea was not long in taking hold of him. He began to think about it practically all the time.

Nothing at all was said about Ruth. Jacy never let on that she knew anything about him and Ruth, and Sonny didn't mention it. After the first date with Jacy he did not once go back to Ruth's. He could not have faced her. At times he missed her, and he often missed making love to her, but he did not go back. Sometimes in the middle of the night he would wake up and feel nervous and ashamed. Late at night he could not help facing the fact that he had treated Ruth shamefully and probably hurt her very much. He didn't understand it, but he knew Ruth loved him. It was unreasonable, but she did; she had put herself at his disposal, and he had left her. It wasn't right and it made him feel terrible, but at the same time he knew he wasn't going to quit going with Jacy. He was being unfair to Ruth, but what he felt for Jacy was beyond fairness. He had a chance to have something he had always wanted, and he wasn't going to pass the chance up.

He and Ruth would soon have had to quit anyway, he told himself. She was old. Her brown hair was not free of gray. Seeing Jacy at close range had made him realize how old Ruth really was. Ruth's thighs were a little thin, and when she sat up her breasts sagged, not much but some, enough to notice. It didn't make much difference, and yet it did. Jacy's body was fresher and smoother, and it even smelled a little better.

All the same, he hated being the cause of Ruth's suffering. The only way he knew how to handle it was just not to go near her, or to say anything to her, or to try to justify what he had done.

To Ruth, his absence spoke very clearly. She knew at once what it meant. Three days after he quit coming a neighbor of hers named Fanny Franklin mentioned that she had seen Sonny with Jacy Farrow. "They better get that girl off to school before she marries one of these roughnecks," Fanny said happily. She knew all about Ruth and Sonny, though she had never mentioned it, and it gave her a good bit of satisfaction to break such news to Ruth.

For a day or two Ruth spent much of her time sitting listlessly in front of the television set, not crying, just sitting. She didn't despair. Sonny had always wanted the Farrow girl—it was natural he would go with her if he got the chance. Still, she thought he might continue to come and see her once in a while, if only for sex. Even if he only did that it would be okay. She just needed to be with him a little while, from time to time.

When he had not come for two weeks, Ruth was forced to conclude that sex with her did not mean that much to him, and then she did despair. She knew he would never come, not ever again. If she saw him at all it would be on the street, and he would do his best to avoid her. She looked in the mirror often, and it told her more plainly than ever that she was old. She hated being old and despised Jacy Farrow for being young. Before long she began to despise Sonny too. The afternoons were long and hot and unrelieved and she would have forgiven him in a minute if he had come through the door. She could not do anything in the afternoons for wondering if he would come, and she could barely handle her disappointment when he didn't. At first she didn't cry, but later she cried a great deal and it only made her look older and uglier.

All the neighborhood women began to come to see her, friendly and smug, but she herself scarcely ever went out—she only went to the grocery store. At times she felt dizzy and almost feverish. She discovered that she missed Sonny sexually, as well as in other ways. From time to time she tried playing with herself, but it didn't work very well. One night in a moment of bitterness she grasped Herman and tried to get him to play with her, but he jerked himself angrily away and she didn't try again. If Sonny was not coming back, there was no point in her wanting sex anymore. It was a door she might just as well close.

The nadir came one day in the grocery store, when she bumped into Jacy. Ruth was in an old dress, her hair was dry, and she had not bothered to put on makeup. Jacy was in shorts, tight at the thighs. Her legs were tanned and her hair shone. They passed one another in front of the pork and beans. Jacy had on sunglasses, but she took them off when she met Ruth.

"Why hello, Mrs. Popper," she said, grinning with delight. "Haven't seen you in the longest time. I thought you must have left town for the summer."

When Ruth got home she began to tremble. She carried the blue quilt across the hot yard and stuffed it in the garbage can. She could think of no reason why anyone should desire her or want to know her or touch her, and she did not expect to touch or make love to anyone she cared about as long as she lived. It was a terrible feeling, knowing she would never really touch anyone again. She lay on the bed all afternoon staring dully at the wallpaper and wishing there were some simple way to die. She tried to remember herself when she was young, tried to recall one time in her life when she had been as attractive as Jacy, but she couldn't think of one. It seemed to her she had always been old. There was no relief in blaming Sonny, because what was there to blame him for? Jacy was exactly the type of girl with whom boys were supposed to fall in love. She herself was just the football coach's wife.

22

ONE SATURDAY MORNING Sonny came in from his tower and found Duane in the apartment, asleep on the couch. While Sonny was taking a shower he woke up and came groggily into the bathroom.

"How you doin', buddy?" he said. "It's a real drive from here to Odessa, especially if you don't start till after you get off work."

"Where's your car?" Sonny asked.

Duane took him downstairs and proudly showed him the car—it was a second-hand Mercury, nice and clean. "Thirty-eight thousand miles on her," Duane said. "Runs like new. I like to drive it so much I thought I'd run home for the weekend."

Sonny was a little relieved. For a few minutes he had been worried that Duane's trip home might have something to do with his relationship with Jacy. Fortunately she was in Dallas that weekend, buying her college clothes.

Duane looked almost the same, except that he was browner. He wore shirts with the sleeves cut completely out, and his shoulders and upper arms were tanned almost black.

"You don't know what sun is till you live out on that desert," he said. "Them folks in Odessa don't even know it's a desert; they think it's God's country." He smoked a lot more than he had, but he was out of school and not in training, and it was natural.

The poolhall was always full of people on Saturdays. It was almost football season and football was what everybody wanted to talk about. The men were glad to see Duane and asked him what kind of football teams they had way out in West Texas.

"Wish you was back here, Duane," several said. "We could use a good fullback this year."

Such talk made Duane feel fine. He had always been very proud of being in the backfield.

When it began to get dark Sonny and he decided to drive to Wichita and drink some beer. They put on fresh Levi's and clean shirts and drove over in Duane's Mercury. He insisted that Sonny drive it.

"Handles wonderful," Sonny said. "Quite a change from that pickup."

They started the evening at a place called the Panhandle Tavern, out on the Burkburnett highway. It was a good place to drink beer, but then nearly any place was. When they left there they stopped in at the big Pioneer drive-in and watched a steady stream of teen-age boys and girls circling around one another in their cars. Finally they went on to Ohio Street and drank in a big roomy bar the size of a barn. There were a lot of airmen there, dancing, playing shuffleboard, guzzling beer. Duane and Sonny drank and idly watched the dancing.

It was pleasant for a while, and then for some reason it began to go wrong. An edge came into the evening. Sonny felt it long before anything was said. He kept drinking beer, but he didn't get high, the way he should have. He should have been comfortable with Duane, too—after all, they were best buddies—but somehow he wasn't comfortable with him at all. The pretty girls on the dance floor reminded both of them of things they didn't really want to remember.

"Still screwin' that old lady?" Duane asked casually.

"Yeah, ever now and then," Sonny said. It seemed to him the best thing to say. Duane hadn't mentioned Jacy all day, but Sonny knew he must have been thinking about her.

"Seen old Jerry Framingham last week," he said. "He came through going to Carlsbad with a load of goats. Said he thought you and Jacy had been going together a little."

"Yeah, we have," Sonny admitted quickly. "Once in a while we come over here and eat Mexican food or something. She's been kinda bored, waitin' for school to start."

He didn't look at Duane but he could tell that something was wrong. Instead of looking at Duane he looked around the room. There were jars of pigs' feet on the bar. Bunches of glum airmen stood around with beer glasses in their hands. There was a jukebox, a Schlitz sign, and a clock that said Lone Star Beer underneath it.

"Way I heard it what you probably been eatin' is pussy," Duane said, his voice shaky and strained. "Not old lady Popper's, either."

"It ain't true," Sonny said. "Whoever told you that didn't know what he was talkin' about. Sure, I been goin' with Jacy, why not?"

He couldn't keep down a pulse of irritation with Duane for having kept so quiet about the matter all day. He had kept quiet about it too, but then it wasn't his place to bring it up.

"I never said I blamed you for it," Duane said. "I don't blame you much. I just never thought I'd see the day when you'd do me that way. I thought we was still best friends."

"We are," Sonny said. "What are you so mad for? I never done nothin' to you."

"I guess screwin' my girl ain't nothin' to you," Duane said stiffly.

"I haven't screwed her, but she ain't your girl anymore, anyway. Hell, you don't even live here anymore."

"Don't make no difference," Duane insisted. He was beginning to seem drunk. "She's my girl and I don't care if we did break up. I'm gonna get her back, I'm tellin' you right now. She's gonna marry me one of these days, when I get a little more money."

Sonny was astonished that Duane could be so wrong. He knew Duane must be drunk.

"Why she won't marry you," he said. "She's goin' off to school. I doubt I'll ever get to go with her agin myself, once she gets off. I never saw what it could hurt to go with her this summer, though. She's never gonna marry you."

"She is, by God," Duane said. "Don't tell me she ain't. She'll never let you screw her, that's for sure. Hell, I was just seein' how honest you was. I knew Jacy wouldn't let you screw her. You ain't that good a cocksman. You never even screwed Charlene Duggs, all the time you went with her."

Sonny didn't know what to say. He was amazed that Duane would bring up such a matter. It was unfair, and the more he thought about it the madder he felt.

"Course I didn't," he said. "You know why? Because you and Jacy had the pickup all the time on Saturday night. Nobody could have screwed her in the time I had left."

"I could have," Duane said smugly. "I could have screwed her in five minutes."

Sonny knew that was true, but because it was true it seemed even more unfair of Duane to bring it up. Suddenly, for the first time in his life, he felt like hitting Duane.

"You know why you could," he said, almost choking. "The only reason you could have was because you was in the backfield. I was in the fuckin' line. That's the only reason Jacy went with you as long as she did, because you was in the backfield."

"That's a lie, you chickenshit," Duane said. "What are you talkin' about? Me an' her was in love."

"You was, she wasn't," Sonny said confidently. "Just because you was in the backfield. She likes me as good as she ever liked you. I'll stay all night with her one of these nights, too—she's done promised."

"You won't either," Duane said, furious.

"Why shouldn't I? She's done told me you couldn't even do it that time in San Francisco. What about that?"

Duane couldn't take that. He came out of his chair and slammed Sonny in the face with the beer bottle he had in his hand. It knocked Sonny backward, but he was soon up and at Duane. It was too much to take, saying he couldn't have screwed Charlene, just because he was in the line. Sonny couldn't see too well, but it didn't matter because in a minute they were both rolling on the floor anyway, punching and kicking at one another. The barmaids and the airmen calmly got out of the way and the boys rolled over against the bar, whacking at one another and bonking their heads on the brass footrail. They got up and slugged a minute on their knees but before they could get to their feet the cops were there. The next thing they knew they were out on the curb, each handcuffed to a cop. One of Sonny's eyes was hurting and he had to hold his hand over it, but otherwise he didn't feel too bad. He and Duane stood beside one another at the police desk, and to their surprise were no longer particularly mad.

"Don't know what happened," Duane said. "Never meant to hit you with that bottle. Reckon we got enough money to pay our fines?"

They did have, barely, and in a few more minutes, without knowing exactly what had taken place, they were on the sidewalk again, walking back up Ohio Street. They walked past the bar where they had had the fight and one of the barmaids waved at them, tolerant, jolly, and apparently amused. It deflated the boys a little bit. Theirs must not have been much of a fight, as fights went on Ohio Street.

"My damn eye sure hurts," Sonny said. "Run me up by the General Hospital— maybe they can give me a shot or something. It's a wonder we didn't tear up that bar."

"I guess they get worse fights than us in there ever night," Duane said unhappily. "When it comes to Jacy I guess I'm just crazy."

By the time they got to the hospital Sonny's eye had swollen shut and was paining him terribly. The momentary good feeling that he had had at the police station was entirely gone, and he was a little scared. It was nice that he and Duane were not going to be enemies for life, but he was still scared. When a doctor finally took a look at his eye he immediately ordered Sonny a hospital room.

"You're not leavin' here tonight," he said.

"You could lose the sight in that eye if we aren't careful, and you might lose it even if we are. In the morning we'll have to have a good look at it."

"Damn," Duane said nervously. "Why'd I have to have that bottle in my hand?"

"Aw, they're always tryin' to scare you," Sonny said. "It feels like it's just swole up."

Duane was really worried, and it made him so nervous and stiff that Sonny was almost glad when he left. He had a shot that made him sleep, and the next day the eye was hurting so badly that he had several more shots and was just in a sort of daze all day. He knew his father was there some of the time. The day after that he had some kind of operation, and when he woke up his father was there, shaking a little but not too badly. It was the first time they had seen one another since graduation night, when Sonny had reluctantly accepted fifty dollars as a graduation present.

"Son, must have been some fight," Frank said.

"Oh, just me and Duane. He gone back to Odessa?"

"Yeah, he had to. Tried to see you yesterday, but they wouldn't let him. He said to tell you he was awful sorry."

"Well, it's over now," Sonny said. "I might have done it to him if I'd been holding a bottle. What'd they say about my eye?"

"They don't know yet," Frank said. "You didn't lose all your sight in it, but I guess you might lose some."

Sonny found it was not so bad having his father around. Frank didn't say much, just sat in the room. He seemed comfortable and Sonny was too. There was only one awkward moment in the three days Frank stayed. It came one night when Sonny was eating supper.

"Son," Frank said, "reckon it would work out if we put the poolhall and the domino hall together? The building's big enough, ain't it?"

It was, but the whole idea made Sonny nervous. "I don't think it would do too well," he said. "The men who play dominos wouldn't want a lot of kids in there shooting pool and making a racket."

Frank said that might be so, and didn't mention it again.

Sonny was in the hospital eight days. He got lonesome, but it was just about as bad when visitors came. Genevieve came one afternoon and brought Billy, who was scared of the hospital and didn't know whether to sit down or stand up. Sonny was so used to seeing Genevieve in her waitress uniform that she looked strange to him in her regular clothes. She came right out and asked about his eye.

"How is it, really?" she said.

"I don't know," Sonny said honestly. "It wouldn't surprise me if I was one-eyed when they take the bandages off. Duane caught me a good hard lick."

"Well, it was awful of you two to fight. You knew he joined the army, didn't you? His mother told me two or three days ago."

Sonny hadn't known it, and was very surprised. For the first time he really wondered about his eye. He had always planned to go to the army too, and it occurred to him that if he was one-eyed the army wouldn't take him. He had never supposed he would be unable to make the army.

The next afternoon the nurse brought in a note.

"A lady's down in the waiting room," she said.

The note just said: "May I come in and see you a little while? Ruth."

Sonny looked at the nurse, who was young and friendly.

"Could you tell her I'm asleep?" he asked.

"Sure I could. But you're not asleep."

"If I go to sleep right now will you tell her I'm asleep?"

The nurse did as he asked, but Sonny was blue anyway. He would not have minded seeing Ruth, but he felt bad whenever he thought about her and he was afraid that if she came up something bad might happen. In a way he wanted to see her—indeed, the more he thought about her the more lonesome he became for her—but it seemed like seeing her would only make everything worse.

The next to last day he was there, Jacy came to see him. She wore a sleeveless green dress and looked a little sad. As soon as the nurse left the room she came to the bed and kissed Sonny for a long time. It surprised him and he embarrassed himself a little by getting a hard-on.

"Oh, I was so worried," Jacy said. "I just had to see you. When do you get out?"

"Tomorrow," Sonny said. "Why?"

"I want us to get married," Jacy said, her dewy mouth close to his. "I really do. Whenever you get out, just as soon as you want to."

Sonny was stunned. "Get married?" he said. He thought he must be having a dream.

"Do you want to?" she asked.

"Oh yeah, yeah," he said. "But ain't you goin' to college?"

"No. I don't care about that. I love you and that's more important. My folks won't like it, but we can run off."

It was an inspiration she had had as soon as she heard about the fight. Sonny was so dear, to fight for her. Running off with him would make her whole summer, and the fact that she did it even though he only had one eye would knock everyone in Thalia for a loop. It would be a lot wilder than Bobby Sheen and Annie-Annie—they were both rich and healthy. She would be running off with someone poor and sort of mutilated. Of course her folks would catch them and have it annulled, but at least she could show Sonny how much she was willing to sacrifice for him.

Jacy sat on the hospital bed and they kissed some more and talked about how wild it would be being married. Life seemed almost too crazy to be true.

The next day they unbandaged Sonny's eye. It wasn't that he couldn't see anything out of it, it was just that all he could see was fog. It was like being inside a cloud. He could tell when people moved around, but he couldn't tell who they were until they spoke.

"Could be a lot worse," the doctor said. "We'll see how it responds before we do anything else."

They gave him a black patch to wear over his eye and told him to come back weekly for checkups, but Sonny hardly listened. Marrying Jacy was all he could think of, and he thought about it on the ride back to Thalia, while his father drove.

As soon as they got home Sonny took the extra eye patch the doctor had given him and showed Billy how to wear it. Billy was tickled to death. Because Sonny did it, he thought seeing out of only one eye was a great way to see, and from then on he wore the spare eye patch whenever he went out to sweep the town.

23

JACY WAS DEAD SERIOUS about getting married: the day after Sonny left the hospital they drove to Wichita and got the license. They had to wait three days, so to be doing something Sonny quit his roughnecking job and arranged for a new job pumping leases, something he could do with one eye. The rest of the time he just stayed around the poolhall thinking about sleeping with Jacy. The prospect helped take his mind off his eye.

Jacy spent the three days imagining the effect her marriage would have on her parents and on the town. Everybody was curious about Sonny's eye, which made it absolutely the ideal time to run off with him. Her folks would simply have a fit. Probably they would call the police and have them arrested and torn out of one another's arms, but at least they would have been married and everyone would know it.

Friday afternoon, when it actually became time for them to run away, she wrote her parents a quick note:

DEAR MAMA AND DADDY—

I know this is going to be a shock to you but I guess it can't be helped. Sonny and I have gone to Oklahoma to get married—I guess it will be in Altus. Even if he is poor we are in love. I don't know what to say about college, I guess we'll just have to talk about that when we get back. We are going to Lake Texoma on our honeymoon and will be home Monday. I guess I will live at the poolhall until we find someplace else to live. Even if you don't like Sonny now I know you will love him someday.

JACY

She left the note on the cabinet, propped up against a box of crackers. Gene found it when he came in from work three hours later. Lois was in Wichita that day and returned late. When she came in, Gene was pacing the kitchen floor, obviously distressed. He handed her the note.

"Oh, goddamn her," Lois said. "I can't believe it."

"Well, we got to get going," Gene said. "I want to catch 'em. Even if we can't get 'em before they marry we can sure as hell get 'em before they go to bed. That way we can get it annulled with no trouble."

"Why bother?" Lois said. "I suppose we could get it annulled anytime—that's what money's for. Why don't we just let her do the getting out—you know she won't stay with Sonny ten days. I just hate to think of what she'll do to him in that length of time. If we don't get that little bitch off to college she's going to ruin the whole town."

Gene was so upset he couldn't take what Lois said. He turned and slapped her, but it was a light, indecisive slap.

"You just change your clothes," he said, shoving her in the direction of the bedroom. "I said we're going to get 'em and by God that's all there is to it. What do you mean calling my daughter a bitch? You're her mother, ain't you?"

"I don't see what that has to do with it," Lois said, but she didn't feel like arguing. She felt sorry for Gene, and pity always made her feel wretched. She already had visions of a horrible scene somewhere in Oklahoma. She stood in the doorway and heard Gene call the highway patrol and ask them to stop Jacy's car. When he hung up he seemed to feel better. A man should react to such an event in a certain way, and he was doing what he should.

"I won't have her living over no poolhall, not even for ten days," he said. "Hurry up and get changed, and don't call my daughter a bitch again."

"No promises," Lois said. "You know what she's doing as well as I do, Gene. She doesn't give a damn about Sonny, she just wants to hurt us and get a little attention while she's doing it. What is that but bitchery?"

"Well, she comes by it honest," he said, looking his wife in the eye. "I know right where she gets it."

Lois merely nodded. "I'm sure you do," she said. She obediently went into the bedroom and put on more somber clothes.

=====

Sonny and Jacy, meanwhile, were off on the realest of adventures: running away to get married. Jacy had an expensive suitcase and enough clothes to last her a week, while Sonny, who owned no suitcase, had a canvas overnight bag and an extra pair of slacks hung on a hanger in the back seat. They were in the convertible, and Jacy drove. Sonny didn't yet trust himself to drive on the highway with one eye.

Jacy was wearing a lovely white dress she had bought at Neiman's the week before, to wear to fraternity parties. She had some new sunglasses, and drove barefoot. It was great fun to be running away to get married—both of them were delighted with themselves. All Sonny had to do was lean back and watch Jacy and imagine the bliss that was going to be his in only a few hours. It was a bright, hot day and there were drops of sweat on Jacy's upper lip. Neither of them minded the heat, though. They stopped in Lawton and had milk shakes, probably the last milk shakes they would ever have as single people. Both of them were hungry and they sucked up every milky drop.

Then they went on to Altus, a popular place for getting married. It was late afternoon when they arrived—Sonny stopped at a filling station and asked where they might find a justice of the peace. "Why there's one right up the road," the attendant said. "What part of Texas you all from?"

They told him and drove on. It turned out to be absurdly simple to get married. The justice of the peace lived in an old unpainted frame house and came to the door in his khakis and undershirt.

"Been having myself a little snooze," he said. "What part of Texas y'all from?"

He surveyed their license casually, got a pencil, licked the point, and filled in what he was supposed to fill in. Sonny would have preferred him to use a fountain pen, since pencil erased so easily, but he didn't say anything.

"I better go get Ma to witness," he said, belching. "I guess I could put a shirt on too, if I can find one."

"Get many marriages up here?" Sonny asked, to be polite.

"Not as many as I'd like," the J.P. said. "Not like I used to when we was a Christian country. Used to be people feared God, but not no more. I don't marry half as many kids as I used to—fornication don't mean nothing anymore. Kids nowadays fornicate like frogs, they don't never think of marryin'. What decent ones is left is mostly hifalutin' kids, church weddin's and recepshuns and such as that. Ma! Got some customers."

An old woman wearing a sunbonnet and gray work gloves came in from the backyard. She was a thin little woman and looked tired, but she nodded politely. "Pardon this getup," she said. "I was out gettin' the last of my black-eyes. Garden's just about gone for this year. What part of Texas you all from?"

The old man had wandered out, but he came back into the living room buttoning a khaki shirt over his belly. He stuffed the shirttail unevenly into his pants and shuffled over to an old pigeonhole desk to find his service.

"Y'all don't mind if I read this, do you?" he asked. "I ain't got a memory worth a damn."

They didn't mind him reading, but Jacy did mind him standing so close to them. He had a body odor that almost made her gag, but he winked at her with mild lechery and seemed to think she found him attractive.

"Wouldn't mind marrying you myself, honey," he said. "You got more meat on you than Ma has."

"Don't be sassing, now," his wife said. "You can wait till I get this sunbonnet off before you start."

He read the service heavily, sometimes stopping to trace his place with a forefinger. When he asked about rings Sonny shook his head. "She's marryin' a cheapskate, Ma," the J.P. said.

When it was over Sonny gave Jacy a quick kiss, but she wanted a long romantic one so they kissed for almost a minute while the old lady wandered off to start shelling her black-eyed peas. As soon as they quit kissing the J.P. came over and placed a wet kiss of his own on Jacy's cheek—it made her furious. Sonny gave him a ten-dollar bill and he stuffed it in his pocket contemptuously.

"Yeah, a cheapskate," he said. As they left he followed them out on the porch. "Hell, you've got a collapsable," he hollered, when they were getting in the car. "Used to be collapsables were twenty-dollar weddin's ever time. Y'all got any fornicatin' friends down in Texas tell 'em to cut it out and come up here to see me. I'll set 'em right with the Lord as cheap as the next man."

"Why he's just awful," Jacy said. "I never dreamed they let people like him do marryin'."

"Anyway, we're man and wife," Sonny said, barely able to believe it. At the first stop sign they kissed again and wiggled their tongues enthusiastically. Jacy was for going to Lake Texoma to spend their wedding night, and Sonny was agreeable to anything.

They left Altus in a high good mood and drove back to Lawton, where they stopped to eat. In Lawton, for some reason, Jacy began to feel a little depressed. A strange thought occurred to her. They were in the parking lot of the restaurant where they were going to eat, so they kissed for a while, as newlyweds should. While they were kissing Sonny got excited and fondled her in a place in which he was very interested. It was all right for him to do it, of course, but a little later, while she was in the rest room of the steak house, it occurred to her that maybe her parents wouldn't have the police arrest them after all. Maybe they would just wash their hands of it and go on watching television. It might even be that they thought she ought to *live* with Sonny, since she had married him.

That was a very sobering thought: to think that they didn't love her enough to want to keep her from living over a poolhall.

Thinking about it took away her appetite, and though she tried to appear gay she really only picked at her fried shrimp. They ordered beer with the meal and drank it self-consciously. It occurred to Jacy that even if her folks sent the cops they might miss them in the dark, or they might even get to the motel before the cops started looking. The thought depressed her more and more.

Sonny noticed that marriage was making Jacy a little nervous, but he supposed it was just worry over her parents. He was sure she would calm down once they got to Lake Texoma. But the strange thing was, the closer they came to the lake, the more nervous she became. He scooted over next to her and patted her leg, but that just seemed to make her more edgy.

When Sonny scooted close to her Jacy really began to feel funny. She realized suddenly that she just didn't want a wedding night with him at all—she had been wrong to think she did. She didn't know whether she even wanted to kiss him anymore or not. Kissing someone who just had one eye was kind of creepy.

Then, just outside Madill, a cop stopped them and everything changed completely. Jacy ceased to feel the least bit nervous.

"What part of Texas y'all from?" the patrolman asked, holding out his hand for Jacy's license. He flashed a flashlight in their faces.

"Newlyweds, ain't you?" he said, when they told him where they were from. They admitted it.

"Well, better follow me in," he said. "I think somebody's lookin' for you."

"But we ain't done nothin' wrong," Sonny said. "Ain't we got a right to get married? How can you arrest us, just like that?"

"I ain't arrestin' you," the patrolman said, peeling a stick of chewing gum. "I just want you to come with me, till we find out. I don't have no idea what you've got a right to do."

"I guess we better follow him, honey," Jacy said. She turned to Sonny and kissed him promisingly. "I'll just be heartbroken if my folks have done this," she added, kissing him again lightly as she put the car in gear.

The patrolman led them to a jailhouse in Madill. He didn't put them in a cell or anything, but they had to sit in the jail for almost two hours and that was almost as depressing as being in a cell. Jacy realized she was tragically in love, and clung to Sonny tightly. They even got in some nice kissing, but in a way it was depressing, at least to Sonny. Jacy's folks were in Lawton and were coming after her. He couldn't figure out the justice of it.

"I thought anybody had the right to get married," he said, several times. The patrolman had gone on about his business. There were only two people besides themselves in the whole jail: one was a prisoner and the other was a redheaded jail-keeper named Elmer.

"Well you might have the right and you might not," Elmer said. "I couldn't say. I ain't gonna hold no gun on you, but if you leave you'll just get caught agin. You might as well wait here as anywhere. If you're thirsty we got a Coke machine you're welcome to use."

While they were waiting the sheriff came in, a fat, white-headed man. He took one look at them and concluded they didn't have any right to do anything.

"Kids, we really oughta lock you up," he said. "Running off from home, making your parents chase all the way up here. I don't know what the world's coming to."

Sonny didn't either, but he knew one thing for sure: he was never going to get to sleep with Jacy. They would never be together in an actual bed, not for a whole night or even part of a night. Somehow his whole life had worked out to keep that one thing from happening, and it was the one thing he wanted most of all. He was not at all sure he would ever get to make love to anyone he cared about, much less to Jacy. In the hot little jail lobby, sitting on the one bench, he couldn't even remember why he had ever thought he *would* get to sleep with her.

It disappointed him terribly and made him feel a little sick and very tired. About ten o'clock Elmer let the one prisoner come in and watch the late movie with him on the jail's old Magnavox TV. That was what they were all doing when Lois and Gene arrived. Sonny was so tired by then that he wasn't even scared of Gene, even though Gene started yelling at him the minute he stepped through the jailhouse door.

"You're fired, you whelp!" he said. "What do you mean, runnin' off with my daughter, tellin' her she's gonna live over a poolhall?"

He would have gone on, but Elmer cut him off.

"Just take him out in the yard to bawl him out, Mister," he said. "I can't hear this movie if you bawl him out in here." It was a Randolph Scott movie, and they had all been sort of enjoying it.

As they went out the door Jacy clung to Sonny, crying bitterly. Mrs. Farrow said nothing at all, but Gene was still mad as cats.

"I'll bawl him out all right," he said. "Think I worked like a dog all my life so my daughter could end up over a poolhall?"

"We was gonna get another apartment," Sonny said, though they had not actually given the matter much thought.

"I bet you was," Gene said. He grabbed Jacy by the arm and jerked her away from Sonny. "Where's your car keys, hon?" he asked.

Snuffling, Jacy fished in her purse and handed them to Lois.

"It's a hell of a note," he said.

"Oh shut up and take her home," Lois put in wearily. "I'm tired of this."

"You bet I will. You take her car. So far as I'm concerned Sonny can walk."

He led Jacy to the Cadillac, got in, and spun the big car off, throwing up dust in the unpaved road that ran by the jailhouse. Lois and Sonny were left standing in the jailyard, by a little cedar bush. It was very quiet all of a sudden, the moon white overhead.

"I would like to apologize for all this, Sonny," Lois said. "It wasn't my doings. So far as I'm concerned you have a perfect right to anything you could get out of Jacy, but I can tell you right now that wouldn't have been much."

Sonny didn't know what to say. He felt awfully tired, and Lois noticed it.

"You're welcome to ride back with me," she said. "In fact I'd enjoy the company. I can understand how you might not want to, though. If you don't just say so and I'll give you some bus money."

Mrs. Farrow didn't seem so bad, and Sonny was much too tired to enjoy the thought of waiting for a bus. "I believe I'll ride with you," he said.

They started back over the same road that Sonny had just driven with Jacy. Mrs. Farrow drove fast, but there was no sign of the Cadillac ahead of them.

"Gene's probably driving ninety," she said. "I bet he's telling Jacy it was all my fault and his, for not loving her more or something."

Sonny didn't know whether he napped or not, but soon they were almost back to Lawton. The wind whipped Mrs. Farrow's hair about her face just as it had Jacy's, when they were driving up. To the west, toward the plains, there were low flashings of lightning and the rumble of thunder. Somewhere over near Frederic it was raining. Sonny noticed that Mrs. Farrow had a little flask that she drank from now and then.

"Here," she said, holding it out to him. "Have a little bourbon—you can have the rest of it, in fact. I've got to drive. It might pick you up."

Sonny took the flask and sipped from it. The whiskey was very sharp on his tongue, but he kept the flask and continued to sip, and after a time he felt a vagueness spreading through him that was almost comfortable. He was surprised to find Mrs. Farrow so likable.

"Not much of a wedding night, is it?" she said. She grinned at him, but it was not an insulting grin.

"No, not much of one," he said.

"Let me tell you something you won't believe, Sonny. You're lucky we got her away from you as quick as we did. Even if you had got to a motel room she'd have found some way to keep from giving it to you. God knows how, but Jacy would have thought of something. You'd have been a lot better off to stay with Ruth Popper."

Sonny was startled. "Does everybody know about that?" he asked.

"Of course," Lois said. "It sounded like a good thing to me. You shouldn't have let Jacy turn your head."

"She's prettier," Sonny said. "I guess I shouldn't have though. I don't guess I can go see Mrs. Popper any more."

"I shouldn't imagine. I wouldn't have you back if you'd left me for Jacy, but then you never know. I'm not Ruth."

They turned south out of Lawton. The bourbon was going down easier and easier. In the west the lightning flashes were closer together, and in the moments of light they could see heavy clouds low over the plains.

"I hope we don't have to put this damn top up," Lois said. She found herself moved by Sonny's youth. He held the bourbon flask very carefully and looked almost comically young. Giving way to an impulse, she reached over and touched his neck. It startled him a great deal.

"Didn't mean to scare you," she said. "I guess I just felt motherly for a second. Or maybe I felt wifely, I don't know. It's strange to have a married daughter who wouldn't go through with her wedding night."

Sonny looked at her curiously and she smiled at him, an honest, attractive smile, as she kept stroking the back of his neck lightly. He drank more bourbon and watched the intermittent lightning yellow the plains. He felt as though life was completely beyond him.

In a little while they crossed Red River, the slap of their tires echoing off the old stone bridge abutments. The water in the channel was shallow and silvery.

"Anyhow, I know why Sam the Lion liked you," Sonny said, and it was Lois' turn to be startled.

"Sam?" she said. "Who told you he liked me? Genevieve?"

Sonny nodded. Lois was silent for a moment. "No, it was more than that," she said. "He loved me, honey."

They were silent almost to Burkburnett, but Sonny noticed that Lois kept wiping her eyes with the backs of her hands.

"I get sad when I think about Sam for long," she said in explanation, her voice unsteady. "I can still remember his hands, you see. Did you know he had beautiful hands?"

They passed by Shepherd Field, with its flickering, rotating airplane beacons and its rows of dark narrow barracks.

"I think he was the only man in that whole horny town who knew what sex was worth," Lois said, her voice a little hoarse. "I probably never would have learned myself if it hadn't been for Sam. I'd be one of those Amity types who thinks bridge is the best thing life offers womankind. Gene couldn't have taught me, he doesn't know himself."

Then they were coming down on the lights of Wichita.

"Sam the Lion," Lois said, smiling. "Sam the Lion. Nobody knows where he got that name but me. I gave it to him one night—it just came to me. He was so pleased. I was twenty-two then, can you imagine?"

Then suddenly her shoulders began to shake and she did a strange thing. She wheeled the convertible off the highway in a screech of brakes and stopped on the hill across from the auction barn. She scooted across the seat and grabbed Sonny's arms, tears running down her face.

"But you know somethin'," she said, her whole body shaking. "It's terrible to only find one man your whole life who knows what it's worth, Sonny. It's just terrible. I wouldn't be tellin' you if it wasn't. I've looked, too—you wouldn't bu-lieve how I've looked. When Sam, when Sam . . . the Lion was seventy years old he could just walk in . . . I don't know, hug me and call me Lois or something an' do more for me than anybody. *He* really knew what *I* was worth, an' the rest of them haven't, not one man in this whole country. . . ."

She lay against Sonny's chest and cried very hard, her face hidden. He put his arms around her and waited. He felt so tired that he could be calm through anything. After a while Lois' body quit heaving. She slipped her hand inside his shirt and touched his chest, and when she finally sat up her face was quite calm. In fact there was something almost gay in her face.

"Hey," she said. "I like you. I don't know if you know what I'm worth or not, but I sure like you and I should like you to have a nicer wedding night than Jacy could ever have given you. I'll take you someplace right now and we'll see to that. Okay? You're not scared of me, are you?"

"No," Sonny said, though he was. But he was glad to go with her, scared or not; he would have gone with her anywhere, just to see what she would do next, what crazy thing life would bring next. Lois got back behind the wheel and drove to a big motel on the Henrietta highway, one Sonny had passed many times. He had certainly never dreamed he would be going into it with Jacy's mother, on his wedding night.

Lois paid for a room and got the key. They were right at the back of the court, and she had a little trouble getting the key in the lock. "Gene and Jacy are home now, wondering why we're driving so slow," she said. She went in and Sonny followed her. She turned on a small bed light and raised her hands to her throat to unclip a black necklace she wore.

"We'll let 'em wonder," she said. "I'll tell them we had a flat and had to get it fixed in Lawton. It's amazing how many good excuses there are."

She was undressing, gracefully and without embarrassment, but she stopped a moment to set the bed lamp on the floor. Her breasts were bare—she was the first full-breasted woman Sonny had seen naked.

"I like a little light but I don't like it in my eyes," she said.

With the lamp on the floor the room was mostly in shadow. As Sonny hesitantly undressed, Lois came and stood quietly by him, smiling, occasionally reaching out to stroke his shoulder or arm or chest. "Shy young men are lovely," she said, smiling. He thought her breasts were what was lovely. When they lay on the bed he quickly reached to caress her, but Lois caught his hands and held them for a moment in the valley between her breasts. She raised up on one elbow, her face just above his, and touched him lightly with her lips before she spoke.

"No, no, now," she said. "You're scared to death of me. Your muscles are all tight." She put her hand on his arms, then on his thigh muscles. Sonny knew they were tight.

"You're scared of me because I'm Lois Farrow," she said. "I'm rich and mean, all that. What everybody thinks of me. But that's not true for you. I may be that way with a lot of men because that's what they want and deserve, but it's still not true. Sam . . . the Lion knew I wasn't any of that, and I want you to know it too. See my hand? It's not like that, and hands are what's real. Put yours right here on my throat."

Sonny did—her throat was warm, and she lowered her face and kissed him. After a while she took his hand off her throat and played with his fingers, kissed them. She kissed him and played with him until he began to play too. He relaxed and became as serious and playful as she was. She seemed really glad to be with him, crazy as it was. What surprised him most was the lightness of her movement—her body was heavier than Ruth's, yet she seemed weightless, so light and easy that they might have been floating together. He came right away, without remembering her at all, and it was only a little later, when he did remember, that he wondered if he had come too soon. She seemed secretly pleased, even delighted, and she took his hands again. They played a little more—Lois continued to touch him lightly with her lips or her fingers.

"You've got a big inferiority complex you ought to cure yourself of," she said.

A little later she spoke again. "It's not how much you're worth to the woman," she said quietly. "It's how much you're worth to yourself. It's what you really can feel that makes you nice."

Dressing, she looked at her watch. "God, it's two," she said. "I guess I better tell them we had a flat and had to *walk* to Lawton." She giggled a little and raised her arms to lower her slip over her head. "The excuse never sounds quite so good afterward," she added lightly. She walked over and asked Sonny to button her dress, and then watched him strangely while he put on his shirt.

"Your mother and I sat next to one another in the first grade," she said. "We graduated together. I sure didn't expect to sleep with her son. That's small town life for you." She grinned and stroked his chest again as he buttoned his shirt.

"What will we be?" he asked, when she stopped at the poolhall to let him out.

"Very good friends for a long time," Lois said. "Even I couldn't get away with taking on my daughter's ex-husband on a regular basis. They'd have me committed. Why do you look so sad? You're fine, Sonny."

"I was just thinking of Mrs. Popper," he said. "I guess I treated her terrible."

"I guess you did," Lois said.

He sat in the car a moment longer and then looked at her gratefully. He started to speak but Lois slipped partly across the seat and covered his lips with her palm. When he closed his mouth she took her palm away and kissed him.

"Don't ever say thank you to a woman," she said. "They'll kill you if you do. You let the ladies say thank you."

24

T HE NEXT MORNING Sonny woke up feeling in love with Lois Farrow, but by the time a long week had passed he was back to missing Jacy and wishing he had been able to stay married to her. One night at the café Genevieve told him Lois had asked her to tell him they had taken Jacy to Dallas and would stay there with her until school started. The news did not improve his spirits.

"What do you think about it all?" he asked Genevieve.

"I don't know about it *all*," Genevieve said, "but the one thing that stands out nice and clear is that Lois' little girl took you for a nice ride. Boys in this town don't seem to have much sense when it comes to girls like her."

While they were talking all the football boys trooped into the café, laughing and cutting up. They were making a big thing of how sore and bruised they were—the first workout had been that afternoon. They played the jukebox and sat around talking about what a horse's ass the coach was. Sonny felt left out and even more depressed. He had always been on the football team and had done the same things they were doing after workouts, but suddenly he wasn't on the team and the boys didn't even notice him—he might have been out of high school ten years.

After a while he went over to the picture show and watched a funny movie with Dean Martin and Jerry Lewis. The movie took his mind off things, but afterward, when he was buying a bag of popcorn from Old Lady Mosey, he got another disappointment. She told him they were going to have to close the picture show sometime in October.

"We just can't make it, Sonny," she said. "There wasn't fifteen people here tonight, and a good picture like this, Jerry Lewis. It's kid baseball in the summer and school in the winter. Television all the time. Nobody wants to come to shows no more."

Sonny said he would be sorry to see the place go, and it was true. He went outside and sat on the curb, waiting for Billy to get through sweeping out. Since Sam's death Billy had grown nervous and restless, and was only really happy when he was with Sonny. If Sonny wasn't there to meet him after the show, he would go sweeping off somewhere and be lost half the night, so Sonny had got in the habit of being there. He and Billy would go walking together, Billy carrying his broom and occasionally sweeping at a leaf or a paper cup someone had thrown out. Sometimes they walked as far as the lake. Sonny would sit and watch the water while Billy swept the dam.

Once a week Sonny went to Wichita to have the doctor look at his eye, but the doctor seldom told him anything new. "Looks like sometime this fall I'll have to send you to Dallas. Better be saving your money. If the doctor down there decides to operate it'll cost you plenty."

So far as Sonny was concerned the Wichita doctor was costing plenty himself, but for once money was not too big a worry. His pumping job paid him enough to live on and he was able to put what the poolhall brought in in the bank. The pumping job was a lonely kind of job, but that was okay: he was not in the mood for people anyway. He spent his mornings bumping over the country roads in the pickup, going from one lease to the next, checking the rod lines, greasing the pumps and motors. Often he took Billy with him—Billy loved to go. When dove season came around Sonny bought a shotgun, an old L. C. Smith .12 gauge singleshot; occasionally, to Billy's surprise, he would take a shot at a dove or a jackrabbit, but he seldom hit anything.

He thought about Ruth a good deal, always painfully. After football season started he thought about her even more—Coach Popper's name was on every tongue. It looked like Thalia was finally going to win the district, and opinion was divided as to whether the team owed its success to the coach's coaching or to Bobby Logan's quarterbacking. Sonny felt strangely reluctant to go to the games, and stayed home from the first three or four. He felt a little guilty about not going, but somehow he just didn't want to.

Finally, in early October, the game with Chillicothe came up and Sonny broke down and went. It was a game that seemed likely to decide the conference crown—custom demanded that every male in Thalia go. At first Sonny enjoyed himself, and regretted having missed so many games. The night was cool and clear and the grass on the football field looked greener and softer than it ever had when he played. The assistant coach asked him and Jerry Framingham to run the first-down chain, and they accepted. When the band played the Thalia school song it was a little thrilling: it touched something in Sonny and made him feel as though he was part of it again, the high school, football, the really important part of life in the town.

It would have been better if he had never felt that way, because as soon as the game started he realized he was not part of it at all. Bobby Logan was part of it, and Coach Popper was very much part of it. He strode up and down the sidelines, scowling fiercely at the referees—everyone knew the coach was there. Even the linesmen were part of it, even the freshmen and sophomores on the bench—at least they were suited out. But Sonny wasn't part of it, and neither was Jerry, who had been out of school so long that he was used to not being part of it. Sonny couldn't get used to it. He kept wishing he was out on the field playing. Running the chain, measuring first downs, that was nothing: he might have been invisible to everyone but the referees. He was an ex-student—nothing. A feeling came over him sort of like the feelings he used to get in the mornings, only the new feeling was worse. Then he had felt like he was the only one in town, but standing on the sidelines, holding the chain, he felt like he wasn't even *in* town—he felt like he wasn't anywhere.

As the game went on the feeling became worse, even though Thalia was winning. Bobby Logan was quarterbacking beautifully: he got Thalia a seven point lead and they still had it when the fourth quarter began to run out. The whole town began to believe that Thalia had won the conference, and Sonny began to believe that he was not there. The people in the stands were wild, their eyes glazed, they saw nothing but the boys on the field. When the game was over and Thalia had won, it was chaos. The cheerleaders, the band, and a mob of high-school girls rushed out of the end zone to greet the dirty, victorious heroes. The girls hugged the boys and clung to them as they walked off the field. The

Quarterback Club, the local gamblers, farmers, lawyers, well-wishers of all sorts crowded around Coach Popper to congratulate him, strewing the green, cleat-torn grass with cigar butts and chewing-gum paper.

Jerry Framingham was as excited as the rest of them: he was going off with some of his truck-driving buddies to get drunk, so Sonny was left to carry the chain back to the football bus. The boys were all crowded around the bus, hugging and kissing the girls who met them on the field. Sonny put the chain with the rest of the equipment and walked back through the crowd to his pickup, feeling like he had been completely erased. People he had known all his life were all around him, but they simply didn't see him. He was out of school.

Back at the poolhall, Billy was gone, sweeping somewhere, probably, and the poolhall was dark and empty. Sonny began to cry. Every minute or two he would think how silly it was and would stop for a little while, but he couldn't stop completely. He was out and could never get back in. He would have got drunk but there was no liquor. The only person who could have made him feel real was Ruth, and he couldn't go to her. Or Lois, but he couldn't go to her either. Or Sam the Lion, but he was dead. Finally he went to hunt for Billy and found him down by the jail. Billy, it turned out, was able to bring Sonny back. They started walking together and Sonny felt okay again. He had started talking to Billy almost as he would have talked to Duane, sometimes even more freely than he would have talked to Duane, and though Billy never answered he was always friendly. Feeling like he wasn't there had made Sonny think about Ruth, and when he really thought about her he felt ashamed of himself. He realized that for years she must have felt like she wasn't there; he was probably the only person who had ever made her feel she *was* there, and he had quit her without a word and left her to feel the old way again. It would have been a bad way to behave even if it had got him Jacy, but it hadn't, and it had probably left Ruth feeling hopeless. He had just begun to realize how hard it was to get from day to day if one felt hopeless.

As they walked, Sonny took off his eye patch and let Billy wear it. They walked north from the jail, past the Masonic lodge and the Jehovah's Witness church. To the south, back toward the drive-in, they could hear horns honking as people celebrated Thalia's victory. Once in a while a dog barked at them as they walked by, but most of the dogs in Thalia knew Sonny and Billy and didn't give them any trouble. They circled past the cemetery and Sonny waited in the road while Billy swept the cattleguard. They didn't often pass the cemetery, because Billy knew that Sam the Lion was there somewhere and he was always reluctant to leave. For once Sonny did not particularly mind. Billy swept the cattleguard and got it very clean—from the pastures to the north they heard the moan of a coyote and when Billy was satisfied they walked on, past the rodeo pens and back to the dark poolhall.

25

A WEEK BEFORE the picture show closed down Duane came home from boot camp. He drove in on Sunday morning and word soon got around that he was leaving for Korea in a week's time. Sonny learned that he was home Sunday night, when he and Billy were having a cheeseburger in the café.

"Wonder where he is?" he asked. "He hasn't been to the poolhall."

"I kinda doubt he'll come," Genevieve said, frowning. "His conscience is hurting him too much about your eye. I think he's gonna stay at the rooming house this week."

"Well, maybe he'll come in," Sonny said. "There ain't much to do in this town. I couldn't live in it a week without going to the poolhall, I know that."

"I think it's all silly," Genevieve said. "Why don't you go see him? Be a shame if he goes to Korea without you all seein' one another."

Sonny thought so too, but he was nervous about going to see Duane. He kept hoping Duane would show up at the poolhall and save him having to make a decision; but Duane didn't. So far as anyone knew, he spent the whole week watching television at his mother's house. A couple of boys saw him out washing his Mercury one afternoon, but he never came to town.

As the week went by, Sonny got more and more nervous. Several times he was on the verge of picking up the phone and calling—once he did pick it up, but his nerve failed him and he put it back down. If Duane didn't want to be bothered there was no point in bothering.

Friday night there was a football game in Henrietta, but Sonny didn't go. He heard the next morning that Duane had been there drunk. All day he considered the problem and finally decided that he would go see Duane at the rooming house and let the chips fall where they may—it couldn't hurt much to try. If Duane didn't want to see him all he had to do was say so.

About five-thirty, as it was beginning to grow dark, Sonny got in the pickup and drove to the rooming house. Duane's red Mercury was parked out front. A norther had struck that afternoon and sheets of cold air rushed through the town, shaking the leafless mesquite and rattling the dry stems of Old Lady Malone's flowers. Sonny rang the doorbell and then stuffed his hands in his pockets to keep them warm.

"H'lo, Mrs. Malone," he said, when the old lady opened the inside door. The screen door was latched, as always. "Duane here?"

"That's his car, ain't it?" she said, edging behind the door so the wind wouldn't hit anything but her nose and her forehead. "He's here if he ain't walked off."

She shut the door and went to get Duane. Sonny shuffled nervously on the porch. In a minute, Duane opened the door and stepped outside.

"Hi," Sonny said, finding it hard to get his breath because of the wind. "Thought I'd better come by and see you before you got off."

"Glad you did," Duane said. He was nervous, but he did look sort of glad. He was wearing Levi's and a western shirt.

"Want to go eat a bite?" Sonny suggested.

"Yeah, let me get my jacket."

He got his football jacket, the one from the year when the two of them had been cocaptains, they got in the warm pickup, and drove to the café. Conversation was slow in coming until Sonny thought to ask about the army, but then Duane loosened up and told one army story after another while they ate their hamburger steaks. It was pretty much like old times. Penny waited on them—she had had twin girls during the winter, put on twenty-five pounds, and was experimenting that night with purple lipstick. Old Marston had died in February of pneumonia—he had gone to sleep in a bar ditch in the wrong season. Genevieve had hired a friendly young widow woman to do the cooking.

"Guess we ought to take in the picture show," Sonny said. "Tonight's the last night."

"A good thing, too," Penny said, overhearing him. "Picture shows been gettin' more sinful all the time, if you ask me. Them movie stars lettin' their titties hang out—I never seen the like. The last time I went I told my old man he could just take me home, I wasn't sittin' still for that kind of goings on."

"Yeah, we might as well go," Duane said, ignoring her. "Hate to miss the last night."

They went to the poolhall and Sonny got his football jacket too. Then they angled across the square to the picture show and bought their tickets. A few grade-school kids were going in. The picture was an Audie Murphy movie called *The Kid from Texas,* with Gale Storm.

"Why hello, Duane," Miss Mosey said. "I thought you was done overseas. Hope you all like the show."

The boys planned to, but somehow the occasion just didn't work out. Audie Murphy was a scrapper as usual, but it didn't help. It would have taken *Winchester '73* or *Red River* or some big movie like that to have crowded out the memories the boys kept having. They had been at the picture show so often with Jacy that it was hard to keep from thinking of her, lithely stretching herself in the back row after an hour of kissing and cuddling. Such thoughts were dangerous to both of them.

"Hell, this here's a dog," Duane said.

Sonny agreed. "Why don't we run down to Fort Worth, drink a little beer?" he asked.

"My bus leaves at six-thirty in the mornin'," Duane said. "Reckon we could make it to Forth Worth and back by six-thirty?"

"Easy."

Miss Mosey was distressed to see them leaving so soon. She tried to give them their money back, but they wouldn't take it. She was scraping out the popcorn machine, almost in tears. "If Sam had lived, I believe we could have kept it goin'," she said, "but me and Jimmy just didn't have the know-how. Duane, you watch out now, overseas." Outside the wind was so cold it made their eyes water.

Sonny insisted they go in the pickup. He knew Duane would go to sleep on the way back and he didn't want the responsibility of driving the Mercury. The wind shoved the pickup all over the road, but the road was still a lot better for their spirits than the picture show had been. Rattling out of Thalia reminded them a little of the time—it seemed years before—when they had gone to Matamoros. As soon as they reached a wet county they stopped and bought two six-packs of beer. The cans spewed when they were opened and the smell of beer filled the cab.

By the time they crossed the Lake Worth bridge they had gone through a six-pack and a half and were feeling okay. Soon they came to the Jacksboro highway bars and Sonny pulled off at a place called the Red Dot Tavern. Inside, a lot of tough-looking boys with ducktails were playing shuffleboard, and a couple of women with dyed hair were sitting at the bar with their middle-aged sweethearts. The ducktails looked at the boys belligerently, but no direct challenges were offered.

"All we can do here is get drunk and get whipped," Duane said. "Let's see what the prospects are on South Main."

They drove slowly around the courthouse—the only courthouse they knew that had a neon American flag on top—and parked far down Main Street, where the bars were. The wind whipped around the big granite courthouse and cut right down the street, as cold as it had been in Thalia. The boys went in a hash house and had some chili and crackers to fortify themselves, then let the wind blow them down the street to a bar called the Cozy Inn, where a three-piece hillbilly band was whomping away. One middle-aged couple was dancing, and a few more were sitting in the booths or at the bar. The barmaid, a friendly old woman in her mid-fifties, wiped off their table with the end of her apron and then brought them some beer.

"Where you boys from?" she asked. "Thalia? Ain't it windy up there? I wouldn't live that close to the plains for nothin'. My oldest sister lives out in Floydada."

In a few minutes the band ended its set and the three young musicians straggled off to the rest room to relieve themselves.

"Maggie, you sing us a couple," one of the older customers said.

The barmaid didn't much want to, but the other couples took up the cry and finally she went over and picked up a guitar, shaking her head and deprecating herself.

"I ain't much of a singer," she said, but she strummed a minute or two and sang "Your Cheatin' Heart." Everyone thought she was real good, the boys included. Her voice was rough but strong—it filled the Cozy Inn better than the three side-burned young honky-tonkers had. She sang like she meant every word; it was not hard to believe that she had run afoul of a cheating heart or two somewhere in her life. After that she sang "Making Believe," and would have put the guitar down and gone back to the bar if Duane hadn't gone up and stopped her. He liked her singing.

"I'm goin' off to Korea tomorrow, ain't no tellin' when I'll get to Fort Worth agin," he said. "Sing one more."

"Why sure, if that's the case," the woman said. "Both my boys was in the service. I was right proud of 'em."

"These is for the soldier boys," she announced, not wanting the rest of the crowd to think she was singing out of vanity. She sang "Filipino Baby" and everyone applauded loudly; encouraged, she finished with "Peace in the Valley" and went back to the bar to draw someone a Pearl. Sonny felt suddenly depressed. The old barmaid had reminded him that he wasn't in the army. It seemed a fine thing to be going off to Korea and Sonny wished very badly that he could go.

When the band came back the boys left and stood on the cold street a minute, both slightly wobbly from the beer.

"We sure ain't findin' no women," Duane said. "Want to look some more or do you want to take the easy out?"

"It's too cold to prowl much," Sonny said.

With no more ado they turned up the street toward the easy out, a whorehouse called The New Deal Hotel. It was about the nicest whorehouse in that part of the country, but a little expensive on that account. Since it was Duane's last night the boys decided to splurge. When they got to the hotel a bunch of high-school boys from Seymour were standing on the sidewalk shivering, trying to get up the nerve to go inside. It was easy to tell they were from Seymour because of their football jackets.

"Yep, it's a whorehouse all right," Duane said. "You boys coming up?"

"How much do they charge?" one boy asked, his teeth chattering. "We're afraid to go up for fear we ain't got the money."

"They start at about ten bucks," Duane said, and the boys' faces fell. They had been hoping for five.

Sonny and Duane went on in and up the green-carpeted stairs, leaving the Seymour boys to count their money. The madame was a quiet, polite woman who looked and dressed like the saleswomen in a Wichita Falls department store. Sonny's girl was a polite, thin-nosed brunette from Corsicana, named Pauline. Everything was splendidly comfortable in the New Deal: the rooms were warm, the beds wide and clean, the carpets good. The girls were pleasant, but so efficient that afterward it seemed to Sonny that he and the girl had barely touched. Before he was even thawed out he and Duane were going back down the green stairs, each ten dollars poorer and neither much less horny.

The Seymour boys were all gone, the streets almost empty. While they were walking back to their pickup the city street-sweeper chugged by and Sonny remembered Billy and hoped Miss Mosey had seen he got home out of the cold.

"Well, I guess the next piece I get will be yellow," Duane said philosophically.

By the time they got back to the Lake Worth bridge, he was asleep. Sonny didn't care—he enjoyed the drive, and was in no hurry. With the wind blowing against him he couldn't make much time, but he didn't need to. North of Jacksboro he stopped the pickup and got out to take a leak, and Duane woke up and followed suit. It was about five o'clock when they pulled into Thalia. The posterboards in front of the picture show were naked. It seemed to Sonny it would have been better to have left *some* posters up, even the posters to *The Kid from Texas*.

"Got about two hours till bus time," he said, when they were at the rooming house. "Want to go down and have some coffee?"

"Yeah," Duane said. "Wait till I go in and get my gear."

In his uniform Duane looked a lot different. When he got back in the pickup he casually handed Sonny the keys to the Mercury. "Here," he said. "Why don't you look after that car for me?"

Sonny took the keys, embarrassed. "Your Ma don't need it?" he asked.

"I wouldn't want her drivin' it, no better than she can drive. You might help her run the groceries home, if you have time."

Sonny didn't know what else to say. In the warm café they both got a little sleepy and ended up playing the jukebox to keep awake. Genevieve wasn't there. Her husband had gone back to work in August and she had hired a girl named Etta May to work the night shift.

When the bus pulled up out front, both boys were glad. Sitting and waiting was hard on the nerves. The bus driver came in to have a cup of coffee and Sonny and Duane walked across the street to the yellow Continental Trailways bus. The wind made their eyes water, and took their breath—they had to turn their backs to it. Duane leaned his dufflebag against the front of the bus.

"Hear anything from Jacy?" he asked suddenly, since there was just two minutes left to talk.

"No, not a thing. She hasn't been back to town since August. I guess she just stays in Dallas all the time."

"I ain't over her yet," Duane said. "It's the damnedest thing. I ain't over her yet. That's the only reason me and you got into it, that night. Reckon she likes it down in Dallas?"

"It's hard to say," Sonny said. "Maybe she does. Reckon you and her would have got it all straightened out if I hadn't butted in?"

"Aw no," Duane said. "They would have annulled me too, even if we had. You all never even got to the motel?"

"No," Sonny said.

The bus driver came out of the café and hurried across the street, tucking his chin into his shoulder so his face would be out of the wind. Duane picked up the dufflebag and he and Sonny shook hands awkwardly.

"Duane, be careful," Sonny said. "I'll take care of that Mercury."

"Okay," Duane said. "See you in a year or two, if I don't get shot."

He got on and waved quickly from the window as the bus started up. A ragweed skated across the dusty street and the bus ran over it. Sonny put his hands in his pockets and walked back across the street to the pickup, not feeling too good. It was another one of those mornings when no one was there.

26

OF ALL THE PEOPLE in Thalia, Billy missed the picture show most. He couldn't understand that it was permanently closed. Every night he kept thinking it would open again. For seven years he had gone to the show every single night, always sitting in the balcony, always sweeping out once the show was over; he just couldn't stop expecting it. Every night he took his broom and went over to the picture show, hoping it would be open. When it wasn't, he sat on the curb in front of the courthouse, watching the theater, hoping it would open a little later; then, after a while, in puzzlement, he would sweep listlessly off down the highway toward Wichita Falls. Sonny watched him as closely as he could, but it still worried him. He was afraid Billy might get through a fence or over a cattleguard and sweep right off into the mesquite. He might sweep away down the creeks and gullies and never be found.

Once, on a Friday afternoon, Miss Mosey had to go into the theater to get something she had left and she let Billy in for a minute. The screen was disappointingly dead, but Billy figured that at least he was in, so he went up into the balcony and sat waiting. Miss Mosey thought he had gone back outside and locked him in. It was not until late that night, when Sonny got worried and began asking around, that Miss Mosey thought of the balcony. When they got there, Billy was sitting quietly in the dark with his broom, waiting, perfectly sure that the show would come on sometime.

All through October, then through November, Billy missed the show. Sonny didn't know what to do about it, but it was a bad time in general and he didn't know what to do about himself either. He had taken another lease to pump. He wanted to work harder and tire himself out, so he wouldn't have to lie awake at night and feel alone. Nothing much was happening, and he didn't think much was going to. One day he went to Wichita and bought a television set, thinking it might help Billy, but it didn't at all. Billy would watch it as long as Sonny was around, but the minute Sonny left he left too. He didn't trust the television. He kept going over to the picture show night after night, norther or no norther—he sat on the sidewalk and waited, cold and puzzled. He knew it would open sooner or later, and Sonny could think of no way to make him understand that it wouldn't.

One cold, sandstormy morning in late November Sonny woke up early and went downstairs to light the poolhall fires. Billy was not around, but that was not unusual. Sonny sneezed two or three times, the air was so dry. One of the gas stoves was old and he had to blow on it to get all the burners to light. While he was blowing on the burners he heard a big cattle truck roar past the poolhall, coming in from the south. Suddenly there was a loud shriek, as the driver hit the brakes for all he was worth—the stoplight was always turning red at the wrong time and catching trucks that thought they had it made.

Sonny went back upstairs and dressed to go eat breakfast. He couldn't find either one of his eye patches and supposed Billy must have them. It was the kind of morning when a welding helmet would have been a nice sort of thing to wear. The sky was cloudy and gritty, and the wind cut. When he stepped outside Sonny noticed that the big cattle truck was stopped by the square, with a little knot of men gathered around it. The doctor's car had just pulled up to the knot of men and the old doctor got out, his hair uncombed, his pajamas showing under his bathrobe. Someone had been run over. Sonny started to turn away, but then he saw Billy's broom lying in the street. By the time he got to the men the doctor had returned to his car and was driving away.

Billy was lying face up on the street, near the curb. For some reason he had put both eye patches on—his eyes were completely covered. There were just four or five men there—the sheriff and his deputy, a couple of men from the filling stations, one cowboy, and a pumper who was going out early. They were not paying attention to Billy, but were trying to keep the truck driver from feeling bad. He was a big, square-faced man from Waurika, Oklahoma, who didn't look like he felt too bad. The truck was loaded with Hereford yearlings and they were bumping one another around and shitting, the bright green cowshit dripping off the sideboards and splatting onto the street.

"This sand was blowin'," the trucker said. His name was Hurley. "I never noticed him, never figured nobody would be in the street. Why he had them damn blinders on his eyes, he couldn't even see. What was he doin' out there anyway, carryin' that broom?"

"Aw, nothin', Hurley," the sheriff said. "He was just an ol' simpleminded kid, sort of returded—never had no sense. Wasn't your fault, I can see that. He was just there—he wasn't doin' nothing."

Sonny couldn't stand the way the men looked at the truck driver and had already forgotten Billy.

"He was sweeping, you sons of bitches!" he yelled suddenly, surprising the men and himself. They all looked at him as if he were crazy, and indeed, he didn't know himself why he had yelled. He walked over on the courthouse lawn, not knowing what to do. In a minute he bent over and vomited by one of the dusty, stunted little cedar trees that the Amity club had planted. His father had come by that time.

"Son, it's a bad blow," he said. "You let me take care of things, okay? You don't want to be bothered with any funeral-home stuff, do you?"

Sonny didn't; he was glad to let his father take care of it. He walked out in the street and got Billy's broom and took it over to him.

"Reckon I better go try to sell a little gas," one of the filling-station men said. "Look's like this here's about wound up."

Sonny didn't want to yell at the men again, but he couldn't stand to walk away and leave Billy there by the truck, with the circle of men spitting and farting and shuffling all around him. Before any of them knew what he was up to he got Billy under the arms and started off with him, dragging him and trying to run. The men were so amazed they didn't even try to stop him. The heels of Billy's brogans scraped on the pavement, but Sonny kept on, dragged him across the windy street to the curb in front of the picture show. That was as far as he went. He laid Billy on the sidewalk where at least he would be out of the street, and covered him with his Levi's jacket. He just left the eye patches on.

The men slowly came over. They looked at Sonny as if he were someone very strange. Hurley and the sheriff came together and stood back a little way from the crowd.

"You all got some crazy kids in this town," Hurley said, spitting his tobacco juice carefully down wind.

By the time Sonny got back to the apartment Genevieve was there. She was crying but when she saw Sonny she made herself quit. She stayed for about an hour, made some coffee, and tried to get Sonny to cry or talk or something. He wouldn't. He wandered around the apartment, once in a while looked out at the gritty sky. Genevieve saw it was going to take some time.

"Sonny, I got to go to the café," she said. "People keep eatin', come what may. Come on down when you feel like it. Dan'll be glad to pump your leases for you when he comes in this afternoon."

Sonny didn't know what he would feel like doing that afternoon, so he didn't say anything. When Genevieve left he turned on the television set and watched it all morning: it made a voice in the room, anyway.

About the middle of the afternoon he began to feel like he had to do something. He had the feeling again, the feeling that he was the only person in town. He got his gloves and his football jacket and got in the pickup, meaning to go on out and pump his leases, but no sooner had he started than he got scared. When he passed the city limits signs he stopped a minute. The gray pastures and the distant brown ridges looked too empty. He himself felt too empty. As empty as he felt and as empty as the country looked it was too risky going out into it—he might be blown around for days like a broomweed in the wind.

He turned around and drove back past the sign, but stopped again. From the road the town looked raw, scraped by the wind, as empty as the country. It didn't look like the town it had been when he was in high school, in the days of Sam the Lion.

Scared to death, he drove to Ruth's house. It was broad daylight, mid-afternoon, but he parked right in front of the house. The coach was bound to be in school. Sitting in the driveway was the coach's new car, a shiny red Ford V-8. The Quarterback Club and the people of the town were so proud of his coaching that they had presented him with the car at the homecoming game, two weeks before.

Sonny went slowly up the walk, wondering if Ruth would let him in. He knocked at the screen, and when no one answered opened the screen and knocked on the glass-paneled front door.

In a moment Ruth opened it. She was in her bathrobe—that was about all Sonny saw. He didn't look at her face, except to glance.

"Hi," he said.

Ruth said nothing at all. She was surprised, then after a moment angered, then frightened.

"Could I have a cup of coffee with you?" Sonny asked finally, lifting his face.

"I guess," Ruth said, her tone reluctant. She let him in and he followed her through the dark, dusty-smelling living room to the kitchen. They were awkwardly silent while she made the coffee. Neither knew what to do.

"I'm sorry I'm still in my bathrobe," Ruth said finally. "It gets harder all the time to get around to getting dressed."

But then, as she was pouring the coffee, anger and fright and bitterness began to well up in her. In a moment they filled her past the point where she could contain them, and indeed, she ceased to want to contain them. She wanted to break something, do something terrible. Suddenly she flung Sonny's coffee, cup and all, at the cabinet, then she flung her own, then flung the coffee pot at the wall. It broke and a great brown stain of coffee spread over the wallpaper and dripped down onto the linoleum. Somehow the sight of it was very satisfying.

"What am I doing apologizing to you?" she said, turning to Sonny. "Why am I always apologizing to you, you little . . . little bastard. For three months I've been apologizing to you, without you even being here to hear me. I haven't done anything wrong, why can't I quit apologizing. You're the one who ought to be sorry. I wouldn't be in my bathrobe now if it hadn't been for you—I'd have had my clothes on hours ago. You're the one that made me quit caring whether I got dressed or not. I guess just because your friend got killed you want me to forget what you did and make it all right. I'm not sorry for you! You would have left Billy too, just like you left me. I bet you left him plenty of nights, whenever Jacy whistled. I wouldn't treat a dog that way but that's the way you treated me, and Billy too."

Sonny was very startled. He had never thought of himself as having deserted Billy. He started to say something, but Ruth didn't stop talking long enough. She sat down at the table and kept talking.

"I guess you thought I was so old and ugly you didn't owe me any explanations," she said. "You didn't need to be careful of me. There wasn't anything I could do about you and her, why should you be careful of me. You didn't love me. Look at me, can't you even look at me!"

Sonny did look. Her hair and lips looked dry, and her face was paler and older than he had remembered it. The bathrobe was light blue.

"You see?" she said. "You shouldn't have come here. I'm around that corner now. You ruined it and it's lost completely. Just your needing me won't bring it back."

Sonny didn't know. Her eyes seemed like they had always seemed, and having her so mad at him was suddenly a great relief. He saw her hands, nervously clasped on the table. The skin on the backs of her hands was a little darker, a little more freckled than the white skin of her fingers. He reached out and took one of her hands. She was startled, and her fingers were stiff, but Sonny held on and in a moment, disconcerted, Ruth let him hold her hand. Their hands knew one another and soon warmed a little.

When Sonny wove his fingers through hers Ruth looked at him cautiously and saw that he was still and numb, resting, not thinking at all. He had probably not even heard the things she said, probably would not remember them—he was beyond her hurting. It was as if he had just come in and they had started holding hands. She would have to decide from that, not from all the things she had said, nor even from the things that had happened, the pain and humiliation of the summer. What if he had valued a silly young girl more than her? It was only stupid, only the sort of thing a boy would do.

She could forgive him that stupidity, but it was not about forgiveness that she had to decide: it was about herself, whether she could stand it again, whether she wanted to. Even if the springs in her would start again it would only be a year or two or three before it would all repeat itself. Something would take him from her and the process of drying up would have to be endured again.

"I'm really not smart," she thought, and with the fingers of her other hand she began to smooth the little black hairs at the back of his wrist. "I'm not smart, and if I take him back again it will all be to go through again."

She didn't know whether she was brave enough to accept it, but she turned his hand over and traced the little lines in his palm, traced them up to the wrist. She pressed the tips of her fingers against the blue veins at his wrist, and followed the vein upward until it went under the sleeve of his shirt. It irritated her that her fingers wanted to go on, to go up the arm to his elbow and over the smooth muscle to the hollow of his shoulder. All at once tears sprang in her eyes and wet her face, her whole body swelled. She knew she was going to have the nerve, after all, and she took Sonny's young hand and pressed it to her throat, to her wet face. She was on the verge of speaking to him, of saying something fine. It seemed to her that on the tip of her tongue was something it had taken her forty years to learn, something wise or brave or beautiful that she could finally say. It would be just what Sonny needed to know about life, and she would have said it if her own relief had not been so strong. She gasped with it, squeezed his hand, and somehow lost the words—she could not hear them for the rush of her blood. The quick pulse inside her was all she could feel and the words were lost after all.

In a moment she felt quieter. She put his hand on the table and stroked his fingers with hers. After all, he was only a boy. She saw that the collar of his shirt was wrinkled under his jacket.

"Never you mind, honey," she said quietly, reaching under the jacket and carefully straightening out the collar. "Honey, never you mind. . . ."

About the Author

LARRY MCMURTRY is the author of numerous bestselling novels, including *Streets of Laredo*, the sequel to *Lonesome Dove*, and *Buffalo Girls*, *The Evening Star*, *Some Can Whistle*, *Anything for Billy*, *All My Friends Are Going to Be Strangers*, *The Desert Rose*, *Cadillac Jack*, *Somebody's Darling*, *Moving On*, and *Texasville*, the brilliant sequel to *The Last Picture Show*.

Mr. McMurtry also wrote *Horseman, Pass By*, which was made into the movie *Hud*, and *Terms of Endearment*, which inspired the film that won the 1984 Academy Award for Best Motion Picture. The son and grandson of Texas cattlemen, he brings the voice of authenticity to his writings about the West.